NEVADA RAIN

a beautifully dark novel

For Carrie ♡
Enjoy the journey
Love
Grant Wolfe

GRANT MONTGOMERY WOLFE

Library of Congress Control Number: 2012907837
ISBN: Hardcover 978-1-4771-0515-3
Softcover 978-1-4771-0514-6
Ebook 978-1-4771-0516-0

This is a work of fiction. Names, characters, places and incidents either are the product of the author's imagination or are used fictitiously, and any resemblance to any actual persons, living or dead, events, or locales is entirely coincidental.

This book was printed in the United States of America.

To order additional copies of this book, contact:
Xlibris Corporation
1-888-795-4274
www.Xlibris.com
Orders@Xlibris.com

Author of the highly acclaimed novel
Dyer Straits: Memoirs of a Killer

"Spellbinding. Captivating. I want more!"

"Impossible to put down. Move over, Stephen King. A breathlessly paced psychological thriller and a must-read. Stays with you well after the end."

"Each page ignited a horror that tore between reason and reality. The first-person narrative drove my mind to some very dark corners. You are a very talented man."

"A novel you can't help but believe. The vividness of his hallucinations make your head turn, eyes focus, and smell react with the same keenness as an animal on the hunt. To have to put this book down to stop your heart from racing is truly a gift given by the author."

In loving memory of Big Chase

More than just a friend

And for Papa's little darlings, Sebastian and Keira

The sunshine in my life

I don't even know your name,
but I love just the same.
If you let me be your slave,
your love I'll cherish to my grave.
And if you die before I do,
I'll end my life to be with you.

—Gregg Allman, "Please Accept My Love"

EPILOGUE

The Destiny Hotel

THE sounds of celebration and Diamond Bob's talented quartet of musicians shake the very foundation of the hotel. It is almost midnight, and the revelers are in full anticipation of the clock turning in a new year.

Johnny is sitting on the radiator beneath the window of room 8 that looks down onto the back alley. It burns the bare of his legs. He is staring unbelievably at the naked body lying on the bed that only moments before was so full of life.

A growing stain of red screams from the mattress on which Rebecca is lying.

Rebecca's body is still, hands resting by her sides—one fisted in anticipation, the other, holding the feather. *His* feather. Her eyes are closed, a significant trickle of blood sieving from the corner of her mouth. Freckled breasts rigid as if they were responding to his touch; however, the oozing hole in the center of her chest tells all.

She is just as she wished to be. "*When the time comes and there is no other way out.*" Her physical life was taken by her lifetime love. A vow made. A promise kept.

"*I promise, Becca. For us,*" he had told her.

So while they listened to the Eagles' "Heartache Tonight" emanate from the portable radio, Johnny had shot her in the heart, through and through.

In his hand is the .38 caliber his father had left him what seems like eons ago. It is still hot, the residue of cordite sticky on his fingers having been fired only moments before. Looking away, tears slide down his cheeks, gather at his chin, and drip onto his bare chest. His battered eyes focus on the calendar above the bar fridge, the one that has been open to November 1960 for the past fifty-some odd years. Smiling back at him is the Marilyn Monroe look-alike perched on that year's Cadillac, pink as a cancer ribbon.

Lifting the gun to eye level, he inspects the chambers. There are three bullets, side by side, waiting their turn—all he needs is one. Using the tip of the barrel, he wipes the tears from his chin. It digs in, searing flesh. Johnny doesn't feel a thing. His eyes are forced back to the bed. *How could it have come to this?* he wonders, formerly convinced that if they had ventured into Canada, they would escape the reaches of their pursuers.

They were wrong.

Now the most wonderful thing ever to happen to him in his life lay dead not ten feet in front of him, destroyed by his own hand. The same hand that will join them in the afterlife they so adamantly believed in.

Tired and growing weaker by the second, he slips off the radiator, bare feet landing softly on the carpet. The raging storm rattles the window. Turning, he parts the curtains, revealing his reflection in the darkened glass. He is unrecognizable to himself. He lifts the sill; winter's breath breaches the room, a beastly howl that whips against the four walls. The calendar pages flutter. Snowflakes sizzle against the radiator, hissing, hissing, hissing.

Behind him, the money they pirated lifts into the air, curling and rolling about the room. Fifty thousand, give or take. Some of the bills settle on the bed, on Rebecca's naked flesh. Johnny lowers himself, pushing his face into the storm. His long dark hair immediately covered with cold flakes.

They feel good against his hot skin.

Streetlamps sway to the will of the wind. Poplars and evergreens lining Government Road bend to its superiority. The local shops have closed long ago. Most of the streets leading to the edge of the river are deserted. A half block away, behind the Esso station, he can see a trio of men standing beneath the glow of a streetlamp, smoking cigarettes, huddled against the cold. *Rebecca was right,* he thinks. *There will always be someone lurking in the shadows.*

Reversing back into the room, he wipes at the snow on his face. His long hair is stuck to his shoulders and back like the slippery tentacles of an octopus. Money dances about room. The calendar flips with life. December's days are almost up. The Marilyn Monroe look-alike is still smiling at him. In that moment, from the open window comes the sound of a distant siren. *Still enough time to do what needs to be done,* he knows.

He dream-walks to the portable radio, hobbling, wincing, turning it loud. The DJ is wishing everyone in the foothills and Calgary a happy New Year. Stepping toward the bed, the weight of the gun is immeasurably heavy by his side. Another siren splits the night. His time is up. "*It's now or never,*" he tells himself.

Looping a finger over the trigger, he sits on the edge of the bed. Rebecca's blood is still flowing. Her beautiful face, that of a sleeping angel.

Lying next to her, he takes her hand in his, squeezing it oh so gently, and kisses her mouth, finding it still possesses the warmth of life. Intertwining his fingers in hers, he whispers, "Forever and a day," then points the snout of the barrel beneath his chin as though he has practiced the motion a hundred, a thousand times before. Closing his eyes, he can see Rebecca calling out to him, running toward him, flowing red hair dancing in a mischievous gust, her young body gleaming in a field of sunlight. "Come to me, Johnny. Come to me, my love."

Now there are voices in the hallway. Bodies scrape the wall. Then there is a pounding on the door that sounds like winter thunder. "Hello in there! This is Officer Morrow of the RCMP! I need you to answer me!"

"Maybe... you should... you know, break the door in," Johnny hears.

The heavy fist of Officer Ken Morrow pounds against the wood once more. "If you don't answer, I'm coming in!"

"I think you should wait for more police. It could be dangerous. I can hear a siren," another woman's voice says.

"To hell with that. Someone could be seriously hurt in there. Stay back, everyone!"

There is a moment of anxious silence before the door explodes with such influence, wood splinters and the dead bolt is sent trolling across the carpet. Officer Morrow's body crashes through the opening, gun at the ready.

Diamond Bob's band slip slides into a festive crescendo.

The twenty-year veteran stops dead in his tracks confronted by the sanguineous scene on the bed and the money fluttering in front of him.

"TEN! NINE! EIGHT! SEVEN! SIX!..." rises through the floor.

"Jesus Christ! No, son, don't do it!" Morrow howls, forced forward by the bodies clambering behind him.

"Oh my god! Oh my sweet Jesus!" someone cries out.

Mr. Jingles, Margaret Lovely's feline companion, saunters into the room, sniffing at the air and swiping a paw at one of the bills floating closest.

Officer Morrow is forced to take another step forward. Using his body weight and arms, he tries to hold everyone back. In a calmer tone, he says, "Don't do it, son. Give me the gun. Everything will be all right. You'll see."

"FOUR! THREE! TWO!"

Johnny squeezes Rebecca's hand, oblivious to the horrified faces staring at him. All he sees is Rebecca's lovely, upturned smile. The clock strikes midnight just as his trembling finger draws on the trigger. The last sound he hears is the hammer dropping.

A thunderous roar resonates within room 8 and from one floor below. "HAPPY! NEW YEAR!"

I've just closed my eyes again
Climbed aboard the dream-weaver train
Driver, take away my worries of today
And leave tomorrow behind

Oh, dream weaver
I believe you can help me through the night
Oh, dream weaver
I believe we can reach the morning light...

* * *

BOOK ONE

Black and White

1

Bay Ridge Cove, Main
6:00 p.m., Eastern Standard Time

A STATIC-FILLED "5 Days in May" emanated from the Panasonic radio perched next to the toaster. With busy hands, Rebecca White scrubbed the breakfast dishes her brother Ben and father Ray had left earlier that morning. Her eyes search the bay for the *Red Witch*, a fishing vessel they worked on hoisting lobster traps. Having changed into denim shorts and red tube top, preferring the lighter wear, divergent to her school's strict dress code of black slacks and white button-down blouses, she felt far more complacent.

For reasons she could not fathom, the powers that be had extended the school year to eclipse the first week of July, a first, and the teachers were still doling out homework as though it was the beginning of the first semester.

The window above the sink presented a view of the entire bay and the houses that surrounded it. Rebecca knew she wasn't alone in her daily search. That the wives of other fishermen also stood at the windows of the houses surrounding the bay, waiting with trepid anticipation.

Since most of the boats that went out at 5:00 a.m. weren't equipped with two-way radios and 90 percent of the men who worked on them couldn't swim a stroke to save their lives, the wait was one met with a rational fear. A fear that was substantiated each time the sun set and another tale of tragedy was born. Whispered about after church and toasted loudly at the local watering hole where many a hero was born and the tragedies that befell the town, became legends upon themselves.

The sea is a merciless mistress, never giving up her dead, and had left many of the women in Bay Ridge Cove to fend for themselves. Most remained, raising their brats best they could, Bay Ridge being the only home they knew. They took any jobs offered, which were few and paid little. The ones with enough sense to leave, as far as Rebecca was concerned, could have only found a better life for themselves, or so she imagined. Willingly inspired to believe. Any place must surely be better than the mundane, insufferable life Bay Ridge Cove had to offer.

Notwithstanding the love she felt for Ray and Ben, she be damned if she was going to play housemaid, nurse and cook to them for the rest of her life. Secretly secured beneath her bed was the suitcase her mother used when she visited her sister in Florida. An Aunt Rebecca had never met. The only evidence of this alleged aunt's existence was her mother's annual paid-for trip and the Christmas card they received, always arriving post haste, signed Kathryn. The suitcase was a hopeful reminder that someday, when the time was right, she would leave Bay Ridge Cove, its endless supply of fishermen and the benign wives who bore them their children, never to look back.

Within the suitcase was a full week's worth of clothing. Two hundred dollars she'd saved babysitting the Hooper twins for the past couple of years and a five-by-seven framed portrait of her mother. The keepsake was taken by Rebecca just months before Deseray White succumbed to a massive coronary. Captured was her mother sitting among a background of summer bright marigolds with a smile as bright as the sun lighting the bay.

The calamitous incident occurred five trapping seasons ago. Rebecca was twelve, on her way home from Our Lady of Peace grade school. Halfway to the top of Dover Bluff Road, a foreboding sense of inaptness overwhelmed her. Running as quickly as her feet would allow, she burst through the front door. The main floor was choked with the redolence and smoke of burnt bread.

Dropping her schoolbag, she dashed into the kitchen to find her mother lying peaceful like in front of the oven, still wearing oven mitts. On the floor next to her was a perfectly golden loaf of bread and the pan it had escaped from. The oven door was open, revealing blackened loaves from which smoke escaped. Having enough sense to shut the oven off and open the kitchen window, she knelt beside her mother, tears streaming. Deseray White's once sparkling blue eyes were dull and vacant, and her skin had already taken on the pallor of death. Even the fiery red of her hair seemed to have lost its luster. Rebecca shook and shook her mother without response. Their house was the only one on top of Dover Bluff Road, so she could not call out to a neighbor for help. For several minutes she pleaded for Deseray to wake, but to no avail. Finally, with no response, she dialed 911 and pleaded through sobs for the operator to send an ambulance right away. "My Momma is on the floor and she won't wake up. Please hurry."

Deseray White, pronounced dead on the scene at the splendid age of forty-four, was laid to rest three days later at the Rosewood Cemetery. She was wearing the very dress and shoes she passed away in. A green knee-length one-piece with pearl buttons up the front and a pair of beige pumps on her feet. Rebecca's mother always dressed in her best attire whenever she baked. It made her feel *womanly,* she continuously told her.

Before her mother's passing, Rebecca was struck with a strange sensation while sitting in class. It crawled up her body from her toes to the last strand of red at the top of her head, lighting her mind with tiny firefly sparks. There was no pain associated with the experience, and she told no one about it. She went about her school day at Our Lady of Peace where she was the captain of the school's field hockey team as though the episode had not existed. Just some kind of weird growing pain, she resolved. She was, after all, entering the stages of puberty and had already received her monthly cycle. Deseray told her that her body would experience changes, and she took this as one of them.

Other than her immediate family, the residing priest, and the women from the church bazarre, few attended Deseray White's funeral. Kathryn, the aunt in Florida, sent a banquet of memorial flowers. Rebecca found herself immediately resentful that so few would show to pay their respects.

Refusing to attend Sunday services, she would turn the other cheek when any of the women tried to persuade her otherwise. God had taken her mother, her best friend, away, and that was a reality she just could not forgive.

Clandestinely, however, since the very day of the funeral, mother and daughter continued a relationship that could only be described as spiritually enlightening. For twelve-year-old Rebecca, the initial visitations were nothing less than frightening. But over time, the bond that had held them so close when Deseray White was alive prevailed, initiating an alliance that brought them closer than ever before.

For two years since that day, the strange prickling sensation rested until one Friday evening, mid July, when three of her friends were killed in a head-on collision making their way to Newcastle to see the latest Brad Pitt flick. An outing that was supposed to include Rebecca, but she had come down with a rare summer cold, she told everyone, and was bedridden for several days. The abnormal prickling, like ants beneath the skin, stayed the course for the entire duration of her supposed illness.

Nowadays, whenever the sensation struck, which usually occurred just prior to another local tragedy, she isolated herself in her room, feeling guilty, guilty, guilty. Sometimes for entire weekends, which was why she was fretful for Ben. Whenever he was near lately, the sensation took hold of her, prickling at her arms and legs, crawling over her flesh. Still, she told no one about her special abilities. Her father, in his small-town ignorance, would tell her she was crazy in the head. Simple Ben would think she was trying to play some kind of weird game with him. To tell them she was continuously visited by her deceased mother, that they carried on lengthy conversations, would have resulted in her being sent away to an asylum. She was smack-dab sure of it. Confiding in schoolmates, even those she considered close friends, would cause her to be ridiculed and made the brunt of cruel jokes. That's just the way it was in the pious-minded population of Bay Ridge Cove. Take it or leave it.

* * *

The generic bubbles from the soap her father always purchased had all but disappeared, leaving a septic sludge to finish the black iron pan used to fry bacon in. Lifting the heavy skillet from the stove, she used an already-abused SOS pad to scrub away the congealed grease then placed it on the drying rack with the rest of the dishes. With a bare foot, she kicked at the dishwasher that seemed to be mourning the death of her mother. Since that terrible day, it refused to go through the rinse cycle, forcing Rebecca to do the dishes and pans the old-fashioned way. Retrieving a drying towel hanging from the cupboard below, she dried her hands. The same towel she had been using for the past two years, full of holes and ragged on both ends. Like everything else that needed to be fixed or replaced, such as the broken window in her bedroom, the step leading to the second floor that mewled like a cat whenever someone stepped on it and the stubborn dishwasher, Ray continued to preach, "It can wait until next season." A season, Rebecca was certain, would never come. However, when the nineteen-inch Zenith gave up the ghost three months prior, Ray White was first in line the following morning at the local Kmart, returning with a thirty-two-inch Hitachi flat screen that must have cost the stars, moon, and a kidney.

Not that Rebecca minded so much, watching television or reading being the principal curriculum of the nonexistent social life she endured. But if he had purchased a smaller version, the money saved could have gone toward fixing the things that needed fixing. Her mother would have insisted upon it. But these days, Ray White lived by Ray White's rules, and there wasn't anything this side of an act of God that was going to change him. He'd become distant since her mother's passing and was drinking far more than he should, or did. Another reason why Rebecca despised the abhorrent Jim Bounty.

Her eyes searched the bay again. Standing on the laundry post, pruning its wings with its yellow bill was a dimwitted seagull completely oblivious to the cliff sparrows dive-bombing it from only a few feet above. The little birds dove in unison, swooping inches above the gull's crown before looping into the air to start the process over again. Rebecca smiled at their antics, her only concern, that the lone gull would not defecate on the recently washed sheets she'd hung before she left for school.

A strong, clamorous breeze rushed in from the reaches of the Atlantic. The laundry whipped and snapped. The little birds struggled to hold their flight, then a moment later, dropped beneath the verge of the cliff and returned to their homes. The laundry would have to come in before the breeze morphed into a full-blown gale which it was apt to do when the sun started its westerly decline.

Nestled between Portland and Newcastle, Bay Ridge Cove was a quaint, benign village horseshoeing high-rolling cliffs that lessened toward the Atlantic. The four winds gathered here, releasing their wrath toward the houses as if they meant to blow them down, down, down. The bay was known to its generations of fishermen and their families as the Devil's Breath, for many a vessel had been caught in its tempered waves and thrown into the jagged toes of the worsening cliffs.

A tale of tragedy lived in every household. Nonetheless, the very reason the sons and fathers of Bay Ridge Cove went out to the sea each morning from May till August was what kept houses heated in winter and food on the tables when times were lean. Trains of the sought-after crustaceans passed just outside the bay each year, filling the traps of men who wagered their lives against the treacherous winds and the shifting currents of her temperaments.

Sometimes the wind grew so strong at night Rebecca believed the roof was surely going to lift away from the four walls and land in Oz. But the century-old house was stubborn, always standing its ground, having lived through more than a hundred years of the worst weather the moody mistress could throw at it.

Numerous boats had entered the bay and were heading toward the wharf, their bows low in the water, indicating the hauls were good. There will be many a beer tipped at the Wind Breaker Hotel and a few stories added to past legacies of the sea.

Rebecca hummed the song her mother hummed when it was she who stood at the window waiting for the boats to come in. There were no words to the melody, and as far as Rebecca could recall, she had never heard it played on the radio. Her mother once told her that it was a tune taught to her by her mother and was passing it on to Rebecca, hoping that one day she would recite it to her own daughter. So that it would be passed from generation to generation of red-headed McClintock women.

Closing her eyes, Rebecca's mind took her back to a happier time. To the memory that always gave her reason to smile. To forget for a trice that up until then her life was anything what she imagined it would be when her young mind was filled with thoughts of fame and fortune. It drifted into view, as vivid as one of the postcards sold at the pharmacy.

She is ten again, standing in the bright yellow kitchen wearing her favorite blue dress while her mother prepared dinner. Her thin legs are warmed by the oven, and she is dizzy with fantasy. She begins to spin, arms stretched wide, music playing from the Panasonic. Closing her eyes, she brings forward the images only seen on her favorite TV show, Vegas, *and in the magazines her mother reads. The concrete structures of New York, Boston, Chicago, Los Angeles, and the steel and glass palaces of Las Vegas fill every crevice of her mind. She spins faster and faster. Long red curls lift from her shoulders, her arms begin to tingle. She chases away all but the images of Las Vegas, for it is her most favorite place in the whole world. She can see clearly the main strip with all its dancing lights and thousands of people searching for dreams, for great financial gains and love rekindled.*

Then she imagines herself, not as an adolescent, but as a grown woman, standing in front of the rhythmic fountain preceding the Bellagio, classical music pouring from an unseen source. She is flowing in a gown of glittering gold, and there are dozens of photographers taking her picture. Lightbulbs flash, and everyone comments on how beautiful she is. The cameras can't get enough of her liquid green eyes and the graceful red locks caressing her upper body like an ardent lover. She is a star. Her name is the headliner on every marquee for miles around. Throngs of fans call out her name. She smiles and waves, and they are jubilant just to be near her.

"Becca… Becca," her mother's voice shakes her from the images, and she stops spinning. Her head goes swoosh. *Several long, pretend moments pass before she is able to focus.*

"You shouldn't spin so fast, sweetheart," her mother says sweetly. "You're going to make yourself sick one of these times." She takes Rebecca to her bosom. "Where were you today, daughter?" she asks, stroking Rebecca's hair.

"My most favorite place in the whole world, Las Vegas. Oh, Mommy, do you think I'll ever get to go there?" Rebecca looks up into her mother's beautiful freckled face, her deep green eyes pleading.

Deseray White takes her by the shoulders, holding her at arm's length, and, looking deep within, says, "It's all up to you, Becca. There isn't anything in this world you can't accomplish if you put your mind to it. If Las Vegas is truly where you would like to go to someday, although I don't know why, then yes, perhaps someday you'll get there… perhaps someday."

Those were the final words Rebecca heard in the fond memory. They were always the final words she heard, for the memory was always the same. It faded back to the only home it knew, where it slept, to be awakened when Rebecca required its moralizing tonic.

Opening her eyes, Rebecca directed them to the place on the floor where her mother was taken so young. As always, tears sluiced the plumps of her cheeks. Wiping at them with the back of a hand, she promised herself once again that someday, she would make it to Las Vegas. She would become the success she had only experienced in dreams and in the memory she clung to dearly.

Static hissed from the Panasonic. Giving it a hard smack on its top, she unplugged it, waited for a moment, then plugged it back in. A strange warble of sound emanated before Rod Stewart's autonomous voice spilled from the small speaker. "Tonight's the Night" filled the kitchen. It is one of Rebecca's all-time Stewart favorites, so she turned up the volume and sashayed back to the window above the sink.

Weaned on rock-and-roll classics, and luckily for her, the only station the radio picked up was a retro station airing from Portland that played the best hits of the '60s, '70s, and '80s. Again her eyes search the choppy waters of the bay beyond the cliff.

The gull had vacated the premises and, at first glance, did not leave any soiled gifts behind for which Rebecca is grateful. The laundry snaps like a whip. Beyond it, she can see the *Red Witch*, bouncing as it enters the bay. A great sigh of relief bursts Rebecca's worry. As always, because Jim Bounty took chances, the *Red Witch* was the last boat to come ashore. It would take two hours to weigh the catch on the giant scales of the cannery. It was time to prepare dinner.

Being a Friday, fish was the course du jour. Rebecca hated fish, resented the foul stench of it that over the years had permeated itself into the carpet, wallpaper, and curtains. She was absolutely certain that if the floorboards were ever pried, there would be thousands of fish skeletons found beneath them. It was permanent in all of Ray's and Ben's clothing, and no matter how hard she tried, no amount of bleaching could eradicate the rancid smell.

Rebecca had eaten fish in every way you could possibly imagine. Fried, boiled, baked, stewed, barbequed, stuffed, poached, and grilled. Put in a pie, casserole, chowder, Creole, puff pastry, and even raw. But what she hated even more were the lobsters that were the very mainstay of her family's survival. She had consumed so many of the bottom-feeding crustaceans she was constantly astounded that her skin hadn't taken on a green-orange pigmentation.

Gone were the days when the house smelled of fresh-baked bread because, try as she may, Rebecca was far less the baker her mother was. For whatever reason, she just couldn't get the recipes right. The dough did not rise sufficiently and always came out tasting like cardboard. So after dozens of attempts, she stopped altogether. Now the bread they ate came in a colorful bag of Wonder.

Rebecca opened the fridge and removed the pair of mackerel she was to make a chowder with and placed them on the cutting board. Then she gathered the other ingredients: potatoes, onions, celery, and carrots. Checking the quart of whipping cream, she gave it a sniff to be sure it hadn't soured. To her regret, it hadn't. Reaching beneath the cupboard, she retrieved a five-quart pot then took a butcher's knife from its wooden block and removed the mackerel from the plastic bag. They were still partially frozen, making them easier to clean. With two well-practiced strokes, she lopped the heads off behind the gill plates and put those into the plastic bag. They would join the other dismembered gaping maws in the freezer that were to be used as bait in the lobster traps.

Next, she removed the tails and fins. Slitting the bellies, she removed the stinking innards and discarded them into the garbage, the smell causing her stomach to wrench. She tried to ignore the stench by focusing on the music. "Love Me Do" lifted her spirits. Dancing in place, she moved her hips and commenced with the task of preparing yet another fishy concoction.

By the time she had cleaved all of the vegetables and fish into bite-sized pieces, bile had risen in her throat and it took all of her will not to toss the oily mess out the window.

Turning on the stove, she filled the pot to a third with water and dropped the ingredients in. Then she scrubbed her hands and waited for the water to heat. When it began to churn, turning grey from the oil of the mackerel, she added the cream, salt, and white pepper to taste, tossed in a couple of bay leaves, then set the stove to simmer.

Another glance out the window revealed that the *Red Witch* was halfway across the bay, its crimson red bow low in the water. Jim Bounty had painted the vessel red so that anyone with half-decent eyesight could easily spot it should they ever need assistance on the unpredictable Atlantic.

Rebecca's distaste for Jim Bounty held true for her female schoolmates as well. During the off season, Mr. Bounty would plant himself on one of the benches outside the school perimeter and watch the girls during field hockey practice. He gave them the creeps and on more than one occasion was seen fondling himself.

He was as big a man, as her brother, with a face only a mother could love. Pocked, with deep festering sores and a ruddy complexion from too much drink. Over the years, he had spent many a Saturday night in the drunk tank, having gotten soused on tequila chasers and picking fights with one or more of the younger fisherman at the Wind Breaker Hotel. He became especially ornery if it was hockey season and the Bruins were playing below the standard of what they were capable. With so many nights spent in the same lockup, the local law enforcers had nicknamed the cell the Bounty Hooskow.

However, Jim Bounty not only kept Ray and Ben employed, he was Ray's childhood mate and long-time drinking partner. A relationship Rebecca was none too pleased about, but they'd been friends for more than forty years, forcing Rebecca to bite her tongue whenever Ray brought him home for dinner, which was customarily accompanied by another all-night drinking contest.

With supper simmering on the stove, a laundry basket tucked beneath her arm, Rebecca went outside and retrieved the sheets from the clothesline before they were sent to the land of lost bedding. Once they were all neatly folded and placed in the basket, she set it aside and walked toward the edge of the cliff. A salt-flavored wind pushed at the length of her hair. She stood as close as she dared, for the drop was more than a hundred feet where the sea foamed white with rage, crashing into jagged rocks below.

Swallows swooped and looped as they fled the safety of their clay homes nestled in the cliff's facade, twittering their disdain for the sudden intrusion

All around her, the landscape was a carpet of green, declining toward the ocean. Houses scattered in a patchwork of white dotted the topography, their black ash roofs looking like scorches against the green. Laundry was being gathered by the wives of fisherman who also anticipated that a much stronger wind was just on the horizon.

Rebecca spread her arms. The ocean's breath encompassed her body, and for a brief moment, she thought she heard her name being whispered by the great Atlantic stretched out before her. If she ever did leave Bay Ridge Cove, she imagined, the smack of salt in the back of her throat would be one of things she would truly miss.

One of the local legends, born in 1850, was that of a young blacksmith who was scorned by the lover he had been having an affair with. Purportedly, he leapt from the very threshold Rebecca was standing on. It was said that he cried out his lover's name as he plummeted to his death, his body never to be found, swallowed by the unforgiving sea. When Rebecca first heard the saga, she was told that each year, on the anniversary of his demise, he could be seen standing on the cliff calling out her name.

However, even with the rare gift Rebecca possessed, she had yet to see, let alone hear the apparition that had come to be known as the Ghost of Dover Bluff Heights.

Dozens of seagulls circled the *Red Witch* as it neared the docks in hopes that unused bait would be tossed into the waters, giving the scavengers an easy feast. The scene always reminded Rebecca of the movie *Finding Nemo* and the greedy gulls who proclaimed that anything edible was "mine, mine, mine, mine."

Garbed in yellow slickers, the men on board resembled corn niblets. Rebecca waved, though the distance between them was far-reaching, and there was no conceivable way they could see her standing at the cliff's summit. Again the ocean seemed to whisper her name.

Once the lobster weighed vessel was safely moored, Rebecca gathered the basket of wind-dried laundry and made her way back to the house, humming. Just knowing Ben and Ray had returned safely put her in a euphoric, carefree mood. So much so that she ignored the telltale itch rising just beneath the surface of her skin.

* * *

2

Perhaps Someday

ONCE the laundry was neatly folded and stacked in the linen closet upstairs and the chowder was checked and stirred, Rebecca grabbed a can of Coke from the fridge, retired to the living room, and plopped herself down on the couch. The ignored itch had relented, so she considered it no further. Popping the tab on the soft drink, she took a long refreshing swallow, found the remote wedged between cushions, and turned on the Hitachi. The huge black screen took a second before it turned into the blue background of a news station. CNN was airing. A pretty blond anchorwoman was summarizing yet another suicide attack against the American and allied forces in the city of Kandahar. The screen switched to a scene where a Humvee, badly damaged in the attack, sat smoldering in the middle of a street while triumphant onlookers, laughing defiantly, paraded around the carnage, some holding signs that read, Death to America.

Rebecca quickly changed the channel. There was no need to hear how many more body bags were going to be shipped home from Afghanistan. She did not want to see the faces of young men who were giving their lives so selflessly, so needlessly, as far as she was concerned. Finding a station airing an *X-Files* rerun, she settled in. Candidly resting her feet upon the coffee table, she nearly scattered the texts of her homework. The assignments were stacked haphazardly next to the model Tall Ship Ben had given her for her fourteenth birthday. He'd cleverly crafted the gift from a block of pine he'd found at the local lumber yard, whittling away in his spare time, and away from the house so that Rebecca knew not what he was up to. He'd used the shells from giant sea scallops for sails and fishing line for the guide ropes. It was the most precious gift she had ever received. Wiggling her toes, she decided she would paint them a radical blue once she showered and readied herself for dinner.

Agent Scully was running through a laneway, her Glock high over one shoulder.

She was wearing a dark blue pantsuit and black pumps. Her hair was bobbed, and the camera zeroed in on her stoic face as her eyes searched the darkness.

Anyone blind in both eyes could plainly see that the dark pantsuits made Jillian Anderson look ten pounds heavier, Rebecca thought. She made a mental note. *When you're famous, stay away from fashion-crippled producers.* Grabbing a throw cushion, she tucked it behind her head and watched the rerun from between her toes. The homework could be postponed for the time being. She had the whole weekend to get it done, and since she would be babysitting the Hooper twins come Saturday, the algebra could wait till then.

However, she was anxious to set her teeth into the theatrical version of *Romeo and Juliet*, but she would delay the read until she had the house to herself. Ben would go out for the night, and she was quite certain that Ray would not be coming home with him.

With a good weigh in, and this being a Friday, and with the prompting from his so-called friend Jim Bounty to "go have a few," Ray would skip dinner and head straight for the Wind Breaker. Rebecca just hoped that she wouldn't have to rescue him like she has had to do in the past. It was embarrassing for her to walk into the bar among the men who kept the town's economy alive. To drag her father's sorry ass off his bar stool, him protesting and calling for the men to come meet his "beautiful daughter."

Nonetheless, embarrassed as she might be by Ray's postulating antics, she didn't quite mind that the men found her presence enlightening. They measured her a refreshing intrusion to their mundane existence and were eager to share with her the tally of the day and the *near misses* they had encountered. She was, after all, a young woman, one that would soon be seeking the esprit de corps of a future husband, at least as far as they were concerned.

Gathering a lock of hair, she twirled it between fingers while watching the images on the big screen and imagined herself there. "*Perhaps someday,*" she heard her mother's voice remind her.

A half hour passed. Scully and Mulder had captured their foe, once again. Rebecca still had the better part of an hour to kill before anyone, if anyone, came home. It was an opportune time to take a shower. Checking the chowder to find that it was as perfect as it could be, she turned off the stove, squiggled her nose at the awful aroma rising from the pot, then went to her room where she stripped down to her panties.

Lying on her bed were a collection of stuffed animals, most of which Ben had won for her at the carnival whenever it came into town, usually twice a year, once in the spring and again in the fall. They had clever names like Arial the Alligator, Pete the Dragon, Sam Snake, and Geoffrey the Goldfish. Bandit the Bear, her most beloved of the collection, had been made for her by her mother, a gift for her tenth birthday. The one-foot-tall Bruin had since then lost one of its eyes and its color had faded over the years, yet Rebecca would still not retire for the night unless it was securely tucked to her bosom.

She powered the radio sitting on the nightstand. Like the Panasonic in the kitchen, it took several seconds for the static to clear before the music kicked in. She danced about the small room, rotating her hips, raising her hands above her head, and snapping her fingers to Madonna's "True Blue." When she passed the window overlooking the bay, a breath of wind whispered against her legs, the break in the glass allowing its entry.

"What are you naughty boys looking at?" she asked the plush spectators sitting on the bed. "You shouldn't watch. Your minds might get corrupted." She laughed, turned, and caught a glimpse of herself in the mirror above the dresser. She stopped dancing and admired her body. It had matured beautifully over the past couple of years. *Good things come to those who wait,* she had been reminding herself since the age of fourteen and the other girls had already begun to develop. Presently, whenever the girls showered after field hockey practice, it was *she* who embraced envy.

In Rebecca's mind, the reflection showed a young woman well on her way to becoming a starlet.

Her hair had grown well below her shoulders. Breasts stood mature without the need for mirror tricks the areolas centering each one perfectly. The flat of her belly was well toned, and she knew it drove the boys crazy whenever she wore tank tops. Her legs were long, slender, and her entire body was a wash of freckles, like Julianne Moore's she always imagined. She was taller than most, another asset, and she considered her face to be unique if not beautiful. "I can't miss," she said to her reflection and turning enough to admire the well-defined curvature of her backside.

Dancing toward the bed, she turned the stuffed animals so they were facing the closet wall. "You boys don't need to see any more," she scolded.

A much stronger wind whistled through the break in the window, causing the sheer of curtain to dance and gooseflesh to rise on her legs and arms. She decided right then and there that she would demand Ray replace it. Moving back to the mirror, she stood there for a moment. Giggling. She said to the young woman staring back at her, "You're bad, Rebecca White."

She closed her eyes, and imagined that her hands were those of her lover. She could imagine him easily through the window of her mind. He was tall, with long dark hair and eyes that were grey-blue, like the eyes of a wolf. Copper flesh covered a body that was void of hair. He had been a part of her deep conscience as far back as she could remember. They had grown together, him as a young boy, a cerebral playmate she could conjure whenever she needed him. As a young teenager, he was her confidant. She would share all her worldly secrets with him. Now like her, he was a young adult and her ardent lover.

Rebecca imagined him taking her face in his hands, kissing her, gently at first, then with intense purpose. Before she knew it, the fantasy conquered her.

Starting between her thighs, her hands traveled the whim of her body and across the flat of her belly until they gladdened the under flesh of her breasts. Cupping them in her hands, she squeezed gently, her nipples responding in kind. Breathing with *him* now, they were one mind, one heart, one soul.

Rebecca had learned long ago how her body responded to certain touches. Pleasing herself was a far better alternative than the clumsy antics she had experienced in the backseats of cars. Though she had gone all the way twice, she came way from each experience still believing she was a virgin. The boys were all hands and greedy mouths.

Selfish, quick to the point. *Surely, true lovemaking lasted for more than a few, short, grunting seconds.*

Momentarily gratified, Rebecca retrieved a towel from the dresser, went into the bathroom, turned on the water, and waited for the spikes to turn hot. She locked the bathroom door, though she was quite alone. Wiggling out of her panties, she cast them onto the lid of the toilet with a thrust of her big toe. Drawing the shower curtain aside, she stepped into the steam, closed the curtain, and summoned her dream lover to satisfy her. He never turned her down.

Blindly, Rebecca retrieved the bar of soap from its caddy and worked it over her abdomen before sliding the ivory bar to her thighs, then along her backside. She lathered her breasts until they were covered with exploding little bubbles of delight. Turning, she rinsed her backside, the hot water wonderful. Bracing herself, the Ivory bar made its way to the orange wisps of her womanhood. With the most affecting touch, she swabbed her genitalia waking within the wanton longings of her sexuality.

The image of her nameless lover returned, and she readily went to him. He took her in his arms. Their bodies pressed, flesh to hot flesh. His long hair fell upon her face. He looked into her green eyes, the length of him pressing. Strong hands touched her in all the right ways, and he kissed her deeply before they tumbled to the earth.

Her fingers became his, stroking quietly. Quick little explosions of paradise enveloped her body. Toes curl, flesh quaking. Then he was in her, deep, fulfilling, driving hips hard against hers. Rebecca's mind ignited. She liberated a long sigh of sexual gratification, climaxing time and time again. She held him there until the water grew cold and his image began to fade. Then he was gone, returning to the recesses of her mind, until it was time once more for them to be together.

Someday, Rebecca understood, frigid water rinsing her body and the remains of their intimacy. *Someday I will find my one true love and we'll be together forever and a day and we will rewrite the history of romance.*

* * *

Dressed, Rebecca went downstairs and settled herself in front of the TV, her toenails painted blue. It was seven o'clock, and it wouldn't be long before Ben, and possibly Ray, would be home. She considered getting started on her homework then pushed the thought aside. *Plenty of time,* she told herself.

Ten minutes later, she heard her father's Buick pull onto the gravel driveway. A moment passed before a single door slammed, signifying that she and Ben would be eating dinner alone.

Ben's heavy footfalls pounded on the front porch. The door opened, and he stepped inside. The wind followed him into the house and shook the interior.

Rebecca turned to see him standing there with that boyish grin of his.

"Hi, Becca," said Ben. He was wearing a red flannel jacket and khaki work pants that were tucked into his gum boots. His dark hair was every which way, his chin covered with the long day's growth.

Rebecca looked to his boots, the smell of chum filling her nostrils from twenty feet away. "How many times do I have to tell you to take your work boots off outside? They'll stink up the house worse than you do."

"Sorry, Becca," said Ben regarding his boots. Toe-heeling them, he tossed them onto the porch. Closing the door, he took an exaggerated breath, filling his chest until it looked like it would explode. "Mmmm. Sure smells good."

"That's your opinion," replied Rebecca. "I suppose Ray is at the Wind Breaker, *again*."

"Yeah, sorry, Becca. I tried to talk him out of it, but he just won't listen."

"I gather you had a good weigh in?"

"Yeah, you wouldn't believe it. We ran into a huge train. Lots of berries though." Ben scratched the top of his head. "Don't worry, Dad won't be too late. We're going back out first thing in the morning. I made Jim promise to bring him home." He moved to the couch, socks full of holes, his hands thick and chaffed red.

Rebecca hated the thought of having Jim Bounty in her house again, but if it meant that Ray would be returned home safely, she reluctantly accepted it. "You better not let Helen catch you smelling like that. She'll never marry you." Rebecca had to bite her tongue to stop herself from laughing. Helen Peterson had been Ben's sweetheart for the past three years. Ben was always chiding on how he was going to ask her to marry him. She worked at the local bowling alley, renting out shoes, and, when needed, cooked in the small kitchen serving up hot dogs, burgers, and fries. Secretly, Helen had confided to Rebecca that she was waiting on pins and needles for him to pop the *big* question.

"Oh, she'll marry me all right. What woman in their right mind wouldn't?" Ben loomed over her, motioned to place his hands on her shoulders.

Rebecca grabbed him by the wrists to ward him off. "I don't think so, lover boy. You get upstairs and wash those mittens before you bring them anywhere near me. And for God's sake, change out of those clothes. I'm surprised the lobsters didn't follow you home. While you're cleaning up, I'll get supper on the table."

"No wonder you don't have a boyfriend. You'd probably nag him to death."

Rebecca thought about her episode in the shower, smiled, and said teasingly, "Who says I don't already have one, huh?"

Ben's eyes lit up. "Really, Becca! You have a boyfriend? How come I haven't met him yet? Does he go to your school? I bet he's the football quarterback..."

Before he launched into a hundred questions, Rebecca mercifully interrupted his rambling. "Okay, you caught me, I don't have a boyfriend. Probably won't have one for quite some time. The boys my age are far too immature for my liking. I think I'll just keep it single for the time being." She propelled hard eyes at him. "Now get upstairs and take a shower! I've smelled seagull shit that smells better than you do."

Ben roared with laughter. "You always say the nicest things, Becca. No wonder I love you like a sister."

Rising from the couch, Rebecca pointed to the stairs. "You get up there and don't come down until you're whistling clean, Mr. Benjamin White. Or I'm liable to throw out the chowder I made and you'll have to fend for yourself."

"Have I ever told you how cute you are when you play mother hen?" That said, Ben climbed the stairs, taking them two at a time, his weight causing them to mewl.

Rebecca smiled even though her tingling had renewed the moment Ben stepped through the front door, inferring that troubled waters lay ahead.

* * *

Ben took his usual seat at the table. He had changed into a denim shirt, clean jeans, if you could call them that, and had, by the smell of him, drowned himself in aftershave. In front of him was a steaming bowl of chowder, loaf of bread, and container of margarine. Greedily he plunged a hand into the loaf and pulled out a half-dozen slices. "Mmmm, mmm, I've been thinking about this all day." Hungrily, he scooped a spoonful of the creamy substance into his mouth, not caring that it was hot enough to scold his gums.

"Jesus, Ben," complained Rebecca from in front of the sink. "What did you do? Shower in Aqua Velva?"

Ben laughed, dribbling chowder down his chin. "You did say whistling clean, didn't you? Well, here I am, washed and polished. Here, have a sniff." He held out one of his mittens.

Rebecca took her place at the table, and leaned close enough so that she got a good whiff. "That's better. Not by much, but better." She didn't have the heart to tell him that his hands still smelled of bait. It couldn't be helped. Ben had been trapping since he was sixteen years old. The rank would always be on him no matter how hard he tried to erase it. It came with the job. And just like the demanding sea beckoned every male in Bay Ridge Cove, so too was the redolent atmosphere each man inherited. "I suppose this means you and Helen are going out tonight?"

Ben swallowed. "Yup. We're going to see the new *Saw* flick. Helen loves to have the pants scared off her. Know what I mean?" He winked. "Hey, how come you're not having any chowder?"

"Please. Just preparing it was enough to make me puke. If I put any of *that* into my mouth, I'd have to kill myself. Then where would you be? Don't worry, I'll have a sandwich or something later. As far as Helen's pants are concerned, that's more information than I need to know."

"Suit yourself. Means there's more for me." Dunking another slice of day-old bread into the broth, he slurped it back. "You don't know what you're missing. Tastes as good as Mom's used to. Well, almost." He drained the bowl, lifting it to his mouth until every chunk of mackerel was jammed between his cheeks, then asked for another.

At the mention of their mother, Rebecca imagined Deseray standing by the stove where she spent most of her days when she wasn't washing, ironing, or cleaning the house. Absently, Rebecca refilled Ben's bowl and set it in front of him. "Do me a favor, okay, Ben?"

"Sure, if I can, you know I will."

"Be careful tonight. You know how dangerous the road from here to Portland can be. There's so many trucks and hardly enough room for them all."

"Thanks for your concern, but I'm the best driver I know, just ask me." He spooned more chowder into his mouth, reached for more bread.

"Ben, I'm serious. Please be careful."

"Okay, okay, I will... I promise. Jeez, what flew up your skirt?"

"Nothing. It's just that." She paused for a moment. How would she explain this sudden concern without sounding like a complete lunatic? Then it came to her. Being a fisherman, Ben was prone to superstition and bad omens. "There's a full moon tonight, and, well, you know as well as I do, strange things happen during a full moon. Usually bad things."

Ben's spoon stopped halfway to his mouth.

Rebecca could see that the wheels were suddenly turning.

"You know," said Ben. "I've been feeling something strange all day, and I couldn't quite put a finger on it. How could I not know it was a full moon? Okay, I'll be extra careful tonight. Jeez, maybe I shouldn't go out at all."

Suddenly, the house trembled, ancient boards groaned, windows rattled. A freight train of a gust whipped and roared, then, just as quickly, retreated. Rebecca's blood rushed to her feet, firecrackers igniting the lengths of her arms and legs compelling the suffocating fear to intensify. Still, she knew she could not stop Ben and Helen from going out, no matter how strong her feelings were. She couldn't protect Ben every minute of the day. Nobody could. If she were to suddenly admit to him that she considered herself gifted, he might distance himself from her. Maybe even fear her. Something she couldn't live with, she loved him that much. "Of course you should go out. Helen would be very disappointed if you didn't. I just think you need to take every precaution. So that you come home safely. You know, because of the full moon and all the silliness that comes with it."

Ben's eyes narrowed. "Jeez, thanks, Becca. Now I don't know what to do."

"You're going to go out and have a good time, that's what you're going to do."

"You're right. Shit on the full moon." He drained his second bowl and considered having another, but he'd eaten all of the bread; and if he didn't pick Helen up on time, it wouldn't be the full moon he need be afraid of. Helen's temper was far more to fear than any superstition. Rising to his full height, he stretched, patted his belly, and put his bowl in the sink. "Make sure you save what Dad doesn't eat," he said, and placed his hands on Rebecca's shoulders and gave them a brotherly squeeze.

Rebecca aversely ignored the smell. Smiling, she looked up at him. "Say hi to Helen for me, okay?"

"I'll do better than that. How about I invite her over for dinner tomorrow? We could have ourselves a barbeque. Supposed to be a nice day. I'll pick up some ribs and corn, and I'll get Helen to make a dessert. Maybe a chocolate cake, or even better, a nice blueberry pie."

The thought of having barbecued ribs set Rebecca's gastronomic juices flowing. She couldn't remember the last time she enjoyed ribs smothered in sauce. Having Helen for company would be a greatly appreciated change to the usual threesome. "That sounds like a great plan. Helen and I could girl-talk. Maybe plan some things."

"Good. It's settled then. Make sure you tell Dad when he gets home. Now I better get going. Helen gets off in a few minutes."

"Have fun."

"We will." Lowering his face, Ben kissed his sister on the forehead. "See you later, alligator."

"After a while, crocodile."

Ben was out of the house in a blink, the Buick roared to life, gravel crunched, then he was gone.

Rebecca cleared the table and put the remaining chowder into a Tupperware bowl, and stored it in the fridge. The house was eerily quiet. If there was one thing Ben could do, it was to fill a room with his presence. She missed that every time he went out, for the house atop Dover Bluff Road had its peculiarities. It could be eerily quiet one moment, then filled with the haunting sounds of its age and the voluble breath of the Atlantic next.

Having to eat, Rebecca grabbed an apple, went to the living room, and turned on the Hitachi. She stared at the screen, chomping bite-sized pieces of the fruit while channel-surfing, not really concentrating on what she was doing. Her mind was elsewhere, horrible thoughts running their course. After five or so minutes, she decided she needed to do something to deflect the unwelcome missives. Discarding the half-eaten apple, she picked up *Romeo and Juliet* and made her way to her room where she would not be disturbed when Jim Bounty dropped Ray off. Whenever that was going to be. Knowing her father, there was no doubt Jim would be invited in for a nightcap. An encounter Rebecca wanted to avoid, at all cost.

Turning the nightstand light on, Rebecca lit an aromatic candle with matches she kept in the drawer and set it next to the radio. A gold flame danced to the rhythmic breeze pushing its way through the break in the window. She sat Bandit the Bear next to her. There was no sound coming from the radio even though it was still on, so she gave it a whack. The Doobie Brothers' "What a Fool Believes" filtered through the speaker.

Opening the six-by-nine cover, crossing one leg over the other, Rebecca settled in, the initial paragraph catching her attention.

PROLOGUE:

CHORUS

Two households, both alike in dignity
In fair Verona, where we lay our scene.
From ancient grudge break to new mutiny,
Where civil blood makes civil hands unclean.
From forth the fatal lions of these two foes
A pair of star-crossed lovers take their life,
Whose misadventured piteous overthrows
Doth with their death bring their parents' strife.
The fearful passage of their death-marked love
And the continuance of their parent' rage
Which but their children's end, naught could remove
Is now the two-hours traffic on our stage;
The which if you with patient ears attend,
What here shall miss, our toil shall strive to mend.

* * *

3

Eden Montana
The Double B Ranch
5:00 p.m., Western Standard Time

JOHNNY Black pushed the mouth of the shovel into the needle-covered earth surrounding Anvil Pine, a hundred-foot Douglas fir rooted almost center to the three thousand acres making up the ranch. The great tree had been nicknamed Anvil Pine by Johnny's great-great-grandfather, Jake Black, when the tree was only twenty feet tall. Its roots had grown out and around a massive rock fashioned like a metalworker's anvil. Rock and roots were covered in moss, supplying the tree with a slick green skirt at the base on its northern lateral.

Being a half-breed, his natural mother a full-blooded Cherokee, Johnny had adopted her strong chin, copper complexion, raven black hair, and the proud acquiescence of her people. From his father Buck, he'd adopted height, strength, and grey-blue eyes so soft they appeared to be translucent. Tutored by his father since he was a boy, he possessed an uncanny business acumen, judging fairly and wisely when his father wasn't around to finalize ranch matters.

Linda Birdhumming had given birth to Johnny when she was seventeen, having married Buck Black the proceeding day of her sixteenth birthday. Johnny was sixteen when she died, never recovering from a persisting bout of double pneumonia. When she was alive, she was Johnny's mentor and confidant, instructing him in the ways of her people and how to see the *truth* in others.

Johnny did not believe he could ever feel such loss again. He was wrong.

A single tear escaped the welling of his eyes. He wiped it away with a gloved hand, sniffed. Using the heel of a boot, he put all of his weight down on the verge of the shovel.

The ground cracked and broke free. He tossed the rich black soil over a shoulder and plunged the shovel deep.

Lying on the ground next to him, wrapped in stiff canvas, was Dallas, the eight-year-old golden lab that had been Johnny's constant companion since a pup. Buck Black had given the ball of fur to him on his twelfth birthday, proclaiming, "Every boy needs a dog, Johnny. Had one when I was your age, and I suspect this one will become as loyal to you as mine was." Loyalty was only one of Dallas's attributes. He also held the roles of champion cattle herder, bird dog when Johnny and Buck went pheasant hunting, keeper of Johnny's most private secrets, and lifesaver.

He tossed another shovel full of wet soil onto the growing mound. High above him, riding the air in search of rodents, a hawk screeched. Covering his eyes, Johnny looked up into the brilliant blue Montana sky. Its wings spread sharp, the great bird circled the globe of the sun. It screeched once more, long and cutting. Johnny jammed the mouth of the shovel deep enough so that it stood on its own. He watched the hawk's circling grow wider with each rotation, its seemingly effortless flight almost hypnotic. Johnny closed his eyes, still seeing the great bird circling on the mirror overview of his mind. Calling upon his ancestors for vision, he thanked brother bird for seeking him out.

A memory spilled forward, as clear as if it happened only yesterday.

It was four years ago and the weekend of Johnny's sixteenth birthday. Buck had taken him on a fall camping trip to Wolfe Creek where it was said the trout were plentiful and grew well beyond their average size. It was to be a coming-of-age outing. One that Johnny had been looking forward to for months. They had set camp along the edge of the creek where a small patch of rye grass and clover split the heavy forest bordering both sides of swift-moving waters. They'd had to leave the pickup truck and walk a mile into the dense thicket of trees, carrying their gear on their backs while Dallas, as if knowing exactly where they were headed, bounded happy-go-lucky in front of them.

They'd arrived at their intended destination just as the sun disappeared behind the tips of tall pines. At first glance, Johnny wondered why it was called a creek, for it was at least fifty feet from shore to shore, with boulders and dead wood rising from its rippling surface.

Night fell by the time they'd set up tent and fashioned an in-ground cooking area with rocks they'd gathered at the river's crag. Dallas, snatching scents of the forest's many animals, meandered about the perimeter, his nose held high in the air. But he did not for one second leave Johnny unguarded, for he was as much a protector as a loyal friend.

Dinner consisted of pork chops, corn bread, a can of beans, and Johnny's first taste of beer. Dallas got to eat the leftover bones, some beans, and a half can of Dr. Ballard's beef stew. While father and son ate and drank, the forest awakened with the sounds of night creatures. Owls hooted, small rodents scurried in the brush, and bats, attracted by the fire, flittered above their heads. Once supper was over and Buck had successfully scared Johnny with several ghost stories, they retired for the night. A night that offered Johnny no rest because of Buck's snoring, Dallas's strong flatulence, and the scurrying creatures that seemed to be just beyond the tent's thin walls.

When morning came, Johnny was excited to get started, so they put their tackle together, slipped into their waders, had several cups of coffee and whatever corn bread was left over, and headed to the creek. Buck instructed Johnny to take the south trail for no more than ten minutes and try his luck there. "You have your air horn with you, boy?" asked Buck.

"Right here under my vest," replied Johnny, giving the vest a pat.

"Good, now you give that thing a blast should you get into any trouble." "I'll be fine. Five bucks for the biggest trout?"

"You're on, boy. Synchronize your watch with mine." Buck looked to his Timex. "I got six a.m. on the dot. Be back here in an hour. If neither of us has caught anything by then, we'll try farther up."

Checking his watch, Johnny found that it was five minutes slow, so he adjusted it and began to head south along a deer path well worn into the river's shoulder.

Out of character, Dallas remained with Buck, even when Johnny tempted him with one of his favorite treats. "Fine, traitor," he said and continued his trek into the brush without looking back.

Johnny nearly lost the trail several times, finding himself moving away from Wolf Creek where the forest grew thick and the sound of running water was lost. Nonetheless, using his keen sense of direction, he righted himself, and in a few moments was back on track. When he assumed ten minutes had vanished, he checked his watch and found that he had walked for an extra four minutes. The extra time was well worth it though. A bend in the topography opened, revealing several boulders that created a natural dock leading into the fast-moving waters.

The area rear of the boulders gave way to a hedge of goose berries, leaving ample room for Johnny to cast his fly without having to worry about overhanging branches. At first glance, it appeared that no one else had discovered this spot, until Johnny saw a Styrofoam worm container and a coffee cup wedged within the outcropping of rocks. "Fucking pigs," he muttered to himself then proceeded to put his tackle together. He tied a black Sisco to the four-foot leader then checked the green float line to be sure there were no kinks or knots. With everything in good order, he carefully mounted the rocks until he was standing on the farthest juncture. From this vantage point, he could see the creek and its tiers of white water rapids forcing their way south.

Circling above him, riding the currents, was a hawk, its wings spread fully, talons tucked beneath the triangle of its red tail. It climbed higher and higher on the updraft, screeching each time it completed a full circle. Johnny took this as a sign of good fortune and began the poetic rhythm of casting. After three attempts, he finally got the fly to land next to an outcropping of rock where a deep, still pool lay from which a thin branch breached its flat surface. The fly no sooner struck the water when there was a large swirl and a heady splash. Johnny waited a quick moment until the line firmed, then set the hook.

The trout dove deep then headed into the wash, and pulled harder than any fish he had ever caught. Line spilled from the reel. Johnny kept the rod taut; if the fish had a notion to jump, there was less chance of losing it. Johnny whooped and laughed aloud, the jingle jangle of his voice echoing off the dense forest of pines beyond the river.

Although he had yet to see the full body of the fish, he was sure that he was going to be richer by five dollars once he landed it. *If* he landed it.

The fish made several attempts at freeing itself by crisscrossing the width of the creek then exploded from the surface not ten feet in front of Johnny. The early-morning sun, for a brief moment, captured its coloration. It was a rainbow and weighed, in Johnny's estimation, at least ten pounds. After ten minutes of man against fish, Johnny heard a disturbance in the berry bushes behind him. He craned his neck, thinking it was Dallas coming to join him. Instead, what he saw was the snout, whiskers, and slanted molasses glare of a cougar. Johnny froze. The trout pulled, bending the rod to the breaking point.

The great cat emerged from the bushes, stepping forward, very slowly, revealing the full length of its body. Its tail was low to the ground, quivering like the rattle of a venomous snake. With its lips curled back, it let out a sound Johnny would never in his life forget.

Johnny was trapped. His first thought was to jump into the rushing water, but he realized that if his waders filled, he would surely drown. If he made his way down from the rocks and ran, the mountain cat would surely pounce upon him. Then he remembered the air horn within his vest. Careful not to make his movements too elaborate, he released the rod from his grip. The trout, sensing it was free, pulled the length of graphite into the water, taking it upstream and out of sight.

Not taking his eyes off the big cat, Johnny carefully reached into his vest until his finger found the air horn. The cougar took several quick steps, its eyes locked on Johnny's. What happened next seemed to happen in slow motion. At the same moment Johnny depressed the air horn, the cat ran, leaping into the air, its front paws ready to tear at Johnny's flesh. Courageously and from out of nowhere, Dallas struck the airborne cat on its side with the blunt of his head. The cougar rolled, solidly striking one of the rocks. It let out a roar just as Dallas sunk his teeth into its back. Johnny depressed the lever once more.

The earsplitting blast caused the cat to right itself and slink away. Dallas stood firm in his place, barking and growling. Cat and dog squared off, the cat moving backward, Dallas moving forward, bloody teeth bared.

Johnny found a rock lying at his feet and threw it with all his might. It struck the cat on its front leg. Hissing, the cougar turned and bounded back into the bushes. Dallas chased after it, ignoring Johnny's calls to stay put. Branches snapped, the cat fled deep into the woods with Dallas in hot pursuit.

"Come back, Dallas! Come back!" Johnny yelled at the top of his lungs. Descending the natural dock, he stood at the edge of the gooseberry bushes, terrified that he might not ever see Dallas again, for a domesticated dog was no match for a wild cat, especially one that was wounded.

Several long, agonizing moments of silence passed. Then there was a terrible roar from deep within the forest. Johnny's heart pounded against his sternum. Blood rushed to his feet. His mind conjured an image of Dallas lying on the forest floor torn to shreds. Dropping to his knees, Johnny cried, "No, Dallas, no!" He gave the air horn three long blasts, the international signal for distress. When the echo waned, he heard something moving through the brush toward him. At first, Johnny thought it was the cat coming back to finish him off, until there was a pained whimper and Dallas emerged. Blood covered his back and rear left leg. Quite apparent was a ripped opening of flesh high on his shoulder.

Opening his arms, the loyal lab went to Johnny, tail wagging, soulful eyes filled with the agony of his wounds, and lapped at Johnny's face. "You crazy mutt," cried Johnny and carefully examined Dallas's wounds, keeping one eye on the edge of the berry bushes.

Buck came running along the path. He had taken off his waders and fly vest. In his hand was a gun Johnny hadn't seen before. Buck's face was red from the quarter-mile exertion, and he was breathing hard. When he saw Johnny and Dallas, he stopped and surveyed the area before kneeling next to his son. "You okay, boy? What the hell happened? Why is Dallas covered in blood? Are you hurt?"

After Johnny explained the bizarre occurrence, the three went back to camp. Buck cleaned and sutured Dallas's wounds with ordinary thread and needle. Dallas complained not once. "Looks to me like that cat took the worst of it. You've got some kind of friend there, boy. A real hero."

A real hero. The memory faded.

Johnny found himself knee deep into the hole. He had been digging without realizing it, lost in memory. Above him the hawk screeched. Johnny watched. The bird stopped circling, quiet in the air, its wings fluttering madly above its head. Its keen eyes had spotted its game somewhere among the grasses. It hung for a spell then dropped, sluicing through the air like a loosed arrow, its wings tucked, talons forward. It struck the earth hard, disappearing from sight.

Johnny plunged the shovel back into the softening earth. He had yet to run into a root, and the ground was giving to his efforts willingly.

A train of Black Angus cattle headed toward the creek running east to west through the ranch. They moved slowly, herding their calves, heads bobbing in unison. Most were ear-tagged, ready to be transported to the slaughterhouse in Great Falls. Only a dozen or so of the younger ones would remain on the ranch for breeding, then once they were old enough, and at the proper market weight, they too would be trucked for slaughter.

Johnny had learned long ago not to get too attached to them. "They're steaks on a hoof," Buck had warned. "That's all. So don't go namin' any of them. They're not pets. They're what put food on the table."

The cattle passed and disappeared behind one the ranch's many slopes.

Weighed by its catch, the great bird emerged a prairie dog secure in its clutches. It powered its mighty wings and rose until it was once again supported by the updraft, then headed west to its nest.

Lightning and Thunder, a pair of Appaloosas Johnny had reared since they were folds, came trotting to the cross fence dividing cattle from horses. The commotion Johnny was making with the shovel had caused them to become curious. Stopping at the fence, they reared their heads, neighing for Johnny's affection.

"Not now," he called out to them from the deepening hole. Buck had instructed him to dig the hole at least five feet deep so there would be no desecration of the grave by bears, coyotes, or cougars. "A wild animal will only dig so far, then he'll give up and move on to something less tiresome," he'd said.

Johnny's long hair was slick with sweat, his shirt glued to his back, the muscles of his forearms tight with wear, and he was sure he had eaten a pound of dirt. He stopped digging for a moment, lifted his cowboy hat, and wiped at the perspiration gathered on his forehead. The late-afternoon sun had burned a line across the collar of his skin.

He directed his eyes to Dallas's golden paw protruding from a small opening in the canvass. He couldn't willfully comprehend his friend was gone. Using teeth, he removed one of the gloves, touched the extended paw, then reached into the canvass and smoothed a hand over Dallas's chest. A brewing anger, just beneath the surface of his flesh, increased tenfold. Fresh tears mingled with the sweat on his face. "Fucking bastards," he muttered. "I promise you, my friend. I'm going to find out who did this to you. I swear on my ancestors." He removed his hand from the canvass all bloodied and covered with golden hairs. Reaching for the spirit bag hanging from his belt, he opened the drawstring and placed several strands within it. He pulled the strings tight, fastening the leather pouch back onto his belt and regloved his hand. Reclaiming the shovel, he dug with the coldhearted angst of a man who had just learned how to hate for the very first time.

It was Johnny's father who had discovered Dallas's lifeless, bloodied body on one of the back roads encompassing the ranch. It was just after the lunch hour. In the late morning, like he always did, Dallas had taken to the back roads for his daily workout.

Buck was working the cutter horses when he heard the retort of a rifle echo across the land. Hearing a rifle being used was not an unfamiliar sound. Many times ranchers could be heard shooting at the prairie dogs that threatened, with each summer, to take over a field if they weren't controlled. But the shot Buck heard was from a much larger firearm. He got into his truck and investigated. When he turned onto RR#12, he noticed a blood trail on the side of the road. Slowly, he followed then saw something lying near the ditch just ahead of him. As he neared, Dallas's still body became terribly apparent.

Dallas had been shot once in the chest and, from the blood trail on the shoulder of the road, had walked more than a half mile, the slug still burning inside. Buck put the lifeless Dallas in the back of the truck and drove him to the ranch house. Once there, he carried him to the front porch and called out to Rose, the loyal lab drooped in his arms.

Rose, Johnny's stepmother, a Navajo Buck had married two years after Johnny's natural mother passed, came out of the house and dropped to her knees, instant tears washing her face. "What happened?"

"Someone shot him," bemoaned Buck.

"Why? Why would someone do such a thing? Dallas was a good boy. Never trouble to anyone."

"I don't' know, Rose, but when Johnny finds out, I reckon there'll be hell to pay. I suppose we better find out where he is and tell him the bad news."

"Johnny will be crushed," sniffed Rose.

"He'll be a helluva lot more than that."

* * *

Sweat dripped from his brow. The shovel bit hard into the earth. Johnny envisioned Dallas walking along the back road. He could see clearly his wagging tail, pink tongue, soulful eyes, and the flame of white centering his chest. The way his backside moved from side to side as if he hadn't a care in the world. A pickup truck pulls up. In Johnny's vision, the driver and passenger are dark silhouettes behind the windshield. The passenger rolls down the window and taunts Dallas into paying attention to him. "Hey, boy. Hey, boy." Johnny can see Dallas stopping in his tracks to look up at the truck. Then the barrel of a rifle comes out from the open window, a shot rings out.

Dallas is thrown sideways, twisting in agony. The truck speeds away. Johnny can hear the passenger and driver laughing, laughing, laughing.

He tried to shake the image from his conscience, but the retort of the rifle and the laughter resound deep within the darkest regions of his mind. He had a good notion as to who was responsible. Two of the Thompson boys had been found guilty of shooting a half-dozen horses two years previous. They'd been sentenced to nine months in reformatory; and their father, Maynard Thompson, was fined $5,000 for each head lost, the judge presiding over the case a horse lover himself. The best way to settle the score was to hit Maynard where it counted, in the pocketbook. However, Johnny had to be absolutely sure before he went off half-cocked. The only way to be sure was to hear it from their own lips, so Johnny schemed, pushing the shovel into the earth.

Twenty minutes later, Johnny was neck deep into the grave. Since he stood six feet and a bit, he figured it was deep enough. He threw the shovel onto the gathered mound of earth and drew a glove over his face. The sting of blisters could be felt through the hide. His boots were caked with dirt, and his shirt was wet through and through.

Reaching, he took hold of the canvass. Alive, Dallas weighed no more than seventy-five pounds, but when Johnny lifted the enshrouding sack, he found his heft had nearly doubled. *Dead weight.*

Lightning and Thunder were still tight against the fence, huffing and neighing. In the background, the Little Belt mountain range shone bronze and pewter in the eye of the sun.

Johnny held the body of Dallas close to his own, cradling his friend like a mother would her child. A fresh stream of grimy tears dripped from his chin, dark dots against the canvass. "I know that somehow you can hear me, boy. I want you to know that I loved you dearly. You were the best friend I had, and I know you loved me just as much. We had some great times together, you and me, and in case I didn't tell you enough, thanks for saving my life. If it weren't for you... well... That damned cat would have got the best of me." Drawing the hot canvass to his face, he pressed it against Dallas's chest. "And I know that when it's my time, you'll be the first one to greet me. I truly believe that. So instead of saying good-bye, I'll just say so long. Until we meet again." Gently he laid the body of Dallas onto the cold floor of the grave. After a long final look, Johnny hoisted himself from the rectangular hole.

He lifted the shovel, and sighed deeply. A blinding, endless wash of tears dripped from his face. Johnny Black tossed the first clumps of earth over his best friend.

* * *

Shoveling the final pounds of dirt onto the grave, lost in memoriam, Johnny was unaware that Buck had parked his truck not twenty feet behind him.

"You just about done here, son?" asked Buck.

Startled, Johnny spun on his heels to see his father standing not three feet away. He was wearing his favorite Stetson and a denim shirt, the sleeves of which were rolled up to the elbows. One hand rested on the hunting knife hitched to his belt, the other wiped sweat from his brow. Lorne Greene sideburns gleamed white in the high afternoon sun. The blue in his eyes radiated as if an ice fire burned behind them. His jeans still bore the stains of Dallas's blood. Earlier, he had dropped Johnny and the canvass-wrapped body of Dallas off, telling him that what needed to be done should be done alone. "You raised him good. Now it's time for you to bury him," he said. "Sometimes, a man's gotta do what a man's gotta do. Dallas would expect nothing less from you."

That was more than two hours ago.

Son. How long had it been since Johnny heard Buck Black address him in such a manner? He couldn't recall, that's how long. "Yeah, just about. I need a few more minutes, okay?"

"Looks like you done a fine job, Johnny. You say your good-byes now. I already said mine. Rose is makin' roast for dinner, so don't be too long. We'll have ourselves a kinda farewell dinner in Dallas's honor. I'll be waitin' for yah in the truck." Turning, Buck headed back to the pickup, lighting a cigarette as he walked.

"Okay, Dad. I'll be right there," said Johnny over the agitated state the horses were in. He went to the foot of Anvil Pine and picked up the makeshift cross he had fashioned from two sticks of hickory. Using the flat of the spade, he hammered it into the earth at the head of the grave. Then from his back pocket, he removed Dallas's blue collar and placed it over the cross. Down on one knee, he read the words inscribed on one of the tags, "For love of man or beast." He'd read that endearment somewhere and had it engraved onto the tag. Emotions took hold of him once more. Anger danced with grief. Love and hate intertwined, giving birth to remorse and guilt.

Suddenly, the ground around him was obscured in shadow. A large cumulus cloud, having crept in from the south, positioned itself in front of the sun. Without warning, a westerly wind blew across the ranch. The great Anvil Pine swayed, its great bows wailing the laments of more than a century past.

Johnny stared at the grave and its marker. So intense was the sudden gust, it lifted the collar from its wooden mount. The tags jingled, and for the briefest of moments, Johnny imagined he could hear Dallas howl with the wind. Loosened earth twisted above the newly created grave. Johnny watched it spin and lift away as if it were carrying Dallas's spirit with it. He smiled and looked up to the sky. Righting himself and standing fully, he took in the land that surrounded him from east to west, north to south, the vast fields and the mountains stretched across the flat horizon. "This is the last time I will come to this place," he told himself. Resting a hand atop the cross, he silently said good-bye. *Our time is done here, my friend. Until we meet again.*

He went to the waiting Appaloosas and stroked each of them on their strong necks. Lightning, the larger of the two, closed one eye like he always did. "Thanks for keeping me company," whispered Johnny. The ears of each horse twitched as if bothered by bothersome flies, and they bowed their heads, listened to their master. "You're the only friends I got left. Now go on. Run as fast as you can. Fast as the bewitching wind."

The horses nodded, flared their nostrils, turned, and bolted across the acres, their hooves tossing large clumps of earth high into the air. Johnny watched them for a moment as each in turn took the lead. Leaning into the cross fence, he tipped his hat back and contemplated the events in his life that had changed him forever. He thought about Linda, his beautiful mother, who had been taken from him so young. He thought about Dallas, a life cut short and a true friend, brutally murdered by cowards. He thought about Buck and how disappointed he would be once Johnny informed him he had no intention on grooming cutting horses and herding cattle for the rest of his life. Then he thought about the means in which he would seek retribution against those responsible for killing a defenceless Dallas.

There was something else egging at him though. Something he could not quite put a finger on. It had been reoccurring for some time, pulling at him from the inside as if there were a hook working to set itself free. Was it a sign that maybe it was time to seek out a living of his own? Pulling him toward another path, another direction? Or was it a prelude to the events that had just occurred and would occur? A warning Johnny had ignored and now Dallas was dead? Whatever it was, it was growing stronger, and Johnny had the feeling that, yet again, his life was going to be altered in some way or another, be it good or bad.

A short blast from the pickup shook Johnny from his thoughts. Lightning and Thunder had all but disappeared. All that remained was a distant cloud of dust. Pushing away from the fence, he picked up the shovel and walked toward the truck. Not once did he look back.

* * *

Once Johnny was in the truck, he put a boot up on the dash, leaned back in the seat, and pulled his hat over his eyes.

"You okay, Johnny?" asked Buck, lighting another Lucky Strike, sweat rolling from his brow. He put the truck into gear and pointed it toward the ranch house.

"I'm fine I guess. Best as can be expected under the circumstances." Johnny crossed his grimy arms over his chest, took a deep, settling breath.

"Don't go bein' too hard on yourself. What's done is done, there's no changin' that. I know it's goin' to take some time for you to get over what happened. I also know that if I were in your shoes, I would be schemin' right now on what to do about it. I know I can't stop yah, just be careful. Them Thompson boys can be a mean bunch, especially when one of them's wounded. They ain't right in the head, just like their old man. If you ask me, there must have been a whole lotta inbreedin' goin' on to create such a vile-tempered bunch."

Always, Buck was two steps ahead Johnny. It had been that way since as far back as Johnny could remember. Whenever he got into trouble, or there was good news to share, Buck knew about it before Johnny could explain. "I can handle myself," he said almost defiantly.

"I know you can. Seen it for myself many a time. But them boys don't play fair. You take on one and beat him, you got the whole twisted clan after yah."

Johnny hadn't considered that he might have to take on all six of the Thompson boys. His sight was set on just those responsible. Maybe the Thompsons had nothing to do with what happened? Maybe it was just some passerby, a hunter maybe, who saw the chance for a kill and took it? Johnny doubted it, but still. "That's something I'll have to find out for myself," he said. "Like you keep reminding me, a man's gotta do what a man's gotta do."

"Fair enough. Just be smart about it, okay?"

"Sure, Dad. I won't put the cart before the horse. You can count on it."

"Good. That's the way your mother and I raised yah, bless her heart. God has a plan for every man, Johnny, be they good or bad. You remember that and everything will work out just fine." Buck flicked ashes out the window then punched a number on the hands-free cell fastened to the dash. After a couple of rings, Johnny's stepmother Rose answered.

"Hello," she said.

"Yeah, it's me. We'll be home shortly. Dinner just about ready?"

"Just about. Maybe in an hour."

"Good. That'll give us time to clean up. See yah in a few." Buck hit the hang-up before Rose could say anything further. He knew she would start asking questions about Johnny's emotional state and that was something he felt Johnny didn't need at the moment. Though it didn't show, Buck Black was just as angry about Dallas' murder as Johnny was. Whatever was running through Johnny's mind would have to stay the course, and Buck would have to do his best not to interfere. Not unless he absolutely had to.

Neither father nor son said another word during the long drive back to the ranch house. There was no need to, each of them having their own demons to do battle with.

* * *

4

A Time to Remember

THE table was set with the finest cutlery and white damask. Crystal glasses saved for only the best occasions stood empty at the heads of Rose's best china. A bottle of Cabernet Sauvignon stood tall next to Buck's arm. A platter crammed with roast, potatoes, carrots, and onion centered the long oak table. The prime rib was big enough to feed eight hungry men. All of it sparkled under the light of the antler chandelier high in the vaulted cedar. Pine crackled in the floor-to-ceiling river rock fireplace. Landscapes depicting the ranch in various seasons hung like apparitions of a time long since gone. Like the men who used to sit around the dining room table when the ranch supported a half-dozen hands. When thousands of cattle covered the terrain and had to be herded to slaughter, sometimes hundreds of miles away. Men with names like Joe Red, Big Dan, Slim, and Panhandle; but like the dust-covered oils hanging about the Double B, they are just a memory.

Johnny had showered and changed out of the sweat-drenched clothes. He'd taken the time to blow-dry his hair and ponder, with absolute clarity, the events he feared would stay with him for the remainder of his life. He could still hear the shovel biting into the earth, the gunshot that took the life of his already missed friend.

Seated across from him was Buck. He too had changed and was wearing a charcoal grey jacket over one of his best shirts, the one with rhinestones on the lapels, and, forever present, his white Stetson. Buck Black never took his hat off, not even in church, much to the dismay of Father Harper and the rest of the congregation. He started to carve the roast, loosing several thick slices.

The head of the table was reserved for the ghost of Johnny's grandfather. He'd died sitting in the heavy armchair, choking on a chicken bone. If the story was to be believed, his wife had prepared a beef stew for dinner that evening, served with corn bread and a side of wild mushrooms. Buck's recollection of his father was that he was an abusive sort who would beat his sons and wife for the most nonsensical reasons and was believed to have been sexually abusing his three daughters.

On the fateful night, it was said that when he began to choke, turning blue, the family seated around the table watched until he collapsed facefirst into his stew. How the chicken bone became a part of his meal, no one knows and, to this day, remained a secret. The chair has remained empty since that night.

Rose was in the kitchen tending to the blueberry pies, Johnny's favorite. She wore an apron over the dress she usually reserved for Sunday mass, being a converted Christian (on Buck's insistence) and was trying to console herself by humming. She had tied her long black hair into a single braid that lay over one shoulder and was wearing all of her turquoise jewelry. Pieces she'd collected since she was a young girl. Having been a solemnest participant of a marital agreement between Buck and her tribe's elders, she was only two years older than Johnny and thirty years Buck's junior.

Johnny stared at the spot on the floor next to his chair, where, on any other occasion, Dallas would be waiting for any and all scraps Johnny sneaked to him. He can still see Dallas lying there, looking up at him with wonton eyes, tongue loose and dripping. Sadness pressed forward. Johnny was once again immersed in a turbulent sea of existential dread.

"How many slices do you want?" asked Buck.

Johnny remained fixated on the floor. He did not want Buck to see that a tear had slid down his cheek. Buck would consider it a show of weakness. And weakness was something Buck could not tolerate. "Just one please."

"One? You're usually good for three or four."

"Yeah, but I'm just not that hungry."

"Nonsense. You need your strength. You just spent the last couple a hours working your ass off. Rose has cooked this wonderful meal in honor of Dallas. The least you can do is participate. You wouldn't want to disappoint her or *him* now, would yah? I sure know one thing. Dallas would be none too pleased to see all this good beef go to waste."

Wiping at his nose, Johnny looked into the steel blue of his father's eyes. Eyes that had sealed improbable deals. Eyes that could stop a Brahma bull in its tracks. His father was the toughest man he knew. There wasn't a soul worth a lick of salt in Montana that didn't know of Buck Black's exploits. Once, he'd taken on four men at the Big Sky Saloon and bested them. No one ever fucked with Buck Black without dire consequences.

Johnny's stomach loudly moaned the need for food.

"See, there you go," said Buck. "Even your stomach is telling yah it needs food, so come on, cowboy up."

Taking a deep breath, Johnny swallowed his emotions. Buck was right. If he was going to exact his plan, he would need all the nourishment he could get. Taking on one of the Thompson boys was hard enough. Engaging two would be nearly impossible, unless of course they were drunk, which was what Johnny was counting on. Loose lips sank ships, and Johnny knew enough about the Thompsons to know that once they'd taken to drinking, they would boast about their transgressions to just about anyone with an ear. "You're right, Dad. I should be remembering all the good things Dallas brought to this family. What's done is done. There's nothing that can change it. So I'll have a couple a slices please and a heap of potatoes." Johnny held out his plate. Buck filled it.

"I know you think you've got things all figured out, but why don't you wait a couple a days, see what comes to the surface. Them boys may be tough, but they ain't all that smart. If any of them was responsible, word will soon get round. You can count on it. Call it braggin' rights."

Rose entered the dining room with one of the pies in her hands. She placed it on the table and looked sternly at both men. "You shouldn't be encouraging him, Buck. If those boys are responsible, then they will be punished either by God or by the law. Either way, they'll get what's coming to them." She took a seat next to Buck and placed a napkin over her lap. Her face was set in stone, but she knew deep down no amount of posturing on her part was going to change the wheels that were already in motion.

"You mind your place, Rose. This is between Johnny and me. We'll settle things the way God meant it to be. Remember your Bible? An eye for an eye. Been that way since forever." He went to fill her glass.

"None for me," said Rose, placing a hand over the mouth of the glass.

"Not even to toast Dallas. Come on now, just a little."

Rose never drank. She had seen what it did to her people, to her father, who had given her up unceremoniously for a small chunk of land. The bottle stole their lives and, in the end, had consumed her father, converting him from a well-respected elder to an incoherent, mean-spirited, lascivious letch who wrecked havoc among the community, especially amid the younger. "I will say a special prayer for Dallas tonight. To help guide him into the afterlife."

"Suit yourself." Buck filled his glass to the rim then offered some to his son. "Johnny?"

"Just a little, okay," said Johnny. He held his glass halfway across the table. "Wine gives me a headache, and that's something I prefer not to deal with right now."

Buck filled Johnny's glass halfway, raised his own, and said, "Here's to Dallas. He was a good ole boy. Best damn herder I ever saw. There weren't a mean stroke in him. He protected his home and kept us good company when we needed it. I will miss him."

Both men took a healthy drink. Buck looked deep into his son's eyes. "Got anything to add, Johnny?"

Johnny looked down at the empty space beside his chair. Dallas was gone. The only evidence of his ever being there were golden hairs weaved within the carpet. He swallowed hard, a log burst in the fireplace startling him. He took in his stepmother's face then Buck's, whom he could see was getting impatient. Patience not being one of his father's virtues.

"Well, boy?" asked Buck, clearing his throat.

Raising the crystal to eye level, Johnny looked around the room to the empty seats surrounding the table. "To my friend. I doubt that there will ever be another dog as loyal or as kindhearted. He was one in a million. I will remember him always. An eye for an eye." He put the wine to his lips and took a small amount into his mouth.

"Good on you, son. Well said." Buck drained his glass and refilled it.

"Yes, that was nice, Johnny," added Rose, worry creasing her brow. "Are you sure that what you're thinking about is the right course of action. I mean, you could get yourself seriously hurt. Then all of this is for not. Dallas's memory would always have a blemish on it. Can't you see that?"

"Rose, that'll be enough," said Buck sternly. Filling his mouth with beef, he pointed his fork at her. "Johnny's old enough to make up his own mind about things without interference from you, *or* me, for that matter. Do I make myself clear?"

Rose nodded. Her self-esteem crumpled. Eyes downcast, she forked some potato into her mouth.

Johnny set his glass on the table, hard. "Okay. That's enough," he said emphatically. "If this meal is to be had in Dallas's memory, then that's what it should be about. I'll hear no more from the both of you. Unless it's something good about Dallas. Do *I* make *myself* clear? What I do is my business, and that's that." He could feel his eyes well. He forced the tears back.

Neither Rose nor Johnny could see the smile Buck was wearing on the inside. He'd raised Johnny right in his estimation. Not a coward's bone in him. Stood for what he believed in. Was none too afraid to take on the world if need be. "Sure, Johnny. Whatever you say. Right, Rose?"

Lifting her eyes, Rose focused on the fireplace. She wanted to say so much more, but knew better. She'd felt, on several occasions, what it was like to go against the grain in the Black household. Not that she feared Johnny would ever strike her, but Buck's back hands had had a sobering effect upon her. She'd learned early and often. "I remember when I was first introduced to Dallas," she began. "After he gave me a good sniff, he lay on his back with his paws in the air, insisting I rub his belly." She looked at Johnny. Smiled. "He was still a puppy in many ways. And I'll never forget the time…"

And that's how it went for the rest of the meal. The three exchanged stories of Dallas's heroics and tomfoolery. When dinner was over, every story remembered, and all but a slice of the blueberry pie was eaten, Johnny excused himself from the table and went to his room where he waited. He lay on his bed, tossing one of Dallas's favorite balls in the air, keeping an eye on the digital clock. He thought about the stories he'd just heard. Visualized Dallas over and over. He remembered him as just a ball of golden fur that fit in the palm of his hand. Reminisced the hero who once saved his life. Remembered the time Dallas had had a run in with a porcupine, returning with quills stuck in his mouth. How he sat bravely while Johnny pulled them out.

Each fond memory played over and over, tallying to the hostility lurking just beneath the surface. Johnny grew more and more bitter with each ticking of the clock. After a time, he stopped tossing the ball and just stared at the wall in front of him. He listened to the beating of his heart, the loathing for those responsible mounting with each passing minute. "An eye for an eye," he told himself. Johnny waited. And waited some more.

* * *

5

Midnight, Eastern Standard Time

SOMETHING woke Rebecca from an unintended sleep. Sounds that at the time didn't make sense because she was lost in a dream world of fantasy. Rubbing at her eyes, she tried to focus. The first thing she noticed was *Romeo and Juliet* lying across her chest. Then she saw her stuffed animals at the foot of the bed still facing the closet wall. Bandit was lying next to her, and she couldn't remember having put him there. She yawned and stretched and was about to get out of bed when from the doorway to her room came a voice.

"Well… Hello… Rebecca. Mmm, my, you sleep beautifully." Jim Bounty stood tall in the doorway, filling the entire frame with his girth. He leered at her and smiled. The radio hissed static.

Rebecca shot up into a sitting position. "What the hell are you doing in my room?" was all she could think to say.

Bounty stepped forward. His face was ruddy from drink, his words somewhat slurred and he was still wearing his work clothes. A Boston Bruin's cap covered his grey spikes. There was a slash of blood and fish guts across his McKenna jacket. "Nowsss that any way to greet your uncle Jim?"

"Where's Ray? If you don't get out of my room this second, I'm going to scream!" A shiver charged Rebecca's spine, and she was suddenly very afraid.

"Your dad'sss on the couch, passs out. Poor man can't hold hisss booze like he usssed to."

Rebecca had to think fast before things got out of control. Jim Bounty had a look on his face that reminded her of a love-starved puppy. "Thanks for bringing Ray home. Now will you please leave. Aren't you supposed to be going out first thing in the morning?"

Bounty stepped farther into the room, rubbed his hands on his pants.

Rebecca could smell his liquor-foul breath, the stench of his unchanged clothes, the combination causing her to gag. She took Bandit into her arms and held him close. She pushed herself farther up the bed until her back was stiff against the headboard.

"I'll leave," said Bounty, taking in the fullness of Rebecca's body. "But nnnot before I get a good night kisss."

"GET OUT! RIGHT NOW! YOU'RE DRUNK! NOW GET OUT!... RAY! WAKE UP! DAD!"

"I'm afffraid the start of World War III wouldn't wake him right now. Come on. Give your uncle a little, a little kiss." Bounty moved toward her, his hands held out in front of him until he was standing at the edge of the bed. His fingers were filthy, nicotine stained. "I seen how you tease all the... the boys, with your short shorts and tight little tops. You should, you should be assshamed of yourself. Parading around with next to nothing on. You should be taught a lesson." The smile faded from his face.

"I'll call the police if you don't leave this instant! You'll go to prison for the rest of your sorry life. Please! If you leave now, I won't tell anyone you were here, okay? You're drunk. You don't know what you're doing." Rebecca began to tremble. Was this going to be the end result of all her special feelings, she wondered. That she was going to be raped right here in her own room. She grabbed the closest thing to her, the bent pages of *Romeo and Juliet* and threw it at him. The book hit Bounty square in the face. He looked down at it lying at his feet and laughed.

Oh, God. Please, please help me, God. Where was Ben when she needed him?

"You've grown up really nice, Rebecca. All I want. All I want isss what you're willing to hand out for, for free." He grabbed her by an ankle, pulled her toward him.

"DAD! PLEASE WAKE UP!" screamed Rebecca with all her voice. But the only sound coming from the main floor was the faint snort of her father's ponderous snoring. She held on to Bandit. Bounty pried her legs apart and grabbed at the snap of her shorts.

"Bet you didn't know I fffucked your mother," he hissed. "Now ssstop strugglin. I wouldn't want to have to hit you, but I... I will if I have to."

Rebecca threw Bandit to the floor, pummeled Bounty's chest with her fists. "I don't believe you! Get off me, you bastard!" She spit in his face. "My mother would never have anything to do with the likes of you, you disgusting pig."

Bounty ignored her. In an instant his hand was over her mouth. Rebecca tried to scream again, but to no avail. Then she tried to bite the palm of his hand, but Bounty pressed it so tight against her mouth that she couldn't latch on to flesh. He lowered his face to hers, licked her cheeks, his breath and body odor so foul Rebecca threw up in her mouth. She forced it down, fearing she would choke to death on her own vomit.

Bounty got the snap of her shorts undone, pushed his free hand into her panties. He began to pant, heavily, pressing his full weight on top of her. "I'm going to fffuck you real good, little princess. You're gonna love it, just as, just as much as your mother did."

Tears streamed over Rebecca's face. She tried to twist away from his awful breath and hungry tongue. Her legs were pinned against the mattress. Try as she may, Bounty's weight was too much. She could not move them an inch. She thought if she could at least get one free, she would be able to knee him where it counted. Put an end to his lascivious behavior before things got way out of hand. Not that they hadn't already. What was happening was any woman's worst nightmare come to life, and it gave Rebecca renewed strength. She pushed hard against his chest. Bounty was in the motion of undoing his belt. The harder she pushed, the more it felt as though her wrists would snap.

"Stop... struggling... you little... bitch. You priggy little cunt," said Bounty, his words catching between laboured breaths. Raising a hand, he struck her hard on the side of the head. "That... Wasss... Your... own fault. I promise you... the, the next one... will be much harder."

Little blue lights danced. There was an instant throbbing in her temples. Rebecca thought surely she was going to fade into unconsciousness. She resisted, sucking in quick gulps of air until the little blue lights faded. Fisting her hands, she continued to pound his chest, but it did about as much good as a pea shooter stood in making a dent in a tank. Jim Bounty weighed close to three hundred pounds. Most of it solid, due to hauling lobster traps most of his life. Rebecca's arms grew weak from her efforts. Their eyes locked for the briefest of moments. Bounty's were lost, insane. Closing her eyes, Rebecca prepared herself for the worst.

Then he was off her. It happened so fast, Rebecca wondered if she hadn't dreamed the whole thing. She opened her eyes, blinked tears. Ben had Bounty by the scruff and was hitting him with cannon shots to his stomach. "You fucking bastard!" he roared. "I'm going to kill you! I'm going to fucking kill you!" Ben's hands were like jackhammers, serving blow after blow.

Rebecca gathered herself and reverse-pushed until she was back against the headboard. "Ben! Be careful!" she yelled.

Bounty grabbed Ben by the shoulders and sent a head butt crashing into his face. He was surprisingly agile for his size and age. The Bruin's cap flew off his head. Ben stumbled backward, blood covering his nose and mouth.

"Is that all you got, Ben? I'mmm afraid you'll have to do a lot better thannn that." He laughed like a crazy man, alcohol and lust fuelling his madness.

Ben charged him, head down and wrapped his arms around Bounty's waist. When their bodies collided, the contact sounding like thunder, both men crashed into the nightstand.

The small room went dark, silent. The radio, lamp, and candle were sent crashing beneath the window.

Rebecca could no longer see who had the upper hand. On hands and knees, she moved with caution toward the edge of the bed. When her eyes adjusted to the dark somewhat, she could barely see that Bounty was on top of Ben, delivering hard-sounding blows. Each man grunted with their efforts. Then a spark of orange lit the area around them. The displaced candle had ignited the curtain. A flame curled up the fine lace. Within seconds, it was licking at the ceiling.

Rebecca pressed hands against her head. *This is not happening!*

Ben and Jim Bounty rolled across the floor, impervious to the flames claiming the wallpaper. In seconds, it was swimming across the ceiling in blue waves.

"*Run, Becca, run!*" the voice seemed to come from all around her. It was her mother's. Pleading. Urgent. A thousand questions formed in Rebecca's mind. The south wall was fully engulfed. *What should I do? What can I do? Should I try to help Ben? Or should I try to wake Ray up?*

Faster than Rebecca could believe, the heat in the room intensified and scorched her exposed flesh. Her little refuge from the outside world was black, orange. Bright as a seasoned pumpkin and Coven dark. There was a loud crack overhead. A portion of the ceiling fell onto the bed, narrowly missing her arm. The flaming chunk of house landed on the pile of plush animals. Immediately they began to melt. A green toxic smoke lifted into the air. Rebecca scrambled from the bed. On hands and knees, she worked her way to the door, coughing, struggling for breath, the black smoke drowning her lungs.

With a quick hand, Bounty grabbed her by the hair, his weight still pressing Ben into the floor.

"Let go of me, you bastard!" screamed Rebecca. She managed to clutch Bounty's thick wrist and fiercely bit down until her teeth sank in. Bounty howled. When she let go, there was a chunk of flesh in her mouth. Repulsed, she quickly spat out.

"You little bitch!" Bounty drew back his arm, sent a punishing blow to the side of Rebecca's head, casting her into the dresser. Drawers flew open. The dresser came crashing down. Rebecca veered, just in time. Grabbing a towel from one of the open drawers, she tried to thwart the flames around her. However, the action only seemed to magnify their life; and before she knew it, fire claimed every wall, the ceiling, filling the room in a hellish drone. She looked to the men still dishing out blows. Ben's face was a wash of blood and welts. "Ben! Get up! The house is burning down! OH PLEASE, BEN! PLEASE GET UP!" But Jim Bounty's blows kept Ben pinned to the floor as though he had every intention of burning with the century-old house.

For a brief second, Ben locked his eyes on Rebecca's. "Get out, Becca! Get out!" he yelled and began to choke.

There was a *swoosh*. Rebecca's bed went up in flames. *Run, Becca, run!*

Deseray White's voice exploded in her mind. Rebecca saw the handle of the suitcase beneath the bed and scrambled for it. Just as she pulled it out, the bed collapsed, its wooden frame ravaged by the insatiable flames. She dragged the case across the floor. Her mind was reeling, flesh burning. Her life was coming down to what lay ahead in the next few moments. Decisions had to be made. Quickly. She tossed the suitcase through the doorway. *This is it*. She looked at the men on the floor wrapped in aggressive arms and legs. Black smoke rolled over head, thick, thick, thick, the temperature beyond bearable.

Choking, Rebecca realized, if she did not escape, the smoke would easily claim her.

Bounty was in a prone position on top of Ben, legs splayed, offering Rebecca the perfect opportunity for a good shot. She drew back a leg and, with all her field hockey might, sent what should have been a debilitating kick to his groin.

Bounty grunted, laughed, and sent a thunderous blow to Ben's temple.

Ben shouted from the depths of his lungs. "FOR CHRIST'S SAKE, BECCA! GET OUT! NOW!"

"I can't just leave you," coughed Rebecca, tears streaming.

"YOU HAVE TO! NOW GO!" Ben had Bounty's head, had it in a firm lock, the other arm raining blows into the side of his face.

Rebecca knew deep down this was it. The telling signs she had been experiencing had come to fruition. She would never see her brother again. Her mother's voice resounded. *Run, Becca, run.* Bandit lay on the floor next to the fallen dresser. She scooped him into her arms and cried, "I love you, Benjamin White." She gave her brother one final look before running out of the flame-ravished room and down the stairs toward the ponderous sound of her father's snoring.

* * *

Ray White lay on the couch, his face turned into the backrest. One arm was bent over his head, the other dangled toward the floor. Like Jim Bounty, he was still wearing his work clothes.

Grabbing him by the shoulders, Rebecca screamed, "RAY! WAKE UP! THE HOUSE IS ON FIRE!!BEN NEEDS YOU!" She shook him and shook him, but to no avail. The only response, a loud distorted grunt before he returned to snoring again. Taking hold of his arms, she pulled with all her might, gritting her teeth with the effort. She managed to get him half-turned. Ray White's eyes rolled open, and he sort of half-smiled before he slipped back into a drunken stupor. "GODDAMNIT, DAD! YOU WAKE UP RIGHT NOW! Oh, please, can't you hear me!" Voice weak now from all the yelling and from the smoke she had inhaled. She began to sob. *Stop it right this minute. Now's not the time for crying.* She slapped her father hard on the face, leaving a red mark on his cheek. Ray White smiled then groaned something inaudible, the slap having no effect whatsoever. Grabbing both wrists, she pulled with every ounce of strength she had left. *Okay, Rebecca, you can do this.* She pulled and pulled until the upper half of Ray White's body slipped to the floor. *Thud.*

Suddenly something cracked over head, sounding like a rifle's retort. Rebecca looked up to find that the fire was breathing through a large fissure in the ceiling. Then the ceiling imploded all at once, a large chunk of it, the size of sofa, fell and crashed onto the coffee table, smashing to nothingness the Tall Ship Ben had made.

Realizing she could move her father no further, Rebecca ran into the kitchen and snatched up the phone. She cursed herself that she hadn't thought to call someone sooner. With a shaking hand, she tried to punch 911, but misdialed on the first two attempts hitting the 6 instead of the 9.

Run, Becca, run!

When she finally got the three digits right, she was mortified to find that there was no signal. Somehow the fire had already claimed the phone line. Being the only house atop Dover Bluff Road, and the nearest neighbor a fifteen-minute walk in either direction, Rebecca doubted if anyone realized what was taking place.

Running back into the living room, she tried once more to move Ray, but his more than three hundred pounds glued him to the floor.

The house was full of sound. A roaring beast that was eating everything in its path at a most alarming rate. Its orange tongue lapped at the air from the widening hole in the ceiling. Deadly sparks dripped onto the couch, the big screen.

Kneeling beside her father, Rebecca took his alcohol-swollen face into her hands. He mumbled incoherently. With escape her only alternative, she wept, "Dad. Ray, I'm so sorry. I can't help you. I tried. Really I did. I love you, Dad. I'll always remember you." Standing, she went to the foot of the stairs where she had left Bandit and the suitcase. There was another loud crack from somewhere, everywhere. Rebecca instinctively ducked and closed her eyes. When she opened them, she saw that the fiery beast had claimed the couch, its hell born hunger mere inches from a prone Ray White.

From the second floor came a beseeching cry which was followed by a crash of glass. "BEN!" screamed Rebecca. Smoke rolled over the steps. Orange dark light coming from the upper hall. With a hand covering her mouth, Rebecca attempted to climb the stairs. The rolling black met her halfway and pushed her back. Then lights on the main floor flickered and died. Rebecca screamed, "NO!... NO!... NO!..." She stood there, frozen in the blackness. "*You must leave, Becca. I will guide you.*" Rebecca looked up. Her Mother's ethereal body appeared within the smoke. It hovered there like a dream, a soul light in the living black, her arms stretched out as if to welcome Rebecca into an embrace, tresses of flowing red hair all about her face.

The first instance Rebecca was visited by her mother confirmed what she already knew. That she was different. That she possessed certain gifts no one would accept, *or* understand, especially in the pious-driven community of Bay Ridge Cove. Gifts that would swiftly grow stronger with the passing time. Regrettably, it had taken the premature death of her mother to fortify them.

"Momma? Momma? I'm so frightened."

"*It is time for your journey, Becca. You must leave now. But beware, my daughter. The road holds many obstacles. You must choose wisely. I can only guide you so far.*"

"Will I ever see you again if I leave?"

"*I will stay with you for as long as I can. If we ever do lose contact with each other, remember that I love you.*" Then she was gone, swept by the billowing smoke.

"I love you too, Momma." Reversing her steps, Rebecca picked up the suitcase and tucked Bandit under an arm. Like her bedroom, the main floor was a contrast of light and dark, orange and black. Movement caused her look to the glow emanating from the second floor. A figure, all aflame, teetered on the last riser. A veil of flames as bright as a freshly struck match obscuring the face.

"Ben? Oh god!... Ben?" Frozen with fear, Rebecca watched as the figure took one step, then another. It moved toward her like a present time nightmare.

The flaming figure took two more steps then fell forward. Rebecca moved away from the landing. Tumbling head over heels, Bounty or Ben came to rest, half on the start of the stairs, half on the landing. Burning flesh filled Rebecca's senses. She stared at the burning thing, shivering, her own skin feeling like it was going to melt away. "BEN! BEN!"

It turned its head. Ben's or Jim Bounty's eyes were white, blistering orbs, the flesh around them having been fired away. Rebecca gasped. She looked to the hands and knew with absolute certainty there was no hope for her brother, for on one of them, a signet ring flickered. The same high school honor her father wore. Ben White would not marry his first love, Helen, and he would never grow old, never fulfill his dreams.

Rebecca gazed to the second floor where smoke billowed and whimpered, "Oh god, Ben. I'm so, so, sorry. I love you."

Unable to bear the heat and flames any longer, Rebecca headed for the entrance. She grabbed a denim jacket and runners from the closet as she went. The second she opened the door, a wind spun into the house. It fed the terrible beast, that in a matter of quick minutes had claimed what remained of her family. Stepping into the cool July night, coughing and wheezing, eyes filled with tears, her mother's words echoed in her mind. *Beware, Becca, beware.*

The full of the moon beamed a path toward the cliffs. Ocean air smacked her in the face and gave her a renewed strength. She stood on the front portico for a moment where her brother's gum boots lay askew. Suitcase in hand, she expunged smoke from her lungs and clutched Bandit to her breast. The jacket she slung over the handle of the suitcase. Quickly she slipped into the runners.

Her face, arms, and legs were still hot; and there was no telling how much of her hair had singed away. Rebecca's immediate concern was that no one sees her. She looked to the cars parked on the gravel. The keys were in the pockets of Ben and Jim Bounty, and there was no way she could retrieve them even if she wanted to. *Can't go down Dover Bluff Road,* she reasoned. *People will be coming soon.* Remembering the infrequently used path behind the house, she stepped off the porch and quickly made her way across the gravel driveway and towards the face of the moon.

Something heavy crashed behind her.

Rebecca stopped in her tracks and turned to see that the second floor was fully engulfed. The century house moaned as though it were in agony. The roof over Rebecca's room buckled and caved. She could hear the joists and two-by-fours snapping like twigs. Flames erupted high above the open pitch and licked at the ink blue sky. A gazillion fireflies burst into the night, the beast devouring everything she owned and cared about.

Following the moon path, she ran toward the cliffs. When she could go no farther, she stopped for a moment, opened the suitcase, put Bandit inside, and slipped her arms into the jacket. The path was easily found, a winding black snake that slithered close to the cliff's boundary. With the full face of the moon lighting the way, she was quite certain she would not be seen.

Tall summer dry grasses lashed at Rebecca's legs as she moved, swift as she dared, for the path was no more than five feet from the steep drop to jagged rocks below. *Don't look back, Becca. Don't look back.*

In the distant below, a single siren split the silence. House lights went on all over Bay Ridge Cove. Rebecca would have to seek refuge for the night. Someplace where she knew she would not be found. Where at the crack of dawn, she could hitch a ride with one of the trucks leaving the cannery. *But where?*

She moved silently along the path, the suitcase knocking against her leg, heart hammering heavily. The intake of smoke had weakened her somewhat, she realized; nonetheless, her legs were strong and they obeyed when she asked them to keep moving.

The path began its downward slope toward the wakening town below. Something slithered in the grass not two feet away. *A snake taking advantage of the full moon.* Though she loved all of earth's creatures, snakes frightened her beyond reproach. Quickly she moved. When she estimated she had traveled enough away from the burning house, she stopped to rest for a moment. She set the suitcase on the path and took in the vastness of the bay. It was calm, shimmering under the spotlight of the July moon. A hundred feet below, she could hear the wash of it crashing into the rocks. Sirens grew closer.

The cannery was in full operation, its lights sparkled like pearls along the wharf. A column of white hovered just above the refrigeration building. She could just make out the row of trucks that would soon be transporting canned and fresh lobsters throughout the states. One of them, Rebecca prayed, would be the beginning of her journey.

Standing on the path, she stared at the dark Atlantic. It came to her that it would probably be the last time she would ever see the bay and the full of the moon sitting heavily over Bay Ridge Cove. She thought of her brother and father. Decent men who were happy with the life they had carved. Lives cut short in a most dastardly act of betrayal. Then the sight of Jim Bounty filled her thoughts, all afire, moving slowly toward her, who, in the end, reaped what he deserved, at the expense of her family. Weeping once more, Rebecca felt suddenly cold and frightened. The Atlantic seemed to beckon her, calling her by name, *Rebecca*. Drawing her toward the edge of the cliff. *Come to me.*

"No!" she cried into the night. "Not ever! Do you hear me?! This is my life! Not yours! I can be strong! I will be strong!"

Palming tears, Rebecca sniffed and thought of her beautiful mother. How they danced hand in hand to the sounds of the dysfunctional Panasonic. That's when it came to her. It appeared on the curtain of her mind, for she knew it well. The one place that could offer her shelter for the night. She lifted the suitcase and pressed on, determined not to look back. She would grieve for Ben and Ray another time, for her passage to becoming a starlet had just begun.

A church bell began to ring. *Dong. Dong. Dong.* A string of headlights curved its way through town and toward Dover Bluff Road. The sound of the single bell ringing sent a shiver up Rebecca's spine. So haunting, so lonely.

* * *

Another tragedy had struck the small, tight-knit community of lobster fishermen and their families. A heartrending tale to be told over cold beer. One that would grow with each telling, until those who perished gained as much notoriety as the Ghost of Dover Bluff Heights.

With her legs stinging, the suitcase growing heavier with each passing minute, Rebecca pressed on. There was no turning back. There was nothing to go back to.

* * *

An hour later, having avoided the cars and people traffic heading toward the fire, Rebecca found herself at the doublewide iron gates of the cemetery. The sirens had long since stopped. Though Rebecca knew deep down Ben and Ray could not have survived the conflagration, she still embraced some semblance of hope for them.

A single streetlamp lit the area around her. Scripted into a brass plate, the word ROSEWOOD welcomed her. If the stories her father told held any truth, then there were more than two hundred fishermen buried within its consecrated grounds. Men and boys who scratched out a living riding the temperamental currents of the Atlantic in search of upper-class fare, who so grievously gave their lives to the sea.

The cemetery had been in place since the inauguration of Bay Ridge Cove in 1716. It covered a hundred-acre sight on the outskirts of town where the topography of the land flattened between rolling hills. There were more people buried within its grounds than the current population of Bay Ridge Cove itself. From this locality, it was an easy exit out of town, the interstate only a brief walk away.

Rebecca pulled on one of the heavy gates. In the surrounding silence, it yawned loud enough to literally wake the dead. Rebecca froze, held her breath. When she was sure that no one else had heard the ghastly lament, she stepped through the gate and into Rosewood's function. Finding her mother's gravesite would be easy enough. Rebecca could manage the short distance with her eyes closed if need be, for it was a vigil she maintained religiously. To bring flowers and spend time talking with Deseray White about all the things that were going on in her life.

There were no lights to speak of. The only visible source marking the tombs, that of the moon. She found that being in the cemetery at night was a far different animal than in daytime. Her head snapped this way and that every time a branch moved in the high Elms bordering the asphalt drive. Night creatures fluttered overhead, or so she imagined.

Shadows seemed to move with Rebecca, and she had a frightening notion that she was being watched, which she knew was ridiculous. Nobody visited the graveyard at night. It was hallowed ground that not even Bay Ridge Cove's wannabe street gangs would dare desecrate, for many of the sights were empty, the bodies having been claimed by the sea. It was out of legendary fears, stories born at the expense of the dead and a community's respect that kept people out of Rosewood when the sun went down.

Rebecca followed the blacktop until it made a sharp right. From there she had to turn left and go five rows up before she found the marble headstone of her mother's grave. She left the intimacy of asphalt, her sneakers sinking into the well-maintained lawn edging the section known as Sleeping Meadows. Walking between headstones, Rebecca smoothed a hand over the arches of marble and granite, reciting the names she knew by heart: Norman Blake, Eloise Batterbee, Coplan Baxter, Ulf Sorenson, Vernon

Friend. An uncommon peace fell over her, the tally of the suitcase no longer a burden. There was something about being there, like the familiarity of an old comfortable shoe that had an instant calming effect. It was as though Rebecca knew each of the dearly departed in a way nobody else could. She counted each row as she passed. When she reached the marble effigy of Gabriel wielding a sword overhead, she set the suitcase down against Eleanor Henry's final resting place. Then she paced three sights in and stood behind her mother's marker.

The flowers Rebecca had offered the week previous were still where she had left them, leaning against the smooth black granite, wilted:

DESERAY WHITE
1961–2005
LOVING MOTHER
BELOVED WIFE. FRIEND
IN GOD"S HANDS

Rebecca sat and made herself comfortable against the headstone. She drew her knees to her chin, and rubbed her face and tired eyes with the balls of her fists. The stone was cool through the jacket, and it alleviated the phantom burn still clinging to her flesh.

From her situate, she could see white smoke rising into the night from atop Dover Bluff Road, the flames having been doused by volunteer firefighters. As she gazed at the hilltop, a blazing star burst through the Milky Way, arcing like a portent into the dark chasms of night. *I should make a wish.* "Starlight, star bright. First star I see tonight. I wish I may. I wish I might. Have the wish I wish tonight." Closing her eyes, the faces of the people she endeared most spilled forward. The beaming expression of her mother. The round, wind-burned face of Ray. Ben smiled back at her as bright as a picture, his eyes full of life. And for a wished moment, the four of them were together once more. Then they faded, and *he* came into view, floating from the closet she reserved only for herself. The nameless countenance of her secret lover. Long dark hair floated on his broad yokes. His face drifted forward, pressed deep, and filled every crevice of her mind. His grey-blue eyes beckoned. He smiled, full lips formed a single word, and messaged her name, "*Rebecca.*"

Rebecca opened her eyes. She could still see a white line drawn halfway around the world. The imaging had taken place in the blink of an eye, as if time had reserved itself for that single moment. *Please help me find a way.*

For the next few minutes of her life, Rebecca listened to the sounds of the graveyard. Leaves rustled in trees. Night's breath moved waywardly throughout the acres of marble-and-moss-covered granite. She began to hum the melody she knew by rote. As though the melody were a summon to those around her, she was joined by the vocal declarations of the dearly departed. Their presence enveloped her, and she welcomed them, for she was not unafraid.

The song they sang spoke of a life's end and what lay beyond one's final breath. Of an existence beyond the beyond, to be indulged by the chosen few. Those like Rebecca.

White wet smoke rose in the distant dark as the voices of the dead serenaded her. Several minutes ticked by before a mounting presence coddled her in its shroud. Rebecca stopped humming. Her mother's voice rose from the surface of her final situation, and silenced the dead. It filled Rebecca's mind, not with words, but with expressions of love and comfort.

Rebecca closed her eyes and embraced the pleasant timbre of her mother's spirit as it took her fully, enchantingly.

"Momma... I'm here," she whispered into the crook of her arm. "I'm here."

* * *

6

The Big Sky Saloon
11:00 p.m.

JOHNNY parked the pickup at the rear of the near-full parking lot. Beside him were a row of Harleys genuflecting in perfect accord to one another. He killed the engine, stepped down onto the dirt lot, and slammed the door shut. The truck he left unlocked should he have to make a quick getaway. From where he stood, he could hear music pumping from inside the acclaimed Biggest Bar in Montana. An all-wood structure that was the place to be come a Friday or Saturday night. Blue neon, perched high above the roof, welcomed everyone to the BIG SKY SALOON.

Johnny wore jeans, white T-shirt, and what he liked to call his shit kickers. A pair of sharp-toed leather boots that had seen many fights, and the pair he wore when it came to calf-branding season. Somewhere in the near brush, noises could be heard. Two people going at it like a couple of wildcats, grunting and hissing, the woman calling out to God, the man proclaiming his satisfaction with a plethora of yes's.

Johnny walked the spaces between vehicles, most of which were pick up trucks, and made his way to the bar. The music emanating from within was by the band Wrangler, a family trio who toured the area and was a favorite at the Big Sky Saloon. They were in the third verse of "Two Bridges Road," their harmonizing, perfection. They had been branded the best bar band in the territory. The mother Eva, lead singer, as well as acoustic guitar aficionado, possessed a Joplinesk voice. Long platinum hair surrounded a whimsical countenance and her blue, inquisitive eyes saw you for exactly who you were. Onstage her aura demanded one's attention, and she didn't mind sharing a joke or two.

Rob, Eva's only son, an old soul at the tender age of thirty-three and intelligent beyond his years, was born to play the keyboard and could manipulate a mandolin into weeping. A huge sports fan, he could be found between sets, watching sports updates and nursing Jägermeister Cokes. However, it was the daughter who drew the attention of every male for miles around, much to the chagrin of wives and girlfriends. Surely her voice was to hear what an angel's must sound like, Johnny always imagined. Sue's ability could fill a room without the assistance of a microphone. Brunette hair sculpted a face that did not require cosmetics. *A natural beauty.* Johnny had had a crush on her since the first time Buck brought him to the bar for a beer. A father and son's night out. That was three years ago. Johnny was seventeen and, like most Johnny's age, had not mustered enough courage to ask her out.

The Thompson ranch pickup trucks were easy enough to spot because each were Chevys, blue, and had "The Thompson Ranch" font across the driver side door. But as Johnny neared the leaning steps of the bar, it was apparent that none of the Thompsons had arrived, or if they had, were already gone.

The Montana night was obliterated with stars. Johnny looked up in time to see one arcing across the heavens. He made a silent wish. *Please let me find those responsible for Dallas's death.*

He climbed the timber steps and pulled on one of the double doors just as the music ended. He stepped inside. A wall of cigarette smoke met him head-on. The place reeked like every other honky-tonk bar in Montana. Body odor, beer, promises and letdowns.

Having just completed "Seven Bridges Road," the band stepped down from the stage and separated. The voices of a thousand patrons spoke all at once, drowning the Dixie Chicks recording of "Wide Open Spaces."

Baseball caps, cowboy hats, bandanas, and paid-for breasts mingled shoulder to shoulder in a tension-filled five thousand square feet where, at any moment, on a Friday or Saturday night, a fight might be provoked.

A mountain of a bouncer, the same chap Buck had fought with in the parking lot over a less-than-cordial remark regarding Johnny's native heritage, barely gave him a glance. Buck had bested the bruiser in a matter of minutes, breaking his left arm and nose and knocking out two of his lower teeth. Since then, a respect regarding Johnny's lineage had been established by all staff, even though he was still underage.

Nearest to the entrance, a leaning table was encircled by bikers who wore the colors and moniker of the El Diablos over black leather jackets. A local club known for its violent tendencies when it came to matters regarding the small-time marijuana and prostitute trade.

The MC, a red bandana low on his forehead, bore a jagged scar that ran from the corner of his mouth, up and around his right cheek and ended in a deep, curving gouge at the corner of his eye. He gave Johnny the once-over. The master of ceremonies threw back a shot glass and violently slammed the jigger down. Wiping at his mouth, he said, "Go ahead, say something, Indiana Joe." His band of motley road brothers cackled like hens.

Johnny broke eye contact. Getting into a pissing match with this lowlife was not something he had time for though he knew he could easily best the asshole. He moved cautiously past and searched the bar for a place to sit.

Eva Levesque played the crowd. Hugged those she knew well and shook hands with those who were always telling her that Wrangler should be recording albums instead of wasting their time in places like the Big Sky Saloon. Sue had been cornered by a half-dozen young cowboys vying for her attention. Rob was seated at the long bar, next to the stage, his eyes focused to the bank of sports teeming flat screens.

One of the waitresses, Brandy, moved through the boisterous throng. She carried a tray full of empties and, spotting Johnny, made a beeline in his direction. "Johnny!" she called enthusiastically, stopping in front of him. "I haven't seen you in forever. Where've you been keeping yourself, honey?" She gave him a ruby red smile. A denim skirt rode high up her thighs, a white blouse revealed the crevice of her ample breasts. Brandy was in her midforties, a single mother, and was always available at the end of her shifts to just about anyone with a pickup truck and money to spend.

"Same old story," said Johnny. "Working the ranch. Just keeping to myself."

"Well, you should come by more often. I miss seeing you around here." She gave him a tell-all smile. "You plan on staying for a while. I get off at one."

"I'm not sure. Say, you didn't happen to see any of the Thompsons here tonight?"

"Thank God, no. The less I see of that bunch, the better. The place has been quiet so far, and that suits me just fine. How's Buck? And how's your dog? What's his name again?

"Dallas."

"Yeah, Dallas. How is he?"

Johnny swallowed. "He's fine. And Buck's fine too."

"Good." She stared at him a moment, her eyes roaming. "Listen, honey. I gotta get going. My section's just over there. Find yourself a seat. I'll bring you a beer. Remember what I said about getting off at one."

Under normal circumstances, Johnny might have given the offer a second thought. He hadn't been intimate with the fairer sex in quite a while. The extra long showers were getting tiresome. He told her what she wanted to hear. "How could I forget? You're looking mighty fine tonight."

Brandy blushed. "Well, thank you handsome. I'll be keeping my eye on you tonight. See you in a minute, Johnny B." Turning, she headed toward the table of Diablos and started to gather the empty shooter glasses, stacking them one on top of the other. The MC grabbed her by the wrist and pulled her toward him. Then he whispered something in her ear and laughed. Brandy smiled weakly. She wriggled her wrist free and nodded. The biker made a motion for another round then slapped Brandy's bottom.

All of this took place under the watchful eye of the bouncer not more than ten feet away. He would not interfere unless things got rough. A waitress getting her ass slapped fell under the category of customary at the Big Sky Saloon.

Johnny waited until Brandy was well clear of the table, just in case, before he moved toward the stage in search of a place to sit. Through the crowd, he turned this way and that. Many of the women, intentionally unintentionally rubbed their bodies against his. If it wasn't for what he had to do, Johnny thought. He would not mind staying till close, have a few beers, and maybe a dance or two.

Beautiful, charming, wonderful Sue had freed herself from her cowboy admirers and was headed his way. In a white cotton blouse and skin-tight blue jeans, she was a sight to behold. Like her mother, she had an aura about her that set her apart from everyone else. *Positive energy.* They casually met at one of the heavy beams that supported the roof and several saddles.

"Hi," said Sue , setting Johnny's heart afire. "Johnny, isn't it?"

Johnny was impressed that she had remembered his name. He was quite sure they had only met briefly and quite formerly. An introduction in passing more than two years ago. "Yes," said Johnny, dumfounded.

Sue held out a hand. Johnny took it in his. "Nice to see you again," she said, magazine smile whiter than white.

"I love your music," blurted Johnny like a love-crushed schoolboy. He slipped his hand from hers, surprised to find that his palm was moist. Staring deep into her eyes, he melted and knew not what to say next. Then just as he was about to say something clever, someone called out Sue's name. Johnny turned to see Eva headed in their direction.

Opportunity lost.

"Sue! Sue!"

"I guess I better get going," said Sue. "It was nice to see you again, Johnny."

"Likewise." Johnny smiled. "Could you do me a favor?"

"Sure, if I can."

"Would you sing 'Strawberry Wine' for me. The last time I saw you, you were singing it, and well, I really liked it."

"Thank you, Johnny. I think we can squeeze it in during the next set."

"Thanks. It would mean a lot."

"Consider it done."

Before Johnny knew what was happening, Eva Levesque had come up behind him and wrapped her arms around his waist. "What are your intentions with my daughter, young man?" she asked seriously then laughed, and Sue laughed with her. She let Johnny go and sided her daughter.

Sue made the introductions. "Mom, this is Johnny. Johnny, Mom."

Eva held out a hand. Johnny noticed right away the calluses on her fingertips. *Thousands of hours applying her trade*. He took her hand in his and found it to be surprisingly soft. More than Motherly soft. Giving her his best smile, he said, "It's a pleasure to meet you, Sue's mom."

Eva looked up at him, smiled back, her blue eyes insightful. "The pleasure's all mine, Johnny." Turning to her daughter, she said, "I hate to break up this little shindig, but there's some people I'd like you to meet before we go on again. They own the Ranchman's over in Missoula."

"Sure, Mom. See you, Johnny. I won't forget your request." Looping an arm into her mother's, the two headed toward the long bar where Rob was already spiritedly involved with the owners of the Ranchman's. A tall glass of Jagermeister coke stood sweating in front of him.

Being six foot three gave Johnny advantages when it came to casing his surroundings. He moved toward the parquet dance floor. Once he was clear of the crushing bodies, his eyes searched the booths running along the west side. Most of the red leather seating were taken. However, he could see a heated argument taking place between a couple in the booth nearest to the stage. The guy was pointing a finger precariously close to the agitated woman's face. They were so close, the tips of their cowboy hats were almost touching. Johnny read their lips. The word *bitch* was used over and over as were the words *cheating prick*. If Johnny was reading things right, it would not be long before the booth became available.

Brandy the waitress maneuvered through the crowd. She carried a full tray of drinks in one hand and moved bodies with the other. She stopped to drop off a few highballs then headed straight for Johnny. "Here you go, honey," she said and handed Johnny a bottle of Budweiser.

Johnny went to fish in his pocket for a five.

Brandy put a hand on his arm. "Don't worry about it handsome. The first one's on me."

"Thanks, Brandy," said Johnny, keeping one eye on the booth, the other on the front entrance.

"Something troubling you, Johnny? You seem… preoccupied."

"Just keeping my eye open for a place to sit."

"Good luck. The place is packed. You'd be better off at the long bar. At least there you won't have to wait too long for a beer."

"Something tells me a booth is about to open." Johnny pointed with his chin.

"Oh, them. They've been going at it for over an hour now. I overheard what they're fighting about. She caught him fucking her best friend. He's trying to deny it. I know Keith. He's lying through his teeth. Some men are so pathetic."

"Can't argue with you there."

Suddenly the woman got up, slapped Keith hard across the face, knocking his hat askew. Then she left, crying, and headed for the woman's bathroom. The stunned cowboy adjusted his hat, looked around. Embarrassed, he got up and left the booth, leaving a half-empty highball, the remainder of a Coors light, and a cigarette still smoldering in the ashtray.

"Excuse me, Brandy, but if I don't grab that table…"

"You go right ahead, Johnny. I'll come by in a while. Got to get these drinks off anyway."

Johnny plopped himself down just as a trio of girls were about to claim the booth for themselves. He butted out the cigarette and took a healthy swig of Bud. The pretty trio surrounded him, put off that he had beaten them. "Hey," said the tallest of the three. Like most of the women in the bar, she was wearing jeans and a top meant to show off the maturity of her breasts. "That's not fair. We saw it first." Her friends nodded in agreement.

"Sorry," offered Johnny, but wasn't about to give up the perfect view of the front entrance. "I'll tell you what, why don't we share the booth. So long as you don't mind having me as company."

"Okay," the trio chimed, suddenly all smiles and perky tits. They slid in, elbow to elbow, eyes aimed at Johnny. "Hi. I'm Tawny. This is Faith, the one on the end is Laurie." Each smiled perfect rows of perfectly white teeth.

"Hi. I'm Johnny. Pleased to make your acquaintance." He held out his hand and exchanged social etiquette with them.

The lights dimmed. The stage came to life in a dancing tempo of golds, reds, and blues. A roar of approval and a round of applause erupted. Eva, Rob, and Sue took to the platform and positioned themselves in front of their respective mikes. The drummer, Chris, and lead guitar, Dave, talented locals hired whenever Wrangler was in town, took their positions.

Anxious couples moved to the dance floor and waited for the music to begin.

"Wahoo," screamed Tanya, shaking her head side to side, long brown hair swaying this way and that way. Faith and Laurie bumped bodies, snapped their fingers. "I hope they're good," said Faith.

"They're the best," confirmed Johnny and took a swig of Bud.

"Do you dance, Johnny?" asked Laurie, pushing aside the unfinished drinks the previous couple had left. "You look like you might cut a mean rug."

"I don't mind a spin every once in a while."

Toying with the ends of her blond locks, Faith interjected, "Good. Then I'm first." She gave Johnny the same alluring look Brandy the waitress had given him not minutes before. Johnny wondered if all women practiced that look in the mirror just before they went out. Smoldering eyes, a little flare of the nostrils, and the faintest hint of a tell all smile. Johnny had seen the look a thousand times, and a thousand times it meant the same thing: *I want you.*

* * *

Eva Levesque cleared her throat, the sound of it loud through the speakers. The bar's level of people noise dropped to a hush. Johnny's newfound friend's were riveted to the stage, eyes all aglow.

"Look at all those smiling faces, said Eva. "I'll tell yah what. Just seein' all you folks puts a song in my heart. It's good to be back at the Big Sky. For those of you who just arrived, I'm Eva, on the keyboards is my son Rob, and playing bass is my beautiful daughter Sue. See that smile, cost me thirty-six hundred dollars." She waited until the murmur of laughter subsided before she announced, "On lead guitar is Dave, and back there, out of sight because you ladies couldn't handle his good looks, is Chris. Together we're Wrangler. We're here to make sure the party keeps going until your feet get sore, or until you get sick of us, whichever comes first."

There was a voluminous cheer. Everyone seemed to move all at once.

"This one's a favorite of ours," said Sue, and beamed a thirty-six-hundred-dollar smile. "I hope you like our rendition."

Rob's fingers went to work on the Roland. "Down at the Twist and Shout" kicked into a full Cajun riot of harmony and precision instruments.

"Well, care to dance, Johnny?" Laurie was already slipping across the leather so her friend could get out. When Faith was clear of the booth, she reached a slender hand.

Eyes still focused on the entrance, Johnny knew if he was going to share the booth, there would be no getting around having at least one dance. He took Faith's offered hand, rose from his seat, and smiled.

Not being more than a bragged five foot one, Faith gazed up at Johnny. "My, my. I didn't realize how tall you were. I like that." She proceeded to pull him toward the dance floor, squeezing his hand as though she were afraid he might suddenly disappear on her.

"Don't you go tiring him out," Tawny called after them. "I'm next."

They found a small square of space near the stage. Faith held out her hands and supplied Johnny with a look meant to melt his heart. Taking Faith's hands in his, they slipped into a two-step, easily blending into the twirling, step, step, slide, making its way around the perimeter of the dance floor.

As they passed the stage, Johnny's eyes sought out Sue's. She was belting out the chorus. Their eyes met for the briefest of moments.

Faith, with a gentle elbow to the ribs, reminded him of her presence. *Hey, buddy. The action's here.*

Smiling, Johnny said, "Sorry. No disrespect." He looked deep into Faith's eyes. After a few ticks of the clock and his best I'm-paying-attention-to-you gaze, he felt her relax again. "I haven't seen you in here before," he pointed out, his voice competing with the music and those around them.

"First time." Faith smiled. "The three of us are heading to California for a few weeks. We thought we'd stop in Montana for the night. Found out about this place, and, well, here we are."

"Sounds like you're going to have a good time." They were at a vantage point where Johnny could see the entrance. He let his eyes wander to the double doors. The bouncer was talking to a couple of girls in cowboy hats, flexing his arms in an attempt to impress. Brandy was serving the table of Diablos again, the smile on her face one fashioned out of fear.

As they turned one of the doors swung outward.

"Something the matter, Johnny?" asked Faith, sounding genuinely concerned that he might not be interested in what she had to offer.

Facing the stage now, Johnny could barely comprehend what it was she was saying over the noise of bodies, hard heels connecting with the floor, and speakers that seemed to sway with the music.

Mother, son, and daughter were bringing the house down. There wasn't an empty space on the dance floor. Even with the stage lights, the talented family exuded an inner quality not many people possessed. Energy poured from their bodies in a pure white light.

An electric current rode Johnny's spine. The same charge he had experienced minutes before Buck informed him of Dallas's passing. "Sorry, no. I was just thinking about something." He smiled down at her.

"Me too. You should have a little *faith,*" she hinted, eyes sparkling, her body pressed against him as if he were made of Velcro.

Johnny regarded her face. Faith *was* beautiful. On any other night, he could easily be tempted by her posturing. Instead, he calmly asked, "Why don't you tell me more about the trip you and your friends have planned?"

Faith skewed her head, confusion arching her brows. "Our trip? Well… okay. The three of us go to the same college up in Regina. Last week we decided a road trip was in order…"

Johnny listened as they turned. When they came full circle, two of the Thompson boys, *the* Thompson boys, were standing at the entrance. Oversized, silver Montana buckles preceded them. PBR labels fronted Lammles denim. The taller of the two wore a white Stetson that added inches to his already looming height. His brother preferred the macho look of a clean-shaven head. They were casing the joint. Shit-eating grins plastered on their faces.

Johnny could practically smell the arrogance of them from across the room. The closest either of them ever came to riding a bull was the last steak they'd had. Their attire was meant to impress anyone foolish enough to listen to their BS. Dwight and Donny Thompson. The same bastards who enjoyed shooting horses and, more likely than not, responsible for killing his best friend. Their faces had been captured by local newspapers, a happenstance not even their rich daddy could avert.

The music abruptly stopped. There was a roar of approval. Hands smacking loud. The voices of a thousand faithful, including Faith, hooted and hollered. Everyone, that is, except for Johnny. The bitterness and anger he had been suppressing brewed to the surface, causing the temperature in his body to escalate dramatically. *Keep your cool, Johnny. Now's not the time or place.* A drip of sweat drew a line over his jowl.

The Thompson boys made their way to the long bar, tongues lapping at every female they encountered. The way they were walking, leaning slightly to either side, they had already been drinking. *Good,* Johnny thought. *It will make what I have to do a lot easier.*

Sue's voice filled the speakers. "This one's for Johnny, a good friend of mine. 'Strawberry Wine.'" She looked to Eva and Rob. Wrangler slipped into Deanne Carter's summer sweet ballad.

"And that's when we decided a few weeks in sunny California was in order." Faith had slipped into Johnny's arms.

Half-listening to her story, Johnny said, "Well, I'm awfully glad you three decided to stop by." Instinctively he put a hand on the small of her back and guided her slowly across the floor.

Short as she was, Faith rested her face against Johnny's chest and breathed a contented sigh. "I'm glad too."

By the time the song ended, they had circled the dance floor thrice. Long enough for Johnny to see that the Thompsons were comfortable at their position against the long bar.

Tawny and Laurie had found suitable dance partners by then, much to the delight of Faith, who had decided she wasn't going to share Johnny with either of her friends.

The applause diminished. Johnny could see by the look in Faith's eyes that she was quickly getting in too deep. "Would you mind if we sit the next one out?" he suggested.

"So long as you don't go getting away from me." Raising herself on the balls of her feet, Faith whispered, "I'm well worth the wait."

It never surprised Johnny anymore to find that *today's* women were very aggressive. Far more aggressive than Johnny could ever be, and all of it, a little intimidating. That there was immediate pressure put on the guy to perform and perform well. Not that he had ever had any complaints in that department. It just seemed all very primitive. *Me cave girl. You must please me.*

When they arrived back at the booth, there were three highballs of varying distinction sitting in a row and a fresh bottle of Budweiser on the table. Faith had looped her arm through Johnny's, intent on sitting next to him. But Johnny had other ideas. "Faith, would you excuse me for a few minutes? Nature calls."

"Of course, Johnny. Don't be too long though." She slid into the booth. "I feel another slow song coming on."

Johnny smiled and headed for the men's room, which just happened to be located at the far end of the mahogany long bar. He moved through the dancers. Rob's spirited rendition of "Great Balls of Fire" had everyone jiving.

The Angels were playing the Giants in the thirteenth inning. Red neon advertising Budweiser and Budweiser Lime glowed from the rafters. A buckboard, suspended from the ceiling, held a banner across its facade: WHERE FRIENDS COME TO MEET. The group from Ranchman's stood huddled at the end of the bar. They nursed martinis while captivated by the sound rushing from the stage.

The Thompson boys were talking it up with one of the three bartenders. They laughed, drank beer and slapped each other on the back.

Johnny headed in their direction.

Approaching, his temper soared. He leaned against one of the support beams, and tuned into their conversation. His mother had taught him how to listen with his mind, his heart, when he was just a boy. He concentrated on their voices, feigning that he was watching the people on the dance floor, the captivating performance onstage. His hands were tightly knotted fists that wanted to react. He had to control himself before he did something stupid so he took a deep breath, let it out and repeated the process. He listened.

"Looks like the chances of getting laid tonight are pretty good," Dwight told his brother.

"You got that right. I haven't seen this much pussy in one room since we went to that whorehouse over in Butte."

"Oh yeah. That was one fucking crazy night. You damn near choked that China bitch to death."

"She loved it. I just got carried away."

"Yeah, like you always do. Like you did earlier today. You're one sick fuck you know."

"Fuck you! You're the one suggested it."

"Yeah, but I didn't expect you to go through with it. Not after the last time."

There was silence for a moment. Johnny imagined they were visualizing the events of the day. Then the volume of their voices increased, suggesting they had turned away from the bartender and were facing Johnny's back.

"Sure was funny though, seeing that mutt go flying through the air like that," said Dwight.

And there it was. Johnny had to bite hard on his bottom lip to prevent himself from turning on them right then and there. The heat in the bar rose significantly or so it seemed.

"Yeah, well, don't go telling the world."

"You worry too fucking much, you know that?"

"Yeah... well... just the same. You never know who's listening."

"Look it. Why don't you just order us a couple more beers and focus on why we came here tonight... remember... to get laid."

"You got a one track mind you know."

"So what's your problem? Now order us some beers. I smell some pretty available meat."

Momentary silence filled Johnny's ears. He sensed they were focusing on the women milling about the bar. The next comment to come out of Dwight Thompson's mouth confirmed it.

"Well, bless your mom and dad. Will yah look at the tits on that sweet young thing. Hey, Donny, whatya think? Fifty bucks says I'll be fucking that piece of ass in about three hours."

"You're on," said Donny. "But a hundred says... you see that one in the purple top? The one that's got Fuck Me written across her forehead."

"Yeah."

"A hundred says I'll be tappin' that thing in the truck in about an hour."

Johnny had heard enough. Loaded with emotional ammunition, he glanced over his shoulder, looked the brothers up and down, then went to the men's room.

Standing in front of a urinal, he relieved himself and reminisced about Dallas and what those bastards had done to him, the poison coursing through his veins acid hot. He made a solemn vow to his already-missed companion. *Soon,* he promised. *Soon I'm going to open a can of Montana whoop ass like no one has ever seen before.*

* * *

The next hour passed swiftly. Wrangler was on their third set. Faith had kept Johnny on the dance floor for most of it. She had already consumed four vodka Cokes, a shot of tequila, and was slurring her *s*'s. When the band played "There's a New Kid in Town," she stood tall and planted a knowing kiss on his cheek.

Johnny maintained his semi-interested posture, knowing she would be safer in his company than with one of the drunken predators lurking the bar for just her type: friendly, fairly liquored up, not from around here, and looking for fun.

Many of the cowboys roaming the bar liked to get rough, the bikers, even rougher. The cougars, of whom there were many, played it either way, depending on what the score was. Johnny liked Faith and her friends. He wanted to be sure they made it to sunny California without the memory of an ill-advised night-out tagging along for the ride.

He had kept his eyes on Dwight and Donny throughout. Donny had indeed captured the interest of the blonde in the purple shirt. Dwight had yet to swoon the affections of the buxom brunette. She had danced with him once, but since then had turned down any and all further advancements. During that one dance, however, Johnny and Dwight Thompson had come close enough to touch. Dwight was as big as he was, yet Johnny had a notion it was the smaller of the two who was going to give him the most trouble. Donny Thompson was stocky. Built low to the ground with a hard chin. The warp of his nose told the story of many fights.

Wrangler completed their set with "Mamma, He's Crazy." Then the talented trio headed toward the owners of the Ranchman's to further engage the prospect of playing at their establishment. Dave and Chris took to a table. The dance floor emptied.

Johnny and Faith squeezed next to each other in the booth that was now crowded with bodies. Tawny and Laurie had invited the guys they had been dancing with to join them. Johnny knew the young cattle ranchers. He had sold them horses in the past and knew they were half-decent, possessing no real threat to the ladies, so he didn't mind the extra company.

Meanwhile, Donny Thompson and the blonde in the black hat and purple top had gotten comfortable at a table near the stage.

Johnny couldn't hear them; nonetheless, he could tell by the subtle hand gestures, the closeness of their faces as they spoke, and the fact that their legs were entangled beneath the table that it wouldn't be long before Donny made his move. When Brandy delivered four shots of tequila to their table, it was a signal for Johnny to initiate his plan. There was no doubt the two were going to end up in Donny's pickup, more sooner than later.

"You'll have to excuse me, Faith, but I've got to get some fresh air. The smoke is a little too much for me."

"Then I'm coming with you," proclaimed Faith, rising part way.

"No. Please. I'm a little dizzy. I wouldn't want you watching me. I might puke or something. I guess the beer's not going down too well either. I won't be more than five minutes, ten tops."

"Are you sure, Johnny? I don't mind." She gave Johnny a hurt and concerned look then slowly sat down.

Johnny slipped from the booth, and stood tall. Taller than he actually was. "No, really. All I need is a little fresh air. Stay with your friends. I insist. I won't be long. I promise."

"You go right ahead," piped Tawny. "I know how you're feeling. I don't know how much longer I can take the smoke either." She turned her attention to the young rancher next to her. "I don't suppose you know of a less-poisoned atmosphere we can go to?"

While the young ranchers talked it over, Johnny excused himself one last time and headed for the entrance. He passed the table of Diablos who were still knocking back shooters. They'd managed to gain the attentions of a couple of women who were wearing leather and jeans. Tough chicks, ready for a long night of frivolous partying and promiscuity.

The mountain bouncer wished Johnny a good night when he pushed open one of the doors.

He found the blue pickup easy enough. It was conveniently parked a few vehicles from his own. The air was still, the temperature mild, a perfect Montana night. Stars blazed in the sky like ice diamonds. It hadn't rained in weeks. The air was mixed with the fragrance of baked Montana earth, sweet sage, and the unmistakable heady odor of cattle. Looking to be sure no one was watching, Johnny hopped into the back of the half-ton, squatted next to a square bale of hay, toolbox, spare tire and waited. Acid blood burning.

It was not long before Donny Thompson and his trophy for the night came through the double doors. They were comfortably close to each other and laughing. Johnny watched them through the rear window of the pickup. Halfway across the parking lot, they stopped and swallowed each other's faces for several long moments before Donny steered her to the family pickup. The young woman, obviously beyond the scope of rational thought, staggered sideways several times and giggled at her own drunkenness. When they arrived at the pickup, Donny leaned her against the wheel hub and fished in his pocket for keys.

Giggling drunkenly, Purple Top asked, "Jussst what do you think we… we're going to do?"

"I'm gonna make your dreams come true," boasted Donny.

"Isss that ssso. Wha… What makesss you think you're man enough?"

Before Donny answered, Johnny leapt from his hiding spot and landed not two feet away from the startled Thompson. Purple Top fell forward and landed on her hands and knees, the black hat popping of her head. It rolled to a stop under the front quarter panel. "What the fffuck," she muttered then giggled.

Johnny loomed over Donny Thompson. Jaw set firm, his eyes filled with the abhorrence pent inside, every nerve firing with the authority of a lightning strike.

"Jesus Christ, chief. You scared the shit out of me. Hey?… What the fuck were you doing in my truck?"

Purple Top pushed herself to her feet, oblivious to the fact that her hat was no longer perched upon her head.

In a flat tone, Johnny said, "So you like to kill things."

"What the fuck are you talking about? You drunk, chief? Get the fuck out of here before I put the boots to you."

"You know exactly what I'm talking about." Johnny took a step closer.

Defensively, Donny took a step back. He put his hands up, palms facing outward.

Behind them, Purple Top spoke. "Hey, what is thisss? I'mmm not fucking both of you. Essspecially no fi-filthy fuckin' Indian."

Johnny shot her an indignant look. "Your boyfriend here shot and killed my dog earlier today. That's what this is about."

Purple Top looked shocked. Her mouth fell open. Regarding the man she was about to give herself to, she said, "You… you did what? You killed his dog?"

Unexpectedly, Donny dropped, rolled and grabbed at one of his boots. When he came up, he held a very sharp knife. He pointed it at Johnny's face. Unrepentantly, he said, "So what if I killed your fucking mutt."

Unfazed, Johnny took a step toward him.

"I'll fucking stick you, man. I mean it. I'll cut you up real good."

Johnny reached at his belt, unbuckled it, and in one fluid motion, yanked it free. "You're going to pay for what you did," he said matter-of-factly. He swung the length of leather at his side as if it were a lariat, the silver buckle flashing an angry circle.

Donny jabbed at the space between them.

Purple Top scrambled out of harm's way. "I'm not going to be a part of this," she yelled, sounding suddenly sober. Hatless, she couldn't leave the area fast enough. Her boots scraped across the gravel. She went down to one knee, righted herself, then disappeared among the parked vehicles. A moment later, a white Camero peeled out of the parking lot.

Johnny's eyes watched the body language of his opponent. Anticipating Donny Thompson's next movements would be crucial if he was going to come away without being badly cut. He had never taken a martial arts class in his life, but in his spare time had studied several forms of the discipline through books.

Wrangler's perfect harmonies spilled from the Big Sky. "Well I'm a honky tonk man. And I ain't gonna stop. I love to give the girls a twirl to music of the old juke box…"'

Johnny moved to his right, forcing Donny into the side of the pickup. When Donny's back touched metal, he narrowed his eyes and sprang forward as if he had been shot out of a cannon. His free hand was fisted. The knife hand slashed at the air.

Having foreseen the movement, Johnny stepped to the side. He swung the belt hard. The buckle made contact with Donny's knife hand opening a laceration across the knuckles. Instantly, blood seeped from the wound. "Fuck!" he yelled, but still maintained possession of the knife. "I'm going to fucking kill you, you cocksucker."

Johnny swung the belt again, only this time his aim was higher. The buckle cracked Donny on the side of the face. His cheek opened and he staggered, spit out a bloody tooth.

With the speed of a gazelle, Johnny pounced on him. He grabbed the knife hand, and using all of his two-hundred-plus pounds, forced Donny back against the passenger door. Glassed cracked. Blue lights danced in front of Donny's eyes.

Johnny dropped the belt and seized him by the throat. He dug his thumb and finger into Donny's larynx. Then he pounded the knife hand against the truck. *Once, twice, three times*. Donny conceded. The knife fell to the ground.

Blood ran from the wound on Donny's cheek and dripped onto the back of Johnny's hand. Johnny leaned into him and put his face as close to Donny's as it could get, the tips of their noses a breath away from touching. "I'm going to put you in a fucking wheelchair," he seethed.

Donny's face turned blue. Alien sounds pushed their way through his lips.

Johnny slammed a fist hard into Donny's heart. Knees buckled. When the killer of animals opened his mouth, Johnny slammed his heart again. In a swift, calculated move, he flipped Donny onto his back and came down with his knees, landing hard into Donny's midsection. Air burst from his lungs in one loud whoosh.

With one hand, Johnny pushed Donny's head into the gravel, the other rained blow after blow into his face until it was a bloody pulp. Johnny's heart jackhammered, blood on fire, boiling his veins. His inner voice told him that his opponent had had enough, but his anger, his hatred for this lowlife, this animal killer, prevented him from stopping.

Something cracked. At first Johnny thought he had broken his hand. Then he saw, through flaming eyes, that the left side of Donny's face had collapsed. He stopped the assault. There was, after all, one more Thompson to take care of. He drew a shaking hand across his forehead and wiped at the sweat stinging his eyes. His knuckles were soar, chest heaving. And the band played on.

Donny Thompson lay semiconscious beneath him, moaning, groaning, his mouth open, blood running.

From the corner of his eye, Johnny saw the knife lying near the rear tire, gleaming, just an arm's reach away. Something deep malfunctioned. A cerebral battle ensued. Dark forces against the will of good. *Don't do it, Johnny. He has paid the price. Go ahead, Johnny. Nobody would miss this piece of shit. He deserves it.*

Johnny reached for the knife and held it in front of him. He studied the simplicity of it. His eyes were reflected in the smooth steel. They were dark with evil intent, flat and filled with rage. A rage that had been his crucifix since the telling of Dallas' death.

All rational thought gone, he raised the knife high above his head and leveled his hatred onto Donny's face.

"JOHNNY!"

The shriek came from somewhere behind him.

Johnny craned his neck.

Faith was standing only a few feet away. Hands cupped over her cheeks. "Don't do it, Johnny!"

Johnny smiled, sinister, impenitent. His arm came down in a blur. Steel flashed.

Faith covered her eyes. Wanted to scream. Couldn't.

The blade struck hard, deep into the gravel next to Donny's head. An anger compelled twist of the wrist, and the blade snapped beneath the ground. Johnny stood, the bone handle in hand. Turning he saw that Faith had gone white. "He killed my dog," was all he could say. He was shaking all over, heart still pounding a rhythm hard against his ribs. He threw the handle far into the brush. Slowly he went to Faith. She wrapped her arms around him. "He and his brother murdered my Dallas," he said. "Shot him in cold blood." He rested his head into her welcoming shoulder.

Faith stroked the back of his head and looked down to a bloodied Donny Thompson. "My god. I thought you were going to kill him right in front me.

"I wanted to," he said into her ear. "Believe me. I really wanted to. But he's not worth spending the rest of my life in prison for." After several unvoiced seconds, Johnny's breaths became more even and the bad vibes ebbed.

"So that's why you were eyeing him all night."

Johnny lifted his head, surprised. "You knew?"

"It was kind of obvious from my perspective."

"Sorry. I didn't mean any disrespect."

"I can't blame you under the circumstances, I guess." She pulled away from Johnny and took in his face, her blue eyes sad with the idiom of memory. "I had a dog when I was a little girl. His name was Bingo. He got killed by a truck one day. It broke my heart in two. But it was an accident, acceptable, even though I really never got over it. I can't imagine what you're going through. Knowing that someone intentionally killed your friend."

"Thank you for understanding." He looked at Donny who was still lying flat on his back, moaning incoherently. Blood everywhere. "I'll never understand the cruelty of some men. It seems to me that as a race, some of us are moving backward. Becoming more barbaric."

"I can't argue with you there," said Faith. "What are you going to do about the other one? It's only a matter of time before he starts to wonder what's taking his brother so long."

"I really didn't have a plan once I got here. Things just kind of happened. But since you're here, I wonder if you would do me a favor."

* * *

Faith approached Dwight Thompson who was standing at the long bar, alone, nursing a beer.

Dwight, thinking his fortunes had suddenly changed for the good, straightened. He put on his best *come-hither smile*.

To Faith, it looked more like the grin a serpent just before it took its prey head first. She stopped in front of him, disgusted.

"Hey there, little lady. What's your name?" asked Dwight, leaning into the bar, his eyes roaming her body, taking in every contour.

"My name's not important," said Faith factually. "You're Dwight Thompson, right?"

"In the flesh."

"I think you should know that your brother just got the crap beaten out of him. I think it was some bikers."

"What?!" Dwight straightened. Concern furrowed the corners of his eyes. "Where?"

Faith supposed the expression made him look like a ghoul. "Right outside. Couple of guys really put the boots to him. Then they took off on their bikes. Your brother is lying on the ground, bleeding badly. Thought you should know." Faith enjoyed the role of concerned citizen she was playing.

"Show me," said Dwight. He took a good swig of beer and slammed the bottle on the bar.

"I don't think I want to get involved any further."

"Like hell!" Dwight took her by the arm. "Show me!"

Once they were outside, Faith shook the grip Dwight had on her arm. Dwight Thompson sickened her. Just knowing that he took part in the death of Johnny's friend made everything that was about to happen seem fitting.

"I still didn't get your name, sweetheart," Dwight pointed out, putting his worry for his brother on the back burner for a moment. He followed her through the parking lot, hoping she might be interested.

Turning on him, Faith locked eyes with his. "Look. Who I am is not important. I am not interested. Get that through your thick skull. Consider yourself lucky that I happened to witness your brother getting the shit kicked out of him. Somebody else might not have gotten themselves involved. Where I come from, well, it's the decent thing to do." She maneuvered between vehicles. Dwight followed.

When they came out from between a couple of raised pickups, Dwight saw that someone was leaning over the stretched out figure of his brother. Donny was not moving. "Hey, you! Get away from my brother!" he yelled.

Johnny remained where he was, on one knee, back turned toward Dwight who was headed in his direction. Faith stayed a good distance back. She knew what was about to go down and she was going to enjoy watching it. In her mind, people who randomly killed animals deserved better than what the anomic courts ministered.

Swift of foot, Dwight went to where his brother lay. "I said get away from my brother!" He put a rough hand on Johnny's shoulder.

Johnny pushed himself to his feet and spun. The look in his eyes told Dwight everything there was to tell. "You and your piece of shit brother killed my best friend."

Dwight stepped back, looked down at Donny then back to Johnny. "Bikers didn't do this. You did. Didn't you? That bitch set me up." He lurched at Johnny. Arms like windmills. The hat flipped from his head to reveal a vast area of premature baldness.

Johnny blocked a straight right with his left arm, countered with a right of his own, catching Dwight on the point of his chin. The blow sent Dwight back a step or two. Before he could catch his balance, Johnny, head down, bowled into his midsection. Both men went to the ground, landing with a double thud.

"Get him, Johnny!" encouraged Faith from somewhere nearby.

However, Dwight managed to roll Johnny onto his back, giving him the upper hand. He sent a punishing fist crashing into the side of Johnny's face. Blood filled Johnny's mouth. Just as another blow came, Johnny moved his head. Dwight's right hand made contact with gravel, sending a shock wave of pain into his arm. "Fuck!"

Johnny took the window of opportunity and shoved hard with both hands like he'd seen in books. Dwight was sent reeling. The fight had taken them to the rear of the pickup.

Donny Thompson was coming around. He tried to sit up. Everything in front of him spun. He was aware that there was a commotion near, but in his fogged state, it might as well have been a couple of animals wrestling. He could do nothing except lie down. When he put his hands to his face, they came away red.

Johnny and Dwight stood, heaving, gasping for air. Dwight's right hand was swollen, sporadically cut across the knuckles. The front of his shirt spattered with the blood from Johnny's mouth. Between breaths he said, "I'm gonna... beat you like a dog... for what you did to my brother."

Johnny clenched his fists in anticipation, jaw tight. If there was one thing he learned in all the fights he had had and the books he studied, it was to let your opponent make the first aggressive move. Nine times out of ten, it was the countermove that got the job done.

Dwight lowered his head, charged Johnny, both arms positioned as if he were going to give him a hug.

Johnny saw the weak point of his attack right away. He waited until Dwight was within a few feet. What happened next happened with such agility, and with so much power, that when Johnny's boot made contact with Dwight's solar plexus, he was catapulted into the air and came down hard, the back of his head crashing onto the bumper of the family pickup.

He did not move.

Johnny stepped toward Dwight, ready for anything, every nerve prickling white hot fire. He was barely aware that Faith was moving toward him and that Donny Thompson was sitting again, cursing to himself.

"Wow! I've never seen anything like that before!" said Faith as much out of breath as Johnny was. "You knocked him out cold. Good for you, Johnny." She looked over to Donny Thompson. "They deserved everything they got."

Johnny stood over his opponent, breathing heavily. "There's... something wrong."

"What do you mean?" Faith moved beside him, looked at the still figure.

"His eyes are vacant."

Faith stared into the eyes of Dwight Thompson. What she saw in them made her bowels churn. She had seen that same look on her father when he had succumbed to a sudden heart attack sitting at the breakfast table. She was fifteen then. They were the eyes of the dead. "Oh my god, Johnny! Oh my god! I think you killed him!" She looked to Johnny, grabbing his arm to steady herself and saw in his eyes he already knew.

Johnny was momentarily stunned into silence. The only voice he heard was the one inside his head. *Surely this couldn't have happened. These things only happen in movies and in books. Didn't they?* He felt suddenly heavy, as if an ocean were pressing down on him. He was sweating profusely, his heart doing a rat-a-tat-tat within his chest, and he could not take his eyes away from the lifeless form of Dwight Thompson.

Faith dug her nails into his arm. "What are you going to do, Johnny?" She pulled at him until he finally turned his head.

"I… I don't know." Unhooking himself from the grip Faith had on him, he knelt beside the unmoving Thompson. Carefully, he put a hand behind Dwight's head. His fingers came away sticky and warm. It was then he realized with utter terror that in the fall, Dwight Thompson's head had been impaled by the ball of the trailer hitch. Reversing, he nervously wiped the bloodied hand against the ground over and over until the gore was gone. He looked to Faith. In a voice lacking expression, he said, "I killed him."

Visibly shaken, teardrops spilled from Faith's lashes and dripped from her chin. "It was an accident, Johnny," she said. "I'm a witness. It was self-defense. I'll swear to it on a stack of Bibles."

"Look. I'm in big trouble. There's no need for you to stick around or get involved. Go back to the bar, get your friends, and don't stop until you're in California. I don't know how they do things up in Canada, but Montana is a white man's state with white man laws. And in case you haven't noticed…"

Faith looked from Johnny to Dwight Thompson then back to Johnny again. "Oh, I see. Surely there must be some way…"

Johnny took her roughly by the shoulders and glared at her. "There is no way! Now get out of here! You hear me?! Leave while you still have a chance, before the cops get here. Forget you ever met me." He gave her an assertive shove.

Wiping the tears from her cheek, Faith said, "Okay, Johnny. I'll go, but I won't forget you." She turned, ran through the parking lot and toward the Big Sky Saloon. She did not look back.

Johnny paced. The voices of his reason and doubt raged on. *What are you going to do now? You're fucked. Call the police, Johnny. Like Faith said, it was an accident. Anybody with an open mind will see that. You better run, Johnny. Run as far away as you can. They'll take one look at you and your life will be over. All they'll see is that an Indian killed a white man. RUN, JOHNNY, RUN!*

Donny Thompson tried to push himself to his feet, but his equilibrium still had not sufficiently returned. He fell forward, landed on his hands and knees and glared at Johnny and his dead sibling. "What did you do to my brother? Dwight! Dwight!"

Johnny took one look at Donny Thompson whose voice was growing louder. It would only be a matter of minutes before he attracted the attention of others. Fifty yards away, the doors to the Big Sky opened, the music increased. Several people stepped outside and headed toward the parking lot.

Running to his truck, Johnny jammed the key into the ignition and turned the engine over. Slamming the door, he grabbed his cell phone from the passenger seat called Buck and threw the truck into reverse. Headlights shone on Donny Thompson. He was cradling his brother in his arms, rocking him back and forth, hands covered in blood, face white hot with rage.

Buck Black answered on the third ring. "Hello."

"Dad. I'm in really big trouble."

"Where are you, Johnny?"

"I'm at the Big Sky."

"I had a feelin' you might get yourself in a bind."

"Dad. Listen. I killed someone."

There was silence on the other end for several long seconds. Johnny looked into the rearview. There were people running towards him.

"Are you sure, Johnny?"

"There's no doubt! He's dead! Dwight Thompson is dead! I'm the one responsible."

"Jesus H. Christ on a stick. Okay, son. This is what you're going to do. Meet me at Anvil Pine. How long do you think it will take to get there?"

"About an hour, maybe a little longer."

"Don't speed. I'll meet you there." The line went dead.

Johnny stepped on the gas, hard. Stones flew in a rooster tail of dust and dirt. He almost lost control, righted the truck, then tore out of the parking lot at a dangerous speed. Within a minute, the blue neon of the Big Sky Saloon disappeared, swallowed by night. The obstinate voice in his head screamed, *You're a killer! Run, Johnny, run!*

* * *

7

Somewhere in the Nevada Desert

JESUS Christ, how on earth did you not see this coming? You are truly one stupid chick. You shouldn't have touched the money. If there's one thing Tony Millions loves, it's his money. You knew that. Stupid! Stupid! Stupid! If Mom could only see you now. Boy, would she be disappointed. Believing you're in Vegas, working as a concierge at New York, New York, living in a moderate bungalow in one of the better neighborhoods with a Chihuahua named Jasper. Ha! So now what are you going to do? Not much, that's for sure. With your hands tied behind your back and mouth gagged, there isn't anything you can do, especially from the trunk of a moving car. Where are they taking you? Does it really matter? You've heard the stories before, but didn't believe in them. Thought they were meant to keep you in line. Meant to fuel the fear they enjoyed dishing out. Now they're going to kill you, you know. That's what they do. It's their job.

The car Chastity was in was moving fast. It hit a bump or a deep crevice. Chastity, formerly Janice Keeper, whacked her head and smashed her knees against the hard metal of the trunk. Tears filled her swollen eyes. She could feel blood, warm and sticky, ooze down her battered and bruised legs. She knew they were no longer on paved roads. They'd made the transition from road to sand quite some time ago. Perhaps as long as an hour, but she couldn't be absolutely sure.

She tried once again to loosen the ties that bound her. In her attempt, she ripped a fingernail clean off. The shovel lying next to her dug into a shoulder, its blade tearing through her top, peeling flesh. Beneath the gag over her mouth, Chastity clenched her teeth, tasted blood on her tongue, in the back of her throat. *You are truly fucked girl.*

"Pull in over there by that big cactus, man," ordered Mr. Black, his voice booming within the spacious interior.

"You sure we're far enough out?" asked Mr. Green, eyes focused on the topography of the land, hands ten to two on the steering wheel.

"Do you see anyone else out here, stupid? Stop being so fucking paranoid. Do as I say. Nobody comes this far out into the desert at this time of night. Not unless of course they're out here to do the devil's work."

The Cadillac rolled to a stop.

"Hey? How many people you figure are buried out here?" Mr. Green leaned his body against the door, studied the man sitting next to him. Twirled the gold ring on his pinkie finger.

"Don't know, man. Don't care. We got a job to do. That's all I care about right now."

"I bet dollars to donuts Hoffa is buried out here somewhere." Using his fingers, Mr. Green pushed his greying, corn, silk hair back in place. He was hot even though the air conditioner was blowing at maximum output. Killing always got him all hot and bothered.

"He might be. Now enough with the forty questions. I got me some killing to do. Get little Miss Sunshine out of the trunk. I've got to drain the snake.

"You enjoy killing, don't you Mr. Black?."

"That's why Mr. Millions hired me, man. 'Cause I just don't give a fuck. Now get the bitch out of the trunk and start digging. If she gives you a hard time, give her a whack across the knees with the shovel. That usually shuts them up pretty quick."

"So how many?"

"So how many what?"

"You know, how many have you buried out here?"

Mr. Black stared at the V of light cast by the headlights. A jackrabbit tore across the waves of sand, stopped to look at the blazing headlights for a second, then disappeared beyond the scope of illumination. Mr. Black was silent for a moment, as if he were mentally taking index. Then he looked to Mr. Green and said, "You know, I think around ten or twelve. Not quite sure though. Could be more, could be less." He smiled at Mr. Green. A smile that sent a shiver up Mr. Green's back. Then he opened the passenger side door and stepped into the darkness.

Mr. Green hit the trunk release. This was his first taste of just how formidable and well connected Tony Millions was. His first "cleansing," Mr. Millions called it. There were not many men like him and Ken Barman, alias Manny Richardson, alias Jim Landry, alias Peter Goodman, had met a considerable amount in his life who were, at the very least, cruel, without sense of moral compassion or virtue. Mr. Green knew it the moment he was integrated into what Tony Millions referred to as his posse. Men who would, at the snap of Tony Millions's fingers, commit brutal murder without breaking a sweat. Men who could strip the flesh off someone with a spoon, one inch at a time, and take great pleasure doing so. Men who would cut their own mothers in half if it was what they were required and paid to do.

Mr. Green had been associated with elite killers from the Russian Mafia, the De Silva family in New York, and the irresolute Irish soldiers he'd camped with when he went underground for two years subsequent to blowing up a bus carrying nuns and schoolchildren in Belfast. Mr. Green enjoyed blowing things up and to watch the ensuing chaos. When he was a member of the secret police in South Africa during the apartheid, he relished the free hand given by the governing body. As a member of the death squads, his penchant for killing was fulfilled beyond his wildest dreams. Currently, he was a street owl who watched over the call girls and collected, on a daily bases 60% from the previous night's lucrative industry. The position came with many fringe benefits.

The inclusive Hollywood conceived posse, together with Mr. Green, consisted of a Mr. White, a Mr. Brown, a Mr. Blue, and Mr. Black, the latter having been employed the longest and who was perhaps the most ardent disciplinarian of them all, cool as a cucumber, quick to react. Averse when it came to someone else's pain with skin as dark as a deathwish night. When he looked at you with those hollow eyes of his and grinned those enormous white teeth, you knew the man was devoid of a soul. Conceived by members of Philadelphia's Black Panthers in the sixties, educated in Trinidad and Cuba, he was basketball player tall, slim, and always wore expensive suits, even when the temperature in Vegas climbed past the hundred-degree mark. Until then, Mr. Green had never feared another man, that is, until Mr. Black smiled at him for the first time and stole his audacious demeanor. Mr. Black scared the living shit out of Mr. Green, and that was no easy task.

When he looked into the trunk, lit only by a small bulb, the battered face of Chastity/ Janice Keeper, stared back at him. A contusion the size of an egg crowned her forehead. Blue-black bruises, the shape of fingers, covered her throat. The denim skirt she wore had climbed her legs to reveal blue silk panties and a tattoo: Slippery When Wet. She was breathing heavily, left eye swollen shut. *Tough chick,* thought Mr. Green.

Chastity had endured an hour's worth of knuckle-hard back hands and ten solid minutes of a torturous rubber hose across the backs of her legs before she finally confessed.

Reaching, Mr. Green grasped the shovel and stood it against the bumper. He loomed over her for a moment before seizing her by the top. He yanked her from the compartment. Buttons popped, exposing the fullness of her breasts and the fact that her nipples had been nearly torn apart. Mr. Black had taken a pair of pliers to them, post confession. Mr. Green's grip on the flimsy material slipped, and she fell back into the trunk. *Thud.* He reached in, took a maltreated breast in each hand and smiled down at her. He squeezed roughly.

With her good eye, Chastity fired daggers at him.

"Stupid whore," said Mr. Green. He moved his hands from her breasts to her mound and stroked it as though he were stroking the pate of a cat. His cock grew stiff. He began to breathe heavily. "Too bad it had to come to this Chastity. You and I could have had ourselves one hell of a good time." Seizing her shoulders, he hoisted her from the trunk and dragged the length of her until she dropped and slammed into the sand.

Chastity tried to stand on her own, but her knees were weak and the blood had left her legs a while back. Her entire head ached, arms pained, shoulders on fire. She teetered sideways. Legs buckled. She almost went down. But Mr. Black had finished his business and was there in time to right her. He grabbed a handful of blond cornrows and steadied her with a powerful yank.

Looking up at him, she pleaded with her one good eye, and mumbled incoherently through the duct tape across her mouth.

"What's that?" asked Mr. Black, smiling down at her. "Here, let me help you." He took a corner of tape and viciously ripped it free.

Chastity's mouth went numb. She was certain a good amount of skin had been torn. When she ran her dry tongue over her lips, she could taste the metallic tang of blood. But at least she could speak. "Please. Please don't do this," she sobbed. "Please, Mr. Black!"

Mr. Black had taken off his suit jacket. The .357 he cherished, tucked comfortably within a shoulder holster, gleamed like a dark omen. A scream rose in Chastity's throat and came out in one long, anguished cry, filling the night air.

"Scream all you like, bitch. There's no one to hear you except Mr. Green and me. Well, maybe a coyote or two."

"Please, Mr. Black. I gave the money back. I'm sorry for what I did. Can't you see that?" One good eye looked from Mr. Black to Mr. Green. "I'm so, so sorry."

"Do you hear that, Mr. Green? She says she's sorry."

Mr. Green laughed. "Maybe if she was good to us, we could, you know, we could let her go," he teased.

Chastity pleaded for her life the only way she knew how. "I'll do anything, anything. I'll suck your cock, baby. Anything you want. You can both have me any way you like. Double anal, anything at all. Let me do it for you. Come on, baby. Let me take care of that big cock for you. You know I'm the best. Just untie me and let me prove it to you."

"Do you hear that, Mr. Green? She wants to put that dirty little mouth of hers on my big beautiful cock. What do you think of that?"

"I think maybe you should let her," said Mr. Green, smiling wickedly.

Chastity dropped to her knees, no longer able to stand on her own, wincing as sand bore its way into opened wounds. "You don't have to kill me. You can fuck me sideways. Then just leave me here. I promise you, no one will ever know. I'll disappear. I promise."

"Oh, you're going to disappear all right," confirmed Mr. Black. He took her by the arm, lifted her to her feet, and steadied her. "Pity," he said. "You used to be a real looker. You should see yourself now. You look like you belong in a zombie movie, baby. Mr. Millions wouldn't be able to get a wooden nickel for you." Then he walked her into the V of light heading the Cadillac where a veil of sand flies had gathered and were hovering like miniature aircraft in its beam. Chastity's injuries were magnified a hundred times, the aim of the headlights seeming to cause the pain of her body to intensify tenfold. She tried to open her injured eye. It would not respond. A rush of tears flooded her cheeks.

The shovel balanced over a shoulder, whistling a solemn tune, Mr. Green looked for a place to start the hole. A tall cactus marked the spot. He jammed the shovel into the cool sand as if he were testing it for pliability. Next to his own, the cactus's shadow resembled that of a giant lying in the sand. "This looks as good a place as any I guess."

"Then start digging, man," barked Mr. Black, waves of steam rising from his bald head. He grabbed Chastity by the hair and twisted her around so that she was staring up into the hollow of his eyes. "You should consider yourself fortunate, baby. Not many people get to see their own grave being dug."

Chastity's welted legs trembled. Urine streamed down her thighs, over her feet and seeped into the sand. She looked up at the billions of stars twinkling like Christmas lights. Her mother's face appeared on the wall of her mind. *Oh god,* she thought. *You only have a few minutes left to live. Twenty-two years old and you're going to die. And for what? A measly five grand. Why? Why? Why?*

"'Cause you got greedy," said Mr. Black, reading her thoughts. "You all get greedy. Dumb fucking bitches. And after Mr. Millions provided you with everything you could have possibly needed. A roof over your head, food, and all the drugs you could handle. And how did you repay him, by stealing what don't belong to you. That's how."

"I was stoned, Mr. Black. Higher than usual. I didn't know what I was doing," Chastity tried again. "Please, Mr. Black. Maybe if you could explain. Tell Tony I'll bring in more money than he can count. He can put me on the street with the other girls. I'll only solicit the whales. Only the best hotels. I'll work extra time. I don't mind. Plll-Pllleeeassse."

"Too little, too late." He kicked her on the side of the leg, and Chastity went down hard, face biting into the sand. "Unlike you, I do as I'm told. It's the healthy thing to do, baby."

Chastity rolled onto her side, face covered with desert. It scratched at her eyeballs, and lodged itself in her teeth, into her wounds. She managed to muster some saliva in her cotton dry mouth and spat a white dot in Mr. Black's direction.

"Now there you go being all stupid again. And to think I was considering letting you suck my cock. Pity." He grabbed her bound wrists, and hoisted her to her feet.

Excruciating pain shot up Chastity's arms and shoulders. Something tore deep, cutting her to the marrow. She screamed, "You fucking nigger bastard! I hope you rot in hell!"

"I probably will, baby. But just knowing you'll be there to greet me makes me all warm inside."

Tears spilled down Chastity's cheeks, dripped from her chin and dotted the sand at her feet. She wanted to scream every profanity she'd ever heard at him, but there was no point. Mr. Black was incapable of emotion when it came to doing his job. He was Tony Millions's right-hand man. Personal bodyguard. Known to one and all within their circle as the Black Butcher. As lethal with a knife as he was with the cannon he wore dangling from his shoulder holster. The devil himself.

* * *

Mr. Green lifted a shovel full of sand and tossed it into the air. Then he got into a rhythm. Before he knew it, he was knee deep. He wiped sweat from his brow. Sand had gotten into his shirt, feeling like there were ants crawling all over his body. "How much deeper?" he called over his shoulder.

"A couple more feet ought to do it," instructed Mr. Black.

"How come you're not doing any digging?"

"'Cause there's only one shovel, man. Besides, that's not what I do. Now quit your grumbling and dig, you're beginning to irritate me, and you don't want to irritate me."

Chastity stood in the Cadillac's headlights, numbed with fear, and watched the hole get deeper and deeper.

Mr. Green plunged the round mouth into the hole he had created. By then, the sand had turned color. Shifting from a soft, grainy yellow to a deeper brown due to the moisture trapped several feet down. He stopped for a moment, wiped his brow and looked to Mr. Black. "Hey? Is it true that you were out here digging a hole and, when you got a few feet down, found that someone had already buried a body in the same place you were digging?"

"As God is my witness." Mr. Black boomed a laugh. "No word of a lie, man."

"So what did you do?"

"Hell, the hole was dug, so I just piled one body on top the other. Filled in the hole."

Both men laughed.

Chastity vomited all over her feet.

An hour later, the hole was nearly five feet deep and three feet wide. Mr. Green had lost his suit jacket and unbuttoned the front of his silk shirt. The thick patch of grey hairs on his chest glistened. Tossing the shovel, he asked Mr. Black to give him a hand up.

"Sure thing, Mr. Green." Mr. Black pushed an exhausted Chastity toward the hole. However, instead of offering Mr. Green a hand, he pointed the barrel of his .357 Magnum at him.

"Hey! That's not funny."

"It's not meant to be, man," said Mr. Black, grinning those large white teeth of his. He eyeballed Mr. Green like a predator set to ravage its next meal.

"Come on, point that fucking cannon someplace else. You're scaring the shit out of me."

"Good. Tell me, Mr. Green. Mr. Master race. Did you think your little extortion scheme was going to go unnoticed, man? You been gambling heavily, Mr. Green, and with Tony's money. You've been taking what don't belong to you. Taking liberties with Mr. Millions's girls. Mr. Millions don't like it when one of his employees thinks they can get away with skimming off the top. And if there's one thing Mr. Millions loves more than pussy, it's his money, man."

Mr. Green's face paled. His eyes went wide. "I… I don't know what you're talking about." He looked at the predicament he literally was in, and realized with utmost horror, that he had just dug his own grave.

Mr. Black kept the gun pointed at his head. Smiling, smiling, always smiling. "Sure you do. Mr. Millions is never wrong when it come to these matters."

Mr. Green pushed his sweat-soaked hair to one side and raised his hands in front of his face as though to ward off something evil. Fear controlled his eyes. His hands began to tremble. His bladder filled. "Okay, okay," he admitted. "I didn't think anyone would notice. And so what if I fucked a couple a tramps. That's what they're there for, right? I'm sorry about the money. Really. Look, I've still got most of it. Let me give it back, and we'll be square."

Mr. Black laughed. "Sorry, man. Mr. Millions says I got to make an example. So that no one else gets it in their heads to rip him off in the future."

Mr. Green threw the shovel at Mr. Black's body. It missed by a good three feet. "You fucking, Keffer!" he screamed. Then he scrambled about the hole like a blind mouse trapped in a maze.

"Sticks and stones, Mr. Green. Sticks and stones." Mr. Black looked to Chastity who was rooted where she stood by interminable fear. "I truly do love my work," he told her, smiling. "Like shooting fish in a barrel, baby." He drew the hammer back, and took careful aim. It dropped. The firing pin engaged. There was a bright blue flash. Thunder rolled across the desert. Mr. Green's head exploded. Blood spattered the wall of sand behind him. Chunks of skull, hair, and brain matter flew out of the hole and his body slumped into the corner. Sand spilled on top of him.

Shaking all over, Chastity wretched and fell to her knees, unable to see through the veil of tears obscuring her vision. From a deeply seeded memory, the descanted melody from a lullaby her mother sang to her when she was a toddler, filled her mind:

Where are you going,
my little one, little one.
Where are you going
my baby, my own.
Turn around and you're three,
turn around and you're four.
Turn around and you're a young wife,
going out through the door.

In the last seconds of her life, Chastity looked up into the night and watched a star explode across the heavens. For a brief pulse in time, she was Janis Keeper again from Boise, Idaho. Cheerleader with a promising future in ergonomics, a mother who loved her, and a little brother who would be thirteen now.

The hot, circular end of the barrel pressed against the back of her head.

From close behind, Mr. Black said, "You should be thanking me, baby. I was seriously considering burying you alive."

Taking a deep, courageous breath, the last sound Chastity heard was the click. Everything went white. Janis Keeper fell into the hole.

"I do love my work," said Mr. Black to the night. During the twin killing, his heart rate remained equable. He retrieved the cell/camera phone from his suit jacket, and he aimed it at the macabre scene, took a picture. Later he would sell it to the highest bidder as he did with all the mementos he had taken. People were sick. Some even more so than he. The more grotesque, the more monstrous the photo, the more money they paid. He went to the Cadillac and turned the volume up on the stereo. A piano concerto filled the night. Casually, he walked back to the hole and looked in.

Janice Keeper's bruised and battered body lay crumpled next to the faceless body of Mr. Green, slumped in the corner like an abused rag doll. She had landed bloody facefirst, her bottom sticking in the air, a final message for the world: *Kiss my ass.* Dislodged measurements of desert grave poured on top of them, creating peaks and ridges like miniature mountains of brown sugar.

Just one more irreparable body added to the statistic of missing persons, thought Mr. Black. *Because nobody was going to miss Mr. Green, and by now, as far as the authorities were concerned, Janis Keeper was just an unsolved, like so many before her.*

Mr. Black fit the .357 into its holster, seized the shovel and began to fill the duo-purpose grave. Smiling, smiling. Always smiling.

* * *

8

Run, Johnny, Run

JOHNNY sat with his back against Anvil Pine, its massive branches moving gently above him. His knees were pulled up to his chest, his face buried in the crook of his arms, the length of his damp hair heavy about his back and shoulders. His mind was being pulled in directions he could not comprehend. *Okay, so now what? You can't go to prison, and you will you know even if it was an accident. You'll be raped, beaten, and possibly killed. But you can't remain at home anymore either. There were witnesses. They'll find you. Just stay put. Buck will know what to do.*

Johnny had killed the engine of the pickup when he arrived, just in case. There was no telling whether or not the sheriff's department would begin their search for him right there at home. He knew several of the deputies by name, and it would only be a matter of time before one of them put two and two together from information gathered at the crime scene.

The clear night offered a smidgeon of light. Above him dancing stars seemed close enough to touch. Somewhere in the darkened acres, he could hear the small herd of Black Angus. They were mooing, having been disturbed from their slumber when Johnny plowed the pickup through the fields. He lifted his head. Unstoppable tears bathed his face. *Could a man really cry this much?* He wiped them away with the same hand that had been wet with Dwight Thompson's blood only an hour ago. He thought about his beautiful mother, Linda Birdhumming. Would she be disappointed in her only child if she were still alive? Would she understand Dwight's death was purely accidental? If he could take that one moment back, he would, but there would be no turning back the hands of time, what was done was done. And Johnny was guilty, guilty, guilty, with a capital *G*. He thought about Faith, her hungry blue eyes and her friends and hoped they had left the bar before the authorities arrived. That they were well on their way to California. Then the death face of Dwight Thompson appeared. Blood dripping from behind his head, courtesy of the family pickup.

Johnny shook the visual from thought and concentrated on his surroundings. Shadows played among themselves. For the first time he realized just how many shades of darkness there were. They created a secret world of landscapes unto themselves. A world shattered by color each time the sun rose. He could just see the makeshift cross heading Dallas's final resting place. Somehow, in the darkness, the newly created grave looked as though it had been there for a hundred years. He wondered if bugs and worms and other belowground creatures had already begun to feed off Dallas's host. The morbid thought caused his stomach to churn.

He rose from his spot, and walked around the base of the tree. *What was taking Buck so long?* After several soul-searching trips around Anvil Pine, Johnny spotted the headlights of Buck's pickup far in the distance. From where he stood, they looked like the eyes of some great beast heading across the land, coming to devour him.

* * *

Buck drew deep on his cigarette, pushed his hat back and he wiped at the beads of sweat across his forehead. He noticed his hands were shaking. An acidic storm roiled deep in the pit of his stomach. He'd been agonizing for the past hour on what it was he was going to say to Johnny. If he had indeed killed someone, in his grief over Dallas, then his life wasn't worth a plug nickel. He knew how badly the Natives were still treated; and if Johnny were to go to trial, well, he could only assume the worst. He'd be locked up like an animal, treated as an inferior. Beaten whenever the opportunity arose and forced into a homosexual existence. His chances of surviving such an ordeal were slim to none. No, in Buck's mind, there really was only one choice for Johnny, and that was to run. Run as fast and as far away from Eden, Montana, as he could. He smashed what was left of his smoke in the ashtray.

The headlights picked out Anvil Pine, standing alone like a sentinel watching over the land. Johnny stood next to Dallas's grave and he waved feebly. Buck pulled in next to Johnny's pickup, got out, and walked toward his son.

Seeing his father, Johnny's emotions seized him and he broke down again, tears spilling over his cheeks in a rush of raw, impassioned shame.

"Okay, Johnny, I'm here now," said Buck. "Pull yourself together, son." He took Johnny by the shoulders, lifted his chin with the tip of a finger, the lights of the pickup holding father and son in its embrace.

Johnny wiped at his nose, took a deep, settling breath. "I'm sorry, Dad," he said, his eyes shining with the threat of fresh tears. "It was an accident. I didn't mean to kill anyone." He sniffed, drew an arm across his nose and mouth.

"Now are you sure you did? Maybe you just, you know, really hurt him."

"No, Dad. I checked. Dwight Thompson is dead just as sure as I'm standing here."

"I see. Why don't you tell me what happened. Come, we'll sit down over there." He pointed with his chin toward Anvil Pine and put an arm around Johnny's shoulder. He steered him toward the great tree. Father and son sat next to each other. Johnny stared out into the fields and began his tale of woe, his body trembling as the story spilled from his lips. Buck sat there and listened without interruption. When Johnny was done, Buck stood, removed his hat, wiped at his forehead, and pulled at his jaw. A long, agonizing moment of silence followed.

"Seems to me that you only have two choices, son," said Buck, pacing the area in front of Johnny. "You can either turn yourself in to the sheriff's department come mornin', or you can…"

"Run," Johnny finished for him.

"Right. Or you can run."

"I can't go to prison, Dad. You know that as well as I do."

"I know, son, I know. But if you run, you'll be runnin' for the rest of your life."

"I know. And I'm scared. I wouldn't know where to go or how to get there." Johnny stood, his eyes worried with questions and wiped pine needles stuck to his backside.

"I reckon I already figured what you would decide," said Buck .

"You did?"

"Same thing I'd be doin' if I was in your shoes. Come here. Give me a hand." Buck walked toward his pickup.

Curious, Johnny followed. By now, the Black Angus were silent.

When Buck reached the back of his truck, he dropped the tailgate and pulled out a long sturdy board.

Johnny looked into the back. Lying on its side was a black motorcycle.

"I was going to give this to you on your birthday," said Buck. He stepped up into the truck and righted the Honda. "Put your foot on the board while I get this thing off."

Johnny did as he was told. Buck rolled the bike onto the ramp and steered it down. Johnny grabbed hold of the handles and eased it to the ground. There was a helmet fastened to the seat. Chrome spokes gleamed in the darkness. The sight took Johnny's breath away. He'd been talking for the past couple of years about maybe getting a bike some day.

"It's yours," said Buck. "The police will be looking for a Native driving a pickup. With this, you'll be less conspicuous. You'll be able to travel wherever it is you decide to go. Long as you don't break any traffic laws, you should be relatively safe. It's already registered and has a full tank of gas."

Johnny took in his father's face. Buck's eyes were misted. They both understood this might be the last time they would ever see each other.

Using his boot, Buck set the kickstand. He reached into the pickup and came away with a full knapsack. "I had Rose put some clothes together for you. You'll find a thousand dollars in one of the hidden pockets. Rose said to tell you good-bye. That she'll pray for your soul."

Stunned, Johnny looked from his father to the bike. Then to Dallas's grave and back to the bike. "Dad… I…"

"You're welcome. Now before either of us changes his mind, you better get goin'. You still have six hours of darkness left. I'll pick up your truck in the mornin'. It won't be long before the sheriff is knockin' at the door. I'll hold em' off for as long as I can. Use the back roads whenever you can. America is a big country. Lots of places to hide. Be smart, and you may never be found." He picked up the board, and tossed it back into the truck then slammed the tailgate shut. Turning to his son, he opened his arms. "Come here, give your old man a hug."

Johnny fell into his father's arms. They held each other in a man's embrace. "I love you, son," whispered Buck. "I know I wasn't the best father in the world, but I tried. Sometimes tryin' is more than a lot a people get."

"I love you too, Dad. And thank Rose for everything she's done for me. I'll miss you both, tremendously."

"I'll tell her." Buck patted Johnny's back. "Just one more thing. Give me your cell phone. You might get the urge to call me. That could mean trouble for you if they're able to trace the call."

Johnny handed Buck his phone.

"Where's your spirit bag, Johnny?"

Johnny looked down at his waist. "Shit! I must have lost it during the struggle."

"And your wallet?"

Checking his back pocket, Johnny realized it was torn and the wallet was missing. "I must have lost it too."

"I guess the cops must know what happened by now and who to come looking for. I hope losing your spirit bag ain't a bad sign. You know what your mother would think. Losing your spirit bag meant nothin' but bad luck."

"I know. I know. Let's hope, in this case, the great spirits are willing to forgive." However, he had lost a piece of Dallas and knew that it would bother him for days, for weeks to come.

"Yeah. Let's hope." Buck drew a deep breath. "Okay, now you get goin'. The cops are gonna be here more sooner than later. Best of luck to yah, son. I'll think of you often." Buck smiled best he could under the circumstances, turned, and walked away. When he reached the truck, he lit a cigarette, slammed the door shut, and drove off without looking back. He did not want Johnny to see that for the second time in his life, Buck Black was crying like an old woman.

Johnny watched the truck until he could no longer see taillights. Then he went to Dallas's grave. On a knee, he said good-bye once more. Then he looked deep into the darkened acreage to see if there were any signs of Thunder and Lightning. Whistling loudly, he hoped they were near.

After a few seconds, the sound of heavy hooves pounding the earth filled the starlit silence. The Appaloosas charged toward him. When they reached the cross fence, Johnny wrapped his arms around their long faces and whispered, "Take care. Run free, my friends. I'll miss you. I love you. Now go." Reluctantly the horses snorted, turned, then trotted back into the cover of darkness.

Johnny went to the Honda, put the knapsack over his shoulders, unfastened the helmet, tucked his hair beneath it, and mounted the bike.

It started smoothly. Although the engine was muffled, its start sounded like machine gun fire across the land. The Angus once again chorused a lament. To Johnny's ears, it sounded like they were telling him good-bye.

Slowly he released the clutch. The Honda rolled forward. "Cowboy up," he said to himself. He toe kicked it into second and drove into the darkness, a single beam of light guiding him, painfully aware that he would never be able to return to the Double B ranch.

* * *

9

Good-bye, Yellow Brick Road

REBECCA woke to the cackle and clicks of a crow. Deseray was no longer with her. She'd had no intention of falling asleep, but sometime during the night, when her mind was running rampant with indecisive thoughts, fatigue had overwhelmed her and she could no longer resist its pull.

Her eye lids separated. A fog had moved in off the bay during the night. It hovered at tombstone height like the smoke from a fire, giving the graveyard an eerie, surreal appearance.

The crow was atop the Gabriel marker announcing the dawn. It hopped from its perch and landed on the tip of the sword where it rocked forward, crowing, clacking, clicking. Morning's first rays lit the tree tops in brilliant shades of golds and greens. The contrast from ground to sky remarkable. Tomb stone height, death roamed in a shroud of white. Tree tops and hills illuminated heavenly.

For a brief moment, Rebecca lost herself in its strange beauty. She soaked it in, knowing that in a few moments, the sun's burn would banish the fog back to whence it came.

She was cold, her mother's marker a block of ice against her back. She pulled her knees to her chest, hugged herself, and wrapped the denim tightly around her torso. Her legs were covered in gooseflesh. With brisk up and down strokes, she rubbed at them in hopes the created friction would warm her.

Everything that happened mere hours before flooded back, and hit her with the force of a real-time nightmare. That god-awful night that would remain with her for the rest of her life. *Oh, God. Ben, Dad.* Pulse quickened, heart hammered in her ears. Using the palms of her hands, she pushed herself to her feet. Her legs were stiff, so it took a moment to gain their trust.

Startled, the crow leapt from its perch, its wings sounding in the silence. It headed for the branches of a nearby Spruce, clicking, clacking, cawing, watching.

Rebecca turned to face the top of Dover Bluff Road. Fog lay over Bay Ridge Cove like a blanket of cotton. The lay of the land gently sloped upward. Dover Bluff rose out of the white like a green thumb hammered by the rise of the sun. An isleland pushing its way out from the Atlantic. The house that had stood on its apex for a century, gone.

Rebecca's eyes misted. Although she had no intention of returning, seeing the nothingness where her home once stood, punctuated the finality of things. She took a deep breath, and said, "Good-bye, Dad. Good-bye, Ben. I love you both." On one knee, she caressed her mother's smooth granite marker. "Stay with me for as long as you can, okay, Momma? I'm frightened. I have to leave now before the town gets too busy. I'll watch and I'll listen for you, and I'll understand when it's time for you to leave me." She traced her mother's engraved name with the tips of her fingers and kissed the cold granite. "I'll miss coming here to see you," she whispered. Seeing the weathered bouquet of daffodils and tulips, received on a previous visit, it dawned on Rebecca that there would be no one left to bring Deseray flowers. Somewhere deep within, a part of Rebecca's soul wept.

Stepping through the parting fog, she stopped at the Gabrial marker, retrieved the suitcase and willed herself to be strong. Somehow, all the material remains that were Rebecca White did not weigh as heavily as they had the night before. She grasped the handle with purpose, tossed her head back, and jutted her chin. Drawing her shoulders true, she took a deep, determined breath. *It's now or never.*

The crow swooped overhead. It was joined by another, and another, until they numbered a murder of five against the sky blue backdrop. While they circled the tips of giant Spruce trees, they cautioned a dire omen.

Rebecca put one foot in front of the other. Her weary eyes picked out a path through the fog, the headstones. And thus began her journey. A page turned.

* * *

By the time Rebecca reached the road leading out of town, all that remained of the fog was a tiny wisp of cotton. The sun's full face was above the eastern horizon and the temperature had already risen markedly. It warmed the Sleeping Meadows chill of her bones. She had ducked the sheriff's patrol car twice and taken refuge in some bushes when a parade of fisherman drove past on their way to the wharf. Certain that everyone in town would have heard of the tragedy by then, mortgages still had to be paid and food put on the tables.

Knowing the first trucks to leave the cannery would not appear until at least seven o'clock, Rebecca concealed herself within a thick patch of vegetation bordering the culvert on the north side of the only road leading out of town. *Funny,* she thought, sitting on the suitcase balanced between her legs. The only road leading in and out of Bay Ridge was without name or number. It was simply known as "You take the road out of town and you go…" She had heard her father use that phrase all her life whenever he gave anyone direction.

To pass the time, she envisioned her father and brother doing what they enjoyed most. Hoisting traps while they sang ditties about the sea. She saw them on the ocean, riding the temperamental waves, happy men, proud men, full of light and life.

Nearly a half hour past before the first semi carrying a load of lobsters rumbled up the road. Rebecca was relieving her bladder, hidden from sight. Quickly, she pulled up her shorts. She emerged from where she was hidden and stood on the edge of the pavement. One hand held the suitcase. Raising the other, she hooked a thumb in the air. With a bare leg forward, she smiled.

The approaching Peterbuilt geared down for a moment, and Rebecca thought that she was going to be lucky enough to catch a ride on her first go. But as the forty-foot truck drew even, the driver pushed it into a higher gear and sped by. *Damn!*

She turned to head back into the brush and tall grasses when another truck appeared over the horizon. It's highly polished red cab and nondescript white trailer gleamed in the sun. It was moving fast. Rebecca repositioned herself at the edge of the road, jutting her arm out, and waved it in a quick, jerky motion. The Kenworth drew near. But it did not slow. Just as Rebecca thought it was going to speed past, the driver geared down and applied the brakes. The truck came to halt about fifty yards farther in a puff of road dust and hissing air. The driver engaged the rear spotlight, flashing it three times.

Rebecca ran along the gravel shoulder, the suitcase swinging wildly at her side. When she reached the passenger door, four feet off the ground, she was out of breath and sweating. God Is My Co-Pilot was scripted in white across the door. She looked up at the dark window. For a moment, nothing happened. Then the window powered down, and a voice came out of the darkness.

"Come on in," it said.

In Rebecca's mind, the voice sounded like it might belong to someone who was burly. Someone who smoked. Hesitating, she looked back at the road, to the place where she spent all her life. "Where are you going?" she called.

"Better question is, where ain't I going? Now come on. Do you want a ride or not? I gotta load of lobsters waiting to be boiled."

Reaching with her free hand, Rebecca took hold of the chrome lift and hoisted herself onto the step-up. Yanking the door, she tossed the suitcase to the floor. She looked to the driver and climbed up into the seat. She was surprised to see that the husky voice belonged to a younger man. Thirty, thirty-five at best.

"Well, close the door, girl. Can't go nowhere with it flapping in the wind."

Rebecca pulled on the door and sealed herself in. *Here I go.* Butterflies swarmed in her stomach.

The driver popped the clutch. The transmission engaged. The engine rumbled. Rebecca watched. Legs and hands moved in synchronization, working through the gears, bringing the eighteen-wheeler back to speed limit. Then the driver turned his head, regarded Rebecca's face. "Hi. My name's Jeff." He extended a hand. "Some people call me Roadrunner." Dark unkempt hair projected from beneath a Red Sox cap. His brown eyes were set apart. Cheeks bearing the scars of childhood pox. There was a tattoo of a bluebird on his left wrist and a gold wedding band welded to a finger. He was wearing the same kind of garment Ben and Ray wore often: red plaid work shirt rolled up to the elbows and jeans. The smile below his thick handlebar moustache seemed sincere.

Rebecca took his hand, gave it a quick sociable shake. The fact that he hadn't ogled her legs right away made her feel safe somehow. But there was no point telling this Jeff slash Roadrunner, what her real name was. "My name is Mary," she lied, and let go of his hand Then she pushed her hair back over her shoulders.

"Better put your seat belt on," cautioned Jeff.

Rebecca, now Mary, reached across her shoulder took hold of the belt and buckled herself in.

"So where are you heading… *Mary*?" said Jeff, annunciating her name as if he knew she was lying. "I'm not going pry as to why you're hitchhiking. None of my business. But if you tell me where you're heading, maybe I can get you close."

A map of the United States filled Rebecca's mind. *Thank goodness for geography lessons.* "I'm going to visit my aunt in Florida," she half-truthed. She did indeed have an aunt in Florida. But had no intention of paying a visit.

"I see. Had an aunt in Florida myself once, but she died. Walking with the Lord now. I can get you as far as Kentucky. Then I have to head north. Get this load off in Chicago. Ever been to Chicago, Mary?"

"Um… no."

"I guess for a city it's okay. Don't like spending the nights there though. Too much crime. We truckers have to watch out that our rigs don't get hijacked."

"They do that? In Chicago I mean," asked Rebecca glad that he had so far not mentioned anything about the fire.

"Hell. They do that in just about every city I've ever been to. Just seems more so in Chicago."

"Oh." Rebecca took in her surroundings. Jeff rambled on about some of the restaurants he'd eaten at in Chicago. She had been in a few trucks in her life, but none as nice as this one. Eggplant leather covered the seats, door panels, even the underside of the roof. There was a sleeper compartment behind her. It was curtained off with a stretch of tangerine fabric stating JESUS DRIVES A KENWORTH. The gear shift was topped by a chrome fist. The gadgets cramming the dash gleamed. An antique pocket watch and a large silver cross with chain hung from the CB mounted to the roof. *Jeff the Roadrunner respected his truck.* There wasn't an ounce of garbage anywhere. Rebecca wondered if Jeff was also a neat freak at home.

Fastened to the visor with rubber band was a picture of a black lab and a pretty woman with long brown hair. Both smiling happily for the camera. They looked down at Jeff as he drove.

Jeff caught her eyeing the photo. "My copilots. Them *and* God." He smiled. "That's my wife, Katherine. Everybody calls her Kat. And that handsome fellow is our dog, Ranger. Kat and I have been married ten years. Sometimes I bring Ranger along when I have a short haul, because he's much older now. Can't handle runs lasting more than a couple a days. Weak bladder, God bless him. Say, what kind of music do you like? I've got all kinds."

"I… um… like old rock and roll."

"Me too. I'll take that as a sign you and I are going to get along just fine." Jeff the Roadrunner reached beside him and pulled up a CD. "Here, put this on for me." He handed Rebecca *Janis Joplin's Greatest Hits.*

Rebecca took the green-and-orange disc and slipped it into the player. In a heartbeat, "Piece of My Heart" flooded the cab from every direction. *How appropriate.*

"Pretty cool, huh Mary?"

Rebecca nodded, relaxed. Up till then, her body had been a knot of anxiety reacting to Ray's warnings that most truckers were sexual predators. Women in every state. His cautioning at the moment seemed unjustified. Jeff the Roadrunner was being nice. Anybody who cared as much about their dog spoke kindly of their wife and had a passion for their faith as Jeff seemed to, couldn't be all that bad. *Could he?*

"Where do you and your wife live?" asked Rebecca, having to compete with Janis's powerful voice.

"Ever heard of Kokomo, Indiana?"

"No. I haven't."

"Well, we have ourselves a nice little place there. A big backyard for Ranger. A garden for Kat and a view that would knock your socks off. A hot tub too!"

"Sounds nice. Comfortable."

"Oh, it is. When I drop this trailer of lobsters off in Chicago, I have to pick up some windows in Peoria, that's in Illinois as well. Drop them off in Minneapolis. Then it's back home to good old Kokomo. Going to put my feet up for a couple a weeks. Enjoy the view. There's nothing like having a home to go to Mary, with a wife that can cook like a chef and a loyal dog by your side. Nope, nothing like it."

Just the mention of *home* caused Rebecca to consider what she had left behind. *Would she ever have a place she could call her own again? Did Vegas hold all the answers for her? Would she become famous? God, she hoped so. Or would her journey never end? Directing her from place to place. Never allowing her to settle in. Would she have to run until she died?* While these thoughts rioted through her mind, her arms and legs began to tingle. She looked to the grinning man sitting next her. Then at the pictures above him. *Could he be? Stop that! You're getting all worked up. That's why your body is responding the way it is. Think positive thoughts... Mary.* Her inner voice laughed. *Funny how it always sounded so much like Mother's.*

The tingling abated. Rebecca rested her head against the beautiful diamond leather and gazed at the reflection in the side-view mirror.

Janis's whiskey voice slipped into "Summertime."

An orange ball rose into the blue, and split the mirror like a diamond. Rebecca could almost feel its reflected warmth. Crossing one leg over the other, she focused on the passing stretches of asphalt that seemed to be swaying to the music, and rendering Bay Ridge Cove far out of reach.

No, no, no, no, no, no, no, don't you cry.

* * *

The Kenworth glided along the interstate. Before Rebecca understood where she was, they had left Maine and crossed the border into New Hampshire. It was officially the farthest she had ever been.

Consciously, she folded her arms over her midsection, her stomach voicing the need for nourishment. The sandwich she had had at school and the half-finished apple were the only sustenance she had ingested in twenty-four hours.

"Sounds like someone's hungry," said Jeff.

"I am, a little," admitted Rebecca.

"Good. Me too." He lowered the volume of the last CD they were listening to. *Bruce Springsteen's Greatest Hits*. "I know a great little place not too far from here called Lucy's." He took his hands off the wheel, spread them apart. "Best home-cooked meals around. They give you plates of food this big."

"Sounds good. To tell you the truth, I could eat a horse."

"Well, I don't think they have horse on the menu, but you could always ask."

They laughed. In the short time they were together, Rebecca had come to trust Jeff the Roadrunner from Indiana. He gave her no reason not to. He still hadn't looked at her legs, not as far as she knew, and he continued to talk about what a wonderful life he had back in Kokomo. She could tell that he genuinely missed his wife and dog, asserting himself into her good book.

If the pocket watch dangling from the CB was correct, it was a quarter to eleven. Almost brunchtime. The span of nearly four hours had passed quickly. "Jeff?"

"Yes, Mary."

"I have a confession to make. You've been so nice. Well, I just can't continue with a lie on my lips."

"Oh? How's that?"

"Well, you see. My name really isn't Mary. I just told you that, well, because I was frightened. I've never thumbed a ride before. I hope you understand."

Jeff released one hand from the steering wheel, and held it out to her. "Hi, my name's Jeff."

Rebecca took his hand. "Hi, I'm Rebecca."

"Pleased to make your acquaintance, Rebecca. God does work in mysterious ways. Don't you think?"

"Yes," said Rebecca, feeling much better. "I suppose he does."

Lucy's diner was located on the south side of Interstate 19. A checker red-and-white single-storey building with large windows across its facade. Standing taller than the structure, holding a tray of beverages, was an aluminum statue of Lucille Ball. Red neon for hair and wearing a waitress outfit. Mechanically, the incredible likeness of the comedic diva waved a welcome. To Rebecca, it reminded her of something she'd seen in a '50s B movie. *The Blob*. Steve McQueen came to mind. Blue eyes laughing.

The acre-sized parking lot was jammed with trucks of all makes and colors, idling comfortably, parked in perfect order, row after row.

Jeff swung the Kenworth into the lot, and found a spot between an International and Volvo. He backed the rig in with hardly a glance into the side mirrors. "Well, here we are," he proclaimed, setting the air brakes.

"Before I get out," said Rebecca. "I would like to change if you don't mind."

"Sure, sure. You can change back there." Jeff hooked a thumb toward the sleeping compartment. "While you're doing that, I'll go and find us a table."

"Thanks, Jeff. I'll only be a minute."

As soon as he was out the door, Rebecca retrieved the suitcase. She drew the Jesus Drives a Kenworth curtain to one side and climbed into the back. She left enough of it open so that light entered. The compartment was roomier than it looked. More photos of Kat and Ranger and a framed print of a crucifix hung on a wall. A small mirror hung above the head of the bed. Rebecca assumed Jeff used it to shave. The single bed seemed comfortable enough, and there were several chew toys piled in a corner for whenever Ranger was able to ride with his master. Flipping the latches on the suitcase, she removed a pair of jeans and withdrew a twenty from the money roll hidden deep within a pair of socks. Hurriedly, she slipped off her shorts, folded them in half, and put them into the suitcase. Lifting Bandit, she kissed him where a glass eye should be. The photo of her mother stared back at her. Rebecca placed a palm over it and said, "Wish me luck." Then she relatched the suitcase.

Without removing her runners, she lay on her back and pulled the skin-tight jeans over her hips, fastened the metal snap and drew the zipper. Then she stuffed the twenty into a pocket. Checking herself in the mirror, she finger-fluffed her hair. Much to her great relief, not a strand of it had been singed by the fire. *All in all I look pretty good.* The minimal amount of sleep she had had, had left little bumps of luggage beneath her eyes. A fresh pimple egged from her forehead. Using the index fingers of both hands, she popped the zit and wiped away the erupting white head. *Yuck.*

Deciding it was better to keep her belongings close at hand, Rebecca lugged the suitcase out from the compartment, opened the door, and carefully climbed down onto the tarmac. When she emerged from between the two trucks, she was embraced by the full warmth of the sun. A red pickup was being fuelled by its owner at one of four pumps. She put the suitcase down, took off her jacket, and slung it over an arm. She adjusted her top, which had bunched to one side, and walked to the entrance of Lucy's diner. Along the way she considered herself lucky that she had gotten a ride with Jeff the Roadrunner instead of some lowlife redneck. The kind her father always warned her about.

Male voices filled the interior. Just about all of the tables and booths were occupied with men of diverse shapes and sizes. An old country classic droned from speakers mounted to the four corners. Patsy Cline was singing "Crazy." The walls were painted a cheery yellow. Prints of boring landscapes were placed here and there. Ceiling fans turned slowly, recycling tobacco smoke. The smell of bacon, caffeine, and toast sent Rebecca's stomach reeling. Forty-plus waitresses in burgundy uniforms moved about robotically. Through the open kitchen, Rebecca could see a couple of men who appeared to be Mexican preparing orders. They wore white caps and T-shirts and their arms were tattooed. A line of chits hung from a metal wire stretched across the pickup window. She found Jeff sitting at a windowless table near the back. He waved her over.

Rebecca felt the eyes of every male on her body. She was used to having men ogle her, but somehow, in this environment, it seemed inappropriate. She felt as though she was the main attraction in a strip parlor. If she'd come in wearing her shorts, she thought, they'd be raping her with their eyes. Not that some of them weren't. Eyes downcast, she nearly bumped into a waitress whose arms were loaded with heaping plates of bacon and eggs. "Careful, honey," the middle-aged woman said. "If I drop these, it comes directly out of my pay."

"Sorry," said Rebecca. "I didn't mean to..."

"That's okay, dear," the waitress interjected and turned to serve a table of very large men who were paying more attention to Rebecca than the food about to be placed in front of them.

Creeps.

When Rebecca made it to the back of the diner, she slid the suitcase beneath the table and sat. Consciously, she pulled her jacket over her shoulders. On the table were upside-down mugs resting on paper mats. A metal condiment holder contained ketchup, packets of various sugars, a salt-and-pepper duo, and a carafe of maple syrup.

Jeff was holding a laminated menu that read, Serving Breakfast Since 1952. He peered over it. "Don't mind them. Most of them are good old boys and don't mean any harm. They probably haven't seen someone with your... attributes in a long while. You're a very pretty young woman if you don't mind my saying so. The road can be a fairly lonely place sometimes. When someone with your looks enters their lives, well, they just can't help but stare. Now what are you going to have? I think I'm going to have steak and eggs. Breakfast of trucker champions."

Rebecca snickered. "I'm going to have blueberry pancakes with lots and lots of syrup. Oh, and coffee."

"Sounds good. Listen, I've got to use the little boys' room, wash the dust off so to speak. If our waitress comes by, please order for us. I like my steak medium. And I'll have coffee as well."

"Sure, Jeff." Rebecca watched him get up and leave and head to the men's room. In less than a minute, a waitress came to the table with a pot of coffee held in front of her. The name tag over her massive left breast said her name was Bonnie. Grey brown hair was tossed above her head and held in place by a colorful kerchief. Around her waist was an apron. The Lucy icon silk-screened across the front. Like the menu, a caption rising from Lucy's mouth read, Serving Breakfast Since 1952.

"What'll it be, sweetheart?" asked Bonnie. She set the pot of coffee down, pulled a pad and pen from her apron.

Rebecca gave her their orders.

"Coffee?"

"Yes, please."

Bonnie flipped the upside-down mugs. Filled them to the brim. She noticed Rebecca's suitcase beneath the table, and she gave her a cautioned look. "What are you running away from, sweetheart?"

"Excuse me?"

"The suitcase. The fact you're riding with Jeff means you're either running from something or to something."

"I, um. I don't think that it's any of your business," said Rebecca, trying to sound polite about it.

"Take my advice, girl. Go home. Nothing but trouble out there. I know. I ran away when I was about your age. I've been here ever since. So no matter what the trouble is. Do yourself a favor and go home."

The two locked eyes for a moment. Rebecca saw a lot of remorse and misery in the woman's face and felt suddenly sorry for her. Then she repeated the lie she had told Jeff. "Just so you know, I happen to be going to visit my aunt in Florida."

"Uh-huh. You know there are better ways to get from one place to another. The Greyhound or a train perhaps. What you're doing is, well, it's dangerous."

Rebecca said, "I'll take that into consideration, thank you." She gave Bonnie a polite smile.

"Jeff's a sweetheart. But there are plenty of them who aren't." Bonnie looked around the diner, eyes suspicious. "So that'll be blueberry pancakes and an order of steak and eggs. Steak medium." She scribbled on the pad, stuffed pen and pad back into the apron.

"If you don't mind, yes, please."

"Coming right up." Leaning forward, Bonnie the waitress put a liver-spotted hand over Rebecca's and spoke so that only she could hear, "Go back home, sweetheart. Take the advice of someone who's been there. The world is full of monsters. Monsters who eat young things like you for breakfast." She picked up the half-empty coffeepot, menus, then turned without saying another word.

The dire warning sent a chill up Rebecca's spine. She reached beneath the table and put a hand on the suitcase as though testing to see if it was still there. *Don't listen to her. She's bitter that she didn't make it. Doesn't mean you won't. Stay the course. You're going to be a star.* Rebecca focussed on the empty chair across from her, and toyed with the packets of sugars. Jeff was a good man. She was sure of it. Bonnie had confirmed it. Still, something tugged at her. Not in a good way.

* * *

When Jeff returned, he looked refreshed, tidier. His Red Sox cap had disappeared, hair slicked back, finger-combed. He radiated with the cleanliness of his faith. "Hope I didn't keep you waiting too long," he said, took to his seat and set the cap on the chair next to him.

"No, I'm okay. Our food should be here soon."

"Good, I'm starved." Jeff took in Rebecca's face, and saw that she was troubled. "Is there something wrong?" He clasped his hands together and gave her an I'm-listening smile.

"Just… oh. It's nothing. It's just that sometimes, people should mind their own business."

"Can't argue with you there. Keep what's yours in your own backyard I always say."

Rebecca had heard that analogy before, but from who or when, she wasn't sure. "I'll remember that."

They sipped their coffees in silence. When their orders came, Bonnie and Jeff made small talk. Just some hellos and "It's been a while since we've seen you in here." The lifetime waitress smiled at Rebecca; however, her eyes still cautioned, *Remember what I told you.*

Disingenuously, Rebecca smiled back, nodded. *I understand. Thank you.* That was twice in one day she had deceived someone. *What was happening? Except for a couple of small fibs aimed at her father, she had never openly, and quite comfortably, lied before. Certainly nothing worthy of having to go to confessional for. Was it a built-in defence mechanism? Was lying to people what she needed to do in order to survive her journey?*

As soon as Bonnie went back to serving others, Jeff made the sign of the cross. Then he whispered his thanks for the bounty of food. Respectfully, Rebecca silently prayed with him. As soon as Jeff said *amen,* she poured syrup over the stack of pancakes until it oozed down the sides and gathered in the plate.

They ate without Jeff asking too many questions, which suited Rebecca just fine. When they were done, he said, "That's a pretty good appetite for someone as thin as you."

"It's a good thing they didn't have horse on the menu. I might have ordered it." Rebecca laughed, and it felt good. Her belly was full. The fullness reenergized her. Bonnie the waitress's cautionary advice now seemed distant words spoken from a dream.

"Would you like something else, Rebecca?" asked Jeff. "Maybe some more coffee? Lord knows I could use another cup."

"Yes, please," said Rebecca. "Just half a cup." Though quite awake, the first cup of java having given her a much-needed boost, there was still the night in the graveyard lingering on her skin that needed to be washed off. "If you don't mind, I'd like to freshen up myself."

"You go right ahead. I'll be right here when you're done."

Rebecca stood, reached into her jeans, and withdrew the twenty. She placed it on the table. "I'd like to buy breakfast," she said. "For your being so kind and for giving me a lift. I think it's the least I can do."

"Well, that's very generous of you, Rebecca. But..."

"No buts about it." She waved a hand. A gesture she'd seen her mother perform a thousand times. "I insist. Please." Then she added for good measure. "Call it one good Samaritan doing a deed for another."

"Well, I suppose it's all right. But I'm leaving the tip."

"Deal."

* * *

The bathroom held two stalls, a double sink with mirror and an automatic hand dryer. Painted a soft pink, it smelled of lavender and was kept meticulously clean by the staff. *Probably the only place where they get to be alone for a few minutes.* Rebecca went into one of the stalls and locked herself in. She dropped her jeans, sat on the cold porcelain and went about the business of relieving her bladder.

Alone, Rebecca thought about Ben and Ray. How the town must be going crazy by now searching for her. First speculation would be that she had perished in the fire. Then what? By Monday, and not finding a body, there would be all sorts of stories rumored. Would they hold a funeral for her as well? Would she become a folktale like the Ghost of Dover Bluff? Told to the young men who would soon become fishermen? Tears welled and threatened to spill, but she fought them back. *Don't think about things you no longer have control over,* she told herself. *It will only drive you crazy.* Then the door to the washroom opened and closed, chasing the undesirable thoughts away. Rebecca watched the space beneath the door. No one entered.

"Hello," she said. "Is someone there?"

No one answered. Yet Rebecca was sure there was another presence in the confined space. She placed a hand flat against the door, and listened. All she could hear was the faint buzz of the restaurant coming through the walls and the murmur of the bathroom's exhaust fan overhead.

Business finished, Rebecca wiped, flushed, and pulled up her jeans. Tentatively, she opened the door to the stall. No one there. She stepped into the empty room. Something flashed in front of her, giving her a start. When she saw that it was her own reflection in the mirror above the sink, she laughed.

Slipping from the jacket, she laid it across the sink counter and looked at her reflection. She stretched her arms above her head as high as her fingers would reach, and took a deep breath. Every muscle in her back and shoulders pulled tight. When she exhaled and dropped her arms, a fresh surge of blood rushed into her limbs.

Supported by her forearms, she turned on the faucets and leaned into the sink. Scooping handful after handful of cool water over her face, she took some into her mouth, rinsed, spat it out, then spread some of it up and down her arms. Oh how it felt wonderful.

Without reason, the lighting in the small room dimmed. The air grew thick, cold. Rebecca looked up. Something moved behind her, reflected in the mirror. A shadow that was there then wasn't. Rebecca turned on her heels. *Nothing.* Just the stalls with their open doors. Toilet paper hanging from plastic dispensers. But it was cold. So cold Rebecca could see her breath. "Momma?" she tried. The word coming out in a white plume. "Is that you?"

The automatic hand dryer engaged. The exhaust fan fell quiet. Something touched her shoulder. A slender finger, tapping once, twice, three times. Frost spread over the mirror in a lacing of silver. Rebecca's reflection wraithlike.

She closed her eyes and concentrated on her mother's face, calling to her with her mind. *I'm here, Momma. What do you have to tell me?* When she opened them again, an invisible hand fingered the mirror. It created letters that dripped with condensation.

Rebecca recognized her mother's text right away. Pure love filled her to the very core, warming her. *I love you too,* her inner voice replied. She watched as each letter was created. When the message was complete, the invisible hand momentarily caressed her face.

Rebecca stared at the message for a moment, absorbed in her mother's familiar touch. "Beware the gentle man," it read. "You mean Jeff?" she said to the mirror and her ghostly reflection. "Should I be afraid of him?"

Cold silence her only reply. Slowly, the hand lifted from her cheek. A tickling feather across her flesh. "No, no," protested Rebecca. "Don't leave me so soon. Momma? Momma? I need you." But she was once again all alone.

Rebecca leaned forward, and gripped the edge of the sink. Her face was fragmented in the bleeding letters. *You've got a decision to make, girl.* With a trembling finger, she wrote "I will" beneath the warning. Then she wiped all six words away with the arc of her hand. The hand dryer shut off, the exhaust fan whirred. The lights brightened to normal. The coldness fled in a rush, leaving the mirror dry and clear and Rebecca's heart wounded once more.

She remained in front of the mirror, and for reasons unbeknownst to her, studied the red mark the pimple had left. The freckles around her eyes and mouth seemed to move as if they had a life of their own, reminiscent of baby spiders she had once seen beneath the front porch. They had hatched from their sack, like a thousand red dots moving as one. Her eyes were playing tricks on her. *How easily the mind can be fooled into seeing just about anything.*

Turning on the cold, she scooped more of it into her palms, and let it wash down her face. When she looked up, the playful freckles had stopped their imaginary dance. Again Rebecca thought about Ben and Ray. How by now they would be out on the ocean, hauling traps, laughing like schoolboys. Completely satisfied with the life they had fashioned for themselves. Tears welled, but before they spilled, she knuckled them away. "I must continue to remain strong," she said to the face staring back at her.

The bathroom door opened. A plump waitress with plump ankles and carrying a black purse over one arm stepped in. The resemblance to Ethel Mertz was remarkable. She gave Rebecca the once-over, smiled, and said, "I hope I'm not disturbing you."

"No," said Rebecca. "I was just finishing up."

"Oh, that's fine then." The small woman waddled into a stall, and closed the door behind her. Rebecca gathered her jacket and shrugged into it. Leaning forward, she ran fingers through her hair and threw back her head. Long locks landed perfectly on her shoulders. When she put her hand on the door to leave, she heard the striking of a match and caught the immediate whiff of a freshly lit cigarette. *What do I do now?* she contemplated. It was the question of the moment, the day, the coming of weeks.

* * *

10

Running Scared

JOHNNY drove all night. He stopped in a field just south of Warland, where, by light of the Honda, he rested among a heard of sleeping cattle. There, he easily discovered the money Buck had left him, mostly hundreds plus a road map. Pinching one of the bills, he stuffed it into his jeans. Just knowing that it was there gave him a sense of well-being. He allowed himself twenty minutes or so to relieve himself, stretch his stiff muscles and to think about how far south he was going to head before taking another direction.

Gazing at the map in the beam of the Honda, he elected to go as far as Lander, then head east toward Casper. From there he would decide whether he should head south into Colorado or continue east to Nebraska. Mounting the bike, he continued on.

The early birthday gift hummed beneath him, its vibration keeping him awake through long stretches of dark and lonely interstate. White crosses indicating a journey's end for someone dotted both sides of the duo tarmac. He had encountered several different systems during the six-hour ride, the voice inside his head hammering home that he was a *killer, killer, killer.*

Wherever there was a pass over a river, multiple crosses came to light, marking the tragic end of entire families. On more than one occasion, teddy bears and other stuffed animals had been taped to the support beams of the one lane bridges.

After he crossed the border into Wyoming, Johnny was assaulted by a stinging rain. It had lasted nearly an hour, pelting his helmet until he thought he would lose his mind. He drove through it with reckless abandonment until he made his way clear. Soaked to the skin, he carried on. Driving him steadfast, always at the forefront of his mind, was the constant need to put Eden, Montana, and the law as far behind as possible.

The sun had been up for nearly two hours. Johnny watched it as it split the eastern horizon. An orange ball that rose swiftly into the blue. It warmed his cold wet body. Nonetheless, his hands were cramped and his leg muscles had stiffened. By the measure of the fuel gauge, he saw that it was time to pull over, dry off, maybe have something to eat and reenergize.

Five miles back, he'd passed a sign indicating to motorists that the last stop for gas for 110 miles was just ahead. A road stop offering food and fuel called Florence's Place. *Good,* he thought. He was strung out. The lines on the roadways had become hypnotic. If he continued in the state his mind was swimming in, surely an accident was not too distant into his future.

* * *

Florence's Place sat off the interstate like a wart on a finger. The white building leaned noticeably to the south and was in desperate need of a new coat of paint. Grimy windows offered little view of what the place looked like inside. Time-faded signs offering ice cream cones and fudge sickles stared out from behind the glass. Blue smoke rose from an exhaust fan mounted to the roof where an American flag and state flag drooped in the windless sunlight. A neon coffee cup was mounted above the screen door entrance where a vine of plastic hyacinths clung to an arch of white lattice.

Next to the steps, to the lattice entrance, three vehicles were parked in a row. A green pickup truck. A baby blue '60s Volkswagen Beatle with Peace and Love decal on its rear bumper and a Roto-Rooter plumbing van with an extension ladder mounted to its roof. *Thankfully,* Johnny thought. *No police cars.* Florence's was just the sort of out of the way place state troopers might gather to make small talk and drink coffee.

Four pumps, one out of service, were being manned by a tall, skinny kid with a face marred by acne and a mouthful of orthodontics. A bright red golf shirt fit loose on his thin frame. Thick black hair fell over his ears. Clinging to his legs was a pair of grease-stained shorts. Construction boots, scuffed to the steel across the toes, held his feet; and a red rag lay limp from a back pocket.

Pulling the Honda to the nearest pump, Johnny shut off the engine and deployed the kickstand. Slowly he dismounted, his legs screamed, and for a second he thought he might actually fall sideways. His spine and ass felt as though he'd been on the back of a horse herding cattle for weeks.

The young attendant walked over, and stopped next to the pump. He tried desperately not to show his braces as he spoke. "Filler up?" he asked.

Johnny removed the bug-splattered helmet. His hair fell about his shoulders and the knapsack strapped tightly across his back. It was the only part of him that was truly dry. "Yes, thanks... Peter," said Johnny, reading the name tag pinned to his shirt.

Peter stared at Johnny and the bike for a split second before removing the gas cap. "Nice bike. Looks new. Say, you look like you've gone through some weather. I heard it was going to rain on the radio. Coming in from the north. Have you been driving all night? Sure looks like it." He removed the nozzle from the pump, inserted it into the tank, and squeezed. A UPS semi roared past the station, resurrecting a tornado of dust.

"Yeah," said Johnny. "Came down from Billings. Long ride."

"I'll say. You must be hungry." "Do they serve a good breakfast in there, Peter?"

"Oh, sure. My sister grills up a mean plate of bacon and eggs." He smiled. Ortho steel glinted in the sunlight. "Coffee's good too."

Johnny smiled back. "Good, I'm hungry. So this is a family-run place then?"

The nozzle kicked in Peter's hand. He pulled it out and said, "Yup. Me, my mom, and my sisters. You'll see. That'll be seventeen dollars, please."

Johnny fished the hundred out of his pocket and handed it to him. "I'm sorry, it's all I have."

Peter took the bill, and examined it. Rubbed it between his fingers as though he could expertly detect a phony. Shoving it into the right front pocket of his shorts, he withdrew a wad of bills big enough to choke a horse from the left and counted out the change. "Have a good day and… *enjoy* your meal."

Johnny noted a glint of mischief in Peter's eyes. "I will. And here," he handed Peter three Benjamins. "Thanks for the friendly service."

"Gee, thanks, mister. I don't get many tips out here."

Johnny looked at the pimply teen. "Here's another one. Be cool. Stay in school."

Peter spread his arms as wide as he could and replied, "What? And give up all this. My empire." He laughed.

Johnny mounted the bike, fitted the helmet over his head, and drew up the kickstand. The engine purred to life when he turned the key. He gave Peter a quick wave and slowly drove the Honda toward the café. He parked it next to the plumber's van. From there he could vaguely see people moving about inside. Removing the helmet, he fastened it to the rear seat, slung the knapsack off his shoulders, and made his way toward the entrance.

The screen door groaned when he opened it. Johnny put his hand out to stop it from slamming him in the back. When he stepped into the café, the plumber, wearing a Roto-Rooter cap, turned his head to watch him enter. The other patrons, a Tiny Tim look-alike and a burly gentleman, remained focused on the plates of food in front of them.

Soft blue paint covered the walls. The recorded sounds of mandolins played from a single speaker. Black-and-white prints of Sicily and Rome and the smell of tomato sauce simmering filled Johnny with a sense of welcome. Overall, the place was in sharp contrast to what the outside advertised. Appliances gleamed. The floors shone, and the lone counter was spotless. Each of the checkered cloth tables were anchored by ladder back chairs. A vine of plastic grapes toured the walls. They climbed the spans of windows and ended above a door stating Employees Only.

Several posted signs indicated that it was a nonsmoking environment. An out-of-date cash register and a figurine of the Virgin Mary sat on the counter next to a collection jar for the Prevention of Spousal Abuse that was half-filled with change . A blackboard behind the register advertised the lunch special: Spaghetti Marinara for $7.95. Included in the meal were a side salad, fresh baked bread, and a beverage.

A silent television screen broadcasting the news looked down at everyone.

An oasis in the middle of nowhere.

Two women stood by a Burns coffeemaker behind the counter. Another had her back turned and was working the grill, turning bacon and cracking eggs. Each donned burgundy outfits hemmed just above the knees. They had been in conversation until one of them, seeing Johnny, nudged the other with her elbow. Johnny noticed right away how familiar they were in appearance, though one was older than the other. The same dark hair framed familiar dark eyes. When the cook turned around, Johnny was staring at a trio of Italian beauties. He smiled politely, and went to an available table at the back of the café. He could feel everyone's eyes on him or so he guiltily imagined. Setting the knapsack on one the chairs, he took a seat facing everyone. A menu already sat on the table: WELCOME TO FLORENCE'S PLACE. Johnny pretended to study it, having already decided to have Peter's recommended choice of bacon and eggs.

"How may I help you?" the Sicilian accent drew Johnny's attention. When he looked up, liquid black eyes gazed down at him. *Oh, how I wished I could disappear in those eyes.* "I would like an order of bacon and eggs, easy over, and some coffee please." His eyes caught the name tag pinned to the gentle slope of a perfect breast: "Theresa." When she smiled extraordinarily perfect white teeth at him, Johnny nearly melted. The simple gesture warmed the very chill in his bones. Her beautiful Sicilian face was absolutely perfect. An aquiline nose centered dark eyes. Exquisite cheekbones. Kissable lips leaned slightly to the south. A pellet of a black mole sat just so above her lip. Again the teeth gleamed.

"Coming right up. Can I get you some water?" She scribbled Johnny's order on a pad.

Though Johnny had spent more than an hour racing the rain, he was parched. "Yes, please. Thank you."

Theresa took the menu, went back to the counter, tore off the chit, and handed it to her sister at the grill. Then she said something. Each stole a quick glimpse.

Johnny focused on the soothing blue of the walls. At a framed print of the Leaning Tower of Pisa. His hands were chaffed red, desperately needing the warmth only a cup of coffee could give them. There was a good half inch of water in his boots, and his pants were glued to his legs. Arms felt like alien extensions. He closed his eyes for a moment, and thought about Dallas, and about everything that had happened the night before. The retort of a rifle. The shovel biting into earth. The killing kick. Dwight Thompson's death stare. *"You should have a little faith.'"* Thunder and Lightening dark silhouettes. His father's sad eyes.

When his eyes separated, the mother was standing next to him and holding a glass of iced water and a mug of coffee. She cut a figure that competed with her daughters. If it were not for the few strands of grey and the fifty-something laugh lines around her eyes, she could easily pass as an older sister. A gold crucifix hung at the soft dimple of her throat. Smaller versions from earlobes. She smiled with the same brilliant warmth her daughter had. "There you go," she said. "I am Florence. The owner. You looking cold, yes?"

Johnny nodded. His eyes met hers and he saw in them a woman of kindness. A woman who was content with her life. Living the American dream, even though that dream was a four-pump gas station and a small café on a stretch of nowhere. "My name is Johnny," said Johnny. The two joined hands for a moment.

"Maybe you lika to use the private bathroom, yes? You having change of clothes?" Florence's eyes moved to the knapsack.

"Yes, thank you. I sure would like to get out of these wet things." Johnny took a quick taste of hot coffee, reached across the table, and lifted his knapsack.

"Come, I show you," the kindly owner said, her dark eyes smiling and motioning with an inherited gesture for him to follow.

* * *

The private bathroom was located at the back of the café, just beyond the Employees Only door. There was a shower, toilet with frilly pink cover. A faux marble pedestal sink and an ornate mirror where two cherubs bordered the gilded frame and looked down with heavenly eyes. A heart-shaped soap dispenser and tulip vase that held a single plastic rose. The walls were fuchsia with white moldings. A scale sat on the floor next to a blue mat for feet wiping.

Johnny thanked the owner for her generosity. "I'm very grateful for this."

"You justa leave wet clothes on floor. I take care of them for you. Okay? I put in dryer."

Again Johnny thanked her, closed the door and locked it.

He waited until he heard her move down the narrow hall before disrobing. Carefully, he removed his boots so none of the water spilled onto the floor. Then he emptied them into the toilet. Removing his wet socks, he wrung and hung them on the edge of the sink. Next were the skin-soaked jeans. He took the change Peter had given him out of the pocket, set the bills on the tank of the toilet, and wrung the jeans over the sink until not another drop fell. Then he took off his shirt. Using one of three towels hanging on the back of the door, he warmed his body. Stepping out from his underwear, he ran the towel down and over his private parts. The soggy briefs he put into a side pocket of the knapsack. There was no way he was going to let the kind owner see his unmentionables.

With the towel draped over a broad shoulder, he turned on the faucets, pumped soap into his hands, and scrubbed at his face in an attempt to alleviate the weariness that was threatening to take him over.

When he took good stock of himself in the mirror, he discovered that even though his hair had been under helmet, many species of insects still managed to die entangled in its strands. *Shit, no wonder everyone was staring at me. I would have stared at me too.* He took a stretch of toilet paper, laid it in the sink and picked the creatures out one at a time. When he'd succeeded down to a wasp that had been torn in half, he folded the tissue and flushed the dead remains down the toilet. Closing the lid, he sat his knapsack on top of it. It was the perfect opportunity for him to inspect all of its contents.

Unzipping the main compartment, Johnny plunged his hand in and came out with a denim shirt. Mother of pearl snaps on the cuffs. A second attempt garnished a pair of black Levis that looked almost new. What he needed was a fresh pair of socks. He jammed his hand farther until his fingers reached bottom. He pulled out a black flashlight and checked its charge. It was good, so he rested it on the lid of the water tank. However, on his next search for useful items, his fingers touched something hard, something cold. When his index finger looped into the trigger, Johnny's heart began to pound. *Shit! Shit! Shit!*

There was no need to extract it. Buck had left him a gun. By the feel of it, a .38. He withdrew his hand. *What the fuck was Buck thinking?*

Every killer needs a gun, Johnny, answered the condemning voice that had so far been his constant road companion.

"Shut up!" he said too loudly. He turned round and round in the small space. He caught a glimpses of his face in the mirror. The discovery of the gun had paled him. *Okay, okay. Calm down, Johnny. Nobody knows you have the gun. Just keep it where it is until you get someplace where you can get rid of it. Everything will be fine. Don't even look at it. Forget it's there. You're just some poor schlep who got caught in the rain, remember that.*

For several minutes, he just stood there. Although Buck's blind intentions were born of concern for his only son, he had really put him in a predicament.

Further inspection of the knapsack and its many pockets profited a pair of work socks and clean underwear. No doubt courtesy of Rose.

Johnny dressed quickly and pulled on his boots. The fresh pair of socks sponged what water still remained. He made sure every zipper of the knapsack was closed, and stuck the bills in a front pocket. Then he folded his wet clothes, and rested them in the sink with the droopy wet socks. Checking himself in the mirror, he looked presentable enough. Slinging the knapsack over a shoulder, he was now very conscious of its condemning weight. "Wish me luck," he said to the cherubs above the sink. "I really need it."

When he came through the Employees Only door, Johnny's heart skipped a beat. Seated at the counter, huddled over coffee, were two sheriff's deputies, their side arms larger than cannons. They turned at the sound of the door opening, and leveled Johnny with a precursory once-over.

Johnny froze. Multiplied by ten, the weight of the gun pulled on his shoulder. Without making direct eye contact, he glanced around the small café. *Keep your cool, Johnny.* The Volkswagen owner was gone, loose change sat on the table. The Roto-Rooter employee and burly pickup driver were still huddled over coffees.

Theresa and her sister were at the grill preparing bacon and frying eggs. Johnny's eyes settled on the owner standing behind the counter, smiled, and said, "Thank you for letting me use your bathroom."

"You leave wet clothes?" asked Florence.

"Yes," said Johnny.

"Good. You sit down. You breakfast is just about ready."

Johnny started for his table.

One of the deputies asked, "Get caught in the rain, did yah?" He was still wearing his sunglasses. His partner was not. Each of them stared at Johnny, waiting for an answer, studying him, dissecting him with their trained cognizance.

Johnny said, "Yes, I did. A couple of hours north of here." The words came out like silk, void of the fear that was threatening to strangle him.

"Too bad," said the lawman without shades. "That your bike out there then?"

"Yes," said Johnny, not sure whether he should add the sir part and didn't.

"Where you coming from?" asked the man behind the shades.

Shit! Here we go, Johnny thought. These guys were going to ask him questions until they found out where it was he was coming from and where he was going. If they'd heard about the killing at the Big Sky, and there was no reason why they shouldn't have, they were going to keep up this brand of if-it-looks-like-a-duck interrogation until they were satisfied. What Johnny had going for him, however, was that running into a lone Native in Wyoming was commonplace. He was just one of thousands upon thousands. As he was about to say Sheridon, the benevolent owner spoke, rescuing him.

"Let boy eat!" she said with the conviction of a demanding mother.

"You know this young man, Florence?" asked the deputy without shades.

"Yes, Ciao. Johnny good boy. You let him eat now."

"Fine then," chorused the deputies. "Just being neighborly is all," added the one wearing shades.

There was a scrutinizing moment of silence. The deputies stared at Johnny. Johnny believed he was going to do a Wicked Witch of the West. Melt right into his boots.

"See, I told you it was going to rain," said the one with the shades.

"Yeah, I guess you were right, Tom."

Both men spun in their stools, eyes returning to the sisters working the grill.

The screen door flew open. Peter ambled in, the door slammed him in the behind. "Hi, Officer Dan. Officer Tom. Catch any bad guys lately?"

"Not so far today," said Deputy Tom.

Disappointed for a brief second, Peter cast his eyes to the floor. When he looked up again, he was all smiles. "You guys staying for breakfast. I sure am hungry. Hey, Mom, can I have something to eat?"

Thank you, thank you, thank you. Seizing full advantage of the presented opportunity, Johnny made a beeline for his table, praying that no one could hear his heart hammering. He placed the knapsack on an empty chair and wrapped his hands around the still-warm coffee cup. When he glanced out the window, he saw that the deputies had parked their vehicle next to the Honda. In plain sight, a shotgun sat erect between the driver and passenger seats. He took a long swallow of coffee. It went down smoothly, but when it landed in his empty stomach, it caused a riot to go along with the tangle of nerves squirming like electric worms.

Florence and Peter disappeared behind the Employees Only door. A moment later, Peter came out and said, "Hey, Angelina. Mom says I can have a breakfast bun. So snap to it." He snapped his fingers loudly.

The young woman behind the grill shook a spatula at him and said something in Italian that made Peter laugh and respond, "Oh yeah, in your dreams maybe." Then he sat on a stool next to the officers and mimed them in their posture. The way they both had their hands clasped in front of them, fingers interlocked, eyes straight and true.

Officer Dan reached over and gave Peter's thick hair a tussle. "You still want to be a cop?" he asked.

"Yeah, sure," said Peter. "That or a race car driver. I'm going to have me a whole string of race cars when I get older. Maybe win the Indianapolis 500."

"Knowing you, you'll be doing both quite well."

"Hey, *yeah*. Nothing says that I can't be both."

"Well, you will let me know when you want to start your career in law enforcement?"

"Oh sure, Officer Dan. You'll be the first to know." As if he had a sixth sense about incoming business, Peter leapt from the stool and fled through the screen door. *Slam!*

"Peter!" Angelina yelled at his fleeing back. "Don't let the door slam!"

Johnny looked out the window. Sure enough, a silver Mercedes had pulled up to the pumps. He watched Peter go about his business while he kept his ears tuned to the conversations going on around him.

Angelina sat two brown bags in front of the deputies. Smiling beautifully, she said, "Have a nice day, gentlemen."

The deputies took their to-go orders and wished her a "good day." Officer Dan added a little four-fingered salute. "We'll be back for lunch," he said. "Wouldn't want to miss your mom's marinara." They went through the screen door, careful not to let it slam.

Johnny watched them through the spans of windows. When they stopped at the patrol car, Officer Dan took a glance at the license plate on the Honda. A long-enough glance to make Johnny more insecure than he already was. Then Officer Dan perused the restaurant.

In Johnny's mind, he had looked right at him. Johnny turned away, his attention to the half-empty coffee cup, the silent television, the prints covering the walls. A few long moments passed before he heard the metallic sound of doors closing and tires biting into asphalt. The deputies drove quickly away.

What if they were running the plates right now? They'd be back with guns blazing. You're being paranoid. But you're right about one thing. You can't involve these nice people. You have to leave as soon as the opportunity lends itself. Attending these thoughts, Theresa's unobserved approach startled him.

"Here you go, Johnny," she said, and set his order in front of him. Perfectly done eggs siding three strips of crispy bacon and hash browns stared at Johnny. "Is there anything else you need?"

"I… um… No. This is fine. And thank you."

"Enjoy your breakfast," said Theresa. "Mom's going to put your clothes in the dryer now. Shouldn't take more than a half an hour." A wholesome smile illuminated her face.

Johnny returned the gesture and said, "I really appreciate what your mother is doing for me."

"That's just the way we are."

"Well, there should be more people like you. The world would be a much better place."

"Thank you," Theresa said, and looked at him curiously. "I don't mean to pry. But where are *you* heading? You're not from around here. I would remember you."

Johnny did not know how to respond. Whether to lie or dance around the truth. "To be honest," he said, his eyes locked on hers. "I'm on a road trip. Kind of a self-awareness thing."

"Really! You're so lucky. I'd like to take a trip like that someday." Chocolate eyes moved about the tiny café. They settled on the prints of places she had never been. Then those warm eyes settled on the plate between Johnny's elbows. "Listen to me rambling on while your breakfast gets cold. Please eat. I'm sorry if I sounded nosy."

"No, it's fine. Talking to you I mean. And I hope you do get to take a trip someday. You *and* your sister. Your brother too for that matter. I'm sure the three of you deserve it." Johnny could have talked to her all day and night, but the voice inside his head was telling him, *Eat up and get your ass away from these wonderful people.*

"Now you're just being kind. You go ahead and eat. If you would like some more coffee, I'll just be over there." With an extra pep to her step, Theresa headed to the grill where her sister was busy preparing Peter's breakfast bun.

Johnny dug into his meal. He broke a section of toast, and dipped it into a runny yolk. One eye remained on the road, the other on the plumber who was talking into his cell phone. The burly man pushed his chair back, rose, tossed a ten on the table, and left the café. Florence came through the Employees Only door, and attended the marinara sauce simmering on the stove top.

Full of gas, windows sparkling, the Mercedes drove away under a plume of dust. Peter stood by one of the pumps and wiped his hands on the red rag. He looked off into the nothing distance. Into his future.

As Johnny was about to bite into a crispy piece of bacon, his heart skipped a beat, then another. The patrol car was coming back down the highway, in reverse, at a fairly good clip. It headed straight for the café.

Johnny's forehead moistened. The momentary waltz he was having with autonomy retreated, deflating him. *This is it. They ran the plates, and now they're coming for me.* He dropped the piece of bacon and, for a brief second, thought about the gun not an arm's reach away. When he looked up, he saw that everyone else was watching as well. The plumber hung up on whomever he was speaking with. Seeing that something might be amiss, Peter took hot pursuit after the patrol car, his long legs and skinny arms a blur in the morning sun. His inherited dark eyes wide with anticipation.

Shit! Why here? Why now? Give yourself up peacefully, Johnny. It's the right thing to do. Quickly he decided that that was exactly what he *would* do. There was no point in running further. His journey had come to an end before it really began. His one regret, however, was that it was going to involve these nice people. It would be over in minutes, but would leave a false impression of who he really was and a blemish on their little piece of paradise.

Two booming heartbeats passed before both doors of the cruiser opened. Officer Dan and Officer Tom emerged. They moved as one toward the café, walking the walk. Officer Dan with one hand on his holster. Officer Tom preferring the grip of his baton.

Peter stopped at the rear of the patrol car and said something. Officer Dan turned, pointed at him, said something back. It seemed that everything was taking place in slow motion, like drying glue. Peter stayed where he was, and kicked at a rock next to his foot.

The screen door groaned. The deputies stepped into the diner. Officer Tom looked directly at Johnny.

Get up, Johnny! It's all over. Johnny moved his feet. Pushed with his palms. The yolks of his uneaten breakfast wept yellow tears. Mandolins played on.

Florence stepped in front of the deputies, "Hey. Whatsa going on? You boys forgetting something, yes? Is everything okay, Officer Dan?"

Johnny rose slowly and reached for the knapsack, the gun within calling to him. *NO!* his rational voice screamed. *Don't touch it! Things are complicated enough!* Johnny's life was going to come to an abrupt end. A prison cell waited. A murdering Native did not stand a chance.

Much to his amusement, Officer Dan said, "Everything's okay, Flo. We just want to have a little chat with Mr. Kemp here." He turned. Both officers moved toward the plumber who was avoiding eye contact.

"Sir? Does that van out there belong to you?" asked Officer Tom.

Johnny sat down, quickly, his sudden weight shoving the chair. It squeaked across the linoleum. Relief rushed to his feet, tickled his toes. He could not believe his good fortune.

The plumber lowered his head. "Yes, Officer, it does," he mumbled.

"Then would you mind stepping outside with me and my partner, sir?"

"Sure... um... no problem." Mr. Kemp stood.

Each deputy took up a side, and steered Mr. Kemp toward the door. They went through the entrance. Not a word spoken.

Slam!

Johnny nearly jumped out of his skin. Inexplicably, he grabbed at the knapsack. *What the fuck are you doing, Johnny? You just caught the break of a lifetime. Relax. Breathe easy. You're probably in the safest place on earth, at least for the time being.* He drew his hand away from the knapsack as though it were contagious, and watched the deputies lead the plumber toward their still-running vehicle.

Florence and her daughters rushed to the windows, bodies pressed together. "What do you suppose he did, Momma?" asked Theresa.

"Yes, what do you think he did?" said Angelina.

Florence stared at the scene unfolding right outside her café.

Peter had smartly moved out of the way, his eyes lit with the fireworks of youth. Mouth catching flies. The three men stood next to the open door on the driver side. Waves of heat rose from the vehicle's hood and roof. Officer Dan's head moved up and down as he spoke. Then the plumber produced his wallet from a back pocket and removed two laminated pieces of ID.

"I don't know," said Florence. "Nothing too serious I think. But I know young boys should not see things like this. They get ideas. Go to the door and tell your brother to come in."

"Yes, Momma." Theresa went to the screen door and opened it quickly. In an urgent tone and wildly gesturing hand, she called out, "Peter!... Peter! Momma said come in! Rapidamente!"

Reluctantly, Peter began to move toward the entrance, not taking his eyes off the three men next to the patrol car. When he made it to the steps, Theresa reached out, grabbed him by the collar, and yanked him in.

Slam!

"Santa Maria! One day that door is going to give me heart attack," bemoaned Florence, clutching at her chest.

"Sorry, Momma," chorused Peter and Theresa.

"Hey, did you see that?!" exclaimed Peter. "Cool huh! They're going to arrest that guy!" He went to the window and stood between his mother and sister. Theresa kept vigil behind the screen door.

"How do you know? Maybe they just want to talk to him," Angelina pointed out.

"Because I heard them. That's how. Jeez." Peter rolled his eyes. "Something about unpaid parking tickets. A lot of them."

"Come away from window now," said Florence. "There is nothing... *cool* about it. Have you forgotten we still have guest?" Everyone's attention went to Johnny.

He smiled, nonchalantly picked up his coffee, and said, "I guess it doesn't pay not to pay your parking tickets around here." In his mind's eye, he could see the gun sitting snug within the confines of the knapsack. *Would I have used it? Of course not. Then why are you thinking about it? And not just once. It's the second time in the past half hour. Jesus Christ, Buck. What were you thinking?* The sooner he got rid of it, the better. His eyes shifted from the faces of his hosts to the men outside.

Officer Dan continued his interrogation, hat moving up and down as he spoke.

Johnny thought, *That could be me out there.* Considering himself to be the luckiest person on earth, at least for the time being, he took a deep breath and an even deeper drink of coffee.

What happened next happened without resistance on the plumber's part. In one swift movement, Officer Tom removed a set of cuffs from his belt, took the plumber's wrists, pulled them around his hips, and slapped them on.

It was impossible, yet Johnny would swear on a stack of Bibles that he heard the click, click as the cuffs took hold.

Officer Dan opened the rear door.

With his hand firmly atop the plumber's head, Officer Tom steered Mr. Kemp into the backseat. Officer Dan turned his attention back to the café. There was a huge got-a-bad-guy grin on his face. He gave everyone a little salute. Then he got in the vehicle and slammed the door with relish. Officer Tom did the same.

Under the blistering sun, the patrol car backed away from the diner, turned toward the highway, and disappeared.

* * *

A half hour, two cups of coffee, and a trip to the men's room later, Florence presented Johnny with his warm, dry clothes folded neatly in her arms. "Here you go, Johnny. Nice and dry. Smell good, yes?" She set the bundle on the table.

Johnny took in the air of lemons. His clothes never smelled so good. He'd been doing his own laundry since he was twelve and could never get the knack women had when it came to getting the best smells into clothing. "Thank you again," said Johnny. "I could never pay you back for the generosity and kindness you've shown me." He unzipped the knapsack, picked up the small bundle and eased it into the opening. The gun called out to him. *Killer killer killer.*

"You good boy, Johnny," said Florence. "This I can see. But there is sadness in your eyes, yes?"

Sadness. The word struck Johnny hard. It manifested an image of Dallas all full of life. "I recently lost my best friend," he said.

"I'm so sorry. It is hard to lose someone close. God does have his reasons for taking those we love away from us." She paused thoughtfully. "He just doesn't tell us." She looked out the window. Johnny understood she was remembering her own loss. Florence lifted the cross dangling at her throat, and kissed it reverently.

He wanted to share with her everything that had happened. He wanted to take the pain of memory from this woman. Someone he knew he could trust with the deepest secrets of his life. There weren't many people like her, but when you met one, you knew it right away. His mother was one. But there was no time to discuss their losses and secrets. He had to leave this little paradise. Quickly, he zipped the knapsack.

Florence said, "Where you go, Johnny?"

"I don't know," said Johnny truthfully. "But I do know that I won't get there if I stay here any longer."

Florence rested a hand on his. "You have safe journey. I will pray for you tonight." She lifted her hand, and smiled so tenderly Johnny thought he might cry.

"I will," he said. Then he added, "How much do I owe you?"

"Please. After what happened here, no charge. I buy."

Johnny wanted to protest further, but the kindhearted proprietor turned her back, went to the Employees Only door, and disappeared. He lifted the knapsack and slung it over a shoulder. He might not have had to pay for breakfast, but there was nothing to stop him from leaving a big tip. Fishing in his jeans, he came up with a twenty and placed it next to the coffee cup.

Peter was sitting at one of the empty tables nearest the screen door waiting patiently for the next customer to pull in.

Since the officers' departure, a tow truck had arrived to pick up the plumber's van. A table of three women had also arrived in an SUV only minutes before. Angelina and Theresa were busy behind the grill preparing their orders while the Four Tenors sang from the speakers.

With the weight of the gun pressing against his back, Johnny thanked the little family once more for their hospitality. He told Peter he should give serious consideration to becoming a police officer. When he went through the screen door, he was careful not to let it slam into place. The sun greeted his face, affecting him. *You're one lucky son of a bitch, Johnny.*

Mounting the Honda, he tucked his hair into the helmet. Then he slipped the knapsack across his back. When he turned the key, the bike obeyed. Backpedaling, he aimed it at the highway. However, when he looked north, from whence he came, the belly of the monster he had earlier encountered was drawing near, a matter of a few hours before it unleashed its storming over this little piece of paradise.

Johnny waited for the south lane to clear and wondered if he would ever be able to return and bask in the company of Florence and her family again. He doubted it, but it sure would be nice. *Yes. It sure would be nice.*

Three vehicles, dangerously bumper to bumper flew past. The lane opened.

With the point of his boot, Johnny Black toed the Honda into first, released the clutch, and drove away, the burden of Buck's good intentions, anvil heavy on his mind.

I'm a cowboy.
On a steel horse I ride.
I'm wanted, wanted.
Dead or alive.

* * *

There's No Place Like Home

THREE hours later, Rebecca sat alone at the table where she and Jeff had eaten breakfast. When she informed him that she would be staying behind, that she had had a change of heart and was going to go back home, Jeff smiled, told her that he thought it was a good idea. "There's no place like home," he reminded her.

Rebecca still insisted on paying for his breakfast. Jeff the Roadrunner gratefully accepted, adding, "The good Lord brought us together if for no other reason than to turn you about and send you back home. He truly is a mystery." Jeff put on his Sox cap, wished her the best, and left her to her thoughts.

As time slipped, Rebecca wondered if she hadn't misconstrued the message her mother had given her. That perhaps she should have stayed with Jeff. That maybe it was someone else, someone in her future that she should be afraid of. Sitting alone with her wayward thoughts, she imagined herself as Dorothy. Lost in the land of Oz. Clicking her red ruby shoes together. Captured in the space between dream and reality while Munchkins danced and sang all around her. *Follow the yellow brick road. Follow the yellow brick road. Follow, follow, follow. Follow the yellow brick road.* Another hour passed.

* * *

Dozens of truckers had come and gone. All shapes and sizes arriving in plumes of dust, departing in plumes of dust. Rebecca watched them all. Their body language. The way they greeted each other. Even the meals they'd ordered. Though it was well past the lunch hour, steak and eggs and plenty of coffee remained the preferred choice. On more than one occasion, Rebecca nearly got up from her place to ask if she might catch a ride, but her little voice, her mother's voice, kept her in place.

She was uncomfortably full. She had eaten two scones on top of the stack of pancakes (a stack of flaps to the regulars) and drank three cups of coffee, something she wasn't used to. Her stomach churned. A headache was beginning to form in the back of her head from the nape of her neck up. She asked Bonnie the waitress if she might have some aspirin.

"Sure thing, honey. That we have plenty of. These boys eat 'em like candy," the waitress had said, adding, "Heard you're going home. Good, I'm glad. Your folks will be happy. Of that I'm sure."

Rebecca just smiled, nodded agreeably, thinking, *Wow. That tidbit of information sure traveled fast.*

While she waited for the aspirin, she kept an eye on the trucks that came and went. On the men and at times women, who, by sense of internal direction, and the need to refuel, stopped at the (what Rebecca was beginning to realize) famous truck stop. *Not such a bad life. Everyone seemed to know each other, and there was an unspoken respect among them.*

Bonnie returned with a packet of Bayer and a tall glass of water. "Here you go. Take these. You should be feeling better in no time."

"Thank you," said Rebecca. "Could I have my bill now? I'll be heading back home soon. The food was delicious, and thank you for your advice."

Bonnie's tired eyes lifted into a smile. Her face brightened. What Rebecca had taken for the jaded look of someone who had been doing the same thing year in and year out disappeared. In its place she saw Bonnie for who she truly was. Just one woman concerned for a sister.

Rebecca tore open the packet and popped the white tablets into her mouth, swallowing them down with a healthy gulp of water. While she did this, she noticed one of the truckers get up from his table. He had been sitting alone, eating the favored steak and eggs. He was lanky tall, but not overly so. He wore a weathered brown leather hat that was curled at the sides. A long scraggily beard with slashes of red, grey, and brown throughout drooped from his chin. A black leather vest rested over the denim shirt tucked into jeans. His boots were black, dirty, and ready for the back of a closet. On his fingers were silver rings. His hands looked unbreakable. However, it was his eyes that Rebecca found interesting. They were full of stories to tell. Even from where she sat, she could well imagine this man had had a hard life. The trucker pulled at his beard, looked directly at her. When he moved in her direction, Rebecca's breath caught in her throat.

Maybe he was just going to the bathroom. As he neared, those storybook eyes of his seemed to dance. He regarded the suitcase beneath the table before locking on to Rebecca's face and settling on her eyes.

Rebecca felt a heat rise within. A feeling typically expended privately in the confines of a hot shower. *But why?* The man certainly wasn't much to look at. Not that he was ugly. In fact, some women might consider him ruggedly handsome. In a John Wayne kind of way. In fact, the first word that came to mind when she first laid eyes on him was *redneck*. Yet there it was. That sneaking, warm tremble that emerged on occasion when she was quite alone and lost in fantasy.

The trucker stooped at her table and looked down at her. Rebecca tried to avoid those eyes. Found it impossible.

"Hello," he said. "My name's Brandon Hogg. Most people who know me call me

Wishbone. I noticed you might be going someplace." His voice was gruff. Accumulated years of smoking. Verifying this was a pack of Marlboros jutting from a vest pocket. He held out a strong hand. A silver skull with red-jeweled eyes stared at Rebecca. Visible beneath the curl of a partially rolled-up sleeve was a tattoo. A dagger pointed to his thick wrist. Rebecca's eyes wandered to the oval silver buckle cinched around his waist. PURE COUNTRY. An acoustic guitar underlining the proclamation.

On good manners alone, Rebecca held out her hand. Before she could stop herself, she said, "My name is Rebecca. Pleased to meet you… *Wishbone.*" Lips trembled as she smiled. *What the hell's the matter with you, girl? Get a grip. You know better. You don't know this man from Adam.* BE SMART! BE *careful!* "What makes you think I need a ride?" said Rebecca, her hand slipping from his.

Brandon Hogg put a boot on one of the empty chairs, and rested the tattooed forearm on his knee. He leaned forward. Just beneath the tip of his hat, dark eyes beamed with light. "I've seen you a hundred times in a hundred different places in my travels. Sure you look different, but the need is the same. If I'm mistaken, then please forgive this country bumpkin and I'll be on my way."

Rebecca sat silent for a second. She hugged the suitcase with her knees. She explored his face. Deep crow's-feet and a burst of tiny blackheads surrounded gentle eyes. The skin on his face had been sunburned over and over, and looked tougher than leather. His instincts were good, hands steady. There was something in his way that reminded her of her dearly departed dad. "Well… I… um… Yes, I do need a ride."

Brandon "Wishbone" Hogg smiled. Several teeth were capped with gold. "My rig's just out front. The black International with the air scoop on top. It says Hogg's Haulin' on both doors, so you can't miss it. Got a load I got to get to Virginia. I'll be leaving in ten minutes." He removed his boot from the chair and he smiled at her with those I-got-a-thousand-stories-to-tell-you eyes. Then calmly walked to the front door, opened it, and stepped out into blinding daylight.

Suddenly, things were happening so fast Rebecca's head spun. She watched him leave. He walked with a real man's gait, confident, unassuming. She listened for her mother's voiced advice. None came. Internal alarm bells did not sound. Only silence and physical calm.

Another decision had to be made. And made quickly. If she didn't take the offered ride, there was no telling how long it would be before another came along. Virginia was not quite the route she wanted to take, but hell, she couldn't afford to be picky. At least not yet. She was only a state from home. More sooner than later, when it was realized she had not perished in the fire, the authorities would have a good description of her and would be on the lookout.

Without waiting for the bill, Rebecca pulled the twenty out of her jeans and placed it beneath the half-empty glass of water. Hurriedly, she pulled the suitcase from beneath the table and swiftly walked across the spans of restaurant. Randy Travis' voice piped "On the Other Hand."

The temperature had risen several degrees since Rebecca's arrived. A wall of hot air hit her smack dab in the face. Immediately her brows beaded. Walking toward the rows of trucks, she found Hogg's Haulin' tucked neatly between a blue Kenworth and an older white flatbed with a backhoe loader chained to its stern. She went to the passenger door, set her suitcase on the ground, and knuckled the hot metal several times. At first there was no response. Then just as she was about to try again, the door popped open. The smell of stale cigarettes assaulted her. Brandon Hogg peered down, kind of half-sitting, half-standing. Dangling from his lips was a cigarette from which a curl of blue smoke rose.

"Hi there. I suspected you might show up. Here, toss me that suitcase. Climb on in."

"Thank you, Wishbone," said Rebecca. "May I call you Wishbone?" She lifted the case high enough so that he could get hold of the handle.

"Wouldn't have it any other way," he said, and grasped the handle. He set the suitcase behind him in the sleeping compartment.

Then he cleared some papers off the passenger seat and stuffed them into a caddy that was fastened to the back of his captain's chair.

Rebecca hoisted herself into the cab, and closed the door once she was settled. The air-conditioning was on high, and it gave her a chill right through the jacket. Her internal temperature dropped in an instant. The sweat on her brow dried all at once. The brown velour seat wrapped itself around her frame. She felt suddenly small. The first thing she noticed was a thin layer of dust covering the dash and gadgetry. Indifferent to Jeff the Roadrunner's sparkling clean cab. A grimy yellow curtain separated the sleeping compartment from the front. Like the Roadrunner, Wishbone kept a pocket watch dangling from a visor. Other than the strong nicotine air, there was another smell Rebecca could not interpret. She must have scrunched her nose because Wishbone said, "Sorry about the odor. I haven't given her a good cleaning in about a month. Been busier than a hooker at a sailor's convention lately. Just haven't gotten around to it." Smiling, he put the truck into gear. The cab lifted then rested.

"That's okay. I don't mind," lied Rebecca. She was happy just to be on the way. To put more miles between herself and Bay Ridge Cove.

The International rolled forward. Wishbone kept one hand on the steering wheel. The other held his smoke and the gear shift. When the forty feet of it was clear of the other trucks, he swung it around (give me forty acres) and pointed it at the southern highway.

Rebecca sat there, taking in the odor she couldn't identify. *Perhaps you'll get used to over time,* she told herself. Like the smell of fish and fish-related things that greeted her whenever she arrived home from school. A memory came forward. Variegated with real events and events that could only occur in dream state. Strange how that happened. Certain colors or certain scents could arouse vivid recollections.

She could see herself playing hockey on the school field. Their team had just scored a goal and was up seven to five. Far off in the distance, a dog barked. The bells from the only church in town sounded. Dong, dong, dong. *Her teammates gathered at the home end of the field leaving Rebecca alone on the center line. They raised their sticks into the air and begin to chant:*

Little Miss White
Oh, what a sight

Nowhere to go
Nowhere to hide
She tries to run
Run, run, run
Little Miss White
What have you done?

The dog howled crazy mad. Church bells sounded. Suddenly Rebecca was naked and everyone was laughing. On the other side of the fence she could see Jim Bounty sitting at his usual place on the bench. He too was naked. Erect penis in hand. He stroked it as if it were a pet. Their eyes locked. He called out above the howling dog and orchestra of bells, "I fucked your mother! Just like I'm going to fuck you!" He laughed, and the laughter filled her mind. Then he burst into flames.

Rebecca's eyes blinked open. She hadn't realized they were even closed. Her head pivoted left and right. She let out a sigh.

"Rebecca. Are you all right?" asked Brandon.

The image of Jim Bounty faded, but his final words lingered, "I'm going to fuck you."

"Yes," she said. "Just a bad memory. That's all."

"Care to share. I'm a real good listener." Wishbone switched gears. The truck lurched forward, gaining speed. Cars traveling in the opposite lanes zip by. *Whoosh, whoosh, whoosh.* The engine revved high. Wishbone's legs moved in tandem, and he pushed the gear into place. The International ran smooth. Rebecca could barely feel the road beneath them. "She's old and a little cranky at times, but she's got a heart of gold." Again his legs moved. The transmission slipped perfectly into gear.

Rebecca sent the nightmarish image far away to a place so deep that it may never be retrieved again. At least she hoped not. "Can I ask you something?" she said.

"Sure. Ask away." He took a long drag of the Marlboro, then snuffed it in an already-overflowing ashtray. Blue smoke curled from his nostrils.

"First of all. Would you mind terribly if I asked you to turn down the air-conditioning? I think it's going to snow."

Wishbone's laughter filled the interior. *It's a good laugh,* thought Rebecca. A comforting laugh. One she could listen to all day if need be.

"Sure. No problem. We certainly wouldn't want it to snow now, would we?" He reached toward the dash, and dialed the air conditioner to low. "There, how's that?"

"Much better. Thank you." A moment of silence passed before Rebecca asked, "Why Wishbone? Is there a story that goes with it? Are you like really lucky or something?"

Brandon Hogg's his eyes remained on the road. A smile curled the right side of his face. "That's my handle. You know. What the other truckers call me when they want to contact me."

Rebecca's eyes took in the CB mounted above his head. "I already knew that," she said matter-of-factly. "I was just wondering if there was an interesting story that goes with it. It's certainly a far cry from let's say... Rubber Ducky or Big Bear."

"Rubber Ducky. That's pretty funny. You have a good sense of humor about you, Rebecca. That's good. Most hitchhikers I pick up just sit there and stare out at the road until I get them to where they're going. *Okay.* Here it goes. When I was nine years old, I was sitting at the dinner table with my folks and chowing down on a piece of chicken. I was the kind of kid that ate everything fast. You know, so I wouldn't have to sit there and listen to my parents while they talked about nothing important. Suddenly, and this is according to Mother, because I don't remember what happened, I began to choke. My face had turned all sorts of color. When I stood, I fell to the floor unconscious."

"That must have been awful for you," said Rebecca, suddenly embarrassed that she had asked.

"Well, like I said, I was nine and don't remember much about it. Anyhow. My mother sat me up. Rammed her fingers down my throat. After a couple a tries, she got hold of the object I was chocking on. Out came that part that everyone calls the wishbone. Ever since then, that's what people have been callin' me. Wishbone."

"That's terrible. You could have died. You could have choked to death right there in your mother's arms."

"Well, I didn't." He unbuttoned the top two buttons of his shirt, and produced a small bronzed wishbone at the end of a gold chain. "My dad had it bronzed. Bless his soul. I've been wearing it ever since."

Rebecca looked at the shiny forked object that was no bigger than a nickel. "It's so small. No wonder you choked on it." She ran fingers across her throat as if there was something lodged in it.

Wishbone let the object drop to his chest. "You were right about one thing. It's my lucky charm all right. I'm doing what I love. Not too many people can say that." He reached into his vest, and took out the pack of Marlboros. With one hand, he lifted the lid, thumbed out a smoke, placed it between his lips, then put the pack back into his vest.

"Now how about you?" he said, the cancer stick jumping with each word.

Rebecca lowered her head, disheartened. "I'm afraid my life just isn't that interesting. At least not yet." As she spoke, a visual of her family crept into her mind. For a second, she thought she might cry. Instead, she drew on her strength, lifted her head, and looked far into the distance, to the blacktop that could take her somewhere, anywhere. All the way to Vegas.

"Oh, come on now," prodded Wishbone. "Surely something occurred in your young life that's worth sharing. I promise it'll never go beyond the interior of this cab, all right?" He made a small cross with his index finger at the center of his chest. "Cross my heart and hope to die."

"Well... It's pretty boring, but okay." Rebecca took hold of the tension seizing her frame and forced it away. The faces of her family faded into a pure white cloud of nothingness. She went back in time. To a point in her life when she was considered homely by the students who had already begun to develop. "I beat a boy up once," she said.

"This I got to hear. Go on."

Rebecca began to tell the tale of the only thing she could think of. Of a time when her name was bandied about surreptitiously by classmates she had considered friends.

* * *

12

The Millions Mansion

"HERE comes trouble," said Norman, the blue macaw Tony Millions kept outdoors in an enormous black gilded cage. The large bird swayed back and forth, and moved its head side to side. "They're off."

The pool was empty, pale water lapped at its edges. Palm trees shaded a dozen or so white chaises. Umbrellas stood erect over glass patio sets crammed with empty glasses and bottles. A stack of used towels lay in a heap next to the cabana bar. Empty bottles lined the surface. Champaign buckets held upturned bottles. Everything said a good time had been had the night before. Sinatra crooned from hidden Bose speakers. *"Fly me to the moon..."'*

The sky was Nevada blue. It held the blistering sun high in its God-conceived canvass so that no *one,* or thing, could escape its scornful swelter. It was not quite midday. The temperature, ninety-two degrees. A perfect day for vultures. Beyond the ten-acre property, the desert stretched out to the horizon. An infinite sandbox that concealed many secrets.

Tony Millions was stretched out on a chaise, away from the pool. Mr. Black approached. Tony wore burgundy swim trunks and his feet were receiving a pedicure by a scantily clad blonde named Pamela whose eyes were glazed over in a coke-induced stare. Wads of cotton separated his well-maintained toes. His flesh, tawny from too much sun, looked every bit the casing of a Soprano leather handbag.

Mr. Black wore off-white trousers and a striking blue golf shirt with a red stripe. Rattlesnake boots on his size 15 feet. The belt cinching his trousers matched his footwear. He looked around, hands on hips, and shook his head. His boss was famous for throwing some of the wildest parties in Vegas. Porn stars, rock musicians, models, visiting dignitaries, and billion-dollar hotel owners had all sampled Tony Millions generous venues at one time or another.

They were the perfect alibi whenever Mr. Black and the others were out plying their trades.

The bikini-clad Pamela worked Tony's cuticles, melon-sized breasts swaying in rhythm with the movements of her hands. Next to Tony, a racing form, cell phone, and nickel bag of Columbia's finest sat on a side table. Next to *it* was a neat Scotch and a bag of peanuts for Norman.

Removing his mirrored Pradas, Tony set them on the table. With the towel looped around his neck, he wiped sweat from his brow, face, and balding head. Then his red-veined eyes looked up at the black giant. Instantly, a fresh layer of sweat beaded his skull. "I take it everything went smoothly?" he said, and tossed the towel to the ground.

"Smooth like silk, man." Mr. Black looked to the blonde bombshell. "Leave us for a moment, will you, baby?"

Without hesitation, the former Miss February '05 stood and walked toward the fifteen-room, three-storey house. Both men watched her leave.

"Don't leave me, baby," screeched Norman, its black beak jammed between bars, its thick tongue working the words. "Who loves yah, baby?"

When Pamela disappeared behind double glass doors, Mr. Black continued. "That damn bird has good taste, man," he said.

"Indeed he does. Pull up a chair and take a seat, Mr. Black." Tony pointed to the empty space next to him. Then he picked up the tumbler of Scotch and took a healthy gulp. "Ahh, hair of the dog."

Mr. Black went to a nearby patio set and dragged a padded chair across the concrete. He propped it next to his boss, sat down, stretched out his long legs, crossed them at the ankles, and interlocked his fingers behind his head. "Looks like I missed a good time last night."

"On the contrary. You probably had a better time than I did."

"True, true."

A brief moment of silence fell between them. The CD changed. Sinatra was replaced by a jazzy keyboard entry and Diana Krall's sultry voice.

Tony took another swallow of the forty-year-old Bruichladdich. "I take it Mr. Green was quite surprised?" A signature sneer curled the side of his mouth. He dabbed a finger into the nickel bag, and rubbed the white powder across his teeth. Then he washed it down with another mouthful of amber liquid.

"Like it was his birthday, man. He didn't suspect a thing." Mr. Black pointed his thumb and index finger in front of him as if he were firing a gun. "Pop. No more Mr. Green."

"Happy birthday to me. Happy birthday to me." The blue macaw hung upside down. Its body and head dangled to and froe.

"Good help is so hard to find these days." Tony Millions rested the near-empty tumbler on his bloated, hairy stomach. "And the girl?"

"Messy. That one was one tough chick, man. Too bad she had to be disposed of. Still lots of miles left on her."

"Yes, too bad. But like they say, what had to be done had to be done. Send word through our network that I require some new talent." He paused for a thought-filled moment, and swirled what was left in the glass before he finished it off. "I want the next one to be a redhead and young. Very young. I've got several Japanese clients including an ambassador and a handful of senators who would gladly pay triple for the attentions of an underling. She'll be difficult, I'm sure, but once assimilated into our way of thinking, she'll realize that what we have to offer is not only her best choice but her only choice. Send word that there'll be an extra five large for a pubertal redhead. That ought to speed things up."

Mr. Black laughed. His voice boomed across the acres.

"What's so funny, Mr. Black?"

"You white people. Always so fucking particular. Pussy is pussy, man. Taste the same. Looks the same."

"Ah, Mr. Black. That is precisely why I do what I do and you do what you do. Take a look around you. My wealth was founded on the peculiarities of men, *and* women for that matter. Combine that with America's love affair with Columbia's finest and *voila*. It's the American dream. Every day they come to Vegas for something different. Something they can't get at home. Willing to pay through the nose for. You know what they say, Mr. Black. What happens in Vegas *stays* in Vegas." Tony looked into the empty tumbler, he sighed. "That's the problem with a good Scotch. Here today, gone today." Rising with great effort, he took a peanut from the bag and showed it to Norman. "What do you say, Norman?"

"Vegas, Vegas, Vegas. Norman likes pussy."

"That's a good boy." Tony put the peanut into his mouth and approached the cage. Inching his face as close to the bars as possible, he offered the nut. Norman stopped swinging and gently plucked the nut from between Tony Millions's lips. Then the rare bird went back to its perch and proceeded to shell its treat.

"Make sure this new girl understands consequence."

"You're the boss, man," said Mr. Black, smiling.

Tony picked up the racing form. "Well, Norman, what do you say? Who do you like in the fourth at Belmont. Cisco Kid is five to one. Lonesome Charlie is four and two.

"Norman likes pussy at four and two."

"Lonesome Charlie it is. You see, Mr. Black. Even dumb animals can be trained to do my bidding. All it takes is patience." He fixed eyes onto the soulless mien of his number one hit man. "With Mr. Green no longer in the picture, I want you to handle this new girl… *personally*."

"It will be my pleasure, man."

"Good. Now on your way out. Tell Pamela that I'm still in need of her special talents."

"Sure thing, man."

"And, Mr. Black."

"Yes."

"Try not to damage the new girl too much during the assimilation process."

Mr. Black just smiled, turned, and walked away. Smiling, smiling. Always smiling.

* * *

13

Have Gun Will Travel

BETWEEN the café and Lander, Johnny stopped at a side road leading into a field. It was rich with golden stocks of wheat. The road ended at a fence of barbed wire noticeably sagging from age, its posts weathered grey. There was a space between the fence just wide enough for a tractor to drive through. Johnny waited until there was a lull in traffic before he dismounted the motorcyle and moved it into the field where his activities would go unnoticed.

There, among the seclusion of wheat, Johnny got down on one knee, opened the knapsack, and removed the .38. He held it in his draw hand, and turned it this way and that. Flipping the cylinder, he checked to see if it held a full load. It did. Each copperhead stared back at him. *Oh so deadly.* It felt good in his hand. Not too heavy. Easily manageable. He pointed it, and took aim, just like his father had taught him, hands on the stock, both eyes open.

A strafing crow startled Johnny. It swooped and cawed madly as it strafed the wheat heads. Johnny followed it through the site of the gun. "Bang!" he said. The crow veered right and headed for the interstate. It landed on the shoulder, and hopped hopped hopped its way to the center. Then it started to pick at something that was permanently adhered to the asphalt.

Johnny sat down, stretched his legs and rested the gun next to his thigh. *Got to get rid of it. I could leave it in this field. But what if some kids find it? Take the bullets out. But bullets were easy to come by. Shit, Dad. Why did you do this to me?* He drew his knees to his chin, and closed his eyes. *Think, think, think.*

Suddenly, the air was filled with the heavy rumble of engines moving along the interstate. Johnny recognized the sound right away. The engines of Harley-Davidsons. Scores of them. They slowed and came to a stop right at the side road leading into the field. Right where Johnny was. *Popular spot.*

Once the engines fell silent, the air filled with the sound of voices. Against better judgment, Johnny rose enough so that he could see what was happening.

Nine bikers, decked in leather, stood among their bikes. They talked and laughed. Smoked and talked. All were Caucasian. Pronounced beards directed to the ground. Colorful bandanas surrounded their heads. The logos on their jackets declared that they belonged to the clique - Los Lobos (Lost Wolves). Most of the bikes were chopped. Suicide bars. King and queen seating. One was a trike. Outfitted in leather and street mages. Spokes and chrome engines gleamed in the sun. The gas tanks were custom-painted in purples, reds, greens, and blues, bearing the Los Lobos icon. A wolf's head. Blood dripping from its fangs.

There was only one woman among them. A fairly attractive blonde wearing glued to my flesh jeans. A silver hoop dangled from her nose. Calvary boots covered her feet. She pulled off her leather jacket. Well-rounded breasts stretched a blue tank top to its limits. Down one arm from her shoulder to her elbow was a peacock tattoo, detailed brilliantly in blues and greens. She rested the jacket over the seat of her bike, and removed a bottle of water from a side saddle. She tipped her head back and took a drink.

Johnny consciously watched from his hiding place. Another crow let its presence be known just over his head. Before Johnny could duck, the fairly attractive blonde looked right at him. "Hey," she said, the bottle pointed in Johnny's direction. "There's someone in that field."

The male voices fell silent. "What do you mean there's someone in the field?" one of them asked.

"I just saw him or her. Whoever it was had long hair. I'm telling you there's a person, right over there. Hiding in the wheat, watching us."

Shit, shit, shit. Johnny's heart pounded. He picked up the gun, and put it back into the knapsack which he zipped very slowly. *Now what? If they come looking, they're going to find you for sure. And if they're not happy with what they find, just about anything can happen.*

Heavy footfalls started in his direction. The blonde's voice was closer. "He's right over there. Just beyond the fence. I swear it."

Johnny did what he thought was best. He stood to his full height, smiled and waved. "Hello. I heard you guys pull in. This must be a popular rest spot. I was just catching some zzz's. Been on the road most of the night."

The bikers stopped, looked at each other. Two of them boomed a laugh. "It's just some Indian kid," said the largest of them, grey beard over most of his face. A cigarette was pinched between his lips and it jumped with every word. "What are you doing in there, chief? Jerkin' off? Come on out here so we can get a good look at yah."

Slinging the knapsack over a shoulder, Johnny took hold of the Honda's handles and guided the bike through the wheat. When he was clear, and still smiling his best smile, he stopped and toed the kickstand down. "You guys heading to Landar?" he asked.

The bikers moved toward him packlike. "Where'd you get the bike, chief? Steal it? Looks pretty new." They circled Johnny. Surrounding him like wolves containing their prey.

Up close, Johnny could see the tattoo of a swastika in the middle of the leader's forehead. Just like Charles Manson. "It was a gift," said Johnny. "Well, I guess I'll be on my way now." He started to push the Honda toward the interstate.

"Whoa. Hold on there, chief. What's the hurry?"

The fairly attractive blonde spoke, "Leave him alone, Gangrene. He's just a kid."

"You mind your shit, Sheila," said Gangrene. He pulled at his beard. "Got any money, chief? You see we're a little low on funds. You know how it is."

Johnny looked him up and down. The man was as big as he was. Probably outweighed him by fifty pounds. A visual of the .38 lying in the bottom of the knapsack came to mind. Remembering the change he had in his jeans, Johnny said, "Look, I don't want any trouble. All I have is about forty dollars. You can have it if you'll let me get on my way."

"Oh, we want it all right. Don't we, boys?" Laughter filled the air.

Johnny fished into his jeans and pulled out two twenties. "Here, that's all I have." He held out the bills, fingers nervous.

"What about the carryon, chief? What you got in there?"

"Nothing. Just some clothes."

"Mind if I take a look?" Gangrene took a step closer, and snatched the bills from Johnny's hand. "You sure this is all you have? Something tells me different." Drawing hard on his smoke, he flicked it at Johnny's feet.

Johnny dropped the knapsack from his shoulder, rested it on the seat and unzipped it. He pulled out a pair of jeans and a shirt. If he allowed the biker to inspect the knapsack, they would find the gun. He would lose the rest of his money and probably get the shit kicked out of him. *Then where would I be.* "You see. Just some clothes."

"Mind if I take a look myself?" insisted Gangrene.

Johnny reversed several steps. He shoved his hand into the knapsack until his fingers made contact with the gun. Push had come to shove. He extracted the .38 in one swift motion and pointed it at Gangrene's face. "Leave me alone. You have my money. So leave me alone." Gunhand wavered visibly.

The circled pack widened as each took a step back. Gangrene put his hands in the air as if in surrender. "Hey. Whoa, chief. No need to get bent out of shape here. We were just having a little fun."

Johnny drew the hammer back and declared, "Well, the fun's over. So why don't you get on your bikes and fuck off. I don't want to have to use this. But I will if you force me to." He waved the gun from one biker to the next.

"Fucking crazy Indian," said Gangrene. "You know there are nine of us and only one of you. One of us would get to you."

"Maybe so," said Johnny and pointed the gun at the forehead swastika. "But I would take *you* down before anyone did."

Gangrene said nothing for a heart pulverizing moment as he weighed his options. "Okay, okay. We're leaving. Let's go, boys."

Grunting obscenities the pack returned to their machines. The blonde Sheila looked back at Johnny, put on her helmet, and mounted her bike. She smiled.

At present, feeling rather brave, Johnny pushed his luck. "Just a minute. Give me my money back. My forty dollars." He stepped toward the leader, gun still raised.

Gangrene stopped, turned around. Malignant eyes held the gun in Johnny's hand. He threw the bills to the ground. "You better not leave your guard down, chief. 'Cause if you do, I'll be right behind you." He cleared his throat, and spat a green wad of phlegm. "Fucking crazy Indian."

"That's right. I am a fucking crazy Indian," said Johnny. "So you just remember that the next time you want to harass one of us." He bent to one knee, picked up the twenties and stuffed them into his jeans. "The next one might put a bullet between your eyes."

Gangrene went to his bike, put on his black helmet, stared at Johnny, and murdered him with his eyes. Engines roared to life. *Broom! Broom! Broom!* Each of the members took a final look at Johnny. Several gave him the finger. Sheila smiled again. Then, in a formation of twos they thundered north. In a matter of seconds, they were out of sight, engines waning.

Johnny let out the breath he was holding. Knees knocked. He felt like throwing up. Bravado swam in the bottom of his boots. Adrenalin pumped through him like rocket fuel. "Holy shit!" he said aloud. "I can't believe I just did that." He looked at the gun in his hand. Though the black steel was cold, it sent a heated ripple up his arm.

"Would have I used it?" he asked himself. *Sure you would have,* answered his condemning voice. *You're a killer, Johnny. Plain and simple.*

He returned the gun to the knapsack, took out the map and examined it from where he figured he was to Lander and found a secondary highway he could take. He sure as hell did not want to run into that bunch again. Folding the map, he shoved into the knapsack and zipped it closed. He was scared more than angry. Angry more than scared. Putting on the helmet, he straddled the Honda and flipped the knapsack onto his back. *If it weren't for the gun, the absolute worst could have happened.*

With the heel of his boot, he lodged the kick-start. The 500 cc engine fired to life. *Maybe I'll just hang on to the gun for a little while more. What could be the harm?* Furthermore, it had saved him from a fate that could have left him broke and beaten. *Yes. I'll hold on to it a little longer. Just in case.*

* * *

With the wind at Johnny's back, the Honda seemed to run freely. The secondary highway was less traveled than its counterpart. He kept the bike at a lawful 55 mph. Other bike enthusiasts passed and waved. Johnny returned each courtesy.

The Wind River leading into the Wind River Reserve and the solemnest village of Saint Stephen's came and went. Many thoughts ran through Johnny's mind. Colliding with one another until he was certain that whatever he decided would have a greater proportion for error. The run-in with the deputies at the café was a close call. Now a bunch of bikers were pissed at him. *Should I hold up somewhere for a while? Or should I continue on my way? Hope that there won't be further run-ins with the law or those who would most certainly do me harm? Was Casper really where I wanted to end up? Or considering the circumstance, should I take a different route?*

On and on these questions tripped over one another until Johnny's head ached.

He was still exhausted from lack of sleep. The only thing keeping him from pulling over into another field someplace for a nap was the abject of fear and uncertainty.

Approaching Arapahoe, he could see the escarpment of Mount Roberts to the west. He wished he had the supplies necessary to hide out in the hills for a while. No one would find him there. In a week or so he could carry on. He'd never been on a vision quest. The mountain would certainly provide the required elements.

The Honda hummed. Hawks strafed the plains on both sides for prairie dogs. Large cotton clouds formed pictorials above. Johnny's weary eyes held the road. The helmet and knapsack seemed to gain weight with each mile consumed. Several times he caught himself sleeping for brief, intermittent periods of nothingness, righting the Honda just in time as it drifted into the opposite lane. Thankfully, these drifting stages were void of traffic.

Once he arrived in Arapahoe, he pulled into a gas station to fuel his body. The small station had two pumps, one out of order, and a picnic table sitting in front of one of its large windows. A wood marquee above the entrance announced simply, Gas and Groceries. The gauge on the Honda still read a little more than half-full. He parked the bike next to a beat-up pickup truck. Inside the GMC were a couple of Native teens sharing a smoke between them. Their young faces bore the scars of many fights. Baseball caps covered long unkempt hair. One smiled broken missing teeth.

A bell above the door sounded when Johnny opened it. The interior smelled of stale tobacco. Dream catchers of varying sizes suspended from the ceiling rotated, brought to life by the sudden intrusion of air. Orbiting faces of wolves, eagles, bears, cougars, and Native warriors stared down at Johnny.

A grossly overweight couple, no doubt the owners of the GMC, stood in front of the counter. Their arms loaded with bags of chips, chocolate bars, and liters of Coke. The man looked at Johnny, his face marred with acne. A furry birthmark covered most of his left cheek. His once-proud nose, purple and bulbous from too much drink. A single braid of raven black hair rode the center of his back. He smiled. Like the kids in the truck, most of his teeth were either broken or missing. Dental hygiene not being high on the list of priorities for Native Americans. His wife or sister was equally crestfallen. She was already munching on a Hershey's chocolate bar. Behind the counter stood a young girl in her late teens, Johnny guessed. A head of beautiful blue black hair fell to her waist. She wore a T-shirt depicting a grizzly bear standing knee deep in a river. A salmon dangled from its jaws. Behind her were carton after carton of cigarettes. She started to bag the items, spoke to the man in what Johnny recognized as Arapaho. Once a nomad tribe that now resided in the Wind River Reserve. The man produced a government check from pocket, signed it, and handed it over to the pretty clerk who counted out the change.

Johnny went down one of the two aisles in search of a sugar fix. He found Ho Hos and Ding Dongs, and took two of each.

The bell above the door sounded, announcing the exit of the enormous twosome.

The pretty clerk smiled when Johnny approached the counter. "Hello," she said, her voice sweet, fulsome. "I haven't seen you before. You're not from around here, are you?"

Johnny set the sugar fix items on the counter and said, "No." Then he asked, "Do you have coffee?"

"Yes, just over there." Hazel eyes pointed to a Lotto station. Next to the station was a Bunsen burner with two carafes of coffee simmering, one regular, the other decaffeinated.

The GMC backed from its spot under a cloud of dust that, in the next moment, settled like a blanket over the Honda.

Johnny poured a tall black coffee, and took a small amount into his mouth before he added the lid. The coffee was hot, almost too hot. It rushed to his stomach, heating him from his eyes to his toes and there was an immediate kick of caffeine. He returned to the counter, and asked, "How much do I owe you?"

The girl added the items into the register. "Five dollars and fifty cents." She proceeded to bag the sugar-filled snacks, her eyes fixed on Johnny who was trying his best to pay no attention, but every time their eyes met, he became less evasive. He pulled a twenty out of his jeans and handed it over.

"I hope you don't mind my saying so, but you have the most beautiful eyes I've ever seen." The clerk made change.

"Thank you," said Johnny, accepting it and the compliment. "My mother was Cherokee. My father white."

"I didn't think you were a full-blood. I could just tell. My name is Justine." Politely, she held out a hand.

Johnny took it in his. Their eyes met yet again in a comfortable hold. Justine smiled shyly, blithely. Young teeth already yellowed.

"My name's Johnny," said Johnny. He released her hand, smiled and relieved her of the white plastic bag. "Well, I guess I'll be going now. Have a great day."

"You too, Johnny."

He left the store, coffee in one hand, plastic bag in the other. The bell above the door tinkled and he was careful not to let it slam into place. He looked around the dusty landscape and to his now dust-covered bike. There wasn't another soul or vehicle in sight. He decided to take a seat at the offered table and refuel. Depositing the knapsack on the bench next to him, he tore the cellophane from one of the Ho Hos and stuffed the whole thing into his mouth. Removing the lid from the coffee, he washed the cream filling down in a single gulp. It landed heavy in his stomach. But the sugar rush was immediate. He took another slurp of coffee then started on the remaining Ho Ho with far less enthusiasm.

The wind that had followed him to the station kicked up dirt devils. They twisted just above the ground, and disappeared for a spiritual moment before remerging again. Other than the dancing devils, the desolate landscape offered little to look at, so Johnny watched the sky.

A pair of hawks circled on a draft of air. Next to them, a billowed formation that resembled a fat white rabbit sat on its haunches. A tumbleweed caught Johnny's eye as it blew past the station. It rolled end over end until it vanished to wherever it was tumbleweeds gathered. When Johnny was a boy, his mother once told him that tumbleweeds were the spirits of once-proud warriors roaming the land they so grievously defended with their lives. He watched it until it became a part of the landscape.

The bell sounded. *Tinkle, tinkle.* Johnny turned to find Justine standing in the entrance, the door held by a well defined hip. He hadn't noticed before, because she was half-hidden behind the counter, that she was wearing a pair of denim cutoffs from which a pair of smooth copper legs emerged. Green flip-flops held slender feet. She twirled a long tussle of hair between the fingers of one hand. In the other she held a cell phone. "Mind if I join you, Johnny. It gets pretty boring around here." The defined hip let go of the door and it closed behind her. *Tinkle, tinkle.*

"Sure. I guess so. Have a seat." His eyes followed her legs all the way up to the little bumps of her breasts. Something woke in him that had been dormant for quite some time. His attention returned to the Ho Ho in his hand. *Not now not now not now.*

Justine lifted one leg, then the other and sat across from him. She rested the cell phone on the table, took the length of her hair and moved it so that it hung down the front of her T-shirt. Hazel eyes demanded Johnny's attention. "Where are you heading?" she asked.

Johnny put the sugar snack down and took in the abrupt beauty of her heritage. In her he saw a hunger usually precipitated by the cougars at the Big Sky Saloon. He thought of a lie pretty quick. "I'm on my way to Casper. I have a job waiting for me there."

Justine smiled. "Too bad. It gets pretty lonely here. I'm sure I could convince my dad to give you a job if you were interested." Bottom lip pouted just so. "Then I wouldn't be so aaaalllll alone."

"How old are you?" asked Johnny.

Justine leaned forward. Slender fingers locked beneath her chin. Her eyes narrowed. "Seventeen. Why?"

"Doesn't your dad worry about you being out here all alone? You could get robbed or something. Hell, I could be a robber. You never know, you know."

"But you're not, Johnny, are you? You're something special. It's in your eyes. You're easy to like. I liked you the moment you walked in." She moistened her upper lip with the tip of her tongue, and crooned, "Do you like me, Johnny?"

"Sure. I guess so. You seem nice and everything." Johnny could feel accumulating moisture beneath his pits, down his back. "Boy, it's sure hot out, isn't it?"

"I'm used to it. Sometimes I sit out back and take my top off. Let the sun get at my body. I love the sun on my body."

Johnny swallowed. This seventeen-year-old was seducing him. *How bold of her.* But that was the way it was with teenage girls these days. They were sexually aggressive. Unafraid to instigate the first move. Second or the third for that matter.

The enamored store clerk reached a hand across the table and rested it on his. "Would you like to come out back with me, Johnny? We can sit in the sun. It'll be fun. I promise." She let her hand slide from his then looked around even though there was no one else in sight. An ill-behaved look crossed her face. She took hold of her T-shirt and lifted until her pert breasts came into view.

Johnny's eyes fell on them. Though they were small, the areolas were large, honey colored. Already rigid. "I really should be going," he said, swallowing, aware that there was movement in his pants. "I've got a lot of ground to cover." Buck's thunderous voice roared in his head. "*What's the matter with you, boy! It's there for the taking. Cowboy up. Give her what she wants.*"

Justine dropped the T-shirt, slowly, seductively. She withdrew her legs from beneath the table and stood next to Johnny, killer legs boldly parted. She put a hand on his shoulder, smoothed it over his musculature. "It really does get lonely out here. The boys my age are lame little assholes. I'll lock the store and meet you out back, okay? No one will ever be the wiser." She grabbed the cell phone, leered at him with that oh so knowing directness to her eyes and disappeared behind the entrance door. *Tinkle, tinkle.*

Every part of Johnny stiffened. He jammed the remainder of Ho Ho into his mouth, and took another swallow of coffee. The sun had moved out from behind the rabbit cloud. The hawks were gone. It really was getting hot out. Perspiration tickled his brow. *What are you going to do now, Johnny?* A part of him told him to gather his things, get on the bike, and ride the hell out of there. Another part of him, the part that was growing by the second, ushered a completely different scenario. *Get off your ass and fuck her brains out. Like she said. No one will be the wiser.*

He rose from the table, gathered the remainder of his sugar fixes and returned them to the bag. He slung the knapsack over his shoulders. The half-finished coffee he left on the table, and he went to his bike. With the helmet secured to his head he toed the kick stand and engaged the engine. *Vroom!* Round and round he went in a growing circle of dust, not once, not twice, but three times. There was no one in sight as far as he could tell. No clouds of dust to signal an approaching customer. So he did what any other red-blooded American heterosexual male his age would do. He listened to the throbbing conscious between his legs and steered the Honda to the back of the store. *Besides. I may never get another chance like this again.*

* * *

The area behind the store was home to a grey disposal bin, several broke-down bicycles, an antique Coca-Cola dispenser. Justine's body was stretched out on a collapsible chaise longue. Next to her lay the cell phone. She had removed the T-shirt and flip-flops. Her breasts stood rigid, and glistened splendid in the sun.

Johnny pulled in next to her, killed the engine and removed his helmet. "Are you sure it's safe to do this?" He placed the knapsack on the seat of the bike.

Justine swung her legs and opened them invitingly. She wiggled an index finger at him. "Come here, Johnny. I'm glad you decided to join me. You're going to remember today forever."

Sweating profusely, Johnny went to her like a puppet on a string. *These kinds of things didn't happen all the time, did they?* When he got within a couple of feet of Justine, she reached out, grabbed him by the belt, and pulled him to within inches of her face. "Something tells me you've got just what I need," she said, and proceeded to stroke him with the palm of a hand. "You're so big, Johnny."

Johnny closed his eyes. *This was a dream. Had to be.*

Justine's practiced hand felt wonderful. In seconds he was rock hard, his penis straining against the denim. Johnny opened his eyes and looked down upon her desirous face. Forgotten for the time being was the accidental killing the night before. The deputies who had him within their grasp. The Los Lobos who would beat him to death if they could get their hands on him.

Justine undid the buckle, unzipped him, pulled his jeans to his knees, and took him hard in her hand. "You feel so good, Johnny. I want you to fuck me, but first I'm going to give you something you'll never forget." Just as she opened her mouth to welcome him in, the clacking sound of an approaching diesel truck stopped her short. She let him go. "Shit! I know that sound. That's my dad's truck. Fuck! He usually calls first." She looked at the cell phone lying on the ground as if it had betrayed her. "Fuck! Fuck! Fuck! You better get out of here, Johnny. He keeps a gun with him."

Not needing to be told twice, Johnny yanked his jeans, zipped and buckled. By the time he turned around, Justine was already to the rear of the store. She looked back at him and disappeared. No bell sounded.

He went to his bike. In a blink, he applied the helmet and hooked his arms through the knapsack. The bag of snacks fell to the ground. He left them. Instead of booting the engine, he depressed the clutch and quietly pushed the bike to the side of the store where he waited. Fear and self reproach dripped from the point of his chin..

Bang! Bang! Bang! Justine's father pounded on the front door. His voice thundered. "Justine! Open the door! Why is it locked?!" *Bang! Bang! Bang!* "JUSTINE!"

Johnny heard the jingle of keys.

Tinkle, tinkle. "Where the hell were you? Why was the door locked?"

"I was in the bathroom, Dad," Johnny heard Justine say. "You wouldn't want us to get robbed, would you? Come inside. I just put a fresh pot of coffee on."

Tinkle, tinkle.

The sound of the bell was Johnny's signal to move fast. He straddled the Honda, kick started the engine and popped the clutch. The front wheel left the ground. He leaned forward and righted it. As quick as he could, he throttled the engine and toed the gears through to second and third. In a matter of two heartbeats, he was well beyond the station. He craned his neck and saw a Native man so big they should have named a mountain after him. He stood in the cloud of dust raised, an angry fist high. Mad as hell.

Justine pulled ineptly at her father's elevated arm. Next to them sat a dual-wheel Ford, glistening blue in the sun.

Fast enough to catch me. Both hands applied the brakes as Johnny approached the secondary highway. Dangerous quick, he took the turn, and shook his head. *That was too close. Stupid, stupid, stupid. What the fuck were you thinking? That's just the problem. You weren't. Again. Christ. A girl like that could have all kinds of diseases. Next time your cock tries to make any decisions for you, ignore it. You'll be better off.*

Johnny made a decision right then and there. As soon as the opportunity presented itself, he would hold up somewhere. Some place safe. Where people weren't after him. Where he would not be coerced into another compromising position.

The afternoon sun beat down on his helmet. The asphalt below zipped by. The engine of the Honda sang between his legs while the miles added up. The fatigue that should have had him in its grasp was not an issue. He was terrified alert. His justifiable fears guiding the motorcycle to anywhere safe.

* * *

14

The Telling

IT was the kind of summer day that perpetuated memories of youth to the minds of old men. The kind of day that sent children running to their favorite swimming holes. Rekindled romance and mended broken hearts. Sandcastles in the sky. Fifty-year couples holding hands. Collecting shells on the beach. Ghost stories around a fire. Kites tugging at anxious arms. The kind of day that made you glad there was always a tomorrow. To start de novo and leave behind the shadows of yesterday.

The sun is the mother to all living things. She gave and she took. She inspired poets, artists, and wars and decimated seasons with the snap of her fingers. It had been this way since the inauguration of time.

Johnny could feel the heat rising from the asphalt. It seared his legs. Melted his mind. He'd taken his chances and refueled in Lander where he purchased several bottles of water and a hamburger with fries at a local McDonald's. Luckily for him, there were no signs of the Los Lobos so he'd eaten the meal at one of the offered tables. Five minutes later he was on the road again.

He headed east through Rattlesnake Hills, along the Sweetwater River to Independence Rock. For most part, traffic was light, being the middle of the afternoon. To the south, the Great Divide rose high toward a sky that was as blue as a robin's egg. The sun was at its apex, and it scorched the plains and foothills. The helmet had become an oven. Johnny believed it was literally frying his brains. His clothes were sweat-drenched, and made the long ride extremely uncomfortable. Every time he looked to the wheels of the Honda, he was amazed that the rubber of them hadn't melted away.

He stopped at the Pathfinder Reservoir to examine the map, give the Honda a rest, and let down his hair. A thin breeze broached the water, and offered minimal reprieve from the sun's unforgiving swelter. He found a place beneath a grove of aspens, parked the bike in the shade offered, removed his boots and opened the front of his shirt. Unscrewing the cap from a bottle of water, he let its contents trickle down his chest. Then he poured the remainder over his scalp. Half of a second bottle cooled his throat even though the water was temperate. A quick change of socks and he felt almost human again.

Johnny breathed the moisture offered by the reservoir and thought about the randy Justine back in Arapahoe. He imagined her not-too-distant future. Three kids under her skirt. One in the oven, and a husband who spent more time drunk than sober. Living in a shack or trailer with no way out. Dependent upon Uncle Sam for their livelihood. It was unfortunate, nonetheless, an emblematic future for most young Native women. *Maybe it wouldn't be that way for Justine.* He doubted it, but maybe, just maybe.

With his head in a comfortable arrangement against the cool bark of an aspen, Johnny closed his road-weary eyes. Yesterday seemed like a thousand dreams away and he wished them to stay there. Within the spans of a minute, he slipped into an altered state, his mind's eye seizing a vision.

He found himself standing at the edge of a roaring river, its width no more than a stone's throw away, yet seemed impossible to cross. Above, the sky was blue, yet held no sun. "*Johnny,*" the sound of his mother's voice filled the air around him. She appeared on the opposite bank with Dallas at her side, his golden coat shining, eyes dazzling with the light of life. Linda Birdhumming wore the deer skin of a people past. Long black hair danced about her beautiful face. In their wake, a roiling column of grey climbed, it seemed, higher than the gravity of the blue sky.

Extending her arms, Linda beckoned, "*Johnny, come to me, my son.*"

Johnny stepped into the river, but the storming water nearly toppled him. "I can't," he called out. "It's too rough." He climbed out from the watercourse, angry that he could not cross its rage, and felt movement against his legs. He looked down. Coiled around both limbs were river eels, their slippery bodies writhing inch by horrifying inch towards his torso. With penetrating red eyes, the largest lifted its black oily head and spoke, "*Fear not the gun, but the hand that holds it.*" One by one the eels released their grip, dropped back into the river, and sank into its depths.

Lowering her arms, Linda Birdhumming spoke her mother tongue, the message carried on the wind across the raging river. "*You are not so lost, my son. Someone seeks your help. Find this person, and your life experiences will begin a new moon. She is your destiny. You will meet three strangers. It is from them that your future be told. Be strong, my son. You are of the blood of great warriors.*"

The river erupted. Great waves spawned an impenetrable wall that separated mother from son.

Johnny spread his arms. The vision willed them to be the wings of a great bird. In a single motion, Johnny lifted himself from the river's crag. Higher and higher he rose until he was soaring without effort against the blue. He took stock of himself. The transformation was complete. He was now a golden bird of prey. His new bird eyes searched for Dallas and his mother. They were no where to be found. He circled the earth below, and called to them with his bird voice. A piercing shrill that spilled forward and lingered on the air. Nonetheless, all he received in reply was the roar of water.

From somewhere below, a shot rang out. The bullet ripped into his chest, a searing, enveloping fire. He plummeted to the earth, end over end, winged arms useless, and his bird body pierced the water like a spear. Down he went, deeper and deeper into the black abyss which filled his lungs until the vision became obscure and was gone.

Johnny opened his eyes to find they were moist with the sadness of commemoration. He rubbed at them with the balls of his fists. The vision was strong. As powerful as the one he had had at the foot of Anvil Pine. The great spirits were being generous. *But why?* The revelation left much to decipher.

If what his mother said was true, then he must find this person who seeks his help. Refolding the map, he stuffed it into the knapsack and gathered his thoughts. *I must be on the right track or Mother would have warned me, "Stay the course. Be wise. Be what you are. The blood of great warriors. See things with the eyes of your forefathers. Find this person who seeks you." But what do I make of the raging river? The warning heeded by the river's bottom feeders? And what of the transformation? Do troubled times lie ahead? Am I to be tested in some way?*

Buttoning his shirt, he took a long drink of water, tucked his hair under the helmet, and mounted the Honda. Rejuvenated, enlightened, and somewhat weary of the road ahead, Johnny brought the engine to life. The gun at the bottom of the knapsack seemed to have lost the weight of its intent. He considered tossing it into the depths of the reservoir, but reconsidered. An itch at the back of his mind told him to hold on to it. *You're going to need it, Johnny.*

* * *

Following the North Platte River to Alcova, he stopped at a gas station for a rest and a washroom break.

The bathroom was the size of a walk in closet. The sink filthy with grease. The toilet clogged with paper towel. Excrement had been smeared on the stall walls. A less than unappealing remark regarding local Natives had been penned by authors of bigotry.

Above the sink was a mirror, web cracked in the center as if someone had driven their fist into it. Johnny removed the helmet and sat *it* and the knapsack on the tiled floor. The single urinal where Johnny emptied his full bladder offered discarded cigarette butts, a wad of chewing gum, and a white disk that faintly smelled of lemons. Empty, he went to the sink, turned on the tap, and pooled cool water into his hands. Over and over he splashed his face until the cobwebs of his sunbaked mind were vanquished.

Johnny took inventory of himself. The mirror offered a face that was fragmented into a hundred different partitions. Not only did he look tired, his cheekbones, chin, and forehead had been blistered red by the constant barrage of wind and sun. Crow's-feet etched deep, white lines at the corners of his eyes. *I look ten years older.*

A rogue wind rattled the door. It whistled a baleful, lonely tune as it swept through the area. Johnny killed the flow of water, and waited for it to complete it's lament. As quickly as it had come, the lonely wind died, leaving behind a silence that in its own right was just as inauspicious.

Gathering his helmet, knapsack, and self, Johnny opened the door to find that a state trooper had parked at one of the pumps. The officer stood near the front bumper of his cruiser while a custodian filled the tank. The trooper was tall and muscular. A razor-sharp uniform fitted his frame with authority. *Do not fuck with me.* Mirrored shades flashed with each movement of his head. The definitive sidearm that hung from his belt with defensible influence shone black.

To Johnny's utmost horror, the trooper started to walk in his direction. There was no lock on the door to secure it. *Shit!*

He pressed his back into the door. *What are you going to do now?* Guilt-riddled paranoia got the best of him. *The stall! Get in the stall!* Quick as a snake bite, Johnny went to it, set his gear on the floor, dropped his pants, and begrudgingly sat on the disgusting toilet.

The door opened. Hard boots echoed in the small space.

Johnny heard the unmistakable sound of a zipper being drawn. His heart was in his throat. Mouth dry. Then out of nowhere, a sneeze tickled the inside of his nose. In an attempt to suppress it, he closed his eyes, wished it away. However, it had other ideas. When the full brunt of it filled his sinuses, Johnny plugged his nose with his fingers, but it had its own way and came out in a full, boisterous, sinus-clearing blow out.

"Gazoontite," said the man at the urinal.

"Thank you," replied Johnny, heart beating a loud rhythm. To add to his panic, the trooper insisted on further conversation.

"That your bike out there?"

"Yes," said Johnny, heart now hammering as if there was a blacksmith wailing away on an anvil.

"My son's got one just like it."

"Oh?"

"Yep. Not the fastest bike in the world. But it gets him from point A to point B."

"I know what you mean," said Johnny. "Definitely not a Harley, but it's good on gas." To his relief, the zipper went up. The next sound he heard was that of running water.

"Have yourself a good day," said the trooper, and ripped paper towel from the dispenser.

"You too," said Johnny, sweat tickling his jowls. When the bathroom door opened and closed, the hand gripped tightly around his throat relented. Deciding to stay put for a few minutes, he stared at the graffiti all around him. One person had written, "The only good Indian is a dead Indian." Another person was more poetic,

Here I sit broken hearted
Paid my dime
And only farted
Poems to shit by Redneck BOB

Johnny almost laughed aloud at the backward, derogatory self-implications of it. Although he feared that some corrupt thing might actually reach up and pull him in, he remained on the porcelain god for several minutes more. When he felt enough time had passed for the trooper to have been refueled and well on his way, he went to the entrance and opened the door.

A black SUV was parked at the pumps; however, there was no sign of the state trooper. Johnny emerged from the washroom, knapsack and helmet in hand and went to the main building to see if there might be a pair of sunglasses he could purchase. Another hour in the punishing sun without a pair, he feared he might actually go blind.

Behind the counter, an obese man with grey-black stubble on his face was reading a *Field and Stream* magazine. He barely lifted his eyes when Johnny asked if they sold sunglasses. "Back of the store," he grumbled, turned a page, and flatulated.

A tall rack offered a dozen or so guaranteed UV protective glasses in various shapes and sizes. Most of them looked cheap, hardly worth a second look. Johnny spun the rack until a pair of black glasses with red tinted lenses caught his eye. The price tag read $14.95. He tried them on. Looked in the provided mirror to see how they fit.

Immediately, a cool relief treated Johnny's sunbaked eyes. He looked around the store. Everything was in crisp pink hues. *Perfect.* He took the glasses and a bag of Doritos to the man behind the counter who seemed more annoyed than appreciative that he had a customer. The clerk rubbed at his chin, set the magazine aside, and tallied the total. "Sixteen fifty-seven," he drawled.

Johnny fished a twenty out of his jeans and handed it to him. The clerk turned it this way and that before opening the register and counting change. "You want this stuff in a bag?" he asked.

"No, thanks." Johnny removed the price tag and put on the glasses. With his new eyes, the clerk looked more like a farm animal than a man, and he half-expected him to squeal. Before he exited the store he tore open the bag of Doritos, and shoved a handful into his mouth. Hot lime ignited his taste buds. When he stepped outside, the world he viewed was now sharper, cleaner, less portentous. He imagined it was how John Lennon observed things when he was alive. A surreal world through tinted glasses. He went to the Honda, dropped the gun loaded knapsack and helmet at his feet, sort of half-sat, and finished the bag of Doritos. A mouthful of semicool water washed it all down. He looked into the distance. The words of Lennon's most profound song filled his mind.

Imagine there's no heaven.
It's easy if you try.
No hell below us.
Above us only sky.
Imagine all the p-e-o-p-l-e, living life in peace, y-o-u,
You may say I'm a dreamer,
But I'm not the only one.
I hope some day you'll join us,
And the world will live as one...

The words filled Johnny with a sense of wonder. So much truth lay within them.

So much hope in a time when mankind was on the brink of self-obsolescence. He wondered if Mr. Lennon ever read Charles Darwin's book *The Descent of Man*.

What was it that inspired him to compose words that could unite an entire race if people adhered to them? What Johnny did know was, if humankind did not make an abrupt turnabout in the way it revered things, there was little time left. Signs were everywhere. Racism, religious wars, terrorism, nuclear armament, global warming, famine, pestilence, overpopulation, political genocide. Depleted water supplies. Nuclear radiation in the air. In the oceans. The cannibalism of land. Industrial diseases. Species on the rampant brink of annihilation.

All of it available in living color each night on the six o'clock news. More damage had been done in the past hundred years than in the entire history of man. Put it all together, you got a recipe for disaster. A dish served oh so very cold by the hand of malcontent.

Johnny crumpled the empty chip bag and tossed it into a supplied garbage bin, doing his part to save the world. He refitted himself with helmet and knapsack and straddled the Honda. Thinking for a moment, as he gazed into his doubtful future, he wondered if John Lennon was ever inspired while munching on a bag of Doritos. The thought made him smile and saddened him in the same moment. *Such a terrible loss.*

The gas gauge read half-full. Enough to get him to Casper. The sun's position told him it was past four in the afternoon. Buck had taught him long ago how to tell time by the alignment of the sun and stars. Too quickly Johnny released the clutch. The Honda jerked forward. He revved the throttle, and he righted it. The rear tire kicked up a cloud of dust and stone. Away he went. One thought on his worried mind, *I've got to find the person who seeks my help. I've just got to.*

* * *

In minutes, Johnny passed through the small town of Alcova. He maintained a respectable speed. The road to Casper was in desperate need of repair. Large cracks and potholes big enough to swallow small dogs made the ride defensible. To his best ability, he'd dodged most of them; however, once in a while, one snuck up on him, jarring his spine and kicking the Honda nearly out of control.

To the southeast, the Laramie Mountains stretched all the way to the Colorado border, rigid peaks carving works of art against the sky. Neglected houses cropped up on either side of the road as though they'd been planted by carpenter farmers. In one yard, where a beagle type dog ran back and forth, its tether preventing it from running out onto the road, children played on a tire swing. In another, a woman, bent with age, hung sheets on a line. One house was so dilapidated and weather-beaten Johnny was surprised to see a young girl come running from its front door to wave as he passed. Slowing the bike, he waved back. A sack of a dress hung from her tiny frame. She possessed rich black hair and joyless eyes that touched Johnny to the very core. But it was her smile he found most disheartening. An expression of innocence, disillusionment, one fashioned from despair, as though at her tender age, around eight or nine, she already understood her future held the impoverishment of her upbringing.

Johnny watched her in the side mirror until she became nothing more than a waving speck.

For the next ten miles, Johnny found himself to be alone on the road. His eyes remained fixated on the upcoming potholes that seemed to multiply with each mile passed. Then, within the spans of the following minute, movement fell within his peripheral vision. When he turned his head, he saw that a hawk was flying low to the ground, and maintaining a speed equal to his own. Fascinated, Johnny watched *it* and the road. The vision he had been thrust into while resting beneath an Aspen, came full circle. Linda Birdhumming's voice called out to him, *"You are the blood of great warriors."'*

The red tail hawk looked at him with its golden eye, and elicited such a piercing shrill, Johnny could not only hear it, but could feel it as well. Together they remained, mile after mile, side by side, one watching the other, the hawk's wings spread in elegance, riding the air, Johnny with the vigilant ceremony of someone on the lamb.

Then unexpectedly, the hawk broke free. It picked up speed and rose into the blue, higher and higher before it veered left, and was gone. Once again Johnny was alone. His only companions that of the scorching sun, the desolate landscape and, up until then, his condemning other, reminding him that he was a *killer, killer, killer.*

After several miles of nothing, there came a two-storey house about a hundred yards or so from the highway. Even through Johnny's rose-colored glasses, he could see that its once-white paint had been beaten grey and was peeled back. The only other structure was a barn in front of which stood a lone mustang. With its face forward, the mare picked at dry land for something to eat. Like a sore thumb against the arid earth, a blue watering trough stood center of the depressed pasture.

Johnny slowed to a near stop. Leading into the property was a rutted gravel road overgrown with vegetation. To his amusement, at the beginning of the road was a cedar post atop of which was the same hawk that had held the air beside him for the longest spell. Attached to the post were two signs. Help Needed. The other, Palms Read $10. Both were printed in bold red paint and seemed to have been there for an extended period of time.

He applied the brakes, and made direct eye contact with the hawk. The majestic bird screeched, lifted its wings, and rose a foot into the air from the post. Linda Birdhumming's words succeeded, *"Someone seeks your help."* Slowly, Johnny manoeuvred the bike closer. The hawk remained airborne, stationed in a seemingly tireless, determined effort, its purpose all too clear. *Or else why would it have led me to this very location? Once again the great spirits were being generous.*

Johnny removed his glasses and stuffed them into the breast pocket of his shirt. The hawk remained stationary in the air. "Is this where I'm supposed to go?" asked Johnny.

Brother bird screeched a response, its flushed tongue rattled ceaseless between the sharp hooks of its golden beak. Lifting itself higher, it moved its wings in a sequential rhythm, eyes still locked on the man riding the machine.

Johnny watched it rise. Higher and higher it soared until it caught an updraft. Then it circled above him, sickle-sharp wings spread motionless by its side. Johnny tore the

Help Needed sign from the post and looked up to the house. With care, he throttled the engine, and drove between the tire ruts in the cracked earth. A journey begun.

The mare lifted her head to watch him pass. A white patch covering her right eye ran the length of her face. Her ribs were slightly distended, and her back drooped with the oldness of her life.

Johnny looked up to the sky. The hawk had gone elsewhere.

Sudden movement at one of the windows on the main floor caught Johnny's eye. A hand, he was sure, appeared then disappeared behind the division of a faded curtain. The closer his approach, the more neglected the house appeared. Roof shingles lifted and rippled. A TV antenna, fastened to the back slant of the roof, stood cockeyed, looking very much like the slightest wind would blow it down. Eaves troughs skirting the gable hung loose. Leading up to the front door, wood risers were suncracked and sagged. The screen door mesh had been ripped away. Both doors were absent of color.

Johnny parked the Honda a few feet away from the steps, removed his helmet, knapsack, and rested them on the bike. Holding the Help Needed sign, he muttered, "Well, here I go." With care, he took to the steps, fearing that they might actually collapse under his weight. They groaned and squealed, but held firm. He opened the screen door and held it with a hip. As he was about to knock, the main door opened to an extent; and a hand, withered with age, buckled by arthritis, took hold of the jam. Half a face appeared. Long, steel grey hair sat on a stooped shoulder. White hairs erupted from the cheek and chin of a face that was as old as time. However, it was the left eye that startled Johnny. It was wide with recognition, yet glazed over in an anemic shade of grey.

He held up the cardboard placard. "I've come about the job you offer."

"Yes, I know," came a voice grated with the passing of ages. "I have anticipated your arrival."

"Well, I'm a hard worker," said Johnny confidently. "I don't do drugs and my needs are minimal."

Further the door creaked.

Johnny now stared at a face that held so much acquired wisdom it radiated, and conveyed a telepathic competence Johnny found a little overwhelming. *You are welcome here*. The old woman was a Native American as well. Leathered skin and a hooked nose defined her heritage. Bright and blue as a winter sapphire, the right eye observed. The old woman laughed, her face fell in on itself, a tapestry of inset lines. Only a few teeth remained, fixed in gums that were several shades of pink and red. She took the sign from his hand, folded it in half then in half again and stuffed it in the pocket of the long dark dress she wore. "Before I invite you in, you must give me something that belongs to you." Spectral eye fell on the breast pocket of his shirt. "Your sunglasses will do fine."

Johnny withdrew the glasses and handed them to her. They disappeared into the pocket which held folded the sign.

"You have traveled far," said the old woman. "Come in, come in. You must be hungry. I have rabbit stew simmering on the stove. We can discuss your employment while we eat." She looked him up and down then added, "I am Shoshone in case you were wondering. You may call me Konahee." Opening the door farther, she motioned for Johnny to step inside.

"My name is Johnny," said Johnny.

"Yes. I am aware of this."

Together they moved into the house.

With Johnny's first step into the venerable home, something transpired between his physical self and the divine analogy of his heritage. Flesh prickled with an electrical sensation. It traveled the length of his body, settled between his ears, and fired the molecular partitions of his mind. It was not painful in the least, but instead woke a measure of him he knew not existed, and communicated that he was in the midst of a power far more grander than the wisdom of great spirits. Stewing rabbit filled his senses.

Moccasin feet shuffled vociferously across the hard wood. Konahee walked swiftly for someone her age. They passed a wallpapered room with sofa and chair. A small portable TV and VCR sat on a stand in a corner. Center to the room, an Aztec throw rug lay beneath a rectangular table where a fat black-and-white cat lay stretched out, its head between paws. Ears twitched. It lifted its head, looked at Johnny with half-closed eyes, meowed once, then returned to its nap.

"That is George," said Konahee over a shoulder. "He used to be a great mouser. Now he is fat with the rewards of his adventures and does not earn his keep."

They entered the kitchen, bright and welcoming. *Probably the biggest room in the house,* thought Johnny. A stainless steel pot, the source of the stewing rabbit, sat on a white enamel stove. The fridge was old and squat. Linoleum covered the floor. Against one wall sat an oval table with two mismatching chairs anchored to each end. Next to it, mounted shoulder height against the wall, was a green seventies phone from which a three foot cord dangled. Sun yellow cupboards hovered over the sink and stove. The room was humid with the air of flavor. Johnny suspected Konahee spent most of her time here.

"Please. Have a seat, Johnny," said Konahee. She moved to the stove, lifted the lid off the pot, and gave it a stir with a long wooden spoon. "Almost ready," she proclaimed.

"It smells great," offered Johnny. He took a seat at the table and rested his forearms on its surface, his stomach loud with want of whatever was in the pot..

Konahee rested the spoon on the counter and turned. "I'm glad you think so. We eat a lot of rabbit here. Snares are set up all over the property. That will be a part of your work should you decide to stay."

"You said we. Does that mean there are other people living here?"

"No. Just me and George. Oh, and of course Juno. You must have seen her on the way up to the house. Forgive me if I misspoke. Sometimes the mind and tongue do not share the same room. My sister used to live with me, but she has gone to be with the spirits of our ancestors. Old habits are hard to break. I miss her." She moved toward Johnny, ghost eye seeming to stare right through him.

"I'm sorry for your loss," said Johnny. "Yes, I saw the mare. She's beautiful. But she needs to eat more. She's a little thin."

"You have a good eye, Johnny." Konahee sat at the table. She clasped her hands in front of her, nails lengthy and yellowed. On her forefinger was a gold and turquoise ring which she rubbed with the thumb of her other hand. "You have lost a dear friend recently."

"You see much, Konahee. Yes, I have."

"I am sorry. But that is not what brings you here, is it? You swim in troubled waters. I have seen this terrible thing. Here you will not drown."

Johnny lowered his eyes and said weakly, "Then you know I've killed."

"Yes, I know." Konahee's thumb rubbed the ring with quick, short strokes.

"Doesn't that make you afraid of me?"

"No! I know you are not here to do me harm. You are here to learn the path of your destiny. This will come with the passing of many moons. This you must believe."

The lid on the pot rattled.

"The stew is ready. Would you like some bread to go with it? I baked it fresh this morning." Konahee rose from her place and went to a cupboard where she removed two bowls. In a drawer, she fished out two spoons, a ladle, and bread knife. From another cupboard, she took out a loaf of bread which sat on a colorful plate.

Johnny watched as she ladled stew into bowls. With the knife, she carved several thick slices of homemade bread. He rose from the table. "Let me help you, Konahee," he offered. Collecting the steaming bowls of stew, he set one at each end of the table.

George the cat sauntered into the kitchen, and wrapped himself around Konahee's moccasins, tail ramrod straight, extended belly nearly touching the floor. It mewled. Konahee ladled a piece of rabbit from the pot, blew on it, then dropped it to the linoleum.

The once great mouser snatched it and scampered.

"He and I never eat in the same room," said Konahee and laughed. "I believe he finds my company lacks providence. Let us discuss what needs to be done here." She took a seat at the table.

Johnny waited until his host raised a spoonful of stew to her mouth before he ladled a good mouthful of his own. The meat was tender as anything. Potatoes, carrots, and barley cooked to just firm and seasoned with white pepper, salt, and rosemary to perfection.

"As I'm sure you noticed," said Konahee as she chewed. "The house has not seen a coat of paint in quite some time. There's that, and the barn which is where you will sleep. There's a loft with a bed and dresser. You will also find an oil lamp for when night arrives. It is clean, and the mice never venture there. You can keep your bike in the barn, out of sight. There is a truck at the back of the house should I need you to go into Alcova for things. My property covers a lot of land, almost five hundred acres. I would like a fence built around three acres of it. Nothing fancy, just some posts and wire will do fine. I am afraid that at Juno's age, she might become senile and wander onto the road." She swallowed. "Once the fence is built, you will plant some grasses and clover so Juno can spend the remainder of her days grazing happily. When you need to shower or use the bathroom, it is on the second floor next to the linen closet. There you will find clean towels. If you need laundry done, just bring it to me. I will take care of it. Do you think you can manage all of this in one summer?"

Johnny swallowed what was in his mouth. "I would like to think so. Not much different from the tasks I had at home. This is delicious by the way."

"Good. And thank you. Your pay will be one hundred and fifty dollars a week, plus room and board. Sound fair?" Kohnahee tore a slice of bread in half, dipped it into the creamy broth and popped it into her mouth.

"Yes."

"Good. Then you can start first thing in the morning. You will go to the hardware in town and order the posts and wire needed for the fence. You will also need some work gloves and a proper pair of boots. You can put them on my bill at the hardware. I will keep tabs on the personal things you need and deduct from your salary. After dinner you can set yourself up in the loft."

"Thank you, Konahee. Your offer is more than generous. I'm grateful."

"At times you will notice people coming and going. I have regular clients who come for my readings. I wish not to be disturbed at these times."

"I will honor your wishes. You can count on it."

"Good. Just one other thing, Johnny."

"Yes." More stew made its way into his mouth.

"You will keep the gun you carry out of sight. I do not like guns. Many of my generations have been wiped out by the white man's thunder stick. I know you understand."

It did not surprise Johnny in the least that she knew about the gun. He swallowed hard. "I promise you, Konahee, you will not know that it is here. I fear it as much as you do." *Killer, killer, killer.*

"Then we are settled." Konahee lowered her head and slurped stew into her mouth, the ghost eye fixed on Johnny. "You have much to learn," she said, rolling a piece of meat between tongue and teeth. "Your lessons will begin on the new day." Pulling a piece of bone from between her lips, she held it in front of her dead eye, and turned it this way and that. Then she took a piece of Kleenex from a pocket and wrapped the bone in it and placed it on the table next to her bowl. She gazed at Johnny, dead eye searching his soul. The other drawing him deep into its depths. "You must never speak to anyone of your experiences here, Johnny. Not even to me. Your destiny depends upon it."

"I won't, Konahee," he said. "I promise."

* * *

After two bowls of stew and half a loaf of bread, Johnny pushed the Honda into the barn. Light poured in through the open doors, allowing him to see the precincts he would be calling home for the next few months. A wood ladder led to the opening of the loft. Sunlight spilled from it like a beacon. Sturdy beams held the floor. An old buggy with broken spokes sat in a corner. Other than a pitch fork hanging from one of the beams and the buggy, the interior was baron.

Johnny walked the bike into the shadows of one of the three stalls, and strapped his helmet to it. He went to the ladder, knapsack slung over a shoulder. Testing the rungs for strength, he found them to be worthy of his weight. One foot ahead of the other, he climbed up to the loft, and peeked his head through the opening in the floor.

As promised, a single bed with grey blanket and pillow lay beneath the pitch of the roof. Close by stood a dresser on top of which sat a red lantern and box of wooden matches. A square opening in the southern wall would be the window he could view the property from.

Johnny slid the knapsack a few feet across the floor. Easily he hoisted himself through until his feet were on the last rung. After a brief fight with balance, he stepped up and into the loft. That was something he was going to have to get used to, he told himself. *But how in the hell did Konahee manage the steep climb? She must have had someone else do it.*

His initial testing of the bed divulged it to be comfortable, soft, easily manageable. Smelling as though it had been recently cleaned, the pillow was firm, just the way he liked it. He retrieved the knapsack, removed his clothing and placed them in the top drawer of the dresser. In the bottom drawer, he stowed the gun. *Out of sight, out of mind.*

In the center drawer he found a flashlight and book, the pages of which were weary and curled, *Life of Pi* by Yann Martel. He read the first line of chapter 1. "My suffering left me sad and gloomy." *How appropriate.* Johnny wasn't much of a reader but figured the story would keep him company during stretches of night when he couldn't sleep or on days when the rains came ending the tasks he was set to. Slipping the book beneath the pillow, he checked the lantern for oil, and found it to be full. He stretched and yawned. The tally of the past 24 hours and full belly had caught up with him.

He went to the window, and perused the property. It was flat to the horizon, vast, with sporadic clumps of vegetation. In the distance, something moved. Using the bridge of a hand, Johnny hooded his eyes, and focused until the movement took shape. It was a coyote or a dog and was having trouble walking as it lifted its hind leg every few steps. Toward the horizon it went. Painstakingly it merged with the dry earth until it was consumed by rising waves of heat. The creature would either die of its injury, and become fodder for sky scavengers, or live cautiously thereafter, having learned a valuable lesson. Mother gave and she took.

Johnny went back to the bed, sat on its edge, and was about to pull his boots off when something caught his mind's ears. Knowing the sound as well as he knew his own heartbeat, he went to the ladder and climbed down.

Juno stood in the center of the barn. She had followed him, curious as many horses are.

"Hello, girl," said Johnny and went to her.

Juno lowered her head. Flies buzzed at her rear quarters. Johnny rubbed the furrow of white. "I guess you and I are going to become good friends in the next little while," he told her.

In response, Juno snorted, and clopped the dirt floor with a hoof. Her tail swished at the air in an attempt to thwart the flies. Her eyes were glossy, the umber of her birth, almost black, sweeping lashes, long and brittle.

Johnny thumbed crusted pus from the ducts of her eyes. "There, how's that?

Better?" Being this close to Juno reminded him of Thunder and Lightning and how much he was going to miss them. The mare neighed, revealing blunt teeth slanted with age.

"I'm going to take good care of you," Johnny told her, his eyes searching the barn floor. There were pieces of straw scattered hither scither. Gathering the golden strands, he held them out to her. "Here you go. It's not much, but it's a start."

Juno tested the straw with a sniff then, with her grey whiskered lips, gently plucked the offering from his hand.

Stroking her tangled mane while she ate, Johnny said, "I guess Konahee got too old to take proper care of you." The mare raised her head and nodded. Johnny fell in love with her right there and then. The feeling mutual, he was confident of it.

For the ensuing half hour, man and horse accrued a bond that would survive each of their lifetimes. Johnny walked Juno around the barn, leading her with the smallest gesture of his hand while he whispered words. She responded in kind, rubbing the side of her face against his shoulder, creating sounds with her horse voice that only a true enthusiast understood. She allowed him to check her shoes, gently lifting a leg when Johnny asked by tenderly stroking the hard bone of her fibulas. He discovered nails missing and a stone embedded between shoe and hoof that must have caused her considerable discomfort. Using the nail that was holding the pitchfork, he dug it out, and promised her that even if he had to use his own money, he was going to refit her with new shoes. If he couldn't find a horse cobbler, he would, at the very least, replace the missing nails.

Subsequent to the exercise, Juno left the barn in search of water.

Johnny climbed back into the loft and sat on the bed. With great effort, he removed his boots. Yanking the socks, he rolled them into a ball, wiggled, and stretched his toes. Wet leather rose from the floor. Removing his shirt, he reached for the book under the pillow and propped himself on an elbow. There was still plenty of sunlight left to read by, so he began again the story of a journey he would later find was not too dissimilar from his own. He began with the author's note, "This book was born as I was hungry. Let me explain."

* * *

15

Wolf in Sheep's Clothing

THEY drove all day, changing one interstate for another. Rebecca could never imagine just how many vehicles there actually were. *No wonder the environment was suffering.* She marveled at the concrete jungles of New York State; Newark, New Jersey; and Pittsburgh, Pennsylvania. *Just like my most protected memory.* However, she was disheartened to see that collectively, they each held their own aura of man-made atmosphere. Heavy ceilings of yellows and greens. The choking influence of industry and three-car families.

Each city offered a distinctive flavor and whiff of calamitous opportunity. It poured through the vents each time the International neared a major metropolis. *Live here. Die here,* it proffered in no uncertain terms.

I-91 was a testing ground for motorists' patience. Jammed to crawls at times, and at times open for long stretches of way bourn traffic as if everyone decided to exit all at once. The weather, like the traffic, was intermittent. Clear through New Hampshire, pouring once they entered the state of New York. Then drizzling in places over the land line of New Jersey and Pennsylvania.

Wishbone told her that he was in the vicinity of New York City on the morning of 9/11. That he could see black smoke billowing from the assailed towers even though he was twenty miles away. "That goddamned bastard Bush had something to do with it," he had said.

Every news flash Rebecca had encountered that morning came back to her in striking, horrible reality. Jetliners turned into lethal flying destruction. Slamming pointedly into the towers of Gomorra. Victory on one side, pretentious disbelief on the other.

* * *

By the time they entered West Virginia, Rebecca was feeling off-kilter, disjointed. She'd spent hours from her vantage point inspecting the vehicles below and was appalled to see just how many drivers used their time on the interstates to pick their noses, scratch an itch between their legs, talk incessantly on cell phones, and even text, their faces down, then up, then down again.

Physically, she was secure in the confines of a mighty International. However, her mind recurrently tripped back in time, to each and every spark of disaster. To when the wanton needs of a drunk whose deprived sense of right and wrong got the better of him, leaving a permanent scorch in her life.

The faces of Ben and Ray floated like disenchanted spirits in the deep reaches of her consciousness. They hovered waywardly, their eyes reaching out to her most guarded thoughts, questioning, supposing, charging her with the blame of their demise. Regardless that it was her own sense of guilt, her own sense of betrayal that conjured such imagery, such unwarranted culpability, it troubled her to no end. Washing her mind of the needless shame, Rebecca went back to the better times shared with her mother. Music on the Panasonic. Bread in the oven. Sun leeching through the kitchen window. Gulls floating on the air of the bay. Rebecca nine again, dancing merrily as her mother sang with the likes of the Stones, Led Zeppelin, Blondie, Simon and Garfunkel, Madonna, Joplin, the Beatles.

"Where were you today, Becca?"

"My most favorite place in the world. Do you think I'll ever get to go there?"

"Perhaps someday, Becca. Perhaps someday."

Rebecca remained cognizant for the longest periods. Eyes closed, the ghost of country music played in the background. Rushes of traffic below like waves on a beach, nine years old again, spinning round and round, arms out, lost in the fantasy of a youth long since gone.

The hour neared 7:00 p.m. The sky was between shades of an incoming night and the ruin of daylight, silver blue, with the bland, clandestine gold of a rising moon. Neither she nor Wishbone had eaten since the diner. His gut complained over the hum of the engine while tiny creatures whaled and pulled at the insides of Rebecca's. "I'm hungry," she admitted.

"So am I. There's a Denny's just up ahead. We'll pull in there and have ourselves some supper. How's that sound?"

Rebecca yawned. "Sounds great. If I had to wait any longer, I'm afraid I might start gnawing on the dashboard or something."

A few minutes later, the oval yellow-and-red sign of a Denny's beckoned them from the interstate. Wishbone maneuvered the International through the parking lot, and smartly slipped the rig between the narrow space of two semis. "Supper's on me," he declared, engaging the brakes. "I insist." He reached behind his seat, and retrieved a stainless steel thermos. Boldly bright was the Southern flag wrapped around its circumference. "I'm going to need all the caffeine I can get. I've made this trip a hundred times. Without failure, by the time I reach West Virginia, I'm dead tired and in desperate need of a full thermos."

Concerned, Rebecca asked, "Why don't you just pull over for the night if you're tired?"

"Doesn't work that way. You are naive, aren't you? This load has to be at a certain place by a certain time. It's expected. That's just the way the trucking industry works."

"Sounds dangerous to me."

"You get used to it after a while. Now are we going to sit here and chat, or are we going to get something to eat?"

A quick shrug, Rebecca was into her jacket. She opened the door, careful not to let it hit the truck next to them. Squeezing herself through the opening, a pit bull dashed at the neighboring truck's window. Startled, Rebecca hung in midair, one foot precarious, the other planted firmly on a metal rung. The fifty-pound dog pawed and barked incessantly, its piggy eyes locked. It pressed its blunt head against the glass with such force, Rebecca feared it might actually break through and attack her. Realizing that that scenario just wasn't possible, she dropped to the ground and gave the overly protective canine the thrust of a middle finger.

* * *

Wishbone and Rebecca were guided to a table by a waitress who walked like she had had the energy sapped out of her. A breast tag said her name was Georgia. An explosion of auburn hair looked as though she hadn't seen a stylist in a very long time. She handed them menus. Her eyes voiced, *I'd rather be someplace else.*

The restaurant smelled of a mixed grill. A layer of airborne grease hung from the ceiling, much like the clouds of global gases doming the major cities they had encountered.

The open kitchen offered a view of the cooks who were nonchalantly going about their business. One was Mexican, with longish hair kept in place by a hairnet and with a colourful tattoo on his neck. The other was black, tall, and bald. Gold hoops dangled from his ears. He was wearing an unsecured apron around his midriff and each time he moved, the apron pendulumed like a bell.

Wishbone set the rebellious thermos on the table, nodded to a couple of truckers who nodded in return.

"Do you know those guys?" asked Rebecca, half-turning in her chair.

"Not in the social sense. But you get to know all the faces once you've been on the road for as long as I have. It doesn't hurt to be friendly. You never know when you're going to be in a pickle."

Rebecca opened the menu. Her eyes scanned the entrees. Several items appealed to her senses. But since Wishbone insisted on paying, she was going to keep her choice on the less expensive side. Without giving it much thought, she decided on a cheeseburger with fries and chocolate milkshake to wash it down.

"Well, I'm going to have the eight-ounce sirloin with mashed potatoes and plenty of gravy," said Wishbone. "And I think I'll have a beer."

Rebecca looked at him sceptically.

"Just one to quench my thirst," he assured her.

With menus closed and set aside, they waited for the waitress to return, the silence between them awkward, yet pleasing in a new friend kind of way. Just the thought of a greasy burger and fries sent the little minions mining for sustenance within Rebecca's alimentary canal into double time and a half. The trucker murmur seemed to intensify or so she imagined it had.

Wishbone removed his hat, and styled his slick hair with a quick comb of his fingers. His eyes were red-rimmed, double-bagged, and possessed the shining, deer in-the-headlight sheen of someone who was in desperate need of sleep.

Rebecca was going to comment, but thought the better of it. Everyone in the restaurant seemed to possess the same sleep-deprived directness about them, like trucker zombies.

Several teens were seated at a table near the window. They talked and laughed louder than necessary, and received blasphemous looks from the rest of the patrons. By the amount of food sitting on the table, Rebecca guessed that they were stoned and were rewarding the munchies with most of the items on the menu.

What seemed like an eternity, but was only a few worried minutes, the waitress returned with glasses of water. Pen and pad at the ready, she asked whether or not they would like to order.

Wishbone spoke for both and asked Georgia if she wouldn't mind filling up the thermos with strong black coffee. "The stronger the better."

"Sure thing honey," said the tired waitress, picked up the thermos and left.

"You'll have to excuse me for a minute, Wishbone," said Rebecca. "Nature calls."

"By all means."

Locating the signs that directed patrons to the men's and women's washrooms, Rebecca rose from the table and made her way to the back of the restaurant.

Both stalls were empty. Rebecca chose the least unsanitary, locked the door, and quickly pulled down her jeans. Finished, she wiped with the last of the square tissues available, readjusted, went to the sink, and splashed cold water over tired eyes. Then she inspected herself in the mirror. Her hair was flat on one side from hours spent watching the traffic below. Her eyes were as red-rimmed and puffy as Wishbone's. The mirror told no lies. She suddenly felt as drained as the person reflected within. She repaired her hair best she could, and waited for a few minutes, anticipating. But after a time, it became obvious that no magic finger was going to send her a message. There would be no love touch to caress her skin. No telltale signs that everything was going to be all right.

When she returned to the table, Wishbone was talking to one of the other truckers at another table. Their heads bobbed in agreement to something or other. The thermos had been returned and stood next to the caddy of food and coffee condiments.

The congress of raucous teens had since left. Plates of half-eaten burgers, clumps of fries, and spilled soda pop remained on the table. Feeling somewhat revitalized, Rebecca shook off her jacket, and let it slip between her back and the booth. To pass the time, she watched the cooks move robotically about as they prepared orders from within a lung impairing fog of grease.

Georgia the waitress set her milkshake and Wishbone's Budweiser on the table. She looked at Rebecca, her demeanor haughty. "You and your *boyfriend's* orders will only be a minute," she said.

Rebecca was about to correct her biased reasoning then decided she did not want to get into a Q and A with her. *Besides, I'll never see her again, so what did it matter? Let her have her little invented theories.* She took a long hard-fought pull on the shake, and instantly regretted it. Her brain froze, teeth pinged with sharp resonance as if a dentist was taking a drill to them without the benefit of a numbing shot.

Wishbone returned to the table at almost the same time their dinners arrived. "Sorry," he said. "That guy over there had what I needed to give me a pick-me-up."

"Oh, and what was that?" asked Rebecca incredulous.

"Just a small blue pill. We all use them when necessary. Nothing to be alarmed about. They go with the territory."

"You mean amphetamines?" she asked though she already knew.

"Sure. They're not harmful. So long as they're only taken when absolutely necessary."

Rebecca wanted to lecture him about the evils of drugs no matter how insignificant they might be. However, the burger and fries sitting under her nose vanquished all reasoning. She kept her opinion to herself, took a healthy bite of the burger, washed it down with some shake, then plowed a handful of fries into her mouth.

By the time Wishbone dunked the last bit of roll into what was left of the gravy, his eyes had become pinpricks of dark light. Concerned, Rebecca asked, "Are you sure you're okay to drive? You look pretty high."

"Never better. I told you, comes with the territory. I'm perfectly awake and perfectly able to drive. You needn't worry that pretty little head of yours."

Draining the last of her shake, Rebecca watched his face. Cheeks were flushed. Eyes narrow, and he was drumming the table with his thumb and index finger to a beat in his head.

"I've got to use the bathroom," said Wishbone. "Why don't you go to the truck. I'll pay the tab. Remember, dinner's on me. I'll only be a minute or two." Collecting the thermos, he stood, and smiled down at her reassuringly. "Then we can get on our way."

Rebecca slipped her arms through the jacket and drew back her hair so that it draped over her shoulders. She was full to the gullet; however, the grease of the burger and fries weren't sitting very well.

Seeing that Rebecca looked uncomfortable, Wishbone asked, "What's the matter?"

"Just a little too full I guess. It'll pass."

"Maybe you should use the bathroom again. We've got maybe seven hours ahead of us."

"No, I'm fine. I ate too fast. That's all."

"Okay then. I'll meet you back at the truck."

"Are you sure you want to pay? I mean, I've got money."

"You keep your money. You're going to need it. Besides, just my way of saying thanks for keeping me company all this way." Turning, he headed for the men's room.

* * *

When Rebecca stepped outside, the air relieved some of the queasiness she was feeling though it was still thick with the warmth of the day and smelling of diesel from all the trucks running. According to a clock in the Denny's, it was just past 9:00 p.m.

Walking across the tarmac, she wondered whether or not Wishbone really was okay to drive. *Should I be putting my life into his hands like this?* It was common knowledge that every long hauler used amphetamines. Even the truckers who hauled lobsters from Bay Ridge Cove used them. Or so she was told.

By the time she reached the International, Rebecca decided that, should she notice Wishbone driving improperly, she would simply ask him to let her out. She would catch a ride with someone else. There were plenty of trucks on the interstates 24-7.

She climbed into the cab. The pit bull next door did his best I'll-bite-your-ass-off-if-you-mess-with-this-truck routine, and slammed his head into the window with such aggression, Rebecca felt he was surely going to knock himself unconscious.

The rumble of the engine had a calming effect on Rebecca and seemed to settle further the queasy feeling in her gut. She leaned back, drew the seat belt over her shoulder and strapped herself in. The gadgetry of the dashboard glowed green in the semidarkness. The pocket watch read ten minutes faster than the clock in Denny's. Through the windshield, she watched as truck after truck roared along the interstate. The sky offered little to look at, becoming overcast again. Rebecca sealed her eyes. An unpredicted yawn stretched her mouth.

Realizing she could easily stumble into sleep, Rebecca sat straight, and knuckled the feeling from her eyes. There was no way she was going to catnap while Wishbone drove under the influence of some little blue pill. Rummaging through his music, she found an Oakridge Boys tape and slipped it into the stereo. Baritone harmonies filled the interior.

A minute later, the driver side door opened. Wishbone hopped into the cab with the springing demeanor of a teenager. He deposited the thermos behind him. "Good choice," he said. "One of my favorite tapes. Well, should we get going?" In the dim light of the cab, his eyes were illuminated like opals, well under the influence of the speed-laced drug. Quick hands went to the shift, and put the truck into reverse. With no more than two feet on either side, he reversed out of the squeeze.

Rebecca's hand went to her mouth, another yawn stretching her chops wide. "Excuse me. I don't know why I'm suddenly so tired. Must be the meal."

Wishbone slammed the gear into first, and swung the rig around. He headed for the exit. "The road can get pretty hypnotic if you're not used to it. I'm surprised you lasted this long. Most of the hitchhikers I pick up are out in an hour. You've lasted through most of the eastern seaboard."

"Well, I don't want to fall asleep," said Rebecca. "Not that I don't trust your driving. I just think it would be best if I remained awake."

"I've got another blue pill if you'd like." He pulled onto the interstate, hand flying through the gears, left leg pumping the clutch until the truck was up to speed.

"No, thanks. I don't do drugs. I'll just pinch myself if I find that I'm nodding off."

"Suit yourself. How about some coffee then? You do do coffee, don't you?"

"Usually only in the morning. But I think I could use some, yes, thank you."

Wishbone jerked his chin. "Thermos is right there. Help yourself."

Rebecca unfastened the seatbelt and reached behind the seat. She twisted the lid, removed the cup, and filled it three quarters full. She leaned back, and took a mouthful. The coffee was black and bitter, already lukewarm. Regrettably, she swallowed it down. "This is awful."

"Yeah, I know. Denny's isn't known for a good cup of coffee. But it will help to keep you awake. Have some more."

Rebecca refilled the cup, resolving it would be better to consume the foul liquid in one gulp. She took it down and scrunched her face. "Yuck."

Wishbone laughed, pinprick eyes fixed on the road. "You think that's bad. Perkins is even worse. At least you'll be awake now."

Rebecca secured the cup and dropped the thermos behind the seat, refastened the seat belt, and waited for the kick of caffeine.

Ten minutes later, her eyes began to close on their own. She fought to keep them open only to find that the effort further induced the need to keep them shut. Fidgeting in the seat, her body became liquid warm, mind buzzed. She faded in and out of rational thought.

"What's the matter?" asked Wishbone. Only it sounded like *washthematter.*

"I don't know. I'm… I'm suddenly so… tired." A yawn broke her face wide open. "I feel strange. Like my head isn't attached to my body." Lifting a hand to her face, she found that her motor controls were all out of sync. Instead of covering her mouth, she hit herself in the chin. "Whathehellsthematterwithme." Words came out drunk, unnatural. Eyes half closed, she looked to Wishbone. His face and hands moved as if in a dream. Slow, detached. The music sounded distant, out of tune. She fought with her eyes. No response. They closed further until the interior of the cab dissolved into a white mist. Her head fell to her shoulder, hands landing useless in her lap, mind mooring in a sea of tranquil nothingness.

Brandon "Wishbone" Hogg's lips manifested into a sinister leer.

* * *

16

Dream Lover

JOHNNY'S head jerked, waking him from a book reader's nap, the remnants of a memory lost dream fading quickly from his subconscious. Something about animals. Strange, animated faces charging. The loft was in the blue-black shadows of night. He was still propped on an elbow, the *Life of Pi* upside down by his side, no doubt the catalyst of his dream state. The hand his head rested in was asleep. Sitting, he shook it until the prickles subsided. Stretching, he loosened the stiffness from his muscles, back, neck, and shoulders, all cracking with the effort. He waited for a moment for his eyes to adjust, and focused on the framed dazzle of brilliant stars he could see across the limits of his hideaway.

Only when he planted his feet flat on the floor and stood did he become self-aware that he had to relieve himself. Locating his shirt at the foot of the bed, he put it on, went to the dresser, found the matches, and lit the lantern. Shadows swaged against the slant of the roof. A black giant looked down at the floor, long distorted features. A creature that fed on the bones of children. Unadulterated from the ingeniousness of a Stephen King lullaby.

Barefoot, Johnny moved across the room. Floorboards creaked. A happenstance he had not noticed when he first stepped foot into the loft. *Strange how things sounded different when day gave in to night's whispering ways.*

The hole in the floor gaped black, like a mouth that would swallow him entirely and take him to another dimension. One where darkness reigned. Where he would blindly roam forever and ever and beyond.

Holding the lantern in front of him, a soft, butterlike shaft illuminated the dirt surface below. He set it on the floor, found his footing, stepped two rungs down, took hold of the handle, and carefully made his way south until his foot touched ground. He held the lantern aloft. Support beams doddered. Irregular shadows spilled from stalls. The buggy in the corner was now an enormous flesh-eating cricket waiting to pounce.

Barn walls moved in and out as though the barn was breathing on its own. The night air whispered in his ears. *What are you afraid of?*

"Nothing!" These new surroundings were different, that's all, causing his imagination to get the better of him. Then he remembered what Konahee had said, *"You must never speak of your experiences here."*

Johnny pressed forward, his eyes locked on the entrance of the barn. A brushing of air tickled his neck like a whispered word, soft, meaningless. A chill rose from the far reaches of his inner self to the slip of his throat. Turning abruptly, the lantern squeaked. Nothing but dancing shadows. Nervous laughter spilled from his mouth. *Knock it off, Johnny. You're scaring yourself.*

Once he was outside, the cool night air caressed his face. Konahee's house was shadow dark. Sharp angles cut deep into the blue night. Orion's belt teetered toward the west. Eleven o'clock, give or take a few ticks. *Konahee was probably sound asleep.* Johnny's night adjusted eyes searched for Juno, finding the silhouette of her standing near the blue watering trough. Not wishing to disturb Konahee's slumber by using the interior bathroom, he decided to relieve himself behind the barn.

With the barely effectual glow of the lantern guiding him, Johnny walked to the rear of the barn and the expanse of Konahee's property. He set the lantern on the ground, unzipped, spread his feet, and released a stream of urine that spattered the ground loud and wet. His listened to the sounds of night. Unseen wings beat a rhythm above him. Something slithered across the ground not far from where he stood. The bottoms of his feet prickled with the movement of belowground dwellers. Finished, he tucked himself in, picked up the lantern, and held it high. Small gnats spun in aimless circles. A moth dive-bombed the hot glass, dropping to the ground, its misguided sense of direction the death of it.

Returning to the entrance of the barn, the forlorn song of a coyote pierced the night, its lament humanlike, sounding as close as his shadow. Listening for a moment, Johnny stood quiet in the amber cone. The cry made his heart ache for home. From his bedroom window, he would often fall asleep to the sound of coyote packs roaming the acreage during night hunts. They were a rancher's most unwanted scavengers, often taking down a calf. However, Johnny found their nomadic ways and night songs very similar to what it must have been like for Native tribes in the early days of the white man's rule. Always on the move. Always on the run.

The coyote fell silent, taking with it the memory of home. The darkness of night seemed to intensify, igniting the points of light above. Venus flashed red, white, and blue, and danced with divine life. Johnny was a night sky addict. He and Dallas often sat under the skirt of Anvil Pine, watching, anticipating where the next shooting star would birth from.

Once he was back in the barn, he raised the wick of the lantern, shrinking the shadow demons lurking in the passageways. Up the ladder he went, the arched handle of the lantern locked between his teeth, the heat of the glass threatening to burn his neck and face. His feet moved quickly, perceptively up each rung as if he'd made the trip a hundred times before. Ambiguous light lit the loft, causing it to move in a melancholy rhythm to the swing of the lantern.

Johnny pushed himself through the gap in the floor, set the lantern on the dresser, raised the globe, and doused the wick. He retrieved the flashlight from the middle drawer, switched it on and pointed it toward the pitch of the ceiling. Silver webs hung from each corner like dental floss. Dust mites floated in the beams path. All in all, the roof looked sound. Aiming the beam on the mattress, the orange-blue cover of *Life of Pi* leapt from the grey blanket. His mind was tired, body drunk with fatigue. He took a deep breath, considered the tasks that would commence come morning. If he was to start building a three-acre paddock for Juno, he definitely needed to get some much-needed sleep. He piled his shirt and jeans on the floor next to the bed, and aimed the flashlight at himself. In the neutral light, his body looked tightly strung. A guitar string on the verge of snapping. Smoothing fingers over the ripples of his abdomen, he found them hard, tender to the touch. *Probably from being bent over the Honda for so long.*

He dog-eared the book, slid it beneath the pillow and eased himself under the blanket. It felt good to lie down and stretch his frame. The blanket itched somewhat, but that was something he was willing to get used to. He felt safe all alone, high above the ground as if he were unreachable. A distant part of the world outside. Not the measure of a society that would see him imprisoned, casting a blind eye to the fact that what had happened was a horrible accident. If someone should, somehow, someway, discover his whereabouts, the giant flesh-eating cricket below was there to protect him.

Johnny killed the flashlight and kept it close, just in case. Fingers locked behind his head, his eyes closed on their own. Breathing became shallow, unrestrained. He listened to his heartbeat, and counted as if he were counting sheep. Quickly, sleep overwhelmed him, and spun him into the depths of a dream weaver's spell.

Falling, falling, falling. Through a darkness that was so absolute, so palpable, it felt as though he were descending through an ocean of ink. Slowly he spun and twirled, lungs filling with liquid blackness, ears roaring with the silence of it. Down he slipped, deeper and deeper into the dream void. This ocean of nothingness.

Time lost, the universe opened beneath him, appealing to his senses, for it was credible in its vastness, splendid with the colors indicative to man.

Like a stone dropped from the apex of a skyscraper, Johnny shot toward the mass of revolving planets with the speed of a missile, flesh afire, vision blinded by the ferocity.

He landed hard, feet first, fully aware of his surroundings. He was standing in the very loft he was dreaming in. The viewing porthole, a window so unfathomably deep, he was certain there was another dream waiting on the other side to swallow him into its theatre should he decide to venture through it.

Flesh prickled. He was completely naked. The coldness of the ebony room swadeled him in its liquescence shroud. He dream-walked across the floor, toward the bed, hands stretched out like a blind man unsure of his surroundings. Reaching, he touched the flesh of his own body, lying prone, breathing shallow, caught up in the very circumstance of the dreamscape he was experiencing.

"What are you afraid of?" the words uttered from a corner of the loft. Johnny turned. Shadow puppets danced all around him, touching his dream flesh with their little puppet fingers. He swatted at them, finding that they consisted of nothing more than the soft complexity of spun webs, and yet they possessed a voice. They shrieked a high piercing cry

as his fingers tore at and through them. He and the Dream Master were not alone. He could hear the breath, feel the heartbeat, taste the flesh, and smell the erotic scent of someone else.

"I'm here for you, Johnny," a voice ripe as morning sunlight.

Dream Johnny's eyes sought the source and location of the voice. There he saw it. A figure of discernable dark lines huddled in the far corner.

"What do you want from me?" he asked, his voice sounding as if it were being funneled through a pipe.

The figure rose, discharging light. Shapely dark lines cut into the pitch of the loft. Phosphorous green eyes opened, sharp like broken glass, revealing a face that was strangely beautiful. An urgent chin beneath a mouth that was plump, fixed as if to speak. The nose dipped gently between high, strong cheekbones. Skin the color of weak tea. All of it pinched forward, haloed by hair that was black as man's original sin, from which the points of unrestrained ears appeared. The countenance of an elfin or nymph. A fine pelt of grey-white hairs covered nominal breasts and the crocodile bumps of her ribcage. Between her thighs, a gentle patch of oil black hair lay beneath the flat surface of her belly. Moving toward him on the air of the dream, she was no taller than Johnny's midriff, the scent of her womanhood filling him to the deepest regions of his nature. The nearer she came, the more pronounced each slender curve, each ripple of flesh, every strand of long raven hair became. When she touched his face, his dream body filled with the warmth of sunshine, and he became instantly aroused.

"You carry the mark, Johnny." The voice was now as soft as a nightingale's croon.

"I do? What mark?"

"The signature of your ancestors. The very reason for your purpose on this earth." The hand slipped from his face, traced his throat, and caressed the broadness of his chest.

"Who are you?" asked Johnny, unable to move, paralyzed by her touch.

Phosphorous eyes brightened. The she creature lowered her hand, setting him free from the deadening hold. "I am your deepest wish. The revelation of your dreams, wants, and fears."

Dream Johnny reversed a step, then another.

The she creature followed, pushed at his chest, and smiled. Lips corpulent. Then with a strength someone of her stature should not have possessed, she shoved him hard. Dream Johnny fell into the Dream Master, merging into his own body as if he were the enchanted ghost of a shadow falling back into its living host.

The imaginarium held fast.

With an attack so calculating and so formidable, she was onto him, straddling the Dream Master, pressing him into the mattress. Lava-hot flesh. When she took him in her hand, the single mind of twinned Johnny's bloomed with the celebration of fireworks. Long hair fell about his face, each strand igniting electric impulses against his flesh, genuine and otherwise.

The dream creature slithered up and down his body. The Dream Master and dream Johnny found themselves plunged deep into the pit of her inferno. Back arching, the creature lifted her head. She panted as though starved for air. Dream-fused hands roamed her electric body, stroking her flesh with the wants of a desperate lover.

The she creature wailed, an animalistic implore hurled from generations past.

Soon they were in a rhythm, moving as one, dream lovers ignited in a fire storm, sounds of pleasure and pain shattering the darkness. The creature's body quaked as if she were in the thralls of a death bed fever. Lashing out, she struck him high on the chest and released a sound so primitive, so nonhuman, that the walls of the loft trembled, the bed beneath him rattled, and the dresser danced across the floor. Then with a touch as soft as a snowflake kissing an eyelash, she smoothed fingers over his eyes, closing them with the powers she possessed. Johnny's dream spirit returned to the precincts of never-never land.

The final words he heard before he bolted upright were, "What are you afraid of?"

Sweat dripped from every pore of Johnny's body, legs tangled in the blanket. Fingers remained locked behind his head. The scent and taste of the creature still strong against his tongue. The loft was as it should be. Illuminated by severe starlight structured within the porthole. Sitting, he used the blanket to wipe away the sheen covering his body. When the material touched the area of his torso, the sting of broken flesh staggered him. Blindly he located the flashlight, and engaged the beam. A cone of angled light lit the pitch of the roof. Aiming it at his chest, he touched the tendered flesh. When he held his hand within the flashlight's shine, they were smeared with the stain of his own blood. Inspecting the cleft between shoulder and pectoral, he discovered four perfect scratches, several inches in length, tattooed into his flesh.

The moon song of a lone wolf pierced the night and resonated through the star-blistered porthole. "*You must never tell anyone of your experiences here.*"

* * *

17

The Storm

WHEN Rebecca woke, she had to blink several times before her eyes would focus. Her tongue felt thick, and she had a headache. The first thing to register was that the truck was surrounded by blackness and was no longer moving. A torrential curtain of water pelted the windshield. Several desperate moments passed before she found her voice. "Where… where are we? Why are we stopped?" she asked, unsure Wishbone was even there to hear her.

"We aren't anywhere."

The dome light brightened to life, illuminating the cab. Wishbone was turned toward her, hat sitting in his lap. "It's time for you to pay for the ride I'm giving you," he said, a wolfish smile tugging at the corners of his mouth.

Rebecca pressed at her sticky eyes. "I don't know what you mean. You know I don't have much money. But I can give you some of it." Suddenly her arms and legs began to tingle. *Oh, no.*

"I don't want your money," said Wishbone matter-of-factly, the grin vanishing. "I want what God gave you that pretty little mouth for." He lifted the hat from his lap.

Rebecca gasped. Lying semi-erect was a very large penis. The boys she had had sex with were miniscule in comparison. On it was a tattoo. Snake eyes crowned the swollen head. Rebecca's heart throbbed in sequence with the pain in her head. Looking away, she stared at the silver streaks. The blackness beyond the windshield. *Oh god. Not again. Ray and Bonnie were right after all.* "I thought I could trust you not to be like this," she said, distress choking her voice. "What did you do to me? Give me drugs or something?"

"Well, you thought wrong. And yes, I did give you a little something to help you sleep." Wishbone placed the hat on his head. "What's a little blowjob between friends. Give me what I want, and we'll be on our way." He took the lengthening snake in hand.

Rebecca set her jaw firm, looked directly into his eyes, the headache no longer relevant. "I won't! I've never done that before, and I'm not about to start with a creep like you! You're disgusting! You and everyone like you make me sick." Breathing hard now, she fisted her hands in case she had to use them. And use them she would.

"Look! You're a runaway. And runaways have a certain unwritten code they must follow. Everyone knows that. You either give me what I want or out you go. See if you can find a ride in this miserable shit. Hell, you don't even know what state we're in."

Rebecca looked at the dangling pocket watch. If it read true, she had been out for four hours. She could be anywhere. In any state. North, east, west, or south. Tears welled. She drew on her strength to stop them from falling. She be damned if she was going to let this creep see her cry. "I'd rather eat fish for the rest of my life."

"That's too bad. Then get out of my fucking truck!"

Beyond the glass, shadows swayed. If she had to get out into the foul weather, she was going to at least give him something to remember her by. She looked to her clenched fists then back to Wishbone. Even if she pummeled him with all the strength she could muster, it would do no good. He was just too big a man, and more than likely, she would get badly hurt, forced to do what he wanted anyway. Her gaze fell into her lap for a moment. In her quick mind, as if placed there by a wayward writer, a reckless and devious plot hatched. She smiled at him. A smile she knew would render him impotent to the plan she would execute with relish. "Okay, okay. You win. I certainly don't want to be stranded in the middle of nowhere. But I've never done this before. I'm not sure how to begin."

"That's better," said Wishbone. "I knew you'd see things my way. Like I said, it's the code of the road. Doesn't mean anything. A favor for a favor. Now just scoot over. Lower your head and put it in your mouth. The rest will come naturally. You'll see."

Rebecca slid across the seat and leaned forward.

Wishbone put a hand on the back of her head, and steered her face toward the snake. "Now just close your eyes. Make like you're enjoying a popsicle. And use your tongue. I like a lot of tongue work."

Rebecca closed her eyes and lowered her mouth. He tasted awful. Like sweat and dirt and salt. Suddenly, the smell she couldn't quite get a handle on became oh so apparent. It was the reek of old sex. Of one person's will over another's. Gag reflexes sent rancid bile into her throat. She forced it down.

Wishbone moaned, raised his hips. "That's it, girl."

When she had enough of him, Rebecca bit down and bit down hard. When the sharpness of teeth broke skin, she let him fall from her mouth. Then with a fist, she drew back her arm and punched him in the testicles as hard as she could.

Wishbone bucked in his chair. Unimaginable pain took control of his entire body. He thought he might throw up. Rage negated pain. "You fucking bitch!" He grabbed Rebecca by the hair, and threw her back into the passenger seat. When he looked down, blood seeped from his snake-eyed member. With quick hand he tucked the thing back into his pants.

"There! How's that, you fucking bastard!" Rebecca wiped at her mouth and took hold of the handle. She glared at him. "What's the matter?! Didn't I do it right? Did I not *please* you! I hope it hurts! I HOPE IT HURTS LIKE HELL!"

Wishbone backhanded her hard on the side of her face. One of his rings split her lip. "GET OUT OF MY FUCKING TRUCK!"

Copper filled Rebecca's mouth. She let loose a good amount of pink spittle toward his face. "Gladly!" she cried, no longer able to prevent the tears from falling. She pushed the door, rain covered her arm and leg. Just as she was about to jump from the truck, one of Wishbone's boots made contact with her ribcage. She was cast into the rain, and landed awkwardly on the ground. Hands hit first, sending a lightning bolt of pain up her arms. Instinctively, her body crumpled into a ball, and she rolled several times before she could stop herself.

Gravel sharked through her jeans, tearing at her knees. The area where Wishbone's boot connected hurt like hell. But no ribs had been fractured. That much she knew.

Soaked through and through in an instant, the only sound Rebecca could hear was the rain pounding in her ears. Indifferent to the pain, she pushed herself to her feet and approached the open door. Amber light spilled into the dark, altering the silver streaks into spikes of gold.

Trembling with fear and loathing, Rebecca summoned all of her courage, found just the right words. They came out in a flurry. "Give me my jacket and my suitcase or so help me God, the next cop I see, I'm going to tell him all about you! I know your plate number and what type of truck you drive!"

The International rumbled to life, headlights stabbed at the rain, illuminated the slick blacktop and surrounding forest. Rebecca took the precious moment to view the environment around her. Evergreens rose into the night. The road's shoulder was narrow, and spilled into a culvert. Lightning plunged to the earth, lighting everything electric blue. A thunderous voice quickly followed, and shook the very ground beneath her feet. She looked east, west, north, and south. From what she could tell, there were no signs and no other lights. She tried once more. "Give me my stuff, Brandon Hogg, license plate MHN 059!"

Out came her jacket. It flew overhead, and landed beyond the road's shoulder. Rebecca raced to retrieve it, stumbled into the culvert, righted herself, and picked it up. By the time she drew her arms through, it was already soaked. Seizing long grasses, weeds, and shrubberies to pull herself forward, every inch was a struggle When she was back on level ground she made a bee line to the open door of the International..

She was about to threaten Brandon Hogg further when the suitcase came flying out. It rolled end over end onto the shoulder. Its latches sprung. All of her worldly possessions were strewn into the air. The framed photo of her mother shattered into jagged shards. She scrambled to pick it up before too much damage was done. Grabbing at it in the semidarkness, she felt a spike of glass bite into her hand. Ignoring the laceration, she tucked the photo inside the jacket, wishing it undamaged.

The passenger door of the International slammed shut. The cab went dark. The engine roared as the transmission rolled through first and second gears before picking up speed.

Rebecca watched it leave. The damaged photo of her mother clutched to her breast.

There she stood, alone, mortified, torrents of water drowning her face. When the truck was swallowed by darkness, she found herself in a world where ethereal shadows played tricks on her eyes. *Get your things, Rebecca!* She fastened the buttons on the jacket so the frame and photo would not fall out. On hands and knees she moved along the shoulder, blind with fear, guided by the loathing in her heart.

Lips trembling, teeth chattering, she whimpered, "Oh, Momma, please help me." The wounds on her knees deepened. With every movement made, she pointlessly wiped at her face. Rain-soaked hair dragged the ground, gathering pieces of twigs, pine needles, and anything else it came into contact with.

Then as if answering her plea, a vein of lightning lit the area around her, revealing the opened suitcase, her clothing, and the blood seeping from her hand .

Thunder boomed. It rolled across the belly of the beast until it became nothing more than an imperceptible snore. Rebecca scrambled to where she had seen the suitcase. Once it was in her possession, she padded the ground for her clothes, gathering one, two, three articles. Haphazardly, she stuffed them into the case. Moving to her left, careful that she didn't roll off the shoulder and back into the culvert, she found jeans, a T-shirt, and most importantly, the rolled-up sock containing all the money she had. Next to the sock was Bandit, heavy with water.

Once everything was secure, she removed the photo from her jacket and placed it between layers of the driest of materials. On her haunches, fingers cold, quivering, she closed the lid and tried the latches. Fortunately they still worked. *Click, click.* She took hold of the handle, stood, and found herself to be completely disoriented. She turned one way then the other, unsure of which direction to pursue. *Follow your heart, Becca,* her mother's voice intoned.

Rebecca performed a swift 180, the suitcase nearly slipped from her grasp. Before her, among the needles of rain, was a violet humanlike aura hovering center to the road. With her injured hand, she reached out to it, "Momma?"

This new revelation of her mother's spirit reacted as if performing a transcendent ballet. It changed shape, swooning and twisting and spinning. It circled her and explored her and wrapped itself around her like a ribbon on a gift. "*Follow your heart.*" The rain seemed to whisper.

"Thank you, Momma. I will. But where do I start?"

The ribbon of violet light left her body, and lingered in front of Rebecca for a beautiful, wonderful second. It throbbed with energy, before it burst into a thousand pricks of neon that slowly dissolved then returned to the otherworld. *Follow your heart, daughter.*

"Please don't leave me, Momma. Not now. Not when I need you most." Darkness and pounding rain her only reply.

Rebecca sighed. The brief visitation left her feeling invigorated nevertheless, as lonely as the only person left in the world might feel. She began to walk in the direction she believed to be true. The blanket of darkness pressed down with all the measure of the heavens and the rain bled over her face. Her mind became tangled in thought. *Perhaps I should just find refuge in the nearby forest and wait the storm out. But what if there were dangerous animals lurking in the woods? What if I was so far into them that when a vehicle passed, I wouldn't have enough time to wave it down? And what if this was only the beginning of the storm? It could be hours before it let up. I should just keep walking. There could be a small town just down the road.*

Crack! Another vein of lightning lit the road in front of her, sending shock waves through the air, jarring all thoughts from her confused mind and leaving in its wake the bitter taste of ozone.

Boom!... Boom!... Boom! The beast cried out. Suddenly the rain no longer fell straight, but was instead driving at an angle, pushed by a rogue wind rushing through the trees, no longer soft and bearable, but hard and stinging. Rebecca shielded her nose and mouth. Blood seeped between fingers. The thought of actually drowning gave rise to much trepidation within her righteously worried mind.

With every step, the suitcase became more than just a burden. It became a symbol for everything that had gone wrong. A ball and chain. Each link representing desperately erroneous decisions on her part. No matter how hard she tried to tell herself that things could only get better, she came to realize, with each agonizing footfall, that, in retrospect, there really was no place like home. And home wasn't just a pile of ashes and old memories. It was the land, the ocean, the sky, and the people. It was faith and sorrow, laughter and pain. The past giving birth to the future. *Her* future. And it would always be there, should fate allow her to return.

* * *

After what Rebecca perceived to be an hour of trudging blind on the gravel shoulder, the rain let up. She'd been counting the seconds between lightning strikes and subsequent thunder, a lesson her father had taught her when, as a young girl, the storms came in over the bay and frightened her to no end. "Just count," Ray would tell her. "The more time that passes between lightning and thunder means that the storm is moving away from you."

Eyes customized to the darkness, Rebecca could make out the tips of a seemingly never-ending forest. Every once in a while, she looked heavenward to see if there might be a break in the clouds, maybe an encouraging star or two, but all she saw was the grey-black belly hovering overhead. And so she pressed on. Conscious that should she veer ever so slightly, the result would be a tits-over-tea-kettle plunge into the culvert.

At one point, a large animal came crashing from the forest and passed not too far in front of her. It raced across the blacktop. An unrecognizable shadow that broke into the dense growth, snapping branches in its haste. Rebecca welcomed the brief encounter. Anything was better than the constant barrage of rain and the raucous pounding of her heart. It gave her a sense that perhaps civilization might soon be forthcoming.

An hour, maybe two, subsequent to the animal encounter, the area in front of her lightened. Rebecca stopped. The light grew more intense. She turned to see headlights moving in her direction. *Thank God.* Relieving herself of the suitcase, she stood as close to the edge of the blacktop as she dared, and waved her arms frantically, adrenalin lending her renewed strength. "STOP!... STOP!" she yelled. "OH PLEASE, GOD. MAKE THEM STOP!"

The vehicle raced toward her at an alarming rate. Windshield wipers slapped at the rain. Headlights held Rebecca's drenched body. *Surely, whoever was behind the wheel can see me*. Then she grasped that the vehicle was swaying. It swerved out to the center and back again, repeatedly. Impulsively, she feared for her life. *What if they don't see me? They could run me over.* Too many times she had seen the way her father drove after hoisting a few at the Windbreaker. Stepping away from the blacktop, Rebecca teetered on the verge of the culvert.

The pickup passed without slowing. Male laughter filled Rebecca's ears. Glass shattered only a few feet away. A trice later, a single red taillight snaked its way into the darkness, and thinned to a spark. Then it faded, swallowed by a nocturnal curtain and became *nothing*.

Rebecca cupped her hands to her face and began to weep. Every happenstance of the past twenty-four hours came out in one long purging of emotion. She dropped to her knees, the pain in them irrelevant. A part of her wanted to lie down, die right there. To let the rain drown her. To let some ferocious animal have her for its next meal. *Perhaps I should have perished in the fire with Ben and Ray?*

Don't think like that, the voice came from all around her. It was not her mother's timbre, and it was not her own. It did not come from the interior of her mind, but seemed to be carried on the air, as close as friends whisper, for she felt its vocal breath tickle the flesh of her ear. *I'm waiting for you*.

Rebecca's gift had never before allowed her to be receptive to anyone other than her mother and those who, recently, had serenaded her while she waited for morning to breech the horizon. This new encounter, however brief it was, had the drawing strength of a magnet and the sadness of a poem. It pulled at her mind, her heartstrings, her very soul.

And so she walked on.

* * *

Eventually the storm moved behind her, leaving a less bothersome rain in its wake. Its once-ponderous dander now a voiceless sentiment. *At least that was something*.

Rebecca's arms were numb. Leg muscles tree trunk heavy and cramped. A deep shiver had taken control of her body an hour earlier. Bones and teeth clattered. She had stopped several times to switch hands, the cut along her palm no longer an issue, for her hands had become unfeeling attachments at the ends of dead weight. For the longest period, she had to urinate. When she could hold it no longer, she simply let it go while she walked, the brief warmth of it as welcoming as hot cocoa after a winter's stroll.

Another hour passed. Maybe more. Time had become inappropriate. Rebecca's pace slow, mechanical, hypnotized by the weak rain, she walked as if in a dream, unconscious of her surroundings, legs so weak she could barely bend her knees to lift her feet.

Without warning, something changed. Gravity pulled her forward. It took Rebecca a few moments to realize the grade of the road had altered. She was walking downhill. Something else had changed as well. She was able to make out the individual shapes of trees, the culvert next to her, the rain slick blacktop and the drops that struck it like tiny missiles. When she lifted her wounded hand to her face, a red line across her palm, the sharp cuff of the jacket and the pale of her wrist become oh so wonderfully apparent. *Color. Beautiful, wonderful color.*

When she lifted her face skyward, relief washed over her. There was a break in the moving clouds where a wedge of moon introduced itself. Next to it, a single star flickered. The worst was over. She wanted to laugh out loud, and did. For the first time, in the longest time, the shiver that had threatened to shake her apart relented.

She continued to walk, eyes fixed on the paleness of moonshine and the single star that seemed to move with her. She gained much needed strength from them. Things were going to change. They had to. A song intruded her euphoric thoughts. She giggled at the irony of it and sang aloud, "Rain drops keep falling on my head, but that doesn't mean my eyes will soon be turning red. Crying's not for me, anyone can see..."

As she was about to present the next line to the moon and star, she was airborne, the suitcase cart wheeling in front of her. She landed on hands and knees, the latter pounding into gravel, hands into sticky warmth. Her face touched down on something soft. Something furry. Something stinking and wet.

"Fuck!" It was a profanity Rebecca seldom, if ever, used. Unlike her peers who wielded it freely on the school grounds as if it were a right bestowed upon them once puberty reared. She hated the implication of it. The very sound of it. The interpretation of it. Fornication under Consent of the King.

Raw bowel filled her senses. She tried to right herself only to have her hands sink farther into the warmth. She turned her head. Staring back at her was the glazed-over eye of a dead deer, its beautiful but deadly antlers mere inches from her face. Its neck had been broken so severely that its head was now resting on the side of its upper torso, its long tongue distended within a partially open mouth. She had tripped over its broken rear legs. Because it was still warm, it must have just been killed. Either by Wishbone's oral-sex-for-miles parlor on wheels or the drunken pair in the pickup truck. She remained there for several heartbeats, and sadly enjoyed the warmth the dead animals eviscerated innards brought to her numb, rain-washed hands.

She sought out the suitcase, locating it about ten feet farther on the down grade. Miraculously, it had not sprung open. Using her badly beaten knees as leverage, she reversed until her hands were free of the intestinal quagmire. "I'm sorry," she told the deer. "And thank you." Righting herself, she held out her bloodied hands so the thin rain would wash them of the deer's life blood. Fragments of gore covered the cuffs of her jacket. She took a few moments to pluck them off then inspected her stinging knees. There were eyeholes where there should have been denim. Large rips of flesh looked oh so terrible. Blood seeped over her shins.

Rebecca rounded the death scene. The poor animal's once-graceful form had been revised into a twisted carcass of senseless roadkill. She knew by counting the points of its antlers that it was no more than three or four years old. *So young.* Reclaiming the suitcase, it seemed to be no worse for wear. The rain stopped as though someone had thrown a switch. Above, the clouds had rolled back, to further expose the phase of the moon. It was still full. A white thumb tack against the fabric of night.

Bathed in the pallor of the moon's night light, the landscape below revealed itself. A bowl of forest lay before her. She could make out the horizon where it caressed the earth. Her eyes traced the blacktop. Deep within the forest bowl, something winked at her, then was gone. *Could it be?* Continuing forward, she wished upon all of her wishes for the prick of light to return. Just when she thought she might have imagined it, it reappeared, as tiny as a budget diamond. Wink. Wink.

It *was* a light. A beautiful, wonderful manifestation of electricity set among the trees.

Rebecca's heart tripped with unbounded joy. She wanted to run to it with all the command of her legs, but knew if she did, she would surely fall and further injure her already-aching body. Still, she set a pace, as tired as she was, that required all of her balance and wits to maintain.

Down the slope she went. *Wink, wink.* So delighted was she, so relieved, and so giddy, she winked back. Wink, wink. It did not matter that the light seemed a forever distance away. Where there was light, there were people. There was structure and comfort. *Maybe a hot bath and some food. And maybe a bed.* Oh, what a wonderful concept. If she could rest her tired and achy body on a mattress, she would gladly give the proprietor a kidney. Stride after stride, she relished in the thought of sleeping for a hundred hours, for a thousand years.

The cold shiver that had earlier threatened to quake her body into fragments returned with a vengeance so consuming, Rebecca could feel it rattle the blood coursing through her veins, as it devoured the bliss of her euphoric imaginings.

When she arrived at the bottom grade of the slope, there was a pellet-riddled sign: Township of Valentine 6 miles. The *other* voice, as if by telekinesis, relented, *I'm waiting for you.*

Rebecca's first encounter was that of a small square cemetery without gate or grand marquee announcing some ethereal title meant to comfort those in need of its function. Being the dead of summer, and because the air was still warm with the passing of the storm, a fog had emerged from the earth. It gave the burial grounds an eerie connotation and directness, reminding Rebecca of an aged vampire movie she had seen with friends in Newcastle: *The Bride of Dracula.*

Grave markers leaned this way and that, some the shape and size of pulpits. Others were of your standard variety, rectangular, arched at the crown. There were no trees to speak of, the forest around the site having been cleared decades before. A simple dirt road, traumatized into mud by the downpour, led into a narrow space, then ended abruptly.

Rebecca stopped for a spell. Not out of respect for the dearly departed, but out of necessity to catch her breath and work the cramps out of her hands and feet. She set the suitcase down and took physical stock of herself.

Segments of twigs and pine hung from her hair like little Christmas ornaments. She took a moment and removed what she could. In this new light, she could see just what a mess she was. The cuffs of her jacket were stained red as were the fronts of her jeans. What remained of her knees were bloody pulps of tissue. Her runners had split at the sides, and her hands were as gaunt as chalk. Deer blood was caked into every chipped fingernail. Buried into the cuticles.

The persistent shiver ravaged her.

From where Rebecca stood, she could no longer see the light that had guided her to this point but knew instinctively it was not too much farther.

She took a deep breath, picked up the suitcase, took one step then another. Her toes cramped severely. "Shit!" The discovery of the light would have to wait a few more minutes. Down went the single piece of luggage. She sat on its edge and removed the runners to find that her feet were as pale as the moon above. Most of the blue of her toenails had been washed away. She was surprised by just how much water the runners contained. *Enough to drown in.* Upending them, water spilled as if from a faucet. Once they were emptied, she crossed right leg over left knee so that a figure four was designed and began to massage the wrinkled, cramped digits of her waterlogged feet. "Ouch!" The cross-legged position caused much pain to ignite from her bashed knees. When she was done with her right foot, she carefully reversed the leg position and worked on the left.

Something altered in the air. Rebecca looked up and into the graveyard from which the disturbance seemed to emanate. The ground-hugging fog moved surreptitiously as if it were a living entity. It slithered about the cemetery, and snaked between headstones before it gathered at the high point of the dirt road. Then it rolled in on itself so that a dreamlike vortex was created.

Rebecca sat, mesmerized. If Dracula suddenly appeared, shoes or no shoes, she was going to beat a path to the ends of the earth, wherever that might be.

Furthermore, the air around her came to life, seeming to resonate, as if quasar impulses were being cast from the ground. A warning that the dead were not as dead as everyone believed them to be. It embraced her. Carried with it was the whiff of an electrical charge that vanquished all her worry, and made her feel as though she were housed in a cocoon of tranquility.

"*Don't be afraid,*" chimed a unification of voices. Kaleidoscopes of light burst from the rolling fog. The light transported a confident peace Rebecca had never experienced before. She sensed that it or they, wanted to communicate. "Hello. I'm not afraid. I'm not." tried Rebecca.

"*Greetings,*" the voices sang in perfect harmony.

"My name is Rebecca. Rebecca White."

"*We are aware.*"

"Did you contact me earlier? While I was walking on this road?"

"*Nooo.*"

"Then who are you?"

"*We are the one.*"

"Oh, I see," she said even though she did not. "I'm lost. Can you help me? Do you know my mother?" she asked, somewhat hopeful. "Her name is Deseray."

"*We are unaware. We are of this boundary. We are of the same. The one.*"

"I *think* I understand. Even though you are spirits. You cannot reach beyond your resting place."

"*We are also lost.*"

"I'm sorry," said Rebecca, feeling suddenly egoistic. "Can I help you in any way?"

"*You already have.*"

"I have? How?" Rebecca stood too quick, the movement caused her injured ribs to throb. Her toes wanted to cramp again. She leaned into them until she was almost tiptoed. With most of her weight centered on her feet, the cramping relented.

"You are of the few while we are of the many. Your gift has given us the use of time and space. Thank you."

"You're welcome," said Rebecca, still not quite understanding their meaning.

As though reading her mind, the one said, *"We shall show you."*

The kaleidoscope swelled, and spun faster and faster until it became a sphere of golden light. Merged within were the faces of children, of men and women, young and old, some looking as fresh as yesterday while others bore the masks of decomposition. They pressed their hands against the sphere as if a window existed, each coveting the same vacant stare; mouths of exposed darkness, hollow gazes direct, unwavering.

Rebecca should have been frightened to the core, but wasn't. As ghastly as these lost souls appeared, she felt only serenity and bliss in them, having accepted their otherworldly predicament albeit, like they said, with certain limits. The sight, for reasons beyond her knowledge, caused her to remember a quote John Lennon proclaimed only months before he was murdered by Mark David Chapman. "I'm not afraid of death at all. For me, it would be like getting out of one car and into another." If that were the case, Rebecca thought. If death was really that simple, then these poor souls had given up the comforts of Cadillac for a Volkswagen. "There are so many of you."

"And there will be more."

"I'm sorry."

"Why?"

Rebecca considered for a moment. "I... I don't really know."

"You are virtuous, Rebecca White. The mark is upon you."

"Virtuous? The mark? What do you mean? Do you mean my gift?"

"Time will tell."

There were so many questions Rebecca wanted to ask, but found that each and every curiousness forsook her for the moment.

"He waits for you," said the *one*.

"Who does? Oh, please can you tell me? Should I be frightened? Is *he* dangerous? Oh, please. I beg you to tell me."

The sphere began to shrink. It became less and less a grand spectacle, closing in size, pressing the many faces. In an idiosyncratic moment, it lessened to no more than the measurement of an ordinary dinner plate, looking very much like the man in the moon. *The one*.

Retracing its original path among the headstones, the fog rolled back into its source.

"You will find yourself within yourself. You will find your destiny," chorused the voices. The spectacle faded like a weakening dream.

"No!... Wait!... Please don't go!"

However, the *one* had said all it was going to say. In the blink of a young girl's eye, the golden disk vanished, and thieved with it the warmth that had embraced

Rebecca. Rooted in its wake was an understanding she found enlightening, edifying, and somewhat disturbing.

She slipped into her soggy tattered runners, stood and picked up the suitcase, a single, perplexing thought at the vanguard of her mind. *If the one hadn't contacted me earlier, then who, or what lay in the road ahead? He could be anyone*. The one's statement was boundless. One thing she knew for certain. For whatever rationale or motive, her gift was swiftly magnifying in strength.

* * *

Twenty minutes later, the forest thinned drastically. Open acres of fields took up both sides of the moonshine road, the flavor of wet grass heavy in the air. Ahead she could see that the road took a hard right. Rebecca hurried as fast as her legs would allow. She had a feeling that the light she had seen would soon come into view.

The hard right led to the beginning or ending of a wood fence, depending on whether you were coming or going. It was about five feet high, leaned this way and that, was stripped grey from lack of paint, and was missing more slats than could be counted. On its opposite margin was a grove of willows that stretched as far as she could see. Their thick tangle of branches and foliage made it impossible to see beyond them. However, somewhere, camouflaged within, happy that the storm had passed, an owl hooted its presence.

Rebecca followed the rickety fence to the end of the curve only to find that the road twisted left then right again, like a godforsaken snake. She was about to take another respite when she saw it. A dulcet dome of light hanging above the willows. *The light! The light! Thank God*. The sight vilified her. She hurried along the serpentine blacktop, the suitcase pounding the side of her bloodied leg.

Rounding the immediate bend, the willows ended abruptly, and gave way to a small acreage. The fence hesitated, adhering to a water-drenched road which lead into the property. Here, out in the open, in the somewhat-illuminated dark, Rebecca saw that the light came from just beneath the overhang of a hip barn, its roof buckled, large sections of tile absent. A side door hung askew from its hinges and looked like the slightest breath might set it free. Encompassing the barn, unkempt grasses grew waist high. A pile of long planks, suggesting a project yet to be started or finished, emerged from the verdure.

Farther on, dappled in moonlight, Rebecca could easily make out the shape of a large twin-storey house. Darkened windows dotted the west side. A stretch of veranda sat beneath the pitch of a listing roof. It was here that the fence made a sharp right and disappeared beyond the occupied dwelling. Next to the house, Rebecca saw that a large dog house, *sans* dog, stood questionably. Parked in front of it was the familiar form of a pickup truck.

Oh no. What if the truck belongs to the drunks who had passed me when I desperately needed a ride? And what if there was a dog, and he was watching me from the darkness. Don't be stupid, Rebecca. If there was a dog, he'd be barking mad by now.

Truth of the matter was, Rebecca had had enough confrontations with men in the past twenty-four hours. America's small towns were filled with the limited minds of the opposite gender. Dimwitted, ignorant boys who grew to be dimwitted, ignorant men. Men like Jim Bounty. The wolf in sheep's clothing Brandon "Wishbone" Hogg. Even her ignorant father Ray, too drunk to even realize that their home was burning down around him, could be counted as one. Their courage and stupidity proliferated by the amount of alcohol consumed. Men who considered the opposite sex beneath them. To be kept in line by rule of thumb. *Servus* who should willingly splay their legs whenever approached.

With dawn only a few hours away or so she imagined Rebecca's aching body was in dire need of rest. She trudged up the muddy road and made her way to the barn. She would locate a dry spot, if there was one, and lie down for just a spell. Then leave before anyone was the wiser. The sadness of the barn seemed to dictate that it would be alright if she slept within its shelter.

Reaching the weakened door, Rebecca used her body to push it open. Its hinges sighed. She stepped into the barn and could hear the coo of pigeons nestled somewhere among the beams. Vertical passages of moonlight spotted the flooring here and there, allowing her the necessary guidance to find a place to rest.

The interior smelled of wet hay and mould and seemed several degrees cooler than it was outside. Another shiver enveloped her completely. Although Rebecca was freezing, her flesh was fever hot. She set the suitcase down, and removed her drenched jacket. Then hugged and rubbed her arms in a futile attempt to rid herself of the impaling cold. Stepping into one of the moonlit shafts, she examined her hands. From the wrists down, they were as pale as milk and as wrinkled as those of an old woman's. Each nail still held remnants of deer blood. She draped her jacket over the suitcase, and waited for her eyes to adjust to the odd lighting. Once objects began to take shape, she moved about cautiously, inspecting each delineation of barn with weary interest.

There were stalls on the far side that once upon a time sheltered horses or cows, but hadn't in a very long time. Heavy beams crisscrossed above her. Drops of rain descended from the open wounds of the roof. Tangled in a heap, in the nearest corner, were the long-since-forgotten skeletons of small farm equipment.

The front of the barn was draped in total darkness, so she lifted the suitcase and made her way to the aft side where the smell of wet hay was most potent. A thick support beam jutted from the floor where a mound of old straw sat undisturbed. She set the suitcase down. With sore hands, she tested the mound for wetness and comfort. *All I need now is the warmth of a blanket.* Teeth chattering violently, Rebecca decided that the moist straw was going to be her resting place for the remainder of night. She went to the stalls in search of anything she might use as a coverlet. Intermittent waves of cold racked her body, causing the pain in her side and knees to bite down hard. The need to urinate once again pressed at her kidneys.

Reaching the first paddock, she undid her jeans, pulled them below her knees, and squatted. While relieving herself, she looked around the narrow stall. Several short links of chain hung from a spike driven into a six-by-six beam. A leather horse collar stood in one corner where a sad oat bag hung empty. In her mind's eye, Rebecca imagined a beautiful black gelding standing where she was, its face buried in the oat bag, tail swishing at bothersome flies. She smiled. Rebecca loved horses, the majestic nobility of them, though she hadn't had the opportunity of riding one. Of the romance they suggested. The gentleness and tolerance each of them seemed to convey whether they be racers, workhorses, or made to pull a carriage. They understood what their challenges were and performed these tasks without prejudice. As old as time itself was the love of man and horse.

Finished, Rebecca pulled her jeans, drew the zipper, fastened the snap and was careful not to step into the puddle she had created. Exiting the first stall, she investigated the next. Here, one of the shafts of moonlight schemed the sections of wood monochrome. The stall was completely empty except for a few loose filaments of straw strewn about the floor.

Without warning, the barn became so reticent, Rebecca could hear herself breathing and feel the rhythm of her heart against her sternum. The cooing pigeons had adjusted to her presence and fallen silent. With no sound apart from functioning body parts, the air grew eerily thick, the barn taking on a bygone facade, as though time had petrified during an era of immense sadness.

Another uncontrollable shiver racked her body. With it came the need to vomit, and she did. A purging of everything she had eaten recently steamed from the ground. With the toe of her foot, she disturbed the earth and covered it best she could. Wiping at her mouth, she discovered that even her lips were blister hot. Forgotten for this ill ravaged phase was the wisdom that someone was waiting for her. All she wanted to do was lay down and sleep for a thousand years.

Weaker than weak, Rebecca investigated the three remaining stalls to find that there would be no added comfort to her slumber. She returned to the mound of straw, opened the suitcase, and took a quick glance at her mother's picture. She kissed the tips of her hot fingers, and placed them over the smiling face of Deseray White, so young, so full of life. "I love you, Momma," she whispered. Re-setting the latches, she placed it behind the beam. Then she rolled her jacket into a ball and gathered straw so that it resembled something of a human nest. With the jacket substituting as a pillow, she lay in a fetal position, her hands supporting the right side of her face as if in prayer, and closed her heavy lids.

Darkness shrouded her mind. Deep cold violated her body. Exhausted, ill, Rebecca soon fell into a deep, dreamless sleep. "*I'm waiting for you.*"

* * *

Something tugged at Rebecca's mind. She tried to fight it, but it urged her from the depths of emptiness. One unfocused eye opened, then the other. Immediately, her body juddered. She had moved during sleep and was now facing the rearmost area of the barn. Her mind still trudged through the tunnel of darkness from which she was interrupted. She moistened her dry, hot lips with the tip of her tongue. Her throat was sore, tummy tossing. For a brief instant, she thought she might throw up again. Unexpected tears dripped from her eyes, causing her to see the proximate area through a transparent veil of tears.

The barn. I'm in a barn. Wet straw and mildew filled her sensess. *Alone, alone, alone. The baby Jesus lying in a manger. No, not the baby Jesus. ME!*

Her feelings of solitude were quickly dashed as she sensed a presence. She could feel it, so near it could be her shadow. But knew it wasn't. Whatever it was, it was as tangible as the cold that enveloped her being. All of a sudden, she was frightened, afraid to lift her head or to take another breath. Her heart thumped heavily as if to escape the bone and cartilage containing it. *Oh god. I've been discovered.*

"Don't be afraid. He likes you." The voice seemed to come from a far distance. A young boy's voice. It filled the silence. Resounded everywhere. Or so Rebecca imagined.

She lifted and turned her head. The face above her caused her to bolt upright. Injured ribs screamed in protest. The pigeons above went into a tizzy, fluttered their wings, and swooped from their purchase. They circled the pitch of the roof several times, then returned to the beams, and cooed en masse.

Staring down at Rebecca were whiskey-colored eyes atop a long muzzle, the end of which was black and as big as a doorknob. A long pink tongue lolled from between razor-sharp teeth. The face was attached to a body as big as a sow, with pocket-sized flaming ears. The red-and-white creature shook its massive head.

Using her feet, Rebecca reversed until her bottom touched the support beam. The great beast followed her, stepping onto the bed of straw with its great paws.

"His name is Chase. Please don't be afraid. He's just curious. That's all," the voice flowed from the darkest region of the barn.

Rebecca stared into the great beast's eyes, contemplating what it would feel like to be eaten alive. Then the strangest thing happened. This man-eater derived from the most fulsome nightmares smiled down at her.

Could it be? She blinked several times. Using the balls of her hands, she rubbed at the confusion in her eyes. *It was!* Just a great big beautiful dog staring back at her. Though it appeared to be a Saint Bernard in size and color, its face bore the distended features of a hound.

"Hello. Chase, is it?" she asked, heart still tripping, but no longer afraid.

The crossbreed raised a paw. Its smile widened. Great drips of saliva dropped from its tongue.

"Back up, Chase. I think you're scaring her," came the voice from the shadows.

Obediently, the massive canine retreated, and stopped not ten feet away. There it sank to the floor, and lay one paw over the other, its smile, effusive.

Rebecca looked to the darkness where she thought the voice came from. "Where are you? Who are you? I'm sorry for sleeping in your barn. But you see, I was so tired... And..."

"Don't be sorry." A small boy stepped from the light ruin curtain. Casually, he walked toward Rebecca, and stopped in a path of moonshine, his eyes gorgeous pearls of blue beneath a crop of sandy hair. An oval face, as smooth as porcelain shone, even in the deficient light. On his meissen countenance, he bore the smile of shyness. He wore a denim jumper over a checkered shirt. On his feet were brown shoes, scuffed across the toes. His hands were behind his back in a military at-ease stance. *"It's okay,"* he said. *"I don't mind that you slept in my barn. Did you get caught in the storm?"*

"Yes, I did. Get caught in the storm I mean."

"That's too bad. Come, Chase."

The impressive dog lifted itself from the floor and moved next to the boy where it sat on its haunches, and looked up at him with so much love that it caused Rebecca's thrumming heart to weep.

"Me and Chase. We don't like storms neither. Do we, Chase?" He patted the flat of Chase's head that in height was equal to his own shoulders. The great dog let out a whimpered answer and lapped at the boy's cheek. *"Hey. Do you want to see something really jim-dandy?"*

"Sure," replied Rebecca, throat all afire, hands clammy.

"Turn, Chase," commanded the young boy.

Chase stood and turned.

"Stop!"

Obediently the dog stopped. Rebecca could see large islands of red across its shoulders and rump. Its thick tail was white except for a smudge of red at the base.

"See." The boy pointed to the center of the dog's thick torso.

Rebecca could not believe her eyes. In the middle of its chest, against a background of white fur, was a perfectly shaped heart of red.

"This means he's special," said the boy, arching an arm over his head and bringing it back full circle. *"The most special dog around, that's for sure."*

"I don't doubt that for a minute. What's your name?" asked Rebecca.

Proudly, with a grin from ear to ear, the small boy pointed at his chest with a hooked thumb and said, *"I'm Caleb. Caleb Hart. You already met Chase. He's my bestest friend in the whole world. I don't go anywhere without him. Yup, we're like two peas in a pod."*

Rebecca tried to stand, but found that her legs were so weak they would not respond. Taking several deep breaths, she tried to settle her racing heart. Her body relaxed, but her head swooned. Exhaustion poured over her like wax from a candle. She yawned, long and loud.

"You're hurt. And sick too," said Caleb Hart, his face scrunched with concerned.

"Not really. Just a few scrapes and bruises, and I caught a chill from walking in the rain."

"Did you fall down? I got sick once too. And I fell out of a tree and broke my arm. Jeepers, it hurt."

"Yes, I did fall. Slipped in the mud. Way up the road." Rebecca tilted her head and regarded the devoted twosome. Though they appeared delighted with the current circumstances, there was something oddly tragic about them. "How come you're out so late, Caleb? Won't your parents be angry that you're out here in the middle of the night?"

"Nah. They're asleep. Besides, it's pretty near morning time and I'm six, almost seven. Me and Chase. We come out here all the time. Don't we, fella?"

The big dog raised a paw. Caleb took it in his little hands and said, *"Good boy."* Lifting the offered paw to his face, he smoothed it across the point of his chin. The great dog leaned into Caleb's body and let out what sounded like a human sigh.

The sight was so touching, an errant tear slid over Rebecca's cheek. She knuckled it away. *Such love. Such loyalty.* "You're a very brave and lucky little boy to have a friend like Chase."

"Rootin' tootin.' Hey!" Caleb beamed. *"Would you like to see Chase do tricks? He's very smart."*

"I'm sure he is." Rebecca yawned, cold rattled her body. "I'm just so tired, Caleb and I'm not feeling too well. What I need is to sleep."

"Ah, just one, okay? It won't take very long. I promise." Crisscrossing the center of his chest with a finger, Caleb vowed, *"Cross my heart."*

"All right, I suppose I owe you one trick, being that you don't mind my sleeping in your barn."

"Swell. Are you ready?"

"Ready as rain."

Caleb Hart skewed his head to one side, curious. *"That's a funny saying. Ready as rain. I don't think rain is ever ready. It just comes."*

"You know, I've never thought about it before, but you're right," said Rebecca. "It just comes. Now how about that trick." She yawned again, body shook, face hot with fever.

"Sure. Here it goes... Chase?"

The big dog looked to Caleb.

"Wanna hug?"

Chase reared back, sat on his haunches, and balanced his ponderous weight on rear legs, tail ramrod straight. A feat that would have been very difficult for an animal of his stature to commit to. It raised its paws as if they were extended arms. Caleb took Chase into his open arms. For the longest time, they remained like that. Boy and bestest friend in the whole world wrapped in each other's embrace, their faces exuding the love they shared between them.

Rebecca's eyes filled. The sight made her feel all warm inside, regardless of the incessant shiver trampling her soul into a million shards of ice. It also reminded her just how much she was alone. Barely able to lift her arms to applaud, she beamed. "Bravo! Bravo!"

Boy and dog separated. Chase lay at Caleb's feet. Caleb bent forward in a showman's bow of appreciation. With his face all aglow, he asked, *"Would you like to see another?"*

Rebecca sleeved tears away. The display of emotions left her feeling even more exhausted than she already was. "As much as I would like to, Caleb. What I really need is to get more sleep. You don't mind, do you?"

"Nah. It's okay," said Caleb, a little dejected. *"Me and Chase should be getting back now anyway. You can watch him do more tricks some other time."* His face brightened. *"Maybe after you've rested. That would be really keen. He knows so many that it would take all day to show you."*

Rebecca did not have the heart to tell him that she intended to be long gone come morning. "Yeah, sure, Caleb, perhaps another time." She lay down, and rested the side of her face against the roll of her jacket. Sleep-deprived lids closed without warning. A fever chill racked her body. Managing a few fever affected final words she said, "Good night, Caleb Hart. Good night, Chase. You get back home now and get into bed. You really shouldn't..." The murky waters of oblivion fell upon her. In a wink, she was dead to the world.

"I knew you would come," whispered the six-almost-seven-year-old. *"I've been*

waiting such a long time. The longest time forever and ever. Sleep tight, Rebecca White. Don't let the bed bugs bite." Taking a red ball from his back pocket, Caleb Hart tossed it into the shadows. Chase chased after it, his great body bounding forward, thick white tail looping happily. Caleb followed, skipping merrily, cherub face beaming.

Together, boy and bestest friend in the world slipped into the darkness and beyond the sealed barn doors.

* * *

18

The Feather

JOHNNY sat on the edge of the bed. He had already dressed, preparing himself for the forthcoming work day: white T-shirt, loose-fitting jeans, and his boots until he was able to purchase a pair of work wear. He hadn't slept much. The undiminished *sex* dream had kept him alert. The scratches on his chest reasoned his mind to recklessly opinion that the dream was not a dream at all, but a slip into enchantment. A world where reality and dreams shared the same moments in time. Still reticent within the boundary of his intellect were his visitor's final words, "*What are you afraid of?*"

Would he venture there again? he wondered.

Morning's sunlight poured through the porthole in a shaft of brilliance that was temperate and splendid with the promise of a propitious day. Johnny went to the opening and warmed himself in the spawn of Mother Nature's greatest gift. Resting against the gas blue sky like a finger pointing south was a whisper of cloud. His hawk circled on the updraft, its wings spread silent while it basked in the sun, and played "catch me if you can" with its rectrix.

Juno was about a hundred yards into the property scrounging for sustenance, head low, tail slack between the contours of her rear quarters. She lifted her head, and reared her neck to look back at the barn as though she knew Johnny was watching her.

Reminding himself of the promise he had made to her, Johnny went to the knapsack, withdrew sixty dollars—more than enough to pay for a bale of hay, bag of oats, some new shoe nails—and stuffed the bills into his jeans.

"Johnny?" Konahee's voice drifted up through the hole in the floor.

He peered into the opening. Konahee stood at the foot of the ladder wearing a dress so splendid with the colors of spring that it could have won first prize in an Easter parade. A bright yellow sun hat, usually reserved for aristocrats at horse races, encompassed her shoulders. On her feet were the comfortable deerskin moccasins. "Yes, Konahee."

Looking up at him, Konahee's bejeweled blue eye met his. "I am fixing breakfast. How do you like your eggs?"

"Scrambled, if it's not too much trouble," said Johnny, pushing hair that had fallen forward and back over the yoke of his musculature.

"There is no trouble. You will earn your keep. We will have to do something about that."

Puzzled, Johnny queried, "About what Konahee?"

"Your hair. It will get in the way while you are at work. Cause you to sweat unnecessarily. I have just the thing. You come to the house now. I will have breakfast waiting."

"I'll just be a few minutes. I want to check on Juno first."

Without another word, Konahee slipped from view, her elongated shadow succeeding in silence.

Johnny made the bed, tucked the corners neat, and fluffed the unfluffable pillow. The *Life of Pi,* he rested on its center. He needed to reenergize. The vivacity spent during the dream sex, whether actual or not, had deadened his usual vigor. Sitting on the floor, he faced the bed, jammed his boots under the side rail and began a series of sit-ups, maintaining an equal rhythm until he reached two hundred. Fresh blood fired through his veins. Tiny beads bubbled on his brow. The scratches on his chest pulled taut already having begun the healing process. Breathing deep, he sucked air until his heart returned to a normal cadence. He stood, invigorated, ready to take on the day.

Descending the ladder, he peered over his shoulder. The flesh-eating cricket was as it should be, a horse buggy long retired since its last use. The prebirthday gift that had gotten him this far stood ascetically in the stall where he had left it. In that moment, he had a sixth sense that he might not ever experience its hum beneath him again.

Once outside, he went to the back of the barn. Several feet off the ground, a ladder was posted to the barn's wall. It lead to the window of the loft and ended at the sill. The sun was just above the horizon, a violent conflagration that would soon scorch the land. Juno was still in search of food, dipping her long neck toward the ground, moving waywardly to her left then right. Johnny whistled.

Juno's head shot up. Ears twitching, her tail thrashing the back of her rump. She made a three-sixty, and trotted toward Johnny with all the grace of a show horse, though Johnny knew she must be at, or near her twentieth year.

When horse met man, Johnny's heart soared. He embraced her long face, and tenderly massaged the bridge between her eyes. In turn, Juno snorted contentedly, and lifted Johnny several inches from the ground as if he weighed no more than a carnival teddy.

Johnny laughed. It felt wonderful considering everything he had been through in the past forty-eight hours. Juno whinnied, worked her lips into a horse smile. "I'm going to get you some nice hay and some oats today so you don't have to keep eating these weeds," he told her.

As if grasping every word, Juno nodded and tramped at the ground.

A tear welled in Johnny's eye. Juno's antics reminded him so much of the friends he had left behind. Thunder and Lightning were so intuned to what he told them, often the three would walk around the Double B ranch, communicating to one another in terms that would make the horse whisperer envious. "This is a very magical place, isn't it, girl?"

Again Juno nodded with enthusiasm, and displayed her slanted teeth. Several flies buzzed her rump. Lifting her cauda equina, she jetted a stream of urine into the air. Finished, she whipped her tail. Two of the three flies landed on the ground, legs up, the other absconded for less threatening things to menace.

"That a girl, Juno," said Johnny. He stroked the underside of her jaw. "That'll teach them."

He left her standing in the shade of the barn, and told her how beautiful she was and that it would not be long before she was dining like a horse princess.

Before he went to the house, Johnny checked the water trough to see if it needed filling. It was half-full, but the sides were slick with moss, and its surface layered with an army of winged insects drowned by their own curiosity. Locating a bucket by the side of the house, he returned to the trough and skimmed the insects out. Later, he decided, he would empty it. Clean out the slime. Transport it to a shadier spot, then fill it with clean water. He indeed had a lot of work to do.

* * *

Johnny sat in the chair that was to become his usual place at the table and folded one hand over the other. Waiting for him was a steaming cup of coffee, just the way he liked it.

Konahee stood in front of the stove turning sausages, cracking eggs, and frying wedges of potatoes. She had her back to him. Long grey hair spilled from under the brim of the sun hat. Her withered hands and moccasin feet seemed to be moving to a rhythm only she could hear.

Johnny decided that there was no point broaching the subject of the trough even though it bordered on neglect, because she was old, probably older than he could imagine and she shouldn't be left to feel guilty. Her mind could be slipping, though he doubted it.

"Did you sleep well?" asked Konahee, shaking spice over the potatoes.

"Yes, Konahee." lied Johnny without thinking. He knew full well there was no lying to this woman. She *knew* things.

"It would not be without reason if you did not." She turned her head to look at him. "New surroundings are often the bearer of dreams. Good *and* bad." That said, she turned back to the stove. "I hope you like spicy. Gets the blood circulating. A friend of mine made these sausages from a deer he shot last fall."

"Thank you. I don't mind spicy, and I love deer. My mother used to make roasts and links whenever my father shot a deer on the ranch. Where's George by the way? I expected to find him at your feet begging for food."

"He has already fed. I expect you can find him just about anywhere sleeping it off. He is not only lazy, he is also quite content wherever he plants himself. I often find him stretched across the top of the television, snoring like an old man."

Konahee plated the food enough to feed a small battalion of men and set the plates on the table. Spices and deer meat filled Johnny all the way to his empty stomach. She dragged her chair out from the table and took a seat.

"Boy, that's a lot of food," said Johnny. Five thick sausages piled on top of one another sat next to a mound of eggs and potatoes. Konahee's plate held an equal amount.

"You have much work to do. You need your strength. The days will be long and hot. The nights, perhaps longer." Her dead eye watched him, the blue eye fascinated with a sausage that still spurted fat.

"I didn't mean for me," said Johnny. "I can handle just about anything. Do *you* always eat this much?"

Konahee laughed. "I have the appetite of a lion. It helps me maintain the beauty of my youth." Strands of grey had fallen from their purchase beneath the hat and surrounded her haggard face. Her mouth curled into a broad smile which revealed the gaps between her decayed teeth. She brushed the wayward hair aside. "Don't you think?"

"Yes, Konahee. You are beautiful and wise."

"Yes. I am aware of this."

Laughter filled the kitchen.

Johnny cut a piece of sausage, plopped it into his mouth, anxious to relive the flavor of memory his mother left upon him. Washing it down with a gulp of coffee, he said, "This is delicious. Tell your friend I said so."

Konahee rubbed at her turquoise ring. "You have fond memories of your mother. She was Cherokee, was she not? I can see it in your face. They are of good people."

"Yes, Konahee. She was taken from me by the white man's sickness."

Forking a piece of sausage, wedge of potato, rumple of egg, Konahee jammed it all into her mouth. She spoke between clattering bites. "This friend you lost. He is not so far away. He has only passed from this time to another. Just as your mother has. They walk together now. One day you will walk with them."

"Thank you, Konahee. I needed to hear that. Can I ask you a question?" He shoveled more food into his mouth to which his belly was truly grateful.

"You are curious about my eyes."

Johnny swallowed. "Well, yes. I was just wondering. If it's too personal. I mean if you rather not say anything, that's okay."

Konahee's blue eye seemed to intensify with angry light. "My grandmother was raped by a white lieutenant after he and his men burned her village and murdered all of the young warriors. They did not exclude the male children. The women, they used to their bidding, old *and* young. This eye is a wretched curse, and I would gouge it out of my head if it were not for the fact that I was born with this other one as dead as the children who never came to be." The eye blazed blue fire.

"I'm sorry," said Johnny. "I shouldn't have pried."

"It is good that you know. We share the same affliction. The eyes of the white man." The blazing eye cooled. "Now let us eat our breakfast. It is still early. I want you to walk the distance of my property. Check on the snares. You will find them at the foot of the eastern slope. Be careful of the snakes. They bathe in the sun there and do not wish to be disturbed. When the hardware is open, I will call ahead and tell them you will be coming." She jammed another fork full of food into her mouth.

"Would you mind if I take Juno along? She could use the exercise."

"*And* the company. I'm afraid I have been less and less a companion to her these past few years. She deserves better I know. Even though I am still beautiful, I am not as spry as I once was." She laughed again. The chewed morsels of deer, potato, and egg, fully displayed, blue eye laughing with her now.

When breakfast was over, Johnny cleared the table. Konahee disappeared somewhere in the house. When she returned, she held in her hands a strip of brown leather, two feet in length and the wing feather of a red-tailed hawk. "Sit down," she told Johnny. "This is for your hair."

Johnny sat in his chair, gathered his thick hair, and threw it behind him so that it fell evenly across his back.

With the strip of leather hanging from her mouth, Konahee moved behind him and gave Johnny the feather to hold on to. He looked at it, turned it this way and that. The feather looked as if it had just been plucked. On one side, tiny black dots formed a grey-blue oval ring against the red. On the other, a splash of yellow created what appeared to be a cloud. The blood within the quill, still pink. "I've never seen a feather like this before," he said.

"And you will never *see* another one like it. It came to me on a day when the sky was dark with anger. I was outside. Much younger than I am now, but no less beautiful. Mother's breath was wild in its search of destruction." Her fingers worked as she spoke. "I could hear the sad cry of a great bird but could not see it. It was directly above me, tearing at my heart with its tormented shrieks. I pleaded with it to seek shelter elsewhere, but the wind had a different fate in mind. It was so mighty, that it felled me to my knees, but I would not give in to its furry. I remained where I was, determined to guide the great bird into my protection. Sadly, in my youth, I was not as pragmatic with the ways of our people as I am today. The great bird's death cries evaded me. When I looked up into the dark sky, I saw something floating toward me even though the wind was whipping the air. I held out my hand. The feather you hold landed softly into my palm. I have saved it for this very day. It will go with you when you leave this place. I have learned all I will learn from it."

"My mother used to tell me stories like that when I was a boy. Of the magic ways of our heritage."

"There, I am almost done. Give me the feather." Konahee took it from Johnny's hand, fixed it to the tether and into the single braid that now hung down his back. "Now you will not sweat so much. Go find Juno and check the snares. If we are lucky. I will roast a rabbit for tonight's dinner."

"How will I know when I reach the end of your property?" asked Johnny.

"You will know, Johnny. You will know."

* * *

Johnny and Juno trekked toward the blaze of a saffron sun rising mercilessly into the blue. He had given Juno two sticks of carrots from Konahee's fridge which she ate in silent gratitude.

The air was dry, as subdued as petrified time. They walked side by side, Juno swishing her tail while Johnny's eyes watched for slithering movement on the ground. The newly placed feather felt strange against his back, a constant tickle that sang up and down his spine, an impression he would have to get used to.

Movement in the sky caused him to look up. Large birds, much too large to be hawks, were ensuing each other in a slow, undulating path a hundred or more yards above ground. *Vultures*. And where there were vultures, death was usually at hand.

Quickening his pace, Johnny directed himself toward the area below the circling scavengers. Juno did not seem to mind the pace, prancing next to him as if she had just won a blue ribbon for best in show. Along the way, Johnny gathered some good-sized throwing rocks.

The vultures swooped down one by one, and huddled together like a football team as the quarterback issued the next play. When Johnny felt he was within reach of his throwing ability, he let loose one of the rocks. The stone ricocheted off the ground a foot away from the shoulder-to-shoulder frenzy that was taking place. The scavengers did not move, far more captivated in the feast they had found. Vultures were determinably fearless, especially when there was free fodder for the taking.

Johnny fired another rock, this one striking one of the birds in the back. It raised its featherless head, a drip of flesh hung from its warped beak. It jerked its cranium from one direction to another. Mindless to Johnny's swift approach, it raised its beak and swallowed the torn flesh down in three obscene spasms.

The only method in which Johnny knew how to disrupt the pack was to charge at them, yelling like a madman, firing stone after stone.

Juno felt that this was an exceptional idea and charged forward, head down.

Together, the vultures raised their heads, hopped up and down with their wings spread in defiance, screeching an ungodly sound meant to scare off the would-be attackers.

Johnny would have none of it. He tore into the group, kicking with his boots, sending one of the birds' tits over teakettle into the air. The rest retreated, and hopped along the ground in a widening circle. In unison, they berated Johnny for having disturbed their feast. Brave Juno held them at bay. She tromped the ground whenever one of them tried to move in and reclaim its prize.

Lying on its side, entrails absent, both eyes plucked clean, was a coyote. Johnny went to one knee and shooed away the flies buzzing at its empty sockets, the fresh opening across its hollow abdomen. A quick inspection revealed that one of its rear legs had been broken. Johnny harked back to the creature he had seen through the porthole, limping in the distance. *Mother gave and she took*. There was nothing he could do for the poor beast, thankful that it wasn't the corpse of a human the scavengers had claimed. Quite often, some city pup toyed with the idea that he can just moezy across the vastness of desert in search of himself. However, once the life-sapping intensity of the sun put them in place, they became so lost and brain-beaten they were usually rescued within walking distance of a house or highway. Or not.

The vultures bravado intensified. They challenged Juno, wings spread, sharp beaks snapping at the air as they moved closer.

"Come on, Juno," said Johnny. "Let them eat. It's just the way things are. The way things have always been."

As soon as horse and man were out of range, the slump-shouldered pack rushed in on the cadaver, and ripped at it as if it were the last meal they would ever claim. In a matter of minutes, they would pick it clean, leaving nothing but skeleton for the sun to bleach. Then the brain-eating maggots would appear as if summoned by magic. Mother gave and she took.

* * *

Ten minutes later, Johnny and Juno approached what Konahee had described as the eastern slope. A gentle lift in the land as though the ground had burped and remained so, preserved in time. "You stay here, Juno. I want to check out the other side. Make sure there aren't any snakes."

Juno nodded and took a comfortable stance.

Johnny went to the rim of the lift, surprised to find that it dropped dramatically. Thirty feet or so. Thumbs of slate jutted horizontal like diving boards. His eyes searched the topography. In the distance, great battlements of stone dominated the land, rising like monuments to primordial gods. Resolute kings of their past, present, and future domain. Great warriors rested undisturbed, waiting for Mother's breath to send them elsewhere. Gnarled cacti dotted the landscape for as far as Johnny could see. All of it under a vapor blue dome. He could well imagine nomadic tribes wandering the land before the first settlers came, as though he had stopped at the verge of one world and was looking at its parallel. A world that had violated the proceedings of time. *This must be where Konahee's property ended.*

A prairie rattler, coiled like a lariat, its head comfortable against its pulsing body, rested on one of the ossified rocks as it basked in Mother's beautiful face. Johnny's sudden approach disturbed its slumber. Its coarse tail rose, and rattled a warning that it rather not be bothered.

"Don't worry, friend. I'm not here to hassle you," said Johnny. He maintained a good distance as he sought a path that would lead him to the ground. He could see one of the snares beneath the foliage of some sage. With care, he descended the crest between two thumbs of rock. His boots slipped, held, and slipped again. The newly fashioned braid bounced off his sweat stained T-shirt. *Thud, thud, thud.* Dust rose in puffs around his legs. When he reached level ground, he dusted himself off, waved the cloud of earth from his face, and looked up to the ridge.

Annoyed, the drab rattler introduced its full length. All seven feet of it. It rose from its sunning place. Two feet. Three feet. Four feet. Its black pronged tongue tested the air for danger.

How in the hell did Konahee set these snares? She was full of surprises that one. The one snare was obviously empty, so Johnny explored the sage and thistles, finding one, then two. Both were empty. Ferreting further, he found another, placed within the snarl of some bramble. Within its constricted loop was the foot of a jackrabbit, chewed off in the creature's effort to free itself. Careful not to get pricked, Johnny loosened the wire and removed the foot. Its severed end was already dry, several days old. Rather than discard it, he put it in his pocket and reset the snare. Another five-minute search produced no others. He wondered how disappointed Konahee was going to be not having a rabbit to roast for dinner.

He wiped sweat and grit from his brow, and decided he would purchase some water and a cooler for the workday ahead. It was going to be a scorcher, the sun already blistering his face. "Sure is hot," he said aloud.

"I agree. Absolutely," a voice commented, soft, lilting, a female's voice.

Johnny spun. No one there. *You're hearing things. Mother playing tricks on you.*

"On the contrary, Johnny. You are not hallucinating. My voice is as real as your own."

Blinking rapidly, it occurred to Johnny that the voice was as close as the air he breathed. *What the hell.* He shook his head and rubbed at his eyes.

"Don't worry, Johnny. You are not going mad."

"Where are you? Who are you?" asked Johnny.

"I will introduce myself in due time. For now, this is my preferred communication."

Johnny looked up to the slope. The rattler had returned to its slumberous way. "Are you a great spirit?"

"I'm afraid my existence is not as sensational as all that. Think of me as a unique acquaintance. A friend perhaps."

"An acquaintance? A friend? In what way? I wish I could see you. Show yourself."

"Under the circumstances, you might find my appearance disturbing. Frightening even. Please understand."

"I'm not afraid of anything."

"Yes, I know. Still, I rather not expose myself for the time being. You will know me when you see me. Be careful when you climb back up the crest. It's damned slippery, and those slithering beasts can be hiding just about anywhere."

"Thanks, I guess." Johnny looked up and around. Nothing, nada, nobody. Yet who, or whatever this abnormality was, was able to see *him*. "Can I ask you something?"

"Yes, I suppose so."

"Do you have a name? Like we do?"

"I do not possess the entitlement of name. But you may give me one on the day of our second encounter. This is the way it is. The way it should be. Now I must go. But I will be keeping an eye on you, Johnny Black."

"Wait! Don't go! Holy shit! This is too fantastic. You can't just leave."

However, the cerebral voice fell silent. Gone. Exit stage left. All Johnny could overhear was his voice of reason battling with the very idea that he just might be going a little crazy.

Taking a running start at the incline, the smooth bottoms of his boots slipped;

nonetheless, Johnny managed to take purchase of an abutting rock and pulled himself to its surface. Standing, he took in the land for as far as he could see. The rattler, disturbed yet again, sounded a warning. It uncoiled, inch by inch and slunk over its sunbathing spot.

Juno stood where Johnny had left her. When she saw him, she brayed a whinny and stomped a hoof.

The sun was at its ten o'clock opinion. Johnny went to the aging mustang and guided her to the ledge of rock. Side by side they gazed at the time-lost territory. "I don't suppose you heard anything, eh, girl?"

Juno shook her head.

"No, of course you didn't. It was another way of this magical place. I guess I'll just have to wait and see. Sure was strange though." He perused the territory one more time. Detecting nothing unusual, he said to his new horse friend, "We should be getting back now. I've got a lot of work to do."

Man and horse turned from the eastern crest and began the hot trek back to Konahee's residence.

Far enough away, so that Johnny could not see it, the nameless creature moved swift across the plains, and returned from whence it came.

* * *

Anticipating Johnny and Juno's return, Konahee sat in a folding chair beneath the transom of Johnny's nightly stargaze. In one hand she held a Japanese fan, and waved it at her face. In the other was a walking stick fashioned from the heart of a beech tree, twisted at the shaft and fisted at the top.

From a hundred yards away, Johnny saw her there, sitting directly beneath the ladder, yellow sun hat a beacon against the dark wood of the barn. He waved to her, and quickened his pace.

Juno suddenly bolted. She ran toward Konahee faster than Johnny believed capable. The old mare stopped in her tracks and lowered her head, submitting herself to the attention Konahee bestowed upon her.

To Johnny, it looked like the two were in conversation. Juno nodding, Konahee gesturing with the walking stick. When he was within a stone's throw, Konahee pushed herself from the chair with the aid of the crafted beech wood. "Wait there," she called out to him. She folded the fan and stuffed it into the side pocket of her colorful dress. Juno stepped aside.

Together, horse and master met Johnny where he waited, empty-handed. "I see that the snares were empty," said Konahee. "Too bad. Maybe tomorrow."

"Sorry, Konahee." Johnny fished in his jeans and produced the rabbit's foot. "This is all there was." He held it out to her.

"Oh, I see." She took the severed foot, and examined it close to her blue eye. "May I keep this. It is full of luck. And at my age, I can use all the luck I can get."

"Yes, of course, Konahee. It belongs to you anyway since it was found in one of your snares. That's an interesting walking stick you have by the way."

Regarding Johnny as one would regard a precious object, she retorted, "It was my mother's and her mother's before her. It is seeped in wisdom I am told, though I find it to be nothing more than a crutch for my rapidly declining life."

Something, an uttered itch within Johnny's skull, told him it was much more than just an ordinary stick one would uncover walking in a forest. He was going to ask her how she managed to set the snares, then reasoned he shouldn't question the ways of the mysterious Konahee. If she wanted to make known her secrets, it would be of her own accord.

"I trust you and Juno had a good walk?" she questioned, and slipped the jack foot into a pocket.

"Yes, Konahee. It was… *interesting.*"

"I see." Looking at the ground beneath Johnny's boots, she said, "This is where I want the entrance of the paddock you are going to build to be." Then she banged the beech wood against the ground, not once, not twice, but three times. "Let us walk. Juno, you must be thirsty. Go to your water. Rest. We can manage without you."

Obediently, Juno left, tail swishing at the air.

Konahee led Johnny to the four attitudes where she imagined the paddock to be. She once again banged the earth thrice with the walking aid. At each corner, she had Johnny place a large stone. Above them, the hawk shrilled and circled carefree, its shadow sharp and elegant against the earth. A moderate wind stirred, and triggered the oversized brim of Konahee's sun hat to undulate. "I have called the hardware," she said. "They are expecting you. Ask for Mr. Lector. He is a client of mine and will take care of you."

"His first name isn't Hannibal, is it?" teased Johnny.

Konahee chuckled. "No, his first name is Harvey. He is not akin to the delicacies of humans. I am sure of it. There is only one hardware in Alcova. A large building on Bandy Avenue that is as yellow as my hat." Exploring the side pocket of her dress, she produced a set of keys. "Take the truck and go now. It is full of gas."

Walking back to the house, they overtook Juno who had had her fill of water and was lying on the ground, four legs comfortable beneath her form. She raised her head and acknowledged their presence with a goatish bleat then rested it between folded knees, the girth of her body expanding as she took a deep intake of air.

"I hope you don't mind, but I'm going to pick up a few things for Juno," said Johnny. "She needs some new shoe nails, and I would like to put her on a diet of oats and green hay. Fatten her up a bit. I'll pay for everything myself. It's the least I can do, you giving me shelter and everything."

"If this is what you feel needs to be done, then by all means do so. Juno is already very fond of you. You have a great rapport with animals, and for Mother Earth. This respect is mutual. For this I will put my Juno's health in your hands."

"Thank you, Konahee. You won't be disappointed with the results."

The blaze of Konahee's blue eye studied Johnny. "No. I think not."

Once they were standing at the risers leading to the house, Konahee said, "I will thaw some chicken for dinner. Do you prefer roasted or country fried?"

Knowing how much trouble it was to pan-fry chicken, Johnny said, "Roasted will be great."

"Good. Dinner will be at seven. I am expecting two clients today, so remember what I cautioned."

"Yes, Konahee. You do not wish to be disturbed."

"Good." Kohnahee looked to the cloudless sky where the hawk circled silently. "There will be rain coming out of the mountains."

Johnny followed her gaze. Not a single cloud interrupted the blue of the day, but if Konahee said it was so, he willingly believed her.

The old and wise Shoshone climbed the rickety steps, the walking stick supporting her weight. She regarded Johnny before she disappeared into the house, smiled and spoke not a word. Both doors closed whisper quiet.

Johnny had yet to see the truck he was going to drive. He expected to find a cancer-ridden thing with four bald tires and an engine that was on its last legs. Rounding the house, his mouth gaped.

Sitting on a gravel pad was a burnished Ford Crew Cab. Candy apple red, 350 diesel engine. Johnny opened the door and climbed in. It still claimed that new vehicle smell. The one that was like pheromones to all men. He turned the engine. The 350 block roared. He checked the odometer, 410 miles. Several trips to and from Alcova. Konahee was not only full of surprises but wealthy as well, he assumed. Depressing the clutch, he shifted into reverse and slowly backed from the house. Reverse to first slipped in as smooth as melted butter. Powering the window, Johnny engaged the radio. The sync voice system flooded the cab. Elvis was crooning "Wise Men Say."

Johnny felt nary a jitter beneath him as he drove along the rutted drive leading to the highway. When he passed Juno, the boy in him tooted the horn. Juno raised her head. Johnny waved. "Be back soon," he called out to her.

Juno responded with a whipping of her tail and a great blast of breath that disrupted the dry earth beneath her face.

* * *

During the hour-long drive into Alcova, Johnny thought about the new *friend* he had encountered. *How much time would pass before it revealed itself? Could it be that this new friend was so repulsive in appearance that I would cringe at the mere sight of it? Run away as though the devil himself were chasing me?* He doubted it, *still*. Fingering the four slashes beneath his T-shirt, he deliberated, *And what of the scratches on my chest? Stranger than strange*. A dream that might not have been a dream at all. But that too was impossible. He and Konahee were the only existing people, he was sure of it. Nevertheless, the scratches were true. As real as the friendly voice that had insisted he was not going mad. Then he recollected his mother's words, *You will meet three strangers*. If he had already met two, one being Konahee, the other being the dream succubus who had left her mark upon him. Then it stood to reason that the voice, whatever form it might take, would be the third. And he, Johnny Black, was going to be the bearer, the sole witness, to events that were completely beyond the realm of normalcy.

After listening to a station that played mostly hits from the fifties and sixties, rededicated to the original Rat Pack, Johnny tried to locate stations that played music more in tune to his liking. Country or classic rock. But each time he found one, the Ford's receiver, as if controlled by the hand of a nostalgic ghost, dialed back to Frank and his friends. *All right, Konahee. Have it your way.*

* * *

19

The Bone Shed

H. L. Hardware, essentially a warehouse clad in canary yellow sheets of metal with red trim, took up most of the end of Bandy Avenue, an acre of it reserved for lumber. A young man sitting in a forklift was distributing long stacks of two-by-tens. Johnny parked the Ford in front of the double-glass entrance.

John Deer riding mowers lined the right side of the hardware. Swing sets of varying design and color lined the left. All of it marked down 25 percent.

Harvey Lector, a balding man of substantial girth, noticed Johnny as soon as he entered. He walked up to him and stretched out a rough carpenter's hand. Harvey was wearing jeans and a golf shirt with the businesses icon on it. "You must be Johnny. The young man Konahee told me about. Her great-nephew."

Johnny took his hand and gave it a firm three shake. "Um... Yes. Good to meet you, Mr. Lector." *So now I'm Konahee's great-nephew. Makes sense I guess.*

"Please, call me Harvey. Everyone does." Releasing Johnny's grip, he said, "That Konahee's a remarkable woman. She's been helping me these past two years since the death of my dear wife. Yes, a remarkable woman indeed. So you're here to purchase the materials needed to build a paddock for Juno." With a gesture of his head, he said, "Come, let's write up the items you require in my office where we won't be disturbed."

Following close, Johnny took in the store's inventory. It was a treasure trove to the handyman and outdoorsman, from the smallest nail to paints and auto parts. Fishing tackle and bird seed, patio sets and barbeques, work wear and sections devoted to lighting, gardens and bicycles. Tents and dinghies floated from the ceiling. Cleverly marketed, mannequins decked in waders hung from it as though they were parachuting into the store.

Harvey Lector's office was scantily furnished with desk, computer monitor, phone, two chairs, and a filing cabinet. However, the walls were festooned with a fine display of taxidermy. Bass, pike, salmon, Arctic grayling, several species of trout, and a barracuda were mounted according to size. The barracuda eye level behind Harvey's desk.

"My passion," he beamed. He gestured for Johnny to take a seat in one of the available chairs, and plopped his size into a leather swivel. Then he positioned the computer monitor so that it faced him. "I'll just bring up Konahee's account." Fingers worked the keyboards. "Here we go. Can I get you anything before we start, Johnny? Maybe a coffee or a soda?"

"No, thank you Harvey. I'm fine. Nice barracuda by the way."

"Thanks. Fifty-two pounds. Not an ounce of it a lie," he boasted, face lit with the recall of pulling it in. "Caught it off the southern tip of Cuba, near Santiago. Took me two hours and four beers. Ever been to Cuba, Johnny? Nicest people in the world."

"I haven't had the pleasure. Maybe someday." Johnny rested his hands in his lap, concluding that Harvey did much of his business in office so he could regale his customers with yarns about his adventures.

"Well, it's a far stretch better than say Jamaica, Trinidad, or Mexico. Too much crime. Too many people with their hands out. Overcrowded, and the beaches just don't compare. Meet lots of nice Canadians down there too. Now back to business. How far down do you plan on putting the posts?"

"Four feet should do it."'

"So you'll need ten-footers. How many?"

"A hundred should do. I'll need to rent an auger for a few days."

Fingers worked the keyboard. "Done. Now how about wire? Do you want barbed, double barbed, or barbless?"

"Barbless. Three spools please. And I'll need eight dozens three-foot stakes and a hundred yards of chalking line. Ten pounds of U nails, oh yes, and a small cooler. Something big enough to hold half a dozen bottles of water. Those, I'll pay for myself."

"Now what about the gate?" asked Harvey. "You plan on building one or should we order a nice aluminum one. Say a six-by-six?"

Johnny thought for a moment. He couldn't see Konahee hoisting a heavy wooden gate at her age. An aluminum one might cost more, but it would swing nicely without much effort on her part. "Let's order an aluminum one."

Again the fingers went to work. "Done. Anything else?"

"I need to be fitted with a pair of work boots and some gloves."

"I've got some nice Kodiaks on special. Only $59.95. The work gloves I'll throw in for free."

"Konahee says to put it on her bill."

"What size are you, about a twelve?"

"Thirteen wide."

"I'll have one of my clerks find you a pair. You can pick them and your cooler up at the front counter when you leave."

"Thanks, Harvey. You're being very helpful."

"Nothing I wouldn't do for that woman. She showed me a very spiritual way in which to deal with the passing of my wife. God rest her soul."

"I also need a one-gallon gas container, and can you tell me where I would be able to purchase some hay and oats and some horseshoe nails?"

"Absolutely. Going to fix Juno up, are yah? She's a good old gal. When you leave here, turn right at the lights and follow the road to the end of town. There you'll find a tack shop. Garrette's Tack, Feed, and Saddlery. Can't miss it. Big statue of a white horse out front. He'll have everything you need."

"Thanks, Harvey. I guess that's it for now."

"Good. I can have the posts, gate, and wire delivered day after tomorrow. Now let's load you up with the things you need right away. I'll just print off a copy for Konahee and have one of the clerks fit you with a good pair of boots. Then I'll meet you out back." "Thanks again, Harvey." Johnny stood and reached across the desk. They shook hands.

"I guess I'll be seeing you hard at work tomorrow. I have an appointment with your aunt. Such a remarkable woman."

"That she is," agreed Johnny. *And then some.*

* * *

Loaded with everything he needed, Johnny drove to the tack and saddlery where he purchased four squares of green hay, a fifty-pound bag of oats, and a dozen shoe nails from a young woman who stood no more than four feet ten and outfitted in chaps over jeans, denim shirt, and white cowboy hat. Silk blond hair fell about her shoulders. A wisp of freckles surrounded eyes that were as blue as the day.

"Just pull your truck out back and I'll help load you up," she said, and smiled country white teeth. "I haven't seen you around here before. Did you just move here?"

Johnny explained that he was working at Konahee's for the summer, not sure whether he should continue with Konahee's misdirection and didn't. Alcova being the small town that it was, word would get around soon enough.

"Oh, I see. Say, well, if you ever get lonely out there, why don't you come to the Gooseneck pub. I can be found there Friday nights. They always have good bands Friday and Saturday nights. My name is Donna by the way. Donna Smith. My dad owns this place." She gave him a knowing wink.

"Thanks, my name's Johnny," said Johnny, smiling candidly. "If I happen to be in the neighborhood, I'll look you up."

"Promise?"

"Sure."

Inhaling deep, Donna Smith's already more than ample bosom stretched denim until Johnny thought surely a button would pop. "I'll save you a dance then."

"I look forward to it," Johnny half-promised.

"Good. I'll meet you out back in a few minutes, and we'll get you loaded."

The tally came to forty-three dollars, which Johnny paid out of pocket. Then he purchased a Coke from a dispenser standing in front of the store. Costumed in a straw hat, the horse replica wore a pair of jeans on its rear quarters and an oversized T-shirt: Save a Horse, Ride a Cowboy. Johnny found it not only amusing but a great way to attract customers.

The only other vehicle in the small lot was a cherry red Mustang with a vanity license plate bragging: HWY2HVN.

He drank the beverage in one long swallow, and deposited the empty bottle into a white recycling bin next to the Coke dispenser. Then he pulled the truck into the lot behind the saddler. Donna Smith had already stacked four squares of hay. The fifty-pound bag of oats leaned against one. Johnny parked next to the bales, stepped out of the truck and dropped the tailgate.

"Nice truck," commented Donna.

"Belongs to Konahee I'm afraid." He lifted a square and tossed it into the back. Donna watched his biceps bulge and the muscles in his back ripple against his shirt. Then she took hold of a bale and tossed it without effort.

In less than a minute, everything was loaded.

"You're pretty strong for a…" Johnny stopped short.

"For a girl you mean. I've got six brothers I have to keep in line. Believe me, I can handle myself."

"I don't doubt it for a minute," said Johnny, and wiped at his brow.

"That's a really nice feather you've got in your hair. I've never seen one like it before. Does it have significant meaning?"

Johnny reached behind him and touched the tip of the braid. "Konahee gave it to me just this morning. She's the one who braided my hair."

"Well, it's really nice. I especially like the leather touch. Not too many men can wear a braid without looking… well… you know, less manly. It suits you."

"Thanks, I guess."

Out of the blue, Donna said, "I hear she's some kind of a witch. Konahee I mean. Living out there by herself with her nose in everybody's business."

Johnny did not doubt for a minute that rumors about Konahee were abundant. After all, she was old, lived by herself, read palms, and her looks were, well, peculiar, with one good eye and one that seemed dead, but wasn't. "She's just a nice old lady. Sure, she may be a little eccentric, but things happen when you get old. I wouldn't put too much stock into what other people say. Small town. There's always going to be a story or two to keep the gossip going. And you're a little too old to believe in witches, aren't you?"

"I suppose you're right." Donna thrust both hands into the rear pockets of her jeans. "I'll just get the shoe nails you need." She went back to the store, and returned a minute later with a bag. She had unfastened two buttons of her shirt so the cleft of her double Ds were visible. "Here you go, Johnny." She looked up at him, blue eyes dancing and handed him the paper bag. She smiled. "You won't forget about what we talked about now, will you? Friday nights and all. I can't wait for my friends to get a good look at you. They'll be jealous as all get out."

Johnny felt his face flush. Without meaning to, his eyes, for a nanosecond, settled on opaque flesh. Correcting himself, his eyes jerked up, and locked on to hers. "I'm flattered, really, but we'll just have to see. I've got a tremendous amount of work to do, and well, I can't promise you anything."

His quick little discovery did not go unnoticed. It was, after all, what Donna had intended. *Give him a little sample. Something to think about.* "Come now, Johnny. You don't expect a girl to believe you'll be working night and day. You know what they say. All work and no play makes Johnny a dull boy. Besides, I promise you, you won't regret it. I'm a helluva dancer as well as other things." She moved close, uncomfortably close. Her breasts a breath away from Johnny's T-shirt. "The men in this town just don't know how to treat a girl right. Something tells me you've got everything a girl could ask for."

Stepping back, blood quickening, Johnny said, "I really should be going. It was nice to have met you, and who knows, I just might show up at the Gooseneck one of these Fridays." He jumped into the cab and slammed the door without meaning to. He tossed the bag of nails onto the passenger seat next to his new Kodiaks, work gloves, and Coleman cooler.

Donna Smith went to the open window, and rested her forearms on the frame. "Oh, I do hope so, Johnny. I'll reserve a spot on the dance floor just for the two of us."

The engine fired. *Man, women had become pushy when it came to their sexual needs. Didn't matter what state you were in.* Then he remembered Justine and how forward she was. A sexual dynamo who had no compunction about doing *it* out in the open. And man, they really knew how to goat a man into getting what they wanted with their words and their bodies. Donna Smith hadn't even touched him, and yet, he was all a flutter, knowing full well that if he remained for one moment longer, they would end up in some hidey hole she knew about. Gone forever was the three-date rule.

"Have a great day, Donna," he said, and slowly pulled away. "And thanks for your help."

"I hope to see you soon, Johnny." When Donna Smith removed her hat, the remainder of her hair fell below her shoulders. Perceptively correct that he was admiring her through the side-view mirror, she offered him a courteous wave, and the dazzle of her pearly whites. She had him, and she knew it. It was one of her better performances without being sluttish. She would just have to bide her time. The notable press against his jeans would be well worth it.

Johnny pulled out of the yard, loaded with everything he needed for several days' work. Donna Smith faded in the side-view mirror, a cloud of dust enveloping her. Very much the spectacle of a fading apparition. One with perfect white teeth, a killer body, and an untamed appetite. He was certain he had not seen the last of Donna Smith.

Before he drove out of Alcova, Johnny stopped at a gas station to fill the gas container. Another cost of $2.75, leaving him with $7.25 of the $60.00 he had brought with him. *Talk about cutting it close.* He purchased a dozen bottles of natural spring water with the remainder. The attendant who served him, a young lad of no more than fifteen, had the taciturn personality of a steamed vegetable, leaving him to wonder if Donna White's declaration bore fruit. That the men in this town didn't know how to treat a girl. If the attendant was an example of the male population of Alcova, he didn't doubt it.

As he approached the town limits, Dean Martin crooning through the speakers, he became conscious that a state trooper was following not fifty yards behind, duo cherries liable to come to life. The speedometer told him he was not speeding and he had no intention of doing so. Speed garnished attention, a happenstance Johnny could ill afford. Instead of panicking, he remained within the limit of the law, hopeful it was the reprehensible hand of coincidence that had positioned him and the trooper on the same stretch of roadway.

When the speed limit augmented from 30 mph to 55, Johnny gradually increased the truck's forward progress, the 350 diesel engine begged for more. He kept one eye on the road, the other steady on the trooper through the rearview. Should the twin cherries suddenly light up, he was toast.

Fifteen uncomfortable minutes later, the trooper gained momentum, and closed in on the Ford, but still without the fanfare of siren and lights. As soon as a semi passed in the opposite lane, the trooper pulled parallel. Through mirrored shades, he judged a nervous Johnny, smiled, then gunned the engine. When the patrol car was swallowed by distance, Johnny wiped at the beads guiltily formed on his brow, the voice of malcontent prompting, *Killer, killer, killer.*

* * *

Much to his dismay, when Johnny turned into Konahee's property, the state trooper's vehicle was portentously parked in front of Konahee's house. The Ford ambled up the driveway at a rate usually reserved for a funeral procession. Juno was in her familiar position, standing near the trough, head down, mouthing the ground for food. Proceeding with caution, Johnny directed the truck to the back of the barn where he and Konahee had measured the paddock with stone and the mysterious three-blow baptism of her walking stick.

The patrol car was empty, that was obvious. *He must be in the house with Konahee.* She had told him she was expecting two clients. Perhaps the trooper was one of them. Just because he was a man of law did not immunize him from life's foibles. Someone who required guidance. *Harvey Lector seemed a gratified customer, so why not a cop?*

Johnny dropped the tailgate and unloaded the squares of hay and the hefty bag of oats. Then he went into the barn and retrieved the pitchfork. Once outside, he called to Juno who came running to him as though she knew a feast awaited.

Together they walked to the rear of the barn where Johnny proceeded to dislodge large clumps of hay from a square, enough to satiate the hunger of a patient Juno. "Go ahead, girl," he said. "It's for you. But take your time. This is all you get for today. Tonight, after dinner, I'll give you some oats" He kicked at the bag with the toe of his boot. "You'll be feeling like a new gal in no time."

Juno looked to Johnny, eyes moist with great appreciation. She sided him, rubbed the length of her face on his shoulder, and liberated a contented breath.

"You're welcome," said Johnny, and scratched her bottom lip.

While Juno ate, Johnny unloaded the rest of the truck. The gas-powered auger he leaned against the barn. Removing his boots, he slipped into the Kodiaks then the gloves. The boots were a perfect fit. His hands accepted the deer hide like a second skin. Removing six bottles of water from their plastic hold, he put them into the Coleman. This he sat next to Konahee's folding chair still perched in the shade. Cranking the cap from one of the bottles, he drained half of it, and offered the remainder to Juno who lapped it from his open palm. Deciding it was time to get started, he went to the rear of the Ford, gathered six of the eight-dozen stakes, and commenced with the task of building a paddock.

Walking to each of the four measured corners, he kicked the stones aside and pushed a stake into the soft ground. The tips of the stakes were pink, allowing him to envision the perfect rectangle of a paddock that would soon be erected. Konahee was not only gifted, she had a great eye for distance. By Johnny's experience and knowledge of how much land one acre amounted to, the three-acre paddock to be built was calculated absolutely.

With chalk line in hand, he fastened it to the nearest stake, pulled it taught to the next stake and tied it off. Then he gathered a couple dozen stakes, and dropped them at what he knew to be ten-foot intervals. He repeated this process four times, expending most of the stakes. Then he strained two more into the ground where the new aluminum gate was to be erected. What he required was a hammer. He could spend all day managing things manually, but that would take more time than necessary, and his shoulders were already burdened. Besides, he also needed the hammer to affix Juno's shoes with new nails.

Juno had long since finished the hay and scrutinized him from the cool shade of the barn. Johnny was pushing a stake into the ground when he heard a vehicle approach. Glancing over a shoulder, he watched the patrol car come to a stop just this side of the barn and nose to nose with the Ford. Konahee was seated in the passenger seat, yellow sun hat taking up most of her side of the vehicle, the severe barrel of a shotgun sitting rigid next to her.

The trooper got out, went to the passenger side, and opened the door for her. He was a colossal man with linebacker shoulders and biceps that stretched the material of his grey short-sleeved shirt to its limits. On his right forearm, the tattoo of dagger through a heart gleamed red and blue. A troop hat and mirrored shades obscured his face. Johnny couldn't tell whether or not he was smiling. Accepting Konahee's hand, the trooper eased her from the car.

Johnny stood, wiped sweat from his brow, and wished that the icy fear gripping his spine wasn't noticeable. "Hello," he called out.

The trooper and Konahee walked toward him. "I am pleased to see you hard at work, Johnny," said Konahee. "I trust Harvey had everything you required."

"Yes, Konahee. He was very helpful." Johnny clapped dust from his gloves.

"And how do you like my new truck?"

"It's a great ride. Runs smooth." Seeing Konahee standing there in her colorful dress and hat, it wasn't hard for him to imagine her behind the wheel, laughing her toothless laugh, the wind blowing the outrageous hat about her face as she sped down the highway.

Introducing the trooper, Konahee said, "This is Officer Frank Roland. He is a client of mine."

Trooper Roland broke rank with Konahee and walked up to Johnny, a bear of a hand thrust in front of him. "I saw you on the highway earlier. Konahee called me and told me that her nephew would be seen about town in her Ford and that I should not be suspicious of you. It's nice to meet a relative of Konahee's. You can call me Frank."

His voice was deep, prodigious. Thin lips broke into a smile, mirrored shades shone electric blue.

They shook hands, mano et mano. Frank Roland was as tall as Johnny, his face marked with deep craters and a zigzagging scar that ran from the corner of his mouth up to just below his right eye. Johnny had seen that scar before. One of the bouncers at the Big Sky Saloon had a similar one. It came from having the business end of a broken bottle jammed in your face.

Neatly trimmed salt-and-pepper hair sprouted from beneath Frank Roland's troop hat. At his waist was a thick black belt; telescopic truncheon, handcuff case, container of pepper spray, and Colt .45 hung impressively. His forearm rippled. The dagger danced on undulating waves of muscle. Within the red heart, scribed in the ink artist's best copperplate was a single word: *Madonna*.

Konahee had taken a seat in the folding chair and was watching the two men exchange pleasantries with great interest. The Japanese fan made an appearance. Juno stood next to her, more interested in the sun hat she wore.

"Nice to meet you," said Johnny. "That's quite the grip you've got."

Frank Roland slipped his hand from Johnny's. "Work out every day. A man of my age has got to keep in shape. It's awfully nice what you're doing for your great aunt, spending the summer with her and helping out. Very commendable."

Johnny looked to Konahee who was fanning her face and could see that she was smiling between the rise and fall of the fan.

Frank Roland appraised the perfectly aligned stakes. "Looks like you're off to a good start."

"Yeah, I guess, but what I need now is a hammer. Konahee, I hope you have a hammer?"

The fan paused midswipe. "Yes. I have one. It is in the shed next to the house with some other tools. Just watch your head when you walk in."

"Okay." Johnny turned back to the trooper. "Well, I've got a lot of work to do. It was nice to meet you."

"I've got to be going anyway. Duty calls. I'll give you a lift back to the house then. Konahee, are you coming?"

"No," she said emphatically, her face hidden behind the fan "I will stay here. It is a nice day."

"Then I'll see you next week," Frank Roland reminded her.

"Yes. Next week. Remember what I told you, Frank."

"Yes, and thank you, Konahee. You've been most helpful. As usual."

Johnny and Trooper Roland slid into the Chevy. Johnny had never been in a police car before and was surprised to find just how little room there was, especially for a man of Frank Roland's dimensions. He could not imagine two of them, equal in stature, being comfortable for long periods of time. Other than the CB and shotgun, a miniature computer, and keyboard jutted from the dash. The clear bullet-proof panel separating the front from rear left little room for head movement.

Frank Roland made a three-point turn and rolled the vehicle toward the house. Sensing Johnny's discomfort, he said, "You get used to it after a while. Like a pair of new shoes that don't quite fit right when you buy them, but the longer you wear them, the more comfortable they get. Call it symmetry."

"Well, I don't know how you do it. I guess I wouldn't make a very good cop. I like my comfort zones too much."

Frank laughed. "Sure you would. We could use young, strong men like you on the force. You should think about it. It's a good career, though the pay isn't anything to write home about. But if you can stick it out, you can retire relatively young with a generous pension. And you wouldn't find a nicer lot. We take care of our own. Of course you'd have to cut your hair. Well, here you are." He pulled the Chevy next to the house.

"Thanks, Frank." Hands merged once more. "I'll think about it though I can tell you that I'm very attached to my hair."

"Well, should you decide you're interested, give me a call. Your aunt knows how to get in touch with me. I can get you into the academy as soon as you like. The state is really pushing for new recruits. There's a lot of bad guys out there."

"Yes, there is," said Johnny, guilt causing a slow burn up the back of his neck.

The CB crackled to life. "Base to unit 2."

"Well, I gotta go. You take good care of that aunt of yours. She's a marvelous woman."

"I will, Frank," said Johnny. "You can count on it." Exiting the vehicle and closing the door, he watched Frank Roland pick up the receiver. Subsequently, at a good rate of speed, the Chevy raced along the driveway, creating great plumes of dust in its wake, then turned sharply and back toward Alcova.

* * *

Johnny rounded the house to its eastern side. The shed, a leaning tinderbox no more than eight-by-ten, stood several feet from the side door. Not to his surprise, George the cat was resting on its peek enjoying the warmth of the day. "Hi, George."

George opened one sleepy eye, yawned, then went back to his dreams of being the world's greatest mouser.

Johnny pushed the door inward, forgetting what Konahee had told him, "to watch his head," and walked straight into a gauntlet of animal bones strung from the ceiling. Femurs, fibulas, jawbones, tiny rib bones, wishbones, skulls from small rodents, talons, and bear claws all hung precariously, including the jack foot Johnny had freed from the snare. Most were very old, bleached white by time and rattled like some macabre wind chime. Reaching to settle them, Johnny had to stoop to a lesser height in order to move about. When his fingers made contact, an unfamiliar sensation pricked at his flesh. Donna White's words returned to him, *"I hear she's some kind of witch."*

As though guided by the hand of an unseen, the door closed and pitched Johnny into a darkness so all-encompassing that it blinded him. The air became thick, almost too heavy to breathe. Though he could no longer see the collection of bones, he could sense them as if they still supported the life they once possessed. His head swooned as if he were being held upside down underwater, and his mind filled with a tapestry of colorful scenery and desperate measurements of time.

Clearly, he witnessed a deep forest, lush with vegetation, its resident animals running through the undergrowth, fear residing in their eyes. Bears, deer, rabbits, squirrels, badgers, raccoons, and mice. Snakes of all sizes and species slithered over fallen timber. Frogs by the hundreds appeared and disappeared as they leapt from place to place. The treetops were crowded with the flights of birds screaming in such high-pitched terror, Johnny was certain the sound would remain with him for the leftovers of his life. In groups they ran and flew incoercible to one another, fleeing from something far more distressing than the threat of being eaten by the order of nature's laws. Johnny could hear the rapidity of their heartbeats thrumming like the distant drums of some unknown world.

Within the next trip of his heart, he was with them, bare legs and arms pumping furiously, leaping giant ferns, broken branches, running through mazes of trees, legs lashed, racing through the forest, frantic birds screeching overhead. There was no preconceived destination. No path to guide him. He was just another animal fleeing for his life.

Whatever was causing Johnny and the animals to escape, approached the darkest region of thought, and crept around in there like some ungodly demon. He could sense that it would come into view any moment. Some horrific thing that would cover his mind in a blanket of darkness, disable him from future dreams, rip apart his very soul.

In a single conscious effort, Johnny reached behind him and yanked on the door. Sunlight corrupted the darkness in a blinding flash, and vanquished the terrible thing back to whence it came. Sweating profusely, Johnny could hear his heartbeat hammer between his ears as well as the ethereal screech of frantic birds. Out of breath, he backed out of the shed and stepped into the grace of the sun. Hands on his knees, doubled over like some old man, he stole air into his lungs and remained that way until his heart settled and the pitching sound of terrified birds faded from the interior of his mind. Standing to his full height, he said aloud, "Holy shit! What the fuck was that?" Looking to George who was still stretched across the peak of the shed, he asked, "I don't suppose you heard anything?"

George remained impassive, tail flicked at the air twice before it dropped like a stone.

"No, I don't imagine you did." Trouble was, Johnny still needed a hammer. He peeked into the shed, reluctant to step in. The interior was alight with sunshine, the bone collection swaying ever so gently. Nestled in a corner, he noticed a red handyman's toolbox. Ducking, he moved into the shed as swiftly as he dared. Bones brushed his back, sang against his spine. On one knee he opened the box. Varying screwdrivers layered the top tray. He lifted it and found what he was looking for. A three-pound hammer with wooden handle. Closing the tool chest, he exited the shed, and slammed the door. As Mother looked down upon him, he hoped that it would be a sustained period of time before he ventured there again, for if he had not freed himself from whatever hold the shed offered, he was certain that the tangible hand of evil would have taken him elsewhere. To a place he would soon not return.

* * *

Konahee was still sitting in the lawn chair, fanning her face when Johnny approached. Juno stood in front of the bag of oats, head bent near to the packaging as though she were reading the benefits of the product within. As though reserved to the pen yet to be built, the hawk glided on the air above it.

"I see you found the hammer," said Konahee, blue eye fixed on Johnny.

He put his free arm under Juno's neck, and patted the opposite side. "It was right there where you said it would be." He scrutinized Konahee's face to see if it would betray a knowledge of the episode he had just encountered. It did not. "By the way, George says hello. I found him sleeping it off on top of the shed."

"I am surprised he had the energy to say hello. It usually takes a good portion of rabbit to get him to say anything. And most of the time it is, I want more please, like the orphan Oliver." She laughed at her humor.

Johnny laughed with her and lifted Juno's head so he and she were eye to eye. "I told you, you can have some oats after I have my dinner. And I don't want you sneaking hay. I'll be watching you."

Juno blew a heavy, rippling breath.

"I think she just gave me the raspberry," said Johnny, a fresh wave of laughter erupted, the living darkness that had crept from the deepest fissures of his mind forgotten for the moment.

When Konahee stopped laughing, and with some effort, she pushed herself from the chair. "I will go now. Let you get back to work. I have another client coming in one more hour. Maybe George and I will talk about his lack of responsibility, though I very much doubt it. He is deaf when it comes to talking about work. Remember, dinner is at seven." She folded the Japanese fan, and stuffed it into a pocket.

"Believe me. I won't forget," said Johnny. "I'll probably stop around six thirty so I can wash up."

"Towels are in the linen closet on the second floor."

"Yes, I remember." Johnny paused for a thought-filled moment. "Konahee?"

"Yes."

"You lied to that policeman and Mr. Lector. Told them I was your nephew."

"Yes, I lied, Johnny. But it was a necessary lie. I have my reasons. Now there will be no questions about your presence here." She looked off to the south. A generous stratum of cloud had settled over the Laramie mountain range. "It will rain," she said, turned on her heels, and headed back toward the house. The beech wood stabbed at the earth with every step. Juno quickly followed.

Johnny looked to the mountains. "I'll be damned," he said to himself. It was smart of Konahee to instil in others that he was her nephew, he thought. Officer Roland would think him nothing more than the nephew Konahee said he was and not the killer in hiding he deemed himself to be. He was safe with her and knew in his heart of hearts that she would not betray him, and he, in return, would do what she asked. That the experiences he had so far been a part of and the events he knew were still to come would always remain within the boundary of the trust they were partnered in.

With hammer in hand, he walked to the first of eight dozen stakes lying flat on the ground and pounded it in. A gentle breeze lapped at his face. The spirit of a great warrior rolled across the plain. Above him, the hawk circled in the glare of the sun.

Smiling a profound indebted smile, Johnny Black went to work.

* * *

20

Choose Me

AFTER stripping the roasted carcass of a five-pound chicken to the bone, including heart and gizzards, and consuming a dozen small roasted potatoes, carrots, and pearl onions, Johnny leaned back in his chair and patted his stomach. "Whoa, I'm stuffed," he said, thoroughly impressed that Konahee had kept up with him: potato for potato, carrot for carrot, and equal portions of the herb-encrusted chicken.

George was beneath the table between their feet and gnawing on the chicken's neck.

Konahee's outrageous sun hat sat at her elbow. She had pulled her hair back from her face and secured it with a pink ribbon. She told Johnny that he should be honored George was sharing the kitchen with them. That she and he hadn't eaten together since he was half his size, insinuating George must like Johnny tremendously.

Johnny had showered and exchanged his sweat-soaked T-shirt for a clean one and removed his Kodiaks, exchanging them for his form-fitting boots before settling down to dinner. Before Konahee served the meal fit for a family of five, she gave him an ice-cold can of beer for the completed tasks of a hard day.

The beer and over-the-top meal created within, a gaseous bubble that ventured forward without warning and came out in one long fulminous belch. "Excuse me, Konahee," said Johnny, and covered his mouth.

Not to be outdone, Konahee reared back and released a burp so voluminous her breath hit Johnny square in the face to which they broke out in a galloping laughter.

Once Johnny contained his composure, he asked, "Konahee? Why do you keep so many bones hanging in the shed?"

Konahee wiped at her mouth with a napkin, her blue eye brightened. "Oh, those. Some people collect stamps or tiny glass curios, cars or plates or spoons. I collect bones. It is just a hobby, nothing more." Reaching into the chicken carcass, she removed the wishbone fully intact then put it in her mouth and sucked away what little meat still remained. She held it in front of her ghost eye and said. "Another one to add to my collection."

Johnny rolled her answer around in his mind for a moment, wishing he could tell her about the experience he had had. However, he knew he mustn't. It was a riddle. A happenstance he would have to decipher on his own. "I would like to move Juno's trough closer to the barn where there's less sunlight. If that's all right with you."

"I think this is a good idea, Johnny. She needs to be pampered in her old age. You care about her very much, do you not?"

"Yes, Konahee. Juno is a wonderful old girl. And still very smart for her age. You have trained her well."

"Thank you, but all the credit goes to her I'm afraid. She has always been in tune. Born that way. Like some dogs are smarter than others, even if they come from the same litter. One of Mother's little jokes she likes to play. Same as giving me one good eye and one that is dead. Ha-ha. She does enjoy her little games."

"Do you have a brush I can use to scrub out the trough?" asked Johnny.

"Yes, under the sink. There is a bucket next to the house. Take another beer with you."

"No, I'm fine, but thank you. I'll just help you with the dishes before I get started."

"No. Leave them. There is little time left before it rains. You should get started right away. I will take care of the dishes. Then I am going to watch some baseball."

"*Baseball?* I never would have picked you for a baseball fan. You are indeed full of surprises, Konahee. Who is your favorite team?"

"The Cleveland Indians of course. They are playing the Colorado Rockies tonight in an interleague game. It will be a good game. You may join me once you are finished with the trough if you like."

"I'm afraid I'm not that big a fan. My game is hockey. Fast, lots of hitting. Besides, I would like to get back to the book I'm reading. The one I found in the dresser."

"I have almost forgotten about that book. My mind does wander at times. Remind me. Which book is it?"

"The *Life of Pi*."

"Oh, yes. An interesting journey to say the least. You must tell me what you think once you are finished."

"I will." Pushing back his chair, legs scraped the linoleum. "I guess I better get going. I promised Juno some oats, and I'm afraid if I don't keep my end of the bargain soon, she might take it upon herself to open the bag and jump right in. Thanks again for supper."

"No need to thank me, Johnny. You will earn every meal. I assure you. Go now. Tend to Juno. I am certain she is waiting." Konahee removed a Kleenex from pocket, and wrapped the wishbone in it. "I will hang this one tomorrow. Soon I will need a bigger shed."

Johnny stood and retrieved the brush from under the sink. "Good luck with the game tonight. Go, Indians, go."

"I'm afraid they do not possess the starting pitching they need to win the pennant.

But I will cheer for them nonetheless. I am their number one fan, though they do not know it."

Johnny moved next to her, lowered his frame and kissed her on the cheek. "Thanks, Konahee. For everything. I could not repay you in a hundred years, but I'll try."

Konahee placed a hand on his arm. "By the end of summer, you will have paid me in more ways than you can imagine. Go now before this old woman gets all teary-eyed."

Without another word, Johnny went through the house and stepped outside. Although a couple of hours of daylight remained, heavy cumulus clouds had rolled in from the mountains. They covered the sky in a slate of grey, their bellies fat with rain. The temperature had already dropped several degrees, and the air carried with it the metallic flavor of ozone. A sure indication that the clouds supported the electrical impetus of a great storm.

* * *

Johnny's first concern was to feed Juno. He located her standing next to the squares of hay where a healthy pile of manure sat steaming in the greying light.

When she saw him, Juno reared, and raised her front legs off the ground. Delighted that she would now receive the promised oats, she pushed at the bag with the brunt of her face.

"Okay, okay," said Johnny, as he approached her. "Give me a minute, will yah?"

Launched from the humps of the Laramie Mountains, distant thunder rolled across the sky and spread north until the sound was directly overhead. "Nasty storm coming, Juno. I think I'll move you into the barn." He stuffed the brush into a back pocket and hoisted the bag of oats over a shoulder. "You coming?" He started to walk to the barn's entrance.

Before Juno followed, she tore a good portion of hay from a square. Pleased with herself, she trotted behind Johnny, tail swishing pendulously.

Tearing at the bag of oats, Johnny poured a good two pounds of it into one of the empty stalls. The lighting inside the barn was gloomy, already creating shadows that crept from the corners. Juno had stopped at the entrance as if she were reluctant to step in.

"Well, come on. This is what you've been waiting for, isn't it?"

Juno took one then two steps forward. Head low, she blew a hard breath.

"Don't you want some oats?" asked Johnny.

Juno nodded, and took a farther step.

"What's the matter? It's just a barn. Nothing can happen to you in here. You'll be safe. I promise." Slowly, Juno went to Johnny. He patted her neck and scratched an ear. "Go on. Eat."

The aged mare lowered her face and sampled the oats, crunching each morsel between her teeth. When she lifted her eyes to look at Johnny, they were moist, filled with love.

"I bet you never had oats before, eh, girl?" He stroked her neck, kissed the space between her eyes. "They'll make you strong again and give your coat a nice shine. Now

I want you to stay right here while I clean out your trough." Lifting the bag of oats, he moved it into a separate stall where the Honda rested.

Once Juno was finished, she turned and backed into the stall.

"That's a good girl. You stay put. I'll only be an hour, tops."

Juno nodded.

Johnny went to the Ford, started it, and drove to the trough while ole blue eyes sang, "I Did It My Way." Killing the engine, he got out and dropped the tailgate. With the trough still full of stale water, he imagined its weight was somewhere around two to two hundred and fifty pounds. On one knee, he began to scrub the floating green moss from the sides. The air around him changed as a distant flash brightened the sky in strobing shades. Johnny counted. One, two, three, four, five.

Thunder traveled across the sky. *Still plenty of time to get the job done before the brunt of the storm is upon me*. He scrubbed harder, the moss came away without trouble. When the task was almost completed, Johnny felt the first sporadic drops of rain fall upon his yoke and arms. Looking to the sky, the beast seemed close enough to touch. Long silver streaks tapped his face. Regarding the house, he could see the blue filtrate of the television through the living room window. He wished that the storm would not be severe enough to disrupt the signal and spoil Konahee's night of baseball.

Quickly, Johnny's arm went to the bottom of the trough. He scrubbed with vigorous application until he was sure he had removed the sledge from the base. When he pulled his arm out, it was stained green up to his elbow. Dropping the brush, he took hold of the trough's edge and lifted with all his might. The trough, having been in the same place for God knew how long, was embedded in the ground in a stubborn hold, the first attempt garnishing hardly any movement at all. Johnny filled his lungs; bent at the knees, relying on his legs muscles; and tried once again. There was a ripping, sucking sound as the trough let go of the earth. Johnny tackled the underside. Putting everything he had into it, he lifted the trough until water rushed out. It created a stream that spread a wide berth before the summer dry ground sucked it in. Once it was empty and the ground had quenched its thirst, there was nothing left but a green brand against the earth.

Hoisting the trough into the back of the truck, Johnny moved it closer to the barn where it would collect the rainwater about to drench the area. He checked on Juno, finding her in the stall, standing at ease, the nervous tension experienced abdicated. "I'll be right back," he told her.

As he drove to the house, the sky darkened, lightning cracked, thunder boomed. He went through the front door, removed his boots and left them on the front stoop. When he passed the living room, he found Konahee sitting on the couch with George across her lap. Over her dress was a Cleveland Indian's jersey. Resting on her eyes were Johnny's sunglasses. In one hand was a pennent that she waved at the TV, the other held a can of beer. Johnny wanted to laugh out loud but knew it would be rude. "Gee. You really are their number one fan, aren't you?"

"I told you I was. I do not miss a game," said Konahee, her eyes did not stray from the set.

"Well, I just came in to wash the sludge off my hands then I'll go back to the barn. Will you be all right with the storm coming and everything?"

"I have seen many storms. They do not bother me. It is just Mother losing her temper."

There was a crack of a bat. Konahee lifted herself halfway from the couch then dropped, disappointed. George slipped from her lap, landed on his back, comfortable with the floor. "Just a fly ball," she said. She looked to George who lay flat with one lazy paw in the air. "Besides, I have George to protect me."

"I'll leave you to your game then."

Shaded eyes turned to look at Johnny. "Are you sure you do not wish to join me?" she asked, taking a slurp of beer. "I am going to make popcorn later."

"Sounds tempting. But Juno's in the barn, and I think I should be with her. She seemed a little frightened."

"Oh? I do not know why. That is where she was born. Perhaps it is the storm. Yes, this is what it must be."

"You're probably right. Enjoy your game."

Konahee returned to the game "I will. I hope the storm does not cause you to lose sleep."

"I'll be fine. Oh, I almost forgot to give you this." Johnny pulled the receipt from the hardware store from a back pocket. "This is your copy of the charges for today."

"Just put it on the kitchen table for me. I will look at it later."

"Okay. Well, good night, Konahee."

"Good night, Johnny."

* * *

After washing the green from his hands and arms, Johnny drove back to the barn, the radio in the off position. It would be a while before his taste in music adapted to a new flavor. By this time, the rain was falling harshly. Hard enough that Johnny had to engage the wipers. He had an idea. He pulled up to the barn, parked the truck and went to the rear of the elderly structure where he retrieved the lawn chair.

Juno was a silhouette in the stall. The darkness of the storm had shrouded everything in a condensed cloak of sable. Johnny set the lawn chair in front of her. "I'll be right back."

Climbing into the loft, he took the lantern and matches and descended the ladder. Once he was grounded, he drew the wick, lifted the housing, struck a match, and lit the lamp. The interior of the barn glowed in a honey tinge. Holding the lantern high, shadows danced as he made his way back to Juno.

The giant flesh-eating cricket looked ready to pounce. Lightning cracked nearby, followed closely by a resonate clap of thunder so strident the very ground beneath Johnny's feet trembled. The walls of the barn seemed to take a quick breath. Then the sky let loose a deluge of rain that veiled the barn entrance. Towering spikes leapt from the ground. The Ford appeared nothing more than a blush of metal in the foreground.

Johnny sat in the chair and placed the lantern at his feet. Juno was wide-eyed with fright. He reached up, stroked the white of her face with the flat of his hand. "There, there, girl. I'm here now. Nothing to be afraid of."

Juno snorted, and shook her head as if she were trying to rid herself of an annoying fly. She tromped the ground in front of her, reminding Johnny he had yet replaced the missing shoe nails. "I'll fix those first thing tomorrow," he told her, his soothing voice seeming to settle the old mare. Her eyes softened, and she became less fidgety.

"I'd like to tell you a story about a friend of mine," said Johnny with the gentle cadence of a nanny telling a bedtime story to a toddler. "His name was Dallas, and he was very brave. Just like you..."

As Johnny told Juno the adventurous story of his dearly departed friend, the storm outside raged with all the potency and brilliant strikes Mother's anger could summon.

* * *

Two hours passed before the storm let up, lightning, no more than a distant white flicker, the thunder, a remote grumble. Though it still rained, the relentless downpour was now lessened to the tranquil opinion of a summer shower.

Juno had listened to Johnny's tale, ears twitching each time the sky lit up. Johnny often stopped to pause between narratives, his emotions roused as his mind revisited the precious life and invaluable friendship he and Dallas shared.

Johnny yawned, the day's work and emotional drain getting the better of him.

Juno stepped forward, and pressed the white patch of her face against his as though she were telling him she could feel his anguish. Johnny wrapped his arms around her. "At least I have you now, even though it's only for a short time."

Juno nodded, water dripped all around them.

"Now I want you to stay in here for the night. I'll be right above you. And keep out of the oat bag, you hear."

Juno looked to the ground as though a mischievous thought had crossed her mind.

Johnny smiled. "Now I'm warning you. No more. I've got to get some sleep. Good night." He picked up the lantern. The walls of the barn swayed, and the flesh-eating cricket rocked back and forth. With the lantern clutched between his teeth, he slowly made his way to his hiding place.

The loft was relatively dry except for a water stain beneath the window that had spread five feet wide across the floor. He set the lantern next to the bed, and inspected the blanket and mattress for dampness. To his relief, both were dry. He stretched out of the T-shirt, pulled off his boots and socks and peeled the jeans from his legs. Everything gathered, he stacked them neatly into the middle drawer of the dresser then cracked his tired back. A yawn caught him off guard. He lay on the bed, belly first, and pulled the *Life of Pi* from beneath the pillow. Opening the dog-eared page to chapter 10, he began to read in the dim lighting.

He managed to get to chapter 18 before the words started to swim across the pages, running into each other, creating sentences written in some alien language. "Well, that's enough for me," he said to the walls surrounding him. Tucking the book under the pillow, he reached for the lantern and drew down the wick. In the sudden pitch, he pulled the blanket across his back and listened to the rain splash on the sill. He gazed at the darkening porthole. Eyelids grew heavy. They closed once, twice, three times. His breathing waned, and he could feel himself slip away as if being extracted from his body. "*No. I don't want to go,*" a voice said the moment he traveled from the loft and into the realm of dreams. Darkness enveloped him and carried him to a place that was neither here nor there.

He journeyed incredible distances, his naked body bleeding through the nothingness surrounding him. There was no up or down, only space that adhered not to the fundamentals of gravity. And he was cold. Oh so cold, spinning end over end. He tried desperately to wake himself, only to find the harder he fought, the deeper he traveled. Calling upon his dream voice, he found that it carried the resonance of an apocalyptic explosion. "STOP!" he screamed into the never-ending void.

The plea echoed on and on and on until it too was consumed.

Dream minutes then hours passed. The complexity of the void changed without warning. It became thick, and oozed warmth, and he found he was no longer speeding toward nothing, but instead was sinking slowly as if he were a coin gradually dropping to the bottom of a syrup fountain.

He landed feetfirst on a floor that was invisible to the eye yet existed nonetheless. It was hot on the bottoms of his soles, the heat of it rising in waves. Three doors appeared in front of him each as white as the virginal testimony of a wedding gown. None were of equal size, and none were taller than five feet, the shortest being more like a square window than an actual door. On each, pulsing in red neon was WAY OUT. Beyond each door, female voices spoke, "Pick me, Johnny." "No, pick me, Johnny. Pick me, pick me." "I'm the one you want." "No, I am. You should definitely pick me. I'm the way out." "No, I am." "Don't listen to her, Johnny. She's a fake. So is the other one." "No, I'm not, you are." "Your time is running out," the voices chimed as one. "You must decide now, Johnny."

From high above, a ticking sound emerged from the darkness. Johnny looked up to see its round shape loom close. It was a clock, with human arms for hands. Only the clock was not measured in hours, but instead was measured by seconds. If what Johnny viewed was correct, he only had thirty of them to make a decision. Tick, tick, tick, boomed the clock.

"Quick, Johnny, pick me, pick me." "Don't listen to her, Johnny. I'm the way out." "No, you're not. I am."

Twenty seconds left. Tick, tick, tick.

Johnny went to the tallest door and realized that there were no handles or knobs in which to open them. "How do I get through?"

"Pick me," said the voice from beyond the tallest door. "No. Don't do it," came another from the next smallest door.

Johnny looked to the clock. Ten seconds left. Tick, tick, tick. Then the smallest of doors spoke. "Take a leap of faith, Johnny."

Five seconds left. The clock shook and swelled ten times its original size as if it meant to implode. Somewhere, the shrill of a great bird pierced the dream.

Johnny positioned himself in front of the small door. He took a deep breath, he dove into it. There was an incredible explosion, and he found himself in a retreating white current.

"You made the right decision, Johnny. You are safe now." The voice came from all around like a goddess speaking to him from the heavens. The whiteness held a certain tranquility. He traveled with it for a dream spell, his body carefree as it pulled him to great heights then plunged him into depths so fathomless, distance became irrelevant.

He was merely a solitary grain in the vastness of it, a dream spirit trapped within the confines of the flesh and blood Dream Master fast asleep in the loft.

With his dream vision, after immeasurable time, he saw in front of him the square of another window set askew in the white. Beyond the window there was only darkness, though he did not fear it, for the darkness seemed to be sending him messages of welcome. The white current pulled him directly toward it. Slowly the window spun, and grew in size with each rotation. Elegant hands emerged from the darkness. They beckoned to him. When Johnny was within range, they took hold, and pulled him through.

Johnny crashed into the loft, and somersaulted end over end. When he abruptly stopped, he was staring at himself lying on the bed, the dream offering him a delicate fog of light.

The Dream Master's chest rose and fell in a slumberous rhythm, eyes jerked with REM. The length of the single braid rested across the bulge of his left shoulder. The secured feather, lustrous.

Spirit Johnny stood, reached out, and touched the limp arm of the Dream Master. "Wake up, Johnny. Wake up. Take me from this place." But the Dream Master held fast, committed to see the dream through.

"Johnny?"

The voice derived from the window. Johnny turned. No one there. Then surreptitiously, from out of the darkness, a green mist like the ghost of wishing well poured in over the sill, down to the floor, and collected itself until it took human form. It moved toward him, arms and legs taking shape, fingers and toes. The curvature of a torso. Then the flat of a belly and the ridges of a ribcage covered in fine grey hairs. A face, with phosphorus green eyes and hair pitch as a raven's wing, long and twisted, pushed through. Swirling at her feet caressing her ankles, and filling the spaces between her toes, the green mist seemed to possess life.

"You again," spirit Johnny said.

"Yes, Johnny. I am here for you once more. Take me in your arms, Johnny. Make love to me." Stepping from the mist, the succubus moved toward him, arms outstretched. "Our coupling is essential to your destiny. This is the way it was written. This is the way it should be."

The Dream Master found himself powerless against her desire. Spirit Johnny floated, and took her in his arms. Eyes locked. Lips met. Tender, wanting touches. Tongues danced, bodies touched, hands roamed, and they breathed as one. The succubus raised a leg and wrapped it around Johnny's waist.

Dream Johnny gathered the firmness of her buttocks, and lifted her until she had him in her grasp. She seized his braid, yanked his head back, and plunged her tongue deep within his throat, the heat between her thighs welcoming his arousal.

Spirit Johnny thrust into her furnace, deep and deeper, to the very heart of her dream pulsing sex.

The succubus let out a wail so piercing it shattered the night and trailed into the darkness for a long, waning moment. Together they fell to the floor, their coupling intact.

She stared down at him, green eyes alight and placed her hands flat on his heaving chest. She took him deep until the petals of her starved flower fondled the very origin of his manhood. Clawing at the air, nails ripped tears into the dream. Then the succubus let out a howl so animalistic it rivaled that of any beast. The grey hairs of her torso sparked with light. Then she released a long malevolent sound that carried with it the cadence of an animal in distress. When the cry of surrender ended, she collapsed, released him from her sexist grip, and began to laugh ever so wildly. "What are you afraid of, Johnny?" she questioned, green-fired eyes seeking the answer written on his soul.

The Dream Master's eyes shot open. "Nothing!" Johnny screamed into the pitch of darkness, his flesh cold with sweat. Sitting firm, still panting, he wiped sweat from his brow, and his eyes searched the darkness. All that registered was the black on black porthole. It was still raining, though lightly, delicate drops like frozen peas in a fry pan. Reaching for the flashlight, he turned it on, aimed the beam at the window, to the vault in the roof, and to the four corners of the loft. *Nothing.* Just another vividly real dream. Beaming the light to his chest and the rest of his body, he discovered no fresh wounds to speak of, only the pink remnants of soon-to-be scars. About to kill the flashlight, something shiny wet caught his eye. He aimed the light to the floor. What he saw caused his heart to pound with the wonder of it and his mind to revel in the implications of it.

From the dark water stain beneath the starless porthole, and one in front of the other, wet footprints gleamed in the bright funnel of light. Holding the beam steady, Johnny counted the water-stained digits of each foot, his senses trying to catch up with what his eyes were considering. Four digits fronted each step, and ended abruptly at the bedrail, then continued on, even more evident, to the square hole in the floor and the ladder leading south into the barn.

Echoed within night's restless distance came the ululation of once great warriors.

* * *

21

Bad News

TONY Millions exited the Bolagio Casino at three in the morning with Pamela, his most recent bedmate, on his arm. He was garbed in charcoals and blacks from the crew neck circling his thick throat to the points of his wing tip shoes. Gold chains dangled from his wrists, the lights of the marquee igniting the diamonds on his pinkie. His balding head shone as if it had had two coats of floor polish applied. It was all about style, and Tony was quite confident he had plenty of it.

Valets, dealers, and waitresses from the Wynn to the Luxor knew him as a generous tipper when he had a good night at the tables. They also knew how he made a living, not caring, so long as the munificent tips kept coming. Business was business. It was all about the money, about the suckers who arrived day in and day out to gamble their mortgages or little Bobby's and Jenny's college funds away, smiles on their faces thinking this is it. *This is the time I win back.* But it always ended the same. The stark reality of their misfortune penciled on their three days of no sleep, too much booze, and too many trips to the ATM faces. Should you happen to be one of the fortunate few who hit it big, it didn't matter, Vegas knew you would return to her.

Tony had just spent four hours at the baccarat tables and was up eighty grand, so he was in good spirits, his accumulated winnings added to the line of credit he held at the hotel.

The temperature was a balmy sixty-five degrees. The sounds of Vegas welcomed him. Even the strip's display of dancing lights seemed to acknowledge that he had made it. Having one of the beautiful people on his arm did not hurt either. So far, his personal assistant and great fuck was lucky for him, so he would hang on to her until she no longer proved to be economically viable.

The women of Vegas came in all shapes, sizes, and prices. The truly glamorous reserved for the men who made Vegas click. Men like Tony Millions, purveyor of flesh, of good times. The Fat Cats. The Whales, debutants of the money industry. Tony felt proud to be among them.

He motioned to the parking valet with a flick of his wrist.

Pamela wore a dazzling Stella McCartney that ended just above her ankles, cut low so that her ample breasts preceded her arrival. A daring split revealed a perfect leg, tanned to copper just below the thin blue tether of panty. Tennis and ankle bracelets glittered blue-white. Her hair was in a bouffant, lips painted ruby red, and her generous blue eyes captured the lights of the strip. Twenty laps a day kept her shoulders, legs, and arm muscles toned to gymnast perfection. Tony would not have it any other way. She stunned all the men who watched her while Tony was busy at the tables.

"You still thirsty, baby," asked Tony.

"I could use a nightcap, sure." Pamela smiled at him, her hand moving stealthlike, stroking the inside of his thigh. "But let's not stay out too late," she whispered in his ear. "I'm horny as hell." Knowing that on any given day he could be done with her on a whim, she kept him happy the best way she knew how. With her mouth and her contortionist figure.

"You're too good to me, baby."

"How about we play a little game tonight? You can be the handsome professor, and I'll be the college student who'll do anything for a better grade."

"Sounds dirty. I like it. But you better be very naughty."

"The naughtiest."

Tony Millions's black Lexus pulled up to the curb. "Here you go, Mr. Millions," the eager valet said, and tossed him the keys. Anxious because word had already spread that Tony Millions had had a good night, so he imagined his tip was going to be generous.

Reaching into a pocket, Tony withdrew a thick fold of bills, peeled off a fifty, and palmed it into the valet's hand.

"Thank you, Mr. Millions," said the valet, his eyes drawn to the length of Pamela's displayed leg. "Will there be anything else, Mr. Millions? The fifty disappeared.

"Not tonight. As you can very well see, I have everything I require right now. Do yourself a favor, kid. The next time you address me, you will look me in the eyes, *capice*?"

"Uh, um, yes, sir Mr. Millions. I meant no disrespect, sir." Red faced, the valet went to the passenger door and opened it for Pamela, averting his eyes from the stunning blonde who climbed in, both legs fully exposed. Closing the door, he returned to his station fronting the most extravagant hotel in Vegas, so far.

Seated behind the wheel, Tony did not bother with the seat belt. The windows of the Lexus were tinted black. Before pulling away, he looked down at Pamela's legs. Reaching, he smoothed a hand over her left thigh. "Let's forget the drink and go straight to class. The professor is in a very generous mood." His hand slid up her thigh.

Pamela invitingly opened her legs.

Tony cupped her mound. The heat emanating from behind the thin layer of panty was almost too much.

Pamela oohed and aahed for him. Smiling wickedly, she said, "I'm afraid I didn't do the assignment you gave me, Professor."

"Then you'll need to be disciplined," Tony laughed, and pulled away from the curb, past the musical fountain then turned right at the strip. At three in the morning, hard-core revelers moved about, drunk with the mystique of Vegas. Traffic was light.

Tony kept two cell phones on his person at all times. One for everyday use, the other a direct line to and from Mr. Black. It chirped from the breast pocket of his jacket. "Fuck!" he yelped, and drew his hand away from the comfort of Pamela's thighs. At this time of the morning, it could only mean that something was not right in his world. He retrieved the slim phone and flipped it open. "Yes!" he said, already annoyed.

Mr. Black spoke, "Got some bad news, man."

"Well. What is it?"

"That new girl, man. She drowned."

"What the hell do you mean she drowned!? You've only had her for two days. Weren't you keeping an eye on her?"

"In the pit, man. Mr. Brown put her in the pit. Filled it with water like we always do. He had to take a leak. Told me he wasn't gone for more than two minutes. When he got back, she was floating facedown. I guess she wasn't a very good swimmer."

"Goddamnit, Mr. Black! I told you to be careful with this one. All right, all right. Can't do anything about it now. What did you do with the body?"

"She's in the lake, man. Way, way down with the fishes."

"And you're sure she won't surface?"

"Weighed her down myself. She's fish food. No one will ever find her."

"You better be sure of it, Mr. Black."

"Don't worry, man. She's with Hoffa, and ain't nobody ever gonna find him."

"Tell Mr. Brown that I am not pleased. I'll deal with him on my own. Fuck! Fourteen years old and still a virgin. That's a lot of lost revenue, Mr. Black."

"Yeah, man, I know. Don't worry, boss. We'll find another, quick as can be."

"You better, Mr. Black. Your employment depends on it. *Capice?*"

"Yeah. I understand." The line went dead.

Pamela looked to Tony whose face had grown irritably red. The blue vein running from the dip of his temple pulsed with anger. His eyes had gone hard and a fine sheen of perspiration slicked the cap of his head. It wasn't hard for her to piece together what had happened from the one-sided conversation. However, she knew to remain silent. Tony's number one rule was to stay out of his way and out of his business if you didn't want to end up with the fishes or in a pit somewhere out in the desert. She also knew that it was she who was going to undergo the full measure of his anger. Professor and naughty schoolgirl were out. In its place was going to be a night of pain and humiliation. When angered, Tony became a brutish tyrant in bed. She would have to lay low for the next several days. To hide the bruises he would leave her with and the degradation she would feel each time she went to the bathroom.

* * *

22

Revelation

TWO days later, the posts, wiring, and aluminum gate for Juno's paddock were delivered at ten in the morning as promised. It had taken Johnny that long to auger the holes. Ten hours each day in the hot, sweltering sun. The snares, over the past couple of days, had produced four jacks. Konahee roasted one of them with garnishes of thyme and garlic to delicate perfection. The rest she had dressed and stored in the freezer she kept in the basement.

The new nails had been applied to Juno's hooves, and she reacted like a woman who had just purchased a new pair and wanted to show them off. There was a pep to her step, and she often lifted her legs, bucking and prancing as if she were decreeing, "Look at me! Look at me!"

It was on the morning of the following day when something miraculous occurred. Johnny rose at seven. Having put Juno on a regimented feeding schedule, his first chore was to climb down from the loft and fork hay from one of the bales and to add some oats. Having learned quickly, Juno waited for him at the entrance of the barn.

After piling her morning feed behind the barn, Johnny watched her while she ate and noticed something not quite right. He interrupted her feed, lifted her face, and he pushed her lips apart so that he could examined her teeth. To his astonishment, Juno's teeth were no longer slanted with the coming of old age, but were instead those of a much younger horse, straight and clean. "How can this be?" he asked her.

Juno's reply was a snort and a shake of her head. It was then he noticed her brown eyes were no longer glazed dark. They were rather clear, alert, the pigmentation rich with the blaze of burnt honey. Johnny was taken aback. *Such a thing was impossible.* Stroking her neck, he allowed her to continue her feeding. Then he reminded himself that he was undeniably in the incidence of pure magic, wonder, and happenstance that could only be described as beyond the fantastic. Juno's sudden reversal of age was just another milestone in the journey he had embarked upon, congruence to the succubus who visited when he was caught between dream and reality and the voice of a stranger he had not met yet.

So on the day the posts were delivered, he was not at all surprised to find that the slope to Juno's back had leveled. There was no doubting it, Juno was indeed getting physically younger.

When the delivery truck pulled into the yard, Johnny had instructed the driver to drop the load behind the barn where it would be easy to access. Konahee had come out of the house wearing a mint green dress and the yellow sun hat she favored. Relying on the twisted beech wood, she made her way to the delivery truck, stopped, and asked the driver how Harvey was doing. The driver, the same young man Johnny had seen driving a forklift, told her that he was fine and sent his regards. Konahee reached into her pocket and withdrew a twenty. She handed it to the driver and thanked him for being so prompt.

Once the truck set off, Johnny pulled on his gloves and clipped the metal bands constricting both rolls of posts.

Konahee and Juno stood off to the side and watched while Johnny loaded the posts into the back of the pickup. From his vantage point, he kept an eye on them. He wanted desperately to speak to Konahee about the incidences that were happening. *Surely she must be aware,* he thought, yet she was proving to be a stubborn hostess. During their meals, she spoke not of the magic that possessed not only the land and air surrounding them but also the flesh and blood of her audience whether in presence of real time or in the thralls of conjured dreamscapes.

"Johnny, come here," Konahee called out.

Tossing a post into the truck, Johnny wiped sweat from his brow. "Yes, Konahee."

"You are a hard worker, Johnny. Three men could not have achieved what you have done so far. I am very pleased. Tonight I will cook you a rack of lamb like you have never had before. You deserve it." Her blue eye caught the rays of the sun. It glimmered like a finely polished gem.

Johnny wrapped an arm around Juno's neck, and stroked her tenderly. "Thank you Konahee. I don't mind the work at all. Keeps me focused. There is so much going on with me right now that I need to keep my mind occupied on other things." He watched her face to see if she understood what he was driving at. The blue eye dazzled, the dead eye continued to focus on the ground, face remained impassive. *She would make a hell of a poker player.* "Juno sure is responding well to the diet I put her on," he ventured.

"Yes. I've noticed," said Konahee, not offering anything further. She pointed the walking stick toward the paddock she could see in her mind's eye. "How long before you are done?" she asked, the twisted piece of beech eye level.

"Baring any inclement weather or injury on my part, I should be done by Friday."

Juno snorted, and nodded her head as though she was in complete agreement.

"Friday is good. You may rest over the weekend if you like. Perhaps you would like to get away from this place for a while. There is a pub in Alcova where people of your age gather. I believe it is called the Gooseneck." She looked up to the sky. The hawk silently circled against the sea of blue. "You will not have to worry about the weather. There is a long dry spell at hand, and you are very strong. I do not see you forgoing injury or illness. Be sure to drink plenty of water. The heat can cause all kinds of manifestation." She lowered the stick, and tapped the ground thrice.

Johnny brushed a hand over Juno's white patch. "Don't worry. I've got the cooler full of water along with the sandwiches you made me this morning. I'll be fine. And I've got Juno to keep me company. As far as going in to town is concerned, I'll have to see how I feel by Friday. I might just use the weekend to rest up."

"Yes. I understand. Journeys can be... ," Konahee paused for a moment, "exhausting."

Though the sun hat she wore shaded most of her face, Johnny thought he caught the angled break of a smile. "You are wise, Konahee. And I believe you find enjoyment in the things you know. I am honored that I might learn many things from you." He was suddenly aware that he was no longer speaking with the Anglo vernacular of his father, but as a true blood of his ancestry, the proud Cherokee people that ran deep within his veins.

Konahee's sun energized blue eye seemed to pulse. Directly above, the hawk filled the following seconds of silence with a long pitching shrill. "Yes, you will learn of the things I already know," she said in a flat tone. "When it is time for you to leave here, you will go with knowledge and a map of the preordained path that has been arranged for you long ago." She looked deep into Johnny, connecting with the awareness each held, yet were, for their own reasons, forbidden to speak of. "I will leave you now so that you may return to work. I am tired, and my feet are sore. I think I will take a nap." She turned away.

Concerned, Johnny asked, "Would you like a lift back to the house?"

"No. I will walk," Konahee said over a shoulder. "The exercise will do me good. One never knows when one takes their last walk. So I like to get in as many as I can. Just in case."

The hawk swooped low to the ground at breakneck speed. Its wings knifed the air and it strafed the ground just beyond the three acres designated for the paddock. It trapped something small in its talons, then rose into the east where it disappeared into the heat waves of the horizon. It was a sight Johnny could never tire of. There was something about birds of prey, especially hawks, that held his interest. It had been that way since he was a young boy and would watch the hawks display their grace and skill in the vast skies over the Double B Ranch foraging for food

"Well, I guess I'll have some lunch before it's back to work," Johnny told Juno, stroking her neck as he watched the old woman waddle back to the house. "She's not going to admit to anything, is she?"

Juno shook her head, and neighed, the newness of her youth showed straight and white.

"I didn't think so," said Johnny. He stretched his postdigging weary arm, and plucked a generous fist of hay from the nearest bale. "Here you go. This is for being a good listener."

Juno accepted the offering with the gentle nibbling of a hay connoisseur.

Johnny sat next to the cooler beneath the loft's glassless window. "That's a good girl, Juno. We must never be too greedy." He took out a sandwich and managed a small bite. "See. We must take everything in the spirit it was given."

Juno lifted her head high and kicked at the space between horse and man, who had become, for this passage in time, best of friends.

Johnny removed a bottle of water from the cooler and drained half of it in the amount of time it took to take three deep breaths. He remised about the green mist that poured in through the porthole each night. How it transformed into a succubus who entered his dreams, or not. He considered the voice he had heard far out on Konahee's property and whether or not he should fear the inevitable meeting. And he thought about Juno's sudden reversal of time and about Konahee, the twist of her walking stick and the life in her watchful dead eye. The shifting from one place to another in the bone shed and the darkness that almost had him in its grasp. He imagined that maybe everything would one day piece together and it would all make sense. He could only hope, for the magic he was experiencing was getting more complex with each passing day.

* * *

Johnny continued to load the truck with the pressure-treated posts until the first roll of fifty were stacked in a heap, neat and tidy. Then he drove the truck to the four corners where he deposited a single post. When the last post was dropped, he went from corner to corner and, using the power of his back and forearms, rammed each into place.

Once that was achieved, he righted each post so they were straight and in line with one another. He repacked the dirt, patting the posts firm into the ground with the back of the shovel the bone shed had relinquished. For the next hour and a half, he dropped posts at each of the augured holes until there remained only three out of the hundred. Sweat poured down his back and face, his calve muscles and back tight knots, and his stomach growled the need for nourishment. He looked up to the sun that caste shadows all around him. It was nearly at its noon position. Time to stop for a spell and eat another of the sandwiches Konahee had made.

Sitting in the barn's shade, he plucked another bottle of water and sandwich from the cooler. He stretched the cramps from his legs, and took a bite from the pastrami and rye.

Juno sauntered over, and stopped in front of him, her large frame offering Johnny further relief from the sun. With her head bent low, nostrils pulsing, she sniffed at Johnny's lunch.

"I don't think so," said Johnny. "And since when are horses interested in meat? You'd get sick. Stick to your oats and hay, and leave the meat eating up to me, okay?" Taking a healthy bite, he waved at several flies buzzing his head that were being as much a nuisance as flies could be. With a quick hand, he caught one, crushed it in his palm and dropped it to the ground.

The other flies disappeared quickly.

Johnny had read that insects, like bees and wasps and other stinging types, gave out a warning when they were in distress, signaling to their kind there was danger afoot and to stay away. Just when he thought the same might be said for the common fly, the trio of pests returned and courageously circled the remainder of his sandwich. Johnny popped what was left into his mouth. "Sorry, guys. Not enough to go around." The flies responded with a swift retaliation toward his face then buzzed away, and found comfort on the gleam of Juno's twitching backside.

Johnny took another tall drink of water, pushed himself to his feet, and stretched his arms above his head until several vertebrae cracked. Then he gloved his hands, ready to continue the task set in front of him. Gathering Juno's face into his hands, he cautioned, "Stay in the shade. It's going to be a hot afternoon."

Juno nodded and moved closer to the barn.

Johnny stepped from the wall of shade, the direct unforgiving rays of the sun immediately heating his face. He went to the truck, retrieved the roll of chalk line, walked to the southeast post, and fastened the line to it. From there he walked, unraveling line until he arrived at the northeast post and pulled the line taut. He tied it off. The line drooped but was sufficiently straight for the burying of the remaining posts. Shading his eyes, Johnny checked on Juno who was standing in the dark shade of the barn though suspiciously close to the bales of hay.

With the shovel balanced on his shoulder, Johnny went to the nearest post and proceeded to fill the augured hole. He was working on the fifth post, filling in the void around it with dirt, when *the* voice spoke to him for a second time.

"You are doing quite an excellent job," said the soft, lovely voice from directly behind him. "But that's a given. You always do a good job. Don't you, Johnny?"

Johnny stopped, stretched to his full height and rested his hands on the stock of the shovel. "You again," he said without turning. "I was wondering when you and I would meet again. If I turn around, will you be there, or are you speaking to me from a distant place? Like you did the last time."

"No, I am here. I thought it was time to introduce myself to you. We have much to talk about."

Slowly, Johnny turned. Not ten feet away, on its haunches, was a beautiful she-wolf. She regarded him with eyes that were as grey as his own. Her body was a juxtaposition of color. Chest of white. Dark lines of red and black across muscular shoulders and down her legs. Ears were sharp and painted a whispering shade of blue. A bush of a tail wrapped around her hind legs was a marriage of all the colors covering her body. A pink tongue lolled from between pointed teeth. Johnny let the shovel drop to the ground, stunned into silence. He had seen many creatures that roamed the lands in his young life, but none were as pleasing to the eye as this wolf was.

"You are not afraid. Only curious. That is good for there is nothing for you to be afraid of." The creature's mouth did not move.

Johnny smiled. "Hello," he said. "Nothing surprises me in this place anymore. I can hear you, yet your mouth does not move. How can this be?"

"I speak with my mind. My opinions are carried telepathically to the receiver which just happens to be you."

Wiping sweat from his brow, Johnny looked to the sun then back to the wolf. "Where did you come from? Do you speak to others? Are there more of you… ?"

"Slow down, Johnny. I understand your confusion and will answer your questions best as I can, but there are specific reasons why I sought you out, so you must listen to what I have to tell you. First, where I come from is irrelevant. Please don't ask me why. I just *am*. Second, I only speak to the one who can hear me, and that is you. Our union was written long ago Johnny Black. Long before you were born.

Johnny lowered himself so he was balanced on his haunches. The she-wolf moved closer so that when she sat again, no more than a foot away, the two were eye to eye.

"I don't know if you are aware of this, but you are very beautiful. I could never have been frightened by you."

"Thank you, Johnny." The wolf raised a paw. Johnny removed a glove, and received it into his hand. The fur was as soft as the underbelly of a mink. He smiled at her, and she smiled back, the points of her coniferous teeth gleamed white.

"For a man, you are not hard on the eyes," replied the wolf. "I find most men repulsive. As ugly on the inside as they are on the outside."

"I understand what you mean, but there are those whom I've met who are gentle of heart and mind, though they are few in number."

The wolf growled. A low sound that emanated from deep within. "Man is the destroyer. He takes and never gives back. He will not be happy until everything Mother has given us is gone in the name of progress." She growled again, and snapped at the air. "I have seen great distances, Johnny. One day the earth will once again belong to the animals, but at a great cost to us all."

"I'm sorry," said Johnny.

They looked deep into each other for a momentary lapse in time, each feeling the other's sadness of things to come.

The wolf spoke. "The future of mankind is not why I am here, so let's not dwell on the injustice of it. What will be will be. You asked me once if I had a name. As I do not, and since we are going to be friends, I think you should have the honor of giving one. It is the way it should be." The wolf skewed her head. "Just say the first thing that comes into your mind."

Immediately, Johnny's mind returned to the memory of his mother. The wolf's voice was kind and gentle, reminiscent of Linda Birdhumming's. One that carried great wisdom.

Reading his thoughts, the wolf said, "I would be honored to carry the name of your departed mother. I am now Linda. Friend to Johnny."

"So you can read my mind as well?"

"Only as a matter of goodwill. I mean no harm doing so."

"Then I guess you know how I came to be here."

"Yes. You have gone through so much sadness that my heart aches for you. It is difficult to lose the ones you love. This person you killed by accident, and you should only see it this way, was a killer of innocent life. You should not mourn for him any longer."

"I try not to, but it is difficult, Linda. There is blood on my hands."

"You must think of all the lives you have saved, for if he had not ceased to be alive, there would be many more lost to his sickness. Many such as Dallas, your friend."

"I'll try to see it that way. But there aren't many others who would. There are no parallels between the life of an animal and the life of a human being. If I'm caught and found guilty, I will spend the rest of my life in prison, and that prospect scares the hell out of me." *Killer killer killer.*

"To be afraid is only natural. It is this fear that drives you. It is also this fear that will guide you through the journey you have embarked upon. Just as it is my purpose to be a part of that journey. Your destiny depends upon it."

"You know of my destiny?"

"Yes. It is one of great importance. It may be hard to understand because of the sadness you carry in your heart, but one day it will once again be filled with the passion of an immense love. This you must believe."

"I have already learned to love again. Juno is very important to me, and Konahee is such an amazing woman that it is hard not to love her. She has saved me from those who wish to do me harm."

"Indeed, Konahee *is* a remarkable person, and Juno, for a horse, is a true friend. Regardless, I speak of someone who is already aware of you. Has been since childhood, though you have never met."

"More magic," said Johnny.

"Not magic, Johnny. This person carries a great gift. She is a seer and is also on the run. There is great trouble in her life, and she drowns in sorrow just as you do." Linda the wolf snapped at a fly buzzing her snout. "Your fate and hers has been versed long ago, Johnny. It is your sadness and loss of love that will bring you together. But beware. There is a great tragedy ahead. And yet bound within this tragedy, after the passing of many many moons, another destiny will be revealed."

"A tragedy? Another destiny? Suddenly my life is a puzzle. Can you tell me more, Linda?"

"I have said enough already. To share with you all of my knowledge would be a travesty in itself. You must walk the path chosen on your own." Linda rose and turned. "I will leave you now. You have much work to do."

"Wait. Don't go. How will I know? Where should I go? You can't just show up in my life again and tell me that I have a destiny to fulfill then leave."

The she-wolf did a three sixty and walked up to Johnny, grey eyes held his. "Trust your instincts, Johnny. Follow your heart. You will be forewarned when it is time for you to leave this place. The voice of a king will lead you to her, and a flower will awaken an everlasting love in you. The moment your eyes meet, you will know."

"A flower? A king? An everlasting love?" Johnny was completely confused, his mind tangled in the mystique of the riddle.

"That is all I can tell you. Remember to follow your heart." Linda the wolf turned once more and walked swiftly toward the east then broke into a full trot toward the horizon without looking back.

Hands cupped at his mouth, Johnny called out, "Will I ever see you again?"

"We will speak three more times as friends," the telepathic message told him. "Do not seek me out. I will come to you when time is appropriate. We will not speak of the things we have spoken of today, so it is important that you do not forget what I have told you. Good-bye, Johnny. Until again we meet."

Johnny watched until she disappeared into the heat dancing from the earth. Above him, the hawk had returned, and it circled without effort against the infinite sky of blue

The circle was complete. Johnny had now met the three strangers his mother spoke of. Old Konahee. A woman whose wisdom held no boundaries. Linda the telepathic wolf. The pedantic teller of futures. And the succubus who visited him each night who apparently also possessed a mysterious authority to his destiny.

He looked back toward the barn and pulled the glove over the hand that only moments ago had held the paw of a talking wolf. Juno remained in the shade, her back to him as if she had not wanted to be witness to the meeting between him and the wolf. He went to the next augured hole, and rammed the post into place. The hawk above screeched. The sun baked the back of his neck. The cry of once great warriors resounded in his mind's ear. His thoughts soared with the revelation of things to come, his utter dread equably profound to the welcomed possibilities of them.

* * *

23

Forever Young

BY two in the afternoon on the upcoming Friday, the paddock had been erected and the gate hinged in place. Johnny had toiled in the sun from the dawn of day until the vestiges of evening, always looking over his shoulder for the next opportunity to speak with his new friend. Each morning the lone hawk returned, and soared above, filling the air with its shrill cry for hours on end while Johnny worked. Konahee continued to feed him well, packing him a lunch each morning after they'd finished another breakfast fit for a regiment of men.

Juno's continued fall from old age did not falter. On the morning of the same day, she had gained overnight, ripples of muscle on her rear and front quarters. When Johnny met her for the first time, he had gauged her height at thirteen hands. Now standing between Johnny and Konahee as Konahee inspected the finished product, Juno was no more than twelve hands high, the markings around her eye and face as white as the head feathers of a bald eagle.

Konahee held the walking stick eye level, and measured the height and directness of the posts. For the first time since Johnny's arrival, she chose to wear a red plaid shirt tucked into worn jeans cinched at the waist by a narrow leather belt. Of course, on her feet and head, she wore her favored yellow sun hat and beaded moccasins. The hat rustled at her brow. Behind her, the Laramie Mountains cut whalelike humps against the sky. Konahee's sharp blue eye poured over the rectangle of paddock, and its three rows of tightly stretched barbless wire. "Perfectly straight," she claimed. "You have done a job worthy of a rest." Lowering the beech wood, she leaned into it, and with both hands grasped the fisted top.

Juno nodded and tromped the ground thrice with a hoof in complete agreement.

Admittedly tired, Johnny said, "I think I'll take your advice and use the weekend to rest before I till the soil for seeding." How on earth he was going to get grass to grow in this desert environment was anyone's guess. Nonetheless, if Konahee said it could be done, he was not going to dismiss her tuitions on how this could be achieved. Lifting a work-weary arm, he patted Juno on the bulge of her jaw. "So what do you think, girl? Do you like your new home?" He had to admit even if he said so himself, he had done a good job.

"Why don't you open the gate?" suggested Konahee. "Let us see if she will accept her new home."

Johnny went to the gate, and unhinged the latch. It swung effortlessly wide. "Go on, Juno. I proclaim this paddock ready for your inspection."

Juno took a hesitant step. She looked to Konahee and Johnny before venturing further. Once she was inside, Johnny closed the gate, leaned into it, and rested a boot on the lowest cross-section. "Go on, girl. Have a good run."

Juno craned her neck, the sun catching her eye just so. It blazed with the color of youth. Established deep within was the mischievous glint of recklessness. To Konahee and Johnny's delight, she bolted forward at a full gallop. She remained tight to the posts, tail and mane whipped at the air.

Konahee moved next to Johnny, and she gave the ground at her feet a baptismal three tap. She watched Juno speed around the paddock with a gracious smile on her face and a warm feeling in her heart. "She is happy. You have done well, Johnny. Now witness the fruits of your labor."

Together they watched Juno circle the paddock. When she came even of them, Johnny saw that her musculature had gained further definition and her chestnut coat gleamed with the shine of her formative years.

Throwing her head back as she passed, large clumps of earth tossed high into the air, Juno presented white teeth and neighed with vociferous jocularity. Momentum gained with every furlong.

Johnny looked to Konahee. No longer apparent were the dog days of old age but a woman who resonated with the magic of the place. For the briefest of moments, he was witness to the powers she possessed. A rhythmic aura of purples and blues danced all about her. His flesh tickled with the electrical pulses of it before the swimming colors dissolved back into their host. *More than magic*. Magic was something meant to trick the eye, to make its audience gasp with premeditated awe. This was more than that. This was nothing less than pure spiritual illumination. A living breathing legendary folktale. And he, Johnny Black, a fortunate spectator and friend.

"Penny for your thoughts," said Konahee.

"I was just wondering about things. That's all."

"Oh. I see. You wonder how such things are possible?"

"Well, yes, but I respect your wishes. I will not speak of them."

Juno passed again. Several years had melted away. Her mane and tail as pitch as coal and her body toned to the grandeur of a prized thoroughbred.

"Good. You are strong of will, and I trust that whatever transpires between us will remain here always, within the boundaries of this place."

"And no further," said Johnny. "You have my word."

"Tell me, Johnny. Have you finished the book you were reading?"

"Just this morning."

"What did you think of Pi's journey?"

"A lot to decipher. But I believe I understand."

"Good," said Konahee, and that's all she was going to say of the matter. She raised the beech wood, its fisted end level with Johnny's eyes. "There is still much for you to learn." Luminous blue eye penetrating.

Johnny stared at the knob of wood. It seemed to expand like a forthcoming storm cloud. His mind fogged. Eyelids closed on their own. The fog of his mind dispersed. Clearly he saw the night visitor and the wolf, their faces merged into one. Then Konahee's face appeared enormous against a backdrop that went on forever. The three spoke as one. "*Trust your eyes for they will not deceive you. Listen with your heart, and it will lead you to your destiny.*"

When Johnny's eyes opened, Konahee and her walking stick were gone as if plucked from thin air. Above him, the hawk circled. More than a fleeting moment had passed for the sun was at its decline toward the northwest/ Canada, and cast shadows that were harmonious with the coming of evening.

Juno stood on the opposite side of the gate. Coat glistened, nostrils pulsed with the need for air. She leaned into Johnny's shoulder, and kneaded him with the bridge of her youthful face. The blaze of a vigorous right eye winked at him.

Johnny took her face in hand, and stroked it gently. The images he had witnessed held effectively true within the province of his mind. The message they conveyed echoed with such genuine notification that, for a long period, he could hear nothing else.

Finally, when reality and he were once again walking the same path and the images had faded and his mind had grown silent, Johnny climbed the gate, seated himself on Juno's back, and took hold of her mane. Under the lessening light of a blue Wyoming sky, he dared, "Okay, girl. Let's see what you've got." Leaning deep, he readied himself.

Juno responded with a telling wicker before she bolted forward at breakneck speed, and rounded the paddock again and again.

The tail of hair, feather, and leather slapping at Johnny's back while his mind dared to venture. *Could it be possible? That Konahee, the wolf, and the voracious succubus are one and the same?*

* * *

24

Matters of the Hart

WELL, praise the good Lord and pass the butter. You had us quite worried, my dear."

Rebecca was seeing through slits. She forced her eyes, and took in the room of fog that encompassed her. "Where am I?"

"Why, you're right here with us, my dear."

Rebecca directed her eyes toward the voice. Sitting in a rocker only a few feet away was an elderly woman of indeterminable age smiling back at her. Long cotton white hair fell about her face and shoulders. Her eyes were the color of periwinkle, deep, full of wisdom. A strand of freshwater pearls graced her throat where a mole with long grey hairs sat like a sleeping spider. She wore a shawl over a blue dress splashed with tiny roses. Rhythmically, the rocker moved back and forth.

"How... How did I get here?" The fog lifted. More of the room came into focus. She was lying in a cozy bed, comforter pulled up to her chin. The bed was next to a window from which a delicate lace of curtain hung and where the sun breached at an angle and gave life to dust bunnies. The walls were covered in a cowboy print wallpaper, yellowed from age. An antique of a dresser stood in one corner, and a narrow closet door, partially open, stood next to it. Two bookshelves held plastic toy soldiers, tanks, and antiaircraft cannons. Sitting catty corner into the far wall was an ornate stand and ceramic basin, a washcloth folded neatly over the rim.

"Now... now. Not so many questions so soon, my dear. You were very ill. The main thing is your fever broke and you're on the road to recovery."

"Who are you?"

"Well, I suppose I owe you that much. My name is Hester. Hester Hart." The old woman reached out and placed a blue-veined hand on the edge of the bed. "It's lucky Ed, that's my husband, found you when he did. Lord knows what might have happened if he hadn't. That barn's no place to take a nap. Especially on a night like that one was."

The barn. Rebecca's mind went into recall. What she came up with was vague, like a dream almost forgotten. She remembered something about a boy and a dog. Ben and Ray. A tragic fire. About how cold she was. And the *one*. Many faces crowded together. Had she dreamt all of it? The memory seemed so distant, so out of reach.

Hester Hart spoke, shaking Rebecca from the fragments of happenstance that were trying to press themselves together like a puzzle of indifferent pieces. "Perhaps you would be so kind as to tell us who *you* are? We rummaged through your suitcase and jeans but found nary a stitch of identification. By the way, you look just like your mother. Such a lovely photo. I gather you two are close."

"My mother's dead," Rebecca deadpanned. It was the first thing that popped into her head. With it came, the terrible reality that her brother and father were also gone, swallowed by a fiery beast. That was one aspect of her life she knew for certain.

"I'm so terribly sorry if I caused you a bad memory. I know of your mother."

"You do! How?"

"Let's discuss your mother another time. Right now I'm more interested in who *you* are."

"Rebecca. My name is Rebecca White. How long have I been like this?"

"What a lovely name. It suits you to a tee, what with all those pretty freckles and that fiery hair of yours. Let me see. Now Ed, that's my husband, found you the day after the big storm. So if my math's as good as it used to be, that means you've been with us for five days."

Five days. Rebecca tried to push herself into a sitting position only to find that her body ached all over.

"Now you shouldn't be moving, Rebecca. As I said, you were, and probably still are, a very sick young lady. I imagine you must be very thirsty. Would you like some nice warm broth? I'll get Ed, that's my husband, to fetch you some."

The mention of something nourishing sent Rebecca's stomach into fits. She was suddenly starving. "I'd like that, thank you."

"Good. I'll just go downstairs and get Ed to bring you some. You never mind about all the questions I'm sure are running through that pretty little head of yours. We'll have all the time in the world to catch up once you've rested and put some of my famous chicken soup into your belly. But for right now, broth's the thing for you."

Rebecca smiled. There really wasn't anything else she could do. Hester seemed like a nice old woman even if she spoke with the slightest detriment of Alzheimer's. And if she was as ill as was implied, she should be grateful. After all, her body and mind were sending signals that implied she needed more rest, so who was she to be unappreciative?

The bed she was in was as comfortable as a mattress of feathers, and she was warm, snug as a bug in a rug. Like Hester Hart said, there would be plenty of time to play catch-up.

Rising from the rocker, Hester patted Rebecca on the arm. "Now we'll only be a minute." Turning, she hobbled on stick legs to the entrance of the room. When she opened the door, she turned slightly, smiled, and said, "I believe you are a very special person, Rebecca. Troubled, yes, but special nonetheless." The door closed softly.

Rebecca stared at the cowboy wallpaper for a moment, fighting for recall. Tryst episodes made themselves available. The fiery scene atop Dover Bluff Road. Her feeble attempts at trying to save her father from consuming flames. Ben in a horrible fight. Dead! Dead! Dead! Her mother's voice, *"Follow your heart."* Sitting in a big truck. Jungles of concrete and steel. A large snake that wanted to bite her. Swimming in blood. Hundreds of ghostly faces staring at her. The *one*. The boy and the dog again. Secured in an embrace. *"He's my bestest friend in the whole world."* Deseray lying on the kitchen floor, lifeless eyes staring at another place, another time.

Round and round the images went until Rebecca dizzied. Closing her eyes, she told herself that soon everything would make sense. She just needed the benefit of time. The mind was very obliging when need be.

When Rebecca unfurled her eyes, unwanted tears drowned her cheeks. She sniffed mucus running from her nose. Turning the comforter to her waist, she found that she was wearing a pink flannel nightshirt buttoned to her chin. She stared at her hands, turning them this way and that. Nails were chipped and broken, and there was a healing wound across the palm of her left hand. Using the sleeve of the flannel shirt, she wiped at her eyes, the simple movement requiring all of her will, the material soft against her skin. She ran a tussock of hair beneath her nose. It smelled wonderful. Lavender and chamomile.

Pain or no pain, Rebecca decided to push herself into a sitting position. It hurt like hell, but she was able to see the room in its entirety. The bed on which she was lying was narrow and short. A child's bed. Next to it, against the nearest wall, a wooden rocking horse stood, tugs of rope running from its mouth and joining at the saddle. Though not a connoisseur of antiquities, Rebecca knew instantly it was decades old. A brass lamp with a square shade and an empty glass stood on a side table.

"My name is Caleb. Caleb Hart." The young voice rang true. It filled her mind, and created a visual so clear it might have occurred only moments before. She saw herself lying in the barn, darkness all around. Shafts of moonlight spilling from the roof. The boy standing next to his beloved pet, each bathed in a shaft of moonshine. *"Would you like to see a trick?"*

There came a light rap on the door.

"Rebecca? We're coming in now." The door opened. Hester Hart proceeded toward the rocker and was followed by Ed Hart who was so big he had to duck to fit through the doorway. He carried a tray from which sat a steaming coffee cup, spoon, some bandages, and a tin of Penaten cream.

Like Hester, Ed's hair was a cap of snow, tossed about his head. Dark eyes bulged from behind a pair of black-rimmed glasses. Unadorned suspenders over a grey T-shirt were stretched to the snapping point. On his forearms were tattoos so old that they no longer resembled anything. His grey pants were wrinkled around the knees, and his feet were huge in a pair of Docs. Though he wore a smile, there was an emptiness about him Rebecca felt right away. He moved toward the bed, favoring his right leg. "Hello,

Rebecca," he said in a cavernous tone. "I'm glad to see you're doing better." He set the tray on Hester's lap.

"Thank you, sweetheart." Hester offered him her cheek.

Ed Hart leaned forward, and placed colossus hands on her frail shoulders. Then he kissed her tenderly. "I'll be in the kitchen if you need me." Regarding Rebecca who had been overwhelmed into silence by his size, he added, "It's nice to have you with us."

"Thank you for rescuing me, sir," she said, deciding a man of his dimensions should at all times be addressed as sir. There was something about him that virtually demanded it.

"Now we'll have none of that, young lady. My name is Ed, and that's how I prefer it. No one has called me sir in a very long time."

"Thank you, Ed. I'm forever in your debt."

"Nonsense. Would have done the same for anyone. That's just the way we are."

"Ed, be a dear and put Rebecca's suitcase on the bed and maybe open the window a few inches. I'm sure she would like to see her things, and it's quite stuffy in here. The fresh air will do her a lot of good I'm sure."

"Yes, Mother." Ed stepped to the foot of the bed, reached down, and pulled up Rebecca's suitcase. He sat it on the bed and flipped the latches. Then he went to the window and pushed it open. A gentle breeze flirted with the lace. Carried with it was the essence of roses. "Just give me a holler if you need me," Ed said to his forever wife. Leaving the room, he ducked automatically, and closed the door behind him.

"That smells wonderful," said Rebecca, breathing deep the intruding fragrance.

"My roses. Yes, they're what keeps me going these days. Do you think you can manage this cup on your own? It's still quite hot." Hester picked up the cup of broth and handed it forward.

Rebecca took it in both hands. "Thank you," she said and blew gently over the rim before taking a small amount into her mouth. When she swallowed, the broth warmed her all way to her toes. "This is wonderful."

"Thank you, my dear." Hester rested the bandages, tin of Penaten, and tape on her lap then placed the tray on the floor. Curious eyes stared at Rebecca. "I've washed all of your things. You'll find them neatly folded in your case along with your teddy bear. There's no cause for concern in case you were wondering. I found your money and put it in an envelope, which is also in the case. Now I don't mean to pry, Rebecca, but it's obvious you're running away from something. Care to fulfill the curiosity of an old woman? I'll understand if you don't, but I think you and I both know that your being here was no accident. That there were powers of intervention at work here." She smiled weakly. "Sometimes, when we're deep in the clutches of a bad fever, we say things. Sometimes they don't make a lick of sense. Then there's things we say that are so true it causes one to wonder, to become more objective than they've ever been in their lives." Young and old stared at each other for a long inquisitive moment. Rebecca finally broke the silence. "This room," she said. There's something so sad about it." She took a long swallow of broth. "What are the bandages for?"

"For your knees, my dear. They were terribly torn, but there's no cause for concern. Some peroxide and Penaten cream and they're almost as good as new. I'll change the bandages in a moment. You were saying about this room." Eyes filled with want.

Rebecca reached under the blanket and touched her knees. They were covered with squares of gauze. "You've taken such good care of me. I suppose I owe you at least some kind of explanation." Taking another swallow of broth, she drained the mug and handed it back to the kindly old woman. "I feel much better now. Thank you again." She didn't know if it was the healing properties of the broth or just that her mind was becoming more focused. Whatever the reason, memories flooded back to her. "This is Caleb's room," she said unvarnished.

"Yes, it was. My son's room." Hester drew a deep breath, wise eyes moistened.

The breeze which spilled from the window grew more robust, and lifted the lace of curtain so it hovered in the air. The air of roses strengthened. Succeeding was the embellished laughter of a boy and the bark of a large dog. Obvious to Rebecca, Hester Hart had not heard a thing.

"We put you here intentionally, my dear. Ed, that's my husband, was against it at first. But I convinced him otherwise."

Rebecca drew her attention away from the window and gazed into the old woman's eyes. "But you're so… so…"

"Old. Yes, I am. I'll be seventy-nine this October. Ed is in the spring of his eighties. As I said before, you are a very special young lady, but you know that, don't you?"

"Yes," said Rebecca, her eyes fixated on the nearly seventy-nine-year-old, an earnest understanding saddening her heart.

"Then you've seen him, haven't you? Our beautiful son. You've been in contact with him."

"Yes," Rebecca sighed. "In the barn. Caleb and Chase." *I'm waiting for you.*

"You've also seen Chase? My, my, my." Hester Hart's face brightened. "They loved to play in that barn. I never would have imagined. Poses many questions, don't you think?"

"I suppose it does." Rebecca knew what Hester was getting at. The same question that had been plaguing her for years. Did God really exist? Was the greatest story ever told just that, a story? That six days of miraculous creation was really millions of years of evolution? That science overruled the integrated faith of billions of people?

As though reading her mind, Hester Hart said, "I too have been questioning my faith for some years now, my dear."

"You should be happy to know that Caleb is not alone and seems very content," Rebecca offered.

Hester pushed herself to her feet. The bandages, cream, and tape fell to the floor. Hobbling to the window, she rested her hands on the sill and stared longingly for quite some time. "May I share a story with you, Rebecca, if you think you're up to it? Then you can do the same. And maybe together we can make some sense out of all of this. You see, I've always sensed that our son was somehow still with us. And with you here, well, you've confirmed what I could only feel." Returning to the rocker, she dropped to a knee and picked up the dressings then lowered herself onto the rocker's cushion.

"I guess that would be all right. If it will help I mean. I am feeling much better than I was five minutes ago."

"I'm glad you're feeling better. The sooner we share our stories the better I believe."

Hester closed her eyes for a moment. When she opened them again, they were filled with the restoration of memory. Sharp, full of light.

Reaching behind, Rebecca positioned the pillows so they supported her back and head. The wind blew once more, lifting the lace and causing some of Hester's long grey hairs to dance about her face. Leaning forward, elbows resting on the arms of the rocker, she interlocked her fingers. When she spoke, it was with the resolute practice of a storyteller.

"You see, my dear. It all started during the Korean War of 1951. Ed, that's my husband, was a captain for the American Twenty-fifth Infantry. He was stationed in Kumsong, at the boarder separating North and South Korea. The platoon was 'prised of Negroes and whites, creating much tension among the troops. You see, my dear, back in those days, they were still hanging African Americans in the South."

"That's terrible."

"Yes, it was. Anyway, I was an RN at the U.S. 121 evacuation hospital in Seoul. I was only twenty-one, brash, just out of med school, and felt strongly about supporting the war effort. Ed's platoon along with a detachment of South Korean's was sent to secure a stronghold detrimental to U.S. military strategists. It was the middle of a bitter Korean winter. The men were ill equipped and poorly trained when it came to such conditions." Hester paused to take a settling breath. "The battle raged on for three days with most of Ed's regiment being killed or maimed, including Ed. They were captured when the allied South Koreans turned tail and ran. Those who could walk were taken to a cave the Koreans were using as a prison camp. Those who couldn't were shot on sight. Ed had sustained a badly broken leg but was not about to let the enemy get the pleasure of killing him. With his shin in splinters, he walked the twenty miles to the rat-infested cave. There, he was placed among other captives including men from Australia, Britain, Canada, Turkey, and South Korea. Some of them had already been there for months and were so malnourished they had been reduced to skeletal spirits of their former selves. Among the men was a medical officer from Australia. Harry Hanover. Harry tended to the men best he could. Using strips of cloth from the uniform of a soldier who had died during the night, which was commonplace, and two branches, he set and splinted Ed's leg.

"Well, you can imagine with that many men in such tight quarters and starving to death, the rats soon disappeared. They tried to maintain morale by forming singing groups comprised of soldiers from their own countries. There was a young Negro boy from Philadelphia named Diddy Dowd who managed to save his harmonica from the thieving Koreans. He would softly play ragtime, blues, and jazz, saving the men from tearing each other apart. You see, my dear, some of the men went quite mad from starvation. It was the music that kept the rest of them sane enough to endure such conditions."

"It must have been horrible for them," said Rebecca.

"Inhumane is what it was. Without going into too much detail, I can tell you that those bastards took pleasure in dishing out daily beatings. Giving the men maggot-laced gruel to survive on while they dined on pork, chicken, dog, and horse meat. If you died, you died." Hester swallowed hard, her face flushed with the anger she still carried. "One night, in the spring of 1952, the Koreans dragged Diddy Dowd from the cave. The following morning, all the officers were gathered and taken outside. The Koreans lined them up all in a row. Now Ed, that's my husband, being a captain, was one of them you understand. The commandant of the prison camp paced up and down, yelling at the men in Korean. Then two soldiers dragged the badly beaten and naked body of Diddy Dowd from a tent and dropped him at the commandant's feet. Again the commandant berated the men. Ed said he looked like a man possessed with spittle flying all over the place and eyes alight with the fiery hatred he had for the allied troops. He ordered one of his soldiers to lift Diddy's body into a sitting position. Though badly beaten, face a swollen pulp, Diddy was still conscious. Through one eye he looked at the officers, smiled, and began to sing 'God Bless America.' The commandant yelled down at him, withdrew his sword, and beheaded the young lad. Then he took the harmonica from a pocket and tossed it on the ground, pointing to the officers that one of them should pick it up. A lieutenant from Canada stepped forward because if someone hadn't you see, he was sure the commandant would have had all of the officers murdered. So by offering himself, he saved the rest of the men. He bent to pick the instrument up. The commandant pulled a gun from its holster and shot him in the head. Morale dropped severely that day."

Rebecca cringed, gooseflesh covered her arms and legs. "That was very brave of him."

"Yes it was. When it comes to the US military bravery is in no shortage of supply." She took another breath and continued. "Ed spent nearly two years in that hellhole watching the men around him drop like flies. If you weren't tortured or starved to death, then the diseases that ran rampant within the cave claimed you. History seems to dictate that, as a species, when we need each other most, mankind discovers new ways of butchering each other."

"So true," said Rebecca quietly caught up in the tale. "Maybe one day *women* will have the power to change things."

"That day can't come soon enough. Anyway, to continue. Finally, a prisoner exchange was amended in August of 1953 in Panmujon between the United Nations Command and the North Korean Chinese Alliance. Out of the eight hundred men who were held captive in that cave, only forty made it out alive."

"And Ed was sent to the hospital you were working at."

"Precisely, my dear. Now Ed, that's my husband, was a big man going into the war at nearly three hundred pounds. When I first laid eyes on him, he weighed just shy of a hundred. His hair had turned grey and needed to be shaved off because of infestation. Most of his teeth were missing, and his leg had to be rebroke so that it mended correctly."

"Which is why he still has a limp."

"Yes. The poor dear still suffers great discomfort whenever it rains or when winter is about to set in. For the first three months, he and Harry Hanover, who had also survived, could only manage small amounts of meat, bread, and milk as a diet. Ed and I spoke often, and when I could afford the time, I would read to the men while sitting on the edge of Ed's bed. You see, my dear, even though Ed, that's my husband, was a sight only a mother could love, a part of me knew right away that this was going to be the man I would spend the rest of my life with. That fate had brought us together."

"How romantic, in a tragic kind of way."

"Yes, indeed it was. When Ed's leg was right again and he had regained most of his weight, we used to take strolls in the gardens around the hospital holding hands and dreaming of better days. Now I don't suppose I have to tell you that we fell madly in love."

"I can see it all. Oh, how I wish something like that happens to me someday. Except for the war part and everything."

"I'm sure it will. Now during our romance, I became pregnant. Because of Ed's injuries, he was sent Stateside where he received the Purple Heart and the Medal of Honor from President Eisenhower himself. I soon followed. A single pregnant nurse was something the military frowned upon in those days. We married as soon as we could. Purchased this acreage with the money I managed to save and from the payment Ed received from the U.S. government for defending democracy."

"What about Harry Hanover? The man who fixed Ed's leg. What happened to him?"

"Harry returned to his hometown in Wollongong, Australia, where he was treated as a war hero. He and Ed kept in touch, writing letters and exchanging Christmas cards every year. Sadly, Harry died not four years ago at the ripe old age of eighty-nine."

"So he lived a fulfilled life then."

"Three sons, four daughters, and eleven grandchildren."

"Good for him."

"Yes. It's strange that sometimes no matter how crooked things appear, they have a way of straightening out." Hester cleared her throat. "Would you mind if I stopped to get a glass of water? My throat's a tad parched."

"Of course not," said Rebecca.

"Thank you, my dear. It's a lengthy story and I'm afraid I'm not as long-winded as I used to be." Rising from the rocker, Hester left the room without another word spoken.

Rebecca sensed that Hester not only needed a drink, but that she also needed time to prepare herself for what was going to come. A story Rebecca was sure she already understood, but had to hear. Staring at the window, she watched the breeze play with the lace. Birds twittered as they dipped around the house. Leaning forward, she lifted the lid of the suitcase. All of her belongings were neatly folded one on top of the other. Bandit looked as fresh as the day she received him. There was even a new black button in place of the missing eye. The broken glass framed photo of her mother had been repaired. No doubt by Ed. The picture was slightly dull having been soaked by rain. However, Deseray's bright smile still held true. Rebecca was going to inspect the contents of the envelope resting on a pair of jeans then thought better of it. Surely the money would be there, there was no reason to think otherwise. Closing the lid, she leaned back and listened to the birds larking outside.

Her mind's eye was creating images of what it must have been like for the battle-weary men to survive in a cold, cramped cave when suddenly, piano music filtered throughout the house. Being a student of music in high school, she recognized Mozart's *Minute Waltz* right away. The music deleted the images of broken men, barely alive, competing with rats for space and any morsels left by the dying.

Another minute passed before the door opened. Hester came in carrying a tall glass of water and a box of Kleenex. She took her place in the rocker, pulled out several tissues, then took a short drink. "I hope Ed's not bothering you with his piano playing?"

"No, of course not. He plays beautifully."

"The piano came with the house. Ed took to it like a fish to water. He'd listen to classics on the record player, and before you knew it, he was playing note for note."

"That's amazing. There's this Chinese kid. I don't recall his name, but at the age of eight, he was already playing concertos in places like Carnegie Hall and with the London Symphonic Orchestra. Some people believe he's the reincarnate of Chopin."

"Yes, I've heard of him. I believe his name is Lang Lang."

"That's it. Can you imagine?"

"I do believe I can. Now if you don't mind, I'd like to continue with my story while my memory still serves me."

"Yes. Please do." Rebecca folded the comforter down to her knees. The small room was very warm, filled with the twittering pitches of passing birds and the strong lust of roses.

Hester took another drink, balling the tissues tight in a fist. "Well, as I told you, I had become pregnant. It was a very difficult pregnancy for me. I was sick all the time, and because there was so much pressure against my spine, I was bedridden for most of it. Back then, Valentine was a busy little town with shops, a bank, grocery stores, local bar, and medical clinic. There were three churches to support the mainstay of religion. Pentecostal, Lutheran, and Roman Catholic. Just up the road from here was a lumber mill. Most of the town's men were employed there including Ed, that's my husband. Times were good. People had money. We owned three horses and a whole mess of laying hens whose eggs we sold at market value to the grocery every couple of days. Three times a week Dr. Vandermeir came to check on me. A friend of mine, Ruth Kellerman, would stop by to clean house and run errands when Ed wasn't home. Such a sweet woman. You wouldn't find that kind of support nowadays."

"No, I suppose you wouldn't." There was a stirring at the window. Two barn swallows had landed on the open sill. One had a length of straw in its beak. Their heads darted this way and that, wings fluttered madly. Then they engaged in what sounded like a spousal quarrel for a moment before taking flight again.

"How unusual," said Rebecca.

"Not really. When you've been in one place for as long as Ed and I have, well, the animals and birds become desensitized to your presence. Why, just last fall, Ed, that's my husband, and I came home from a bit of shopping to find a family of squirrels in the kitchen helping themselves to a loaf of bread."

Rebecca snickered at the visual this created. "Sorry, I didn't mean to laugh."

"Don't be. Laughter cleanses the soul. You should never be sorry to laugh, unless of course it's at someone's expense, my dear."

The piano music suddenly stopped. A moment later both women heard a door close.

"Ed's probably gone for a walk," said Hester. "He does that every day. Just walks around the property. Tells me he's gone thinking. About what I don't know. He never tells me. However, I imagine he carries Caleb on his shoulders while reexperiencing the war, so I leave him alone." She dabbed at her eyes with the ball of Kleenex.

"How sad for him," said Rebecca. "And for you."

Hester took another swallow of water, her eyes drifting back in time. "By my eighth month, I was as big as a house. We didn't have ultrasounds like we do today, but the good doctor and I both knew something was wrong. To confirm this, on the second day of June 1954, I got out of bed to use the bathroom and my water broke. Ed wasn't home, so I had to make my way downstairs to call the doctor's office. His secretary informed me that he wasn't in. That he had to go out to the mill where there was an accident. She said she would place a call to him, but it might be some time before he could get to me. So I hung up the phone and called my friend Ruth. Fortunately for me, she was in and rushed right over. By the time she arrived, I was lying on the kitchen floor next to the fridge. I'd managed to get a throw cushion from the couch so at least my head was comfortable, but I was in a tremendous amount of pain.

"Ruth had already delivered several babies in her time, so she knew what to do right away. While she put a pot of water on the stove and retrieved clean linen from the closet, I kept telling her that something was wrong. My contractions were getting closer and closer and it felt as though my insides were being torn. Ruth removed my undergarments and examined me. 'Oh no!' she cried. 'Your baby's a breach! I never delivered a breach before!'

"Well, you can imagine I was scared to death. I did not want to lose this child."

"What did she do?" asked Rebecca, eyes wide with anticipation.

"The only thing she could do. She found the sharpest knife in the house and cut my private parts. Then reached in and turned that baby around. Ten minutes later, at exactly one twenty-seven in the afternoon, our son Caleb was born. Ruth held him upside down and slapped his little behind. The little bugger let out a roar like you never heard before, announcing his arrival into this world. She laid him across my bosom and made a call to the mill. Together we cried like a couple of old hens sitting in my blood and placenta, waiting for the good doctor and Ed to arrive."

"I guess if he was a she, you would have named her Ruth after your friend."

"You know, I never really gave it much thought. Caleb was such a boy right from the get-go. Full head of hair. Big feet and curious hands. But I suppose you're right. I would have named her Ruth had he been a she." She dabbed at her eyes once again. "That wonderful woman was murdered a year later during a botched robbery at the bank. Shot in the face. Didn't stand a chance. She was buried in the cemetery just up the road."

"I'm so sorry," sniffed Rebecca, and reached for the box of Kleenex. She wondered if Ruth Kellerman's spirit had become part of the *one*.

"Me too." Hester paused for a thoughtful moment and stared at the window. When she began again, her body seemed to deflate. "By the time Caleb turned one, he was already walking and talking. Ed took that boy with him wherever he went. There was a bond between them like no other. Ed, that's my husband, decided that a boy, no matter how old, should have the companionship of a dog. So one day he brought this puppy home from the pet shop in Hopkinsville. It was big for a puppy of only six weeks, so we knew right away it was going to be a very large animal once he matured. Chase was this big ball of white and red fur, but there was something very special about him we noticed right away."

"His heart," interrupted Rebecca, her mind's eye seeing the big dog standing in a shaft of moonlight.

"Yes, my dear. Even as a pup, he had this heart-shaped patch of fur on his chest as if it were put there by the hand of God. Chase grew quickly. By the time Caleb was three, Ed would put him on Chase's back, and that dog, as if he were a pony, would walk him around the property. Now I suppose I don't have to tell you that the two became the best of friends. Chase never let Caleb out of his sight and vice versa. One of Caleb's favorite things to do was to watch the lumber trucks pass by. The truckers would toot their horns and Caleb would dance with glee. They all knew Caleb by name and would wave to him. Sometimes they would stop to give him a small token of their affection. One of these gifts was a red ball about the size of an orange. It barely fit into Caleb's hand, but that didn't stop him from teaching Chase how to fetch and retrieve. They would spend the whole day out in the yard playing fetch and waving to the trucks that passed. Under my supervision of course. Chase was not only big but incredibly smart. Ed and Caleb had him doing many different tricks by the time Caleb was five. Caleb's favorite was that when asked, Chase would rear back, give Caleb a hug, and lather his face with kisses. That summer, Caleb had fallen out of a tree and broke his left arm. You think that would limit him from the fun and games he had. Not Caleb." Hester pulled more tissue from the box. Taking another drink, she set the glass on the floor next to her feet. "I can't remember a time when that boy wasn't smiling. He absolutely adored life."

Rebecca's heart sank, already knowing where Hester's tale of woe was headed.

"Ed, that's my husband, began to teach Caleb the basic chords on the piano, and like his father, Caleb took to it. On his sixth birthday, he surprised us by playing 'Happy Birthday,' 'Mary Had a Little Lamb,' and 'Twinkle, Twinkle, Little Star.' By then he had discovered the wonderful places to hide out in the barn and would often have me in fits as to his whereabouts.

"Sometimes I would find him high up on the support beams, walking along as if he were some kind of trapeze artist. If it weren't for Chase staring up at him, I might not have ever found him. To this day I still don't know how he ever got up there." She paused again and took a breath.

"The year was 1960. Business at the lumber mill had declined significantly. Many families were forced to move in search for other means of support. Most of the shops closed, and there weren't enough people left to support the faith of all three churches. Only the Roman Catholic church remained. Ed, that's my husband, had to take a lesser-paying job at the bank as a security guard. We were determined not to lose the home we had built for ourselves, so we crimped where we could, selling the horses and hens for the going rate, which wasn't much I can tell you, and I took in laundry from those who were more fortunate than anybody else.

"Nineteen and sixty fell into '61. Winter turned to spring. By this time, the clear cutting had all but stopped. It became a rare sight to see one of the lumber trucks rumbling down the road." Hester's eyes welled with tears.

Rebecca noticed that her hands were shaking. "If you need to stop, it's okay."

"No. I can't. You see. I've never told this story to anyone else. Paining me as much as it does, I feel that you need to hear it. You do understand, don't you?"

"Yes, I believe I do."

Hester closed her eyes for a moment. Pent-up tears slipped over her face like sad little diamonds. When she opened them again, they were filled with the pain of memory. "It was a sunny promising day in May. A month shy of Caleb's seventh birthday. I was hanging laundry on the line. Caleb and Chase were playing fetch in the yard. Ed, that'd my husband, was at work. I could hear the rumble of a truck as it made its way around the bends up in the road. Caleb heard it too and went to the fence as he always did so he could wave to the trucker as he passed. Chase followed, the red ball fitted into his mouth, and sat beside Caleb. The truck drew near. But something was amiss. I could hear it in the way the driver was gearing up and down. My heart began to hammer in my throat. I dropped the bedsheet I was about to hang and ran. 'Caleb!' I yelled. 'Get away from the fence!' He turned and waved to me, his face as bright as the sun. Wearing that smile he always wore. The truck came around the bend. It broke free of the road, plowing through the fence… and… and…"

"Hester, please. You don't need to finish," said Rebecca, weeping.

Hester's face went blank. "The driver was drunk. If it wasn't for that single moment God chose to take him from us, Caleb would be in his fifties now." She brought her hands to her face and cried.

Tears of compassion flooded Rebecca's cheeks. Together they wept silently. Birds twittered, the lace of curtain danced, the crackle of Caleb's laugher emanated from somewhere outside. It filled the room, and Rebecca's heart.

"Thank you for listening, my dear. I know it was a lot to take in on such short notice, but I had my reasons." Hester wiped the remainder of tears from her face.

Rebecca sniffed. "Did you have any more children?"

"Unfortunately, no. You see, Caleb's birth was so difficult I had to have my tubes tied. I spent a couple of weeks in the hospital having lost so much blood."

"What about Ed? How did he manage after the death of his only son?"

"Poor man went off the deep end for a while. Wouldn't talk to anyone, including me. He carried this anger with him for months, then the anger turned to a terrible sadness. He drank heavily. Practically drowned himself with gin. Sometimes I would find him out in the yard just staring at the road, crying in fits. You see, my dear, no amount of brutality the Koreans dished out could break Ed like the passing of our son did. It took the life right out of him. I thought I was going to lose him. That his mind might not ever be right again. Then one night, in the late spring of '62, while we were in bed, Ed woke me. He said, 'Listen, Mother. Do you hear it?' I sat up and listened. 'Twinkle, Twinkle, Little Star' was being played ever so softly on the piano. Ed rushed out of bed and ran downstairs. I followed. By the time we reached the piano, the music had stopped. Ed looked at me. I saw right away that the hold of such a deep sadness had released him. Ed was himself again. He hasn't touched a drop of liquor since. Caleb's little message to us breathed the life back into him. We never heard the music again and never spoke of that night. Not until you were dropped into our laps. How about we change those bandages? I'd like to hear what it was that landed you on our door step.

During your fever, you spoke of many things, including the name of our son, which is how we knew that you are a very special person. One in a million. Maybe a billion." She rose slightly from the rocker and drew it closer to the bed.

Rebecca swung her legs from beneath the comforter and let them dangle over the side of the bed. "Can I ask you something, Hester?"

"Of course you can, my dear." Hester peeled the wrapping off a square gauze.

"What state am I in? I mean. I know I'm in Valentine. But Valentine what?"

"My, my, you really are lost, aren't you? Why, you're in beautiful Kentucky, my dear. Home of the Derby, bluegrass, Mammoth Cave. Why, did you know that cheeseburgers were first served in good old Louisville, Kentucky, in 1934?"

"Kentucky... huh. No, I didn't know that about the cheeseburger."

There came a knock at the door. "You ladies decent?"

"Come in, dear," said Hester.

Ed ducked and entered the room. Both hands were jammed into the pockets of his pants. A sweat track had formed around the neck line of his T-shirt.

"Did you have a nice walk, my love?"

"Glorious day out there. I'm just going to take a run to Sonjee's. Pick up some coffee and bread. Can you think of anything else we might need?"

Hester thought a moment.

"Mr. Hart?" said Rebecca then remembered about the Ed thing. "Ed. I just want you to know that I think your playing is beautiful."

"Thank you, Rebecca. I guess that means I just doubled the amount of fans I have." He smiled down at her. "Maybe after you've rested some, I'll play a little more."

"That would be awesome, thank you, Ed."

"Check the milk on your way out, dear. With one more mouth to feed, we probably should get more."

"Okay, Mother. Well, I guess I'll let you ladies get back to changing bandages and whatnot. I'll be back in a half hour or so. You know how Mr. Sonjee gets when he starts talking. Lucky to get out of there before the sun sets." He boomed a laugh.

Again, Hester offered him her cheek. Ed leaned down and brushed it with his lips.

Such love and devotion, thought Rebecca. As before, her eyes welled, only for much different reasons. When Ed left, she asked, "Who's Sonjee?"

"Why, he's a Pakistani gentleman who owns the small grocery and café in town, my dear. He and his family moved to Valentine, oh, about ten years ago. He supplies the basics, some meats and toiletries and whatnot. On weekends, he serves curry dishes and other delights from his country. It took some time for most of the townsfolk to get used to the fare. But now, on most weekends, you're lucky to get a seat. Ed, that's my husband, loves the stuff. A little too spicy for me I'm afraid. Now sit still for a moment. I'm going to remove your bandages."

The sound of the pickup truck roaring to life and a door slamming filtered through the open window.

Hester took the corner of one square and tore the bandage off as quickly as anything. It stung, but only for a second. Rebecca looked down at her knee. It was a track of pink lines, and there was a strawberry as big as a quarter.

"There. That didn't hurt too much, did it?"

"No. Not at all."

"You know what they say, quicker is better. If your other knee is as healed as this one, I think we should let the air get at them. Ready?"

"Yes."

Hester took hold of the other bandage and, just as quick, ripped it free. Like its opposite, the knee was a track of pink lines except there were more strawberries, and one of them was still pus filled. "Well, I guess we'll still have to keep this one covered," said Hester. She removed gauze from the packet, opened the Penaten tin, put a dab on the end of a finger, and smoothed it over the wound. Then she placed the gauze over it. Striping lengths of tape from a roll, she fixed the gauze into place. "So now are you going to tell me what it was that brought you to our home? I promise that none of it will ever leave this room. We'll both share our little secrets. Like old friends." She leaned back in the rocker and prepared herself for what Rebecca had to say.

Rebecca remained seated on the edge of the bed. She was comfortable. As comfortable as she could ever remember being. Like she used to be with her mother when they would spend hours in the kitchen talking. Talking and dancing. "Well, I suppose I should start with the death of my mother."

"Deseray?"

"Yes. How did you know?"

"As I said before, my dear. You were quite vocal during your fever. It wasn't hard to put two and two together." She fixed her wise old eyes on Rebecca's. "You were saying?"

Rebecca began with finding her mother on the kitchen floor of their home and the communications shared since that day. From there she spoke of the friends she had lost then jumped forward to the fire and how Jim Bounty had tried to rape her. About the death of her brother and father and how she had spent the night in the graveyard talking to her mother and listening to the songs of the dead. How she decided to seek out a new life, having lost everyone dear to her.

Hester listened without interruption. The expression on her face remained pensive throughout the story Rebecca revealed. When she reached the part where Brandon "Wishbone" Hogg had given her a choice between the storm or fellatio and how she had taught him a lesson he would never forget, Hester said, "Good for you, my dear," clapped her hands together, and smiled proudly. "I don't know if I could have done the same thing if I was in your position."

Rebecca told her of the deer, of the *one*, and of the voice that seemed to draw her to the acreage. By the time she reached the part where she sought solace in the barn, Hester was leaning forward, hanging on to her every word, periwinkle eyes wide as saucers.

"The last thing I remember was Caleb and Chase embracing in a hug. Then I woke up in this room."

"My lord. You've been through so much in such a short period of time. You are even more special than I could have imagined. Do you now feel as I do? That somehow you were destined be here even at the price you had to pay?"

"Yes, I do. I also believe my mother had a lot to do with it. She kept telling me to follow my heart. I believe the heart she was speaking of was you and Ed and Caleb." Rebecca yawned. The telling of the story had left her mind weary.

"I believe you're right, my dear. How wonderfully fascinating." Seeing that the story had tired Rebecca, Hester said, "As I promised you. I'll not tell another soul. To share your sensitivities will be entirely up to you. Now there's something I'd like to show you if you think you can manage. Something I left out in *my* story. Then you can rest those knees for the remainder of the afternoon. As far as your bruised ribs are concerned, the color is almost back to normal. What a nasty little man."

"Okay." Rebecca slipped from the bed and planted her feet on the floor. She tested her weight and found that she was still a little weak, but strong enough to stand on her own.

Hester rose from the rocker and took her by the elbow. "Come to the window for a moment. What I have to show you can be seen from there."

Together they strode the few feet to the window's sill. Hester drew back the lace, the sun felt wonderful against Rebecca's face. Hester looked down onto the property, and pointed. Behind the house, sitting at the forefront of pine trees, was a wide field of red and yellow roses brilliantly enhanced by the daytime star. A white picket fence segregated them from the rest of the yard.

"My roses," said Hester. "An acre and a half of them."

"They're beautiful." Rebecca breathed, inhaled perfumed air. Swallows dipped and dived acrobatically.

"Now look toward the middle," said Hester, her finger guiding Rebecca's eyes. "You see. Right over there in the clearing."

Rebecca's tired gaze followed the finger. Center to the melody of reds and yellows, a square of green existed, as well kempt as a golf course and much in contrast to the rest of the property. Centering the patchwork of green were two white crosses and a park bench. Leading into the green space was a stone pathway that started at the entry of a gate. Rebecca's heart suddenly ached with sadness.

"You see, my dear. Against the wishes of the church, we buried Caleb and Chase here. We were ostracized by the community for doing such a thing for the longest time. Told that without the proper burial by the church, Caleb's soul would never get to heaven. But we couldn't bear to have him away from us, so without the benefit of final rights, we hired a contractor to dig the holes and laid their bodies to rest where we could visit them anytime we wished. I started the garden that year and have been adding to it ever since. Sometimes, sitting on the bench, Ed, that's my husband, and I will spend hours there just talking about all the things Caleb and Chase used to do. Have ourselves a little picnic. Sometimes not. Sometimes we just sit on the grass in silence, waiting, listening. Hoping that he might send us a message that he's doing fine. Then you came along."

Rebecca drew a breath to expel the sadness in her heart. "I believe you did the right thing. I can feel it as well as I can feel my own soul. Their presence is strong, very strong. Especially in the barn. But you know that."

"Yes, my dear. That is why I need to ask you a very big favor. For Ed and me."

Rebecca did not have to think very long to know what that favor was. "If I can I will," she said. "I'll be more than happy to. You and Ed have been so kind."

"Oh, thank you, my dear. You don't know how much it will mean to us. Now let's get you back to bed. You need to rest. Then after that we'll see if we can't get some of my famous chicken soup into you. Should I leave the window open?"

"Yes, please."

With her hand on Rebecca's elbow, Hester steered her back to bed. Once there, she tucked her in as though she were a nanny tucking in a child. "You rest now, my dear. Have pleasant dreams." She raised the comforter to Rebecca's shoulders, leaned forward, and kissed her on the forehead. Then she whispered something very familiar, "Sleep tight, Rebecca White. Don't let the bed bugs bite." That said, Hester Hart picked up the dressings, tray, empty mug and left the room as quietly as a prayer.

Staring at the ceiling, Rebecca hoped she would be able to fulfill the needs of Ed and Hester Hart. To act as a medium between the two worlds was something she had no idea how to achieve, being more of an innocent receptor than a communicator between the dead and those who were not. Nonetheless, she was going to try damn it. She was going to give it all she had. Quickly, she took Bandit from the suitcase, tucked him beneath her arm, and kissed him on the cheek like she had been doing since she was ten. The touch of Bandit's fur filled her with childhood memory and she danced once again with Deseray to the music of her mind.

Contented minutes later, she turned to face the window. Although the rocker sat empty, she could feel the warmth, the desperate need that had been present only moments before. Overwhelmed by a critical urge to rest, Rebecca sealed her eyes. She slipped into a deep slumber, her mind attentive to Caleb's laughter, and the woof woof woof of big Chase, contained within the breeze filtering from Hester's vociferous garden of roses.

* * *

25

Memories Are Golden

BY 6:00 p.m., Ed, Hester, and Rebecca were seated in the large country kitchen enjoying Hester's world-famous chicken soup. The table was Formica, white with gold flecks, and most assuredly was new when James Dean was every young girl's idol.

Centered on the table, resting on a doily, a blue tulip vase held two red grandifloras freshly clipped from the garden. Sunlight gave life to the otherwise dull yellow paint covering the walls. A trio of avocado appliances—fridge, stove, and dishwasher—stood against a wall of cupboards where a short patterned curtain sequined one of four windows. Crisscrossed atop the doorway leading to the sitting area where the sound of the television remained low hung a wood spoon and fork.

Although quite not 100 percent, Rebecca was feeling better and had insisted on joining them for dinner. She'd put on jeans, one of her T-shirts, and borrowed a pair of slippers from Hester. "You were right, Hester," she said, pushing a spoonful of chicken, noodles, celery, and carrots into her mouth. "This is the world's best chicken soup. And the dumplings are to die for. I could never get mine to turn out so plump and full of flavor."

"Why, thank you, my dear. My mother, God rest her soul, taught me how to prepare it when I was just a young girl." Hester still wore her blue dress minus the shawl. She'd pulled her hair back and pinned it so that it sat in a bun at the rear of her head. On her ears were a pair of bejeweled ruby earrings that dangled from her lobes like ornaments. With the proper movement of her head, the sunlight embraced them, and set them on fire.

"Those earrings," commented Rebecca. "They're exquisite. They really bring out the color in your eyes."

Hester moved a hand to an ear and touched one. "Third generation. My grandmother wore them for her wedding. They're Spanish. Her father purchased them for her as a wedding gift in a little antique shop in Boston. That's where my family originates from. I imagine that they're worth quite a lot in today's market. Sadly, I'm the last of the Borrow women. No one to pass them on to." She rested her eyes on the bowl of soup in front of her. "There's so much I have to share... it's just... just not..."

Ed patted her arm. "There there, Mother. Let's not dwell on something we have no control over."

"You're right, my love. Sorry, Rebecca. I didn't mean to sound so morose. Please forgive me."

"Nothing to forgive," said Rebecca, smiling. "Ed?" She turned her attention to the bruin of a man sitting across from her. Ed had exchanged his sweaty T-shirt for a rusty brown Cardigan though it was quite warm in the house. His this-way-and-that-way hair was combed to one side with a fair amount of gel. Each hand, as big as the bowl of soup between them, rested on the table an empty spoon in one. "Yes, Rebecca," he said, swallowing a mouthful of dumpling.

"Hester told me what you went through in the war. I just want you to know that I think you are the bravest man I've ever met."

"I'd say more lucky than anything, but thank you. As much as I hated it, I never would have met this beautiful creature who has fulfilled me more than I could ever have imagined." He had picked up some dinner rolls from Sonjee's and dipped one into the broth, the entirety of it disappeared into his mouth.

Hester's face took on the blossom of a schoolgirl. "Oh, you. Keep it up, and I just might have to give you seconds, maybe thirds."

Rebecca shifted her gaze from one to the other. *What made two people stay in so much love for so long?* she wondered. *Was it the death of their son that bonded them together? Or was it simply that without each other, neither of them would have had a life so complete? That fate had shot cupid's arrow and struck them both with a never-ending love.*

"Penny for your thoughts, my dear."

"Huh? Oh, I'm sorry. I kind of got lost there for a moment."

"They must have been nice thoughts," Ed pointed out. "You had a smile on your face that lit up the kitchen."

"They were!" Rebecca lifted another spoonful of soup and eased it into her mouth. When she swallowed, she asked, "From my recollection, I was quite a mess when you found me. How come you didn't call the authorities right away? I mean. I'm truly grateful. I was just wondering. Weren't you frightened that I might have been some escaped lunatic or something, all covered in blood and looking like something the cat dragged in?"

Ed looked to his wife who nodded in jest. "Well, you see, Rebecca, when I found you the morning after the storm, you were hot with fever and you were walking around the barn with your bear in your arms and you were mumbling incoherently. But something inside me told me you were not dangerous, so I managed to corral you and sit you down on the bed of straw you had obviously made. I told you that you were safe. That everything was going to be okay. Somehow, in your fevered mind, you understood. You wrapped your arms around my neck, and you said... you said... Caleb's six, almost seven." Ed's eyes grew moist behind his glasses. "I knew right away that we needed to nurse you back to health ourselves, that you were special, so I picked you up and carried you into the house. Hester ran you a hot bath, cleaned you up, and we waited for your fever to break."

"Again, I thank you."

"Hester says you're going to try to contact our boy for us. Kind of speak to him for us. Is that right?"

"I'm going to do what I can, but you understand I can't make any promises. It's really up to Caleb you see. I'm just a kind of receptor."

Hester put a hand over Ed's thick arm. "We understand, don't we, my love?"

"Yes, Mother." He looked to Rebecca. "Now we want you good and strong for when you attempt something like that, so you eat all your soup. It'll make you feel like a new woman. Just so you understand, we're not going to rush you about this. You let us know when you're feeling up to it, okay?"

"Thank you for being patient. I'm already feeling much much better, so maybe we can try tomorrow."

"That would be splendid, my dear," said Hester. "Now who would like a nice cup of tea after dinner. I know I could use one." She got up and went to the stove where a copper kettle sat and filled it with tap water. "Maybe you would like to watch some television, Rebecca," she said over a shoulder. "Ed and I love to watch *CSI*."

* * *

After an hour of their favorite show, Ed asked, "Shall I play something on the piano for you?"

Rebecca was comfortable on the couch seated between her hosts. "Nothing would give me more pleasure, Ed, thank you." After dinner, she had become a little chilled, so Hester lent her the use of a pink housecoat that covered her from neck to ankles.

Ed rose and went to the 1920s Davenport upright leaned against the wall where stairs climbed to the second floor. Above the piano were black-and-white photos of the family that once was. Ed with Caleb on his shoulders while Chase stood obediently beside them. Hester and Caleb in the kitchen preparing cookies. Chase looking forlorn as he lay halfway into his dog house outside. A photo of the four of them standing at the entrance to the barn. The photos went on and on covering every square inch of wall. In each of them, Caleb wore the same expression. A young boy who was in love with life.

Askew atop the Davenport were the medals Ed received, framed in gold, constant, indelicate badges of preservation, mementos of a time when half the world was at war with the insufferable North Koreans. Dividing the medals was a poem set in the middle of a gilded frame:

They say memories are golden
well, maybe that is true.
I never wanted memories
I only wanted you.
A million times I needed you

a million times I cried.
If love alone could have saved you
you never would have died.
In life I loved you dearly
in death I love you still.
In my heart you hold a place
no one could ever fill.
If tears could build a stairway
and heartache make a lane.
I'd walk that path to heaven
and bring you back again.

Hester turned off the television via remote, and she and Rebecca gave their attention to Ed who had seated himself on the piano bench and had lifted the gleaming lid. He entwined and cracked his fingers, looked over his shoulder, and asked, "Okay, what shall I play. Since you're our guest, Rebecca, you get first selection."

"Ed can play just about anything, my dear. Go ahead, name a tune."

Rebecca thought for a moment, and chose a favorite she and her mother used to listen to on the old Panasonic. "How about 'Piano Man' by Billy Joel? Or is that too recent for you?"

Ed smiled. His eyes twinkled. "'Piano Man,' eh?" He laid his fingers on the keys and, to Rebecca's joyful surprise, fell beautifully into the intro. Softly he sang the words, which surprised Rebecca even more. He had a nice voice, she thought, and his head moved in rhythm to the music. When he was done, without missing a note, he fell into a finger-snapping toe-tapping piece of ragtime. "This one's for you, Mother," he called out.

Hester rose from the couch and, for a woman of her age, started to dance the jitterbug as though she were a woman half her age.

Rebecca clapped her hands, feet moving to the lively tune. Against common sense, she stood and tried to match Hester step for step. Soon, the two were synchronized, the floor beneath them creaking, the tall lamp next to the couch swaying as if it too were enjoying the music. When the tune was over, both women plopped themselves on the couch a little spent.

"Thank you, my dear. That was fun, wasn't it?'

"Oh, yes," replied Rebecca. "You're quite the dancer, Hester. I could hardly keep up." She wiped beads of sweat formed on her brow with the back of a hand. The energy she'd spent left her feeling a little peaked.

"Ed and I used to go dancing at the army barracks once his leg healed. God, that man could cut a rug. Couldn't you, my love?"

Ed laughed, his shoulders lifting with each tally. "Well, I don't mean to toot my own horn, but there weren't many people who could keep up with me. So what shall I play next?"

"I know, why don't you play one of Caleb's favorites," said Hester. "When Ed played 'Cat on a Hot Tin Roof,' that boy would wiggle his little bum and move about the room like he hadn't a care in the world. Chase would bark and prance around, getting every bit of enjoyment out of Ed's playing as Caleb did. Yes, those two were quite the pair." Her face took on the glow of fond memory.

Ed's fingers coasted across the keys. He lifted his head and stared at the photos as he played.

Rebecca could see them all in her mind's eye. Caleb's face all a glow, wiggling his fanny while big Chase performed his variation of the two-step. A much younger Ed Hart sitting at the piano. Hester cooking in the kitchen, young and beautiful. She could see it all with such clarity that it was almost too much to bare. That all these two wonderful people had other than each other were memories of a time long since past. God, she hoped she could do something for them.

An hour passed swiftly. Rebecca and Hester spent the time listening in comfortable silence, applauding Ed's efforts and just simply enjoying each other's company as if they were old friends who didn't need to say much to delight in the other's companionship.

Ed's upbeat tempo slowed somewhat, a good indication that he was getting tired.

"I think that's enough for tonight, my love," Hester intoned after he had played "Ob-La-Di, Ob-La-Da" by the Beatles with lesser pep than the song required.

"You're right, Mother. I am a little tired. Perhaps we should go to bed. The sun's almost set anyhow."

"I'll just fix Rebecca a nice glass of warm milk to help her sleep, then I'll join you."

"Please," protested Rebecca. "You don't have to go to all that trouble on my account. I think I'll be able to manage sleep without it. If I can't. I can always fix something myself."

"Are you sure, my dear? I really don't mind."

"Absolutely. I insist. You and Ed get some sleep. I think I'll watch a little more television if you don't mind. I'll keep the volume low so that I don't disturb you.

Hester smiled and, with a little difficulty rose from her place on the couch.

Ed got up from the piano bench he'd been sitting at for over two hours, stretched, and arched his back. "You coming, Mother?" He held out a hand.

Hester moved to his side, and took his hand. They kissed, and stared into each other's eyes for a loving moment. Then they wished Rebecca good night and together, still hand in hand, made their way up the stairs.

Once Rebecca heard their bedroom door close, she clicked the remote and waited for the screen to come to life. *Criminal Minds* was showing, so she rested her head on one of the throw cushions and tucked her legs. Even though the episode was a chilling story about two men who went around butchering families, she could not ignore the desperate, albeit ever-loving and completely devoted relationship her more-than-generous hosts dealt with day in and day out. The sadness of it all made the blood rush right out of her heart.

With her head resting on the cushion, mind wandering elsewhere, she whispered quietly, "Caleb. If you can hear me, I have a favor to ask of you..."

* * *

When morning came, it was announced by a trio of crows moving about the pine tops like black-winged chess pieces admonishing each other's flighty moves.

Rebecca sat in the rocker. She had moved it to the window's ledge so she could view the garden and watch the crows that had wrestled her from a deep and restful sleep. It was another beautiful morning, blue sky, no wind to speak of and the warmth of the early-morning sun filled her with joy. She was feeling like herself again. Reenergized, ready for what the day might bring.

Typically, as older people do, Ed and Hester woke at the crack of dawn. The house creaked and moaned under Ed's ponderous weight as he made his way to the kitchen. A few minutes later, the smell of fresh-brewed coffee floated throughout the house.

Between the cackling crows, the pained boards of the century house, and the jazzy rich brew, Rebecca had no choice but to wake.

As she stared at the crosses in the garden and watched the birds move about the tree tops, a doe and her dappled fawn emerged from the woods. They seemed unnerved as they walked the perimeter of the picket fence surrounding the garden of roses. The sun enriched the fawn's rich pelt enough that Rebecca could count the spots across its back. Mother and daughter searched the ground for food, dipping their heads simultaneously, their mouths picking bits and pieces of nourishment. Suddenly, as if startled, their heads bolted upright, but they did not flee. Instead they stared to the back of the house with their deer in the headlight eyes.

After a moment, the back door opened and closed.

Rebecca heard Hester say, "Good morning, my beauties." Then she appeared carrying a grey metal bucket, still wearing her white housecoat and slippers. She approached the deer, and they moved slowly toward her. Immersing a hand into the bucket, Hester held out what appeared to be small pellets of food. Rebecca observed, astonished at what she was seeing. Mother and fawn took the pellets from her hand as gentle as anything. When they were done, Hester poured what was left in the bucket on the ground and returned to the house. The deer ate with gusto. The crows cawed and moved deeper into the woods just as a storm of swallows passed the window and circled the house. *What a perfect day,* Rebecca thought. She remained in the rocker and breathed it all in.

A few minutes later, there was a knock at the door. "Rebecca my dear, are you awake?"

"Yes, Hester. I was just going to come downstairs. I won't be a minute."

The door opened enough for Hester to squeeze her head through. "Good. I've made pancakes with sausages. You do like sausages, don't you?"

Rebecca left the comfort of the rocker and went to the door, close enough to feel Hester's breath and kissed the caring woman on the cheek. "I adore sausages and pancakes. Thank you for being so kind."

Hester blushed, the color rose in her cheeks and around her eyes. She looked twenty years younger. She smiled and said, "Aren't you sweet? Now get dressed. We won't start without you."

"I saw what you did with the deer a few minutes ago," said Rebecca. "It was remarkable. How did you ever get them to trust you?"

"We have a mutual understanding, my dear. They don't eat my roses, and for that, they get oats. It works out well for both parties, don't you think?"

"Magical is what it is."

"Yes, I suppose it is. Now hurry up or the sausages will get cold." Quietly she closed the door.

Rebecca removed the housecoat and draped it over the bed. The bandage across her knee was holding nicely, and the bruise on her side was merely a discoloration of the flesh. She put on the same jeans she had worn the previous day then rummaged through the suitcase for a fresh top, deciding on a pink tank that captioned in bold red: Angel Without Wings. Tucking it into the jeans, she put on her road-weary runners *sans* socks.

She gave her attention to the room. It was bright with morning sun as if new life had been breathed into it. Further opening the window, the full aesthetics of the rose garden entered and was quickly followed by a young boy's giggle. "Bet you can't catch me, Chase." The doe and fawn had left after getting their fill. Swallows lined the picket fence, chirping and exercising their wings. The crows were nowhere to be seen. Instead, a pair of scarlet cardinals had taken their place on the very tip of the tallest pine. *It was going to be a very special day, very remarkable day.* Rebecca knew.

* * *

26

Valentine

AFTER the hearty breakfast that left Rebecca more filled than she had been in a very long time, Ed announced that he was going to Sonjee's. "Do you need anything, Rebecca?"

"Would you mind terribly if I went along for the ride? I'm feeling like my old self, and there's something I need to pick up."

"Not at all. Fresh air will do you a world of good." With some effort, Ed pushed himself from the table. There was a drip of syrup at the corner of his mouth which he wiped clean with a napkin, removed his glasses, and gave them a quick wipe as well. "Would you like to come with us, Mother?"

Hester was at the sink scraping dishes. "No. You two go. It'll give me a chance to catch up on the book I'm reading."

"What are you reading?" asked Rebecca from the table where two yellow roses now stood tall in the blue vase.

"Do you know Bryce Courtenay?"

"I can't say that I do. The name's familiar though."

"Bryce Courtenay wrote *The Power of One*."

Rebecca thought for a moment. "That's right. I saw the movie."

In a haughty tone Hester said, "Well, the movie never did the book much justice in my opinion." She dropped the front of the dishwasher, and began to fill it with the morning's dishes. "I'm halfway through brother fish. Another epic. That's all the man writes. You'd enjoy it. It's about the relationships endured during the harshest times during the Korean War and life afterward for three unique individuals. How did Mr. Courtenay put it? Oh yes, 'friendship is the companion that walks beside love and is often the more enduring of the two.'" She sealed the dishwasher and turned the dial. The old GE rumbled to life.

"That's beautiful, but I don't think I could read it after knowing what Ed went through. I'd be too frightened." Rebecca stood from the table, pushed the thickness of her hair over her shoulders, and looked to Ed. "I'm ready any time you are."

"I'll just go start the truck." He went to Hester and pecked her on the cheek. "Maybe I'll bring back some steaks for dinner. Throw them on the grill. How's that sound?"

"Perfect day for it," agreed Hester. "I'll make sure the grill's nice and clean. What do you think, Rebecca, up for a barbeque? We'll have some nice corn, and I'll make my world-famous potato salad."

"Only if I get to help. I insist on it. And please leave those pans, Hester. I'll do them when I get back. It's the least I can do."

"I'll just let them soak then." She turned on the faucet and placed three pans into the sink with a good squirt of dish soap.

"It's settled then," said Ed. "We'll have ourselves a good old-fashioned outdoor dinner. I'll clean up the old picnic table and set up the umbrella when I get back." He left through the side screen door whistling, an extra little pep to his labored step.

Both women stood in pacified quiet for a moment. The truck roared to life before Hester said. "Rebecca, my dear. Ed, that's my husband, and I were talking this morning and... well... we'd like you to stay for as long as you wish. You're a breath of fresh air much needed in our cumbersome lives. And with your gift... well, who knows."

Overwhelmed by the kind offer, Rebecca did not know what to say. Her face flushed with emotion. "You and Ed have done so much already. And I like you both tremendously, but, you see, after the fire, I decided I wouldn't be a burden to anyone. That I would make a fresh start. Have a go at it on my own. As far as my gift goes, I don't even know if I can help you. I'm certainly going to try, really I am, but you know as well as I do that nothing might happen." The frailty of Hester's makeup seemed to weaken, so Rebecca added, "May I think about your offer? It's a big decision to make."

This pleased Hester. The weakened constitution of her self-worth only moments ago refortified. "I guess we can't ask for more than that," she said, and smiled. "Thank you for considering our offer. We truly do mean it. What it says on your top speaks volumes about the person you are. We believe that, Ed and me. Now you better get out to him before he gets antsy."

"Oh, I almost forgot. I'll be back in a minute." Rebecca ran back to her room and took a twenty out of the envelope within the suitcase then stuffed it in her jeans.

Once she was back in the kitchen, she hugged Hester, and held her tight for several long seconds.

"What was that for?"

"Just for everything." Rebecca didn't have the heart to tell the Harts that she planned on leaving once she attempted the mediation between herself and Caleb. That Vegas had been calling her ever since she was a young girl. A call that Rebecca had every intention of answering.

* * *

On their way into Valentine, Ed and Rebecca passed the local elementary and high schools, their grounds empty except for a row of yellow school buses sitting dormant, waiting for the September bell to announce the beginning of a new school year.

Before they entered the main stay of town, they observed a fire engine being washed in front of the firehouse that had been present since 1934 and, according to Ed, ironically burned to the ground in 1957. The stone marker announcing the date of its erection the only object that had survived the inferno.

"The mayor at the time," informed Ed, "proclaimed that the town should pitch in to help rebuild the station, so he announced there was to be a charity dance at the community center to raise funds. The event was called Valentine's Day in July."

"How poetic," said Rebecca.

"Yes. Anyway, since then, there has always been a dance held at the end of July, only now we shut down Main Street for the day. The whole town attends. Paper hearts are put on display in store windows, and everyone wears something red. Women sell their goods, usually pies, cakes, and knitted things. There's games for the kids, and a stage is set up for local musicians to jam. People dance in the streets from noon till night."

"It sounds like a wonderful time."

"Indeed it is. We all look forward to it the year round."

The first thing to catch Rebecca's eye was the white banner that stretched from one side of Main Street to the other.

Valentine's Day Dance in July
Saturday, July 26, Come One, Come All

Ed drove the truck up one side of Main Street and down the other giving Rebecca a quick tour. Several of the shops along Main Street were for sale or rent and appeared to have been so for a very long time. Yellowed newsprint or black paint covered the windows.

Rebecca took it all in.

Ted's barbershop with a candy striped pole out front. The Bank of America that stood architecturally gothic on the corner of Main Street. Across from it was the saintly white structure of Saint Luke's Catholic Church complete with bell tower and stained glass windows. Next to it was the community center. Catty corner to the church was the sheriff and administration offices, a very nondescript building, and it wouldn't have surprised Rebecca if Andy Griffin of Mayberry came waltzing through the door. A single vehicle of authority sat parallel to a pickup truck that had a mitt full of tickets beneath a wiper blade. There was a used furniture store named Benny's Bargains with a worn green sofa and chair parked outside its large display window. A Chinese restaurant, Ming's, offered Western cuisine as well as dinners for two for $18.99. Stationed outside a used clothing store were two racks of clothes with a sale sign reading, $5.00 & UP. And there was Donna's bakery, the busier of the community businesses with people coming and going at a healthy rate. Many of the stores had already posted red hearts and cutout cupids on their windows in preparation for the Big Day.

The tallest structure was the town's watering hole and hotel, the Elton, hours away from being open for business.

The only gas station belonged to a man named Larry Moffit. A single-storey garage where stacks of tires were on display. It offered regular and unleaded gas from ancient pumps and Pepsi from a vending machine anchored next to the front door. Having seen better days, a blue-and-white tow truck sat parked in front of the service bay.

Seniors strolled the sunny side of town. Dog owners walked their furry friends who berated a skateboarder, zigzagging his way through the human traffic. Couples pushed strollers, and several early rising teens stood on the bank's corner smoking and watching the minimal traffic. It was a typical day in Valentine, Kentucky, population 1,300 souls, give or take.

Sonjee's grocery was located in the center of a town that was beginning to come to life again. A two-storey building of stucco with large windows advertising specials. The top half of the structure was living quarters. Bright yellow curtains covered two windows where a Christmas cactus and a pot of geraniums grew snug against the glass. Plastic tables and chairs sat on a wide covered porch offering patrons shade from the afternoon sun. A midlife couple enjoyed the lift of an early-morning coffee. They laughed about something or other, while the man puffed eagerly from a Colts cigar. A small deck sat off to the side. Wood steps led to the ground where three Pakistani children, a boy and two girls, were playing on a colorful jungle gym.

Ed parked the baby blue '65 Ford in the shade of one of the few elm trees adorning Main Street. He unfastened his seatbelt and turned to face Rebecca. "Just so you know, before we go in, when I was here yesterday, I told Sonjee that I had a great niece visiting with us just in case. Sorry that I fibbed, but I didn't know how else to explain you in case you should come into town, and well, here you are."

"That's okay, Ed. I kind of like being thought of as your niece. It makes me feel special. Is there anything else you told him about me that I should know?"

"Just that you were very pretty and smart as a whip."

Rebecca blushed. "Well, thank you, kind sir."

"Rebecca?"

"Yes, Uncle Ed."

"There's one other thing I'd like to say."

"Okay."

"I know Hester spoke to you this morning about you staying with us for as long as you like. Well, I want you to know that we truly mean it. Nothing would make us happier."

Rebecca put a hand on Ed's arm. "I am truly grateful, Ed, but like I told Hester, I need some time to think about it, okay?"

"I suppose that's all we can hope for." He put a hand over hers. "You'd like it here. Valentine has a way of growing on people."

They exited the truck and went up the steps to the front door where a Help Wanted sign was posted. The couple drinking coffee greeted Ed then continued with their conversation. Ed held the door open for Rebecca. "After you," he said.

"Thank you, Uncle Ed."

The pungent smell of curry hit Rebecca square in the nostrils. Above, a circulating fan moved the air. Red and white streamers hung from one corner of the store to the next. In a designated corner were more plastic tables and chairs. Sitting on each table were red cardboard hearts with the date July 26 printed on them.

Framed photos of the town Rebecca had just toured hung from a wall. A rubber tree stood in a corner. Two aisles of canned and dry good stretched to the back of the shop.

There were several people in the store. When they saw Ed, their faces lit with neighborly recognition. "Good morning, Ed," said an African American woman Rebecca guessed was somewhere in her fifties. Surrounding her round face was a kerchief of amber, and when she smiled, blinding white teeth lit her face as if a light existed somewhere inside her skull. "This must be the niece I've heard about."

Ed made the introductions. "Rebecca, this is Mrs. Helpnot."

"Pleased to make your acquaintance," said Rebecca, and extended a hand.

Mrs. Helpnot took Rebecca's in hers, and it disappeared between flesh that was roughly calloused and sustaining the grip of a wrestler. She looked Rebecca up and down. "My, now aren't we the pretty one. Cuter than a duck wearing a hat."

"Thank you, Mrs. Helpnot."

"Now, child, you call me Mabel. I insist on it. We're not so formal here in Valentine, are we, Ed?" She let go of Rebecca's hand.

"Not at all, Mabelle. How's Barnaby?"

Mabel's smile faded. "Poor darling. I just hope he is better by the time the dance arrives. I'm sure he will be. Haven't missed a dance in twenty-five years. How about you, Rebecca? Going to be around for the big dance?"

Rebecca looked to Ed then back to Mabel Helpnot. "I'm not sure. It's very possible I guess," she said though she knew it to be untrue and hated herself that she had to continue to lie to people who were being so kind to her.

"Well, child, I can tell you that you do not want to miss my crayfish pie. Does she, Ed?"

"Best I've ever had," said Ed. "Will you excuse us, Mabel, I've got a long grocery list, and we don't want to miss too much of this glorious day."

"Oh, of course, Ed. Praise be to the good Lord for a day such as this. I hope Hester is in good health?"

"Indeed she is, Mabel, and thank you for asking." Ed took Rebecca by the elbow and gently steered her forward.

"It was nice to meet you, Mabel," said Rebecca.

"The pleasure was all mine, child. I do hope we shall meet again, and very soon."

When they were out of Mabel's ear range, Rebecca said, "Boy, news travels fast here. I mean, I come from a small town as well, but it would have taken a day or two for the news of a visitor to get around."

"You can thank Mr. Sonjee for that. When there's new gossip to be had, he and the wind are formidable allies. Speaking of which, here he comes now."

Swiftly closing, a man wearing checkered pants, blue shirt under a brown silk vest, open sandals, and a smile from ear to ear bore in on them. An oval birthmark as purple as a plum sat rigid beneath his left eye. Looking thirty something, his cinnamon flesh was wholesome, but he could have been much older. He was flattening his already flat black hair with the palm of a hand. "Ah, Mr. Ed. How wonderful it is that you have graced us with your presence once again in such short time." Thrusting a hand, he regarded Rebecca as if she were a prize he had just won. "If the gods should be striking me blind this moment, I will have had the great honor of seeing such beauty for the last time. The gods have been very generous to you. Only my Masha, mother of my children, can be kinder to my eyes."

Rebecca took his hand. Heat filled her cheeks. "Thank you, Mr. Sonjee. It's a pleasure to meet you. You have a very nice store." Her hand slipped from his, an encouraging blush as bright as valentine erasing her freckles for a moment.

Without taking his eyes away from Rebecca's, Mr. Sonjee asked, "What is it we can be getting for you this lovely day, Mr. Ed?"

"Well," said Ed, "I was hoping you had some nice steaks. Hester, Rebecca, and I are going to have a barbeque this evening."'

"Come. Come. I show you. We are having the nicest T-bones. Best price for you, Mr. Ed." He led them to the back of the store where a chilled display of meats was lit under display lights. Behind the display was a small kitchen and sinks where Rebecca guessed his wife Masha did the cooking on weekends. Mr. Sonjee took his place behind the cooler and put on an apron, the smile on his face unwavering.

Though the display was half-empty, the meats therein looked fresh. There were beef tongues, liver, pork chops and ribs, chicken legs, and three different kinds of steaks all separated by robust garnishes of parsley. A row of two-inch thick T-bones caught Ed's eye. "Those look great, Mr. Sonjee. I'll have three, please."

"Yes, yes. They are being fresh cut this morning. Twenty-six days for the aging. Black Angus. Beautiful marbling. Only the best. I am giving to you for three ninety-nine per pound. My best special." He ducked and slid back a glass panel. Using tongs, he took out three of the front steaks and placed them on some butcher's paper before adding them to a scale sitting atop the display. "I am thinking seventeen dollars is a bargain for such beautiful meat."

"A bargain indeed," said Ed. "Why don't you throw in some of those chops as well. Six will do."

"Yes, yes. Very good choice, Mr. Ed. Very lean. Corn fed." Again he disappeared. A moment later, half a dozen pork chops resting on butcher paper sat across his arm. He showed them to Ed who nodded his approval.

Mr. Sonjee wrapped the steaks and chops and tied the packages with butcher's string. "May I be asking to you, Rebecca, that you will grace this otherwise simple town with your presence at the big dance that is coming? You are indeed an angel," he added, appraising her tank top.

Rebecca smiled, the flush of her cheeks still warm. "I think I might be able to. It depends on if Uncle Ed and Aunt Hester can put up with me for that long."

"She can stay for as long as she likes," Ed pointed out once more.

"Then this is very pleasing to me. I am anxious for my Masha to be meeting you. She should see such beauty. I am wondering, Rebecca. Maybe you should be staying long enough to come working with us? Our weekends are very busy. Yes, yes. Very busy indeed. Sometimes too much for Masha and me. The gods have sent you to me I am thinking. They are saying to hire such a person. It makes good sense indeed." Like all good businessmen of his culture, Mr. Sonjee was seeing that hiring such a beautiful young lady might increase his weekend tally immeasurably.

"I really don't know if I'll be around that long, Mr. Sonjee, but thank you for the kind offer. Do you have any toothbrushes and paste here?"

"Yes, yes. The far aisle you will be finding everything a young woman needs."

"Thank you, Mr. Sonjee." Rebecca went to the far aisle. She discovered several brands of toothbrushes and paste, and selected a pink medium brush and tube of Crest. When she returned to the meat display, there were two other customers waiting to be served. A young teen with Harry Potter glasses who wore jeans and a green Hulk T-shirt. His eyes fell onto Rebecca's face as if it were a love icon designed to initiate his first crush. Next to him, a woman wearing too much makeup for a person her years had an arm through Ed's and was looking at him with great fondness.

"This is my great-niece Rebecca. Rebecca this scallywag is Jason Darby, and this ravishing young thing is Louise Dubauex."

Greetings were exchanged.

When Rebecca smiled at the young Jason, his face churned all shades of red and he thrust his hands deep into pockets and toed at the floor. *How cute.*

Ed spoke, "I'll also need some charcoal for the barbeque. I'll pick it up on the way out. So what's my total today, Mr. Sonjee?"

Mr. Sonjee looked skyward for a moment totaling the meat to the bag of charcoal. "Twenty-eight dollars, Mr. Ed. Twenty-five for the meat and three for the coal. Not a penny more for such beautiful meat. My best deal indeed."

Ed shoved a hand that barely fit into his pocket, and came up with two twenties. He handed them to Mr. Sonjee over the display.

"And I have these," said Rebecca. She held out the brush and tube of Crest.

Again Mr. Sonjee looked skyward. "Five dollars even."

Rebecca fished in her pocket for the twenty and handed it over.

Mr. Sonjee made change for them both. He handed a plastic grocery bag containing the meats to Ed over the display. Rebecca added her purchases. "Such beauty," Sonjee commented once more. "Will you be coming in tomorrow, Mr. Ed. Masha is making tandoori chicken. You've never tasted meat so tender, so divine. And please be bringing Hester and Rebecca. But come early. Everyone loves my Masha's chicken."

Louise Dubauex let go of Ed's arm and leaned forward to examine the meat within the display. Jason, still infatuated with Rebecca, stood in enraptured silence, apparently forgetting what he had come in for.

"We'll have to see about that, won't we, Rebecca?"

"Yes, Uncle Ed. I've never had tandoori chicken before, sounds delicious."

"Then please be bringing an appetite," suggested Mr. Sonjee. "Perhaps we will be talking more about your possible employment with us."

Rebecca could only smile. Again she was forced to lie, and she did not like the way it made her feel. Totally ugly. Inside and out.

"Have a good day, Mr. Sonjee, Louise, Jason," said Ed.

"Yes, have a nice day," added Rebecca. "It was nice to meet you. Good-bye, Jason. Good-bye, Louise."

"May the gods be walking with you on this lovely day," Mr. Sonjee wished before turning his attention to the overly made-up Louise Dubauex.

On their way out, Ed grabbed a ten-pound bag of King's briquettes and tucked it beneath an arm. "What do you think of our town so far?"

"Except for the ocean not being here, it reminds me a lot of *my* hometown. Same type of characters. And the landscape is beautiful."

"You have a Mr. Sonjee where you come from? I thought we were the only ones to boast such a privilege."

"I think every small town has a Mr. Sonjee. They add much-needed character. Like the local drunks. What small town doesn't have its share of them."

They laughed.

* * *

Once they were back in the Ford, Rebecca asked, "Would you mind very much if we stopped at the church for a few minutes?"

"The church? That's an odd request."

"Yes, I know, but there's something I need to do. I'll only be a few minutes."

"Then Saint Luke's it is." He turned the ignition, put the truck in reverse, and backed away from the shady spot. Since there was no air-conditioning in the old Ford, each rolled down their windows, for the temperature had increased significantly having spent fifteen minutes in Mr. Sonjee's store.

There were more people walking Main Street. Men and women of varying ages, some with young children by their sides, just out and about enjoying the splendid July morning. Most of them recognized the old Ford and waved to Ed as the truck slowly passed. The banner hanging across Main Street swayed melodiously in the morning breeze.

Ed pulled into a spot in front of the bank. Immediately, the windshield was hit by a dollop of white-and-black pigeon shit. "Damn," muttered Ed.

Rebecca looked through the windshield. Sitting in a row atop the bank's ornate roof were a dozen or so pigeons bobbing their heads and looking down at the town. "That's supposed to mean good luck," she pointed out.

"Well, that's the kind of luck I can do without, thank you very much."

Rebecca snickered.

"Listen," said Ed. "Since we're here, I'm just going to walk to the post office around the corner. You go and do what you need to do, and I'll meet you back here, okay?"

"Okay. I won't be more than ten minutes." Rebecca got out of the truck and closed the heavy door. Crossing at the corner, she made her way up the steps leading to the entrance of Saint Luke's.

Opening the hefty wood door, she stepped into the vestibule leading into the church, dipped a finger into a marble stand of holy water and made the sign of the cross.

Walking between rows of pews, she made her way to the front where a divine altar of granite and pulpit with microphone stood. The interior was empty and so quiet Rebecca could hear herself breathing. Genuflecting before taking a seat in the front pew, she inspected her surroundings. A confessional stood gleaming beneath stained glass, and there was a stand of candles lit within ornaments of red near the tabernacle. Far in a corner was a modern Yamaha organ. Rear of the altar was a cross fashioned from pine. A white porcelain Christ hung solemnly from its apex and seemed to judge her.

Stained glass windows depicting religious panoramas lined both sides of the church: Christ as an infant in the arms of Mother Mary. A winged Gabriel, sword drawn. Christ the Redeemer, hand over heart, a golden halo surrounding his head. A roman soldier spearing the side of Christ nailed to an unrefined cross. Apostles looking up to him as his spirit rose toward the heavens. In the natural light, all were alive in their glorious, sainted colors.

Rebecca clasped her hands together in prayer and bowed her head. She closed her eyes and whispered, "*God, I know I haven't spoken to you in a very long time. I've been confused since the death of my mother. I guess you had your reasons for taking her away from me. I'm here to ask a favor of you even though you are probably very busy. Would you please take care of Ed and Hester Hart. They are such wonderful people and deserve nothing but happiness for the remainder of their lives. I've never asked you for anything before, so if you could grant me this one kindness, I would be truly grateful. And please forgive me for the lies I've told. Amen.*"

When she opened her eyes, she saw that a priest stood near the altar where a vase of fresh flowers were now exhibited. He seemed to be waiting for her to finish her business with the Lord. Rich black hair and kind eyes radiated from a face that was quite young, handsome even. Moving toward her, he turned, genuflected in front of the altar, then stood in front of Rebecca, hands clasped behind his back. "I haven't seen you before," he said, and smiled. "You're not part of the usual Sunday congregation."

"I'm sorry. I hope it's okay for me to be here?" said Rebecca.

"Of course. Far be it from me to interfere when someone seeks counseling from our Lord. These doors are always open."

"Thank you, Father... ?"

"Father Murphy." He held out a hand, his dark eyes bore into hers.

Rebecca took his offered hand. It was warm and as gentle as his voice. "I'm Rebecca. I'm staying with the Harts for a while."

"Ah, Hester and Ed. Such wonderful people. You must be the niece I've heard of. Mr. Sonjee has a remarkable talent for gossip."

"Yes, he does, doesn't he?" She let her hand slip free. "Well, I'm done with what I came here for, so I guess I'll be on my way." She stepped from the pew, genuflected, and crossed herself.

"Please feel free to come by anytime you wish. The Lord holds no specific business hours. I hope perhaps that I will see you at Sunday mass?"

Rebecca didn't know what to say. She certainly didn't want to lie to a priest. "I'm afraid I haven't been a very good Catholic, Father. This is the first time I've been inside a church in years. I really just came in for a talk with God. It's something I haven't done in quite a while. I hope you're not offended."

"Not at all. We all have our own ways in which we communicate with the Almighty. I hope he had some answers for you."

"I hope so too. Time will tell I guess."

"Ah, time. The great equalizer." Father Murphy looked at Rebecca inquisitively. "Our journeys in life are filled with the paths of time. Some last as long as a fleeting moment while others seem so distant in their measurement that it is difficult to see where they lead."

Was he reading my mind? wondered Rebecca. "Well, it was nice to have met you, Father Murphy, but I really must be going now. Ed is waiting for me in front of the bank."

"Say hello to the Harts for me. Such wonderful people. The world could use more of them."

"I will, Father, and thank you."

"May God keep you safe, Rebecca," he said, his dark eyes sparkling with incontestable faith.

I hope so too. "Have a nice day, Father." Turning, she quickly, but quietly, made her way to the vestibule where she dipped her fingers, made the sign of the cross, pushed on the heavy wood door, and went outside.

The warmth of the sun enveloped her. The sounds of human and vehicular traffic seemed magnified. She looked skyward to the sound of beating wings. A dozen or so cardinals, as red as the print on her T-shirt, passed over the church's summit then landed on mass in a nearby tree.

Her eyes sought out Ed's pickup. He was seated behind the wheel waiting for her, left arm dangling out the window. She made her way down the steps. When she reached the sidewalk, the cardinals took flight, and circled overhead twice before they disappeared beyond her scope. Tiny red dots against the vast blue backdrop. *May God keep me safe indeed,* thought Rebecca, and drew a breath of sweet morning air.

* * *

27

Tender Kisses Good Night

WHEN they arrived back at the house, Hester was seated on the bench among her garden of roses reading a book under the shade of an umbrella fastened to the slats of the bench. She had changed into a flower pattern dress and wore glasses for reading that hung around her neck on links of gold. The gate leading into the garden was open, and a pair of swallows was resting on its arch, squabbling about something or other. Pigeons sat in formation on the barn's roof. The tips of considerable pines swayed gently to the push of a mischievous wind.

Ed and Rebecca got out of the truck and went to the garden.

"Well, that didn't take too long," Hester pointed out. She rested the thick Bryce Courtenay novel on her lap. Removing her glasses, they dangled on the plate of her breast. All around, clouds of disorganized insects buzzed in and out from the rose heads. Swallows dived at them, and picked them off one meal at a time. Not twenty feet away, white as winter's first snowfall, the ceremonial shrines marking Caleb and Chase's final station stood brilliant.

"You know I can't be away from you for too long, Mother," said Ed. He held up the bag, and proclaimed, "We be eatin' steak tonight."

"Good, I've already made the potato salad and cleaned the grill. All you have to do is get the table ready, set up the umbrella, and shuck the corn." She looked up to the sky. Several grey clouds had moved in. "I hope there's no chance of rain. How's your leg feeling, my love?"

"Never better, so don't go fretting about anything. I'll just go and put this meat in the fridge, then I'll tackle the table." He looked to Rebecca. "I'll put your things on the kitchen table for you."

"Thank you, Ed."

Hester patted Ed's stomach. "Well, there's egg salad sandwiches in the fridge in case you're hungry."

"You know me too well, Mother." Leaning, he tenderly kissed her lips.

In jest, Hester raised a hand and gently stroked his face.

Rebecca stood off to the side, a fortunate spectator to the enormity of their love in play once more. She felt happy and terribly sad. Happy that two people could be so romantic with each other after so long and sad that she would be leaving soon. She had to. Something stronger than fate was calling to her.

Ed stood tall and headed toward the house.

Hester admired him until he disappeared beyond the side door. "He's still got a nice bottom, don't you think, Rebecca?"

Rebecca giggled. "I guess so. Though I can't say that I've intentionally noticed."

"You should find such a man some day." Patting the empty space next to her, she said, "Come, sit down. How did you like our little town? Quaint, isn't it?"

Rebecca took a seat next to Hester, and crossed one leg over the other. "It's very nice. And the people are wonderful. And I just love the Valentine's Day in July idea. The whole town seems caught up in it."

"What do you think of our Mr. Sonjee? Quite a character, isn't he?"

"You can say that again. He doesn't even know me, and he offered me a job. Just like that." She snapped her fingers. As if the snap of her fingers could somehow summon nature, a monarch butterfly flittered sporadically under the umbrella and over Hester's shoulder. It came to rest on the larger of the two crosses. Both women watched as it moved its wings rhythmically.

"Beautiful, isn't it?" said Hester. "You don't see many monarchs in these parts."

"This may sound weird, but it seems as though it's paying its respects." In that moment, something moved through Rebecca, warm, playful, frolicsome. Then the sound of Caleb's laughter filled the air around her. "*Catch me if you can, Chase.*"

"Not at all. This area seems to attract all manner of nature. As God is my witness, I once saw it rain, just here, over the garden, while the sun still shone. And another time, while I was out hanging laundry, this was back in the midseventies, a bear came snooping around. The gate to the garden was open, so he waltzed right in. I thought for sure he was going to tear things up. Instead, it sniffed the air for a moment as if it were sampling the roses, then lay down at the foot of the crosses and took a nap. That's the honest-to-God truth."

"Remarkable. But it doesn't surprise me in the least. Caleb's love of life is still very strong. You must believe that." The butterfly took flight, and floated out of the garden. It headed in the direction of the barn without notice from the swallows.

"Oh, I do, my dear. I do. Now tell me more about your trip into our town."

Rebecca told her about meeting Mabel Helpnot and Jason the teenager who fell madly in love with her. About Louise Dubauex who seemed to have an eye for Ed and how most of the stores were already decorated for the upcoming dance. About her brief visit at the church and meeting the nice Father Murphy. When she was done, she told Hester that she was going to do the breakfast pans, and if it was all right with her, she was going to take a bath and change her bandage.

"Of course, my dear. You'll find clean towels in the linen closet on the second floor, and there's bubble bath and bandages beneath the sink in the bathroom. You'll have to wait a few minutes for the water to get hot, but once it does, there's plenty of it." Lifting her glasses, she rested them on the bridge of her nose. "I think I'll stay out here a while longer and finish this chapter. Be a dear and ask Ed, that's my husband, to make me a nice cup of tea."

"Of course. Anything else?"

"No, a cup of tea will do nicely."

Rebecca left the garden feeling reinvigorated. Caleb's little adventure was surely a good sign for things to come.

* * *

Done with the dishes, Rebecca went upstairs to the bathroom and closed the door. She rested her new brush and paste on the sink then turned on the faucet and waited until the water became hot before stopping the drain.

There was a window over the tub facing the rear of the yard, so she looked down into the property. Ed and Hester were seated at the bench. Hester was enjoying the tea Ed had made her, and Ed seemed to be gazing at the burial site, hands clasped and head slightly bowed as if in prayer. It could have been a painting, something Renoir would have created. A still life moment Rebecca felt strongly would remain with her for the rest of her life.

Stripping out of her clothes, she set them on the lid of the toilet and found the bubble bath and bandages under the sink just where Hester said they would be. Upon further inspection, she also found Head and Shoulders, a nail clipper, and a bottle of mint Scope.

Adding a good dollop of soap to the water, she adjusted the temperature to just barely tolerable, sat on the edge of the tub, and with one quick rip, removed the gauze covering her knee. It looked much better than the previous day. Pus no longer leaked from the wound that was now showing signs of restoration. The opposite knee was nearly healed to normal.

Using the clippers, she evened her broken fingernails best she could and clipped her toes. Examining her entire body, she realized she had lost some weight and that her legs were in desperate need of a shave.

Testing the water with a toe, she found it to be tolerable, the bath soap having created mountains of foam that rose above the edge of the tub. She shut the water off.

The mirrored facade of the medicine cabinet over the sink offered a good glimpse of what she looked like. A fresh pimple sat angry at the side of her nose, and she was suddenly embarrassed that people had seen her with such an abomination. Popping it with the tips of her fingers, she wiped the yellow discharge with some tissue. *Yuck.* Removing the cap from the Scope, she took in a mouthful and swished and gargled until the inside of her mouth felt relatively clean. Spitting out the green, she proceeded to brush her teeth.

Once finished, she rinsed her mouth and inspected her teeth in the mirror. Because it had been a while between brushings, a portion of her gums were bleeding. *But oh god, I feel human again.*

An inspection of the medicine cabinet produced a pack of blue Bic Razors. She took one, hoping Ed wouldn't mind too much, then set the Head and Shoulders on the floor next to the tub where she could reach it.

Slowly she immersed herself into the water, razor in hand, and slunk down until the bubbles covered her to her shoulders. Her breasts reacted to the heat, nipples felt as though they could explode. Closing her eyes, she waited for her body to adjust to the temperate water. In her mind's eye, the town of Valentine came to life. She imagined Main Street full of people all wearing red, dancing while a band played on. Streamers and hearts and Cupids decorated every available space of storefronts. Mr. Sonjee had an outdoor booth and was selling meat, holding large fillets of steaks in his hands and calling out, "My very best special for such beautiful meat."

The visual caused Rebecca to laugh aloud. She opened her eyes, pinched her nose and dunked her head beneath the surface until her hair was good and wet. With a handful of blue dandruff-fighting exfoliants, she washed, rinsed, then repeated the process. When she was done, she lifted one freckled leg from the water, removed the protective guard on the razor, and stroked away the red stubble that had sprouted over the past week. Repeating the process on the other leg, she was careful not to get too close to the damaged knee. Tossing the razor to the floor, she closed her eyes and relaxed.

Soon, the image of her dream lover came into view, his virility filling her mind. He was standing tall in a field, a range of mountains in the backdrop, his long hair blowing in a playful wind. Next to him stood a pine tree as tall as the sky. He held out his arms and mouthed the words, *Come to me.*

And so, in the privacy of Ed and Hester's bathroom, Rebecca did, willingly, completely, surrendering to a man she had never met.

* * *

After the delicious barbeque of steak, corn, and Hester's world-famous potato salad, the three sat at a picnic table, stuffed and a little weary from overindulging.

It was seven o'clock, the sun still strong in the sky. The red-white–and-blue umbrella in the center of the table offered them a fair amount of shade and the iced tea Hester made cooled their insides.

During the meal, a few annoying wasps had buzzed the table and were quickly dashed by the surprisingly quick hand of Hester, who put them out of their misery with the aid of a swatter. "Little buggers," she had commented. "I hate to do it, but they just don't get the message they're unwanted."

Ed picked meat from his teeth with a length of straw that was in no shortage of supply all around them. The coals in the grill were still red-hot. Waves of heat and the aroma of already-consumed steak rose into the air.

Crows had gathered at the edge of the pines, and waited for anything they could salvage. They seemed to be fighting among one another as to who would be first to swoop down and get the initial crack at leftovers. Their disruptive cackle echoed loud in the open space.

"Bloody scavengers," said Ed, the straw probing the spaces between his teeth. "Too bad you can't eat them. We'd be in meat for the rest of our lives."

"Ed, that's terrible," said Hester, grinning. "They're one of God's creatures and serve a purpose just like the deer, the worms in the ground, and even those annoying wasps. If they didn't, do you think God would have put them on this earth?"

"I suppose not. Still wouldn't be too brokenhearted if the damn things suddenly became extinct."

"Give mankind enough time. He'll figure out a way," replied Hester in a venomous tone.

"Well, I don't know about you two," piped Rebecca. "But I'm stuffed. That was delicious. And the steaks were cooked to perfection."

Puffing his already-mammoth chest, Ed tossed the piece of straw to the ground. "Well, if I don't mind saying so, I do know my way around a grill." He patted his enormous stomach the sound of which was not unlike the probing of a watermelon. "This didn't come from love alone you know."

Rebecca stood and picked up the plates. "Now I don't want any arguments from either of you. I'm going to clean up, you just sit and enjoy the evening."

"Are you sure, Rebecca?" asked Hester.

"Absolutely. What you can do is come up with some questions you would like me to ask Caleb. I think we'll go to the barn after I've cleared everything. I believe it's time we tried."

Hester's and Ed's faces lifted into beams of joy. "Oh, that would be wonderful, my dear," chimed Hester.

"Are you sure you're ready, Rebecca?" asked Ed.

"Ready as I'll ever be I guess. His presence was very strong today, and I'm feeling much much better."

Ed and Hester stared into each other. There was so much hope, so much desire between them that time seemed to reverse itself. They looked decades younger.

Gathering the plates, utensils, and condiments, Rebecca took everything to the kitchen where she scraped the plates clean and put them into the dishwasher. Through the window over the sink, she looked to the garden and crosses.

The evening sun strafed the roses in a brilliant shaft of light, igniting the horde of insects raiding the red and yellow blooms. The murder of crows sitting among the pines continued their squabbling and intermittent flights from one treetop to another. To Rebecca, their antics seemed more brutish than playful.

Turning on the faucet, she squirted some dish soap into her hands and washed. *Please, Caleb,* she wished. *If there ever was a time to show yourself, let it be today.*

* * *

With Rebecca in the lead, the three walked toward the barn. Ed and Hester held hands, smiling at each other. Rebecca's fingers toyed with the tips of tall grasses. No one said a word until they arrived at the double wide doors.

"You better let me pry them open," said Ed. He stepped in front of Rebecca. "Sometimes after a heavy rain like we had, they have a tendency to get stuck."

Rebecca and Hester stood back.

Ed fit his hands into a narrow gap and heaved with all his weight. At first, nothing happened. "Just as I thought. They're good and stuck." A second try garnished a groan from the wood, and the door swung reluctantly open. "After you, ladies," said Ed , half-bowing.

Hester gushed. "Why, thank you, kind sir. Whoever said chivalry was dead."

By the open door and with shafts of sunlight beaming from the cavities in the roof, the interior and all its contents came to life.

Moving to the center of the barn, each searched with their eyes. The pigeons that had earlier been stationed on the roof were back to their posts, one next to the other on the heavy cross beams. They cooed en masse. The human nest Rebecca had made brought back an instant memory. The first time she was visited by Caleb and Chase. "*I'm six, almost seven,*" his tiny voice resounded.

Ed held Hester by the waist while Rebecca walked the perimeter of the dirt floor. She tried to get a feel or a sense that Caleb's presence was with them. She felt nothing and was suddenly fearful that she would not be able to attach herself to the entity that was Caleb Hart. She went to Ed and Hester. "I'm not getting anything," she said honestly. "It's like the barn is just that, an empty barn."

Hester looked to Ed then back to Rebecca. "Perhaps you should try calling to him? Maybe that will work."

"Let's hope so. Like I said, I've never done this before." Closing her eyes, Rebecca concentrated. "Caleb, are you here? It's Rebecca. Remember me? Your mommy and daddy are with me. They would like to talk to you."

The only reply she received was the sudden silence of the pigeons that stared at her from above. She tried again. "Caleb. I know this is your favorite place to be, so please, if you can hear me, show yourself. We're all here for you, Caleb. You're a very special boy."

For twenty minutes she tried, and managed only silence. The sun had begun its descent. Angled shafts of light leeched from the wounded roof.

"I don't know what to say except I'm sorry," said Rebecca.

"Don't be. You gave it a good try. Perhaps another time." Hester gave her a quick smile though deep inside she was feeling remorseful and a little aggrieved.

"Yes. You tried, and that's all we could ask for," said Ed. He put his hands on Hester's shoulders. "Come on, Mother. Maybe we should go back to the house."

Hester reached up and patted his hands.

Rebecca wanted to cry. In silence, the three walked toward the barn entrance, heads held kind of low, emotions bottled inside.

"*Here I am.*"

Rebecca stopped in her tracks and turned around.

"What is it, my dear?"

"He's here! Caleb is here!" said an elated Rebecca.

All three moved back to the center of the barn.

"Where are you, Caleb?" asked Rebecca.

"I'm up here, silly."

Rebecca looked to the pitch of the barn. Ed and Hester did the same. Standing on one of the support beams, arms outstretched as he fought for balance was Caleb Hart, face all aglow, outfitted in the coveralls and red checkered shirt he had passed away in.

Rebecca had wondered often how this was possible. Clothes and personal items held no soul, so how was it that they became a part of the afterlife? It was the same with her mother. Upon each visit, Deseray White wore the same items she had passed away in. It was as much a mystery as her sudden introduction into the world of the dead. Questions that held no answers.

"Hi, Mommy. Hi, Daddy. Hi, Rebecca. Jeepers, it's swell to see you."

"Caleb says hello," said Rebecca.

With her eyes moist, Hester spoke, "Hello, my darling."

"Hello, son." Ed's voice was choked. "Can he hear us?"

"Course I can hear you. I hear you all the time."

"He says he can hear you just fine," confirmed Rebecca. "Caleb, can you come down so we can talk?"

"I like it up here."

"Yes, I know, but just come down for a little while, okay?"

"Oh, all right." In a blink, he was gone.

Rebecca's eyes searched the barn. "He said he's going to come down," she told the Harts who were now gathered in each other's arms.

"Where are you now, Caleb?"

"Why, I'm over here."

Rebecca followed his voice. Caleb now stood in front of the nest she had made. "He's standing right over there by the straw bed."

"Oh, how I wish I could see him," said Hester, her desire giving lift to her voice.

"Maybe if you close your eyes and listen to what he has to say, your memories of him will be just as strong," offered Rebecca.

Tightly wound in each other's arms, Hester and Ed closed their eyes.

"Caleb?"

"Yes."

"You do know that your mommy and daddy can't see you, don't you? That you're not the same as us?"

"Yes, I know, though I tried really hard. But they're not like you, are they? You're special... and pretty."

"Thank you, Caleb. I think you're pretty handsome yourself. He says he knows that you can't see him. He seems to understand his... his situation."

"Oh, but I can see him. I can," beamed Hester. "Can you see him, my love?"

"Yes, I can, Mother. Is Chase with him?"

"Chase is outside," answered Caleb. *"I'm hiding on him."*

"He says Chase is outside. I guess they're playing hide-and-seek."

"Would you like me to call him? He's such a silly. He hardly ever finds me anyway."

"That would be nice, Caleb."

Moving toward the center of the barn, Caleb looked to his parents. His little hands touched theirs, and he smiled up at them. *"Jeepers, I wish they could see me, Rebecca. It's not fair."*

"He's standing right in front of you, touching you and smiling. He says he wishes you could see him."

"Oh, my beautiful boy. Mommy and Daddy miss you very much." Hester let go of Ed and reached out. Her hands passed through Caleb's body as if he were made of smoke.

"That tickles."

"Somehow he is able to feel you touching him. He says it tickles."

Hester opened her eyes. Ed did the same. Opening their arms, they chorused, "Can we have hug, Caleb? Like old times."

"Sure." Caleb moved into their open arms. *"I love you, Mommy. I love you, Daddy. I'm with you all the time. I kiss you both good night at bedtime."*

"He said that he loves you and that he is with you all the time. That he kisses you both good night each and every night." Rebecca was fighting hard to keep herself from crying.

Without being called, Chase came bounding through the barn wall. He landed on all fours, head swiveling in all directions, the perfect red heart on the side of his massive chest as bright as one of the roses in Hester's garden. When he saw Caleb, he headed straight for him.

Caleb moved out from Ed's and Hester's arms. *"You found me!"* Offering his face, the big dog licked it from brow to chin. *"Give me a hug!"*

Rearing on hind legs, balanced by his tail, Caleb's bestest friend in the whole world presented his outstretched paws.

"Chase is now in the barn," said Rebecca. "He and Caleb are hugging right next to you. Oh, I wish you could see this. It's so… so beautiful." A tear slid over her cheek.

Ed took Hester back into his arms. "Caleb? Can I ask you something?"

Caleb and Chase parted. The big dog circled Ed and Hester and sat on his haunches next to Ed's left leg. He looked up as if he were expecting a command, pink tongue lolling from the side of his mouth. *"Sure, Daddy,"* answered Caleb. He looked up at his father, a great fondness lighting his eyes.

"He said yes. He's looking right at you, Ed."

Behind lenses, a shroud of tears filled Ed's eyes. He lifted the frame and knuckled them away. "Are you all right, son? I mean… you're not in any kind of discomfort, are you?"

"Course not. Me and Chase, we play all day. Except for the dark time."

"He says he and Chase play all day. But there seems to be a period that he calls the dark time."

"What's the dark time?" asked a concerned Hester.

"It's just, you know. A place. I have to go there every now and then. Sometimes during the day. Sometimes at night. It's cold, but I don't mind. Sometimes there's other people there, but mostly not. Chase is always with me though."

"It's just a place. Other than here. He says that he sometimes meets other people like him. But most of the time it's just him and Chase." Rebecca moved to where Caleb and Chase were. "Caleb?"

"Yes, Rebecca."

"One time you played the piano. Do you remember?"

"Yes. But it was hard to do. I had to really try. I like to listen to my daddy play the piano. He's really good. Don't you think? Sometimes I sit right next to him. Sometimes me and Chase dance."

"Do you think you can try again. For your mommy and daddy. They tell me you play wonderfully."

"Oh, that would be so wonderful, Caleb," said Hester.

"I guess I can try again, Mommy. It makes me tired though. Then I have to go to the dark place."

"He said he will try again. But it's hard, and it makes him tired." Rebecca left out the part about returning to the dark place, deciding that it would only concern Hester and Ed needlessly.

The lighting changed as the sun set further.

Caleb pulled a red ball from his back pocket. *"Fetch, Chase."* He threw it, and it went straight through the wall of the barn. Chase bounded after it, thick tail looping with joy, and, like the ball, went clean through the wood.

"He's such a good fetcher. Don't you think, Rebecca? I taught him myself."

"Yes, he is, Caleb. You did a really good job." She looked to Hester and Ed. "He just threw a red ball, and Chase is gone to fetch it."

"It only took that boy a couple of days to teach him to do that," Ed pointed out.

In the next instant, Chase came through the wall with the ball in his mouth. He returned it to Caleb, prancing proudly and dropped it at his feet.

"Good boy." Caleb reached down and put the ball into his back pocket.

The great dog raised a paw, wanting to shake hands, which they did. Suddenly, Caleb's spirit began to fade. *"I'm getting tired now, Rebecca. We've been playing all day."*

"Try to hang on for just a few more minutes, okay?"

"I'll try. But it's hard."

"What's wrong?" Ed and Hester said simultaneously.

"He's getting tired. His spirit is beginning to fade."

"But there's so much more I want to ask him," said Hester.

"There there, Mother. Perhaps another time," said Ed comfortingly. He looked to Rebecca, his eyes pleaded that there would be another time. "Caleb?" he asked.

Caleb looked up to his parents. *"Yes, Daddy."*

"He is waiting for your question," said Rebecca.

"Do you walk with God, son?"

"God? I never met him. I only meet people like us."

It was an answer Rebecca feared and dreaded to hear. She knew she had to lie to the Harts for their peace of mind. *May Father Murphy forgive me.* "He said he's not sure."

Caleb turned to look at Rebecca. *"You told a fib. Naughty, naughty, naughty."*

"Yes, but you do understand, don't you?"

"I guess so. It's what Mommy and Daddy want to hear. They pray to him all the time."

"You're such a smart boy."

"Rootin' tootin'."

"What did he mean by he's not sure?" asked Hester. "And what does he understand?"

"Well, he says he meets other people. Maybe God is one of them. None of us will ever know for sure until our time comes. He understands that his answer might seem a bit problematic, but it's all he knows. He *is* a very smart little boy."

The Harts gushed with pride and put aside for the moment that their beliefs, that everything they revered to be accurate as far as their faith was concerned had now changed.

"Rebecca?"

"Yes, Caleb."

"I knew you would come. I just knew it. Only you could bring us together. But you're going to leave us, aren't you?"

Rebecca did not know what to say, so she just said, "Yes."

"I'll try to do what you asked. You know, play the piano. I play 'Twinkle, Twinkle, Little Star' real good. It's my mommy's favorite. Tell Mommy and Daddy that I will really try." His spirit faded to the point that he was now transparent.

"Caleb is really going to put an effort into playing the piano for you. But he's fading rapidly. If there's anything you want to say, you better make it fast."

"Do you really visit us every night, Caleb?" asked Hester.

"Rootin' tootin'. I kiss you on the cheek. Sometimes you smile even though Daddy snores loud. Sometimes I sit in the garden with you while you're reading. But I don't go near the road. It's too dangerous." He yawned. *"Oops. Pardon me. I really have to go now, Rebecca. Tell them not to be sad anymore. They've been sad for too long."* His body regressed. Only his head remained, floating in the air like a balloon.

"Every night, he says. He also says that he sits with *you*, Hester, while you're in the garden reading. And that he sits next to you, Ed, while you're playing the piano. He doesn't want you to be sad any longer. But he is almost gone now. You better say your good-byes."

Tears spilled from Hester's eyes. "Good night, my beautiful boy. Good night, Chase."

"Good night, son. See you, boy. You keep Caleb safe, you hear."

The grand dog pawed at the air.

"Good night, Mommy. Good night, Daddy. Don't let the bed bugs bite." Then he was gone. Chase stood, ran toward the barn entrance, and barked excitedly just before his sow sized body flew through the air and he too disappeared.

"They're gone now," said Rebecca.

Ed pulled Hester into his arms. "That was really something. Wasn't it, Mother?"

"I'll never forget what you've done for us, Rebecca. You're a godsend."

"I'm just glad I was able to do something for you. But I'm really tired now. It seems that Caleb was drawing energy from me. Perhaps we should go back to the house. I think I'll make it an early night if you don't mind."

"Not at all," said Ed. "I can imagine something like this was draining. Although I don't know if I'll be able to sleep tonight. Too many things going on in my head."

They left the barn. Ed drew the doors shut.

The sun was near to its final plunge yonder the horizon. Shadows emerged all around. A few early stars flickered in the heavens. The first quarter of a new moon held its place in the eastern sky. The crows had resigned to wherever it was that crows went to at night, and the air was still, silent, except for a hoot owl somewhere in the woods. They walked through the tall grasses in silence. Ed held Hester's hand. Hester's grey head rested blithely on his enormous chest.

Rebecca's thoughts focused on what she was going to do next. She hated to leave, but knew that if she stayed any longer, she might end up a permanent resident, she liked Hester and Ed Hart that much.

There was no threat of rain. The temperature was perfect. It was going to be a good night to travel.

* * *

Rebecca lay under the comforter, fully clothed, and listened to Ed softly play the piano. It was several ticks past 9:00 p.m. Oncoming dark spilled through the open window. She imagined Caleb sitting next to Ed, his head bobbing to the music and Chase prancing around the room, the vision forever ensconced in her mind.

Certain that everything she owned was securely locked within the confines of the suitcase waiting at the foot of the bed, she had slipped under the covers and bid her time. Her jean jacket rested on the arm of the rocker. Dead tired, she fought the urge to close her eyes, for if she had, she was certain that she would not wake until morning.

Her plan was to wait until Ed and Hester were sound asleep. The miraculous incident in the barn would keep them awake well beyond their habitual attitude she knew. Regardless, they were old, and old people needed their rest. Then she would quietly sneak out of the house and begin the next chapter of her journey.

* * *

It was several hours before the piano music ceased. A few minutes later, Rebecca heard the stairs groan under Ed's lumbering weight as he ascended the steps. He and Hester spoke in low tones. Then she heard the door to their room close, the sound of which was followed by the squeak of springs as they crawled into bed.

In the silence that followed, Rebecca waited, anticipating that it would not be too much longer before the sounds of sleep became apparent. Ed Hart snored like an erupting volcano. She wondered how Hester got any rest, but she supposed that it was like getting used to the sound of a passing train in the dead of night. After nearly sixty years of marriage, Hester had become accustomed to the nights sounds of her forever love.

It was another hour before Rebecca was certain that Ed and Hester had fallen asleep. She threw back the covers back, slipped out of Caleb Hart's little bed, put on the jacket, lifted the suitcase, and quietly opened the door.

Ed's deep snuffle was magnified tenfold. Slowly she descended the stairs. When she reached bottom, she looked up into the darkness. "Good-bye, Ed. Good-bye, Hester. Thank you for everything." She made her way into the kitchen where the small watt bulb of the stove kept it alight. Just as she was about to open the side door, she felt guilty about not leaving them some sort of explanation, so she found some manila paper and pen in a drawer and quickly wrote a note.

Dear Ed and Hester,

I'm sorry for sneaking off like this, but I know that if I told you about my plans, you would have tried to talk me out of it. I must follow the call that has been urging me for quite some time now. I hope you understand. I will never forget you and Caleb and his best friend Chase. What we shared together was more than special. I promise that should I find myself in Kentucky again, I will drop by to see my most favorite people in the world. Have a great time at the Valentine's Day in July celebration.

Love,

Rebecca PS. Listen for the music.

She set the note beneath the vase of roses centering the kitchen table. Taking one, she put it in the breast pocket of her jacket. Its perfume filled the area beneath her chin, her delicate nose. When she opened the door and stepped outside, the night air wrapped itself around her as if to whisk her away.

The sky was an explosion of dazzling lights. The moon, a bright Colgate smile that beamed down upon her. Somewhere nearby, covert crickets orchestrated their night song.

Rebecca headed for the road, suitcase banging against her leg. However, the light attached to the barn seemed to beckon her once again. An idea came to mind. It would be the perfect farewell to a boy she had only met in death.

She moved swiftly across the field, tall grasses lashed at her legs. The redolent flavor of roses filled her senses. When she got to the barn, she entered through the side door.

Although the moon was only in its first quarter, enough of its shine bled from the divisions in the roof, allowing Rebecca to make out the interior and do what she had to do, what she needed to do. She went to the nest she had made on that stormy night, and remembered the first time she laid eyes on Caleb and his "bestest friend in the whole world." There, she set the suitcase down and opened it. Removing Bandit the bear, she hugged it, kissed it on its snout, and whispered, "I'm going to miss you, but you're needed here." When she sat the stuffed bruin against the support beam, a solemn tear slid over her cheek. She backhanded it away, and took a deep breath. She fastened the locks on the suitcase and lifted it from the dirt floor. She knew it was impossible, but it seemed lighter somehow, as if the weight of her youth had been abruptly taken away.

Before exiting the barn, she called out, "Good-bye, Caleb. Good-bye, Chase. Jeepers, it was swell to meet you."

And so, Rebecca White, in the dead of night, with nothing to guide her except for an impaired sixth sense, the crest of a smiling moon and a call that had been beckoning her since childhood, began a new and uncertain chapter in the journey she called her life.

Another page turned.

* * *

BOOK TWO

Fallen Angel

28

In God We Trust

TWO days and three rides later, Rebecca found herself in a Flagstone, Arizona, McDonald's, one state away from her destination. She sat at a table where, through a pane of glass, she could take in the mostly full parking lot and people watch.

The rides she managed to obtain were from exceedingly diverse personalities. A trucker whose handle was Hemp because he smoked a lot of pot, even while driving, which made Rebecca a little nervous and somewhat paranoid. Nonetheless, he got her to where he promised, Tulsa, Oklahoma, before dropping her off, claiming that he had a crop of *primo buds* he needed to check on.

The second was from a group of college students, three girls and four boys in an old Volkswagen van who were exploring the country for the ultimate party. They took her to the Texas–New Mexico border, paying her way whenever they stopped for food or gas. Rebecca had insisted she pay her share, only to be chided by the driver, a husky young man named Mark McElroy whom she kind of liked. Her money was no good, he told her, considering Rebecca to be a good omen. They'd insisted that she join them in their search, which she graciously declined, citing that she too had a destiny and it didn't include spending the rest of the summer drunk and stoned to which they all laughed. During this brief friendship, Rebecca had procured a new pair of runners at a gas station which Mark insisted on paying for as well.

Third was from a forty two-year-old woman in a station wagon that had no business being on the road. She called herself Sky, christened so by parents who had attended Woodstock in '69. Conceived while the likes of Jimmy Hendrix, Crosby, Stills and Nash, Joe Cocker, and Janis Joplin filled the air around Max Yasgur's farm with sound while the sons of America were sent to an unpopular war. She had pink-and-blue hair and wore bug-eyed sunglasses, even at night when they drove through New Mexico.

On the backseat of the wagon was a six-string acoustic her father had insisted she learn to play autographed by Carly Simon, dated 1972. Also seated in the back was the spirit of Harry Chapin, though Rebecca made no mention of him. He remained with them through New Mexico, singing with the radio tuned to a station airing music from the decade of peace, love, and war protests. Then he simply vanished sometime in the early hours of dawn. Rebecca had the notion that he often took rides in the backseats of peoples cars so he could listen to the radios and relive the days of his time.

When they'd arrived in Flagstone, it was near lunch hour, so Rebecca asked to be let out at the nearest restaurant which just happened to be a McDonalds. Sky drove away under a plume of blue exhaust emanating from the rear of the unbalanced wagon. She never did tell Rebecca where she was headed.

It was a hundred-plus degrees in Flagstone, so the cool interior was as welcoming as an oasis in the middle of a desert. Rebecca lifted the suitcase and placed it on the table in front of her, flipped the latches, and retrieved the envelope that contained all of her money. To her surprise, she found an extra two hundred dollars and a note from Hester Hart. She held the square piece of paper close and read.

Dear Rebecca,

I knew you were going to leave us soon, so I took the opportunity while you and Ed were shopping in Valentine to add a little more to your possessions. I know it's not much, but I hope it helps. I can't tell you what a pleasure it was having you with us. You were like a breath of fresh air in the lives of two people who were otherwise going through the passages of old age with nothing to look forward to. I hope you find what it is you're looking for. Should you ever feel the need to return to us, our door will always be open.

Forever your friend,
Hester

Rebecca's eyes moistened. Folding the note, she put it back into the suitcase under the picture of her mother. Sniffing tears, she took a ten from the now-beefy roll, stuffed the rest back into the envelope, closed the suitcase, and tucked it under the table.

For a moment she thought about Caleb, a lovely boy who would always remain six, almost seven, and his bestest friend in the world, Chase. That they would forever be each other's companion in a world of the nonliving. Kindred spirits to freely play among the roses and hide from each other in the only place they knew as home. How so unfair it was that two such wonderful people like Hester and Ed had to endure the grief-filled life that was bestowed upon them in an unjust instant. She hoped that her gifted deeds gave them something to hold on to other than each other. That maybe one day, Caleb would once again find the strength needed to tickle the ivory keys for them.

After ordering a number one—Big Mac, fries, and a medium Coke—she returned to the table and dug in, keeping her eyes on the patrons for the next ride that would take her possibly all the way to Vegas. She reminisced about maybe using some of the extra money and take the Greyhound, then decided she would need all the money she could get her hands on in order to survive her first few days in Sin City. She would just have to bide her time and hope that her next ride was just around the corner.

When she'd dunked the last of her fries into the cup of ketchup, she noticed a silver Freightliner cab without trailer pull into the parking lot. The driver, a belly of a man with snow white hair and wearing a T-shirt that captioned Jesus Is Lord, stepped down from the cab. His round face was accented by rosy cheeks that were puffed as if he had a mouthful of apples. Even from the distance between them, Rebecca could clearly see the gold chain and cross he wore around his neck glinting in the merciless sunlight. He wore a smile on his face and bore the aura of a saint. The pleasant man pulled a hanky from a back pocket and wiped at his forehead while he ostensibly surveyed the sky.

She watched him enter the restaurant. For a brief second, their eyes met as he sought a place to sit in the increasingly busy establishment. Rebecca smiled, and he smiled back respectively. Then she noticed that the pinky finger of his plump right hand was missing. She looked to the tray and its empty containers, feeling, for reasons unbeknown to her, sorry for him. *How had he lost that finger?* she wondered.

A few minutes later, the trucker stood in the middle of the restaurant, balancing a tray in his hands while his eyes searched for a place to sit. He went up one aisle and down the other, his belt busting belly jiggling like a bowl of Jell-O when he moved. As he approached Rebecca's table, she felt that it would do no harm in offering him her spot since she had already finished the number one brunch. "Excuse me, sir."

He smiled down at her with the kindest blue eyes she had ever seen.

"You can have my place. I've finished my lunch." She smiled back.

"God bless you. Thank you very much. Kind of crowded in here." He noticed Rebecca still had a half-full container of Coke. "But you haven't finished. You still have some drink left. I'll tell you what. I'll take you up on your generous offer if you keep a tired old man company while you finish your drink. I could use some pleasant conversation."

"Deal," said Rebecca. It was the perfect opportunity for her to learn where he was heading.

The trucker placed his tray of large coffee, fries, three containers of ketchup and cheeseburger on the table, and squeezed his large frame between the table's edge and the permanently fastened seat meant for people half his size. "Boy, they sure don't make it easy," he said, and they laughed. "My name's Henry. Henry Klondike. Like the chocolate bar." He extended a hand.

"I'm Rebecca," said Rebecca, and received his large hand into hers. "Pleased to meet you."

Henry then took the lid off his coffee, added two packs of sugar and a thimble of cream, blew over the rim, and took a sip. "Boy, that's some good coffee they're serving up these days." Unwrapping the burger, he took a healthy bite. "I see by your suitcase, Rebecca, that you're either coming into Flagstone or just passing through. Which is it if you don't mind my asking?"

"That's very observant of you, Henry. Still going."

"Well, you're too young and too pretty to be in any kind of trouble with the law, so I'm guessing that there's either been trouble at home or you're on a quest of some sort." Soft blue eyes twinkled with life.

"I suppose you can call it a quest," offered Rebecca. "How about you? Do you live here, or are you just passing through?"

"On my way to Cedar City, Utah. Got a load to pick up there. Then it's off to Wyoming. Say, you wouldn't happen to be going that way, would you? We could ride together. I sure could use the company, and I'm certain the good Lord brought us together for a reason. Praise be his name." He lifted the crucifix, and touched it to his lips.

Rebecca reflected for a moment. If her geography was correct, Cedar City, Utah, was just a stone's throw away from Vegas, at least on a map anyway. There seemed to be no reason not to trust this man of God. She was on a good roll as far as rides were concerned, and her internal radar was not giving her reason to not trust the person seated across from her. "To be honest, Henry, I'm on my way to Las Vegas."

Henry looked at her, puzzled. "Now why would a nice young girl like you want to go to that din of sin? Far as I'm concerned, that place should be bulldozed. It's an affront to God I tell you."

Rebecca could see that he was getting upset. His already-robust cheeks had turned a shade of scarlet, so she told him a small lie. "I'm visiting friends for the rest of the summer. You can set your mind at ease. I have no intention of getting involved in the sleazy part. Just going to spend my time there lying around my friend's pool. Then it's back home."

Henry took another chomp of burger and dipped a handful of fries into the ketchup. He loaded his mouth until his cheeks looked like they would literally burst. When he'd chewed and swallowed, he asked, "And your parents are okay with that?"

"They let me hitchhike across the country, didn't they? Besides, I'm old enough to take care of myself, and you yourself said the good Lord must have brought us together for a reason." She knew she was being sassy; however, all she wanted was a ride and not a lecture on the dos and don'ts of life as far as Henry Klondike understood them.

Henry calculated Rebecca for a moment. The fingers of his left hand drummed the table. After a brief spell he said, "Well, the good Lord does work in mysterious ways. He wouldn't have had you land in my lap without good reason. I guess if it's okay with him, then it's okay by me. Praise be His name."

"Good, I'm glad. You seem like a very nice man, and I was hoping to get to Vegas by tomorrow."

"Tomorrow you say. Well, I have a great idea. I have a friend who lives not too far from Cedar City who just happens to owe me a favor. I bet you dollars to donuts that if I asked him, he'd be willing to take you all the way to Vegas. It's only a couple-hour drive, and like I said, he owes me a big big favor."

Rebecca's heart soared. "You'd be willing to do that for me? Do you really think your friend would take me there? That would be so awesome. I can't believe my luck. I'm so glad I asked you to sit at this table."

"You must have an angel watching over you. Rebecca. I'll radio him when we get close enough. He has a two-way at home and always has his ears on. I'm sure he'd be willing to oblige an old friend."

Rebecca could feel her face flush. This was too good to be true. Two days ago, she was in Valentine, Kentucky, and now she was a state and a couple of rides away from her objective. "I don't know what to say, Henry. Thank you. Thank you very much. Of course I'll help pay for gas. I have some money."

"Out of the question. I was going in that direction anyway. You hang on to your money. Vegas can be expensive even if you're staying with friends. Just promise me you'll call your folks. Let them know you're safe. There's a pay phone in the entrance.

I'm sure they'd be glad to hear from you." Stuffing the remainder of burger into his mouth, he took a good drink of java.

Somewhere behind them, a child scolded his mother for not allowing him to have a toy. "You're not being fair. You're mean. I hate you. Daddy always lets me have a toy. I'll be good. I promise..."

"I'll call them right now while you finish your lunch. I'll be back in a minute." Rebecca got up from her seat, fished in her denim shorts for change, then went to the pay phone at the entrance. Lifting the receiver, she pretended to drop in change just in case Henry Klondike was watching, then carried on a one-way conversation with the dial tone for several minutes before returning to the pleasant man of god.

"There. All done. I told my mother about you and your kind offer, and she said to thank you. So on behalf of my mother, thank you."

"Good," said Henry Klondike. H wiped at his mouth with a napkin. "I'm just going to use the bathroom, then we'll be on our way. Wait for me by that silver Freightliner out there." He rose with difficulty, picked up the tray, and emptied it in one of the garbage disposals then disappeared into the men's room.

Rebecca retrieved her suitcase, feeling a little out of sorts that she had to reduce herself to such low levels just for a ride; however, what had to be done had to be done. She stepped outside into the hundred-plus degrees. As she approached the Freightliner, her arms and legs began to tingle. She ignored the warning, feeling completely safe with the God-fearing Henry Klondike, figuring her internal radar, her reliable sixth sense, was jammed, like it had been since she left Bay Ridge Cove. There cannot be any other explanation, she told herself. The man she had just met was as gentle and meek as a lamb. She was absolutely sure of it. She waited by the passenger door where she rested the suitcase on the ground. There was a large yellow decal on the door just below the handle, IN GOD WE TRUST.

* * *

Henry Klondike entered one of the stalls and locked the door behind him. When the man using the urinal had washed and left, he pulled out his cell phone, scrolled for the right number and waited. Someone picked up after the third ring. "Yes."

"It's me, Preacher," said Henry in a slippery tone. "I have a little gift for you."

"Good," said the voice on the other end.

"Still five large, right?"

"Correct."

"Meet me at the rest stop just before Saint George Park in four hours. You're a friend of mine. Peter Brown. You owe me a favor. You're going to give her a ride."

"Four hours. Favor. Friend. Got it."

The line went dead.

The Preacher closed the cell and returned it to a pocket. He looked at the four fingers of his right hand, the hard lesson he had to pay for a debt not paid on time.

* * *

29

Taken

REBECCA sat comfortable, and admired the mountainous landscape while Henry Klondike kept a sharp set of eyes on the road, both hands on the wheel. His large stomach jiggled as the truck rumbled and rolled through twists and turns, peaks and valleys.

The interior was in harmony with the exterior. Grey-blue leather seating, a meticulous slumber area, and spotless blue carpeting on the floor. Across the dash were little figurines of Jesus with a hand over his heart, Mother Mary kneeling in prayer, and a crucifix made of bronze. Jesus hanging, head down, a trickle of red dripping from his ribcage. *Just like the Roadrunner's truck,* thought Rebecca.

Windshield was cracked along the passenger side, and branched like a vein of lightning from where a stone had left a chip the size of a golf ball.

Rebecca yawned. She hadn't gotten much sleep the night before, preferring to stay awake while Sky drove through New Mexico with her sunglasses on.

"Tired?" asked Henry.

"Yes, I am. I didn't get much sleep last night."

"Well, why don't you put your head back and have yourself a little nap? It will do you a lot of good. You'll see."

"Sounds like a good idea. You won't mind?"

"Of course not. Besides, I've got God to keep me company. He doesn't say much, but he sure is a good listener." Henry smiled reassuringly.

"Would you mind if I put my feet up on your dash?"

"Whatever makes you comfortable."

Rebecca toed off her new runners, put her feet up and crossed her ankles. She kind of half-turned, so that her head was comfortable, and watched the landscape zip by. Contented, in a matter of minutes, her eyelids drew closed, and she slipped into a dream filled slumber.

She found herself walking along a white sandy beach all alone, the sand hot on the bottoms of her feet. She was naked, the salty air toying with her hair, the sun's warmth caressing her body, invisible seagulls screeching high above. "Becca, beware." Her mother's voice seemed to come from the ocean. She stopped and took in the endless blue water. It was calm with points of light dancing like diamonds. "Momma?" Feeling suddenly exposed, she covered her privates with her hands. "Momma, I'm here. Can't you hear me? I'm so alone."

Unexpectedly the ocean erupted. Titanic waves churned the sea in upon itself. The wind grew stiff and the sky darkened, obliterating the sun. A bitter cold enveloped her, sending a chill throughout her being. Veins of blue-white lightning sparked from the oblique darkness. Her mother's ghostly voice once again echoed a dire warning from the churning waters. "Beware the gentleman, Becca... beware. Run. Run as fast as you can, daughter. I must leave you now. You have traveled beyond my reach."

Rebecca began to run as fast as her feet would carry her. The beach seemed endless, an infinite path of white sand. She moved along the shoreline, stretching her long legs, waves lapping at her feet. Then she sensed something behind her. Something evil. It seemed to be keeping pace. Somehow Rebecca knew that if she slowed, it would take hold of her, strangle her in its wicked grasp, for she could feel its fingers brushing the back of her neck. She ran for an endless span of time, the dream not wanting her plight to end. Then when she thought she could run no further, she saw them, Ben and her father waving to her frantically in the distance. "Don't look back, Becca," they pleaded.

Rebecca quickened her pace, feet slapping hard against the rushing waves. As she was about to fall into her father's arms, something stung her. The pain so intense it caused her to stop dead in her tracks and fall into the sand.

Evil's hand was upon her.

She was stung again and again. The pain unbearable. She cried out, "Help me, Dad! Help me, Ben!" But when she looked up, Ben and Ray were gone, erased by the dream. The sand moved beneath her, falling away, taking her with it. Down, down, down she went, inch by agonizing inch until only her face and hair remained. "Please help me!" she screamed into the storm.

The shadow hand of wickedness pushed her deeper. Sand filled her mouth, stifled her cries.

Then she was gone.

Rebecca woke, eyes blinked, and she gasped, dream sand stuck in her throat. It took a second or two for her to remember where she was.

"You okay, kiddo?"

Wiping at her eyes, she turned to look at Henry Klondike. "I'm fine I guess. Bad dream."

"Must have been a doozy. You were fidgeting and jerking this way and that. I was just about to reach over and shake you out of it. Good thing you had your seat belt on.

I was afraid you were going to bounce yourself right out of the truck. Do you want to talk about it? Sometimes talking helps make sense out of things."

Rebecca looked down at the seat belt across her chest. For some reason, she couldn't remember having put it on. *But I must have.* All around, the landscape had changed dramatically. Plateaus of desertlike terrain stretched east and west. "Where are we?"

"Just north of the Hualapai Indian Reserve."

"How long was I asleep for?"

"A good two, two and half hours.

"That long. The dream seemed to last only a few minutes."

"That's the funny thing about dreams. Some only last seconds, but seem like hours, while others have a tendency to run on and on, changing when you least expect it."

"Speaking of running. That's what my dream was about."

"Oh. How so?"

"I don't remember all of it except that I was on a beach, running away from something. Something bad." She left out the part that she was completely naked.

"Running, eh? Sounds to me that your journey to your friend's house in Vegas might have something to do with it. As far as the bad part is concerned, I for one can't remember a dream I had that didn't include something sinister in it. Seems to be the natural order of dreams. They can take something good and twist it and turn it until it resembles something wicked. Doesn't mean anything though. There are no monsters lying beneath our beds or bogymen in our closets. The good Lord sees to that… amen." Lifting the crucifix, he kissed it for a second time since they'd met.

"What about all the evil in the world today? Don't you think God could or *should* do something about it?"

"Ah, you see. That's the thing about God. He gave us this." Henry tapped the side of his temple. "The greatest gift he could bestow upon us. The ability to think and to make decisions for ourselves. Evil exists in our world because *we* decide it should. But don't you worry. He's up there keeping track. Those who decide to reap havoc on his children will pay for it in the end. You mark my words. Remember your Bible. 'Vengeance is mine,' sayeth the Lord."

"That's one way of looking at it, I guess.

"It's the only way. 'Keep the faith and you shall be rewarded with everlasting life in my kingdom,' he says. You see, we're constantly being tested, Rebecca. That's what life is. His test of us to see if we are worthy of his promise of eternal bliss."

Rebecca did not want to get into a whole lot of religious innuendos, so she steered the conversation in another direction. "I hope you're right."

"I've never been more sure of anything in my life."

"Hey. Isn't the Grand Canyon near here somewhere?"

"Sounds like you know your geography. It's a couple of hours to the east. I don't know what all the fuss is about though. If you ask me, it's just a big hole in the ground."

"You know what they say, beauty is in the eye of the beholder. What's ugly to some people is beautiful to others. Take art for instance or babies or the sun or a flower. It's how they make us feel inside. For some, the sun is just a big orange ball in the sky. For others, it's much more than that. And not everyone likes Picasso, yet there are those who believe he was a brilliant artist. See what I mean? In a way, you were right. It's all about choices."

"You're pretty smart for someone your age. How old are you anyway? You never said."

Rebecca added a year. "I'm eighteen."

"Eighteen and all grown-up, eh? Ready to take on the world." He gave her a fulsome smile.

"Well, not the world, but I'd like to put a dent in the good old US of A by the time I'm twenty-five. By the way, how much farther is it before we meet up with your friend?"

"A little more than an hour. Give or take. I got a hold of him on the radio while you were sleeping. He said he'd be happy to give you a lift to Vegas. We're going to meet him at a rest stop."

"You never did tell me his name. I think it's important that I know who's giving me a ride, don't you?"

"Of course. Where's my manners? It's a wonder I remember to wake up some mornings. His name is Peter, like the apostle. You'll like him. He's a real *gentleman*. A God-fearing man, just like me."

"If he's anything like you, then I feel safe already. I can't wait to meet him. What's his last name?"

"Brown. Mr. Peter Brown," said Henry, and recalled with painful clarity the last time he met up with Mr. Brown and what it had cost him.

* * *

Henry Klondike, alias the Preacher, pulled the Freightliner into the designated rest stop, a one-acre green space crowded with shade trees and several picnic benches. There were two other cars parked in the lot. A green RX7, its windows tinted, and a blue station wagon loaded with kids, its license plate indicating it originated from Michigan. "Well, here we are," he said.

"Is your friend here yet?" asked Rebecca. She stretched her arms and legs, relieved to see that there was a cedar building that offered travelers a place to freshen up and use the facilities. She'd been holding herself for the past hour.

"Sure is. That's his car over there. The green one."

"Oh, good. I hope he wasn't waiting too long." As she spoke, the driver door of the RX7 opened and a man in his midforties, kind of short but solidly built, got out and waved. He wore beige trousers, a nice white, short-sleeved cotton shirt, and sunglasses. He had a full head of dark hair and a smile from ear to ear. The gold watch adorning his left wrist looked terribly expensive. Diamonds flashed in the observing sun.

"Come on," said Henry. "I'll introduce you to him."

Rebecca retrieved the suitcase, opened the door, and stepped down from the cab. The air was dry, hot. She filled her lungs with it. Although she'd enjoyed the ride, the air within the cab of the truck had grown stale, and on more than one occasion, she'd gotten a whiff of Henry's quiet flatulence. She gave the man waiting by the car a friendly smile and wave.

Henry came to her side of the Freightliner. "Here, let me carry that for you." He took the suitcase from her, and they walked across the sunbaked parking lot. One of the kids in the station wagon with a head of flaming red hair and a face covered in freckles rolled down a window, aimed a squirt gun at them, and let loose a stream of water. "Gotcha," he proclaimed victoriously.

The Preacher set the suitcase down, offered his hand to Mr. Brown. "Long time no see," he said. They shook hands, eyes locked. "This is Rebecca," said Henry, acquainting the two. "Rebecca, this is my friend Peter."

Rebecca extended her hand. "It's very nice to meet you, Mr. Brown. I can't tell you how much it means to me that you'd be willing to give me a ride to Vegas."

Peter Brown took her hand and gave it a gentle squeeze. "Oh, please. It's not that big of a deal. I'd do anything for my good friend here. We go way back, don't we, Henry?"

"All the way back to the good ole days," said Henry, the stub of his missing finger itching with memory.

"And I insist you call me Peter, Rebecca. If we're going to spend the next couple of hours together, we should be on a first-name basis. Don't you think?"

"I agree, absolutely… Peter," retorted Rebecca, gushing.

"Here, let's put your suitcase in the trunk, then we'll be on our way." Peter fished keys from a front pocket, and with a press of a remote, the lid popped.

Henry picked up the suitcase, and laid it flat into the compartment. "Well, I guess that's that then. It was a pleasure having your company, Rebecca."

"I can't thank you enough, Henry." She went to him, and wrapped her arms around his large frame. "You're a very nice man. Drive safely, okay."

* * *

An obese woman wearing black spandex and a yellow top several sizes too small exited the woman's side of the cedar building. Heavy breasts rode the bulge of her stomach, distended nipples pointed to the ground, breasts flopped like the full utters of a cow each time she took a waddled step. On her platform feet were a pair of pink flip-flops that were stretched to such limits they appeared that they would snap free.

A moment later, a stick of a man in jeans and Mickey Mouse T-shirt emerged from the men's side. A long grey beard as thin as a ruler pointed to his chest. His once-red hair shot out from his head like a fireworks display gone wrong. He was barefoot, long skinny feet in desperate need of a bar of soap. Quickly he caught up to the obese woman, said something no one could hear because of the rumbling coming from the Freightliner, laughed, produced an already-half-finished cigarette from behind an ear, lit it, and headed to the car full of kids. Regarding the trio standing next to the RX7, he sort of half-smiled large yellow teeth, then climbed into the front passenger seat. A moment later, blue swirls of smoke lifted from the open window.

The whale of a woman waddled to the station wagon, panting as if she'd just run a marathon, opened the driver side door, and planted her four hundred pounds between the seat and steering wheel, her weight causing the vehicle to tilt.

The smoking man made directional gestures with his hands, turned his attention to the kids sitting in the back, said something, then flicked the smoke out the window. The engine whined to life, and the kids went suddenly silent, all except for the redhead. Aiming his squirt gun at Peter Brown he yelled, "BANG! You're dead."

"Cute kid," said Peter.

The wagon reversed on four bald tires, the sound of strained shocks and struts squealing for clemency. When the wagon turned north, all that could be heard in the following silence was the rumbling of Henry Klondike's Freightliner and a high whisper speaking from the tops of the trees.

"Before we go, I've got to use the bathroom," said Rebecca. "I'll only be a minute."

"Sure, you go right ahead." Peter smiled. "Henry and I will catch up on old times." Peter checked his watch. "But if you're not back in ten minutes, we'll send a search party."

Rebecca laughed. "A sense of humor. I like that. It'll make the drive to Vegas fun." She headed toward the outbuilding.

Once she was inside, Henry said, "So what do you think? Gorgeous, right?"

"She's a looker all right. Mr. Millions will be pleased."

"So you have something for me then?"

Peter Brown reached into the green sports car and handed Henry Klondike a thick manila envelope. Within was five large of his own money. Punishment for "lack of better judgment," Tony Millions had told him for allowing the previous girl to drown. "Now don't go spending it all at one track."

Henry fanned the bills then shoved the envelope into a back pocket. A consummate gambler, he already envisioned placing his bets at Churchill Downs. Five grand could go a long way at the track, and he was feeling lucky. "What I do with it is none of your fucking business."

"Now is that any way for a man of God to speak?"

"Fuck him," grunted the Preacher.

"I'm surprised that crucifix you wear around your neck doesn't catch fire every time it touches flesh. You're a prick you know. Parading around as a righteous man of God when you're nothing more than a money-hungry predator like the rest of us."

"Not as bad as you thought, eh, Mr. Brown?" Henry sneered, cleared his sinuses, and spat a green mass of phlegm onto the asphalt.

Mr. Brown raised his sunglasses with an intended middle finger so that the Preacher could see his killer black eyes. "You just remember that."

The two men eyeballed each other for a disparaging moment, Mr. Brown liking the idea of burying the Preacher somewhere out in the desert while the Preacher imagined cutting off all of Mr. Brown's fingers. However, business was business, and both men were being paid well for their erudite expertise.

"What about family?" asked Mr. Brown, lowering his shades. "Did you learn anything?"

"If I read her right, she's a runaway. No parent would allow their kid to hitchhike across America. Not in today's world." He laughed. "Too many predators out there. She also said she had friends waiting for her in Vegas. Again a lie."

"Good. That makes my job a lot easier."

* * *

Rebecca pulled her shorts up, glad to be off the smelly hole in the ground, no doubt courtesy of the woman from Michigan. At the sink, she turned on the hot, soaped her hands, and washed. When she was done, she checked herself in the mirror. Except for a little puffiness beneath her eyes, she looked good. Ready to take on Vegas. She would have to take a menial job, probably as a waitress someplace or a cashier at a grocery. Stay at a hostel until she saved enough money to rent a room or two. But it would be a start, and when she got older, the sky was the limit. And who knew? Maybe she would meet Mr. Right along the way. There was something about the dream she had had that was bothering her however. It had returned to her in small segments. Deseray's warning. Drowning in sand. The awful, over and over again, stinging. Ben and Ray there to help but couldn't. She imagined that sooner or later it would all make sense, but right now, she was only a couple of hours from Vegas and that's all that really mattered.

When she exited the building, Henry and Peter were still communicating by the rear of the nice sports car like old friends should. A maintenance crew had arrived and were unloading a rider mower and several weed whackers from the back of a flatbed hitched to a white pickup. The men were Mexicans, dressed in white overalls, colorful bandanas and they eyed Rebecca as she made her way to her next ride.

"There, all done and ready to go," said Rebecca, stopping between Henry and Peter and feeling rather pleased with herself.

"Good. Then we'll be on our way." Peter turned to the Preacher. "Well, Henry, it was good to see you again. Let's get together real soon."

Joining hands, Henry said, "You bet. Next time I'm in the neighborhood, I'll stop by for a few days." He turned to look at Rebecca. "Godspeed, Rebecca. I know he'll be watching over you."

"Thank you, Henry. I don't know where I'd be if I hadn't met up with you. Good-bye."

Henry Klondike turned and walked back to the idling Freightliner. A prickle of guilt jabbed at him, for he knew what was in store for his latest passenger. Regardless, the padded envelope in his back pocket quickly banished all culpable judgment of himself.

Rebecca did not have to be told twice to get in the car. Opening the passenger door, she climbed in. What she liked right away was that there was plenty of room for her long legs. Contoured seat hugged her body, and the tinted windows kept the sun's glare at bay. Reaching over her shoulder, she took hold of the seat belt and fastened herself in. *Click.*

Peter Brown slid in, and closed the door, the key in his hand finding its home with measured practice. The engine purred to life. He looked at Rebecca through sunglasses. "All set?"

"As ready as I'll ever be," said Rebecca, enthusiastic gooseflesh giving her a chill.

"Good. Then let's get you to Vegas. What kind of music do you like?"

"Classic rock if you have any."

With the touch of a finger, the console between them slid open. Within were an array of CDs. "Go ahead. Take your pick. I'm sure there's something in there you'll find to your liking."

Rebecca's eyes scrolled the titles: the Beatles' *White* album, Aerosmith, Garth Brooks, Roy Clark, Snoop Dog, Nazareth, Ice Cube, Karen Carpenter, the Rolling Stones, LeAnn Rimes, U2, Queen, Motown Favorites, and so on. "That's quite the selection you have," she said.

"I have an open mind when it comes to music." Mr. Brown disengaged the hand brake, shifted into reverse, and backed out without using the rearview mirror. They were on their way.

Rebecca chose the Stones CD, and slipped it into the player. "Under My Thumb" filled the interior. Twirling a long lock of hair between fingers, she moved her head to the beat while Mr. Brown's hands drummed the steering wheel. Her mind was so full of favorable thoughts, she didn't notice they were headed in the wrong direction. When "Under My Thumb" neared its ending, Mr. Brown modified the volume to a lesser degree of noise.

"By the way, I made some sandwiches for the ride. Nothing fancy mind you. Just ham and cheese. You hungry?"

"That was very nice of you, thank you, but I'm not hungry right now. Maybe later."

"Well, would you mind reaching in the back and getting me one. I haven't eaten yet today, and my stomach is complaining big-time."

"Sure," said Rebecca. She unfastened the seat belt and half-turned so that she was squeezed between seats. "I don't see them. Where are they?"

"They must have fallen off the seat. Check the floor. They're in a brown paper bag."

Rebecca pushed her torso through the narrow gap, exposing the firmness of her buttocks. "I still don't see them," she said, head this way and that, hands probing blindly.

Mr. Brown increased the volume, a malignant smile carving his face. "Sympathy for the Devil" resounded from the Bose rear speaker system. He stared at her perfect ass for an enjoyable second. The needle went in, clean and quick.

Rebecca gasped, thinking she had been stung by a bee. "Ouch!" Without warning, her head filled with white sticky clouds. Everything seemed to be moving in the wrong direction. Up was down. Down was up. The sports car spun. She tried to move, found that she was no longer in charge of her motor skills. "Whaaatthe fffu..." The words came out all slurred as if she were drunk, as if they were coming from a faraway place.

Before her face touched down, she was gone, mind and body succumbing to the elixir of Mr. Brown's potent syringe.

Please allow me to introduce myself
I'm a man... of wealth... and taste
I've been here for a long, long year
Stole many a man's soul and faith

And I was around when Jesus Christ
Had his moment of doubt and pain
Made damn sure that Pilate
Washed his hands and sealed his fate

Pleased to meet you
Hope you guess my name
But what's puzzling you
Is the nature of my game...

* * *

30

Orchid

A WHISPER of rain. The cool judgmental hand of encompassing darkness on naked flesh. The smell of tobacco smoke. Heart thumping between her ears in rhythm with the headache she had. The ignored prickles traveling the length of her arms and legs. *Too late, too late, too late*. Unable to move. Lying on something cozy. Not alone.

These were the first things to register for Rebecca as she sobered from the drug-enduced state cogently forced upon her. She tried to call out. Couldn't. Something's covering her mouth. Desperately, she tried to reacquaint herself to a distorted past, the voice inside her head recalling sticky webs of memory. *You were in a truck. No, a car. Nice man. Number one with cheese. Fat woman. Peter the apostle. Beware the gentleman. Godspeed, Rebecca. The Rolling Stones. Run, Rebecca, run. Falling, falling, falling. Rocked to sleep in a cradle absent of everything.* Rebecca wanted to cry. Could not. Too frightened.

"I wonder what's going through your mind right now, baby."

The voice came from right next to her. A deep, guttural sound, like the voice of a giant in a nightmare fairytale. Eyes jerked left to right, right to left. Terror seized her in its formidable grasp. Rebecca screamed, only the sound did not pass her lips. Her body began to shudder uncontrollably. Arms and legs restrained. Soft rain on glass.

There was a click. Malleable light draped the area next to her, and revealed a small square of window. Her eyes went to the giant of a man sitting in a chair next to the bed in which she was imprisoned. He was smiling great white teeth, skin as black as char. Head as bald as a boiled egg. Nice dresser. She looked up at her hands then down at her feet. They were tethered to posts, legs spread eagle, hands numb. Areolas ripe with fear. Her womanhood exposed, vulnerable. *Oh god, I'm going to be raped by the giant sitting in the chair.* Then the tears came. They blurred her vision. Washed her cheeks. Rolled into the cleft of her throat.

"Now that ain't necessary, baby. You're here now, with us. That's the first thing you need to learn."

Rebecca's fright shifted in the time it took to blink. Rage became the catalyst of a fury instantly born. She pulled hard against the tethers, back arched, body twisting. The bed rattled. The wildness of her eyes shot daggers at the giant, lungs heaving sharp bursts of instant loathing. If she could be heard, she would have screamed blue bloody murder.

"Save your strength. You're going to need it." Mr. Black stood as tall and menacing as he truly was. The smile fell from his face.

Rebecca continued to writhe and whither on the bed. However, she was still weak from the effects of Mr. Brown's cocktail and her efforts began to sharply decline. Fear and hatred were not enough to sustain her struggles, so she collapsed weakly, nonetheless, maintained a steady glower of fury directed at the giant's eyes.

"There. Now that's a whole lot better." Mr. Black took a half step, his shins connecting with the bed rail. He lowered his frame. The valley of teeth returned. Reaching a plenteous hand toward her, he stroked Rebecca's hair. She turned away and spoke in unrecognizable anger through the silver tape across her mouth.

"Now I'm going to take the tape off. You would be smart to be quiet. Not that anyone can hear you, it's just that loud noises piss me off. And believe me, baby. You don't want to get on my bad side." He took a corner of tape. "Now this is going to hurt. But it will be over quickly." He ripped it free.

Rebecca felt some of her lip go with it. She gasped, extended her lungs to their fullest. She wanted to cry out in pain but wouldn't give her captor the pleasure of hearing her scream. Instead she drew her bottom lip into her mouth and sucked the blood from it.

Forgotten for the moment was her vulnerability. Tear-filled eyes took in the room from corner to corner. Except for a couple of chairs, the bed on which she was lying, and the small shaded lamp on a side table on top of which was a black leather pouch, there were no other furnishings. She could also see the dark mouth of a hallway, a door. The square of window decorated with the legs of a light rain. She was in a house or dwelling, that much she knew for sure. Again, she struggled with her bonds.

The giant black man standing next to her took hold of her face and twisted it so they were eye to eye, then he spoke. "My name is Mr. Black, Rebecca. If that is your real name. Not that it matters. We will find out who you *really* are soon enough." He released his grip.

In her seventeen years, the foulest of words to have ever escaped Rebecca's lips were *shit* and *damn* and the occasional F-word; however, growing up with two men who often enough swore with displeasure or pain gave her the ammunition she needed now. Courageously, she spat at him and screamed, "Well, you're a fucking bastard, Mr. Black!" The spittle missed the giant's face, leaving a white dot on the breast of his expensive suit jacket.

Mr. Black regarded the irregularity against the blue. "Now look what you've gone and done. And just when we were beginning so well." Repulsed, he removed the jacket, and thumbed away the spittle.

Rebecca stared at the holster that draped his shoulder and the black grip of the large gun comfortable within. Fear once again ruled the moment. In an instant, her entire body was covered with a slick sheen of it. A scream rose from deep, deep, deep; however, just as she was about to give it a voluminous birth, somewhere a toilet flushed, unnerving her and causing her to swallow the verbal tirade she was about to hurl.

With care, Mr. Black shouldered the Yves Saint Laurent jacket over the chair. "Ah. That would be Mr. Brown. You do remember him, don't you?"

Rebecca did not respond, though the mention of his name created an instant memory of the man she so stupidly trusted. Several anxious heartbeats passed before she heard footsteps in the darkened hallway. Then like a ghost returning from the other side, Mr. Brown appeared out of the dark and stepped into the light, still wearing sunglasses. He smiled down at her. "Hello, Rebecca," he said. "Nice of you to join us." He moved to the foot of the bed, removed the sunglasses, and tucked them into the breast pocket of his shirt. He stared at the private area between Rebecca's legs.

Up until then, Rebecca had not seen his eyes. They were as black as a shark's. Reflected within were points of amber light that spilled from the lamp.

"That is truly one of the prettiest vaginas I've ever seen," he said. "Wouldn't you agree, Mr. Black?"

"That's the first thing I noticed, man. Like the petals of a beautiful flower."

A woman's worst fear, anger, and disgust came out of Rebecca's mouth in one long purging. "If you bastards think you're going to rape me, you better kill me first! I won't let you! I'll fight you with every ounce of strength I have! You'll have to fuck a corpse, and I'll even fight you then!" Her body thrashed about the bed like a fish out of water. Eyes jerked from one man to the other.

"Now who said anything about raping, baby," declared Mr. Black. "I can see why you might think something like that could happen, being in the position you're in, but believe me when I say that we are not interested in raping you, though I wouldn't mind getting intimate with what you got." He released a creeping chortle. "Maybe in time though, eh, Mr. Brown?"

"She'll beg for it. Just like they all do."

"Never! You hear me! NEVER! NEVER! NEVER!" Rebecca pulled with all her valor, the leather restraints cut into her wrists.

"Feisty," said Mr. Brown. "But I'd expect nothing less from a redhead." He drew a chair, placed it at the foot of the bed and took a seat. With one leg crossed over the other, his reflective eyes devoured Rebecca's body.

Mr. Black seated himself on the mattress, and ran the tips of his fingers over Rebecca's belly, left breast and he pinched the nipple so hard Rebecca felt the pain all the way to her toes. Eyes clamped, fresh tears spilled over her cheeks.

"I have three rules," deadpanned Mr. Black.

Rebecca opened her eyes, seeing the giant through a transparent veil of pain. She could smell his cologne, physically feel the omnipotence of his stature. *He was in control,* she now understood. Mr. Brown was just a pawn in whatever sick game they were playing. Despairingly, she asked, "What do you want from me?"

Mr. Black ignored her. "Rule number one." He drew back a hand and as quick as a lightning strike, smacked her.

Rebecca's teeth rattled in her head, blood filled her mouth, cheek burning red-hot, the blow traumatizing her into momentary silence.

Mr. Brown remained seated, amused, a lecherous smile curling his lips.

Mr. Black received the long middle finger of his right hand into his mouth, and sucked on it as if it were a liquorice. When he pulled it out, it gleamed wet. "Rule number two." He jammed it hard into Rebecca's cunny, and pushed until it could go no farther.

Rebecca's back arched, the sharp edge of his fingernail tore flesh. Bile rose and spilled from her lips. "You fucking bastard!"

"I'm that and then some." Mr. Black laughed. "This young lady"—he pushed even harder, twisted—"belongs to us now." Removing the finger, he brought it to his lips and ran a thick, rolling tongue against it. "Tastes just like honey, Mr. Brown. Like the nectar of some exotic flower. That gives me an idea, baby. From now on, you'll be known as... Orchid. Rebecca no longer exists." He roughly grabbed her by the hair, large titian eyes bore into hers. "What is your name?" He wrenched her neck until she thought it would snap.

Clenched teeth, Rebecca screamed, "My name is Rebecca, you bastard!" She spat at him again, a spray of pink dots that landed on the front of Mr. Black's silk shirt.

"Now that wasn't nice. Was it, Mr. Brown?"

"Not nice at all, Mr. Black. Maybe I should get my cutters and teach her a lesson. She wouldn't miss a baby toe. They're useless anyway, but the pain will be excruciating."

"Not just yet, Mr. Brown. I have a better idea." He released her hair, removed the gun from its holster, turned it and held it as if it were a hammer. "You'll soon learn, Orchid, that I am the master of pleasure and pain." He looked at her right kneecap. "Now remember that you brought this upon yourself." He held the butt end of the .357 a foot above her knee.

Rebecca shut her eyes, tensed, prepared for the worst.

What came next was a pain that absorbed her entirely. Her mind went blank with it. Every nerve in her body succumbed to it, sending jagged messages of suffering until finally, she wretched the number one with cheese down her chin. She opened her eyes. Tears would not come. The pain insisted upon it. Reluctantly, she looked down at her knee. It was completely altered.

"Get me a towel, Mr. Brown."

Mr. Brown disappeared into the darkened hallway. When he returned, he carried a white terrycloth draped over an arm as though he were a waiter in some fancy restaurant.

Mr. Black took it from him and wiped the mess from Rebecca's chin and throat with a gentle touch. "There, now that's better, Orchid, or is it Rebecca. I ask you again, baby. What is your name?"

Rebecca stared at the gun hovered above the opposite knee. *Tell him what he wants to hear. Don't be stubborn. It'll cost you. If you're going to get out of this somehow, you'll need both knees.* "Orchid," she surrendered in a timid tone.

"There. Now that wasn't so hard now, was it?" Mr. Black reholstered his gun, and handed the towel to Mr. Brown. "Now where was I? Oh yes, rule number three." He drew back his large hand again, and struck her harder than the first time. "Refer to rule number one."

Rebecca's eyes rolled back in her head. She willed herself not to pass out. Tiny blue lights appeared in front of her, dancing round and round, until, one by one, they disappeared. "Please don't hit me again," she whimpered.

"Now that's entirely up to you, baby. Like I told you. I *am* the giver of pleasure and pain. What you've just experienced is nothing compared to what I'm capable of." He looked to Mr. Brown. "Get me some ice and a fresh towel."

Mr. Brown rose from his seat with the vomit-stained towel bundled in hand and disappeared once again.

"Now I'm going to untie your ankles, Orchid," Mr. Black told her. "Keep still and be a good girl. Struggling will only result in more pain, and I'm sure you don't want to experience anything further, do you, baby?"

Slowly, Rebecca shook her head.

"Good. We're off to a fine start, you and me."

By the time he removed the tethers from her ankles, Mr. Brown had returned with a towel filled with ice.

Rebecca stared at the red welts surrounding her ankles, the flesh rubbed raw. At least she could move her leg about. Drawing it toward the other, she could still feel Mr. Black's cutting finger, understanding she was bleeding inside but could do nothing about it.

Mr. Black took the towel and seated himself next to her. Unfolding it, he removed one of the cubes. "Now I want you to take this into your mouth and bite down when I say so. I'm going to pop your kneecap back into place, and I'm sorry to say, it's going to be quite painful. Now open your mouth."

Rebecca remained tight-lipped. However, when she looked down at the disjointed bulge of her knee, she decided it would suit her better to have it repaired, no matter how much it hurt. Then she could devise a way of getting the hell out of there. Eyes narrowed, she drove home the loathing she felt for the man sitting next to her and opened her mouth.

Mr. Black put the square of ice in. Then, he applied pressure to the underside of the kneecap with his thumb and held her leg still with the other hand. "Ready?" he asked in a gentle voice.

Rebecca closed her eyes and nodded. She directed her mind's ear to the discreet rain tapping against the window, and recalled the kitchen of her youth where her mother baked and she danced to the music emanating from the old Panasonic.

"Now!"

She bit hard against the ice, smashing it into a thousand shards, the pain wiping the slate of her mind clean. Her eyes shot open, bulging, everything around her pulsed white. Her good leg kicked at the air again and again while Mr. Black held the right leg in place with his powerful hands. Body bucking, arms yanking at the restraints binding her wrists, the entirety of her experiences up to then rushed forward. "YOU FUCKING PRICK! GOD DAMNED YOU TO HELL, YOU BLACK BASTARD! MOMMA, PLEASE HELP ME! PLEASE, PLEASE, PLEASE! Her screams resonated off the walls of the tiny room, burning tears set her face on fire.

Mr. Brown laughed from the threshold of the darkened hallway.

"There, it's over now, Orchid," said Mr. Black. "You'll feel like new in just a few short minutes." He wrapped the swollen knee in the towel. "Better?"

The ice felt good against the throbbing. Blinking tears from her eyes, Rebecca sniffed and sniffed, the shards of ice in her mouth melted into a soothing sip of water. Debilitated by pain, she nodded. "I need a drink of water," she said in a raspy voice.

"Of course, Orchid." Mr. Black shifted his weight. "Mr. Brown."

"Coming right up."

Mr. Black stood, went to the foot of the bed, pushed the chair Mr. Brown had occupied out of the way, bent marginally, and came up with Rebecca's suitcase. He held it aloft with one finger as if it weighed no more than a canary.

Rebecca's heart pounded at the sight of her captor holding everything she owned. "That's mine!" she adamantly proclaimed.

"Don't worry, baby. Everything is still there. Your money. The letter from Hester. Your clothes. Everything. You look just like your mother by the way. Though I don't think she is in any position to help you. Am I right, Orchid?"

Rebecca did not answer. Instead she looked to the rain skating south on the window. *Don't tell this bastard anything.*

"No matter, Orchid. We'll soon find out everything we need to know."

Mr. Brown came back into the room holding a tall glass of water. Mr. Black handed him the suitcase, exchanged it for the glass. "You know what to do with it."

"Of course, Mr. Black." Mr. Brown whistled as he left the room, the tune as familiar to Rebecca as her own heartbeat. "Pop! Goes the Weasel" echoed in the hallway. For an inexplicable instant, the sound of Mr. Brown whistling the popular children's melody terrified her beyond all rational.

Mr. Black read the look on her face. "You have every right to be frightened, Orchid. I may be a bastard as you so eloquently pointed out, but Mr. Brown"—he shook his head—"that man's just plain nasty." Edging the water to Rebecca's lips, he cautioned, "Take small sips, okay? We wouldn't want you tossing your lunch again."

Rebecca leaned forward, and took in a small amount of water, held it in her mouth, let the coolness of it mollify the cuts within. When she swallowed, it had the bitter flavor of her own blood. She took another, then another until the glass was empty. The cool liquid felt good in her empty stomach. "Are you going to kill me?" she asked, choking on the words.

Mr. Black stroked the inside of her thigh, stopped just short of touching her vagina. He held his hand there for a long unnerving moment before he took it away. "Killing you is the furthest thing on our minds, baby. Killing you would be profitless. You see, we are in business together, Mr. Brown and I. You could say we are in the entertainment industry. People pay us well for services rendered. As I understand it, your wish is to get to Vegas. Well, I'm going to see to it, in time, that you get there."

Rebecca's mind darted in motley direction. *Kidnapped. Held against her will. Stripped of her dignity and name. Beaten. The entertainment industry. Services rendered.* All of it sounded like an episode of the show she loved and that *she* was cast as the suffering victim. Her eyes grew wide, the reality of her situation slapped her in the face. The word lit her mind as big as a neon billboard. PROSTITUTION. *Ben. Ray. Momma, please help me.* "You'll never get me to do what you want! I'd rather die first!"

"That's what they all say, baby. And in time, they've always shown just how willing they were to oblige us. You're no exception, Orchid. You have a mind. And I'm more than capable of bending it to my will." Great white teeth made an appearance. "A month from now, should the need arise, you'll suck my beautiful cock and enjoy it. This I promise you."

Mr. Brown returned. In his hand was what looked like a pair of pliers. Dragging the chair next to the bed, he sat opposite to Mr. Black. He held the instrument so Rebecca could see it, and turned it this way and that so she understood just how sharp it was. "Is she ready?"

"No time better than the present," said Mr. Black. He retrieved the black leather pouch from the side table, and slowly unzipped it. It opened like a book. He set it on the bed next to Rebecca's leg. Within the pouch were two syringes and three vials filled with clear liquid.

Rebecca's heart raced, adrenalin pumped like rocket fuel, cold sweat urgently covered her body. Hopelessly, she struggled against her restraints.

"You see, Orchid," said Mr. Black, removing one of the syringes and holding it in the air. "I need to know everything about you. I am sorry that I have to do this so soon after you've recovered from Mr. Brown's cocktail, but it's a necessary evil." He detached a vial, jabbed it with the needle, and drew the amount needed for the interrogation. When he depressed the plunger, a stream of liquid arced into the air and landed on the mattress. "This is sodium pentothal. A kind of truth serum. However, it also possesses other benefits. Not only will you tell me everything I need to know, but the pain in your leg will no longer be an issue."

"Please, please, please don't, Mr. Black," cried Rebecca. "My name really is Rebecca."

"Sorry, baby. My employer pays me too well not to. An hour from now, we will know all about you. What your favorite food is. Where your family lives. Whether you like cats or dogs. The last time you had your period. Even the name of the boy who first popped that beautiful cherry of yours." Looking to Mr. Brown, he said, "If she struggles, cut off that baby toe."

"It'll be a pleasure." Mr. Brown took hold of her left foot and pinched her little toe between the razor edges of the cutters.

Knowing full well Mr. Brown would obey Mr. Black in an instant and enjoy doing so, Rebecca pushed her thoughts to a faraway place. The tension in her body subsided. She focused on the ceiling. Light rain on glass. She could do nothing else.

Mr. Black slapped the top of her foot. A vein rose. "Just a little pinch," he warned.

Easing the needle in, he drew back the plunger until a cloud of pink appeared within the syringe, then, using his thumb, injected Rebecca with 10 cc of pentothal.

In seconds, Rebecca felt all warm inside, and she was suddenly drowning in a tickling delight. Her focus zoomed in and out. The ceiling dropped then rushed away. The tap tap tapping of rain sounding like the hands of little people, knocking on the window, wanting to get in. *My name is Rebecca White. My name is Rebecca White. My name is Rebecca White.* Slipping awareness went from one man to the other. They swam all distorted, like Saturday morning cartoon characters from another world. Even the little redheaded girl standing at the foot of the bed appeared to be floating.

In the next moment, Rebecca White felt the urge to laugh, the pain in her leg no longer relevant, her mind appropriated to someone else. And so she laughed.

* * *

31

The Hurting Room

THE following morning, while Rebecca slept, still unconscious from the all-night interrogation, Mr. Black stood at the foot of the bed and, with his cell phone, took a photo. He'd learned many important aspects of Rebecca's life, none more important than the fact that she had no immediate family and the letter writer was a woman named Hester Hart who lived in Kentucky with her husband Ed and their son Caleb. Rebecca had fought hard not to answer, harder than most, but Mr. Black was a master of getting information, and in the end, she gave it all up.

The room was alight with the morning sun. It streamed through the window near the bed, coating the floor in a square of warmth. The rain had left the ground cool, so there was a low-lying mist surrounding the house, the fifty acres encompassing it and the shore of Crystal Lake.

The 1,500-square-foot bungalow was built to very specific design. Though it appeared as your everyday run-of-the-mill cottage on the outside, it was fortified with unbreakable windows, heavy oak doors, laser graphic technology, and a soundproof basement. For a decade, it had been the last stop for dozens of young girls before they were introduced into the sex trade industry, their spirits broken, dreams and hopes methodically taken away. The entire setup, from the flesh mules like Henry Klondike to the street owls, its business was designed to profit from a well-organized system that saw to it there was always new flesh on the market. Time and time again.

More than thirty thousand children and teens went missing every year in the United States. Half of them intercepted by estranged parents. Eighteen percent runaways, eager to return when darkness reveals a world rife with dangerous vulnerability. They are the fortunate ones. The remainder slip between the cracks, becoming the unsuspecting prey of murderous pedophiles, the white slave market, and those like Mr. Black and Mr. Brown.

During Rebecca's drug-induced state, Mr. Black had once again tethered her ankles, fearing she would do more damage to her swollen knee during the night. He had to be careful with this one. Tony Millions would be none too pleased should permanent damage occur. Jobs like his weren't readily available at the local employment office, and Mr. Black did enjoy his role as devil's advocate.

He watched her breathe for a moment, how quiet it was, how her nostrils flared ever so slightly. She was a beauty all right. Body and face unadulterated. By the time he was done with her, she would fetch top dollar, which would delight his employer to no end. Mr. Black's bonuses for assimilating her to the needs of the well-to-do would be astronomical. Ten percent every time she spread her legs. The thought of the wealth she would bring gave Mr. Black cause to smile.

He went to the kitchen where Mr. Brown was fixing breakfast. Scrambled eggs with bacon and toast, enough for three. A full carafe of coffee rested on the counter.

"How's our sleeping beauty this morning?" inquired Mr. Brown.

"Still out, man, though I don't think it'll be too much longer before she wakes up. She'll be hungry, and she'll need to use the bathroom. Allow her to put some clothes on. Let her walk around the house. Make her feel at home. Do not mention anything we discovered last night. Leave that to me. I'm going to catch a couple of hours of sleep after breakfast. I'll take over when I wake up. Then I want you to get the pit ready."

"I hope she swims better than the last one," said Mr. Brown, remembering what it had cost him when fourteen-year-old Kimberly Gagne drowned.

"I have a feeling this one swims like a duck. She comes from a fishing town. Probably learned how to swim before she knew how to crawl."

"Well, I'm not going to be responsible this time if she doesn't!" said Mr. Brown emphatically.

"You'll do whatever it is I tell you to do, man, and don't forget it." Mr. Black reminded Mr. Brown by glancing down at his loaded shoulder holster that if need be, he would kill him in an instant. "But no worries, Mr. Brown. I'll keep an eye on this one. Your money will be safe, man." He inspected the eggs in the cast iron pan while scrolling for Tony Millions's private number. "Remember to put Tabasco on mine," he said. "Lots of it."

"I know, Mr. Black. I'm not stupid. I've been fixing you breakfast for quite some time now. You take Tabasco on almost everything. I get it."

Mr. Black ignored him and sat at the table where he could see the lake, the dock, and the eighteen-foot Crestliner through the bay window. He could also see where the pit was. Mist poured into its sucking vortex. He thumbed the single digit that connected him to Tony Millions. The signal linked, which wasn't always the case from where they were. When it rained like it had the previous night, the signal sometimes got swallowed on its way out.

The cell on the other end chirped twice.

"Ah, Mr. Black," answered Tony Millions in his morning-after-the-night-before crackle. "As I understand it you have some good news for me."

How his employer always seemed to be one step ahead of everyone puzzled Mr. Black. "True, man. You are going to be very pleased. The Preacher came through for you with flying colors, again. She's a real beauty, seventeen and hot in between. I'm picture-messaging you right now." He hit Send with his thumb.

A quick, silent moment passed. "Well done, Mr. Black. She'll be the jewel in my crown. At least for a while anyway. What happened to her knee? And why is her mouth swollen."

"She was being uncooperative, man. Don't worry, the swelling will go down in no time."

"See that it does. How long?"

"Give me a month, man. Then she'll be all yours."

"Be sure Mr. Brown understands he's not to touch this one. As for you... ," he paused, "you do what's necessary to ensure that she gets to me safe and obedient."

"Don't worry, man. This one's going to be real special. I can tell. Men will be tripping over their dicks to pay for a piece of what she's got."

"I'm glad to hear that, Mr. Black. Keep me up to date on her progress."

The line went static.

Mr. Black folded the cell, and returned it to a pocket. He poured himself a cup of coffee, and stared out the window. It was going to be a glorious day. He could feel it in his bones. The mist would soon be off the lake. The sun would dry everything in a matter of hours.

"What did he say?" asked Mr. Brown, as he spooned large amounts of egg onto a plate.

Mr. Black blew over the rim of his cup before taking a sip of hot java and, while watching ghostly waves lap at the shore, said, "Our boss told me to tell you that if you touch her, and we both know what I mean by touch her, I get to kill you... man." Smiling, smiling, always smiling.

* * *

Heavy lids retracted. The unfocused room came into view. Rebecca tried to concentrate. *Dizzy, dizzy, dizzy*. Sunlight swirled in a rhythmic dance. She felt nauseous, hungover, as if she would throw up any moment. The boisterous thump of a headache pushed against her skull, threatening to implode. She closed her eyes, and wished the sensation away. The need to urinate pressed hard against her kidneys. Sounds ushered from somewhere. Pans clanged. Hushed voices. The smell of cooked bacon was almost too much. She dry-heaved. *What the hell had happened?* She forced her eyes. The room zoomed in and out then settled. The pain in her knee caused her to look down. Cuts in her mouth, naked, ankles tied to bedposts. She looked up. Arms secured above her head.

Think, think, think, Rebecca. Her mind drew on clouded memory. At first she could come up with nothing; however, just when she thought all was lost, it all came back to her. It rushed forward, a stampede of indignation. Mr. Black. Mr. Brown. Kidnapped and beaten. A painful assault on her womanhood. Number one with cheese down her face and chest. My name is Orchid. Prostitution. The prick of a needle. "*You are going to tell us everything*." The opaque face of a young girl.

Terror gripped her in its clammy hands once more. Headache intensified to an unbearable status. *Oh my god. Oh my god.* She wanted to scream. Knew it would not do any good. She looked around the room, pulled at her bindings. *Maybe If I reasoned with these bastards, they would let me go. Convince them I wasn't what they wanted. Huh. Fat chance. They chose you specifically. From the moment Henry Klondike stepped into the McDonald's and into your life, you were theirs.*

She looked to the window and the beaming shaft of sunlight. Over the pounding in her head, she heard the sound of a chirping bird. Her senses picked up the murky scent of water. Having grown up surrounded by it, she knew right away that there was a large body of it nearby. She was a good swimmer. If she could get out of the house without being noticed, she could swim for miles if she had to. There were no bars on the windows. If she could just get free of her bindings, she could use one of the chairs, break the window, and run like hell. There was no way Mr. Brown or Mr. Black could keep up with her. After all, she was the fastest girl at her high school.

Twisting her wrists, she tugged at the leather bindings. A picturesque Bay Ridge Cove filled her mind. *Home*. She'd made the biggest mistake of her life leaving. Not listening to the signals that were always accurate in their message. Nevertheless, she couldn't focus on what she could not undo. She had to put all of her resources into getting the hell out of there. An added worry was just how much of her life did she tell them. Had she put others in danger? She hoped not. "Oh, Momma, please help me," she whispered.

Five, maybe ten minutes passed before the effects of the previous night finally wore off. The headache cheapened to a dull roar. Rebecca tried to zero in on the conversation she was hearing. Nothing. Just the sound of plates and pans. If she didn't get to a bathroom soon, she was going to wet the bed. "Hello! Can you hear me? I need to use the bathroom!" There was silence for a few moments. Then she heard someone move about.

Footsteps echoed in the hallway.

Mr. Brown appeared. He carryied a plate in one hand and a glass of orange juice in the other. He smiled as he approached the bed. He was dressed casually in jeans and a blue Polo shirt. His shark eyes lapped at Rebecca's body. "Good morning, Orchid," he said, and set the plate on the bed, the juice on the side table.

"I need to use the bathroom, now!"

"Of course you do. Let me just untie you and I'll show you where it is." He went about the task of loosening her bonds. "No funny business, you hear. I wouldn't want to have to start the day off by hurting you."

Rebecca nodded weakly.

"Good. You may take some clothes out of your suitcase and put them on. It's just in front of the bed."

Free, Rebecca swung her legs over the side and stood. There was specific pain in her knee when she put her weight down, but it wasn't enough to stop her from going to the foot of the bed and removing a pair of jeans and T-shirt. She pulled on the jeans while looking at the picture of her mother lying flat among her possessions.

Mr. Brown stood directly behind her. "You've got a beautiful body, Orchid," he said. Impervious for a randy moment to Mr. Black's warning, he reached around her, and took her breasts in his hands. To Rebecca, they were blue cold, as reticent as his dead eyes.

"Leave me alone!" She spun on him, slapped at his hands, forgetting for a trice the situation she was in and just how scared she was.

"You're a feisty little cunt. I like that. You'll do very well. Very well indeed. Now do you want to use the bathroom or not?"

Rebecca drew the T-shirt over her head and let it fall. She did not like being called that, that disgusting word at all. Anger obstructed the access of her fears. She eyeballed Mr. Brown who did not blink, his black eyes absent of emotion, the corner of his lip curling. For several long seconds, they stared at each other until, finally, Rebecca rescinded, aware she had just had a staring contest with unremitting evil. *Round one to Mr. Brown.*

"That's right, Orchid. I am that bad." He took her by the arm, squeezed harder than need be, and ushered her into the hallway and to a door that was partially open. "Now do your business and make it quick. And be quiet about it. Mr. Black is taking a nap, and you definitely don't want to wake him. I'll be right here with this." He pulled out from behind his back what looked to Rebecca like a long flashlight without the light. Slapping the palm of his hand with it, he said, "Any funny business and I'll have to use this on you."

Rebecca wasn't sure what *it* was. What she did know however was that she did not wish to become acquainted with *it*. Pushing the door open, she stepped into the small room and pulled it closed, aware that there was no lock on the handle to keep Mr. Brown at bay should he decide he wanted to come in. The small room consisted of a bathtub with shower, curtained by a transparent drape of plastic. Personal hygiene products lined the edge of the tub. A vanity sink with mirror. Two burgundy towels hung on a rack. The ceiling held a small light domed in floral glass. Toilet, but no window. Which meant no way out. Unable to hold it any longer, she dropped her jeans and sat on the cool porcelain. She cupped her face in her hands. The sum of all her fears came full circle, filled her eyes.

"Help me. I'm lost."

Rebecca's head jerked. The plighted voice of a young girl seemed to come from directly in front of her. Little fingers as tactile as a breath touched her eyes and brushed the tears away. "I'm afraid that I'm in no position to help you," whispered Rebecca.

"My mom and dad don't know where I am. Please, won't you help me find them. I'm sure they're close by."

Fresh tears welled in Rebecca's eyes. "I'm sorry. I'm so sorry."

The shower curtain moved ever so slightly as though an errant breeze had suddenly breached the small room. Rebecca sensed that the spirit of the young girl was gone in search of her mom and dad, loved ones she would never find. A crack developed on Rebecca's heart knowing that Mr. Brown and Mr. Black were responsible for her untimely death. *Those fucking bastards.*

Mr. Brown knuckled the door. "Come on now, Orchid. The delicious breakfast I made you is getting cold."

Frustrated, hurt, and irate, Rebecca cleaned herself and pulled up her jeans. She felt as though she were standing on a layer of thin ice, cracked all around, and that beneath, deep within the frigid waters, Mr. Brown and Mr. Black waited. Quickly she went to the vanity, and opened the front in search of something, anything she could use as a weapon. All she discovered was a toilet brush, several roles of paper, tampons, and a blow-dryer. *Useless.*

"If you don't open the door, I'm coming in."

Rebecca slowly opened the door, regarded Mr. Brown with a loathing as deep as her soul. "I'm done."

"That's better. Now let's get some food into you." He held the black thing and puffed on a cigarette.

There was something oddly familiar about the contraption in his hand, but Rebecca couldn't quite put a finger on it.

Mr. Brown blew several smoke rings. "Do you smoke?" he asked to which he was answered by the shaking of Rebecca's head.

"Good for you. Nasty habit. Somehow I can't seem to kick it." He drew on the smoke. Blue curls settled about his face and clung to his hair.

It would not have surprised Rebecca in the least if he suddenly sprouted fangs and turned into a werewolf.

"After you," he said, and pointed the black cylinder in the direction of the hurting room.

Once there, Mr. Brown ordered her to get on the bed. Seeing the plate of food caused Rebecca's stomach to growl. Reluctantly, she sat. "I suppose begging you to let me go wouldn't do me any good," she said.

Mr. Brown took a seat in one of the chairs, rested the cylinder on his lap, dropped what was left of the smoke on the floor, and smashed it with a shoe. "You're right, Orchid. Begging would not do you any good. Now why don't you enjoy the meal I've made you. I'm quite the chef as you'll find out. Call it a gift."

"How do I know you didn't put something in it?"

"I guess you'll have to trust me on that."

"Trust *you*. Ha! I don't think I'll trust another man for as long as I live." She rubbed at her sore knee. She wasn't going to give this bastard the satisfaction of watching her eat, then reminded herself that she would need all of her strength if she were going to make a break for it. She rested the breakfast plate on her lap, and said, "Your mother must be very proud of you."

"My mother." He gave a little laugh. "That bitch left me when I was three. Consequently, I grew up as a ward of the state. Passed on from one home to the next. Do you know the things that happen to children when they're passed from one home to the next?"

"So that explains it."

"Explains what?"

"Why you're a monster."

The little laugh returned. "Let's get one thing straight between you and me. I do what I do for the money. Nothing more. You, my sweet little Orchid, are nothing more to me than a commodity. To be sold for your worth."

"You won't break me."

"I beg to differ. Do you think you're the first? Mr. Black and I have been doing this for quite a while. We have a system as you'll soon find out."

Rebecca thought about the young girl. She looked to the window then to the door. She had to get the hell out of there. *And quickly.*

As if he were reading her mind, Mr. Brown said, "Thinking about escaping? I would too if I were in your shoes. It's only natural." He offered that malevolent smile of his, black eyes flashed.

Rebecca looked away, and picked up the fork. Oh, how she would like to jam it into those dead eyes of his. Pop them out. Step on them until they were nothing more than a smear on the bottom of her shoes. *There must be another exit someplace in the house. Had to be.* Bad knee and all, she believed that if she got the smallest of head start, she could outrun Mr. Brown with ease. She came up with an idea. If Mr. Black was indeed napping, then she only had Mr. Brown to worry about and that he, like most people, was inherently curious. She stared at the window, keeping Mr. Brown in her peripheral vision. She stared and stared, unblinking, for what seemed like an eternity as if she were seeing something that fascinated her. Anger, fear, adrenalin, and hope fuelling her next move.

Finally, Mr. Brown asked, "What the hell are looking at?" As soon as his eyes shifted to the window, Rebecca, and with all her might, flung the plate of food as if it were a Frisbee in the direction of his face then bolted from the bed. The pain in her knee stabbed deep. She did not care. She brandished the fork as if it were a knife, and made it to the hallway faster than you can, say run, rabbit run.

The edge of the plate had caught Mr. Brown in the forehead, opening a small gash. "Shit! You fucking bitch!" Wiping egg from his face, he bolted from the chair in hot pursuit.

Rebecca's long strides took her halfway into the hall in a heartbeat. When she passed the bathroom door, she saw that the hall took a sharp right. Quickly, she looked over her shoulder. Mr. Brown was less than ten feet behind her. *Run, Rebecca, run!*

Making the turn as fast as she could, she nearly tripped over her own feet. Then bang! She was down, lying flat on her back, the fork jarred from her hand, tiny blue lights popping. She'd run smack into a wall that was Mr. Black. He looked down at her. Thick brows furrowed over irate eyes. "You woke me up, baby," he said in a dangerous tone.

Mr. Brown stopped short. "Nice try, bitch," he said, and wiped a smear of blood from his forehead.

Rebecca kicked out with her good leg, her aim bruising the air. "You fucking bastards!"

Hands on his hips, Mr. Black instructed, "Hit her with it."

Smiling, Mr. Brown pointed the end of the black cylinder at Rebecca's shoulder, and touched her with it.

Rebecca's body convulsed as the cattle prod gave her a jolt. Arms and legs went numb, eyes felt as though they were melting. The electric charge surged through her teeth, curled her toes, and her head felt as though it were a balloon floating away, intoxicated with the thrumming of her own erratic heartbeat.

Still in his briefs, Mr. Black stepped over Rebecca, took her by the hair, and dragged her through the hallway, back to the room, back to the bed. He lifted her off the floor, and dropped her on the mattress as if she were as weightless as a child's toy. "Tie her up again," he told Mr. Brown, and glared at him with hard, cold eyes.

While Mr. Brown secured her wrists and ankles, Mr. Black took Rebecca's chin in a powerful hand lowering his face to hers, and kissed her hard on the lips. Then he grabbed the front of her T-shirt and ripped it from her body. "Have it your way, Orchid," he said.

Topless, Rebecca began to moan as the effects of the cattle prod began to wear. Her flickering eyes tried to focus on Mr. Black. He seemed much larger somehow. She tried to say something only to find that her thick tongue would not respond.

Mr. Black stood to his full height.

To Rebecca, he looked like a human skyscraper rising from the ground, his eyes the windows to a very dark soul.

"I'm going to get dressed," he told Mr. Brown. "Tape her mouth again, and for fuck's sake, clean up that mess. We're going to start her on her special diet *now* instead of later."

Mr. Brown wiped at his injured forehead again. "The bitch cut me."

"Yes, I can see that, man. The next time you let your guard down, I'll cut you in so many ways that by the time I'm done with you, you'll look like you've been run through a windshield. Understand?"

"Yes, Mr. Black." Mr. Brown went to the side table, opened the drawer, and removed a roll of silver duct tape. He tore a five-inch strip and forced it over Rebecca's mouth.

When Mr. Black left the room and Mr. Brown was sure he was out of earshot, he pulled a switchblade from his pants and pointed it an inch from Rebecca's face, the tip of it almost touching her nose. "That stunt was very courageous of you," he said with the calm demeanor of a sadist. "You try something like that again, Orchid, and I'll rape you with this knife."

* * *

When Mr. Black returned, he was wearing a red dress shirt, grey slacks, and Western-style boots. Rebecca watched as he approached the bed. In one hand he carried his little black kit. In the other was a spoon and wax candle.

After cleaning the mess of broken plate, toast, egg, and cigarette butt, Mr. Brown had seated himself in the chair at the foot of the bed. He hadn't said a word to Rebecca the whole time Mr. Black was gone, which suited her just fine. The threat of raping her with his knife had left her horror struck with the implications of it.

Mr. Black took a seat on the bed and rested the leather pouch, candle, and spoon on the side table. "Before we get started," he said. "We're going to have ourselves a little talk. Actually, I'm going to do all the talking and you're going to listen. First, let me tell you that I understand about losing family. It must have been terrible for you to watch yours burn up like that. I mean, of all the ways to go, getting crispy in a fire would not be one of my first choices."

The memory of that night rushed forward. Rebecca breathed laboriously through her nose. Eyes filled with tears. All remaining strength rushed from her body as if she had been punched in the stomach.

Mr. Black continued, "I suppose you now know that running away was your first mistake. Bad for you. Good for us. Isn't that right, Mr. Brown?"

"Indeed, Mr. Black," said Mr. Brown from the foot of the bed. "Very profitable for us."

Rebecca murmured through the tape, tugged weakly at her restraints.

"Now from what we gathered, the only people you have left in your life are the Hart family down in good old Kentucky."

Rebecca's eyes widened at the mention of the Harts. *Oh god. What have I done?*

"That's right, Orchid. We know all about Hester and Ed and little Caleb. So you listen and listen good, baby. I'm going to tell you this once and only once. If you do not perform well for us, I'm going to send some of my people down to Kentucky. People you would not wish on your worst enemy. And they will see to it that the Hart family comes to great harm. Do you understand? A simple nod will do."

Blinking tears from her eyes she nodded. Mr. Black hadn't mentioned anything about the aunt she had in Florida which she was thankful for. At least she hadn't given her up as well.

"That's good. What do you think, Mr. Brown? Do you think she's being honest with us, or is she trying to snowball us?"

"Hard to tell right now. However, I don't believe she could ever forgive herself if let's say little Caleb were to suddenly disappear, never to be seen again. I think our friends in Mexico would pay highly for the proprietorship of a child's kidneys."

"I believe you're right. Fifty thousand a kidney is the going rate. A hundred thousand for a heart, excuse the pun." Mr. Black let out a short-lived laugh and took Rebecca's chin in hand again. He squeezed her cheeks with so much authority, Rebecca believed his fingers were going to impale her flesh. "The sale of organs is a very profitable business, Orchid. You wouldn't want something like that to happen to young Caleb now, would you?" He let go of her face.

Rebecca's head dropped, eyes closed. Although these bastards had no idea that Caleb had already passed, she had no doubt that there were people who would do terrible things to Hester and Ed, and that was something she just couldn't live with. What was left of her fiery spirit vanished in that moment.

"I see by your body language that we are now on the same page. That's good. Isn't that good, Mr. Brown?"

"Exemplary," replied Mr. Brown, smiling, knowing the first step of assimilation was complete. The straw now sat firmly on the camel's back.

Mr. Black rose from the bed and went to the side table where he withdrew a lighter from his slacks and tipped the candle at an angle. "I want you to watch this, Orchid. You'll be doing this on your own in a couple of weeks."

Rebecca opened her eyes and turned her head.

Mr. Black lit the candle. He allowed the melted wax to adhere to the surface of the table before he stuck the candle in. In a quick moment the wax hardened. From his shirt pocket he took out a small square of foil paper. Carefully he unfolded it, and removed what looked to Rebecca like a small cube of white sugar. He placed it in the bowl of the spoon and held the spoon several inches above the flickering flame. Soon the cube began to melt until it looked like clear syrup. When it bubbled, he set the spoon aside, opened his leather kit, and removed a syringe. "Don't worry," he said. "I only use clean needles." Dipping the point of the needle into the spoon, he drew back the plunger until the bowl of the spoon sat empty. Holding the syringe in front of his eyes for a moment, he sat at the foot of the bed near Rebecca's tethered feet. "Do you remember what your favorite candy was when you were a little girl?"

Rebecca just stared at the syringe in his hand, fists clenched. A newfound fear took her in its hold and squeezed the breath from her lungs.

"No matter, baby. You'll soon have a craving for this as powerful as anything you have ever wanted in your life. In time it will control you. Soon after that, you'll sell your body and soul for it."

All Rebecca could think about was how terrified the young girl must have been when they had her in their grasp.

Mr. Black set the syringe on the mattress, took her right foot in hand, and slapped the bruised area from the previous night's pentothal-laced interrogation. "This is where you should apply the needle. We don't want you walking around with track marks up and down your arms. Now just a little prick."

The needle went in just above the anterior puncture. Mr. Black's thumb slowly depressed the plunger, his eyes locked on Rebecca's. Smiling, smiling, always smiling. "Heroin has always been the preferred choice of street people."

Hot liquid filled Rebecca's vein. It moved through her body with the velocity and assault of a charging rhino. Her mind swooned. *Bang! Bang! Bang!* pounded her broken heart. Tiny little creatures danced about her flesh, tickling her in places that were private. Mr. Black's body seemed to move as if it were made of rubber. Mr. Brown's face erupted into a bouquet of flowers. Ones with the eyes of a shark. Eyelids drew heavy, closed on their own; however, there would be no sleep, only feelings of euphoria, tangerine dreams, and plastercine skies.

Mr. Black blew out the candle, wiped the tip of the needle clean, and placed the syringe back into the little black pouch. He took a long, hard look at his newest acquisition before he said, "Mr. Brown, you may get the pit ready now."

* * *

32

Sold

TONY Millions sat in front of the blue screen of his computer, silk robe opened in the front, waiting for the first bids to come in. He had picture-text Rebecca's photo to a dozen wealthy clients who would pay large sums of money for the privilege of being the first to sex the new girl who would soon be a part of his stable.

Codes were used so that snooping Feds would just see encrypted numbers and letters that wouldn't mean shit to them. It was puerile in its simplicity, nonetheless, proved to be foolproof.

Most of the clients were of Asian persuasion, old and couldn't get enough of good old American pussy. They flew to Vegas on private jets, gambled two or three million dollars away as if it were pocket-change then licked their wounds in Tony's house of ill repute. The photo of a redheaded Rebecca White tied to a bed would fetch him top dollar, though not as much as the fourteen-year-old virgin would have. *Pity*.

A 3-D image of the Wizard of Oz filled the screen. "You have mail," it told him. Tony entered his three-digit password. The wizards' face spun, shrinking to a red dot. The first bid was in. "FT MRK@ I HAVE SEEN YOUR LATEST ACQUISITION AND AM VERY INTERESTED. PLEASE BE ADVISED. 010010201."

The first bid of five grand was good. It made Tony smile. However, he was sure it would go higher. He cued the message then hit Delete. While he waited for others, he removed a gold container from the front drawer of his ornate mahogany desk, unscrewed the lid, and dipped the tip of his pinky nail into the white, sniffing a portion into each nostril. He tilted his head back, closed his eyes, and waited for the euphoric effects of the high-grade cocaine to further brighten his already-blissful day.

"You have mail." Tony looked to the ghostly face of the wizard floating against the blue. "Thank you," he said, snickering to himself. *What a great country we live in*.

"FMMRP@ VERY INTERESTED. 040100020."

Vegas' proprietor of flesh rubbed his hands together. The early bids were giving him a hard-on. He lifted the receiver from the house phone and called down to the pool. After three rings, the maid picked up. "Si, Meestor Millions."

"Is Seniora Pamela by the pool?" he asked, deleting the bid. He could hear the blue macaw squawking in the background. "*Norman likes pussy. Norman likes pussy.*"

"Si, señor," the Latino maid answered.

"Send her to my office."

"Si, señor. Anyting else I can do for you, señor?"

"Give Norman some peanuts."

"Si. Anyting else?"

"Nada, Rosita." Setting the receiver into its cradle, he took another amount of coca into his nail and sniffed. The face of the wizard became very bright as another bid came in.

"FBMRW@ 4011000301."

A few minutes later, there was a light rap on the thick walnut door.

"Come in."

Pamela entered the richly furnished office. She wore a white bikini. Just enough material to cause a man's mind to melt. Her hair was still partially wet from her morning laps and drooped past her shoulders. "Is there something I can do for you, Tony?" She walked across the lush blue carpet, and gave Tony what he liked, plenty of hip action.

Tony swiveled in his chair so that he and his confined erection faced her.

"Oh, I see," said Pamela, and smiled. "It will be a pleasure, baby. I love sucking your cock." Reaching, she undid the drawstrings and dropped the skimpy top to the floor. Perfect breasts stood firm. Blue eyes luminous, she knelt between Tony's open legs, and released his swollen member from the boxers. "And how is Morgan the Organ today?"

* * *

33

The Pit

THE sun was well beyond the reach of the window when Rebecca's first journey into the perilous world of altered states yielded. What remained was an itch deep beneath the surface of her skin. She realized with great sadness and mortification that the dark road that lay ahead would be filled with self-loathing and righteous trepidation. That this was not a nightmare she would soon wake from. It was the sum of a young girl's fears. As real as the tethers that held her at bay and as palpable as the murky depths of unmitigated evil. Mr. Brown and Mr. Black and those like them were advocates of a source far more pious than the hordes of virtuous men. *Money.*

She was relieved when she tried to wet her lips to find that the tape had been removed. The tip of her tongue probed for damage. A repeated stinging told her that her captures were not gentle when the tape was removed. She took visual stock of herself. The assaulted flesh of her foot was tender and bruised green. Two red dots remained where the needles had gone in. The beginnings of a track that in time would distinguish her as a user. Her exposed breasts, daunting reminders that at any given time should either Mr. Brown or Mr. Black choose to have their way with her, she would be defenseless.

For an hour, she stared at the empty room. The walls became grey with the oncoming of dusk. Though the chairs were empty, she could still see the imposing figures of Mr. Brown and Mr. Black, staring as if she were some kind of prize. The flameless candle remained erect on the side table. Hours had passed since her last taste of self-worth.

In what little borrowed time she had, lying there in the silence of the hurting room, Rebecca turned to her faith despite everything she had gone through. She closed her eyes, and allowed her thoughts to ascend to a higher plain. In a child's whisper and with the last vestiges of her precipitously failing faith, she prayed, "God. It's me again. I can only hope you are listening. As you can see. I've made a terrible mess of things. I'm in desperate need of your guidance. Please, please help me. Help me find a way out of this mess. Away from these men who only intend to do me harm. I promise that I'll return to Bay Ridge Cove and face whatever consequences await me for leaving there in the first place. If you find that you do not have time for me, could you at least help the young girl who died here. Her spirit is lost. It needs to find you." She paused for a moment. "And my friends, Hester and Ed. Could you see to it that no harm comes to them. For that I would be truly grateful. I guess that's all I have to say. Please help us. Amen."

When she opened her eyes, Mr. Black stood next to the bed. He towered over her, shoulder holster gleamed black, the gun within looked like certain death. Watching her, his eyes etched into a smile. "That was very touching, baby," he said, and placed a hand over his heart. "Kind of gets to you right here. Funny thing is though, Orchid. I spoke to him only a couple of days ago and asked him to send me a beautiful young redhead, and voila, here you are. As my good friend the Preacher would say, God does work in mysterious ways."

Rebecca's heart wrenched. She looked away from him, her eyes rested on the votive candle that only hours before ignited her into a world where reality, truth, and logic were turned inside out, rebirthed as make-believe, lies, and irrationality.

Mr. Black tugged at the bind of her left foot. "You must be hungry, Orchid. Mr. Brown has fixed us a wonderful dinner. I hope you like spareribs." He reached to the bed posts and untied the remaining binds.

Rebecca's arms dropped to the mattress, and she was suddenly aware of cooked meat emanating from the hallway. She watched Mr. Black move across the foot of the bed. He unleashed the foot that had yet to be corrupted. Resting hands on his hips, he pointed a wagging finger at her. "Now we don't want any trouble from you. Mr. Brown is still angry about the cut you gave him. If you promise to be good, you might even get dessert. Now that's only fair, isn't it, baby?"

She nodded. "Can I put a top on?"

"Of course, Orchid." Mr. Black stepped back, and allowed Rebecca to rise from the bed. Arms still lacked the life of blood. She shook and flexed her fingers until her skin began to prickle with verve. Her knee was still sore, but manageable. She went to the foot of the bed, thinking if she could get her hands on the gun; and that's as far as her thoughts took her, for she could not imagine herself using it, except maybe to throw it. She moved the photo of her mother, and retrieved the T-shirt captioned Angel Without Wings. Quickly she slipped it over her head and turned to face, Mr. Black. "I need to use the bathroom first."

"After you, baby," said Mr. Black. He directed her with an outstretched arm. "If you try to run again, Orchid, I will shoot you as sure as I'm standing here. You wouldn't be the first, and you most certainly wouldn't be the last. I can always ask God for another favor. He is always quite obliging."

Rebecca's eyes fell to her tarnished foot. A quote from the Bible floated in the swill of her mind, "Suffer the children to come unto Me." Turning on bare heels, she walked into the hallway, Mr. Black close behind. *Oh, God, please help us,* she pleaded and, for the first time in her life, wondered if God, the god she was raised to trust, to offer her faith to, to love unconditionally, more times than not said no.

* * *

Mr. Brown was putting the last cobs of corn on a plate when they entered the kitchen, the walls of which painted a frosty white. The fridge, stove, and dishwasher—all of which were steel—gleamed with obstinate care. Classical music hissed softly from a mini stereo perched on the black-tiled counter. The cattle prod she would soon learn to hate sat at the ready next to a toaster. Two stainless steel pots, one much larger than the other, sat on the stove.

Baked ribs and the sweet smell of boiled corn filled the air. *Dinner in hell with the devil himself,* thought Rebecca. *How avant-garde.*

Through the window, she could see the grey waters of a lake and a dock that stretched out from the shore. The contours of a boat, secured to the dock, bobbed in rhythm to the lapping waves. On the table were three plates of ribs, rice, and corn, steam rising from all of it. A bottle of soya sauce and a bottle of Tabasco sat on a white doily next to a saucer of butter and shakers of salt and pepper. Glasses of milk headed each plate.

The cut on Mr. Brown's forehead had been cleaned to a thin red line. He wore a burgundy apron that captioned: "I beat my eggs on a regular basis."

"You sit here," he said, and pulled out the center chair as if he were a gentleman of refined upbringing.

Rebecca sat, as did Mr. Brown and Mr. Black. Steamed rice warmed her face. Anchoring her plate, a knife and fork gleamed under the overhead light. Her hands remained in her lap, the length of her hair hiding her face. She remained fixated on the plate of food, not wanting to make eye contact with either man. Her empty stomach rumbled a series of gurgles and whines.

"Go ahead, Orchid, eat," said Mr. Black. He reached for the Tabasco, removed the red top and shook dozens of drops onto his rice and rack of sauce-smothered ribs. "I know you're hungry. You wasted your breakfast on Mr. Brown here." He looked across at Mr. Brown, merriment played in his eyes. Lifting the flank of ribs, he tore off a section of meat. "Mr. Brown makes excellent ribs. Go on, baby, try them." Then in a voice that was more demanding, he commanded, "I insist!" To add further authority to his posturing, he removed the gun from its holster and placed it next to his arm.

Nestled between the hulking form that was Mr. Black and the devil-may-care Mr. Brown, Rebecca felt dwarfed, completely defenseless. Hands shook on her lap. Slowly she raised them, rested one then the other on either side of the plate. Her eyes remained downcast. She sniffed a wandering drip of mucus. Having been in their grasp only a short while, she was as biddable as an impressionable child who would relent to their instruction because of a threat she had no doubt they would carry out.

She raised the corn, brought it to her mouth and bit into it. Juices flew in motley direction. She took another bite, then another, until her mouth was full of sweetness.

Mr. Black dropped a bare bone onto his plate. "Now that's better, Orchid. I told you Mr. Brown was a good cook. My compliments, Mr. Brown."

"Thank you, Mr. Black. I do try to be accommodating." Lifting his milk, he took a good swallow, then wiped at the moustache it had left on his upper lip. "Try the ribs,

Orchid. You'll find none better anywhere. Besides, you need to keep your strength up." He was quiet for a moment, then asked, "Tell me, Orchid. How well do you swim?"

Rebecca wanted to be sick with all the niceties they bantered about as if they were a married couple and she were a revered guest. Dropping the cob onto her plate, she lifted her eyes and focused on the lake. "I swim just fine," she said matter-of-factly, and wondered what the question was leading to. Were they going to take her out on the boat and make her swim acres of water until she could swim no more? Pluck her from the chopping waves just before she gave in to exhaustion? So that she might be, what, grateful? That certainly was a possibility, *wasn't it*?

"That's good," opinioned Mr. Brown.

"That's very good," affirmed Mr. Black.

They regarded each other with secretive knowledge. As if they knew of a grand reward Rebecca would receive for just knowing how to swim. She picked up the knife and fork. In the reflective surface of the knife, she caught a glimpse of her eyes. They were vacant, hoary, and lacked the shimmer of green they possessed only days before. The area around them sallow for want of sleep. The one dose of heroin she had had, had already left its mark upon her. She dug into the ribs, the knife in her hand begging for her to drive it into the flesh of Mr. Black or Mr. Brown and to hell with the consequences. Instead, she picked up the sauce-lathered meat and tore into it like a depraved street urchin. She called upon her desperate anger to give her continued strength.

* * *

When all the meat was stripped from bone, the cobs naked of their golden fruit, and only a few grains of rice remained on each plate, the meal was declared a social success by Mr. Black. "There, you see, Orchid. There's no reason why we can't be civil to each other during your stay." He followed that up with a picking of his great white teeth, and sucked the meat from them while Mr. Brown cleared the table. He loaded the plates and utensils into the dishwasher, and whistled a cheerful ditty while doing so.

Rebecca remained forlorn. Though her belly was full and she had regained some strength, she had an inkling that the night was far from over. She could see it in their eyes whenever they looked at her. Deception and deviousness masquerading as smiles and benevolence, Mr. Brown and Mr. Black being masters of their avaricious natures.

"I noticed that you had some toothpaste and a toothbrush in your suitcase," offered Mr. Black. "Would you like to use them, baby? You must keep up your appearances."

Rebecca nodded, her gaze still focused on the dip and rise of the boat that had become, over the course of the meal, a silhouette on the water, lit only by the reaches of a near full summer moon.

"Come with me then." Mr. Black lifted the gun and slipped it home, then he rose to his full height, and stepped behind Rebecca's chair. In one swift movement, he dragged it out from the table. "After you, baby," he said.

Bay Ridge Cove brave Rebecca turned on him. "Stop calling me that! I'm not your or anyone's baby!"

Mr. Black grabbed her roughly by the arm and yanked her from the chair. "You are whatever I say you are... *baby.* If I choose to call you a bitch or whore or even an apple. You *will* accept it." He squeezed her arm until he knew it hurt. "Do I make myself clear?"

Rebecca ground her teeth. Though the pain he was administering to her arm was almost unbearable, she would not give Mr. Black the satisfaction of knowing that he was hurting her. She locked eyes with his. Mr. Brown continued to whistle merrily. "You disgust me. You're nothing but a bully. The both of you!"

"Sticks and stones, baby, *ouch*. Now are you done with your little tantrum?"

"Fuck you, you black bastard!" She knew she was going to pay for that one and did.

Mr. Black slapped her hard across the face. "Still a little fight left in you, *eh, baby*? I tried to be nice. But you won't have it. Well, I have just the thing for that." Drawing her forward, he grabbed her by the hair and steered her out of the kitchen. "I will own you, Orchid," he whispered maliciously into her ear. "After tonight, you'll know what it means to be truly terrified."

* * *

They returned to the hurting room where Rebecca would spend the next harrowing month. She located the toothbrush and paste in the bottom of the suitcase while Mr. Black stood ominously above her.

"Now take your clothes off," he demanded

"What for? So you can humiliate me more?"

"If you don't take them off, I will. And I won't be gentle. Or maybe I'll get Mr. Brown in here to do it. I believe he likes you. Would like to get close to you. As close as your deepest secret. Know what I mean, baby? Now take them off!"

Grudgingly, Rebecca set the brush and tube of Crest aside and lifted the T-shirt over her head. She dropped it onto the mattress. Turning, she unzipped her jeans and pushed them down to her knees, kicked out one leg then the other. "There, you happy now? Getting a good look?" Grabbing the hygiene products, she squeezed the tube so hard she thought it might burst open.

Mr. Black's eyes roamed her body, a reprehensible look of satisfaction heightened his tawdry features. The whites of his eyes and the audacity of his piano key smile, made him look like a jack-o'-lantern in the bewitchment of a Halloween night. "That tight little body of yours is going to make me a lot of money, Orchid. Every time you spread your legs, I'm going to hear a cash register go off."

Flesh-goosed by cold and fear, a just reminder of her predicament, Rebecca placed her occupied hands over the gentle wisp of her womanhood. With what little frankness remained, she said, "You might be able to control me physically and perhaps psychologically, Mr. Black, but I guarantee you, you will never control my spirit."

"We'll just see about that. Remember, the Harts are counting on you being cooperative."

The mention of the Harts again put to rest her daring gumption. The promise of a terrifying night that lay just ahead toyed within the asylum of her most profane thoughts. *What were they going to do to me next?* With a last breath of bold faith, she said, "You'll pay for all your sins, Mr. Black. You'll be judged and spend the rest of eternity in hell with your bastard friends."

"You're probably right, baby. But right now I've got a job to do. So let's get going." He put a powerful hand on her shoulder, steered her into the hallway and God only knew where else.

* * *

Once they were outside, Mr. Black pulled the gun from its holster and pressed it against the back of Rebecca's head. "Keep going, Orchid," he said and applied pressure. His boots crunched, the fulsomeness of his heavy breath evil on the back of her neck.

The ambient casting of the moon caused the stirring lake to dazzle with pricks of light. Billions of stars watched with twinkling awareness as Rebecca walked forward, feet sensitive to each stone, each twig, and every spiny weed they encountered. Darkness caressed her nakedness with the cowardly glove of an inauspicious lover. Although the night air was warm, she shivered uncontrollably. "How much farther?" she asked, not daring to look back, a hundred possibilities of what was to come oppressing her thoughts.

"Not much farther. You'll know when you get there."

Rebecca continued forward, the sound of waves lapping at the shore, anything but peaceful. A night hawk tore through the air above her, its high-pitched cry pierced the night with haunting sentiment. With each step, her eyes adjusted to the gloom, enabling her to make out more and more shapes. A chair. Several large rocks clustered to form a circle. Waist-high shrubs scattered hither scither and what looked like a square box that seemed to emanate a low motorized hum.

Then she saw it. A sphere of darkness on the ground not twenty feet away, approximately eight feet in diameter. Its intended function stopped her dead in her tracks.

Mr. Black shoved her from behind. "Keep going. You're almost there."

Rebecca refused to move. The hole in the ground looked like the wells that fed the homes surrounding Bay Ridge Cove with water. "What is that!? Is that a well!? You're not putting me in any fucking well!"

"Actually, we prefer to call it the pit. And yes, you're going in whether you want to or not."

Terrified, Rebecca dropped to the ground, knees dug into the earth. "Please don't put me in there, Mr. Black. I'll do anything. I won't give you any more trouble. Just don't put me in there."

"Sorry, baby, but we have to teach you conformity. We find this method very effective." He slippped the gun back into its holster, and grabbed Rebecca by the hair. He stood her up. "You're going in if I have to throw you in."

Rebecca dug her heels. Ever since she was small, she'd always had a fear of cramped spaces. Even a room without a window reasoned much anxiety. Just the thought of being in a well caused her to wretch. She grabbed at her stomach, tears filled her eyes. "Please, Mr. Black. I'm begging you. Don't put me in there!"

"We know all about your fears, Orchid." Pulling her by the hair, he dragged her to the edge of the pit.

To Rebecca it looked like a hungry mouth that would swallow her into its depths. Bare feet teetered on the rough perimeter. "Oh, God, please help me," she whimpered.

Mr. Black whispered in her ear, "God has no place here, baby. I'll check on you from time to time. It's a good thing you're a skilled swimmer." He shoved her roughly with his knee.

Rebecca fell forward, arms and legs flailed in the air, lungs releasing a primal scream. Down she went. Into the darkness. Into her own personal hell, the free fall seeming to last forever. She hit the surface of water face and hands first, the speed of her fall sending her deep into its reaches. Hands struck bottom, hard. Pushing off, she turned herself so that her feet were planted on the cold, clammy bottom. Her face broke through the surface. Gasping for air, she spit and choked, wiped at her eyes, at the hair that was tangled about her face. The frigid water cut right through her, shocking her into silence. However, much to her relief, she found that the water was only up to her shoulders, enabling her to stand without too much trouble. She looked up. Mr. Black stood looking down, his silhouette cutting into the myriad of stars which surrounded his head.

The fall was at least forty feet, Rebecca estimated. The pit or the well or whatever the hell you wanted to call it was built with cobblestones that glistened within the scope of the habitual moon. Looking up from the depths, she became dizzy, the stars and Mr. Black rotated as if they were some dastardly kaleidoscope. She closed her eyes, and treaded the cold black water around her.

"I hope the water isn't too cold," Mr. Black called down to her, voice echoing off the stone walls. Then he stepped back and was gone. Heavy footsteps receded from the well.

Numbing cold merged with Rebecca's deepest fears. Heart hammered in an alarming panic. Cold air barely filled her lungs. She could feel the walls close in on her though they were not. If it wasn't for the grey light the moon distributed, she would be in complete and utter darkness. Blindly she stepped back until she came into contact with the slippery stones, teeth chattering irrepressibly. *Think of something nice.* Her mind created visuals of puppies and kittens. Rainbows arching over fields of sunflowers, her dream lover standing among them, long hair blowing about his face. Oh, how she would like to feel his secretive arms about her. Still, the walls seemed to close on her.

Instinctively, she hugged at her bosom in an attempt to warm herself. Something pushed against the backs of her legs. A jet stream of water not unlike the propelled water in a hot tub. "LET ME OUT OF HERE!" she screamed. Her tormented voice echoed off the walls, resounded within the confines of her mind. Then in a despairing whimper, she pleaded, "Please, Mr. Black. Please let me out."

Suddenly, and with absolute mortification, she realized the water was up to her chin and rising. Somehow it was being flooded into the well. *The box that hummed. It must be some kind of pump. Drawing water from the lake.* Her body became buoyant, forcing her to tread water. In less than a minute, she was lifted off the cold, clammy floor.

The water rose higher and higher until it filled half the well. It took her to a section where she could actually see the various colors of the cobblestone. Moving her arms and legs in unison, she expunged water that had found its way into her gaping mouth. She tried to resolve her turbulent breathing by taking in deep gulps of air, the desperate need to survive overriding her claustrophobic fears. She closed her eyes, and imagined herself lying on her back in the warm buoyancy of the Atlantic Ocean, arms drifting at her sides, fingers splayed apart, face pointing up to the stars. The only thing keeping her afloat, the slight back-and-forth movement of her submerged legs.

Several minutes passed before her rapid breaths mollified and her heartbeat returned to a lesser state of agitation. She knew that if need be, she could remain like this for hours.

During the next half hour, Rebecca listened to the music of her memories. Despite the cold, she was able to conjure images of the good times spent with her mother in the summer-filled kitchen atop Dover Bluff Road. The ruminations were crisp and clear, and they lent her imaginary warmth. She smiled despite her watery state of affairs. *Fuck you, Mr. Black.*

As if reading her mind, he appeared at the cusp of the well, his imposing figure casting a dark shadow over Rebecca's body. "I thought you might like a little company," he said, and flashed those great white teeth. In his hand, he held what appeared to be a gunnysack fastened with rope. "I told you, Orchid. We know about all your fears."

Renewed terror seized Rebecca by the throat, for she could see the sack contained life. *Snakes!* she realized. *Oh my god! He's going to put snakes in here with me!*

When she was four years old, a simple garden snake had latched on to her hand while she was picking flowers in her mother's garden, leaving a small laceration on her palm. Traumatized by the incident, the mere mention of snakes sent her skin crawling. To be in the same room with one caused her to jump and run about as if she were having a fit of hysteria.

Righting herself, she moved to the nearest wall, and watched with utter horror as Mr. Black unraveled the rope and tipped the sack upside down. Laughter thundered in Rebecca's ears. "Mr. Brown sends his regards." He walked away.

Dark serpentine shapes, four in all and each longer than the other, spilled like black demons into the well and splashed into the surface with deadly intentions.

Rebecca screamed. She thrashed about, slapped with her hands, and kicked with her feet until it seemed a storm of great intensity had entered the well. She slipped beneath the surface, and blew countless bubbles through her mouth. So terrified was Rebecca, she urinated copiously.

One of the snakes coiled itself around her left arm. She kicked her feet until her head was above water once again, and grabbed at the snake. "GET OFF ME!" Water filled her mouth. She coughed and choked and spit it out, all the while trying to remain above the surface. The snake would not budge. Instead it constricted further, becoming a part of her flailing extremity. Another snake slipped over her face and head, and yet another wrapped its oily body around her throat.

Rebecca's eyes bulged. Something in her snapped, augmenting her into a primitive mad woman. A wailing banshee. The world's most proficient snake killer.

She screamed blue bloody murder in some alien language and pounded her arm against the wall over and over, irrespective of the pain until the snake slipped off and slithered away. Grabbing at her throat, fingers ripped at the tightening reptile with Herculean strength. She slipped beneath the surface again, only this time she managed to take a deep breath before doing so. Spinning in the water, she struggled with the snake that would surely cut off her air passages. Finding its head, she pulled at its length until she could get it to her mouth, then in a fit of extreme odium, bit its head off.

The body of the headless reptile let loose and fell into the depths of the well. Rebecca let the head drop from her clenched teeth. The shriek of utter madness she let loose beneath the water sounded like a blunted roar in her ears. However, her rage did not stop there. She reached up, tackled one of the remaining three by its tail, rose from the water, and using it like a whip, flung it against the wall over and over until the creature went limp in her hand, its head smashed into a pulpous mess. She let it loose, and it drifted down, brushing her leg as it sank to the bottom. The two that remained tried vainly to escape Rebecca's wrath by climbing the walls, only to fall back into the water.

Rebecca would have none of it. She took to them like a hound takes to a fox, and repeated the killing ceremony, her mind temporarily lost, until all four snakes lay at the bottom of their watery grave.

She looked up to the convention of stars, and screamed, "My name is Rebecca White! Do you hear me, you bastard?! My name is Rebecca White! You'll never take that away from me!"

* * *

Two, possibly three hours passed since the incident with the snakes. Rebecca had watched the configuration of stars change as the world traversed its nightly orbit. The moon had since moved on, retiring the pit into a darkened state, lit only by the twinkling points of light above her.

Her legs were numb, almost too numb for her to move. Nevertheless, she found within herself an obstinate vigor that otherwise did not exist, enabling her to stay afloat. The old Rebecca would have surely drowned; however, this was the new Rebecca, forged by hatred and the deeds of those whose only accountability was the necessity of ill-gotten gains.

Dead tired, she had kept herself conscious by biting her bottom lip until her eyes bled tears. Each of her ten toes cramped painfully, though Rebecca welcomed such discomfort, for the pain also rendered her sentient when she wasn't biting her lip. She lay floating on her back, weak arms stroking the water that had long since filled the passageways of her ear ducts, causing her to hear sounds she knew not existed.

Ponderous groans and bleats. Squeaks and clucks. Ringings and pingings. Toots and gurgles. It was these sounds she felt that if anything were to drive her over the edge, it would be these persisting, unmelodic cacophony of noises only she could hear.

Every now and then, a night bird shadowed across the mouth of the man-made shaft, screeching a mournful note as if pleading clemency for the woman in the well. She wasn't absolutely sure, considering the resonant noise in her ears, but every now and then, she thought she heard the same crunching Mr. Black's boots made when he walked about. *Surely, he would not let me drown,* she thought. *His goal after all was to make money through the sex trade industry. What good would it do him to let me drown? None.* He'd have to start the process all over again, and that just didn't seem rational. No, he would not let her drown. She was sure of it.

* * *

Another hour passed, or so it seemed. Barely afloat, eyes, nose, and mouth, were the only parts of her body that remained above water.

Something stirred beneath her, and she thought that it was one of the snakes come back to life to torment her further. Suddenly, the water next to her parted, and gave way to the top of a head that soon became a face and then shoulders, rising from the depths of the well. It was the young girl she had seen in the hurting room, features sallow, ghostly eyes pleading. She could have been Rebecca's younger sister if she'd had one.

"*Can you help me?*" Water purged from her mouth. "*I'm lost. I can't seem to find my way home. I miss my mom and dad. Maybe you could call them and tell them where I am. I know they must be worried. I shouldn't have run away. I'm really sorry that I did. I'm so cold.*" The girl raised her arms and hugged the pale bumps of her bare shoulders, slim fingers clutched inconsolably.

In case Mr. Black was close, as Rebecca suspected, she spoke with a softness she knew only she and the girl could hear. "What's your name?"

"*My name is Kimberly. Kimberly Gagne.*" The spirit smiled innocently. "*But everybody calls me Pinkie, because one of my little fingers is a lot shorter than the other one. See.*" She held out both hands. The little finger on her right hand was an inch shorter than the one on the left and was bent at an odd angle.

"My name is Rebecca," said Rebecca. "But you can call me Becca. How old are you, Pinkie?'

"*Fourteen. I'll be fifteen in a couple of months.*" More water poured from her mouth.

Rebecca pretended not to notice, obviously she had drowned. Most likely in the very well she drifted in. Now Kimberly was lost. Caught in limbo. Completely unaware that she had passed on. Left to roam the last place she knew when she was alive. "I'll try to help you, Pinkie. What are your parents' names? Where do they live?"

"*My dad's name is Martin, and my mom's name is Yvonne. We're French. Although I don't speak it. Only my parents do, usually when they're fighting. We live at 133 Belmont Street in Sacramento, California. Do you really think you can find them for me?*"

"I'll try my best, Pinkie."

"*Thank you, Becca. You're very nice. Maybe we could be friends.*" More water spilled from Kimberly's mouth.

"I'd like that very much," said Rebecca, and forced a smile. "When did you leave home?"

Kimberly Gagne's spirit tilted her head to one side, pondered the answer. "*I think it was yesterday. Yes. That's right. It was yesterday. I got a ride from this really nice man who talked about God a lot and wore this big gold cross around his neck. He drove a big silver truck, and he told me he would take me to... take me to. That's strange. I don't remember.*"

"That's okay, Pinkie. It doesn't matter. What matters is that we get you home safe and sound," Rebecca lied, felt awful about it and mentally cursed the artful Henry Klondike. How do you tell a person who has passed on, who doesn't know they have, that they're dead? Little Caleb Hart, in his own way, knew that he was no longer the same, that there was a reverent difference between himself and his parents.

Kimberly Gagne's spirit faded. "*I've got to go now, Becca. I've got to keep looking. Between the two of us, we should be able to find them.*" She reached a hand, and gently stroked Rebecca's face. "*You're very beautiful, Becca.*" She sank ever so slowly until the top of her head disappeared beneath the surface, followed by the length of her outstretched arm until the tips of her fingers slipped under, and left the area flat as glass.

Tears spilled from Rebecca's eyes and into the deadly mirror of water. Anger charged her with renewed strength. Those bastards had let that poor girl drown and thought nothing of it. She realized that because she and Kimberly resembled each other, she was a replacement for Mr. Black and Mr. Brown's hard-hearted neglect. She righted herself, moved her hands back and forth, scissored her legs, and tilted her head from one side to the other repeatedly until the water in her ears let loose.

Several minutes passed before she became conscious she was moving closer to the opening of the well. *Thank God,* she thought then rescinded the consideration. What good *God* could allow such things to happen? *Suffer the children indeed.*

Mr. Black's ominous silhouette appeared over the hole. "Had enough, Orchid?" His baritone voice boomed in her ears.

She wanted to scream at him that he was a murderer, but he already knew that. Instead she said, "Why don't you join me. The water's fine." She laughed. A crazy, lilting kind of laugh, the sound of someone who teetered on the slippery edge of sanity.

In under five minutes, her head was level with the ground. Mr. Black reached out to her. "Here. Take my hand."

Rebecca lifted a weary arm over her head.

Mr. Black took her hand in his and, with a powerful pull, drew her from the pit.

With water dripping from her body, tangled ropes of lake water hair, Rebecca remained on her hands and knees, exhausted, mucus running from her nose. A knifing shiver ran roughshod through her body as she wretched. Lifting her head, she looked up at Mr. Black who stood over her, legs spread, hands on his hips, the whites of his eyes and teeth shining in the darkness. "I hate you," she stammered through trembling lips.

Mr. Black laughed, reached down, took her by the hair, and yanked her to her feet. "What's not to love, baby. I'm a beautiful man. Ask anyone." He let go of her hair, went to the chair situated not five feet from the well and retrieved a towel. He wrapped it around Rebecca's shoulders. "There. How's that? Better?" Hands placed on her shoulders, he steered her back toward the house. "It's time for another taste of that good old feeling," he told her. Smiling smiling always smiling.

* * *

Once Rebecca was tethered to the bed, Mr. Black opened his little black kit of suffering while Mr. Brown watched from the foot of the bed. He administered the heroin with practiced efficiency, leaving her to lose herself in its potent grasp.

Later that night, she would be introduced to a new form of discipline. A cage of wrought iron with padlock, no larger than a sofa, tucked away in a corner of the damp basement. Rebecca would spend that night and many others listening to her heartbeat, to the mindless boggle of voices in her head brought on by the hot liquid traversing within, and to the floorboards creaking above her.

Days and nights would become the same for Rebecca. She wallowed in and out of reality, becoming nothing more than an empty vessel. Each day she was returned to the pit, left to the point of near drowning before she was plucked from the icy waters. Nights in the cage humbled her, converted her to the will of Mr. Black's designs. It was there she was frequently visited by the spirit of Kimberly Gagne, always searching for her parents, lost in the in-between world forever.

Rebecca's taste for food diminished as the drug became her only wanton necessity. In a short matter of time, she learned how to melt the heroin, charge the syringe, and delight in the prick of the needle. She lost weight, but hardly enough for there to be a concern.

The tops of her feet became tracked with tiny red welts, fashioned in the form of a Y, to which Mr. Black treated with ointment. The threat of assured unrepentant harm done to the Harts ever present.

Once he was sure Rebecca was truly under the influence, Mr. Black commenced with instructions on the ways a man should be pleasured. He rewarded her constructive efforts with gestures of kindness, and punished her when she became doggedly stubborn, depriving her of sleep and by means of Mr. Brown's cattle prod.

Weekly, Mr. Black contacted Tony Millions and told him of her progress, to which the self-proclaimed affluent architect of Vegas's more sordid side was delighted. For the final bid to bed Rebecca was seventeen thousand, offered by Mr. Wong of Hong Kong. More than double Tony's original investment of the fourteen year old virgin Kimberly. And that was to be just the beginning.

Rebecca White—formerly of Bay Ridge Cove, daughter of a home misplaced, captain of her field hockey squad, and otiose dreamer—slipped through the cracks forged by nefarious hands and landed in the palm of inequity.

Abandoned by faith, mind retooled, her body was converted into a haven for the social requirements of libidinous men, leaving her to feel like a wayward ship crashed against the jagged rocks below Dover Bluff Heights.

Before long, much to the delight of her abductors, Orchid became the moniker she capitulated to. *Assimilation complete*. Another page turned.

* * *

34

The River

THE end days of August brought with them a season of cold nights and windswept days, the weather causing much havoc in many areas of the states. Hurricanes, tornadoes and floods, the high cost of petrol, and a slumping economy were bringing the mighty US of A to its knees.

Konahee stood in front of the stove stirring a two-gallon pot of rabbit stew. It was nearing 6:00 p.m. In an hour, Johnny would arrive for dinner, hungry from the toil of the day. Her beloved Cleveland Indians were out of playoff contention, and she knew deep down it would be several more years before they championed themselves into a position where they would contend well into the playoffs.

Adding the herbs, a blend of thyme and rosemary, several pinches of salt, and white pepper to taste, she poured the cream and set the stove to simmer.

It was Johnny's birthday, and he'd come to love Konahee's rabbit stew more than anything she had to offer him. She had also baked three loaves of sourdough bread to compliment the stew, knowing that between them, they would, at the very least, consume the better part of two.

The special day seemed to have faded from Johnny's memory. He'd made no mention of it during breakfast, but instead went about his continuing task of painting the barn. However, Konahee knew, and she'd spent the morning baking him a chocolate cake with orange icing and wrapped for him a gift of valued significance. A smooth stone of turquoise she had had in her possession since she was in the springtide of her youth. He was going to leave on the morrow, that much she knew for certain, and never again would the two break bread, their short time spent together warmhearted memories that would last each of them the rest of their predestined lifetimes.

Johnny stood on the scaffolding he'd rented from HL Hardware, applying a second coat of paint to the weather-dried barn. The sun was at his back, hammering him with its setting heat. If it weren't for the cool winds descending from the Laramie Mountains, he would not be able to sustain more than a couple of hours at a time perched on the two-storey platform. His stomach was telling him that it was almost dinnertime.

Earlier in the day, he'd been visited by Linda the wolf after what had become a morning routine of riding the youth-inspired Juno, galloping around the paddock now green with blades of grass and clover. It was the second such meeting since their first, leaving Johnny with the sad knowledge they would only meet twice more.

The beautiful wolf had snuck up on him, her preferred method of meeting, while Johnny tended to the thirsty needs of the sweat-coated Juno.

"Good morning, Johnny," she'd said, startling him.

Johnny emptied the bucket of water into the blue trough. Without turning, he said, "Good morning, Linda. I had a feeling I might be seeing you soon." He turned to greet her. Linda was lying on her haunches, eyes narrowed against the wind, the tip of her tongue protruding from between powerful jaws, the luxurious fur across her back undulating. Seeing the wolf, Juno finished her need for water and sprinted to the end of the paddock. Johnny bent so that they might shake hands, instead, Linda raised herself and licked his face.

"What was that for?" he asked, putting a hand to his face.

Linda's words filled his mind. "Today is a special day, Johnny. Surely you must remember your own birthday?"

Johnny hadn't. To him, the day had become like any other, just another day that included a full day's labor and the magical aura of the place. He had become complacent in his tasks and welcomed whatever mysterious events might be offered. "I completely forgot," he said. "Wow, that makes me twenty-one. Legal in every state." Realizing this, he thought of the bike and his father and how he wished he could be with him even if it was just long enough to tell him that he was doing all right.

"Do not worry about your father, Johnny. He is well. You have my word on it."

"Thank you, Linda. That's good to know."

The beautiful wolf raised and stretched, and dug her paws into the earth before seating herself on hind legs. "Is there anything special you would like to do now that you know it is your birthday?" She snapped at a wind-carried insect.

"You mean with you?" Johnny scratched the top of his head.

"Answering a question with yet another question. That is very guarded of you. Yes, of course with me. I do not see anyone else around. Well, except for Juno, but she has a distaste for my company. We could go for a walk and talk."

"I don't know if I should. I have to start putting the second coat of paint on the barn." He looked to the structure. The first coat of red had all but vanished, absorbed by weather-dry planks. All that remained of his week's long labor was a dark, nearly colorless stain, as if the barn had been dipped in pink water. Then again, he'd reasoned, how could he refuse time spent with a talking wolf. "Okay," he said. "The barn can wait an hour. It's still early. We can walk to the end of the property and back. How's that sound?"

"Lead the way," encouraged the wolf. "I'm all ears."

Johnny had closed the gate to the paddock. Man and wolf embarked on an hour's long journey to the end of the property where they stopped for a period in time to admire the rugged landscape, the sea of desert, and watch the spirits of once-great warriors tumble across the land. They spoke of a civilization past, mentor and student sitting on the edge of a flat rock, the sun at their backs, a hawk soaring overhead, its piercing cries filling the air around them.

* * *

Johnny dipped a brush into the five-gallon pail of paint. The second coat was holding, though he knew it would need a third to get the exact color Konahee wanted. He rolled his tired shoulders. He had gained a great deal of muscle mass since his arrival. His biceps bulged, and his chest had become thick, hardened plates over a stomach that rippled like a washboard. Hands billeted the calluses and blisters of hard labor and held within them the gripping power of a vice. It was as though his body was responding with the coming of age, now that he was twenty-one.

A crow landed on the roof of the barn. To Johnny's recollection, it was the first crow he had seen since he first drove up the driveway more than a month ago. It cawed down at him, clicking its black beak and fluttering its ebony wings. It was joined by another and another. In seconds, there was a row of the yakking birds, beating the air with their wings.

Johnny counted eight in all. A murder complete. A bad omen. "Shoo!" he yelled up at them. "Go away." He looked around the platform for something to throw, but found nothing.

In unison, the murder hopped to the edge of the roof, their obsidian eyes stripping Johnny of his bravado, leaving him to feel something he hadn't in his twenty-one years. Fear. If these creatures who dined on carrion were to attack him, which it looked like they were about to do, he would be defenseless. Consciously, he put the brush down, and kept his eyes on the moving mass that continued to reprimand him with their caterwauling.

From above came a piercing cry. Johnny looked into the fading blue. The hawk, Johnny's daily visitor, hung in the air in attack formation as still as a statue except for the rapid movement of its wings and its calling challenge to the crows. One by one, the scavengers launched themselves from the roof, and rose into the air, the challenge accepted.

Johnny took the opportunity to relid the pail of paint, deposit the brush into a coffee tin filled with Varsol, and climb down the scaffolding.

Once grounded, he lifted his face to the sky, fearing that irremediable harm would come to the courageous bird of prey. Crows as a single unit were cowardly, but as a murderer's row, they possessed the brash disposition of a pack of wild dogs.

Johnny watched helplessly as they bore into the hawk, a single cloud of ominous black. There was a great clash of talons and beaks. Black feathers exploded and spiraled to the ground. The hawk emerged from the mass of black and climbed high into the air. For a moment, the crows seemed confused, as one of their own fell awkwardly through the air. One of its wings had been severely damaged, and protruded from its body like the mast of a ship. It spun unceremoniously to the ground, and landed with a thud, the impact killing it instantly. The remaining crows dispersed, circled the air in frantic pandemonium.

For several trips of Johnny's heart, the hawk remained high, its wings carving the updraft. Then like a stone, it dropped, gathering tremendous speed, silent. With the power of a lightning strike, it collided talons first into one of the crows. The impact destroyed the bird in an eruption of sable feathers. It fell in three pieces to the ground, and landed mere inches from its brethren of darkness.

George appeared from a hole in the barn, raced to the carcasses, picked up one of the three pieces, and fled back into the barn. *Dinner served.*

The six remaining crows retreated toward the mountains in a cacophony of ill tidings as the hawk rose into the air once more, ready to defend again if need be.

"Thank you, brother bird," Johnny called out. The fearless hawk screeched a reply, turned on the air, and headed south.

Johnny jumped into the pickup, engaged the engine, and headed to the house. *What a strange and frightening birthday gift.*

Upon entering the house, he could hear Konahee busy in the kitchen and he could smell the thick aroma of rabbit stew and fresh-baked bread. He called out that he needed to wash the paint off his hands before sitting down to dinner and took to the stairs, mounting them two at a time. Vigorously he washed his hands and face then changed into fresh clothes Konahee had left draped over the tub: blue jeans and a denim shirt she managed to get to smell like springtime. It had become customary for him, and Konahee to dress for dinner as if it were a social event. Konahee would often be garbed in outrageous attire and her favored yellow sun hat, except on the nights the Indians played. Those nights were reserved for a baseball cap, Cleveland jersey, and Johnny's sunglasses.

He inspected himself in the mirror,and pronounced himself clean and tidy except for a sweat pimple that had erupted on the side of his nose. After a quick pinch and wipe, he ascended the stairs as if it were Christmas morning, feeling somewhat more mature because it was his birthday and anxious to sink his teeth into Konahee's tender, herb-flavored rabbit.

To his immense surprise, the kitchen was festooned with blue ribbon which hung from the four corners and was taped to the bottom of the globe mounted over the table.

Konahee stood at the stove, her back to him, the pointed cap of a kid's birthday hat, red and green in color with yellow feather sitting askew atop her grey head. A flamboyant pink dress adorned with dozens of green dragonflies covered her body.

Johnny's jaw dropped.

Konahee turned to greet him. "Well, are you going to just stand there with your mouth hanging open, or are you going to sit down?" There was a glint to her blue eye Johnny hadn't seen before.

Still flabbergasted by the unexpected surprise, Johnny looked to the table where a cake with orange icing and three blue candles stood looking delicious. At his place was a pointed cap. Birthday Boy in blue across a shine of silver. "You did all this for me?" he asked, his skin tingling with ingenuous joy.

"Of course. Today is your birthday, is it not? Now sit and put on your hat. Dinner is just about ready."

Johnny went to his place at the table, sat, and fixed the snug cap to his head, the elastic digging into his chin, but he didn't care. Not since he was six years old could he remember a time when his birthday was celebrated with such festive proclivities. His heart soared with new love for this mysterious and pleasantly eccentric woman. "If you tell me this is a chocolate cake, I'm going to kiss you."

With serrated knife Konahee cut into one of the sourdough loaves. "Chocolate is also my favorite. So you can save your kisses for another. I have not been kissed in so long, the shock of it might kill me anyway." She laughed heartily, the sound of it filling the kitchen, and Johnny's heart.

Forgotten for the time being was the alarming incident with the crows.

Konahee dished out two large bowls of stew and set them on the table with the bread and a bottle of beer for each of them. Once seated, she raised her bottle and made a toast. "It has been a long time since I've enjoyed the company of another. You are an exceptional young man, Johnny. I thank you for everything you have done for Juno and me. I wish you continued strength on your journey. Happy birthday."

Overcome with emotion, Johnny found it difficult to suppress the tears welled in his eyes. A single drip escaped and carved his cheek. He knuckled it away and said, "Thank you, Konahee. I will never forget this day. You have brought much wisdom and kindness into my life." They clinked bottles, and took healthy swallows of ale.

Once dinner was over and Konahee had sung "Happy Birthday" while he blew out the candles, Johnny cut into the cake, and placed large wedges onto mismatched saucers. The first piece he put into his mouth was heaven. The second, ecstasy, and the third, an amalgamation of the first two.

"I have something for you," said Konahee, reaching into a pocket. The small gift was wrapped in blue foil and no bigger than a throwing stone. She placed it on the table in front of him.

"You didn't need to get me a gift. The dinner and the cake and well, everything were more than enough."

"Nonsense. It is your birthday. To receive a gift is tradition still, is it not? Take it as a token of an old woman's gratitude." She looked at him with all the love a mother might bestow upon her son, the blue of her eye shimmering with emotion.

Johnny set his fork down and took the blue foil gift into his hand. It weighed no more than an ounce, yet, the moment he touched it seemed to exude lofty properties, as if it held within it the prodigy of infinite wisdom. With care, Johnny tore the tape and unraveled the gift, revealing a smooth oval rock of turquoise. He held it in his fingers, eyes curious. "It's very beautiful. Thank you Konahee. I will treasure it always."

"My mother gave it to me and her mother to her," explained Konahee.

"Then I can't accept it. It has been with you far too long."

"No. It is time for me to pass it on. I want you to have it since I do not have children of my own." Reaching, she closed a hand over his so that the stone was concealed within the bond of their hands. "One day the stone will reveal its true purpose. You will feel it in your heart and know." She smiled wide, blue eye ablaze, dead eye fixed on Johnny's face and removed her hand. "Now let us have more cake."

Johnny fingered the stone into a front pocket. Through the jeans he could feel its life, as if it were animate with spiritual energy. He cut two more sections of cake.

George the cat sauntered into the kitchen, belly low with the fullness of the day's harvest. In a single belly full bound he leapt onto the counter, curled his tail around his backside and meowed.

Konahee turned in her chair, "What is it, George?"

The cat pointed at the pot on the stove with its face, nose pulsing, vertical ears twitching back and forth.

"It looks to me that you have had enough to eat already. Perhaps I will give you some rabbit during the game tonight, but not before. Now be off with you." She waved a dismissive hand.

George scooted off the counter, landed on the floor with a dull thud, tail rigid, ran into the hallway, and disappeared.

"Where does he go?" asked Johnny, somewhat bemused.

"He will sulk for a while then turn up when he thinks I have grown soft." Konahee laughed. "Usually he is right."

"So there's a game on tonight?"

"Yes. Cleveland is playing Baltimore. Two teams going nowhere fast, but I will watch it anyway. Since this is your birthday, I think you should go out tonight. Go to the Gooseneck. Be with people your own age. The company of an old woman and a horse must have gotten boring for you by now. You can use my truck as long as you promise not to drink."

Johnny thought for a moment. It *was* true. He hadn't been off Konahee's property except to go into Alcova and pick up supplies. Perhaps he would run in to the very amicable Debbie Smith as she so often promised whenever he went to Garrette's Tack and Feed. Swallowing the cake in his mouth, he said, "You're right, Konahee. I should be with people my age on my birthday. It would be good to get out and stretch my legs a little. And I promise I won't drink."

"Good. I will keep a light on so you can see where the house is when you come home tonight. Put the lantern on the front porch to guide you back to the loft. Be careful on the road. Too many of our people overindulge then get behind the wheel of a crowded vehicle. There have been many deaths on the road between here and Alcova."

* * *

Johnny checked on Juno before he left. She came to the gate with blades of green grass drooped from muzzle, her eyes bemusing her delight in having a field of never-ending edibles.

The sun neared its drop behind the mountains, igniting clouds that had gathered at their peaks in striking shades of orange, pinks, and plumbs. Johnny stroked the length of Juno's face, and told her how beautiful she was. Juno responded with a nod of her head and a flicker of her now elegant tail. "I'll see you in the morning," he told her then went to the loft and retrieved the lantern and matches. Once he was back at the house, he set them on the front stoop.

He had showered after dinner, and Konahee had rebraided his hair, relishing him with compliments on how very handsome he was and that he would be a great catch for some lucky girl one day. Then she'd retired to the living room after exchanging her birthday hat for her Cleveland baseball cap and slipped the jersey over her dress, completing the ensemble by resting Johnny's sunglasses on the bridge of her nose.

Boots polished, Johnny made sure everything was tucked in just the right places. It was his birthday after all, and some female company wouldn't do him any harm, even if it was just meaningless conversation.

The game was already on when he left. Without taking her shaded eyes from the screen, Konahee had simply said, "Have a good time tonight."

* * *

Headed to Alcova with the all rat pack station to keep him company, Johnny wore a smile on his face as reaching as Konahee's property. Children played in yards, all wrapped in colorful fall sweaters, and chased one another in circles, the setting sun casting their shadows long against the earth. They stopped their activities long enough to wave as Johnny slowed the vehicle and waved back. They had become over the weeks friends of a sort, acknowledging one another whenever Johnny drove into town. He'd found that this simple gesture of recognition was also prevalent with most of the people he'd met in Alcova. When they found out that he was Konahee's nephew and helping out, they'd treated him like one of their own. Always a friendly smile and a hello or a wave from a passing vehicle.

There was one occasion, however, when Johnny had stopped to fill the truck after picking up more paint thinner and brushes at the hardware and a few grocery items.

It was midday on the previous Tuesday. A group of teens, girls and guys alike, bored with the humdrums of a small town, made nuisances of themselves by verbally taunting him from the open windows of the station wagon they were in. They'd circled the gas station twice, cutting Johnny deep with racial vernacular, "Dirty, fucking redskin ass fucker! Big chief blowjob! Shit eater!..."

Johnny had ignored them best he could, but when one of them yelled, "Your mother gives the best blowjobs in town!" Johnny set the hand pump to auto fill, turned, and stared them down. He was wearing a tight white T-shirt that framed his muscular torso and powerful arms. Upon seeing what they were up against, the churlish group became silent, windows went up, and the station wagon made a U-turn for Main Street.

He had smiled at their false bravado and wondered how long it would be when the color of a person's skin wasn't the facilitator of racial profiling. That all races were created equal when it came to the masses of good and the communities of bad. That it didn't matter what your heritage was. Good and evil resided in all cultures. He truly believed it. He wished that within his lifetime, he would witness a world where man found within the betterment of sharing and of friendships instigated by a simple hello. It was what his mother had always hoped for.

* * *

The parking spaces in front of the Gooseneck pub were full, so Johnny drove to the rear and found a spot beneath a fire escape next to a large waste bin. The digital clock read 9:17 p.m. The area was lit by a set of lamps festooned to red brick. A rear metal door announced KITCHEN. Sitting on steps leading to the ground, a skinny, dark-haired teen with a stained apron around his front pushed back the length of his hair and smoked a cigarette, looking like he'd rather be anywhere else.

With the window down, Johnny could hear a country band playing. Most of the vehicles were pickups except for a red Mustang with the vanity plate HWY2HVN Johnny knew only too well. Debbie Smith had already arrived. He did not know how to feel about it, though he'd half-expected it, so he decided to play it by ear. He killed the engine, engaged the security alarm and walked to the front of the pub, festive about it being his birthday.

A sandwich board erected on the sidewalk announced that the music emanating from the building was by a group called the Jimmy Pickens Band. A colorful photo of five musicians; a country pretty brunette and four men, all wearing cowboy hats, was taped beneath the glittering headliner.

Johnny opened the door, liberating the lead singer's rendition of Patsy Cline's "I Fall to Pieces." Murmuring voices spilled out into the street. A couple was exiting, and the three nearly plowed into each other. "Excuse me," said Johnny.

"Don't mind us, chief," said a hard-looking cowboy, his stumbling date laughing, tripping over her own two feet. "Chief," she snorted. "That's"—snort, snort, snort—"funny, Bill."

"Gotta get this little woman home before she changes her mind." He gave Johnny a wink. "Know what I mean?" He gathered the intoxicated woman to his chest, walked her to a gleaming black Jimmy parked by the curb and opened the passenger door. "Bye bye, chief." The woman waved drunkenly, slid in and fell on her side. Her date for the night slammed the door, rounded the truck and a second later, tires yelped.

"I... fall... to pieces. Each time I hear your name..."

Johnny walked into the Gooseneck, welcomed by a carcinogenic wall, the lively rhythm of voices, and two bouncers who were cross-armed and very big. Neither asked for identification. The wood floor hummed beneath his feet. The stage was lit in reds and yellows, the rest of the bar by antiquated lamps that were mounted to sturdy beams. It appeared as though whoever owned the place couldn't decide on English decorum or Western influence and had decided to combine the two.

Comfortable leather booths lined one wall, and square tables of some kind of hardwood made up the floor. Paintings of England's countryside were placed here and there, aged appropriately by the stingy light of the lamps. Too many in number to count, books of varying sizes and age sat on ornate shelving meant to impress the tourists who stopped in for a cold one.

Cowboy hats of all different styles and colors—painted on blue jeans, silver buckles, and boots, was exactly what Johnny expected and looked forward to. It wasn't difficult to see that the women outnumbered the men three to one. Barely legal waitresses, all dressed in black skirts and white tops, carried trays of beer and apps through the pressing crowd. Two bartenders, both large men in black vests and white shirts, tended to the patrons lined three deep along the bar. Three flat screens hovering above broadcasted the Cleveland and Baltimore game.

The lead singer ended her Patsy Cline impersonation, thanked the crowd for their applause with a smile and wave then smoothly slipped into "Wide Open Spaces" by the Dixie Chicks. Beautiful young women and reluctant young men moved to the dance floor. Because the girls outnumbered the guys, many were comfortable with a sister in which to trip the light fandango.

As always, due to his height, Johnny could see over the heads of most people. To his relief, he was glad to see that the patrons were heterogeneous in age and race and that everyone was having a good time. He remained near the door, eyes scanning for familiar faces. Though the Gooseneck and Big Sky Saloon were in drastic contrast to one another and there was not a biker in sight, the undeviating smell of beer, the blue haze of smoke and country ambiance resurrected within that fateful night. *You killed my dog.*

A pretty waitress, older, with an athletic body and carrying a tray of empties, stopped and asked, "Can I get you a drink, handsome?"

Shaken from the unchangeable reverie, Johnny blinked and said, "I'll just have a Coke or Pepsi with a lime, please." He gave her his best smile.

"Big spender. I imagine you'll be here for quite a while." Vast brown eyes left his for a fleeting moment, so they might take all of him in. "I haven't seen you in here before. You looking for anyone in particular?" She smiled that all-too-familiar smile.

"Not really. I'm visiting and thought I'd drop in. Somebody told me this was the place to be Friday and Saturday nights."

"Well, it is. The music's always great as you can hear. The food's not so bad, and everyone knows everyone else, so there's not much trouble." Suddenly there was a spark of recognition in her eyes. "Say, you must be the guy working out at Konahee's place. Her nephew, Johnny, right?"

"How'd you know?"

"Well, for one thing. I haven't seen you before. Two, you're Native, and three, you're as gorgeous as Debbie said you were. And those eyes. Beautiful." She winked at him.

Johnny felt the blood rush to his face.

"And modest too. I like that in a man. Say, what are you doing around… ?"

"Oh no, you don't." Appearing out of nowhere, Debbie Smith and her double Ds stepped between them. "This one's mine, Shirl. Find your own man." She looped an arm through Johnny's, and looked at him as though she already owned him. "It's about time you showed up. I was beginning to think you didn't like me." From under the brim of her white hat, bright blue eyes dazzled, and the press of her breasts stretched the fabric of her red shirt to the limits. Turning to Shirl, she said, "I'll have a rum and Coke please." Then she added, "Sorry, but finders, keepers."

Shirl the waitress, rightly confounded, turned on her heels and headed for the bar.

Debbie steered Johnny through the crowd, arm locked on to his impressive bicep.

Johnny took in all of the faces surrounding him. "What about our drinks?"

"Shirl knows where I'm sitting. Come on, I'll introduce you to some of my friends."

Debbie Smith and three of her friends had procured a booth near the stage and next to an upright speaker. Still clutching his arm, she made the introductions. "Heather, Tom, Brenda, this is Johnny. The guy I told you about."

Johnny smiled and said, "Hello. Pleased to meet you." He shook hands with Tom, a dark-haired young man, midtwenties with a bad case of acne, and a silver hoop through his left ear. His handshake was weak, clammy, and he displayed two missing teeth when he smiled.

Johnny and Debbie squeezed into the booth. With the speaker so close, they had to elevate their voices in order to hear each other. Brenda and Heather also wore Western hats, one black, the other brown. Brenda, a cute, slightly overweight brunette, remarked, "So you're helping out your Aunt Konahee."

"Yes. Just for another month or so."

"Then what are you going to do?" asked Heather, taking a sip of her Budweiser. She had freckles across the bridge of her nose, pouting lips, and deep green-blue eyes. Like Debbie, she was the personification of a healthy country girl: large breasts, wholesome face, and the brassy glow of someone who spent much of their time outdoors.

"I'm not sure yet," said Johnny. "I'm still weighing my options."

"Is Konahee as crazy as everyone says she is?" asked Tom.

"My aunt's a wonderful old woman," said Johnny, and gave Tom a hard look. "And you're the first person I've heard mention that she's crazy. People shouldn't go around spreading rumors. Other people get hurt that way." Johnny clenched a fist that did not go unnoticed by Tom who slunk against the booth. "Sorry. I didn't mean anything by it." He tried a smile, but the only look he managed was one of uneasiness. His confidence as the stud at the table was obviously lessened when Johnny moved in. So to reenforce his manhood and to make it clear that Brenda was spoken for, he reached across the table and took her hand in his.

To cut the tension, Debbie said, "You know what, Johnny. A bunch of us are going to go down to the river where there'll be a bonfire. You should come with us. It'll be a lot of fun. I promise."

Without revealing that it was his birthday, Johnny said, "You know, I can't think of a better day to enjoy a fire by a river. It's been a long time since I've done that. So long as your friends don't mind."

Brenda pulled her hand from Tom's and put it on Johnny's shoulder. "We don't mind at all, do we, Heather?"

"Absolutely not." Heather beamed Johnny a smile as big as the great outdoors.

Tom nodded in agreement, his manhood taking another shot and hoped Johnny wasn't going to throttle him for the less-than-cordial comment he had made about his aunt. *Stupid. That guy could kill you just by looking at you.*

Shirl the waitress stopped at the table and delivered their drinks. "That'll be three seventy-five. The pop's free." She smiled at Johnny.

Johnny reached into his pocket to pay, Debbie quickly placed a five at the edge of the table and told her to keep the change and buy something nice for her son. *Ouch.*

Put off once again, Shirl the waitress turned and left in a huff, muttering "Bitch!" under her breath, the heels of her pumps clacking against the floor as she pushed her way through bodies.

No one spoke for a moment. Then pointedly, Heather giggled. "Shirl's had more men than a dog has fleas."

"You can say that again," agreed Brenda, and the three girls had a private laugh among themselves.

"That was kind of mean," said Johnny, and took a sip of Coke. He gave Debbie a dubious expression. It was a side to her he hadn't seen before, and he wasn't sure he liked it. One thing he knew for certain was that Debbie Smith was not going to be the great love of his life.

"Yeah," agreed Tom. "Just because she has a kid. I mean. Give her a break. Could be any one of you."

"We're way too careful. Aren't we, girls?" said Debbie, eyeing each of her friends.

Heather and Brenda nodded. "I sure as hell wouldn't want to end up like my mom did," surrendered Brenda, unintentionally revealing an aspect of her mother's impulsive past.

"Me neither," said Heather. "That's why I carry my own condoms at all times."

Everyone sort of looked at each other. It was obvious to Johnny that the women of Alcova, outnumbering the men, took to heart any advantage they might gain by chastising one another in order to fetch the attentions of a single male.

A food server stopped at the table and unloaded a heaping platter of nachos, heavy with peppers and ground beef. From her apron she extracted a thick wad of napkins and set them in front of Tom. "Thanks, Reanne," he said to the leggy blonde. His eyes wandered long enough to steal a look.

"Are you guys going down to the river later?" asked Reanne, and pushed a wing of hair over a multiringed ear where a diamond stud sparkled with the same intensity as the one in her nostril. She held Johnny's eyes for a fleeting moment then looked to Debbie for an answer.

"Absolutely. Aren't we, Johnny? Are you going too, Reanne?"

"As soon as I get off work. It's going to be a blast. I hear it's going to be the biggest fire this year. I've got tomorrow off, so I'm going to get hammered. Maybe get laid if I'm lucky."

"Amen to that, sister," said Heather, raising her beer. "Here's to getting laid tonight."

The four friends raised their beers and clinked. Hesitantly, Johnny raised his

Coke and joined them, not really hoping for anything more than a little camaraderie and fun.

Tom stole another look at Reanne's legs.

"I know someone who's not going to get laid if he doesn't keep his eyes focused where they should be," promised Brenda, wiping ale from her lips, dagger eyes stabbing Tom where it counted.

Reanne smiled. "Well, I guess I'll see you guys down at the river." Then she disappeared behind a door leading into the kitchen.

The music concluded. The raise of voices grew soft. The pretty singer reached down, picked up a beer, and held it high. "Sociable!" Holding drinks high, the crowded bar responded in a single chorus of voices, "SOCIABLE!" The singer took a good drink then set the bottle next to the mike stand. "Here's one for lovers of all ages. My favorite Deanna Carter tune, 'Strawberry Wine.'"

The four-piece band slipped into the ballad. Moderately played instruments drifted through the speakers as gentle as a summer's rain. Couples rose from their seats. Chairs scraped the floor. The singer took the mike stand in her hands as if she were caressing a lover, pressed her lips to the microphone, and in a voice as tender as a first kiss, began,

Strawberry wine... seventeen.
The hot July moon
Saw everything.
The first taste of love, oh bitter sweet
Like fruit on the vine
And strawberry wine...

The song took Johnny back to the Big Sky Saloon, Sue Levesque's limpid blue eyes, the trio of college students from Canada, the fight to end all fights, and the beginning of a journey that took him to this very moment.

"I love this song," said Debbie, and squeezed Johnny's arm. "Come on, handsome. You owe me at least one dance for standing me up so long." She nudged him with her hip.

"I guess I do owe you a dance, don't I?" said Johnny, the reverie slipping from his conscience.

Heather and Brenda gave each a look that implied a certain unspoken knowing.

"You want to dance?" Tom asked Brenda, voice pensive.

"With you? You'll be lucky if you even get to cop a feel tonight the way I'm feeling right now. You've got a lot of ass-kissing to do as far as I'm concerned."

Tom lowered his eyes, took a good portion of nachos, jammed them into his mouth, and mumbled something as he chewed.

Johnny slid from the booth.

"Now now, you two," said Debbie, moving her small frame across the leather. "You better have kissed and made up by the time we get back." She took Johnny by the arm, and led him toward the mobbed dance floor.

They found a small space. Debbie pulled Johnny close, reached up and wrapped her arms around his neck. Johnny rested his hands on her hips. She looked up into his eyes, baby blues sparkling sweet from beneath the rim of her hat. "I've got a confession to make," she said as they slowly turned.

"Oh. What's that?"

"I hope you don't think I'm being too forward, but I've got a terrible crush on you, Johnny Black."

"I'm flattered." Johnny's internal temperature rose.

They moved about the dance floor in silence, Debbie's blue gaze fixated on Johnny's face while she mimed the words to "Strawberry Wine."

After three trips around the floor, the music faded to silence and the lead singer told everyone they were going to take a fifteen-minute break. "Then we'll be right back. So don't go anywhere."

The dance floor emptied, voices elevated.

Arm looped through Johnny's, Debbie steered him back to the booth, the mien on her face meant for everyone to understand that the hunk at the end of her arm was hers. Within seconds, the smoke in the room thickened into a rolling cloud of blue that enveloped the spans of the bar and clung to the spotlights above the stage. Tom and Brenda were holding hands again. All was right in the love department.

Johnny and Debbie took to their places. "I see you two made up," said Debbie.

"Yeah, I can't stay mad at him too long. He'll get a complex. He's so emotionally crippled, but somebody's got to love him." Smiling at Tom, she squeezed his hand.

"So when do you want to head down to the river?" asked Heather to no one in particular.

"How about one more drink then we'll head out," offered Brenda.

"Sounds good to me," said Debbie. "What do you think, Johnny? One more for the road then we'll head out. You can come in my car."

"Sounds great, but I've got Konahee's truck and I don't think I should leave it in the lot out back."

"Okay, then I'll go with you. You can drop me off later."

They ordered another round, finished the plate of nachos, and the girls went to the ladies' room to freshen up before heading to the river. Tom told Johnny that he would see him later and left him sitting alone in the booth. Johnny finished a third coke with lime and gave Shirl the waitress a tip of twenty dollars and apologized for the crude remarks made. Shirl in turn told him that if he became bored with Debbie Smith's company, she would be available at the end of her shift. "I get off at one handsome. I'll wait until one thirty." Johnny used the washroom, left the interior bar and waited for Debbie at the entrance.

* * *

The August air was typically cool. The vast sky brilliant with immeasurable stars. Full-faced, the moon peered down from the Western horizon.

"Nice truck," commented Debbie, as they approached the red, all rat pack Ford.

"Yeah. It handles nice and is quite the workhorse." Johnny unlocked the doors with a press of the remote.

"Just a minute, okay?" said Debbie. "I want to get something from my car."

Johnny started the engine. When Debbie returned, she climbed into the passenger seat, a blanket folded over her arms, and was *sans* hat. Straw-colored hair hugged her face and shoulders. "Okay, let's go," she said, bouncing in the seat like a child who has just been given the keys to the chocolate city. "I'll navigate." She leaned across the space between them, and planted a kiss on Johnny's cheek.

"Thank you," he said. "That was just what I needed. What's the blanket for?" Reversing the truck, he had one eye on the blanket, the other on what he was doing.

Mischievousness danced within the blue of Debbie's eyes. "In case, you know, we get cold or something."

The rear door of the Gooseneck opened. A young man, apron around his midriff, tossed a full garbage bag into the Dumpster, lit a half-finished smoke, and blew rings into the air.

* * *

The glow of the bonfire reached high into the night. Johnny parked the truck amid a row of maybe thirty or forty vehicles, about a hundred yards from the shore of the Plateau River. Even from their distance, they could see old glory wavering on the draft, held high by a pole firmly planted in the ground, the reflection of the fire causing it to look like it was all aflame.

Music drifted from the beach. With Debbie on his arm, Johnny carried the blanket and they walked the well-traversed path towards the fire and the river beyond.

Orange sparks zipped unceremoniously toward the stars like fireflies gone mad. Several large breeds of dog ran back and forth along the river's edge, manoeuvring between throngs of bodies.

Judging by the forms moving in and out of the fire's influence, Johnny estimated that there were probably as many as a hundred people milling about. Stretched across the bank, groups of men and women danced, sang, drank, kissed, and drank, the light of the fire illuminating the blanch of every cowboy hat. Huge logs for seating had been placed in a hexagon around the roaring flames, every inch occupied. Dozens of coolers in bright beach colors sat this way and that. Folding chairs and white plastic chairs formed circles around men wooing women with their guitars.

The scene reminded Johnny of a vampire movie he once saw where a coven of female vampires, outnumbering their prey four and five to one, attracted men to a specific location and feasted upon them.

Debbie let go of Johnny's arm. "Come on," she said and began to run toward the melee. She'd gained ten feet before Johnny took after her. Five strides of his long legs and he was even. He put a hand on her shoulder to slow her progress. "Hang on a minute. What's your hurry?'

Debbie turned, and in a flirtatious tone said, "Because there probably aren't many private spots left."

"I wouldn't mind sitting around the fire for a while. Listen to some music." He considered telling her that it was his birthday. Maybe she would back off some. Let him enjoy the night the way he wanted to. "Today is a special day for me," he tried.

Debbie turned completely around, eyes impossibly bright. "If you tell me it's your birthday, Johnny Black, I'm going to scream."

"It is my birthday, but I don't want it to become common knowledge. I'm telling you because, well, I had to tell someone. And I really would like to sit around the fire, meet some people, listen to the music."

Debbie's lips leaned into a pout. "Just promise me you won't make me wait too long." Making herself taller, she kissed him softly on the mouth. For several long counts, they remained like that. Then Debbie pulled back and said, "Happy birthday, Johnny. You should know that I usually get what I want. It just might be the most memorable birthday of your life."

* * *

They joined a group sitting in a circle close to the quivering flag where the heat from the fire could be felt against their backs. A man in his fifties, face lathered orange by the flames, strummed his guitar from the comfort of a stump. A can of Budweiser sat at his feet, and a cigarette burned from the top fret of his guitar. With a voice redolent from years of drink and smoke, he started to sing an old Hank Williams tune.

Johnny unfolded and spread the blanket next to an old Native with long grey hair and deep wise eyes that were drowning in the shine of alcohol. He sat cross-legged on the ground, feet bare and his flesh bore the wrinkles of countless seasons, blasted bronze by the sun. The sides of his tannery pants were fringed with dark leather that ran from his hips to his ankles. Around his neck and bare chest he wore several strands of colorful beads. A medicine bag dangled on a tether at his waist. He smiled and said, "Nice night." A Mickey appeared from between his crossed legs, and he took a swallow. Then he offered it to Johnny and Debbie as they took a close position on the blanket.

"No, thanks," said Johnny. "I promised a friend I wouldn't drink tonight. But you're right. It is a nice night."

"Well, I wouldn't mind some." Debbie reached across Johnny, took the bottle, and tipped it back. "Whoa!" she said, handing it back and wiping at her mouth with the back of a hand. "That's got quite the kick. What is it?"

The old Native tucked the bottle back between his legs, and stared at the Stars and Stripes and the river beyond. "Just something my father taught me."

"Well, my name's Debbie," said Debbie. "And this is Johnny. I don't know who you are though. I haven't seen you around here before."

"Who I am is not important. It only matters that we get to share this moment in time, Johnny and Debbie. That is what is important." His distant gaze shifted to Johnny. "You are Cherokee. But not a full-blood."

"Yes. My mother was Cherokee. My father is white."

"I am also Cherokee. Did your mother teach you the ways of our people?"

"As much as she could. She died when I was young."

The old man took his medicine bag between fingers and rubbed it with his thumb. "You mourn the loss of a true friend. I am sorry. In this life, true friends are not easy to come by."

Johnny closed his eyes for a brief moment. Dallas's golden face filled the void, pink tongue lolling, whiskey eyes brimming with life. The fire cracked like a gunshot, shaking him from the preserved memory. Looking at the old man with new curiosity, he said, "He will always be my best friend."

The old man smiled, eyes remained impassive. "Your friend will always be by your side in this life's journey and in the afterlife."

Johnny nodded. There was an understanding between them that could only be interpreted between peoples who were knowledgeable in the ways of the old ones.

The aged Cherokee was a Shaman. A drunken one at that; however, he was still to be respected as the most revered seer among his people, and that included Johnny. Still, he felt sorry for him and his compulsion. Like many Native Americans, he had given into a life anatomically engineered by the depredating forces of alcohol. "You see much," said Johnny.

"When I need to."

"You never told me you recently lost a close friend," admonished Debbie, and rested her head against his shoulder, her eyes filled with genuine pain for Johnny. "That must have been terrible for you."

"I really don't like to talk about it. It hurts too much. Besides, I wouldn't want to spoil the atmosphere."

"I understand. No more talk about lost loved ones."

The Budweiser-drinking guitar player finished his woeful H. W. tune to a smattering of applause. The wind picked up, blowing pieces grit into everyone's faces. With it came a whiff of marijuana. Old Glory snapped like a whip. Three dogs—a shepherd, black lab, and something whose parentage was as good a guess as anyone's—broke into the circle, chased one another to the delight of everyone, then, just as hastily, departed, the thing of many breeds taking up the rear.

The old man laughed. A rolling sound that came from deep within. His gaze followed the animals until they disappeared beyond the scope of the fire. One of the admiring females called out, "Sing 'Sharin' the Night Together.' You know, by Dr. Hook." The entertainer took a sip of Bud, crossed one leg over the other, smiled, and picked at his guitar. In his most Hook-like rendition, he began to sing.

Are you feelin' kinda lonely, girl
Would you like someone new to talk to
Oh yeah, all right...

"How did you know Johnny had recently lost someone close to him?" Debbie asked the old man, not knowing the lost friend was a cherished pet.

The wise Indian looked skyward, his eyes seemed to search the stars for something. "Call it a gift," he said and smiled.

Fascinated, staring at him with greater interest, Debbie asked, "So are you just passing through Alcova?"

"I drift from here to there. I arrive when least expected, and I go when I am no longer needed." He tipped the bottle to his lips, and savored the home brew for a second before swallowing it down.

"That's a strange way to go about life," offered Debbie.

"Not really," said Johnny. "You have to understand our peoples in order to truly comprehend our ways. By our heritage we are nomads. It is natural for some of us to move about. All lives are born to journeys." He held up his hands and spread them a foot apart "Some travel short distances from here to there. Some are never-ending." He looked up at the night sky. "Like a comet chasing its own tail."

"That's sooo deep," crooned Debbie. "You sure know how to impress a girl, Johnny Black."

The trio sat in silence, Debbie clutching Johnny's arm, Johnny watching the old man, the old man gazing far beyond the banks of the river. The Budweiser-drinking crooner sang and played. For the time being, all was right in the world, at least as far as Alcova, Wyoming, was concerned.

The fire behind them roared with sound as more logs were added to its inferno. Several people ran butt naked into the river, splashing about and tossing a football. Bare bottoms, shrunken penises, and jiggling breasts glowed pale from the deep dark water.

* * *

Heather stood on the gentle slope leading to the river. She tipped a can of Budweiser to her mouth, its plastic ringed mates dangling from her right hand. She was ready to party. Eyes scanned the bodies for her friends. There was something she desperately needed to share with Debbie. She'd run into Debbie's latest ex at the beer store, and he told her that he wanted to reconcile their relationship and was on his way to the river to see it through. That could mean big-time trouble if he caught Debbie with Johnny. Corey Goodman, if anything, was the jealous type and he'd already been drinking, doubling the chances of a physical confrontation.

Walking quickly toward the fire, she could just make out the coif of Debbie's blond hair and Frank Kemp playing the guitar. She tripped over nothing and spilled some ale on her top. *Shit.*

"Hey, you two," she said, coming at Johnny, Debbie, and an old Native from behind.

Debbie turned. "Hi, Heather. Where's Brenda and Tom?"

"You know them. They're probably doing it someplace in the backseat of his car."

"I hope one of those are for me," said Debbie, eyes fixed on the five remaining Buds.

"Oh sure. Here." Ripping a can from the rings, she handed Debbie a beer. Sitting next to her friend, she looked at the old Indian rigid next to Johnny. "I see you've made a new friend? Hi. I'm Heather."

"Hello, Heather," the old man said, still staring at the far shore of the river, seeing something no one else could, his eyes shining like new pennies.

"Listen," said Heather. "You and I have to talk, girl."

"Okay. Go ahead. Talk." Debbie took a good swallow of beer, before she detected the panic in Heather's eyes.

"Not here." She looked to Johnny. "I don't mean to be rude, but I've got to borrow Debbie for a few minutes. Girl stuff."

"That's okay. I understand," said Johnny, the stone in his pocket suddenly warm.

Heather stood, pulled Debbie to her feet. "Come on. It's important." Quickly they moved closer to the river, toward the naked football players, turned right, and disappeared into the darkness.

"I wonder what that's all about?" asked Johnny.

The Shaman looked to Johnny, his face serious. "I am sure whatever it is, it is important enough for them to leave us to ourselves." Uncrossing his legs, he plugged the top of the mickey with a cork, set it flat on the ground, and pushed himself to his feet. "Come with me, Johnny. There is much we need to discuss." He walked east, away from the fire and the quivering Stars and Stripes.

Johnny rose to his feet and followed.

When they were far enough away, the old man found a log large enough to sit on and motioned for Johnny to join him. The terrain had changed to soft sand with sprouts of sporadic grasses. Though it was dark, the faint orange glow of the huge bonfire offered adequate lighting. The stone in Johnny's pocket had grown cold.

Young and old sat a foot apart, the silver shine of the river moving in silence before them, the strum of guitars barely audible. The voices of bonfire revelers sounded like bees caught in a jar. Three silhouetted figures darted past, head to tail, head to tail, head to tail. The Shaman pushed his hair from his shoulders and laid his hands flat on his knees before sinking his bare feet into the sand so that it covered him up to his ankles.

"It is time for you to leave, Johnny."

"Leave. You mean leave here. The river?"

"No. It is time for you to continue with your journey. You must leave Konahee and abandon the work you have started."

The fact that the old man knew of Konahee did not surprise him. "I can't just pack up and leave. I have an obligation to her. She's helped me so much."

"She will understand. You have been told there is another who waits for you. You must leave with the rise of the sun come morning."

Johnny mulled this over for a moment. How on earth was he going to explain to Konahee that he could no longer stay with her and finish the work he started? "Are you sure I have to leave come morning? Couldn't I stay for say another month to complete the work she needs done?"

"No!" the Shaman's voice boomed. "If you do not leave tomorrow, the course of your destiny will be disrupted. This single act would change the outcome of many lives." He placed a hand on Johnny's shoulder, looked deep into his eyes. "You bear the mark. Of this you are aware. Do not give in to the needs of the one for the sake of so many, Johnny. Your coming of age is the beginning of a new path. Do not stray from it." His hand slipped from Johnny's shoulder, and his distant gaze returned to the silver shine of the river.

The three dogs barreled past them once more, only this time the mutt taking up the rear stopped, sniffed at the air, and stared at the two sitting on the log. It walked toward Johnny, square head low to the ground, elongated tongue slack from exertion. Bent forward, Johnny took the mutt's head into his hands, and rubbed its ears. "Hey, fella. You're a strange one, aren't you? How am I going to…" When he turned to look at the Shaman, the old man was gone. In his place was a blue smoke that hung in the air like the coil of a serpent. "Jesus H. Christ on a stick," Johnny muttered, mimicking his father's favorite blasphemous anathema. He should have been at the very least astonished; however, the episodes he experienced at Konahee's had mollified him to such manifestations.

Guitar compositions drifted more voluble as a wind swept across the girth of the river. The breath of it banished the smoke, leaving in its place deep footprints in the sand and the old man's rolling laughter as it waned into the night like the jubilant bellow of a great spirit. "Did you see that?" Johnny asked the strange-looking dog.

The thing of many breeds looked up at Johnny, confused, head tilted to one side, red irises cross-eyed.

"I didn't think so."

* * *

Johnny took a roundabout way back to the pickup so he would not be seen, having to climb up and over an eroded platform where dozens of clay nests had been fashioned into its façade. Debbie Smith was with friends, and they would see to it that she got back to her Mustang safely.

A great spirit, he believed, had impressed the necessity for his leaving Konahee. And he knew in his heart that he would have to adhere to the nature of its telling.

Still, as he backed the truck away from the river, clinging doubts occupied his thoughts. He was safe at Konahee's. If he exposed himself to the outside world, there was a greater chance of being apprehended by the law, whom he felt were still on the lookout for a Native driving a motorcycle. There was no letting up when it came to murder. Even one perpetrated by accident.

* * *

An hour later, Johnny turned onto Konahee's property, drove slowly toward the house and parked the truck. An interior light was on enabling him to locate the lamp he had left. A second match later, the wick came to life. Walking toward the barn, a circle of pale light to escort him, the smell of thirty gallons of red paint filled the air. Halfway to the silhouetted structure, a sound came from nearby. First thoughts were Juno had somehow gotten out of her paddock. That with the strength of her youth having been reborn, she'd jumped the barbed wire and was roaming the property. He stopped to listen. "Juno?" The footfalls, he realized, were from a source not as heavy as a horse and were stealth like in their approach. Like something was trying to sneak up on him. "Who's there?" he whispered, then remembered how the she wolf enjoyed sneaking up on him. "Linda? Is that you?"

Her voice filled his mind. "Do not be alarmed, Johnny, it is only me." She appeared in the reaches of the lantern, and moved slowly toward him until she was completely visible within its glow. "Sorry. I have a dreadful sense of humor." She sat on her haunches, a smile drawing the corners of her mouth.

On one knee, Johnny set the lantern on the ground. "What are you doing out so late, Linda? Not that I'm not glad to see you."

"I've come to say good-bye."

"Then you know that I am supposed to leave tomorrow. Somehow I'm not surprised."

"Yes, Johnny. Your purpose here has come full circle. The old man was right. It is time for you to leave." Her right eye slowly closed as if the light was bothering her. Then a tear spilled, rolled down her snout and dripped onto the ground.

"You're crying," said Johnny.

"Nonsense," the wolf rebuked. "Wolves do not cry."

Johnny now knew with utmost confidence, no matter what doubts he may have had earlier, that his departure was imminent. He was being guided by sources far beyond his sensibilities. "I will miss you, friend."

"And I will miss you, Johnny." Moving forward, she raised a paw and lapped at his face, her tongue warm and moist.

Johnny took the offered paw in hand. "Of all the things I've experienced here, you are perhaps the one who has had the most influence on me."

"I am honored that you feel that way. Remember to stay the course, Johnny. The knowledge you carry is as true as Mother's rising. " The wolf pulled her paw away, both eyes moistened by her wounded heart. "I must go now."

"But how will I know whether or not I'm on the right path, Linda?"

Turning, the she wolf walked into the darkness, words resonant in Johnny's mind, "You will know, Johnny. You will know. Remember what I have instructed and your journey will not falter." Then she was gone.

Johnny stood and lifted the lantern. His eyes searched deep into the darkness for his friend; however, like the old man, the Shaman, the great spirit, she had disappeared from his life in less time than it took to break a heart.

* * *

Once he was in the barn, he climbed the ladder, and lifted himself into the loft, the lantern drawing three irregular shapes against the pitch of the roof. One of these outlines was that of a wolf sitting on its haunches, its face tilted high. Another was of a serpent coiled around the base of a tree. The third was that of a great bird, wings spread full. Within the following beat of Johnny's pained heart they vanished.

He sat on the edge of the bed, face cupped in his hands, his emotions in a frenzied state of being, the lantern light an amber circle that embraced him. He did not know whether to cry, be elated, or whether he should be terrified by the prospect that come morning he would have to leave this place of magic. He tried to rub the peculiar weary thoughts from his mind when something sharp pricked at his theatre. He looked up. The green mist spilled from the star-blistered porthole and rose until it modified into a curvaceous form swimming foglike in the middle of the loft. Without fully shape-shifting into the succubus who had controlled his dreams, or not, it spoke to him in a tender voice. "Good-bye, Johnny. You and I have completed our appointed station in this life. Forever we shall not meet again. Within yourself be true. Go swift on the wings of your brother." It poured into the floor, a green puddle that reclined toward the window and rose up the planks. Before it vanished over the sill, the green intensified to a radiance that was so overwhelming, Johnny had to close his eyes. When the severe shine left his face, he opened them. Four digit footprints receded from the star blaze. A trice later, they too vanished and the melodic declarations of once great warriors filled the night.

Johnny doused the lamp. Fully clothed, he rested his head against the pillow, believing sleep was going to be difficult to achieve. However, within the hour, his eyelids settled, and his spiritual awareness succumbed to the repertoire of recent, and not so recent past events. For the first time since his arrival, he surrendered to a dreamless void. The turquoise gift within his pocket as cold as, well, a stone.

* * *

35

Never Say Good-bye

MORNING came, a brilliant offering of Mother's first light. It shone a path of warmth onto Johnny's face, waking him instantly. He bolted upright, blinked several times and yawned. He could not remember ever having a better sleep. He sat in the beam of warmth for a few moments, booted feet planted firmly on the floor, the events of the night before playing like a tape on fast-forward. *It's time,* he told himself.

Gathering the knapsack, he filled it with the remainder of his clothes, exchanged his shirt for a T-shirt and moved through the chest of drawers a quick as he could, leaving the bottom drawer last. The work boots, though they had gotten comfortable, would have to remain in the loft. Taking sixty dollars of his money, he stuffed it into his jeans. The keys to the Honda he slipped into a back pocket. If the Shaman was right, and there was no reason for him to think otherwise, then timing was of the essence.

It had been weeks since Johnny laid eyes on the gun, preferring to put it out of his mind altogether. Opening the bottom drawer, he took it into his hand, its deadly weight cold with its purpose. As much as he feared doing so, he stuffed it into the bottom of the knapsack, closed the zipper, and slung it over his shoulder.

Descending the ladder, he stopped for a moment to take a last look at the little hideaway that had been his secret haven and spiritual den; an experience he would never forget. Yet nothing compared to the fond relationship he had with Juno. A sudden sadness touched his soul. He had to say good-bye to her. The hardest good-bye of them all he knew, for the rejuvenated mare was as much a part of his life as Dallas had been, and in some ways even more so. She was the absolute sum of what Konahee's place of magic represented, nothing less than extraordinary.

When his boots touched the earth, he could feel Konahee's presence as if she were sending out a charge of biorhythms. Turning, he found her standing in the center of the barn, twisted shaft of beech wood clutched in her hands, favored sun hat covering the grey of her head, the blue of her eye caught in a slant of sunlight. She wore a full-piece deer hide, just like his mother had in his dream. They stared at one another, each waiting for the other to speak first. After a pregnant silence, Konahee said, "It is a good day to travel."

"How long have you known?" asked Johnny, trying to keep the sadness from his voice.

"Since long before the day you arrived." Konahee stepped toward him with some difficulty.

Noticing her struggles, Johnny said, "You are tired, Konahee. You shouldn't have walked all the way here. I would have come to *you*."

"I enjoyed the walk. It is a beautiful morning."

Concerned about the uncompleted work, Johnny asked, "Who will finish the work I started?"

"I will put my sign back out. Someone will come by. Someone always comes by." Looking at Johnny approvingly, she added, "Though I do not believe whoever it is will match you in tenacity. Three men could not have accomplished what you have in the time given you. I am in your debt."

"It is I who should be thanking you, Konahee. You gave me shelter and food when I needed it most. I will always be grateful for that."

Konahee waved a hand in the air to dismiss him. "Do not try to sweeten an old woman's tired heart. I have heard it all before." She laughed, a sound married with mirth and melancholy.

In the moment, Johnny did not want to say good-bye. Remembering that she had spent the night watching baseball, he asked, "Who won the game last night?"

Konahee's face lit, her smile revealing the deteriorating state of her gums and teeth. "My Indians did. Six to three."

"Good for you, Konahee. Maybe next year."

"No. I do not think next year or the year after that. But they will try. That's all I can ask for at my age." She breathed deep, the blue of her eye held Johnny's in its wise regard. "I will miss you, Johnny."

"You will be in my thoughts every day, Konahee. You *are* a remarkable woman. And a great cook."

This remark pleased Konahee to no end. She held out a withered hand, and motioned for him to come to her.

Johnny moved into her opened arm as if he were surrendering an embrace to his mother. Leaning forward, he was a mighty willow bending to the wisdom of the wind and he kissed her on the cheek.

Konahee blushed and whispered smoothly into his ear, "Never lose the feather, Johnny."

"I won't, Konahee. I promise."

The old woman straightened best she could, the ghost of her dead eye glistening with a tear. "Now let us speak of your transportation." Pulling away from him, she turned toward the entrance of the barn.

"My transportation? I have my bike," he said to her back.

"No! You will take my truck," she said pragmatically.

"Your truck? I can't take your truck, Konahee."

"You must! I insist upon it!" In a swift, agile movement far too immediate for a woman of her years, she turned on him. "Do not easily dismiss the wishes of an old woman." Eye blazed with blue fire for a hair in time, then she smiled. "Besides, I can always have Harvey Lector buy me another one. It is only a truck. Your motorcycle is a good trade. And besides, it would only get you into trouble. This I know." She reached into a pocket, and offered an envelope. "This is for you. Minus the money for your boots. Just as we agreed."

Overwhelmed by Kohahee's submission of her new truck, Johnny took the padded envelope, and stared at it as if it were something completely alien to him.

"You will find a lunch and bottles of water in your cooler. It is already in the Ford. I was up early this morning."

"Konahee. I can't take..."

Raising a finger to her lips as if to quiet a child, Konahee said, "You go say your good-byes to Juno now. She is waiting for you. I will walk back to the house." Once she was past the entrance, frame bent, beech wood tapping the ground, a telling aura of multihued light poured from within to further reveal the sovereignty she possessed.

There was no point in arguing. Not for a second. Johnny had learned that much. As wise and magical as Konahee was, she was also as stubborn as a child refusing to eat its brussel sprouts. He dropped the knapsack and secured the envelope in a side pocket, then went to the Honda, where it had sat dormant for more than a month. Retrieving the keys, he placed them on the seat next to the helmet. Funny, he thought, how the birthday gift he had received in earnest would be taken away the day after his actual birthday. The face of his father's rough features came forward. *"Cowboy up, Johnny!"* Johnny smiled, took a deep breath. *Thanks dad. I will. Time to face Juno.*

* * *

Everything was aglow with Mother's great smile, the rebirth of life, of color, when day banished night to the dominion of its own slumber. The air was as still as a painting and the big Wyoming sky screamed blue laughter. Shades of purple and coral rose from the plains of the eastern horizon. To the south, the coppery humps of the Laramie Mountains cut mammal-like skeletons into the blue. Juno was waiting for him, pressed into the gate, head low, the usual blaze of her youthful eyes dulled to flat mattes of sorrow.

Johnny carried on his shoulder a fresh square of green hay he'd stopped to pick up from the back of the barn and dropped it at his feet, a portion breaking free. "Hello, girl," he said, unable to camouflage the regret in his voice. Slipping the knapsack off his shoulders, he set it against the gate, reached down, and picked up the loose hay.

With nimble lips, Juno took it from him. Johnny stroked the white mark of her face. "I didn't want to leave like this. But we both knew this day was coming."

Juno nodded. Tears slipped from her eyes and sketched lines over the bridge of her face. Johnny's heart thumped, filling him with the fevered rush of heartache. Once again, a part of his soul was ripped free. His eyes clouded with his own sadness. "I will never forget the time we had together. You are a true friend." With the back of a hand, he wiped the misery from his face and noticed that his hawk's shadow was circling the ground. He looked up to find it circumnavigating Mother's face, its wings urgent on the draft of a new day.

Juno snorted, and bumped Johnny's arm. "All right, all right." He took her by the ears and thumbed the velvet interior. "You'll forget all about me when somebody new comes a long."

Juno shook her head. Johnny forced a smile and rested his face against hers. "Well, if you do make a new friend, I want you to know that it's all right by me." He looked into her the sorrow of her eyes.

Man and horse spoke in the silent language of true friends and said their good-bye.

Juno reared her head and suddenly bolted, the thick of her tail snapping like a whip. Green clumps of earth were sent into the air, Mother's rapture brandishing her coat in blazing sequences of chestnut.

"You run, girl. Always run," whispered Johnny. "I'm going to miss you most of all." For a woeful moment he stood in silence, and watched her run full out toward the far end of the paddock. She did not look back.

The memory of a much older Juno came to mind. How she was bent with the final stages of her life. A test for him, there was no doubting it. It had all been a test. One for the mind, body, *and* spirit. Now at the new beginning of an old end, an inescapable journey awaited him.

The hawk filled the quiet of Johnny's thoughts with a cry so piercing it shattered all reverie from his mind. Hooding his eyes, he watched it swoop toward him at an alarming rate of speed. In the moment he decided he needed to duck, the great bird came to a threshold in midair and took to the post nearest to him. It tucked its wings into its speckled body and stared at Johnny.

"Hello, brother bird."

The hawk released a gentle warble of sound.

"I guess you've come to say good-bye as well. I'm glad. We kept good company together. I never did get the chance to thank you for ridding me of those crows. So thank you."

The hawk spread its wings and rose into the air, just as it had when Johnny first arrived, only this time it was saying farewell. It loosed such a mournful beseeching, tears spilled over Johnny's flesh. "Good-bye, brother bird," he said, and wiped at his face, yet again.

Rising high above the scope of Mother's face, Johnny's bird friend became a speck against the blue canvass. He could still hear its ghostly cry. A sound Johnny was sure he would often hear wherever his journey took him. Brushing hay dust from his jeans, he took a final look at the magical architecture of Konahee's land, lifted the knapsack, and headed in the direction of the house, a final farewell still to be expressed

* * *

Konahee sat relaxed in a green-and-white lawn chair next to the Ford, the length of her twisted walking stick horizontal across her lap. Her head bobbed beneath the sun hat and as Johnny grew near, he realized her eyes were closed. He sat the knapsack on the ground next to the driver side door.

"Konahee?" he asked gently, afraid that he might startle her.

"I am awake, Johnny. I am only resting my eyes. I heard you coming for a while now." When she pealed her eyes, the blue of her good eye looked tired, old. "I guess you will be leaving now."

Johnny went to her, lowered himself and rested a hand over hers. "Will you be all right, Konahee? I hate to leave you like this."

"And it pains my heart to see you go, but you must. This is the day of reckoning. It has been foretold by a higher source than you or me." Placing a hand over his, she rubbed the turquoise ring and warned, "Be careful, Johnny. Many obstacles await you."

"I will, Konahee. And as promised, I will never speak of my experiences here." With heavy heart, Johnny rose to his now-full, imposing size. Lurking beneath the surface of his consciousness, trepidation of the unknown, of the known, and of what lay down an unforeseeable road pressed forward.

George came rushing out from behind the house and leapt upon Konahee's lap. She scratched him between the ears. "You go now, Johnny. We have talked long enough. There is nothing more to say."

Lifting the knapsack, Johnny opened the truck door and tossed the sum of his possessions into the rear compartment. Reaching in, he gave life to the engine, then turned to regard his host for a final time. He would not, could not, say goodbye.

Konahee's weary gaze quickened to a blaze of blue fire beneath the brim of her outrageous hat. A tear dripped from the plainness of her ghost eye. "Johnny?"

"Yes, Konahee." He thought she might give him some final council of what the future might hold. Instead, all she offered was, "Go be what you are within, Johnny Black. The mystic of great warriors runs through your veins."

* * *

Johnny pulled away from the house. The tank was halfway full, enough to get him to Casper or back to Alcova. He would have to decide in which direction the next stage of his life was going to take before reaching the T in the road.

Driving slow, and not looking back at the house, his mind wrestled with what he was going to do. When he reached the T, he looked left then right, stopped the truck, and reached into his jeans for a coin. *Why not,* he told himself. *Life is a coin toss,* Buck Black once told him. *Heads or tails, it came down to what you make of it.* Balancing the quarter on his thumb, heads would take him north to Casper, tails would steer him south and back to Alcova. He flipped the coin. It seemed to take impossibly long, flipping end over end until it landed in the palm of his hand. Tails it proved. Alcova it was.

When he came upon the stretch of houses sitting like dilapidated memories of yesterday, he stopped, took a bottle of water from the cooler, twisted the cap, and took a cool drink. Each of the yards were void of children; however, their collection of play things lay hither skither across dry lawns: a bicycle with training wheels, several colorful balls, a scooter, a plastic lawn mower and a large cardboard box disguised as a two-little-people clubhouse. The beagle-type dog tethered to a rope ran back and forth near the tire swing. It barked incessantly at nothing like small dogs do. The rubber swing moved to and fro without the benefit of a handler, as if the ghost of a child were causing it to do so.

Oh, how Johnny wished he could turn back the pages of time like Juno had. He would go to that swing and pump himself until he rose high into the air, and all he had to worry about was eating his brussels sprouts without fear of the future. But that was wishful thinking. Impossible dreams. The kinds of things old men dared to contemplate when death was knocking at the door. He pulled away from the houses and drove on.

The silence of the cab was causing him to think too much about what lay ahead, so he turned on the radio. A young Elvis, singing "Viva Las Vegas," filled the interior. Johnny wasn't much of an Elvis fan; nonetheless, the upbeat tune improved his capricious mood. Fingers drummed the steering wheel, and his left foot kept rhythm with the bass. Through the side mirror, he watched the blacktop zip by, adding miles and miles of distance between Konahee's sanctuary and his inescapable future.

When Elvis concluded, the radio went silent. Johnny waited. After a minute or so, he turned it off, waited a few seconds, he didn't know why, it just seemed the logical thing to do, then turned it on again. At first static hissed all around, then to his surprise, Elvis started singing "Viva Las Vegas" again. *Must be a mistake by the station,* thought Johnny. *DJ asleep at the wheel.* He stabbed at the control with a finger, but instead of tuning out, Elvis's voice amplified. It rose to such a crescendo it hurt Johnny's ears. Powering the windows while fidgeting with the controls, all he got was Elvis. "Viva Las Vegas. Viva... Viva... Las Vegas." When it ended, it started again. *This is no mistake by the radio station. This is a Konahee thing.* Then he remembered what Linda the wolf had instructed, "*The voice of a King will lead you to her and a flower will awaken an everlasting love in you.*"

The voice of a King! Elvis! Las Vegas! Of course. He didn't have to be hit over the head with a hammer to realize the significance of what was happening. Slowing the Ford, he pulled onto the shoulder and stopped. Extracting the map, he saw that Las Vegas was only two states away. *If that's where my search begins, then so be it.* Folding the map, he took another swallow of water and said to the monotonous Elvis, "Okay. I get it. I have to go to Vegas." The radio fell into a taciturn mode. "Thank you." There were worse places he could have ended up he supposed. Vegas and the thousands of tourists who flocked there daily might be the optimum place for him to hide while searching for the preordained love of his life. Depressing the gas pedal, the Ford tore onto the highway at breakneck speed. With the wind sharp at his face, Johnny said, "I'm coming whoever you are. Stay safe. I'm on my way."

As though Elvis Aaron Presley were sitting in the passenger seat next to him, the King orated in his famous vernacular, "*Well, how about a little thank you... thank you very much.*"

* * *

36

Hot Child in the City

SHE is an oasis of glass and steel in the middle of desert, fortified by man's contagious misfortune. She smiles at you when you see her, and she bids you welcome. She wears a gown of lights and guards more secrets than any other place in the world. Her smile is infectious. It seduces you. You can't help yourself. You fall in love with her the moment you meet. You drink from her, devour her offerings, and she makes you promises of promiscuity and good fortune. She is everything your normal world is not. When she holds you in her arms, you become forth giving, willing to risk it all for just another dance with her. She has many lovers, nevertheless is a woman unencumbered by love. Her initials are LV.

She is a goddess, and you flock to give her reverence. The price you pay to worship her comes from somewhere, anywhere. Little Timmy's college fund. Susie needs new braces. Social assistance. Christmas cheer. Credit card rating at 19 percent. Just one more roll of the dice and everything will be all right. But she intentionally cuts you and laughs while you're bleeding. And you pay homage to her once more.

The affair ends. She smiles as you part, knowing it won't be long before she holds you in her arms again. You vow never to return. But you do anyway. You can't help it. When she makes love to you, nothing else exists. She is a siren and you beckon to her call, adding to the secrets she bares with anonymous arrogance. She is Sin City. There is no other place like her on the planet.

* * *

Seated on the bed in Tony Million's mansion, Orchid awaited the arrival of Mr. Wong, who was being picked up at the airport by Mr. Black. The room she had been segregated to for the past three days was decorated in shades of green and taupe. Drapes of golden silk jacketed the windows overlooking the pool and gardens. The bed was queen-size, burdened with a half-dozen pillows covered in gabardine cases. The floor, a marriage of hardwood and throw rugs. Expensive Grecian vases beatified marble pedestals. Two leather high backs sat askew, facing each other. Center of them, a chess set fashioned from crystal stood regal. In the walk-in closet were her suitcase and an array of sexy lingerie and evening gowns that fit her slender frame to a tee. At Tony's insistence, she had tried them on, and found that each piece fit her frame as though they were tailored for her and her only.

A Venus de Milo figurine lamp cast a soft glow.

A three-piece en suite offered privacy.

Orchid's dinner. Medium rare steak, baked potato, and carrots sat untouched on a TV tray. A seventeen-inch LED television broadcasted the evening news. The only door to the lavishly appointed room was locked. As always. And of course, there was no method at her disposal to communicate with the outside world.

In her trembling hand was a spoon, on her body, a pink negligee and nothing else. White stockings lay on the bed next to her. Mr. Wong did enjoy his fantasy theatre she'd been told. She was to play the role of a randy fifteen-year-old who had a penchant for senior men.

With much trepidation she watched the heroin melt. Animated by her breath, the candle flickered. Lying unfed on the nightstand, the syringe waited to be fuelled.

When she'd arrived in Vegas, it was nighttime, and though she had been drugged to keep her complacent, she still marveled in the lights that seemed to pulse with life. At the splendid architecture of places like the Luxor, Caesar's Palace, MGM Grand Hotel, the Eiffel Tower, and the Wynn. Cranes rose into the night, the beginnings of new billion-dollar hotels and million-dollar condominiums.

Regardless of the magnificence all around, and much to her disappointment, the streets were not filled with the beautiful people garbed in luxurious gowns and thousand-dollar suits as advertised on television. Instead, what she'd witnessed were overweight American families dressed rather casually, roaming the streets as if lost, dragging their two-point-one children to places they shouldn't know about at their age. Sure she saw the odd limo go by and there had been groups of young revelers staggering drunkenly up and down the main strip, but for the most part, everything she had ever dreamed about came to an abrupt end as the true face of Vegas became apparent. It was all a big misconception. A Hollywood falsehood.

The heroin pooled, Orchid's hands trembled, not so much because she was panicked, but because it had been more than ten hours since she'd been allowed to satisfy her wanton craving. Far too long for a user. Snuffing the candle, she rested the hot spoon on the nightstand, the smell of melted wax occupying the air around her. Using thumb and index finger, she drew the plunger, and transferred the clear liquid into the syringe until the basin of the spoon sat empty. Holding it in the light, she depressed the plunger until an arc rose from the needle. Wasted heroin dotted the nightstand. With a swipe of a finger, she erased it and tasted for the first time the bitter expense of her imposed habit.

Lifting a leg, she rested the heel of her foot on the edge of the mattress. A quick slap to raise a vein and the needle went in. *Oh so smooth.* She did not deliver the full amount, leaving 5 cc in the syringe should she need a nightcap after her paid-for favors with Mr. Wong.

A now-familiar warmth filled her, and her mind reeled, spinning her into a web of compliance. Dropping the syringe onto the nightstand, she fell back into the bed, head seeming to take forever to land. Smiling at nothing, she lifted one of the silk stockings and stretched it over her foot, her leg. It felt nice, like a whisper against her skin. Leg held aloft, she examined its shape. It's a beautiful leg she believes, the camouflage of white concealing the raised designs of her addiction.

Taking the sister stocking, she ran it against the polish of her teeth then slipped her foot in and drew it up to her thigh. The Venus de Milo lamp smiled at her, the ceiling seemed to slip away, leaving her to gaze at a sky of diamond lights and runaway comets. The voices from the television sounded like they were emanating from the pillows that surrounded her. She was flying without the itinerary of destination.

Minutes melted away in a slow dance of time running backward. An hour passed. Then another. She found herself following a white rabbit down a dark and dingy hole. It pulled a pocket watch from the tartan jacket it wore. "I'm late, I'm late, I'm very, very late," it told her. Together they arrived in an animated land of candy-coated trees, marshmallow houses, and gummy bear skies. The Mad Hatter stood before them, arms folded across his chest, foot tapping the ground. "You're late," he admonished in a cartoon voice.

"No, shit," said the rabbit, drew a gun, and shot the Mad Hatter between the eyes. He turned to look at Orchid. "I never liked him anyway."

The Mad Hatter fell dead on the ground, his preposterous hat rolling from his head.

Orchid laughed so hard tears streamed from her eyes. Opening them, she discovered that she was lying on the bed, real tears wetting her cheeks, body electric, pulse running overtime, the rhythmic pounding of her heart rat-a-tat-tating against the wall of her sternum. There was music playing. Violins and keyboards and the faint strum of an acoustic guitar. It was music of the mind, and it quickened to an ear-splitting crescendo. She heard a hauntingly familiar scream from faraway, realizing a moment later that it was her own tortured voice. Rolling on her side, she pressed hands firmly against her ears. Someone somewhere was trying to convince her to buy Cottonelle toilet paper.

Minutes or hours passed. She wasn't sure. The room had darkened, the sun having drifted off to set alight the other side of the world. She was sobering. All that remained of the heroin's influence were tiny creatures dancing on her flesh and the flaming tickle of her privates. She sat up, pulled her knees close and regarded the ruinous design she could see beneath the sheer of stocking. *These are not my feet.*

A knock at the door startled Orchid. Moving quick, blood rushed from her head, and she fell forward. Righting herself, she sat on the edge of the bed, one stocking leg over the other, the final hallucinogenic effects of the heroin slip slip slipped away. Guilt ridden, she hid the spoon and syringe in the drawer of the nightstand. The candle stood alone, a forlorn reminder. Already she wanted more.

The lock disengaged.

Mr. Black, followed by Tony Millions and a small oriental gentleman with a crown of cotton white hair and dressed in a shiny blue suit, stepped into the room. Following Mr. Wong was a pretty Asian woman, face a placid moon, her hair an eruption of curls and decorated with tassels that glittered in the light. She wore a golden cheongsam of silk, slit up one side to reveal a rather shapely leg.

Tony, Mr. Wong, and the pretty woman walked toward Orchid. Mr. Black kept his station by the door, a sentinel dressed in white. The woman moved to the window as though she was gliding on the air, the sleeves of her gown reaching beyond the cusp of her wrists, finger nails painted fire dragon red. *Was she going to watch,* Orchid wondered. *Anything was possible with these people.*

In a bright Hawaiian shirt and Bermuda shorts, Tony said, "This is Orchid." In his hand was a tumbler of Scotch with lemon twist. On his feet were a pair of yellow thongs.

"I am very impressed," contented Mr. Wong in perfect English as if he were the benefactor of a Yale or Harvard education. "You are more beautiful than your picture."

Orchid remained impassive. Just because she was going to have to have sex with him didn't mean she had to be courteous. Performing the role of a teenage slut was going to be humiliating enough.

"Say hello, Orchid," Tony more or less demanded in a diplomatic tone. "Mr. Wong has come a long way and has paid a great deal of money for your attention. So be polite."

"Hello, Mr. Wong," said Orchid in a small voice, and crisscrossed her legs, a movement not unnoticed by Mr. Wong.

"Very splendid. Well worth what I paid you, Tony."

The Asian woman remained by the window, aloof.

Tony located the remote, and changed the station to an all-symphonic channel. He noticed the tray of uneaten food. "You haven't eaten, Orchid. Rosita's feelings will be hurt. I hope you're up to breakfast in the morning. She's going to prepare salmon eggs Benedict." He picked up the tray and joined Mr. Black by the door and gave it to him. "We'll just leave the two of you alone then. Should you require anything, Mr. Wong, do not hesitate to ask. My house is your house. You be sure to take good care of our guest, Orchid." He held his hands as if in prayer, and bowed slightly at the waist. "Mr. Wong." Then he and Mr. Black disappeared behind a closing door.

Mr. Wong smiled teeth capped with gold and somewhat bucked. He removed his jacket, took a place in one of the leather high backs, picked up a crystal bishop, examined it, then placed it back on the board.

Orchid noticed the simple gold band on his ring finger. It took her a heroin fogged moment for what Tony had said to register, *"We'll just leave the two of you alone."* Slowly she turned to the woman facing the window who had not moved. Everything fell into place. The way she was dressed. Her congenital silence. The way she seemed to drift across the room. As if the woman was reading Orchid's thoughts, she turned to look at her, a judgemental look drawing her face into a mask of duplicity.

"Mr. Wong?" asked Orchid. "Does your wife know what you're up to? Paying for the affections of young girls."

The unforeseen question threw the small man. His head dropped in an admission of guilt, and his eyes clouded with troubled memory. After a moment, he asked severely, "Who are you to speak of my wife? No one, that's who! You are paid to perform. And perform you will." He stood, took off his tie and unbuttoned his shirt to bare a chest that had long since caved in on itself. "I want you to tell Daddy what a bad princess you've been and that you need to be punished," that said, he unbuckled the black leather belt cinching his pants and drew it through the loops in one swift movement, the leather snapping like a whip.

Orchid flinched. *Seize the moment or he's going to beat you into submission.* "Your wife is very beautiful," she said to him, hoping that like most Asians, he was, deep down, very spiritual.

This did not seem to faze the little man. He slapped the palm of his hand with the belt. "I want you to get on the bed," he ordered. "On your hands and knees so I can see you from behind. You *will* tell me that you've been bad."

The woman moved from the window and drifted to the side of the bed, eyes filled with shame. She spoke to Orchid in Mandarin, yet somehow, in Orchid's ear, the words were translated into English. "*Forgive my husband. He has developed poor habits over the years. He was once a very honorable man. Full of joy. At peace with himself. Now he is an empty shell. Anatomically and mentally destroyed by the demon opium. I am ashamed for him and for me.*"

Orchid positioned herself on the bed as she'd been told, her eyes pleading the woman for something, anything that might help her.

"*Tell him that Lilly would not approve,*" said the moon faced woman.

Mr. Wong made his way to the bed, belt dangerous at his side.

Orchid craned her neck and looked directly into his eyes. "Lilly would not approve!"

This stopped the little man in his tracks. "What did you say?"

"I said Lilly would not approve."

Mr. Wong's knees buckled. The belt fell to the floor, face bleached white as the blood rushed out. "No one knows that name except for me and my"—he cast his eyes to the floor—"wife. I demand to know how you are aware of this."

"*Tell him I am always with him. Tell him that I did not die in vain. That it was a terrible accident. The brakes of the car I was in gave out. Nothing more. He should not blame himself.*"

"Lilly's accident was nothing more than that," said Orchid. "You have been blaming yourself since her death. But it wasn't your fault."

Mr. Wong seemed to lose his balance. He teetered, then dropped to his knees.

"She wants me to tell you that she is always with you." Orchid turned fully around, sat with her legs folded beneath her, and gathered the sheet to cover her own shame.

"*You speak with the dead?*" he asked from his knees.

"I think you should sit down, Mr. Wong. The answer to your question is yes.

Sometimes. I never know when. It just happens." The night in Caleb's barn spilled forward. "Most of the time I'm not even aware that I'm in contact with one unless it's obvious. I have a gift. I have had it since I was a young girl."

On hands and knees, Mr. Wong dragged himself to the leather chair and crawled into it, face pale, breath short little bursts. He stayed like that for a moment and just stared at Orchid. When he opened his mouth to speak, the dialect of aggression was no longer present. Humbled, he said, "I would not believe you if not for... I was told when I was a young boy by my mother that my grandmother possessed such a gift. The third eye. My mother never spoke an untruth in her life." He sealed his eyes. A fond memory created a scene on the curtain of his mind. "Lilly is a nickname I bestowed upon her because on our first date, I had given her a bouquet of white lilies to mark the occasion. I had called her Lilly ever since, but only in privacy. Tell me, child. Is my wife with us right now?"

"She is. She's wearing a gown of gold silk, and there are tassels in her hair. I'm sorry for your loss," she added.

Mr. Wong cupped his face in his hands and openly wept.

Lilly's spirit moved to the leather chair, took a place next to her husband and rested a hand on his shoulder as if to comfort him. Several moments passed before Mr. Wong lifted his head and wiped at his eyes. "It was Christmas Eve," he began. "I was working late and told her that I would meet her at the party we were to attend. She told me that she had bought a new dress that would make me the envy of all men." He paused as if the sudden recall cut him to the core. Remorse quivering his voice, he continued, "The weather was terrible. A snowstorm had moved in. I told her to take a taxi, but she insisted she would drive herself. She was so independent. So young. So vibrant with life. This was in 1964. The garment you describe is what she wore that horrendous night. It changed me forever. How will she ever forgive me?" He wept again, his face looking as though the past few seconds had aged him ten years.

"Tell him things do not have to be the way they are. That I can forgive him if he abandons his pursuit of the demon dragon and discontinues his lecherous ways. Tell him that I long for the day we are reunited. Tell him that I still love him."

Raw emotion rose in Orchid's throat, choking her in its sadness, in its humility. There was nothing more heartwrenching than the partition of love. Two lives changed in a split second. Like Ed and Hester's. The world their oyster one moment, the next, total and complete devastation. It was this undesirable happenstance that had caused Romeo and Juliet to end their lives.

A tear slid down Orchid's cheek.

Mr. Wong rose from the chair and moved toward Orchid with the physical tranquility of a man who wished only good intentions. Reaching a hand, he wiped the tear from her face. "I have offended you in the most disrespectful way. If I were in the time of my father, I would be executed for my actions. Please tell Lilly that I have been lost without her and have drowned myself in the well of malcontent. I am sorry."

"You just did," Orchid told him. "She's standing right beside you. She can't speak to you, but she is able to understand you just the same as understanding me. Do you understand?"

"Yes." Returning to the chair, he dropped into it, the weight of his transgressions pressing him down.

"Lilly wants you to end your chase of the dragon and to stop your lecherous ways. She wants you to know that she still loves you... regardless."

Mr. Wong's head swiveled in an attempt to catch perhaps a glimpse of his deceased love. "Lilly, I never should have let you drive that night. I should have left work and picked you up. Things would have turned out differently. I have no excuse for my actions since then. Please forgive me. I will honor your wishes. No more from the white dragon will I partake, and I will never lay a hand on another human being as long as I live. I swear it on my mother's grave. I love you, my wife, and have missed you every day."

Lilly nodded, a smile of contentment shining across her moon face. Regarding her husband, she stroked his white hair with the sweep of a ghostly hand. *"I have been waiting more than fifty years to hear those words."* Looking to Orchid, she said, *"Thank you, young lady, you have done us a great honor. Our house is now clean."* Her spiritual presence began to abate. Slowly she returned to the other world, a wraithlike hand caressing the pate of her husband's head, a final indication that she was ever there. Then it too vanished.

"She is gone now," said Orchid. "I believe she is finally at peace."

Hastily, Mr. Wong rebuttoned his shirt and fixed his tie. Snatching the belt from the floor, he turned away from Orchid. Embarrassed, and with as much dignity as he could, he reassembled his suit. When he turned to face Orchid, his demeanor had taken on the glow of contentment, his eyes shining with the youthful acuity of a much younger man.

Love had come full circle.

"How can I ever repay what you have done for me? You should not be doing this. I have much influence. If you like, I will tell Tony to cease with whatever hold he has over you. I know very well how Mr. Millions operates." Lowering his head in shame, he admitted, "I was perhaps his most ardent customer. But no more! He will listen to me. Tell me, child. What do you wish?"

Orchid's mind immediately returned to the Harts. It may be true that Mr. Wong could influence Tony into letting her go, but at what price? It was made perfectly clear on many occasions that Mr. Black would pay the Harts an unexpected and costly visit. And that was something she wasn't willing to risk, even though it might mean her freedom.

Gathering the remote, she clicked off the music, and tossed it toward the empty high back. It missed and clattered to the floor. "All I ask is that you never mention what occurred here today. Not to anyone. It would be dangerous for me if people found out about the gift I possess." She looked toward the drawer containing the tools of her addiction, the chasing of her own demons. A living itch had developed just beneath the surface of her skin.

"What about your family?" enquired Mr. Wong. "Surely you can return to them, regardless of the tensions that may exist between you. There is nothing stronger than the chain of family."

"I have no family left," admitted Orchid. "I'm safe here. Well, safer than being out on the streets."

"The world *is* a hungry animal. I am sorry for the losses you have had to endure. But you are young and possess an extraordinary talent. This combination should be enough to see you through this dark stage of your life. Tell me what your real name is, child?"

Orchid wrapped the sheet around her shoulders so that it covered her completely. The question drew a blank where there should have been an obvious answer. She blinked several times in response, her washed mind searching for a name. *Rebecca*. It floated on a familiar voice as if her mind were a huge cavern and the conversant voice a wind roaming within. "My name is Rebecca," she said tentatively, the word sounding strange coming from her own lips.

"And my name is Benjamin. I want to help you, Rebecca. As I said before, I have much influence. I can take you away from all of this. All you have to do is say so. It would be of great comfort to me if I knew you were safe."

A sinister scene unfolded on the stage of Orchid's mind. She could clearly see Mr. Black silently walking through the Harts' house, climbing the stairs leading to the master's bedroom, opening the door without making a sound, his giant shadow cutting a figure across the bodies in the bed. There's a flash of steel. He moves to the sleeping Harts and, in two quick slashes, ends their lives. Reluctantly, she dismissed Mr. Wong's offer of amnesty. "I can't leave. Please understand." She formulated a quick lie. "I'm indebted to Tony. Don't ask me why or how."

"I see." Mr. Wong rubbed the point of his chin with thumb and index finger. Reaching into the inner pocket of his suit, he withdrew a small gold case. From it, he removed a business card and walked toward Orchid. "Please. Take this." He held it out to her. "Very few people have this number."

Orchid looked around the room as if there was an audience watching the transaction before plucking the card from his fingers.

"That is my private number and my personal lawyer's number. If you should need anything, and I emphasis the word *anything*, you call and I will make it happen. If for some reason I cannot be reached, then call my lawyer, he will locate me. Promise me this, and I will forget for the time being that you are just another cog in Tony Millions's grand scheme of things."

Orchid palmed the card without reading it. "Thank you, Mr. Wong. If you keep your promise about not telling anyone of me, then I promise to you that I will call you if I need your help."

They smiled at each other. A pact was made, each of them knowing neither would violate the other by dishonoring the agreement.

Mr. Wong asked if he could sit next to her on the bed. Orchid agreed that it would be all right. He noticed the candle and melted wax on the nightstand, but said nothing. He had smelled the melting of heroin when he'd first entered the room and seen eyes painted with the glaze of someone who was still under its stimulus. Like opium, it had left its devilish signature.

Taking both of her hands into his, he regarded her as a father would regard his most precious daughter. "We still have much time to pass," he said with quiet piety.

"Perhaps you would do me the honor of sharing with me the wonders of your gift and tell me more about my wife. Any little thing will do."

* * *

An hour and a half later, Mr. Wong left Orchid to herself. The stride in his step as he walked out of the room that of an invigorated young man. Orchid remained on the bed for a few minutes before putting the card within the sock pocket of her suitcase. She was hurting. A knife plunging deep within, twisting to amplify the pain. The cutting hunger of her addiction. It would not let up until the craving was satisfied.

Walking to the window, she looked to the pool. Water glowed iridescent green, lit by submerged lights. Tony, Mr. Black, Mr. Brown, Mr. Wong, and two of his body guards were huddled near the cabana. Mr. Wong seemed to be doing all the talking and was being very animated with what he was saying. Norman sat on his perch, blue head tucked into a wing, fast asleep for the night. The sky was blue-black, starless, the lights from the Vegas strip so overwhelming they obstructed the shine of twilight faces.

Someone knocked on the door. Orchid turned away from the window, the knife plunging deep. Whoever it was didn't wait for a reply. The door opened. Pamela walked in wearing a white poolside robe that covered her from shoulders to toes.

"Are you all right, sweetheart?" Closing the door, she strode across the room, stopping at the bed. "I know your first time can be tough. Did he hurt you in any way?"

"No," replied Orchid, taking a seat in one of the wingbacks. "He was very nice. Gentle," she lied.

Pamela sat on the bed, crossing one leg over the other, hair looking as though she had just come from the beauty parlor. Skeptically, she said, "Nice and gentle are two words that aren't usually associated with Mr. Wong. But you *are* beautiful. Perhaps, to him, he saw you as a person of virtue and didn't want to mark your body in any way. Can't say that I blame him. You are gorgeous. That color really brings out the green of your eyes and enhances the fiery red of your hair."

"What do you want, Pamela? I'm tired and I just want to go to sleep."

Reaching into the robe, Pamela removed a small silver cylinder. Unscrewing the cap, she stuck the painted nail of a pinkie in and removed a clump of white. She sniffed it into one nostril then the other. "You want some, sweetheart? It'll take the edge off."

"No, thanks. I really just want to be left alone."

Rising from the bed, Pamela stood next to Orchid, baby blues intoxicated in a tidemark shine. The belt of her robe loosened enough for Orchid to see the tanned flesh of bountiful breasts. Pamela toyed with her hair. "I understand if you don't want to talk about it, but sometimes it helps. Men are brain-dead when it comes to the emotional sensibilities of women. All they care about is when they're going to get it next and from whom. They're nothing but pigs, the whole lot of them. We girls have to stick together."

"Thanks for your concern. I'm fine, really. I just want to take a shower, get his smell off me, and go to bed."

Leaning forward, breasts practically falling out of the robe, Pamela sniffed the air around Orchid's head. In her ear, she whispered, "You smell like roses to me. Any time you feel the need for, well, a woman's company, you let me know." Brushing lips across Orchid's cheek, she breathed. "I know what a woman needs."

Orchid drew her face away, mouth twisted in disgust. "Is that all you people think about around here, sex?" She pushed on Pamela's shoulders. "Leave me alone! You hear! Get out of my room!"

"My, my, my. Aren't we the little firecracker."

"Out!"

"You'll see. You'll come around. So many men are going to have what you've got between your legs you'll think you're a revolving door. You'll soon welcome the attention of a woman." Turning, she went to the door, the belt of her robe coming fully undone, revealing the fullness of her exquisite body and the shaved plump between her thighs. In a voice redolent with angst, she said, "Believe me, sweetheart. I know firsthand." Opening the door, she left, the skirt of her robe sweeping the floor.

The lock engaged. *Click.*

Orchid's face fell into her hands. She wept until no more tears would come, the knife in her stomach twisting again and again. She looked to the night table. *Make it go away. Make it all go away.*

Picking up the remote, she surfed until she found an all-seventies broadcast. Pink Floyd's timeless masterpiece spoke softly to her through the small speakers.

There is no pain, you are receding.
A distant ship smoke on the horizon.
You are only coming through in waves.
Your lips move, but I can't hear what you're saying.
When I was a child I had a fever.
My hands felt just like two balloons.
Now I've got that feeling once again.
I can't explain, you would not understand.
This is not how I am. I... have become... comfortably numb.

Removing the loaded syringe from the drawer, Orchid sat centre of the bed and drew her knees to her chin. She removed the stocking of her left leg, and searched for an unblemished spot, hating herself. Nonetheless, it was a necessary evil. The knife within was ripping her apart. Slapping the area, insentient to the pain, a vein rose.

OK Just a little pinprick.
There'll be no more aaaaaaah!
But you may feel a little sick.
Can you stand up?
I do believe it's working, good.
That'll keep you going through the show.
Come on it's time to go...

The needle slipped home. Immediately, the pain in her stomach vanished, its insatiable hunger gratified for the time being. Orchid's eyes rolled in her head. The syringe dropped to the floor, the music sounding as if it were coming from another dimension. For a brief hazy second, she saw the face of the man she had loved all her life. *Help me. Oh, please help me.*

When I was a child,
I caught a fleeting glimpse.
Out of the corner of my eye.
I turned to look but it was gone
I cannot put my finger on it now.
The child is grown.
The dream is gone.
I... have become... comfortably numb.

* * *

She is floating on a carpet of feathers. It is dark. Much darker than night. There is an unknown melody playing from long-forgotten instruments. Higher and higher she climbs, reaching a ceiling so soft she breaks through to find herself in a universe filled with lost hopes and dreams. She cries out for the souls that seem to be all around, having lost their way to a final destination. "Shhh," a voice whispers. "There's no reason to cry." Suddenly there is a hand covering her mouth, terminating her agony. Eyes without a face, dark as pitch. She tries to move, but finds she is weighed down by the burden of her fears. Something sharp cuts a line across her throat. "Don't scream. Don't move. Or your next breath will be the last breath you ever take." She knows the voice as well as she knows her own. A penetrating force enters her, filling her with such revulsion she begs the dream to take her elsewhere. But the dream keeper holds her in its suffocating grasp. Choking, choking, choking. She is flooded within by a demon seed. She can feel it working its way to the very nucleus of her being. The music ends. There is only silence and pain. The weight of the devil has departed, leaving her to feel shame. Somewhere in the darkness, a door closes.

Gasping for air, Orchid forced her eyes. The area between her legs was damp, and there was something wrapped around her throat. In the darkness, she grabbed at it. Abominable terror wreaked havoc, causing her to tremble in its most vulgar wake. For in her hand was the familiar length of stocking she had removed in order to satiate the demon that had taken residency within. Her face fell into her hands now, understanding that the dream was not a dream at all. Tears would not, should not, could not fall. She had been raped, and she knew by whom. *"I'll rape you with this knife,"* he once told her.

* * *

37

Best-Laid Plans

TONY Millions sat at the head of the conference table in a room that he dominated. Appropriately, sitting to his right was Mr. Black. To *his* left was Mr. Brown and Mr. Blue. Just back from Columbia, where arrangements for a shipment of three hundred kilos of cocaine was contracted, sat the inscrutable Mr. White, completing the enigmatic quintet, each of them armed with their own personal methods of persuasion: Mr. Black preferring the power of his .357 while both Mr. Green and Mr. Blue cherished their Sig Sauers. Mr. White, elite in the method of strangulation, had on his person at all times a garrote made of fine piano wire. He had used it successfully with stealth performance ten times in his career as an expensive contractor and three times, completely decapitating his agreed-upon obligations.

Beneath the table where Tony Millions sat, and well within his reach, was a 9-mm Glock holstered within a sleeve of leather. Tony Millions trusted no one, and should any member of the posse decide to take it upon themselves to take him out while they were having a private session (Tony had his fair share of enemies, people with money who would like to see him out of the picture), he maintained the upper hand by always having the benefit of surprise.

A carafe of coffee centered the oval table, the sun blistered the floor-to-ceiling windows, cutting a sharp radiance across the far wall where an expensive replica of Edvard Munch's *The Scream* hung over a faux fireplace. Behind the knockoff was Tony Millions's safe where large sums of money, stock certificates, and his own personal stash of cocaine were kept.

Tony was wearing a polo shirt, light slacks, and nothing on his feet, the three-carat diamond of his pinkie ring dazzling in the sunlight. Steam rose from his coffee cup. "First order of the day," he commenced. "How was your trip to Bogota, Mr. White?"

"Hot, but very profitable."

"Good. And how is my friend Mr. Gutierrez?"

"He is in good health and sends his regards. He sent you a gift to show his appreciation for your continued business." Reaching into his suit pocket, Mr. White removed a small package and slid it across the table.

"Another Rolex to add to my collection no doubt. Anyway, back to business. When will the shipment arrive?" Leaning back in his chair, he locked his fingers behind his head.

"In three weeks. Do you want to know the particulars?"

"Amuse us." Tony Millions snorted, a habit with those who danced often with the *White Lady.*

Mr. White took a swallow of coffee before continuing. "Five vessels will depart Columbia for Miami. Four will be decoys. The U.S. Coast Guard, throughout Internet, will believe that one of these decoys carries our shipment. The boat carrying the actual goods will enter the port of Miami in broad daylight, its manifest stating it's carrying medical supplies. Meanwhile the Coast Guard will be chasing the four ghost ships all over the Caribbean. By the time they realize they've been duped, it'll be too late. From there, *our* customs agent will see to it the medical supplies pass inspection. Then they will be moved to a shipping container bound for LA, where the Crips will apprehend it, step on it, tripling its value, and wait for your instructions. In a few months, your original investment of ten mill will, well, you do the math."

"Excellent." Tony leaned forward, and placed the palms of his hands flat on the table. "I want you to fly to LA when the shipment arrives and handle the distribution personally. I trust the Crips about as far as I can throw them, but they're a necessary means… for now." Looking each man in the eyes, and one by one, he reminded, "We're swimming in unprecedented waters here, gentlemen. Three hundred kilos is our biggest shipment ever. It is also my largest investment. I will take it personally if there are fuckups." He let that sink in for a moment. "Mr. White, as soon as you're ready to traffic, fifty kilos goes directly to the Santangello family so they can flood the east side of Chicago. Toss in an extra kilo as a gift from me personally." Pausing for a moment, he pushed himself from the chair, domineering his posse. "I want the entire shipment expedited within two months, gentlemen. It's going to snow all over America early this year."

There were smiles all around. Each man looked to the next. A tremendous amount of money was to be made if things were handled properly.

"Second order of business," continued Tony. "As you know, Mr. Wong's visit yesterday was more than a little profitable." He dropped back in the chair.

Each man nodded, faces set in stone though each of them was imagining how much they were going to benefit from Mr. Wong's generous offer, the common anthem within the posse being share and share alike.

"For whatever reason *or* reasons," continued Tony, "Mr. Wong has graciously offered me the sum of one million dollars to keep our little Orchid's chastity virtuous, the greedy slant-eyed fuck. He and his entourage will be staying at the Venetian for the next week on my dime. The money will be transferred to one of my accounts in the Caymans by noon tomorrow. Once this is confirmed, we are going to transport our little Orchid to the Shangri-La Palace and the loving arms of Madame Olivia."

A short-lived chuckle filled the spaces between each posse member.

"Madame Olivia will hold her for safekeeping until I decide what's best for our little Orchid. If we happen to make a little money, no scratch that, a lot of money while she's there, so be it. Mr. Wong is scheduled to fly back to Hong Kong this coming Saturday. Mr. Blue?"

"Yes, Tony."

"You are to see to it that he does not reach the airport. His sudden demise must look like the actions of someone who can no longer live with themselves. He is addicted to opium and prefers the affections of young women. It is to be believed he could no longer live that lifestyle. I do not want the long arms of Mr. Wong's associates to reach my backyard. That would be detrimental for all of us. Once you've disposed of our Mr. Wong, you are to disappear for a couple of days."

"Consider it done," said Mr. Blue, a knowing smile embellishing the creases around his eyes. Drawing a hand through his slick black hair, cold blue eyes went from one man to the next.

"Good. I'm counting on you. No fuckups or we're all dead men."

"He's as good as in the ground, Tony. Don't give it a second thought."

Taking a slurp of coffee, Tony watched the faces of each man over the rim. His shrewd mind, as always, way ahead of the game. "Now I suppose you're all wondering what's in this for you."

"Yeah, man," said Mr. Black, smiling. "That little bitch must have fucked his brains out to give you a million. Who would have thought?"

"To tell you the truth, Mr. Black, there's something else going on here. I just can't put my finger on it. Mr. Wong can afford any woman, or women he wants. Anytime. Anywhere. So why our little Orchid? That is the question of the day, my friends. Anyway, that's for me to worry about. Now back to the topic of money. Mr. Black and Mr. Brown, you will receive fifty thousand each for your rolls in bringing our little Orchid to us. Mr. White, you will benefit when the transaction of our next shipment is completed, 10 percent. I will give you twenty-five thousand to keep you comfortable in Miami. *Capice?*"

Mr. White nodded.

"Mr. Blue, you will receive fifty thousand for the disposing of Mr. Wong. That leaves me with eight hundred and seventy-five thousand net profit. Isn't America beautiful?" Tony's eyes moved over his men. "Add your regular earnings to your usual percentage from the sale of my shipment, and well, gentlemen, Christmas is going to come early this year for all of us."

Smiles all around. Dollar signs for eyeballs. Grown men reduced to ragamuffins who could not get enough of what was in the cookie jar.

"Now that I have your full attention," said Tony, "There's the matter of our dearly departed Mr. Green. You all know why I had to rid us of him. He was greedy, and his greed was only going to make us vulnerable. Create a fissure in the solidarity of the posse. We could not have that. However, in order for this association to function appropriately, we still need another member. Therefore, I have arranged for a new Mr. Green to join us. He will be arriving from Chicago in two days."

"What are his qualifications?" asked Mr. White.

"He is an ex-Navy SEAL fed up with a dysfunctional government. Frank Santangello highly recommended him, *personally*. He is murder for hire I've been assured. Mr. Santangello has already been the benefactor of his expertise. Three times he has contracted him to strengthen the Santangello hold in Chicago's east end. Apparently, his knife skills are second to none. I want you, Mr. Black, to pick him up at the airport. I'll give you the details a little later. Any questions?"

Heads shook.

"Mr. Brown, I want you to do the collections today. Make sure each girl is rightly forthcoming with what they earned last night. Then I want you to go to the club. See what's up. Make sure the girls are staying in line, that sort of thing. Assure the bartenders aren't skimming off the top. You know. The usual."

The club, aptly named Club Paradise, and the Shangri-La Palace were legitimate businesses Tony sustained for tax reasons, maintaining a businesslike forum on the surface for the gaming commission and other governing sectors who always had their hands and dicks out. Club Paradise featured topless dancers, slot machines, expensive alcohol, waitresses with legs up to here, and an ambiance of sex, sex, sex.

The Shangri-La Palace, located five miles south of Vegas, was a destination many male clientele ventured to when closing out the night at one point in time or another during their stay. *Viva Las Vegas!*

Mr. Brown nodded. Should he receive a blowjob while at the Shangri-La Palace, which occurred more times than not, that was fine by him. A hundred-dollar bag of coke went a long way. He loved these little side jobs. Once the new shipment was ready for sale, he could unload a good quantity of it right there at the club, after he stepped on it once more for a little side cash of course.

"Good. Now it's almost lunchtime. I suggest you go about your business for the day. Mr. White, I don't expect to hear from you until the shipment is safely in your hands. Try not to gamble too much. It will most certainly come out of your share, I assure you."

Mr. White looked down at his hands, casually shook his head. His silence could have meant many things. However, he and Tony knew that as soon as he landed in Miami, he would be spending most of his time in front of a blackjack dealer.

Chairs scraped the flooring.

"Hang back for a moment, Mr. Black. There's something I need to discuss with you in private." When the last body exited the room, Tony simply said, "When Mr. Blue completes his task and returns from a short-lived vacation, you know what to do. It's a shame to lose him, but there are to be no loose ends."

"What about his share?"

"Is that all you ever think about? Money?"

"It's what makes the world go round, man."

"Very well. It will be yours, as always."

"Then it will be a pleasure."

"Just one more thing, Mr. Black."

"Yes."

"Take our little Orchid along for the ride. I want her to understand the reality of her situation. That way, Mr. Blue will think you're out in the desert to dispose of her and not him. This should facilitate within Orchid that if she does not conform to her new life, certain death is her only other option. I'll make sure Mr. Blue perceives things our way. I'll tell him that it's come to my attention Mr. Wong may have told her things that could be disadvantageous to the posse. Things that if they got out would mean prison for all of us. And since Mr. Blue has already spent fifteen years in Sing, Sing, his dutiful conscience will get the better of him. It's the perfect setup. Don't you think?"

"You're a real bastard, man," said Mr. Black, smiled and headed for the door.

"Thank you, Mr. Black," said Tony. "Coming from you, that's a superlative compliment."

When Mr. Black was gone, Tony opened the small gift. It was indeed a new Rolex, platinum, with plenty of diamonds. Value no less than fifty grand. Slipping it onto his wrist, he opened a drawer within the oval table to expose a cylinder of coca and sniffed a fingernail full into each nostril. It was time to pay Orchid a much-needed visit. *Sniff. Sniff.*

* * *

Sitting on the lid of the toilet, wearing one of the robes supplied, Orchid pulled her knees to her chin. Tangled hair dangled freely over the slopes of her shoulders. Music drifted through the closed door. She examined the wounds of her nearly numb feet, thinking how quickly her life had changed. The tracks screamed back at her, bright red, even though she had continued the care Mr. Black had shown her. Plenty of vitamin E, conveniently supplied in the medicine cabinet. What in the beginning had been blots of purple and green decorating the fonts of her feet were now golden scars in the form of traitorous vines. She could cry no more.

The deepest of her nightmares, or any woman's for that matter, had come to full connivance; and she was trapped in the web of it, never to escape.

Sitting on the bed in the adjoining room, a half-eaten breakfast of salmon eggs Benedict grew cold. Rosita had dropped the meal off with a friendly smile and encouraging words, "You must eat. It will keep you going."

Orchid had spent hours in the shower, the water as hot as she could stand it, scrubbing the tangible dream from her flesh until welts rose. When the water turned cold, she'd turned off the taps, sat in the glass stall and cried, shivering in the stark, cold reality of what had happened. She *had* been raped. Black eyes, pinpricks of demon light. Mr. Brown's eyes. *"I'll rape you with this knife."*

Thumbs smooth over the designs on her feet. She had eaten in an attempt to thwart the hunger pain in her belly, a constant issue that was slowly tearing her apart from the inside out. With no heroin left to satisfy the insatiable appetite of her compulsion, all she could do was sit on the toilet and rock and hope that it would soon go away. *"Don't scream. Don't move. Or your next breath will be the last you ever take."*

The words came back to her again and again, the obsidian eyes of her rapist filling the tapestry of her mind, culminating with the fiery pain in her stomach. Suddenly, a sound tripped over the music, her angst. She listened intently to see if it would repeat, but it did not. Planting her feet on the floor, she cinched the robe and pushed damp hair over her shoulders. She stood and found she was a little lightheaded, the knife in her belly twisting. She went to the banjo mirror covering most of the wall.

She was a fright.

Sallow eyes. Gaunt complexion. Her beautiful red hair reduced to tangles and knots. Even the freckles around her eyes seemed to have lost their luster. She tried a smile on the person looking back at her; however, the person in the mirror wasn't in a particularly good humor and only stared back at her accusingly. *Look what you've done to me.*

Just as a fresh onslaught of dry tears threatened to spill, she heard it again. A sound mixed with the muffled music, like glasses clinking. Opening the door, she stepped into the lavishly appointed prison. A short breath of surprise caught in her throat. Standing in the center of the room was Tony Millions, a putter in his hands, a glass lying on the floor. On its way toward the glass was a golf ball. It missed its mark by nary an inch. "Damn it," he said then looked up to see a startled Orchid. "Pardon my French, but you look like shit, sweetheart. Just look at those once-pretty feet of yours. Mr. Black's methods are a little... shall we say... disturbingly altering."

"What are you doing here?" She would not look down and give him the satisfaction of seeing her wallow in self-degradation.

"Hasn't anyone told you? This is my house." He swung the putter so that it rested on his shoulder. "We need to talk," he said matter-of-factly.

Orchid moved toward him. Out of the corner of her eye she caught the steely glint of the knife sitting on her breakfast tray. Would she have the courage to use it? she wondered. *You bet you would,* replied the little voice that didn't sound anything like her mother anymore. "Perhaps you can start by telling me just how many people have a key to this room?"

"Why do you ask?"

"Because someone came in here last night and raped me, you bastard!"

Tony did not seem at all fazed by this outburst. He walked toward the glass, retrieved the golf ball, and took another shot. The ball sailed right into the glass. *Tinkle, tinkle.*

Orchid was now near enough to the bed that if she moved fast enough, she could grab the knife and charge her host. Jam the business end right into his throat. She would probably not get out of the house alive, but exacting her revenge on the man who began this journey through hell would be of great satisfaction.

"That would not be very smart of you," said Tony, as if reading her thoughts. He went to the bed and picked up the knife. "It's good to see that you've eaten something." Holding the knife in front of her as if he were going to use it, he said, "These things could kill someone. I'll have to reprimand Rosita for leaving sharp instruments with you." Slipping the knife into a side pocket, he leaned the putter against one of the high backs. "You say you were allegedly raped. Would you mind telling me by who?"

Orchid paced in a tight circle, hands fisted by her sides, knife within driving her voice. "Mr. Brown did, you prick! As if you fucking care!"

"Now there you go. Mr. Brown does not possess a key to this room. Are you sure it wasn't just a bad dream brought on by all the junk you've been putting into your system? That heroin is nasty stuff. We'll have to remedy that. It has turned you into a less-than-appealing person whose hold on reality has become distorted."

"I didn't imagine I was raped! I *was* raped!" She shot green daggers at him. However, Tony Millions's smug response was a good indication that it really didn't matter whether she was raped or not. These people had no souls. Her claim was falling on deaf ears.

"Come and sit down before you fall down, Orchid. I promise I will look into the matter. If I find that Mr. Brown did indeed violate you, then I will deal with him, personally. I can't have my men going around taking what does not belong to them." He motioned with his hand for her to take a seat in one of the high backs. "Please. Sit down. I insist." *Sniff. Sniff.*

Orchid knew the matter to be closed, and doubted Tony Millions was even going to give it a second thought. He didn't give a shit. It was in his eyes, referring to her as something that could be bartered with. Her rapist would go unpunished, and she would have to live with the consequences of his prurient actions. This was a world that she and everyone knew existed, but no one talked about and she had landed right in the middle of it. As her anger was about to peak, something within shattered, the anger derailed, leaving her deflated. She went to the high back and dropped herself in. What else could she do?

Tony sat in the opposite chair, took the putter, and twirled it as if a baton. "Now isn't this better? Just the two of us. I'd like to be your friend, Orchid. In time you would find that I can be a very generous benefactor. Just ask any of my girls. I'm a prince among thieves. Well, and murderers. It's just business. There's a lot of money to be made if one knows what one is doing."

"You forgot rapists," she threw back at him.

"Now there you go again. Let's put that matter aside for the time being, shall we, and move on to a topic more to my liking. Money." A well-practiced smile drew his thin lips so tight that they almost disappeared. "Speaking of money." The lights in his eyes demanded her attention, an inherited gaze from his father who was a ruthless Wall Street broker. "Did you know that your guest paid a very large some for whatever you did last night?"

Orchid shook her head. She'd hoped he wouldn't go there, that the fact she'd been raped might have deflected the rendezvous with Mr. Wong. She was wrong, yet again.

"Well, he did. And I can't say that I can remember a time when he was so... *pleased*."

Orchid lowered her eyes.

"Don't be ashamed. What you and Mr. Wong did is between the both of you. In time, when we think you're ready, you will receive your share. Until then, you will remain under my watchful eye. I will feed you. Shelter you. Clothe you, and like I said, hope to be your friend."

"How generous of you."

"Yes, well." He snorted, looking at Orchid like a man would look at his most prized possession. "I would like to know what differentiates you from the dozens of other women I've supplied him with. You come across as a frightened and guileless young lady. On the *other* hand... it appears that you are not the innocent person you are perceived to be. Mr. Wong is infatuated with you. The question is why?"

"I don't know what you're talking about. I did what I was supposed to do and nothing more." Eyes remained in her lap.

"Look at me, Orchid! I have an uncanny knack for reading people. I know instantly when someone is lying to me. The eyes are the windows to the soul they say."

Orchid lifted her head. When she looked at him, it was with disdain.

"Now tell me. What's the big secret between you two?"

"We had sex. That's all," she replied, hoping the adamant tone in her voice was convincing enough.

"I see. You must have spoken to each other. You were together for almost two hours and pardon me for saying, but I don't believe our bygone Mr. Wong could keep it up for that long. What did you talk about? The weather? The universe? Politics maybe? Religion? What?"

Orchid remained silent. Tony's eyes were locked on to hers. She had already lied, and he knew it. Forcing her eyes away, she looked to the chessboard, the crystal pieces shouting her next attempt at a lie. "We played chess," she said.

"Chess! You played chess!?" He looked down at the board and laughed. "That's a first. So you're a good chess player, are you?"

"I used to play with my brother."

"Yes. Your brother. That was a tragedy. Him burning up like that."

Orchid's heart immediately began to pound. Malleable hatred lifted her eyes, and they screamed at him with the green fire lying within.

"Sorry, sweetheart, you raised the subject, not me." Tony sighed, pushed the air out of his lungs in one short burst. "Here we go, getting off on the wrong foot again." He looked at her, eyes narrow, then they seemed to smile, altering in the blink of an eye to the warm facsimile of a father who was conversing with his daughter. "Look," he said, voice warm, reassuring. "I just want to know what you and Mr. Wong spoke of last night. I know that Mr. Black's willingness to pay your friends the Harts a visit would have prevented you from spilling the beans as they say. So unless you played chess as you say you did and not uttered a word to each other, highly unlikely by the way, then there must have been some kind of communication between the two of you."

Orchid straightened. "If you must know, we talked about his wife."

"His wife?" Tony's eyebrows twisted into a single thought. "She died decades ago."

"Yes. I know. I'd noticed his wedding ring. I raised the question. He didn't answer at first. After I... ," she paused for effect. "After I went through with my end of the deal you've cajoled me into, he asked if I could play chess. I needed something to take my mind off the fact that I just had sex for money. Then during our first game of chess, he just opened up to me. It was very sad."

"I'm sure it was," said Tony, reading her eyes. What he saw in them was deception wedded with some truth. "How many games did you play?"

"Just two. I won the first game only because I think he was distracted by talking about his wife. It only took him ten minutes to win the second game." *Good*, she thought, he was believing her.

"You know, I don't mind a good game of chess myself. You might even say it's how I run my little empire. Reading your opponent. Staying several moves ahead. Being defensive when need be and cutting your opponents throat when you have the chance. It's how every big business in this wonderful country is run. Perhaps you would do me the honor and play me some time." *Sniff.*

The knife in Orchid's stomach twisted, causing her to clutch at the robe. "I need to go to the bathroom," she said, voice shaking. In a sick way, she welcomed the knife. It gave her an excuse to end Tony's prying, and she was positive he was about to ask her to play a game of chess. She had played with a friend once, but she was terrible and it wouldn't take Tony too long to figure out that there was no way she could have beaten Mr. Wong.

"I told you that heroin was nasty stuff. Look what it's done to you. I think the best thing for everyone concerned is that we wean you off it as soon as possible. I have big plans for you, Orchid. In ten years you'll be able to retire to a very comfortable life. All you need be is cooperative. Starting today, you will receive only half of what you're accustomed to. And in smaller doses so that it lasts you through the day and you don't experience fits of withdrawal. Then eventually, we'll cut that in half, and before you know it, you'll be as good as new and earning yourself a lot of money. The process shouldn't take any more than three weeks, a month tops. During this time, I'm going to send you to a friend of mine. She'll take good care of you. You'll make some new friends. Everything is going to turn out for the best. Trust me." He twirled the putter once more.

The knife dug deeper. "I really need to go to the bathroom. Please!"

"It's a shame. I really must speak to Mr. Black about his methods. They're costly, time wise. I guess our little meeting is over then. I'll have Pamela bring you what you need for the time being. Thanks for the talk. I think I've learned what I need to know for now. You really should take better care of yourself. You're a fright. Go on now. I'll leave you to the comforts of this beautiful room." Using the putter, he pushed himself from the chair.

Orchid stood and was headed for the bathroom when Tony said, "Just one more thing, Orchid."

Turning, Orchid said, "Yes."

"I want to see what all the fuss is about. I mean I've seen the photo of you, but I'm certain the picture did not do you justice. Please open your robe."

"What?!" she asked, incredulous.

"Just open your robe so that I can see the body that's going to make me a ton of money. Mr. Black and Mr. Brown tell me you have the body of a goddess. I on the other hand have only seen that photograph in a less-than-appealing environment. I would like to see it with my own eyes. Put an end to the mystery you could say." He swung the putter at an imaginary ball, his eyes occupied with the appeal of Orchid's body.

Reluctantly, Orchid untied the robe. There was no telling what he would do if she didn't comply, having already experienced the power Tony Millions possessed. Drawing the collar over her shoulders, she let the ties fall and parted the robe so that the fullness of her front was exposed. "There! You happy! You're all sick! You know that?" Quickly she gathered the robe, turned, and ran to the bathroom.

Tony Millions left the room with four words echoing in his altered state of mind, *Money in the bank*. She was indeed a goddess.

* * *

38

Between You and Me

BY Friday morning, Orchid had been given the privilege of sunning herself by the pool under the watchful eyes of Tony Millions and Mr. Black of course. The newest affiliate of the posse had arrived and was currently being introduced to Club Paradise by Mr. Brown. The new Mr. Green bore a striking resemblance to Rembrandt. His goatee and hair as orange as, well, an orange. He preferred turtlenecks under a casual jacket even in Vegas's sultry temperatures. Through the window of her prison, Orchid had seen him when he'd arrived, but only for a moment. He was talking to Mr. Brown and Tony Millions one moment, then the three disappeared somewhere in the house. Even from sixty feet, Orchid could see that the man towered over the other two and outweighed them by a hundred pounds. His eyes blazed an almost transparent blue in the bright Nevada sun. Her fear of him was instantaneous.

Orchid watched Pamela from the comfort of a chaise as she backstroked the length of the pool in a red single-piece bathing suit. A tall sweating glass of iced tea with lemon wedge sat on a small glass table next to her. Encouraged to wear one of the bathing suits Pamela offered, she instead assigned herself to a pair of jean shorts and her Angel Without Wings T-shirt. The sun felt wonderful on her face. She had spent the past few days cooped up in the room with the satellite radio and the anticipated need of her next fix for companionship.

Music played from a hidden source. Jazzy piano accompanied by a tenor saxophone. Norman was swinging upside down in his cage, head rocking side to side, catcalling, and whistling. His antics brought a much-needed smile to Orchid's face. Her appetite had gained momentum, and she'd eaten the entire breakfast of omelet, home fries, toast, coffee, and muffin Rosita fixed for her. It felt good to feel full again.

Tony's interest in what she and Mr. Wong did, or did not do, on that eventful night seemed to have diminished. He had only visited her once more, asking if she was certain she had fulfilled her role as Mr. Wong's entertainment for the evening. It was then that he told her she was going to get certain privileges, like sitting by the pool for a few hours. He never did ask her to play a game of chess.

Orchid now realized the good cop, bad cop role he enjoyed playing was his way of maintaining control over others.

Tony was sitting at a table for four under an umbrella, puffing on a cigar and drinking a Scotch though the clock had not hit noon yet. His outfit for the morning bordered on tacky. Bright Hawaiian colors mixed with red and white checks. You couldn't miss him in a total blackout. His watchful eyes were preoccupied with Pamela's every stroke.

Mr. Black, in a soft yellow suit and reflective sunglasses, stood in military stance near the rear. Snakeskin boots completed the expensive outfit, the .357 beneath the jacket snug as a bug in a rug. Every time he looked at Orchid, sunlight reflected from his eyes like demon fire.

One of the rear sliding glass doors opened and Rosita made her way toward Tony Millions, a newspaper folded in her arms. Mr. Black followed her, hand at the ready. It would not be the first time a staff member offed their boss.

"Meestor Millions," she called out in her best Mexican English, "Dee newspaper and racing form ees finally here."

"Good." Tony sort of half-rose from his chair and, extending his hand, took the papers from her. "Thank you, Rosita."

"Si, Meestor Millions. Eees dare anyting else you need? More Scotch maybe?"

Tony laid the newspaper open on the table. When he saw the headline, a smile lifted his thin lips. He hadn't watched TV. He drew on the Cohiba, releasing a dragon breath of smoke through his nostrils. "Another Scotch would be exactly what the doctor ordered, Rosita." Looking to Mr. Black, who was standing close by, he said, "It would appear Mr. Blue has carried out his mission. I knew I could count on him. Come, have a look for yourself."

Mr. Black went to the table, removed his sunglasses, and read the headline of the *Vegas Mirror*: Billionaire Shipping Magnet Benjamin Wong Dies of Apparent Suicide. There was no reason to read the follow-up. It was indeed the work of Mr. Blue. He was a master at his vocation. Making things appear like something they're not. He'd used the same method with a certain Southern senator not a year ago. Both he and Mr. Wong had been tossed over their balconies without the trace of influence. An alleged suicide note, signed by the deceased left for family.

Tony gulped his Scotch. "To Mr. Blue," he toasted. "I'm going to miss his quiet hand. He really performed his tasks well. Is the hole dug?"

"I had Mr. Brown dig it yesterday. He wasn't too happy that I took him away from the club for the afternoon, but I persuaded him with the usual compensation. Money and the fact that I wouldn't kill him if he dug the hole. He really put his back into it, man."

Norman screeched, "Who loves yah, baby?"

"And what of our Mr. Green? What was he doing while Mr. Brown dug the hole."

"He stayed at the club. He seemed to know his way around the business end of things. I didn't see the harm leaving him on his own for a few hours. He was quite a hit with the ladies."

"Yes, Frank Santangello warned me about his empowerment over women. That's something we'll have to keep an eye on. We can't have him taking liberties with the dancers. If he feels the need for company, he can get it at the Shangri-La Palace and pay for it like everybody else. Make sure he understands this."

"You're the boss, man. What about her?" Mr. Black looked in Orchid's direction.

"You know, she's got me stumped. I know she didn't have sex with the dearly departed Mr. Wong though she says she did. Something transpired between the two of them, that I'm sure of. But what? What was it that caused him to offer us a million for her safekeeping? I'm fucked for an answer." He looked to Orchid. "I wonder how she's going to react to the news of his death. That might tell us something. Let's find out, shall we?" Resting the cigar in an ashtray, Tony set the empty glass down and pushed himself to his feet. The newspaper he folded under his arm.

They headed in Orchid's direction.

Orchid's eyes were sealed. She was trying to focus on the few good things that had transpired since her flight from Bay Ridge Cove, her mind pleasant with demonstrative reverie. Deseray's beautiful face. The ghostly smell of fresh-baked bread. The six-almost-seven Caleb Hart who had stolen hers. His budding companion, Chase, whose heart was as big as his love for his best friend. Even the flamboyant Mr. Sonjee brought a secret smile to the almost-forgotten person residing within. *My name is Rebecca White,* the voice sounded as though it were a testimony given by someone else.

The merciless Nevada sun blistered the tops of her raw feet. A forgiving breeze whispered from the desert that stretched as far as the eye could see. In the background, water swished with each stroke of Pamela's arms.

Suddenly, Orchid felt overwhelmed as though a shadow had passed before the curtains of her eyes. Before she opened them, something cool landed in her lap. Mr. Black and Tony Millions stood over her. Peering into her lap, the Vegas headline, in bold revelation, screamed. Her eyes grew wide enough to serve dinner on.

"That's right," said Tony, an almost-jubilant effervescence to his tone. "Mr. Wong, it would appear, has taken it upon himself to end his own life," he paused, enjoying every second. "And so soon after you two had been intimate with each other.

Orchid's heart literally wrenched, a jolt of raw emotion twisted with the ever-present knife. Straightening, she lifted the paper and stared at it, dizzy. A lump formed in her throat. *How terribly sad. He must have decided after visiting with his wife that he could not be without her anymore and gave up everything he had for love. How tragically romantic.* Tears formed in her eyes. Looking to Tony and Mr. Black, she lied, "I don't understand. "What would make him do such a thing?"

"We were hoping you could shed some light on the matter for us," said Tony, a sick sort of smile stretching his lips.

In the background, Pamela climbed the ladder and emerged from the pool. She retrieved a towel and roughly dried her hair. Seeing Tony and Mr. Black standing over Orchid, the way they were was not a good sign. Instead of getting involved, she slipped her feet into a pair of thongs and went straight to the house. She nearly knocked Rosita over who was coming out of the house and carrying a neat Scotch for her employer.

"How am I supposed to know why he did what he did?" said Orchid. "I have no control over other people's lives, you've seen to that." She spun out of the chaise, the newspaper fell to the ground in loose sections. With her face mere inches from Tony's, she said, "You know what your trouble is, Mr. Millions? You're paranoid. The whole rotten bunch of you. As if I could have had anything to do with what he did. I suppose I just snapped my fingers and made it all happen." Snapping her fingers in front of Tony's nose, she supplied, "I'm sorry that he's dead, but you're barking at the wrong tree. For all I know, you had a hand in this… not me."

This was a side to Orchid Tony hadn't expected. Instead of bowing to his whim, she had gained a rather-thick skin. *Not after tonight though,* he thought. "Me thinks thou doth protest too much. But I'll let it go for now. You should go back to your room. Your skin has already turned pink. We wouldn't want you getting skin cancer or anything. Rosita will be up with your lunch in a few minutes. Run along now, little Orchid."

"Fine by me. I don't care too much for the company I'm with anyway." Storming off, a moment later, the sliding glass door slammed.

"Don't leave me, baby," screeched Norman.

Rosita had been standing off to the side. She knew when to interrupt and when not to. "Here ees your Scotch, Meestor Millions." Stepping forward, she offered the crystal tumbler.

Tony took it from her, "That will be all, Rosita."

"Den I weel begin lunch." She hurried back to the house.

Tony stared out over his property, the gardens and the desert looming endless nearby. Taking a strong swallow of Scotch, he savored it on the flat of his tongue, listened to the music for a moment, swallowed, and said, "I want Orchid's ordeal tonight to be a most memorable one. I want the little bitch so frightened that her only recourse of action will be to bend to my will. There's something she's not sharing with us. I want to know what it is. Snap her fingers in my face will she. We'll soon see about that."

"I have a good idea how to handle this, man," said Mr. Black, smiling great white teeth. "Leave it to me."

* * *

Orchid climbed the spiral staircase, eyes cast south, so when she bumped into Pamela standing next to the railing with a towel wrapped around her head, she was taken aback. "Oh. Sorry," she said. "I didn't see you." Moving aside, she started up the curling steps.

Pamela took hold of her arm, water dripped from the red V between her thighs, dotted the carpet between her feet. "Wait a minute, Orchid. I'm glad I bumped into you. There's something I need to tell you."

"I don't feel like talking right now thank you very much." Orchid tried to pull away, but Pamela held firm.

"It's important," said Pamela, eyes pleading.

Orchid sighed. "Okay. What is it?"

Pamela let go of her arm. "I was watching the news this morning. I think you know what I'm talking about."

Benjamin Wong's apparent suicide in Las Vegas would have been all over the news, worldwide. "You mean Mr. Wong?"

Pamela looked to the second floor, listened to the sounds of the house to be certain that what she was about to say would be between the two of them. "I don't know why I'm telling you this. There's something about you I like. I think it's because I know I can trust you. Forget about the other night. I was stoned, really stoned, and well, sometimes I get a little adventurous. As I said before. You're going to need a friend in this business."

Orchid's silence a loud signal for her to continue.

"Mr. Wong's death isn't what it appears to be," whispered Pamela.

"What!" Orchid's voice came out too loud. She looked around, listened. *Nothing.* "Sorry. Are you saying what I think you're saying?" A rush of anxiety coursed through her body. *Somehow they had murdered him.*

Pamela nodded. "Be careful, girl. Tony thinks there was something between you and Mr. Wong. He doesn't know what, and it's driving him nuts. Did you know Mr. Wong gave Tony a million dollars to keep you from having to have sex with other men?"

Orchid was stunned. *A million dollars.* "Are you sure?"

"Absolutely. The money was deposited in his offshore account two days ago."

"How do you know all this?" asked Orchid, unable to come to terms with the fact someone would pay that much money for her. But she did know why. And now it all made sense.

"Because Tony Millions talks in his sleep," said Pamela matter-of-factly, a smile lifting her beautiful mouth.

Tony and Mr. Black's voices filled the quiet of the first floor.

In a quick tone Pamela said, "Go to your room! You and I never had this conversation. And remember. Be careful."

Orchid nodded and climbed the stairs with as much stealth as possible. When she reached her room, she slowly turned the knob not to make a sound, slipped in, and gently closed the door behind her. With her back against the wood, she exhaled, not realizing she had been holding her breath the whole time. Perspiration dotted her forehead. Hands trembled. A mournful tear slid over a cheek. A knife twisted in her stomach, but it was not the knife of her hunger, instead, it was the knife of self-persecution. *They murdered the poor man for his money. And it was all because of me.*

* * *

39

Streets of Gold

JOHNNY sat in the single room he had rented when he arrived in Las Vegas a week before. With a pillow propped under his head, he watched baseball on the small TV supplied by the landlord. One Ms. McGregor, a woman of immense dimensions, undeterminable age, and short temper who had fed him the riot act. "No parties. No smoking. No pets. No cooking. No guests after eleven. Pay the rent on time or out you go." A reminder of which hung taped in bold letters to the inside of the paint-starved entrance.

The three-storey boarding house was located on Baltimore Avenue amid a complex of white two-storey low rentals and a twenty-minute walk to the Stratosphere Hotel. Rooms were rented by the week. Johnny had paid her enough to get him through the remainder of September.

The room was painted in a glossy green-blue latex and so small, it was almost claustrophobic. A small window allowed him to see the backyard of a neighbor who kept three Junkers parked side by side where weeds grew without care. A print of the Stratosphere Hotel hung over the bed like some bizarre religious symbolism of Vegas's faith. Chest of drawers held his clothing and gun, which was kept wrapped within a pair of jeans should the landlord ever come snooping around while Johnny was away. The linoleum flooring was scarred with cigarette burns even though certain death awaited those who disobeyed Ms. McGregor's six commandments. A single bathroom centering the main floor was shared between himself and five other tenants whom Johnny could hear through the paper-thin walls whenever they were home.

Each night, while he sought sleep, he could hear the light tick-tick-ticking of a mouse's tiny feet as it traversed back and forth across the room, the evidence of its nightly expedition, small pellets of excrement left for him to clean up in the morning. But it would have to do. It was all he could afford and still remain incognito.

Johnny managed to get a job rather easily, working on the new $3.8 billion mega complex Cosmopolitan, cleaning up after the carpenters, electricians, and plumbers and getting paid a hundred dollars a day under the table for doing so. No paycheck meant that he could continue to remain anonymous. Everyone knew him simply as Johnny. He started at seven, Monday to Saturday, the workday not ending until the last of the skilled labor got in their trucks and drove home. Fridays were only half-days, something to do with union policy. The job was easy enough, moving about the site with a wheel barrel, picking up sections of partitions, two-by-fours, and discarded wiring which he tossed into large metal containers. Any discarded copper wiring or plumbing was quickly salvaged by invisible hands. He was well liked among the workers and was constantly asked to go out and "toss a few" with them at Club Paradise, which, to date, he had respectfully declined.

Each night, after a quick meal, he walked the main strip of Vegas, his eyes always searching; but since he had no idea who he was searching for, the walks became a lonely, monotonous quest as tens of thousands passed without giving him a second glance. He was often propositioned by members of Vegas's legal sex trade industry. Mexican immigrants flicked business card–sized advertisements of women who could be hired for private affairs, their seductive photos and number displayed for all to see. The streets were littered with them as if they were Vegas's rendition of confetti.

Being a Friday, the night would be no different. He turned off the television, put on his boots and T-shirt, checked to make sure the turquoise stone was still in his pocket, and headed for the main drag.

He parked Konahee's Ford in the underground parkade of the new Planet Hollywood, formerly the Aladdin.

Riding the escalator to the main floor casino, the musical carillon of slot machines filled the air, culminating with a sound system that was as pure and efficient as Bose. The Tragically Hip's "New Orleans Is Sinking" rocketed through speakers. Hundreds of people moved about in a paradox sea of persistent misfortunes and arbitrary good luck. Only a hint of cigarette odor was prevalent even though many of the patrons were smokers. Massive exhaust systems kept the casino breathable for those who did not.

"Cigars. Cigarettes." A beautiful blonde passed. She carryied a square tray of carcinogenic brands and roses strapped to her shoulders. A revealing black uniform glittered with sequence. Looking bored, she sauntered between rows of slot machines, repeating the call of, "Cigars. Cigarettes." Spotting Johnny, she moved toward him. "A rose for your lady friend perhaps?" she asked, flashing a smile, offering him a whiff of perfume and a glimpse of her robust breasts.

Seeing the red roses, Johnny made mention of them since it was going to be a flower that would rekindle a love lost. "Those are very pretty, but unfortunately I don't have a lady friend at the moment." The blonde, whose name was Kansas according to the name tag pinned to her chest, looked him up and down, and declared, "That's too bad. That must mean there's a lucky girl out there somewhere waiting for you to sweep her off her feet." She smiled. "A cigar perhaps? I carry only the finest brands."

It was then Johnny noticed the wedding ring glittering from her left hand. "Sorry, I don't smoke."

"Well, good luck to you then." Turning, Kansas continued with her minimum wage trade. "Cigars. Cigarettes."

Johnny moved past blackjack tables and a large wheel which consisted of varying denominations of bills. Behind the betting table was another gorgeous employee dressed like a showgirl. Large plumes of feathers protruded from a headpiece and she had glittered breasts that were out to here. Five young men flashed their money, ogling her as they placed their bets. The wheel was gently spun. "Good luck, gentlemen," she said, smiling gregariously.

Johnny stopped to watch. Although he had been in and out of casinos for a week, he had yet to drop a nickel into a slot or take a chance at any of the tables. The five men, in total, had bet $55. The wheel slowed to an agonizing stop. One of the five pumped his fist into the air and whooped. He had just doubled his $5 bet. However, in the time it took to butter toast, the casino was up $50. As Don King would say, "Only in America."

He left Planet Hollywood to the sounds of Dobie Gray's "Drift Away" and the ringing of a bell as someone hit a jackpot.

Dark was quickly approaching. Someone flipped a switch to reveal the absolutism of what Vegas was all about. Trillions of lights lit Las Vegas Boulevard like an excessively decorated Christmas tree. People from all walks of life poured in and out of casinos, fish drawn to the desirability of a colorful lure. The bell tower of the Bellagio rang in the time: 9:00 p.m. The voice of Canada's French diva Celine Dion filled the air. Jets of water erupted from the pool fronting the billion-dollar hotel and began to sway to the sound of "My Heart Will Go On."

Cameras flashed. Impatient drivers honked their horns, caught in a maelstrom of traffic.

A block away, the monuments of Caesar's Palace stood like white granite guardians of the gods.

Johnny moved through the throngs of onlookers. The ballet of fountains precipitously exploded one hundred vertically impressive feet into the air sounding like a cannon shot. Though he had seen the sight several times already, he was still quite captivated by the watery show. He carried on, passing the shorter facsimile of the Eiffel Tower. Several guests exiting the stanchions of steel drank from straws deep within plastic replicas of the posh hotel. A sandwich board near the entrance advertised one could be had for $19.95.

The sight made Johnny thirsty. Still, he pressed on in his search, ignoring the flicking taunts of Mexican immigrants who lined the sidewalk, earning a penny for each provocative card they handed out.

Arriving at Flamingo Avenue, he took the escalator to the catwalk and crossed over the traffic-jammed asphalt below. A Japanese couple stopped him and asked him in broken English if he would take their picture to which Johnny kindly obliged. Once the photo was taken, another memento to add to their already hundreds, the couple respectfully bowed and examined the picture captured in their digital Minolta.

Bill's steak house and saloon offered sirloin steak and baked potato for $9.95. Outside the Flamingo, a line had formed to purchase tickets for the Vinnie Fabarino show, an Italian comedian who could strip paint with his acidic tongue. If you were unfortunate enough to be seated in the VIP seating, you were in for a long, humiliating night. But it was all in good fun.

The voice of Fat Elvis pumped through grainy speakers. A heavyset black attendant, wearing a pink Flamingo T-shirt, was keeping the line entertained with colorful jokes and anecdotes. Johnny stopped to listen. Once the attendant finished with a somewhat-tasteless witticism of his own race, he continued with a story about a father who had given his eight-year-old son one hundred business cards of barely clad women, encouraging him to sell them to his schoolmates for fifty cents a piece. *Only in America*, thought Johnny. He continued on.

By the time he reached Harrah's, he was parched. Portable kiosks selling everything from cheap jewelry to T-shirts, magnetic signs, and a photo of *you* on a Harley lined the entrance. At the carousel stage, where the bartenders were alleged to be the best cocktail acrobats in the world, the Boogie Time band played.

Johnny's eyes searched the crowd, his instincts telling him he would not find her there.

Sitting in a wheelchair next to one of the jester mannequins bookending the glass entrance, a scruff of a man looked defeated. Around his neck was a cardboard sign: Vietnam Vet. His ragtag clothing smelled of vomit and sweat, and he had no arms or legs to speak of. A filthy tube ran from the inside of his pants to a saddlebag dangling from an arm of the chair. In his nonexistent lap sat a Dodger's cap. Through a mat of yellow and white facial hair, he looked up at Johnny, his eyes watering. Johnny fished into a pocket, and withdrew a five-dollar bill. *Karma*, he thought. He placed it in the cap where nickels, dimes, and pennies gleamed. The veteran looked down at the bill and said in a voice void of the derring-do he must have once possessed, "God bless you, son."

"You're welcome," said Johnny and turned away, for he could not bear to look at the decrepit stump of a man any further. With aggrieved heart, he went through the glass doors.

To his left, a crowd had gathered outside an open bar and were listening to female twins dueling it out on a pair of baby grand pianos. Johnny peered over the heads of onlookers for a moment. Drunken patrons, most of whom were young women, danced about the floor in a parody of flailing arms and twisting, jiving legs, their inhibitions lying at the bottom of a cocktail glass or bottle somewhere.

The smell of cigarette smoke was more prevalent in the older casino. One of the twins made eye contact with Johnny and smiled while voicing her rendition of "Piano Man." Johnny smiled back; however, the ivory-tickling blonde went about her business of entertaining the crowd. *Not the love of my life*.

Moving on, he passed banks of penny slot machines and a sports betting lounge. A waitress in her fifties, trying to look thirty-something, stopped and asked him if he would like a drink. "Yes," said Johnny, throat desert dry.

"Where are you sitting?" she asked, meaning which machine.

Johnny quickly noticed a Texas Tea slot was unoccupied. He said, "I'll be right over there," and directed her with his eyes.

"What'll you have?" she asked, pen and pad ready on her tray.

"I would like a Budweiser please."

"Coming right up, sweetheart." The middle-aged waitress turned and disappeared.

From past days, Johnny understood drinks were free so long as you were gambling, so he sat at the Texas Tea slot machine, slipped a five into it, bet one credit per line, and hit the spin reel. Right away, four dancing armadillos lined up, doubling his investment.

An elderly woman, with a puff of cotton white hair and the prongs of an oxygen tube dangling from her nostrils, was sitting at the machine next to him. Glancing over, she commented, "That's a nice start, young man," then cupped her hand over her mouth and coughed.

"Thanks," said Johnny. "To tell you the truth, I've never gambled before."

The old woman lowered her hand, sucking the oxygen she was being supplied with. "Then you'll have very good luck. All novices have good luck. But don't get hooked like me. You'll go broke before you can say you'll go broke. I've been playing these damned contraptions since the mob owned this place, and I can count the amount of times I've hit a big one on the fingers of one hand. But I keep trying."

"I'll keep that in mind," said Johnny, offering her a smile. "I hope you have better luck."

"Thank you, young man." Pushing the reel button, she palmed the screen and won a hundred credits, which pleased her to no end. Hitting the cash-out icon, she collected the ticket valuing $7.75 She left Johnny to his game, dragging the oxygen tank behind her like so much luggage. She went straight to another machine.

The waitress returned with a full tray and handed Johnny his beer. "Here you go, dear." She stood there for a good five seconds before Johnny realized she was waiting for a tip. Shoving a hand into his pocket, he came up with a George Washington and handed it to her.

The waitress stuck it in a glass with a wad of other Washingtons which were standing as rigid as soldiers. "Good luck," she said and left.

Johnny took a long swallow, closed his eyes, and savored each drop. When he opened them, an Elvis impersonator was strolling the carpeted walkway as if he were the king himself. A couple of hot young girls stopped to speak with him, and the guy curled one side of his lip and said in perfect Elvis vernacular, "How would you like to love me tender tonight?" Everyone laughed, including Johnny. He could easily see how one got caught up in Vegas's bewitchment.

Finishing his beer and without gambling his winnings, Johnny cashed the ten-dollar ticket at one of the automated cash machines, *karma*. Leaving Harrah's, he walked farther east along the busy boulevard aptly named Las Vegas.

Another night would pass, and just like the others, Johnny would go back to his dismal room, wondering if he was ever going to find the gifted one who so desperately needed him.

* * *

40

All in a Night's Work

FOR the remainder of that day, Orchid contemplated what it meant to have the kind of knowledge Pamela had given her. It certainly could mean death for the both of them. Pamela had taken a big chance trusting her. It most certainly could be useful in the future, but for right now, it would remain a secret. Even if given the opportunity to blackmail Tony Millions, she wouldn't know where to begin.

Lunch had consisted of enchiladas that burned in her stomach for the remainder of the day. The half ration of heroin she was allowed had calmed the hunger within, but only for a short time. She became restless and paced the room for hours on end listening to music and wondering what it was Pamela was trying to warn her about. "Be careful," she had said. And more than once. Comprehending the men she was dealing with, it could mean anything.

After dinner—lamb, rice, and a medley of vegetables—Orchid pushed one of the high backs toward the window and just sat there, amazed with the incredible view offered. Giant azaleas, flowering cactus, hibiscus, and pods of enormous ferns surrounded the entertainment area. Beyond stretched the Nevada desert, its terrain almost golden in the waning sunlight. If not for the circumstances she was in, the room and its view could be compared to one of the more expensive lodgings the big hotels offered.

Still in jean shorts and the Angel Without Wings T-shirt, she put her feet up on the windows ledge and examined the bruises of her calamity. *Will my feet ever be the same again?* She couldn't imagine it. They were a fright, looking like some mad doctor's failed experiment. Closing her eyes, she rested her head, and listened to the music more with her mind's ear than anything else.

If I should swallow anything evil
put your finger down my throat.
If I should shiver, please give me a blanket.
Keep me warm
Let me wear your coat…

Soon she fell asleep.

"Where am I?" Complete darkness. Feet immersed in something sticky cold. Naked.

"You are with us," hundreds of voices speaking as one.

"Who are you?" She turned round and round in the void, eyes searching, sticky goo squishing between her toes.

"We are the one, the many, as before."

"Yes. I remember you. Am I dreaming?"

"Only with your heart."

"Can you help me?"

"We are only messengers. As before."

"I thought you were bound to your residence."

"Only you could have made our travel possible."

"Then what is it you have to tell me?"

"He searches for you."

"Who? Who searches for me?"

"Your salvation. He is near."

"Are you sure? I am lost forever."

"He will find you."

"But it's so dark and I'm so cold. How will he ever find me in the dark?"

"He knows who you are."

"But how?"

"You are his guiding light. His destiny."

"Will he love me?"

"Yesss," the voices sang. "Forever and ever. He would die for you."

Footsteps in the darkness. Coming closer and closer, choking the air with evil intent.

"WAKE UP, REBECCA!"

Orchid's eyes shot open in time to see hands coming at her face. She tried to yell; however, her mouth was covered immediately with tape. Two silhouettes standing before her in the dusk of night, the green iridescence of the pool lighting the background. Mr. Black and Mr. Blue.

"Good evening, baby," said Mr. Black.

Orchid tried to get out of the chair. Mr. Blue shoved her roughly. The chair nearly toppled. He took hold of her hands, and secured them with a white plastic tie, binding them together at the wrists.

Orchid's eyes, wild with uncertainty, darted from one to the other, muffled screams filled her mind.

Mr. Black took hold of her ravaged feet and, in one quick motion, secured them with another tie.

Struggling, Orchid was helpless.

Mr. Blue drew a black sack over her head, and whispered, "Mr. Millions says your time is up, sweetheart. We're going for a little drive."

Orchid was hoisted into the air, carried out of the room, down the spiral staircase, and through the front door.

Mr. Black popped the trunk to the Cadillac. Orchid tried to kick out with her feet, but powerful hands held her at bay.

"One, two, three," said Mr. Blue, and she landed awkwardly into the compartment. Something hard jammed into her back. Before Mr. Black slammed the trunk, he said, "Don't worry, baby. I'll make it quick. You won't feel a thing. I promise."

Orchid was not quite sure where she was until the engine fired up. *They've put me in the trunk of a car. Now they're going to take me someplace and kill me.* Terrified like never before, tears fell like rain from her eyes. It was difficult to breathe, but not impossible. A thousand thoughts ran roughshod through her mind. The car lurched forward. She could hear music coming from the rear speakers and the voices of her executioners speaking in hushed tones. Whatever she was lying on was digging in, and she was sure she was bleeding, the warmth of it running beneath the T-shirt and down her back.

An hour passed, maybe two. She wasn't sure. The sound the tires were making had changed long ago, and she got the impression they were traveling on something soft, like sand. *Oh my god. They're taking me into the desert. They're going to kill me and bury me and my body will never be found. I guess the one were wrong.*

"Don't be afraid, Rebecca."

The voice came from next to her as if there was someone else in the trunk with her. Young, female. Orchid mumbled incoherently through the tape. The stale air in the trunk grew cold, chilled her exposed legs.

"You must listen to me, Rebecca. I have something very important to tell you.

Orchid listened with baited breath.

"My name is Janis Keeper. I ran away from home in Boise, Idaho. I don't know how long ago. Big mistake. Tony Millions stole my life. Mr. Black pulled the trigger, but it was Tony who gave the order."

"Look for the screaming man. Memorize these numbers. Thirteen left. Twenty-four right. Nine left. This combination leads to Tony Millions's personal possessions. Money, bonds, and drugs. These are the things that drive his warped world. Every Tuesday, Thursday, and Saturday, without fail, Tony goes to the Bellagio to gamble."

Then there was only silence. Janis Keeper's enchanted presence vanished as mysteriously as it had arrived.

Orchid repeated the numbers in her mind over and over until they were tattooed there. *But what good would they do me?* she wondered. *I'm going to die. Murdered for all the wrong reasons.*

The Cadillac suddenly slowed and came to stop. Orchid heard the doors open then close with a slam. The engine was still running. A moment later, the trunk opened, and she was hoisted out by her legs and shoulders and made to stand on her own.

"Here we are, Orchid," said Mr. Black. He removed the hood and tore at the tape. Orchid's flesh screamed pain.

"You fucking bastards!" she aimed at the two men bookending her. Then she saw it, horrific in the beams of the Cadillac's headlights. Just like the well she had been thrown into time and time again. A dark shadow in the desert sand where a mound of earth was piled next to. The sight caused her to shudder irrepressibly. It was going to be the grave where her flesh would rot, bones turn to dust, and no one would ever know.

Reaching into a pocket, Mr. Black removed a pair of wire cutters. On one knee, he cut the ties binding her feet. "I borrowed this from Mr. Brown. Nasty little thing. No wonder he likes it so much."

With her feet free, Orchid kicked at him, but missed completely and fell awkwardly in the sand. "I fucking hate you. I'll fight you with my last breath."

Mr. Blue grabbed her by the arm and stood her up. "I think your fighting days are over, young lady. Your tomb awaits your arrival." Leading her to the edge of the rectangular hole, Orchid thrashed out with her legs every step of the way, and made contact with his shin, but only once. It hurt him, and she was glad to have inflicted at least some kind of pain to the bastard.

Standing at the precipice, Orchid refused to look into its waiting darkness. Her gaze followed the headlight beam to the fringes of night. This far out in the Nevada desert the countless stars above dusted the night in a blanket of diamonds. That's when she saw them. People moving about aimlessly as if they were lost. A dozen, maybe more. Young women, middle-aged men, none of whom seemed to be aware of each other. Spirits of the walking dead. Lost in limbo. *Like Kimberly Gagne.*

Mr. Black moved behind her and spoke in no uncertain terms. "I promised to make this painless, and I will."

Orchid turned her head so that she was looking into his devil-may-care eyes. "Just how many people have you buried out here? You're not a man. You're a fucking animal. Your parents must be very proud." The muzzle of Mr. Black's .357 pressed against the back of her head. She closed her eyes and thought of her family, her entire body tensing as it readied for the bullet that would splatter her brains all over the desert. So frightened was she that she urinated, the warmth of it running down her legs and onto her bruised feet. But she would not cry. She would not give them the satisfaction.

"Any last words, Orchid?" asked Mr. Black.

"Yes. Just three. Go fuck yourself!"

There was a thunderous roar which momentarily deafened Orchid, the report of it echoed across the plains.

Mr. Blue fell facefirst into the hole.

Orchid opened her eyes, not believing what they were seeing. Mr. Blue lay in the hole, half his face missing, right leg jerking in death spasm. Sinew, brain matter, and skull fragments decorated the farthest wall of the burial plot and slid into the hole like lumpy porridge. She dropped to her knees, and vomited. Lamb, rice, and vegetables splashed onto Mr. Blue's back. Her mind was completely flummoxed. *What had just happened? Mr. Black just shot Mr. Blue instead of me.* She turned her head wiped at her mouth and looked up at him. There was a great big shit eating grin on his face. The gun in his hand black death and smoking.

"Surprised?" he said, and tucked the gun back into its holster.

Orchid blinked several times, still confounded. "You killed Mr. Blue." Looking into the darkness, the roaming spirits were moving toward her as if the sound of the gunshot had beckoned them.

"That's right, baby. It's that simple. He was a loose end that needed tying." He took her by the hair, and forced her to inspect the macabre scene. "I want you to take a good look at him, Orchid. Tony Millions thinks you're worth salvaging. I, on the other hand, think you're not worth the effort, but he's the boss, so I do what I'm told. Now you remember this, baby. Because I guarantee you, if you do not cooperate, it will be *your* brains splattered all over the place. But not before Mr. Brown and I torture you, a lot. We'll take turns raping you until you think you're going out of your mind. Then I'll fly to Kentucky, personally, and do the same to your friends." He held her there for a long unpleasant moment, letting the scene penetrate deep. Then he spun her so that she was looking into his devil eyes. "Now wait right here." He went to the Cadillac, and retrieved the shovel from the trunk. He shoved it at her. "Here. Start filling the hole."

"What?"

"You heard me, bitch! Fill in the hole and be quick about. I would do it, but I detest physical labor."

"But my hands." She held the shovel clumsily.

"You'll manage, baby." He smiled wickedly, retrieved his cell phone, and took a picture of the faceless Mr. Blue. "I'll be in the Cadillac waiting and watching, so don't get any stupid ideas in that pretty little head of yours. I can just as easily bury you on top of him." He went to the Cadillac and slid in. Classical music floated into the night.

The walking dead had gathered around Orchid in a spectral circle and were gazing into the freshly dug grave as if they were reliving the moment of their own demise. They still bore the wounds of their passing: cut throats, faces obliterated, missing fingers. Two of them, a man and a woman, had been disemboweled, their intestines hanging like sausage castings. Another was a young woman about Rebecca's age. If it were not for the fact that a third of her face was missing, she would have been pretty.

She kept looking at Orchid and nodding while the others seemed to be more interested in the body of Mr. Blue. Orchid understood she was looking at the disembodied apparition of Janis Keeper.

"I'm sorry," she whispered to the gathered dead. "I wish I could help you. But as you can see, I'm in big trouble here." Each seemed to accept this and, as one, dispersed. They drifted back into the desert night, a single file of the damned, and vanished beyond the scope of the Cadillac's headlights.

A hostile gust swept across the plain, and stormed shards of sand into Orchid's face and legs. She closed her eyes and waited for it cease. When it finally did and she unclenched her eyes, she witnessed orbicular white lights, the remaining life forces of the lamented, the wrongful dead, drift waywardly across the plain.

Rounding the mound of earth, she gripped the shovel best she could and pushed it into the sand. She aimed the first, second, and third shovelfuls at what remained of Mr. Blue's face, unable to look at the mess Mr. Black's cannon had made for another second. *That could be me,* she kept telling herself as the mound of sand grew smaller. Sweating with the effort, the shovel slipped in and out of her grasp. But she did not stop. Death was seated in the car not twenty feet away.

Soon Mr. Blue's body was completely covered; however, the image would remain with Orchid for the remainder of her life and be the facilitator of nightmares to come. *Thirteen left. Twenty-four right. Nine left. Thank you, Janis Keeper. I'll try to do right by you.*

* * *

41

Baby Blue

LOCATED south on Highway 6, the Shangri-La Palace, a Spanish villa, boasted terra cotta roof, pink stucco frame, buttressed windows and an arched all wood double door entrance which was stained red. Surrounded by a six-foot fence of wrought iron, its titled grounds were sparsely landscaped. A cactus here, cypress tree there. A single hibiscus with elegant pink blooms looked out of place. A large sign festooned above the double wide entrance welcomed patrons and trumpeted: *Through these doors are the most beautiful women in Nevada.*

With the sun rising from the east, the slope of the tiled roof resembled that of the scaled belly of a fabled dragon, Orchid thought.

All around the come-hither oasis for as far as the eye could manage was a sea of desert. All of it crowned by a universe of blue and its watchful golden eye.

Mr. Black pulled into the looping driveway and parked the Cadillac in front of the entrance. Viewing Orchid in the rearview he said, "Wait right here." As if on cue, the front doors swung out, and Madame Olivia stepped into the sunshine. She wore a dazzling blue Vera Wang though it was only 10:00 a.m. and was smoking a cigarette, blowing jets of blue through her nostrils. Locks of golden hair rode the erupting designs of her breasts. Her eyes were pitch, like doll's eyes, set deep within a face that had been perfectly schemed by the hands of plastic surgeon; demure with the overriding promise of wickedness. An adult version of Cindy Lou Who. Silver stilettos added inches to her tallness.

Orchid watched from the rear seat, numbed by her experiences, unquestionably complaisant by the threat of certain death.

Mr. Black left the Cadillac climbed the rises of concrete, received Madame Olivia's hands in his, and kissed her on both cheeks.

Orchid could read his lips, "This one will give you plenty."

Dwarfed by Mr. Black's looming shadow, Madame Olivia drew on the cigarette, doll eyes narrow as she gazed at Orchid through the glass. She offered an effusive smile and nodded her head while Mr. Black spoke. Dropping the cigarette, she snuffed it with the silver tip of a stiletto.

Orchid looked away, and smoothed a hand over the suitcase Tony Millions so graciously allowed her to keep. Within, the framed memory of her mother rested not three inches away among the totality of her seventeen, almost eighteen years. This was going to be an introduction into a world she could not, or even dared to imagine. Forged into submission, her lonesome heart wept strident against her breastbone.

She was beaten, yet again, her life another page turned. Paragraphs of humiliation of hopelessness. Still, a part of her remained unresolved, for somewhere deep within the turmoil abyss of Rebecca White's inner self, there burned a desire to triumph over Tony Millions's domination and whatever pains he was going to inflict upon her.

Mr. Black smiled and waved her out of the Cadillac.

Orchid hated that big ivory smile of his. It was so dishonorable, so somatic. Taking a deep breath, she opened the door and lugged herself and the suitcase from the comfort of the backseat. The simple cotton dress she wore shone virginally in the early sun. She stood, not moving, the suitcase dangling by her side, her eyes cast to the pavement.

"Come here, dear," the alluring woman in fashionable blue finally said. "There's nothing to be afraid of here. I'm going to take good care of you."

Orchid took a stride, then another. Madame Olivia ascended the steps and held out a gleaming set of red nails and fingers that were adorned with more diamonds than Orchid had ever seen in her entire life. She waved as if to summon a child. "Come on in out of the hot sun. It's nice and cool inside. I'm Olivia by the way, however, my girls call me Oli, and as I understand it, you go by the beautiful name of Orchid."

Orchid nodded. "Yes." She looked to the man who had given her the pseudonym; he was smiling like the jackal he was. Reaching a hand, she took Madame Olivia's. It was warm, soft. Nothing like she expected.

"You have beautiful hair, Orchid. And those freckles. I've never seen so many." Steering Orchid toward the entrance and Mr. Black, she assumed, "You and I are going to become great friends. You'll see."

Orchid advanced with the saunter and decisive movements of someone who was in a trance.

"I'll leave her to you then, Madame Olivia," said Mr. Black. "I have other things that need taking care of." Resting a heavy hand on Orchid's shoulder, he simpered, "You're in good hands, baby. Oh, before I forget." He reached into his suit pocket and removed a small black kit, not unlike the one he had used with alacrity in the house of pain. Handing it to Madame Olivia, he cautioned, "Twice a day and only the amount I discussed with you over the phone. Tony wants our little Orchid clean ASAP."

Madame Olivia palmed the kit, and slipped it into an invisible side pocket.

Knowing what was in the little black pouch caused the knife within Orchid's stomach to twist with want.

Oli looked to Orchid's feet. Open sandals revealed the signature of her dependency.

"We'll soon take care of those, sweetheart. They will be as good as new in no time." She looked to Mr. Black with disdain. "You undoubtedly had a hand in this."

Mr. Black shrugged, held the palms of his hands out as if he were making an offering. "My hands are tied. You know how it is. You have your instructions, so clean her up."

"Come inside, Orchid." Oli placed her hands on her shoulders, and eased her toward the yawning double doors. "I suddenly don't care for the company."

"Ouch! Suit yourself Madame." Mr. Black stared down at the Mistress of the Shangri-La Palace, his eyes venting malice.

Oli was not swayed by his soulless glare. "And fuck you too, Mr. Black."

Laughing, he said, "I'll keep in close contact. Tony will be paying you a visit tonight. Make sure Orchid is… presentable." He went to the Cadillac, and slid his monstrous size behind the wheel. A second later, five hundred horses roared to life.

Orchid stepped into the enormous villa supposing the rift between Mr. Black and the Madame had been theatrically presented for her benefit. Oli sealed the doors behind them.

The air was cool, filled with the perfume of flowers. The welcoming room a paroxysm of pinks. Pink walls, pink shag carpeting, lamps with pink shades, Roman chaises with rich pink coverings, and giant throw pillows scattered about, each of them a different shade of blush. A fake palm tree stood in a corner. In sharp contrast to the room, a mirrored bar extending half the length of the far wall stood out like a throwaway from the fifties. Faux leopard skin decorated its facade. Liquor bottles crowded a shelf. High boy seating with pink fur and wrought-iron legs stood askew to each other. Within the mirror, aft to the leopard skin bar, the Shangri-La Palace glittered gold. In bold black script beneath the title was the pledge: Your Fantasy Is Our Obsession.

All of it blueprinted to sexually entice the male and sometimes female customers.

Standing behind the bar, a beautiful Oriental girl, cloth in hand, cleaned the inside of a martini shaker. Blue-black hair hung just below slim shoulders and was cropped straight across her forehead. Her small frame looked lost in the men's T-shirt she was wearing. She smiled sweetly when Orchid's eyes came to rest on hers.

"That's Li Ling," said Oli. "She helps me maintain the place… among other things. You'll meet the rest of the girls later. We had a busy night last night. Lots of big winners. We expect the same tonight."

"Hello," said Orchid in a timid voice and rested the suitcase on the floor next to one of the bar stools.

"Unfortunately, the poor girl's a mute," continued Oli. "Regardless, she can understand you just fine. She nods and speaks with her eyes. Li Ling?" Oli's eyes demanded the young girl's attention. "Once you've finished with the bar, would you please tend to the bedsheets in rooms 3, 4, and 5."

Li Ling smiled and nodded. Her eyes sparkled as if doing laundry was the greatest chore one could possibly have bestowed upon her.

Oli continued. "We're quite self-sufficient here, Orchid. We have our own laundry facilities and a kitchen that would cause Emerald Lagossi to bam in his pants. We have a theater room. A solarium if you're into growing things. Which the girls are. A hot tub room and an exercise room. All our supplies arrive Tuesdays by truck, and weekly, the girls and I like to go into the city to do a little clothes shopping. You'll like that. We really make a day of it. Listen to me rambling on. I've completely forgotten my manners. You must be thirsty. Li Ling, fix Orchid a nice cold iced tea please."

The pretty Asian smiled with her eyes, disappeared for a moment behind the bar and came up with a can of Nestlé iced tea. Another fast movement and she had a tall glass in her hand filled with ice. Emptying the can, she added a wedge of lemon that appeared out of nowhere.

Orchid stepped forward, glad for the opportunity to quench her thirst. "Thank you," she said, taking the glass from Li Ling. With a greedy yearning born deep within, she took a very satisfying drink.

"As I was saying, Orchid, we have the necessary amendments required to earn a very auspicious living."

The iced tea landed hard in Orchid's stomach and awakened the knife. The thick cologne of flowers and pink pink pink oh my god pink caused her to suddenly feel nauseous. She had not eaten since the night before, unable to get the visual of Mr. Blue's head splattered everywhere out of her mind. Her head swooned. Oli continued to speak. "My girls make a very profitable living. As will you. We have a dental plan, eye care, and financial portfolios that would make an investment broker, well, you know." She continued to go on as if she were selling a condo with fringe benefits. "Our business hours are a little irregular, but you'll get used to them."

Orchid put the cold glass to her forehead and managed a seat in one of the chairs. It was all so much so fast. And it was all about control. It had been from the very beginning. From the moment Henry Klondike smiled heavenly God fearing eyes at her.

"Orchid? Are you all right, sweetheart? Don't fret. I know it's all rather fast and a lot to take in, but I want you to know that from this moment on, your life is going to take a turn for the better. Isn't that right, Li Ling? We girls take care of our own."

Li Ling's head bobbed with enthusiasm, her eyes as bright as an eight-year-old girl who had just been given the keys to the Barbie kingdom.

The head mistress studied Orchid for a quick moment. "Perhaps I should just show you to your room for now. So you can get comfortable. Take a nap. Yes, I think that would be best. We want you looking rested when Mr. Millions comes this evening." Examining Orchid from the digits of her feet to the perfect shape of her throat, ears, and apple green eyes, Oli smiled. The wickedness within camouflaged by a flash of teeth and the motherly charm of benign eyes. "You'll love your room," she said brightly. "I hope you like stuffed animals. Your bed is covered with them. There's a beautiful view of the landscape and mountains, and the sunrises are spectacular. There's even a private bath and shower. I want you to feel at home here, Orchid. If you're hungry, I can get Li Ling to bring you up a sandwich later. Then when the girls arrive, you'll be all that much better to meet them."

Stuffed animals? Window with a view? Just like home. Information garnished while I was under the influence of Mr. Black's sodium pentothal–loaded syringes no doubt. "I think that would be best. I am tired." If she spent another five minutes in the fragrantly claustrophobic room, Orchid was sure she would vomit.

"Good then. Come along. Bring your drink with you." Oli went to a side door.

Orchid slipped from the chair. "Thank you for the drink, Li Ling." The demure Asian girl's face brightened into a, *your welcome* smile.

Orchid estimated her to be in her early twenties, though it was hard to tell with Asian people. Retrieving the suitcase, she followed Oli through the door.

A narrow flight of steps curved at the upper landing. Pink sunlight led the way. Oli hiked the Vera Wang so her heels would not catch. "I know it seems a little cramped, but what's at the top is well worth the climb." She continued on.

Orchid boosted the suitcase with a knee. The incline was steep for a house, the climb taking everything Orchid had left to get to the top. Again, the result of lack of sleep, for each time she had closed her eyes the previous night, Mr. Blue's missing face filled the void with convincing reverie.

The staircase led to a red carpeted hallway patterned with twists and turns of coral. There were a half-dozen arched maple doorways. All closed. Stucco walls, ten feet high were adorned with paintings of Spanish landscapes, mariachi bands, and villas. Beside each doorway stood white marble pedestals atop of which were vases filled with colorful silk flowers. Pink sunlight bled from three rose-tinted skylights.

"Nice. Don't you think?" asked Oli.

"Yes. Which room is mine? I'd like to lie down."

"Your room is at the end of the hall where you can have all the privacy you need. My room is this one." She pointed to the room nearest them. "If for any reason you feel the need to talk, my door is always open."

They moved down the hallway. Oli opened one of the massive doors without effort. "This will be your bathroom. I have my own."

Orchid peeked. The lavatory was lushly appointed with rich creamy colors, thick burgundy bath towels, a separate shower stall, dual sink with ornate oval mirror, and a jetted soaker tub as big as a Volkswagen. The flooring was constructed of pink tiling, with throw rugs placed just so. Motif candles sighted everywhere. Even the toilet was covered in a shag of pink, and the toilet paper holder was made of elaborate brass molding. Everything very much over the top.

"It's nice," she remarked with a sigh.

"It's all yours, Orchid. However, because Nevada is experiencing its worst drought in history, all I ask is you refrain from letting the water run unnecessarily. We're very conservation-conscious here." Regarding the worried look on Orchid's face, she tried. "Please don't be distressed. This is your new home." Seeing Orchid's difficulty with the suitcase, she offered, "Here. Let me take that for you."

Orchid squeezed the handle as if giving up the suitcase to Madame Olivia meant she was handing over the miniscule sum of what remained of her life. Reluctantly, she let it go.

"Come," the mistress of the house said, and carried the suitcase as if it weighed no more than a hummingbird. She led Orchid down the extent of the hallway. When they arrived at what was to be Orchid's room, Oli opened the door exclaiming, "Well, here it is. I know you'll be happy here."

Sunlight nearly blinded Orchid as the door swung open. When her eyes adjusted, the first thing she saw was a queen-sized canopy bed wearing a thick comforter of aubergine to match the skirt and silk partitions hanging from its frame. On the bed were a dozen stuffed animals all within hugging size. Everything from bears to fish, a bumblebee, two giraffes, and an alligator, the sight of which caused her thoughts to venture to a recent past and to her beloved Bandit and the Harts.

Tiffany lamps sat on side tables that bookended the bed. A digital clock radio stood on the one nearest to the window.

Above, center to the room, a double tier Chrystal chandelier captured the sun's rays in a dazzling display of refracted light. A Louis XIV armoire and credenza sat majestically against two of the floral walls. An enormous oil painting depicting a scene from the Spanish civil war with horses clashing and swords drawn by sneering men hung from the wall nearest the bed. French doors, shouldered by sheer drapes of cinnamon led to a balcony. Beyond Orchid could see the rolling mounds of the Charleston mountain range.

"Lovely, isn't it?" Oli moved graciously across the room, and set the suitcase in front of the bed.

"It's beautiful," replied Orchid, dumbstruck by the omnipotence of it. Though it was obviously decorated by a woman's hand, there was something very masculine about it. The horses in the painting were so lifelike it looked as though they would leap from the canvas and charge across the room. Stepping farther, Orchid's feet sank into the butterscotch carpet, thick and supple as sponge cake.

Oli went to the wall where the credenza stood, placed her hand on the wallpaper; and much to Orchid's surprise, opened to reveal an enormous walk-in closet where colorful garments hung all in a row. Beneath the garments was a rainbow of fashionable shoes. "These are all for you, Orchid. Size 7 dress and 9 shoe, right?" She removed an avocado evening gown. "We would like you to wear this tonight." She held the gown in front of her like a saleswoman would, draping it over one arm, brushing her cheek against the chiffon. "It's so soft and so light, you'll feel like you're wearing nothing at all. And the color will ignite those eyes of yours. There's a pair of saffron pumps in the closet that will go beautifully with this. We must have you looking your best when the customers start to arrive. Of course we don't expect you to participate your first night. All we want from you is to observe the other girls, learn how to entice the guests into spending large amounts of money, and simply look wonderful doing so. We have two couples and three businessmen scheduled. Then there are always at least two or three young studs who venture our way with their winnings so they can have their utmost fantasies fulfilled." She laid the garment across the comforter. It landed in a whisper of elegance.

Orchid's head spun in phantasmagoria loops. If it wasn't for the reality of the situation, she thought she might have just been thrust into an elaborate dream. She went to the suitcase, sat on its top, cupped her hands to her face, and began to weep, her body shuddering with each intermittent breath.

Oli went to her and stroked the top of her head with the soothing touch of a matronly caregiver. "There, there, my dear. No need to cry. Tell me. What's got you so upset. I've been assured that you would be most… *cooperative.*" On one knee and using the point of a finger, she lifted Orchids' chin.

Orchid sniffed and wiped at her eyes. "I will. It's just… ," she sniffed. "Just that I'm not used to this type of lifestyle."

In a seriously sinister tone, Oli said, "But you *will* be cooperative. Won't *you*, my dear?"

Orchid looked into her doll's eyes, seeing the wickedness lying just beyond. The manner in which she said my dear as Hester had, appropriately disturbing.

"Yes, I will," said Orchid, the night before reassembling in her mind in a flash of gore.

"Good. Believe me, it will be much for the better for you if you are." Oli stood, placed her hands on her hips. "I'll leave you to your room for now. The other girls will be arriving shortly. Familiarize yourself with it. Have a nap if need be. I'll send Li Ling up with a nice roast beef sandwich and a glass of milk. How does that sound?" She smiled down at her mollified recruit, the Shangri-La Palace's newfound cash cow.

"That would be nice. I am hungry."

"That's the spirit. Oh… and should you feel the need for, well, you know, do tell me. I'm going to show you a discreet method of application so your feet can heal. All right?"

Orchid looked to her feet. "Yes. Thank you, Oli." Although her tears had dried, her heart was filled with self-loathing. The thought of being a whore terrified her to no end. However, the little voice inside her head was telling her that it was better than dying or being responsible for terrible harm, if not death, coming to the Harts. The *one,* albeit in a dream, had told her that her saviour was near. She could only hope he found her soon.

As if the next words out of Oli's mouth would soften Orchid's trepidation, she said, "My girls earn on average two thousand a week. You can't earn that kind of money just anywhere, sweetheart. Our methods are clean, and all precautions are made so that no diseases enter the Shangri-La Palace. Kind of makes you think, doesn't it? You mull that over for a while." Turning, she headed for the arched door. When she opened it, she said over a fine shoulder, "Li Ling will be up momentarily." The door closed and there was a click, validating Orchid a captive once more.

* * *

She turned on the radio then finished the sandwich Li Ling had provided. The milk she took out onto the balcony. Slipping out of her sandals, the air felt good against the tracks of her addiction; and the concrete platform, though rippled, comforted the pads of her feet. The warm desert air well against her face. Below, a green lizard troddled across the cracked desert earth, climbed one of the few cactuses, and perched itself atop. It sat there with its long tongue flickering, and its eyes rotating dizzily while it took in the day.

With one hand holding the railing, Orchid finished the milk to the last drop and wiped at the moustache. Sighing heavily, she emptied her lungs. A solitude tear spilled over her cheek. In the same moment, a desert breeze lifted the ends of her hair and warmed the breadth of her throat. She closed her eyes, breathed it in, and allowed her mind to wander on its own. Fragments of the dream she had had filtered through tangled worry. *"He knows who you are,"* the voices of the *one* prompted. *"He is your salvation. He would die for you."*

A screeching penetrated her thoughts and she opened her eyes. A hawk circled high on a draft, its wings sharp and still. Orchid watched it circle over and over, climbing higher toward the scorching sun until it became no more than a dot against the blue background, its cry almost lost in the distance. "Whoever you are," she whispered to herself, "I hope you find me soon."

Returning to the elegantly frightening room, Orchid put the glass on a nightstand, increased the volume of the radio, and lay on the bed among the stuffed animals. Blindly she reached for comfort, her hand finding the black-and-yellow bumblebee. Tucking it beneath her arm, she held it close to her breast. She fought with all the resolve she could manifest against the hunger that was eating away at her self-control, twisting a knot within her damaged soul. A commercial was advertising time shares. She listened intently to the drone of a male voice. When the commercial concluded, the DJ, a woman, returned and announced in a sultry voice, "'Baby Blue' by Chilliwack."

Music rode softly on the air waves. In an attempt to lose herself, to forget for a trice her predicament, Orchid closed her eyes and sang along, immersing herself in the love ballad, the bee fierce against her breast.

Have you got something to tell me
Please come up and tell it to me
Please come up and tell me
Baby Blue

Have you got a tear or two
Well, come on up and tell me do now
You can tell it all now
Baby Blue

Really, baby, don't be shy
It's all right for me to talk to you
So let it all come out and let it all come through
Baby Blue

Someone has been cruel to you...

Orchid fell deep into the world of dreamless cinema, tears spilling from her eyes, the words of the *one*, the many, and the ballad guiding her into darkness, *"He is your salvation. He would die for you. Someone has been unkind to you. Let it all come through. Baby Blue."*

* * *

42

Dream Girls

LAUGHTER shook Orchid from the depths of sleep. She forced her eyes. There came a soft knuckled rap at the door. More giggles. Sitting, she wiped at her face, her eyes. Neil Diamond's "New York" alto in the key of G serenaded her, the illuminated digits reading 3:00 p.m. Mr. Bumblebee had rolled out of her grasp and sat staring at her, confused. The evening gown, a testimony of things to come lay across the bed, anxious to feel the closeness of her body.

There was a click, the knob turned slowly, then the heavy door opened wide. Wearing schoolgirl smiles, three women, all young, two of them gorgeous twins, stood at the threshold, arm in arm. "May we come in?" asked an olive-skinned beauty. She had thick black hair and wore a short denim skirt with blue halter that was having difficulty holding enormous breasts. Carmel eyes twinkled with the varnish of honey. White gold glittered from her fingers and toes. Without Orchid's permission, all three entered the room and headed straight for the bed.

Orchid sat ridged, noticed the twins were walking funny then saw that their feet were encased within Rollerblades. One was wearing red shorts and white top while the other wore white shorts and red top, their blond hair cut into the same fashion, short, pulled back and gleaming with hair gel. Cherry red lips sat beneath cerulean eyes. "Hi," they giggled in unison. "I'm Brit." "And I'm Brat."

"And my name is Gypsy," said the olive-skinned beauty. We're here to welcome you." All three took a place on the bed next to a startled Orchid and stared at her in silence. "Hello," Orchid finally said.

Wrapped in each other's arms, the twins giggled simultaneously.

Seeing that she was still half-asleep and scared, Gypsy took Orchid's hands in hers. "Don't be frightened. We didn't mean to scare you. We were anxious to meet you and wanted you to know that we're so glad you're here."

"Thank you," offered Orchid.

"God, you're so beautiful," said Brat. "Isn't she, Brit?"

"Yes. Very pretty. Those green eyes are going to melt a lot of hearts." In a synchronized movement, each twin tucked one leg under the other, their Rollerblades moving in harmony to Heart's "Rockin' Heaven Down."

Moving her face close to Orchid's, Gypsy said, "Don't mind them. Between the two, there's only one hamster spinning the wheel." Then she leaned in and kissed Orchid on both cheeks. "Welcome, Orchid. I know you're going to love it here." Her eyes were warm, sincere. In them, Orchid could see her reflection. *'Be co-operative,'* Madame Olivia's subliminal voice reminded her. "I'm sure I'm going to like it here," she said managing a smile. "This room is so beautiful and Madame Olivia seems nice."

Each of the girls looked at each other. Something was spoken between them that Orchid picked up immediately. Voiced in their predisposed eyes was a flicker of unpleasant reverie.

"Well, yes. Nice is one way to describe Oli I guess," said Gypsy.

Brit and Brat tut-tutted. Brit asked, "What's your specialty, Orchid?"

"Yes, please do tell us. We're dying to know," countered her sister.

"My specialty?" asked Orchid, ignorance causing her voice to lift.

"Yes," prompted Brit. "You know. Do you do couples? Like us. Or threesomes? Do you like toys? Are you into anal or just regular? Personally I *love* anal. But Brat doesn't. It's the only thing we disagree on."

"Take it easy, girls," said Gypsy. "This isn't twenty questions you know. I'm sure if Orchid wants to share her signature dish with us, she will in good time. Right now we've got to get her ready for this evening as per Oli's request. I'm thinking just a little green eye shadow and a touch of blush for the lips." Resurrecting the avocado gown from the comforter, she stood and held it abreast. "This is going to look sooo scrumptious on you. Come on, Orchid, we'll help you, won't we, girls?"

"Oh yes," chorused the twins. "We just love to play dress up."

Gypsy wiggled ringed fingers. "Come with us, Orchid. You're in good hands. I promise."

Orchid took hold of the extended hand, and allowed Gypsy to pull her from the security of the bed where Bumblebee sat, still looking confused.

"Brit? Get those pumps Oli wants her to wear," said Gypsy, her eyes sad for Orchid's damaged feet, reliving the days when her own had brandished the same invasion.

The dishwater blonde stumbled to the walk-in closet and retrieved the requested shoes. Gypsy looped an arm through Orchid's. "I know who's going to be getting all the attention tonight." Lips parted, the tip of her sexy tongue washed the crest of her upper lip. "You're going to look good enough to eat." Arms looped, she ushered Orchid toward the door. The twins followed unsteady.

Orchid peered over her shoulder to the animals bunched together on the bed, and wished she could be one of them. To spend her life numb to the world's Tony Millions, Madame Olivia's, and Mr. Blacks. To never feel pain or hurt again. To be pampered and hugged by loving arms for the remainder of her life, like Bandit had been. Because once she went through the bedroom door, she knew there would be no reprieve from the life that was about to be thrust upon her. *Not unless... unless my saviour finds me soon. Because if he doesn't, I know I will drown in this morally empty pool.*

The women exited Orchid's room to the sound of Sir Paul McCartney's "Wings."

Stuck inside these four walls,
Sent inside forever,
Never seeing no one,
nice again,
like you... momma... you.

* * *

Within the privacy of Orchid's lavish bathroom, the girls undressed and dressed Orchid, then Gypsy applied a smidgeon of makeup to her eyes and lips while Brit stroked a brush through her hair. Brat had lifted her frame onto the sink and was humming an unrecognizable tune. Orchid slipped her feet into the saffron pumps, the new leather cutting into the tops of her feet. She winced. None of the girls made mention of the bright designs though it was obvious she had been dancing with the needle.

Much to Orchid's disbelief, Brit set the brush on top of the toilet, went to her sister, positioned herself between opened legs, took a breast in hand, and kissed her passionately, the probe of her tongue thrusting in and around Brat's receptive mouth.

"Don't mind those two," said Gypsy. "They're a couple of nymphs. It must have really been something growing up in Willow Creek, Oregon, with three sisters, five brothers, no mother, and an overly affectionate father. Get what I mean?"

"Oh," was all Orchid could think to say, her eyes still riveted to the twins entwined in each other's arms in an arousing display of sisterhood. When they stopped kissing, each turned to look at Orchid, impish smiles, deep blue eyes shining with rapture. "My sister tastes so good, Orchid," said Brit. "You should try her some time."

"I've never been with another woman before," admitted Orchid.

"I guess that answers one question," said Gypsy, and gathered the makeup. "Turn around, Orchid. Let's get a good look at you."

Orchid rotated as if she were a model presenting a new fashion. The pumps were beautiful even though they were causing discomfort.

The twins clapped. "Pretty as a peach," said Brat.

"Yes," Brit added excitedly. "Pretty as a peach."

"I don't think pretty quite covers it," said Gypsy, admiring her handiwork. "Simply gorgeous is more what I had in mind."

"So this is the new girl. Cute." Standing with her body against the jam was a woman Orchid estimated to be in her forties; piggish face, Clairol blond hair and easily weighing two hundred and fifty pounds. A Little Bo Peep frock ended at the dimpled flesh of her knees. Black leather boots added inches to her squat physique. Solitary brown eyes homed in on Orchid's.

"Hi, Tinker," chorused the twins.

"Good afternoon, Tinker," said Gypsy, sounding miffed. "Where have you been? You should have been here to greet our new friend. Isn't she lovely? Orchid, Tinker. Tinker, Orchid."

"Hello... Tinker," said Orchid.

The heavy woman moved into the room, broad, unhampered breasts jiggled. She extended a pudgy hand. "It's nice to meet you, Orchid. Sorry that I wasn't here to welcome you officially, but I had a meeting with a certain politician who does enjoy his midafternoon sessions."

Orchid accepted the hand, hers disappeared in the doughy mitten. Tinker's grip was vicelike. "It's nice to meet you as well," said Orchid, and pulled her hand free, afraid that the bones might be fractured.

"So you're the one replacing Chastity." Tinker placed her viscous hands on her wide hips. "I hope you can live up to her enthusiastic standards."

Orchid looked to Gypsy, eyes questioning.

"Chastity was a girl who was with us for several years," explained Gypsy. "She simply disappeared, not too long ago. Probably made enough money then called it quits. She spoke of her mom and brother a lot, so I'm guessing she went home."

Brit and Brat gave each other a look that said otherwise.

Orchid picked up on it. The word disappeared, and the twins' angst-ridden stare were a tell-all. *Disappeared into a hole out in the desert someplace more likely.*

"Well, Oli wants us all downstairs," said Tinker. "So let's go, girls. On the double." She clapped her hands, shoo-shooing like a mother hen ushering her chicks.

Brat slipped off the counter, Rollerblades hard on the tiles.

"Oli would be none too pleased with you marking up the floors like that," reprimanded Tinker. "You know the rules. No rollerblading on the second floor. I wonder what planet you two are on sometimes. Really, girls."

"Sorry," giggled the twins. "We'll take them off."

Orchid, Tinker, and Gypsy waited until the twins removed their Rollerblades. Then as a newly formed family, they headed to the stairway and the welcoming room below.

* * *

43

Cheers

MADAME Olivia was seated at the leopard skin bar when the girls burst through the door in a heap. Violin and harp music spilled from hidden speakers. Li Ling, wearing a one-piece leather outfit, the zipper lowered to just below the dimple of small breasts, arranged champagne flutes enough for all. Electric blue eye shadow lent an Egyptian countenance.

Oli turned in her chair. "My, my. You look positively ravishing, my dear. I knew that dress was going to look good on you, but it has exceeded my expectations. Come here, girls. Let's toast our new friend."

The quintet went to the bar, Brit and Brat carried their Rollerblades. Gypsy had Orchid by the arm and steered her toward the Madame then she took a key from her denim skirt and handed it over. Tinker took up the rear, managing her weight and high heels with the grace of a duck with a bad leg.

"Li Ling? Pop the cork on one of our finest champagnes, please." The girls gathered around Oli in a skirmish. "Your makeup is perfect, Orchid. Just enough to allow those beautiful eyes of yours to shine. And the avocado of the dress really makes those freckles of yours jump right off your skin."

"Thank you, Oli. Gypsy did the makeup."

"We helped too," piped the twins, holding on to each other as if one could not be without the other.

"Yes, I'm sure you did," said Oli, looking hard at the Rollerblades dangling in their hands.

The cork popped. Liquid gold flowed. Li Ling poured each glass to the rim without spilling any of the French Crystal. Oli handed each girl a flute, and raised her own to eye level. "To Orchid," she chimed. "May your time with us be," she paused, "magnanimous. Prosperous and fun. Cheers." She lifted the flute to her lips, and took a healthy sampling of the expensive grape.

The girls followed suit.

Orchid had never tasted champagne before. When she took a small sip, bubbles tickled her nose and tongue, the Crystal flowing down her throat like cascading silk.

Tinker gulped her entire glass greedily, wiping at her lips with a pudgy hand. "Mmm," she exclaimed, jiggling her ponderous breasts. "Champagne gets me all horny."

Everyone laughed except for Orchid. She wasn't used to such openness when it came to sex. In Bay Ridge Cove, it was a topic left to the boundaries of closed doors and secretive musings.

"What's the matter, Orchid? Don't you like the champagne," asked Oli. "I assure you, you'll taste none finer."

"It's fine. I just never had it before. It kind of took me by surprise."

"And so it should. That bottle costs three hundred dollars. Surprise is the least it should do for you."

When the bottle was empty, Orchid's head swooned in directions she could not comprehend. She giggled unintentionally. "Excuse me," she said, and reached for Gypsy's arm to support herself. "I think I'm a little tipsy."

"You had better sit down then," instructed Oli. We don't want our new star injuring herself on her first day, do we, girls?"

"Un un." The twins shook their heads, sniggered at Orchid's intemperance.

Tinker swallowed the last drops in her glass, each one landing flat against her extended tongue. "Well, I'm ready to take on an entire fleet," she declared. "When do the first customers arrive?"

Oli checked her diamond-clustered Rolex. "Should be arriving any moment now. Unfortunately for you, it's a couple who want to experience a threesome with another girl. And they specifically asked that she be young, slender, and possibly exotic. A Mr. and Mrs. Humphrey. Marriage is on the rocks and all that. They figure a new experience will juice up their sex life. When I told them what we offered and how much, they specifically requested Gypsy. Too bad, so sad." Turning her attention to Orchid, she said, "You see, Orchid, we try to get as much information from our clients as possible. Makes things easier up front. When they come through that door, it's like we already know them, intimately."

"Lucky bitch," snorted Tinker with an air of indifference.

"Heyyy, that'sss not nnnice," Orchid slurred, complaining on Gypsy's behalf.

"It's okay, Orchid," assured Gypsy. "We call each other bitch all the time. It doesn't mean anything. Come with me. We better sit you down." She led Orchid to the Roman chaise where she eased her down until she was comfortable. Touching her face as if it were something new, Orchid said, "I'm… I'm kind offf tingling alllll over."

"It'll go away in a while. You just rest your head for a minute. I'll get you a glass of water." Using Orchid's knee for leverage, Gypsy pushed herself to her feet and smiled down at a drunk Orchid.

She wasn't sure, because of her current state, but she thought Gypsy had given her knee a loving squeeze. "Thhhank you, Gypsy. You're vvvery nice tooo do thhhat for me." She giggled, again trying to mask the drunkenness with the back of her hand. "I think I like being drunk," she said to the giant pink throw cushion across from her.

Gypsy went to the bar and asked Li Ling for a bottle of Evian. When she handed it to Orchid, Orchid unscrewed the top and took a long quenching gulp, the ice-cold water soothing the fiery pain in her belly that had been present ever since the girls introduced themselves.

"Ttthank you, Gypseee. I really needed ttthat."

"You'll be as sober as a judge in no time, you'll see."

As Gypsy was about to take a seat next Orchid, the massive front door opened. A man in his forties, with a thick head of curly black hair and moustache entered.

All the girls turned toward him, money smiles bright.

"Excuse me, ladies," said the man in a Texas drawl. "I'm not sure if I should have knocked first, but my wife told me to just come on in. I'm looking for Madame Olivia." He stepped further into the welcoming room. "Come on, honey. This was your idea, remember?" A slender woman wearing bug glasses and jeans over a pink tabard though it was ninety-plus degrees outside, followed her husband, and stopped just behind him. "Hello," she said shyly, running fingers through titian hair.

Oli slipped from the stool. "I'm Madame Olivia." Extending a hand, she moved toward husband and wife. "You must be the Humphreys, Mack and Linda."

Hidden behind her husband, Linda nodded. Mack Humphrey extended his hand. "Yup. I spoke to you yesterday on the phone."

"Please do come in. These are my girls." Oli stretched her arm as if she were showcasing a new automobile. "These are the twins, Brit and Brat. And this plump little darling is Tinker. Sitting on the sofa is Orchid, and that beauty standing next to her is Gypsy, the partner you've requested. The bartender is Li Ling, and she would be happy to fix you anything you want. On the house of course."

Linda Humphrey moved from behind her husband, and gave Gypsy the once-over; toes, legs, hips, and breasts. "I'd like a white wine spritzer, please," she said, her eyes deeply involved with Gypsy's.

Orchid watched and listened with fuzzy interest. The twins joined her on the chaise while Tinker moved off to the side.

"And for you sir?" smiled Oli. "Perhaps a Scotch? We carry only the finest brands."

Mack Humphrey ran a finger through the collar of his well-fitted shirt. "You know, a neat Scotch sounds like just the ticket."

"Then please, join me by the bar." Oli looked to Gypsy, and nodded so slightly Orchid wasn't sure she nodded at all that the subtle gesture was just a result of the champagne buzz.

Gypsy went straight to the wife, took her by the hand, and walked her to the bar where she took a seat and prompted Linda Humphrey to do the same.

By the time Mack and Linda were comfortable, seated on either side of Gypsy, Li Ling had their drinks ready. Gypsy's attention remained solely on the wife. "I understand this is the first time you and your husband have ever done something like this."

"Yes," said a meek Linda Humphrey. She lifted the spritzer without sampling.

"Well, I want you to know that I'm very glad you considered the Shangri-La Palace for your first time. And I'm terribly excited that you chose me to make your fantasies come true. I promise. You won't be disappointed." Moving her face close to Linda Humphrey's, Gypsy brushed the blush of her cheek with the fullness of her lips. Mrs. Humphrey did not move except to finally take a sip of her drink.

The husband took a short swallow of Scotch, his eyes fixated on Gypsy's halter busting 38 double Ds.

Oli put a hand on his shoulder. "I trust you're pleased with your selection."

"Absolutely. Positively," he said, nodding like a kid in a candy store. "What about condoms?" he asked.

"No need to worry, Mr. Humphrey. We have everything necessary to see you have a good time and come away from your experience as clean as you came in."

Gypsy reached and placed her hand between his legs, and stroked his already-hardening member with her fingers.

Oli, all business, asked, "So you'll be paying with your Visa as per our phone conversation?"

Beads of sweat rose on Mack Humphrey's forehead. From a back pocket, he took out his wallet and blindly thumbed through it. "Two thousand, right?"

"Correct," said Oli, gingerly taking the credit card from his fingers. "For an extra hundred, you can have a video of your experience with us. Would you like that?"

Mack Humphrey said, "I don't think…"

"Yes, we would," his wife interrupted. "I'm mean, you never know when we're going to need it. It might be fun watching us, you know."

"Okay. We'll take the video."

"I think that's best considering your current situation. The camera is already set up. I promise you'll have the only copy. All Gypsy has to do is turn the camera on. It's very discreet. I assure you. You won't even know it's there." She handed the Visa to Li Ling who lifted an automated teller onto the bar and swiped the card. A few seconds later, she nodded. By this time, Gypsy was stroking Linda's arm while her other hand worked the inner thigh and cock of her husband. "You're so beautiful," she told the wife. "I can't wait to hold you in my arms. I'll be everything you've ever dreamed of and more."

Mack Humphrey downed the Scotch. His wife set her empty glass on the bar. Gypsy took both their hands and slipped off the stool, slowly, seductively. "Come with me," she said in a sultry tone and led them to another chamber of the villa.

"Enjoy yourselves in my little paradise," Oli said after them. Then added, "Take all the time you need."

Gypsy's display had sobered a newly schooled Orchid whose mind was trying to wrap itself around the cost of Gypsy's affections. *It was so simple,* she thought. *Just the right choice of words and the Humphreys were like putty in her hands.*

"Are you feeling better, Orchid?" asked Oli.

"Yes, I am, Oli."

"Then come with me. It's time you were introduced the rest of the palace."

The twins, wrapped in each other's arms, giggled. "Enjoy," said Brit. "The tour," finished Brat.

Tinker went to the bar looking a little reclusive and asked Li Ling for a light beer.

Orchid lifted herself from the pink chaise, her mind so preoccupied with what had just transpired, she scarcely felt the knife within give her stomach a new slice.

Harps and violins played on.

* * *

Oli led Orchid through the same hallway Gypsy had taken the Humphreys down. The first door they came to was labeled Toy Room. Oli opened it so Orchid could see what it contained.

Blushing immediately, her eyes absorbed shelf after shelf of dildos and vibrators of varying shapes, sizes, and color. Sitting on the floor, looking like a bicycle with several major parts missing, was a contraption with pedestals for the knees to rest on and a straight black bar for the handle. Further inspection of the alien thing revealed a ten-inch dildo attached to a mobile lever. Orchid had never seen anything like it.

Oli explained, "This is the newest form of self-utilization. The girls just love it. You simply balanced yourself on the pedestals, pull the handle forward and the dildo, well, you know. It's like an exercise machine with a bonus."

"I could never do… I mean. The girls really use it?"

"I couldn't keep them away from it when it first arrived."

The next door they came to was marked Supplies. "In here are boxes of condoms, tampons, an emergency kit, fire extinguisher, mops, vacuum, and the like. Most of our male customers come here ill prepared, so it's up to us to determine size and preference."

"Preference?"

"Yes. Preference. My, you are naive, aren't you? Surely you understand that not all men are created equal."

Lowering her eyes, Orchid said, "Yes. Of course."

"Well, some men prefer to use lubricated condoms, while others are into specific colors. Then there are those who like to use French ticklers. You do know what those are, don't you?"

"Of course," admitted Orchid, though she'd never seen one, just heard about them from the other girls at school.

"Good. For a minute there I thought I was going to have to give you a quick 101 course on the methods and safety of contraceptives."

"I'm not that naive."

"Good. I'm glad to hear it. Number one rule in our business is safety. You'll be no good to me if you pick up a venereal disease."

"No, I don't imagine I would be." Orchid's mind went back to the night Mr. Brown had raped her and prayed she hadn't picked up something horrible from the bastard.

"I'm glad you understand that."

Further down the hall, they came to six doors, three on each side numbered and marked Private. Oli opened room number 1. It was the size of a second bedroom, lit only by the sun's rays filtering through sheer drapes. Centering the room was a double bed stripped to the mattress. On each of the four posts were leather restraints for the wrists and ankles, tools of confinement Orchid knew only too well. Standing against one of the blue walls was a wooden cross that also held the leather handcuffs of restraint. Hanging on another wall were the tools for those who were into S-M: leather whips, hoods, belts with silver spikes, leather underwear, bras, gloves and a tether with buckle orange ball fashioned to its center.

Orchid stood aghast, mouth open in shocked silence.

Oli pushed the door farther with the point of a finger. "You seemed surprised. Don't be. You wouldn't believe how many men of influence request this room. Including those who are in positions of trust with their constituents. Schoolteachers, council members, doctors, lawyers, police, even a priest or two."

"Priests?" Orchid reversed out of the room.

Oli closed the door. "Why, of course, my dear. All men are the same once you get their pants off. Their dicks do all the thinking for them. Why, just last month we serviced a bishop in this very room. According to Tinker, the man prayed to God for forgiveness all the while she was whipping him into a frenzy. He couldn't get enough. Tinker whipped him until she was exhausted. Then he wanted her to cut him in certain places, but we don't do stuff like that. No mutilation being one of our rules. He left in a huff. Swearing that he would never come back, but you know what, he will. I guarantee it."

"You don't expect me to whip somebody, do you?"

"Not right away of course. But in time, you'll realize that it's just part of the services we offer and nothing personal. That's the key. Not to take things personally or get emotionally involved. It's just a job that pays very well I should remind you."

Orchid followed her to the next two doors. "These are just your average rooms with bed, dresser, and minibars, in case your client should get thirsty. This room, room number 4, is the room you will be assigned to for the time being. Would you like to see inside?"

Orchid's innards shuddered, awakening the knife within. It stabbed her deep. She grimaced.

"Are you hurting, Orchid?"

"Yes, just a little," she lied.

"Do you want me to take care of it?"

"No, it's okay. I'm good for now."

"That's my girl. You fight it for as long as you can. That Mr. Black should have his balls cut off for the methods he uses."

Orchid could not agree more.

Emanating from door numbered 5 were the sounds of people lost in rapture.

"Let's eavesdrop for a minute, shall we?" suggested Oli.

"I don't think we should." Again Orchid blushed. "It wouldn't be right."

"Fiddle sticks. Listen. Mr. and Mrs. Humphrey are very involved. Gypsy really knows how to make a couple feel needed. The wife is always easy to persuade. Every woman fantasizes about having sex with another. It's the husband that's usually harder to convince. The male ego and all. Most can't handle their wives getting better pleasure than what they can manage. And believe me, Gypsy certainly knows her way around the female anatomy."

"I don't want to listen anymore. I feel like I'm invading on their privacy." She moved farther down the hall.

"Suit yourself." Oli followed until they were both standing in a room that opened up at the end of the hall and was appointed with a half-dozen burgundy wingbacks. Duncan Phyfe tables situated each chair and large crystal ashtrays centered each table. Another bar, made entirely of cherrywood, stood gleaming against the westmost wall. Next to it stood a humidor with row after row of fresh worldclass cigars contained within. A floor-to-ceiling fireplace took up another where the massive taxidermy head of a buffalo hung above the mantle looking anything but its former self but no less menacing. Thick swags of Persian carpet angle covered the hardwood floor. The south wall was made entirely of glass and led to the solarium Oli spoke of, its fascia hazed with humidity.

"This is the smoking room. Exclusively for our more prestigious guests where they can smoke, sip cognac, and tell lies."

Orchid looked up at the partial domed ceiling. From corner to corner, oil-varnish bright, was the scene of a great battle between charioted Romans crushing underfoot masses of peasants pathetically armed with pitchforks and wooden stakes. It was so lifelike it could have been painted by the master hand of Michelangelo.

"Impressive. Don't you think?"

"The colors look alive. It's frightening."

"If I told you how much it cost, you wouldn't believe me. Let's move on, shall we? There's too much secondhand testosterone in here for my liking. Can you smell it? It's a combination of conspiracy, bigotry, self-righteousness, pomposity, and fear." Oli pinched her nose. "Men do so like to leave their signatures behind."

All Orchid could sense was the leftover emissions of expensive cigars. She followed Oli to the solarium. The door opened with a swish, releasing a thick wall of moisture wedded with the floriated perfume of hundreds of flowers. Together they stepped through, the door automatically swished closed.

Orchid stood in awe at the beauty potted row after row. To her left, hundreds of orchids—purple, white, blue, and peach—lifted their dragon faces to the fettered sun. To her right, a rainbow of roses glistened with moisture, their heads boldly high. Up the center was a long table of Japanese lilies trumpeting worship. Against the south wall a dozen bonsais clipped to magnificent glory stood ancient, tiny trees, decades old.

"This is so beautiful," said Orchid, breathing in the culminated fragrances.

"The bonsais are solely Li Ling's. Her grandfather taught her the technique of caring and cultivating. The large maple tree in the middle is seventy-five years old and priceless. The twins and Gypsy take care of the rest. It's a good hobby to have during downtimes. Do you like to grow things, Orchid? Because if you do, I will order some seedlings of your choice from a florist we deal with and you can start your own little garden."

"I would like that, Oli. Doesn't Tinker, you know, have a hobby?"

"Tinker is a different matter all together. She is what we call an independent. What this means is that she works outside these walls as well as applying her specialties here. You see my dear, having someone with Tinker's, well, let's say dimensions is a necessity in this business. Most of our black customers and a lot of French Canadians prefer the affections of a plump and surly escort. More cushion for the pushin' I've been told.

Orchid chuckled. "I've heard that expression before."

"You should consider yourself fortunate, Orchid, that Tony has assigned you to the Shangri-La Palace and not to the streets. It's a tough go out there. The competition is immense. Men flock to Vegas for three things: to gamble, to consume as much alcohol as possible, and to have sex. The streets of Vegas are maligned with women offering themselves at cut-rate prices. It's a cutthroat business, and other than the casinos, the sex industry is Vega's number two income." Her eyes roamed Orchid's body. She smiled. "When do you get your menstrual cycle, Orchid?"

"My period?"

"Yes, my dear. Your period. You see, Tony Millions owns another establishment. Club Paradise. Excluding Tinker, each of the girls dance there when they have their periods. It's additional income for them. Do you like to dance, Orchid?"

Orchid did not like where this was going. "You mean they strip for money?"

"Why, yes, my dear. But only topless. Gypsy and the twins easily make a couple of grand during their cycle."

"I don't know if I could do that. Take my clothes off in front of a lot of men. I've always felt that kind of thing was so degrading for a woman."

Oli placed a firm hand on Orchid's shoulder, dug her red nails in and turned her so that Orchid was looking right into her dark eyes. Amid all the sculpted beauty, wickedness reared its ugly head. "Let's get one thing straight right here and now, you little bitch! You belong to *me* and Tony Millions. You will do whatever we ask of you without complaint. Do you hear! Because if for one moment you do not comply with our wishes, there's plenty of space remaining in the desert where you'll rot. And the Harts, tsk-tsk-tsk. Do I make myself perfectly clear?" Breaths hard, eyes reflecting pure evil, she let go of the painful grip she had on Orchid's shoulder.

Orchid lowered her eyes and said, "Yes, Oli." There was nothing else she could say.

"Now there's a good girl." Evil intent retreated back to the domain of her black soul and was replaced with a spurious smile. "Now we'll go to the games room and then the kitchen. But I must warn you. The kitchen is Li Ling's territory, so do not go rummaging around in the fridge or cupboards for anything. If you are ever hungry, all you have to do is ask for something. Li Ling would be more than happy to prepare it for you. Brat made the mistake of getting something for herself a year ago. Li Ling blackened both her eyes and broke an arm. It was a solid month before she made any money for us. If it were not for the fact that she had a twin sister, she would have ended up on the street or in the desert someplace. You see, my dear, Li Ling is proficient in martial arts. She is not someone to fuck with. Am I making myself clear in this matter?"

"Yes, Oli. If I get hungry, I'll ask."

"I'm glad we're seeing eye to eye on these matters, my dear. The violation of our rules can be most devastating. This much I can assure you. Now let's visit the games room, shall we?"

During the tour of the rest of the house, all Orchid could think about was that soon she would have to surrender her body for money and, when the time was right, remove her clothing for all mankind to see. She couldn't comprehend which was the lesser of two evils.

The knife dug deeper.

* * *

The games room consisted of a pool table, ping-pong table, card table, dart board, fifty-inch flat screen, reclining chairs for comfort, hot tub, and adjacent sauna. Orchid was shown where five other bathrooms existed, each one decorated with a woman's, just so touch. The kitchen was a gourmet's dream. Stainless steel appliances, Viking hood range, black granite island and counters, walk-in freezer, and more cupboards than Orchid could count. All of it in pristine condition. "Who takes care of all this?" asked Orchid. "Everything is so clean." Her hands were at her stomach, the knife twisting.

"Why, we girls do of course. Each of us has their list of chores that we modify every week so they don't become monotonous."

"I see." Orchid's sickness tore at her insides. "I think I need to have you show me this new way of taking my poison. My stomach is on fire, and I don't think I can hold out any longer. It hurts too much."

"Of course, my dear. Do you think you can make your way back to your bath?"

"Yes. I can manage."

"Then I'll meet you there in five, ten minutes tops. Okay? I'm just going to check on the girls, see how the Humphreys are doing, if they're still here." She left Orchid to herself, each departing stride announced with self-confidence.

Orchid stood in silence for a moment. If there ever was a chance to run, it was now. *But where would you go, my dear?* The voice inside her head sounding just like Oli. *We'll find you, then you know what happens after that. You'll not see your next birthday. I guarantee it, my dear.*

Sighing heavily, she left the kitchen and made her way to the welcoming room where the twins had a young man cornered at the bar and were running their hands over his shoulders, down his thighs and whispering God knew what into his ears. Oli was nowhere to be seen, nor was Gypsy or Tinker. She asked Li Ling for a bottle of water, measuring the pretty bartender in a new light. This sweet, seemingly fragile creature held within her tiny frame the means to inflict substantial harm when called upon. "Thank you," she said when the small, mighty Asian handed her the water.

Her riposte a sweet smile.

Orchid went to *her* private bathroom, sat on the toilet lid, and waited. To pass the time, she counted the tiles on the ceiling, concluding fifty-six in all. That done, she toed off the pumps and examined her feet. Some of the sores had broke and were bleeding. Taking a long strip of toilet paper, she cleaned them best she could. Just as she flushed the blood-stained paper, Oli stepped into the room with the little black kit Mr. Black had given her clutched in hand. She set it on the counter, and opened it to reveal a set of syringes and several balls of foil. Orchid could plainly see that one of the syringes was already loaded, and she began to arbitrarily salivate as if she were looking at a juicy steak.

Oli pulled it from the kit and depressed the plunger so that a minimal amount of heroin shot into the air. "Turn around, Orchid, and lift your dress up above the knees please."

Orchid turned, lifted the dress, and peered over a shoulder so that she could see what Oli was up to. "My knees?"

"Yes." On one knee, Oli slapped the back of Orchid's left leg where the patellar tendons connected. "This is a method I learned long ago and is the preferred method of prostitutes who are addicted to this shit. But we'll soon take care of that, won't we, my dear?"

"God, I hope so. I hate it."

"There, there now. Don't move. I would hate to miss the vein."

The needle slipped in. Orchid felt the rush of heroin course its way throughout her being. Immediately, the pain in her stomach subsided and her head swooned, but not nearly as mood altering as on previous occasions.

"Sit down for a minute or two," instructed Oli.

Orchid let the dress fall and sat on the toilet's lid, all smiles now and hating herself.

Oli lifted her chin with the point of a finger, examined her eyes. "There. Do you feel better?"

"Yes, thank you, Oli." Orchid put her hands to her face. For a quick moment, it felt as though there were tiny creatures running unbridled, like the signals she used to get when trouble was about to rear its ugly head. In the next instant, they abandoned her face, tickled her in her most private place for a brief second or two, then were gone.

"You never did answer my question earlier. About your menstrual cycle. When are you expecting your next one?"

Orchid had to really think for a moment. Days and weeks had become disjointed, blending into one another. "If I'm right, it should be next week, Thursday, possibly Friday."

"Then I will have the girls make sure you are well prepared."

"Prepared?"

"Yes, prepared. The twins will show you how to combine dancing with the pole. We have a room I haven't shown you yet where they practice their dancing."

"Oh." For a brief second, Orchid imagined herself sliding up and down a brass pole, stage lights exhibiting her body that, without warning, erupted into a thousand creepy crawly lobsters.

"It'll be fun. You'll see." Combing fingers through Orchid's hair, she coached, "Now I don't expect you to inject yourself. Far too awkward. When it's absolutely necessary, you just ask me and I'll take care of you. When you crash from this dose,

I'm going to give you some Percocet. It will ease the pain I know only too well when the hunger attacks. Now do you think you can go to the welcoming room and just sit at the bar looking pretty?"

"Yes. I can do that." Lobsters crawling from the stage and dropping into whiteness.

"Good. More customers will be arriving shortly, and I want you to listen and observe. Have a drink if you want, though after the incident with the champagne, I suggest you stick to iced tea."

"What if someone wants to, you know, hire me?"

"Just tell them you are already spoken for for the evening. But that you will be available come Monday. Steer them to Gypsy or the twins. If they happen to be black or have an outrageous French accent, refer them to Tinker."

"I can do that."

"I have no doubt, my dear. That's why we chose you. In a month, you'll be our star attraction. Men are going to pay through the nose to make your acquaintance."

In Orchid's altered state of mind she reminisced Mr. Black's prediction, *"A month from now, should the need arise you'll suck my beautiful cock."*

* * *

44

Scent of a Woman

ORCHID sat at the bar. In the past four hours, she had consumed ten iced teas and had eaten the dinner Li Ling prepared for her. Garlic shrimp, pearl rice, steamed broccoli, and a heaping helping of chocolate ice cream. She'd used the facilities on the main floor thrice. The effects of the minor amount of heroin Oli had injected had long since departed, leaving her feeling burnt inside, but she managed to maintain a smile for the customers who arrived every hour on the hour.

The sounds of Kenny G's sax floated sensually through speakers.

The twins were kept busy, mostly with young studs who had money to burn. Two thirty-something women had arrived shortly after Gypsy's tryst with Mack and Linda. They were drunk, wealthy, and looking for someone to complete a threesome they had always talked about since their college days. The cost for fulfilling their fantasy, an astounding twenty-five hundred dollars to which they paid gladly, adding two martinis on top of whatever it was they had consumed to liquidate their resolve.

As Oli had alluded to, a Frenchman from Laval, Quebec, arrived and immediately sought the attentions of Tinker who promised for everyone to hear, "I'm going to fuck your brains out, little man. Come with me." The rail-thin Frenchman followed her like a puppy who had just been given a bone made of gravy.

Consequent to each session, the twins, Gypsy, and Tinker showered then altered their outfits., except for Tinker who opted to remain in her Little Bo Peep ensemble for the night, declaring it to be her luckiest outfit. At present Brit wore a white peek-a-boo blouse that made visible the gentle slopes of her breasts and the pink flesh of her areolas. Red lace covered her tight little bottom. Completing the fuck-me outfit was a pair of red spiked, open-toed pumps that added several inches to her average height. Brat had changed into a more conservative outfit; green tartan skirt, white blouse, not quite as revealing as Brit's, but nonetheless sensual; and private girl school loafers from which white knee-high stockings rose.

Gypsy, like Orchid, now wore a beautiful soft blue gown fit for a night on the town; azure sequence around the neckline, shoulders, and cuffs. Transparent pumps revealed impeccable feet.

Everyone was waiting for the next customer to arrive, comfortable on giant throw cushions while Oli regaled them with a story of how she got started in the business.

"You see, my darlings. I had been molested so many times by my father that by the time I was fifteen, I had no choice but to leave home—ha, home—and try to make it on my own." She was sitting on the Roman chaise, the girls all ears, listening intently to a story Orchid suspected they'd already heard. "I lived with a girlfriend of mine whose parents were kind enough to take me in. I took a job as a part-time cashier, but the money wasn't enough to sustain a half-decent living. I soon learned that the boys at the local high school were willing to pay me twenty dollars for blowjobs. Well, the oral sex escalated to romps in the backseats of local men who worked at the Ford plant. By the time I was seventeen, I was making three hundred a day. Back then, that was a lot of money for a young girl. I remained single throughout those years, my distaste for men birthed by my own father. I..."

The massive front doors opened, and put to an abrupt end Madame Olivia's sordid tale. Mr. Black walked in, looking sharp in a shimmering gold Armani, his face all business.

Orchid looked away.

Trailing Mr. Black was Tony Millions, dressed in black slacks, blue dress shirt, and spit-polished Salvatore Ferragamos. What little hair he possessed slicked back. All smiles, he made his way to Oli who stood to greet him, extending her hands. "Madame Olivia. How good it is to see you again." Taking her hands, he kissed her on both cheeks.

Mr. Black remained statuelike by the entrance.

"It's nice that you pay us a visit, Tony. It's been weeks since we've seen that handsome face of yours."

"I've come to check on our new recruit. How is she doing?" His gaze fell on Orchid.

"She's doing wonderfully. But let her tell you. Orchid. Come here please."

Gypsy, Brit, Brat, and Tinker were all smiles; however, they knew their place and remained silent.

Orchid turned in the stool, slipped to the floor and reluctantly went to Oli and Tony Millions, a derivative smile on her face. Oli put an arm around her shoulders. "Beautiful, don't you think?"

"I could not agree more," said Tony. He gave Orchid the once-over, obsessed her flesh with his twisted little mind.

"Say something, Orchid. Don't just stand there," reprimanded Oli.

"Hello, Mr. Millions."

"Hello, Orchid. It's a pleasure to see you so soon. Madame Olivia has done wonders for you already. You look absolutely ravishing. Are the girls treating you well?"

"Yes. They've been very nice."

"And what about your living quarters? Do you find the room adequate?"

"The room is fine. It's beautiful."

"Well, there you have it then. Beauty for the beauty." Leaning, he placed a kiss on her cheek.

Repulsed, Orchid wanted to back away, but there was no telling what the consequences would be if she did, so she allowed the man who had plunged her into this contemptuous world his way. At least for the moment.

Tony Millions offered his cheek.

Orchid returned the gesture. She would later scrub his taste from her lips with an SOS pad if need be.

Relishing in her discomfort Tony sneered, "There, that wasn't so bad now, was it?" Orchid shook her head.

Tony moved closer to the mainstay of his stable and asked, "And how is everyone? Making lots of money no doubt."

"Yes, Mr. Millions," they said in unison. Tinker took a swallow of water and supplied "We've already had a very busy day, and it's only nine o'clock. I think this might be one of our biggest Saturdays ever."

Tony clapped his hands, "Splendid! Keep up the good work my lovelies. I believe a bonus is in store for each of you." He turned back to his business partner. "Madame Olivia, I would like to speak with you in private, if you don't mind."

"Of course, Tony. We can adjourn to my office. Girls, the place is yours. I'll be back momentarily."

Once they were gone, Orchid returned to her place at the bar and asked Li Ling for an iced tea. She knew they were going to talk about her. She just knew it. To what extent was anyone's guess. But it could not be good. Her eyes went to Mr. Black who had not moved. Hands behind his back, eyes without emotion, smiling, smiling, always smiling.

Oli opened a window, took a seat behind her desk, lit a cigarette and blew smoke towards the ceiling.

Tony took an easy going position on the available sofa. Above hung an oil painting. Madame Olivia naked and lying on a thick shag of pink. One hand covered her womanhood, the other held a leash at the end of which sat a nude Li Ling, spiked collar snug around her throat. The pretty Asian held a flute of champagne close to ruby lips, the hoops in her nipples steel grey.

"What can I do for you?" asked Oli , night's shadows bleeding through the bay window.

"Do you think our little Orchid will comply? And please be honest." He cracked his knuckles, a habit his collaborator found unnerving. Her father often did the same thing just before he ravaged her. A betrayal of trust that began when she was too young to remember.

"Absolutely. She will start working for us on Monday. I've made that more than clear to her. She knows what the consequences are."

"Excellent. And when will she start dancing at the club?"

"If she's correct about her cycle, by next weekend. I'll have the twins coach her on how to strut her stuff on the pole. Hopefully, the wounds on her feet will have healed somewhat by then. Really, Tony. Mr. Black has to alter his methods of control. Not only is Orchid savagely marked, but she's a junkie. It makes my end of our business very challenging. Sure I'm going to wane her off the heroin, but I'll be turning her into a painkiller addict doing so. I don't know which is worse. Having a girl with needle marks or someone whose mind is so numbed she will not be able to perform up to our standards. You *know* how long it took me to break Gypsy from both."

"You do make a valid point Olivia. I'll consider it." Tony inspected his cuticles for a quiet moment. There would be no consideration of the matter. Heroin controlled the mind, the body, the spirit. "Tomorrow, I'm going to send Mr. Brown to take pictures for her new identification."

"Have you chosen a name?" Oli took a long drag of her cigarette, smashed it in an ashtray, gave her Rolex a quick glance then set her hands flat on the table.

"Yes." Tony smiled, pleased with himself. "For authorities sake, she will be known as one Tiffany Rose. And as in Gypsy's case will be provided with two sets of identification. One stating that she originates from Baltimore, Maryland for when you girls go to the casinos. The other for when she dances at the club with valid Las Vegas residency. Age, twenty-three. She is mature enough looks wise and can pull it off."

Oli rolled the name over and smiled. "Tiffany Rose. I like it. It has a certain elegance, suits her beauty to a tee."

"I'm glad you agree. Well, that's all I need to know for now." Tony stood, and with the backs of his fingers, brushed nothing from the fronts of his slacks.

"Just one more thing, Tony," said Oli in a serious tone.

"What is it?"

Pencil-thin eyebrows raised in a guarded arch she said, "About Mr. Wong. I know you had a hand in his untimely demise. I fear that his people will put two and two together. Then we'll be in the deepest of shit."

"You worry too much. I've already severed the ties that bound us to his alleged suicide. Mr. Blue sleeps with the scorpions and snakes. He'll never be missed. You let me worry about the fallout, if any. It's not the first time I've expunged someone of Mr. Wong's influence as you very well know. And so far"—he patted his chest—"not a scratch."

Oli had liked Mr. Blue immensely. He had a quiet reserve about him and was not always looking for freebees from the girls like Mr. Brown and Mr. White. "I'm going to miss him," she said, and swiveled in the chair so she faced the darkness, her displeasure with the news painstakingly obvious.

"Then I believe this little tête-à-tête is over. Good night, Madame Olivia. I will be in touch. Mr. Brown will be here by noon tomorrow. Expect him." Tony went to the door, opened it, and pulled it closed.

Oli stared into the waning desert. She had a bad feeling about the mimetic suicide of Benjamin Wong and now the murder of Mr. Blue. Tony was managing his component of their little empire nonsensically. Too much Cocaine and Scotch. Believing himself untouchable. Something was going to come back and bite them all on the ass. She just knew it.

* * *

By 3:00 a.m., the doors to the Shangri-La Palace were closed for business. The girls had serviced eight more customers. Five young men, one of whom was getting married in a weeks time and three businessmen from Apple who had arrived at midnight, all bearing wedding bands and sporting wods of cash. They'd ended their cheating night of indulgence sipping cognac and puffing on Cohibas in the smoking room.

Orchid's hunger had returned, the knife deeper than deep. She fought it best she could, but by one in the morning, she had requested Oli supply her with the painkiller Percocet. Two ten-milligram pills later, the pain subsided, and her head buzzed with white noise. She spent the resulting two hours consuming large quantities of water in an attempt to quash the thirst and lightheadedness the Percocet had impressed upon her.

After a quick cleanup, the twins and Tinker changed into civil clothes and left for their perspective homes. Oli and Li Ling said their goodnights, and disappeared to the second floor leaving a still pharmaceutically disoriented Orchid and Gypsy to themselves.

Gypsy went behind the bar, poured herself a glass of wine, and turned off the music, ending the warm, soothing tones of Sarah McLachlan's rendition of "Unchained Melody."

"Would you like some?" she asked Orchid, waving a half-empty bottle of Châteauneuf-du-Pape.

"No, thank you, Gypsy. I think I should just get to bed. I'm feeling a little woozy." Rising from the stool, Orchid felt off center, equilibrium gone. Dropping back onto the stool, she rubbed at her forehead.

"You look like you could use some help. Just let me polish off this glass and I'll take you to your room. Okay?"

"Thanks, Gypsy. You've been so kind to me." An unanticipated yawn stretched her lips. "That was a long day, wasn't it?"

"Oh, you'll get used to it. Time is irrelevant. It's the money that matters. I should be able to retire in about five years. I won't even be thirty yet."

"Really? How much do you make if you don't mind my asking?" Stifling yet another yawn, she sent it back to wherever yawns came from.

"It's a sixty-forty split. Orchid. The house gets sixty and we get the remainder. Why, tonight alone, I've made a prosperous two grand. Sure, it's not like that every night, but the good nights outweigh the slow ones. Then there's the dancing. If you really turn the men's cranks, five hundred a night in tips is easy money. Our accountant really knows his stuff and keeps most of it out of the hands of the government." Taking a long swallow of the grape, Gypsy emptied half the glass. "And you only spend about thirty minutes in total onstage per night."

"You really don't mind taking your clothes off in front of all those people?"

"It's a piece of cake. The spotlights block out most of the faces except for the ones seated along the stage. All you have to do is concentrate on the music, let your mind drift. Your body will take care of the rest. If some customer tries to get frisky, he gets his head bounced off the sidewalk. We're very well protected. Tony Millions wouldn't allow anything to happen to one of his cash cows." Downing the remainder of wine, she flipped a switch. The welcoming room darkened, cast in pink shadows, lit only by a single low-watt bulb emanating from the plastic palm tree.

The sudden pitch into fragmented darkness felt cool against Orchid's skin somehow.

"Come on," said Gypsy. She moved out from behind the bar, took Orchid's hands, and helped her from the stool. "Let's get you upstairs and comfortable."

* * *

They entered Orchid's room. Music drifted from the clock radio. Journey's "Lights"

When the lights,
go down, in the city,
and the sun shines on the bay,
Oh, I want to be th-e-r-e in the city…

Orchid's head was reclined on Gypsy's shoulder. Moonlight bled through the French doors in a ghostly pallor. Five miles away, the multifaceted shine of Vegas bore semblance to the Northern Lights. "It's been a long time since I've been in this room," said Gypsy.

Orchid lifted her head and looked into her eyes. They were adrift with memory. "You stayed in this room as well?"

"Yes, but I don't like to talk about it. Too many bad memories."

Orchid could feel her sorrow. *Gypsy must have experienced the same indignations I had.* Allowing herself to be steered to the bed, and with Gypsy's assistance, sat on the comforter and slipped out of her pumps. She wiggled her toes. Irritated dots, all in a row stared back at her. "You know," she said looking up at Gypsy. "You have such beautiful skin. I've never asked you what your nationality is."

"My mother was Hispanic. My father was white and a mean drunk. But let's not talk about that, okay? *Now* is all that matters. Let's get you out of that dress. Stand up for a second."

Orchid, pushing with the palms of her hands, rose from the bed. Moonlight enhanced the perfect body hidden within the material. Reaching, she drew the zipper as far as she could.

Gypsy's ringed thumbs hooked the straps and drew them over Orchid's shoulders. The dress fell to the floor in a heap. Orchid stepped out of it, stumbled and landed in Gypsy's arms. Their eyes coupled empathetically. Gypsy's practised fingers traversed the ridges of Orchid's spine. A warm pleasurable shiver ran its course. It had been far too long since she felt safe in someone's arms, even if it was another woman's. She'd only kissed a friend of hers at a sleepover once and remembered that she enjoyed the intimacy of it even though it hadn't gone any further. *If sleeping with Gypsy was going to bring some reprieve to this nightmare,* she thought in her current state of mind, *then so be it.* She allowed herself to be taken.

Gypsy's hand moved to the nape of Orchid's neck, and massaged oh so gently. Orchid closed her eyes and parted her lips invitingly. When Gypsy's closed over hers, Orchid was momentarily released from the prison of her circumstance.

Two silhouettes in the moonlight. Lovers for a secret moment in time. Sisters who had tasted the same indignations Tony Millions and his henchman doled out. *Yes,* thought Orchid delighted by the sweetness of Gypsy's curious tongue. *This is so right. So very much needed.*

Gypsy moved from Orchid's mouth to the base of her throat. She kissed it softly and in the same moment unzipped her own evening dress. When she stepped out of it, the bathing moon revealed perfect breasts swelled with desire. Orchid placed her hands on the small of Gypsy's back and drew her down onto the bed among the stuffed animals, arms and legs intertwined. Gypsy's mouth covered one of Orchid's areolas, her tongue teasing, lips sucking tenderly. A violating current born of darkest sin travelled from her breast to the heat of her sex. She became very wet and tore Gypsy's panties from her body.

The Latino beauty guided her into a world of remorseless pleasure. She slipped Orchid's panties off, moved a hand between her thighs, and toyed with the wisp of her womanhood. When first one finger, then another entered Orchid's holiest of holies, she climaxed heavily and requested more with the thrust of her hips. Their kisses became more heated, the sound of each fevered breath drowning out the radio. Lost in each other, they writhed to a tempo orchestrated by the shine of the moon. Gypsy began a journey along Orchid's breasts, to her midriff, the tip of her tongue barely touching flesh, teasing, giving further life to the fire within.

Orchid splayed like a flower bloomed, seized Gypsy by the hair, and guided her to a hunger she had never before appreciated.

"You're so beautiful, Orchid." When her capable tongue found Orchid's tender, engorged nub, Orchid sighed and climaxed again, fingers tearing into the comforter. "Oh god. Love me, Gypsy. I need you so badly."

For time misplaced, Gypsy mentored the love-deprived student. Orchid became educated in methods of pleasure she knew not existed.

When finally the moon banished the room to total darkness, they fell asleep in each other's arms while the radio played on, completely unaware that Li Ling and Oli had watched the entire episode from the open door.

We'll be shadows in the moonlight
Darling, I'll meet you at midnight.
Hand in hand we'll go,
Walking through the milky way...

* * *

45

A Rose by Any Other Name

WHEN Mr. Brown arrived the following day, precisely at noon, with a .35 mm Nikon slung over one shoulder, the celebrated mood the girls were in vanished, for they knew all too well one of them was going to have to pleasure him. He wore a white short-sleeved shirt opened in the front to reveal curls of jet-black hair and a gold Saint Christopher medallion. Brown khakis covered his stumpy legs, the smile on his face pathetically vain.

"Whose turn is it?" asked Brat in a whisper.

"Why, I believe it yours, sis," answered Brit, having to suppress a giggle with the back of a hand.

They were all seated in the welcoming room minus Tinker, who did not work Sundays, being a Catholic and all. Li Ling was in the kitchen preparing lunch. Pitas stuffed with chicken, sautéed vegetables and sides of fruit salad.

Orchid could not understand why they just didn't refuse to service him. *The bastard.* Oli had instructed her to dress conservatively, so she had put on a simple beige top over jeans. She was still tingling from her lovemaking with Gypsy who was seated on a throw cushion across from her, caramel eyes twinkling with preserved memory. She had also opted for the Percocet instead of her morning dose of heroin, which pleased Oli to no end. So far, the little pill held at bay the insatiable hunger lurking within.

Oli greeted the rightfully hated Mr. Brown. "Right on time," she said without giving him the benefit of a kiss on both cheeks. Her hair was coiffed and held by a tortoise shell clip. Long pale legs emerged from beneath the hem of a blue business skirt, its jacket fitting her frame like a glove. On her feet was a pair a blue suede shoes.

"As always." Mr. Brown smirked. "Let's get this over with. I left Mr. Green on his own. He may have been a Navy SEAL, but he doesn't know his way around the club business worth two shits."

"Wait outside my office. Orchid doesn't know why you're here, so I'll have to explain it to her and convince her that it doesn't really mean anything, just goes with the territory."

Mr. Brown checked his watch. "Fine. But don't keep me waiting. You know how I hate to be kept waiting." He left in a huff, swinging the Nikon like a purse.

Madame Olivia despised Mr. Brown as much as anyone, always entering her world with the air of being in charge, strutting his stuff like some rooster bursting with testosterone. Joining the girls, who had been watching her with keen interest, she said, "Orchid? I would like to have a word with you if you don't mind," her eyes conveying the directness she flaunted with regularity.

"Sure, Oli." Orchid uncrossed her legs and pushed herself out of the pink throw cushion, to find she was slightly unsteady from the effects of the Percocet, something she was going to have to get used to. "Where?"

"Let's go into the kitchen and keep Li Ling company for a few minutes."

"Okay."

Oli led the way, posture ramrod straight, the heels of her blue suede shoes sounding hard against the tile.

Orchid followed, the voice of trepidation asking a thousand questions as to why Oli wanted to talk to her.

Once they were in the kitchen, Oli told Orchid to take a seat in one of the stools fronting the granite island. Li Ling smiled, while stuffing pitas with chicken salad. A large bowl of cut-up fruit blazed with color.

Oli paced the floor for a moment, the point of a finger tapping ruby lips as though she were contemplating something.

"You look very nice today," offered Orchid.

"Thank you, my dear." Oli stopped in front of her, arms folded across her chest. "Mr. Brown is here today to take your picture."

"Oh. I was wondering why he came with a camera."

"Yes, well, the reason for this is so that we can provide you with new identification. Two sets. One name. Different addresses. Driver's license, social insurance number, birth certificate. Items like that."

"But why? I don't understand. Why would I need two sets of identification?"

"For one. You haven't a stitch of your family history with you. For all anyone knows, and by anyone I mean the authorities, you're Jane Doe from the North Pole."

Orchid did not know how to respond, so she allowed Oli to continue.

"One set will prove that you are from Baltimore Maryland, age twenty three. A tourist. It is this Baltimore address you will use should you be asked to prove your age when we go shopping and then to the casinos for lunch. The other will state that you are a resident of Vegas should the authorities come snooping around. We just want to be safe. And you want to be safe."

Safe. Orchid nearly laughed out loud.

Oli continued, "You'll be dancing at the club soon. The authorities don't bother us here, however, they do have a tendency to show up at the club on occasion. Usually a rookie full of piss and vinegar. The identification stating that you reside in Vegas will be the one you show them should the occasion arise. Do you understand?"

"I think so. But what if they find out my I.D. is fake. Then they'll find out"—she looked at Li Ling over her shoulder—"that Tony Millions kidnapped me." It was a bold statement, but she tried it on for size just the same. *Must be the Percocet talking.*

Oli's dark eyes flashed with anger: however, she maintained a calm diplomacy, her voice unruffled as she said, "I should remind you, Orchid, your life, as they say on that insurance commercial, is in our hands. So is the Harts for that matter."

Orchid lowered her eyes. When she looked up again, she asked, "Who will I be then?"

Oli smiled. "Tony has chosen a beautiful name for you. Tiffany Rose. Isn't it pretty? Suits you to a tee."

"I guess so." She rolled the name over in her mind. *Tiffany Rose. Tiffany Rose. Tiffany Rose,* deciding that if she had to have a new ID to save her neck, there certainly were worst names they could have come up with. *Don't forget your savior is near. This will all be over soon. Keep playing their little games.*

"Now don't get me wrong." Oli placed her hands on Orchid's knees. "You will always be Orchid to us here and at the club. Tiffany Rose is just in case. Mr. Brown has an associate who is a master at reproducing authentic-looking identification and we have friends at the DMV and the police department who will key in your new data on their computers should anyone decide to go sneaking around. You see my dear, many law enforcement members, including judges and high profile lawyers come to the Shangri la palace to get what they can't at home and they'll do anything to remain anonymous. Secrets secrets secrets. It's what makes Vegas go round. Now let's go to my office. Mr. Brown is waiting with his camera and, as he so unnecessarily reminded me, hates to be kept waiting."

Orchid slipped from the stool. "Okay, Oli." Turning to Li ling who had all the pitas in a row on a silver platter, she said, "I'll see you later. I'm looking forward to lunch. You're a very good cook."

Li Ling offered a genuine smile, her eyes expressing thanks for the compliment.

Located down the hall from the games room, Mr. Brown waited in front of Madame Olivia's office.

"How's *my* Orchid today," he taunted.

Orchid did not look at him when she said, "Fine! For all you care." The night he raped her as fresh in her mind as the bowl of fruit sitting on the granite countertop in the kitchen.

Oli produced a key from her jacket pocket and opened the door. Sunlight and warmth rushed through.

Orchid and Mr. Brown followed. The first thing to catch Orchid off guard was a large oil painting depicting Oli and Li Ling in a rather compromising position.

Oli saw the surprised look on Orchid's face, sat at her desk, and said, "Beautiful, isn't it? Powerful and tranquil with naughty intentions." A sun-designed aura gave her the look of a saint, which she was most definitely not.

How inappropriate, thought Orchid, standing in the middle of the sky blue room.

Mr. Brown said, "Stand against that wall, Orchid. I don't want you to smile. Just look into the lens of the camera, nothing more." Removing the Nikon from its case, he uncapped the lens and checked the charge.

Orchid went to the wall, leaned her back into it, and stood plank straight. She looked to Oli. "Is this okay?"

"That's fine, my dear. You just stand there and let Mr. Brown do his thing."

Mr. Brown positioned himself so that he was six feet from Orchid. He lifted the camera to his eyes, and held it perpendicular. "Now don't smile. Don't move. Look as plain as possible."

Orchid shot him hot daggers.

Mr. Brown lowered the Nikon. "Now enough of that. Everyone knows how much you love me." He returned the camera to his eye. "Good. Now hold it." Blue light flashed. "Now one more just in case."

Orchid remained still, though a blue dot existed where Mr. Brown's face should have been. Another flash. The room faded then came back into focus.

"There, all done." Mr. Brown slipped the camera back into its case. "Just for the record, Orchid. When's your birthday?"

"December 13."

"Fine then. We'll keep it that way." Looking to the grand guard of the palace, he said, "Madame Olivia, nice to see you again. I'll have Orchid's new identification for you in a couple of days. Don't bother getting up. I know my way around." He left, the door sweeping him into the hall.

"There. That wasn't too bad now, was it?" Oli pushed the chair back, stretched her arms high over head, fifty-three-year-old elbows popping. "Have a seat on the sofa, my dear."

"I guess it was all right." Orchid went to the sofa, her eyes glued to the painting, and took a seat. She rested her hands in her lap, the effects of the Percocet wearing off, the all-too-familiar devouring of her insides returning.

"Do you approve of my painting? Sometimes it catches people off guard. If you haven't guessed already, my dear, Li Ling and I are lovers. Have been for almost ten years now. We abhor men. Funny, isn't it? Hating men, yet making a living from their deceptive ways."

The confession came as no surprise to Orchid. She said simply, "I kind of thought you two were an item. But she seems so young."

"That's the beauty of Orientals. They hide their age very well. Li Ling is forty-six years old. Can you believe it?"

"Really! I would have taken her for early twenties. She looks so youthful."

"I believe it's because of the love of a good woman. You should know all about that." A knowing twinkle lit her eyes.

Heat rushed up Orchid's body, colored her cheeks. "Oh? I don't know what you mean."

"Come now, my dear. Our room is just down the hall from yours if you remember. Your door was open. You and Gypsy were quite involved."

Orchid's entire face reddened. "You and Li Ling heard us. I… I…"

"There's no need to feel guilt or shame, my dear. You were beautiful together. You're a natural-born lover."

Swallowing hard, Orchid said, "You mean you saw us."

"We couldn't help ourselves. Like I said. Your door was open. We were hot as hell, so we kind of watched for a while. The two of you in the moonlight. I've never seen anything more beautiful."

"It just happened. I needed someone."

"Understandably so after all you've been through. The death of your mother, then losing your brother and father in a fire. It must have been horrible for you. Then there's everything Mr. Black and Mr. Brown did to you. I'm sorry for your losses and the degradation they put you through, not to mention turning you into a heroin addict, however, that will soon change."

"You know all that?"

"Of course, my dear. Tony Millions and I are business partners. There is nothing that happens regarding our little enterprise that we're not aware of. And there isn't anything that takes place in the palace that I'm not aware of. I know the twins do coke every once in a while, especially when Mr. Brown and Mr. White visit. I know that Tinker does her thing, then regularly visits the church for confession. I guess it eases her mind somewhat. Makes her believe she'll still get into heaven. And like you, I know everything about Gypsy's past. Not too dissimilar to your own. It's my business to know these things. I am also pretty sure your little rendezvous with Gypsy last night was probably your last, unless of course you're being paid to do so. Deep down you're straight as an arrow, preferring the affection of men. Last night was just a necessity in your time of need. I can read people like a book. And as sure as I'm sitting in this chair, I know that you're hurting right now. Am I wrong?"

"No."

"Would you like me to take care of it, or do you think you can get by for a while longer?"

"I can manage for a while longer."

"That's my girl." Pushing herself from the chair, Oli stood, opened a drawer, removed a pack of Viscounts, and tapped out a cigarette. "Shall we join the others? Lunch should be ready. I'm going to step outside and have a smoke. Nasty vice, but what are you going to do?" Fishing in the drawer, she produced a slim gold lighter. "It won't be too busy today being a Sunday, but you never can tell. Men's dicks don't accord themselves to any calendars that I know of."

Orchid stood, seeing Oli in a new light. "I am hungry," she confessed, and gazed at the painting, the domination of it. It frightened her.

"Good. I'm so glad we're seeing eye to eye, Orchid. Six months from now, you'll be one of us, making tons of cash and living like a queen ought to."

* * *

Mr. Brown stood within the circle the girls had positioned themselves in. Hands on his hips, he looked each of them in the eye. "So who's the lucky girl today?" Not receiving a direct response, he said, "Come on now, I haven't got all day."

Slowly Brat stood, and jammed her hands in the front pockets of denim shorts. "I guess it's my turn."

"Lucky you," said Mr. Brown. "Well, let's go, girl. I've got an itch that needs scratching."

Tossing the Nikon onto the Roman chaise, he headed to the hallway.

Brat followed, reluctantly. The thought of putting his *thing* in her mouth, again, sickened her. *He better have what I need to get me through it,* she thought.

Mr. Brown opened the door to room number 1. Li Ling had already changed the sheets, turned the covers, and vacuumed.

Brat followed him in, hesitantly, and with the press of a hand closed and locked it. "Did you bring me some candy?" she wanted to know before things went further.

"Now what kind of friend would I be if I didn't." Reaching into his khakis, he took out a nickel baggie, went to the nightstand, tapped out a couple of lines and straightened them with the edge of a finger. "There you go. Knock yourself out, kid."

Brat reached into her shorts, took out a twenty, and rolled it between fingers until it became a paper tube. Walking to the nightstand, she leaned forward and snorted both lines, drawing them deep. When she turned, Mr. Brown's khakis and boxers were already down around his knees and he was pulling on his diminutive cock. She waited a moment for the coke to kick in. Then she positioned herself in front of him, dropped to her knees, took him in hand, and massaged until he was fully aroused, Columbia's finest banishing all inhibitions.

"Tell me how big it is! Tell me how much you love to put it in your mouth," demanded Mr. Brown.

"It's so big, Mr. Brown." Brat looked up at him. "I just love sucking on your great big cock." Inside she was laughing hysterically. Fully erect, Mr. Brown's member was no bigger than a breakfast sausage. She took him in her mouth, massaged his ping-pong- testicles.

In less than a minute, Mr. Brown's body shuddered. "That's it, Brat!" he cried. "Oh, you fucking bitch!"

Brat let him slip from her mouth. The few drops of semen produced, she caught in the palm of a hand.

"Thanks, baby," said Mr. Brown in a pant. "You're much better than your sister. You loved it, didn't you?"

Brat rose. "Of course, Mr. Brown. Who wouldn't?" She went to the side table where a box of Kleenex sat and deposited the spent semen into a tissue.

While he redressed, Mr. Brown looked to the bed and its leather restraints. "You know what I would like to do to you someday, Brat?"

"What's that, Mr. Brown?"

"I would like to strap you to that bed and whip the living shit out of you, then fuck you in your tight little ass. How's that sound?"

Brat wanted to scratch his eyes out, but that would only lead to her death. Mr. Brown would strangle her with his bare hands and think nothing of it. Hating herself, she said, "I guess we could do that. Sure. Providing you bring me a treat."

"I'm looking forward to it. Well, I've got to get going." He unlocked the door and began to whistle. "Pop! Goes the Weasel" echoed from the hall

Immediately Brat went to the nearest bathroom, scrubbed her hands with soap, and gargled the taste out of her mouth with a heaping helping of Scope.

When she joined the others, lunch had been served and there was no sign of Mr. Brown or the camera. "Is he gone?" she asked unsure.

Brit piped up, spoke around a mouthful of pita. "Yeah, he's gone. And good riddens to bad trash."

Orchid looked at Brat, a forkful of fruit halfway to her mouth. She noticed that her hands were trembling. "I don't understand how any of you can do those favors for him. I hate him. I hope one day somebody puts him in his place. If anybody tried to make me do *that* to him, I would bite it off and spit it in his face," the incident in Wishbone's truck relived for a split second. The fork went to her mouth. Melon, orange, and banana exploded, soothing the fire within.

"We all hate him, Orchid," offered Gypsy. "He thinks he so much this and that." She and the twins began to laugh.

"I don't see what's so funny," said Orchid, unamused.

Brat sat next to her on one of the throw pillows, produced a thumb and index finger, brought them close until they were only inches apart. "You see this?" she asked.

"Yes."

"Well, that's about the size of his dick. And I'm being generous." She snickered.

Brit said. "Yeah, it's like a little mouse wearing a turtleneck."

Everyone laughed at Mr. Brown's expense. Orchid imagined a little mouse wearing a sweater.

The front entrance opened. Oli stepped in, waving a swirl of blue smoke from her face. She had intercepted Mr. Brown on his way out and told him in no uncertain terms while enjoying a third cigarette and the midday sun, that he was to pay for all future favors like everyone else. "Lots of space in the desert," she reminded him in reference to the late Mr. Green.

"Well, I'm glad to see everyone in such good humor. What's so funny?" She moved across the room and stood in front of the bar.

Convulsing with laughter, Gypsy said, "We were just talking about Mr. Brown and his inadequacies."

"Oh, that. Personally, I've never seen the thing, and have no inclination of ever doing so. I told you, Orchid. All men are not created equal. Mr. Brown's gruff exterior is compensation for being derisory in the meat department."

Brit and Brat nearly wet their panties. "Yeah," said Brat. "It's like when God gave out dicks, Mr. Brown was last in line and thought he said sticks and asked for a twig."

Orchid was now laughing as hard as the others, tears rushing to her chin. "That's funny," she said, catching her breath. "Asked for a twig."

"Where is Li Ling?" questioned Oli.

"I think she's still in the kitchen, cleaning up," said Gypsy. "We offered to help, but she shot us that look she gets when she thinks we're trespassing on her territory."

"Best to leave well enough alone then," said Oli, adding. "When you're done with your lunches, I would like you to tidy up the smoking room. Those think tanks from Apple left ashes everywhere and broke a couple of my finest crystal. I should have added it to their bills, but they spent a lot of money and promised to be back once their little convention is over."

"How did we do last night?" chimed the twins.

"We did very well. One of our best Saturdays in years. The house took in just over twenty thousand, so you girls really made some outstanding money."

"Yippee!" the twins yelped like a couple of grade students, the math of such earnings incalculable in their feeble little minds.

"I'm going to the kitchen," said Oli. "Would you mind joining me there for a moment, Gypsy?"

"Yes, of course." Unfolding her legs, Gypsy pushed herself from the pillow then looked to Orchid. "Eat up, Orchid. You look like you could use the nourishment."

Orchid smiled, a fleeting glimpse of their lovemaking filled her thoughts. A phantom tickle affected her most private area. She finished the last of the fruit. However, another hunger reared it's ugly head and stabbed her deep.

"I don't imagine it will be too much longer before the first customer arrives," said Oli. She rounded the bar and slipped a CD into the hidden stereo. Speakers hissed for a second before Gino Vennelli's "Powerful People" filled the welcoming room.

Well, it's a lonely afternoon
With nowhere to go but my room
Someday, when there's time
I'll think about these things on my mind...

Heading for the kitchen, Oli crooked a finger as though summoning a child. "Follow me please, Gypsy."

The twins put their plates aside, stood, caressed each other's hips, and began a seductive waltz. They stared into each other's eyes as though impassioned by a great love.

Orchid watched, still stymied as to how sisters could act like that with each other. *It must have been really something growing up in that household.*

* * *

Once in the kitchen, Oli tugged on her suit jacket and paced in front of the island. Li Ling stood by the sink where a fresh pot of coffee brewed, half-finished pita in one hand, bottle of water in the other. Li Ling hardly ever ate with the others. She smiled at her lover and Gypsy. The Latin beauty stopped within arm's reach of Oli. "Well?"

"You did splendidly last night, my dear. Your little session with Orchid really brought her closer to our way of managing things. You've earned her trust and made her feel needed. Just what I was hoping for."

Gypsy half-curtsied. "Thank you, Oli. It was my pleasure. I don't suppose you have what you owe me in one of those pockets."

Madame Olivia produced twenty-five twenties from a pocket which were folded in half and held in place by a red elastic band. She tossed it. "Don't spend it all in one place."

The wad of bills disappeared into a denim pocket. "Anytime you need me to... Well, let's just say, *persuade* Orchid. You let me know. Only next time, though I really enjoyed myself, her little pussy is so juicy and tight, it'll cost you a thousand."

Li Ling glowered at Gypsy who saw it and said, "Oh, relax. Like you wouldn't want a taste of what she's got between her legs."

"Just stay close to her for now," said Oli. "She's still a flight risk even though she has no place to go."

Gypsy's response was a *whatever* wave of a hand. She left the kitchen.

Oli smiled. Gypsy had come a long way since she, like Orchid, had been taken from the streets and assimilated to a lifestyle most women abhorred. Her descent from heroin had taken nearly two months of rehabilitation and the convalescence from her addiction to painkillers thereafter, almost a year. Now she was a cunning, manipulative, money-hungry bitch, like everyone else. Oli did not doubt for a moment that Gypsy would one day become a very profitable Madame of her own little brothel. Turning so she was facing Li Ling, she said, "I'll have a cup of coffee please, my darling."

Li Ling set her lunch down, poured her mistress a cup, and handed it to her across the island.

Oli blew her a kiss before taking a sip. "I love you," she said.

Li Ling smiled, and placed both hands over her heart. "I love you too," her eyes implored.

The corners of Oli's red lips lifted into a scandalous smile.. A blue suede shoe slipped from a foot an struck the floor. She stretched her toes. She was very pleased with the way things were unfolding. *Orchid was going to bring in more money than the twins combined,* she believed. Still, in the back of her mind, the whole Mr. Wong thing scratched at her. And not in a good way.

* * *

Orchid assumed the duty of vacuuming. Brit and Brat picked up broken crystal and cigar butts while Gypsy polished the tables and bar. In ten minutes, the smoking room was ready for the next group of men with money to burn.

"What do you think of our solarium?" Gypsy asked Orchid while wrapping the cord around an upright Hoover.

"It's beautiful. I told Oli that I would like to grow something. Maybe some chrysanthemums or peonies or maybe marigolds." Immediately the portrait of her mother came to mind, sitting in front of a wrangle of orange blooms, splendid in a blue summer dress, legs folded beneath her.

"Peonies would be nice," agreed Brat.

"What about daffodils?" said Brit. "They're nice."

They were standing in front of Orchid, wearing identical outfits. They had changed after lunch. Yellow T-shirts. Purple mini skirts. Pink Van runners. Orchid could not tell them apart. *It's no wonder men paid high prices for their services,* she thought. They were every young man's wet dreams come true.

Being Sunday, it was time for the orchids, roses, and lilies to receive their twice-a-week spraying. Led by Gypsy, the four women entered the solarium, the door swishing closed. Humidity kissed their faces. Brit, Brat, and Gypsy took spray bottles from a table near the door. "You can just watch, Orchid," said Brat. She went to the lilies and began to mist the heavy heads.

"Yeah," added her sister. "It's real easy. Just a light spray or the flowers will become too heavy and break off. Especially the orchids. They're very delicate."

"Come with me, Orchid," said Gypsy. "I'll show you how to dead-head the roses so they'll produce new buds."

"I know how to do that," replied Orchid.

"You *do*. Good. Then you can start with the Mother Teresas and go from there. They're the pink ones, there." She pointed with the spray bottle to a bushing of pink roses.

"Okay." Orchid went to the Mother Teresas and began to pinch off the withered heads, thumb and index finger trembling. She fought hard to steady them; however, the need for a fix was getting the better of her. "What should I do with the dead ones?" she asked, one hand already full.

"Just drop them on the floor," said Gypsy. "We'll sweep them up later."

Orchid dropped what she had in her hand and moved to the next bush. With care she spread the thorned branches and looked deep within for any that might be hidden. She knew it was important to get them all if you wanted to establish a complete set of new blooms.

Halfway through the roses, the door swished open. Oli stepped into the solarium. "I just received a call," she said. "Three men are on their way. They'll be here in less than ten minutes. So chop, chop. You can finish later."

Orchid stopped what she was doing and moved up the aisle to where Oli stood. "I don't feel very well,' she said under breath so the other girls wouldn't hear.

"Very well. I'll take care of you in a moment. Brit, Brat. It's your time to shine."

"Yes. Oli," they chorused from deep among the flowers. Spray bottles went back to their purchase. The twins left in a rush, anxious to fulfill their duties.

Gypsy started sweeping the dead heads and said she would be out in a minute.

"Don't take too long. I have a good feeling about these gentlemen. They sounded like big money."

Orchid didn't know what big money sounded like, but she did have an idea. The money that flowed into the palace daily was astronomical. "I'm hurting, Oli. I need you to help me, please."

"Meet me in your bathroom. I'll be up in an minute or two. Your timing could not be worse, Orchid. You should have had me take care of you earlier. Really, my dear."

"I'm sorry, Oli. I tried to hold out for as long as I could," she said, and presented shaking hands. "I can't control them."

"Go on then. I want to be in the welcoming room when these gentlemen arrive so I can squeeze them for what they're worth."

Lowering her eyes, feeling shame for God knew why, Orchid opened the door and headed for the second floor.

Oli went to Gypsy who was bent over, broom in one hand, dust pan in the other. "I want you to work on the gentleman who called. His name is Larry Kennedy. He's bringing his twin sons. It's their twenty-first birthday. This man is made of money. I could feel it when I was talking to him, so I did a little research. I was correct in my assumption. Larry Kennedy is New York City's crown prosecutor. Third cousin to *the* Kennedys. Born into wealth. He says he's not interested in our services for himself, only his sons, but I feel if you used your methods of persuasion with him, he would fold like a house of cards."

"Leave Larry Kennedy to me. He won't be able to resist. I'll take him for what he's worth."

"That's my girl. Maximum payments on everything. Before and after drinks. Cigars if he smokes. I've already instructed Li Ling to put together a platter of cheeses and our finest caviar. We could use a few more Larry Kennedys as our regulars."

"He's as good as gold as they say."

The sound of a car entering the circular drive could be heard through the glass.

"That must be them," said Oli. "Get cleaned up and meet us in the welcoming room. Put something on that says I'm a conservative slut."

"I know just the outfit. I won't be five minutes. What about, Orchid?"

"She's hurting, so I'm going to fix her up. I'm going to suggest she remain in her room, at least until the Kennedys have left. Tomorrow's her big coming-out party. She'll need her rest." Oli smiled with lascivious intent. "That one's going to spend more time on her back than a corpse in a coffin."

* * *

Orchid waited in the extravagant bathroom, the hunger within intensifying with each passing minute. She had heard a car pull into the driveway so she went to the window overlooking the entrance to the Shangri-La Palace.

It was another scorching day in Nevada. Waves of heat rose from the driveway, rolls of desert sand stretched to the east as far as she could see. A black limousine pulled up to the main doors and parked. Three men got out. The oldest wearing a dark suit, the other two much younger with curly blond hair and looking as much alike as the twins did. They spoke for a moment before disappearing from her sight. The limo driver emerged, took off his cap, and lit a smoke. He looked to the sky, his gaze falling on Orchid's face.

Orchid smiled and moved away from the window, feeling embarrassed for no other reason than that she was now a component of everything that went on in the Palace.

For something to do, she sat on the toilet and considered everything that had taken place in such a short period of time. Her flight from Bay Ridge Cove. The people she'd met while on the road. The bastard Henry Klondike who started her freefall into a world she had only read about and seen on TV. She wondered how much he had been paid for his role in her abduction. The house by the lake. Her first introduction to the hungry beast that now controlled her. Tony Millions and the coked-out Pamela. Mr. Black and his hateful smile. The despicable Mr. Brown who had taken advantage of her condition and raped her. Mr. Blue's murder in the desert that could have easily been her. The safe combination the vengeful spirit of Janis Keeper had surrendered. The tryst between her and Gypsy. These piecemeal memories reminded her how stupid she had been in her decision making. *Stupid. Stupid. Stupid.* Then her mind wandered to a better time, bringing forward the cherub face of Caleb Hart and his bestest friend in the world, Chase. She imagined the two running around the Hart property, Caleb tossing Chase's favored red ball and him bounding to retrieve it. She aimed a delusory smile at her damaged feet. It was foolish to leave the aging Hester and Ed. She knew that now. But why hadn't her special gift given her some kind of warning. *Maybe it had. You just didn't pay attention. Stupid girl. Too anxious to get to, where, here.* Cupping her face in her hands, she spoke quietly through her fingers. "Why did you leave me so soon, Momma, when I needed you most?" The widespread tracks of her unrecognizable feet screamed, WHY? WHY? WHY?

There came a light knock at the door. "May I come in?"

Orchid raised her head, wiped at an errant tear. "Yes, Oli. I'm just sitting here."

Oli entered the bathroom, black kit in hand. She closed the door. "Still feeling rough?"

"Yes. Terrible. I hate to say it, but I need what you have in that case."

"Take your jeans off please."

Orchid stood and, without feeling shame, dropped her jeans and stepped out of them.

Oli noticed that the blue panties she was wearing were worn in the rear to the point she could see flesh. "Poor little, Orchid," she said. "We'll have to get you some new under garments when we go shopping this week."

Craning her neck so she could see, Orchid said, "Believe it or not, they're my best pair. I didn't bring the ones Tony left for me. It seemed wrong somehow."

"I understand completely, my dear. Now hold still." Taking the prepared syringe, Oli went through the routine of ensuring no air bubbles existed. Heroin squirted, landed in the sink. On one knee, she slapped the area above Orchid's left calf. "You know something," she said as the needle pricked in. "I think you should rest for the remainder of the day. Perhaps take a nice long soak in that beautiful tub. Then have a nap in that handsome bed we've supplied you with. Dream about all the money you're going to start making tomorrow."

Orchid was still looking over her shoulder, a thick portion of red hair pushed to one side. The sound of a hot bath sounded enticing even though she had already showered. Heroin rushed, and fed the voracious beast within. Inhibitions lost, her eyes thinned, satiated once more. "Don't you want me to learn? From the girls I mean."

"You're a smart girl. What have you learned so far?" Oli stood and returned the used syringe to the kit then zipped it close.

"That the right choice of words can will a client into spending a lot of money, depending on what they're into."

"And what else?"

"That our bodies are only instruments to the trade and not to get emotionally involved."

"There. Spoken like a true pro and you haven't even entertained anyone yet. It is also important to make our male clients feel that they have performed admirably. Give them a swelled head sort to say." She sniggered. "When you achieve this, they'll keep coming back for more. Believe me. Every man desires the requisite need that they have performed well. A reassuring word fortifies their silly little egos. Believe it or not, that thing that dangles between their legs is sensitive and prone to mood swings."

Orchid chuckled and sat on the toilet. Legs marginally spread, the heroin crept along her flesh like so many spiders. She looked to the jetted tub. "Is it really that simple, Oli?"

"As simple as making a peanut butter sandwich. Now would you like me to run you a bath. I'd be happy to."

In her heroin state, Orchid took into account that Oli and Li Ling had spied on her while she and Gypsy were involved with each other. *What if she asked to wash my back?* "No. I can do it on my own, thank you."

"Fine. I'll leave you to it then. Just one more thing to think about, my dear Orchid. The future Bay Ridge Cove offered was of an unstable life spent in turmoil. Married to a fisherman, who would probably beat you when times were bad. Three kids pulling at your skirt and one in the oven. Laundry up to the eyeballs. Barely sustaining a life, living in a tar paper shack growing old before your time. Now what kind of life, would that be for a beautiful young woman such as yourself? You think about that. Get some rest. Your new life starts on the morrow." Picking up the kit, she smiled notoriously and left Orchid to her thoughts.

Oli made everything sound so simple while painting a nasty picture of what Orchid's life might be like. She slipped off the toilet, fought for balance, and went to the tub where a bottle of lavender bubble bath stood next to an assortment of soaps. She turned on the faucets, adjusted the heat, and poured a good amount of lavender into the frothing water. Removing her panties and top, she tossed them to the floor, sat on the edge of the tub and watched as a purple cloud of bubbles formed. Her mind established a visual of herself, much older, ragged from being overworked, a brood of children demanding her full attention. In her present state of mind, Oli's forlorn tale of a life wasted rang true. *Maybe Oli is right.*

When the water was deep enough, she turned off the faucets, stepped into the tub, submerged her body and turned on the jets. The cloud developed into a purple storm. Head comfortable, she closed her eyes and allowed her mind to venture on its own. Immediately, her dream lover filled the void, tall and handsome as ever. Only in this imagined scenario, instead of being alone in a field, he stood among a crowd bathed in dancing lights and seemed to be searching for her, calling to her, "*Rebecca. Where are you?*" In his hair was a feather within a twist of braid. Beautiful grey eyes searched the faces of those around him. In jeans and T-shirt, he looked so much bigger than before. Larger than life even, so real she could smell the very essence of him. "*I'm here,*" she heard herself whisper.

His incisive eyes fell upon her. "*I'm coming, Rebecca. I'm coming for you.*"

In her narcotic state, bubbles dripping from her hands, elbows, exploding across her breasts, Orchid reached out to him. "Find me soon, my love. I'm all alone and drowning."

* * *

46

The Dreamer

JOHNNY woke with a start. He was lying on the bed in his underwear, having fallen asleep while watching an Evangelist plead for money from his congregation.

It was the only station available.

The small room was much warmer than it was outside. He sat up, rubbed at his eyes. The dream he had just had was powerful in its telling. In it, he found himself to be walking Las Vegas Boulevard as he did every night, the streets teeming with people from all walks of life. The lights of the Vegas Strip danced all around to music emanating from everywhere. *"Keep searching, Johnny. You will find her,"* ten thousand voices sang out. Then the dream pulled at his very soul. In a instant, he was flying above the city, bird of prey eyes searching the ground. "I'm coming," he called out over and over. "I'm coming. I'm coming." Screams rose into the night. *"Keep searching, Johnny! Keep searching!"* He dream flew on. Over the Wynn, the Venetian, the Paris Hotel, and the construction site of the new Cosmopolitan.

From far below, a woman's voice, young despondent, rose above the music, above the pleading thousands. *"Find me soon, my love. Find me soon, my love... I'm all alone and drowning."*

Johnny drew his legs over the side and pulled on his jeans, his boots. He went to the dresser, took out a clean T-shirt, slipped it over his head, and tucked it in. Killing the television, he unchained the door and stepped into the long hallway.

A very large man he had not seen before was coming toward him, floor boards creaking underfoot. He was dressed in shorts, running shoes, and an old short-sleeved shirt. There was something odd about the man's appearance. As he drew near, Johnny grasped, with utmost empathy what it was he was seeing. The man's bald head bore a half-dozen holes, each a half inch deep or so they seemed. The thick brows of a boxer sat over gentle eyes, and his ears were cauliflowered. Immense hands looked as hard as stone. He was sweating copiously. Johnny got a whiff of a recently smoked cigarette. "Hello, he said. "Hot out, isn't it?"

The man stopped and in a gruff voice answered, "Da. It is being very hot today. Better to find a nice cool hotel to spend a day like today, yes?"

Try as he might, Johnny could not help but stare at the man's head. "You're probably right," he agreed.

The man said, "You are wondering what happened to me. Da?"

"I'm sorry if I'm staring," said Johnny. "How did that happen to you?"

"Da, this is the result of crossing the Russian mob. They call it the Siberian corkscrew."

"I'm sorry," said Johnny, truly feeling for him.

"Da, it is better than being dead, yes?"

"I suppose."

The strange man moved on. When he reached his room, he looked back at Johnny. "Stay in the shade, yes. Look with your eyes wide shut." A moment later, Russian music leaked from beyond the closed door.

Quickly, Johnny used the singular bathroom to wash the cobwebs from his mind. *Look with your eyes wide shut*. He had never heard that expression before; however, the meaning seemed obvious. It was a message he had received from others. Search with your heart and your mind. *But how did the Russian know I was looking for someone?* Stranger than strange. And yet, considering everything he had experienced recently, it wasn't. Not really. He dried his hands and took stock of himself. *I will find you. I promise.* He would begin again his search for the gifted one starting at the Golden Nugget. A district of Vegas he had not ventured to yet. *Old town Vegas*.

When he stepped outside, the scorching sun set his flesh on fire. He looked around the dilapidated neighborhood. A couple of black kids, no more than eight or nine, were rolling a tire down Tam Avenue. They laughed when the tire jumped a curb and slammed into a tree. An old Chinese man pushed a grocery cart leaden with green garbage bags full of bottles and cans. Inside the cart was a mutt with mangled hair, viewing the world through one eye. A taxi sat idling, its driver perched on the hood and having a smoke. Leaning against the front stoop of the local convenience store, a shamble of a man, matted facial hair hiding his shame, held a baseball cap while he sucked on something in a brown paper bag. A large black woman exited the store, looked down at him, and dropped some change into the hat. The man raised the paper bag. Johnny clearly heard him say, "God bless you, auntie."

This is a side of Vegas nobody sees, Johnny knew. *The slums of the world are all the same. Out of sight and out of mind.* He got into Konahee's Ford, turned on the air-conditioning, the radio, and headed for old town Vegas. Super Tramp's "Dreamer" filled the interior. "I will find you, whoever you are," he told himself. "You will not drown. I promise."

Dreamer
You're nothing but a dreamer,
Can you put your hands on your head
Oh no...

Another day would pass. The DJ kept warning of a much-needed storm heading for the greater Las Vegas area. Johnny would go back to his room, dejected once more. The stone that always remained in his possession relinquishing no telltale signs. But he would keep on searching. He had to. It was a matter of life and death. Of that, he was certain.

* * *

47

When It Rains, It Pours

ORCHID'S day of reckoning arrived with a burst of thunderclap, jolting her from the void of a dreamless sleep. She had taken two Percocet before going to bed, which had caused her to crash heavily into a world of white noise. Now her mind thick with the hangover of it. She sat upright, eyes focused to the French doors and the sound outside. It was raining, heavily. The red digits of the clock radio informed her it was 8:37. Reaching, she turned it on.

Janis Joplin's "Piece of My Heart" tore through the static caused by the storm.

Didn't I make you feel, like you were the only man
Yeah... and didn't I give you nearly everything a woman possibly can
Well, honey, you know I did
And each time I tell myself that I, well, I think I've have enough
Well, I'm gonna show yah, baby, that a woman can be tough...

Orchid drew the comforter aside, pulled her knees to her chin and wrapped her arms around her shins. She hugged herself in an attempt to impede the alarming shiver traversing within. To think she was going to have sex with a total stranger for money in a few hours was unfathomable. Tears leaked from heavy eyes. Sniffing, she wiped the flow of mucus secreting from her nose. For the first time since her abduction, she cavorted with the idea of ending it all. She could leap from the balcony to the ground below. *But what if the fall didn't kill you? You might end up a paraplegic or a vegetable for the rest of your life. Locked in some hospital room. Eating your meals through a straw.* Quickly she destroyed any thoughts of suicide. It was not Rebecca White who had conjured such anarchistic musings. It was the drugs, her fall from grace, forged by an anxious mind that had been worried into submission. Grabbing at several stuffed animals, she gathered them all around her.

Take another little piece of my heart now, baby
Break it
Take another little bit of my heart, my heart, yeah, yeah, yeah
Power
Take another little piece of my heart now, baby
Well, you know you've got it
Shine if it makes you feel good…

She found herself singing to Janis's heartwrenching, empowering tune. *So appropriate*. Well, she was going to show them. She was going to show them all just how tough she could be. Leaping from the bed, she went to the walk-in and retrieved her suitcase. Opening it, she removed the photo of her mother, and held it tight to her naked bosom. She turned and watched the rain pour from the grey sky. "You're not going to be very proud of me, Momma. But I've got to do things that disgust me in order to survive. I know deep in my heart that I will be taken away from all of this. If you're still watching over me. Please close your eyes. I will be shamed enough for the both of us. I love you, Momma." Raising the photo to her lips, she kissed her mother's face. "I *will* get out from under these people. You'll see."

Returning the photo to the suitcase, she snapped it closed. *I know you'll understand*. Li Ling would serve breakfast soon. She put on jean shorts and a red checkered shirt. Slipping into a pair of white runners, she examined her reflection in one of the French doors to find she bore a resemblance to a recluse from the Ozarks. *Perfect*. She ran a brush through her hair, teased it until it spread wide off her face. She winked at the woman staring back at her. "Time to shine. Thanks, Janis."

* * *

The first client did not arrive until 4:00 p.m., which was not unusual considering the rain continued until well into the afternoon. He was a good-looking man, midthirties, well dressed in a casual suit, and had a head of luxurious brown hair most women would kill for. All of the girls were seated at the bar, Orchid centering the twins, Gypsy, and Tinker. Li Ling stood at her usual place behind the bar in a shimmering pink bodysuit.

Soft jazz breezed throughout the welcoming room.

In a black dress, spaghetti straps accentuating athletic shoulders, Oli greeted the would be spender. "Welcome to the Shangri-La Palace," she said. "I'm Madame Olivia, the Palace's proprietor."

The client beamed a smile of perfect white teeth. "I'm Michael," was all he offered.

"Please, follow me, Michael. We haven't seen you here before. Would you care for a drink, on the house of course."

"A beer would be great." His eyes wandered to the women seated at the bar.

Oli slipped an arm through his, and steered him toward her girls. "What type of beer? We have Heineken, Pilsner, Budweiser of course, and Guinness. If you prefer the dark ales."

"A Heineken would be fine."

"These are my ladies. Say hello to Michael, girls."

In unison, legs crossed, they chimed, "Hello, Michael." Gypsy made the introductions. "We're so glad to meet you. My name is Gypsy. This plump little darling to my right is Tinker, and this gorgeous creature is Orchid. The twins names are Brit and Brat, but you'll have to figure out which is which."

Li Ling popped the cap from a bottle of Heineken and poured it into a pilsner glass. Oli handed it to the client. "So tell us, Michael, what brings you to our humble abode."

Michael mulled the question for a moment. "Well, to tell the truth, this is the first time I've visited a place like this. A friend of mine recommended it, highly. Said it was just what I needed. You see, I'm recently divorced, well, six months now, and I've tried the bar scene, which didn't work out too well. It seems I've forgotten how to socialize with the opposite sex. So here I am."

"Well, you've come to the right place," said Oli. "I promise you, you won't be disappointed."

"That's what my friend said." He took a sip of beer.

Gypsy, wearing a black negligee and black pumps, slid from the stool and moved next to the client. "So what do you do, Michael?"

"I'm a dentist."

"Well, I'm so glad to meet you, Michael the dentist." She slid a hand to his shoulder, drew little circles with a finger. "Let me take your jacket so you can be more comfortable."

Michael took another swallow of beer, beads of sweat just above his brow.

Gypsy moved behind him, relieved him of his jacket then ran a gentle finger down his spine. She handed the Scottish tweed to Li Ling. "Please take care of this."

Smiling brightly, Li Ling took it from her and folded it over an arm.

"Please have a seat," said Gypsy, and offered a stool.

Supporting the pilsner glass with the flat of a palm, the new client took to a seat. "This is a really nice place," he said, taking it all in.

To mimic the words glazed within the bar mirror Gypsy said, "Your fantasy is our obsession."

"Yes, I can see that."

"So what do you have in mind?" interrupted Oli.

"I'm not sure. What are the prices? My friend told me you're a little on the expensive side."

"Our prices vary. Depending on what you require. If you're looking for a threesome with the twins, you're looking at spending twenty-five hundred. Tinker here is our resident S-M specialist if you're into pain."

Michael looked at the doughy woman seated next to him and cringed. "No disrespect, but no, thanks." He took another swallow of Heineken.

Just then, the double wide entrance opened. Two large black men stepped into the welcoming room, obviously under the influence. They semi-staggered across the room.

"Duty calls," said Tinker, jumped off the stool, and made a beeline for them.

"You're just what we're looking for," the largest of the two observed. "We gonna make an Oreo cookie out of you."

Tinker steered them to the bar. "I like the way you think. I can take everything you've got to give and then some."

"How much?" the smaller of the two asked.

Oli was going to offer them another drink, but thought better of it. She spoke to them for a moment before the smaller of the twosome took out his wallet and handed her a credit card. Slipping the Visa through the automated teller, Oli waited a few seconds then nodded to Tinker that it was okay to continue. The three disappeared down the hallway, laughing, each man with a handful of Tinker's enormous bottom.

"When it rains, it pours," remarked Oli. "Now back to you, Michael. As I was saying, the twins are twenty-five hundred, for both of course. If you would prefer just one, reduce the cost by half."

Brit and Brat giggled, then kissed. "You wouldn't believe the things we like to do Michael," said Brat. "You'll stay hard for a week," prompted Brit.

Oli continued, "Gypsy is twelve hundred."

Michael turned in his chair so that he was facing a quiet Orchid. "How much for you?" he asked.

Orchid looked to Oli. "You'll have to ask Madame Olivia."

"Ah, you like our little Orchid, do you? Isn't she beautiful? A rare flower indeed. Fifteen hundred to taste the nectar of our little Orchid. Did I mention that our prices include a video if you like and carte blanche of the bar?"

Orchid swallowed. Self- effacement colored her cheeks. *This is it.*

Gypsy took a place on the stool next to Michael, crossed one leg over the other and ran a finger down the dentist's shoulder and arm. She leaned forward so that he got a good glimpse of her breasts. "You can have us both if you would like, Michael. We'll rock your world."

Michael mulled the offer over for a moment. His eyes went from the bountiful mounds of Gypsy's breasts to Orchid's face. Running fingers through his thick mat of hair, he said, "I can swing fifteen hundred."

"A fine choice, Michael," said Oli. "I'll just need a credit card please."

"Is it all right if I pay cash?"

"Or you can pay cash," beamed Oli.

Michael the dentist dug into his front pocket and came up with a very large roll of twenties. "I got lucky at the craps table," he said unnecessarily, counted out fifteen hundred, and slid the bills across the bar to Oli's waiting hands.

"I wish all my clients paid cash. Less paperwork." She knew Michael's tale of divorce was a fabrication. Anyone who paid cash had something to hide. And it was usually a wife. "Orchid, you may take our new friend to room four when he's ready."

Michael swallowed what was left of the German ale, and set the empty bottle on the bar. "If it's all right with you," he said to Orchid. "I'm ready now. A video isn't necessary. Do you have contraceptives?"

Orchid nodded, looked to Oli then to Gypsy and back to Oli again who smiled approvingly. Everything she had learned from the girls over the past few days came rushing forward. "I'm glad you chose me, Michael. I knew you would pick me the moment you walked through our door. You won't forget our time together, that I promise." Rising from the stool, she took him by the hand, leaned her head on his shoulder, and whispered. "I'm so hot for you." Leading him into the hallway, to her designated room, she looked back at her adopted family who were all smiles. *Momma, if you're still with me somehow, please turn away. I'm only doing this because I have to.*

* * *

48

Promises, Promises

INSIDE an abandoned warehouse on Vegas's east side, Rick Warren sat in a chair, hands tied behind his back, ankles bound to its legs. On his head he wore a gunnysack cinched with rope. A red stain seeped through the material where his mouth was.

Mr. Black stood in front of him, black gloves covering both hands. Mr. Brown and Mr. Green stood off to the side, so they may watch Mr. Black ply his trade. He drew a fist back and sent it crashing into the jaw of Rick Warren, nearly knocking *him* and the chair over. "When can we expect the money, man?"

Rick Warren played the ponies. So much so that he had managed a tremendous debt to the wrong sorts of people. Other than supplying America with coke and being a purveyor of the flesh industry, Tony Millions also loaned money to those who could not get it elsewhere. At 25 percent interest of course. "I don't have it. Please. I need more time," whimpered Rick.

Again Mr. Black drew his fist back and sent it crashing into the side of Rick Warren's head. This time the chair did tilt sideways, and Rick Warren fell to the cement floor.

"Pick him up," Mr. Black told the spectators.

Mr. Brown and Mr. Green righted the chair.

"My hands are getting sore, man. Perhaps I should use a bat."

"No, please don't. I'm begging you." Rick cried. "I'll get the money. I just need a couple of weeks." Blood dripped from the sack, his body shook uncontrollably.

"Mr. Millions already gave you two weeks, man. You promised to pay it then. And still no money. Mr. Millions has a reputation to maintain. I'm sure you understand." He drove his fist into gunnysack where he thought Rick Warren's nose to be. Cartilage and bone crunched. Rick Warren's head shot backward before falling forward. "You're not going to pass out on me now, are you, Rick?" He shook the man's shoulders. Inaudible sounds emerged from the sack. "What's that? I can't hear you. Did you hear what he said, Mr. Brown?"

"I believe he told you to go fuck yourself," said Mr. Brown, smiling.

Mr. Green agreed. "That's what he said all right. I heard him plain as day."

"He did? Now that wasn't very nice, Rick." Mr. Black drew back his fist, gritted his teeth, and was about to send the punch of all punches into Rick Warren's already-broken nose when Tony Millions pulled his Lexus into the warehouse.

Mr. Black's fisted hand fell to his side.

Killing the engine, Tony emerged, dressed in a dark suit. He walked over to Mr. Black. "When can I expect my money?"

"He says he needs a couple more weeks, man."

"Oh, he does, does he? Mr. Brown, please remove the hood."

Mr. Brown untied the rope, and drew the sack off Rick Warren's smashed face.

Barely conscious, Rick lifted his head, both eyes closed, mouth resembling chopped liver, nose on the other side of his bloody face.

Tony circled the chair like a predator, and grabbed a handful of Rick Warren's sweat-drenched hair. Leaning forward so that he was close to Rick's ear, he said in an acerbic tongue, "Now you listen to me, asshole. If I don't get my money in two days, Mr. Black here is going to take your son Billy. How old is he, six? Take him out into the desert and bury him up to his neck so the buzzards can feast upon his ears, pluck out his eyes, and tear out his tongue for dessert. A very slow and excruciating death indeed. If by chance, the buzzards don't come, he won't last a day in this heat. He'll go out of his mind while the scorpions and snakes find solace within him. While Mr. Black is doing this to poor little Billy, these two men are going to go to your house and rape your wife in so many ways she'll beg them to kill her. Now! Do I get my money in two days or not? Your family's lives depend on your response."

Rick Warren tried to open his blue black eyes, couldn't. "Yes. Two days," he whimpered.

Tony let go of his hair and wiped his hand on his trousers. "There. Now that wasn't so hard now, was it, Rick? Just so your memory does not fail you." He looked to Mr. Brown. "Please do your thing."

"Yes, Tony." Reaching into a pocket, Mr. Brown produced his-well practiced wire cutters. He walked up to Rick, steadied one of his tied hands, and spread the fingers. Placing the razor edges over the little finger, he removed it from the hand before his heart took its next beat..

The pinkie fell to the cement floor. Rick Warren bucked, the agony more than he could bear. The chair skittered and scattered, sanguine squiggles decorated the cement canvas around him. Red spittle flew from his mouth, tortured screams echoed from the walls. The chair fell sideways.

"Untie him," said Tony. "We don't want him bleeding to death. Who would pay his debt?" He laughed.

Mr. Brown bent low and untied the screaming man's hands and feet.

"He can find his own way home," said Tony. With a casual gait he went to the Lexus, got in, and backed out of the warehouse.

Mr. Black, Mr. Brown, and Mr. Green returned to Mr. Black's Cadillac and drove away.

Rick Warren lay on the floor shrieking from the deepest depths of his lungs, clutching the hand with only three fingers and a thumb.

* * *

49

Turn on Your Heart Light

OVER the next five days, Orchid learned the strippers' poetry of the brass rail, gliding upon its metallic smoothness, upside down, turning slowly, eyes beseeching to faces that weren't really there to watch her. The twins taught her how to entice men into throwing money by touching herself in the most provocative ways. She became as proficient as they were in a short span of time, much to the delight of Oli and Tony Millions.

By the time Orchid's menstrual cycle came, she was, in a way, truly grateful, because it meant she hadn't been impregnated by Mr. Brown.

She had slept with nine men and two women, the money, totaling fifteen thousand and fifty dollars, which she only saw four hundred of, the remainder having been "invested in your future," Oli told her. Now dependent upon the painkillers, preferring the numbness they provided to the mind sizzle of heroin, she went about her new vocation with a detached vagueness.

Oli insisted she still needed a minimal daily injection so she could be weaned off the narcotic without the sickness of a cold turkey quitting. Orchid's feet had all but healed. All that remained of the bruising were light pink dots that could easily be mistaken for indifferent freckles. The area behind her knees however had turned into blotches of green rawness that were easily masked with a little skin toner.

Gypsy remained close to her as per Oli's instructions, befriending her as an older sister would, sharing stories, most of which were fabrications of a vivid imagination to keep Orchid entertained. Neither spoke of their pasts or how they came to be employed at the Palace. It just wasn't allowed. "Someone is always watching, always watching and listening," Gypsy constantly reminded her.

They had all gone shopping early Wednesday morning, venturing into the Vegas Orchid had always imagined it to be. Architectural monuments to the gods of money rose high into the blue Nevada sky. Giant marquees advertising only the best in the entertainment industry dazzled her. She marveled at the structural geniuses of the Paris Hotel, the bygone design and size of Caesar's Palace and the Luxor. The Disney-like turrets of Camelot, and the miniature complexity of New York, New York. But it was the immense construction site of the new Cosmopolitan and its futuristic scheme that held a strange interest for Orchid. As they walked past the sight, she was drawn to it as if she were made of metal and the monolithic buildings were hulking, glass magnets.

With her own money she'd purchased a dozen pairs of panties, a couple of T-shirts—one captioning, What Happens in Vegas Stays in Vegas—and a red Velcro wallet that fit neatly in her back pocket to hold her new identification. Tiffany Rose from Baltimore. Tiffany Rose from Vegas. They had brunch at the Bellagio. A veritable feast for the eyes and palate. Then drinks at the Venetian where Brit and Brat gambled while the rest of the women walked the casino floor, sipped twelve dollar martinis, and admired the grandeur.

With the new identification Mr. Brown supplied, identifying her as Tiffany Rose from Baltimore, Maryland, getting into the casinos was not an issue. She was fitted for several outfits which she would wear while dancing at Club Paradise. They were all very risqué and paid for with funds from the Shangri-La Palace's "mad money" Oli called it.

Orchid's favorite, if you could call it that, was a shimmering red two-piece with gold tassels edging the skirt, reminiscent of a cheerleader's outfit she had once seen on television. Price: $250.

When they'd arrived back at the Palace, and since it was still too early for clients to arrive, she was encouraged into fashioning each outfit for Oli's approval and to the envious applause of the other girls. Having taken to the brass pole like a fish to water, the music she would dance to she was told, would be the fundamental burlesque works of the seventies and eighties; Rod Stewart's "Hot Legs," David Bowie's "Let's Dance," "Pretty Lady," and "On the Dance Floor." Music she knew oh so well.

That night, when the last of the clients departed and Oli and Li Ling had retired for the night, she and the girls watched *An Officer and a Gentleman* in the games room. After the movie, Orchid went to her room. Although she had taken another painkiller, knowing her cycle was about to commence, dreams of past and future better times would not come. For the upcoming initiation into the world of ogling men, stage lights, smoke-filled parlors, and the degrading act of taking her clothes off, had terrified the sleep from her.

* * *

Mr. Black arrived at 7:00 p.m. Friday to escort Orchid to the club. He stood by the entrance in a peacock blue suit, waiting patiently, hands folded behind his back.

Oli had given Orchid a medium sized valise to carry her outfits in. The Palace was busy. The rain had stopped. It was a beautiful post-rain evening with the sun perched deep into the west looking like a radiant disk of gold. The Apple convention had concluded, and the three executives who had ventured to the Palace a week prior returned with five coworkers who wanted to end their trip with a veritable *bang* before returning to the mundane lives they had forged.

Orchid sat on her bed, loaned case packed and ready to go. She was told to dress casually, so she wore jeans, her What Happens in Vegas Stays in Vegas T-shirt, and white sneakers, no makeup. Her hair was gathered at the back, held in place with a blue bungee, looking very much like the tail of a prime rooster. She hadn't prayed to God since her assimilation into the flesh industry, and as she closed her eyes to pray, a doubting voice said in no uncertain terms, "*You're wasting your time, Rebecca. There's no one there to hear you.*" So she sat on the bed and stared at the Spanish painting until the horses did leap from the canvass, and charged her in a crashing of hooves. It was the combination of drugs and an overactive imagination, but it scared her to death nonetheless.

A few minutes later, Oli entered the room without knocking. "Mr. Black is here to take you to the club, Orchid. We mustn't keep him waiting. Mr. Black is a man of little patience."

Orchid took hold of the powder blue case and stood, her legs shaking with consternation.

"Come now, my dear. No need to be frightened. You'll do very well. I'm betting the star of the evening." Oli moved toward her. "Here, put these in your pocket. They'll help take the pressure off." She handed Orchid a baggie containing three Percocet. "Take two twenty minutes before you go on. You won't even know there's an audience. Just dance as you've practiced and let your mind devote itself to the music. Your first set won't be until nine. That will give you a chance to observe the other girls."

"Thank you, Oli," said Orchid, stuffing the baggie into a front pocket. "Will you be up when I get back?"

"With the bunch we have downstairs, things could go on all night, so yes, I'll be waiting for you to return. Now come. Let's go."

With valise in hand, Orchid followed Oli out of the room and down the stairs to the welcoming room. It was indeed busy. The bar was crowded with men and drinks. Gypsy, Brit, Brat, and Tinker were in fine form, pressing their bodies against perspective clients, whispering sweet nothings in their ears. The philharmonic symphony was almost lost in the male babble.

Li Ling shook a martini jigger and smiled at Orchid as she made her way across the room. A couple of the businessmen glanced in her direction then quickly turned their heads when Mr. Black cautioned them with his soulless eyes, and that faithless smile of his.

Orchid and Oli approached. "Ready for the big show, baby?" he asked.

Orchid's eyes fell to the blue valise. "Yes," she said timidly.

"Now, Mr. Black, I expect you to take good care of our little Orchid," Oli told him in no uncertain terms. "If anything should happen to her, I'll personally hold you responsible."

"Don't worry, Madame Olivia. She's in good hands. I'll bring her back safe and sound."

"You'd better." Oli took Orchid by the shoulders, turned her so that she was facing her, and kissed her on the cheek. "That's for good luck. Knock them dead, sweetheart."

"Thank you, Oli. I'll do my best."

"I know you will, dear. Now go make some big-time money."

Mr. Black pulled on the arched door and swept a long arm out into the sunshine. "After you, baby. Your chariot awaits."

Orchid stepped out into the dry air, the evening sun warm on her face. A bird twittered from within the blooming hibiscus. Sunning itself on one of the concrete risers, a deadly bark scorpion seemed pressed into the step. Mr. Black's ominous Cadillac sat parked directly in front of the entrance looking like some evil thing brought to life from a Tarantino script. It had recently received a coat of wax, and Orchid could see her reflection in the shine of metal as she approached.

Mr. Black stepped ahead of her and opened the rear door, smiling, smiling, always smiling. "Better than the trunk," he cruelly reminded her.

Orchid slid in, the powder blue valise she rested on her lap. She looked back toward the villa. Mr. Black closed the door. Oli stood at the entrance, a cigarette between her fingers, blue smoke curling at her face. She waved and smiled, noticed the scorpion sunning itself, and shooed it away with the point of a shoe. The scorpion landed on its back, righted itself, and spun in circles, its pinchers high, stinger curled toward its back.

When Mr. Black entered the Cadillac, the vehicle leaned for a second, then readjusted. The engine came to life. Mr. Black drew an arm over the seat, regarded Orchid over his shoulder. Big white teeth brighter than bright. "Mr. Millions will be arriving at the club to watch you perform. So you better put on a good show."

Without response, Orchid continued to stare through the window as the Cadillac pulled away. Oli pinched the cigarette she was smoking between fingers and went back into the Palace. *Through these doors are the most beautiful women in Vegas.*

Orchid regressed, for in a strange way, the Shangri-La Palace had become a safe haven for her. No harm would fall upon the Harts as long as she cooperated and she was alive. Who knew what the hand of fate was going to deal next? *One day at a time,* she told herself. *One day at a time.*

Another page turned.

* * *

50

Shine a Light

CLUB Paradise, located at Paradise Boulevard, a block south of the Hard Rock Café and five minutes to the airport, looked gloomy, and it gave Orchid a solitary chill. Mr. Black parked the Cadillac at the back of the building near the stage entrance where a heavy metal door with PRIVATE stenciled on its facade stood under a weak light. Every space was contained with all manner of transportation from old pickups to hundred-thousand-dollar luxury cars.

Orchid waited for Mr. Black to open the door for her. When he did, he said, "Here you are, baby. Time to shine a light." Taking her by the arm, he steered her to the metal door and gave it solid three knocks. A moment went by before the door opened. A bald and bulging man wearing a black T-shirt with Club Paradise in pink neon appeared. Tattoos covered both arms, and Orchid believed he had one of the meanest faces she had ever seen and she had seen more than her fair share in a short period of time.

When the doorman saw it was Mr. Black, he smiled a missing front tooth, and said, "So this is the new girl. Come on in." Holding the door with one arm, he shook Mr. Black's hand with the other, his sickle eyes giving Orchid the once-over. *Real nice.*

By now, Orchid could recognize the telltale signs of someone who was under the influence of amphetamines. Tinker regularly took speed tablets. The bouncer maintained the same pinprick light to his eyes. Wishbone Hogg reincarnate, only bigger.

They entered a narrow corridor feebly lit by a string of bulbs and the transparent reflection of colorful stage lights. A stool with folded newspaper sat by the door. Music pumped through speakers. The weighty murmur of men could be heard just under the verses of Journey's "Babe."

Mr. Black put his hand flat against Orchid's back, urging her forward. The metal door closed with a slam, causing Orchid to nearly jump out of her skin. The small suitcase fell to the floor, and popped open. Quickly she knelt down, gathered the extra tampon, the bottoms to one of her outfits that had escaped, and snapped the lid closed, her face and ears flush with embarrassment.

"No need to be embarrassed, baby," said Mr. Black with a snicker. "And why are you so jumpy? From what I hear, you've taken to the brass pole like a pro."

Ignoring the remark, she continued forward. The speakers fell silent. Cheers erupted and the entire structure seemed to vibrate, including Orchid.

Young or old, rich or poor, the sight of a woman taking her clothes off to music encouraged the inherited fundamentals of the Neanderthal to come forward in all men.

The bouncer fell in behind them. "Place is packed tonight," he said to an indifferent Mr. Black who had no intention of getting into a conversation with the hired musclehead. Ignored, the bouncer raised his tattooed middle finger, turned, and went back to his station by the rear entrance.

Suddenly, a door at the end of the corridor burst open. More color was added to the dimness of the hallway. A pretty blonde with red glitter eyelashes and legs up to here stepped through. Against her chest she held a blanket and a yellow bikini top. Lined within the thin fabric of her bottoms were dozens of bills. Immediately apparent was the wafting flavor of dry ice. *Vanilla.* The dancer hurried to another door, the spikes of her silver shoes clacking. Looking quickly to Orchid and Mr. Black, she smiled and disappeared.

The raucous bedlam of male voices returned to an enthusiastic murmur over top of which a baritone voice announced that there would be a fifteen-minute pause between acts and that Club Paradise was pleased to offer a two-pound platter of wings for only $7.95. Then the Undisputed Truth's "Smilin' Faces" filled the club's interior.

As Orchid approached the open door, the clucking of female voices spilled into the hall. Standing in the doorway for a moment, she stared into the dancers' dressing room. It was set up like a salon, housing individual vanities with makeup lights, and was much larger than she had anticipated. There were a dozen stations in all, seven occupied by leggy, mostly topless dancers who stopped what they were doing to stare at the plain Jane standing at the threshold. "Come on in, honey," said a beautiful black woman with long red hair.

With the press of a hand, Mr. Black ushered Orchid farther into the room. "Ladies, this is Orchid," he said. "Orchid, these are the girls."

Orchid took in their faces. "Hello," she said, no longer shocked by the frankness of naked flesh.

The blonde who had just finished her act said, "Here, you can take the spot next to me." With a tube of lipstick in hand, she pointed to an unoccupied vanity. The money she had made for her last set was in a small stack next to a makeup case. "Come on. Don't be shy. We're all friends here. Nobody's going to bite you. Not unless you want them to."

The comment provoked a rash of giggles.

Another of the girls, a slim dark-haired Asian apparelled in an I Dream of Genie outfit, said, "Must be that time of the month. Where'd Tony find this one? In the lost and found?"

Mr. Black narrowed his eyes. "Best to keep your comments to yourself, Ming."

"Sorry. You know me. Can't keep my mouth shut. Sorry, Orchid. I didn't mean anything by it. Sometimes I say the first thing that pops into my head. It gets me into all sorts of trouble. But my shrink says I'm improving."

Orchid went to the offered vanity and set the small case on its surface. There were pictures lining the mirror. Shots of a pretty brunette with family members Orchid guessed. An old woman in a wheelchair, the brunette hugging her shoulders. The same brunette between a couple who looked in their fifties, the woman bearing a striking resemblance to the brunette. A little boy standing at the end of a dock holding a fishing rod in one hand and a small mouth bass in the other. The same brunette sitting on a Harley in leather jacket and chaps.

"I'm Bethany," said the blonde. "That's Gabriella's place, but it's her night off. I'm sure she won't mind you using her table to get ready."

"Are you sure?" asked Orchid. "I wouldn't want to impose." In the short time she was at the Palace, she had unintentionally gained an echo of Madame Olivia's tart vernacular.

The beautiful black woman got up from her stool, surgically enhanced breasts preceding her. She went to Orchid and placed her hands on her shoulders. "I'm Jasmine. And no, you wouldn't be imposing. Like Bethany said, we're all friends here." With minimal force she pressed Orchid onto the stool. "There now. Comfy?" Without waiting for an answer, she went to Mr. Black, reached up, and looped an arm around his neck. "Where have you been, baby? It's been a long time." Reaching, she grabbed hold of the bulge in his pants. "What you been feeding this thing?"

Mr. Black smiled. "If I told you, you would only get jealous."

"Well, the next time it needs feeding, you let me know. I hate to think it was receiving subpar nourishment."

"I'll keep that in mind," said Mr. Black, and pushed her aside. "Now I want you girls to take care of Orchid. Her first set will be at nine. She still needs to select her music, so you can help her with that. Mr. Millions is coming as well, so be at your best." Taking hold of Jasmine's arm, he said, "I want her well adjusted by the time she goes on. Okay, baby?"

"Sure, sugar. Just leave things to me."

"Good. I'll leave you ladies alone then. Remember, put on a good show for the boss. He expects nothing less from you." That said, Mr. Black left the dressing room and closed the door behind him.

As though her head was on a swivel, Orchid took in the girls, one by one, the brightly lit room, the outfits hanging on a mobile rack, and the door that stated Restroom. There was a brief moment of silence before Bethany said, "First thing we're going to do is take that bungee out of your hair. It's too pretty to keep all bunched up like that." Rising from her stool, she stood behind Orchid. "Do you mind?"

"I guess not," said Orchid. Watching Bethany in the mirror, the topless dancer untangled the bungee and set it aside. Then she took her hair and spread it out so that it fanned across Orchid's back and shoulders. "There," she announced. "Pretty as a picture."

The remaining girls stood and gathered around Orchid in a flesh-exposed huddle. "I'm Heather," said another blonde. "And I'm Lola," said a tall lithe of an Amazon with a bouffant of silk white hair. "I'm Lorrie Anne," said yet another. "And my name is Jesse," said the smallest of the bunch, who was wearing a glittering gold top and bottom, ash grey hair to the small of her back. Through the mirror, Orchid could see a tattoo on the inner part of her thigh, "Five inches to heaven."

They all smiled down at Orchid, leaving her to feel for a trice, impotent and very plain.

"Okay, girls," said Jasmine, clapping her hands. "Let's not frighten her. Back to your stations." The girls dispersed and continued with the task of applying more makeup and adjusting hair that as far as Orchid could tell did not need adjusting. "First things first," said Jasmine. "We only dance to seventies and some eighties. Most of the patrons prefer good old rock and roll. Sometimes Toby, he's our main DJ, will let you slip in some country music if you like. Some of our guests are oil people and prefer the twang of my dog died last night and my wife is cheating with another man. They're pretty easy to spot in their jeans, oversized buckles, and cowboy hats. That aside. Do you have anything in mind for your first set?"

There was a quick knock at the door before a black bouncer poked his head in and announced, "Five minutes, Ming." The door closed.

"Shit!" said Ming. "I still haven't made my face yet. Shit!" Quickly she began applying rouge to her cheeks and purple mascara to her eyes. "Here, let me help you," said Bethany. She went to the candid Ming, turned her in the stool, and asked, "What color lipstick?"

"Black," answered Ming.

Bethany opened a drawer, found a tube of black, and proceeded to color Ming's pouted lips.

"Now as I was saying," continued Jasmine. "Do you have any songs in mind, Orchid? You'll have to get them to Toby quick as a rabbit so he can down load them onto his software."

"I like the Stones," said Orchid, looking up at Jasmine.

"That's as good a start as any. Which song?"

Orchid thought for a moment. The first song that appropriately came to mind was "Beast of Burden." "How about 'Beast of Burden'?"

"Oh no, girl. Too angry. How about something like 'Angie,' only used it for the last song of your set. It's soft, yet strong and conveys a message of purity. The men will eat it up. Just a second. I'm going to get a pen and paper." She went to her station, found what she needed, and set a small pad and Bic pen in front of Orchid. "Okay, let's really put our heads together."

Ming jumped out of her seat, went to the mobile rack, and grabbed a blue blanket. "See you girls in ten minutes," she said, and rushed through the door.

The DJ's voice announced, "And now, gentlemen. For your viewing pleasure, I give you our little darling from the Far East, Ming." Hoots and applause ensued. David Bowie's "China Girl" wafted through the speakers.

Five minutes later, Jasmine and Orchid had selected four songs: "Bang a Gong," "Every Breath You Take" by the Police, "Back in Black," and her closing number, "Angie," which Jasmine told her she should perform to on a blanket. "Better tips," she explained. She leaned forward so that she had Orchid's ear. "Listen. We all know it's your first time. News travels fast in this profession. Don't be afraid. Let the music guide you." Standing to her full height, she filled the mirror in front of Orchid. "Now what do you plan on wearing for your first set? Vibrant colors are important."

Orchid opened the borrowed case. Sitting on top were a pair of pink tights with matching top. "How about these?" she said, holding the pieces for Jasmine to see.

"No. Not for your first set. Maybe the second or third, certainly not the first."

Orchid put them aside and dug into the case, finding the cheerleader's costume. "What about these?'

Jasmine looked both pieces over. "Yes, definitely those. You'll shine on the stage. The men won't be able to take their eyes off you. Don't let them have too much at first. Tease them with your dancing, then when 'Every Breath You Take' begins, give them a sample of your beautiful breasts. Once you've done that, work the pole, and give them lots of eye contact. Always lots of eye contact. It makes them feel like you're dancing just for them. The money will quickly follow. I go on just before you. Watch me and learn. I've been doing this for a long time. Beats the hell out of four hundred a week for a job not appreciated with brats and a husband waiting for you to come home. You'll see. It's easy money, girl."

Orchid's stomach cramped. "I've got to use the bathroom if you don't mind."

Jasmine pointed a red nail to the door marked Restroom. "There's also a shower if you feel the need to freshen up. You can get pretty sweaty on that stage."

"Thank you, Jasmine." Orchid fished into the case and retrieved a fresh tampon. She went to the bathroom, which was a lot cleaner than she had expected with two stalls and, much to her surprise, held a urinal. The tiled walls gleamed, and a deodorizer filled the room with the scent of flowers. Entering one of the stalls, she dropped her jeans and exchanged tampons, flushed, then went to the sink to wash up. Cupping cool water over her face, she caught glimpses of herself in the mirror. *This is it,* she told herself. *If you haven't hit rock bottom yet, you're going to before the night is through.* Taking the Percocet from the baggie, she put both into her mouth and swallowed with a small amount of water pooled in her hands. An automatic hand drier came to life when she put them beneath it.

Returning to the vanity somewhat restored, Jasmine had a selection of makeup lined on the table. "Sit down, honey. I'm going to make you look like star."

Orchid took a seat. Jasmine studied her face for a moment, turning her head this way and that. "I think light cinnamon for the eyes, a touch of cherry for the lips, and magenta to raise your cheekbones. But not too much. We don't want to hide those freckles."

Orchid watched as Jasmine began applying makeup. First to her eyes then cheeks and finally her lips. In a matter of minutes, she was transformed from pretty, in that Bay

Ridge Cove girl kind of way, to looking like someone on the cover of *Vogue* magazine. "There. All done. What do you think?"

Such was a face Orchid hadn't seen before. "I look so mature," she said.

"If I wasn't standing right behind you, I wouldn't believe the change myself. You're a knockout. The men are going to drool all over themselves. What do you think, girls?" She spun Orchid in the stool. Everyone oohed and aahed, telling her how beautiful she was. However, the beauty was only skin-deep, for inside, Orchid felt detached, dissimilated, dirty even. More sullied than she felt when she had to sleep with someone. On her back she could go away, pretend to be somewhere else. Someone else. On the stage, there was no place to hide.

Jasmine helped her into the outfit. When she saw the pink dots on Orchid's feet and the bruises behind her knees faintly hidden with skin toner, she said, "How long?"

Feigning ignorance, Orchid said, "How long what?"

"Come on, girl. You don't get marks like those from falling down the stairs. If you don't want to tell me, that's fine, I understand, but if you're going to poke yourself, please don't do it in my presence. I've been off the needle five years now and the thought of it makes me literally sick to my stomach."

Orchid whispered, "I'm almost clean. Madame Olivia is weaning me off the stuff."

"Well, that's good to hear. The sooner the better. How is the Dragon Lady by the way? Haven't seen her face in here for at least a year, maybe longer. Not since she convinced the twins there was more money to be made lying on their backs. Trust me, girl. There's only half a sandwich in that picnic basket. I'm surprised they can tie their own shoes. But each to his or her own as they say. Now what about footwear? Black pumps would be perfect. Did you bring a pair?"

Orchid thought for a moment. She couldn't remember packing shoes. "I guess I forgot," she said, the first buzz of Percocet kicking in.

"Shoes are very important. They add height and a touch of class to your act." She looked down at Orchid's bare feet. "I think we can fix you up. You're about a size 9, right?"

"Yes, correct. Size 9."

"Lola?" Jasmine asked over a shoulder. "You're a size 9, right?"

Lola turned in her stool. "That's right. Why?" she asked, primping her hair with a chopstick.

"Orchid forgot to bring pumps with her. Would you mind loaning her a pair of yours? Black preferably."

"No problem." Lola went the costume rack, bent forward, and came up with a pair of black pumps. She dusted them off with a strong breath and a swipe of her hands. Handing them to Orchid, she said, "They're not in the best shape. I even forgot I had them. But they'll get you through your first night. Here you go."

Orchid slipped her feet into them. They were well broke and felt very comfortable. "Thank you, Lola. I appreciate it."

"Now this is important, Orchid," said Jasmine. "When you perform with the blanket, it's vital that you take your shoes off. Let the men see you do it. It drives them crazy."

Orchid could not get over the woman she was seeing in the mirror. Her own mother wouldn't have recognized her. "If that's what you think I should do"—she looked down at her feet snug in the pumps—"men sure do get off on the strangest things, don't they?"

Jasmine laughed. "You don't know that half of it. But you'll soon learn."

Ming came through the door in a huff and tossed the blue blanket to the floor, her eyes black pits of anger.

"What's the matter?" asked Jasmine.

"What's the matter? I'll show you what's the matter." She tossed a small amount of bills on her station. Most were ones. "Seventeen fucking dollars! That's what's the matter! Bunch of tight wads in there tonight." Dropping herself onto the stool, she buried her face in the crook of her arms. "Fucking pricks," she said loud enough for everyone to hear. "I've got fucking rent to pay. How am I supposed to pay the rent with seventeen fucking dollars?"

"Maybe you'll do better on your next set," offered Lola.

"Yeah," added Jesse. "You know how it is. Night's young. Give them a chance to get liquored up.'

"Yeah. Ming. Don't fret," chimed Bethany and Lorrie Anne. "You'll do better next round. You'll see."

Heather, quiet until then, said, "Maybe if you didn't buy expensive clothing and eat at the finest restaurants all the time, you could afford to pay the rent."

"Fuck you and the horse you rode in on, Heather," Ming said wickedly from the crook of her arm. Then she raised her head. "I'd better do better, or my landlord is going to toss me out on my ass next week. Or worse, he's going to want half a dozen blowjobs in lieu of rent. The thought of putting that ugly man's cock in my mouth is sickening. I'd rather sleep on the streets."

"Now calm down, Ming," said Jasmine, hands planted firmly on her hips. "You've had slow beginnings before. We all have. The money will add up in the end. You'll see. But you better calm down before your next set. You're quite ugly right now."

Bethany, Lola, Lorrie Anne, and Jesse all agreed that the night would only get better. Heather remained indifferent.

Jasmine looked to her watch. "Okay, it's eight o'clock. I'm going to bring Orchid out front. You girls calm Ming down." Hoisting a white shirt covering her stool, she put it on and fastened the buttons to halfway. "Come on, Orchid. Mr. Millions is probably already here. Lots of eye contact. Lots of smiles. It's time to introduce you to the lion's den. And don't forget your music."

Orchid tore the songs that would plunge her deep into the world of carnal men from the pad. *Play the game. He searches for you.*

"Good luck," chimed everyone except for Ming who was still bemoaning underbreath about the paltry earnings from her last set.

* * *

Tony Millions and Mr. Black sat in the leather booth usually reserved for VIPs and whenever Tony visited the club. They had just arrived. In perfectly tailored suits, Mr. Brown and Mr. Green stood rear of Tony and Mr. Black, their hands folded low, eyes casing the club like a couple of G-men.

Lights bounced from the empty stage while "Stairway to Heaven" bled through speakers. Elevated five feet from the floor Toby the DJ stood tall in his glass booth. The club was thick with male conversation as they awaited the next act to begin. Four waitresses, in black mini skirts, white blouses, and red bowties tended to the tables, pearly whites preceding them. All ten slot machines were occupied. Two bartenders filled orders with expeditious apropos while they made small talk with the patrons seated at the rail.

Tony took a sip of his Scotch. "How was Orchid when you dropped her off?" he asked Mr. Black.

"She seemed compliant, man. Don't worry. The other girls are taking good care of her. She'll perform well. I guarantee it."

"Madame Olivia seems to share your sentiment. I on the other hand still have doubts. There's something we're not seeing with that one. A hidden agenda if you will. As though she carries within an enormous secret. Something that lies beneath her conscious exterior." Taking another sip of Scotch, he looked to Mr. Brown. "What's your take on our little Orchid, Mr. Brown?"

Mr. Brown leaned forward and rested his hands on the leather. "I agree with Mr. Black. From what I've seen and heard, Orchid has transgressed to her new life with flying colors. You've got nothing to worry about."

Tony rolled this over a moment, spinning the Scotch within the tumbler. Regarding his new Rolex, he said, "I guess we'll soon find out, won't we?"

Jasmine and Orchid appeared through the exit door behind the stage. All eyes fell upon them as they moved to the DJ booth. Orchid noticed Tony and his henchmen right away. She didn't make eye contact, but instead climbed the steps leading to the glass booth. In blue silk shirt, and blue jeans, Toby looked down at her. An Afro, from which a white pick stood, circled a face that was flat yet sharp at the same time. Long black whiskers, tied in place with pieces of red ribbon, fell from his chin. "You must be Orchid," he said with a smile. "Have you got some music for me?" He reached a slender hand. Four gold rings spelling *love* shone from fingers.

"Yes, I am," said Orchid and handed him the piece of paper. The Percocet were really starting to kick in. She could feel the effects in her face, hands, and feet. Behind her, standing on the second riser and looming over a patron who had already had too much to drink, Jasmine's eyes sought the attention of a bouncer nearby.

Toby's eyes scanned the selected songs. "Is this the order you want them in?"

"Yes, please, Toby," said Orchid.

"Good choice of music. Are you sure you haven't done this before?"

"Jasmine helped me." She looked behind her just as the drunken patron reached out to grab a handful of breast. Jasmine pushed him away. Almost immediately, a brute of a black man and easily weighing three hundred pounds, most of which was gymnasium muscle, grabbed the overtly friendly drunk by the collar and, without a word, ushered him out of the club with his arm bent halfway up his back.

Jasmine joined Orchid on the top step. "So what do you think, Toby, beautiful, isn't she?"

Toby set the list on one of his electronic gizmos. "Stairway to Heaven" ended. "Just a second," he said then put his face close to the mike hanging from the ceiling. "Gentlemen, gentlemen, gentlemen." His voice boomed throughout the club. "It's that time once again. Set your eyes on stunned. Fresh back from her *Penthouse* debut, Club Paradise is pleased to welcome one of your favorites and mine, Jesse. Put your hands together and let her know how much she was missed." Dry ice floated across the stage. Most of the patrons applauded. Overhead lights went dark for a moment. "All I Want to Do Is Make Love to You" by Heart aired through the speakers. When the lights brightened again, Jesse was hanging from one of two brass poles, ash grey hair flirting with the material of her glittering gold hot pants. Jesse slipped from the pole, her eyes locked on the faces surrounding the stage. The white fog lifted in a swirl, covering all but her face. Leaning forward, she crawled across the stage like a beautiful predator stalking its prey.

"Wow," said Orchid, face all abuzz. "That's very dramatic."

"Taught her everything she knows," said Jasmine, pleased with herself.

Toby asked, "So do want dry ice for your act, Orchid?"

She thought for a moment. *Dry ice might hide the fact that I'm going to be terrified on that stage. Between the Percocet and the fog, I just might make it through the night without looking too foolish*. "Sure. Why not."

"That a girl," said Jasmine. "Jump in with both feet. I'm on after Jesse. Pay attention. I'll leave my blanket on the stage for you since you don't have one of your own."

"You know. I didn't know what to expect when I got here. I thought maybe you girls might make things difficult for me. But you know what? You're all nice. Well, excluding Ming. "

"Hey. We're just women trying to make a living. No biggie. Nine to five, Monday to Friday, just isn't our thing. We don't get involved with the patrons, and most of us are drug free. And don't fret about Ming. She's a drama queen. Has to make a big fuss about everything. Toby here takes good care of us, and if there's any trouble, well, you saw what happens. On top of all that, on average, we earn about five grand a week, each."

"Whoa," was all Orchid could summon, for the amount was over the top. Just like the Palace. She looked to the bouncer standing near the entrance, whose thick arms were folded across his chest, mean eyes scanning the crowd, face etched in stone.

For a brief second, Orchid's gaze met Tony Millions who smiled and raised a tumbler. Then he lifted a stubby finger and waggled for her to join him. Mr. Brown and Mr. Green watched Jesse as she, on hands and knees, approached a group of young men, moving toward them ass first and slapping a cheek hard, much to their drunken delight. Flashing a breast, she disappeared back into the white mist. That little display of naughtiness ushered the opening of many wallets. The men seated on three sides of the stage held varying denominations of bills high enough for Jesse to see, who, in turn, using only her teeth, plucked them from their waiting hands.

Jasmine had witnessed Tony's beckoning gesture. "I better get you over to *him*," she said with an air if distaste. "Can't keep the boss waiting."

"Well, it was nice to meet you, Orchid," said Toby. "I'll keep the lights soft so they won't bother you too much. And I'll really give you a good intro."

"Thanks, Toby. I appreciate everything you're going to do for me." She looked toward Tony who was still watching her. "I guess I better get this over with," she sighed, face buzzing.

When they arrived at Tony's booth, he motioned for Orchid to sit next to him. She could smell his expensive cologne from three feet away. Without desire to be too close, she took a seat at the very edge of the booth. Jasmine fell in next to Mr. Black and looped an arm around his shoulder. Orchid looked to the faces surrounding her. They were blurry, almost comical because of the Percocet. So obvious were they in their suits and cool, self-possessed demeanors, Orchid thought, they might as well be wearing signs that read, ORGANIZED CRIMES R US.

"Well, if you were not sitting right next to me, I would not have believed it," said Tony. "You are quite the striking woman, Orchid. A far cry from when we first met." Draining the Scotch, he motioned for a nearby waitress to bring another.

Orchid lowered her eyes. "I guess I owe you a thank-you for that, so thank you."

"Madame Olivia tells me that you have adapted into our little business nicely. That you've found a second home at the Shangri-La Palace. I am as proud of you as a father would be of his only daughter."

Orchid felt she might throw up. To think that this bastard even considered them as close as father and daughter literally made her sick to her stomach. Putting a hand to her mouth, she swallowed the rising bile. "Sorry," she said. "I must have eaten something that's not agreeing with me."

"Don't sweat it, sweetheart. I understand if you're a little nervous. That stage can be overwhelming at times. But I know you will do just fine."

A stunning waitress set a Scotch in front of Tony. Jesse was halfway through her act. Jasmine put a hand over Mr. Black's. "Gotta go and get ready," she said.

"You look ready to me, baby."

"We women are never quite ready. You should know that by now." She looked to Orchid. "Remember what I told you and you'll do fine." She slid out of the booth.

"Thank you, Jasmine," Orchid said to her fleeting back. The Percocet had caused her throat to go dry. "May I have a drink of water, please."

"Sure thing, sweetheart. Anything else?" asked Tony.

"No. Just water." Tony's face zoomed in and out. Orchid almost laughed.

"Mr. Brown? Fetch Orchid a bottle of water. And bring me a cigar. Make sure its fresh."

"Sure thing, Tony."

Orchid watched her rapist leave. She'd give anything to see him suffer. Her eyes fell upon the face of Mr. Green. To date, it was the closest she had seen him. A strong jaw supported girlish lips, a bent nose, and ethereal blue eyes. His forehead was as thick as a brick, and his red hair and goatee added a sinister advocacy to his features. There was something about him that terrified her. He caught her staring and smiled, his lips no longer girlish, more contemptuous was what Orchid now considered.

She looked quickly away, a cold shiver exorcising up and down her spine. If it wasn't for the down syndrome effects of the Percocet, she would have gotten up and run for her life, for he frightened far more than Mr. Brown and Mr. Black combined. *But why?* Focusing on Jesse, who was nearing the end of her set, she leaned into the palm of a hand and rested her buzzing face.

The dry ice was no longer present. Marigolds of light swept the stage in a dizzying, dazzling dance. Jesse was upside down on a brass pole, the muscles of her legs securing her there. Ash hair swept the stage. She cupped an impish breasts and pinched the nipple much to the delight of those down front. Led Zeppelin's "All of My Love" slipped into the final chorus then ended.

The club erupted in a cacophony of "More! More! More!" Satisfied patrons having been duly entertained by Jesse's sexually charged performance and by the music from back in the day.

Toby's practiced voice reminded them to show their appreciation and help boost the economy with a little bit of spending. This ushered the opening of many wallets. Jesse quickly collected their hard-earned dollars. Once she had gathered all of it, she looked out to Orchid, gave her a thumbs-up, and mouthed, "Good luck."

"What's the matter, Orchid?" asked Tony. "Don't care for the company?"

Orchid half-turned so that she was looking at him from only one eye. "It's not that at all," she said. "I need to watch. So I can learn. You wouldn't want me to look stupid up there, would you?"

"No, of course not," said Tony, his smile reassuring. "You and I both know you're going to do fine." Raising his Scotch, he tilted it toward her. "As they say in show business, break a leg." He swallowed half of the contents.

Mr. Black did the same with his cola, smiling arrogantly. He was not big on drinking, his rationalization being that it fogged the mind and made you slow, and he was always on duty. 24/7.

Mr. Brown returned with Orchid's water and Tony's cigar. Handing Tony the cigar, he lit it before setting the water in front of Orchid. A thunder cloud of smoke billowed across the table.

"Would you like me to open it for you?" asked Mr. Brown, his malevolent black eyes twinkling with certain knowledge, laughing at her.

Orchid wanted to tell him to fuck off, instead, she grabbed the water from the table, twisted off the cap, took a drink, and narrowed her eyes at him, the silence between victim and abuser as loud as a war.

Tony drew on the cigar, releasing a funnel of blue smoke toward the ceiling. He'd already noticed the dilation of Orchid's pupils when she first sat down. That was good. Loosened inhibitions, though her dislike of Mr. Brown remained unyielding, unaffected by the drug. He couldn't blame her though, for there was no doubt in his mind that Mr. Brown had indeed raped her. "That will be all, Mr. Brown," he said with authority, waving him back to his post. Reaching across the table, he put a hand on Orchid's forearm, applying a pressure usually reserved as a sign of affection. "Pamela and I are throwing a little get-together tonight. Just a few friends. Cocktails. Hors d'oeuvres. That sort of thing. Perhaps you would be kind enough to join us. So that I can show you off. After your sets of course. I can have Mr. Black here drive you."

Orchid looked down at his hand, her skin crawling where he was touching her. Wanting to reach out and scratch his eyes, she said, "I don't think tonight's a very good idea. Madame Olivia is expecting me back once I'm done. I'll be tired and just want to go to bed. Thank Pamela for me, but for now I think I'll stick close to the Palace." It was bold of her to say, but she didn't care, the Percocet were lending her courage. Yanking her arm from Tony's grasp, they locked eyes.

Tony smiled. He was not used to being turned down, especially from the workers. He gave her kudos for showing a little moxie.

Orchid was first to look away.

Tony seized the moment. "You know that I can insist you attend. Madame Olivia would understand. This I assure you."

Orchid wondered how far she could push him. If he really pressed that she attend, she would go, knowing she had no other choice; but maybe, just maybe, she could convince him that it wasn't in his best interest. Taking a swallow of water and as succinct as she could put it, she said, "If the reason you want me there is to show me off, then all I can tell you is that I'm going to be tired, probably cranky. As you very well know, it's that time of month. I'm certainly bitchy during my period, and I don't make a good drunk. If that's what you want, then fine, I'll go. Your choice."

"Did you hear that, Mr. Black? Our little Orchid is all grown-up. Thinks she knows what's best for her."

Expanding his perpetual smile and folding his large hands in front of him, Mr. Black said, "What are you going to do, man? Sounds like she's made up her mind to be unsociable."

"Yes. It does," said Tony. "No matter. I'll decide whether you are to attend once I've seen you dance. You *will* perform well for us, won't you, Orchid?"

Taking another swallow of water, she took in the faces around her. Screwing the cap back onto the Avian, she let the Percocet do all the talking. "I'm going to do what I've been told to do and nothing more. Once my sets are over, I have every intention of returning to the Palace. Even if I have to walk. Now if you don't mind, I'm going to the DJ booth to watch Jasmine." Scooping the bottle from the table, she stood. "Anything else?" she fearlessly asked.

Mr. Black was about to reprimand her; however, Tony raised a hand to silence him. "Let her go," he said.

Spinning on borrowed heels, Orchid went to the DJ booth where she stood on the steps, terribly pleased with herself.

Toby smiled down at her. "I didn't expect to see you so soon."

"I hope you don't mind my standing here. I didn't care for the company."

"Can't say that I blame you. Just a second." Leaning his face toward the mike, Toby announced, "Gentlemen. It's that time again. How about a little hot chocolate to sooth your souls? Put your hands together for our very own Jasmine."

Applause filled the club. The bagpipe intro to "Centerfold" filled the room, and the men around the stage fell silent, their hungry eyes ready for the next flesh act. Pulsating red, white, and blue lights embraced the hard wood flooring.

Jasmine, in a purple teddy over a glittering silver two-piece, appeared through the door, walked the steps leading to the stage with blanket in hand, and spread it between the brass poles. Silver stilettos added to her lofty stature. Taking to one of the poles, she swung round and round effortlessly, her head reversed, molasses eyes riveted to those nearest.

Dancing in place to the music, Toby asked, "So are you ready for your maiden voyage?"

Orchid looked up at him and smiled. "If I'm not ready now, I'll never be." The pinnacle charge of the Percocet was leveling. She was no longer viewing things through the zooming lens of a dysfunctional camera.

Toby's thin eyes went to the club owner and his entourage, flashing what looked to Orchid like pure hatred. "Don't do it for them, Orchid. Don't let them have the satisfaction of knowing that you're under their control. Forget they're even here."

"I'll try. Thanks, Toby. Sounds to me that you don't care for their company either."

"Hey, I got a job to do, rent to pay, and *he* signs the paychecks. I know what they're all about, believe me. I've been working here for four years and have seen many things, including other girls like you, pressed under their thumb and forced into a lifestyle of their bidding. They'll all get theirs one day. You'll see. God will smite them. It's only a matter of time."

"The sooner the better," agreed Orchid.

"I just hope I'm not in the way when he does. God can get pretty nasty when he's pissed." Toby gave her the thumbs-up, lit a cigarette, and proceeded to dance.

Orchid watched Jasmine perform for twenty minutes teasing the crowd with her body language, offering visual pragmatism to their fantasies. On the brass pole, she was as lithe as a butterfly floating on the wind. On the blanket, she made love to an invisible paramour, driving the audience into a frenzy. Orchid could actually feel the testosterone in the club multiply tenfold. Money flew onto the stage as the last song of her set ("Lady") neared its conclusion.

"Okay, you better get ready, Orchid," said Toby. "Go to the stage door and wait until I'm finished with your intro. Just lose yourself in the music. You'll do fine. Good luck."

"Thanks, Toby." Descending the steps, Orchid made her way to the exit door, hungry eyes on her backside, and pushed through it. There she waited. "Lady" came to an end. The club erupted with cheers and whistles. So nervous was Orchid that her knees actually knocked, regardless of the drug coursing through her body. A moment passed before Jasmine, holding a fist full of money, came through the door. "Okay," she said. "You're up. Just remember what I told you and everything will be fine. I'll see you in the dressing room when you're done." Kissing Orchid on the cheek, she added, "That's for good luck. Knock 'em dead, kiddo."

"Would you mind staying with me until it's time for me to go on? I'm really nervous."

"Sure," said Jasmine, looking down at the money that was by far more than seventeen dollars. "I can count this later. Ming is going to be pissed. Too bad, so sad." Drawing an arm around Orchid's waist, now sisters of the flesh industry, they waited.

"Gentle, gentlemen, gentlemen," boomed Toby's voice. "And I use that term loosely. How about a little back-to-back action. Club Paradise is pleased to offer for your viewing pleasure its newest star. She's a redhead with bad intentions. Never before seen on a Vegas stage. Put your hands together and give her a big Paradise welcome. I give you the unforgettable... superlative... Orchid."

"Bang a Gong" shook the speakers.

"Well, here I go," Orchid sighed.

"The blanket's on the edge of the stage. Don't use it until your last song. Be brave. Now go on."

Orchid pushed through the door. The stage was covered in a layer of dry ice, its vanilla flavor filling her senses. Soft blue lighting lit the stage as Toby promised and somehow felt warm against her flesh. When she climbed the steps, pushing the thickness of her hair over her shoulders, there was a wave of applause and whistles that filled the club to the rafters.

Stepping into the fog, she nearly tripped over the blanket she couldn't see. For a moment, she just stood there, her eyes searching. The men seated around the stage ogled her. Someone booed, the negative rant quickly followed by, "Don't just stand there. Do something."

Orchid let her mind drift. She returned home to the privacy of her bedroom. Music played. The faces of the men around the stage became the faces of the stuffed animals sitting on her bed. The visual made her smile and caused her green eyes to radiat with the light of complacency. Her presence on the stage became surreal. While a part of her was back home, something deep within, something primal, something morally corrupt surfaced on the stage. Sashaying to the nearest pole, she wrapped an arm and leg around it, then proceeded to twirl like a top. Her head dropped so that her hair hung freely, a flaming sweep within the fog.

Animal faces all smiles now.

Descending the pole, Orchid eased herself to the floor. On hands and knees she crawled forward through the miasma, an animalistic scowl flashing from prismatic eyes, hair blanketing the yokes of her shoulders. She hissed like a serpent and moaned like a feline in heat, snapping at the air with her teeth. Attacking the face nearest, sharp nails slashed at the air and came within a slim margin of removing flesh. The club fell silent, her audience mesmerized by what they were witnessing. From his private booth, the smile on Tony Millions's face was that of grandiose incredulity, his Scotch varnished eyes dollar signs.

Out of necessity to survive, and to guard those she cared about, Rebecca White, daughter of a simple fisherman, prisoner to the sex trade industry and now drug abuser, was born a prodigy of the stage.

Another page turned.

* * *

BOOK THREE

Destiny's Child

51

Christmas Eve

DECEMBER 24 was an overcast day with intermittent periods of rain, the temperature, an un-Vegas-like fifty-four degrees. Hotel rates were up due to the holidays as was the influx of fortune-seekers.

Six-year-old Billy Warren had been missing for three months. The story had been well documented by state media for the first month. Las Vegas police, sheriff's offices, state trooper detachments, and volunteers had led an exhaustive search, scouring desert terrain, abandoned buildings, playgrounds, and anywhere else a six-year-old boy might have taken refuge or been lost. State pedophiles were investigated. Nothing. Two months into the investigation, the media coverage became less attentive, ratings needing fresh meat for the masses to chew on. Now the story received only an honorable mention on the late-night news. Billy Warren's file had been demoted from search and rescue to recovery.

Distraught parents, Rick and Karen Warren, had pleaded through the media for their son's safe return, though Rick Warren knew without a doubt what had transpired, his gambling debt to Tony Millions the fate of his only son.

Entrepreneur that he was, Tony Millions harvested little Billy's heart, liver, and kidneys, selling them to an associate of his in South America for a substantial profit, the knife skills of Mr. Green indeed having come in handy. The remainder of Billy Warren's dismembered body had been broken down to nothing more than sludge in a fifty-gallon drum of hydrochloric acid; a young life terminated because of a father's debilitating disease.

Assuring the virtue of his wife, and to save his own neck, Rick Warren would not divulge this information to the police, which in turn had kept him in Tony Million's good books, so that he, when need be, could borrow further monies for his gambling proclivities. Within the span of time his son had been missing, Rick Warren was once again indebted to Tony for another twenty-five large. A debt he would not be able to repay.

Before the onset of the new year, he would join his son on the missing persons list, his wife Karen abducted and traded throughout the white slave market in Romania time and time again until she was too old and worthless. Tony Millions's continual pressing of his unremitting dictum, *Never leave loose ends.*

Mr. White had returned from his business venture, the results of which had been distributed to all points north, south, east, and west. The Santangello family of Chicago was more than pleased with their share of the three hundred kilos and flooded the east side, taking control, once more, of the fought-after territory.

The posse was intact once again. Three kilos of Columbia's uncut finest sat secure in Tony Millions's safe. It was indeed going to be a merry Christmas.

Due to the in-climate weather, Tony's annual outdoor Christmas party would have to be held indoors, the guests to attend including members of the gaming commission, council members, hotel owners, captains of commerce, and stars of Vegas's entertainment industry. A four-piece band, Last Dance, was hired for the entertainment.

Tony was in the kitchen with the catering company's head chef, reviewing the menu for the midnight feast, when his cell phone chirped. "Yes."

It was Mr. Brown. "I'm at the Palace."

"Just a minute." Tony excused himself and went into his study where Norman hung upside down in his cage. "Who loves yah, baby?" it mimicked when Tony entered the room. Tony sat on the edge of his desk, wiped nothing from his pant leg with the tips if his fingers, and said, "Okay. We can talk now."

"Subjects A and B are home. Mr. Green is keeping a close eye."

"Good. Escort Orchid to the club then carry on. Once A and B are secure, go back to the club and wait until Orchid has completed her sets then bring her here."

"Anything else?"

"Leave no trace."

"Do I ever?"

"Good evening, Mr. Brown." Closing the cell, Tony returned it to a breast pocket. Looking to his watch, he saw that it was 7:00 p.m. The guests would start arriving within the hour. By 10:00 p.m. Karen Warren (subject A) would know of her son's fate before disappearing from American soil. Rick Warren, subject B, come Christmas morning, would be resting comfortably on the bottom of Lake Mead, cement shoes to weigh him down. Fish and other marine life would leave no trace. It was going to be a silent and very deadly night.

* * *

Rebecca's eighteenth birthday came and went with a small celebration at the Palace that included champagne, cake, dancing, and gifts of panties and drive-the-men-crazy bras for whenever she danced at the club. This coming of age was also the night she had intercourse, unknowingly, with a priest. Cost a silencing $2,000. This tidbit of information was kept from her until the session was over. Orchid, Tiffany Rose, and a forgotten Rebecca White spent the remainder of her birthday vomiting in the shower. *Happy fucking birthday.*

During the weeks leading to the holidays, the Shangri-La Palace had become a beehive of activity. Clientele arriving by 11:00 a.m. and continuing, more or less, nonstop throughout the days.

The welcoming room was decorated for the season, complete with an artificial Christmas tree where colorfully wrapped presents sat at its skirt. Garlands, streamers, and lights were hung just so and a fist of mistletoe dangled from the entrance. Old-time periodic favorites poured through the speakers: Elvis's "Blue Christmas," Burl Ives's "Silver and Gold," Frank Sinatra's "White Christmas," etc., etc., etc.

The ladies of the Shangri-La Palace were dressed in their finest attire. A secret Santa had been held the prior week. Orchid had drawn Madame Olivia, and she had bought her a new gold-plated lighter with her nickname *Oli* inscribed on it. It was going to be the first Christmas in Orchid's life where she wasn't surrounded by family and friends. This irregularity caused her enough reflective grief that she'd spent the morning crying in her room. To make matters worse, it was that time of the month, and she dreaded the thought of having to spend Christmas Eve dancing for drunken buffoons. Her only reprieve was that the club would be closed by eleven, being the holidays, then she would be whisked to Tony Millions's mansion where she would join the others in celebration.

It had taken Madame Olivia's disciplinary charge and two months to wean Orchid away from the heroin. For two weeks, as she neared the end of her addiction, her nights had become filled with demonic possession, body shakes, hallucinations, and sheet-drenching nightmares. If it weren't for the painkiller, which she was now abusively dependent upon, she thought she would surely go mad. When the end came, it was as though she had broken through an invisible barrier and was irrefutably freed from her own personal hell.

Madame Olivia assured her that her wanton need of Percocet would be dealt with over a matter of time and before she could say, "I'm not a junkie anymore," she would be clean of it as well.

Orchid sat on a bar stool, one leg crossed over the other and dressed in a flowing amethyst gown cut low to expose the freckles leading to the budding curvature of her breasts. Her hair had grown inches and hung loosely across the open back of what Oli had called "the nicest evening gown I've seen in a long time." Completing the ensemble was a pair of mint green open-toed pumps. At her feet was the valise containing her costumes for the night. She was sipping a margarita while Li Ling mixed drinks behind the bar. Seven German men had arrived via limousine and were intent on getting drunk before taking part in the world's oldest profession.

Gypsy, Brit, Brat, Tinker, and Madame Olivia mingled with the Heineken-drinking Europeans. There was a certain festive atmosphere in the Palace, leaving Orchid to feel far more homesick than she already was.

Dressed in a brown suit, white shirt with silk tie, Mr. Brown stood near the entrance. He had just finished speaking to someone on his cell, all the while staring at Orchid and creeping her out. It was usually Mr. Black who escorted her to the club, but he was at the mansion with Tony helping with the preparations for the big bash.

Mr. White was at the club distributing thousand-dollar bonuses to the dancers as well as five-hundred-dollar bonuses to the waitresses, bouncers, bartenders, and DJs. Inscrutable as Tony Millions was, he knew how to take care of his *family*. Like everything else in Vegas, money was the lifeblood pumping through the hearts of the God-bless-us-everyone gluttony.

Orchid finished the margarita just as Mr. Brown moved toward her.

It was time to leave.

"Are you ready?" he asked, stopping next to her, obsessive black eyes fixated on the V cut of the dress.

"Stop staring, you pig," deadpanned Orchid. Slipping off the stool, she picked up the valise and said, "Let's go."

"After you, dollface."

Oli noticed Orchid was leaving. "Just a minute, Orchid," she called out over Elvis Presley's "Jingle Bell Rock."

Mr. Brown continued to the entrance. Oli was in a very festive mood. She had been drinking champagne since the first guests arrived. In a white Oscar de la Renta, she looked every bit the part of what she was. Prada stilettos covered her feet and a pair of red chopsticks held the coil of her hair in place. Diamonds glittered from her ears, wrists, fingers, and left ankle; and she was noticeably wobbly. Wrapping her arms around Orchid, she supposed for the third time in the last hour. "Merry Christmas, my dear."

In a sad tone, Orchid said, "Merry Christmas, Oli."

Oli held her at arm's length, eyes swimming with the influence of alcohol. "Come now, darling. Don't be sad. It's Christmas. You know. Rejoice in our Lord's birth and all that shit." She released a throaty laugh. "The night will fly by, then you'll join the rest of us at Tony's and we'll all have a merry old time. You'll see."

"I guess so."

"Did I tell you how ravishing you look this evening?"

"Yes. And thank you." Orchid feigned a smile.

"There. Now that's better." Kissing Orchid on both cheeks, she wiped the resulting residue with a thumb. From the entrance, Mr. Brown looked impatient, checking his watch, leering in a most un-Christmas-like manner. "You better get going. Mr. Brown is giving us the eye. I'll see you in a few hours, okay?"

Smiling, Orchid nodded, grudgingly turned, and joined Mr. Brown at the entrance. He held the door open and bowed. "After you, sweetheart."

Cool air swathed Orchid's face, arms, and legs, giving her a chill. Stepping into the grey evening where Mr. Black's Cadillac sat waiting, something tugged at her, stopping her mid stride as she was about to step down from the entrance. It birthed from deep within, drawing her forward as if she were a tether and someone was pulling the other end. Without warning, a delinquent gust forced the hair from her shoulders. Filling her lungs with it, Orchid smiled with genuine fervor. Something good was going to happen on this otherwise ruinous day. The errant draft was whispering it to her mind's ear in a voice that only she could hear.

From behind, Mr. Brown said, "Okay. Let's go, Orchid. I've got work to do."

* * *

It was nearing 9:00 p.m. when Johnny decided he would join his friends for a few beers at Club Paradise. Spending Christmas Eve in a strip club was not his idea of holiday cheer; nonetheless, it would be a far better alternative than just sitting in his rented room, alone, the TV and the shenanigans of the mouse his only company. His exhaustive search for whomever, a search he was more and more contemplating on ending, could wait a day. It was after all the holidays, though he didn't feel very celebratory, being away from home. It would be the first Christmas in a very long time where he didn't wake up with Dallas lying by his side. Or to sit around the tree, listening to his father retell tales of back in the day when he was a young stockman and the land was untamed.

He'd showered and rebraided his hair, affixing the feather and tether near the end of the braid so that it sat over his left shoulder. Jeans, a new dress shirt, black, with pearl buttons up the front and on the cuffs would be his attire for the night. He had amassed a good amount of money working at the Cosmopolitan project. During his wearisome search one night, he'd stopped at a men's clothing store and treated himself to the shirt.

Taking a hundred from the two thousand stashed beneath a loose floorboard, he stuffed the bills into a pocket.

According to the guys at work, Club Paradise maintained a strict dress code. No T-shirts. No baseball caps. No threadbare jeans. No shoes, no service. After he polished his boots, he cinched his belt, clicked off the television, gathered his keys, and left the small rented room, locking the door behind him.

Christmas music emanated from several of the rooms, filling the otherwise-dingy hallway with joy, hope, and peace on earth. As he made his way to the front door, the turquoise stone in his pocket began to vibrate as if it were responding to the music. He stopped, pulled it out, and held it in his hand, looking at it curiously. To his surprise, he found it to be extremely cold and pulsing with life. An errant shiver ran up his arm as if his veins had been injected with iced water; however, by the time the rhythmic palpitations extended to the rest of his body, it was as warm as liquid sunshine, filling his being with a certain vitality. *More Konahee magic,* he thought. *But what did it all mean? Perhaps it was her way of saying merry Christmas.* Closing his hand around the stone, just in case she was somehow listening, he brought it to his lips and whispered, "Merry Christmas, Konahee."

As though the message had been transmitted and received, the stone ceased with its animated dance and returned to being nothing more than a colorful rock. Slipping it to the pocket, Johnny opened the door and stepped outside. He was instantly slapped by a rogue wind, carrying with it the force of mule kick. Johnny stumbled backward, an arm across his face. The wayward wind filled the hallway with a ghostly lament, sounding very much like Jacob Marley. Johnny's spine tingled. Then the grieving wind abruptly stopped as though Mother had flipped a switch. *What the hell was that all about?*

Momentarily stunned by what he perceived to be an omen of sorts, he stood on the leaning stoop. Whether or not the traceable portent was good or bad, he imagined he would soon find out.

Christmas lights strung on the balconies of surrounding apartment complexes were all aglow, the faint sounds of festive music carried on the air. *Christmas was in full swing. No matter how poor one was.*

The street and sidewalks were still slick from the last cloud burst, a recurring theme for the day. The night sky held a grey, leaden weight, and the air was moderately cool. Humidity 68 percent according to the television in his room. There were few people out. An elderly couple held hands, strolling nonchalantly in the glow of streetlamps, forever in the prime of their youthful love. The owner of the corner store was closing shop, his stooped figure villainous in the shadows of light. A medium-sized mutt with extended ribs roamed back and forth between buildings in search of its Christmas meal.

Johnny called out to it, "Here, fella," but the stray only cowered and disappeared behind one of the low rent structures.

Once he was in the truck, Johnny engaged the engine and pulled away from the curb. "Feliz Navidad" was playing on the radio. He headed south on Baltimore until he reached the Stratosphere Hotel all decked out for the holidays where people exited cabs and limos. An African American employee, dressed as Santa, welcomed the gamblers as they hurried to their capricious fates.

Vegas went all-out during Christmas and New Year's, the season attracting the loners of the world, romance-bound couples, the mega rich, and the destitute, thinking their luck might change because of the holidays. Everything cost more, and why shouldn't it? It was Christmas after all, and wasn't that the season for giving?

Easing his way into the knot of traffic on Las Vegas Boulevard, he approached an extreme limo with hot tub in which a half-dozen half-naked partiers were enjoying the five-hundred-dollar-an-hour ride. He waved and honked as he passed, maneuvering the Ford through the stop-and-go traffic. When he reached Desert Inn Road, he turned left, found Paradise Road, hung a right, and headed to the Club. From there he could see it in the distance, blue LED lights bright and welcoming. Johnny imagined his coworkers were already past the do-not-drive stage.

Unable to find a space out front, he drove the pickup to the rear of the blue lit structure and found a suitable spot near the exit door. Smoking a cigarette, tattoos for sleeves, a bouncer stood between a Mercedes and a Porsche. Johnny parked across from the Mercedes just as the sky opened up and a light rain fell from the darkness. He locked the doors, engaged the security alarm, and headed for the main entrance, the smoking bouncer giving him the once-over as he passed.

* * *

Orchid sat at her designated station readying herself for her first set. She had changed out of the luxurious evening gown. Her salute to the Burl Ives classic were a pair of red suede pumps, gold satin miniskirt and silver vest. A few minutes later, her eyelashes, lips, and hair sparkled with silver glitter.

Tony Millions had insisted that all the dancers' costumes for the night were to be reflective of the holidays. Jasmine and Ming were each garbed in Santa's little helper outfits. Jesse wore the green and brown of an elf complete with pointed ears. Lorrie Anne, the white flowing ensemble of an angel. Bethany, Lola, and Heather had already finished for the day and were by then comfortable in their family's homes.

Mr. White had appeared earlier presenting each of the dancers envelopes filled with cash. Orchid's was waiting for her when she arrived. It sat in front of her, next to the handbag containing the Percocet she would need to get her through the night. Unlike the other girls, she had not bothered to count its contents.

"What are you going to do with your bonus, Orchid?" asked Jesse from her station.

"I don't know. Save it I guess," said Orchid insouciantly.

"What's the fun in that? You should pamper yourself. Maybe go to an all-day spa. Buy something completely unnecessary."

"What are you going to do with yours?" asked Orchid, turning in her swivel so she was facing Jesse.

"I'm going to give mine to the SPCA. I know it's not much, but I can't help feeling sorry for all those stray dogs and cats. I'll get some comfort knowing that I've at least helped somewhat."

"That's nice. Maybe I'll do the same. Although I've never had one as a friend, I just love dogs. They're so dependable. Great companions, and their love is unconditional." For a brief moment, Orchid envisioned Chase and Caleb and how the two of them were inseparable, even in death.

"What are you thinking about?"

"Your mention of dogs made me think of a couple of friends of mine."

"Oh." Jesse could see the sadness in Orchid's face. "Do you miss them?"

"Very much. Yes."

"Well, why don't you call them? Here. Use my cell phone." Reaching into her purse, Jesse extracted a slim pink phone and tossed it.

Orchid caught it between her palms and looked down at it. There was no one to call. "I can't right now, but thanks. You see, my friend is a little boy and he would be in bed by now. I'll call him tomorrow. When I know he'll be up. Wish him a Merry Christmas." She tossed the phone back.

"That's nice that you have a young friend. What's his name?"

Before Orchid could answer, the dressing room door opened. Jasmine breezed into the room wearing only the red-and-white bottoms of her outfit and with a blanket rolled into a ball against her chest. In one hand was a thick wedge of money, dangling in the other, high-heeled shoes. She went to her table, sat down, dropped the money, and toweled the blanket around her midsection. The shoes clattered to the floor. "There must be three hundred dollars here," she beamed. "They're feeling mighty generous tonight." She looked to Orchid. "Toby says you're up in ten."

"Okay, thanks, Jasmine."

Lorrie Anne and Ming got up from their tables to admire the stack of money sitting in front of Jasmine. "Oooh. You did really good, girl," Lorrie Anne commented.

"I just hope there's still some money left for me when I go on," said Ming, a little miffed.

"So what's his name?" Jesse coaxed, applying a slick coat of blue to her lips. "Your little friend? I'll bet he's really excited about tomorrow."

Orchid swivelled back to the mirror so she could study her face. The woman staring back at her had aged years in a brief period of time. She had become a hand-me-down, passed from man to man like some tarnished trophy granted to the highest bidder, mutated into a living, breathing mannequin of the flesh industry. *Who are you? Is Rebecca White gone forever?* Opening the handbag, she removed two tablets of her nouveau addiction and answered Jesse's question. "His name is Caleb, and he's the nicest little boy you could ever meet."

"That's nice. I hope you get to see him real soon."

With ten minutes to go before her set, Orchid went to the bathroom. Locking the door, she swallowed the mind-numbing provisions of her dependency without the benefit of water, tears of remorse dripping from her chin. She sat on the toilet and waited.

* * *

Johnny found his friends easily enough. They were seated in a booth, back from the tables and a good thirty feet from the empty stage. Much to his surprise, they were each wearing suits. "Spirit in the Sky" pumped through speakers dangling from the ceiling. The energy in the smoke-filled establishment was on high alert. One armed bandits lined one wall and were being primed with money. Leggy waitresses carried full trays. The bar was three deep with thirsty patrons where a pair of bartenders acrobatically flipped liquor bottles into the air. Standing alone at the end of the bar, a Caesar in hand, was a man dressed in a white suit who seemed to be eyeing everyone. Johnny suspected he might be the owner or very least the manager.

"Hey, amigo!" cried Hector Sanchez when he saw Johnny. "Sit down! Sit down! We were wondering if you were going to show up tonight." He smiled two rows of gold-encrusted teeth, picked up a shot glass of tequila, and downed it.

"Hi, guys," said Johnny. "Nice place. No wonder you come here so often. I feel a little underdressed though. You didn't tell me you were coming so formal."

Hennrick Schmidt, a German immigrant who had been working on the Cosmopolitan project for the past two years as a pipe fitter smiled and said, "Don't worry about it. You look fine."

Johnny took a seat. On the table were nine empty shot glasses, three bottles of Heineken, and an ashtray holding a thick cigar. Smoke curled in a ballet of blue rings and loops.

"What'll you have, Johnny? I'm buying the next round," said David. "You just missed the last act. Really nice. Dark and smooth like melted chocolate. I swear she was giving me the eye." David Manning, an electrician, had been working on the Cosmopolitan for as long as Hector.

"You wish," teased Hector, punching him in the arm. "What woman, unless she was blind and brain-dead, would have anything to do with your ugly ass." He laughed heartily, his huge stomach jiggling, stretching the already-stressed buttons of his dress shirt to the popping point. Picking up the cigar, he rolled it between fingers then drew on it until smoke billowed in front of his sun-drenched face.

Johnny's eyes scanned the bar, settling on the DJ booth where a young black man with red ribbons in his beard was dancing in place to the music. "Thanks, David. I'll have a Budweiser," he said.

"One Budweiser coming up, though I don't know how you can drink that shit." He caught the attention of their waitress who immediately came to the booth. Hector, Hennrick, and David had been tipping her quite generously since they'd arrived.

The pretty brunette flashed perfect white teeth. "Another round, boys?" she asked, hazel eyes coming to rest on Johnny's sculpted shoulders and face.

"Yes, and bring our friend here a Budweiser and tequila."

Johnny raised a hand in protest. "No tequila for me, thanks. The beer will do fine, really."

"Ah, come on, Johnny," said Hennrick. "It's Christmas Eve. Get bent like us. You can take a taxi home."

Hector returned the cigar to the ashtray and pulled at his thick moustache. "Yeah. Come on, amigo. You have a lot of catching up to do."

Since neither of Johnny's friends were married, or had families in Vegas to be with on Christmas, all they had were each other. Their way of celebrating Christmas was to get plastered together.

"All right," said Johnny. "But just this one. Since it's Christmas and all. Tequila doesn't really agree with me."

Hector laughed. "Tequila doesn't agree with anyone, amigo. She is a mysterious bitch who leaves us wondering what happened come mañana."

Suddenly the lights dimmed. The waitress left to fill their orders. Dry ice flooded the stage in a swirling fog. Soft blue lighting poured into it. The ruckus sound of male voices fell silent.

"Spirit in the Sky" ended.

The DJ put his face close to a suspended mike and said, "Gentlemen, gentlemen, gentlemen. Are you ready?" Silence replaced with cheers, whistles and catcalls. The entire club vibrated. "Are you sure your eyes can handle what they're about to see?" The cheering grew louder. "Then put your hands together for your favorite redhead and mine. Once again, Club Paradise is proud to give you its newest star. I give you the delectable... *Orchid*."

Tina Turner's "Private Dancer" spilled from the speakers.

* * *

Orchid stood behind the stage door waiting for her name to be broadcast. In her hands she held a leopard-patterned blanket. The Percocet was kicking in. *Courage.* Toby's voice boomed. "Private Dancer" began. Pushing her way through the door, she sashayed up the steps leading to the stage, dropped the blanket, went to her hands and knees, and crawled through the white fog, invisible to those watching.

When the DJ announced that the next performer's name was Orchid, the stone in Johnny's pocket began to vibrate once again. In his mind, Linda the wolf's words compelled, "*A flower will awaken an everlasting love in you.*" His attention fell upon the stage. The waitress returned with the drink orders and set them on the table. So focused was Johnny on the pale silhouette emerging from the white mist, he barely heard Hector toast, "Merry Christmas, amigos." Blindly, he reached for the tequila, put it to his lips, tipped it back, and let the gold liquid run down his throat, his heart pounding, the stone vibrating as if it were an alarm.

Emerging from the mist, Orchid stopped at the stage edge, green eyes scanning the faces near to her. She then reversed, slipped into the shroud of white and slowly rose, her body bathed in blue, an apparition rising from its resting place. Her audience erupted with cries of wonder. Flowing across the stage, hands on gyrating hips, she took to one of the brass poles. Slowly she climbed its length until she was five feet from the floor. Legs wrapped, back arched, the length of her hair flirted with the mist. Round and round she went, her mind chemically sated, the white mist enveloping her in a vortex.

Johnny had finally found her. He knew it as well as he knew his own face. "*You will know her when your eyes meet.*" His heart soared, filling him with instinctive awareness. A certain warmth coursed through his being, rendering him spiritually and emotionally conscious of its meaning. It was love in its purist narration, whispering words of harmonious bliss. So overwhelming were these sensations that his heart literally pained for the woman on the stage. The gifted one he was to liberate. But how could he attempt a rescue of her? He looked to the bouncer standing by the entrance and to the man in the white suit. Surely they weren't about to let him walk out the front door with her. *Think, Johnny, think. You are only going to have one shot at this, so make the right decision.*

Orchid slipped from the pole, flouncing suggestively from one end of the stage to the other. Someone held up a twenty. Down into the mist she went. On hands and knees, she crawled toward the young man who was smiling from ear to ear. Turning sideways, she offered her hip. The patron gently tucked the bill into the waistband of her skirt just as "Private Dancer" came to an end.

The stage erupted with golden light, allowing Orchid to see further into the faces staring back at her.

Dry ice bled from the stage, vacuumed by invisible vents. Standing, she walked toward its center to cheers and catcalls. Someone yelled out, "Marry me, Orchid!" Green eyes scanned the crowd. The Beatle's "Long and Winding Road" ebbed eloquently from above. That's when she saw him. His was a face she had known all her life. Their eyes locked. An awareness, birthed by a lonely heart flooded her soul. Her entire being tingled. It was kismet. It was misplaced dreams reborn. It was enigmatic love.

The constricting chains imprisoning her free spirit shattered like fine crystal. He had found her, just as the *one* had predicted. Within the distant stare, she could see he was as much caught up in the moment as she was.

Realizing she wasn't moving to the music, she began to dance, putting to rest the impatient murmurs rising from the crowd, her eyes conveying a message only he could decipher. *Help me. Please, please help me.*

An idea formed in Johnny's mind. "Have either of you got a pen and paper?" he asked his friends.

Each quickly gave their pockets a patting. "As a matter a fact, I do," said Hennrick, withdrawing a small black pad and pen from a breast pocket. Handing them to Johnny, he asked, "What do you need it for?"

Johnny flipped the notebook open. "I just thought of something and I want to put it down so I don't forget," he lied. He covered the pad with an opened hand so neither of his friends could see what it was he was going to write. He messaged, "IF YOU ARE IN TROUBLE, MEET ME OUT BACK IN TEN MINUTES. RED PICKUP TRUCK. I'M HERE TO HELP YOU. I BELIEVE YOU KNOW THAT." As an afterthought, he concluded, "MY NAME IS JOHNNY." Tearing the page from pad, he folded it and handed pen and pad back to Hennrick. "Thanks," he said. Turning his attention back to the stage, he watched the beautiful redhead move, her eyes engaged with his, sending him messages of hope.

Ten minutes later, Orchid's performance came to an end. Money littered the stage.

Rising from the booth, Johnny took a twenty from his jeans and concealed the note within. "Excuse me for a minute," he said to his friends and rounded the tables until he was standing in front of the stage and the woman he was already in love with.

Topless, Orchid collected the money scattered about the stage, one eye on what she was doing, the other watching as her dream lover walk toward her. He was everything she had ever imagined. Tall, strong, with the same grey-blue eyes that had melted her heart time and time again. However, it was the feather dangling from his braided hair that rang true, for she had see it more and more in her secret dreams as if it symbolized everything he was.

Johnny held out his hand. Their eyes caressed. No words were exchanged. Orchid took the offered twenty.

Their fingers touched ever so gently; nonetheless, the emotional current exchanged in that single moment was immeasurable. She smiled at him, and he returned the gesture in kind before turning from her and heading back to his friends.

Orchid picked up the blanket, silver vest, and made her way down the steps through the door to the dressing room and went straight into the bathroom without saying a word. Dropping all of the money into the sink, she singled out the twenty she knew in her heart held the first communication of a love never-ending. Releasing the note, her pulse raced as she read its message. Somehow, deep within, ever since she was a child, she just knew his name would be Johnny.

Without sitting, Johnny took forty dollars from his pocket and set the money on the table. "I'm buying the next round, but I'm afraid I have to call it a night," he said to friends he would never see again.

Hennrick, David and Hector gave him the hundred-yard stare. "What do you mean you have to go, amigo?" asked Hector.

"Yeah, Johnny. You just got here," said David.

Hennrick just looked at him and smiled knowingly.

"Something I have to do. I can't explain. I'm really sorry. You'll have to celebrate Christmas without me."

"Come on, amigo. Nothing can be so important not to spend Christmas Eve with your friends. Sit down. Have another beer."

Looking into the eyes of his coworkers, he said, "I wish it were that simple, but I really must go. Have a very merry Christmas." He extended his hand.

The three friends looked to one another. "A handshake just won't do, amigo." Hector rose. Hennrick followed suit as did David. Heartfelt hugs were exchanged. Hector said into Johnny's ear, "Whatever it is, amigo, I hope everything turns out for the best. Go do what you have to do. And Feliz Navidad, my friend."

"Thanks, Hector," said Johnny and turned away.

Exiting Club Paradise, he stepped out into the drizzly dark night. *I finally found her. And on Christmas Eve no doubt. Thank you, Linda.* Making his way to the Ford, he sat behind the wheel and waited in the shadows of electric blue candlelight, rain running south on the windshield, a part of him still not believing he had found her.

Hurriedly, Orchid used soap and water to scrub the glitter from her eyes and mouth. The anxious state she was in had completely wiped away the effects of her nemesis. With a clear head, she opened the bathroom door and retrieved her evening dress.

The girls stared at her, curious. "What's up, sister?" asked Jasmine from her dressing table.

"Nothing, really. I just want to get comfortable for a while. My next set isn't for another hour and a half and this outfit is chaffing me." Dress in hand, she returned to the bathroom, locked the door, kicked out of the remainder of her costume, and slipped the flowing gown over her shoulders. Folding the bills into a thick wad, she quickly checked her appearance in the mirror.

Minutes had already passed. She knew she must hurry. Barefoot, she exited the bathroom, walked casually to her table and eased her feet into the pumps lying beneath the stool. The money she had collected from her final performance went into the white envelope containing her bonus. Everything went into her handbag. "I think I'll go for a short walk," she said to no one in particular.

"But it's raining out," said Jesse.

"You'll ruin your nice dress," added Jasmine.

Ming had no opinion. She was too busy checking her makeup in the mirror. Lorrie Ann had already departed being the next flesh show.

"I'm just going for a couple of minutes. I need the fresh air. The smoke in there really got to me. I feel a little sick to my stomach."

"Just a second," said Jasmine, rising from her place. "I have an umbrella in here someplace." She went to the rack, moved things around, and came up with a white collapsible umbrella. "Here you go. At least you'll save the dress."

Taking it from her, Orchid said, "Thank you, Jasmine. I won't be more than a few minutes."

Regarding the handbag, Jasmine queried. "Do you really think it's a good idea to go for a walk carrying all that money? It may be Christmas Eve, but there's still a lot of bad people out there. You could get mugged. Or worse."

The clock in Orchid's mind was ticking in succession with her rapidly pounding heart. Whispering so that only Jasmine could hear, she said, "I don't trust Ming, and you shouldn't either. She's jealous of all of us because we make more money than she does, and besides, I'm going to stay close to the club." *Tick-tick-tick-tick*.

"If you say so. Just be careful, okay?"

"I will." Turning, she went through the dressing room door.

Johnny patiently waited, his eyes fixed on the rear exit door. Ten minutes had already passed. The rain was coming down harder now, thick veins of it running south on the windshield. The owner of the Mercedes had come and gone. The rear exit bouncer had poked his head through the door a couple of times. He'd looked in Johnny's direction, stared at the silhouette he could see through the windshield, decided nothing was amiss, and closed the door. *What do I do if she doesn't come through that door?* Having no plan B, he waited. He would wait all night if he had to.

In her haste, Orchid had completely forgotten about the bouncer guarding the rear exit. Slowing her gait, she approached him. He was sitting on a stool, a *Penthouse* magazine opened in front of him. "Where are *you* going?" he asked.

"I'm just going to step outside for a few minutes," said Orchid, stopping in front of him.

The steroid abuser folded the magazine and looked her over. "I'm under strict orders not to let you leave the building, so I think you better turn around and go back to the dressing room."

Orchid thought quickly. "Look, your name is Mike, right?"

"Yeah, so?"

"Well, listen, Mike. The smoke really got to me in there, and I'm feeling a little nauseous. I'm just going to walk around the club and come right back. See, I have an umbrella and everything."

"Mr. Millions told me that no way I should let you leave the building." Mike folded his thick arms over his chest.

"I understand that. You're just doing your job. But I think Tony would be none too pleased if I got sick and couldn't perform. I won't tell anyone you let me out. Nobody needs to know. I won't be two minutes, promise. All I need is a little fresh air."

"Sorry, sweetheart. No, can do."

Orchid looked to the folded Penthouse and the swollen member within his jeans. "Not even if I give you a little Christmas bonus when I get back?"

"Keep talking."

"I'll suck your cock, Mike. Like no one ever has before. I love sucking cock. It's what I'm paid to do. I've been watching you, and, well, I like what I see. It'll be our little secret. That's a pretty good deal if you ask me. The best blowjob of your life for letting me out for a couple of minutes."

The big man unfolded his arms, scratched the top of his head, his eyes undressing Orchid. He looked down the stretch of hall. "All right. I'm going to give you two minutes to get some air. If you're not back in that time, I'm going to come looking for you, and you'll owe me more than just a blowjob. Understood?"

"Thanks, Mike. You won't be sorry. I'm the best. You'll see." She rounded Mike the bouncer, went to the door, pushed it open, and stepped out into the rain.

Johnny's heart truly skipped a beat when the rear exit opened. There she was, beautiful, carrying an umbrella which she dropped to the ground when she immediately saw the truck. In pumps, she ran across the tarmac splashing through the puddles.

Reaching, Johnny opened the passenger door and engaged the engine.

Orchid jumped in.

They walked into each other's eyes for a forever silence.

Reaching, Orchid wrapped her arms around his neck, squeezing with all her strength for only a second, but to Johnny, it felt like a lifetime. When she released him, her eyes went to the exit door. "Go! Go! Go!" she cried.

Johnny dropped the shift, awakening 350 horses. Rear tires slipped on wet tarmac before catching, then the Ford roared out of the parking lot and on to Paradise Road.

Each stared at the rain, wipers slapping the only sound between them. A single triumphant tear slowly carved the plump of Rebecca's cheek. However, deep down she knew her troubles were not over. Not by a long shot.

Several long pounding heartbeats passed before Rebecca reached over and took Johnny's hand in hers. "Thank God you found me, Johnny. I've been waiting for you all of my life."

Little did they realize when Mike the rear exit bouncer heard the tires squawk against tarmac, he opened the door in time to see the truck leaving the parking lot. Not seeing Orchid, his eyes immediately went to the Wyoming license plate. Returning to his station, he wrote the sequence of numbers and letters down on the cover of the *Penthouse* magazine, aware he had done something terribly wrong and would pay the ultimate price. *Stupid stupid stupid.*

* * *

52

A Time for Killing

BEFORE we go any further, I need to know who you really are," said Johnny, keeping his eyes on the road. The rain was letting up. He adjusted the toggle controlling the wipers to a lesser degree of motion.

Rebecca breathed a sigh of relief. For months she imagined she would never hear her true identity spoken again. She said, "My name is Rebecca White, and believe it or not, this may sound strange since we've only just met, but I'm in love with you, Johnny. Always have been. Always will be."

I'm in love with you, Johnny. Six little words he longed to hear. "I've been searching for you for months now, Rebecca," admitted Johnny. "Don't ask me how, at least not right now, but I knew you were out there and needed my help."

"Yes, I know. I've known for quite some time. Just knowing that you were out there somewhere kept me sane in an otherwise insane situation."

"I understand. I've been told you carry a gift. So it's true then?"

Rebecca turned her head so she was looking in the rear compartment where a large golden lab sat comfortable, pink tongue dangling from its mouth. However, now was not the time to tell him of his spirit companion. Looking at her savior, she smiled. "Yes, I *am* one of the gifted. Sometimes it's a curse and other times a blessing. I just never know when or what to expect."

Johnny let his concentration leave the road for a moment and looked into the fathomless depths of her green eyes. In them he saw the same formulation Konahee's held. Seeped in magic and mystery. He also saw the love she felt for him, and it made his heart melt in serenity. Returning his focus to the rain-drenched macadam, he saw there were all but a few cars heading south on Paradise Road. "Well, what do we do now, Rebecca White?"

She put a hand on his shoulder. "I need to get my belongings. Do you know where the Shangri-La Palace is located?"

"Sorry, no, I don't."

"Well, do you know how to get to Highway 8?"

"That I do know."

"Once you're on the highway, I'll direct you. It's a big Spanish mansion about twenty minutes south of Las Vegas. There are some things I need to explain to you before we get there. So you'll understand the whys of it all. So you'll understand why you found me in a strip parlor." Moving her hand from his shoulder, she hung her head, shamed by what she was about to tell him.

From the corner of his eye, Johnny saw the sudden change in her demeanor. Without taking his eyes off the road, he said, "Rebecca, I want you to know that no matter what you tell me, I'll understand. What happened in our past lives is irrelevant to our future together. What really matters is that we found each other. I already have feelings for you I thought I would never admit to again. I know in my heart that my destiny is to keep you safe and share my life with you for as long as I live."

Kissing him gently on the cheek, Rebecca said, "Thank you, Johnny. You don't know how much that means to me." Silent for a moment, she collected her thoughts, assembling the dark periods of her memory. "I guess... I guess I should start at the beginning."

And so, as they drove through the Nevada rain, in the direction of Rebecca's house of infamy, she told her story from the beginning, starting with the night she lost the remainder of her family and how she began, on what she believed, was a quest to nirvana.

* * *

By the time they reached the Shangri-La Palace, Johnny was seething. The story she reminisced tore a hole in his heart the size of Montana. His eyes were misted with tears of hatred for the man she called Tony Millions and his henchmen. *If I ever get my hands on them, I will tear them apart. Inch by fucking inch.*

Stopping the truck outside its gates, the mansion loomed foreboding in the dark rain. All the lights were off. He put the Ford in neutral and yanked on the parking brake.

"What do we do now, Rebecca?"

"Everyone has gone to Tony's big Christmas party. There's an alarm system, but I'll be in and out so fast by the time the security company shows up, we'll be long gone. The door to the solarium is never locked."

"I'm not letting you go in there by yourself."

"It'll be faster if *I* just go. You don't know your way around. I do."

"Now that I've found you, Rebecca, I'm never letting you out of my sight. I'm going with you, and that's all there is to it."

The look in his eyes told her there would be no arguing the matter, so she said, "Okay, let's go then. Stay close behind me."

"I'll be like your shadow." The stone in Johnny's pocket began to grow warm.

Exiting the running truck, they made their way up the driveway and to the south side of the house. By the time Rebecca opened the glass door, they were soaked to the skin. She stepped inside, Johnny on her heels. The stone was now hot. No alarm sounded. *Must be silent,* thought Rebecca. Hurriedly, in the shadows of the house, they moved out of the solarium through the great room and into the hallway. "Once we get into the welcoming room, there's a flight of stairs we have to go up," whispered Rebecca, not knowing why.

"I'm right behind you."

Reaching back, she took his hand. As soon as they stepped out of the hallway, the lights in the welcoming room powered, startling them. Standing near the bar and wearing a white housecoat was Li Ling. In one hand was a large butcher's knife. The other was closed in a hard fist. A look of surprise widened her eyes when she saw who the intruder was. Stepping forward, she pointed the knife toward them.

Rebecca and Johnny stood frozen in place. They hadn't been together for more than a half hour and already they'd slammed into their first road block. Maintaining a firm grip on Johnny's hand, rain dripping from her hair and face, Rebecca stepped toward Madame Olivia's lover. Halting within an arm's reach, all she could hope for was that Li Ling was willing to listen to reason. "Li Ling," she tried. "I've come to get my things. I don't belong here. I'm here against my will. Forced to do things I didn't want to do. My real name is Rebecca." She pulled Johnny forward. "I'm in love with this man. I want to spend the rest of my life with him. I know you understand love. I see it in your eyes whenever you look at Oli. I want that for me too. Do you understand?"

Li Ling lowered the knife, unfisted her hand, and looked to Johnny then Rebecca. Her eyes alighted with compassion, understanding. Smiling, she nodded and stepped aside.

"Oh, thank you, Li Ling," said Rebecca. "You don't know how grateful I am. How we are. We're just going to go to my room and get my suitcase, then you'll never see me again. Okay?"

Johnny was wondering why Li Ling hadn't said a word. As if reading his thoughts, Rebecca said, "Li Ling is a mute. A very nice one at that."

The smile on Li Ling's face grew wide.

Rain dripping from the feather and his chin, Johnny said, "Thank you, Li Ling. You're doing the right thing. I just hope there won't be any trouble for you." The stone in his pocket cooled.

Li Ling shook her head, eyes telling them to hurry.

Rebecca pulled Johnny to the door leading to the staircase. Opening it, they took the stairs two at a time. All the lights on the second floor suddenly brightened. *Thank you again, Li Ling.* They moved down the hallway as quickly as two startled cats. When they entered Rebecca's bedroom, Johnny stopped in his tracks. *Was this the room she was forced to have sex in?*

"What's the matter, Johnny?"

"I'd like to burn this place to the ground," he said.

"So would I. Believe me. But let's just get my stuff then we're outta here." Kicking off her shoes, she drew the dress over her head and tossed it onto the bed.

Embarrassed, Johnny turned, but before he did, he had caught a glimpse of her imposed addiction, several discolored blotches on the back side of her knees. He would never mention them.

Naked, Rebecca hit the wall with her hand. The closet opened, revealing the outfits that had lent credibility to her nights as a lady in waiting. Taking hold of the suitcase, she popped it open, removed a pair of jeans, and struggled into them. A plain white T-shirt she slipped over her wet skin, and stole a quick moment to look at the photo of her mother. Something tugged at her, like before, but she couldn't decipher its meaning. Closing the suitcase, she pushed her feet into a pair of pink Vans. "You can turn around now, Johnny."

Johnny turned. Standing in the middle of the room was the most beautiful woman he had ever seen even though her hair was dripping and she looked completely the part of a runaway. He went to her, taking the suitcase from her hand. Their eyes met. It was a moment they would never forget. For Johnny, love had come full circle. For Rebecca, the love she had always felt for him bloomed into an everlasting reality. On tiptoes, eyes riveted to his, she kissed him on his waiting lips. Johnny drew her close, feeling her life force pounding rhythmically against his own. The world stood still for a trice in time. When they parted, he said, "Okay. Let's go."

Hand in hand they made their way through the house, stopping to thank Li Ling once more. Through the front door they crashed, two lovers on the lamb, a perilous future waiting in the shadows.

Johnny placed the suitcase in the rear of the cab and, unbeknown to him, next to the spirit of Dallas.

They jumped in and slammed the doors, anxiety fuelling every ounce of their being.

"Where do we go from here?" asked Rebecca.

Johnny made a three-point turn. "We're going to go back to my place for the night. It's against the rules, but if we keep quiet, no one will know. We'll be safe there. Come tomorrow, we'll decide the next direction in our journey."

Rebecca put a gentle hand on his arm. "Johnny?"

"Yes, Rebecca."

"Merry Christmas."

* * *

Tony Millions, Mr. Black, and Madame Olivia stood in Tony's study. Norman hung upside down in his cage and was swaying back and forth to the music emanating through the closed door. Tony had received a call from Mr. White informing him that Orchid had fled. Most likely with a big Indian seen leaving the parking lot in a red pickup. All of it witnessed by one of the bouncers. Tony told him to come back to the mansion, making it abundantly clear that he was not pleased. He also told him to fire the bouncer for letting her out of the building and to take back his bonus money.

"What are you going to do now, man?" said Mr. Black. "She might go to the police."

"Somehow I doubt that. I'm sure the only thoughts going through her mind right now is to get as far away from us as possible. Apparently she left with a big Indian in a pickup truck." He turned his attention to Madame Olivia. "Did Orchid ever have a client who was a big Native?"

"No. We've only ever had one Native come to the Palace, and that was well before she arrived."

"I wonder who he is? Probably someone who saw her dancing at the club. We'll find out soon enough." Turning his attention back to Mr. Black, he asked, "Did you plant the tracking devise like I asked you?"

"Yes. Mr. Brown put it where she'll never find it. It fit perfectly in the back of the framed picture of her mother."

"Good. Let's just see where they've gotten to." He went to his desk, opened the drawer, retrieved a square PalmPilot, and powered it. The small screen came to life. A tiny red dot pulsed, moving slowly across the map of Las Vegas. "They're still on the move." He showed Mr. Black and Madame Olivia the devise. "Isn't technology wonderful? Looks like they're heading away from the Palace Olivia. Our Orchid would not run without the photo of her mother, hence the tracking devise. It pays to stay one step ahead. What concerns me however is that she got past Li Ling? Any ideas, Madame?"

"No. But I'm sure going to find out."

The trio watched the screen as the red dot moved north toward the Stratosphere Hotel. A few minutes later, it stopped. "Bingo," said Tony. He hit a few keys. The PalmPilot told him they had stopped on Tam Avenue. A seedier part of Vegas.

"I'll take care of them," deadpanned Mr. Black.

"No! I want you to stay close to home. This is Mr. White's problem. I want the two of you to mingle with the guests. Send Mr. White to me when he arrives.

"You're the boss, man," said Mr. Black. "Still, I would like to have seen the looks on their faces when they're found."

"What are your plans for them?" asked Oli.

Tony pulled on his chin and sniffed. "I'm afraid I've done all I can with our little Orchid. I hate to lose her, but what are you going to do? If I give her another chance, I'm quite certain she'll only run again. I'm sorry, Olivia. Orchid and her newfound companion will have to be eliminated."

* * *

As quietly as he could, Johnny opened the door to his room. The house was silent except for the sound of "The Little Drummer Boy" drifting throughout the hallway. Hitting the light switch, he closed the door, and engaged the dead bolt. He dropped Rebecca's suitcase onto the bed that had been his only comfort and where on any given night he dreamed of flight.

Spirit Dallas bounded through the closed door as if it were made of smoke and went to a corner of the room where he lay down, crossing one golden paw over the other.

Rebecca couldn't believe the tawdry condition of the room. She dropped her handbag next to the suitcase. "This is where you've been living while you were searching for me?"

"I know it's not much to look at, but it was affordable and the location was right. We'll be safe here. For the time being anyway."

"Where do you eat?" Rebecca sat on the bed.

"Here and there. There's lots of places to choose from." He sat next to her, picked up the remote. "Would you like to watch some TV?" He clicked on the set. It took a moment for the screen to come to life. When it did, *It's a Wonderful Life* was airing. George Bailey was telling his lifelong sweetheart Mary that he would lasso the moon for her.

Looking to the Labrador resting in the corner, Rebecca said, "There's something I think you should know."

"Okay, I'm listening."

Taking his hands in hers, she said, "You have a very special friend with you. I can see him as well as I can see you. You once had a friend. A golden lab. He has probably been with you since he died. What was his name?"

"Dallas! You can see Dallas?" Johnny's heart thumped in his chest. An emotional warmth rose from his feet to the top of his head. "That's some gift. Where is he?"

Rebecca looked to the corner of the room. "He's lying right over there, content as can be. He must have been a wonderful friend to have sought you out. I rarely see the spirits of animals, but when I do, it's because they had a very special bond with their human companions."

Johnny rose from the bed, his eyes riveted to the corner of the room. "Can he hear me?"

Orchid skewed her head. "I'm not sure. Why don't you try?"

Johnny was so overjoyed, a tear trickled over his cheek. "Dallas." He moved toward the corner of the room.

Spirit Dallas raised his head, tail wagging.

"He can hear you, Johnny. He's looking right at you. Wagging his tail. This is so wonderful. I wish you could see him."

"Oh, but I can, Rebecca. I can see him clearly in my mind." Johnny put a hand out. "Come here, boy."

Spirit Dallas pushed himself to his feet and went to the outstretched hand, tail looping as he licked the tips of Johnny's fingers.

Tears filled Rebecca's eyes. To see them together brought back fond memories of Caleb and Chase. "He's licking your hand," she told her newfound love.

"This is so unbelievable. I can almost feel him. Thank you, Rebecca."

On haunches, spirit Dallas proceeded to lick Johnny's face, molasses eyes full of love for his human friend.

Wiping the tears from her eyes, Rebecca said, "Would you like to tell me about him?"

Without taking his eyes from where spirit Dallas stood, Johnny said, "Dallas is sort of the reason I'm in the trouble I'm in."

"You're in trouble? With whom?"

"With the law. You see, Rebecca, this isn't easy for me to admit to, but I feel I should. These two men. They shot and killed him. I sought retribution. To make a long story short, I killed one of them. It was an accident, but it happened, and I'm on the run. Have been for months now. So if you don't think you could handle being with me, because I'll always be running, I'll understand."

"Then I guess we're both running. I won't leave you, Johnny. No matter what happens." She paused for a thought filled breath. "There's something else I need to discuss with you," she said in a serious tone.

Johnny stood. "What is it, Rebecca?"

"Come and sit down." She took the remote and killed the power to the television.

Johnny sat next to her. Spirit Dallas returned to the corner of the room.

"These men I told you about. They're going to be looking for me. They won't just let me run away. I've seen and know too much, and I'm worried about some friends of mine. They threatened to kill them if I didn't do as I was told. These are bad people, Johnny. I've seen them kill one of their own just because it suited them. I'm frightened that they'll carry out the threats they made."

Johnny took her hand and fell deep into her eyes. "First of all, there's no way they're going to find you here." He brushed strands of damp hair away from her face. "These threats they made, I'm sure that's all they were, idol threats. As bad as these people are, they can't just go around killing people when they feel like it. They'd eventually get caught. Then where would they be? Out of business. What they're probably doing right now is planning another abduction to replace you. I'm sure your friends will be all right."

"I'm afraid I'm not as certain as you are."

"Do you know how to get in touch with your friends?"

"I don't have a phone number, but I can get the operator to get it for me and I can call them."

"Then that's what we'll do. We can't stay here too long. So in a few days, when we've found another place to stay, you'll call them to be sure they're all right, okay?"

"Okay, Johnny." Rebecca yawned, semicomfortable with Johnny's reasoning.

"You're tired. It's been one hell of an emotional day. Why don't you try to get some sleep? You take the bed. I'll sit next to you on the floor."

"I don't know if I could. There's something else I have to tell you." She cast her eyes to her lap then to her handbag.

Johnny waited for her to continue.

"I told you that they forced heroin on me. What I didn't tell you is that when I came clean, I was addicted to painkillers. My body is telling me that I need to take some. Right now. Or I'm afraid I'm going to get sick." She also needed to change her tampon. "If I could just use a bathroom for a moment."

Johnny looked to the handbag. "I'm glad you told me. Now I know what to expect when we get you off the stuff. The bathroom's just down the hallway. I'll take you there, but we'll have to be as quite as mice. The walls are as thin as paper, and by the sounds of it, there are still some people awake. Hopefully no one will decide to use the bathroom while you do." Picking up the handbag, he gave it to her. "Come on. Let's go. But let's take our shoes off first. We'll make less noise that way."

After removing his boots and setting them next to Rebecca's pink Vans, Johnny unlocked the door and peeked his head into the hall. Seeing that no one was about, they quietly made their way to the bathroom. Rebecca went in, closing the door. Johnny stood against the wall, arms folded against his chest, the stone in his pocket growing warm. *Shit.*

* * *

Mr. White turned onto Tam Avenue, the PalmPilot in his free hand. He was wearing a black jacket over a black T-shirt, black pants, and black runners so that he blended into the night. He found the address easy enough and parked the black Escalade across the street from what was obviously a rooming house and about ten feet behind the red Ford. The PalmPilot did not give him their exact location in the house and he couldn't just go knocking on doors. *Damn it. I'm going to have to sit here until one or both of them comes out of the house.* He patted the holster concealed within his jacket. Although his preferred method was to strangle his victims, Tony had given him a Walter PPK and told him to make the kills quick and clean. "A bullet to the head leaves no doubts," he had said. So Mr. White waited in the light rain, his eyes focused on the paint-starved entrance. "Merry fucking Christmas," he said to the pale, rain washed reflection of himself.

* * *

Farther down the hall, a door opened. The big Russian, Siberian corkscrews in his head, stepped into the hallway. He saw Johnny and, slightly staggering, went right to him. "Johnny my friend. Merry Christmas." He held out a paw of a hand.

Johnny took it, the smell of vodka on the Russian's breath very strong. "Merry Christmas," said Johnny, suddenly nervous.

"Da. It will be a good year, yes." He squeezed Johnny's hand then let it go.

"I hope so."

"You are all wet, my friend."

"I got caught in the rain."

"Da. I see. Better than snow. Yes."

"I suppose you're right."

The big man looked to the closed door. "Someone is using, yes?"

"Um. Yes. A friend of mine."

A smile as wide as a canyon grew on the big man's face. "A special friend I think, yes."

"Yes," admitted Johnny. "You won't tell Ms. McGregor, will you?"

The bathroom door opened. Rebecca peeked into the hallway. "I *thought* I heard you talking to someone. Hi. I'm Rebecca," she half-whispered to the big man standing in front of Johnny.

The Russian took in Rebecca's face. "And what a beautiful friend you are. My name is Vladameer Koslov. And I am at your service, pretty lady." He gently bowed, took Rebecca's hand, brought it to his lips, and tenderly kissed it. "You don't have to worry. I will say nothing. What kind of a man would I be to get in way of such love, yes?"

"Thank you," chorused Johnny and Rebecca.

"Da. You are welcome, but you should get out of hallway, yes. Before someone not so nice sees you. Go. Go now."

Johnny thanked the Russian once more, then he and Rebecca returned to the room. Once the door was closed and locked, Rebecca asked, "What happened to that poor man? I've never seen anything like that before." Plopping herself down on the bed, a strong visual of the man she had just met sent a shiver up her spine. "It looks like he was tortured."

"I think he was. By the Russian mob. He told me once that what happened to him was called a Siberian corkscrew. I don't know what it involved, but it must have been excruciatingly painful." The stone in Johnny's pocket was getting hotter by the minute, a sign he now knew meant there was trouble afoot. Problem was, he didn't want Rebecca to know. Whatever it was, he would deal with it. Konahee had prepared him well, and working at the Cosmopolitan project had only added to his strength. Rebecca White had gone through enough in one day. He would take on the world for her if need be. It was his destiny.

"He must be so lonely," said Rebecca, saddened by the thought.

"I think he enjoys his life now. You saw how pleasant he was. It's certainly a far cry from where he came from."

"I suppose you're right. We have our own problems to deal with anyway." She looked to the empty corner of the room. "I wonder where he went."

Johnny followed her eyes. "Dallas is gone?"

"Yes. And I never know where the spirits I meet go. I mean they must have a place, right? They just don't vanish into thin air then reappear again when they feel like it. I'm convinced there's an after place. A plane we go to when our mortal life cycles have ended. Where we can be with our loved ones and our pets and carry on in a different way. A young boy once told me that there were lots of people where he was though the only one I could see was him and his dog. Why that is, I just don't know. In a way I'm glad. I don't think I could handle seeing the disembodied spirits of everyone."

Johnny thought for a moment. "Maybe not all of us get to go to this plane. Maybe only people and animals who have certain criteria get to go. You know. Like if they're taken before their time is supposed to be up. Their life cycle interrupted. You said you met a young boy. Was his death wrongful?"

"No. It was an accident. He and his dog were killed by a drunk truck driver."

"Maybe we're on to something then. If we die before we're supposed to, we go to this place."

"It's possible, but I've also met many others, several times, all together. They couldn't have all died wrongful deaths. No. I think it's something more than that. I used to be in contact with my mother. Then one day she simply never showed up again." The Percocet started to kick in. She yawned, face buzzing with its all-too-familiar attitude.

Johnny went to her and put an arm around her shoulder. "I'm sorry about your not being in contact with your mother, but maybe one day you will be again."

"I hope so. I miss her tremendously." She yawned again, long and winded.

"You *are* tired. You need to sleep, Rebecca. One day the answers will come. There's no point staying up all night trying to figure it out. Tomorrow's Christmas, and after you wake up, we're going to go to the Denny's down the street and have a big breakfast. Okay?"

"Will it be open?"

"If there's one thing I've learned during my stay here, it's that everything in Vegas is open all the time. Like New York. It's a city that never sleeps." He kissed her forehead.

Rebecca wrapped her arms around his neck, squeezed tight, and whispered in his ear, "You're the best gift I could have ever received. I love you, Johnny... Johnny... Huh? I don't even know your last name, and here I am professing my love for you."

"It's Black," said Johnny.

She tried it out. "Johnny Black. Kind of suits us, doesn't it? Black and White I mean. It's poetic. Well, I'm in love with you, Johnny Black." She yawed again. The effects of the painkillers and the emotional day causing her eyes to close.

Johnny eased her head toward the pillow. Rebecca responded by curling into a ball. He pulled the blanket over her. "I love you too, Rebecca White," he said, brushing the hair from her face. He sat on the floor next to the bed and watched until her eyes closed and she began to breathe the breath of sleep. Once he knew she was out for the night, he took the time to change out of his wet clothes; Black T-shirt, dry jeans, and clean socks. He transferred the hot stone and truck keys. The persistent flame of the stone told him to gather his things just in case. He stuffed his clothes into the knapsack, went to the loose floorboard, pulled it away from the wall, retrieved the gun, and the remainder of his money. Stuffing the bills in a side pocket, he returned to the side of the bed with the gun tucked into the waistband of his jeans.

* * *

Mr. White checked his watch. It was 3:00 a.m. Christmas Day. All the lights in the house were off. The rain had stopped. In his mind, he ran through his options. He could sit here all night and wait, or he could use the spare gas can in the back, set the house on fire, and wait for everyone to come running out. He liked that idea; however, in the subsequent chaos, someone might see him and his vehicle. He needed to be as stealth as possible. Any more fuck-ups and he might end up lying next to Mr. Blue in the desert. His stomach growled. He hadn't eaten. All his stomach contained was the nutritional values of three Caesars. He decided he would take a quick walk around the house. He might get lucky.

Exiting the Escalade, he looked up and down the quiet street. Decorative lights still shone from balconies of apartment complexes and the corner store. He heard a sound behind him, quickly he turned to see the rear end of a dog running between buildings, its hips narrow from starvation. His right hand automatically went to the holstered gun. Chuckling, he crossed the street, opened the dilapidated gate, and crossed the spongy lawn. Once he was beside the house, he saw that there was soft lighting emanating from the rear, illuminating the metallic ghosts of three junkers in the neighboring yard. *Could I be so lucky?* he wondered.

In the darkness, he moved with the furtiveness of a cat on the prowl, unaware that spirit Dallas was close on his heels, low to the ground, hackles raised in defense.

He found the source, a single square window shaded yellow from the low-watt bulb located inside. Without making a sound, he took an angle from which he could see beyond the scarred window frame. There they were, in the flesh. The Indian was awake. The girl, lost in sleep. What concerned Mr. White was the gun he could see protruding from the waistband of the big Indian's jeans. His first thoughts were, *Who was this fucking guy? And why does he have to be so big?* What Mr. White had going for him however was that the guy was young and young people made stupid mistakes. *Advantage to me.* Now that he knew where they were, he would just walk in, burst into the room, and pop-pop! *I am a very good shot.* Take out the Indian first, then quickly get to the girl and put a bullet in her brain. By the time anyone decided to do anything about the sound of murder, he would be long gone and on his way to a cold dinner and Tony Millions's gratitude, he hoped.

* * *

Rebecca was in the grasp of a telling dream, walking in a field, the sound of a whimsical breeze playing all around. In the distance she could see a massive pine tree. The dream enabled her to float toward it, moving on the air as though she were an ethereal phantom. There was no sun in the clear sky, yet warm sunlight poured upon her. In a dream moment, she was standing in front of the evergreen giant, its roots growing over an oddly shaped boulder. Not far from its skirt was a single white cross, a dog collar hanging from its apex. A piercing cry caused her to look to the sunless sky. Circling the updraft was a hawk, its wings spread wide. It cried a mournful oration. Rebecca watched it as it drew higher and higher until it was no more than a dot, then, nothing. When she looked down again, there were six more crosses set askew next to the giant pine. On one of these blindingly white icons of death was a single word. She floated closer. When she saw what was written, she cried aloud, the dream allowing her to fall to her knees, for on the cross was a single name: JOHNNY.

From out of a dream within a dream, a dog began to whimper.

Rebecca woke with a start. Looking down at her was spirit Dallas, his eyes warning danger, whimpering with fear.

"Johnny!?"

"I'm right here," said Johnny from the floor.

"There's something very, very wrong." Rebecca sat up, noticed the gun.

"I know." He pushed himself from the floor and put a vertical finger to his lips.

Bellowing a forewarning, Spirit Dallas jumped from the bed and leapt through the wall.

"Where did you get the gun?" said Rebecca as quietly as she could.

"I'll tell you later. Get off the bed and stand over by that wall." He pointed with his chin.

Rebecca, now trembling with fear, threw the cover back and, moving as quickly and quietly as she could, planted her back firmly against the wall.

Johnny stood next to her, pulled the gun from his jeans, and held it to his ear. He drew the hammer back. With a finger steady on the trigger he flipped the light switch.

Darkness enveloped the room, rendering them blind. Rebecca put a hand to her mouth to prevent herself from screaming. Johnny listened to the sounds of the house. In the silence he could hear their panicked breathing.

What happened next occurred in slow motion. The door burst open with a crash. Johnny flipped the lights on long enough to get a visual of the man pointing a small gun in the direction where he had been sitting on the floor. Rebecca swallowed her breath. Johnny killed the light, aiming the .38 where he thought the man's head was. A shot rang out, which was immediately followed by another, not quite as telling and was succeeded by a heavy thud not three feet away.

Johnny flipped the switch.

Prone on the floor was a man dressed all in black, the back of his head blown out, one eye still open, the other, the recipient of the bullet, now a deep bloody hole. Brain matter clung to the door and wall. A small-caliber gun lay next to the killer's open hand.

"Mr. White," said Rebecca with such calmness that it surprised even her, for she felt like screaming blue bloody fucking murder.

Johnny pulled the truck keys from his pocket and tossed them to her. "Get out, Rebecca! Go to the truck! Now!" It was then he noticed the bullet hole in the wall not three inches from her head.

Barefoot, Rebecca ran into the hallway.

Johnny tucked the hot .38 into his jeans, grabbed the suitcase and knapsack, and slung the latter over a shoulder, the stone still warm in his pocket.

The house woke with people sounds. He looked for the briefest of moments to the footwear sitting next to each other near the bed. They would be the only remaining evidence of he and Rebecca having ever been there. He fled into the hallway, running as quickly as he could, Vladameer Koslov's voice behind him, "What has happened? Johnny! Johnny!"

In her haste Rebecca had left the front door open. Johnny flew through the opening, down the steps, and across the street. Behind the Ford was a black Escalade. Rebecca had had the common sense to start the truck and open the driver side door. Johnny tossed the suitcase and knapsack into the rear compartment, hoisted himself behind the wheel, dropped the gear, and hit the gas. The truck lurched forward. Pulling the gun from his jeans, he shoved it at Rebecca. "Put it in the glove compartment!"

Rebecca held the gun, but only for a second. The three-pound hunk of metal was still hot. She opened the glove compartment and tossed it in, closing the opening with a slam. Although it had saved their lives, she did not want to look at it further.

Johnny looked back to the house. The lights of each room blazed in the dark. There were people standing on the stoop, looking in their direction. "Fuck! Fuck! Fuck!" he yelled, striking the steering wheel with a hand.

Rebecca stared straight ahead, terror bleaching her face ghostly white, fingers digging into the dashboard. The bastards had found her, and it didn't take any more time than it took to go shopping. *But how?*

Johnny turned the pickup onto Las Vegas Boulevard and headed west, staying within the speed limit, thinking exactly the same thing. *How in the hell did they find us? That's impossible. We weren't followed. I'm sure of it. I kept checking.* Looking to Rebecca, he asked. "Do you know how they found us?"

Rebecca eyes were frozen to the road in front of them.

"Rebecca! Look at me!"

Slowly Rebecca's head turned.

Johnny saw the look of utter fear on her face. He asked again, his voice less menacing, "Do you have any idea how they found us?"

All Rebecca could do was shake her head. Tears began to spill down her face, her body trembling deep within, threatening to shake her to pieces.

Johnny almost drove through a stop light. He hit the brakes and watched as a police cruiser moved through the intersection, its driver giving the truck a quick once-over. They were directly in front of the Wynn Hotel, the street and sidewalks slick with the last rainfall. "Rebecca. Please snap out of it. I need you right now. We have to figure out how they found us so quickly. Rebecca. Please. I need you."

Johnny's pleading tone brought her back to reality. "Johnny!" She wiped at her face, pushed her fear aside, mind back to function mode. "Find a place where we can stop for a few minutes. Someplace where no one will see us."

* * *

Tony and Mr. Black stood in the middle of his study watching the PalmPilot. Norman was fast asleep, blue head tucked beneath a wing. Mr. Brown and Mr. Green had returned from their task, gotten drunk, and were passed out in separate rooms on the second floor. Tony's guests and Madame Olivia had left around two thirty. He had been keeping an eye on the PalmPilot while entertaining. The pulsing red dot hadn't moved for hours, then suddenly, it began moving south. "Looks like Mr. White has completed his task and is heading home with Orchid's suitcase," said Tony. He was about to snap the digital contraption closed when the red dot stopped. "What the fuck?"

"Looks like Mr. White has stopped to do a little Christmas gambling, man."

"He wouldn't do that! I told him once he eliminated the Indian and Orchid to return straight away! He wouldn't dare disobey my orders! Not after losing her in the first place." Reaching into a pocket, he pulled out his cell phone, eyes still on the PalmPilot, and thumbed Mr. White's cell. A connection was quickly made. After five chirps, Mr. White did not answer. Tony was about to close the phone when the line opened; however, he was not greeted by Mr. White's voice, but the sound of breathing. Quickly he closed the phone. "It's a good thing these things aren't traceable. Something is not right. I'd bet a million dollars that the person who picked up just now was a cop. I could smell him over the line."

"I told you I should have taken care of this, man. There wouldn't be any mistakes. They would be dead by now. The Indian must have gotten the upper hand."

"Yes, but how? Mr. White is usually very good at keeping a low profile when it comes to these matters." He looked to the PalmPilot. The pulsing red dot hadn't moved. He thumbed a few keys. "Well, now's your chance. They're stopped near the back of Harrah's. Take this with you." He handed the PalmPilot to Mr. Black. "I want them dead, do you hear! Dead! Dead! Dead!" Picking up a tumbler of Scotch from his desk, he took a long swallow. "That little bitch has just cost me one of my best men and who knows how much trouble. I'm going to have to grease a lot of palms."

Pocketing the PalmPilot, Mr. Black looked to his employer whose face was red with anger. "I'll be there in fifteen minutes, man. They'll be dead in sixteen. And I won't even get any blood on my nice new suit."

When Mr. Black left the study, Tony Millions opened a drawer, took out a small container of cocaine, brass cylinder, and tapped out two even lines. Leaning forward, he ingested Bolivia's finest through each nostril. Sniffing the uncut cocaine, he pulled habitually at his nose. He thought of the big Indian, described to him by Mr. White, picturing him in his numbing mind. He dropped into the chair, and drained the tumbler of its contents. "You're going to get yours now whoever the fuck you are. Merry fucking Christmas."

* * *

Johnny had pulled into the parkade behind Harrah's into a darkened corner and away from the other vehicles. There he killed the engine. They sat in silence for a few moments. The stone in Johnny's pocket still warm. "Okay. What do we do now?" he asked.

Without answering, Rebecca pulled her suitcase from the back, laid it across her lap, and popped the lid. "These men. They have a lot of people in their pockets and probably have access to a lot of things. Like you said. There's no way they could have found us so fast." She looked at the suitcase's contents. "I bet you they planted something in here. It's the only way they could have found us, right?"

"You're not only beautiful, but smart too. You're right. It's the only way they could have found us." He paused in thought for a moment. "What's the one thing you couldn't do without? The one thing they knew you would keep close to you?"

Together they looked at the photo of Rebecca's mother. "Of course!," she proclaimed, taking the frame and turning it over.

"Take off the back," said Johnny. "And do it quickly. If you're right, then they're still tracking us."

Rebecca's fingers worked quickly. When she flipped up the clasps and lifted the back, there it was, black and slim, no bigger than a stick of gum. "What do we do with it?" she asked.

Johnny took in their surroundings. There was no movement in the parkade. He could see the rear entrance of the hotel where a taxi was parked, its driver reading a newspaper. "I've got an idea," he said. "Give me the thing."

Rebecca handed over the tracking devise. "What are you going to do?"

"I'm going to send them on a wild-goose chase." Reaching behind him, he grabbed the knapsack and took out a hundred dollars in twenties. "You stay here. I'll be right back." Getting out of the truck, he moved across the asphalt at a quick pace. When he got to the taxi, he tapped on the window.

The Asian driver powered it down. "You need cab?"

"Yes," said Johnny. "But I'm playing a little joke on some friends of mine. How would you like to make a hundred dollars."

The cabbie smiled. "Yes Yes. Its been slow night."

Johnny gave the smiling cabbie the money. "I want you to take this and drive around the city for a half hour." He handed what looked to the driver like a thin strip of plastic.

"What is it?"

"It's a special key that belongs to a friend of mine. He's looking for it. It's kind of a game. Do you know what I mean?"

"Oh yes. A game. I drive. One-half hour. Then what?"

"Then you go to New York, New York, and give the key to the person at the front desk, okay? Tell them to hold on to it. That someone will pick it up in a minute or two."

"Okay. I go now." The cabbie powered the window and pulled away from the arched curb, then disappeared down the back entrance, brake lights illuminating each time the vehicle came to a speed bump.

Johnny went back to the truck where Rebecca waited anxiously. The suitcase and knapsack were tucked back into the rear seating. "I was watching you. Did you give that man the tracking devise?"

"Yes. I told him to drive around Vegas for a while then drop it off at New York, New York. I gave him the hundred to do it. If someone *is* following us again, they're about to be taken for a ride." He smiled, smug with his decision.

"Johnny. You didn't. These men are ruthless. What if they catch up to the driver? They'll be so mad, they'll probably kill him!"

The smile fell from Johnny's face. "Oh shit! I didn't think about that. I was only thinking about saving you. What did I do? Oh no, Rebecca. I might have just killed that man." He banged his head against the steering wheel.

Putting a hand on the back of his head, Rebecca said, "You were trying to protect me. You just didn't think things through. Let's hope that that man gets to the New York Hotel before they catch up to him. They wouldn't dare make a scene there. Not with all those people around."

Lifting his worried head, Johnny said, "I hope you're right, Rebecca. I couldn't live with myself if I knew I was responsible for the death of an innocent man." He looked at his hands, his mind's eye beholding the blood of Mr. White and Dwight Thompson on them.

"Promise me the next time you get an idea, you share it so that we can think it through together, okay?" Rebecca leaned forward, kissed him on the cheek. In *her* mind, she saw the white cross with his name on it, a revelation she would never burden him with. Whatever journey they were about to undertake and for however long, knowing it would end in tragedy, would remain an enigma that only she would bear. To lift his spirits, she said, "You know the cabbies in Vegas drive like maniacs. They'll probably never catch him. I'm sure he'll be all right." Moving back to her seat, she fastened the seat belt. "What we need to do now is find ourselves a room for the night. Maybe even for a few days. Someplace out of the way. The police will be looking for this truck by now, and the traffic is almost nonexistent. It will stand out like a stop light in a snowstorm. Do you know of any nice, sleazy motels where we'll be able to hide for the time being?" She smiled, though it was one fashioned by frayed nerves and indelible fear.

* * *

Mr. Black was nearly to the Harrah's Hotel when the pulsing red light began to move again. Had he continued toward the back of the hotel, he would have seen the red pickup pulling out of the parkade. The predator was that close to its prey. Instead he followed the direction the PalmPilot was dictating, the black machine moving surreptitiously through the streets.

He turned north on Flamingo Avenue, the PalmPilot telling him that his quarry was only a couple of blocks ahead, but all he could see was a taxi in the distance.

Mr. Black looked left, right, and behind. No sign of the red pickup. When the taxi in front of him turned left, so did the pulsing red dot on the PalmPilot. *They must have ditched the truck and taken a cab to throw us off. Clever. But not clever enough.* Maintaining a reasonable distance from the cab, he followed it through the downtown core of Vegas as it seemed to have no discernable destination. For nearly half an hour, the cab looped and turned, circled and drove in various directions, pissing him off to no end. Then finally, it pulled into the entrance of the New York, New York, Hotel, stopped, and just sat there. Mr. Black could not see anyone else in the cab except for the driver who then got out and went through the automated glass entrance. He put the Cadillac in park, killed the engine, and followed the driver into the posh hotel.

The Asian driver walked right up to a young lady working the front desk, spoke, and handed her something. Then he left, smiling as if he'd just heard a good joke, got back into the cab, and drove away. It didn't take rocket science for Mr. Black to understand that he had been duped. They'd found the device. He smiled inwardly, giving the Indian and Orchid kudos for having come up with such a clever plan. Tony Millions would be pissed. *But what are you going to do?* He walked up to the pretty brunette who was garbed smartly in a blue dress suit and said, "That gentleman just gave you something"—he looked to the name tag—"Jordon." He waited for her to offer further direction.

"Yes. A key. Something about a game being played. Told me someone would be by in a minute or two to pick it up. That must be you. Your friends must have a strange sense of humor to play a prank this early on Christmas Day."

"You have no idea. May I have the key please." He offered his great white teeth.

"Certainly." Jordon handed him the slim tracking device. "Do you mind my asking what the key is for."

In a serious tone, Mr. Black said, "If I told you, Jordon, I would have to kill you." Then he let out a booming laugh, turning the heads of several people who happened to be walking by.

"That's funny. You had me going there for a second. Well, I hope you get even with them," she said, and smiled sweetly.

"Believe me, sweetheart. I will." He turned to leave.

"Sir."

Mr. Black turned on his heels. "Yes."

"For what it's worth. Merry Christmas."

"And a very merry Christmas to you, Jordon." Leaving the hotel, he pocketed the troublesome gadget, returned to the Cadillac, sat behind the wheel, pulled out his cell phone, and hit number 9.

Tony Millions immediately picked up. "Mr. Black. I trust you have good news."

"On the contrary, man. You're not going to like what I have to tell you."

* * *

Furious from Mr. Black's calamitous news, shaking with uncontrolled anger, Tony Millions slammed the cell phone on the top of his desk. "That fucking bitch!" he yelled within the confines of his study. He turned this way and that, knocking items around, kicking at the air in a pitiful, childish tantrum. He had to let loose his frustrations.

He went upstairs to the master's bedroom where Pamela lay sleeping, a pink night mask covering her eyes. He flipped on the light switch. He had disrobed, leaving pieces of his suit in clumps on the stairway and now stood in the doorway completely naked, erection pointing toward the bed.

Disturbed from her four-martini, and three hundred dollars worth of nose candy slumber, Pamela removed the mask from her eyes. When she saw Tony standing there, breathing heavy, the ire on his face, the rage in his eyes, not to mention that Morgan the Organ was aimed straight at her, she turned the covers from her naked body, and pleaded, "Please, Tony. Not in the face."

* * *

53

The Park Pines Motel

JOHNNY pulled the truck into the lot of the Park Pines Motel and in front of the rental office. The two-storey motel offered free cable, kitchenette rooms, and favorable privacy. There were only three vehicles in the lot and two bicycles fronting blue-painted doors. A red neon sign above the office, the Y burnt out flashed VACANC. A strand of red Christmas lights with several bulbs missing hung haphazardly beneath the neon. It was the type of place one would see in a *slasher* flick where the psychopath office manager, one by one, murders his guests as they arrived. Perfect for their requirements.

"I guess this is as good a place as any," said Johnny, killing the engine. "Besides, we're getting low on gas."

"I love it. It's out of the way and very très chic." Rebecca laughed, then yawned, then laughed again. "I better get myself into a bed quick."

Beyond the grimy window, Johnny could see an old man leaning on the counter watching something high and in the corner. Removing his wet socks and much to his dismay, remembered he didn't have any identification. "I don't have ID. These places always ask for ID."

"Don't worry, I do. Just call me Tiffany Rose from Baltimore Maryland and follow my lead. I'll explain later. And by the looks of the guy behind the counter, a little cash in his hand might go a long way."

"There's something I need to know before we go in there."

"Oh. What is it?"

"Dallas. Is he with us?"

Rebecca needn't look for the answer. She had not seen spirit Dallas since he vanished through the wall of the rooming house barking like the end of the world was near. "I'm sorry, Johnny. Dallas is gone. He's been gone for a while now."

"Do you think he'll come back?"

"Honestly, Johnny, I can't answer that. The whole purpose of his visiting you might have been for one reason and one reason only. To stay with you so that he could warn us of impending danger."

"I hope not. But if that's the case, it was nice to know he was around.

Rebecca put a hand over his. "Just because I can't see him doesn't mean he's not with you."

"I guess you're right. He'll always be with me here." Johnny put a hand to his heart. "I sure do miss him." They looked into each other's eyes for a moment before kissing.

"Okay, *Tiffany Rose*," said Johnny, thumbing the area beneath a dazzling green eye. "Lead the way."

Barefoot, they left the truck, opened the screened door, and stepped up to the counter. Wearing a red plaid shirt under black suspenders and threadbare jeans, the old man took his eyes off the television mounted in the corner and smiled missing and broken teeth. His white hair was cropped military short. A used hanky protruded from the plaid shirt, and there was a cigarette burning in a glass ashtray in front of him from which a curl of blue rose to the ceiling. "Merry Christmas," he said in a phlegm-filled voice. "What brings you two to my humble abode so early on Christmas Day?" Picking up the smoke, he took a quick puff, then smashed the remainder among other partially smoked butts, the inhaled smoke exiting his nostrils in a twin blast of blue.

Johnny let Rebecca do the talking since she was the one with the ID.

"We thought we would spend the Christmas holidays traveling." Looping an arm through Johnny's, she added, "Stop here and there. Spend a couple of days in each place and see the sights. We got tired and saw your sign. You do have a vacancy, don't you?" She smiled a beautiful smile. One she knew would pull at the old guy's heartstrings.

"As a matter a fact, I have several." He looked up at Johnny. "Would you like a king-sized bed? Queen-size bed or a double? Are you planning on doin' any cookin'? 'Cause if you are, I can get you a room with small kitchen for an extra ten spot a night."

"How much are your rooms... um ?"

"Call me Poppi, little lady. Everybody does. Got thirteen grandchildren. Rooms are 39.50 a night, includes tax. You won't find cheaper anywhere. Guarantee it."

"Very reasonable. You must be very proud to have so many grandchildren."

"Oh, I am. Though I don't get to see them as often as I would like. Spread out all over the States. This place kinda keeps me pinned down. They'll call me in a few hours after they open their gifts. That's about all I can look forward to I guess. How long you plan on stayin'?"

"Oh, I don't know. Perhaps three, maybe four days."

Poppi pulled out a registry. "I like doin' things the old-fashioned way," he said, and opened it. "Hate them damn computer things. They're the devil's work I tell yah. Still gotta keep track of things though, damned government. They should all be strung up by their toes if yah ask me. Bunch a thieves."

"We'll take a room with a queen-size. Hopefully one on the second floor overlooking the parking lot. Johnny is very protective of his truck."

"Second floor it is. Got the perfect room for a nice couple such as yourselves.

Number 21. Right on the end. New sheets and everythin'. How will you be payin'? I take Master Card. Visa. American Express. Don't take no checks though. Got burned too many times."

"Is cash okay?" said Rebecca, setting her handbag on the counter.

"Cash is king far as I'm concerned. No paperwork. Fits real nice inside the pocket. I do however need to see some ID. You know how it is. Government policy and all."

"Yes, of course," said Rebecca, fishing for her Velcro wallet and removing the driver's license and social insurance card for one Tiffany Rose of Baltimore. "Will these do?"

Poppi picked up the license, looked at the photo. "*Say*, you folks have come a long way. That's a real nice picture, um, Tiffany. Real nice. Most driver license photos don't do justice. Yours looks just like you. Pretty as a picture as they say." He tried out her full name. "Tiffany Rose. Now that's a name that suits you just fine."

"I'd like to pay for three nights if that's okay with you." The grandfather of thirteen was as lonely as they came, and Rebecca felt sorry for him. She was, however, exhausted and desperately needed to sleep. Nearly getting killed will do that to a person. She made a promise to herself that once she was rested, she would go out of her way to help fill the void in his life with some conversation. Withdrawing a thick wad of twenties, she placed them on the counter.

"That's fine by me. That'll be. Let me see now." Poppi regarded the smoke-blemished ceiling as if it were a calculator. "That'll be a hundred and eighteen dollars and fifty cents by my calculations."

Rebecca counted out the money.

"Now if you'll just sign here." Poppi turned the ledger around, pointed to an empty line, handing Rebecca a pen and her fake ID. He looked up at Johnny again. "You know, young fella. If you're concerned about somebody maybe stealin' your truck, you can park it behind the office so's it's out of the way. That's where I live. Nobody goes back there. And if they do, they get a blast of rock salt up their asses."

"Thanks, Poppi," said Johnny. "I think I'll take you up on that offer. I do love my truck."

"Can't says I blame you. She's a beaut."

Rebecca finished signing *Tiffany Rose* to the ledger and the address she had taken the time to memorize on the driver's license. Same as she did for the identification stating she was a resident of Las Vegas and was glad that she had. "I guess we'll just get the keys and be off."

"Course." Poppi gave her change and a brass key on the end of a blue plastic fob advertising the name of the motel. "You rest comfortably now. There's a restaurant just down the road called Big Bob's diner. Foods real good and cheap too. Best breakfast this side of them fancy hotels."

"We'll remember that," said Johnny. "Thanks, Poppi." He and Rebecca turned to leave.

"Oh and folks. Once again. Have a merry Christmas and welcome to the Park Pines Motel."

* * *

Once they were back at the truck, Rebecca yanked the suitcase out from behind the front seats. Johnny sat at the wheel. "Why don't you let me bring that up for you? It's heavy and you're tired."

Standing in the open passenger side of the truck, Rebecca said, "Thanks, Johnny, but I need to do a few things before I go to bed. You know, freshen up. Girl stuff."

"Oh. I see. Then I'll just park the truck and be right up. Won't be more than a minute or two."

"See you then. Oh, and see if you can't park the truck so the rear is hidden somehow. Because of the Wyoming licence plate."

"Good call."

Rebecca closed the door. Suitcase in hand, she walked toward the flight of stairs leading to the second annex of the motel where a metal-capped lamp fastened to a tall post lent her enough light to manage her way.

Johnny started the truck, pulled away from the office, and headed for the rear, headlights beaming a path and illuminating weeds that had pushed their way through the cracked blacktop. There was ample space behind the office, and a thick hedge of bushes next to a decaying pine. He reversed the truck and parked it until he knew the plate was hidden within the overgrowth of the hedge. *That was very smart of Rebecca,* he thought. He grabbed the knapsack, retrieved the gun from the glove compartment, stuffed it into the knapsack, locked the doors, and headed for room 21.

Rebecca unlocked the blue door. Finding the light switch, she set the suitcase and purse on the queen-sized bed that was, as promised, nicely adorned with a fresh set of linen. Opening the suitcase, she removed a pair of clean panties, nightshirt, toothbrush, paste, and hairbrush. Before closing the lid, she glanced at the picture of her mother, thinking how terrible it would have been for her and Johnny if they hadn't found the tracking devise. They could both be in the trunk of Mr. Black's Cadillac, headed out to the desert where they would be executed, left to decompose in a shallow grave, their time together ending before it had a chance to flourish. A splinter of sadness broached her heart. She would spend every waking moment with Johnny, her childhood companion, her ill-fated lover. Walk hand in hand with him on their journey, loving him every instant, never disclosing the knowledge she carried until the end which could be tomorrow, next week, next year. For time could be joyous. It could also be cruel.

She took in her surroundings. Sitting askew over the brass rails of the headboard was a print of some mountains. A small round table with two chairs sat in the corner near the bathroom. In front of the bed, perched on a small dresser was a portable television. Above the television was a velvet painting of Elvis singing into a mike, the white collar of his gem-studded jacket pulled up around his ears.

Placing the suitcase in front of the bed, Rebecca went to the bathroom, grooming products in one hand, small purse in the other. There, she saw in the mirror the toll of the night. Her hair was a tangled mess. The usual light of her green eyes, dulled as if they had been thieved of life. Resting the paste and toothbrush on the sink, she began to stroke the tangles out of her hair.

A moment later the door to room 21 opened, causing her heart to skip a beat. Although they were miles away from the reaches of Tony's men, her nerves were still completely tattered. When she saw that it was Johnny, she let out the breath she was holding. "I'll be out in a minute," she said, toeing the door closed.

Johnny dropped the knapsack next to the suitcase, opened it, removed the gun, put the safety on, and slipped it beneath the pillow on which he would lay his head. He stared at the Elvis painting for a moment, hearing in his mind the premonitory lyrics of "Viva! Las Vegas" that had taken him to this very moment. Clicking on a small lamp sitting on one of the nightstands, he went to the blue door, set the dead bolt, and killed the main light. The comfort of the bed called to him, so he sat on its edge, stretched, and yawned just as the sound of running water emanated from the only other room.

Uninvited, the night's events began to unfold in his mind. Not wanting to revisit them, he took the remote and clicked on the TV. It took several moments for the black screen to come to life. When it did, the colors were running into each other. He channel-surfed until he found a station that wasn't news. Since it was early Christmas morning, the only other programs were cartoons. Leaning back, he rested his head against the .38 caliber pillow and watched. Tom and Jerry were up to their same old antics.

Granting that adrenalin was still pumping through his system, Johnny's eyes began to grow weary, and he caught himself just before they closed.

The toilet flushed. The bathroom door opened. Rebecca stood in the lighted doorway, a white T-shirt dropped to her knees, the light behind her causing the flimsy polyester to be transparent. In her arms were jeans and the T-shirt she had been wearing, on top of which was the purse Johnny knew contained her addiction. She was even more beautiful than he could have imagined. Gone was the temptress he saw on the stage. In her place was a young woman whose beauty could put any flower to shame. Staring at her for a moment, he looked away, somewhat embarrassed.

Rebecca flipped the light switch, plunging the bathroom into darkness. Making her way to the bed, she set the clothes and purse neatly on the nightstand. "Do you need to use the bathroom?" she asked, her eyes on the televised cartoons.

Johnny clicked off the set. "Right now, I just need to sleep. I'll freshen up later. Did you take more pills?"

"Yes, but only one. It'll help me sleep without the after effects." Sitting on the bed, she tucked one leg beneath the other, her hair falling about her face. Pushing it back, she yawned and took Johnny's hand. "We have a lot to talk about."

"I know. But for right now, I think the most important thing is to get some sleep. You can tell me about the whole Tiffany Rose thing in the morning. I'll stay on top of the covers so you can have some privacy."

"That's sweet of you, but I would rather fall asleep in your arms. I'll feel safer."

Johnny reached out to her. Rebecca eased her way into his arms and rested her head on his broad shoulder. Johnny put an arm around her, pulling her tight, feeling for the first time in a very long time the press of someone who truly loved him. Rebecca tilted her head, kissed him on the cheek. "I love you, Johnny Black."

Walking into her eyes again, he said, "And I love you, Rebecca White." Reaching, he clicked off the lamp, wondering what, as his friend Hector would say, mañana was going to reveal.

Within the sleeping shadows of room 21, coupled in an embrace everlasting, they listened to the sound of each other's breathing until their eyes closed and darkness took them down. One heart. One mind. One soul.

Another page turned.

* * *

54

The Contract

TONY stood at the head of the table, a golden robe cinched at the waist. In his hand he held a crystal tumbler of nearly finished thirty-year Balvenie. Mr. Brown, Mr. Black, and Mr. Green waited for him to say something. Tony cleared his throat, swallowing Scotch-flavored phlegm.

It was noon, and the only thing he had ingested were three tumblers of Scotch and a snootful of cocaine. Still furious, though he had taken his frustrations out on Pamela who now hid in the master's bedroom nursing her bruises, he slammed the table with a fist. "One of my best men is no longer with us because of this fucking Indian." He eyeballed his men. "Who the fuck is this guy? First he kills Mr. White, then he gives you, Mr. Black, the slip." He pointed an accusatory finger at Mr. Black's face. "You're supposed to be the best. And yet two kids, and let's not lose fact that that is exactly what we're dealing with here, a couple of kids, slipped right through your fingers. FUCK!" He slammed the table again.

Mr. Black narrowed his eyes. He did not take kindly being talked to this way, but he would remain silent for the moment and let him rant.

Tony looked across the table to Mr. Brown. "As soon as the DMV opens, I want you to get in touch with our friends and find out who that truck belongs to, *capice*?"

"Yes, Tony," said Mr. Brown, the smirk on his face intended for Mr. Black.

"Good. Once we find out the identity of this guy, I want his whole fucking family dead. Do you understand? Men, women, children, even their pets. I want them to suffer so this bastard understands who the fuck he's dealing with. Kill one of my men will he. Well, he's going to find out just how ruthless we can be."

"What about Orchid's friends in Kentucky," asked Mr. Brown. "Shouldn't we send a message to her as well?"

"You leave the Harts to me. I have other plans for them. I want *you*, Mr. Black, to scour Vegas. Orchid and her new companion could not have gotten very far. If I were them, and I had just killed someone, I would have tried to find a place to hide as soon as possible, to establish what course of action need be taken next. Whether to run or stay put. As soon as they pop their heads out from their hiding place, we'll nail them. I'll have our friends in the police department keep an eye out for a red pickup driven by an Indian.

"They could be a thousand miles from here by now, man," Mr. Black pointed out.

"I don't think so. They must be scared shitless, and in my experience, scared people hide, they don't run right away. A running rabbit is easier to spot than one that's hiding in the bushes. They now know we're after them. They'll stay put. At least for the time being." Pointing a finger at Mr. Black again, he said, "You find them, Mr. Black, or you'll be seeking employment elsewhere. Do I make myself clear?"

Mr. Black folded his hands together and placed them on the table. "I don't think I like your tone… man."

"Well, that's too fucking bad! I give the orders around here, not you! I can have you replaced with a phone call. You *are* expendable, just remember that. All of you are for that matter. You, Mr. Black, will focus on finding our little Orchid and this Indian. When you do, I want you to bring them to me before we exterminate them. Mr. Brown?"

"Yes, Tony."

"Get in touch with the Preacher. Tell him we need a new recruit. Same price as always."

"I'll get in touch with him as soon as this meeting's over."

Mr. Green spoke. "What am I to do, Tony?"

"Assist Mr. Brown for the time being. I'll need you back at the club once it opens tomorrow. I want you to talk to the other girls. Find out anything Orchid might have told them. We might get a clue as to where they'll run to once they decide to flee."

"You got it."

"Good. You know your assignments. Get it done, gentlemen. This meeting is over."

"What about replacing Mr. Blue?" asked Mr. Brown.

"I haven't got time for that right at the moment. When I do, I will find a suitable replacement. Now get the fuck out of my office!"

Mr. Brown and Mr. Green stood. Mr. Black remained in his chair. Once his co-conspirators were gone, he stood and pointed a long hard finger at Tony Millions face. "You pay me well for the work I do, but if you ever point that finger of yours at me like that again, I'm going to bite it off. Do I make *myself* clear… man?"

"Just do what you've been told to do. Now! I have other business to attend to."

"As you wish. Just remember what I said. I'll bite it off and eat it for lunch." Mr. Black stood to his enormous height of six feet ten inches, a tug of a smile lifting one side of his face. "I'll find them," he said then left the room.

"Don't come back until you do!" said Tony to the closing door. Plopping himself in the chair, he emptied the remainder of Scotch, pulled a cell phone from the desk, and keyed the area code for Chicago, then the number.

"Yes," a voice on the other end answered.

"I wish to speak with Mr. Santangello. Tell him it's Tony Millions."

"Are you crazy?" the voice said. "It's Christmas and he's with his family."

"Just get him on the line. Tell him I will make it worth his while."

"He's not going to like being disturbed."

"Just do as I ask." *Sniff*

The line fell silent. After what was a long, impatient wait, Mr. Santangello's voice filled the silence. "This better be good, Tony. I was just about to sit down to lunch with my grandchildren."

"I need a job done."

"I see. And this could not have waited until tomorrow?"

"No. The sooner the contract is filled, the better."

"What are you offering?'

"Fifty, no, make it seventy-five per head."

"That's generous."

"I want only your best men."

"I understand Mr. White is no longer with you. News travels fast. Too bad. He was good."

"Shit happens."

"Yes, it does. Give me the particulars, Tony, and I'll see what I can do."

Tony gave him the names of the Harts and the town in which they lived. "I want them to suffer," he added.

"For seventy-five each. I'm sure we can arrange something."

The call disconnected.

Tony Millions smiled, sniffed, looked at his empty tumbler, and decided he needed a full one. *Things were going to turn out fine,* he thought. *They always do for me. Always.*

* * *

55

Sea of Love

REBECCA woke, still nestled in Johnny's powerful arms and to the sound of a crow purchased on the rooftop directly above. Sunlight leached through a crack in the drawn curtains. Elvis looked down at them. Young laughter came from outside. Rubbing at her eyes, she wondered what time it was. "Johnny?" She cupped his face in her hand.

"I'm awake," he said, opening his eyes, losing himself in her beauty. "I've been watching you sleep for quite some time. Did you know you snore? Just a little."

"I do? I'm sorry. I hope I didn't keep you up."

"No. It wasn't your snoring that woke me. It was a dream I had."

Rebecca nuzzled her face against the musculature of his yoke. "Care to share?"

Johnny tried to remember what it was that had woken him, but it was all a white fuzz, except for a small piece of the dream where he was flying. "To tell you the truth, I don't remember much. Hardly anything at all except for the flying part."

"Oh. One of those. Well, if you do happen to remember later, I'm a really good listener." Kissing him on the cheek, she contemplated, "I wonder what time it is?"

"I was just thinking the same thing."

The cackling crow ceased with its rooftop raucous.

"I'm hungry," said Rebecca, the need for nourishment and the desire for more Percocet cramping her stomach.

"Me too." Johnny yawned.

"Do you think Big Bob's diner is open?" asked Rebecca.

"We can ask Poppi. If it is, it'll be a good place to talk. You take a shower. I'll go and ask if the diner is open."

Looking down at their naked feet, Rebecca said, "I know one thing. We need to get ourselves some shoes." She wiggled her toes. Johnny did the same. "We can't go around barefoot all the time. People will think we're weird or something." Smoothing the bottom of her right foot over his, she added, "How long do you think we'll be safe here?"

"I don't know. But for today, I don't believe we have anything to worry about. The truck is out of sight, and deep down I don't feel like we're in immediate danger." The stone in his pocket was cool, indicating things were okay, for the present.

"I agree. I feel safe right now too. Safer than I have been in a while." A moment passed. "Johnny?"

"Yes."

"Last night. You did what you had to. You shouldn't feel guilty about it. I would be dead right now if it wasn't for you." Lifting her head from his shoulder, she turned her body so that she was comfortable atop of him. Looking deep into his wolf eyes, she said, "I'll never forget what you've done for me." Kissing his mouth warmly, her eyes remained open so that she could see his handsome face. "I do love you, Johnny Black. Thank you." Using the palm of her hand, she pushed herself into a sitting position, one leg tucked beneath the other.

About to respond in kind, three loud, startling bangs interrupted their short lived, easy disposition. Johnny bolted upright. His first instinct was to shield Rebecca. One powerful arm drew her behind him. The other reached for the gun beneath the pillow. When they realized the noise was just some kids lighting firecrackers, nervous laughter filled room 21. "You see," said Rebecca once she managed her breath. "You were sent to protect me, even if it's from some fireworks." She kissed him again, a deep, penetrating show of affection. "Time to take that shower. You go and see if you can find out whether or not Big Bob's diner is open today."

Johnny watched her rise from the bed. *Beautiful.* "I hope it is. I'm so hungry I could eat a couple of kids lighting firecrackers."

Rebecca chortled, went into the bathroom, purse in hand, flipped on the light and closed the door.

Johnny swung his legs off the bed, stood, stretched, and said to the velvet Elvis in his best imitation of the King, "How about a little thank-you-very-much for bringing us together."

* * *

According to the young girl acting as clerk who had introduced herself as Nichol ("Everybody calls me Nikki") while Poppi took a nap, Big Bob's diner was about a half mile south of the motel and was always open, she explained. "Big Bob's not much for the holiday season," she told Johnny. She had rounded the front counter to reveal the fullness of her fifteen years beneath a Rolling Stones T-shirt and jean shorts. Framed within a crop of blond with pink highlights flourished a narrow face, bright baby blues, desirable lips and nose diamond. Libido in full gear. Before Johnny left, he learned it was just past noon. The promiscuous part-time clerk also informed that Poppi was going to deep-fry a turkey for the guests and to be sure to, "come by around six."

* * *

Showered, Johnny left his hair loose as per Rebecca's request and toweled himself dry. His feather, its length of tether and turquoise stone rested atop the toilet tank. Since they did not possess a blow-dryer and one wasn't supplied by the motel, he would have to rely on the sun. With no toothbrush of his own, he borrowed some toothpaste Rebecca had left on the sink and finger-brushed his teeth. Finished, he put on clean jeans, black T-shirt, collected the feather and tether and inserted the birthday gift deep into a front pocket.

When he exited the bathroom, Rebecca was running a brush through her hair and waiting for him on the $39.95 per night bed. She was wearing a pair of Levis and a T-shirt that read, Angel Without Wings. Midday sun poured through now open curtains igniting the lustre of McClintock red.

"Come and sit down," she said. "I want to try something different with your hair."

Johnny sat next to her. "Nothing too crazy I hope."

Rebecca examined his wet hair for a moment before running the brush through. He was so handsome, she thought. "That feather is obviously important to you," she said, looking at it clenched in Johnny's hand. "It's so unusual. Where did you get it?"

"It was given to me by a friend of mine. Her name is Konahee. She helped me when I needed it most," he offered, hoping Rebecca would not pry further, for he had every intention of keeping his promise. To never to speak of the events that took place while he was in seclusion at Konahee's place of magic.

"Oh, I see." The brush stopped. "May I have it please?"

Johnny handed it over.

As soon as the feather was in her hand, it appealed to her gift, as though it held within an abundant secret. Turning it over, the marking that for all intents and purposes looked like an eye stared back at her. Leveling Johnny's with her own, she saw the direct resemblance he obviously did not. "It's beautiful," she said.

"I can't explain, but it's important that I keep it with me always."

"I understand. I'm going to put a small braid in your hair so that it hangs down this side of your face." Running a finger over the left side of his jaw, she added, "And I'll put the feather in it so that it dangles in front of your ear." Handing it back to him, she continued, "This Konahee must be a very great woman. I'd like to meet her some day if it's possible." Taking three even lengths of his slick hair between fingers, she proceeded to create a triple braid.

"Who knows where we'll end up," said Johnny. "I certainly wouldn't want to bring her any trouble. We have enough to deal with on our own, no sense bringing people we care about into the mess we're in."

"Of course. You're right." Rebecca thought of the Harts hoping they were safe.

"So are you going to explain to me about the whole Tiffany Rose thing?"

"Not much to tell really. When I was abducted, I did not possess any form of identification." Fingers stopped working, her eyes went to the floor. "It burned in the fire. I didn't have the opportunity to retrieve it." She looked up again. "I was supplied with two sets identifying me as one Tiffany Rose. All of it very authentic. Passports, drivers licenses, the works. I can be Tiffany Rose, age 23 from Baltimore or Tiffany

Rose from Las Vegas. As you've seen, they have already come in handy. In a way it's a good thing since you don't have any of your own. We don't know where we're going. Either set could come in handy." Nimble fingers went back to work.

Johnny was going to express his remorse again for her losses then thought it better not to resurrect the sorrow she held close. "Well that's one good thing we have going for us."

"We also have each other Johnny. Together we're a formidable twosome."

"Yes we are, aren't we."

Once Rebecca finished the braid and the feather dangled just so, she gave her handiwork the once-over. "There. All done. Perfect if I do say so myself. Go look in the mirror. You're as handsome as a penguin in a tuxedo."

Johnny went to the bathroom to inspect his new look. He liked the braid. It was simple, yet manly. The slightly bowed feather curled just beneath his chin. He smiled. The pageantry of his Cherokee heritage smiled back. His stomach growled the need for food. To maintain his strength would be paramount, for the road ahead was going to be dangerously rough. There was no telling just how far the reach of this man named Tony Millions encompassed. However, for the time being, there was just the two of them, Johnny Black and Rebecca White, two lost souls who, by preordained influence found each other, and that's all that really mattered.

* * *

They resolved it was safer to leave the truck parked behind the rental office and walk to Big Bob's. The highway was void of traffic being Christmas Day, so, hand in hand and barefoot, they walked the half mile in the middle of the road while the sun dried their hair. The asphalt cozy warm on the pads of their feet. Rebecca had taken a hundred dollars from her savings and stuffed the bills in her jeans. She'd also taken a Percocet to offset the demons that had been demanding so much more.

"I hope you don't mind my asking. But do you have any money, Johnny? Just so we have a better picture of our finances."

"As a matter a fact, I have almost two thousand dollars."

"So do I. Well, that's one good thing. We're not broke. Tomorrow we'll find some place close to buy shoes, my treat."

"I hope Big Bob doesn't mind us being barefoot. A lot of places won't even let you in the door without shoes."

"Let's hope he has a good heart."

"What if he doesn't?"

"Then we'll order some food and eat outside. Kind of like a picnic. Surely he wouldn't mind. It is Christmas after all."

They walked the rest of the distance in silence, the December sun temperate on their young faces, their love of one another flourishing with every step taken. One drew strength from the other, heartbeats in perfect harmony, past and future irrelevant, at least for the time being.

Big Bob's diner was a single-storey building that had suffered the same fate as the Park Pines Motel, not enough clientele to afford rejuvenation. Built in the fifties, it remained a rumination of its former self, exterior blue paint almost nonexistent, the windows thick, burdened with decades of road dust and too much sun. It was set off the highway facing east, its asphalt parking pad cracked and lifted as though something were pushing from beneath. Weeds zigzagged from cracks, some pretty, Rebecca thought, their purple flowers bright. A wisp of blue smoke rose from a chrome stack that was charred black on top and gave the air a flavor of grease. The only semblance of recent times, a neon sign announcing, BIG BOB'S.

A bell above the door tinkled when Johnny opened it. "After you," he said, a chivalrous smile brightening his already-handsome features. For a pleasing second, Rebecca saw the dream lover of her veritable imagination.

She stepped in, Johnny followed and made sure the screen door did not slam. Rebecca's eyes wandered. A soda shop counter with red vinyl stools ran from one end to the other. Behind it was a rectangular opening where she could see a large man moving about in the kitchen. Four tables and two booths fronted the stretch of window. Taped to the walls in various sizes and colors were bristle board cutouts advertising daily specials. The only other person in the place was a woman, forty-something, Rebecca guessed, her hair coiffed and wearing a flower-patterned dress. She was sitting in the farthest booth, sipping on a cup of coffee or tea. Propped against the wall next to her stood a fifties Wurlitzer jukebox waiting for a quarter or two. The woman smiled. Rebecca returned the gesture in kind.

"Let's sit at this table," said Rebecca, moving to the nearest square of maple where three chairs waited and took a seat. Johnny sat across from her. A red laminated menu was wedged between a sugar dispenser, salt and pepper shakers, and a small bowl of creamers. They looked to the offered items taped to the wall, none of which cost more than $7.95

A single door leading to the kitchen swung open. A balding man, as big as Johnny and twice as broad, pushed his way through while wiping his hands on a dish rag. He moved toward them smiling and said, "Welcome to Big Bob's. As you can plainly see"—he looked down at the girth of his enormous stomach—"I'm Big Bob."

"Hello," Rebecca and Johnny chorused. Rebecca added, "Merry Christmas, Big Bob."

"And a merry Christmas to you, both. Not that I don't mind the business, but what brings you folks to my fine establishment today of all days. I didn't even here you pull up."

Johnny said, "We walked. We're staying at the Park Pines and were told you serve the best breakfast around."

"Can't argue with you there. My steak and eggs are famous in these parts. Say. How is Poppi? I haven't seen that old coot in about a month."

"Poppi's fine," Rebecca assured him. "I'll tell him you said hello." She noticed the gold band choking his ring finger.

"You do that, young lady. Now. What can I get for you? Coffee's free."

Whether or not Big Bob noticed they were barefoot, he made no mention of it.

Rebecca said, "I would like a cheeseburger with fries and gravy." Pausing for a trice, she added, "And a chocolate milkshake please."

"I like a girl who can pack away the food. And what about you son?"

"I think I'll have your famous steak and eggs of course. Steak medium rare please and a coffee."

"Oh, I'll have a coffee to start with too," piped Rebecca.

"Two coffees coming right up. Steak medium rare. How do you want your eggs?"

"Over easy please."

"What about white or whole wheat?"

"White will be fine. Thank you, Big Bob."

Big Bob went to the counter, poured two mugs of coffee, and returned, setting them on the table along with two spoons and napkins. "Do you want me to get started on your orders, or would you like some time to enjoy your coffees and this magnificent view." He laughed, his stomach rolling like a great storm, the triple folds beneath his almost-nonexistent chin jiggling to the rhythm of his mirth.

With nothing but time to kill and things to talk about, Johnny said, "We're not in any hurry, so why don't you give us some time to enjoy our coffees and, like you said, this magnificent view."

"Fine by me. I don't imagine I'll be getting much business today anyway."

"I hope you don't mind my asking," queried Rebecca. "But how come you're open on Christmas Day? Don't you have any family to be with?"

"To be honest. I haven't been much on this time of year for going on four years now." His face took on the slack of sad memory, his eyes, vacant orbs of loneliness. "I've got a son someplace. We don't talk much. He's never in one place for very long. The last time I saw him was at his mother's funeral." He tried a smile, the band around his finger suddenly dull.

"I'm sorry," said Rebecca. "I didn't mean to pry, and I'm sorry that your wife passed away."

"Me too. I loved that little woman. She helped me run this place for twenty years. We thought opening Big Bob's was going to be our ticket to an early retirement. Boy, were we wrong. Oh sure, in the beginning we had a pretty prosperous place. Lots of traffic until the state decided to put in a highway. Damned near put us out of business. Nowadays, most of it comes from the guests staying at the Park Pines. Like you two. So I stay open three hundred and sixty-five days of the year. I've got nothing better to do anyway. Not since my Maggie passed away. Listen to me." He forced a smile. "It's Christmas Day. You don't need to be hearing me lament. Enjoy your coffees and just let me know when I should start your orders. I'll be in the kitchen. Just give me a holler." Out of habit, the big man wiped his hands on the apron, smiled again, slowly turned, and headed for the kitchen.

When the door swung shut, Rebecca added a creamer to her coffee and said, "That's sad. I feel sorry for him."

"Yeah. Me too. Losing someone you love, well, you know as well as I do, it's hard to take."

For a brief pause in time, they each reflected on their losses until Rebecca broke their reverie. "I guess we should talk."

"Yes, we should."

Rebecca put her hands around the mug and took a sip, her eyes marking Johnny's. "Your truck. The police will be looking for it."

"I know."

"Is there any way that someone might know the license plate? Like did you have to give it to your landlady or anything?"

"No. All she cared about was the rent being paid on time. I hardly ever saw her."

"Well, that's one good thing. As long as we stay off the main roads, we should be all right, at least for the time being. Do you still feel safe?"

Johnny's hand went to the dormant stone in his pocket. "Yes. At least for now. I think we should stay put at the motel for a few days. It's well out of the way from everything. It'll give us more time to consider where to go next. What about you? Do you feel safe?"

Rebecca's feet searched beneath the table until they found Johnny's, her eyes smiling. "I feel safe if you do. Whatever we do, we do together. Watch out for each other. Tony isn't going to let go of what we did to one of his men very easily. They'll be looking for us. With the police looking for us and them looking for us, it isn't going to be easy to hide."

Johnny lifted his cup to his lips and took a long drink of the hot black java. "Yeah, I suppose you're right. But I've been running for a while now. Maybe together we can elude them, find some place out of reach. It's a big country. Lots of places to hide."

"Maybe Mexico. Or Canada! I understand Canada is beautiful. Plenty of places to hide up there. I guess that's something we'll have to decide pretty quick. But not right now. Right now I just want to enjoy this coffee." Reaching across the table, she took one of his hands. "We'll get through this, Johnny. Between us, we have almost four thousand dollars. That should be enough to feed us and take us wherever it is we decide to go. For a while anyway."

"And what about when the money runs out? What do we do then?"

"I haven't though that far ahead, and you shouldn't either. Let's just take it moment by moment. Let kismet continue to guide us. It's taken us to this moment, and I feel that it will be with us for a while. We were meant to be together, Johnny. Fate can be a powerful adversary."

Johnny wanted to say that fate could also be cruel, instead, he smiled at the beautiful young woman sitting across from him. "I want you to know that I will protect you the best I can."

"I know you will, Johnny. And I'll stay by your side no matter what."

"I know you will." A thought occurred to him. "At least we won't go hungry tonight."

"Why? Are we coming back here?"

"No. According to the clerk, Poppi is putting on a deep-fried turkey for the guests. Have you ever had deep-fried turkey?"

"No. Is it good?'

"You're in for a treat. My dad prepared it once. It's better than roasted."

"Well, that's something to look forward to then. I guess we'll have a Christmas dinner after all. It'll be our first. What a nice way to start our relationship. Don't you think?"

"Yeah, I guess it is pretty nice. Maybe we'll have kids someday, and it'll be a story we can share with them."

Rebecca had never thought of having children; however, the white cross bearing Johnny's name came to the forefront of her thoughts. She would have ten children with this man if it were not for the telling of his future. "It would make a wonderful story someday," she said to her love, smiling confidently, though fate had already sealed Johnny's.

* * *

After finishing the hardy meal, they had more coffee, paid the bill, thanked Big Bob, wished him a merry Christmas once more, and told him the meal was terrific and that if he was so inclined, Poppi wouldn't mind him showing up for some turkey.

As they were about to exit the restaurant, Rebecca looked back at the woman still sitting in the booth, drinking from a mug. She said to Johnny's back, "That's so sad." The door closed behind them. Johnny turned to her. "You mean Big Bob?"

"No. That woman who was sitting in the far booth behind us. She was so lonely. Imagine spending Christmas Day like that. Just sitting in a restaurant with no one to talk to. Maybe we should go back in and just say hello or something. Brighten her day. We have each other. She appears to have no one."

"Rebecca, there *was* no woman in the booth behind us. Other than Big Bob, we were the only others."

They turned to look through the windows. Rebecca saw the woman. Johnny saw an empty booth. Big Bob inserted some coins into the jukebox. The Wurlitzer came to life. Through the restaurant's facade, they could hear the beginning of "Sea of Love."

Come with me,
my... love
To the sea,
the sea of love.
I want to tell you,
Oh, how much, I love you...

Rebecca took Johnny's hand in hers.

It was the second time in less than twenty-four hours Johnny had witnessed the *gift* Rebecca possessed. Remarkable as it was, there was also something he found frightening about it. "We should get going," he said, looking down at her. "Walk off this big lunch. Leave the two of them alone."

* * *

56

She Talks to Angels

BY 6:00 p.m., Johnny had taken a second shower, for no other reason than to clean his road-dirty feet.

Rebecca watched the news while stroking the brush through her hair hundreds of times until it was shining, full of life, wondering when the time would come, for she was certain that it would, she would make love to the man in the other room. She had taken another painkiller. Only four remained, causing her to deliberate the deviations her body would undergo once she ran out.

Johnny pulled the black T-shirt over his head and flipped the length of his wet hair out from the back, deciding he would attend the dinner formally, and leave the tether and feather in the safety of the little motel room. He was looking forward to the deep-fried turkey and hopefully, friendly faces. They both needed an emotional break from the dangerous events that had occurred since their meeting. For the time being, they were still safe, he was certain of it.

Inspecting himself in the mirror, the eyes of the person staring back at him were those of someone whose heart was deeply involved with the woman in the other room, a woman he would die for. They were also the eyes of a second-time killer who would kill again if need be. Tucking the T-shirt, he cinched the belt, hoping nobody was going to mind that they were going to arrive at Poppi's Christmas dinner barefoot. Opening the door, he saw that Rebecca was still sitting where he had left her. Barely audible was the sound of the newscaster's voice as he spoke of the unsolved disappearance of an entire family, the Warrens.

Police are not closer to solving the bizarre disappearance of Rick Warren, his wife Karen, and their six-year-old son Billy...

Rebecca set the brush on the bed. "Isn't that awful? A whole family disappeared. Just like that."

"Yes, it is." Johnny went to the bed and sat next to her. She was even more beautiful than twenty minutes ago, he honestly believed it. "Unfortunately, it happens all the time. There's a lot of pretty bad people out there, you and I both know that. Was there anything about what happened last night?"

"Not a word. You'd think there would be at least some mention of it. Better for us that there isn't anyway." Picking up the remote, she aimed it and killed the screen, wondering if Tony Millions's influence had anything to do with it. Turning, she looked up into Johnny's face, seeing the worry he was desperately trying to hide. "I guess you want me to braid your hair again."

Johnny put the tether and feather on Rebecca's pillow. "No. I think I'll leave them here for the time being. Who knows what kind of people will be at the dinner. I already look like an Indian. No point in adding fuel to the fire. Just in case."

Rebecca looked to the unusual feather resting atop the pillow. "Are you sure?"

Johnny followed her eyes. "Yeah. Just for tonight. You can put it back in when we come back."

The eye, as far as Rebecca could tell, was staring directly at Johnny's face. "Okay. Just for the next few hours, then it's going back where it belongs. And once it's back in, it's staying there. You and *it* need to be together. Like peaches and cream. That much I'm sure of."

"Well, are you ready to face the other dinner guests?"

"I am if you are."

Rebecca raised herself so they were face-to-face, mere inches apart. "Let's have fun tonight, Johnny. It's important that we do."

"I know."

They stared deep into each other for a devoted moment before their lips touched, a promise made that they would put aside their troubled times and just be with each other.

Rebecca broke the kiss, cupping his strong jaw in her hand. "I hope you don't mind my saying it again, but I love you, Johnny Black."

Taking her lovely face in his hands, he lost himself in the depths of her green gaze. Drawing thumbs across soft lips, he kissed her, tenderly, taking her into his powerful arms, loving every second of their closeness. Rebecca welcomed his mouth, giving back with a passion far beyond her eighteen years.

As they kissed, the owners of the fireworks broke the silent bliss between them. *Bang! Bang! Bang!*

Reluctantly they parted.

"I guess that's our signal the party has started," said Johnny.

Rebecca's eyes brightened. "Shall we join them?"

"I guess now is as good a time as any."

They left room 21 and locked the door. Velvet Elvis kept watch over their meager belongings; almost four thousand dollars in cash, the .38 tucked beneath the pillow, and a part of Johnny that was more important than he could ever imagine.

They made their way down wooden stairs, Johnny in lead should Rebecca lose her balance. At the back of the rental office, where the truck was conveniently out of sight, they could see the blue flame of propane and the huge steel cauldron where, in about an hour, a crispy tender bird would be lifted from. There were people sitting in lawn chairs, six by quick count, and Poppi was talking to one of them. From their distance, it was difficult to tell whether the goliath human was man or woman.

Two young boys on bicycles appeared out of nowhere, one from the east, the other from the west. They came to a skidding stop. Each scallywag had gripped tightly in their hands, yellow and black checkered firecrackers. "Hey," a slightly bucktoothed, freckled-faced eight- might be ten-year-old said, then added with unabashed approval, "Holy cow. You sure got like a gazillion freckles. I got some, but, wow! You must have the most in the whole wide world." Mischievous eyes roaming, he introduced himself. "My name's Garth. This is Tommy."

"Hi," the boy named Tommy said from beneath a Giant's baseball cap. Jamming firecrackers into the pocket of his grey hoodie, he held out a polite hand.

Orchid took it and gave it a gentle shake. "Hi, boys. My name is Tiffany."

"Yeah, we know," Garth and Tommy chorused, Tommy slipping his now-sweaty palm from hers.

"My dad told us," Garth said proudly.

"So are you boys having a good Christmas?" asked Johnny, lowering his height so he could better communicate with the two curious-looking boys. He held out a hand that both boys stared at for a gosh-darn-that-sure-is-a-big-hand moment before all three exchanged pleasantries.

"I got this new bike from my mom," said Tommy, looking at the gleaming two-wheeler he was sitting on. "I picked it out of the Sears. It's way cool. Got five speeds."

"Well, I got a new watch, only my dad doesn't want me to wear it while I'm playing 'cause I might lose it or something," said Garth in an almost my-present-is-way-cooler-than-yours tone.

"A new watch and a new bike. You boys must have been very good this year," said Johnny.

The boys looked at each other and exchanged a smile suggesting otherwise. Then Garth looked down at Rebecca's feet.

"Hey. How come yous guys don't got no shoes?"

Johnny looked to Rebecca who was looking at her feet and said, "Because we like to feel the ground beneath our toes."

"Oh," the boys chorused, a thought-filled moment of silence ensuing.

"Yous guys coming to the party?" Garth suddenly asked, still looking at Rebecca's feet. "My dad's gonna play the guitar and sing."

"Yeah," said Tommy. "And my mom made sweet potato pie. Do you like sweet potato pie? My mom makes the best." He waited for an answer, a toothy smile from ear to ear.

"I love sweet potato pie," said Rebecca though she had never had it.

"Me too." Johnny rubbed his stomach. "I could eat a whole pie by myself. And if you say your mom makes the best, I could probably eat two."

This pleased the Giants fan to no end. "You really think you could eat two, mister? Wait till I tell my mom. She'll have to cook more."

"I promise I'll leave some for everybody, even though I could certainly eat two."

"Yeah. You sure are big enough," said Garth who was now looking up at Johnny wondering if he would ever achieve such height.

Floating across the tarmac, the sound of an acoustic guitar filled the air, followed by a male voice in good baritone pitch, "Out in the south Texas town of El Paso... I fell in love with a Mexican girl..."

"That's my dad!" beamed Garth. "Come on. He's a real good singer." Setting both feet on pedals, he turned the bike and was off. From twenty feet away, he challenged over a shoulder, "Let's go, Tommy. I'll race yah."

Not wanting to lose a race to his friend, Tommy, whose mom made the best sweet potato pie in the world as far as his nine years of experience were concerned, pulled his cap down, leaned into his bike, and said, "See yah." The rear tire of his Sears-ordered present slipping sideways, then he too was off in a blur of pumping knees. Two firecrackers fell from his hands.

Johnny went to the lost, nerve-shattering bang sticks, picked them up, and put them in a back pocket. "These might come in handy," he said, standing to his full height. They looked toward the gathered guests where the sound of good times was just beginning.

Garth and Tommy were now neck-and-neck and seemed intent on plowing into the back of the enormous person crushing a lawn chair.

"They were cute," said Rebecca, looping an arm through Johnny's. "Those boys. I bet you were like them. Rambunctious, carefree."

A snapshot of a memory came to mind. Johnny was eight and had received Lightning, his very own horse as a gift from Buck who told him in no uncertain terms, "Treat him right and he'll do all right by you." It hovered there until Johnny blinked, then it was gone. "Thinking about it, I guess in a way I was. How about you?"

"I guess I was what you would call a tomboy, when I needed to be anyway."

"I bet you were. I bet you could beat up all the boys."

"I could take care of myself. So you better watch yourself." Looking at him, her face truly radiated for the first time since her daring rescue. They were already extremely comfortable with each other. Like Ed and Hester, she reminisced. Balling a hand into a fist, she jabbed him in the ribcage.

Raising a defensive hand, Johnny said, "Ouch! Okay, so you can take care of yourself."

"And don't you forget it," retorted Rebecca, shaking a fist in triumph, not seeing the stone she was about to step on. "Ouch! Shit!" she cried, hopping up and down, clutching at her big toe.

"Oh, you're tough all right." Johnny laughed, holding her arm so she wouldn't fall sideways.

Rebecca steadied herself, the bottom of her big toe stinging. "You can stop laughing now," she said in a serious tone, but could not stop a much-needed burst of laughter escaping from within.

"Yeah, you're tough all right," chided Johnny.

They walked across the parking lot where only three vehicles were parked. None younger than ten years off a dealership's lot. The early-evening sky was clouding over; however, the temperature remained a moderate sixty-five and would do so for several more hours according to the weather report Rebecca had listened to.

The red neon VACANC sign seemed to be broadcasting the uninterrupted, stoic lives of the guests at the Park Pines Motel. The odor of hot oil and a cooking Tom was thick in the air. Sitting in a white plastic chair and wearing an all-black ensemble from his boots to the Stetson was Garth's dad, an acoustic balanced on his crossed legs. He began to sing "Silent Night" in a beautiful voice. Those around joined in.

Johnny and Rebecca stood to the back of everyone until the song was finished. When the entertainer was through, there was an appreciative applause. Reaching toward a boot, Garth's dad came up with a can of beer, tipped it toward everyone, said thank-you, and took a long swallow.

Johnny and Rebecca moved into the gathering.

"Hello," said Poppi, noticing them for the first time. He was wearing a brown plaid shirt with red bowtie beneath his chin. In one of his hands was a can of Old Milwaukee. "I'm sure glad you folks made it. Merry Christmas. It's not much, but there's plenty of food for everyone. And plenty of beer too." Raising the can to his lips, he took a swallow. "Let me introduce you around. Hey, everybody. This is Tiffany and…" He turned his attention to Johnny. "Sorry, son, I never did get your name."

"It's Johnny," said Johnny.

Poppi looked over his guests. "This is Tiffany and Johnny. All the way from Maryland. They'll be staying with us for a couple of days." He proceeded to introduce everyone, starting with an enormous woman smoking a cigarette and chomping on a wedge of pie. "This bundle of love," said Poppi, "is Lou Belle. She and her son have been regulars here for going on eight months now. Lou Belle makes the best sweet potato pie you ever had. Don't you, Lou Belle?"

The enormous woman, whose thick legs were trapped in black spandex and with feet that seemed impossibly too small to carry such a burden, moved just enough to shift some weight. Concealing her upper body and tire-sized breasts was a red top big enough for two people to camp under. The lawn chair groaned. With little effort, she swallowed what was in her mouth. In an unexpected high voice, she said, "How do you think I got in such great shape?" She let out a full-throated laugh, coughed, and took a drag of her cigarette before saying, "Pleased to meet you, Tiffany and Johnny. Merry Christmas. I hope you're hungry. We've got enough food to feed an army."

"Nice to meet you," said Rebecca, who was now going to be Tiffany for the remainder of their stay. "We're starving. Aren't we, Johnny?"

"I could eat a side of beef," said Johnny.

Lou Belle looked Johnny up and down, the folds of her doughy throat rolling. "By the looks of you, I don't doubt it for a second." Turning to Rebecca, she added, "Now you on the other hand. Too skinny. Why, a strong wind would blow you over. We've got to get some food into you before you vanish so you too can have this magnificent form." She held up what was left of the wedge, laughed at herself again, and dropped the smoke next to one of her tiny feet. With great effort, she drew a knee, lifting a leg no more than three inches from the ground, and dropped it on the cigarette with a thud.

In his mind, Johnny questioned how this woman ever got around. "Well, it was nice to meet you, Lou Belle," he said. "And merry Christmas. I'm sure we'll talk again before the night is through."

"You can bet on it, honey. I'd like to hear the story behind you two. I get the feeling it's a whopper."

Poppi introduced everyone else. The entertainer's name was Lenny Hooper, single father to Garth Hooper, the bucktoothed boy who was so proud of his singing dad. They'd arrived the week before, Lenny's hopes of landing a gig as a nightclub singer still somewhere in the future.

An elderly Jewish couple, the Feinsteins, huddled close together in heavy coats, only nodded when they were introduced.

There was Mary Madigan, a still-pretty fifty-year-old Irish dancer, and Nikki's mother, who was on her third beer and ready to tell her life story to anyone who would listen. They'd arrived four months ago, just passing through, intent on starting life over again due to a nasty divorce, find employment and a place for themselves. Now they seemed a permanent fixture at the Park Pines.

Poppi stopped at the bubbling pot where a cooler rested on the ground next to a picnic table covered in white plastic. On top of the table sat three sweet potato pies, two large Tupperware containers, a pan of corn bread, paper plates, and plastic knives and forks wrapped in Christmas napkins. Rebecca and Johnny peered into the frothing oil. All they could see was a length of chain and the tips of the Tom's legs.

"Smells delicious," remarked Rebecca as Lenny Hooper plucked the guitar strings and began singing "Sitting on the Dock of the Bay."

"You're in for a treat, Tiffany," said Poppi, leaning forward and flipping the lid on the cooler to reveal dozens of beers in layers of ice. "How about a cold beer," he said into the open cooler.

"Sure," said Johnny. "Thank you, Poppi."

"I better not," said Rebecca, not wanting to further elevate the effects of the Percocet.

Poppi handed Johnny a Pabst Blue Ribbon. "I've got some soda pop in here someplace." He moved the cans around. "Here we go. How about a cream soda, Tiffany?"

"That would be great. I love cream soda. Thank you, Poppi. You sure are a good host."

"We do what we can. What we can't, them's for other people to deal with."

"That's a good way to look at things, and I agree completely," said Rebecca, taking the soda.

Simultaneously, she and Johnny popped the tops.

Taking a long swallow, Johnny savored the ale before letting it run down his throat. "Ahh. That's pretty good beer. I've never tried it before."

"Only the best for my guests," said Poppi. "Cheers." The three touched cans, each taking good swallows of their beverages.

"I hope you don't mind, Poppi," said Rebecca. "But we invited Big Bob to join us. I hope that was okay?"

"Well, that was mighty nice of yah. I haven't seen Big Bob in about month, poor bastard. I don't 'spect we'll be seeing him though. Not tonight anyhow."

Rebecca pressed. Perhaps she could learn something about the woman in the booth. "Oh. How come?"

Poppi took another swallow and backhanded the froth away. "You see," he began. "Big Bob lost his wife Maggie four years ago this very day."

"Yes. He told us. So sad."

"Yup. She and Bob always came to my turkey dinners. She was sitting in one of the booths drinking a cup of coffee, waiting for Bob to close the restaurant. Had a stroke. Died right there in the booth. No, we won't be seeing Big Bob tonight. He'll stay at the restaurant, plug some quarters into the jukebox, and listen to their favorite song over and over. "Sea of Love." Strange enough, it was the song that was playing when poor Maggie had her stroke. Yup. If you drove out there right now and put your windows down, that's what you'd hear coming from the restaurant. It's a shame is what it is. That man adored Maggie."

Rebecca's hand searched for Johnny's. Finding it, she squeezed it tight. "That's such a sad story. He must be so lonely."

"I reckon he is. That Maggie was some kind of woman. Never had a bad thing to say about anyone. Always smilin'. Saint of a woman. Devoted to her husband, their church. Wouldn't harm a flea. She used to stop by and we would just talk. Yah know. Yup, she's missed all right." He took another drink, the passing imagery of fond memory watering his eyes.

"I'm sorry for bringing it up," said Rebecca. "I didn't mean to cause you any grief, especially today. I'm sorry that I did."

"No matter. I think about 'em every Christmas Day anyway, hoping one year Big Bob will show up."

"Maybe he will. Maybe even tonight," said Rebecca, trying to sound optimistic.

"It's nice of you to think that, but sadly, I doubt it. No. That poor man's still in mourning, and I 'spect will be for the rest of his life. That restaurant's what's keeps him going. It's all he has left other than a son who don't care."

Tommy and Garth halted their bikes next to the picnic table. "Hey, Poppi," said Tommy. "Mom wants to know when the turkey is going to be ready."

"Tell Lou Belle in about twenty minutes," answered Poppi, looking into the crackling pot.

"Can we have another pop?" asked Garth, smiling in retrospect.

"Sure. Help yourselves, boys. But it's the last one before dinner. Don't want you two filling up on junk, yah hear."

"Thanks, Poppi," the boys chorused, climbed off their bikes, and proceeded to dig into the cooler. When they found what they wanted, they climbed back on their bikes and circled the lot. A moment later, four firecrackers cracked simultaneously. *Bang! Bang! Bang! Bang!*

"They seem to be enjoying themselves," said Johnny. "I never had firecrackers when I was a kid. Aren't they illegal?"

"Yeah," said Poppi. "But I'm not going to spoil their fun. Those two don't have much of a future, so far as I'm concerned, they should enjoy all the good times they can get. Lord knows there's goin' to be plenty of bad times the way things are."

"Maybe not," offered Rebecca. "They could be diamonds in the rough. Grow up to be doctors or lawyers. Maybe one of them will discover the cure for cancer. There's plenty of opportunity out there."

"I hope you're right, Tiffany," said Poppi, emptying his beer and crushing the can. He went to the cooler, retrieved another, and popped the tab. Foam billowed. Poppi slurped it up, watching the boys go round and round. "I'd like to think they wouldn't slip through the cracks. Too many of 'em do."

"Think of the glass half-full, Poppi," encouraged Rebecca, watching the boys laugh, going around and around, eyes full of Christmas spirit, their legs pumping furiously. "I'm sure those two will be fine."

"Let's just hope no one takes a drink from that glass," said Poppi before taking another mouthful of beer.

Rebecca altered the conversation. The sad story about Big Bob and Maggie and questioning the future of two young boys was putting a damper on things. She wanted the night to be as pleasant as possible for her and Johnny. "Who's the young girl over there, Poppi? Sitting by herself."

"That's Nikki," he said, turning to see his sometime clerk sitting in a plastic chair near the pickup truck. She's Mary Madigan's daughter. Pretty little thing. Smart too. I believe you already met her, Johnny."

"Yes. This afternoon. She told me where the restaurant was located. Should we get her to join us?"

"Don't see why not, but you know how teenagers can be. Everythin's black-and-white and don't make a lick of sense."

Nikki Madigan was sitting away from everyone, knees drawn to her chin, eyes watching everything through the cracks of folded fingers. When she saw Poppi, Johnny, and Rebecca approach, she raised her head. She had already decided she didn't like the new girl on the block; however, she would put up with her, she'd decided, if it meant getting close to the best thing she'd seen in jeans in a long time. Still outfitted in the Rolling Stones T-shirt, jean shorts, and white sneakers, she lowered her knees, her eyes devouring the approaching stud.

"What are you doin' over here all by your lonesome?" asked Poppi. "It's Christmas. Come and join the rest of us."

"Merry Christmas, Nikki," said Rebecca, offering her hand. "It's nice to meet you. I'm Tiffany."

Casually, Nikki held out a hand. "Merry Christmas, Tiffany." Then with more enthusiasm and a twinkle in her blue eyes, "Hi, Johnny! Merry Christmas!"

"Hello again," said Johnny. "And a very merry Christmas to you too."

"I really like what you've done with your hair," offered Rebecca, smiling, knowing the right compliment in the right place did wonders for moody teenagers. She was, after all, one herself in some respects.

"You do!" Nikki's already-striking eyes brightened further, lighting her face. *Maybe this new girl isn't so bad after all.* Reaching, she ran thin fingers through the pink framing her face. "I did it myself. I'm going to be a famous hairstylist in New York or Los Angeles. Do all the stars' hair and make lots of money. You have really nice hair, Tiffany." Standing and moving closer to Johnny, she thrust her hands into the back pockets of her shorts where a last joint lay waiting to be smoked.

"Thank you," said Rebecca. "It's getting a little long though."

With her eyes focused on Johnny's face, Nikki said, "Maybe you'll let me give it a trim. I'm really good. Ask anyone."

"I'm sure you are," said Rebecca, seeing that the future hairstylist already had an adolescent crush on her man. "Maybe before we leave."

As though reading her thoughts, Nikki moved closer to Johnny, looping an arm through his. "So what brings you to the Park Pines?" She steered him away from Poppi and Rebecca. "Do you sing? I bet you do. I sing sometimes. When I'm in the mood…"

"That girl is gonna give some guy more than he can handle," Poppi said to Rebecca when they were out of earshot.

"If she isn't already," said Rebecca, a little miffed at the sight of Nikki's arm looped through Johnny's. "Shall we join them?" She put an arm through Poppi's who instantly blushed like a heart-sweetened teen.

"Everybody together. Just as it should be on Christmas Day. Lead the way, pretty lady. I'm all yours."

* * *

Poppi led the little gathering in a prayer of thanks before doling out crispy slices of turkey. Rebecca and Johnny had taken the ceremonial time to reflect about the people they loved and lost. Everyone fit around the table snugly, except Lou Belle, who had a chair of her own. Rebecca on Johnny's left, Nikki on his right and pressed against him. Lenny, Garth, and Garth's best friend for the time being taking up one side of the table. Poppi sat at the head; Mary Madigan squeezed next to him. The Feinsteins sat on the opposite end, faces set in stone, eyeing everyone almost suspiciously.

The Tupperware containers were opened, and the salads passed around. Poppi removed tin foil from the corn bread, cut it into squares, and using plastic tongs, gave everyone a piece. Lou Belle two.

Rebecca couldn't wait to try the turkey. Cutting a small piece, she popped it into her mouth. "Mmm, this is amazing, Poppi. It's so juicy and tender."

"Thank you, Tiffany. I do make a mean turkey if I do say so myself. Try some of the potato salad. Mary here made it."

"And I made the Caesar salad," piped Nikki, hoping to impress.

"Well, it's all very wonderful," said Johnny. "I didn't know where we'd be today. I'm glad it's with you, nice folks. I can't think of a better way to spend Christmas than with some music, drink, good people, and my Tiffany." Raising a fresh beer, he added, "I'd just like to say, on behalf of Tiffany and myself, thank you for everything and merry Christmas."

A celebrated toast was sealed with the raising of drinks. Garth and Tommy were drinking iced tea and, when the toast was made, clanged their glasses with a little too much enthusiasm, causing some of the iced tea to spill on the table. They laughed wholeheartedly poking at each other with their elbows.

From nearby, Lou Belle asked, "So what's your story, Johnny? How did you two get together? And please, don't leave out any sordid details on our account." She took a monster-sized bite from the drumstick she was holding.

Johnny looked to Rebecca who nodded for him to take the reins on this one. Nikki sort of rolled her eyes. Everyone was all ears. Johnny had to fabricate a story and do it quick. Rebecca smiled, enjoying the discomfort she could plainly see etched on his face.

"Well, let me see. We met just over a year ago around the Thanksgiving holidays. I was on my way to see my brother in Arlington when my car broke down on the highway. I tried for hours to get someone to stop and help me, but no one did. Just when I thought I would have to walk miles to the nearest station, Tiff pulled over and asked if I needed some help."

Tommy quickly asked, "Didn't you have no cell phone?"

"No, I didn't, Tommy. I know it's almost a sin not to in today's day and age, but I never found I had use for one."

"Not until your car broke down," Garth pointed out and everyone laughed.

"Why wouldn't anyone stop?" Tommy quickly asked.

Garth answered for Johnny. "Are you dumb or something? It's 'cause he's an Indian. Isn't that right, Johnny?"

"Unfortunately, yes. There's still a lot of racism out there."

"What kind of Indian are you?" asked Garth, his eyes wide, twinkling with the need for knowledge.

"I'm Cherokee."

"Wow! That's really cool. Did you ever scalp anybody?"

"I'm not *that* kind of Indian." Johnny laughed. "But I bet you some of my ancestors did."

This impressed the boys to no end. They began firing all manner of cowboy and Indian questions one would expect from a couple of eight-year-olds.

Poppi raised his hands in the air. "Whoa, boys. Let the man finish his story. Go ahead, Johnny."

Relieved he didn't have to answer Garth's and Tommy's inquisitive inquisitions, Johnny said, "As I was saying, Tiffany pulled over and gave me a lift to the nearest station, and no, she didn't have a cell phone either. We talked for a while, and when she dropped me off, we exchanged numbers. I was anxious to talk to her again, so I called her the next day to thank her once more and we kind of made a date. We've been together ever since. Now I know it's not the most romantic story, but it is to me."

"Do I hear any wedding bells?" asked Lou Belle.

"Yes, Johnny. Please do tell," said Rebecca, loving every moment of it. "*Are* there wedding bells in our future?"

Taking a swallow of beer, Johnny replied, "I guess there could be, but not right now. I prefer things the way they are for the moment. Say this corn bread's really good." Heat rising up through his shirt. "It reminds me of the bannock my mother used to make."

"Made it myself," said Poppi.

"What's bannock?" asked Garth, his nose scrunched in distaste at the mere sound of it.

"It's Indian bread, cooked in a pan or on a griddle in lard. I haven't had it since my mom passed away."

A silence fell over the table.

"So where are you two headed?" asked Lenny Hooper, rescuing everyone from the uncomfortable moment.

"We're just traveling from here to there," said Rebecca. "Take in the sights while we're young. Create some memories, that sort of thing."

"Don't you have jobs to go to?" inquired Nikki, placing a hand on Johnny's forearm.

"Yes, of course we have jobs, *Nikki*," said Rebecca, staring at the paw resting on the muscles of Johnny's arm. "We took a month holidays, and well, here we are."

"Sounds pretty romantic if you ask me," said Poppi. "Just travelin'. Not a care in the world 'sept for each other."

"Say, Poppi. Did you get to talk to your grandchildren?" Rebecca wanted to know.

"Sure did. All thirteen of 'em. Phone started ringing at around ten, didn't stop till one. I had to take a nap. Those kids wore me out with all their questions and telling me what they got for Christmas and such."

"That's nice. They must love you very much."

"And me them, though I 'spect most of them will be all grown-up before I see them again."

"Hey, Dad. Can I be excused?" asked Garth.

"Me too, Mom!" added Tommy.

Lenny regarded his son's plate. All that remained was a bit of salad. "Sure, son. Have some fun. But don't go too far. We still have some Christmas songs to sing."

Lou Belle pulled the drumstick from her mouth. "You may be excused too, Tommy. But like Mr. Hooper says, stay close, it'll be dark soon."

"Thanks, Mom."

The boys were off in a shot, each grabbing a bike and disappearing to the front of the motel. A moment later firecrackers sounded.

"I wish they would stop that," said Nikki. "I practically jump out of my skin every time they set one of those things off."

"Let them have their fun," said her mother. "You know how boys are. If you can't hear them, then they're up to no good. Better that we know where they are. And for God's sake, will you stop pawing at that young man's arm."

Nikki's hand slipped away. She'd hardly touched the food on her plate. Forking some turkey into her mouth, her eyes conveyed to her mother that she didn't care for her interference.

"Mr. Feinstein," inquired Rebecca. "What brings you and Mrs. Feinstein to the Park Pines? Are you just arriving or on your way home?"

Everyone's attention turned toward the quiet Feinstiens.

Mr. Feinstein wiped at his mouth with a napkin and looked to his wife through bespectacled lenses, his thick grey eyebrows closing in on each other in consternation. "Vell," he started. "Ve are comink to Las Vegas for you know, how you say, relaxation. Ve own small store in San Diego. Sellink mostly hardware. Ve not havink vacation in fifteen years. Sellink hardware all your life is gettink very boring, yes. Ve are both in our sixties, yes. Time for, how you say, lettink hair down. Ve leavink tomorrow. Gettink room at Caesar's Palace."

"How long do you plan on staying in Vegas?" asked Johnny.

"Das good question. Ve close shop for von month. Ve stayink until money runs out or hittink big jackpot, yes." He laughed, his shoulders moving up and down beneath his heavy coat.

Mrs. Feinstein spoke, "You see. Ve not havink honeymoon forty years ago. Too much vorking. Then our children come. Von, two, tree. So ve vork, raising tree sons. Put through college. All doctors. All married. Five grandchildren. Now it is time for us, you understandink?"

"Absolutely," said Rebecca. "Everybody needs a little time on their own. I hope you have a nice stay and win lots of money."

"Ya. Das vould be good." Mr. Feinstein smiled. "Maybe breakink bank, yes." He laughed again, eyebrows crisscrossing in a comedic twitch.

Everyone laughed. When the short-lived jollity was over, Mr. Feinstein said, "Ve must go to room now. Ve are tankink you very much for vonderful dinner."

"Please stay," said Rebecca, looping an arm through Johnny's. "It's still early. We're going to sing more songs. Aren't we, Lenny?"

"A whole bagful," the wannabe entertainer agreed.

"Yes," said Lou Belle with a mouthful of turkey. "Please stay a little longer."

"Das is very goot of you to say," said Mr. Feinstein. "But ve are needink rest. It has been long day. I am needink beauty sleep." With that said, he helped his wife from the table, supporting an arm. "Ve are vishink you goot night. And how you say, the very best in new year. Ve will be leavink first tink in the mornink. It vas nice to be meetink you. Ve hope your journeys are prosperous." The Feinsteins turned together and headed for their rooms, arm in arm, huddled close together.

"Well, that leaves nine of us," said Poppi. "Anybody for more turkey? Johnny, you look like you could still pack down a heaping plateful." He began to carve from the breast.

Not knowing how long it would be before he would have deep-fried turkey again, if ever, Johnny held out his empty plate. "Thanks, Poppi. Sure is delicious."

Poppi served everyone except Nikki a second plate. When the turkey was nothing more than a carcass of bone and the Tupperware containers were all but emptied, and only one pie remained, Lenny Hooper picked up his guitar and began to sing "Blue Christmas" in his best Elvis impersonation.

* * *

By ten, the weather began to turn. A strong wind swept through Park Pines, kicking up dust and debris, yet there wasn't a cloud in the sky, prompting Poppi to call it a night.

Garth and Tommy insisted they weren't tired, however, were convinced that it was time to hit the hay. With her son's help, Lou Belle managed her great size from the lawn chair. She and Tommy went to their room, the ground quaking beneath each thunderous step Lou Belle took. Nikki had disappeared earlier, bored to tears with the music and small talk and the fact that between Rebecca and her mother, she wasn't going to get anywhere with the likes of hunky Johnny.

The effects of the last Percocet Rebecca had taken was on its last legs.

Mary Madigan wished everyone good night, asking should anyone see Nikki, to "please send her back to her room."

Lenny packed his guitar. Its case emblazoned with stickers from cities all over the US of A. Finishing the last of his beer, he put a hand on his son's shoulder and said good-night, leaving Johnny, Poppi, and Rebecca to clear the tables and chase down paper plates and napkins the wind had distributed in all directions.

Once everything was straightened out, Poppi said, "Come to the office for a minute. I have something for you."

Rebecca and Johnny followed the grandfather of thirteen into the office. Poppi disappeared into the back for a minute, then reappeared, carrying a small portable radio wrapped in its cord. "Here. I want you to have this until you leave. The rooms don't offer much in the way of entertainment, so this should help." He handed Johnny the RCA.

"Thank you, Poppi," said Rebecca. "We'll put it to good use."

"Now if you two need anything at all, don't hesitate to ask. Think of the Park Pines as your home away from home."

Rebecca noticed how suddenly tired Poppi looked. With his eyes captured in the shine of alcohol, he seemed smaller. "You should get some rest, Poppi. You look tired."

"You know. I'm thinkin' of doin' somethin' I haven't done in years."

"Oh? What's that, Poppi?" asked Johnny, cradling the radio in one arm.

"I'm gonna close business for the night. Turn on the No Vacancy sign and make friends with a bottle of Kentucky vintage. It's not like people are beatin' down the door anyhow."

Rebecca and Johnny looked to each other, each carrying the same thought. That Poppi was a very lonely man who adored a family he never got to see. "I think that's a good idea, Poppi," said Rebecca. "But don't drink too much, alcohol can't replace what you're missing."

"Sound advice, young lady, but I'll manage just fine. Never knew a bottle of bourbon that didn't help pass the time away. Now if you don't mind, I'm gonna lock up and say my prayers. You two enjoy the rest of the night. You might have to give that radio a slap or two to get it proper."

"I'll remember that," said Johnny. "Well, I guess we'll be on our way."

"Mind settin' the lock on your way out. Just give the knob a turn to the left and it'll set when you close the door."

"Sure, Poppi."

"Good night, Poppi," wished Rebecca, though she was concerned for the kindly motel owner. A tug of memory caused her to say, "Don't let the bed bugs bite."

Poppi chuckled, unclipped his bowtie, turned, and shuffled his way to the back of the office, disappearing.

Rebecca and Johnny went to the front door. Johnny turned the knob, holding the door open for Rebecca. When he pulled it closed, the lock clicked into place. He tested it anyway, turning the knob and pushing inward. The door didn't budge. "I guess he's pretty safe." He turned to find Rebecca staring across the parking lot. "Everything okay, Rebecca? I mean, Tiffany."

"Huh? Oh yes. Everything's fine. I was just thinking about what a wonderful night it's been. How fate took a handful of strangers, brought them together, and created what would become a fond memory." Turning to face him, her green eyes flashed under the light of neon.

"Yeah. I had a really good time too. It was the kind of distraction we needed."

A moment later, the office lights darkened and the red neon NO lit in front of the VACANC, capturing Rebecca and Johnny in its glow.

Rebecca went to Johnny, pressed her body into his. Taking his hands, she kissed him with all the passion she could summon. They stared into each other for a century, mouths hungry, the desire for each other creating a wave of heat that poured over them, hearts beating in perfect rhythm. Everything around them, everything they'd been through, seemed to vanish to another place and time and it was just them, two people in love, standing beneath the twinkling sky. When their lips parted, Rebecca whispered, "I love you, Johnny. Thank you for tonight."

Johnny looked deep into the glitter of her eyes. There was so much hope in them, so much trust, so much yearning to be loved. "You make me feel like there's so much hope."

"There is, Johnny. As long as we have each other."

"And fate."

"And fate."

They walked across the tarmac in silence, stars blazing an infinite trail above. The sound of a television emanated from one of the rooms. There was no sign of Nikki. Hand in hand, they made their way to the second story, the old steps creaking under their combined weight.

When they reached room 21, Rebecca said, "Why don't you plug the radio in and find a good station? I'll be in in a few minutes. I just want to look at the stars for a while."

"I'll look at them with you."

"That's sweet of you, but I would like to be alone for a few minutes. I hope you understand."

Reluctantly, Johnny unlocked the door. After everything that had happened, he didn't want to leave her out of his sight; however, she would only be a few feet away and it would only be a few minutes. "Okay," he said. "Don't be too long though."

"I won't." On tiptoes, Rebecca rested her hands on his broad shoulders and kissed him. "Mmm," she said. "You still taste like turkey and beer."

"You don't taste so bad yourself. See you in a few minutes." Opening the door, he disappeared, and closed it behind him.

Rebecca went to the railing, leaned into it, elbows pressed deep into the wood, her hands clasped as if she were about to recite a prayer. She looked up into the blue-black sky shimmering with life. Her first thoughts were those of her family. Poor simple Ben. Never knowing what it truly meant to be loved. Her father, made of steel, yet was helpless against the romantic grip of alcohol, leading ultimately to his demise. Then there was her mother. Her best friend in the whole world. God, she missed her.

A shooting star arced a path through the middle of the Milky Way, seemingly destined to hit the horizon, instead, died, thinning as it hit the earth's ozone, a firefly of blue, then, nothing.

The reasons her mother lost contact were just as confusing as the on-again, off-again gift she must adhere to whether the precognitive insight into the future were good or bad. Everything that was happening seemed to be an attempt at weakening her resolve. She had Johnny now, and that's all that seemed to matter for the time being, for however long it would last.

As a young girl, she once wished upon a star that she would receive a new bike for her birthday. The following day, when she officially turned eight, her father had presented her with a brand-new bike from the hardware she had fallen in love with when Mr. Gilbert put it on display. Now as she stared into the heavens, she wished for only one thing. That the time they had together, whether be distant or brief, be the most memorably enlightening time she could imagine. She knew trouble lay ahead, bad trouble, and that they would always be on the run; nonetheless, it was going to be moments like the one they had just shared that would fulfill her. There wasn't much more she could ask for.

Suddenly, music drifted from room 21. Led Zeppelin's "All of My Love" serenaded her through the thinness of the door. She listened to the words and how appropriately adequate they seemed for the time.

From her vantage point, she could just make out the front of the pickup hidden behind the office building. *How far could they make it?* she wondered. *A big Native American and a redhead driving around in a bright red truck weren't exactly going to be able to stay incognito for very long.* She felt like crying. Not because she was sad or because of the desperate situation they were in, but simply because she needed to. At the tender age of eighteen, she was already a vindictive woman driven to thoughts of revenge by the exploits she was forced to endure over the past six months. Oh, how she would love to get even with Tony Millions. Tears spilled from her eyes and down her chin. Several long breaths passed before something in the air chased the malignant thoughts away. It rose up from just below, filling her nostrils with its pungent essence. *Marijuana*. She leaned over the railing to see if she could locate its source; however, the balcony over shot the lower units by a good eight feet.

There was only one person in the group that fit the description of someone who smoked pot. "Nikki?" she said over the railing wiping the tears away. "Is that you?"

A moment passed before she was answered, "Yes, Tiffany, it's me."

"Your mom says you should go back to your room."

"Oh, she doesn't really care what I do. She pretends to, but doesn't, not really."

"Stay there. I'm coming down."

"Okay."

Descending the steps, birthed from her worries, a brilliant idea rushed forward.

Nikki was leaning against the building, a puff of smoke around her face as she inhaled deeply. "Do you want some, Tiffany? It's really good shit." She held out the joint pinched between fingers.

"No, thanks, Nikki. What I would like is to talk to you about your abilities as a hairstylist."

* * *

When they finished talking, Rebecca returned to room 21, locking the door behind her. Johnny was lying on the bed, fully dressed, listening to the radio in the dim lighting of the table lamp. A young Michael Jackson's "I'll Be There" was playing. "Hi," he said. "The radio only gets two stations. This one and a country station."

Rebecca went to the bed and sat on its edge. "I was just talking to Nikki. We made some plans for tomorrow."

"Oh. What sort of plans?"

"You'll see. I don't want to spoil the surprise." She yawned. "I don't know about you, but that big meal has made me tired. More than usual."

"It's some kind of chemical in the turkey. Makes you tired."

"I've heard that. How about you? You tired?"

"Yeah. Sort of. What I am is stuffed. That was a lot of food."

"It sure was. I'm going to take a minute and brush the turkey out of my teeth." Leaving the comfort of the bed, she went to the bathroom.

Johnny stretched, the joints throughout his body popping like little firecrackers. Leaning on his side, he rested his head in the palm of a hand, gathered the feather and tether from Rebecca's pillow and laid them on the nightstand. She could amend them come morning. It had been a while since his hair hung loose. It felt good. Staring at the bathroom door, he thought he was the luckiest man on the planet to have a person such as Rebecca in his life even though the circumstances were less than cordial. *A lot less.* He sang with the radio, keeping his voice low, for Johnny was a lot of things, a singer he was not.

A minute or two passed before Rebecca emerged in blue polka-dot panties and nothing else, her jeans and T-shirt bunched in her arms. The Bee Gees "Stayin' Alive" was playing, so she danced her way to the bed, much in the same manner when she danced for libidinous men. *Crazy sexy.* "Move over," she said. "So I can lie next to you."

Johnny rolled, opened his arms, and welcomed her. "You're *so* beautiful," he said.

Brushing strands of hair away from his face, Rebecca's body conformed to his. They held each other for a long moment before she lifted her face and kissed him. "I can't think of a better way to end this wonderful day than to make love to you, Johnny, but now's not the time. I'm kind of indisposed. I hope you understand."

Johnny walked into the depths of her green eyes. "I'm happy just being with you, Rebecca. I'll wait as long as I have to." He kissed her deeply, eyes closed, holding her as close as possible without crushing her. The room seemed to float away, music sounding as though it was being broadcast from another dimension. Reaching, he clicked off the light. Darkness covered them in its tranquil blanket.

They stayed like that, holding on to each other, mouths exploring, Johnny's arousal pressing hard against Rebecca. When he removed his T-shirt, flesh met flesh. With a wandering hand, Rebecca unfastened his pants. Her stomach cramped with desire for more drugs. She ignored it best she could.

"You don't have to do that," said Johnny, his voice horse.

"Shhh, I want to." She had learned many things at the Shangri-La Palace. Taking the full of him in hand, she stroked him gently. Not a word spoken. For an eternity of pleasure, she fondled him. They remained like that, wrapped in each other's arms, locked in a paramour's kiss, stealing each other's breath, hearts beating a harmonious rhythm.

Sometime later, and Christmas Day another year away, they fell asleep, having exhausted each other to the lyrics of "She Talks to Angels."

She never mentions the word addiction
In certain company
Yes, she'll tell you she's an orphan
After you meet her family

She paints her eyes as black as night, now
Pulls those shades down tight
Yeah, she gives a smile when the pain comes
The pain gonna make everything all right

She says she talks to angels
They call her by her name
She talks to angels
Says they call her by her name...

They had fallen into such a deep, comfortable slumber, Johnny was unaware the stone in his pocket was growing warmer minute by minute.

* * *

Mr. Black could just make out the motel. If it were not for the NO VACANC neon, he might have driven right by the place. He pulled into the lot, and parked the Cadillac in front of the office. The Park Pines was going to be his last checkpoint for the night as he was tired and still pissed off at Tony Millions for being such an asshole.

The lights of the Cadillac brought to life the otherwise-dark office. He looked for signs of life. Except for three vehicles parked in the lot, none of which was a red pickup, the place appeared deserted. He killed the engine. The office went dark. Emerging from the Cadillac, he went to the front door and tried it. It was locked. *Strange,* he thought.

Only three cars in the lot and yet there was no vacancy. There was a buzzer next to the door. He tried it, hearing the ding-dong from within. He waited, hands thrust deep into the pockets of his suit. Just as he was about to return to the Cadillac and call it a night, the office lights came on and an old man in a housecoat, not looking too happy, made his way to the front and opened the door. "Can't you read… ," Poppi began to say then stopped short, the size of the black man standing in front of him wrenching the words from his mouth.

"Sorry to bother you," said the giant, smiling big white teeth. "But I'm looking for friends of mine."

"Oh," said Poppi, rubbing at his bourbon-weary eyes. "Kinda late to be lookin' for friends, don't yah think?"

"Yes, well, I do apologize for disturbing you, sir. I won't take a moment of your time. These friends of mine. One is a Native American and the other is a pretty redhead by the name of Tiffany Rose. They told me last week that they might be stopping at this motel on Christmas day."

Poppi looked the giant over. Every fiber of his being was telling him that something was not right here. That this giant of a man was nothing but trouble with a capital *T*. "Sorry," he said. "Can't help yah. Nobody fittin' that description has stopped here."

"Are you sure?"

"Look, mister. I said they didn't stop here, and I meant it. I may be old, but I ain't senile. Now if you don't mind, I'd like to go back to sleep. I'm closed for the night."

"Would you mind if I looked around?"

Poppi's hackles went up. "You callin' me a liar, son. I told yah. They ain't here. And I don't want you disturbin' my guests. So I suggest you be on your way, b'fore I call the police. Good night." He pulled the door and locked it.

Mr. Black stood there a moment. The old man shuffled his way to the back of the office then the lights went out, leaving him in the glow of red neon. There was movement behind him, and he turned to find a young girl in shorts and a Rolling Stones T-shirt standing next to the Cadillac. "Can I help you, mister?" she said, glossy eyes communicating that she was high on something.

Mr. Black moved toward her, looking like the devil himself under the neon. "Hello, young lady. Yes, well, I'm looking for some friends of mine. A big Indian and a redhead. The girl's name is Tiffany Rose. You haven't seen them, have you? They would be driving a red pickup truck. We were supposed to hook up two days ago."

Nikki looked up into the black man's face. Though he was smiling an enormous trust-me flash of teeth, there was something untrusting there. Size alone, he could force someone into betraying their own mother. *Holy shit! Where the fuck did this guy come from? A nightmare. That's where.* Red flags burst into flames in her fogged mind, causing her to believe with absolute certainty that if she divulged any information in the least, this man would kill them all. People like *him* didn't stop at places like the Park Pines, and she doubted very much that Tiffany and Johnny were this giant's friends. "Well, I practically live here, and I haven't seen anyone like that. You must be at the wrong motel."

"Are you sure?"

"A big Indian and a redhead. Well, *yeah*. Do I look like stupid to you, mister? I think I would remember them."

Mr. Black wanted to strike her with the blunt knuckles of his fist, grab the pretty little thing with killer legs, stuff her into the Cadillac, and bring her to the house where the pit awaited its newest arrival; however, that's not what his agenda dictated for the time being. *Too bad. She would have made a great addition to the Shangri-La Palace. A nice replacement for Rebecca*. And the wheel went round and round. Instead, he opened the Cadillac door and slipped into the seat, the interior light casting an iniquitous glow about his face. When one saw the Cadillac, death was near. Mr. Black, for all intents and purposes invisible until he thieved your soul. "Well, thanks for your time," he said. "A pretty young thing like you shouldn't be out this late at night. There's a lot of bad people out there, baby."

"I can take care of myself," Nikki said boldly, standing with her hands on hips, feet a foot apart, the point of her chin thrust audaciously into the air.

Mr. Black imagined her lying on a quilted mattress, legs spread to reveal the comb of her untrained vagina. "I'm sure you can. I'm sure you can." Staring at her legs for a moment, he closed the door and fired the big black machine, his intuition gnawing at him. *Something wasn't right here, and yet was right here. Furthermore, the old man and the young girl were hiding the truth. They had seen them*. That much he was sure of. He would soon return, more guarded in his approach. But before he did, there were a few other issues that needed his attention.

The Cadillac moved away from the Park Pines Motel, slowly, a giant leach slithering across tarnished flesh, Mr. Black guiding it back to Sin City.

Nikki watched it leave until its red taillights were specks in the dark, now knowing that Tiffany and Johnny were in some kind of trouble. *Friends indeed*, she thought. Walking across the parking lot, hands stuffed into the back of her shorts, she wished never to see that man again. He'd scared the shit out of her, but she stood up to him, the effects of the marijuana lending her courage. *No wonder Tiffany asked me to cut and dye her hair. She's in some kind of trouble and needs a disguise*. Looking to room 21 where Tiffany and Johnny slept or did other things, she tried to imagine what they might have done to warrant the attentions of the giant black man. Running roughshod through her mind, many scenarios made themselves present. Stopping in front of room 3, she opened the unlocked door, and paused for a moment before stepping into the room where her mother lay snoring. *This was bigger than big. Fucking terrifying*. A tension-filled chill tickled her spine, and wrapped itself around her throat, abominable fear insisting that the giant could actually snatch her breath away.

The usually humdrum Park Pines Motel had just became a very interesting, possibly terrifying place to be.

* * *

57

Mr. Brown

THE truck belongs to a Konahee Wolf as far as the DMV is concerned. I had a friend of mine hack into the records. She lives just outside Alcova, Wyoming." Mr. Brown was seated at the end of the conference table, munching on the tuna sandwich Rosita had prepared for him.

Tony Millions, in casual khakis and beige golf shirt, stood at the opposite end, fisted hands knuckling the surface of the table, a smile drawing his lips. *Sniff.* "Good. At least one of you is doing their job." Moving from the table, he went to the Screaming Man and stood silent for a moment, staring at the expensive knockoff like a true connoisseur of the arts. "This is what I require of you, Mr. Brown. You are to depart immediately. This Konahee must be the Indian's mother or the very least a close relative. Close enough that she would lend him her truck. I want you to find her. I want you to kill her and anyone else you find there. I want there to be suffering, Mr. Brown. So much that they'll be thankful once you've killed them." He turned to face Mr. Brown, his eyes as serious as a heart attack. "I want a souvenir of the event so that when we do catch up to this Indian and Rebecca, we'll have something tangible to terrify him with."

"I can do that. What about Mr. Green? Should I bring him along?"

"No! You are to go alone. Mr. Green will stay close to home. Mr. Black is out there somewhere, searching. I haven't heard from him since yesterday. And if I know Mr. Black, it won't be long before we have the two of them in our custody. Should you not have returned by then, I'll need Mr. Green to help with the," he paused for a second, "punishing."

Mr. Brown raised the sandwich to his mouth but did not take a bite. This new assignment he would perform with relish. He hadn't tortured anyone in some time, and his was a skill, if not kept honed, could become sloppy in its artful design. Torturing someone took a certain finesse. A certain inbred quality few people possessed. Mr. Brown knew he had it the first time he skinned a cat alive, cutting off its two front paws so that it pushed itself in circles until it bled to death. He was eight at the time. Dropping what remained of the sandwich onto the plate, he said, "I'll leave right now." Pushing himself from the chair, he confirmed, "By nightfall, this Konahee Wolf and whoever else I find will be crying for their mothers. You can count on it. I do however expect full compensation for what I'm about to do."

"Of course, Mr. Brown. You can expect the usual, plus 10 percent."

"For an extra 10 percent, I'll bring you this Konahee Wolf's head on a silver platter."

"I expect nothing less from you, Mr. Brown. Thank you."

Mr. Brown turned and left the conference room. Thoughts of a good old-fashioned bloodletting excited him beyond reproach. He would bring an ice pick and a power drill for this particular job. Pain beyond anything imaginable would be his fulfillment and for whomever resided at this Konahee's household, absolute horror, disillusionment, and suffering. Oh, how he loved to see the looks on their faces when he cut a finger off or pushed the point of a pick into a vital nerve, the indictment of pain reflected in their eyes, their screams for clemency. He absolutely got off on it. Notwithstanding that this Konahee Wolf was eighty-six years old, according to the DMV, made little difference. Young or old, a job was a job, pain was pain, and Konahee Wolf was going to bear the most vilest nature of it.

* * *

Tony Millions turned the Screaming Man like a book, dialed the three-digit combo, and opened the safe. He stared at the stacks of bills, bonds, and kilos of cocaine. Life could not be more fortuitous as far as he was concerned. Lifting a stack of bills, he held it in his hand, testing its heft. Fifty grand in denominations of hundreds was proportionate in weight to a kilo of coca, yet the latter, because of a binging society, far more exclusive.

Returning the money to the safe, he locked it and closed the copied oil, hoping Pamela was feeling better. All the scheming and talk of murder had aroused Morgan the Organ.

* * *

58

Restless Hearts

AT 11:00 a.m. the following day, Johnny woke, exhausted by the temptress hands and hungry mouth of Rebecca's unabashed desires. Right away he realized he was alone in the bed. Terror gripped him in its hold when he saw that the bathroom was also empty. Bolting upright, a note rested on the pillow where her head should have been. Lifting it, he stared at it for a nervous moment before his eyes consumed the words. It read simply,

Don't worry, Johnny.

I have gone into Vegas with Nikki and her mother to buy us some shoes and a tooth brush for you. You were sleeping so beautifully I didn't want to disturb you. I'll be back soon.

Be prepared for a big surprise.

Love,

R

Dropping the note, Johnny swung his legs and stood. He didn't know if he could handle any more surprises. Without Rebecca's presence, the room seemed as lonely as he suddenly felt. He went into the bathroom and relieved his full bladder. It was careless of Rebecca to have gone into the city without him. There was no telling where Tony Millions's men might be. His only reprise of the situation was that it was Boxing Day and the shops of Vegas would be crammed with would-be sales aficionados.

Standing in front of the mirror, his face reflected the worry within. His mouth was as dry as cotton and his usually steady hands trembled. Shaking them, he told himself that Rebecca would be fine. She was, after all, with two others; and he doubted that even if one of Tony Millions's men did recognize her, they wouldn't dare act with malice with so many people around. However, there would be nothing to stop them from following Rebecca back to the motel where they could wait in the camouflage of darkness and make their move. This thought only added to his fears, initiating a sinking feeling that dropped his stomach to his feet, rendering him nauseous with worry. *Stop it, Johnny. You're worrying yourself to the point of hysteria and probably all for nothing. Rebecca's fine. Deep down you know this to be true. So stop scaring yourself needlessly.*

Turning on the taps, he splashed handfuls of water over his face until the cold of it numbed him. Hot water was in short supply at the Pine Ridge Motel. A few minutes of tepid water in the shower was all the old place could manage. Squeezing an inch of toothpaste onto a finger, he proceeded to work his mouth until the dry film of the night before was cleansed away. Spitting out the froth, he rinsed and dried his face with a hand towel. When he looked at himself in the mirror again, he was a cleaner, more awake Johnny, except the intent look of concern was still exhibited in his grey eyes.

As another round of worrisome thoughts was about to overwhelm him, Rebecca's voice fragmented the bindings of his pessimistic opinions.

"Well, hello, sleepyhead," she said from the other room.

Johnny hadn't even heard the door open. Turning to look at her, his jaw literally dropped, his eyes blinked several times to be sure he wasn't dreaming. "Rebecca?"

"You like?" She turned completely around for him. On her body, the body he had recently become familiar with, was a new dress, yellow, with rosettes, that ended just above the knees. Feet were encased in black Doc Martins. Red laces rose above her ankles. But the face belonged to someone else. Rebecca's long red hair was gone. In its place was a short jet-black mane, scissored up and over her ears. Sharp black spikes pointed to the ceiling. Even her eyebrows had been dyed. Black mascara dwarfed her eyes. In her hands were shopping bags. "Well, don't just stand there with your mouth open. Say something, silly."

Johnny's mouth formed several words that barely escaped his lips. "Your beautiful hair. It's gone. Why?" He stepped out from the bathroom. "I mean. I think I know why. It's just a shock. You don't look like you."

"That's the whole point, isn't it? Not to look like me. Now I'll be able to do things without being recognized. You still love me, don't you?"

"Of course." Stepping toward her, he said, "I should be angry with you for going to Vegas without me. What if you were seen? What if someone like Mr. Black followed you here? That was pretty reckless of you."

"Well, nobody did and he didn't. I've made you mad, haven't I?"

"I have every reason to be angry. Are you forgetting about the other night? How close we came to being killed?"

"Of course not. But I couldn't go another day without shoes and neither could you. So I did what I had to do. Now I'm back safe and sound, so please don't be mad at me anymore. It doesn't look good on you."

Exhaling a breath of frustration, Johnny said, "Just promise me the next time you get an idea like that, you discuss it with me, okay?"

Rebecca smiled her best smile. "Okay, Johnny, I promise. No more disappearing acts without your permission."

"That's not what I mean. You know that. Jesus H, Christ on a hockey stick. I can't protect you if I don't know where you are."

"My big brave Johnny. My love. My savior." Dropping the bags, she held her hands in a come-hither gesture. "Give the new me a kiss. I'm sorry and I won't do it again."

Johnny took her hands, kissed her, his eyes open, not believing the dramatic change a little dye had made, how tense she must have been during her shopping spree, though she was feigning complacency.

When they seperated, Rebecca said, "I bought you some boots and socks and a toothbrush. I hope I guessed your foot size right. The boots are size 13. Was I close?"

"You have a good eye," said Johnny, putting aside for the moment the worry still swirling deep within. It was reckless and careless what she had done, but she was back now, and that's all that really mattered. "That's exactly what my size is." He peered into one of the bags. Standing upright were a pair of brown Boulets. Rising from the second bag, the air of food caught his senses. "Whatever is in the other bag sure smells good."

Picking up the bags, she said, "Come. Let's sit on the bed. I thought you might be hungry, so I picked us up some breakfast. I hope you like egg McMuffins and hash browns?"

"What growing boy wouldn't."

They sat on the bed. Rebecca proceeded to empty the contents of the bags, removing a package of white socks then boots.

They were the most beautiful boots Johnny had ever seen, depicting an Indian stitched into the leather across the legging with a headdress of feathers surrounding a stoic face. The leather shone impressively.

"Try them on," urged Rebecca.

Tearing the package of socks open, Johnny slipped a pair over his feet, took hold of the left boot, and jammed his foot down hard until he and the boot were one. It was a snug fit; however, working on the ranch all his life, Johnny understood it took good boots time to stretch and adhere to the foot. He put the right boot on and stood. "They're magnificent," he proclaimed.

"I'm so glad you like them. They were expensive, but you're worth it. Next time you see Nikki, you should thank her, she helped me pick them out. She also did my hair. She's very talented for a fifteen-year-old." What Rebecca wasn't willing to share with Johnny, at least not right away, was that Nikki had confided in her that a very large black man driving a Cadillac had visited the motel shortly after she and Johnny retired for the evening. Nothing was going to spoil the moment.

"I will. You both have great taste. And Nikki did a great job on your hair. If I didn't know you were a redhead, I would believe it was your natural color."

"Well, thank you, kind sir. I kind of like the change. It makes me feel different somehow." Reaching deep into the bag, she retrieved the toothbrush, a battery-powered Oral B, blue handle with rotating head. She handed it to him. "Now you won't have to use your finger anymore."

Johnny put the toothbrush next to him on the bed, more interested in the smell coming from the second bag. Practically drooling, he offered, "We should celebrate with breakfast."

"You men. Always thinking of your stomachs." Taking a McDonald's bag from the smaller of the two, she handed Johnny two yellow-wrapped McMuffins and a red container of hash browns. "I would have brought you coffee, but I was afraid it would have cooled by the time I got here, so I got you a bottle of Coke instead." She lifted a ten-ounce bottle from the bag, handing it to Johnny who had already unwrapped one of the McMuffins and taken a hardy bite.

"Thank you," he said between chomps. Unscrewing the cap, he took a healthy swallow to wash the ham, egg, processed cheese, and toasted muffin down.

Rebecca took out her own breakfast sandwich, unwrapped it, and joined him in the midday feast.

They ate in silence, sharing the Coke between them. Every other minute, Johnny got up from the bed and tested his new boots, walking the perimeter of the room, smiling like an eight-year-old who just got his first two-wheeler.

By the time they were finished, Johnny's insatiable appetite was contented, for the time being. Scrunching the wrappings, he tossed them into one of the empty bags with the empty Coke bottle. Turning to give Rebecca a thank-you kiss, he noticed crumbs had gathered at the corner of her mouth. Gently he brushed them away, and kissed her softly. "Thank you, Rebecca," he said. "I love the boots, and now I'm going to take a shower and brush my teeth, *properly*."

"First, I want to rebraid your hair. I like the whole Fabio look, but you and the feather belong together. That much I'm sure of."

A few minutes later, the feather was secure, back where it belonged, dangling at the side of Johnny's strong jaw. "I guess I'll take that shower now." He pushed himself from the bed.

"Would you like some company? You know, I'll wash your back, you wash mine. I've finished my monthly." She winked, giving him an insouciant smile, green eyes shining like polished emeralds

The thought of holding Rebecca's naked flesh in his arms was almost more than he could bear. A lump grew in his throat. Tiny beads of perspiration formed on his brow, the fiery rush of diffidence coloring his cheeks.

In Rebecca's mind, it was the perfect opportunity to make love to him, not knowing how long they had together and whether or not they would ever have a moment like this again. Mr. Black had come too close. Leaning forward, she untied the laces of her new boots, toeing them from her feet, then removed the white ankle socks. Her toenails had also been painted black. Standing, and in one fluid motion, she drew the dress over her head, and dropped it onto the bed. She went to the clock radio, turned it on, increasing the volume so they would be able to hear it in the bathroom, but not loud enough to disturb anyone. When the old radio came to life, Elton John's "Good-bye, Yellow Brick Road" filled the space around them. "Well," she said, standing there in pink panties, hands on her hips. "Do you want company or not?"

Johnny's eyes poured over her body. Immediately, the surge of desire thrilled his loins. "I would like nothing better," he said. "Are you sure?"

Rebecca went to him, wrapping her arms around his upper body, kissing him tenderly on his broad chest, the press of her areolas sending shivers down Johnny's spine. Looking into his beautiful eyes, she said, "I've never been more sure of anything in my life. I want you to make love to me, Johnny Black. I want to feel you inside of me."

Scooping the new Rebecca into his arms, as if she weighed no more than a pillow, he pressed his mouth against hers, softly at first, then with more want, more need. The fiery breath of a furnace surged throughout his being, igniting a passion far more intense than anything he had ever experienced in his life. Carrying her into the bathroom, he set her gently on the lid of the toilet.

The press of Johnny's erection filled the front of his jeans. Rebecca unfastened them, drew the zipper down, and tugged at them until they were resting on knees.

Using his feet, Johnny inelegantly toe-heeled the boots, stepped out of the jeans, and kicked them aside.

"I have something else to tell you," said Rebecca.

"Oh. What's that?" Johnny replied, his breaths already rapid.

"I didn't take any of my, well, you know, this morning."

"You didn't? I'm so glad. The sooner you're off those things, the better. How do you feel?"

"I feel okay, I guess. Just a little craving, like a smoker needs a cigarette I imagine."

"Well, hold on best you can, okay?"

"I will. With you being strong for the both of us, I think I'll be able to kick it in no time."

"I'm glad to hear that. But no matter how strong I am, it's you that needs to be resistant."

"I know, Johnny. I promise I'll do my best."

They stared at each other for a moment, the longing for each other palpable. Rebecca smoothed a hand over his inches before pulling his boxers to the floor. "I want to please you, Johnny." Leaning, she took him in her mouth, teasing, circling the sensitive flesh of his impressive manhood with her tongue. What the girls at the Palace called a French oral lesson.

"Oh god, Rebecca," breathed Johnny, his eyes closed, mind free from all the recent events they had endured. Hands atop her head, he ran fingers through her newly fashioned hair, his heartbeat a storming rhythm so amplified he could hear the pulsing of it in his ears.

Rebecca drew him deeper into her mouth, savoring the taste of him, massaging his testicles with practiced aptitude. An act she never would have considered before she was schooled in the art of seduction at the Shangri-La Palace. A few minutes spent in heaven later, she felt him shiver with the covet of release. Liberating him from her voracious mouth, she smiled. "I want you, Johnny. I want you so badly it hurts." Rising slowly, she kissed his stomach, teasing his hot flesh with the point of her tongue.

"I want you too, Rebecca. I've never wanted..."

"Shhh." She put a finger to his lips. "Let's not say another word. Just let it happen."

Johnny thumbed her panties, kissing the inside of her thighs, feeling the heat of her against his face.

Together they went to the shower, drew the curtain, turned on the faucets, and stepped into the small space, closing the curtain so they were in a world secret unto themselves. Music spilled from the adjoining room. Two lovers about to embark on a journey of discovery, not the fugitives of their blighted pasts chased by the hounds of malice. Theirs would be a joining of souls, so desperately in need of the other that when they became one, the intimate birthing of their providence would be theirs and theirs alone to preserve.

I was standing
All alone against the world outside
You were searching
For a place to hide

Lost and lonely
Now you've given me the will to survive
When we're hungry... love will keep us alive...

* * *

59

Welcome to My Parlor

WELL into the evening, as shades of darkness descended over the town of Alcova, Mr. Brown stopped at a gas station on the edge of town. He asked the attendant who exited the rundown shop if he knew of a Konahee Wolf, that she had ordered a new vacuum cleaner from his company and he was having trouble locating her.

"Oh sure," the young attendant said, pointing to toward the open highway. "Just follow the road out of town for about a half hour or so. You'll pass several houses, then nothing for a while. Hers will be the next property you come to with a big barn on the north side. There'll be two signs attached to a post. One saying Help Needed, the other, Palms Read for $10."

"You know this Ms. Konahee well then?" asked Mr. Brown.

"Not really. Just know her by reputation. She hardly ever comes into town."

"Oh, what reputation is that?" asked Mr. Brown, inquisitive about the woman and whomever he was about to murder.

"Some people say she's a witch," the young attendant said so quietly Mr. Brown had to strain to hear him.

"A witch. You've got to be kidding. You don't really believe in such things, now, do you, son?"

"Not really. I know they're just stories, but you know, some strange things happen there I've been told."

Mr. Brown laughed. *Small towns,* he thought. Where gossip held no bounds. Thanking the young man, he gave him a fiver for the information, got back into the RX7, and headed out of town.

Just as the attendant had said, he passed several rundown houses where numerous children played on ill-kept lawns, obscure silhouettes against the darkening sky, an unseen dog barking, then there was nothing but dry fields on both sides. Ten minutes later, he came to the property of Konahee Wolf. The Help Wanted sign was gone; however, the Palms Read sign was still adhered to the post. He could see the house farther up the driveway where a single light was on and also the bulging shape of a barn. The rest of the house was cloaked in darkness. Slowly he made his way toward it, headlights of the RX7 lighting the way through the diminishing light. He would ask her if she was open for business, he decided, a sure way to get him into the house. Once inside, he would take stock of the situation, whether there were others he had to deal with, take rule over the occupants, if any, which he doubted by the looks of things, then go to work. Take all night if need be. The place was far away from everything, no one would hear the screams replicated by his well-schooled trade.

Parking the car in front of the house, he got out and looked at the night sky. Diamond dust swept the universe. The gun he would use to secure the situation was tucked into the small of his back, wire cutters secure in a back pocket. Drill and pick still in the trunk. Quickly he went to the side of the house, found the phone line, and with cutters, severed any communication to the outside world. Returning to the front door, a figure appeared in the lighted window. A shadow really, small in stature, standing as still as a statue.

Smiling, Mr. Brown waved. The figure disappeared. It didn't move sideways or backward, it just seemed to vanish right before his eyes. Mr. Brown gave his head a shake. *Shadow tricks. Stupid rumors. Witch. Give me a break.* Walking up the stoop, wrenching his neck until vertebrae cracked, he knocked on the door. He could hear someone moving about, moving toward him. The door opened slowly. No one was there.

Mr. Brown stepped into the house, the air within thick with the smell of stew. "Hello," he called out. "Ms. Wolf. Ms. Konahee Wolf. I know it's late, but I passed by your property and saw the sign. I would like to have my palm read."

"Come in, please," said a woman's voice from deep within. "I've been expecting you, Mr. Brown."

* * *

60

The Promise

REBECCA woke, still concealed in Johnny's arms. After their lovemaking, to which they had exhausted each other long after the water had grown cold, they crawled into bed, their passion for each other unfulfilled, so they made love again, for hours it seemed, until they fell into each other and gave into sleep.

Johnny was breathing peacefully, his broad chest rising and falling beneath her. Kissing his mouth, she prodded, brushing the tips of a finger over his lips, "Wake up, sleepyhead."

Groaning, Johnny opened his eyes to see Rebecca's face hovering over his. Pulling her close, he kissed her softly. "Hello, beautiful. What time is it?"

Looking at the clock radio that was forecasting good weather for the Las Vegas area, she said, "My god, it's almost six thirty. We've slept most of the day away. No wonder I'm so hungry." Rolling from him, she rested her head in the palm of a hand, elbow pressed deep into one of the pillows. "You were magnificent."

"Thank you, but I did have a little help if you recall. You weren't so bad yourself." Johnny sat up, stood, and stretched his arms over his head, shoulders popping, tendons fully extended, muscles rippling like waves.

Consuming his sculpted body, Rebecca said, "We'll have to do that again and again and again."

"You won't get an argument from me. I'm kind of hungry myself. Should we go to Big Bob's diner?"

"Sure. I could eat a great big steak with all the fixings. All that excessive curricular activity has left me famished. Not to mention sore in some places."

"Me too. I'll take your steak and top it with a cheeseburger, fries, and a chocolate milkshake. Then I think I'll have a great big piece of pie."

"My, my. You are hungry. We should shower and brush before we go."

"Yes, but not together. We might never get out of there again. You go first."

"And what's wrong with that?" said Rebecca, and sitting, her perfect breasts tingling as though each freckle were a feather.

"Nothing, it's just that Big Bob's closes at ten if you'd noticed, and I'm afraid that if we start up again, we won't get the chance to eat."

"Someone's awfully confident in themselves."

"It's not me. Well, I guess some of it was me, but it was you who kept me going. You were really something."

The ladies at the Shangri-La Palace had schooled Rebecca in the art of prolonging sexual encounters as well as how to deflate a man in a matter of seconds. She blushed, not from embarrassment, but from the fact that she was a more learned partner than Johnny was and that he understood this, yet would not attribute or suggest, he simply accepted. For this, she loved him even more. Rising from the bed, she went to him, wrapping her arms around his midsection. On her tiptoes, she kissed him. First on the mouth, then on his neck and chest. Gazing at his handsomeness, she said, "Thank you for not thinking ill thoughts of me, Johnny."

"I told you. What happened in our pasts doesn't matter. It's today and tomorrow. That's all I care about." Smiling at her, his eyes conveying a love so penetrating, Rebecca felt every ounce of its dominion fill her heart. A single tear rolled down her cheek.

"I'll love you always, Johnny Black."

After they washed the sex from their bodies and brushed, Rebecca put on jeans, T-shirt, and her new Doc Martins. Johnny also put on jeans and the new black dress shirt he wore the night he first laid eyes upon her. Squeezing his feet into his new boots, he proclaimed himself ready to eat half the menu. Retrieving the gun, he deposited it into the knapsack. "Just in case whoever cleans the rooms comes by while we're out."

"Good idea. I'd forgotten it was even there."

"Well, let's get going. It's a long walk."

"Let's drop in to see Poppi first for a minute," suggested Rebecca. "Thank him for last night."

"Sure. It *was* nice, wasn't it?"

"I'll never forget it. It meant so much to me, just sitting around with you, listening to music, and well, not having to run for the time being. I wish every night could be like last night."

"Me too. But you know it can't be, right? Eventually we'll have to move again."

"I know," said Rebecca, conscious that Mr. Black had come within a hundred quick steps of discovering them.

Once they were outside, Johnny locked the door. It was that time between daylight and dark when everything seemed to belong to the shadows of twilight. Garth and Tommy were on their bikes circling the parking lot, laughing as one gained distance on the other. Garth looked up and saw them. "Hi, Johnny. Hi, Tiffany." He waved, nearly losing control of his bike.

Johnny and Rebecca waved back and made their way down the stairs. Both boys came to a stop in front of them. "Hey. Where are you going?" asked Tommy. That's when he noticed Rebecca's newly fashioned hair. "Hey. You cut and changed the color of your hair. How come?"

"Just for a change. We girls are always changing things. Do you like it?"

"It's okay I guess. I think I like the red better. You're still pretty though."

"So where are you going?" repeated Tommy.

"Just out for some dinner," said Rebecca. "And thank you for the compliment."

"Oh," said Garth. "We already ate. My dad took us to Big Bob's for supper. I had a cheeseburger and fries."

"And I had a clubhouse and fries and a large Coke. Sure was good." Tommy's satisfied smile lit his face. "I'm so full I could burst," he added.

"Well, it's a good thing you're riding your bikes," said Johnny. "So you can work off that big meal.

"That's what my dad says. He doesn't want me getting fat like most of the kids my age he says. Damn computers he says. Makes everybody lazy."

Johnny winked at Garth. "Your dad's a smart man. You should always listen to your parents. Remember, they've already experienced life, so they know things. Now if you boys will excuse us, we're going to say hello to Poppi, then we're going to stuff ourselves." Johnny patted his stomach. "Oh. I almost forgot about these." Reaching into his back pocket, he removed the firecrackers the boys had dropped the night before. "Here you go."

"Gee. Thanks, Johnny," said Tommy, a quick hand snatching the firecrackers.

"You're welcome. Now if you'll excuse us, we should get going."

"Sure. Okay," said Garth then saw Rebecca's new Docs and added for good measure. "I like your boots. See, Tommy, I told you they had shoes." Hooking an accusatory thumb, he added, "*He* said you guys were probably poor. That's why you weren't wearing any shoes yesterday."

"Well, I can tell you we're not poor and thank you, Garth," said Rebecca. "I accept all compliments from handsome young men."

Considering the source of the compliment, Garth blushed severely. He had an immense crush on the beautiful girl whose name sounded like a song. His eyes went to the ground and he kicked at an invisible stone.

Tommy punched him in the shoulder. "Come on, handsome. Bet you can't catch me." And they were off, Tommy's legs pumping furiously, putting a good gap between himself and his lovestruck friend.

"They're so cute," said Rebecca, looping an arm through Johnny's.

"When I was their age, I could never be so open when it came to pretty women. I would just stand there and gush like an idiot."

"Well, after this afternoon, I'd say you've come a long way, baby."

The first signs of the infinite universe dazzled with life. The closest stars were already out, blue pricks of light confirming the earth was nothing more than an ecological blue particle of matter in the grand scheme of things. Rebecca stopped for a moment to take it in. "You know," she said, looking up into the coming of night, "I wonder what the other life-forms up there are doing right now. Are they like us? With families, jobs, problems? Do they think like we do? Do they fall in love like we do?"

"So you believe that there's others besides us."

"There has to be, Johnny. Just look up there. It's our vainness that keeps most of us thinking otherwise."

Johnny looked up, pulled Rebecca close. The firecrackers he'd given Garth sounded. *Bang! Bang!* "So you don't believe there's a god or a heaven we go to?"

"I kind of used to. And in some ways still cling to the idea that there might be. I even pray sometimes, just in case. You see, my mother was Catholic, so I was introduced to the Bible at an early age. As I got older and my gift became more apparent, it seemed to me that no god would allow us to suffer so much. That creating a place like heaven was just a way to simplify man's fear of death. But I know that death isn't the final stage for us. We exist somehow beyond it. I don't know how and I can't claim to understand the whys of it. We just do. To tell you the truth, I'm really quite confused about it all. If there really is a god. And in *his* own way has a hand in what happens to us, well, after all the suffering I've seen and the way the world is and has been for a very long time, then *he* has a warped sense of humor, bordering on sadism. What about you, Johnny? Do you believe in a god?"

Without hesitation, Johnny said "No. Although I've always leaned toward the belief that once we die, our spirits carry on in some other way. It's what my mother's people believed, and now that I've met you, well, you've kind of given that belief an incredible amount of leverage. As far as there being others up there." He looked skyward. "I guess man won't know for sure until they introduce themselves." Still holding the stars with his eyes, he said, "Maybe when *we* die, you and I can find each other, be together forever as they say."

"Then let's make a promise, Johnny. Right here and now. Under the stars. That when one of us dies, they'll watch for the other. Maybe we'll die together. I don't know for sure. But if I go before you, I promise to wait with you. Always by your side."

Johnny looked away from the sky and fell into the green of her gaze. "And I promise that if I die first, I will wait with *you*. I'll always be with you, Rebecca. I swear."

They kissed. A solemn promise made as two eight-year-olds circled the timeless bond made between them. Blue light streaked across the sky, leaving a white tear in the heavens as a meteor fell to the earth. When they parted, each of them held in their hearts hope. Joining hands, they walked the short distance to the motel office where they could see Poppi sitting in a chair, the top of his grey head barely noticeable over the counter.

Opening the door, Johnny allowed Rebecca to go in first.

Poppi raised his head, his eyes widening when he saw the transformation Rebecca had gone through. "Oh. Tiffany. I wouldn't have known it was you if you weren't with that handsome young man of yours. Looks like Nikki had her way with you. She does my hair too. How has your stay been so far?"

Johnny and Rebecca went to the counter. "Everything is fine," said Rebecca. "That's why we came to see you. We wanted to thank you again for last night. We had a wonderful time."

"Yes," agreed Johnny. "The food was great. So was the company."

"Well, I'm sure glad to hear it. So how come the change, Tiffany?" he asked, the late-night visitation by a giant still fresh in his mind. "You had real nice hair. Real nice. If I didn't know any better, I'd think you were tryin' to disguise yourself or somethin'.

You folks ain't in any trouble, are yah? Don't need no trouble round here." He watched their eyes.

"Trouble. No, of course not," lied Rebecca. "It's like we told you. We're just passing through. Taking in the sights. As far as my hair goes, I just thought a change might be nice."

"I kind of like it," added Johnny, putting an arm around Rebecca's waist. "It's like I'm dating someone new."

"Well, I'm glad to hear there's no trouble with you," said Poppi though he knew there was. Giant black men don't show up in the middle of the night asking for one of your guests if trouble wasn't afoot. "So where you two off to then?"

"We're going to Big Bob's for some dinner," replied Johnny. "We're starving."

"Well, that's just fine. Ain't no better place for two hungry people to go to than Big Bob's. He sure knows how to stack a plate."

"Well, I guess we'll be on our way," said Rebecca. "Thank you again, Poppi. For everything."

Looking them both in the eyes, Poppi said, "You be careful out there now. Never know. Things have a habit of changin' real quick."

"We will, Poppi," replied Rebecca, understanding perfectly.

"See you tomorrow." Johnny smiled.

Poppi plopped himself back into the chair. He liked Tiffany and Johnny. Yes, there was some trouble with them, and it came in the form of a giant, but his sixth sense was telling him they weren't the cause. He decided he would keep his shotgun close at hand should the giant return. Give him an ass full of buckshot if need be.

Once they were outside, Johnny asked, "What was that all about? It sounded like Poppi knew we were in trouble. Is there something you're not telling me?"

"Let's walk for a while, Johnny." She took his hand in hers. "I'll explain on the way."

* * *

By the time they were seated in Big Bob's diner, Johnny didn't know who he was angrier with, Rebecca or himself for thinking they were out of harm's way. There were two others seated at the counter, a couple of teenagers, a boy and a girl, no more than fifteen or sixteen, working on a plate of fries and sharing a large soda between them.

After they placed their orders with Big Bob, a steak, medium rare for Rebecca with stuffed potato and vegetables, and a double cheeseburger for Johnny with a large order of fries and a chocolate milkshake, Johnny looked hard into Rebecca's eyes, his disappointment evident. Keeping his voice low, he asked, "How long were you going to keep this from me? My god, Rebecca. Don't you understand that everyone at the motel is now in danger? What were you thinking?"

Rebecca lowered her eyes like a child that's been caught with their hand in the proverbial cookie jar. Sniffing back a tear, she said, "I was thinking how nice it would be to have some time alone with the man I love. That obviously Mr. Black hadn't discovered we were there or you would be dead and I would be left alone to suffer the worst kinds of indignity, not to mention torture." She lifted her eyes.

In them Johnny saw regret, hurt, and anguish. "You realize we'll have to leave the motel as soon as we get back. Where we're going next, I have no idea. I am, however, a little dismayed by your lack of faith in me. Haven't I protected you from harm so far? I might have gotten the upper hand on this Mr. Black." He put his face in his hands and rubbed at his suddenly weary eyes. When he looked at Rebecca again, she was smiling.

"My big brave Johnny. You would take on the world for me, wouldn't you?" Reaching across the table, she took his hands. "I know how strong you are. Stronger than most men, but this Mr. Black, you don't know him. He's a killer, Johnny. Plain and simple. It's his vocation. He enjoys it immensely."

"I'm not afraid of anyone."

"I know, my love, I know," she said, parodying the endearment Hester Hart held for Ed, that's my husband. "And I adore you for your courage. But I'm afraid that if push came to shove, Mr. Black would kill you. I'm sorry if I seem a little disloyal to your abilities, but this man who is after us is a killing machine and paid handsomely for doing so. If you only knew the stories I've heard about him. Not to mention the fact I've seen him in action firsthand."

"Still, I could get lucky."

Rebecca lifted his hands to her lips, and kissed each knuckle. "Let's hope that if Mr. Black does catch up with us, you have the luck of the Irish and then some."

Just as Johnny was going to admonish her further, the stone in his pocket grew terribly cold. So cold, it burned his leg through the jeans. Suddenly distressed, he quickly pulled his hands away from Rebecca's.

"What's wrong, Johnny?"

Reaching into his pocket, he removed the stone and held it in the flat of his palm. It was no longer the aqua blue of turquoise, but instead had turned raven black. Fear gripped Johnny's spine. He dropped the ice stone onto the table.

"What's that?" asked Rebecca.

"I never told you about it. It was given to me by the woman who allowed me to hide on her property. Konahee. She's in trouble."

"How do you know? It's just a stone."

"It's not just a stone. It's been helping us. It used to be blue. It has certain… powers. You of all people should be able to understand. You'll have to trust me. We have to leave. Right now! I know where we're going next, and I hope I'm not too late." Taking forty dollars from his jeans, he laid the bills on the table next to the stone. Taking Rebecca's hand, he practically yanked her from the chair. "Come on!" The stone he left on the table. It had said everything it was going to say.

"But I'm still hungry," complained Rebecca as Johnny pushed through the door.

"We'll get something when we stop for gas. Now let's go! Konahee is in danger, and other than you and my father, she is the most important person in my life."

* * *

They ran the full distance, in the cool darkness of night, from Big Bob's to their motel room. Panting, Johnny unlocked the door and pulled Rebecca into the room. "Now hurry. Get all your things together. If we hurry, we can get to Konahee's before morning."

"Let me catch my breath for a minute." Rebecca stood in the middle of the room, heaving.

Johnny checked the knapsack to be sure he had everything. He went to the clock radio, killing the voice of Don Henley who was into the second chorus of Hotel California.

Breathing normally again, Rebecca went to the bathroom, collected their toothbrushes, hairbrush and paste. Returning to the small room, she lifted her suitcase onto the bed, unlatched it, checked it quickly, and stuffed the brushes and paste into a sock compartment. That's when she noticed the small business card tucked into a corner. She had forgotten all about it. Removing the card, she turned it over so the number of Mr. Benjamin Wong's lawyer stared back at her.

"What's that?" asked Johnny, standing anxiously by the door.

"Remember I told you about Mr. Wong and how Tony Millions had him killed. Well, this is his business card. It has the number of his lawyer on the back. Mr. Wong told me that if I was ever in trouble to call him."

"Well, he's dead now. I don't think he can help you from where he is."

"Yes, but his lawyer's not. First chance I get, I'm going to call him and tell him that Tony Millions had his boss murdered."

"How's that going to help?"

"I'm not sure, but it might." She put the card into the suitcase with her purse, looked at the picture of her mother for a brief moment, and closed and secured the lid, proclaiming herself ready for whatever lay ahead.

They hurried to the truck, tossing their belonging into the rear compartment. Johnny fired the engine. The gas tank was half-full. He looked to Rebecca. "I want you to be ready for anything," he said in a serious tone.

"I will be." She rested a hand on his shoulder.

"Good. Because I'm expecting the worst." He threw the truck into first.

Poppi came barreling from the rear door, dressed in pajamas, a nasty-looking shotgun in his hands.

Johnny stopped the truck. "It's just us, Poppi," he said through Rebecca's open window.

Poppi squinted. "Oh, it's you, Johnny. I was afraid someone was tryin' to steal your truck." He lowered the shotgun.

"Thanks for keeping an eye out. Tiffany and I are just going to go into Vegas, gamble a little bit. I'm feeling a little lucky."

"Oh. I see. Well, you folks be real careful out there. Vegas is chock-full of the wrong kinds of people, if you know what I mean."

"We will, Poppi, and thanks," said Rebecca.

Poppi stood in the shine of headlights as Johnny drove swiftly away, ready to defend his little piece of paradise if need be.

They left the Park Pines where they had had such a memorable time, the tires of the Ford biting into the highway. Johnny pointed it north and off they went, another journey begun, neither knowing what to expect once they arrived at Konahee's place. Whatever it was, it was not going to be good. Johnny was certain of it.

61

Ashes to Ashes

THEY'D stopped for gas, once, Rebecca purchasing a cold roast beef submarine and coffee to wash it down. Johnny had been so worried he'd lost his appetite and went without food even though Rebecca urged him not to. "You need your strength," she kept telling him; however, Johnny would not, could not eat he was that concerned about Konahee, the woman who had shown him so much generosity, allowed him to be privy to things he would have otherwise scoffed at if he hadn't experienced them himself.

They turned into Konahee's property, the headlights of the Ford lighting the Palm's Read signage and the beaten road leading to the house that was as dark as pitch.

The sky over Wyoming was without stars, adding to the foreboding feeling Johnny had as he drove the Ford to the front of the house. A dome of light lit the facade of the old structure. It looked vacant. The barn nothing more than a black outline against the blanket of darkness encompassing the property. According to the digital, it was 3:17 a.m. He killed the engine. "There's a flashlight in the glove compartment," he told Rebecca. "Take it out and check to see if it still works."

Rebecca did as she was asked while Johnny reached into the back, retrieved the knapsack, and removed the gun.

A small beam of light hit Johnny in the face.

"It works," said Rebecca.

"Good. Point it someplace else, okay?"

"Oh, sorry. Johnny?"

"Yes," he said, checking the chamber, not knowing why, it just seemed the right thing to do.

"I have a strange feeling about this place."

"A good strange feeling or a bad one?"

"I don't know. I just feel, it's hard to explain. I've never felt like this before. It's like all of my senses have been ignited somehow. Like they're on fire."

"Does it hurt?"

"That's just it. It doesn't, but it does. I don't understand it at all. It's something new to me. I don't mind telling you that I'm frightened, Johnny."

"You're not the only one. Give me the flashlight. You stay here in the truck. If I'm not back..."

"No way. I'm not staying here by myself. I'm going with you."

"You might not like what we find."

"I don't care. We do this together."

"Okay. Stay close to me."

"You don't have to worry about that."

Exiting the truck, the power of the small flashlight led the way. Johnny went up the stoop first, opened the door, and shone the beam of light to the stairs leading to the second floor. Rebecca stayed on his heels. Together they entered the residence of Konahee Wolf.

"Konahee!" Johnny called out. "It's me, Konahee, Johnny!"

The house responded with silence.

They moved further, cautiously, Rebecca holding on to the back of Johnny's shirt.

"Oh my god!" she screamed. "What's that? On the floor! Is that blood?"

Johnny pointed the light to the floor. Slashes and twists of blood were everywhere. On the floor and up the walls. A large puddle of crimson lay right at their feet. "Oh no! Konahee!" A surge of anger seared Johnny's mind. "Konahee! Konahee! Answer me, please!" His distraught voice echoed off the walls. "Oh god. We're too late."

"Let's get out of here, Johnny," urged Rebecca, clinging to his back, so frightened by the blood everywhere she wanted to cry forever.

"No! I have to find her. Don't you understand that?!" He began to weep, running into the hall toward the kitchen, through the bloodletting on the floor, flipping on lights as he did.

Rebecca followed, slipping in the sticky gore. When she reached Johnny, he was standing in the middle of the kitchen, his eyes wide with fear. "What happened here?" she said, seeing that all hell had broken loose in the room.

Pots and pans and utensils were scattered on the floor. Blood was everywhere. On the small table where Johnny had taken his meals. A bloody handprint was smeared on the white of the refrigerator door, the cupboards. Ruptures of blood had even hit the ceiling. A gallon of stew was spread out in front of the stove. They stood in shocked silence, tears streaming over Johnny's face.

Rebecca swallowed her fear. She had to be strong for him in this tormenting moment. "Johnny. Johnny. Let's go. Whatever happened here is over. We have to leave. Whoever did this might still be here."

Johnny looked to the gun in his hand. "Well, if they are, I'm going to kill them." There was pure malice in his voice. He drew the hammer back.

"Johnny. You're frightening me. Please! Let's just go. You can't help your friend now."

"I have to find her."

"She might not be here anymore. Whoever did this might have taken her with them." Rebecca had to try anything to get him out of the house. Back into the truck, far, far away from the macabre scene. That's when she noticed something under the table. She pointed. "Johnny, look! What's that under the table?"

Johnny's followed the direction of her finger, eyes wild, mind avarice with thoughts of murder. Lying in a small pool of blood was a finger. An index finger. Bending his frame low, he reached under the table and picked it up. When he stood, he was smiling.

"What the hell are you smiling about?! Have you lost your mind?"

Johnny moved toward her, holding the digit in front of him. "On the contrary. This finger doesn't belong to Konahee. This is a man's finger. See?" He held it out to her. He had a good notion as to what had happened; however, he had to be sure.

"Okay, okay. It's a man's finger. Get rid of it."

"Don't you see." Johnny tried to explain without revealing the secrets he knew. "If this is a man's finger, then Konahee might be all right."

"Yeah, or maybe she got lucky, cut her attacker's finger off with one of those knives just before he or they killed her."

"We have to check the rest of the property. I have to be absolutely certain before we leave here." He dropped the finger to the floor. "Come on. There's still a good chance Konahee is alive."

* * *

While Rebecca and Johnny inspected the rest of the house, a black SUV was making its way toward the town of Valentine, Kentucky. Behind the wheel was one Luigi Vitelli, Frank Santangello's number one hit man, ruthless in his enterprise, and as stealth in his approach as a midnight breeze. Sitting next to him was Victorio Bandini, just as hard-hearted in his skill as a contract killer, however at three hundred pounds, far less covert. Their predawn approach assured them that the Harts would all be home and fast asleep. It would be an easy kill to which they were going to be paid handsomely.

"We should be coming to a cemetery soon according to the Internet printout," Victorio pointed out. "Once we pass the graveyard, our target will be the first house on the right."

"I like this Internet. It makes our jobs more easy than the old days. You can find out anything about anyone. Saves a lot of time."

"Slow down, I see something coming up."

Luigi slowed the SUV to a moderate 15 mph. "I see it. That's the cemetery all right. We should arrive at our destination in less than five minutes. Hey, did you know people are just dying to get in there?"

Both laughed. Victorio Bandini so hard, his enormous gut rolled up and down, side to side.

Luigi depressed the gas, bringing the SUV to a speed of 50 mph.

"Hey, what's the hurry? They'll be there. Tucked safe and sound in their beds."

Turning his head, Luigi looked to the fat man. "I want to get the job done before sunrise. I want to be able to…"

"Watch out!"

Luigi Vitelli's head snapped back to the road. What happened next happened in deadly seconds. Caught in the headlights of the SUV was a small boy and a very large red-and-white dog. Luigi spun the wheel. Tires caught a rut in the road, sending the vehicle sideways along the icy blacktop. Luigi tried the brakes but to no avail. The shiny black vehicle slid and darted over the embankment, hitting the hard winter ground with such force it flipped once, twice, three times, before coming to a rest upside down, its tires spinning freely.

Luigi and Victorio were in the habit of not wearing their seat belts. The fat man was sent through the windshield, his life terminated when his head hit the unforgiving trunk of a pine tree.

Upon impact, the driver was launched forward as the steering wheel came up, catching him just under the chin and snapping his neck like a twig.

With the Hart residence still several hundred yards away, no one would discover the wreckage until morning.

* * *

After they checked the rest of the house finding no one, Rebecca and Johnny took their search outside. "We'll check the barn first," said Johnny, aiming the flashlight in front of them.

"Okay, I'm right behind you." Rebecca's nerves were still frayed by their ghastly discovery.

As they made their way past the Ford, Rebecca heard a sound, like a baby crying. "What's that?"

"I hear it too. Stop for a second."

They listened. Apparently the crying was coming from behind the house.

"Come on," said Johnny, grabbing Rebecca's hand and pulling her with him.

"What the hell is a baby doing out here? I really don't want to find out, Johnny."

"It's not a baby. It's George."

"Who the hell is George? Johnny, stop!" She dug her boots into the earth. "Wait a second. Who is this George?"

"Don't you remember? I told you. He's Konahee's cat and sounds distressed. Now come on." He pulled on her arm, the beam of light jumping up and down as they half-ran to the back of the house.

"MEOWWW," George's cry sent shivers up and down Rebecca's spine.

Johnny pointed the flashlight at the shed. Sitting on his haunches atop of it, his paunchy face pointed to the sky, George let out another distressed mewling. When Johnny hit the feline with the beam of light, George's eyes shone green. It leapt off the shed, not making a sound, and disappeared into the shadows, tail ramrod straight.

As one, they approached the shed door. "You wait here. I'm going to take a look inside." Releasing the hammer on the .38, Johnny tucked it into the front of his jeans, took hold of the handle, and pushed. The door opened a crack then stopped. He tried again, managing another inch or so. When it would open no farther, he put the flashlight in his mouth and tried with both hands, leaning into it with his shoulder. Stubbornly, the door opened, the beam of light igniting the small space. The first thing Johnny saw was the face, or what was left of it. "Jesus H. Christ on a hockey stick," he muttered, flashlight wedged between his teeth.

"What? What is it Johnny? Is it Konahee?"

Removing the flashlight from his mouth, he directed the beam so he could see what was left of the person lying on the ground. The man was naked. His legs had been preventing Johnny from opening the door. They were bent awkwardly, broken beyond repair, fibulas rupturing flesh. The man's upper torso had been ravaged, torn to shreds, exposing raw ribs. The cavity where his intestines should have been was a gaping, bloody hole. Genitals, ripped free. His right arm was missing. Only a bloody stump remained. The index finger of his left hand had been severed. However, it was the face that caused Johnny to nearly lose his lunch. The man's throat, mouth, and nose had been torn away. All that remained were dark eyes that seemed to stare back at him.

Konahee's collection of bones began to sway, sounding like wind chimes. Johnny beamed the light at them. Hanging by a tether, among the motley collection, was the man's arm, still dripping. Johnny reversed several steps until he was outside again.

Rebecca moved toward him.

"No, Rebecca. Stay away. You don't want to see this."

"It's Konahee, isn't it?"

Johnny turned to face her, pointing the light at her midsection. "No. It's a man. Or what used to be a man."

"Do you know him?"

"Even if I did, I probably wouldn't recognize him."

"I have to look, Johnny. What if it's one of Tony Millions's men? The truck, Johnny. The truck. Think about it. What if somehow they found out you were driving Konahee's truck and they sent someone to kill her, just as they threatened to send someone to the Harts. To teach you a lesson for rescuing me. I have to see for myself."

Her reasoning was sound, thought Johnny. If Tony Millions possessed the power Rebecca said he did, then it was possible that the man lying in the shed was one of his killers for hire. "Okay. Take a look. But I hope you have a strong stomach."

"After what I've just seen in the house, I think I can handle it." She went to him.

Together they stood in the doorway. The inside of the shed was pitch, musical sounds emanating from within. "Are you ready?" asked Johnny.

Rebecca drew a breath. "Yes."

"You'll need to duck your head." Johnny aimed the flashlight into the shed. The interior lit up like a lantern.

Head low, the first thing Rebecca saw was the empty cavity and missing genitals. Bile rose in her throat. She swallowed it down and looked up for a second to find the arm dangling among dozens of swaying bones. For reasons unknown, the ghastly discovery didn't faze her at all. Forcing her eyes, she looked at the face that wasn't actually there. When she saw the eyes, she knew. The demon dark fixation was not unique to her. "That's Mr. Brown," she acknowledged as calmly as anything.

"Are you sure?"

"Of course I'm sure. I'll never forget that bastard's eyes." Her calm demeanor was replaced by an anger so hot it burned the area between her legs. Summoning a good amount of phlegm into her mouth, she leaned forward and let loose. "You fucking bastard!" she cried, hating absolutely. "You finally got what you deserved! I knew you would, you fucking pig! I hate you! Do you hear me, Mr. Brown?! I fucking hate you!" She sent a vicious foot at his face. One of the demon eyes popped from its socket and just dangled.

George the cat, who had been watching between loose boards darted into the shed, mouthed the eye, pulled on it three times before detaching it from the optic nerve and returned from whence he came.

Grabbing Rebecca by the shoulders, Johnny spun her around. Her green eyes were feral. "I never told you this, Johnny, because I was afraid to, because I thought you would think ill of me. But that son of a bitch raped me." She fell into his arms, weeping, dispelling the hatred one tear at a time.

Johnny backed her out the shed and pulled the door closed.

When Rebecca looked at him again, it was with frightened, curious eyes. "What or who could have done that to him? He's torn to shreds. Who is this Konahee, Johnny? I thought you told me she was an old woman."

"She is Rebecca. I swear to you."

"There's no way an old woman could have done that! Not that he didn't deserve it. No *person* could have done *that*."

"I know."

"Then what is it you're not telling me."

"I can't Rebecca, please. I made a promise. One just as binding as the promise I made to you last night."

"That's why I felt so strange when we arrived, isn't it? Because this place holds some kind of power or magic, doesn't it? This Konahee. What was she? Some kind of medicine woman or something? Believe me, I'll understand."

"I'm glad you would. I can't say anything more." He held her eyes, hoping she would understand and not pursue the matter further. "There's something you need to think about. If Mr. Brown ended up here, then your friends might be in as much danger."

Rebecca thought for a moment, the faces of the Harts vivid in her mind's eye. "Oh my god, Johnny, you're right! I have to call them. I saw a phone in the kitchen. I'll get the operator to locate them, and I'll make a collect call."

"You'd go back in there."

"For the Harts, I would do anything. Come on." She yanked on his shirt.

Johnny led the way to the side entrance, the beam of light zigzagging back and forth, the .38 in his other hand ear high. The old door groaned when he opened it.

They'd left the lights on in the kitchen. Rebecca rushed past him, watching her every step toward the phone, avoiding the gore best she could.

Clicking off the flashlight, Johnny followed her in, drew the hammer back on the .38 just in case Mr. Brown wasn't the only one sent to Konahee's.

Rebecca lifted the phone from its cradle and, looking back at Johnny, put the receiving end to her ear. The line was dead. She depressed the dial tone button over and over; however, no amount of tampering was going to raise an operator, it was as dead as Mr. Brown. "Shit! Shit! Shit! It's dead." She slammed the receiver back into its cradle.

"Mr. Brown probably had something to do with it. I'm sure if we checked, we'll find that the line has been cut."

"Then we have to get to another phone. I have to talk to them, Johnny." Moving across the kitchen, she stopped in front of him. "We'll go into town. Find a phone booth."

"Okay, but I have to make sure Juno is okay first."

"You mean the horse?"

"Yes. I have to check on her. It'll only take a minute."

"Okay, but let's hurry."

They left the kitchen through the rear exit, Johnny leading the way back to the truck, Rebecca close behind. Once they were inside, Johnny turned the key. The engine fired. He made a three-point turn and headed in the direction of the barn, the headlights of the Ford illuminating the barn's great face and the scaffolding still clinging to its side. Halfway there, the dashboard lights flickered and the truck began to lose power. "What now?" said Johnny, staring at the flickering dash.

"What? What is it?"

"I don't know. The truck's losing power." He depressed the gas. The Ford lurched forward a few more feet then died, rolling to a stop. Johnny cranked the key. Nothing. He tried again and again; however, the Ford would not respond. Throwing it into neutral, he set the brake and hung his head over the wheel.

"Did we run out of gas?" asked Rebecca, powering the flashlight so they could at least see each other.

"No. There's plenty of gas." Turning his head, he looked at her. Rebecca wore the expression of someone who had just been betrayed.

"What are we going to do?"

"I don't know. I don't understand why it won't start."

"Maybe we should give it a moment," suggested Rebecca.

Johnny knew that no amount of waiting was going to miraculously cure whatever was ailing the new truck. It was another Konahee thing. They were meant to remain on the property. Why, he had no idea; however, to mollify Rebecca's suggestion, he agreed to wait a few minutes. Try again.

They sat in silence, the beam of the flashlight illuminating the space between them. When a fitting amount of time passed, Johnny tried again. Nothing. Not even a click. "It looks like we're stuck here. For the time being anyway."

"I don't want to be stuck here, Johnny! This place frightens me. I want to talk to the Harts. Can't you fix it?"

"I'm not a mechanic, and please try not to be frightened. I'm right here with you. We'll have to wait until morning which is only a few hours away."

"I don't want to wait here."

"Yeah, well, we don't have a choice, do we? The truck's dead, and it's pitch-dark. What do you want to do, hitchhike in the dark? It's best to just wait until the sun's up, then we'll have a better appreciation of our situation. Maybe the truck will start then." Pulling the keys from the ignition, he shoved them into his jeans.

"So we're just going to sit here?"

"No, we're not. Give me the flashlight."

She handed it to him. Johnny opened the driver side door. "Come on."

"Where are you going?"

"I'm going to check on Juno."

"Are you crazy? What if whatever did *that* to Mr. Brown is still out there somewhere. And you still don't know where this Konahee person is."

"I'm quite sure whatever did that to Mr. Brown doesn't mean us any harm. Think about it. He shows up to murder Konahee. Tony Millions's way of teaching me a lesson for taking you away from him. Only it's Mr. Brown who ends up dead."

"You mean torn to shreds."

"Yes. Torn to shreds. You're right for thinking that this place is laden with magic, and please don't ask me to explain further, I can't. All I know for sure is that we'll be safe here. You have to trust me on it. You do trust me, don't you?"

"Of course I trust you. What about Konahee then? Where would an old woman be hiding?"

"I don't know. It's a big property. She could be anywhere."

"Shouldn't we check the barn then."

"We will. But first I want to make sure Juno is okay. You coming?"

"Do I have a choice?"

Side by side they walked toward the back of the barn where Johnny had constructed the paddock, the weakening flashlight offering them little luminosity. The only sounds they could hear were those of their footsteps crunching underfoot the sprouts of dry grasses. There were no cricket songs. No night birds twittering in the dark, just a silence so loud it caused Rebecca's skin to crawl.

When the beam of light reached the paddock, and much to Johnny's dismay, they saw the gate was open. Johnny hurried toward it. "Juno! Juno!" he called out. "It's me, Juno! Where are you, girl?" Scanning the area with the weakening light, he saw no movement. Not even a shadow. Just the blue water trough, empty and the darkness beyond.

Rebecca caught up to him, the tone in Johnny's voice telling her something was amiss. "What's wrong, Johnny?"

"It's Juno. She's not here."

"Are you sure?"

Though the beam of light did not cover the entire acreage, Johnny knew in his heart that he would not find her. "She's gone," he deadpanned.

"Just like Konahee."

"I'm afraid so," he said, staring into the empty paddock.

"I don't pretend to understand what's going on here, Johnny, but I don't mind telling you, I find it all a little creepy. First, we find Mr. Brown torn to shreds by I don't know what." Her voice raised several octaves now. "Then we can't find this Konahee person who you say is very old, and now her horse is missing. The truck won't start, and I'm fucking cold! I'm afraid to find out what's going to happen next."

So was Johnny, but he wouldn't entertain the thought any further. "We'll go to the barn and spend the next few hours in the loft I stayed in. We'll be safe there, I promise." He hit her with the beam of light. Rebecca's arms were crossed in front of her chest, and like a woman scorned, she wore a malignant countenance.

What he did not need at the moment was for Rebecca to suddenly become frenetic, though she had every right to be. He tucked the .38 into his jeans. "I need you to focus, Rebecca. Stay with me. Everything will be all right. We'll go back to the truck and get your jacket if you're cold."

"I don't want to spend the rest of the night in some loft! I want to talk to the Harts! I want all of this to be over with, Johnny! I want..."

That's when they heard it. A sound that came from deep within the darkness of Konahee's property. Powerful in its animation like the violent intentions of a runaway train.

"What's that?" asked a suddenly vigilant Rebecca.

"It's the wind," said Johnny, listening as the sound bore across the land. "Come on. We don't have a second to lose." Grabbing her hand he pulled her with him. "We'll go to the truck! Come on!"

The flashlight's beam bounced in front of them as Rebecca tried to keep up with Johnny's pace, the thunderous voice of the wind growing in fury as it rushed toward them. Ten yards from the truck, Rebecca tripped on something and fell to her knees. Johnny stopped, hitting her with the beam. Rebecca looked up at him, tears of frustration filling her eyes. Johnny scooped her into his powerful arms and stood her up. "Are you okay?"

"I'll live," she said, looking down at herself.

"Good." Roughly, Johnny took hold of her arm, and ran her the rest of the way to the truck. By the time he opened the driver side door and unceremoniously tossed Rebecca in, the air was filled with stinging desert sand. He jumped into the truck, slamming the door closed. Rebecca had crawled to the passenger side, the sound of her intrepid breathing filling the cab. Resting the flashlight between them, so a dome of light was created, Johnny apologized. "I'm sorry for being so rough, but we didn't have much time."

"What's happening, Johnny?"

"I don't know." He stared into the darkness through the windshield. The roaring wind was closer, audible even in the confines of the cab. Desert sand rained on the truck. In seconds, the windshield was covered in an impenetrable layer of Mother Earth.

Sliding across the seat toward him, Rebecca said, "I'm scared, Johnny."

Opening his arms, he allowed her to cradle her head against his chest and held her as close as he could. "I'm not too proud to tell you, so am I."

Rebecca's heart pounded with growing fear. Johnny continued to stare at the windshield, the edifice of sand sounding like millions of nano-sized creatures trying to breach the interior. "It's just a windstorm," he tried to assure her, though he wasn't at all sure if that's truly what it was. "We'll be safe in here. Close your eyes if you have to."

Rebecca did just that, closing them so tight her teeth hurt.

That's when it hit. The full brunt of the wind was upon them, shaking the truck in its strength, sounding like the howling of a distressed beast. The flashlight flickered, then died, leaving them in darkness absolute. Reaching for it, Johnny slapped it a few times in the palm of his hand, but to no avail. "Shit," he muttered under his breath. The Ford seemed to lift several inches on one side before it dropped. Rebecca was squeezing her eyes so tight tears erupted and ran down her cheeks.

Johnny tried to comfort her by covering her head with his hand. "It'll be over soon," he said close to her ear. "I'm sure of it."

"I wish I were as confident as you are," she whispered more to herself, not moving from the guarding comfort of Johnny's protective arms.

To Johnny's surprise, the digital lighting of the radio came to life without the benefit of battery. Elvis' voice poured through the speakers.

Love me tender
Love me long
Never let me go
You have made my life complete
And I love you so.

Rebecca's eyes shot open. A green hue of light spilled from the dashboard. "I thought the truck was dead," she said, voice competing with the whaling of the wind and Elvis' love ballad.

"So did I."

In the dim lighting, Rebecca saw that the keys weren't in the ignition. She looked up at Johnny, the jade of her eyes glowing in the artificial light. "More magic?" she said.

"I believe so."

Love me tender
Love me true
All my dreams fulfilled
For my darling
I love you
And I always will...

Wrapped in each other, eyes engaged deep, they listened to the Konahee magic of Elvis. The wind howled like an angry god, the truck alive in its wake. Johnny leaned forward; they kissed. Unbeknown to them, as their lips pressed tight and they drank each other's breath, a mysterious impenetrable bond was fashioned.

They parted when the radio fell silent and the dashboard light diminished, pitching the cab into darkness once more. Much to Rebecca's relief, with the silence came the cessation of wind. "Is it over?" she asked under the cover of darkness, respite washing over her.

"I think so," said Johnny, listening. His hand searched for where the flashlight should have been. Finding it, he banged it against his hand. Not to his surprise, the small device came to life, the beam of light reflecting off the sand-drowned windshield.

In its entirety, the storm had lasted for no more than a few minutes, or in the time it took for a King to serenade star-crossed lovers.

"Maybe you should try the keys again," tried Rebecca. "So we can get out of here."

Johnny did. Several times. The Ford remained lifeless.

"So now what are we going to do, Johnny?"

"We'll stick to our original plan and go to the barn. Wait for morning to come." Leaving the keys in the ignition, Johnny tried the driver side door. Sand spilled onto his arm. He had to give it a mighty push before it opened. Scanning the immediate area around the truck, he was amazed as to just how much sand there was. So much desert had been displaced by the wind, it had gathered deep above the wheel wells and up the side of the Ford. Opening the door as wide as he could, he took Rebecca by the hand and helped her out of the truck. "Be careful. The sand is deep."

Rebecca stepped down, new boots sinking inches into what felt like quagmire.

Johnny scanned the area around them. For as far as the flashlight would allow them to see, small rolling dunes of sand had gathered as if the windstorm had blown an entire desert onto Konahee's property. Rebecca tried a couple of steps, finding the task difficult.

"We should get to the barn," urged Johnny.

All Rebecca could see of the barn was a stark silhouette against the cloud-covered night. "It'll take us an hour to get there in this," she overstated.

"I'll carry you then."

"Fine, but I want to get my suitcase first. I'm not going anywhere else without it. Who knows, the way things are happening around here, the truck just might disappear, then where would I be?"

Johnny couldn't argue with her reasoning. Stranger things *had* happened. "Well, if you're going to get your suitcase, you might as well grab my knapsack while you're at it."

Rebecca crawled back into the truck and, with the aid of the aimed flashlight, reached into the rear of the cab, retrieved everything she needed, awkwardly slipped her arms through the sleeves of the jacket and grabbed the knapsack. She handed it all to Johnny.

Johnny set the suitcase onto the sand, and slung the knapsack over his shoulders. Rebecca backed out of the truck, closed the door, and sank up to her ankles.

"Feel better now?"

"I can think of a thousand other places I'd like to be, but yes, I feel better now that I have my things."

"Good. Let's get to the barn."

"You don't really have to carry me. I think I can manage." She lifted one boot from the sand then the other.

"Are you sure?"

"Can't be any more difficult than walking on a beach. But you'll have to carry the suitcase."

Johnny lifted the suitcase. "You hold the flashlight." He handed it to her. "Take my arm so you don't fall."

Looping an arm in his, she aimed the beam of light in front of them. They began to trudge through the sand, toward the ghostly structure of the barn.

"You know," said Rebecca. "Even though I was scared shitless, it was kind of nice having Elvis sing to us. Very romantic, considering what was happening. I hope your friend is all right."

"I'm sure she is. If there's one thing I learned while I was here, Konahee can take care of herself."

When they were close enough to the barn, Rebecca aimed the flashlight at it. The barn's facade came into full view looking like a sad face. There were large vertical gaps where there should have been planks. She scanned the area around it. Protruding from the sand were barn boards, ripped away by the wind's fierce breath. Scattered all around was the scaffolding, felled in dozens of pieces, the blare of the wind having been so capacious, they didn't hear it crash to the ground. Looking to Johnny, she said, "Are you sure it's safe in there?"

"Can't be any less safe than it is out here. The barn may be old, but it was well built. Come on. Aim the light at the doors so I can open them." Johnny set the suitcase down and went to the double wide doors.

Rebecca pointed the light.

There was just enough sand piled in front of the doors to make them difficult; however, with the muscle Johnny had gained, the task seemed almost effortless. The great door yawned, the sad face coming to life.

Rebecca flashed the interior. Parked in the middle of the barn was a green RX7. *The* RX7. She gasped. "That's Mr. Brown's car."

Johnny stopped pushing on the door, his eyes followed the beam of light. "Well, I guess he had to get here somehow. Funny how it never occurred to either of us there wasn't a vehicle parked close by." Picking up the suitcase and moving to Rebecca's side, they cautiously stepped in, Rebecca clinging to Johnny's arm.

"I hope the keys are in it so that we can get out of here."

"Even if they are, do you think it could get through all that sand? It's a sports car. Not an ATV."

"We can try, can't we?"

"I guess we could. But don't get your hopes up."

They moved to the driver side door. Johnny opened it. "Here, give me the flashlight."

Rebecca did, her eyes taking in the shapes and shadows of the interior. Her memory kicked in and she could see Mr. Brown sitting at the wheel, instructing her to get him a sandwich. Stung by a bee. Big mistake. She chased the image away.

Slipping the knapsack from his shoulders, Johnny crawled halfway into the vehicle and inspected the interior. The ignition was empty. He checked both sun visors and glove box. Nothing. All he found were black gloves, maps, an empty Starbucks coffee cup, some cellophane wrappers, and a dozen or so CDs. Finding the release for the trunk, he pushed it. There was a click from behind as the trunk popped open, giving Rebecca a start. "Shit, Johnny. You could have told me you were going to do that."

Withdrawing his frame from the small space, Johnny said, "I'm sorry."

"Yeah well, I almost peed myself."

"Sorry. I'm afraid I didn't find any keys."

"Did you check everywhere?"

"Everything except the trunk." He hit it with the light. Each stared at the open hatch for a moment.

"You look," said Rebecca, her eyes riveted to the open lid where anything or anyone could be concealed. "I don't want to. God knows what you'll find in that bastard's trunk."

Johnny beamed the light into the open compartment. Except for the spare tire and a length of half-inch rope, it was empty. "There's nothing here," he said with some relief. "It's empty."

"Please tell me you know how to hot-wire cars."

"Sorry. Not one of my strong points."

Rebecca wanted to cry. They were stuck there for who knew how long. And where the hell was this Konahee person? She couldn't have just disappeared off the face of the earth. *Could she*?

Johnny closed the trunk, and flashed the beam of light all around him. The black buggy was where it should be. The ladder leading into the loft stood strong. His motorcycle still leaned against one of the stalls. Unfortunately, he no longer possessed the key. When he flashed one of the sturdy support beams, much to his surprise, Konahee's walking stick was leaning tall against it.

When Rebecca saw the motorcycle, a certain hope filled her. "Please, please tell me you have the key to the bike."

"I'm sorry. I gave it to Konahee when I left."

Rebecca's head dropped, all hope washed away. Everything seemed to be going against them. *But why*? "So what now?"

Johnny had moved to the walking stick. He looked at it, curious. "I guess we'll go into the loft. When the sun comes up, we'll decide what we're going to do next."

"What's that?" asked Rebecca, seeing that Johnny was looking at the strange length of wood.

"It's what Konahee used to get around."

"Seems to me this Konahee person gets around just fine. How else would Mr. Brown's naked body get put into that shed. You told me she lives alone. And you don't think that Mr. Brown drove his car into this barn and just left it, do you?"

"I can't answer that except to say Konahee is truly one of the most," he paused, thinking of the right word, "remarkable people I've ever met, excluding present company."

"Well, thanks for that. I'd say this Konahee is a little more than remarkable. I'd say she possesses certain gifts I'm just starting to get a handle on. I guess I shouldn't be bold enough to think that my gifts are unique. Obviously, Konahee's gifts far exceed my own."

Johnny left the walking stick where it stood. Walking to Rebecca, he said, "I don't know about that. Your gifts and her gifts are just different." He hit the ladder with the beam of light. "I'll go up first. If I'm right, there should be a lantern up there. We'll leave your suitcase and the knapsack down here for the time being."

"I told you, I'm not going anywhere without my things. You'll have to carry it up."

They went to the ladder, Rebecca lugging the suitcase while Johnny dragged the knapsack and pointed the beam into the opening. Removing the .38 from his jeans, he handed it to Rebecca. "Hold this for a minute. I wouldn't want to accidentally shoot myself."

Rebecca took the gun in her hands, felt the cold, stark life of its intended purpose.

Inserting the flashlight into his mouth, Johnny climbed the first three rungs of the ladder. "Give me the suitcase," he said, the words slurred, sounding like he was drunk.

Rebecca lifted it toward him.

With the light in his mouth and only one hand to climb the ladder, Johnny began his ascent into the loft, the light diminishing below, leaving Rebecca to stand in waning darkness. "Hurry," she called up to him. "I don't like being in the dark."

Johnny disappeared into the square hole.

Standing alone at the foot of the ladder, Rebecca's mind began to play tricks on her. Suddenly, there were moving shadows all around and she thought she heard the sound of footsteps other than Johnny's. Squeezing her eyes, her fingers took a death grip on the .38. A whispered plea escaped her lips. "Hurry, Johnny. I'm frightened." She could hear him moving about above her, floorboards creaking under his weight. What seemed like an eternity passed before she heard, "Okay. You can come up now."

Opening her eyes, a soft yellow glow poured through the opening, lighting the rungs of the ladder. Johnny's handsome face hovered, his hair dangling long, the feather twisting at his chin. In one hand was an old-fashioned lantern.

Shoving the .38 into a jacket pocket, she put one foot on the first rung and began to pull herself upward, leaving the mind play of shadows and sounds behind. When she reached the top, Johnny took hold of her arms and drew her the rest of the way.

In the glow of the lantern, the loft looked comfortable enough, Rebecca supposed, a single bed and dresser the only furnishings. A glassless square of a window looked out into the darkness. "So this is where you hid. Comfy."

Johnny held the lantern, the light emanating from within, giving his face a jaundice manifestation. "I know it's not much, but for right now, it'll suit us just fine." He had placed Rebecca's suitcase at the foot of the bed.

Rebecca reached into her jacket. "Here. I don't want to hold on to this thing longer than I have to." Between thumb and index finger, she held the .38. at arm's length.

Taking it, Johnny jammed it into the waist of his jeans and set the lantern atop the dresser. Light bounced off the lean of the roof, creating a butter colored dome all around them.

Rebecca yawned. Her entire body seemed to deflate with sudden fatigue.

"Are you okay?"

"I'm suddenly very tired. I feel strange."

"It's been quite an experience for you. Why don't you sit on the bed and rest? It's comfortable enough."

In a matter of seconds, Rebecca's body had become perplexingly weak. She practically dragged herself to the bed, sat down, and yawned again. "I don't know what's the matter with me. I feel like I could sleep for a hundred years." Leaning into the mattress, she pulled her feet up so she was in a fetal position. When her head touched the pillow, her eyes closed, and she entered a dreamless slumber in the time it took to take her next breath.

Johnny went to her, staring down at her beautiful face, understanding that her sudden need to sleep was more than just exhaustion, it was this place and it had her in its grasp. *But why?* That's when a familiar, friendly voice filled his mind.

"I wish to speak with you, Johnny. Come down from the loft. Rebecca will be safe. I will be waiting for you."

Taking the lantern, pitching the loft into darkness, he made his way down the ladder and held it aloft.

Sitting next to Mr. Brown's car was Linda, covered in blood. Dangling from her teeth were a set of keys. She dropped them to the ground. "It is good to see you again, Johnny."

"It's good to see you again, *Linda*."

"Let's no longer pretend. We both know who I am."

"Yes, Konahee. I know. I've known for quite some time. You were also the green mist that visited me nightly."

"Green mist? I know nothing of a green mist." Konahee wolf-snapped at the air.

"You mean to tell me you weren't... you and I never... never mind."

"Remember, Johnny, your experiences here were forged for reasons you cannot grasp. This green mist you speak of. Perhaps it was only in your dreams."

Johnny understood. Whether Konahee was telling another, *necessary* nontruth to hide the intimacy they shared, or whether she really did not know of the succubus who had left her mark upon him, it was this place, coveting more secrets than Vegas.

"Why did you bring us here, Konahee?"

"It was necessary. This is much a part of your journey as well as Rebecca's. She, more than you, needed to be here. Now the circle of life will be complete."

"The circle of life? What do you mean?"

"I will not explain further, except to say that a predestined course culminates while your friend sleeps. Tell me, Johnny. Was your search worth the reward?"

"Yes, Konahee. We are very much in love."

"That is good." Konahee Wolf eyed the keys on the ground. "Those keys belonged to Mr. Brown. When you leave here, you are to take what was his."

"I'm sorry he came here. It was my fault. I'm glad you're all right."

Konahee Wolf snapped at the air again, a low growl emerging from deep within. "Do not blame yourself. Everything is as it should be. Mr. Brown was pure evil. I could taste it in his flesh. I found great pleasure in ending his life. I took his nasty little tools, clothes, and identification far out onto my property and buried them where no one will ever find them. It will be a long time before anyone discovers who the man in the shed is. Now our time is short. So you must listen to what I have to say."

"I'm listening."

"First, let me tell you Juno is fine. I can feel your concern. You need not worry. I gave her to Frank Roland, the officer you met. He has a young son who loves her."

"I'm relieved to hear that. But what about, you know, the fact that she isn't old anymore?"

"Frank Roland is many things. A good father. Defender of the innocent and a pillar of strength in the community. But what he is not is a horseman. To him, Juno is as she always was. Just a horse."

"And what about George?"

Konahee Wolf's cackling laughter echoed in Johnny's mind. "George can fend for himself. He always has. He will probably outlive us all."

"And what about you, Konahee? How will you be?"

"This body is the final stage of my lineage. I will remain what I am. I am stronger and will live many more seasons. So you need not worry."

"I'll try not to. Can I ask you a question, Konahee?"

"I know what you wish to ask. And I believe you have earned the right to know." A moment of silence filled the space between their minds before Konahee Wolf continued. "My family has walked this earth for more than four thousand years. We are the shape shifters of the world. Sadly, there are few of us left. Now you know." The wolf lowered her head in a show of sadness. For the second time since their meeting, a single tear rode the length of her snout. When she raised her head again, her eyes demanded Johnny's attention. "Now listen and listen carefully. The new year is upon us. With it comes a divine trust between you and Rebecca. From this bonding trust your true self be revealed. It has been written on the wind long ago. You and I are not so different."

"I understand, I think," said Johnny, though he didn't. Not really.

"Rebecca has faith in you, Johnny. The promise made between you is the key to your providence. You will understand more when you leave this place."

"But how will Rebecca and I leave? Mr. Brown's car will never get through all that sand."

Konahee Wolf went to the support beam where her twisted length of magic stood. "Take my stick, Johnny."

Johnny went to it, taking it in his free hand, feeling the life it possessed shiver up his arm. "Now what do I do?"

"Go to the entrance of the barn and slam the stick into the sea of sand three times. Close your eyes and wish the wish that is most important to you right now."

Carrying the lantern and length of beech wood, Johnny went to the open door. Konahee Wolf followed and sat on her haunches next to him. She closed her eyes. "Do it now! With all of your candor and all of your belief."

Johnny pounded the earth thrice, wishing for an escape. For himself and Rebecca, so that their journey may continue. As hard as he willed, nothing happened. "Nothing's happening," he said dejected.

"Wait. You young people. Always in such a hurry. Do you think magic can take place at the mere sound of your voice. There are certain elements far beyond your ability to comprehend that unfold when certain bodies are brought together."

They waited in silence. Without warning, the ground beneath Johnny's feet began to tremble. Then it happened. The masses of sand began to part, like the Moses parting of the sea, creating a path as far as the lantern would allow Johnny to see.

"Thank you, Konahee," said Johnny, expecting nothing less from her.

"You are welcome. Now. Throw my stick as far as you can."

With one hand, Johnny did just that. Konahee's walking stick sailed through the air end over end, planting itself upright in the sand like a lightning rod.

Opening her eyes, Konahee Wolf said, "I must leave you now, Johnny. Our time together has come to its final purpose. We shall never meet again." She raised her body, stood on all fours, and turned to leave.

"Where will you go, Konahee?"

"First, I will go to the river and wash the evil from my body. Then I will go into the mountains. I have always liked the mountains. They are full of rabbits. Mother will provide for me, so you needn't be concerned for my well-being."

"I will never forget you, Konahee."

"And I will think of you always, Johnny. Go back to your loved one. You must leave this place. Now!"

"I will."

Konahee Wolf tilted her massive bloodied head, grey eyes demanding his attention. In her final telepathic words, she said, "Before the new year arrives, you will kill again, Johnny." Then with a swish of her colored tail and a grey blue leap into darkness, she was gone from his life taking a piece of his heart with her.

Johnny returned to the loft, the keys to the RX7 now in his possession and in time to see Rebecca stir from her enchanted sleep. If something took place while he was talking with Konahee, there appeared to be no physical evidence of it.

Rebecca sat up, rubbed at her eyes. "What happened?" she asked in between subsequent yawns.

"You fell asleep." Konahee's last words resonating in his mind. "*You will kill again, Johnny. You will kill again.*"

"I *did*? That's strange. I don't remember."

Setting the lantern on the dresser, Johnny went to her. *You will kill again, Johnny. You will kill again.* "You complained how tired you were and fell asleep."

Noticing the keys he was holding, she asked, "Where did you find those?"

Johnny lied out of necessity. "I guess I didn't look hard enough the first time. When you fell asleep, I decided to go back down and take another look. They were just lying on the ground, near one of the back tires. They're the keys to Mr. Brown's car."

"You mean you left me up here by myself?" Rebecca pushed herself from the bed.

"It was only for a moment, and I was right below you. Nothing would have happened to you. I wouldn't allow it. So try not to be mad, okay?" He shoved the keys into his jeans.

"I guess. At least that's something. But how are we going to drive out of here with all that sand outside?"

Johnny did not know how he was going to explain the parting of the sand. "I have a feeling this place will allow us to leave."

"You mean more magic?"

"If that's what you want to call it, yes. I believe we were brought here for a reason. It might be as simple as finding Mr. Brown and taking ownership of his car. Think about it. Now we can move around less conspicuously."

"Until Tony realizes Mr. Brown isn't coming back. Then he'll put two and two together and understand we took his car."

"*Maybe*. But he won't know right away. This will give us the advantage of time we need to put some distance between us."

"And what about the Harts? Have you already forgotten about them?"

"No. Of course not. As soon as we can, we'll get to a phone booth and call them. But I have a feeling they're fine."

"I wish I was as optimistic about it as you are. They could be dead for all we know."

"You shouldn't think that way." Johnny smiled. At an attempt to give their situation some much-needed reprieve, he added, "You'll go red before your time."

"Ha-ha, very funny. I'm just so worried about them. You don't understand how much they mean to me."

"I think I do. Which is why we're going to leave now, find a phone booth, and call them." He lifted the suitcase. "There's a booth in Alcova. You can make the call from there. Now let's go."

Once they were out of the loft, Johnny opened the trunk to Mr. Brown's car and deposited the knapsack and Rebecca's suitcase next to the spare tire then closed it with a slam. The sound echoed from the walls of the barn like the persistent roll of a thunderstorm. When he looked at her, Rebecca was staring at the car.

"I'm not sure how comfortable I am getting in that thing," she said, unblinking.

"I know how hard this must be for you. Try not to think about what happened. It's just a car. An inanimate object. It had nothing to do with what happened. That was all Tony Millions's and Mr. Brown's doing. And well, it's the only way we're going to get anywhere. At least for the time being." He went to her, placing his strong hands on her shoulders, squeezing them with just the right amount of assurance. "Everything is going to be fine. Look at me, Rebecca."

She looked up to him. In his eyes she saw strength, trust, and the shine of his love for her. Drawing a deep breath, she looked to the car again. "You're right. It's just a machine. Nothing to be scared of." Turning her face back to Johnny's, she said, "Besides, I have you to take care of me. Right?"

"Always." Removing the keys from his pocket, he dangled them. "Well?"

"Well, what are we waiting for? Let's get in." She went to the passenger side, opened it, stopped for a breath to look inside, then climbed in.

Squeezing his body behind the wheel, Johnny adjusted the seat, put the key into the ignition, depressed the clutch, and turned it. The engine whined to life. "Here," he said, withdrawing the .38 from his waist. "Put it in the glove box."

Rebecca took the gun and popped the small compartment. A light came on, revealing several maps and a pair of black gloves. Storing the gun out of sight, she slapped the compartment closed.

It took Johnny a moment to get used to the clutch. Once he was comfortable, he made a three-point turn and drove out of the barn.

Immediately, the headlights picked up the red Ford, Konahee's walking stick, and the path miraculously created. Seeing they were going to have no problem driving from the property, Rebecca said, "I don't suppose you know how the sand just up and moved for us."

"Let's just say it was one more act of kindness from a friend and leave it at that, okay?"

"I guess. That's some friend you have there."

"Yes, she is." Johnny kept his eyes on the walking stick as the RX7 moved slowly through the sand. It seemed to be brighter than usual, like it had just received a fresh coat of varnish.

"And I don't suppose you're going to tell me how that stick got out here. Last I remember, it was leaning against one of the beams in the barn."

As Johnny's mind manufactured another believable lie, flames erupted at the base of the stick, violently lapping at the shaft.

Before Rebecca uttered another word, a blue electrical arc loosed from the stick's twisted knob, striking the barn's double wide doors, setting it alight. "Holy shit! Did you see that!"

In seconds, the barn's sad facade was engulfed in an intense wall of flame.

Johnny stopped the car.

"What are you doing?!" shrieked Rebecca. "Don't stop! Let's get the hell out of here!"

A second and third arc struck Konahee's Ford and the house. Like the barn, they were baptized in a furnace of flame, manipulating the canopy of night into day.

Grabbing Johnny by the shoulder, Rebecca screamed, "Drive, Johnny, drive!"

Regardless of her plea, Johnny was caught in the mystique of what was happening. Staring through the windshield, he was mesmerized, as the first and second floor of Konahee's house filled with the orange burning that would erase all evidence of him ever being there. A forth, and final blue bolt, zigzagged through the air, hitting the bone shed, turning it into a conflagrating ball of amber turbulence.

Rebecca's eyes widened, terror seized her in its nefarious grasp. In front of her, a great rolling ball of orange rose into the predawn night and leveled the bone shed to the ground. It had taken mere seconds for the century-old wood of the house to turn into a blazing cathedral of pyre. When she realized Johnny was not doing anything to take her away from it all, she slapped him hard across the face. "Johnny! Snap out of it! You get this fucking car moving, and I mean right now!"

Johnny turned to look at her. "Don't you see? This is all for us. So that no one will know we were here."

"I don't fucking care! You put your foot on the gas and get me the hell out of here! I don't want to end up like my brother and father did! I'm terrified of fire!" Her voice collapsed, and she pleaded, "Please, Johnny, please."

A thick black column twisted into the night.

Rebecca's pleading tone and the sting in Johnny's cheek steered him back to reality. "Yes. We should get out of here," he said way too calmly for Rebecca's liking. "I'm sorry if I frightened you." Lifting his foot from the clutch, and much to Rebecca's relief, the RX7 started moving again. Nonetheless, she began to weep. Crowding her mind's eye, the images of her brother and father burning to death was restored fully in its savagery. Cupping her face in her hands, tears dripped between her fingers.

"I'm sorry, Rebecca. That was thoughtless of me. Please don't cry." Gears were shifting. The tires of the sports car dug in and it picked up speed.

Sniffing, Rebecca wiped at her eyes, black mascara down her cheeks. She stared at the fully engulfed house. "Ashes to ashes," she said to herself.

"Huh?"

"Nothing. It's not important."

Johnny noticed the black tears. "You might want to do something about your face."

"Why?"

"Look in the mirror. Your makeup is running."

Rebecca turned the rearview mirror and saw that she looked like a raccoon from hell. Using the sleeve of her jacket, she removed the mascara best she could and laughed at herself.

Johnny turned the car onto the rough road leading to the highway. Behind them, the house collapsed upon itself in a hellish roar and a burst of orange so bright it ignited the interior of the RX7.

Rebecca wanted to look back. Something inside told her not to, whispering what she had just experienced should be left to rest. She had learned much during the short visit to Konahee's place. *The things Johnny must have experienced were inconsolable.* She certainly had a much-better understanding of what it must have been like for him during his hiatus. His friend's gifts, though an all-together different creature than her own, far exceeded the ability to see and speak with those who have passed on. Konahee's were that of a timeless magic, likely inherited, using the elements around her to do her bidding. The wind, earth, and fire bending to her will. And what she obviously did to Mr. Brown, a feat usually perpetrated by a wild animal, was something even more perplexing than Rebecca could imagine. Johnny knew though. And these secrets would remain unshared. Just as he promised. Sniffing and wiping black tears, she drew strength from the man sitting next to her. "I'm sorry for slapping you."

"That's okay. I deserved it. You pack quite a wallop."

"You mean for a girl."

"Not at all. My cheek still stings."

"I had to do something. As magical as it may have been to you, I was terrified. I thought you were just going to sit there and let the fire take us."

"I wouldn't have let that happen. I was just caught up in the moment. It won't happen again."

"I wish I was as confident as you are."

"You have to trust me no matter what."

"I do trust you. I think that's my problem. I've never put too much faith in the men in my life, especially after my recent experiences. You, being who you are—trustworthy, courageous and fearless—is somewhat of a relief, though I still suspect there's a lot more to Johnny Black than I know."

Johnny said nothing. Headlights picked out the silent highway. He slowed the vehicle, down-gearing to a crawl. "At least now you know why I couldn't tell you about my stay here. What you experienced was just one of many things that occurred here."

"I can only imagine, and yes, I do understand. You did after all promise Konahee you would not reveal anything, and you haven't. You should be proud of yourself. I don't know if I could have kept such secrets to myself."

The RX7 came to a stop. Johnny looked deep into the darkness that would lead them back to Alcova. "You'll be able to make that call in less than an hour. Why don't you close your eyes?"

"Are you kidding? My heart's still pounding." She gave life to the surreptitious stereo. Jeff Healy's "Angel Eyes" flowed from all around. "What I need is to listen to some music so I can relax." The thought of taking a painkiller had entered her thoughts several times in the past hour; however, she drew on an inner strength and remained abstinent. Increasing the volume, she leaned back, and looked to the man she loved. A feeling so intense in its all-consuming opulence filled her to the very well of her soul. "I do love you so, Johnny Black." Closing her eyes, she fell hostage to the late great bluesman.

So tonight, I'll ask the stars above
How did I ever win your love
What did I do
What did I say
To turn your angel eyes my way...

Johnny popped the clutch, spraying a rooster tail of dust, tires screeching as they tore into the highway. He pointed Mr. Brown's sports car toward Alcova, the insatiable fire forbiddingly amber in the rearview mirror as it consumed everything that was Konahee Wolf.

* * *

A pair of fire engines roared out of town, sirens blaring, at almost the same instant Johnny and Rebecca drove in. Harvey Lector at the wheel of one. Daylight cracked the eastern horizon. Rebecca remained with the music, impervious to the rush of emergency vehicles all around. Johnny maintained the legal speed limit, avoiding eye contact, and headed where he knew a phone was located. Not far from the Gooseneck Pub.

A state trooper roared from a side street, roof lights screaming red and blue, but Johnny couldn't tell whether or not it was Frank Roland.

The phone booth was located under the domed light of a streetlamp. Johnny turned off the stereo, digital reading 6:27 a.m.

The sudden absence of music caused Rebecca to open her eyes. "Did anybody see us?" she asked, fully alert.

"Oh, I'm sure we were seen, but they've got more important things to tend to. That fire is going to keep them busy for quite a while I imagine. Still, we shouldn't take any longer than necessary."

Parking the sports car under the cloaking canopy of an elm, Johnny killed the engine. They were fifty feet away from the booth. Anyone passing would get a clear look at the person inside. "I know the Harts are okay. I can feel it."

"I hope you're right. I don't know what I would do if I found out I was responsible for any harm coming to them. I wouldn't be able to live with myself."

"Do you need some change?'

"No. I've got some leftover from shopping. Would you mind opening the trunk. There's something I want to get out of the suitcase."

Reaching below the dash, Johnny found the rear latch and popped the trunk. "What do you need? I'll get it while you phone the Harts. Like I said, we should be as quick about this as possible."

"That business card I showed you. The one Mr. Wong gave me. It's in the sock compartment. I'm going to make two calls."

"What good would that do?"

"I don't know. Let's just say I owe it to Mr. Wong. He and I connected in a way you wouldn't understand. I think the least I can do for him is to have his people know that he didn't kill himself."

"Okay, you get to the phone booth. I'll find the card. Anything else before you go out there?"

"Yeah. What time do you think it is in China?"

Plugging the machine with two quarters, Rebecca hit the key for the operator while keeping her head low. The glass of the booth had a film of morning dew, and more than one sleazy artist had lent their talent with the pertinacious point of a black marker. A pickup passed; however, its driver didn't even glance in her direction. He seemed more focused on catching up with the parade of vehicles heading to the fire.

"Operator," said a mechanical voice. "What city please?"

"Yes. I would like to make a collect call to Mr. and Mrs. Edward Hart. The city would be Valentine, Kentucky."

"Do you have a proper address?"

"No. I'm sorry." Rebecca cursed herself for not knowing the address. "It's a rural route address. That much I'm sure of."

"One moment please. I'll see what I can find." Silence filled the line. Rebecca was getting more anxious by the second, her eyes scanning the length of the street while she waited. The small town had come to life. There were a number of vehicles appearing from side streets, the news of the fire having spread fairly quickly.

Several apprehensive heartbeats passed before the operator came back on line. "I have only one listing by that name. A Mr. Edmond Hart. Valentine, Kentucky, post office box 1119."

"Yes. That's it."

"I'll be connecting you now. Collect call to Mr. Edmond Hart. Whom may I say is calling please?"

"Rebecca. Rebecca White," she said, trepidation causing her voice to rise.

There was a moment of silence before the line whispered a distant ring. There was another and another. Rebecca's heart began to pound. Then there was a click before Hester's weak voice came on line. "Yes. Hello."

"I have a collect call from a Rebecca White. Do you wish to except the charges?"

"Rebecca! Oh my, yes. I'll accept the charges."

"Your call is open, miss."

"Hester." It's me Rebecca."

"Rebecca, my dear. How wonderful it is to hear from you. Ed and I, that's my husband, were just talking about you yesterday and wondering how you were doing."

"Then everything is all right with you and Ed?"

"Of course, my dear. It's funny that you should call though, but I'm not surprised you did. There's been a terrible accident. Sometime during the night. Not a half mile from where we live. Two men killed in an auto accident. The sheriff and his deputies are there now. I just got off the phone with Mabel Helpnot, you remember her, well, she works the dispatch sometimes, and you know what she told me?"

"No. What?"

"That the sheriff found a cache of guns inside the vehicle among other things. Imagine that."

Rebecca swallowed hard, for she had no doubt the dead men had been sent to do no good. That somehow Tony Millions had his hand in this. Fortunately for the Harts, divine intervention had prevailed. But what was to stop him from sending more men? She tried to maintain a nonchalant opinion. "Sounds pretty scary. I'm so glad you're okay. I was worried about you."

"You needn't worry about us, my dear. We're as safe as two bugs in a rug. Now what about you? How are you fairing?"

"I'm fine, Hester," she said, though far from it. "I've fallen in love."

"You have! That's wonderful, my dear. What's his name? Does he love you back?"

"Yes. And his name is Johnny. Johnny Black."

"Johnny Black and Rebecca White. Now if that doesn't sound like a match made in heaven I don't know what does. Will you be coming to visit us? Is that why you're calling. Please say yes. We do miss you so."

Rebecca's eyes misted. Nothing would be more pleasing than to be in the comfortable hospitality of Ed and Hester Hart, but it couldn't be. Not now. Probably never.

"I'm sorry, Hester. I can't right now. Johnny and I are heading to Canada where we'll start our lives together."

Silent disappointment filled the line. "Canada's beautiful." There was an audible sniffle. "Did you get the note and money we left you? Of course you did. What a silly question."

"Yes. And thank you. The money got me through some difficult times."

"I'm glad we could be helpful."

Rebecca could hear Ed's sudden voice in the background before Hester said, "It's Rebecca, dear. She's called to say hello." There was a muffled conversation before Hester came back on line. "Ed says hello, and if it's money you need to get you here, then just tell us where you are and we'll wire the funds to you."

How was she going to tell them that she could never return to them? She couldn't just come out and say, "Oh, by the way, those men who were killed were sent to murder you and it's all because of me." She thought hard for a few seconds. "It's not the money, Hester. Johnny managed to get a job in Alberta, on the oil rigs. We have to be there in two days. His employers were very adamant about it. He'll be making good money. Maybe when we're settled, we'll be able to afford to fly out for a visit, but for right now, we have to get there before any of that can happen."

"I understand. Times are tough all over. Like Ed, that's my husband, says, economy's in the shitter. I'm just glad your man was able to find employment even though it's taking you away from us."

The farther the better, thought Rebecca.

Johnny gently knocked on the glass.

Rebecca turned. The look on her face told him everything he needed to know. The Harts were fine. He held up the business card.

"Rebecca, Are you still there?"

"Yes, Hester. I'm still here."

"Good. I thought we were disconnected for a moment. I have some wonderful news for you, my dear."

"Oh. What's that?"

"Well, last month was our anniversary. And you'll never guess what happened."

Rebecca waited for the news.

"Our Caleb. He managed to play "Twinkle, Twinkle, Little Star" on the piano. We were sitting down to dinner, and well, he just played. I'm sure we have you to thank for that."

"That's wonderful, Hester. I wish I was there."

"So do we, my dear."

Rebecca's eyes filled with tears of joy for her friends. "Hester, I have to go now. Johnny's waiting for me."

"I understand. You will call us again, won't you, my dear?"

"Yes, Hester, I will. As soon as Johnny and I get settled. I promise. You and Ed take good care of yourselves. I miss you both tremendously."

"We will, my dear, and the feeling is mutual. You know how, Ed, that's my husband, and I feel about you. Anytime you feel the need to talk, we're only a phone call away.

My goodness. In my excitement to hear from you, I almost forgot to wish you a merry Christmas."

"Merry Christmas, Hester, and I hope the New Year brings further contact with your lovely boy. Good-bye. Give Ed a big kiss for me. I love you both."

"Good-bye, my dear, and I will. We'll think of you often."

There was a pause in time as both parties were reluctant to hang up. Then there was a click, the line was closed. Rebecca replaced the receiver, head hanging in remorse.

Johnny knocked again. "We have to hurry," she heard him say through the glass. "Before the sun comes up."

Opening the door, she took Benjamin Wong's card from him. "I'll only be a couple of minutes."

"Are you okay?" he asked.

"I will be. I'll tell you what happened once we're on the road again." Leaving the retractable booth open, she plugged more money into the machine.

"I'm going back to the car and out of sight," said Johnny, turning.

"I'll be right there." Hitting the operator button again, she turned the card over. The name Jim Han was written in black ink as well as the long series of numbers that would connect them. By her account, and remembering her geography lessons and time zones, it was 9:00 p.m. or thereabout in China.

"Operator," a somewhat friendlier voice said.

"Yes. I would like to make a collect call to this number please. To a Mr. Jim Han." She rattled off the eleven digits.

"Whom may I say is calling please?"

"Rebecca White," she said, not knowing if Benjamin Wong had had the time to inform his lawyer of her existence before he was murdered. *What if he hadn't? I would be no better off than I am now. I have to at least try.*

A phone rang on the other end of the world and was picked up on the third ring. "Jim Han," a voice said in perfect English.

"I have a collect call from a Rebecca White. Will you accept the charges?

"Rebecca White!" There was a pause, causing Rebecca's heart to sink. "Yes. I will accept the charges."

"You may proceed," said the operator.

"Mr. Han, my name is Rebecca White. I need to speak with you."

"Yes, Ms. White, We are well aware of who you are. Your call has been anticipated by us."

Relief filled Rebecca. "I need to tell you about Mr. Wong and what really happened to him."

"Yes. I am listening, Rebecca. Please continue."

"Well. He didn't kill himself like the newspapers said. He was murdered."

"We had our suspicions. Unfortunately, our sources were unable to verify."

"It was Tony Millions. Well, not him personally, but he did give the order to one of his men."

"And you know this for a fact?'

"Yes, Mr. Han. What happened to Mr. Wong was directly attributed to the wishes of Tony Millions. For the money he gave him."

"This is very useful information, Ms. White. We are indebted to you for this call. Now tell me, Ms. White. What is it that we can do for you? Mr. Wong left us with instruction that should you ever call, we were to offer you our assistance in any way. How may we be of service to you?"

It didn't take Rebecca more than a second to ask, "I have some friends who are in trouble because of me. Tony Millions has already sent men to kill them, only it was they who were killed in an accident. I'm afraid that he will send more men. Is there anything you can do to help them?"

"What are their names? We will assist you any way we can."

Rebecca told him of the Harts and where they lived.

"Leave this information with us. We have many associates in the States. I'm sure we can be of assistance. Now what about you personally, Ms. White? What is it you desire? We would be most accommodating."

"All I care about is that the Harts remain safe. I have everything I need right now, thank you." Rebecca knew she could ask for anything and it would be granted; however, she preferred to remain as far out of the circle of organized crime as she could get. If this Mr. Han could prevent further retribution by Tony Millions or whomever, then that was good enough for her. "I'll keep your kind offer in mind, Mr. Han, but for right now, I'm fine, really."

"Be sure to keep possession of this number, Ms. White. We will always be at your service."

"I will, Mr. Han."

"Good-bye, Ms. White. Thank you for calling."

"Good-bye, Mr. Han."

The line went dead.

Hanging up the phone, Rebecca stepped out from the booth, somewhat relieved. *Could Mr. Han really help?* There was a carrying breeze in the predawn air. She looked at the card once more before tearing it up into dozens of tiny pieces and allowing the wind to carry them in its swirling draft.

When she got back to the car, Johnny said, "Not a moment too soon. The sky is getting brighter. We have to get out of here. Where to, madam?"

Closing the door, Rebecca pulled on the seat belt, seeing that the ink of night had surrendered to the coming of day. The sun would fully breach the horizon in less than half an hour. "Right now I don't care, Johnny. Just get us as far away from here as possible. I'll tell you about the phone calls on the way."

Shifting the RX7 into first, Johnny moved from the shadows of the elm and aimed the car south toward Colorado. "I hear Denver's nice this time of year."

* * *

62

The Wishing Tree

BY the time the sun reached 10:00 a.m. Midwestern time, Johnny's eyes had become hypnotized by the road, the toll of the past twenty-four hours having taken effect. They were just outside of Cheyenne, near the Wyoming, Colorado, border. There was only one cloud in the sky as far as Johnny could see, looking like a splatter of white against a palette of blue, the cars sharing the road, mere flashes of metal.

To his right, a great Cottonwood stood in the middle of what he figured was eighty fenced acres, give or take. He decided it was time to pull over. Removing his cramped hand from the stick shift, and easing his feet from the gas and clutch, the RX7 shifted down. "I've got to pull over, Becca. I'm tired."

Rebecca looked at him and smiled sweetly. "That's the first time you've called me Becca. I like it. It's what my mother and Ben called me. I understand you need to rest. Besides, I'm not sure if I want to go to Denver. It'll be a lot colder there."

Johnny stopped on the graveled shoulder, yawned, and shook his head. "See that tree over there in the field?"

Rebecca *had* noticed it. It seemed out of place in the middle of basically nothing. A giant with black branches for arms and thick, ground-hugging roots for legs. There was something odd about it though. Something Rebecca couldn't quite place. "Yes. It's pretty hard to miss."

"Well, there's an opening in the fence. We just passed it. How about we park the car, walk to the tree where we'll be out of sight and where I can take a nap? You too if you need one. We can decide where to go once we've rested."

"Sounds very romantic. You can rest your head on my lap."

"Romance is the last thing on my mind. But your lap does sound comfortable." He waited for a semi to pass before he backed the vehicle and came in line with the opening in the fenced property. The dirt road leading into the field was rutted with tire marks.

Putting the RX7 into first, he eased it through the opening and stopped on the other side. Killing the engine, he pocketed the keys.

The leafless tree was in their direct line of sight and about three hundred yards in. Johnny stared at it for a moment. It must be his tired eyes playing tricks on him, he thought, because he was seeing things hanging from the trees' massive branches. "Is it me, or are there things hanging in that tree?"

"I see them too."

"Give me the gun."

"Why?"

"Even though this place looks out of the way and safe, I'm not taking any chances with our safety."

Opening the glove compartment, Rebecca removed the .38 "Here," she said and, with care, handed it over.

Johnny tucked it into the waistband of his jeans. "Okay, let's go."

Simultaneously, they exited the car, minds trying to comprehend what it was they were looking at. The air around them smelled sweet, even though the field was nothing more than dead, weathered grasses.

Rebecca breathed it in. "Do you smell that? It smells like… like, potpourri."

Johnny filled his lungs. "Yeah. But where's it coming from? There's nothing near here except for sunburned grass and that cottonwood.

"I don't know. Strange, isn't it? Let's find out."

At their feet was the beginning of a well-beaten footpath that wound its way to the base of the tree. Above them, a crow passed, wings spread, talons tucked, making clicking sounds with its black tongue and beak.

"Looks like this is a favorite spot for a lot of others." Rebecca reached for Johnny's hand. "Come on. Let's find out what all the fuss is about."

They stayed on the path, Rebecca pulling on Johnny's arm. The closer they got, the more Rebecca became filled with a sense of euphoria. The tree seemed to be drawing her to it, as if it had a purpose, as if their being there was meant to be. Once they were close enough, the items hanging from the great cottonwood's branches began to take shape. Rebecca stopped and stared in wonder. Hanging from the branches were dozens and dozens of pairs of footwear. Different shapes and seasons. "Look at that, Johnny. It's beautiful."

Johnny didn't see a tree with shoes hanging in it as being beautiful, more bizarre was what he was thinking. "What do you suppose it means?" he asked as they began to walk toward it.

"I think I get it. Don't you see? This is a place where people come and dream and make wishes. It has to be. All those shoes. They represent all the wishes made here. It's like some kind of wishing tree. Old and wise."

"I think you're right. Has to be. Why else would they be there?"

"This is so amazing. I wish I had a camera."

"The tree might not like it. You know, taking its picture."

"You mean like I would be stealing its power if I took its picture?"

"Yeah. Something like that. For whatever reason, people believe this tree holds the answers to their dreams. It's become a talisman of good fortune. Many of the old ones of my people believed that if you took their picture without their consent, then you stole their spirit from them. Same thing could apply to this tree. After what we experienced last night, we should be open to other and all possibilities. Every legend, they say, has some semblance of truth to it. Who are we to argue?"

"Then I'm glad I don't have a camera. I wouldn't want to be responsible for changing something I'm not supposed to." She put her arm around Johnny's waist, and they stood there for a quiet moment, looking at the tree, each of them already wondering what they were going to wish for.

They walked the remainder of the distance and stood at the mighty cottonwood's footings, instantly feeling the mystique of the centuries-old tree. The sweet smell seemed to be emanating from all around it. Running shoes, dress shoes, hiking boots, sandals, and even steel-toed work boots twisted and swayed above them. By the looks of some, they had been there for years, decades even, disfigured by the elements. There were other items hanging among the smaller branches as well. Men's and women's necklaces, colorful bandanas, neckties, scarves, an array of hats, and Johnny noticed that there was even someone's red toupee and war medals nailed to a limb. Not a single branch was spared. They all hung there like perennial ornaments, testimonials to the great tree's formidable wisdom.

With their eyes searching throughout the branches, as the warming sun rose behind them, Rebecca said, "This is one of those things that happen to you in life you never forget. I mean, what happened last night was mysterious and at times scary, and certainly memorable, this is something that touches me right to my soul. Do you feel that way too, or is it just me?"

Johnny didn't know how to explain what it was he was feeling. It was certainly something; however, it wasn't touching his soul, it was more like the thick blanket of ambiguity bearing down on him. *Did everyone feel something different when they came here?* "I know one thing, I'm still tired. Do you think the tree would mind if I had a nap at its feet?"

Rebecca knew without a doubt they were meant to find this place. That it was going to play a major role in the grand scheme of things. She was as certain of it as she was certain Mr. Black was still out there somewhere, hunting for them. "I think you should. I believe you were meant to. Like this chapter in our journey was somehow already written by a foreseeing author. It was meant to be, just like you and me finding each other."

"That's pretty deep."

"I feel deep right now. But before you lie on my lap, I'm going to give the tree something and make a wish." Rummaging through the pockets of her jeans and jacket, all she came up with was the wrapper to the Three Musketeers bar she purchased when they'd stopped to fuel in Laramie. She looked at her Docs. *No, not them. I need something that will truly show the tree that I'm serious.* "Everything I have is in my suitcase."

"I hope you're not suggesting I..."

"No. Of course not. You're tired. You stay here. Sit by the tree. I'll be back in five minutes." She didn't wait for Johnny to stop her before she was off and running down the path.

Johnny looked up into the tree again. The personal effects swaying created an illusion, making the tree appear as if it were breathing. "I hope you can make her wishes come true," he said then, crossing his legs, sat against the trunk that was wider than the breadth of his arms. Elbows on knees, he closed his eyes. The first thing to come to mind was what Konahee Wolf had told him before disappearing from his life forever. "*You will kill again, Johnny.*" She seemed so certain of it, and now, so was he.

Opening the driver side door, Rebecca popped the trunk. Several cars zoomed behind her. She paid no attention to them as she walked to the rear of the RX7. Reaching into the trunk, she flipped the latches to her suitcase, already knowing what she was going to offer the tree. She had made up her mind from the short time it took to run from the tree to the car. She would miss it dearly; however, she had three wishes, deciding it was going to take something dear to her if there was a chance of any of them coming true. Lifting the framed photo of her mother, she said, "I hope you understand that I have to do this, Momma." Deseray White stared back at her. Kissing the picture, Rebecca tucked it between her legs, closed the suitcase, and slammed the trunk. A car whizzed by. The cry of a hawk filled the air; however, when Rebecca looked up, she could find no trace of it.

With the only physical thing she had to remember her mother pressed against her breast, she ran back to the wishing tree.

Johnny could hear Rebecca's arrival long before she made it back to the cottonwood. Opening his eyes, he watched her return, running as though she were being chased, holding something tight to her bosom.

"What took you so long?" he said when she reached him, all out of breath.

"Ha... ha." She sat next to him and took a deep, calming breath before removing the photo of her mother from the jacket.

Seeing what she was holding, Johnny said, "You're going to offer the picture of your mother to the tree? Isn't it all you have left to remember her by?"

"Yes. But I have big wishes. I know she'll understand. Besides, I have enough memories of her to last me a lifetime." She looked fondly at the photo. "You should offer something as well."

"I don't have anything."

"Sure, you do." Reaching a hand toward his head, she told him, "Sit still for a second." Taking hold of some loose hairs surrounding the feather, she came away with three.

"Ouch."

"Big baby. I'll put them inside the frame, then you can make a wish."

"If you say so."

"I do. This is important, Johnny. Don't ask why. It just is." Taking the back off the frame, she inserted the long black hairs then closed it again, kissing the picture of her mother once more. Resting the frame next to her, so that it sat askew against the tree's trunk, Deseray White looked up to the sky, smiling in the sunlight. Stretching her legs, Rebecca said, "Come and lie down, my love."

Johnny put his head against her lap, straightened his legs, and crossed his boots at the ankles. Pulling the .38 from his waistband, he laid it next to him, fingers gently touching the smooth tungsten grip.

Rebecca gazed into his grey eyes. "Now close your eyes and get some sleep. You need it."

"What about you? Aren't you tired?"

"A little. I'll just sit here for a while." She began to stroke the side of his face. "Kiss me before you fall asleep." Leaning into him, their mouths caressed for several long beats.

"Thank you," said Johnny when they parted and closed his eyes. Using his inner voice, he made his wish. It was a simple wish, though Johnny had his doubts that a tree could make someone's wishes come true. *Then again*. All he wished was freedom for them both.

Rebecca watched Johnny's eyes. "I love you," she told him.

"I love you too," he said, his eyes still closed.

She watched the rise and fall of his chest. Within a few minutes, he was sound asleep, eyes moving about as he succumbed to the dream world. Continuing to stroke his face, she looked deep into the tree's decorated branches. In a voice as soft as the breeze kissing her face, she made her wishes. The first, not for herself, but for the Harts. "I wish that no harm come to Ed and Hester Hart. That they live the remainder of their lives in peace." Her second was for a continued relationship with her mother. Blindly, her fingers traced the frame. "I would like to speak with my mother again if you please, even if it's just one more time." Her third and final wish was for Johnny. She looked down at the gun, then into his sleeping face. "I know that my love and protector will die. My wish is that when the time comes, it be as quick and as painless as possible."

As though the mighty cottonwood were responding in kind, the breeze strengthened, causing the items above to sway unceremoniously.

From high above the branches, the unseen hawk split the silence with a cry so high in pitch it pained Rebecca's eardrums. Closing her eyes, she waited for what she knew would be another magical encounter. Immediately, she could feel the forces of it all around, closing in on her, taking her in its lullaby hands, a thousand voices whispering their wanton desires, drowning in the fathom of her clairvoyant mind.

She began to free-fall into the white noise of the many, escaping into the illusory world of unrestrained liberty, one hand on Johnny's chest, the other tangled in the thick carpet of his hair, the voices of the many following her to a most illusory place.

The dream catcher offerings above continued to stir as the unseen hawk flew into the path of the sun, its winged shadow crossing their darling faces. Dancing with the mystical energy encompassing the sleeping lovers, the feather in Johnny's hair twisted and twirled with animated life. Dreams of intrepid flight would be his escape. A clockwork of dark events Rebecca's only comfort, as the wants, needs, and desires of the many serenaded her.

* * *

63

A Fine Thin Line

PAMELA set Tony's coffee on his desk, next to the last powder line of what used to be three. She was wearing a red silk robe, her hair loose across the front, and resting on the rise of her breasts, the Christmas gift of bruises still sore, hidden behind the expensive material. He had bitten her left breast so hard blood was drawn. She had screamed while he laughed, and she loathed him for it. However, leaving was out of the question. She'd heard about his past relationships and what happened when one of them tried to leave him. You didn't leave Tony Millions. He left you, and only when he was done with you. Or you ended up with sand in your mouth.

Coffee and cocaine were going to be Tony Millions's breakfast of champions for the day. He paced back and forth, robe open to reveal white jockey shorts, and T-shirt. A cell phone was pressed to his ear. He had just placed another call to Mr. Brown, the fourth, and was going to come away with the previous three's results, no answer.

Closing the thin device, he tossed it on the desk. The cell phone spun several rotations before coming to a stop. "Why the fuck doesn't he answer?" *Snort.* "I should have heard from him by now!" *Snort.* He pinched the end of his nose. "If he fucked up a simple little task like killing an old woman, I'll have his fucking tongue cut out!"

Norman stirred in his cage. "Who loves yah, baby?" it screeched.

"Shut up, Norman! Not now!"

Norman turned upside, whistled once, and fell silent.

A frightened Pamela tried to console Tony who was getting redder by the second. "You'll hear from him," she said, smiling artificial enthusiasm. "You know Mr. Brown. Always dramatic. He's probably on his way here right now."

"I do not like this! I do not like this one little bit! I gave him strict instructions to contact me when the job was done. If he *is* being dramatic, I'll cut his balls off. I don't need this shit! Not after what happened to Mr. White." Pacing again, he saw the single white line next to the coffee cup. Stopping in front of it, he leaned forward, put a finger to the side of his nose, and ingested it, throwing his head back. *Sniff, sniff, sniff.* Picking up the coffee, he put it to his lips, slurped some, and swallowed the coke down. When he looked at Pamela, his cheeks were flushed, eyes swimming in the watery light of intoxication.

Rosita appeared in the open doorway, hands folded in front of her.

Tony saw her immediately. "What is it, Rosita? Can't you see I'm fucking busy here!"

Pamela moved so she wasn't in the line of fire.

The maid lowered her head, not making eye contact. In a compliant servant's voice, she said, "I need to know what you want me to prepare for lunch, Meestor Millions."

"LUNCH! LUNCH! I can't think about lunch right now! Go away!" He looked up to the ceiling and spoke to it as though it were listening. "Can you fucking believe it? My men are disappearing one by one, and she wants to know what's for lunch." He started to laugh, launching a hard, wicked sound. It lodged in his smoker's throat, and he began to choke, a heavy hacking noise that caused Norman to drop to the bottom of its cage.

"You should take it easy, Tony," said Pamela, playing the dutiful girlfriend. "Maybe you *should* eat something."

Tony moved to the desk, placing his hands flat on the polished oak, choking coughs leaving him breathless. He stood there, heaving, face swollen red, tears leaking from his bloodshot eyes. Several seconds passed before he felt reasonably together. Raising his head, he wiped at the tears with the back of one hand, a twisting sneer curling his lips.

Pamela knew that expression all too well. It meant trouble for someone and most likely her.

Dutifully, Rosita slipped away.

"Who the fuck are you to tell me to take it easy," he hissed. "No one. That's who. And I'll eat when I'm good and fucking ready. Now get me a Scotch. I've got issues to deal with that your nimble brain could not begin to comprehend."

"Yes, Tony." Pamela went to the door, happy to do so. As she was about to leave Tony to his tantrum ways and unfinished business, he said something that made her stop dead in her tracks, an icy hand gripping at her throat.

"You keep yourself handy today. Once I've solved these issues, I'm going to want to get in a little exercise."

* * *

Once Tony and Norman were alone, Tony picked up the cell phone again, scrolled Mr. Brown's number, waited, and plopped himself in the black leather swivel. He didn't need to hear the fifth ring to know Mr. Brown was not going to answer. Slamming the phone, he stared at it. "Fuck!" He thought about smashing it against the wall then reconsidered. He was going to need it. *Think, Tony, think. Examine, dissect. So far, everything I've done to retrieve little Ms. White and her new friend has backfired. Mr. White's dead. No doubt by the hands of this big Indian. Mr. Brown does not answer my calls, and I haven't heard anything from Mr. Black, meaning he has yet to solve the whereabouts of these two jackrabbits. So how the fuck do these two kids keep eluding the most proficient help money can buy? So I was told. Certainly not by coincidence.*

"You don't believe in coincidence," Tony's other voice told him, sounding very much like his father's.

No, there's something else at work here.

"You've known it since her relationship with the honorable Benjamin Wong."

Yes, something wasn't quite right there. It's as though she's being protected. But by who or what? And why? That Indian friend of hers got lucky, that's all. Mr. Black will find them.

"You better hope so. No loose ends, Tony."

That's right. No loose ends.

"Because loose ends have a habit of coming back and biting you on the ass."

I won't let that happen.

"This girl. There's a reason why she hasn't gone to the authorities. Perhaps she's wanted for something. Then again, it might be the Indian she's with. Maybe he's the reason for their flight."

You might have something there.

There was a light rap on the door, ending Tony's vociferous thoughts, at least for the moment.

Pamela did not wait for Tony's permission to enter the room. She opened the door, tumbler of Scotch in hand and went to Tony who was sitting not too comfortably in his chair. "Here's your Scotch, Tony."

"Just sit it on the desk. Can't you see I'm thinking."

"Yes. Sorry. I won't disturb you any further."

"Good. Now go away. Go sit by the pool or something and wait for me."

Turning on heels, Pamela exited the room, and closed the door so it didn't make a sound.

Reaching across the desk, Tony lifted the Scotch and took a good swallow. *Ah, that's what I needed. Now maybe I can think straight.* He set the tumbler in front of him.

"You should maybe lay off a little, Tony."

The only advise I want from you is how to solve the issues at hand. Nothing more.

"If you say so."

I do.

Silence filled the interior of Tony Millions's usually active mind, so he took the moment of nonthought to have another drink. *Maybe it's time I bring in our new Mr. Green. Navy SEALs, even ex–Navy SEALs, are capable of locating and destroying if need be.*

"Aren't you afraid he might disappear as well."

I'll just send him to Wyoming. Maybe he can find out what the fuck is up with Mr. Brown.

"And then what, Tony?"

Depends on what he finds.

"Are you really that deluded?"

Are you going to help me or not?

"'I'll tell you this. Do you really think you should be putting all of your eggs in one basket? I mean, Mr. Black is already in pursuit of Ms. White and the Indian. You've sent Mr. Brown to exterminate some old woman, and Frank Santangello's men are on route to the Harts. If you send Mr. Green out there, you'll be alone. The remainder of the posse segregated. That's not good management of your men, Tony. You're used to having someone around you."

No one can touch me. And what the fuck do you know about good management?

"I'm just saying."

Well, mind your own fucking business.

"You brought me in on this."

And now I'm going to tune you out.

Flipping the cell phone, he scrolled the number for Mr. Green who answered on the second ring. "Yes, Tony. What can I do for you?"

"You haven't heard from Mr. Brown by any chance, have you?" *Sniff.*

"Not a word."

"How soon can you come to the house?" *Sniff.*

"I can be there in a half hour. What about the club? It'll be opening soon."

"You let me worry about the club. Get your highly paid ass over here." *Sniff. Sniff.*

"Yes, Tony."

Tony ended the call and slapped the cell closed.

"Not one of your better plans," his father's voice said.

"Leave me the fuck alone!" Tony shouted, picked up the Scotch and drained the glass. *Sniff, sniff, sniff.*

* * *

By the time Mr. Green arrived, Tony Millions had already had another Scotch churning in his empty stomach. A half-empty bottle of Balvenie and two tumblers sat in front of him. Taking the time to change into what he liked to refer to as his power suit, a black Armani jacket over a light knit, equally black turtleneck, he sat at his desk, hands folded in front of him.

Mr. Green stood close to Norman's cage, looking down at the blue macaw who was perfectly intent on staring back at the red whiskered giant and still not uttering a word.

The study door closed, Rosita retreating once she had ushered Mr. Green into Tony's study.

"Why don't you take a seat, Mr. Green?" said Tony as soon as they were alone. "Can I pour you a drink?"

"If it's all right with you, I would like to remain standing. Keeps the blood circulating." Being a Scott who enjoyed his motherland's finer exports, he added, "And two fingers if you don't mind."

Tony was not about to have this new Mr. Green dictate how the meeting was going to commence. When Tony gave orders, it was *he* who maintained the upper hand. "Please, Mr. Green." He motioned with an extended arm toward one of the padded chairs. "I insist." He then tipped the bottle of Scotch, poured two perfect fingers in one tumbler, and refilled his own glass.

Mr. Green still wasn't sure whether or not he liked his new boss, the man enjoyed his power trips a little too much for his liking. Nonetheless, he had sniffed out a good opportunity to earn extra cash and show this wannabe wop just what he was made of. Looking into Tony's red-rimmed eyes, he said, "Sure, Tony. I'm anxious to hear what you have planned for me." He went to the appointed chair, sat, crossed one leg over the other, and leaned forward.

Pushing the tumbler of Scotch toward him, Tony said, "Have a drink, Mr. Green." Lifting his own glass, he drained it in one swallow and pointed it toward Mr. Green's face. "I have a job for you."

Mr. Green picked up his drink, tipped it, and took a hardy Scotsman's swill. "I'm all ears. But first I would like to discuss how much I'm going to earn for this job."

Tony smiled at the audacity of the man. "You don't even know what the job is and already you want to know what I'm going to pay you." He laughed, throwing his head back, and closing his eyes for a quick moment. When he looked to Mr. Green again, his face was a statue of solemnity. "That's pretty voracious of you, Mr. Green. I like that in respect, being a man of opportunistic ways myself. Money makes the world go round. The more of it you have, the more of it you own."

"Isn't that the honest-to-God's truth. So how much?"

Ignoring Mr. Green's demand to negotiate wages, Tony said, "It's a simple task really. You *are* good at tracking people, are you not?"

Mr. Green nodded and swallowed another ounce of Scotch.

"Good. I want you to find out where Mr. Brown is. As you know, I sent him to Wyoming to do a job. Now I've lost contact with him. I want you to go to this place, this Konahee Wolf's place, and find out what happened. See if Mr. Brown carried out the task I sent him on. Report back to me as soon as you find evidence of his whereabouts. While you're there, you might as well keep an eye open for Rebecca and this Indian. They'll be driving a red pickup. It's possible they returned to the Indian's home turf. Do that, not only will I pay you two grand plus expenses, but I have another idea I'm considering where you could earn much more if you think you can handle it."

Looking Tony dead in the eyes, Mr. Green said, "I'm always up to the task. I'm sure Mr. Santangello assured you of my abilities. You'll find that hiring me was a good omen on your part as long as you continue to pay me well."

"That's good, Mr. Green. You'll only cement my trust in you with that kind of attitude. But before we discuss your future wealth, you go to Alcova, Wyoming. You should get there by this evening. Snoop around. Contact me when you find something."

Getting paid two grand for finding Mr. Brown, who was probably laid up someplace with one of Alcova's finer members of the opposite sex getting his dick sucked, was easy money. One of Mr. Green's finer attributes while employed as a Navy SEAL was search, locate, and destroy if need be. "I'll find Mr. Brown. For an extra grand, I'll rough him up if you like. You know, send him a message that you're not pleased with the way he performed his duties."

"I'm getting to like you more by the minute, Mr. Green. When you do find him, I'll give that thought serious consideration."

"Then we're done here," said Mr. Green matter-of-factly, tipped the tumbler to his lips and knocked back the Balvenie.

"For the time being, Mr. Green. On your way out. Please inform Rosita that I wish to see her."

Rising, Mr. Green extended his hand. "You'll hear from me by this evening."

Tony Millions did not accept the Scotsman's hand. Instead, he reached for the bottle, poured another shot, and said, "Do not disappoint me, Mr. Green."

* * *

64

From the Mouths of Babes

BY midday, Mr. Black had positioned himself a hundred or so yards north of the Park Pines Motel where he could watch the activity of the guests through a pair of binoculars while remaining anonymous. There was no doubt in his mind that if he could get someone to talk to him, he would be able to gather some valuable information concerning the Indian and Rebecca. His searches of other motels in the vicinity, in case the Indian and Rebecca were playing hopscotch in their attempts to evade him, had proved to be fruitless.

He had already witnessed the young, sassy girl come out of her room, walk across the lot, long legged and pretty, and go to the main building. Mr. Black's visual thoughts had seen him stuff her in the trunk, bound and gagged, ready for assimilation. *Maybe once I've finished with the task at hand.*

Shortly afterward, an obese woman, chomping on a chocolate bar, rumbled from her room, managed to fit herself behind the wheel of an old Plymouth station wagon, backed out of the lot, and headed toward Vegas. She had passed Mr. Black without a glance, her attention focused on the last morsel of chocolate she could muster from the Sweet Marie wrapper.

The temperature had risen by several degrees each hour on the hour, unusual, even for Nevada's winter climate. A sky as blue as lapis lazuli held the sun's position directly overhead. The air-conditioning kept Mr. Black comfortable. His choice of music, Beethoven's fifth executed by the philharmonic symphony, keeping him footloose and fancy free.

At the moment, there were two young boys riding their bikes in the parking area. They, Mr. Black decided, would be his informants. Boys at that age were invaluable sources of information, be the information truth or lies or a combination of the two. *Spiders, snails, and puppy dog tails.* Question was, how would he approach them? The old man who ran the place had a sharp eye and no doubt would call the police should he set eyes on Mr. Black again. A happenstance he could ill afford.

He watched as the young cyclists stopped. One of them pointed up the road, gesturing with his arm. The other, clearly and adamantly, shook his head. The lad who was doing the pointing flapped his arms up and down, no doubt calling the other a chicken, the catalyst to many a dare. Much to Mr. Black's delight, the daring boy took to the shoulder and headed toward the parked Cadillac. It took a moment, and only a moment, for the other to follow in hot pursuit.

Setting the binoculars on the seat next to him, Mr. Black lowered the driver side window and turned the volume down on the stereo. When the lead rider came even with the Cadillac, Mr. Black called out to him. "Excuse me there, son. I was wondering if you could help me?"

The boy stopped directly across the road from Mr. Black, and looked at him curiously. "What's the matter? Did your car break down or something, mister?" His partner in crime caught up to him, halting his bike with a screeching of tires. He looked to Mr. Black and shook his head. "My dad says we shouldn't talk to strangers. Come on. Let's go back to the motel."

Mr. Black exited the Cadillac. "Your dad's right, young man. You shouldn't talk to strangers." Crossing the road, his great size seemed to paralyze the boys in place. "There's a lot of bad people out there," he said, approaching slowly.

"Sure, mister," the more adventurous lad said. "You sure are big. You a basketball player or something?"

"No, I'm afraid my life isn't that exciting. Listen, you seem like a smart young man. Perhaps you could help me. I seem to be lost. I'm looking for friends of mine. We seem to have gotten separated. He's a big Indian type and he's with a girl named Tiffany Rose. They're driving a red pickup truck. You didn't happen to see them, did you?" He pulled a twenty from a pocket. "It's important that I find them."

Both boys looked to each other. The one who did not want to wander up the road shook his head. The other looked at the twenty in the giant's hand then at the ground. "Sure, I saw them," he blurted. "We both did."

"You shouldn't tell," said his friend. "I'm going to tell my dad."

"Hey, twenty bucks is twenty bucks. Sure, I saw them. They stayed at the motel. For Christmas. Had turkey and everything. Now they're gone." He shrugged his shoulders, eyes fixated on the bill in the giant's hand.

Mr. Black gladly handed the twenty over, predator senses on full alert.

The young lad snapped it from his fingers. His friend put feet on pedals and quickly headed back in the direction of the motel.

"They didn't happen to say where they were going, did they?" asked Mr. Black , smiling down at the boy on the bike. "It's really important that we hook up. Now think hard."

The boy made a face like he was thinking, scrunching his nose and closing one eye. "Nope," he said, shaking his head. "They didn't say anything like that. They were just here one day, gone the next."

"Well, thanks. What's your name, young man?"

"Me? I'm Tommy."

"Well, thanks again, Tommy," said Mr. Black, smiling, then turned and crossed the two-lane highway, leaving Tommy richer by twenty bucks and with a story to tell.

Tommy shoved the twenty into a pocket, one foot on a pedal, and turned the bike as he watched the big man get into the shiny black Cadillac. There was something about the smile on the giant black man's face that bothered him deep down. *I hope I didn't do anything wrong. Maybe I shouldn't have told. Stupid, stupid, stupid.* He watched the black machine make a three-point turn and head back toward Vegas, its dark windows and silent departure causing a chill to rise up his spine. His little heart thumped in his chest. Sweat beaded his forehead. He *had* done something wrong. He was certain of it.

The smile on Mr. Black's face was fashioned by confidence and admiration. Confident that within a short amount of time, he would catch up to his prey, admiring them for having eluded him for as long as they had. Not in all his formidable years as purveyor of death for money had two people evaded him with such stealth. *No matter.* He was so close he could smell their fear, their angst, knowing he was closing in, a mere breath away from ending their lives.

His foot pressed hard on the pedal. The black machine roared, and shot forward along the blacktop like a bullet released from a gun. He would be on top of them before the day was out. Of this he was certain. His assassin disposition never failed him, and it was telling him the Indian and Rebecca were within his grasp. It was only a matter of time. A few ticks of the clock really, for he knew exactly where to go now.

* * *

65

Payback's a Bitch

JOHNNY'S eyes opened, the sun hot on his face, his hand blindly, automatically, protectively feeling for the .38 lying at his side. Lifting it, he slipped it back into the front of his jeans. Looking to a still-sleeping Rebecca, her hand resting on his chest, a somnolent smile on her face, he once again believed he was the luckiest man on the planet. If he could spend eternity with her, just as they were in this moment, he would. But their brief encounter with solace was over, they must continue their evasive travels. There was no telling just how close Mr. Black or whoever was to catching up with them. Taking her hand and squeezing it gently, he kissed it, loving the warmth of it. "Rebecca, wake up."

Rebecca's eyes fluttered, releasing her from the dark, telling dreams that had been her companion while she lay beneath the wishing tree. Immediately, the sweet potpourri scent surrounding them filled her lungs, dismissing the final detail of unfinished dreamscapes. Smiling at Johnny, she squeezed his hand. "How long have you been awake for?"

"Not long. Did you have a good rest?"

"Yes. And you?"

"Slept like a baby." Shading his eyes, he looked to the sun. "By all accounts, it looks like we've been asleep for almost five hours."

"Five hours! Really! That would explain why I'm so hungry." She looked to the items steadily twisting above her. "Did you dream, Johnny?"

Johnny sat, rested a forearm on a convenient knee. He had dreamed, but for the time being, all he could summon was the fragmented pieces of movement from one dream to the next. "Yeah, I did. But I couldn't begin to tell you what it or they were about. What about you?"

"I did too. But like you, I can't remember." Unfortunately for Rebecca, images of dark times ahead were quite vivid in her mind. While she slept, Johnny's death had been scripted in various scenarios, the road ahead, a serpent waiting to swallow them whole. Putting her arms around his neck, she drew his face close and kissed him, assessing the expression on his face, seeing the love he felt for her. The love he would always feel for her.

After a splendid moment, Rebecca pulled away, the need to travel quickly rubbing at her conscience. There was no telling how close Mr. Black had gotten in the hours they slept. "We have to leave, don't we?"

"I'm afraid so."

"Would you mind giving me a second or two alone? I'll catch up to you."

Johnny looked to the open field. There was a lot of nothing except for the RX7, the drone of a passing car, and the black silhouettes of a murder of crows lining the weathered rails of the bordering fence. Standing, he looked at the photo of her mother, understanding he had to allow them a last moment. "Sure. You do what you have to. I'll walk slow." He looked into the tree. *Rebecca was right. This place, like Konahee's place, is something I will never forget.* Without saying a word, he left Rebecca to her thoughts, to her mother, and took to the path and toward the next leg of their journey.

Rebecca's eyes fell to the photo of her mother resting next to her. Silently, she wished the powers of this place grant them some clemency from what she knew lay ahead. Kissing fingers, she placed them gently on the Kodak face of Deseray. "I love you, Momma," she whispered. "I'll miss looking at your face, but I'll always see you in my mind. I wish there was some way you could make everything all right, just like you used to." Rising, she wiped debris from her backside. Gazing into the tree twisting with life, she took in a deep breath of the sweet air abounding this magical place. "Thank you for letting us rest with you and listening to our wishes. If not for me, then for Johnny. I do love him so. He deserves better." She watched, waited, and listened.

The wishing tree responded with a breath of life, its branches dancing with the hopes of the many. They spoke to Rebecca once more, filling her receptive mind with their magniloquence. Looking to the field, Johnny stood tall in the sun, walking slow, his long gleaming hair and attentive feather gently playing about his face. Taking to the footpath, feeling rather melancholy about leaving this place, she did not look back.

In a short time, she caught up to him. The woman, she had become aware and frightened by the approaching inevitability of their situation; however, the young girl who still resided within needed to have some fun. When she was within ten feet, she quickened her pace to nearly a jog, leapt on his back, and wrapped her arms around his neck.

Johnny caught her legs, supported them with his hips.

Rebecca kissed his cheek, the feather tickling her chin. "I told you I wouldn't be long."

"So you said what you needed to say?"

"Yes. I just hope it was enough."

"Me too." Hoisting her bottom so she was sitting more comfortably, he picked up the pace.

For a trice, neither spoke, relishing in the afternoon shine warming their backs, the sweeping breeze on their faces, feeling nothing more than what they were, two young people in love. Reaching into his shirt, Rebecca smoothed a palm over his bronze flesh. "I love how you feel. You're so strong and yet you have the soft skin of a baby." She giggled in his ear, the sound of it music to Johnny's heart. "And you're sexy as hell." She nibbled on his lobe. "What more could a girl ask for?"

"Well, there's that whole-provider, roof-over-your-head, food-on-the-table, and two-cars-in-the-garage kind of guy."

"Yeah, but they're a dime a dozen. With you, I get adventure, travel, and incredible sex."

"I guess I can't argue with you there." Craning his neck so he could see a portion of her face, he asked, "Becca?"

"Yes, Johnny."

He came to a stop. "I really am sorry you had to experience so many terrible things."

Rebecca's heart warmed. "Let's not go there. And thank you. Put me down for a minute."

Johnny released his grasp so she could slip off his back. Rebecca rounded him, gazed at his face, every part alight with sunshine, the feather playfully twisting. Reaching, she took his handsomeness in her hands. Behind his loving eyes, she could see the pain he was feeling, possessing the knowledge of her treacherous past. "I love you so, Johnny Black. You're everything I've ever dreamed of and more. I wouldn't change anything for all the tea in China. Just being with you is enough for me. I accept whatever lies ahead of us as long as we're together." Resting her face against his chest, the rhythmic beat of his heart sang to her, the .38 dug into her midsection.

"Then it's enough for me too," said Johnny.

They kissed deeply, passionately, in the middle of the field, the high sun and their love for each other filling them with dizzying warmth, the moment forever inscribed to memory. Breaking gently apart, Rebecca brushed a finger over his lips. "Forever mine," she told him.

"Always," said Johnny, looking into eyes that were brimming with light.

"Good. Now do you think you can carry me the rest of the way?"

"I could carry you from here to anywhere."

"Then turn around and let me get back on your back."

Turning, Johnny readied his hands.

Rebecca sprang from the ground, and latched on to his neck. "To the car, James."

"Your wish is my command." Johnny took to the path once again, Rebecca bouncing on his back, weighing nothing more than a pillow in his strong arms.

* * *

The murder of crows were in a restless dither, hopping from one place to the next along the fence rail when Johnny and Rebecca arrived. A semi pulling a Budweiser trailer portraying the Christmas Clydesdales roared past, causing the black mass to take flight in a cacophony of strange sounds. Turning, Johnny deposited Rebecca on the hood of the car. When he turned to face her, he took her hands in his and looked into her face. "Well, that was fun. So where do we go from here?"

Rebecca looked east and west. "I think we should keep heading west, toward the coast, through Idaho. Nobody ever goes to Idaho unless they have to. Maybe find some place to stop and eat. I'm starving. And I would like to brush my teeth, freshen up a little."

"I could use something to eat myself. But first we should put some miles behind us. I've got this itch that's telling me we haven't traveled far enough out of harm's way. The time we spent here, though it certainly was an experience to remember, might have given whoever is chasing us the upper hand."

As if on cue, a long black car approached from the east, slowed when it came parallel to the RX7. Johnny and Rebecca froze. Rebecca stared at the slow-moving vehicle as Johnny's hand went to the .38. Neither could see the driver through tinted windows. Time stopped for a moment. Rebecca's breath caught in her throat, her heart missing several beats.

Perspiration rose through Johnny's pores, covering him in a veil of cold, his finger on the trigger, ready to bring the weapon to life if need be.

Much to their relief, the car sped up, its driver waking the horses of the '74 Plymouth. Silently, Johnny and Rebecca watched until it was out of sight. Not until the highway was clear of all traffic, did Johnny relax his fingers on the .38.

Rebecca let out a nervous laugh. "I guess that's something we're going to have to get used to, looking over our shoulder all the time."

"Like you said. With me. Every day's an adventure. Let's get out of here." He eased her from the hood and they returned to the interior of the green sports car.

Comfortable behind the wheel, an almost smile lifting the mouth Rebecca loved to kiss, Johnny said, "Buckle your seat belt, Becca."

"You buckle yours, Johnny. I believe we're in for a hell of a ride."

* * *

Three hours took them to the Wyoming, Idaho, state line, winter darkness swiftly approaching. All that remained of the day was a crested sun, blistering the horizon pink and purple as it receded to the other side of the world. Above them, a massive gathering of dark clouds billowed wide for as far as they could see. The road was sparse of traffic except for semis racing east and west, passing whoever was in the way with roaring, shifting gears and decked out lights.

AC/DC's "Hell's Bells" filled the interior.

"Johnny?"

"Yes," said Johnny, contemplating on whether or not it was going to rain.

"I don't know about you, but I've had to go to the bathroom for the past hour. My kidneys hurt."

Johnny had to go himself; however, it was far more important to put some miles behind them than to stop and take a break. But now that they were in Idaho, he agreed it was a good time to stop. Ahead in the distance, on the right-hand side, he could see a blob of shimmering lights indicating a gas station and, hopefully, restaurant. "We'll pull into whatever *that* is just ahead of us." Checking the gas gage, he saw it was bordering on quarter full. "We could use some gas too. Here. Put this in the glove compartment." He pulled the .38 from his jeans.

Rebecca took it as though she'd been given a glass of milk. It was a part of her life now. It came with Johnny, and she knew it would play a major role in their lives. The effective dreams she had had while resting beneath the wishing tree told her as much. She stuffed it into the compartment.

A smattering of rain dotted the windshield.

"I was hoping it wasn't going to rain. I guess we're going to get a little wet." He engaged the wipers.

"I don't care if we get soaked. As long as there's something to eat there and a bathroom."

Approaching the structure of white lights, it became more apparent that what lay ahead was a truck stop as the flat shapes of semis parked all in a row began to take form. It began to rain harder, the sky above them dark and yet the vanishing sun was still coloring the horizon, creating a magnificent contrast of light as day gave swiftly into night.

"Look at that sunset. It's so beautiful."

Johnny had seen many spectacular sunsets from the ranch and Konahee's place of magic. This one was right up there as one of the finest. "Might be a good omen."

"We could certainly use one," said Rebecca, awestruck by the fusion of color across the horizon.

Johnny took the exit road where a green-and-white fluorescent sign promised food, gas, rooms, and showers. "Looks like we hit the jackpot." Downshifting, he slowed the RX7 to the posted speed of fifteen miles per hour.

"I'm going to have a steak. Medium rare. With mushrooms and fries and lots of gravy. And I hope they cook everything in grease." Rebecca's stomach churned at the mere thought of it.

"I'll take your steak and wash it down with two cheeseburgers and a milkshake. Chocolate, maybe strawberry. Then I might have some desert. I am after all a growing boy."

They came to the first row of semis. Diesel stink penetrated the interior of the car, the mélange of running lights resembling a Coca-Cola postcard Johnny had seen when he still bore the eyes of youth. "Looks festive. Don't you think?"

"I don't think the holidays are supposed to smell like this. They should all be fined for polluting."

Rebecca killed the volume on the stereo ending Trooper's "We're here for a good time." Raindrops tapped the windshield, sounding louder than necessary in the sudden quite. The RX7 moved slowly along the service road. Even in the rain, most of the trucks gleamed chrome, rumbling in place, shinny exhaust stacks intermittently spewing black diesel into the air.

What happened next was kismet in its most rudimentary form. In the blink of an eye, Johnny and Rebecca's evening took a sudden turn, and not for the better.

Rebecca's heart drowned within her chest when she saw it. *My eyes are lying to me. There can be no other explanation.* They were not. Her mind regressed to that very moment in time when she was thrust into a life of debauchery. Sitting in a McDonalds. The crucifix. That trusting smile. His soft-spoken manner. In God we trust. Lies, lies, all of it lies. Flesh pricked with anger. "I don't fucking believe it!" she cried, her eyes riveted to the running silver Freightliner.

"What is it!" asked Johnny, suddenly alarmed by the tone in her voice.

"That fucking bastard is here! I don't fucking believe it!"

"Who? Who's here? Mr. Black?"

"No! Harvey Klondike. The bastard who sold me to Mr. Brown."

Johnny stopped the car, tires biting into wet macadam. "Are you sure? Where?" He moved his head back and forth, trying to see what Rebecca was seeing between the raindrops and slapping wipers.

"That's his truck." A hard finger made contact with the windshield. *Tap, tap, tap.* "Right there. The silver Freightliner. I know it like I know my own name."

Johnny's eyes settled on the silver semi. In that instant, something happened. A primitive stew of anger, hatred, loathing, and the most potent of the four, the *need* to kill someone, consciously and with malice, took hold of him. For a horrible moment, he could imagine her sitting high in the passenger seat, not knowing what life-changing experiences lay ahead. A vision of innocence.

Then she was gone, the rain melting her away.

"Are you absolutely sure?" Boiling blood surging.

Rebecca turned on him. Her breaths coming out in short bursts, seething with anger, her eyes reflecting disbelief. "I'm telling you that's his fucking truck! I spent enough time in it, listening to that bastard preach to me to know it when I see it! Don't you believe me?"

"I'm sorry. Yes. Of course I believe you."

"What are we going to do?"

Johnny sat motionless for a moment. "*You will kill again, Johnny,*" Konahee Wolf's voice resounded. The person who pulled the trigger, ending Mr. White's life came rushing forward. "I'm going to kill him," he said so softly Rebecca wasn't sure she'd heard him correctly.

"What?"

"I said I'm going to kill him." He looked at her.

In his eyes, Rebecca saw the tantamount expression of a man who had crossed the line of morality. "You can't just kill him, Johnny."

"Why not, Becca? He's a predator. He sold you like you were a piece of meat. And I'm sure you weren't the first. But I'm sure as hell's going to make sure he doesn't kidnap anyone ever again." Putting the sports car into first, he eased his foot off the clutch. The RX7 rolled forward. Turning into the parking lot, he found a space between two pickups, and far enough away from Henry Klondike's silver Freightliner.

The rain began to fall harder, the last remnants of daylight slipped away, plunging everything into the shroud of night. Johnny killed the engine and turned in his seat. "Give me the gun."

Rebecca was now terribly frightened. "You can't just walk in there and shoot him, Johnny. That would be stupid. The place is full of truckers. You would never make it out of there. Then where would we be? Calm down for a second. Your anger is causing you to think irrationally." She jammed a boot against the glove compartment. "I'm not giving you the gun," she said adamantly. "You don't even know what he looks like."

Johnny pounded the steering wheel with his fists in frustration, retrospect tears falling. "He deserves to die, Becca."

"I'm not arguing that he deserves anything less. I'd like nothing better than to know he's dead and won't do to another girl what he did to me. All I'm asking is that you, we, think this through. Step by step. So there are no mistakes." She could hardly believe she was going to collaborate murder. However, the flower cultivated by immoral hands saw no other alternative. The man deserved to die.

They sat in silence, staring at each other. Johnny's thoughts went to the running Freightliner. In his murderous mind, a flawless puzzle began to piece itself together. "You were right, Becca. I don't know what he looks like, but you do. How courageous do you feel?"

"Why? What do you have in mind?"

"Do you think you could get him to his truck? I mean, do you think you could go in there, confront him, scare him enough that he runs to his truck?"

Rebecca thought about it for a moment. "He could be sitting with someone else. Another trucker perhaps."

"Okay. He wouldn't recognize you the way you look now, right?"

"You're right. He wouldn't recognize me."

"Then just go into the restaurant and see what the situation is, then come back and tell me. If he's alone, great. If he isn't, then I'll have to think of something else."

"I hate the thought of going in there alone, Johnny."

"You have to be brave, Becca. I'll be with you all the way in spirit. You can do it. I know you can."

Summoning all of her courage and hatred for the man whose fate rested in her hands, she took a deep breath. "Okay, I'll go." Before she could change her mind, she opened the door, stepped out into the rain, and swiftly made her way to the restaurant.

Johnny watched until she disappeared, hit the trunk release, and got out of the car. Quickly he went to the partially opened trunk, lifted it, and moved the suitcase and knapsack aside so he could retrieve the length of rope he had seen. Coiling it into a small roll, he stuffed it into a back pocket and returned to the dry interior. He sat and waited, rain dripping from his hair, eyes preoccupied with the double-glass entrance of the restaurant.

The eatery was nearly full to capacity. Truckers of all sizes, loners, the elderly, and entire families, a real casserole of humanity refueling for the next leg of their destinations. Christmas music droned from the ceiling. A dancing Santa stood just beyond the entrance. Garlands of plastic pine were placed here and there. A six-foot white Christmas tree with blue balls and red lights stood in a corner with faux presents at its skirt. Middle-aged waitresses garbed in drab, sickly beige uniforms dragged themselves from one table to the next. It only took a moment for Rebecca to lay eyes on the abhorrent Henry Klondike. He was sitting at a table for four, away from the window. In front of him was a partially eaten burger and fries and a cup of coffee, but more importantly, he was alone.

A waitress carrying a tray under one arm and wearing as weary smile stopped in front of Rebecca. "Just seat yourself, sweetheart. We're not that formal around here."

"Thank you," said Rebecca. She stood there a moment, her eyes riveted on the man who would sell her again in an instant if he thought he could. Her hatred of him affected the courage she needed to press forward. In that instant, he looked right at her, smiled, lifted his burger, and took a bite, the crucifix dangling around his thick neck gleaming beneath the fluorescent lighting. The satisfaction of knowing he would soon be dead gave Rebecca the necessary strength to turn and leave the restaurant; otherwise, the preserved memory of his transgressions would have kept her frozen her in place.

Leaving the restaurant, hatred in full gear, she splashed through puddles, rain drowning her face, and made her way back to a waiting Johnny.

Watching her exit the restaurant, Johnny promptly opened the passenger side door, slanted rain dotted the upholstery.

Rebecca threw herself in and slammed the door. She was shaking, cold, wet, and breathless. She looked at Johnny, her eyes wild with the recall of having faced her abductor. "He's… in… there," she confirmed between breaths. "And… he's… alone." She swallowed the catching of her breath.

"Good. I know that was hard for you. But what you have to do next is going to be even harder. Are you up to it?'

"I… think so. Now that I've seen him. I understand we cannot allow him to ever profit from the flesh market again." She blew a final episodic breath. "His days of abducting young girls are over. I'll see to it, so long as you're sure you can go through with whatever it is *you* have planned."

"You just get him to his truck. I'll take care of the rest."

"What do we do when it's over?"

"We're going to do what we came here to do. Eat, use the bathroom, and get some gas. No one will be the wiser, I promise. By the time anyone discovers the body of Mr. Klondike, we'll be long gone. You have to remember, he's a predator, and from what I know, predators are loners. Nobody's going to miss him."

"So you just want me to get a table and wait for you."

"Exactly. Act normal. Like you're just passing through. A regular tourist. No one will remember us. Too many people pass through here. Order me a steak. Rare this time. With a baked potato and a Coke. Once he leaves the restaurant and goes to his truck, I'll join you in a matter of minutes."

"Promise me you'll be all right. That bastard's a pretty big man."

"So am I. It'll be over before you know it. He's as good as dead. That much I promise you. He won't know what hit him."

"I love you, Johnny Black."

"And I love you, Rebecca White."

Quickly they kissed, sealing Henry Klondike's fate.

"Now get in there and see to it that he wants to leave in a hurry. I'll be waiting for him."

Exiting the sports car, Rebecca walked swiftly across the rain-drenched tarmac, courage in full stride, revenge fuelling a desire to want Henry Klondike dead dead dead. The sooner the better.

Johnny calmly walked to the silver Freightliner. He looked over a shoulder, and saw no one who could bear witness. Climbing the chrome steps, he opened the driver side door and slipped into the comfortable chair. The truck rumbled beneath him. Sealing himself in, he crawled into the sleeper compartment, withdrew the length of rope from his jeans, crouched as low as he could manage, and waited.

Rebecca entered the restaurant scanning the place for an empty table, the drone of conversation and the smell of grease filling her senses. Everyone was wrapped up in their own little world. No one paid attention to her. Henry Klondike was near to finishing his meal. *Maybe he'll just finish his meal and go to his truck. But what if he rented one of the cheap rooms. Planned on staying here for a couple of days. I can't take that chance. I've got to do something to get him moving.*

An elderly couple was getting up from their spot, three tables back of him. She walked nonchalantly past the Preacher, eyes fixed on his fat, disgusting face and the icon of his artificial faith dangling from his throat. He smiled at her, not recognizing her and why should he, like Johnny said, to him she was just a piece of meat. Smiling back, Rebecca wanted to scratch his eyes out. Cut off the remainder of his fingers.

The silver-haired couple rose from their seats, the man leaving a fiver for a tip. They walked past, husband holding his wife's arm for support. Rebecca sat down, and positioned herself so that she viewed the back of Klondike's head. It only took a moment for a waitress to come to the table, pocket the five note, and hand Rebecca a menu. "Can I get you something to drink first, honey."

"Um, yes. A couple of Cokes please."

"Someone will be joining you then?"

"Yes. My boyfriend."

Watching the waitress scribble on her pad, an idea formed in Rebecca's alert, revenge plundered consciousness. However, in order for it to work, Henry Klondike would have to abandon his place and return. She would have to depend on the after effects of the coffee he was drinking. "Do you think I could borrow some paper and a pen please"—she looked at the name tag—"Mildred."

"Would the back of one of these do?" Mildred, flipped the pages of the order pad.

"Yes, that would be perfect. Thank you."

The waitress tore off a clean page. "I think I have an extra pen in here someplace," she said, fishing in the apron. "Ah, here it is. Promise to give it back though."

"Oh, I will. And thank you again."

Mildred stuffed the pad into the apron, cleared the table, and gave it a quick wipe with a cloth that appeared out of nowhere. "I'll be right back with your Cokes."

Rebecca put the menu aside, and turned the small sheet of paper over. One eye watched Henry Klondike, the other trained on the blank page. Tapping teeth with the ballpoint, she thought of exactly what needed to be said. It was short to the point and, more importantly, highly accusing. She began to print,

I KNOW WHO YOU ARE
I KNOW WHAT YOU DO
KIDNAPPING YOUNG WOMEN
I'M WATCHING YOU, HENRY KLONDIKE!

All she had to do now was wait. Tucking the condemning note under a leg, she opened the menu and pretended to read its offering. A minute later, Mildred returned, carrying two large Cokes, and set them on the table.

"Thank you," said Rebecca. "And here's your pen."

Mildred took it from her. "Are you ready to order yet?"

"I think I'll wait for my boyfriend before I do. He'll only be a few minutes. He's gassing up. Long drive ahead of us."

"That's fine then. Let me know when you're ready. I've got other tables to attend to." She lifted a foot and scratched the back of the opposite calf with it. "Don't know how I'm going to get through my shift today. My legs are already falling asleep."

"Maybe you should take a break," offered Rebecca.

"Those three words don't exist around here, honey," she said and returned to her minimum wage duties.

Rebecca's kidneys painfully reminded her that she needed to use the restroom. As though fate was in cahoots with the plans she and Johnny were about to instigate absolutely, Henry Klondike stopped Mildred and held up his coffee cup.

Good, Rebecca thought. *The more caffeine the better.* Her own needs could wait a little longer. Laughter erupted from one of the booths where three truckers sat. Mildred filled the Preacher's cup. Rebecca people-watched for what seemed an eternity, the need to urinate pressing, pressing, pressing. Finally, the caffeine kicked in. Klondike rose from his seat and made his way to the men's room, back of the restaurant and down a hall.

Taking a deep breath, Rebecca pulled the note from under her leg and went to his table. With sleight of hand, she slipped it under his coffee cup, then returned to her place, legs shaking, heart racing a mile a minute, kidneys punching her sides. She waited.

Several hour long minutes passed before Henry Klondike returned. Rebecca watched him over the top of the menu. Raising his coffee cup, it stopped in midair. His head jerked left and right. Rebecca could clearly see his ears turn red. Picking up the note, he stared at it for a second before crunching it up and stuffing it into a pocket. Quickly he rose, almost knocking the chair over, tossed a couple of bills on the table, and looked around again, his anxious eyes looking past a disguised Rebecca.

The Preacher left the restaurant like a man being chased by his demons.

Smiling, Rebecca put the menu down and went to the ladies' room for a much-needed break, satisfied that she had successfully steered him toward Johnny.

Johnny waited in the dark confines of the sleeper cab behind a width of curtain, the cord wrapped around both hands, perspiration covering his face. He knew that only fifteen or so minutes had passed, yet it seemed like an eternity. The truck was making all kinds of sounds as the engine idled in place. *How long should I give her?*

The rain had let up, all that could be heard above the noise of the engine was a soft tapping on the roof.

Suddenly the cab leaned south, and the driver door opened. Henry Klondike took his place behind the wheel, muttering profanities a man of God should not be uttering.

Rebecca had done her job.

Quietly, Johnny drew the curtain back.

Before the Preacher could put the truck into gear, Johnny looped the cord around his throat, braced a knee against the back of the seat, and pulled the nylon with all his might. "You'll never kidnap anyone again, you fucking prick," he voiced.

Klondike's hands went to his throat, legs thrashing, choking on his profanities, spitting, gurgling and knocking several religious figurines from the dash. He would never take another breath.

Johnny pulled hard, the tendons in his neck straining, heart hammering within. The cord dug into his hands. In that moment and the next, Johnny Black from Eden, Montana, no longer existed. He became a nameless killer, ruthless, precise. In his rage, he said matter-of-factly, "This is what it feels like to die. Can you feel it, Henry Klondike? Your life is slipping away. You deserve nothing less. Oh, and by the way, Rebecca White and all the others send their regards." Killer Johnny pulled so hard something in Henry Klondike's throat popped. His arms became less animated, legs jerked, body went taut, then, in the next moment, his arms dropped, his life interrupted by sudden death.

Johnny took no chances. He maintained his murderous conduct for another solid minute, pulling harder and harder to be sure the Preacher was dead, dead, dead. When he finally let loose, his arms were sore from the effort, his lungs starving for air. Climbing into the front, he stared at the dead man's face, waiting for killer Johnny to return to the darkness from which he was born.

Henry Klondike's eyes were open, full of blood, distended tongue hanging stiff from a face that had turned a soft shade of blue. His bowels had let loose, filling the cab with a disgusting air.

Johnny stuffed the cord into a pocket and put a finger to the Preacher's neck. He had to be sure. There was no pulse. Ripping the crucifix from the fat man's swollen throat, he reckoned Henry got what he deserved. A violent end to a sleazy life. Nonetheless, he knew there were a surplus of Henry Klondike's roaming the streets for girls like Rebecca. At least now, there was one less.

Taking him by the shoulders, Johnny rolled him out of the chair so his body wedged between seats. Stepping back into the sleeper cab, he took hold of the Preacher's lifeless arms, pulled him into the small space, and took a satisfied look at the man he had just murdered, then closed the curtain. Before leaving the silver Freightliner, he killed the engine. It would be days before anyone discovered the rigid remains of the predator Preacher Henry Klondike.

Once he was outside, Johnny welcomed the light rain on his hot face. He stood there, between trailers, staring at the gold chain and cross in his hurting palm. Surprisingly, he was relatively calm. Too calm for having just murdered someone, he thought. Looking into the dark sky, silver lines fell all around him. "*You will kill again, Johnny.*" With all remaining strength, he threw the golden Jesus and its broken chain of faith as far as he could.

* * *

Rebecca happened to look up just as Johnny entered the restaurant. He was a little wet, yet looked no worse for wear, his telling eyes scanning the restaurant.

She waved.

He saw her immediately and moved toward her. The eyes of many truckers watched the tall Indian invade their space. A thick, resentful murmur rose among them.

Stopping at the table, Johnny said, "I'm going to use the bathroom."

Rebecca saw the abrasions on his hands and took hold of his arm. "Are you all right?"

Johnny nodded. A drop of rain fell from the tip of his nose, the feather. "I'll be right back. Order our food." He left.

In a span of seconds, a thousand scenarios ran through Rebecca's mind. All of them ending with the same conclusion. Henry Klondike was dead. That much she was certain of. Although it wasn't implied, it was inked in Johnny's eyes. From the moment he walked into the restaurant, they emitted a definite approbation that spoke volumes to her. Now her concern was for Johnny and what effect murdering for a third time was going to have on him.

Mildred returned to the table. "I saw that your boyfriend has joined you. Are you ready to order now?"

"Yes, thank you. Two eight-ounce sirloins. One medium rare, one rare. A baked potato for the rare steak and fries for the other. Oh, and gravy please, for both."

Mildred scribbled on her pad. She saw that Rebecca had nearly emptied her Coke.

"Would you like more Coke? Refills are free."

"Yes. That would be great." Rebecca handed her the menu.

"We're really busy, so it'll be a few minutes before your steaks are ready." Again the shoe went up and eased the numbing feeling in the opposite leg.

"That's okay. We're in no hurry."

"Well, that's good. Most people who stop here are in a rush to get someplace. Especially during the holidays. Did you have a good Christmas?"

"One of the best that I can remember," said Rebecca, fleetingly recalling the small gathering at the Park Pines Motel, deep-fried turkey, song, and lovemaking. *God, it seemed so long ago.*

"That's nice. Well, I'll get your orders in and be right back with your Coke."

"Thank you, Mildred." Breaking eye contact, her thoughts ventured. *How did Johnny kill him? With his bare hands? It certainly looked like it.*

After using the toilet, Johnny removed the death rope from his pocket and put it in the waste receptacle beneath a paper towel dispenser, pushing it way down until it disappeared among a sea of used paper towels. Then he went to the sink, turned on the cold, and held his injured palms beneath the numbing water. The abrasions on his hands weren't that bad, not once he cleaned the minimal blood from them. Face cupped in his hands, the sounds of Harvey Klondike's choking last breaths echoed in his mind. He chased the haunting memory away, filling his mind instead with song. "Strawberry Wine" and Sue Levesque's genial aura crowded his psyche. *Home. A thousand years past. A journey begun.*

One of five stall doors opened. Johnny watched as a thin elderly gentleman with gold-rimmed glasses on the end of a slender nose emerged. On his head was a red Santa hat. He began to hum merrily, still enraptured in the festive season. Noticing Johnny, he said, "Hello, young man. Merry Christmas and all the best in the New Year."

"Merry Christmas," replied Johnny. "And all the best to you, sir."

The merry gentleman went to the next available sink, squirted soap into his palms, and cleaned up.

Tearing paper from a dispenser, Johnny dried his face and hands. "Well, have a nice day," he said.

The old man turned. "Pays to be humble, son. You remember that. It'll get you far. Got me all the way to ninety-five and, God willing, to a hundred."

"Thanks, I'll remember that." Johnny left the men's washroom, the cheerful gentleman's advise interrupting the music in his head. Self-effacement would never be a relevance he could ever possess. Not after the exploits of the past couple of days.

* * *

When he sat at the table, Rebecca seemed lost in thought, green eyes unblinking. It took her a moment to snap out of it. Seeing Johnny sitting across from her, she asked again, "Are you all right?"

In a low tone Johnny said, "He won't be bothering anyone ever again."

Rebecca half-smiled. Knowing Henry Klondike would never profit from the avails of innocence again filled her with morbid joy. Looking to Johnny's hands, she noticed the abrasions across the thick tissue of his palms. "You're hurt."

"It's nothing. Don't worry about it. Did you order?"

"Yes. It'll be a few minutes. Maybe more. They're pretty busy."

Johnny took a long quenching drink of Coke. "You were lost in thought when I sat down. Care to share?"

"I've been thinking about a lot of things, but mostly about Tony Millions and how we could hurt him."

"Oh, how so?" Leaning forward, voice low again, he said, "You're not going to ask me to kill him, are you?"

Rebecca shook her head, leaned forward so they were close. Whispering, she said, "We can rob him of the things he loves more than women. Money and his drugs."

Johnny sat back, pondered the unthinkable proposal for a second. "That's pretty risky, don't you think?"

"Yes. It would be. But he wouldn't be expecting it. If I know Tony, he's probably going round the bend right now. Drinking himself into a stupor and snorting cocaine like there's no tomorrow. Mr. White's dead, and he'll soon learn the fate of Mr. Brown.

So far, everything he's done to get rid of us has backfired. His so-called posse has been reduced to Mr. Black and Mr. Green. It must be driving him crazy."

"You're thinking with your emotions and not your head, Becca."

"Maybe so, but that doesn't mean it wouldn't work."

"So what makes you think we can just walk into his house and rob him?"

"Because I know the combination to his safe."

Johnny thought about this for a moment. It was true. This man Tony would not expect them to return to Vegas. Especially not to walk into his house and steal from him. Not even Mr. Black, who could be anywhere, would expect it. "How in the world did you get that kind of information? It's not the kind of thing men of Tony's position would easily give out. I know I certainly wouldn't and neither would you for that matter."

Rebecca told him of the night she was taken into the desert where she believed she was going to be killed. But Mr. Black, instead, had turned his weapon on Mr. Blue. She told him of the visit she had received from the spirit of Janis Keeper while locked in the trunk of Mr. Black's Cadillac, hooded and restrained. Information received by another life lost by the will of Tony Millions. That in her afterlife state, Janis Keeper was asking for redemption.

Just as she ended the story, Mildred the waitress sat their dinners in front of them, assuming the rare steak was for Johnny. "Can I get you two anything else?"

"No, thank you. Looks great," said Rebecca, the smell of charred beef rising beneath her nose. When they were alone again, she asked, "So what do you think?"

"I think you're crazy and reckless, but that's just me." Cutting into the steak, he filled his mouth with much-needed nourishment. Murdering Henry Klondike had drained him of all energy.

"I've been called worse." Pouring ketchup onto her plate, Rebecca dipped a fry and popped it into her mouth. "I know something else," she added for leverage.

"Oh, what's that?" asked Johnny, savoring the meat and digging into the baked potato.

"I also know that tomorrow night, Tony Millions will go out to gamble. He's an addict about it. It won't matter that his world is falling apart around him. To him, gambling is like breathing. It's a necessity he can't do without."

"Are you sure?"

"Absolutely. He'll take his girlfriend Pamela with him. He enjoys being seen with beautiful women. He can't help it. His ego is bigger than Texas. The rear entrance to his mansion is always unlocked. That'll leave only the maid and his parrot Norman to worry about. We could easily deal with the maid if we have to. This is personal, Johnny. It's something I have to do. For me and for all those who are buried out in the Nevada desert. Like they say, payback's a bitch, and right now I feel like the queen of bitch city." She smiled.

There was something in her eyes Johnny hadn't seen before. *Malevolence.* It disturbed him; however, he knew instantly he would do what she asked of him. He would do anything for her. No matter what the consequence. Theirs was a partnership preordained by the hands of time, that in life, as well as in death, they would always be together. He swallowed what was in his mouth along with his sense of righteousness.

"Okay, Becca. I'll do what you ask. I just hope we don't get killed in the process. You are crazy, you know that, don't you?"

"Yes, but you still love me."

"Unfortunately for the both of us, I do."

For the remainder of their meal, they devised a simple plan. They would drive back into Nevada that night and spend the balance in some out-of-the-way motel near Reno. The following day they would make their way back to Vegas and remain out of sight until the time was right, Janis Keeper's ghostly declarations the sole key to their plans coming to fruition. Their only concern for the time being was the whereabouts of Mr. Black. Johnny would have to keep one eye on the road, the other on what or who was behind them.

* * *

66

Free Falling

MORRIS McCracken, a.k.a. Mr. Green, sat in a booth at the back of the Gooseneck pub, nursing a beer and watching the pretty waitresses bring drinks to a sparse group of patrons scattered throughout the bar. Country twang spilled from speakers.

Local watering holes were great sources when one needed information. He had learned some valuable yet disturbing news about Konahee Wolf and the whereabouts of Mr. Brown. Tony Millions was going to be none too pleased. Flipping his cell phone, he scrolled for the number and engaged the line, just as his waitress, a forty something still supporting great legs and trying her best to look twenty something, stopped to see if he needed another beer. Mr. Green shook his head and smiled. "No, thank you, dear. However, I would like a cheeseburger and fries."

"Coming right up," said the leggy waitress. "Would you like gravy?"

"Is it homemade, or does it come from a can?" The cell phone continued to ring in Mr. Green's ear.

"We make it from scratch."

"Then by all means."

Shirl the waitress, who had once eyed Johnny for a night of pleasure, returned to the bar, and linked Mr. Green's order to the kitchen.

After six rings, Tony Millions finally picked up. "Mr. Green." His voice sounding as though he'd been drinking for the better part of the day. "I gather you have some information for me."

"That I do, but you're not going to like it."

"Well, I'm waiting."

"Last night, there was a fire at this Konahee Wolf's residence. House, barn, and get this, even her red pickup was burned to ashes, meaning our two friends had returned." He let this sink in for a moment before continuing. "Now rumor has it that only one body was found in the ashes. A man's body. At least that's what's believed. This Konahee person and our two friends are nowhere to be found."

"What the fuck is going on here! What about Mr. Brown?"

"Well, when I arrived, I stopped at a gas station on the edge of town. One of the attendants remembers seeing Mr. Brown and his car. Said he had asked for directions to this Konahee Wolf's place. No one has seen him since. I'd bet dollars to donuts that the body found when the fire was extinguished is our associate, Mr. Brown. I'd also bet that our two friends are now driving his car. It makes sense. Somehow they got the upper hand. *Again.* And since this Konahee person can't be found, I'm betting she is probably with them."

"FUCK!"

"Yeah, tell me about it. So what do you want me to do now? Maybe I should team up with Mr. Black. Together we could…"

Tony interrupted him. "I've been trying to contact that black cocksucker all day. He won't answer my calls. I don't know what's going on here, and quite frankly I don't like it. Not one little bit." There was a pause. "Can I count on you, Mr. Green?"

"As long as you keep paying me well, I will adhere to your instruction."

"Good." Another pause. Morris McCracken heard ice tinkle. "Tell me, Mr. Green. You're a scumbag and scumbags are usually associated with other scumbags. Do you happen to know a few good men who would like to earn some extra cash? A lot of extra cash."

"Of course."

"How soon do you think you can round them up as they say?"

"Within forty-eight hours. Maybe sooner. Being the holidays, you'll have to pay them very well."

"Money is not a concern. Get them to Vegas, Mr. Green. Those are your instructions for now. Once they arrive, bring them to my home."

"And what of our friends?"

"Let them run for the time being. Having an old woman with them will slow them down. Old people have certain requirements. They'll have to stop more often than they would like. We'll catch up to them. You can bet on it."

"There's something else you should know."

"Oh? And what's that Mr. Green?"

"Everyone I've spoken to here in Alcova agree on one thing."

"Being?"

"That this Konahee Wolf is some kind of witch. Someone of mystical powers."

Tony laughed hard. *Sniff, sniff.* "Preposterous. She's an old woman. That's all. Every small town in America holds the same story. Gossip and hearsay perpetrated by wild imagination and people with nothing better to do than to create tall tales. A means in which to bolster the local economy. Nothing more. You get your men here, Mr. Green. Be sure they carry their passports just in case our rabbits cross into Mexico or Canada. *Witch.* Now I've heard everything." He laughed again. *Sniff. Sniff. Sniff.*

The line went dead.

Closing his cell, Mr. Green deposited it into the breast pocket of his tweed jacket.

Taking a long swallow of beer, he emptied the mug. He thought of his grandmother he only knew as a boy in the small village of Tain near the Tarbat Ness and how she used to tell him of things that would happen before they did. His mother had referred to her as a seer. The locals, a witch. She died at the age of one hundred and one, her last words to him on her death bed, "You are plagued by a darkness that surrounds you, young Morris." Those words rang true when, at the age of seventeen, Morris McClracken stole his first life.

One thing Mr. Green knew for certain was that rumored tales of what most people considered bizarre usually held measures of legitimacy. Regardless, he would gather his small band of irrefutably prurient men. It's what he was being paid to do.

Shirl stopped at his table carrying a plate heaping with fries and a loaded cheeseburger, gravy on the side. Setting it in front of him, she asked, "Can I get you another beer?"

"Why not. I could be here for a while."

Shirley Kellerman liked what she saw. She hadn't had sex in over a week, and the man before her looked like he could provide her with a memorable night. "I get off at nine," she said, offering him a predictable smile. "Perhaps I'll join you if you're still here."

Mr. Green looked her up and down. *Why not?* A little small-town pussy might be just what the doctor ordered. Smiling up at her, he said, "I look forward to you getting off. Again and again."

* * *

Tony Millions sat slumped in his chair, head in hand, an empty tumbler of Scotch before him. The last line of coke he'd ingested had given him a bloodied nose. Now his head boomed with a headache that was threatening to split his skull in two.

"I told you, you were making a mistake," his father's voice inferred.

"Leave me alone. I don't need you right now."

"I'm afraid I can't do that. All that shit you're putting into your body is causing you to be stupid, Tony. Irrational."

"This is my show and I'll run it however I see fit."

"You should take a good look in the mirror. You might not like what you see."

"I'm as fit as ever."

"So you say."

"Yes, I do."

"Mr. Brown is dead you know."

"So what of it. If he got himself killed, then he was sloppy. There's plenty of Mr. Browns in the world."

"Forget about the two you chase, Tony. No good will come of your continued approach to this matter. You are not as unrivaled as you believe yourself to be."

"Fuck you!"

"Fine. Don't adhere to my advice. But let me tell you this, Tony. You and you alone will bear the consequences of your actions."

"So you say."

"Yes, I do."

Tony Millions's head boomed. He became dizzy. Tried to stand. Couldn't. The room spun around him. Norman became a blur of color just before he passed out in his chair, a trickle of blood leaking from his nose, his father's voice following him into a bleak void of nothingness.

"You're a fool, Tony. And you will surrender to a fool's demise."

* * *

67

December 28
A Beautiful Day

JOHNNY and Rebecca had spent the night in a rundown motel just outside of Reno called the Blue Moon. Their search for a place to stay was a lengthy one due to the fact that most of the motels wanted a credit card for damage deposit. Just as they considered spending the night in the car, they came upon the Blue Moon, as derelict a place if there ever was one. The manager, a grumpy old geezer named Carl with the manners of a goat, gladly accepted the cash without question, the money no doubt lining the inside of his pocket, for the Blue Moon was an out-of-the-way place where Johns and Jane Does exchanged funds for pleasure at $39 per night.

Road weary, Johnny and an emotionally drained Rebecca needed a good night's sleep; however, once they were inside the windowless room, their desires for each other choreographed a time of sexual proclivities.

They had made love, exhausting each other, every inch of flesh tasted, ravaged, consumed. Their erotic appetites a symphony of indulgence, both animalistic and spiritual, as if they had performed a sacrosanct ritual of rights. Then finally, in the wee hours of morning, they had fallen asleep on top of the covers, Rebecca's head on Johnny's chest, his heartbeat for a lullaby, while Johnny slept, one eye open, the .38 close by.

Once they woke, showered, and performed the necessary hygienic tasks, they went to a side café aptly named Cee Cee's where they ate rubber bacon, eggs, and toast and drank several much-needed cups of dishwater coffee.

They were on US 95 south, an hour into the drive, and nine hours, as the crow flies, from Vegas, the December sun bright and warm. Barring any misfortunes, they would be in Sin City by 8:00 p.m. They had just passed through Fernley, a nice enough town with a population of 8,543 according to a designated sign. The radio was on. Rebecca mouthing the words to "Girls Just Want To Have Fun."

Something bright caught Johnny's peripheral vision. His eyes stabbed the rearview mirror. Pulling in behind them were three state patrol cars, lights flashing. "Shit!" He looked to Rebecca.

"What is it? What's the matter?"

"The police! They're right behind us!"

Slowly, Rebecca turned, her face alternating to a lighter shade of pale. Sure enough, there they were, close enough to touch. "What are we going to do?"

"I don't know. We can't outrun them, that's for sure. I guess the jig is up as they say."

In the same moment Johnny was going to gear down, the patrol cars broke their single file pattern, veered off the highway, onto the shoulder, and passed without a glance in their direction.

"Holy shit, that was close! I thought we were done for. Never to see each other again." Johnny wiped at the perspiration gathered on his forehead.

Rebecca placed her hand on his arm. "I think maybe someone is watching over us."

"Well, if they are, I hope they keep both eyes open." He noticed that there was no traffic coming in the opposite direction. Abruptly, the traffic ahead slowed considerably, forcing Johnny to gear down. Another half mile, everything came to a complete stop.

The clock kept ticking.

"I wonder what's the matter?" said Rebecca, feeling all of a sudden pessimistic.

"There must be an accident up ahead. That would be the reason for the police." He deleted the volume on the stereo. A stony silence filled the interior.

They came to a halt behind an orange Mustang. Johnny powered the window, stuck his head out to see how far the delay extended. All he could see were the roofs and brake lights of a sea of vehicles. Still, the northbound lane remained empty. Pulling his head in he said, "Must be pretty bad. I can't see anything except for a line of cars."

Approaching from the rear, the wailing sounds of several emergency vehicles coming out of Fernley filled the still air around them. Rebecca turned in her seat; however, a large dark green Escalade had come bumper to bumper aft of them and she could only see the frustrated look on the driver's face as he took a drink from a Starbucks coffee cup.

Aggravated drivers, male and female, emerged from their vehicles to see what was the matter.

"Looks like we're going to be here a while," said Johnny as a motorcycle patrolman passed on the desert shoulder, lights flashing, siren blaring above the Harley engine.

"Should we turn around? Maybe there's another route to take."

"I don't think so. According to the map, this is the quickest route."

Two ambulances and a fire truck zipped past, sirens screaming.

"Let's just wait it out. Now that the emergency vehicles have arrived, it won't be long before the traffic is moving again."

They had purchased a small travel cooler, some cans of pop, chips, and chocolate bars the last time they stopped for gas to hold them over until they reached Vegas.

Unfastening her seat belt, Rebecca reached into the back, opened the cooler, and retrieved a cola. "Do you want one?" she asked, wedged between seats.

"Sure. Orange please."

Opening the cans, she handed Johnny his, then consciously reattached the seat belt. "Wouldn't want to get pulled over for a misdemeanor," she said.

Taking a swallow of orange, Johnny smiled. "Yeah, that would really be careless on our part if we got pulled over for something as silly as an unbuckled seat belt."

Suddenly, those who were outside their cars rushed back in. The Mustang in front of them inched forward. Two tow trucks flew by at a high rate of speed.

"There, you see. We're starting to move already."

"Good. At this rate, we should reach Vegas next week."

"Maybe next month."

They laughed, good and long. Something they hadn't done enough of and needed to do more often.

Rebecca turned on the radio. Amanda Marshall's voice interrupted the distilled silence. Leaning back in the seat, she took a drink of cola, allowing herself, at least for the time being, to lose herself in the music like she had done many times in the past, for she had a deep, intuitive feeling about what lay ahead. While they had enjoyed a brief moment, laughing at each other's quips, death's claiming hand had reached in through the open window and tapped her on the shoulder.

Somewhere there's an angel
Trying to earn his wings
Somewhere there's a silent voice
Learning how to sing
Some of us can't move ahead
Paralyzed with fear
And everybody's listening
'Cause we all need to hear

I believe in you
I can't even count the ways that
I believe in you
And all I want to do is help you to
Believe in you…

Lowering the volume, Rebecca said, "I do, you know," a charming smile on her freckled face.

"You do what?"

"Believe in you. This song. The words. They ring so true for me. For us. We should make it *our* song. If we're ever separated and one of us hears this song, we'll think of the other. Pretty romantic. Don't you think?"

"Yeah, I suppose it is. Okay, we'll make it our song. We needed one anyway. All great couples have a favorite song. Why not us? We're a great couple."

"I couldn't agree with you more." Rebecca could still feel the icy touch death had placed on her shoulder. "Johnny?"

The traffic moved ahead by twenty or so feet. Easing his foot off the clutch, he depressed the gas. "Yes."

"There's something bad ahead. Something terrible has happened."

"I know."

"I don't want to see it, Johnny. I've seen enough death to last me a lifetime."

"Then close your eyes and keep them closed. Listen to the music. I'll tell you when we've passed through it." He increased the volume.

Rebecca took one more drink of cola before sitting the can in one of the cup holders. She closed her eyes, her face turned toward Johnny, a sad disposition drawing her mouth.

It was twenty long minutes before intermittent traffic began to flow in the opposite direction. The Mustang rolled forward. The parade of vehicles began to move, though no more than ten miles per hour.

The air coming through the open window changed, taking on the heavy, redolent odor of radiator steam, burnt rubber, road flares, and shattered dreams.

A tizzy of swirling lights lay just ahead. Flare smoke rose into the air like a hundred genies emerging from bottles. Johnny could see the hull of a tractor trailer, on its side, stretched across both lanes. It's steaming engine was being doused with water from a hose emerging from the rear of a fire truck. A man sat at the rear of an ambulance, face buried in his bloodied hands, a paramedic there to console him. Another ambulance was positioned thirty yards off the highway, next to the carnage that no longer resembled a vehicle, twisted and flattened from impact. A half-dozen white tarpaulins of varying sizes were placed on the dual-lane blacktop of US 95. Emergency crews hastened from one place to another, erecting death curtains, their faces grim, the high noon sun beating down on it all.

The lines of traffic, in both directions, veered off the highway. Troopers holding orange-coned flashlights waved drivers away from the scene and onto desert sand. Nonetheless, vehicles slowed to a crawl, the morbid minded in need of a better look.

"See us, Rebecca."

A woman's voice, as close as a best friend's whisper, startled Rebecca into opening her eyes.

"What are you doing? I told you to keep your eyes closed." Johnny sounded angry. "You don't want to see this."

"Believe me. My eyes aren't open because they want to be. Someone is contacting me." With trembling fingers, she killed the stereo.

"Contacting you. Who?"

"Be quiet for a minute. I don't know who. It's a woman. Let me listen."

Johnny watched as Rebecca's eyes searched the macabre scene.

"See my children. Torn from life. See us now and you will understand." Then the voices of children spoke. *"We know you can see us, Rebecca."*

Rebecca looked to the ambulance parked in the desert sand. From the thick arid atmosphere, four children appeared, the youngest a boy, no more than two or three, the eldest a pretty young thing barely into puberty. The middle two were twin girls, eight or nine. All had blond hair, piercing blue eyes. They held each other's hands and, like the contented spirit of Caleb Hart, all were smiling.

Seeing that Rebecca was focused on something, Johnny asked, "What is it, Becca? What do you see?"

"Children, Johnny. I see the children who were killed here today. It's so sad, and yet, they appear to be happy."

The traffic came to a complete stop again. Though he could not see them, Johnny imagined what Rebecca was seeing. An overwhelming sadness gripped his heart. Tears filled his eyes and spilled down his cheeks. He couldn't bear the thought of lives ended so young, so innocent. Backhanding the tears away, he took a last drink of orange and tossed the empty can into the back. "How can they be happy? I don't understand, Becca. I don't understand any of it."

Blindly, Rebecca reached for his hand, squeezed it tight. A woman with flowing blond hair emerged from the white tarpaulin lying on the sand. She moved toward her children, as beautiful in death as she was in life, and stood behind the twins. She placed her hands on their shoulders, her eyes making direct contact with Rebecca's. "*Understand,*" she offered.

The line of cars began to flow again. Rebecca stared at the family of comfortable spirits for as long as she could. *Understand*. The word echoed in her mind over and over. In under a minute, they were beyond the carnage, beyond the death scene, a clear blue sky above, an open highway for as far as the eye could see.

Johnny watched with one eye in the rearview as the accident site grew small and became nothing more than a blemish on the horizon. Looking to Rebecca who seemed lost in thought, he said, "Becca? Rebecca? Snap out of it. I need you to help me understand."

"Huh?" Rebecca's eyes blinked several times before she came back to earth. "I'm sorry. What did you say?'

"I said I don't understand. I need you to help me understand. How can children who were just killed be happy. It doesn't make a lick of sense to me."

Putting a hand over the one guiding the gear shift, she said, "I think I know now. Remember the little boy Caleb Hart who I told you about and how in death he was still so full of life. And his dog Chase."

"Yes, of course I remember. How could I forget."

"Well, I believe that, like the family who were just killed, as long as they were still together, their love of each other being so strong, that death was just a passage into another time, another place. So long as they were *together*, their existence, wherever this place may be, will always be one of serenity. Does that make any sense to you?"

Johnny thought for a moment. He still didn't know how Rebecca could manage seeing the residual happenstances of death and not go completely out of her mind. However, what she was saying did make sense in a morose kind of way. That true love conquered all, even in the dark throws of death and what lie beyond. His features softened with the light of acceptance. "I think I do understand now that you've explained it. So what you're saying is, that if you and I died together, our love will never falter. That we'll be just as happy wherever it is we end up. So long as we're together."

Rebecca smiled. "Yes. I believe it with all my heart. Death is a stage, a platform if you will. What we know of life, as we exist today, is a bridge, a stepping stone, before we're passed on to *be* somewhere else. We would be just as happy in the afterlife as we are now." Taking a drink of cola, she added, "In a way, it's kind of beautiful when you think about it."

"It's poetic is what it is. That death is really the beginning of a new life. Still, I don't know how you do it. Seeing those who have passed on to the next stage. I'd be afraid to open my eyes in the morning."

Rebecca's mind entertained an episode of unimaginable consideration. She understood now. The woman told her as much. *Understand*. All the signs were there. They had been all along. She was just too blind to see them. Too afraid to conjure them. Johnny would die. Yes, it was true. Except that his death would be decreed by the wishes of her own making. And she would go with him. Should they ever come to the point where they were trapped or would be separated forever, they should end their lives. Commit the ultimate act of duplicity. No one, not Tony Millions's men or the police who still searched for Johnny could reach them in the next stage of their love. Convincing Johnny would be difficult. She had to make him realize, make him believe, ending their lives, if that's truly what their journey dictated, would be better than the alternative. "Johnny?"

"I lost you there for a moment. Didn't I?"

"Yes. And for good reason. Remember the promise we made under the stars at the Park Pines?"

"Of course."

"I need you to listen to what I have to say. Not just with your ears but with your heart as well."

"Okay, I'm listening."

"Do you truly believe that our love can be timeless? That once we've crossed over, we'll always and always be together?"

"Yes. You've convinced me. Like you said, I believe it with all my heart."

"Good. That's important. What we're about to do, rob Tony Millions. There could be residual consequences. In fact, I know there will be. If his men ever caught us, and believe me when I say that they haven't stopped searching. If they do catch up to us, I fear the worst for you and me. They would kill you, that's a given. And as for me, they would probably turn me into a junkie again, force me into a life of debauchery, and that's something I don't ever want to experience again. I'd rather die first."

"You're not saying what I..."

"Let me finish, please. Then there's always the law, Johnny. If they find you, you will spend the rest of your life in prison. If they don't kill you first. I don't know what would happen to me, being an accessory and all. My point is, is that we would be separated from each other for God knows how long. Forever probably. I could not live with that. Could you?"

"No, I guess I couldn't."

"I want you to promise me, Johnny Black, that when the time comes, we should end our lives together."

"I was afraid that's where you were headed. I don't know if I could do that, Becca. What you're asking is that we make a murder suicide pact?"

"Yes, Johnny. It's the only way. Then we would be together forever without having to keep looking over our shoulders every minute of the day, not knowing when or how." She opened the glove box and removed the .38. "This would be the best method. A bullet to the brain. Quick and, more importantly, painless for both of us."

"You think it would be painless for me to put *that* thing against your head and pull the trigger?"

"I know it would take a tremendous amount of courage on your part, but you are the strongest and most courageous man I've ever known. I know you can do it. If not for me, then for us. Promise me, Johnny. I could not bear the consequences of being captured or you spending the remainder of your life in prison or worse."

Johnny's body deflated. The road in front of him seemed to rise and fall. A tidal wave of scenarios ran through his mind in a matter of seconds. Then Konahee Wolf's voice spoke to him. "*There is a great tragedy ahead. And yet, bound within this tragedy is another destiny revealed.*" He felt trapped between the love he had for Rebecca and the precognitive telling of his future. He knew they couldn't run forever. That eventually, the torrent waters of their pasts would catch up to them. Deep down, ever since he laid eyes on her, he knew theirs would be a marriage of trepidation, of an everlasting passion. After all, theirs was a fated journey written long ago.

So he had been told.

Turning his head, he took in the depths of Rebecca's imploring green eyes. "Okay, Becca. For you. For us. I promise."

"Thank you, my love." Mollified, she smiled, reached out, and turned up the volume, good and loud. Classic Elton John filled the interior. "Now let's go rob that bastard!" she said, her voice tainted with the conviction of Tony Millions's victims. "You and me, Johnny. Until the end. And a new beginning. Where every day is a beautiful day. Forever and ever. Like Romeo and Juliet."

He must have been a gardener who cared a lot
Who weeded out the tears and grew a good crop
And we are so amazed we're crippled and we're dazed
A gardener like that one no one can replace

And I've been knocking but no one answers
And I've been knocking most all day
Oh, and I've been calling, oh hey, hey, Johnny
Can you come out to play
Johnny?
Can you come out to play
In your empty garden,
Johnny...

* * *

68

Thieves in the Night

IT was just past eight thirty when they entered the bright lights of Las Vegas, having made good time even though the accident had robbed a good measurement of it. Rebecca had slept for a while, spending the remainder of the eight-hour trip perusing the maps Mr. GBrown kept in the glove compartment. Johnny had kept himself alert by listening to music and drinking four cans of caffeine and consuming all of the chocolate bars. They had stopped at a gas station just outside of Elgin to refuel, use the restroom, and purchase a lightweight black plastic flashlight for the task ahead. The one Johnny had had was left on the dresser in the loft of Konahee's barn to burn with everything else.

It was a clear, cool night. The kaleidoscope shine of Vegas's downtown core rose deep into the obscurity of darkness. From their vantage point on the Oran K. Gragson Highway, they could see arriving jet liners banking toward the McCarran International Airport, their landing lights white glittering dots against the nocturnal backdrop.

Johnny asked, "Now that we're here, what do we do?"

"It's still too early to even attempt an approach. Tony Millions won't leave his house until at least ten. Then he'll stay out until two, three, or four in the morning, depending on whether he's winning or losing. That will give us plenty of time to sneak in, take what's his, and get the hell out of there." She pointed. "There. Take the fareway and head into the downtown area. We'll stop and get something to eat. I'm starved."

Johnny took the exit, the caffeine in his system edging him forward to what lay ahead. Traffic was moderate. Taxis vied for every inch. "Okay, we still haven't discussed what we're going to do or where we're going to go once the job is done."

"We'll talk about that over dinner. I have some ideas. Those maps I was looking at. There's so many places." Green eyes smiled. "Where would you like to eat? New York, Paris, the MGM, or maybe you're in the mood for a little Chinese. Dinner's on me."

"Aren't you afraid someone who knows Mr. Brown might recognize this car? I mean, think about it. How many green RX7s have you seen in all our travels? None. That's how many. And as for dinner, I think we should stay low-key, maybe go to the old part of Vegas. Binions or the Golden Nugget. Have one of their all-you-can-eat buffets."

"First of all, Tony Millions's men were thugs, hired hit men who handled his affairs. The only social life they had came from the attention they received at the Shangri-La Palace and Club Paradise. Believe me when I tell you these men were about as popular as the plague. Apart from being visible at the club, the only one who ever made public appearances was Mr. Black, when he would sometimes escort Tony to the casinos. Now we know Mr. Black is out there somewhere looking for us. Everywhere except here, where it all began. The rest of Tony's men, except for Mr. Green, are dead. Tony Millions will probably keep him close at hand."

"I hope you're right."

"I know I am. But let's not throw caution into the wind. I haven't seen the old part of Vegas. It might be nice. I understand Freemont Street is dazzling this time of night."

Johnny took the off-ramp to Las Vegas Boulevard where the traffic was crawling at a snail's pace. The new Cosmopolitan where he'd spent months as a laborer stood magnificent in the mélange of colorful lights. It took them twenty minutes to reach Spring Mountain Road where they stopped at a light. A large crowd was gathered in front of the Treasure Island Hotel and Casino where a staged pirate raid was being theatered aboard a cleverly conceived ship. Across the street, on the southeast corner, the Wynn Hotel stood bronze, forty-five stories high. Its jungle of foliage lit by well-placed spotlights. Rebecca and Johnny looked to each other. Not a word had to be spoken for they each knew it would be the last time they would ever see the splendorous wonders Las Vegas had to offer.

It was another twenty minutes before they entered old Vegas where the less-fortunate masses went to gamble, drink for free, and dine at the well-established and affordable venues.

Johnny found parking on Ogden Avenue, away from the main attractions of older casinos but no more than a five-minute walk to Freemont Street. They left the vehicle and walked arm in arm to the outdoor strip featuring an overhead canopy of lights, souvenir booths, and the promise of good fortune. Hundreds of tourists crammed the cabaret-like atmosphere, waiting for the next all-American light show.

They stopped in front of Binion's Horseshoe Hotel and Casino. Menus of the three restaurants were set behind a glass partition for all to see. The café offered burgers and Binion's famous bean soup with corn bread. Benny's Bullpen boasted a sports bar and cigar lounge. There was no mention of food. Last but not the least was the menu for the Binion's Ranch Steakhouse. Their eyes moved down the menu. Listed were a tourist's delight of steaks served to one's liking, prime rib, Australian lobster tail, to which Rebecca scoffed at, salmon, and the Ranch's signature dish, chicken fried lobster.

The menu also bragged about the restaurant having the most spectacular view of the great Las Vegas Valley.

"That chicken fried lobster sounds good to me. How about you?" said Johnny as they moved to one of the casino's glass-tinted entrances.

Rebecca squeezed his arm. "I never told you this, but if I ever see another lobster, I'll probably throw up. It's all I ate for most of my life. That and fish. Why, just the smell would probably cause me to go into convulsions."

"Okay, I guess the lobster is out. How about a nice thick slice of prime rib then?"

"Now you're talking. I'm so hungry I could probably put down two pounds of it, not to mention Yorkshire pudding, baked potato, and side salad. Of course everything must be covered in gravy."

"Fine. Then prime rib it is."

Rebecca had taken one of the maps, a map of Canada, out of the glove compartment and was carrying it in her free hand along with the handbag containing more than a thousand in cash and duo identification.

Johnny opened the door and they were welcomed by the musical chorus of slots singing their greedy, mechanical songs and the reek of tobacco smoke. "After you, madam."

"Well, thank you, kind sir."

They entered the casino. An older gentleman in black tuxedo, red bowtie and wearing a dexterous smile greeted them. A brass name tag pinned to the left lapel of his suit and just above his heart introduced him as Ernie. "Good evening," he said, the smile proficiently affixed to thin lips.

"Hello," said Rebecca. "Could you tell us how to get to the Ranch restaurant, Ernie? We're starving."

"Certainly, miss, or is it missus?" Ernie glanced at her ring hand.

"Miss, for now." Rebecca smiled at Johnny who was looking at a pyramid of money encased in an acrylic box that had caught his eye. Tugging on his arm, she said, "Maybe missus someday. Right, my love?"

Johnny looked to the maitre d' then down at Rebecca. "Only if you promise to pay for dinner."

"I said I would, didn't I?"

Ernie nodded toward a set of escalators. "Take the escalator to the second floor. There will be a set of elevators on your right-hand side. Take one to the twenty-fourth floor. That is where the restaurant is located. The cuisine is splendid. Our chefs work wonders, and the view, magnificent this time of night. Do you plan on gambling while you're here?"

Rebecca and Johnny looked at each other. Rebecca said, "I don't know. It might be a good way to pass the time. What do you think, my love?"

"Sure, why not. We are in Vegas after all."

Ernie piped his accomplished spiel. "The Binion still boasts the highest payouts in all of Vegas. It's been doing so since 1951. Benny Binion, the original proprietor, would have it no other way. His sons continue his legacy."

"I bet you've been here quite a while," said Rebecca.

Ernie puffed his chest and proudly proclaimed, "Since 1960. Haven't missed a day's work since then." He reached into the inside pocket of his tux. "You seem like a nice couple." He handed Rebecca four vouchers. "Two of these will get you 20 percent off your meal. The other two, you can cash at the cashier window for a little gambling money. Consider it comps from the hotel."

"Thank you, Ernie. It's very kind of you."

"Don't mention it. We pride ourselves on our visitors enjoying themselves. There's a lot of competition out there. Like I said, Benny would have it no other way."

"How much money is that I'm seeing?" asked Johnny.

"That is our famous pyramid of one million dollars. You can have your picture taken with it if you like. Of course, there's no charge."

"That, I've got to see up close."

"Well, come on then." Rebecca pulled on his arm. "It was nice meeting you, Ernie, and again, thank you."

"Think nothing of it, miss. Enjoy your meal."

Rebecca pulled Johnny farther into the casino. People from all walks of life moved about in an almost-predatory manner, considering which machine to plug with money next. The carpeting was old and threadbare and bore the scars of many cigarette burns. Waitresses of varying ages carried trays of beer and highballs. Men on ladders were stringing New Year's Eve streamers and other colorful accouterments from the twelve-foot ceiling. A shrilling bell began to sound, alerting anyone within earshot that a jackpot had been prized. The woman sitting in front of Wild Seven's slot shrieked with astonished joy. "I won! I won!" Instantly, a small group of onlookers gathered around her.

Johnny steered Rebecca toward the pyramid of money. "Let's get our picture taken with it."

"I guess we have the time. It'll be a nice memento of our visit here."

The pyramid of cash stood within a cubicle on a poker table where security cameras and a photo lens hung strategically from the ceiling. Garbed in a grey uniform, an overweight security guard stood nearby. A banner festooned against the backdrop declared ONE MILLION DOLLARS in bold red letters. Disinterested with her career, a Mexican girl stood next to the cubicle, concentrating on the length and color of her nails.

Rebecca released Johnny's arm and went to her. "We would like to have our picture taken, please." The girl wore a name tag like Ernie. "Juanita," she added.

Juanita half-smiled, clicked her red-tipped nails. "Of course," she said. "Will it be the both of you?"

"I don't see why not."

Johnny moved next to Rebecca and draped his arm around her waist. "I never thought in my lifetime I would ever see a million dollars in cash, never mind having my picture taken with it." He was grinning ear to ear.

Juanita the minimum-wage photographer said, "Just stand behind the money, pose any way you like and wait for the red light to come on."

Hand in hand they moved behind the stack of money. Rebecca set her purse and map on the poker table.

"How should we pose?" asked Johnny.

"I know. Why don't I leap into your arms like we just won it? I'll put a really cheesy expression on my face and you can look overjoyed.

"Sure. Why not?"

"Are you two ready?" asked Juanita.

"Just give us a second." Rebecca reversed a couple of paces. "Promise you won't drop me?"

"How could I? You don't weigh any more than a flea."

"Okay then, here I come. Taking two quick strides, she leapt into Johnny's waiting arms, and hammed it up for the camera. Johnny did the same. The red light came on. A memory captured.

Johnny released her from his grasp, but not before he kissed her for prosperity's sake.

"That was nice," said Juanita, a genuine smile pulling at her lips. She pointed with her eyes. "You can pick up your picture over there at the customer service desk in about twenty minutes."

"Thank you, Juanita. That was fun. Wasn't that fun, Johnny?"

"A regular riot. Now let's get to the restaurant. Winning a million has made me extremely hungry."

On their way to the escalator, Rebecca noticed an elderly gentleman with leathery features and dressed in an out-of-date Western-style suit. On his head was a white Stetson. He was making his way toward a bank of nearby slots, smiling and tipping the brim of his hat to those nearest. Rebecca had a suspicious notion she was looking at the hotel's original founder, Benny Binion himself. When the smiling apparition waltzed straight through a tier of one-armed bandits, Rebecca smiled. Even in afterlife, Benny Binion cared enough to stick around.

They took the escalator to the next floor and rode the elevator to the twenty-fourth level with an Oriental couple, dressed in what they must have considered the correct tourist apparel, jeans, heavy sweaters, and runners. The man had a large camera slung over a shoulder, and the woman was holding on to a glittering silver handbag big enough to conceal a microwave. They nodded and smiled in a way that implied they spoke very little English.

Immediately upon arrival, the foursome were confronted by a sandwich board announcing the day's special. A six-ounce filet mignon with lobster tail, choice of rice pilaf or stuffed potato, and a selection of four side salads which could be had for the bargain price of $18.95.

The Oriental gentleman made a gesture with his hand that Rebecca and Johnny enter the restaurant first to which Rebecca replied, "Thank you."

A podium, stacked with menus, stood at the entrance. Next to it, a sign asked patrons: Please Wait to be Seated.

From their vantage point, the restaurant appeared to be all but empty except for a table of four middle-aged women, one in a wheelchair, and a young couple sitting face-to-face and off to the side. Typically, the square tables were draped with damasks of fuchsia and surrounded by plush seating. Tea candles centered each one. Soft spotlights cast a celestial mood. An expanse of windows, top heavy with Burgundy swags were floor to ceiling high. The view unimpeded. The entire atmosphere very romantic.

Several brief moments passed before a pretty blonde waitress wearing her hair in a ponytail, white blouse, black skirt, and comfortable black shoes greeted them and asked if they would like a seat near the window. "The view's incredible," she reminded them.

"That would be wonderful," beamed Rebecca. "Yes please."

The waitress picked up two menus from the podium and guided them to a table overlooking the entirety of the Great Las Vegas Valley.

Johnny drew out one of the plush chairs and made a motion for Rebecca to sit.

"My, my. And they say chivalry is a thing of the past." Rebecca sat, and placed the handbag and map next to her on the empty seat.

Johnny sat opposite of her. Two crystal water glasses sparkled with life. The waitress offered the menus and informed them that her name was Wendy, asking if they would like to start with something from the bar. "We have an extensive wine selection," she postulated, the lights of the city below flickering in her blue eyes.

"I know I would," confirmed Rebecca. "What's your house wine?"

"We have a wonderful full-bodied Cabernet Sauvignon from the Napa Valley. You can purchase by the glass, carafe, or if you dare, by the bottle. It goes excellent with our USDA prime age beef."

"That sounds wonderful. I'll have a glass please." Looking across at her chivalrous soul mate, she prodded, "What about you, Johnny?"

Not being much of a drinker, Johnny hummed and hawed, not sure what to have or even if he should have anything at all, considering.

Seeing he was undecided, Wendy interrupted his ambiguity, suggesting, "We offer a wide selection of ales and lagers. We import from all over the world. May I suggest a nice pilsner perhaps?"

"I suppose a nice cold beer wouldn't hurt. Why don't you surprise me?"

"I think I know what a man of your stature would like." Again the blue eyes flashed and her smile revealed perfectly aligned, dental perfect teeth. "I'll be right back with your drinks. Please take your time selecting from our menu. The Ranch prides itself on offering a comfortable atmosphere where one can relax, enjoy the view, and feel like they're at home." Turning on black pumps, she was gone, the length of her ponytail swaying with each step.

"Make sure I give that girl a great big tip." Reaching across the table, she took Johnny's hand in hers. "Isn't this so incredible? Just look at that view. I don't think I've ever seen anything more beautiful in my life. It's as though the stars have fallen from the sky and landed right down there." Her green eyes were shining like the rarest of gems. A full winter's moon, hovering over the western horizon, allowed them to trace the shadowed humps of the Sierra Nevada's stretching across the Northern Hemisphere.

"It is something, isn't it? But I have to disagree. And this may sound a little cliché, but the most beautiful thing I've ever seen is sitting across from me."

Rebecca truly blushed, the pigmentation so ripe it nearly caused the freckles of her face to disappear. As they looked into each other's eyes, forgotten for the time being was the cold, harsh reality that, in a short time, they would risk everything and break into Tony Millions's home, robbing him of his most illicit possessions.

"I haven't told you how proud I am of you."

Looking down at their hands, Rebecca asked, "What for?"

"For not taking any more of the drugs I know you still have in that purse. I've never been dependent on anything like that, so I can only imagine how very difficult it is not to be tempted."

"Yes, it's difficult. And it hurts sometimes, but less so with each passing day."

"I'm glad."

"Me too."

Wendy returned. Balanced on a tray was a rich red wine in sculpted crystal, a pilsner glass of golden ale, and a pitcher of water. She set the wine in front of Rebecca and the ale next to Johnny's outstretched arm. Then she filled the crystal glasses with ice water. "I believe you'll like this ale, sir. It comes from Germany and has a wonderful flavor of honey and Bavarian malt." She waited for Johnny and Rebecca to sample their beverages.

Mutually, they hoisted their glasses, toasted silently, and sampled the suggested cocktails. "Mmm," declared Rebecca. "This is delicious."

Wendy the waitress turned her attention to Johnny.

"You made a good choice. I'm not much of a connoisseur, but I know what I like, and I like this very much. Thank you, Wendy."

"You're welcome, sir. Now shall I start you with an appetizer?"

"We haven't looked at the menus yet," confessed Rebecca. "Perhaps you could suggest something."

"It would be my pleasure. Our chefs prepare a delicious oyster Rockefeller."

Rebecca made a face that did not escape Wendy's eye.

"*Or* we have a homemade bruschetta served with wedges of Italian pane parrozzo. If that isn't to your liking, may I recommend satays of Thai chicken served with a side of peanut sauce. It's a little on the spicy side, but personally, it's one of my favorites."

"What do you think, Johnny? Care for a little Thai?"

"I can already taste it. Sounds great. We'll start with an order of that please."

"Splendid. I'll put your order in and give you a few more minutes to decide on your entrées."

Johnny said, "I don't think we need any more time to decide. We'll have two of the biggest servings of prime rib you offer. Stuffed baked potatoes for the both of us with all the fixings, and I would like an extra Yorkshire pudding with mine. What about you, Becca?"

"I would like gravy on top of my potato, please," she said, garnishing a wide-eyed stare from Johnny. "What type of salads do you have?"

"We have an Italian, American, an Oriental served with mandarin oranges and nuts, and of course a Caesar."

"I would like the Italian please."

"And you, sir?"

"I think I'll have the American."

"Very good. Shall I bring the salads once you've finished with your appetizers?"

"That would be fine," said Rebecca, picking up both menus and handing them to her.

Wendy the waitress set off to serve another table of three that had just arrived, ponytail sweeping her back.

"I feel so sophisticated," said Rebecca. "I've never been to a place as nice as this, except for a couple of buffets at the Bellagio. And our waitress is so professional. She didn't even need a notepad to take our orders."

"Yeah. And you know what? I've never been called sir in my life, and already within the past ten minutes, I've been called sir several times."

They raised their glasses. *Clink clink*. "Here's to us, my love. And like the song says, whatever will be, will be."

Johnny smiled. "And here's to not getting our asses shot off."

They each took a drink.

Retrieving the map, Rebecca set it on the table. "Speaking of not getting our asses shot off." She unfolded it this way and that until the province of Alberta was revealed. "I think I've found the perfect place for us to run to once the job is done."

"I had a feeling you might. Okay. Where?"

With the tip of a finger, Rebecca pointed to the most southern district of Alberta. "Right there. You can hardly read it. But there's a town just south of Calgary called Destiny. As soon as I saw it, I knew that it must be the place we should to run to. It's so... so... consequential. Like it was meant to be. Like we were meant to be. It wasn't just fate that brought us together, Johnny. It was destiny. And besides, I already told Hester Alberta was where we were heading. I guess you could say I already had a preconceived notion."

"Now why doesn't that surprise me." Beyond the green of her eyes, Johnny could see an almost-religious fervor, as if the light of her soul was shining through them. Up until then, their journeys it seemed had been scripted by sources that existed far beyond the realms of practicality, guiding them from one moment to the next. The term *destiny* had been reared by Konahee many times over, whispered to him while he slept. Even in the telling dream, he had had of his dream spirit mother. "*She is your destiny.*" Gazing at the map where Rebecca was pointing, he said, "It would take us more than a day to get there, and that's only if I drive nonstop. Then there's the whole border thing. I don't have the necessary papers to get across, and since 9-11, the border guards are extremely strict when it comes to people moving back and forth. They suspect everyone. Your fake I.D. might get *you* across, but what about me?"

"I haven't thought that far ahead yet. Just give me some time. I'll think of something. So what do you think?"

"Do I need to remind you that I think you're crazy?"

"Maybe I am. But to what extent? Therein lies the real question." Crossing her eyes, she stuck out the length of her tongue.

Johnny laughed, a little too loud. Those seated around them turned their heads. Once he collected himself, he said, "Okay, you've convinced me, yet again. Destiny, Alberta, here we come." They toasted once more and kissed over the table, the winter's moon witness to a fate sealed, a legacy born by the liberation of their love.

Their meals were exquisite, from the Thai chicken to the melt-in-your-mouth prime rib to the decadent triple chocolate cake they shared. Rebecca had had one more glass of wine while Johnny nursed his beer. She paid the bill with cash and left Wendy the waitress a tip of fifty dollars. With spare time to kill, they went to the casino, picked up their photo at the information desk, and played the slots until the hour and their formidable courage were in sync.

* * *

Dressed in his lucky blue shirt and black slacks, Tony Millions swung open the Screaming Man, fed the Franklin wall safe its three-digit combination, and inspected his ill-gotten gains as though they might have somehow disappeared. Tony trusted no one.

Earlier in the day, he had tried unsuccessfully to make contact with Frank Santangello, wanting to confirm whether or not the assassins had completed their task. However, the manservant who picked up the phone informed Tony that Mr. Santangello was not available to take his call and that he should wait for the boss to contact *him*. Another unanswered call to Mr. Black left Tony feeling quite solitary. *Is it possible the Indian got the better of Mr. Black? Preposterous. The Black Butcher is the best.*

Tony's defensive mechanisms had gone into full detachment. Sitting at his desk for the remainder of the afternoon, he consumed the better part of a bottle of Scotch, not to mention two hundred dollars' worth of Columbia's finest.

Pamela stood in the doorway of the conference room looking exquisite in a full-length sequence Vissachi, teal, the cut of which barely concealed the bite mark Tony had left her with. A lengthy fissure enhanced the eye-pleasing curvature of her left leg. White stiletto heels added inches to her splendour and her hair shone with the electrical light of a hundred brush strokes, nails shaded cinnamon. A Gucci handbag, blue, completed the expensive attire.

Tony closed the Franklin, spun the dial and fixed the faux painting back into place, the effects of alcohol he had consumed not fully waned, and he sidestepped toward Pamela. "Are you ready?"

"Yes, Tony."

"Good. I'm feeling really lucky tonight. Wait for me in the car."

"Maybe we should take a cab. You're not quite sober yet."

"Who are you? My fucking mother. I'm fine. Just wait for me in the car."

"Yes Tony."

He stopped at his office, keyed in the code on his computer, and powered the hidden security camera in the conference room, the infra red lens of which was pointed directly at the Screaming Man. The camera recorded not only images but sound bytes as well. No one, not even Mr. Black, knew of the hidden recording device.

The hour neared 11:00 p.m. The night air cool, the sky unmarked by clouds. Tony's Lexus was parked at the double-columned entrance of the mansion. He engaged the engine, and smoothed a hand along the velvet flesh of Pamela's exposed leg. "I've got a good feeling about tonight."

"I hope so. You haven't had much luck lately," Pamela reminded him.

"Maybe so, regardless, I've got this ingressive conception that everything is about to change for the better." He put the Lexus into drive, circled the triple tiered fountain, looked up at the towering palm trees surrounding his property and headed for the casino.

* * *

It was just past midnight when Johnny stopped the car a hundred yards away from Tony Millions's mansion. They had had fun gambling at Binions, cashing in several tickets for a sum of four hundred dollars to add to their personal wealth. From their vantage point the mansion property was obscure, except for the iridescent lights of the pool rising into the darkness.

"We should take our shoes off," said Rebecca, lifting her knees, untying the laces of her Docs and removing her socks. "So we make as little noise as possible. Rosita will have retired for the night by now, but she has great hearing."

Johnny had to open the door to toe-heel his boots. "What do you expect to find once we get in there?" he softly asked.

"Money, drugs. Probably stocks and bonds. Why are you whispering?"

"Because the devil himself might be listening."

"Trust me. The devil is at the casino by now, gambling. Now pop the trunk so you can empty your knapsack. We'll put whatever we steal in it."

Johnny tossed his boots into the backseat, and away from the million dollar photo of them hamming it up. He removed his socks and stretched his toes. Although tired from all the driving, fear and adrenalin heightened his inner self, reasoning him to be alert and aware.

Hitting the trunk release, he removed the .38 from the glove compartment, took the flashlight they had purchased, stepped out into the cool night, and tucked the firearm into the small of his back, the asphalt road cool on the bottoms of his feet.

Barefoot, Rebecca rounded the car and looked down into the space, then at Johnny. An idea quickened in her nimble mind; however, now was not the time or place to share it. "We'll put your clothes in my suitcase. There's plenty of room." She hoisted it out and opened it.

Johnny unzipped the knapsack, and removed all items. Rebecca lay his clothes flat across her own and with some effort close the lid and set the latches. "There. Snug as a bug in a rug."

A set of headlights approached from behind. Rebecca froze. Johnny held his breath. A silver Mercedes came to a stop next to them, its driver powering the passenger window. "Are you in need of assistance?" a woman's voice asked. Then her glamorous face appeared close to the open window.

"No, thank you," said Johnny. "Lover's quarrel, that's all."

The woman's eyes calculated for a dubious moment. "That's fine then. I understand young love. Hope you can work it out." The window went up; the Mercedes continued down the road.

"We've got to do this as quick as possible. The people who reside in this neighborhood are suspicious of everyone to the point of being paranoid. It wouldn't surprise me in the least if that woman was on her cell phone right now calling the police to investigate. We certainly don't look like we belong here. No disrespect, but you're a Native. Your breed just isn't seen in these parts, not to mention my own scanty looks."

"Then we should move the car," said Johnny, holding the empty knapsack by his side.

"Where?" Rebecca's eyes scanned the darkness.

"You let me worry about that. I'll meet you at the back of the house in five minutes. Here, take the flashlight, I see pretty good in the dark, being a Native and all." He smiled.

Rebecca slapped him on the shoulder. "Stop that. I told you I meant no disrespect."

"Get going. And don't do anything without me."

"I won't," she said and hightailed it into the darkness.

Johnny tossed the knapsack on the passenger seat, climbed in, started the engine, and followed the same path as the Mercedes.

Rebecca made her way through the unkempt part of the estate, running as fast as she could, nearly blind, the bottoms of her feet taking a beating from the thistle and dried fescue. In quick time she found herself next to the cabana and pool area.

Johnny was already standing in front of the sliding glass doors.

Out of breath, she went to him, and turned on the flashlight, the beam of it pointed to the ground.

Quietly, Johnny asked, "What took you so long?"

"Let... me... catch... my... breath." Hands on hips, she settled her racing heart. "How did... you get here... so fast?"

"I figured if I parked right in front of the house, no one would think anything of it. I'm sure Mr. Brown parked there on more than one occasion. Besides, we'll be in and out in a matter of minutes, right?"

Breath stable, Rebecca said, "That's the plan. Keep your fingers crossed just in case." She tried the sliding door. It opened with a rush of air into the mansion. "Don't say a word while we're moving about. Like I told you, Rosita has very good ears."

Johnny made a motion to his mouth as if he were turning a key and locking his lips.

It took less than a minute to locate the conference room once they padded their way through the kitchen and formal dining room, then finding themselves in the marble foyer. Rebecca tried the brass knob. The door opened soundlessly. She directed the light into the room, and they stepped in. Gently, Johnny sealed the door behind them.

* * *

Rosita had heard a noise, recognizing it right away. Someone had opened the sliding doors leading to the pool area. She climbed out of bed and turned off the movie she was watching. Opening the bedroom door, she listened. She knew every sound the house made, and was taken aback when she clearly heard the sound of bare feet padding through the house. Calling the police was out of the question. The mansion held too many secrets. She made her way to the spiral staircase, her heart a beating drum. A beam of light entered the foyer. There were two of them. One much smaller than the other who was holding a gun. *Best to let them take what they want, and not get myself killed.* Without sound, Rosita went back to her bedroom, locked the door, and covered herself with the comforter from head to toe. She crossed herself thrice, and beseeched Christ our Lord for protection.

* * *

The conference table and eight sturdy chairs came to life in the flashlight's beacon. A much grander more imposing chair headed the table. Rebecca could well imagine it was where Tony Millions issued orders to the posse. She directed the light to all four corners of the room. Shadows danced. They saw the painting above the faux fireplace in the same instance. In the unnatural light, it was utterly frightening.

Rebecca passed the flashlight to Johnny. "Hold it steady," she told him. Reaching, she took the edge of the frame in hand and drew the painting toward her. It opened like a book. Staring at her was the metallic face of a safe. She let her mind drift back in time. To Mr. Black's trunk. To Janice Keeper's haunting instructions. "*Memorize these numbers. Thirteen left. Twenty-four right. Nine left.*"

Trembling fingers entered the combination. There was a click. Turning the handle, she opened the safe to reveal a cubicle occupied with money stacks, a thick wad of bonds, and three kilos of cocaine wrapped in grey polypropylene. "Bingo," she bolstered a little too loud for Johnny's liking. "There must be fifty thousand dollars here! Thank you, Janice." She turned. In her hands were two thick bundles of money. "We're rich, Johnny!"

"Becca. Keep your voice down," scolded Johnny as unobtrusively as possible.

"Don't worry, my love. No one, not even Rosita, can hear us in here."

"Still. I don't mind telling you I'm pretty creped out by all of this. I've got this suspicious feeling. Like we're being watched or something." He looked around the room as if there were sets of eyes in every corner.

"My big brave love. There's nothing to worry about. The walls are soundproof. We'll be out of here before you can say, I hate white rabbits."

Johnny tucked the firearm into the waistband of his jeans. With a sense of urgency, he unzipped the knapsack and held it open.

Rebecca removed the banknotes, passing them to Johnny who, in turn, quickly stuffed them into the knapsack. When she handed him the last bundle, she said, "What should we do with the bonds? They're no good to us."

"Just leave them and let's get the hell out of here."

"No! That bastard has to pay for what he did to me and the others." Her eyes were those of an untamed animal in the beacon of light. Lost in the moment of retribution, like a lion who attacks its trainer because he had used the whip one too many times. Fanning the bonds, she took a dozen or so in her hands, tore them into little pieces and dropped them to the floor.

Johnny witnessed the violence of her actions, and realized with great sadness that no amount of imagining on his part could ever completely substantiate the suffering she had gone through.

When rebecca tore the last of the bonds, she said, “There. I feel much better now.” She tossed him one kilo of cocaine then another and another until the Franklin safe sat empty.

“Can we please get the fuck out of here now?”

“Just one more final touch. See if you can’t find a pen and paper.”

“What the hell for? Come on, Becca. We got what we came for. Let’s go. Please!”

“No, Johnny!” she said severely. “I want that bastard to know exactly who did this to him. “Here!” She held out an opened hand. “Give me the flashlight! I’ll find it myself!” She practically tore the flashlight from Johnny’s grasp, aimed it at the table and to the small bar set up in the corner, the light causing the crystal decanter of Scotch and tumblers to glitter. Nothing. She went to the end of the conference table, and drew the principal chair from its position. A small curved drawer was set into the wood. Opening it, she found what she was looking for. A small pad and fountain pen sat next to a brass cylinder. Removing the required items, she set them on the table. Johnny stood next to her, the knapsack sealed and slung over his shoulders. “Can I help?” he asked solemnly.

“Here! Hold the flashlight.”

Johnny took it, and directed the beam to the notepad.

Removing the cap from pen, she gave it a shake so the ink flowed to the tip. In perfect script, she wrote with a proud hand simply,

Fuck you, Tony
Love,
Rebecca White

When the self-accusing note sat alone in the opened safe, she declared triumphantly, “Okay! Now we can leave! Destiny, Alberta, here we come!” Throwing her arms around Johnny’s neck, she squeezed him close.

“Thank goodness,” said Johnny. “For a moment there, I thought I was going to have to carry you out of here by force.”

“You know what they say, my love. Hell hath no fury like a woman scorned.”

“Amen to that. Now can we please get the fuck out of here?”

Releasing her grip of him, she looked at the empty Franklin, the confetti of bonds at her feet, understanding that it took the death of a young woman to supply her with the knowledge needed to get a little even with Tony Millions. *Thank you, Janice Keeper.* “Yeah Johnny. Let’s get the fuck out of here.”

They exited the house the same way they had entered and made their way to the columned entrance, Rebecca leading, Johnny’s eyes suspicious of every shadow.

Once they were in the RX7, he tossed the money and drug-laden knapsack into the backseat. The .38 he returned to the glove compartment. Quickly they put on their socks and footwear. Johnny started the engine. A victory smile lit Rebecca’s face. “We did it!” On went the seat belt. “And thank you, my love. You gave me the courage I needed to pull that off, even if I was a little terrible in there. “I love you, Johnny Black,” she said with as much conviction as she could manage. “Canada, here we come!”

Johnny stretched the seat belt over his chest and slipped the gear into first. "I love you too, Becca. Forever and a day."

"Yes," she agreed. "Forever and a day."

They strolled into the vast depths of their love.

Rebecca saw the paramount glow of adoration surface from within. It made her yearn for him. To hold him in her arms, whisper to him that she loved him a hundred times over, to feel the all-encompassing needs of his body against hers.

Johnny witnessed the pyre blaze of her passion. It came forward like an ethereal dream, possessing him completely, forever. Reaching, he cupped her face in his hands. No words were exchanged. Within a breath of each other, love spoke its secret language.

Rebecca turned on the stereo. "Candle in the Wind," Elton John's lamentation for his longtime and dearly missed friend, cried through the speakers.

It seems to me,
you've lived your life
like a candle in the wind
Never knowing
who to cling to
when the rains set in
Oh, I would have loved to have known you
But I was just a kid
your candle burned out long before
Your legend ever did...

They left the wealthy neighborhood to those who dwelled in its ambiance. Never to look back. Never to hear the siren call of Vegas again, the sinfonietta that had brought them together. A further journey now commenced, leading to the long and distant road that would guide them to the sanctioned entry of their providence. Hoping beyond wishes, that their love of one another and fate would conduct them to a safer haven.

Another page turned

* * *

69

Who Loves Yah, Baby

BY 3:00 a.m., Tony was up fifteen thousand. He knew his luck was going to be restored, it was only a matter of time. They had changed blackjack dealers on him three times, and each time Tony bested them. The pit boss, a sharply dressed bull of a man, had moved close enough to let Tony and the dealer know he was watching.

However, it did not take long before the pit boss's attention moved from the table to the V cut in Pamela's Vissachi. It was a game she enjoyed playing while Tony focused on the cards dealt. She knew how to make men want her when it suited her needs. It was how she attached herself to Tony Millions and his money in the first place. A far better alternative, even considering the beatings, than fucking every Tom, Dick, and Harry, who knocked on her door. Her days of spreading her legs on the stage floor of a strip club were a thing of the past.

At five hundred dollars a played hand, it didn't take Tony long to accumulate the stack of chips that stood in front of him. In the four hours he was seated at the end of the arched table, he turned twenty-one nineteen times. The three players, two wealthy old broads and a true-blue Texan who had been seated with him during his ace game left, the Texan first, the gals about an hour later. Victims of the dealer's ability to best them, leaving Tony and the dealer to duel it out. *Mano et mano.*

Pamela stood next to him, Chardonnay in hand. Between leisurely breaks to powder her nose, the alcohol, and Tony's winnings, she felt more and more at ease; for if he had lost, there was no telling the physical harm he might have inflicted upon her once they were home. He was spiraling downward at an alarming rate. Only his vanity was keeping him afloat. However, not even Tony's vainglorious self could keep him away from the crash. With most of his men dead or missing, and Tony drowning himself with booze and cocaine, Pamela seriously contemplated if it wasn't time for her to leave and find another whale to latch on to. Regardless of the possible consequences.

Tony motioned her closer.

"All this winning has made me horny," he told her.

"Then I think you should cash in your chips and let me take care of Morgan for you," she whispered in his ear.

The warmth of her breath aroused him. Morgan the Organ began to stir within the press of his pants. "One more hand before we leave," he said confidently. Pushing a stack of chips valued at one thousand dollars to his marker, he told the dealer, "Okay. Make my last hand another winner and you'll be rewarded handsomely."

"I'll try, Mr. Millions," said the dealer, turning an ace up.

Pamela squealed, set her drink down, and wrapped her arms around Tony's shoulders, playing the role of caring mistress to a tee, her eyes glued to the table, waiting for the next card to be turned.

The dealer drew a king for himself.

Pamela clucked. "That's not good, Tony."

He looked to the dealer, eyes narrow, mentally wishing for a face card. He tapped the table with a point of a finger.

The pit boss watched.

The dealer slid a card from the shoot, turned it over onto the ace. It was the jack of spades. "Blackjack," he called out. "Congratulations, Mr. Millions." He pushed a three to two double stack of chips toward the others.

Pamela leaned forward. "Let's get out of here, baby. Let me take care of that bulge of yours."

Tony tossed a five-hundred-dollar chip to the dealer, thanking him for a pleasurable and prosperous evening.

Once he cashed two thousand in chips, adding the remainder to his line of credit with the casino, he tipped the valet a fifty and squeezed himself behind the wheel of the Lexus. He was beyond himself with the need for Pamela's special treatment. By the time they reached Blue Diamond Road, he was sweating profusely. Pamela had Morgan the Organ gripped tightly in hand.

"You're a filthy, dirty little bitch, aren't you?" Tony told her.

Pamela squeezed him harder, pulling the foreskin back to reveal Morgan's swollen head. "Only for you, Tony," she said, her mind on more important things like when it would be a good time to separate herself from this loser. Nonetheless, she had to be careful. Even in his free fall, Tony was still a very dangerous man.

Tony's body shuddered. Sweat dripped from his forehead.

Pamela released him.

"You fucking bitch! You know me far too well."

Pamela stuck a finger into his mouth, let him suck on it for a while. Then she tucked Morgan the Organ back into Tony's slacks and drew up the zipper. "He can wait until we get home."

Reaching between Pamela's legs, Tony's fingers toyed with the silk pedals of her blossom. "I'm going to fuck you good tonight. You won't be able to walk properly for a week."

"I can't wait, baby," said Pamela as the Lexus pulled into the circular driveway of the Millions mansion.

The first wrong thing Tony noticed was that the foyer lights were on. "We didn't leave the lights on, did we?"

"No, Tony. They were off when we left. I'm sure of it. Maybe Rosita turned them on again."

Tony pulled to the front of the house, threw the Lexus into park and killed the engine. His eyes searched the lighted windows that should all be dark. Reaching beneath the seat he withdrew a 9-mm Walther P99 and opened the door.

Once outside, he looked around. Everything seemed to be in place. But the air smelled of wrongdoings. He motioned for Pamela to get out of the car. Together they walked to the front door. Tony tried the handle, surprised to find it unlocked. "I don't like this. Something smells. Stay close behind me." He raised the weapon shoulder height.

With extreme vigilance, he opened the door, ready to bring the German firearm to life if need be. Foyer light spilled onto the steps and Pamela's gown. The first thing to register was the sound of a woman in distress. Pushing the door to its full extent, they found Rosita sitting on the bottom rung of the staircase, face in her hands, housecoat wrapped tightly around her frail body. "Rosita!" Tony bellowed. "What has happened? Why is the door unlocked?"

Rosita lifted her wet face to see her boss and Pamela standing in the doorway. "Oh, Señor Millions," she cried. "Two men. Dey come in. I am so scared, but I watch dem. Dey go to your meeting room… And dey…"

Instant anger flushed Tony's face. He cut her off midsentence. "What do you mean two men?" Moving toward her, he lowered the 9 mm. Pamela remained by the door. What she wanted to do was turn and run as far away as possible. There was no telling what Tony was going to do next.

Rosita made the sign of the cross. "Ieee, Santa Maria. Si. Two men. With the flashlight. Dey come into the house. I am being so scared. I don't know what to do."

"Did you see who it was, Rosita?" asked Tony, anger mounting with each passing second.

"No, señor. Too dark. One big. One small. Dat all I see."

Tony ran to the conference room, flung the door open, and hit the lights. "NOOO!" he shrieked, his voice resounding throughout the mansion. The safe was open, empty. Three million dollars in bonds lay beneath the Screaming Man, torn into small pieces. He went to the painting, tore it from its mount and flung it across the room. It landed hard against a wall, but remained intact. Immediately he turned his attention back to the safe.

Pamela appeared in the doorway, a hand covering her mouth, Rosita cowering behind her. "Oh my god! You've been robbed, Tony."

Tony's head snapped so viciously, every vertebra in his neck and upper back crackled like bubble wrap. His eyes were those of a wild animal. Blood rushed to his face, a stop sign with eyes. "You fucking, stupid bitch! What was your first clue? Of course I've been robbed." Turning his attention back to the safe, he noticed a small square of paper within. Plucking it, he stared at it, not believing what he was reading. His body slumped as if it had lost all skeletal support, and he began to laugh. Softly at first, then with the force of someone on the verge of losing it. Stepping back, he stared at the note until his ass hit the conference table. Resting the firearm on its surface, he said, "That fucking little bitch!" Insane laughter erupted. "I don't believe it!"

"What is it, Tony?" Pamela asked from the doorway, absolute fear causing the bite mark he had left her with to pulse with warning. For Tony was, more often than not, at his worst when he was laughing. "What little bitch?"

Tony let the note slip from his fingers so that it spiraled to the floor. "That little whore Orchid. Or should I say Rebecca White as she has so lovingly stated. She and that Indian of hers had the balls to come in here and steal from me. ME! But how the fuck did she get the combination?" He looked to Pamela.

"Well, don't look at me, Tony. I had nothing to do with it. I don't even know the combination." Deep within, where no one else could hear, she was laughing. *Good for Rebecca. It's about time someone got even.* She just hoped the Indian and Rebecca were far, far away by now. Tony's revenge on them was going to come right out of the Bible.

"If I suspected you did, I would kill you where you stand," hissed Tony. "Besides, you are not smart enough to be involved in this." He began to laugh again. "She and that Indian pulled a fast one on us. Backtracked, just like an Indian would while Mr. Black is out there somewhere probably running in circles by now. All my money! My cocaine! Those bonds! Gone!" His voice shook with rage, with disbelief. "Leave me alone!" he roared, and stared at the handwritten note at his feet.

Pamela reversed her steps, a terrified Rosita still clinging to her gown. Closing the door, she decided the safest place to be was locked in a room someplace, out of Tony's anger range. "Go to your room," she told Rosita. "Lock the door. Stay there until morning."

Without a second thought, they disappeared, Rosita running to her bedroom, Pamela choosing one of the five bathrooms as shelter, all of Tony Millions's forgotten winnings stuffed within her handbag.

Tony went to the bar, poured himself a triple Scotch. Gulping half of it down, he took a breath then finished it. Pulling out his cell phone, he scrolled for Mr. Green's number, catching his breath, ready to take out his anger on anyone.

Mr. Green answered on the third ring. "Yes, Tony," he droned, sounding like a man who had just been disturbed from sleep.

"Did you contact those friends of yours?" he asked in an ireful tone.

"Yes, Tony. They'll be arriving in Vegas a few hours apart from each other tomorrow. The latest arriving at three."

"Good. See to it that you all come straight here."

"Yes. Tony."

"These friends of yours, Mr. Green, if you fail me in the job I have for you, I will pay them enough money to turn around and murder you, and I should add… not very nicely."

"If there's one thing I am, Tony," Mr. Green reminded him, "is loyal, so long as the money is right. There's no need to threaten me."

"Then get some rest, Mr. Green. You are going to need it." Closing the cell, he picked up the decanter of Scotch, tucked the Walther P99 into the waist of his trousers, and went to his office where he engaged the computer. Sitting in the dark, while Norman stood placid in his cage, he watched the blue screen come to life. Pouring another three fingers, he entered the code, bringing to life the events that took place while he was gambling. A dark, grainy image appeared, time running present at the bottom. He fast forwarded the recording until the conference door opened and light poured into the room. Watching, listening, and downing much Scotch, the shadow figures of Rebecca White and the Indian proceeded to do their dirty work. The images played out for a full five minutes, the sound at times barely audible. He watched as the Indian stuffed a backpack with *his* money. Then the new-look Rebecca White tore his bonds into shreds. *Clever*, he thought. *Changing her appearance like that.* He actually admired her for a moment. When the three kilos of cocaine disappeared into the backpack, Tony's annoyance rose to such a crescendo that a vessel popped and his nose bled, drops of crimson dotting his pants. Tony paid no mind to it. The daring couple disappeared from the lens's view for a minute then returned to the safe. Rebecca deposited the love note. They hugged and spoke. Tony increased the volume with a stroke of the curser. Something about hell hath no fury and all that nonsense. Rebecca looked right at the hidden lens. A smile grew wide on Tony's face. Blood continued to paint his leg. Before they left the conference room, he clearly heard Miss White say, "Destiny, Alberta, here we come."

Lifting the Scotch, he began to laugh. Softly at first, then rising to a pitch not unlike the parody of a shrieking woman. In one satisfying breath, he drained the glass and finally wiped at the blood dripping from his nose. "Yes, little Ms. White! Destiny, Alberta, here we come indeed." Laughing with inevitable certainty, he smashed the empty tumbler against the nearest wall.

The sharp explosion caused Norman to bolt upright and draw its wings into a blue-gold arc of color. He could see his master in the dark. Angling his head, he looked at Tony with the opulent black disk of his left eye. "Who loves yah, baby," he croaked, sounding very much like his mentor.

* * *

70

December 29
Last Dance

KNOWING they were heading to a territory hampered by a frigid winter's climate and all they had were clothes suitable for mild temperatures, Johnny and Rebecca purchased parkas, gloves, winter boots, and woolen socks at a Gap in Boise. Right away, Rebecca changed into the new winter gear. Johnny remained comfortable in the clothes he was wearing. Working outdoors most of his life had earned him a thick skin. The cold had to be extreme before he sought the warmth of heavy clothing. He'd also purchased a six-inch skinning knife with scabbard from a nearby sporting goods store, reasoning they couldn't always carry the gun with them and it made him feel secure. The knife fit snugly within the confines of his right boot.

Because the road ahead was going to be unpredictable at best, they took the RX7 to a nearby garage and had the mechanic there install winter tires while they sat across the street at a McDonald's and ate lunch.

"How are you doing?" inquired Rebecca, seeing that Johnny's eyes were blanched with fatigue.

Swallowing a good portion of the Big Mac he was chewing, he said, "I'm not going to lie to you, I'm pretty damned tired. I'm going to have to stop soon and take a break. Sleep for four or five hours, then I'll be good to go."

"I'm sorry if I'm pushing you too hard."

"I know you are. I also know that it's necessary. The farther away we get from Nevada, the better."

"How far do you think it is to the border?"

Johnny had to think for a moment. He had studied the map, memorizing the route they would take; however, maps could not determine delays, rest periods, mechanical breakdowns, or anything else that might postpone them from reaching their destiny.

"If all goes well, and once I've had time to rest, I think we can get there in about fifteen hours, give or take."

Rebecca seemed to mull this over. "Fifteen hours to freedom," she said.

"I hope you're right. I hope Tony Millions has learned a lesson or two and given up the chase. But from what you've told me of the man, my suspicions are that he's not one to take what we did to him very lightly."

"I would have loved to have seen the look on his face when he discovered an empty safe. He must be beside himself right now. I just hope he doesn't take his anger out on Pamela. She was good to me in a weird kind of way." She dipped some fries into the small container of ketchup.

Johnny took another bite of burger, and washed it down with Coke. "I'm still very concerned about some things."

"Oh. What's that, my love?"

"This Mr. Black. Since the near miss at the Park Pines, there's been no sign of him. That bothers me. If he's as good as I believe he is, why hasn't he caught up to us yet. Or maybe he has. Maybe he's close by and watching us right now. Playing a sick little game. Knowing he can take us any time he wants. Getting some kind of perverted pleasure from it."

Instinctively, Rebecca's head turned in all directions, the fine hairs on the back of her neck rose to attention. She looked out the windows, at the cars passing by and the ones parked in the lot. A light snow had begun to fall. "Thanks," she said. "You just scared the hell out of me."

"I'm sorry, but we can't assume we're in the clear. That's usually when things happen, when people let their guards down."

"I think you've seen too many movies. If Mr. Black had caught up to us, I don't think we would be talking to each other right now. He's a killer. Plain and simple. Money drives his tasks. He's not one for playing little games. Trust me. We would be dead by now."

"Still, I'm not letting my guard down. Not for a minute. And neither should you for that matter." Looking around as though everyone within ten feet had some kind of connection to Tony Millions, he said, "Maybe once we've crossed the border we can ease up a little. Until then, I think we should still be very aware of everything and everyone around us."

"Okay. I won't let my guard down," Rebecca half-promised.

Johnny took another bite of his Big Mac. Chewed. After a moment, he looked deep into the meaning of Rebecca's eyes. "You won't, will you? Stop looking over your shoulder? Two sets of eyes are better than one."

"I won't. But for right now, I think we're in the clear."

"Listen to me, Becca. I'm sorry if I'm not as optimistic as you are. You should not forget what brought us to this point in the first place. We've been running since we met. I don't mind telling you that I'm scared for the both of us."

"You've forgotten about one thing, Johnny. Whatever happens next was always meant to happen. We're being guided by the will of untold influences. I truly believe that. Like I told you before. I've known you since childhood. Loved you before you knew I even existed, knowing in my heart that one day we would meet." Reaching across the table, she rested a hand over his, her green eyes bearing the depths of her own fears. "Am I still frightened? Of course I am. I'm fucking terrified. But I'm not going to let it ruin the time we have together." She tried a smile.

"Good. I'm glad you're still scared. Scared makes you think. Scared makes you believe in other things. Scared keeps you safe." He paused for a thoughtful instant. "You make it sound as though you know something I don't. Do you? Is there something about our future you're not telling me?"

"No," she lied. "Not really. Mixed messages. That's all."

A short period of silence fell between them. Johnny took several more bites of his burger. Rebecca fished for the last of her fries. Small children raced around the tables, giggling with excitement, brandishing toys they'd received in their kid's meals.

"What else do you have concerns about?" Rebecca finally asked.

Johnny lowered his voice as though to confess to a priest. "What are we going to do with all that... you know."

"I've thought about the *you know* quite a bit while you've been driving. It's no good to us. We'll just get rid of it."

"How?"

"I saw this in a movie once where this couple stole a whole bunch of *it* and you know what they did? When they found themselves on an open highway, the girl ripped open the packets and let the wind take care of it. That way no one will be able to get their hands on it and there'll be less of it available on the streets."

"I think I saw that movie. They die in the end?"

"Yeah, but it was just a movie. What else is bothering you? You might as well get it off your chest. I can see in your eyes that there's something else troubling you."

"Well, there's the whole getting me and the money across the border thing. How do you plan on achieving that?"

"Better that I show you than tell you. Once we're out of Boise, we'll find a nice side road someplace, and I'll show you what I've come up with."

"Your plan doesn't include me shooting our way across, does it?"

"No. Nothing as dramatic as that," she giggled, seeing in her mind's eye Johnny hanging from the open window of the sports car, gun ablazing. "You'll have to trust me. What I have planned will work. You'll see."

They finished their lunch, went to the garage, picked up the car, then stopped at a Kentucky Fried Chicken outlet, purchasing a bucket of chicken, coleslaw, and more pop for the drive ahead.

Rebecca had retrieved the knapsack from the trunk. It rested on her lap, Johnny's knife beneath a leg while he drove north out of Boise on the I-15 and toward the Salmon River Mountains and Yellow Stone National Park. The sparse landscape was submersed in a fine layer of snow, dormant lands anticipating spring's rejuvenation. The sky ahead of them heavy with castles of cumulonimbus cloud.

"Looks like we've got some weather coming up," said Johnny. "You know I'd feel a lot better if we got rid of the cocaine now."

Rebecca turned in the seat so she could see through the rear window. From what she could tell, there were three cars behind them and a semi pulling a load. "Slow down some. Let those cars pass us. I don't think there's anyone behind them."

Johnny slowed to a speed that would force the other drivers to pass. Rebecca took out one of the kilos of cocaine and, using the knife, made a slit from corner to corner.

The first car sped by, its irritated driver flipping him the bird. Johnny smiled and shrugged his shoulders. The second and third car passed without incident. The semi approached quickly, its driver signaling before it overrode them in a gust of eighteen wheels. The light RX7 rocked in its wake.

Johnny glanced at the rearview. There was no one behind them for as far as he could see. "Okay," he said. "The coast is clear. Get rid of that stuff."

Rebecca powered the window enough so that her hands could reach through. She lifted the kilo toward the opening. Immediately, the suction of air began to dislodge the fine powder. Pushing it farther through the open space, she broke the package open. Cocaine poured from the bag in a swirling vortex, like an unleashed storm of snow. "What should I do with the empty package?"

"I'm not one for littering, but these are extreme conditions. Just let it go."

The empty package lifted into the air like a rebellious kite. Rebecca repeated the process with the remaining kilos until her fingers numbed and the air behind them glittered. The interior of the RX7 became screened in a fine layer of powder. Pulling her hands in, they were pink and white with a residual glove of cocaine. She held them in front of her as if they carried the plague. "What do I do about these?"

Fingering the main controls to his left, Johnny powered both widows. Frigid air rushed in. "Brush off as much as you can and try to hold your breath for a minute. There's enough cocaine in here to get us high for a week." He dialed the temperature control to full heat.

Taking a deep breath, Rebecca held her hands out the open window, shaking, clapping, and wiping the dust off best she could. However, the cocaine trapped inside the vehicle took its effect. Her face tingled and she began to feel euphoric. Drawing in her hands, she said, "This didn't happen in the movie." She pulled the fur-trimmed hood of the parka over her head.

Johnny looked at her, and she saw right away that he too had been affected. His eyes held a shine to them she had not seen before. He let out the breath he was holding. "Yeah, but if I remember correctly, they were driving a convertible with the hood down. The cocaine blew directly behind them. There was nothing to trap it."

"I didn't think about that. Are you okay to drive?" she giggled.

"I think so," said Johnny with a silly grin to complement his shining eyes. "My face is tingling and my mouth is numb."

"I think it's best we find that side road and take a break. Once the effects of the cocaine wears off, I can show you what I have planned." Slipping the knife back into its scabbard, she handed it to him. Awkwardly, he returned it to the inside of a boot.

Scanning the highway and the dormant fields of snow on either side, Johnny said, "I don't see anything."

"Wait a minute. There's a sign coming up. Slow down so I can read it."

Johnny clutched, dropped a gear, and eased his foot from the accelerator.

Through the haze of cocaine, Rebecca read the signs aloud, "Fifteen miles to

Mountain House. Seventy five to Twin Falls and another two hundred miles to Pocatello.

Just past the posting, the carcass of a young roadkill deer was being feasted upon by a murder of crows. "That's so sad. As I understand it, there are more deer killed by cars than by hunters." In her mind's eye she revisited the night where, on a dark side road, she had immersed her hands past the wrists into the gory opening of a deer's abdomen for warmth.

"Yeah. I heard that too. So what are we going to do? There doesn't seem to be a side road anywhere near here. Not that I can tell anyway. We might be right next to one, but if it's covered in snow, it'll be hard to find."

Rebecca shook the cocaine-induced image from her mind, lifeless eyes, lolling tongue, seven points drifting deep. "We'll see if we can't find a deserted road near Mountain House. Then you're going to teach me how to drive this thing."

Johnny looked at her, the silly grin vanishing from his face. "You want me to teach you how to drive?" he asked, incredulous.

"Yes. It won't take long. I already know how to drive an automatic, it's the standards I don't have a clue about. Then I can share the driving time with you, and you can rest when you need to."

Johnny considered her reasoning. "You know, that's not a bad idea. But why do I have this feeling that there's an ulterior motive up your sleeve?"

"Who? Me?" She giggled again. "Well, maybe. Maybe not. You'll just have to wait and see."

They continued north, both windows down, until the mist of cocaine diminished and its effects had worn off. By the time they reached Mountain House, it was snowing, again, though lightly. They stopped at a gas station, refueled, and used the facilities where Rebecca scrubbed until her hands were raw. They asked the clerk if there was a service road nearby.

"Oh, sure," he told them. "Just keep going north on I-15. Once you get out of town, you'll see an old water tower. There's a back road just past it where the railroad goes through. But be careful back there. A couple of kids got themselves killed by a train last year."

"We will," Rebecca assured him. "We're just going to have a little winter picnic."

"That's nice," the clerk said and wished them well.

Once they were back in the RX7, refueled, refreshed, and ready for anything, they headed toward the tower.

The road was found easy enough. It broke off the highway, and disappeared into a cluster of evergreens burdened with snow. A thick layer of it covered the road. There was a railroad crossing posted at its entrance.

Immediately, Rebecca and Johnny saw the double crosses nailed to a lodge pole pine and the now-black wreath encompassing them. Neither spoke as the clerk's warning resounded in their thoughts. Johnny looked to his left, away from the crosses. Rebecca closed her eyes, wishing she never saw them.

When they reached the railroad tracks, about fifty yards in, Johnny stopped and put the brake on. Large flakes of snow gathered on the windshield. He turned in his seat. "Okay, Becca. What's this big plan you have?"

"Pop the trunk for a minute."

Johnny reached for the release and pushed the button. "Now what?"

"Let's go outside for a minute."

"I'm not sure I like where this is headed."

"Oh, don't be a chicken. Come on." Opening the door, she stepped out into the snow, new boots crunching.

By the time Johnny reached her, Rebecca had already taken the suitcase out. Looking into the open space, she pulled the hood over her head. "I'm going to get you across the border with you hiding in the trunk."

"Well, that confirms it. You are crazy. You think I could fit into that little space?"

"Give it a try. Ball up into the fetal position. It wouldn't be for long. I'll let you out once we're a few miles away from the border."

Reluctantly, Johnny lifted one leg then the other and climbed in. "The things I do for love," he muttered to himself. Lying on his side, he pulled his knees to his chest. Remarkably enough, though it was tight, he managed to fit.

Rebecca clapped. "There! I knew it. Now I'm just going to close the trunk for a second."

Before Johnny could protest, the lid closed with a clunk, immersing him in total darkness. His muffled voice bled through the trunk. "Okay. You've made your point. You can let me out now."

Rebecca went to the driver side and pushed the trunk release. By the time she returned, Johnny was already out of the small space. He stared at her in disbelief. A large flake of snow landed on the bridge of his nose. "So your big plan is to hide me in the trunk until we're past the border. What about the money?" The snowflake melted, ran down the side of his nose and onto his upper lip. He licked it away.

"We'll put the knapsack in there with you. No one is going to question a young girl with a suitcase in the backseat on her way to visit her sick aunt in Calgary. I can be very convincing you know."

"Yes, I do know. And what if they do decide to inspect the car. Then what?"

"Then I guess we'll be up shit creek without a paddle. But it's worth a try and the only alternative. Surely you can see that."

"Yeah. I guess it's the only way. Still, I want you to know that I'll being doing it under protest."

"Duly noted." She went to him, wrapped her arms around his waist, and laid her head against his chest. She gazed up at him, her eyes partially hidden by the fur trim of the parka. Snowflakes fell between their faces. "We'll get through this. You'll see. All you have to do now is teach me how to drive a standard. Nobody is using this forgotten road. I'll learn quick. I promise."

Brushing several flakes that had landed on her eyelashes, Johnny lowered his face and kissed her. The sound of wings cutting through air could be heard directly above them. They looked up to see a crow as black as soot land at the top of one of the evergreens. It raised its head and cawed a mournful, lonely lament that seemed to carry on forever. It was joined by another crow, then another, until the tips of the trees surrounding them each held a black raucous figure.

"Well, there's a good sign," said Johnny sarcastically.

"It's just some birds. Nothing to be afraid of. Silly superstitions. That's all. Okay. Show me how to drive this thing. I've been watching you, so I have a fairly good idea what to do already."

They got back into the idling car. Johnny turned on the wipers, erasing the thin layer of flakes that had gathered. "Okay. The first thing you must remember is that first is one up. Second is directly below." He pushed in the clutch and went through the first two gears. "Now when you're putting it into first and second, you must release the clutch slowly and add a little pressure to the gas at the same time. If you release the clutch too quickly, this will happen." He put the gear into first, popped the clutch. The RX7 jumped forward like an epileptic rabbit then stalled. "That's really the hardest part about driving a standard. Becoming one with the clutch, gas pedal, and gear shift." Starting the engine again, he pushed down on the clutch. "Now third, fourth, and fifth are easy. You can release the clutch fairly quickly. They're located here." He put the gear into third. "Here." He moved into fourth. "And here." He shifted up and over into fifth. "Now reverse is over and down. And like first and second, you have to release the clutch very slowly, apply a little gas. How you doing so far?"

"Sounds easy enough. How do I know when to change gears?"

"You listen to the rise and fall of the engine. It will tell you when you need to shift into another gear. Now in this kind of weather, you really have to be patient with the clutch or you'll jackrabbit and fishtail all over the place. This particular vehicle was built for speed. The engine will want to go. What you have to remember is that you are in control of *it* and not the other way around."

"Got it."

"Now I'm going to drive up the road aways. I want you to watch every move I make. Then you can try it out yourself. Pay close attention."

"I will."

Rebecca watched and listened as Johnny smoothly slipped into gears. The car moved forward effortlessly. Once they jumped the railroad tracks, Johnny moved the shift into third just as the engine whined for release. However, Rebecca heard another sound within the rise of the engine. It was hidden in the upswing, like a subliminal message. The voice of a young boy urging, "*Come on, Billy. We can beat the train.*" Casually, Rebecca looked to her left and right. All she saw was snow, trees, and the rails of the vanishing tracks.

"What are you looking at?" asked Johnny.

"Oh, nothing. Just the landscape. It's so beautiful back here."

"Well, you're supposed to be paying attention," he admonished. "It wouldn't look very good if you pulled up to the border station not knowing what you're doing. They would pull you over for sure."

"You're right. Sorry. Okay, I'm focused now."

Johnny kept the car at an even thirty miles an hour for about a mile where the road took a sharp left. Unbeknown to them, as the car made fresh tracks in the snow, the gathering of crows were flying directly above them and out of their line of sight.

He stopped the car and made a three-point turn so the RX7 was facing the route they had just taken. The crows, en masse, landed in the nearby trees eclipsing the road, their polished eyes cast downward, watching, watching, watching. "You think you're ready to give it a try now?"

"I think so. Piece of cake. Right?"

"*Right.*" Johnny smiled. "Okay. Let's switch places and see what you've learned." He killed the engine, put the car into neutral, and pulled the parking brake.

They swapped seats, Rebecca having to adjust hers so her feet could reach the pedals.

"Are you comfortable?"

"*Yes!*" Rebecca said firmly and with confidence, nodding her head.

"Can you see out of the side mirrors properly?"

"Yes, I can see fine," she said, looking left and right.

"Good. Now push in the clutch, release the brake, and start the engine."

Using the weight of her booted foot, Rebecca pushed the clutch as far as it would go, released the brake, and fired the engine. "Okay. I'm ready."

"Now remember. Nice and easy."

Jamming the gear into first, she raised her left foot and depressed the gas. However, she allowed the clutch to come up too swiftly, and the car responded with a leap forward.

"Push the clutch in!"

Rebecca did, the car came back under control. "Sorry."

"A little gentler this time." Johnny was smiling. "It's okay that you don't get it right the first couple of times. Nobody does."

"Well, that makes me feel a lot better."

"Try again."

Rebecca went through the motions of clutch, gas, and gears. Much to her surprise and Johnny's, she got the clutch right on her second attempt. She headed back toward the train tracks, turned around, and followed the tire tracks left in the snow, disturbing a family of deer that had emerged from the woods. Each animal stared at them as if they were something foreign, something that didn't belong before returning to the camouflage of evergreens. Subconsciously, Rebecca told them to stay away from the roads and continued the back-and-forth route until her feet and shift hand were synonymous with the lifting whine of the engine. An hour later, she was driving the RX7 like a pro. It had stopped snowing by then with the sun breaking through the dense clouds and adding several degrees to the coldness.

Stopping the car ten yards from the railroad tracks, she applied the emergency brake and killed the engine as though she'd been doing it all her life. "Aren't you proud of me?" Her eyes bright with the accomplishment.

"Absolutely. You're good to go. But let's not forget you had a very good teacher."

"Touché"

"So what do you want to do now?" Johnny yawned.

Rebecca could see it was time for him to take a break. His eyes were bagged, red rimmed, and on their way to closing. "Why don't we eat some of that chicken and coleslaw? Then I think it would be a good idea for you to take a nap. You need it. It's obvious nobody came back here anymore. It's as good a place as any."

"I am kind of hungry. And a little tired," he admitted.

"Then we will have a picnic in the snow. The landscape is beautiful, the air refreshing, and the sun is nice and warm. Let's enjoy the moment. Turn on the radio."

With the jab of a finger, the speakers came to life. Bob Marley was jammin'.

Rebecca turned up the volume, unfastened the seat belt, opened the door and stepped out into virgin snow, boots crunching like peanut brittle. She left the door open so they could listen to music while they had a picnic. She began to dance, closing her eyes, losing herself in the reggae beat, the warming sun so gentle on her face.

Johnny retrieved the bucket of chicken, coleslaw, and cooler from the backseat. By the time he stepped outside, Rebecca was in full rhythm to the reggae genius. He watched her for a moment, the way she moved and how it reminded him of the first time they met. It was a part of her life that would remain with her forever. The lights. The stage. The roaming eyes. As strong as she was, he understood that once upon a time and very recently, she had been broken. Watching her sway and move, lost in the freedom of her spirit, added further testament to just how stalwart she really was. Even in heavy parka and boots, he found her to be very sexy.

They were parked far enough away from the tracks that should a train happen to pass, they were safe. Johnny put the cooler and bucket on the hood and reverse jumped. By the time his bottom hit metal, he was already a bite into a leg of chicken. "You know, this stuffs not half bad. Believe it or not, I've never had it before."

Rebecca stopped dancing and opened her eyes. "You're kidding right? You've never had Kentucky fried chicken before?" She went to him, joined him on the hood and plucked a thigh from the bucket.

"Seriously. This is the first time. I mean I've had home style fried chicken, but it didn't taste anything like this. The Colonel was a genius." Reaching into the cooler, he popped the top on a can of Coke. "You want one?"

"Yes, please."

Johnny gave her the one in his hand and opened another. "Cheers," he said. "What should we toast to?"

"How about world peace?"

"Sure. Why not? It's as good a toast as any I guess. Here's to world peace." They clinked cans. The reggae tune came to an end, replaced by the drone of a boxing week commercial for hot tubs and pool tables.

Rebecca dropped the hood of her parka and ran a hand roughly through the spikes of her hair. "I hope the winter in Canada is like this. The temperature is perfect. Not too cold."

"Don't get your hopes up. My dad told me the winters in Canada can be brutal. We could be going into a vicious cold. I hope you're ready for something like that."

"So long as we're together and far away from harm, any type of weather will do." Leaning, she kissed Johnny's greasy mouth. The radio DJ introduced the next song. The grievous melody of "Knights in White Satin" aired from the open door.

Knights in white satin, never reaching the end
Letters I've written, never meaning to send
Beauty I'd always missed with these eyes before
Just what the truth is, I can't say anymore...

"Dance with me, Johnny." Rebecca slid from the hood, deposited her partially eaten thigh into the bucket and brushed crumbs from her hands. She reached out to him.

"What? Here? Now?"

"Sure. Why not? It's as good a place as any. I promise not to step on your feet."

Dropping the chicken bone into the bucket, Johnny licked the grease from his fingers and allowed Rebecca to pull him from the hood. He drew her close, and wrapped his arms around her waist. They looked into each other's eyes, turning slowly in the snow.

"This is nice. Don't you think?" said Rebecca.

"Yes, it is. Maybe you're not so crazy after all." He lowered his face, and they kissed for a long moment, tongues meeting, probing, dancing, eyes open, regarding each other with wondrous temptation. With one hand on the small of her back, Johnny used the other to unzip her parka. When the front fell open, he reached in, caressed her waist, and thumbed the soft flesh beneath her top. "I love you, Becca," he told her, his eyes imprisoned by the green of her gaze.

Overwhelmed, Rebecca's welled until tears spilled and liquid love gathered on the plump of her cheeks, dripped from her chin. "I'm forever yours, Johnny."

Gazing at people, some hand in hand,
Just what I'm going through they can't understand.
Some try to tell me, thoughts they cannot defend,
Just what you want to be, you will be in the end...

They stopped turning, held each other, the totality of their hopes, dreams, and fears felt in the embrace. Rebecca rested her head against Johnny's chest while his hands remained comfortable on the slide of her waist. It was at this point and time when they came to believe that moments like this were going to be far and few, if any. As silently as their wings would allow, the crows gathered in the treetops, and surrounded the suckling young hearts, their intentions more telling than curious. Deep in the woods, an otherworldy fog appeared and began a rolling course toward the heedless Johnny and Rebecca.

Time slowed for the brash young lovers. The secrets of their love revealed in the bleak surroundings of a back country road, leading them to a place in their hearts neither believed possible.

'Cos I love you, yes, I love you,
Oh, how I love you, oh, how I love you.
'Cos I love you, yes, I love you
Oh, how I love you, oh, how I love you...

Johnny brushed the wetness from her cheeks and kissed her eyes. "We're going to be all right. Aren't we, Becca? At least for now?"

"I wish I had all the answers, my love. I wish I could tell you yes, but I can't. Let's just take this moment and the next and enjoy them for what they're worth. Let's imagine that we're the only two people left in the world. Just you and me, Johnny. Living in the right now. Can you do that with me?"

"Yes, I can do that," he said, and kissed her again and again.

They continued to dance, slowly, no one to fear, no one to bear witness to their dilemma and a love never ending.

Impassioned lovers
Wrestle as one
Lonely man cries for love
And has none
New mother picks up
And suckles her son
Senior citizens
Wish they were young...

When the song ended, so did their time alone in the world. They stared into each other. "Thank you for the dance, kind sir," said Rebecca.

"It was nice just being the only two people in the world for a few moments. We should probably get back to our picnic before those birds swoop down and steal it on us."

Rebecca looked into the trees all around, seeing that as many as hundred crows had gathered. "I didn't even notice them. I was kind of caught up in the moment."

"I can honestly tell you that I find their presence a little alarming. Like a bad omen." *A great tragedy lies ahead.*

"They're just curious," said Rebecca, finding the gathering of scavengers and their silence surreal and, admittedly, a little spooky. "But you're right, we should get back to our picnic. They do look hungry."

Comfortable on the hood, they ate chicken, coleslaw, and enjoyed the winter white picnic for a half hour while the crows kept tacit vigil. When Johnny could eat no more, he suggested it was time to rest. They gathered the near empty bucket, Coke cans returned everything to the cooler and put it in the trunk.

Once they were inside the car, Johnny started the engine to warm it. Killing the music, he readjusted the seat to suit his legs and leaned back. Rebecca did the same, and stared at the mass nestled in the trees. *Maybe Johnny was right.*

He let the engine run for five minutes before turning it off. "Are you warm enough?" he asked.

"Yes, I'm fine."

"Then let's get some rest. There's still a long way to go."

Within minutes, as the telling murder watched and the fog drifted toward them, they fell asleep.

It wasn't the death rumble of an approaching diesel engine that woke Rebecca. Nor was it the plaintive cackling from the treetops. It was the sound of a young boy's voice that drew her from deep within the hold of a peaceful slumber. "*Come on, Billy. We can beat the train.*" Rebecca opened her eyes to find that a fog had rolled in and was hugging the landscape in its haunting, hoary shroud.

Two boys emerged from it on the far side of the tracks, obviously brothers. Each with the same brown hair, bright dark eyes, and podgy noses. The elder was no more than twelve, his sibling just a couple of years his junior. They wore T-shirts and jeans, the bigger of the two urging his brother forward with an animated arm. Rebecca sat up. The unearthly scene played itself out.

"Come on, Billy. We can beat the train."

"I don't want to."

"Don't be a chicken shit. The train is still far away."

"I'm not a chicken shit."

"Then come on." Older brother ran to the tracks, and crossed them. *"See. Nothing to worry about. Now come on!"*

Younger brother hesitated for a moment, looked both ways as though he were ready to cross at an intersection, then ran toward the tracks. Rebecca watched and listened in horror as the small boy stumbled forward, tripping over a rail. When he tried to get up, he couldn't.

"My foot's caught Gary!" he cried.

"Stop kidding around. Get over here. The train's coming."

"I'm not kidding around. My foot is stuck under the rail." He began to cry. *"Help me, Gary! I can't get it out!"*

Gary went to him, pulling on his arms. *"Shit, Billy. The train's coming."*

"Pull harder, Gary! Pull harder!"

"I'm trying! I'm trying!"

The approaching train blasted a triple warning, spewing black diesel into the air and appearing out of the fog like a hungry beast from a Brothers Grimm fairytale.

Johnny woke with a yawn.

Gary tried desperately to lift his brother free, holding him beneath the arms, face straining with the effort. He too began to cry. The train's engines roared. *"MOMMY!"* Little Billy shrieked. Rebecca squeezed her eyes tight as she could, not wanting or needing to bear witness.

"That's a hell of an alarm clock," said Johnny, yawning. He looked to Rebecca who was squeezing the tears from her eyes. "Becca, what's wrong?" The freight cars chugged by. *Clickitty-clack, clickitty-clack.* He looked to the train, understood. The fog only Rebecca could see vanished. "You saw something again, didn't you? About what the clerk told us. About what those crosses represent."

Rebecca wiped at the tears with the back a hand. "Yes, Johnny. It was terrible. I felt so helpless. The boys who were killed here last year. They left their signature behind. I imagine they must relive their tragedy every time a train goes by.

"I'm sorry. No one should have to see things like that. I wish there was a way you could control your gift."

"At times like this, so do I." She drew the hood of her parka over her face, more to hide the self-incrimination she felt than for warmth.

Johnny started the engine. The digital clock read 3:15. They had been asleep for several hours. He turned on the radio to lighten Rebecca's mood. "Love Me Do" by the Beatles filled the interior.

As a single entity, the crows lifted from the treetops, gathered en mass high into the atmosphere, and flew deep into the woods.

Johnny and Rebecca watched the wheat-laden freight cars move past them, taking several minutes before the mile-long train's caboose appeared. When it was safe to continue their journey, Johnny said, "I had a dream about my father. I think I'll call him once we get into Montana."

"I think that's a good idea. He's probably very worried about you."

Slipping the gear into first, Johnny eased his foot off the clutch. The RX7's tires crunched through the snow and they lumbered over the tracks. They came upon the crosses nailed to the tree, white as sugar against the dark vertical trunk, phantasm memorials to Gary and Billy.

Johnny looked to Rebecca whose eyes remained on the crosses until the car traveled beyond her line of sight. "You'll have to get used to seeing those for quite a while once we're in Montana. There are white crosses all over the highways. Are you going to be able to deal with the possibility that you might be witness to many *signatures* as you put it?"

Rebecca raised her knees, tucked them beneath her chin. *Am I going to be able to deal with whatever lay ahead?* For a moment, she felt as vulnerable as she was the first time she was thrown into the pit. "I don't know, Johnny. I just don't know."

The RX7 fishtailed. New winter tires gripped the highway. Another leg of their mysterious passage begun, each deliberating what the next stretch of road to Destiny, Alberta, was going to expose.

* * *

71

Ignoble Bastards

SITTING in his office, watching Norman's antics, Tony had made several calls. The first call was to Nazeem Kahdar who just happened to reside in Calgary, proprietor of several auto body shops and also a major player in the flesh industry. Nazeem supplied weapons to the cities' Hispanic, Jamaican, and Lebanese gang members vying for territory in the cities northeast. He was surprised to hear from Tony. It had been more than a year since he'd paid the Shangri-La Palace a visit.

"Tony, my friend. It is good to hear from you. It has been far too long since I have enjoyed your hospitality. What can I do for you, my friend?"

"I'm sending some associates of mine to Alberta for a few days. I need you to supply them with the necessary applications so they may complete the task I've sent them on."

"I see." A bartering silence ensued. "I can do that."

"Good. A Mr. Green will contact you."

"I will be waiting. When can I expect to hear from this Mr. Green?"

"Twenty-four hours, give or take."

"I see. And what can I expect as compensation for my urgent generosity?"

"How about a week in Vegas. I'll put you up in the best suite the Bellagio has to offer. Women coming out of your ass. All on me of course."

"Is Gypsy still in your employment?"

"Yes, of course. One of your favorites. She asks of you often."

"Then I accept your generous offer."

"Good. I will contact you again once my associates' tasks are completed."

"I look forward to it, my friend."

Each man considered the value one had for the other and, in the same instance, ended the call. A verbal contract for murderous amenities was made. A deal sealed. To neglect your end of it was very frowned upon by those who looked down on you.

The second call was to Olivia. Tony wanted to be certain the preparations for the New Year's Eve gala, held at the Palace this year, were in order. Olivia assured him they were. The caterer was hired. The liquor purchased and Hijinks, a five-piece '70 and '80s cover band, were going to set up the following day. She also added for good measure that the girls were looking forward to having a lucrative night. Guests, who numbered more than a hundred. will be "overwhelmed by your generosity," she assured him. She also boasted the New Year would be more than fortuitous for both and that she looked forward to him visiting, claiming it had been "far too long." When she asked if there was news of Orchid's whereabouts, Tony went silent for a moment. She could almost hear the clenching of his jaws. He had been wound too tight lately. Rumors abound within the sordid walls of Club Paradise that he was losing it. Drinking and snorting with reckless abandonment. *Perhaps the party would put him in a lighter spirit,* she hoped. He was, after all, 49 percent of the Palace and her personal cash cow. "Sorry, Tony. Perhaps I shouldn't have broached the subject. Forget I even asked. Take it from someone who knows. Once you have completed your business today, get a massage and buy yourself a new tuxedo for the party. It will do you a lot of good."

"Don't be so fucking needy, Olivia," suggested Tony, a slippery tone in his voice. "It doesn't sound good coming from you. If you want to suck on my cock, just say so."

"I'm just concerned, Tony. So are the girls. There is no need to be hostile or vulgar. We are only trying to be helpful."

"I'll take care of things on my end, Olivia, just make sure you do the same. I'll see you at the party." He'd closed the cell phone, sat behind his computer, and retrieved the candid viewing of him being robbed. Seeing Rebecca White looking directly at him had caused his heart to pound like a fist in his chest. He froze the image. *Even with her short dark hair, she still possessed the beauty of innocence and mystery.* However, there was more to her than just appearances. Something about her he could never put his finger on, and it was driving him crazy. He'd stared at her image for an hour, wondering what mysterious qualities she possessed. Then he'd shut off the computer and poured himself another Scotch.

He made a call to a car rental company and reserved for a week a large SUV for Mr. Green. Needing cash, he put on a light jacket and drove to his bank where he withdrew one hundred thousand. Then he decided to stop at the club, since there was no one left to watch the place and because he'd had to depend on the managerial skills of the bartenders, which were weak at best. He had to be sure things were running smoothly.

The club was to near capacity, pleasing him to no end, and decked out for the holidays with garlands, enough tinsel to sink a ship, and a well-lit Christmas tree standing next to the stage. When the DJ noticed Tony, he announced over the speakers, "Mr. Tony Millions is in the house."

Tony spent an hour there, nursing a drink, getting hugged and kissed by the dancers, brownnosed by the waitresses and bouncers, and told by everyone that things were going great. People who knew him wished him all the best, season's greetings, shook his hand, patted him on the back. By the time he'd left, he had a buzz going and was feeling much better about how the club was operating, making reservations with himself that he would soon pay another visit.

When he returned to his mansion, he Googled the town of Destiny, Alberta, learning it had once been a coal mining town that flourished for several decades and died. Today it had a population of seventeen hundred and was thriving on tourism dollars accumulated during the summer months.

Sitting in front of the computer, he replayed Rebecca White's daring deed over and over. It was four o'clock, a bottle of Scotch and a half-filled glass sat at his elbow. He had changed into an all-black ensemble. Crew neck, trousers, and loafers. Black got you what you wanted. Black made people pay attention. Black made others feel inferior. He was expecting Mr. Green and his accomplices at any moment.

The hundred grand stood in neat stacks of twenty-five-thousand-dollar increments toward the edge of the desk. The sight of money always made people pay attention. *Always.* He had no idea who these new recruits were and liked it that way. He had been forced to rely on Mr. Green's talents and ability to sway others. *So be it,* he thought. Should Mr. Green prove capable, Tony would move him up in the ranks while assembling a new posse. Perhaps these friends of his would demonstrate enough daring do to be considered as well. Mr. Black was history. That was a given.

An unfinished plate of shrimp Creole and braised short ribs sat on his desk. He had taken several bites of the lunch Rosita prepared, opting for the liquid attributes a bottle of Scotch offered instead. Glaring at the screen, he watched the Indian stuff *his* money into a backpack, the grip on his glass growing tighter, anger rising with each bundle lost. He had come up with the perfect revenge for the Indian that involved a knife and the hair on his head. Raising the glass to his mouth, he noticed his hand was shaking. "You'll get yours, my friend," he told the screen.

There was a knock at the door.

Tony hit a key. The screen went blue. Aiming his voice at the door, he said, "Yes. What is it?"

The door opened enough for Rosita to poke her head through. "Meestor Green and two mens are here to see you," she said, her eyes immediately going to the unfinished lunch.

Only two, Tony thought. Nothing he could do about it at the moment. "Fine. Give me a minute before you show them in."

"Shall I take your lunch away?" Rosita stepped farther into the room, hands folded in front of her.

"Yes. Please." Tony turned so that he was facing her. Throughout everything he had been through, Rosita had remained loyal to him. For ten years, she put up with his tantrums, verbal abuse, and brief encounters with insanity whenever he decided to walk that very thin line. Looking at her now, he realized she was the only true friend he had left at the moment. He spoke to her in apologetic tones. "I'm sorry for not eating. What I did have was very good. Thank you, Rosita. I believe in the new year we will have to discuss a wage increase for you."

Rosita's complacent eyes lifted into a smile. "Tank you. Tank you, Señor Millions." She moved quickly to the desk, and removed the unfinished plate of Creole. "God bless you. I weell be saying prayer for you tonight."

"That would be good, Rosita. I could use a prayer, possibly two. After you show Mr. Green in, I do not wish to be bothered. Not by anyone."

"Si, Meestor Millions. No one to disturb you." Bending slightly at the waist, the obedient servant reversed out of the room.

"Remember. Give me a minute before you show them in."

"Yes. Si. I understand." said Rosita, still smiling about her future good fortune and closed the door.

Tony took another swallow of Scotch, and set the empty crystal on his desk. A few stabs at the keys and the digital replay of the five-minute burglary was ready to start. He pushed himself from the chair, and habitually wiped imaginary crumbs from his lap and front. A practice his father maintained until he died. He then went to Norman who was obediently sitting quiet. When he put his face to the cage, the blue macaw leaned forward so they were beak to nose. "What do you think, Norman? Will Mr. Green and his friends find retribution for me?"

Norman bobbed its head as if it were saying yes, yes, yes. Then it croaked, "Norman likes pussy."

"Of course you do. Who doesn't." Tony put a finger through the guilds of the cage. Norman took the tip into his mouth and gently prodded it with the nub of its black tongue. Tony turned his attention to the stacks of money sitting all in a row. Since there were only going to be three and not four able bodies to tempt, he picked up one of the stacks and put it in the drawer of his desk. Standing behind it, he made himself as intimidating as possible and poured another Scotch. Taking a drink, he swished it around his mouth as if it were wash, waited, then swallowed.

After an appropriate minute, there was a heavy knock at the door.

"Come in!" said Tony in an authoritative tone.

Mr. Green opened the door and stepped into the office. He was followed by two men, one very large, bald, and with a lightning bolt vein running from his left temple toward his shiny skull. A thin, bleached scar ran vertical from just above his left eyebrow, skipping the eye itself and continuing halfway down his cheek. *Courtesy of a knife fight,* imagined Tony. The other was small, almost girlishly so, with slick black hair pulled back and a glint of evil in his lifeless eyes. Pencil-thin lips and ears that were too big for his small head made him look almost comical. A silver hoop dangled from his right ear. *As queer as a three-dollar bill. No matter.* Each man was dressed casual. Light jackets over button-down shirts and khakis. Tony motioned for them to join him by the desk.

"Gentlemen," he said, addressing the new recruits. "I'm pleased that you could make it on such short notice. I trust your flights were comfortable." The two men nodded, their attention visibly devoted to the money sitting in front of them. To Mr. Green, Tony said, "It was my understanding that you were able to enroll three for the task I have set for you."

"Originally, yes, there were, however, my friend out of Boston had second thoughts due to the threats his wife made on him."

"I see. Women." Tony smiled. "Can't kill them and you can't kill them. No matter. I'm sure these associates of yours are more than capable of handling the job."

The strangers nodded in agreement. Neither spoke, waiting out of respect for their benefactor to address them first. Killer protocol.

"You'll find that my friends here are more than capable," said Mr. Green.

"Good. I'm glad to hear it." Tony's eyes settled on the big man. "I do not wish to know the full extent of your identities. First names will suit me just fine. You are?"

The big man spoke, accent pure Russian. "Da. I am Yuri," he said, military sharp. He extended a bear of a hand. Tony reached across the desk and shook it. The big Russian gave Tony's hand three hard jerks, nearly crushing every bone.

"It's a pleasure to make your acquaintance, Yuri," said Tony, pulling his hand free, his eyes falling on the smaller man. "And you are?"

"Tim. But most people call me Cracker."

They shook hands.

Tony noticed that on the back of Cracker's knuckles were tattoos: HATE and LOVE. Cracker had obviously spent time in prison. "Sounds sinister. I like that. Somehow I believe there is a very interesting story behind it that I would like to hear once you have returned." His eyes settled on each of the three, holding their attention, impressing upon them that he was in charge. "Now that the social niceties are over, let's get down to some business, shall we?"

Yuri spread his feet apart and placed hands behind his back.

Tony surmised he wasn't old enough to be KGB, but had at one point in his life spent some serious time in the Russian military. Used to taking orders, which suited Tony just fine. Cracker's dead black eyes were drawn back to the money. *Good*, thought Tony. Greed made people pay attention. "You have been brought here to perform a specific task. Mr. Green has assured me that you can be relied upon without question. In front of you are three stacks of twenty-five thousand dollars. There will be another twenty-five thousand waiting for each of you once the task is completed to my satisfaction."

All three nodded. Avarice smiles. Tony spun the computer screen so it was facing them. Touching a key, the digital surveillance began. "I want you men to pay close attention to what you are about to see. Memorize the faces. Listen to their voices. It will be your job to see to it that these two thieves are exterminated. By any means you see fit and as promptly as possible."

The recorded images played. Tony swallowed more Scotch, retrieved three other glasses, and poured two fingers into each. When the recorded images came to an end, Tony said, "So what do you think, gentlemen? Can you oblige me by ridding the world of those two?"

"They're just a couple of kids," Cracker pointed out.

"Do you have an age bias about who you murder, Mr. Cracker?'

"Hell, no. For fifty grand, I'd kill my own mother."

"Good. Because I wouldn't want to send you all the way to Alberta only to find you are not willing to hold up your end of our business transaction."

"I have no problem," Yuri assured Tony. "They have taken from you what does not belong to them. For fifty thousand dollars, I will be making it my business to see that they regret it."

"Oh, they have done much more than that, my Russian friend. They may look like kids, but believe me when I tell you they are just as unscrupulous as you three are. The Indian is going to be a handful. And then some. Which is why there are three of you." Tony hit a key. The computer screen froze. He pushed the glasses of Scotch forward. "Now they have an almost twenty-four-hour head start on you. If you take into consideration time spent resting, eating, et cetera, et cetera, they should be in Alberta by early tomorrow." Opening a drawer, he retrieved a pad and pen and scribbled on it. "I have reserved a car for you at the Avis rental on east Sunset Road. I trust each of you have your passports and driver's licenses."

"Da."

"Yes" and "Yes."

"Good. Now I don't imagine that you, Yuri and Mr. Cracker, are in possession of weapons."

Both men shook their heads.

"Good. Better that you don't. You are to appear as nothing more than three tourists. Mr. Green, you will leave whatever weapons you have in your possession with me."

"Yes, Tony." Reaching, Mr. Green withdrew a chrome-plated Smith and Wesson from his waistband. He put it on the desk next to the stack of money that would soon be his. Then he leaned forward, pulled up his pant leg, and unclasped the hunting knife strapped to his shin. This he set next to the Smith and Wesson. "I hate to leave it behind," he said. "We've been through a lot together."

"Don't worry, Mr. Green. I've already arranged for you and your friends to be amply supplied once you get to Alberta." Pushing the piece of paper toward Mr. Green, he said, "When you arrive, you are to contact this man. His name is Nazeem Kahdar. We have an understanding. He will instruct where and when to meet. Now I took the liberty of procuring as much information about the town of Destiny that I could. Not only is it fucking cold there, but the mainstream of populace is of the blue-collar type. Electricians, plumbers, oil rig workers, and cribbers. There is a high population of retirees and single mothers living on welfare that establish the remainder of the town's inhabitants. The local hotel is the main source of extracurricular activity. This is where you will be able to gather pertinent information regarding our two friends. Once you've obtained what you need from my friend Nazeem, purchase the clothing required to blend in. The way you three look right now, you would stand out like a New Orleans blues quartet at a Klan meeting. Heavy parkas and jeans and you'll fit right in. I will of course reimburse you once you return. This is to be an in-and-out operation, gentlemen. Leave no trace of yourselves. And better yet. No trace back to me."

"What about the money and the cocaine they took?" asked Cracker.

Tony let out a dry laugh. "I don't imagine you will find any evidence of the cocaine. They probably disposed of it as soon as they could. Now the money is another matter entirely. If you are able to retrieve any or all of it, you will find that I can be a very charitable benefactor. Now as of a few days ago, they were driving a green RX7. Somewhere along the line, they ditched the old woman, Mr. Green. I'm quite sure of it. Probably dropped her off at a reserve someplace. I will give you the plate number to the RX7 before you leave. It is possible, however, that they have switched vehicles. If they haven't, then they will be that much easier to apprehend. Now as per the video, we now know that the Indian's name is Johnny. I well imagine the girl will be using the fake identification we supplied her with, identifying herself as one Tiffany Rose."

The three men nodded, eyes alight with dollar signs. *Easy money.*

"I'm glad we're all on the same page." Raising his glass, Tony motioned for the others to do the same. When glasses were elevated, Tony said, "As an added bonus, I will pay the one of you who brings me the scalp of the Indian Johnny an extra ten thousand. A trophy I would like to have as a reminder to others that Tony Millions is not a man to be fucked with." He smiled wickedly. "As far as the girl is concerned, do with her what you wish. If you should find yourselves in a position to have a little fun with her, then by all means, do so, with my blessings, though I don't imagine raping a woman is within your makeup, Mr. Cracker."

"Maybe not. But I wouldn't mind watching." Thin lips broke into such a salacious smile, a cold shiver crawled along Tony's spine.

These were indeed ignoble bastards. My kind of people. "Just one more thing, gentlemen. There is to be no communication between you and me. I do not wish to hear back from you until the matter is settled. Until the last nails have been driven into their coffins as the saying goes. Agreed?"

"Da."

"Yes" and "Understood."

"Then the matter is settled. *Salute,* gentlemen." Tony drained his glass in one swallow as did his newly acquired henchmen. A verbal death contract for money established. The insidious covenant, as far as Tony Millions was concerned, secured. Johnny the Indian and Rebecca White would not live long enough to bring in the new year. Of that he was certain.

* * *

72

Home Is Where the Heart Is

REBECCA had taken over the driving duties from Idaho Falls all the way to Great Falls, Montana, while Johnny spent a good portion of the nine-hour drive dozing, eating what remained of the chicken, and listening to music. Her need of the drug Percocet ate at her more times than she liked; nonetheless, she remained focused on the task at hand. To get them as far away as possible from Tony's unrestrained authority.

The temperature had plummeted the farther north they ventured, the landscape in all directions burdened with heavy overlays of snow. As long as she kept the RX7 just below the posted speed limits, the sports car remained straight and true.

It was just past 11:00 p.m. when she pulled into a twenty-four-hour truck stop, the gas gauge reading dangerously low. There were at least twenty or thirty semis idling all in a row along the far side of the five-acre parking lot. The smell of diesel breached the vents. Johnny was asleep. She gave him a nudge. "Johnny, wake up."

"Um. Yeah. I'm awake." He rubbed at his eyes and looked around. "Where are we?"

"We're in Great Falls, close to your home if I'm not mistaken. Just a hop skip and a jump to the border."

"Oh, *yeah*. I know this place. Foods pretty good here."

Rebecca pulled up to one of the pumps, killed the engine, and set the brake. "I'll get the gas. Why don't you collect all of our trash and get rid of it?"

"Sure, Becca."

Exiting the car, she wrapped the coat around her body and pulled the hood over her head then proceeded to fill the tank. Johnny gathered the bucket of bones and pop cans and took them to the nearest garbage bin. While the tank was being filled, Rebecca felt it would be a shame for Johnny not to see his father since they were so close to Eden. A simple phone call between a father and son who had not seen each other in months and would probably never have the chance to see each other again, she knew, just wasn't good enough.

Looking around, she noticed a bank of telephones near the entrance to the restaurant, one of which was being used by a heavyset man in a checkered jacket and baseball cap who had his back to her.

Johnny came up behind her, placed his hands on her shoulders, and gave her a start. Rebecca quickly spun around, the hood of her coat tipping back from her head. "Jesus, Johnny. Let a girl know the next time you plan on sneaking up on her."

"What would be the fun in that?"

She hit him in the chest. In many ways, he was still just a boy in an oversized body. "Just don't do it again, okay? My nerves have been damaged enough already."

Wrapping his arms around her, he pulled her close. The gas pump kicked, indicating the tank was full. "All right," he said. "I won't sneak up on you anymore." Lowering his face to hers, they kissed for a long breath. "You did really good getting us here. I'm very proud of you. Now how about we go into the restaurant and have ourselves a bite to eat. They make a mean hot turkey sandwich."

"Always thinking of your stomach. You go ahead of me and order me a coffee and a plate of fries. I'm going to pay for the gas. See you in a minute. There's something I want to discuss with you."

"Okay. See you inside." Kissing her quickly, he made his way across the tarmac and to the entrance of the diner, the man on the phone giving him the once-over as he passed.

Returning the pump to its caddy, Rebecca started the car and parked in front of the station kiosk, paid for the gas, and picked up a pack of Wrigley spearmint gum with the change.

Entering the restaurant, she avoided the eyes that were burning a hole through her clothing. Country twang emitted from ceiling speakers. Each of the booths was occupied by truckers of all ages and girth. A stretch of tables crowded the spans of windows. Johnny was seated at one of them, sipping a tall Coke. She removed her coat, and sat across from him where a steaming cup of coffee waited.

Johnny smiled. "I see you got the same reception I did."

"Yeah. I felt like I was being visually raped. Gave me the creeps. I really have learned to hate these guys. They think they have the right to leer at anything in a skirt. That every woman in the world creams their jeans for them. Bunch of redneck dickheads. Makes me sick." She took a settling breath. "Sorry. I was venting."

"No need to apologize. I understand completely. When I walked in, I thought they were going to take me out back and lynch me."

"Did you order already?"

"One plate of fries coming right up."

"I'm not really that hungry, but a plate of fries will tie me over until we stop for breakfast, hopefully in Alberta." She lifted the cup, blew gently, and took a sip.

"So what is it that you want to talk about?"

"You know how you said that you wanted to call your father once we were in Montana."

"Yes."

"I have an even better idea. I think we should get in touch with him and meet him someplace."

"Don't you think that could be dangerous? I mean. What if his phones are tapped or something?'

"It's been months, Johnny. The police have probably backed off by now. *I* could make the call. Have him meet us someplace nobody knows about. Wouldn't you like to see your dad again? We're so close. You might not get another chance like this."

Johnny thought for a moment. Rebecca was right. There may never be another chance for him to see Buck again. "I suppose we could meet him at Anvil Pine. It's a place on the ranch where Dallas and I spent a lot of time. It's also the place where I buried him."

Rebecca's potent dream came rushing back. The pine tree. The big rock. The crosses. Johnny's name loud and clear. Pushing it away, she looked at him over the brim of her cup. His eyes had come to life at the mention of seeing his dad again. "Then that's where I think we should meet him. I'll make the call just in case, but I don't believe we have anything to worry about."

"What will you say to him? He doesn't know you from Eve."

"Leave it to me. I'll word things without mentioning your name so he understands what I mean."

Their orders came. The waitress set their food on the table along with the bill. Rebecca squeezed ketchup on the fries. Popped one into her mouth. Johnny dug into the gravy-smothered bread and turkey like he hadn't eaten in a week. When he swallowed, he said, "It would be nice to see home again. Even if it's just a quick visit."

"Home is where the heart is," said Rebecca, smiling. "I realize that now, though I could never return to my own."

They finished their meals, left money for the bill plus tip, and went outside to the bank of telephones. Rebecca plugged the coin slot with quarters. "What's the number?"

Johnny recited it. She punched it in. Three rings chimed in her ear before a man's sleep-disturbed voice answered, "Yes! Who is this! Do you know what time it is?"

"I'm sorry to wake you, Mr. Black."

"Again. Who the hell is this?"

"My name is Rebecca. And I think you should meet me at Dallas's resting place in about an hour. I believe you know why."

There was a long moment of silence. Rebecca thought Johnny's father had hung up. Then in a gruff voice, he said, "In an hour. I'll be there." The line went dead.

"Well?" asked Johnny, standing close. "What did he say?"

"He said he would be there."

Johnny's face lit up like a child who has seen his first Christmas tree. "I didn't think I would ever see my dad again. Thanks, Becca." Leaning forward, he took her face in his strong hands and kissed her waiting lips.

When they parted, Rebecca looked splendidly into his eyes. "That's what girls do for the guys they love."

"Come on," said Johnny, anxiously taking her by the arm and pulling her toward the car. "I'm driving."

"Of course you are," intoned Rebecca, stumbling, trying to keep up with Johnny's long strides. "I don't have the first clue on how to get there anyway."

* * *

Johnny avoided Eden, zigzagging through back roads he knew better than the back of his hand and the one where Dallas had been shot and killed. It was pitch-dark, the headlights of the sports car stabbing at frozen asphalt. Music kept him focused. The night was moonless, and blistering with the light of so many stars they filled the universe. A generous layer of snow covered everything: the gullies, the narrow roads, and the dormant pastures of ranches. Shadow herds of cattle, huddled together against the cold, could be seen on both sides, the snow covered ground exposing them in its star bright illumination.

When they reached the entrance to the Double B ranch, Johnny stopped for a moment, and killed the radio. He was home again. During his journey, he had imagined many different scenarios into the future; however, none of them included ever seeing his home again, yet here he was, the headlights illuminating the beamed entrance. The road leading into the property had been cleared. Johnny was glad to see that his father had kept the maintenance up or the RX7 was going to have a difficult time. "Well. Here we are," said Johnny nervously, not knowing why. It was his home after all.

Rebecca's eyes followed the path of light before darkness devoured it. "It's enormous."

"This is nothing. It's going to take us about twenty minutes maybe more to get to Anvil Pine. And that's only if my dad went ahead of us. We'll be able to follow his tire tracks. If he hasn't"—he looked at the acres of snow then to Rebecca—"it's going to be a tough go. This thing isn't exactly a four-by-four. We might even have to walk some of it."

"I'm confident he's there already, Johnny. I can feel it. Probably as nervous as you are. I imagine your dad thought he would never see you again."

"Well, there's only one way to find out." Easing his foot from the clutch, the RX7 fishtailed slightly before the tires gripped and they moved forward into the vastness of Johnny's once upon a time residence.

They located the tracks his father had left easy enough, the pickup having left deep ruts for the RX7 to grip. A blazing dome of stars poured into the horizon in front of them. Deep snow drifts swam like dessert dunes all around. Rebecca imagined for a moment that they were inside a giant snow globe and someone was about to shake it. "See. I told you he went ahead of us," she said smugly.

"It's a good thing. The wind is picking up. You definitely don't want to walk out there once the wind picks up. The snow can cut right through you like razor blades."

Rebecca shivered at the thought of it. She had experienced many hard winters back in Bay Ridge Cove; however, the frozen tundra she was looking at appeared paper cut sharp, as if it had teeth, as if it could bite you. And yet, in the same instance, the barrenness of it manifested an impression of utter loneliness. Wrapping arms around herself, she said, "You better put your coat on. It looks frozen out there."

Engaging the brake, Johnny reached into the back and pulled his coat out. Opening the door for extra space, he turned in his seat, slipped his arms through, and pulled the lapels close to his collar. Gathering the length of his hair, he drew it out so that it rested across his back. The feather dangled freely. He closed the door. "You ready to meet my dad?'

"I'm looking forward to it. He raised a wonderful son."

"Yeah. Well, you'll see. He'll either like you right away, or he'll make you feel unwanted. He can't help it. That's just the way he is." Releasing the brake, he pushed the clutch and glided the shift into first. The newly purchased tires gripped the tracks left for them, and the green sports car trudged forward with a jerk and a slide sideways.

"His son fell in love with me right away," Rebecca reminded him. "I'm sure I can manage your father. But just in case, I'll wait in the car until you let me know it's okay, okay?"

"Okay."

Following the ruts, they wandered in and around deep shifts of drifting snow. Suddenly the wind blew a desperate breath, causing the small car to quake in its path. Rebecca had one hand on the dash for leverage while she watched the darkened landscape for signs of Johnny's father. The heater was working overtime, preventing ice from forming on the windshield.

A few minutes into the drive, Rebecca felt a presence with them. Her peripheral vision caught movement. Looking to the ground next to her, she saw Dallas running alongside of the car, his ears flapping, tail rotating in tight circles. "We have company," she said.

"We do?" Johnny looked all around. "Who?" He killed the radio, liberating John Fogerty's "Bad Moon on the Rise" to the air waves.

"Your friend Dallas. He's running alongside of the car right next to me. I guess he wants to welcome you back home."

"He is! That's awesome and not surprising considering."

"It's times like this that I'm glad I have this gift." She looked out the window. Because they weren't moving very fast, spirit Dallas had no trouble keeping up with them.

Ahead in the distance, Johnny could see a shimmering light where he knew Anvil Pine stood tall against the backdrop of night. The light disappeared then reappeared again several times. "There's my dad," he pointed out. "He's signaling us. Letting us know he's there."

"Where? I don't see anything."

"Wait a second. There! Straight ahead."

Rebecca had to squint to see the on-and-off again dot of white. "Oh, now I see him." Another strong wind erupted from out of nowhere, shaking the car, sounding like the lament of a long-lost spirit and sending a chill up Rebecca's spine. She shook it off. "Isn't this exciting, Johnny? You're going to get to see your dad again."

"To tell you the truth, I don't know exactly how to feel about it. Sure, I'm glad I'm going to get to see him, but he must have gone through a lot while I was on the run. Dealing with the law and everything. Not knowing where I was or if I was okay. It must have put quite a strain on him."

"I promise, once he sees you, all of that will be forgotten. Parents love unconditionally, or at least they're supposed to. You'll see."

They drove until the single dot of light became the double beams of Buck Black's pickup truck. Forms began to take shape, the headlights revealing the monstrous height of Anvil Pine, the boulder held in its grasp and the cross section of fence subdividing the cattle section of the ranch and the acres where Johnny's horses roamed.

A thin sheen of nervous sweat gathered on Johnny's forehead.

The driver side door opened. Johnny's father stepped out and moved to the front of the truck where he stood as tall as ever, his shadow immense against the green backdrop of Anvil Pine caught in the headlights of the RX7. He was wearing a heavy suede coat, lamb's wool trim around the collar, and a white Stetson. He had grown a goatee as white as the drifting snow. In his left hand he held a cigarette. Even from thirty feet away, Johnny could see he looked older somehow. He stopped the car, set the brake, sat for a moment, and just stared.

"What are you waiting for, Johnny, an invitation? Go see your dad," prodded Rebecca.

"Huh? Yeah, okay. Just give me a second." Checking his face in the rearview mirror as though he were preparing himself to go out on a date, he opened the door and stepped into the snow.

Father and son stared at each other for what seemed like a millennium in time. Country music emanated from the interior of Buck's pickup. Anvil Pine stood like an arrow pointing to the stars. The midnight rendezvous had ferreted the attention of Thunder and Lightning. They came to the fence, nodding and snorting great plumes of white into the cold night.

Johnny looked from his father, to the makeshift cross where Dallas was buried. He took several steps forward, inciting his father to do the same. Spirit Dallas walked cautiously behind Johnny, tail in full wag, tongue drooping from his mouth.

"Hello, son," said Buck, flicking the cigarette to the ground where it rolled and drifted away. "You look good. I didn't think I was ever going to see you again."

"Hi, Dad. It's really good to see you. You look... good too." Johnny could see that his father's eyes were shot red, shimmering with the residue of fresh tears.

When they were close enough, they fell into each other's arms and hugged for a long grateful moment. The full tantamount of Johnny's fears rushed forward; and he shuddered in his father's arms, a child in need of the comforting reassurance of his father, eyes shut tight, loving him though he was a man hardened through and through.

A ghostly wind rushed across the acres, taking Buck's favorite hat with it.

He didn't move. The Stetson sailed into the air, narrowly missing Thunder's long face before it rose into the night and was swallowed by darkness.

The last time Buck Black hugged his son, he believed he would never see him again.

From the interior of the car, Rebecca watched the two men, in the emotional height of the moment, embrace and weep. Dallas circled the legs of both men once and came to a stop on its haunches right next to Johnny's boot, looking up to him with so much adoration it made Rebecca want to cry. She had seen that look before. In another place, in another time, it seemed, between a boy and his bestest friend in the world, captured in malleable light within the sanctity of their barn.

With a great sadness in her heart, knowing that this moment was truly going to be the last time Johnny and his father would ever see each other, Rebecca closed her eyes, leaving the two alone, the silence of her own tears spilling into her hands. The faces of her family flashed as vividly as if they were standing right in front of her. She held them there for a long loving moment, then let them go until she needed them again. Smiling, she wiped at her eyes. When she looked up, Dallas was sitting in the driver's seat. Rebecca laughed and sniffed the running mucus from her nose. "Hello, Dallas," she said.

Spirit Dallas raised a paw, his eyes projecting the verity that he was grateful. His Johnny, his friend, was home.

"You should be with Johnny, Dallas. And you're welcome. I would also like to thank you for saving our lives."

The loyal lab nodded its head and reverently closed its eyes. Rebecca and Dallas shared a solemn moment between the living and the dead. Then Dallas lifted his head, turned in the seat, and leaped through closed the door. He appeared on the other side, sauntered back to Johnny and took his usual place, by his friend's side.

Rebecca straightened, and continued to watch the welcoming between the two men unfold, waiting for the signal from Johnny that meant it was time to meet his father.

Buck extended his arms, held Johnny by the shoulders, his upper lip quivering with emotion. "You've put on some muscle. Good on you, son. At least now I know things weren't too rough for yah." Drawing a hand, he wiped tears away and sniffed, the usual hard glint of his steely eyes now soft, clouded with the love he had for his only son.

Johnny wanted to tell him everything; however, he knew that it would be in everyone's best interest if he didn't. "I hope my running wasn't too much trouble for you, Dad." He ran a forearm across his wet eyes.

"The sheriff's deputies kept me busy for a while. Put a trace on the phone and everythin. Told me they were gonna charge me with aiding and abetting a fugitive. I told them to go ahead and charge me. Then I told them to fuck off. And they did. I still carry a little weight with the old boys. Thankfully, one of them's the mayor and another is the district attorney. Then after a couple of months, they eased up. Sheriff Baxter still drops by every once a while to check up on things. See if I've heard from yah. I tell him the same thing every time. Go fuck yourself. He doesn't like it much, but there ain't a damn thing he can do about it and he knows it."

"What about the Thompson's dad? Did they give you any trouble?"

"Oh, sure. Old man Thompson threatened a wrongful death lawsuit. His lawyer advised him against it. Dwight's brothers, though I have no proof, came out to the ranch one night and shot a bunch of cattle. Fucking cowards. I let word out that if I ever caught any of them on my ranch again, I'd shoot first, ask questions later."

"I'm sorry, Dad."

"There ain't nothin' for yah to be sorry for, Johnny. It was me told yah to run. I still stand by my decision. The main thing is you're all right and no worse for wear."

"How is Rose, Dad?"

"Left me two months ago. Came home one day after ordering some feed, and she was gone with all her stuff. Haven't seen or heard from her since. No matter. I like being alone."

Johnny looked deep into his father's eyes, and saw in them a broken heart, though he'd never admit it. No. Not Buck Black. To admit such a thing was against his character. Nonetheless, the eyes were the mirror to the soul, Johnny now knew, and his father's conveyed within a prism of loneliness. "I'm sorry she left. Are you sure you're all right?"

"Get to eat when I want. Sleep as late as I want, and there's nobody to tell me to pick up after myself. Life couldn't be better, except of course if you were back home. But we both know that's not possible, don't we?"

"Yeah. I've got to keep going."

A prolonged silence ensued before Buck said, "Say, that's a mighty fine feather you got there. Real *unusual*."

Johnny's hand went to its softness. "A friend gave it to me. Someone I met while I was running. Someone special."

"I see," said Buck, noticing the eye. "Someone special you say."

"Very."

"At least you weren't lackin' for company. Speaking of someone special, you gonna introduce me to the young lady I spoke to on the phone? That's her in that fancy car you're drivin', ain't it?"

"Yes. Her name is Rebecca. And we love each other. But before I introduce you to her, I need to tell you that the gun you left me has saved me a couple of times. Rebecca too for that matter. So much has happened, Dad. You wouldn't believe me if I told you."

"No, I don't imagine the past five months have been a picnic for you. I've imagined all kinds of things, and not a lot of them good. If you want to tell me, then that's fine. If you don't, I understand."

"Thanks, Dad. I think it's best if we leave things the way they are. All you need to know is that I'm happy and that Rebecca and I are going to start a new life together."

"That's fine, son. Never let it be said that Buck Black got in the way of true romance. If you're happy, then I'm happy. Now about the gun. Keep it close at hand, Johnny. I imagine it still has a lot of savin' left in it."

"I will, Dad." Johnny turned and gestured with a wave for Rebecca to join them.

Rebecca hesitated for a moment before opening the door and stepping out into the snow. The sudden change in temperature cut right through the parka. Boots crunched loud as she left virgin footprints in the icy surface and made her way toward Johnny, his father, and Dallas who was still sitting in place. Music was playing "I'm Movin' On" by Hank Snow. Though she couldn't see them, the air was heavy with the smell of cattle. Johnny's horses were beginning to get agitated from lack of attention. They snorted boisterously, rearing themselves against the cross fence and knocking it with the hard shanks of their hoofs.

Rebecca took a position next to Johnny, looped an arm through his, her eyes settling on Buck Black's. She smiled sweetly. "Hello, Mr. Black. It's a pleasure to meet you."

"Dad. This is Rebecca. Rebecca, my dad."

Buck took a step forward and extended a hand. Right away he saw the young woman his son had fallen in love with was special. It was in the resonance of her green eyes. They possessed the steely light of mettle, much like his own, and the warmth of a kind heart. If what Johnny said was true, then she too had gone through some tough times. He liked her right away.

To Rebecca, Johnny's dad reminded her of the rough tough cowboys she had seen in movies. John Wayne big, and though his face had been seasoned by the hottest summers and most biting winters, he was handsome in a hard life kind of way. His staring blue eyes dazzled in the headlights, and he seemed to be looking right into her. Johnny's description of him couldn't have been more true. Buck Black was as tough a man she had ever seen. Letting go of Johnny's arm, she took a step forward, and accepted Buck's hand. "I'm sorry you lost your hat."

Buck took her hand between each of his, Rebecca's disappeared. "I'm awful glad to meet you, Rebecca. And don't worry about the hat. Stores are full of 'em."

"It was Rebecca's idea that we come here tonight," said Johnny.

"Is that right?" Buck smiled with genuine gratitude. "Well, thank you, Rebecca. You don't know how grateful I am to see my son again. I can honestly say that I didn't think I would ever see Johnny again. I'm forever in your debt, young lady. I'm just sorry we had to meet under these circumstances and way out here in the middle of nothin'."

"Well, the circumstances can't be changed, but as far as I'm concerned, it's as beautiful a place as any to meet."

"Optimistic. I like that. Shows you got gumption. And if you don't mind my sayin', pretty too. It's no wonder Johnny fell in love with you."

"You have a wonderful son, Mr. Black, and thank you... There's nothing I..."

Buck interrupted. "Call me Buck, please." He let go of her hand.

Rebecca moved next to Johnny, relooped her arm, and looked up at him then back to his father. "Well, as I was saying... Buck. There's nothing I wouldn't do for him and I know he feels the same way I do. You should be very proud of him. I know I am. Your son saved me from a very difficult life. I know you don't know me from Eve, but you can be certain that I'm very much in love with him."

"I know, I know. I can see it in your face. I used to look at his mother the same way, bless her warm heart. Sometimes you gotta go through hell before you realize that heaven is right in front of you. I never realized what I had until Johnny's mother died."

Rear of them, Thunder and Lightning whined for attention. "I don't suppose your visit is gonna be a long one," said Buck. "We better go see them before they take down the fence." He turned and started toward the horses.

When his father was out of earshot, Johnny asked softly, "Is Dallas still here?"

"Yes, Johnny," said Rebecca, clutching his arm tightly. "He's sitting right next to you. Looking at you with so much love I could cry."

Johnny looked down. Seeing Dallas in his mind's eye, he remembered every furry stroke of his golden body. "Hi, boy. I'm glad to see you too."

Spirit Dallas pawed at the air then moved with Johnny when he and Rebecca started after Buck, never taking his eyes off him.

Thunder and Lightning, their faces lit ghostly by the lamps of the vehicles, began to grunt happily, the sound emanating from deep within. Buck was already stroking the white nose of Lightning when Johnny, Rebecca, and Dallas stopped in front of Thunder. Reaching with both hands, Johnny held the horse's face. "There, there, Thunder. I'm happy to see you too. It's been a while."

Thunder lifted its head abruptly and gave Johnny the raspberry, it's lips contorted, revealing large white teeth and the rolling point of its tongue.

Rebecca laughed, reached up and scratched an ear. "Your friends are beautiful and funny, Johnny. It's no wonder you miss them."

"They're just acting up because you're here."

Leaning her face into Thunder's neck, Rebecca stroked the musculature leading to his quarter leg. She could feel the pulse of his emotions, winter fur quivering at her touch. "There, there, Thunder," she whispered into his ear. "I'm awfully glad to meet you too."

Thunder's tail swished at the air, and he let out a deep, relaxing breath.

Seeing that Thunder was receiving all of Johnny and Rebecca's attention, Lightning broke from Buck's affections and moved sideways until it bumped against Thunder, moving him several steps from Johnny's comforting grasp. At sixteen and a half hands high, Lightning lowered its head so that he and Johnny were eye to eye. Lightning's amber glare was moist with crusts of ice clinging to lashes. Johnny took his head in his arms and whispered, "Hello, old friend. I've missed you."

Lightning let out a long pluming breath and settled its head into the crook of Johnny's neck and shoulder.

"You know, it's the damndest thing," said Buck, moving next to Johnny. "I was out here earlier in the day checking on the cattle, makin' sure the coyotes were keeping their distance, and those two were kicking it up like nobody's business. Never seen them act like that before. At least not on a cold day. Now that I think of it, it was like they knew you were coming." He shook some ice crystals from Lightning's mane. "And you know what else? I kinda knew that I was going to be hearing from you very soon. I just kinda had this feelin' for the past couple of days, even though I had it set in my mind I would never see you again. Like I was getting a message." He paused for a moment, looked at the ground, and rubbed his chin inquisitively. When he looked up again, his steely eyes locked on to Johnny's. "Somehow I knew you wouldn't be alone."

Johnny lifted his love embrace from Lightning's neck and looked to Rebecca who was smiling approvingly and scratching the bridge of Thunder's nose. "Well, Dad. To make a long story short, it was probably Rebecca who sent you that feeling. Don't ask me how because I really don't understand all of it myself, but Becca is special. She has a gift. A gift that has saved our lives more than once already."

Buck looked past Johnny to Rebecca who smiled at him passively. Without taking his eyes from her, he said, "You know. It was your mother who convinced me of those who were gifted. Told me stories 'bout your grandmother and the old ones." His eyes moved so that he was looking directly into Johnny's again. "If what you say is true, and I know that it's entirely possible, then you're lucky you found her."

"Yeah. I know, Dad. I don't know where I would be if we hadn't found each other."

There was a contemplative moment between them. A streak of blue exploded from the blaze of stars above, arcing toward the earth, catching the attention of both men who looked up to watch it fall. Father and son knew instinctively it was the last shooting star they would share together.

Spirit Dallas moved from Johnny's side and went to Rebecca, tail wagging gently. He sat in front of her, looking at her as though he were expecting something to happen between them. "What is it?" she asked softly.

The faithful lab looked back to Johnny and Buck. He whimpered a long, melancholic sound that nearly tore Rebecca's heart in two. When he looked back to Rebecca, he had already begun to fade. It was time for him to go back to the other side.

Rebecca watched as he became less and less, the final measure of him to disappear, the length of his outreached paw and the gratuitous glint in his caramel-colored eyes. A gust of wind blew as if it were signaling his withdrawal to another world, where six-almost seven-year-old boys played with their pets and loved ones reunited. Where heart of hearts roamed freely to live another lifetime, an alternative journey begun. Quickly Rebecca wiped the tears that had escaped and rested her head against Thunder's face.

The cold wind subsided. Strained country music played in its wake, lending a surreal atmosphere to the reticent meeting.

Buck broke the silence. "Before I forget. I brought you some more money. Thought you could use it." He turned to go back to the truck.

"Dad? Dad? It's okay. We don't need any more money."

Buck stopped abruptly and turned back to Johnny. "You don't need any money. Everybody needs more money."

"You keep it, Dad. Rebecca and I don't need any."

Rebecca moved to Johnny. "Thank you, Buck, but Johnny's right. We're fine as far as far as our finances go."

Buck stared at them for a quick moment, rubbed at the whiskers of his goatee. "You say you're fine for money. The way I see it, you two are on the lamb. You can never have enough when you're runnin'. It would make me feel a whole lot better if you took it."

Johnny opened his mouth to protest; however, Buck raised a hand, stopping him short. "Now I won't take no for an answer. Maybe you do have some money. God knows where you got *it* and that car from, and I ain't gonna ask. But like I said, it would make me feel better if you did." He turned again and headed for his truck. The clandestine meeting between father and son was over.

Johnny patted the space between Lightning's ears. "Run," he told him. "Run free, my friend. I won't forget you. Not ever."

Lightning held Johnny's eyes for a moment, turned from the fence, kicked his rear legs high, then bolted into the darkness.

"Go, Thunder," said Johnny.

Thunder hesitated for a second before he too bolted from the fence and disappeared beyond the scope of artificial light.

Rebecca and Johnny listened until the horses were far enough away so that all they could hear was the haunting breath of night sighing through the branches of Anvil Pine and the sad verses emanating from Buck's truck:

She's had eighteen years
to get ready for this day
She should be past the tears
She cries some anyway.

Looking toward the ground around him, Johnny asked, "Is Dallas still with us?"

"Sorry, Johnny," said Rebecca, resting her head on his shoulder and wiping a tear from her eye. "Dallas went back to the other side only moments ago. I did thank him for saving our lives in Vegas."

"Oh." Johnny looked to the makeshift cross and the collar centering its apex. "Well, it was nice to know he was here for a little while. Do you think he knows how grateful we are for what he did?"

"You can count on it," she said confidently. "I guess we should take the money your dad wants to give us. He'll worry if we don't, and I don't think you want your dad worrying about us."

"Yeah. I guess you're right. I've given him enough cause to worry." He put an arm across her shoulders. "I sure do hate leaving him like this though. He's all alone now in that big house. I'm going to worry about him."

"Your dad doesn't strike me as the type of man who will just sit back and let old age take over. He'll be fine, Johnny. Honest. I can feel it."

"I guess that makes me feel a little better. Do you think we should tell him where we're going?"

"No, Johnny! He'll be better off not knowing. If he knew where we were headed, he might try to find you and that could cause all kinds of problems. Not just for us, but for him as well. We don't know where Mr. Black is, and you sure as hell don't want him in your father's life."

Buck returned, carrying an envelope in front of him. "Here. You take this now." He pushed the envelope toward Johnny; however, it was Rebecca who accepted it.

"Thank you, Buck. We'll make good use of it. Won't we, Johnny?"

"Yes. Thanks, Dad. We appreciate it."

"Think nothin' of it. I just hope it helps getting you two to wherever it is you're headin'." A fatherly idea crossed his mind, though he already knew what the answer would be. "You know, it might not be a bad idea to stay at the house tonight. Get a good night's rest before you head off again."

"That's very kind of you, Buck," said Rebecca. "But it would be best if we didn't. I hope you understand."

"I guess I kinda do."

Another cold gust gave Rebecca a shiver and blew Johnny's hair about his face. The notion of spending a night in his own bed was a comforting one; nonetheless, Rebecca was right, it was out of the question.

"I suppose I should let the both of you get goin'," said Buck, looking fondly at his son. "Bad weather headin' this way from the north. Wouldn't want you catchin' a cold on my account." Moving close to Johnny, he stuck out his hand. Johnny accepted it and the two held on to each other for a father-and-son moment. Johnny saw that his father's eyes had taken on the liquescent shine of sentiment again. "Don't worry about us, Dad. We'll be fine."

Buck let go of Johnny's hand, grabbed him by the shoulders, and hugged him hard. "All I've ever wanted from you is to be the very best man you can be. Go be a man, Johnny. I love you, son. I hope the both of you find happiness wherever it is you end up."

"I love you too, Dad. I'll miss you."

Buck held him at arm's length. "Until we meet again, Johnny. Now if you don't mind, I would like to speak to your lady friend for a minute. Alone." He looked to Rebecca who was having difficulty keeping her emotions in check. "Do you mind, Rebecca?"

"No, of course not," she said. "Wait for me in the car, Johnny. I'll be right there." She handed him the envelope.

Johnny looked to his father again. An understanding was exchanged. Without another word, he headed back to the cramped confines of the RX7.

Stepping close to Rebecca, Buck Black put his hands on her shoulders and regarded her with the eyes of someone who needed affirmation. He smiled. Rebecca smiled back. "If what Johnny says is true, then you are of a special breed, young lady. I can't pretend to understand it at all 'cause I don't, being a man of simple ministrations. You say you love my son."

"Yes, Buck. More than you can imagine."

"Then promise me you'll take good care of him. He's all I got left."

"I will, Buck. You have my word."

"Then that's all I need to know. You go to him now. And Godspeed, Rebecca."

Enveloping her arms around Buck's thick chest, she stretched her frame as tall as it would reach and kissed him on the cheek. "I'm glad I had the opportunity to meet you, Buck. I now know where Johnny gets his strength from. Good-bye." She let him go.

"Good-bye, young lady," said Buck Black, and wiped at the wetness in his eyes for he knew he would never see his son again. At least not in the way he hoped. Turning, shoulders slumped, he went to his truck, closed the door, killed the soft twang of music, and lit up a smoke, fresh tears wetting his gruff face.

For a brief moment, Rebecca stood in front of Anvil Pine, her shadow long and narrow across its facade. She looked to the single cross emerging from the snow-covered ground, where it would soon be joined by another with Johnny's name inscribed on it, knowing with absolute certainty that Buck Black *would* see his son again. It would be on the day he buried him at this very special place.

Buck's truck moved forward and around the RX7.

Rebecca went to the car, got in, closed the door, and fastened her seat belt. "Your dad's a very nice man," she said to Johnny who was watching the pickup in the rearview.

"Yeah. I know."

"So where to now?"

Slipping the gear into first, Johnny turned so he was following the taillights of the truck. "I think we should go back to Great Falls and find a motel where we can spend the night. Get a fresh start to the border in the morning."

"Sounds like a good plan. What did you do with the money your dad gave us?"

"It's in the glove compartment. We can put it with the rest of the money once we're settled at a motel."

"Okay." Rebecca was quiet with her own thoughts for a moment. "Johnny?"

"Yes, Becca."

"You don't have to worry about your dad. He's going to be fine. He's stronger than you know."

Johnny made no comment. He continued to follow the red taillights until they reached the area of the ranch where they would have to exit. Buck Black stopped the truck. Johnny pulled even. Through the glass, father and son looked at each other. Buck drew hard on his cigarette, the orange glow illuminating his rough features.

"Wait a second!" said Rebecca, and reached into the backseat. She retrieved the million dollar photo. Quickly she opened the door and went to the pickup.

Buck powered the window. "What's this?" he asked as Rebecca handed him the photo.

"It's for you. A kind of keepsake."

Buck looked at the picture and sniffed fresh tears. "Thank you, Rebecca. Thank you very much. I'll treasure it always."

"You're welcome." A moment of silence passed between them as though neither wanted to say good-bye again. Buck stared at the photo. Happier times frozen forever.

"I guess I should get back to the car," said Rebecca.

"Be safe, young lady."

"You too, Buck."

The window went up. Rebecca returned to the car and settled in.

Johnny honked the horn once. Buck did the same. In the semidarkness, they smiled at each other. Not a good-bye. There could never be another good-bye. More like "Until we meet again, Dad. Yes, son. Until we meet again."

The pickup continued toward the ranch house, swallowed by the encompassing arms of night.

Johnny watched until he could see it no further. Reaching for the stereo, he gave it life.

And the cats and the cradle
And the silver spoon
Little boy blue and the man in the moon
When you comin' home, son
I don't know when
But we'll get together then, Dad
You know we'll have a good time then...

A single tear slid over Johnny's cheek. They exited the Double B ranch.

Lost in thought, Rebecca stared at the darkness. Blindly she reached for his hand, taking it, holding it forever tight, seeing vividly the cross with his name on it rooted next to Dallas's

They left the place where Johnny grew up and where his mortal self would be laid to rest. Home. Forever home. Using the back roads from which they came, the fated lovers headed northwest toward Great Falls, Montana.

Another page turned.

* * *

73

December 29

AFTER a hardy breakfast of flapjacks and sausages at the local IHOP, Rebecca and Johnny started their trek toward the Canadian border. During the night, as predicted by Johnny's father, a system had moved into Montana, dropping several inches of snow. Fortunately, in the wee hours of morning, snowplows had removed the surface snow from the highway and the squall had given in to a beautiful sunny day. They were listening to a station broadcasting all the way from Seattle.

"We're doing it, Johnny! We're really on our way!"

"Let's not put the cart before the horse. We still have to get across the border."

"It'll be a snap. You'll see."

"Still. The thought of me in the trunk while you talk our way across is a bit frightening. Scratch that. Is very frightening."

"I have no ill feelings about what we're going to do. If I did, do you think I would even attempt putting us in danger?"

"I don't know. Would you?"

"Of course not. We would just find some other place to hide. So you can relax. As far as my intuition goes, we're going to be fine. At least for the time being." She increased the volume.

I can't light, no more of your darkness
All my pictures, seem to fade to black and white
I'm growing tired and time stands still before me
Frozen here, on the ladder of my life

Too late, to save myself from falling
I took a chance, and changed your way of life
But you misread, my meaning when I met you
Closed the door, and left me blinded by the light

Don't let the sun go down on me
Although I search myself, it's always someone else I see
I'd just allow a fragment of your life to wander free
But losing everything, is like the sun going down on me...

For nearly three hours, they drove toward the invisible border dividing Canada and the United States into their respective countries. When they came to a posted sign informing them that they were only twenty miles to the Port of Piegan border station, Rebecca said, "It's time for you to get in the trunk. See if you can find someplace where we can do it without being seen."

Johnny found the shell of a BP station that had long since seen better days. The single-storey building had succumbed to a fire, the windows smashed out and white stucco scarred black around the window frames. Its facade had been spray-painted with graffiti. Pulling off the highway, he drove to the back of the building where a gathering of crows and magpies lifted into the air having been disturbed from their feasting on the carcass of dead cat. They came to rest in the bare branches of a nearby poplar.

A green disposal container sat empty. A stack of used tires stood four feet high, reminding him of the almost-sexual rendezvous he had had with a very amorous Native girl named Justine. Popping the trunk, Johnny left the RX7 running. "I guess this is where I get in," he said with a half smile.

"It won't be for long. I promise. Once we're across the border, I'll find a place to let you out. Now give me a good luck kiss."

Johnny leaned toward Rebecca. They kissed. "Give me the gun," he said. "I'll put it in the knapsack."

Opening the glove compartment, Rebecca handed him the .38. "Do you think we should get rid of it? Just in case."

Johnny thought for a moment, his father's words coming back to him. "*I imagine it still has a lot of savin' left in it.*" "No. I don't think that's a good idea. If we get caught, we get caught. It's not going to matter if we have a gun with us or not. Besides, you've already assured me that that won't happen. And if we should run into Mr. Black again. Well, it would be comforting to know that I can defend us against him."

"Yes, you're right. We keep the gun." Unfastening the seat belt, she reached into the back, retrieved the knapsack full of money, and handed it to Johnny who unzipped it and laid the gun on top of the bills. "Well. Here I go." Opening the door, he stepped into the cold air.

Rebecca followed him, sinuses assaulted by the decomposing body of what used to be an orange tabby. There was little snow behind the once-upon-a-time gas station. Nonetheless, the air was bitterly cold and it sharked into her face.

Stepping into the trunk, Johnny lay on his side with the knapsack held to his chest. He smiled up at Rebecca. "Try not to hit too many potholes. Okay?"

"I'll do my best."

"See you in about an hour."

"No more than that. I promise."

"I love you."

"I love you too, Johnny." Taking hold of the trunk lid, she closed it with a locking click. "You comfortable?" she asked through the trunk.

Johnny's muffled voice replied, "As best as can be expected."

Hearing Johnny's voice coming from the interior of the trunk took Rebecca back to a time when she too had been placed into the cramped space of a trunk. Shaking the image, she looked into the tree where the birds of salvage sat waiting for them to leave. She had never seen a magpie before and found the black-and-white birds pretty, though they were nothing more than scavengers, like their black cousins. Gently, she placed her hand on the trunk and whispered, "Be safe, my love. I'll see you soon."

Once she was behind the wheel, she checked herself in the mirror, fastened her seat belt, and slipped the gear into first. The RX7 rolled forward without a hitch. Driving to the front of the white elephant, she waited for a semi to pass then took to the highway, changing gears until she was traveling at the posted rate of speed and headed to the border station, mind traveling just as fast as she was, a twisting knot of fear constricting her stomach.

Cocooned in absolute darkness, Johnny could feel the cold of the trunk filter through his coat and jeans. He listened to the rise and fall of the engine. Rebecca was doing fine. He closed his eyes. The volume of music increased. Eric Clapton's "Pretending" He let his mind wander. Instantly, it created the spectral memory of Dallas, his father, Thunder and Lightning, and finally, his mother, Linda Birdhumming. *How an instant in time had changed everything.* He would still be at home if it were not for the immoral actions of the Thompson brothers and his own manner of vengeance. Then again, he never would have met Rebecca. *Kismet truly was a strange bedfellow.* With happier times running through his mind, he listened to the music and hoped with all his judicious might that they make it to Destiny, Alberta, without incident, providence once again guiding their purpose.

That's when she said she was pretending
Like she knew the plan
That's when I knew she was pretending
Pretending to understand
Pretending, pretending
Pretending, pretending

Satisfied but lost in love
Situations change
You're never who you used to think you are
How strange

I get lost in alibis
Sadness can't prevail
Everybody knows strong love
Can't fail...

* * *

It was almost 3:00 p.m. by the time Rebecca reached the Port of Piegan border crossing. Signs in French and English welcomed travelers to Canada. All five stations were open, and there was a long line of trucks, cars, and mobile homes waiting to cross. She selected the third station from the left and pulled in behind an older model station wagon. Turning off the music, she hoped Johnny understood they were about to cross over.

Finding the handbag, she removed all identification announcing her as Tiffany Rose, born and raised resident of Las Vegas Nevada. When she opened the passport and its photo of a redheaded Rebecca, she froze with sudden doubts about how easy it was going to be to cross. Hopefully the border guard could see that she and the photo were of the same person or there was going to be more trouble than she could handle.

The station wagon moved one vehicle length, leaving only three more before it was her turn to lie through her teeth. "Johnny!" she called out loudly. If you can hear me, bang on the trunk!"

Thump! Thump! Thump! was Johnny's response.

"We're almost to the border station, so it's very important that you be as still as possible, okay?"

Johnny replied with a muffled "Okay" and, just in case, hit the trunk lid one more time. *Thump!*

Rebecca took a deep breath to settle the queasy feeling she suddenly had. She focused on the two flagpoles bearing the Canadian maple leaf and U.S. Stars and Stripes separating the people traffic coming or going from one country to the next.

The station wagon moved ahead another car length.

Checking herself in the rearview mirror, she pulled the hood over her head so it covered her now-short black hair. She looked at the passport again. With the hood covering the dye job, she could easily be seen as the person staring back at her. Satisfied, her gaze went to the guard occupying the station she was about to enter.

Behind the glass was a large black woman who was inspecting the passports of a couple who were stopped parallel to the window. The large woman made a motion with her arm, and Rebecca realized that she was ordering the couple to move to one of the inspection stations. *Great,* thought Rebecca. *You chose the line where the guard was either having a bad day or she was just plain overzealous in her job. Can't change lanes now. That would certainly raise the suspicion of anyone watching.* She went over her story about having to visit a sickly aunt in Calgary. As she mentally examined what she was going to say, she realized it sounded a little suspicious, even to her. And if it sounded like a lie to herself, then it was certainly going to sound skeptical to anyone else.

The station wagon pulled up to the window. The driver, a man, handed the portly woman his passport. Words were exchanged.

Think, Rebecca, think.

After a long minute, the gate arm went up and a green light told Rebecca it was now or never. Nervously she moved ahead, swallowed the lump in her throat, and told herself to calm down. When she was directly in front of the boarder guard who had watched her approach, Rebecca powered the window and smiled. Cold air rushed at her face.

Passively, the guard whose name was Louise Parrera according to the photo ID she wore, asked, "What's your purpose for entering Canada?" She held out her hand for Rebecca's passport.

Still smiling, Rebecca handed the fake passport over and explained, "I'm on my way to visit my fiancé in Calgary. So that we can spend New Year's together. We're getting married in May. I couldn't get a flight out being the holidays so I decided to drive."

Louise Parrera examined the passport and took a good, long look at Rebecca. "Are you carrying any weapons or alcohol? Do you have anything to declare, Ms. Rose?" Eyes moved to the backseat and settled on the suitcase.

"I did buy my fiancé a new tie. I have the receipt here someplace. And no, I don't have any weapons or alcohol." She began to fish through the pockets of her coat.

"That's fine, Ms. Rose. And how long will you be staying in Canada?"

"Just for a week. Though I wish it were longer. I miss him terribly. We've had a long-distance relationship for two years now." *You're blabbing. Stop it!*

Louise made a few key strokes on her computer. She looked at Rebecca again, closed the passport, and handed it back to her. "Enjoy your stay," she said with a hint of a smile. The gate arm went up. Another green light told her to proceed.

"Thank you. I will." Rebecca took the passport, sat it on the seat next to her, powered the window, and eased her foot off the clutch. In the time it took for her to get her heart started again, they were in Canada. Sighing with great relief, she saw that the couple who had been directed to the inspection station were standing outside their vehicle, arms crossed. A heavyset guard, and a leashed German shepherd circled the Dodge with vigilance.

Rebecca continued at a moderate rate of speed, tears of relief covering her cheeks. Triumphantly she called out to Johnny. "We made it, Johnny! We're through! We're now in Canada! I'll get you out as soon as I find a suitable place!"

A thump emanated from the trunk and was followed by a stifled "HURRAY!"

Cranking the music, Rebecca took to Highway 2. The station out of Seattle sizzled with static, so she searched for another, finding, according to a DJ's blurb, "The Eagle." 100.9 out of Okotoks. When he was done, he told his listeners that it was -15° Celsius in Okotoks, Destiny, and Turner Valley. Then he introduced the next song, a classic by Canada's own, Burton Cummings. Fittingly, "Break It to Them Gently" filled the small space.

According to a green–and-white distance marker, Calgary was 267 kilometers away. Some quick math and a mental map of Alberta told Rebecca Destiny, their destiny, was somewhere between a two- and three-hour drive.

Unbeknown to the running lovers was that Mr. Green, Yuri, and the killer Cracker were less than half a day's drive behind them.

'Cause I'm runnin' with a gun and it isn't any fun as a fugitive
Fightin' for my life and I don't know if I'll make it alone
Runnin' with a gun and it isn't any fun as a fugitive
God, I wanna go home
Lord, I wish I was home…

* * *

74

Destiny

WITHIN an hour, Rebecca reached an area christened Crow's Nest Pass. This was where Highway 2 became less trafficked. Everywhere she looked there were forests after forests of evergreens and snow. The sky remained blue, an odd cotton ball of cloud dotted it here and there. She knew that somewhere nearby, the Canadian Rockies would reveal themselves. It was time to locate a side road to release Johnny from his confined space. She took to the number 9 highway.

With a keen eye, she spotted a side road covered in snow that ventured far into a forest on her left side. Gearing down, she left the highway and proceeded to go deep into the woods. Feeling she was sufficiently out of sight, she applied the emergency brake, popped the trunk, cranked the heater to maximum, and hurried out of the car. A chilling wind met her head-on, the sound of it rushing through the trees.

Johnny was out of the trunk by the time she reached him, shaking so badly from the small deep freeze, he looked as though he would jump right out of his skin. Dropping the knapsack, he opened his arms.

Rebecca fell into them. They held each other for several heartbeats before either spoke. "I'm so sorry for taking so long, my love. I had to be sure we weren't going to be seen."

Teeth chattering, Johnny said, "The... the... the main th-th-thing is th-th-that we ma-ma-made it." A broad smile lit his face.

With brisk strokes, Rebecca rubbed his back, his neck, his arms. On tiptoes, she kissed his blue lips. "Come on. Let's get you into the car where it's nice and warm." She lifted the knapsack, deposited it into the trunk and slammed the lid. Walking Johnny to the passenger side, she opened the door and helped him in. Peter Frampton's "Do You Feel Like We Do" spilled into the wilderness.

Once Rebecca was behind the wheel, she lowered the volume on the radio, looked to Johnny who was staring at the landscape. "We'll just sit still for a while and let the heater raise your temperature."

After a few minutes, the chill in Johnny's face and teeth ceased their biting dance. "Holy fuck, it was cold in there. I've never felt a cold like that in my life. For a while there I thought I might freeze to death and you wouldn't even know, you were playing the music so loud. What a surprise that would have been for you."

"Again, I'm sorry, Johnny. You don't know how frightened I was that we would get caught somehow. I had to be sure."

Closing his eyes, Johnny adjusted the seat so he was almost lying and rubbed the feeling back into his cheeks with the palms of his hands. "It's a good thing I love you as much as I do or I might be a little bit angry. But I do understand. You had to be sure. It's a good thing we bought these down-filled coats, or you might have found a Johnnysicle when you opened the trunk."

"That's funny, in a morose kind of way. The main thing is you're fine. And we're in Canada, Johnny. We get to start anew. Just us and nobody else. Tony Millions's men will never find us here." Even as she spoke the words, a knowing awareness told her otherwise. But she had to keep Johnny on a positive note, reassure him that everything was going to be all right. Though she knew with all her heart that his time on this earth was drawing to an end. And as promised, she would go with him.

Johnny opened his eyes. "You know, I'm already feeling 80 percent recovered."

"That's great, my love. We'll stay here until you're fully recovered then it's off to Destiny. It's no more than two hours from here. We're on the number 9 highway, and that will take us to the twenty-second highway, and from there it's just a hop skip and a jump to our new lives. And you know what?"

"What?"

"According to a sign I saw, there's this place called Head-Smashed-In Buffalo Jump. Does it mean what I think it means?"

"Yes. In the old days, Natives on horseback would direct herds of buffalo toward the edge of a cliff where they would just go over and kill themselves instead of turning around and charging their pursuers. Nobody ever said buffalo were very smart. It was an easy hunt, and the meat would feed the villages for the whole winter, not to mention the hides provided for warm clothing. You see, at one point in time in history and not so long ago, there were herds of buffalo as large as the state of Texas. Westerners would just shoot them randomly for no other reason than they got to kill something. Nobody thought about the consequences. Just like the fish of the oceans today, they're a vanishing species. I'm surprised they didn't teach you that in school."

"What I learned in high school could fit in a shoe box. I sucked at math, language arts, and science. I did however come away with a good geographical understanding of the planet."

"Then how did you get so smart?"

"I guess from reading. I did a lot of that back in Bay Ridge Cove. Did you know that where we're going there's this anomaly called a chinook wind that raises the temperature dramatically. It can be well below zero one day and the next, be warm enough to wear T-shirt and shorts. If my memory serves me correctly, this indifference of weather only occurs in Alberta and Sweden. Isn't that something?"

"I wouldn't mind if it started blowing right now. I guess we both learned something we didn't know before." Johnny's body temperature was rising quickly though his feet still felt like they were encased in ice. "I think we can go now. I'm feeling much better."

"Are you sure?'

"Yes. I can't wait to get to Destiny and start over. Just you and me and our *good* memories. Where we can put all the bad behind us." He looked at the dash. "You better stop at the next gas station. We're a little low on fuel, and I'm kind of hungry."

"How on earth am I going to afford that appetite of yours? We'll be broke within a month." She laughed and Johnny laughed with her. Another much-appreciated moment.

Rebecca made a three-point turn, front tires catching in the snow and spinning before they took hold. Reaching, she took Johnny's hand in hers. "Remember always that I love you, Johnny Black. No matter what the future holds for us."

"I will, Becca. As I've promised. Forever and a day." Adjusting the seat so he was sitting, he reached for the volume of the radio and turned it loud.

The long and winding road
That leads to your door
Will never disappear
I've been down that road before
Don't leave me waiting here
Standing at your door...

Rebecca guided the RX7 onto Highway 9 and headed east, the winter sun a golden disk above, the vast kingdom of natural wonder all around them. Not two hours away, the avaricious sum of their destiny awaited.

* * *

They stopped at Pincher Creek to refuel the car and Johnny's appetite. The people they encountered were friendly to a fault and had a healthy glow about them that reminded Rebecca of athletes she had seen during the last Olympics. "Do you think everyone in Canada is as friendly as they were?" she asked Johnny who was stuffing his face with hot dog and fries.

"Not all people are nice, Becca, you know that as well as I do. But my dad always told me that Canadians were among the nicest people in the world." Taking another bite from his hot dog, he said, "Let's hope the people of Destiny are just as friendly."

Once they were on Highway 22, they passed through the before-mentioned Head-Smashed-In Buffalo Jump. From there, the highway snaked through snow-covered hills that rose and fell all around.

According to the digital, it was 5:35 when they crossed a stanchion bridge over a partially frozen Highwood River and into the village of Longview. A quaint spot with an Esso gas station, liquor store, restaurants, local watering hole, firehouse, school and gift shop, each ablaze with colorful Christmas lights. Daylight was swiftly surrendering to the looming night. It was here that the Rocky Mountains revealed themselves in all their majestic glory. With the sinking sun nestled at their summit, the conventionally white rugged peaks were painted in contrasting shadows, cutting a dazzling sharpness into the waning blue sky. The foothills leading toward them were aligned with forests of spruce and pine, like legions of soldiers heading for the escarpment of ancient rock.

Rebecca killed the radio. "Oh my god, Johnny. Will you look at that? They're so big and so beautiful. Much bigger than anything we've seen."

Johnny whistled. "Wow. It looks as though you could just reach out and touch them."

Ahead of them, a white RCMP cruiser was parked on the edge of town just in front of a green-and-white sign announcing that they were only sixteen kilometers from their destination and nineteen kilometers from a town called Turner Valley.

"Watch your speed, Becca. That's a radar up ahead."

As soon as they were on the outskirts of town, the posted speed of 50 increased to 80 kph and the highway rose dramatically. Rebecca geared to fourth. Since the RX7 was only equipped with mph, she had to equate what the accurate rate of speed was. "That's something we'll have to get used to," she said. "Converting metric to what we're used to. They do things differently up here."

"You're right. I almost forgot. Liters for gallons. Kilograms instead of pounds and so on. It's a good thing for us I was pretty good at math."

"Okay, smarty. How fast should I be going?"

Johnny thought for a moment. "It's about forty-five miles an hour give or take."

Rebecca looked to the speedometer. She was coasting at a reasonable 40. "I'll just keep here. That way we won't give anyone reason to pull us over."

"Good idea. So how did you know how fast to go once we were over the border?"

"That was easy. I just kept up with the car in front of me. I had no idea if I was speeding or not and figured if anyone was going to get pulled over, it would be the person in front of us. When there was nobody in front of us, I kept the vehicle at the rate of speed U.S. highways conform to. Couldn't be much different, right?"

"See. There you go. Being all clever again. So what should we do once we get to Destiny?"

"I think we should convert about a thousand dollars to Canadian. But the banks are probably closed by now, so we'll have to wait until tomorrow. When we arrive, we'll find a nice motel and stay there for a few days before we decide our next course of action. Maybe there's a house we could rent for a while. We'll just pay cash for everything."

"Okay, if you say so. But when the banks open in the morning, you go in. They may not be receptive to someone who looks like me. Ask a lot of questions."

"You worry too much. People are different up here. There's not a lot of bigotry like there is in the good old US of A. You'll see. Canadians see each other as equals, no matter what the skin color. At least that's what I've heard."

"I hope you're right. Things are going to be difficult as it is. We don't need anyone looking down at us or questioning our activities because I happen to be part Indian."

"You'll win everyone over with your charm and good looks. You'll see. I'll probably have to fight the women off with a whip and a chair."

"I hope you're right, but somehow I get the feeling we're in cowboy and redneck country. And those boys just don't like my kind. Never have, probably never will."

* * *

Ranches for as far as the eye could see and towering pushes of earth that rose and fell measured the landscape between towns. The odd oil derrick, evidence of what boosted Alberta's economy, stood like hulking hammers. Scattered among many of the fields were rolls of hay, their rounded bulks dusted in snow. Another mile into the drive, the sun melted over the horizon, converting the topography into blue-black shadows.

As the up-and-down-again highway fell into another valley, Destiny came into view. Like Longview, Christmas lights painted the town in a kaleidoscope of color.

The speed limit fell to seventy then quickly to fifty kilometers.

Rebecca slowed the vehicle more so than needed. She wanted to take it all in, though night's awakened shadows cloaked their surroundings in a spurious mask. The headlights of a logging truck, fully loaded with stripped pine, and traveling well beyond the speed limit appeared in the rearview. Rebecca paid it no mind and continued at a leisurely pace.

They came upon a herd of fenced-in animals standing stationary in the snow that were difficult to identify because of night's shadows and their size. Too big to be deer and too small to be horses. The headlights of the RX7 gave life to a large white sign. Scripted in black letters was Elk Meat For Sale. Across from the farm was a hospital, and small community of houses lit with the celebrated radiance of Christmas.

A community board welcomed them to historic Destiny and announced a food drive that had already occurred on December 17 and 18. From there, into town, streetlamps were decorated with bright candy canes, reindeer, and Christmas wreaths. Highway 22 became Government Road where plumes of smoke rose from chimneys. Garbed in colourful lights, Giant evergreens stood rigid. The entire scene beckoned a welcome to all who entered its limits.

Rebecca took to the shoulder, and stopped the car. The logging truck roared by, its driver hell-bent for leather. From out of nowhere, red and blue lights flashed. A white cruiser chased the reckless driver into town.

"We're here, Johnny! Isn't it beautiful? I imagined all along what Destiny might look like, and true to my suspicions, it's exactly how I perceived it to be. I can't wait to see it when the sun rises."

Johnny's focus was on a couple of horses grazing snow-covered ground on a large property with house and barn. Turning to her, he said, "I'll be a lot more comfortable once we find a place to rest our heads. But you're right. It is beautiful. Pretty as a postcard."

Taking to the road again, they came to the flashing lights of a crosswalk. Rebecca geared down and came to a stop. A man wearing a dark parka so thick and encompassing it looked as though it had swallowed him was walking a black Newfoundlander and Yorkie. The sight comical to say the least. The Yorkie wore a set of reindeer antlers on its small head and the Labrador had a Christmas tie around its neck that twinkled green, red, and blue. Once the unusual trio crossed, Rebecca proceeded cautiously, for the policemen had caught up to the speeding driver of the logging truck and was speaking to him through an open window, cruiser lights blaring red and blue.

As soon as they passed, Rebecca spotted an illuminated motel sign that read, The

Cowboy Trail Motel. *Johnny was right. This was cowboy country. And where there were cowboys, there were truck driving, womanizing, ignorant rednecks.* Engaging the signal, she turned into the parking lot. Vehicles of one sort or another were parked in front of small units. "You wait here. I'm going to see if they have a vacancy, though it doesn't look promising."

"I think that's a good idea," he said, the marquee above bright and telling. "Me being an Indian and all."

Rebecca slapped him on the shoulder and kissed his cheek. "I'll only be a minute or two. And stop worrying. It's only a sign. A way to attract tourists." She left the engine running and went to the office.

Once inside, she saw that there was no one behind the desk and that a small sign said, Ring Bell for Manager. On the counter was a silver bell so she tapped it a couple of times. When appropriate time passed, and she thought she should do it again, footsteps echoed from somewhere behind the counter where a curtain hid an entry into another part of the motel. It parted. A small woman, probably well into her sixties, stepped up to the counter. "Can I help you, miss."

"Yes," said Rebecca. "I was wondering if you have a room to rent?"

"Sorry, dearie. Booked right through to next week. You might try the Destiny Hotel. It's just down the street on the southwest corner. Where the four-way is. They might be able to help you, though it is almost New Year's."

"Thank you," said Rebecca. "The Destiny Hotel. Just down the street."

"Yup. You can't miss it. Been there since 1937."

"Well, thank you again. Sorry to have bothered you."

"No bother, dearie. I hope you find what you're looking for."

"So do I." Rebecca left the small office and returned to the car.

"Any luck?" asked Johnny.

Rebecca buckled in. "Not here, but there's a hotel just down the street. At the four-way stop. They might have something, though the woman here said it might be difficult because it's almost New Year's.

"I hope we don't end up having to sleep in the car. It's awfully cold out."

Rebecca looked at him, and wondered how long their intrepid flight to Destiny, Alberta, was going to prolong the inevitable, for she knew nothing in this world could stop fate once it had you in its command. "We'll be okay. I told you. This is where we need to be. Destiny, Alberta, is where the next step of our journey begins. This much I'm certain of. Be a little more optimistic, Johnny. We'll be fine." She volunteered a beautiful smile. "We'll find a room. Don't you worry about it."

"Okay, if you say so."

"I do. Next stop, the Destiny Hotel."

They arrived at the only four-way stop in town. The hotel was situated on the southwest corner, just as the manager of the Cowboy Trail Motel had told her. A large marquee advertised that Diamond Bob and the Boys were going to play on New Year's Eve and that there was no cover charge. Katty-corner to the hotel was a real estate office, pizza parlor, and the town clock, which was not functioning. It read 9:35.

Each of the businesses, in harmony with the houses they had passed were lit with brilliant displays of Christmas lights, creating a picture-perfect holiday missive. Searching for a place to park, they found that all the spots assigned to the hotel were occupied. "I guess I better circle the block."

"The hotel must be busy," said Johnny. "Try over there in front of that pharmacy. I think I see a spot."

Rebecca turned left onto Center Street, locating a narrow space in front of a Pharmasave. Pulling even with a pickup, she measured the distance she had to work with. "It's going to be a tight fit."

"You want me to park?"

"I think I can manage." Slowly she maneuvered the RX7 between the pickup and a newer version of the Volkswagen. With only inches to spare, she managed it on the first attempt. "Are you impressed?" she asked, killed the engine and set the brake.

"Very. I couldn't have done better myself."

For a few moments, they people-watched. Some held shopping bags. Others were just out for a stroll. Johnny was relieved to see that several were Natives. Almost directly across the street was yet another pharmacy and a fifties-style restaurant called Marv's Classic Soda Shop. There was a bakery. A Pop's barbershop and like the competing pharmacies, another pizza parlor, each past preserved, looking every bit the part of their former days. "It's so quaint," breathed Rebecca. "I can't wait to take a stroll through it all."

"We better get to the hotel before someone steals our room on us."

Rebecca popped the lid on the trunk. Johnny removed the .38 from the glove compartment, jammed it deep into a pocket, then retrieved the suitcase before exiting the vehicle.

Rebecca leaned into the trunk and opened the knapsack while Johnny stood watch, and collected what she estimated was a thousand dollars give or take. "This should do us for the time being," she said, stuffing the bills into her jeans. Johnny flung the knapsack over his shoulder. Rebecca closed the trunk, looped her arm through his, and they proceeded toward the recently renovated Destiny Hotel.

Each person encountered either nodded a greeting, said hello or season's greetings. Rebecca and Johnny opined each and every courtesy with greetings of their own.

"See. I told you the people would be different here."

"Yeah. So far so good. Let's keep our fingers crossed and hope they're this friendly all the time, that their good cheer isn't just because of the holidays."

"There you go again, being all pessimistic."

"Sorry. I can't help myself. I faced a lot of animosity while growing up. Still do. People can't help themselves. They take one look at me, and their minds are made up."

"Well, it's going to be different here. I just know it. You'll see. And if someone should look at you with indifference, they'll have me to deal with."

The Destiny Hotel stood large on the corner of the four-way stop, outshadowing all other businesses that made up the corporate limits of the historic town. When Johnny opened one of the large double doors, they were met by a cacophony of voices and, much to their surprise, instead of country music, a more recent tune greeted their ears. Tom Petty's "American Girl" filled the entrance. On the wall to the right were glossy photos of bands that had, one time or another, entertained the masses. Trooper, April Wine, Nazareth, Doug and the Slugs, Chilliwak, Matt Minglwood, and the like.

"Wow," said Rebecca. "That's a pretty impressive lineup. Do you think they still tour here?"

"I don't know. It's possible I guess. If they do. Then at least we won't be starved for entertainment."

In keeping with community spirit, the bar was festooned with all the colors of Christmas. Blue, silver, and gold garlands surrounded the windows, kitchen, and tables. Blue and red LED lights strung along beams and mirror of the impressive bar flashed intermittently. A white Christmas tree stood decorated near a fireplace with colorful gifts resting at its skirt.

Seated on a stool, in black golf shirt and jean, was the doorman. Older than most of that profession, he wore a grey goatee, and salt-and-pepper hair. Tattoos covered both arms. On the middle finger of his right hand was a large silver ring, a three-dimensional bust of a wolf. Hard cowboy boots rested on a rung of the stool. Though he was diminutive in stature, behind silver-rimmed glasses, dark eyes spoke volumes about his ability to handle the crowds. He looked Johnny and Rebecca over as they entered, smiled, and greeted them with a dazzling display of teeth and a friendly, "Season's greetings. Enjoy your evening." Directly behind him was the open kitchen where three cooks grilled steaks and burgers and tossed salads.

Johnny asked the doorman to whom they would see about renting a room. "Go and see the bartender. Her name is Brook. She'll take care of you. And again, have a great night."

Most of the tables were occupied with people from all walks of life. Waitresses carried trays topped with pitchers of beer, highballs and plates of food. A bank of Vegas-like slot machines lined one wall, and a woman shouted with glee as the light above her machine flashed red and yellow. "I got bells! I got bells!" she cried to the people bookending her.

Hand in hand Johnny and Rebecca walked into the friendly setting.

The horseshoe bar, crafted from sturdy oak, centered the width of the hotel. Although obvious the establishment had gone through a recent makeover, tarnished four-by-six paintings mounted to the ceiling depicted bygone landscapes before builders moved in.

Behind the bar stood a young woman almost as tall as Johnny, model slim, with long jetted hair and dark complexion. She was drawing beer from a tap into a pitcher.

Rebecca set the suitcase on the floor. "Excuse me. But are you, Brook?"

The pretty bartender, who could have been Johnny's sister, flashed a perfect smile and said, "Yes. I'm Brook. How can I help you?"

"Your doorman said we should see you about renting a room."

"You're lucky. We just had a cancellation about an hour ago or else we're booked solid. I'll just finish up with this drink order, and I'll be right with you."

"Thank you Brook."

Johnny's attention was diverted to a bank of televisions at the hotel's south end.

A hockey game had just started between the Toronto Maple Leafs and the Montreal Canadians. "Maybe after we get our room, we should have a drink and watch the game. I haven't seen a hockey game for quite some time."

"I'm sure there's a TV in the room. Besides, I'm really tired and I need to take a shower. I feel dirty from all that driving and I'm quite sure I don't smell very good." She sniffed the air around Johnny, smiling. "And neither do you for that matter."

"All right, all right. Maybe they have off sales and we can get a six-pack. I really think I deserve a beer after what I've been through."

"Now that I can live with. A cold beer sounds like just like the ticket."

Brook the bartender returned with a ledger and pen in hand. "I need you to fill out here and here. And I need to see your driver's license and credit card." She smiled, eyes of Sienna brown shone like agates.

Rebecca began to fill in the spaces. "I don't carry a credit card. We were hoping cash would be okay. We plan on staying here through New Year's."

Brook held Rebecca's eyes, not suspiciously, more like she was speculating. "Normally we need a credit card, but I'm going to trust my judgment. Cash will be fine, however, I still need to see some form of identification."

"Yes. Certainly." Rebecca went to one knee, opened the suitcase, retrieved her handbag and removed the Nevada driver's license and passport. "Will these do?"

Brook took the ID and briefly looked them over. "You cut and dyed your hair."

"Unfortunately yes. Tried it on a whim. My boyfriend doesn't like it much. Says it makes me look too bitchy."

Johnny smiled, shrugged his shoulders.

"I also have a social security card if those aren't enough," said Rebecca.

"These will do fine, um, Tiffany. You two *have* come a long way."

"Yes. And we're both really tired."

"How long will you be staying with us?"

Rebecca looked to Johnny. "At least four days. Is the room available for that long?"

"You're lucky. It isn't booked again until next week."

"Oh, that's good. It'll give us enough time to find a house to rent. We plan on moving here. Permanently. Do you know of any houses to rent?"

"Not offhand, but there's always someplace or another to rent in Destiny. You shouldn't have any trouble finding one."

Do you have off sales?" asked Johnny.

"Of course. What would you like?"

"Six cold beers please. It doesn't matter what kind."

"How about a half-dozen Kokanee? It's what most of the men around here drink."

"That sounds great. Six Kokanee it is."

While Rebecca filled the questionnaire, Brook the bartender disappeared behind a large metal door and returned a few moments later with six beers in a white plastic bag. She set them on the bar. "Here you go."

"Thank you," said Johnny and thought. *If I did have a sister I bet she would be just like Brook and in more ways than one.*

"How much do we owe you?" asked Rebecca. She set the pen down and turned the ledger so it faced the pretty bartender.

Brook withdrew a calculator from the apron she wore and added the tally. "Let's see. It's fifteen dollars for the beer and seventy-nine dollars plus tax per night for the room. Since you're paying cash, I'll need to get a two-hundred-dollar damage deposit from you." She added it all up, hitting the keys on the calculator with lightning speed. "That'll be five hundred and forty-six dollars and eighty cents please."

Rebecca reached into her jeans and withdrew the wad of bills. "I hope American is all right. We haven't had the chance to change it into Canadian yet."

"Not a problem, however, it'll be on par with our money."

"We don't mind. Do we, Johnny?"

"A few cents here or there isn't going to matter," said Johnny, one eye back on the game.

Rebecca counted out four fifties, a bunch of twenties and tens. When she reached the correct amount, she added an extra twenty and told the bartender it was for "being so kind."

"Thank you," said Brook, and pocketed the twenty. "Here's the keys. A set for each of you. Now to get to your room, you go through those doors over there." She pointed a long finger. "You'll come out into a back lane. Turn right on the walkway and you'll come to a metal door. This key opens that door." She held up one of two keys. "Go up the stairs, room 8 will be on your left-hand side. It backs onto the alley so there's not much of a view. But it's clean and the mattress is new. And there's a television and small refrigerator to keep the beer cold." She handed the keys over.

Johnny lifted the bag of beer off the counter. "Thanks, Brook."

"Yes. Thank you, Brook. You've been very helpful."

"Not a problem. I hope you'll be at the New Year's Eve party. The music is great, and we'll have door prizes and a draw for a trip to Las Vegas."

"It all sounds very enticing," said Rebecca though a return to Vegas sounded more gruesome than enjoyable. "Hey, do those bands we saw coming in still play here?"

"I'm afraid not. Nowadays, the hotel's entertainment comes from local groups like Diamond Bob and the Boys. But you'll find they're all quite talented. The area is chock-full of musicians *and* artists."

"Oh. I see." Rebecca had never in her life attended a concert. Her hopes of perhaps seeing one of the original seventies legends close-up were quickly dashed. Forever the optimist, she smiled. "Well, if everyone is as talented as you say they are, then I guess we can't ask for more than that."

"Believe me. You'll be quite surprised. People come from all around for the entertainment we offer."

"Well, I guess we'll get to our room now."

"You two enjoy your stay. If there's anything else you need, don't hesitate to ask. I'm here most nights."

"We will." Rebecca closed the suitcase and lifted it from the floor. "We might come down for some dinner after we've cleaned up."

"Well, we serve only grade A Alberta beef. Our steaks literally melt in your mouth."

"We might just take you up on that," said Johnny.

"Perhaps I will see you both later then."

"Yes, you just might."

As Brook the bartender was about to turn, she remembered something. "Oh, I almost forgot to tell you. We have a full-time resident. An elderly woman named Margaret Lovely, who lives in room 12 with her cat Mr. Jingles. You might find either him or her wandering the halls sometimes. We send up her meals, and she doesn't bother anyone, so we don't mind that she lets her cat out every now and then."

"We'll remember that," said Rebecca. "Thanks again, Brook."

The new occupants of room 8 followed her directions and left the bar. Three older cowboys stood at the rear entrance and were smoking. Though the cold was sharp enough to cut glass, the trio wore only denim shirts, jeans, and leather boots. Beer enriched bellies rode the crests of silver buckles. A haze of blue smoke swirled within the closeness of their stockman hard faces.

Ranch tough like Buck, thought Johnny.

The tallest of them tipped his hat. "Good evening."

"Nice night," replied Johnny.

"Sure is. You folks just visitin'? Haven't seen you around here before."

"Yes," piped Rebecca. "We just got into town."

"Well, you enjoy your stay. Destiny is a beautiful place to be this time of year. Ain't it, fellas?" The other two men nodded their agreement, and drew on their cigarettes, deep crow's feet branching from the corners of their eyes.

"Yes," agreed Rebecca. "We're beginning to realize that. Everyone has been so nice, and the town is beautiful."

"Well, it's just the way folks are around here. Well, most of us anyway." He tipped his hat once again. "Well, like I said, you enjoy your stay."

"Thank you. Well, I guess we should get to our room. It was nice meeting you."

"The pleasure was all ours, little lady. Good night."

"Good night."

They went through the metal door, climbed the stairs, and found room 8 in the middle of the dim hallway. Using his set of keys, Johnny unlocked the door. It opened on its own accord as if there was someone on the other side gesturing a welcome. "Well, here we are," said Rebecca, and carted the suitcase in the room.

Both were quite surprised to see it was very well appointed, the furnishing and carpet looking new. In the middle of the room was a double bed with four pillows and a thick comforter. The bed was sided by cherrywood night tables where small lamps rested. Centered on the shelf of a large armour was the television set, its remote, on a small table close to the window overlooking the back lane. Beneath the window stood an old steam radiator. The small fridge was white and stood against the wall where the entrance to the bathroom was located. Above the small fridge, looking completely out of place, was a calendar from 1960, its page turned to November. The photo of a Marylyn Monroe look-alike, clad in a red two-piece, was perched on the hood of that year's version of the Cadillac, pink as a cancer ribbon.

Rebecca flung the suitcase onto the bed. Johnny did the same with the knapsack and bag of beer. Then he went to the door and locked it.

"This is really nice." Rebecca took everything in.

"Yeah, and the price is reasonable." Johnny retrieved the remote, sat on the edge of the bed, turned on the television, and thumbed until he found the hockey game. The drone of the play-by-play broadcaster's voice spilled from the television's small speaker. "I wonder why they still keep that calendar hanging?"

"Who knows. It might have sentimental value to the owner." Removing her overcoat, Rebecca draped it over an available chair. "I know one thing. I would like one of those beers."

Johnny reached into the bag, pulled out two Kokanee, twisted off the caps, and handed one to Rebecca who settled next to him, finding that the mattress was quite comfortable and in the same moment alarmingly questionable. She raised her beer. "Here's to a brand-new beginning, Johnny. Just you and me and Destiny."

They clinked bottles, and stared at each other for long comforting moment before taking deep swills of the cold ale.

Rebecca toe-kicked her boots from which a damp, fulsome odor rose.

Johnny scrunched his nose. "Pee-u."

"They are a little ripe, aren't they? Probably from all the sweating I was doing at the border crossing." She took another swig of beer. "Why don't you take your coat off? Stay a while."

Setting his beer on the nightstand, Johnny shrugged out of his overcoat, removed the .38, and slipped it beneath a pillow. Then he reached down, lifted the leg of jean over his right boot, extracted the knife, and sat it next to the beer. A cheer erupted from the television. The Leafs had drawn even with the Canadians.

Leaning forward, Rebecca peeled off her wet socks and wiggled instantly cold toes. "You were right about one thing. It sure is cold here. But it's a different kind of cold. A dry cold instead of the humid colds we had in Maine. I think I'll take that shower now. Get the chill out of my body, not to mention kill the odor of my feet." She rose from the bed, set the half-empty bottle of beer on the floor, and began to unbutton her top. "Why don't you put the rest of the beers in the fridge and join me?"

Johnny looked from the television to Rebecca who stood near the bathroom door, top open, the curves of her breasts modestly exposed. The sight of her made everything in his being stir with want. "I don't know if I'll ever get used to it," he said.

"Get used to what?"

"Just how beautiful you are."

Rebecca felt her face flush. "Well, thank you, kind sir. So what do you think? Wanna fool around?" Running fingers through her spiked hair, she unfastened the clasp to her jeans, drew the zipper, and winked.

Johnny emptied the beer in one long pull. "To hell with the hockey game." When he rose from the bed, Rebecca dropped the shirt and slipped into the bathroom, anticipating another glorious round of lovemaking.

Johnny put the remaining beers in the fridge and removed his boots. He entered the bathroom; Rebecca was on the toilet seat, jeans down to her knees. "Give a girl a hand," she said, raising her legs.

Johnny took hold of the ends, pulled them the rest of the way, and tossed them in a heap, not taking his eyes from her body. The sight of her sitting there wearing only panties added inches to his already-swelling member.

Rising from the porcelain seat, Rebecca removed her panties and allowed them to slip to the floor. Naked, she gazed up to her true love, unbuttoned his shirt, and drew it down and over his shoulders. "I'll start the shower." Drawing the blue synthetic curtain aside, she adjusted the faucets to steaming, stepped in, and closed the curtain. "Hurry, Johnny," she said through spiking water. "I'm waiting."

In less time than it took to put on a clean pair of socks, Johnny was out of the remainder of his clothing, his manhood at full alert. He drew the curtain aside, and saw that Rebecca's body was already slick with soap. Stepping into the tub, he sealed them in and joined her beneath the spray.

Rebecca's eyes immediately went to his member. Stepping toward him, she took him in her hand, and stroked him gently. "Make love to me, Johnny Black."

Johnny pulled her close, kissed her neck and moved slowly toward her breasts until his mouth overtook a rigid nipple. Taking it between his lips, he teased it ever so gently with the flourish of his tongue.

Rebecca sighed and placed her hands atop his head. With an urgent press of her palms, she guided his hungry mouth south.

Johnny explored her flesh, jets of hot water spiked off his back. When his mouth came into contact with the wisps of her mound, Rebecca invitingly parted her legs. Receiving the nub of her sex into his mouth, he relished in the delicious flavor of it. Rebecca tossed her head back, the stretch of her toes curling inward, hands pressing the back of his head hard into her mound. Eyes closed, body trembling, mind numb for want of more, she cried, "Oh god, Johnny! Oh god! Oh god!" He drank her down.

After an eternity of heaven, Johnny rose, kissed her mouth, and plunged his artful tongue deep into her throat. When they parted, Rebecca turned, placed her palms against the shower wall and offered him the soapy smoothness of her buttocks.

Johnny leaned forward, placed his hands on her hips, then with a quick thrust, was deep into her heat.

Biting her bottom lip, Rebecca felt every pulse of him as he rotated, wanting to cry his name a thousand times over. When he drew back and plunged hard into her again and again and again, she thought she would pass out from the sheer pleasurable pain of it all.

After what seemed like a millennium in time and countless orgasms, she felt him shiver, the pulse of his manhood in sync with the pounding of her own heart. "Oh, my beautiful Becca!" he cried, and filled her with the potent seeds of his loins. He remained within for several long moments until his breathing returned to normal. When he fell from her passion, he whispered into the nape of her neck, "I love you, Becca."

Rebecca straightened and turned to face him. "I love you too, Johnny. I will always love you." They held each other. "There will never be another," she whispered in his ear. Taking the bar of soap from its caddy, she washed his chest with one hand, the other holding him tight until he softened.

They cleansed each other's hair with provided shampoo. When they were done and the water had turned tepid, they left the shower and dried their hair with the supplied blow-dryer. Not bothering to dress, Rebecca rebraided the feather into his hair, still tingling with the electrical palpitations of their lovemaking. With the feather in place, Johnny scooped her into his arms and carried her into the adjoining room. Clearing the suitcase and knapsack from the bed, he laid her on the comforter as if she were the most precious treasure on the face of the earth. Lying next to her, he took his forever love into his strong arms.

The hockey game was in its second intermission. Don Cherry was lending his proficient opinions on the two-two draw. Holding Rebecca tight to his chest, Johnny told her he will always be with her, now and forever. With the softest of touches, they traced each other's faces, kissed softly, and breathed the breath they shared until falling asleep in a tangle of arms and legs. One heart. One mind. One soul.

* * *

While Johnny and Rebecca peacefully slept, Mr. Green, Yuri, and Cracker made their way across the border, taking the number 2 highway north and passing through Fort Macleod, Claresholm, Stavely, Nanton, and High River before they reached the city limits of Calgary. They had driven nonstop since leaving Vegas, each taking their turn at the wheel. It was almost midnight according to the digital in the dash.

While Cracker drove, Mr. Green opened his cell phone, entered the number for Nazeem Kahdar who promptly answered on the second chirp.

"Yes."

"This is Mr. Green."

"I have been suspecting I might hear from you soon."

"Do you have what we need?"

"Yes, of course."

"Where should we meet?"

"Go to the airport. Meet me on the roof of the parking terminal in one hour."

The line went dead.

Mr. Green closed the cell, returned it to a breast pocket. "Follow the directions to the airport," he told Cracker.

From the backseat, Yuri asked, "What are we to do once we have what we need?"

Mr. Green replied, "It's too late to start hunting our quarry, so I will drop you off at separate hotels downtown. We are not to be seen together. I will pick you up in the morning at ten a.m. Don't be late. We'll stop and buy proper winter clothing somewhere. Then we'll head to Destiny, separate, and wait them out. I have every intention of finishing what the others couldn't by tomorrow evening."

"Da. That sounds good," agreed the big Russian.

"And what about you, Cracker?"

Cracker turned his head and smiled. "You're the boss on this one. I can't wait to get my hands on that sweet little Rebecca. She'll live a thousand deaths before I'm done with her."

* * *

75

Death Becomes Him

IT was 3:00 a.m. when the last of the lights in the Millions's mansion went out. The assassin had been watching it from a safe distance for more than four hours. Exiting his car, he walked casually toward the 15 room structure, a black silhouette in the shadow of night. *It was unusually cool,* he thought. Not a breeze or a cloud in the sky above Nevada. He would enjoy killing Tony Millions. The money he was going to attain for the hit he could easily retire on at his age.

He entered the house through the pool side doors without making a sound. The mansion was as quiet as an empty confessional. He moved through the first floor with as much stealth as a feather in a wind. Upon reaching the spiral staircase, he removed his weapon from its holster and screwed the silencer to its business end. Up the stairs he climbed, stopping for a moment because he thought he heard a sound. *Perhaps the live-in maid*. He would have to kill her too if she got in the way, then realized it was just the air-conditioning kicking in. Smiling, he continued the climb.

Once he was on the second floor, he paused to listen. The sound of Tony Millions's snoring filled the upper level. If the woman he spent his nights with was with him, he would kill her as well. Two for the price of one. *What a bargain*.

With the confidence of the killer he was, he entered the master's bedroom, night's inky shadows and opalescent pool lights lending him enough visibility to mark his target.

Tony Millions was not alone.

The assassin moved toward the bed, silenced firearm rigid by his side. *This was too fucking easy*. What he wanted, what he needed, was to see the look on Tony Millions's face just before he pulled the trigger, splattering his brains all over the headboard and wall.

Walking casually, he stopped at the nightstand, clicked on the lamp, and sat on the edge of the bed right next to the comfortable wanna-be wop, who, in turn, mumbled incoherently. The woman Pamela stirred; however, she did not wake, neither did his target for that matter.

Pointing the gun directly at Tony Millions's sleeping face, the assassin crossed one leg over the other. With a strong hand, he shook one of his legs. "Wakey, wakey," he said, voice animated.

"Huh? What? Leave me alone, Pamela." Tony's cocaine-strung-out eyes blinked. The first thing he saw was the sleek black .357 pointed at his face. Then he saw the whites of his assassin's teeth. He bolted upright. Pamela rolled, tossing beneath the sheets. "Mr. Black! What the fuck do you think you are doing?"

Rolling toward Tony, Pamela opened her eyes. A silent scream grabbed at her throat.

Mr. Black put a finger to his lips, his eyes cautioning her to be quiet.

Pamela straightened, large breasts jiggling, nipples rigid with fear. Seeing the silenced killer in Mr. Black's hand, she moved as far away from Tony Millions as she could without falling from the king-sized bed. She grabbed at the satin sheets and pulled them to her chin.

Tony Millions, wearing silk jockeys and nothing else, opened his mouth to speak further. Like a striking snake, Mr. Black's hand connected with his cheek. "Surprised, man? You should see the look on your face. It's priceless. A real Kodak moment."

Tony Millions swallowed hard, Adam's apple rising and falling as though a piece of meat was stuck in his throat. "Who sent you? I'll double whatever it is they're paying you."

Mr. Black smiled, like he always did just before he ended someone's life. "You can't afford what they're paying me, man. I told you when you first brought me in. It was always about the money. Besides, I never did like you. You're a little man in the grand scheme of things and a fucking coward. I hate cowards. Did you think you could murder a high-ranking member of Hong Kong's elite society and get away with it? Did you? You little white people who think you are so fucking big. Always so fucking greedy. You've become a loose end, man."

Tony's eyes watered. His bladder released. Urine stained his thighs, the bedsheet. "Please, Mr. Black, don't kill me," he cried like the coward he always was. In his mind's ear, his father's voice boomed. *"I told you it would come to this, Tony. Now you're going to die."*

"Look at you, man. Crying like a baby. You had to know in our business that this was going to come sooner or later. Or are you so conceited you thought you were indispensable? Tsk-tsk-tsk. You of all people should know better. What is it you've always said? Leave no loose ends." Mr. Black smiled again. "Frank Santangello feels the same way. He sends his regards."

Tony's eyes went wide. Unremitting terror seized his throat. *"Good-bye, Tony,"* his father's voice intoned. Tony Millions attempted a scream. However, the only sound to escape his lips was the croak of a dying frog.

Mr. Black squeezed the trigger. The .357 made a deadly sound. *Pfff.* The hollow point he was using for the special occasion left a neat hole in the middle of Tony

Millions's forehead. The back of his skull shattered into hundreds of loose pieces of bone and brain matter, that splattered the headboard, the area above it.

A naked Pamela dropped the protective fabric of silk, leaped from the bed, and wiped Tony's brain matter from her face and arms. She stared at Mr. Black, terrified, eyes like saucers, tears covering her cheeks and dripping onto her breasts.

"Now what am I going to do about you, baby?" Mr. Black pointed the silent killer at her beautiful face.

"I hated that fucking bastard, Mr. Black! I'm glad you killed him! He was a no good piece of shit! You don't know what he put me through." Her body began to shudder.

Even in the dim lighting, Mr. Black could see the bruises on her thighs, the pink oval remnants of a bite mark on her left breast. Tony Millions got great pleasure doling out punishment on the women who shared his bed. It was what Mr. Black hated most about him. Though ruthless as they came, Mr. Black loved women. Unless of course he was paid handsomely to dispose of them. "Still, the question remains, baby. Should I kill you, or let you go? You can clearly see the position I'm in. You might go to the police."

"I wouldn't do that. Take me with you, Mr. Black. *Please!* I've always liked you you know. And I know you like me. I've seen the way you look at me. I'll fuck you every day of your life in ways you never dreamed possible. Please, Mr. Black! Please!" She wiped at the tears dripping from her chin and sniffed like a child. *"Please Mr. Black."*

Mr. Black thought for a moment, and scratched his chin with the hot end of the silencer, loving the smell of cordite. Pamela did have a great body. Perhaps the most fuck-worthy body he has ever seen and he had seen plenty. Her secretive wounds would quickly heal, and she would be flawless once again. In a day he would have more money than he would know what to do with deposited into an account in the Caymans. Frank Santangello and Mr. Wong's people had been very generous. Mr. Black loved the Caribbean and, at his age, intended to spend the remainder of his life stretched out on a beach. *Why not have a little company?* "How soon can you be ready?"

Pamela let out the breath she was holding and sniffed the mucus running from her nose. She smiled, blue eyes twinkling with utter relief. "I can be packed and ready to go in twenty minutes. Thank you! Thank you, Mr. Black! I promise you won't regret your decision."

"Make it ten minutes, baby. And try not to disturb Rosita. I would hate to have to kill her. She was always good to me. Now hurry. And don't forget your passport. The world is waiting for us." Mr. Black looked at a dead Tony Millions sprawled on the bed, brains sliding south like a snail from hell. Blood trickled from the dime-sized hole in the middle of his forehead, eyes frozen in disbelief, mouth gaped in a silent scream. "Good night, and good riddens you greedy little man." Mr. Black stood and emptied his .357 into the chest of Tony Millions just for the hell of it.

* * *

76

December 30
Fate's hand

HAVING been exhausted by the recent stresses they had gone through and the sex they had performed, Rebecca and Johnny did not wake until eleven fifteen the following day to a grey light filtering through the curtains. The television was still on and the CBC station was airing the weather report. Somehow, through the night, one of them had managed to pull up the comforter. Rebecca sat up and listened, shaking Johnny awake.

"A storm system is moving into southern Alberta. It should arrive sometime this afternoon and last for several days, bringing with it temperatures well below the norm and heavy snow. Possibly as much as thirty centimeters.'

Grabbing the remote, she turned off the set.

Johnny yawned himself awake. "Hey, beautiful."

"Did you hear that?"

"Hear what?"

"According to the news, there's a storm heading this way. A really bad one."

Wiping at his eyes, Johnny sat up. "Then we'll have to keep each other warm. Won't we?" Reaching, he took the nearest available breast in hand and squeezed it gently.

Rebecca reached beneath the comforter to find that he was as stiff as a metal rod. Using a finger, she traced the length of him. "My, my. Is that for me?"

"Of course. Who else would it be for?"

"How about a quickie then?"

"You read my mind."

Rebecca drew the comforter, and mounted him. With one, hand she guided him to find that she was still a little sore from their lovemaking in the shower, so it took some effort on her part to accept his size. Hands on his shoulders, she drew him in, inch by magnificent inch, until she became slippery wet.

Johnny placed his hands on her hips, drew himself to the rosettes of her breasts and kissed one, then the other. Rebecca moved her hands from his shoulders, seized the headboard, and in a single moment they were in perfect rhythm, flesh over flesh, eyes embraced.

"Oh god, Johnny! Oh god!" Hips faster now, body trembling with want of release.

Johnny thrust deep. Rebecca cried out, and in concert they climaxed. After a breath-catching moment, she released him, rolled, and with the use of her feet, pushed the comforter to the edge of the bed. "God, that was good. Better than good. If I had a cigarette, I'd smoke it. I guess I'll have to take another shower." She slid off the bed, legs still quivering.

"You go first. I'm going to see if I can find a station that plays music."

"See you in a few minutes," she said, and looked back at him, mischievous light emitting from her eyes.

After showering, still tingling in her most private places, Rebecca stood in front of the sink, and wiped steam off the mirror. She inspected what she could see of her body. The blackness of her hair had become less obtrusive, its true color showing in places having been washed so many times recently. The green of her eyes were more radiant than usual. *Incredible sex will do that to a girl.* When she examined her legs, she saw they needed the strokes of a razor and that her toenails needed clipping. *A coat of red polish wouldn't hurt either.*

While brushing her teeth, she hummed the melody taught to her by her mother. She was happy. At least for the moment, for the telling signs of her gift could only mean bad times were just ahead. Dismissing the negative thoughts, she capped the toothpaste, took another look at herself in the mirror, smiled, and went back to Johnny who was still lying on the bed, his eyes focused on the television.

He turned to look at her. *God, she was beautiful.* "You know, I can't find a station anywhere that just plays music. We'll have to remedy that as soon as possible."

"I'm sure there must be a store in town that sells radios." She went to the suitcase and removed a clean top and jeans. While she dressed, she said, "So what would you like to do?"

"Well, I'm kind of hungry."

"Oh, there's a big surprise. Shall I alert the media?"

"Ha-ha. Very funny." He rolled onto his side. "I wonder if the bar serves breakfast."

"It's almost noon, Johnny. Breakfast is over. You'll have to set your sights on something else." Pulling the zipper on her jeans, she holed the brass button.

"I suppose one of those melt-in-your-mouth steaks Brook promised would do all right."

"Then you better shower and get dressed. After we eat, I would like to walk around the town for a while, pick up a few items, and exchange some of the money we have."

Johnny stood, and stretched powerful arms over his head, every vertebrae sounding. "Why don't you go to the bar? I'll take a quick shower and be right down. We're far enough out of harms way. You'll be fine. I'm sure of it."

"Okay. Should I order your steak right away, or do you want me to wait for you?"

"You might as well order for me. I'll only be a few minutes." He took her in his arms and kissed her. "See you in bit. See if you can get a table next to a window so we can people watch."

"Okay. Make sure you lock the door."

"Yes, Mother. Anything else?"

"Yes. Make sure the cleaning lady doesn't find that gun, the knife, *or* the money."

"No one will. I promise. I'll guard them with my life." He picked up the remote, killed a Family Feud rerun, and went to the bathroom where he started the shower.

Rebecca put on her coat and boots, grabbed the handbag, filled it with more money, left the hotel room, and made her way to the bar, the blossom between her thighs still pleasingly throbbing.

* * *

She sat near one of the large windows in the comfort of a wingback chair. Shrugging out of the overcoat, she let it drop behind her. The handbag loaded with cash she kept close to her elbow. John Denver's, Annie's Song emanated from speakers above. More than half of the tables were occupied with customers, some eating, some still waiting for their orders to be filled. Most were drinking beer. Centering the bar was a table of six senior men drinking ale from one of two pitchers. Rebecca had a notion they were regulars and probably gathered each day to reminisce about the good old days.

The VLT machines were occupied by several Natives and a couple of elderly women. An attractive waitress wearing a burgundy top and black jeans approached Rebecca with menu in hand and a vibrant light to her blue eyes. Crimped, sun-kissed hair hung to the waist of her jeans.

"Hi," she said smiling and handed Rebecca the menu. "I'm Keely and I'll be serving you today. Can I get you something from the bar?'

"No, thank you. It's a little too early for me. I would like a cup of coffee though."

"Coming right up. Should I give you a few minutes to look at the menu, or do you know what you would like?"

Rebecca handed the menu back. "Yes. My boyfriend will be joining me in a few minutes. He would like one of your rib eyes, medium rare, with a baked potato. No, make that fries, smothered in gravy and a side of mushrooms. And I would like a cheeseburger with a side salad."

"What size steak do you think your boyfriend would like? We offer two sizes."

"The biggest you have."

"Big eater is he?"

"You don't know the half of it. He might just have two."

"And what type of dressing would you like with your salad?'

"Italian will be fine."

"Would your boyfriend like something to drink?"

"Yes, of course. He would like a large iced tea."

"One coffee, one iced tea, and possibly two steaks." She smiled cutely. "I'll be right back with your coffee."

"Thank you, Keely."

Turning so she could view the outdoors, Rebecca saw that the sky was heavily laden with cloud. Across the street, the Esso station and liquor store were busy with customers arriving and leaving. An Asia fellow wearing black glasses and bundled tightly in a heavy coat stood by an air hose, and smoked a cigarette.

The town clock stood rigid on the northeast corner like a black sentinel, still reading 9:35. From what she could see, there were few people walking about, and it looked oh so cold.

"Here's your coffee." Keely set the cup in front of Rebecca, and produced a wicker basket containing cream, sugar, and plastic stir sticks. "As soon as I see that your boyfriend has arrived, I'll bring the iced tea."

"Thank you, Keely."

"Not a problem. Are you staying at the hotel?"

"Yes. For a few days anyway. In room 8."

"That's nice." She looked toward the kitchen. "Your food should be ready in about ten minutes. If you need anything else, just throw something at me."

Rebecca snickered. "This will be fine. Thank you."

Keely the waitress turned on her heels and went toward the bar, crimped hair swaying like a pendulum.

Rebecca did not notice Johnny enter until he was standing next to her, knapsack slung over a shoulder. "Room for one more."

"I always have extra room for a handsome gentleman."

Johnny rested the knapsack and his overcoat on an empty wingback and took a seat opposite Rebecca. "I'm starving. What are you having?"

"A cheeseburger with salad. I ordered you fries with gravy and mushrooms to go with your steak."

"You know me so well."

Rebecca looked at the knapsack, lowered her voice so only Johnny could hear. "I suppose we're sharing this table with fifty thousand dollars and a loaded gun?"

Leaning halfway across the table, he said, "Yes. But who's to know." He smiled, and for the first time, Rebecca could see the young boy she entertained as a cerebral playmate.

"And what about the knife?"

"Back in my boot."

Rebecca shook her head. "Taking chances, aren't you?"

"Maybe. But I didn't know what else to do with them. Don't worry. It'll be all right. And like I said, no one knows about the you know what except us."

"Let's hope so."

"Here's your iced tea." Keely set a tall glass filled with ice and tea next to Johnny's elbow.

"Thank you." Johnny smiled at the pretty waitress.

"Not a problem." Turning sideways, so only Rebecca could see, Keely winked her approval. "I can see why he might eat two steaks."

"I told you. Johnny, this is Keely. Keely, Johnny."

"Nice to meet you, Johnny."

"Likewise. Can you tell me where I might be able to buy a portable radio?" he asked.

Keely thought for a moment. "You might be able to get one at the Pharmasave. But if you want a good selection, you should drive to the Wal-Mart in Okotoks, get one there."

"I'm sorry. We're not familiar with the territory. Where's Okotoks?"

Keely pointed at the window. "Just go through the four-way stop and head east. Okotoks is about twenty minutes away. When you come to the first set of lights, turn left. You can't miss it."

"Thank you, Keely." Rebecca smiled.

"Your orders will be ready momentarily." When she left, she gave Johnny and anyone else who was watching plenty of hip action.

"Feel like going for a drive after we eat?" asked Johnny.

"Not really. I think I'll do like I said. Just walk around town for a while. Pick up a few items. I'm sure you felt the stubble of my legs this morning."

"Didn't bother me at all. Kind of tickled."

"Well, that's nice of you to say, but they bother me. And I would like to paint my nails. Then I'll wait for you back in the room. Make sure you get a good radio. I think we can afford it."

"Only the best. Do you think it's safe for us to separate? I told you I was not going to let you out of my sight."

"That's very brave of you, but we're okay, at least for now. I can feel it." It would be good for them to separate for a little while, she thought. When they were together, all she could think about was Johnny's impending death and that she would have to end her own life. But for right now, she was certain they were safe. Her gifts had been dormant since they crossed the border.

"If you're sure."

"I am. Besides, we need a *really* good radio. Something that will drown out the noises that will be coming from our room later."

A burst of laughter erupted from the table of elderly gentlemen. Each raised their glasses. One of them said, "Here's to Urbin. We'll miss you, old friend. Nobody could tell a good story like you could. And nobody had more dance partners than you did. You really knew how to cut a rug."

"To Urbin," chorused the others, glasses held high.

"So what do you want to do once I've returned with a radio?"

"How about we dance the afternoon away in our room? Have a couple of beers and dance some more? Then you *know*."

"That would be all right I guess." Johnny smiled teasingly for he could never get enough of her. He took a long pull from the iced tea just as Keely set their protein-filled breakfasts down.

"Will there be anything else?" A flash of teeth, eyes genuinely smiling.

Johnny looked at his half-finished drink. "More iced tea for me please."

"And some ketchup?" added Rebecca.

"Yes, of course. How stupid of me." Crossing her eyes comically, Keely went to the next table; plucked a chrome carriage of salt, pepper, vinegar, mustard, and ketchup; and set it in front of Rebecca. "Sorry. I don't know where my head is at sometimes. I guess I just cut my tip by half."

"No need to apologize," said Rebecca, snickering again. She took a liking to Keely the waitress and her refreshing sense of humor. "We all have those days, don't we, Johnny?"

"Life wouldn't be the same without them." He squirted ketchup onto his fries.

"That's kind of you. Well, if there's nothing else, I've got to get those guys another pitcher of beer. A friend of theirs passed away yesterday, and they plan on getting pretty drunk, as usual. Enjoy your lunch." With a sweeping of her crimped hair, she went to the table of elderly men and asked, "Another round, boys?"

After their meals, Johnny slung the knapsack over his shoulders and put on his coat. "Are you sure you don't want to come with me? You know how I feel about us separating."

"I know. But it won't be for long, and like I said, there's some things I need to get, not to mention exchange some of the money. We'll be fine." She smiled confidently.

Johnny shrugged. "Okay then. If you're sure?"

"I am."

"Then I'll see you in about an hour." Rounding the table, he kissed her cheeseburger-flavored mouth, smiled that beautiful smile of his, and left through the rear entrance.

Rebecca had another coffee, enjoyed the atmosphere of the small-town bar, then paid the tab about ten minutes later, leaving Keely a generous tip. She used the bathroom before she began her tour of Destiny. When she stepped outside, the cold air bit into her face. It had started to snow. An unfamiliar tingle rode the length of her spine.

Crossing the street, she went into the Alberta Treasury Bank, exchanged five hundred dollars American, then went to the Pharmasave where she picked up nail clippers, a bottle of red nail polish, and razors. She then went to the Bali Bling store on the corner, deciding she would start her tour from there. She widow-shopped the displayed jewelry, knick-knacks, and colorful garments. Seeing nothing that she absolutely could not live without, she went next door to the Blue Rock Gallery.

There she was greeted with a friendly hello by the proprietor, an attractive middle-aged woman who asked if she would care for "a coffee or maybe a tea." The gallery smelled of perfumed soaps. The tranquil sounds of waves crashing against a shore echoed through the premises, reminding Rebecca of home.

"No, thank you. I just ate and already had two cups of coffee, which is my limit. You have a beautiful store here."

The woman thanked her, explained proudly that she and her husband had just recently purchased the shop, and told her to take her time browsing about, adding that much of the art was by locals.

Rebecca toured the store, eyeing the different genres of canvassed art, shelves of colorful ceramics, and the source of the fresh, clean smell that had filled her the moment she walked in. One section, at the back of the shop, was dedicated to soaps of varying colors and design, incense, and votive candles, all of which had been crafted by locals.

She made her way to the front of the galley and was looking at some beautifully glazed plates and stained glass art when a black Lincoln Navigator slowly passed and parked just up the street. Rebecca could see the license plate, Nevada. *Huh. That's quite a coincidence.* Much to her horror, her body prickled with its internal warning and the tingling of her spine returned, only it possessed the beastly conclusiveness of a raging fire. As if to add credence to the message, the plumps of her cheeks blazed with plausible stinging. *No! No! No! It can't be!* However, when the passenger door opened and Mr. Green stepped out and onto the sidewalk, quickly followed by two men she hadn't seen before, her heart tripped, internal temperature tripled, and she had to cover her mouth to stifle the scream that wanted to escape.

The three men were wearing recently purchased parkas, jeans, and boots, their faces, all business.

They had found her. Again. *But how? How?* She knew there existed a certain inevitability to the journey she and Johnny had embarked upon, but for it to come to a conclusion so soon was unthinkable. Flashes of her terror-filled past months raced across the canvas of her mind. She was all alone. *JOHNNY!* Legs almost abandoned her, and she teetered on the brink of a complete breakdown. Tears of absolute resignation filled her eyes. *Oh god, what have I done?* Finding her legs, she backed away from the window, drew the hood over her head, and watched. With large flakes descending around them like downy feathers, Mr. Green, with great plumes of frozen breath, gave directions to the other men. Then they separated. Mr. Green headed straight for the hotel.

Panicked, Rebecca turned abruptly, and stumbled into a display.

"Are you all right, miss?" asked the kind owner. "You suddenly look pale."

"Um. Yes. Sorry. I have to go. Thank you." She waited for Mr. Green to go into the hotel before she left the store and headed straight to the metal door leading to room 8. Two at a time, she took to the stairs and locked herself in, body quaking within the aura of her most loathsome fears.

The cleaning lady had already come and gone. Throwing the Pharmasave purchases and handbag on the carpet, Rebecca plopped herself down on the bed and cried into the palms of her hands. *How on earth am I going to be able to warn Johnny? Certainly Mr. Green was in the hotel asking questions. Would anyone give us away? She hoped not. And how the fuck did they find us here in Destiny, Alberta? And so fucking soon. What was it that gave us away?* Though she knew without a doubt troubled times were ahead, she didn't believe fate would deliver them within the spans of twenty-four hours. That she and Johnny would have at least some time to share the love they had for each other before the proverbial shit hit the blades of the fan. She was wrong. *Again. Shit. Shit. Shit.* She thought and thought and thought until her mind grew numb. Could not come up with an answer. She supposed the good thing was all the rooms were occupied and there was a heavy metal door needing a rented key between her, Mr. Green, and whomever those other two men were. As all these thoughts ran rampant in her mind, she knew with absolute certainty this was it. It was over. They could run no more. Fate *had* dealt its final task.

* * *

Mr. Green approached the bartender and stood right next to Keely the waitress. "Excuse me," he said, offering a smile. "I was hoping you could help me. I'm looking for a couple of friends of mine. One is a big Native named Johnny and the other is Tiffany, a girl with short dark hair. We were supposed to meet here yesterday, however, I got hung up in Montana. Have they checked in?"

Keely, being a great judge of character, did not like the looks of this guy. There was something very wrong about him, so she stuck around to listen.

"Not that I know of," said the bartender. "Keely? Have you seen anyone matching that description?"

"Nope. Maybe one of those Natives playing the machines is your friend."

Mr. Green glanced at the bank of VLTs. There were four Natives all in a row, none of whom was Johnny. "Perhaps they checked into the hotel last night, and you're not aware of it. Do you think I could see your ledger?" he asked.

Keely interjected. "Sorry. That's against hotel policy. We don't know you from Adam, and we reserve the right to our guests' privacy. I hope you understand."

"I see. You wouldn't happen to have a room available, would you?"

"Sorry. We're booked solid. You might find your friends at the Cowboy Trail Motel just down the road. If not there, then there's another hotel in the next town just west of here called Renegades. They could be there. Or they might be down in Longview. That's south of here. Or maybe there in Okotoks or even Calgary. It is almost New Year's. Rooms are scarce. We've been booked solid for two weeks now. They could have had trouble finding one."

"I see. Well, thank you for your time."

"Sorry, we couldn't help you." Keely watched Mr. Green leave the hotel then turned to the bartender. "I didn't like the looks of him."

"Me neither. Gave me the creeps."

Mr. Green stepped outside. The snow was coming down heavier, propelled into a turbulent rave of white by a mountain birthed gust. Pulling out his cell, he called the Russian first.

"Da."

"Anything, Yuri?"

"Not yet. No car. No people. In this shit, it is hard to see anything."

"Keep a sharp eye. They're here, and probably closer than we know."

"Da."

Mr. Green then called Cracker, receiving the same response. Nothing. He went to the Navigator, deciding to check out the other hotels in the area, a knowing itch scratching at the back of his mind.

* * *

There came a soft knock on the door. Rebecca was still lost in thought, tears wetting her face. She wasn't sure she had heard anything at all until whomever it was knocked again. Wiping at the tears in her eyes, she went to the door, stressed heart thrumming an insane beat. "Yes? Who is it"

"It's Keely Tiffany. The waitress you met," came a voice from the other side.

Rebecca turned the lock, opened the door slightly, relieved to see Keely and no one else.

"I need to speak to you," the waitress said, her eyes giving rise to her consternation.

Rebecca opened the door wide and said, "Come in" then quickly investigated the hallway. An orange tabby was sitting by one of the doors as if waiting for it to open. Quietly, she closed the door, and relocked it.

"You've been crying," said Keely.

"That obvious, huh?"

"Look. I don't usually stick my nose in other people's affairs, but I'm a very good judge of character, and I could see right away that you and your boyfriend were good people. I have to get back to work. No one knows I came up here, so I'll make this quick. There's a man looking for you. He's tall with red hair and a red beard. I didn't like the looks of him, so I didn't tell him anything when he started asking questions about you two. Are you in some kind of trouble?"

"You shouldn't get involved," said Rebecca and moved to the bed. She turned, eyes pained. "The less you know, the better. But thank you for not saying anything."

"What are you going to do? I didn't like his eyes. There was something very sinister in them. Shouldn't you call the police?"

"That's not an option. Don't ask me why, it's a long story. And the less information you know, the better you'll be for it. I'll wait for Johnny to get back before we make any decisions. He should be back any time now."

"Okay. I wish you both the best of luck. If I can do anything for you, just ask."

"Thank you, Keely. All I ask is that no one finds out that we're here."

"I won't tell a soul. I've got to go now."

"Just a second." Rebecca retrieved the handbag from the floor, dug out a wad of twenties. "Here. Take this."

"No, no. You don't have to pay me off. I said I wouldn't tell anyone and I meant it."

"It's not to pay you off. It's for being nice and for being concerned. Nothing more. Please. Take it. I won't take no for an answer."

Keely took the press of twenties and stuffed them into her jeans. "Thanks, Tiffany."

"I should be honest with you, Keely, since you've been honest with me. My name isn't Tiffany Rose. It's Rebecca White. I hope you would keep that information to yourself because if that man finds us, our lives won't be worth a plug nickel. I suppose I can tell you this much. So that you understand. So that you don't think we're criminals or anything. That man and others kept me as a, well, let's just say I did things for money that I'm terribly ashamed of. Do you understand? But with the help of Johnny, I was lucky enough to have escaped."

Aghast, Keely covered her mouth and spoke through fingers. "You mean like you were kidnapped and made to..."

"Yes," said Rebecca, her eyes cast to the carpet. "As well as others."

Keely lowered her hand. An unspoken bond filled the space between the two women. "Don't worry, Rebecca. They won't get any information from me or the other girls. I'll see to it. My god! What you must have gone through. It must have been terrible."

"It was far more than that, Keely."

* * *

Johnny parked the RX7 at the rear of the hotel. He had purchased a Samsung radio at the Wal-Mart in Okotoks. He got out of the car, shopping bag in hand, and immediately heard his name being called through the heavy snowfall. When he looked up, Rebecca was hanging halfway out the window.

"Johnny!"

"What are you doing?"

"Never mind that! Get rid of the car, Johnny! Right away! Hide it as best as you can! And be very careful."

Johnny stared at her for a moment. He was about to ask why when the answer hit him like a freight train. There was only one reason why she would want him to hide the car. Somehow Tony Millions's men had found them, again. "Okay. Get back inside. Don't leave the room unless it's on fire."

Rebecca drew the window closed. Johnny slipped into the car, knowing immediately where to hide it. He had seen a trailer park on his way out of town where there were a couple of empty lots, one of which had a large tarp partially covered in snow lying on the ground. Starting the engine, he backed out of the spot and drove.

Rebecca shook all over. Not because of the cold air that had entered the room but of her judicious fears. Sitting on the bed, she pulled the comforter around her shoulders, rocked back and forth, her mind racing, the pulse of her angst like a bass drum between her ears. *What if they find Johnny before he has a chance to make it back to the room? They would kill him. That's a given.* She would be left to fend for herself, with what, nothing but the razors she had purchased. She couldn't stay in the room forever. Eventually they would catch her, and she would be helpless against their will. Tony Millions wanted her back. If for no other reason than to prove that his control over her was boundless.

Fresh tears emerged from her eyes, dripped from her chin, and dotted the comforter. She took in the four corners of the room that suddenly seemed to be pressing in on her. *Just like the pit.* Without warning, a man, wearing a white cowboy hat, blue denim shirt under a black vest and jeans, appeared from out of the wall nearest the bed. He could have been Johnny's father's twin brother. His hair and long sideburns were as white as snow, his face, ruggedly handsome. He smiled at her, tipped his hat, then began a two-step without partner and to music only he could hear. Stepping forward, using the area in front of the bed as a dance floor, he stepped back again and circled.

After that, and just as he had appeared, he danced toward the door leading to room 8, twirled and smiled and slipped beyond it.

So the hotel has a spirit. Probably more than one. It did not surprise Rebecca in the least. Her gifts were in full swing again. The gathering of elderly gentlemen came to mind, and she wondered if the dancing man wasn't their recently passed friend Urbin. Sniffing mucus, she wiped at her eyes. In the next moment, she heard the sound of a key being inserted into the lock that was keeping her safe. The door flew open. Much to her relief, Johnny stepped into the room, all out of breath, closed, and locked the door, twice. He had a bag in one hand, knapsack in the other. Neither spoke as he moved to the bed and deposited both items next to Rebecca.

They looked to each other.

"Mr. Black?" questioned Johnny.

"No." Rebecca stood, fell into his chest, and wrapped her arms around his shoulders, fresh tears washing her worried face. Taking a moment to compose herself, she said, "Mr. Green and two others." She sniffed. "They arrived in a black Navigator while I was window-shopping. Oh god, Johnny! What are we going to do? What have I done? I brought us here! It's all my fault!" More tears fell.

"You can't go blaming yourself, Becca. I don't think it would have mattered where we ended up. Somehow they seem to know our every move." Cradling her head against a shoulder, he said, "Did they see you?"

"No. I was hidden behind a window full of artwork."

"And you're absolutely positive it was Mr. Green?"

"Yes, Johnny. From the moment I first laid eyes on him, I was terrified of him. Now I know why."

"Shit!"

Outside, the wind howled, rattling the window, fraying what was left of Rebecca's nerves.

"Oh my god, Johnny! If they found us here..." she didn't finish. "What are we going to do? Did you hide the car so they won't find it?"

"Yes," said Johnny calmly. "They'll never find it. Not in this weather. These two other men. What did they look like?"

"One was very big, bigger than you, bald, with a long scar on his face. The other was very small, with an earring in one of his ears, which looked out of place because they were too large for his head. But he had these eyes, Johnny. Eyes that scared the hell out of me. They were all wearing heavy parkas and jeans."

"Where did they go?"

"Mr. Green directed them, and all three separated. Then Mr. Green came right to the hotel and began to ask questions."

"Do you think anyone told him where we were?"

"I don't think so. You know that waitress who served us earlier today?"

"You mean Keely?"

"Yes. Keely. Well, while you were out shopping for the radio, she came to tell me that there was a man asking questions about us, but that she steered him away and she promised that no one working at the hotel will tell of our whereabouts. That she would see to it."

"Well, at least that's one thing we have going for us. Extra time."

"To do what, Johnny?"

Johnny gazed at the floor, paced back and forth. When he looked at her again, his eyes bore the same look he had just before he murdered Henry Klondike. The look of someone who teetered on the very edge. Reaching for the knapsack, he unzipped it, withdrew the .38, and checked to make sure the safety was still on. "Take this."

"What?"

"Take it, Rebecca!" He thrust it at her.

Rebecca took the gun, turning it in her hand. "I don't know how to use it."

"It's easy." He took it from her and sat next to her. "First you flip this little toggle here. That will take the safety off. The gun won't fire unless you do that. Then you draw the hammer back like this. Point and pull the trigger. It doesn't have much of a kick back so whatever you aim at, you'll hit." He disengaged the firing pin and gave it back to her. "You said that all three separated?"

"Yes," said Rebecca, staring unbelievably at the weapon in her hand.

"That makes sense. They could cover more ground that way." He stood, pulled up his pant leg, and removed the skinning knife from his boot. Opening his coat, he tucked it into the small of his back. "If anyone other than me comes through that door, shoot first, ask questions later." He zipped the overcoat.

Rebecca didn't like what she was hearing. Where are you going, Johnny? What are you going to do? Please don't leave me here by myself! I'm frightened! Please, Johnny! PLEASE!" Fresh tears filled her eyes.

Lifting her from the bed, his grey eyes all afire, he placed his hands on her cheeks, thumbed away the tears then kissed her mouth. "They may know we're here, how I don't know, we'll try to figure it out later, but what they're not expecting is for us to fight back. I'm not going to just sit around and wait for them to find us. I'm going to take these fuckers out one at a time."

"You can't do that, Johnny! They're professional killers!"

"Well, I'm about to find out just how good they are." Turning for the door, he stopped and looked back at a terrified Rebecca. "I love you. Remember what I said. If I'm not back by nightfall. Shoot whoever comes through that door."

* * *

77

Cat and Mouse

JOHNNY stepped through the metal door and into the ire of a white storm. The temperature had dropped further. There was a delivery truck parked at the loading zone. A bulky young man in layers of clothing wheeled boxes of French fries through the receiving doors.

He made his way to the front of the hotel, stood at the corner, and surveyed Center Street with his keen, feral eyes. There was very little people traffic. Those who were out for whatever reason leaned into the biting wind, the hotel, for several, a hard fought destination. None fit the description of the men Rebecca had described. There were many vehicles parked on the north and south sides of the street. The black Navigator was not among them, at least as far as he could tell. He began to walk in a westerly direction, hoping to be recognized, hands thrust deep into pockets, the collar of his coat turned up to protect his neck.

A white RCMP cruiser, wipers slapping a quick beat, passed him and turned onto Government Road, it's driver ignoring the stop sign. *I'll have to be very careful.* As he moved along the sidewalk, the scabbard for the knife rubbed rough against his back.

In less than ten minutes, he passed the town offices and library. Farther up the road, located on the north side, a small strip mall came into view, its storefront Christmas lights dulled by the maelstrom. Standing in front of the local post office, in a dark overcoat, his arm moving to and from his face as he smoked a cigarette was a man who was certainly big enough to be one of Johnny's targets. He headed straight for him and as he grew close, knew without a doubt that he was one of the men hired for murder. The verifying deep scar running along his face told Johnny as much. He took a deep brave breath and walked right past him.

* * *

From a distance of about thirty yards, Yuri the Russian could see a tall Native who fit the description of one Johnny, heading in his direction. Mr. Green had specifically told him and Cracker that if either of them should locate one or both parties, they were to contact him immediately. That they would deal with them together. *To hell with that,* Yuri told himself. He had murdered for money in the Russian Republic, Poland, Yugoslavia, Czechoslovakia, and another four since arriving in the United States. He could certainly handle one Indian. Besides, Tony Millions might be extra generous to the one who cared not about the how but got the job done. Yuri Dimeniachuk could certainly use the extra cash. He had had a string of bad luck with the ponies lately.

The Indian walked right past him without giving him a second look, the feather in his hair like a beacon in the storm. This was going to be easier than he hoped. The peaceful town of Destiny, Alberta, was about to get a rude awakening. Tossing the cigarette, Yuri followed his prey.

* * *

Johnny led the Russian to a bridge on the outskirts of town where a small, dense wooded area of poplars, evergreens, and birch edged a river frozen except where there existed a strong undercurrent. Broken branches lay hither skither along a deeply rutted deer path. Within the thickness of woods, the storm was far less menacing.

Johnny took to the path, fully aware that he was being pursued, the knife against his back alive with want of use. It didn't surprise him that the big man knew what he looked like. Johnny's murderous design depended on it. The deer course took an abrupt right. He continued farther for another hundred yards and backtracked twenty feet, carefully placing his steps into the imprints he had made, then stopped, jumped as far away from the path as he could and camouflaged himself behind a broad pine. At his feet lay a large, hard-looking arm of birch. He picked it up, and turned his body sideways. Withdrawing the knife from its scabbard, he put the length of it between his teeth and with one eye, waited for his prey. Hidden deep and with the storm howling, no one would witness or hear the sound of murder.

* * *

The Indian had disappeared deep into a thicket of trees bordering a river. Yuri pursued, reached into his coat, and withdrew the silenced .45 he was given by the associate of Tony Millions, Nazeem Kahdar. Like most Russians, Yuri despised Pakistanis, Hindus, and East Indians. They were a filthy stain on the earth as far as he was concerned. If he had his druthers, he would kill them all. But he had kept his mouth shut during the transaction. He was being paid too much money to allow his bigotry to spoil things. He held the .45 at his shoulder, ready to bring it to life, and followed the fresh footprints Johnny had made. The farther into the undergrowth he moved, the voice in his head began to ask questions. *Why would the Indian be out in this kind of weather? And alone? And why would he choose this particular area to suddenly take a stroll`? Could it be that he knows I am following him? Tony Millions did say to watch out for this one.* The big Russian stopped in his tracks, the flesh on the back of his neck prickling. Too late.

A tree branch snapped.

The Russian spun.

* * *

Johnny swung the club of birch with all his might. It connected solidly with the side of the big man's face, falling him to one knee. The big man looked up, swung the gun in an arc, and fired. The silenced retort of the .45 sounded like a whisper in the wind, the slug kicking off the very pine Johnny had secreted himself. With a vicious kick of his leg, the gun was knocked free of the Russian's grip and out of reach. The big man tried to get up. Johnny hit him again, the club of wood shattering when it made contact with the back of his bald head. Blood burst from the wound like a spigot. Nonetheless, the big man continued to rise.

Removing the knife from his mouth, Johnny lunged forward, his intended target, the exposed throat.

Yuri anticipated the Indian's next move, blocked the assault with an arm, and kicked outward, the hard boot connecting with Johnny's knee. He fell backward. With amazing agility for a man his size, the Russian was on top of Johnny, pinning his arms by his sides. He slammed the knife hand into the frozen tundra again and again and again, breaking a couple of fingers until the blade was set free. "So you vant to dance, Indian? Ve dance." Blood ran from the back of the Russians head and into his face, covering his cheeks and throat and inking the scar bright red.

"I'm going to kill you!" Johnny told him.

"I don't think so!" the Russian spat back. In a blink, he let go of Johnny's right arm, made a fist, and slammed it into Johnny's jaw. Then he reached for the knife, his tremendous weight keeping Johnny in place.

With his one arm free and, remembering an article he had read in one of the martial arts books, Johnny thrust upward, thumb straight out, aiming for the big man's right eye. It hit home. Johnny pushed, ripping his thumb sideways. The eye popped out of its socket, supported only by its optic nerve.

The Russian's hands immediately went to his face. "You fucking bastard!" he cried, his fingers trying to locate the swinging eye.

Johnny thrust a hard knee into the Russian's testicles, rolled quickly and reclaimed the knife.

Yuri fell sideways, one hand holding the eye, the other clutching his groin.

Johnny was on his feet, an animal intent on ripping its prey to shreds, the steel of the knife flashing before it sank into the Russian's side. He withdrew the bloodied knife and attempted another thrust; however, the Russian trundled to his right and Johnny missed.

Before the hitman could manage his feet, Johnny was on top of him. Insensible to his injured hand he yanked the Russian's head until his throat was exposed and swiftly drew the blade across. A sound not unlike air being released from a balloon emanated from the newly created smile in the Russian's gullet. Johnny stood, lungs starved for breath, the knife dyed crimson, blood dripping from its sharpness.

All around, trees sighed as the wind strengthened.

Homicidal Johnny watched the Russian's life blood spurt from the mortal wound, layering the snow-covered ground with savage squiggles and loops. Finally, Yuri collapsed, hands at his throat, dead before his bloodied face hit the ground.

Standing over the Russian, hair and feather tossing wildly, Johnny wanted to scream like a primitive beast that had just laid claim to its quarry. He stared at the big man lying motionless on the ground then at his hands. They were raw and red, and for certain, two of his fingers were broke. He dropped the knife. *What are you going to do now?*

Konahee's wind-carried voice supplied him with the answer, "*Use the river, Johnny.*"

The river and its steep bank were less than twenty feet away. He hoisted the Russian's legs and, using all remaining strength, dragged him toward it, tracing a slick smear of gore in the snow. When he reached the verge of the bank, he turned the Russian so he was perpendicular to the edge and, with one mighty push, rolled him over.

Yuri Dimeniachuk's corpse tobogganed the icy slope, and splashed into the swift-moving current with the telling weight of a boulder. For a moment it did not move. Then like a piece of driftwood caught in a vortex, the potent current pulled him upstream until his undulating body came to a bulking mass of ice. Johnny watched as the body hit and spun before the strength of the mighty river took the Russian under, trapping him beneath the thick island of ice like so much debris.

Following the trail of gore back to the knife, Johnny picked it up and, using clumps of snow, cleaned the blade and his raw, wounded hands. The fact that it was going to snow for the remainder of the day and probably tomorrow, Mother would conceal the big man's bloodletting. After a quick search, he located the .45, thought about keeping it for a moment, then went back to the river's periphery and threw it into the current where it sank like a stone.

Hidden within the thick collar of the parka was a hood. Johnny released it, drew it over his head, and shoved his raw hands into deep pockets. With a sore jaw, two badly injured fingers, his mind wandering, the vengeance madness satiated, he headed for the hotel and back to a distraught Rebecca.

* * *

78

We Belong to the Light

STYMIED by the lack of information he was receiving, Mr. Green drove from the Renegades Hotel in Turner Valley back to the town of Destiny. He'd managed to get a room with two double beds and bar fridge for $69 per night. Circling the hotel several times, he parked across the street from Grillos Pizzeria and flipped open his cell. He tried Cracker first. "Where are you?"

"I'm standing in front of a place called Koop's. About five minutes south of the hotel. I think they fix cars or something."

"Seen anything?"

"Just an Indian woman pulling a cart, some teenagers, and a lot of fucking snow. No one matching this Johnny *or* Rebecca's description. Hey? How long are you going to keep us out here? It's fucking colder than a nun's cunt."

Mr. Green looked at his watch. It was three thirty. Darkness would soon fall. Shops in small towns closed early during the winter season. The only place he could see that would remain open was the hotel. The weather reports he had been listening to said the snow was going to get worse before it got any better. There would be no reason for the Indian and Rebecca to venture the streets once everything shut down.

"Give it another hour. Then I'll pick you up."

"They might not even be here yet. They could have stopped someplace on the way up. You know. To enjoy their freedom. Spend some of that money they stole."

"Trust my intuition, Cracker. It hasn't let us down in the past, and it's not now. They *are* here. I can feel it in my bones."

"Okay. Just don't forget we're out here freezing our nuts off."

"One hour." Mr. Green disconnected the call, scrolled for the Russian's number, and hit Talk. The line connected. It chirped and chirped and chirped. Yuri did not pick up. *What the fuck?* Mr. Green did not like this at all. Not one little bit. He backed from the parking space and headed to where the Russian should be.

* * *

During his return to the hotel, identity concealed by the hood, Johnny had seen the black Navigator with Nevada plates pass him on Center Street. As soon as he was able, he took to the side avenues and quickly made his way to the rear of the Destiny Hotel. Using his good hand, he fished for keys, opened the heavy metal door, and took the stairs two at a time.

Reaching room 8, his attention was distracted for a moment by the cat Brook the bartender had told them about. It walked up to Johnny, tail straight in the air, and curled its body in and around his legs while it purred for attention. Johnny bent low, scratched it between the ears. "It's nice to meet you too."

Two rooms down, a door opened and an elderly lady with frizzled grey hair poked her head into the hallway. "Mr. Jingles. Don't bother the guests. Come. I have a nice treat for you."

Mr. Jingles looked at her, meowed, and ran toward the open door where it fled into the room.

"I'm sorry if he bothered you, young man. He's such a social creature."

"It's okay. He didn't bother me at all," said Johnny, fondly remembering George.

"Well, have a nice day, young man."

"You too."

The permanent resident of the Destiny Hotel smiled and closed the door.

Inserting the key into the lock, Johnny turned the knob and stepped into the room. Sitting on the bed where he'd left her, gun firm in hand, Rebecca aimed it at him. "It's me, Rebecca," he said, closing the door and setting the deadbolt.

Rebecca gasped when she saw Johnny's swollen face. Her feelings of anxiety immediately transposed to one of worry. "Oh my god, Johnny! You're hurt!" She went to him, stopped cold when she saw the fingers of his right hand completely bent out of shape. "Your fingers! What happened!"

Johnny removed his coat, carefully.

"Here, let me help you." Rebecca freed one arm then the other, careful not to make contact with the broken fingers. Once it was off, she let it drop to the carpet. Together they went to the bed where the dormant pain in Johnny's body finally surfaced.

Looking at her, he removed the skinning knife from the small of his back, and tossed it on the bed next to the gun. "I did it, Becca. I killed one of them. The big one with the scar on his face. He's as dead as sure as I'm sitting here."

"He hurt you, Johnny," said Rebecca, her eyes inspecting every inch of him. "Are you in pain?"

"Just a little. I'll live." He took a deep, settling breath. "It wasn't easy. He was very strong. And for a moment while we were fighting, I thought I might never see you again. At least not in this life."

"What happened? What did you do with the body?" Taking his injured hand, she gently stroked the damaged fingers.

"You don't need to hear the details. Just know that he probably won't be found until next spring. One down. Two to go."

Abruptly, the hallway filled with voices.

Each held their breaths, Rebecca's fingers searched for the gun, her eyes riveted to the door. The voices waned, then they heard the sound of a door closing. She let out the held breath. "Just some hotel guests. I imagine we're going to hear a lot of that over the next little while, tomorrow being New Year's and everything."

Johnny let loose a nervous laugh. "The big question is, what do we do once it's over? Run again?"

"Honestly, Johnny, I don't know," though she did. "We can't fool ourselves into thinking that Tony will ever stop sending men after us. You can't kill them all, my love."

"I know," said Johnny, pained, knowing that no amount of preparation on Konahee's part could aid him in taking them all on. He looked to the gun. "I do know however, that I'm not ready to put that thing against your head or mine. We'll figure something out."

Rebecca smiled even though she wanted to cry until the very end of time. They held a silent moment for several anxious heartbeats. "What we need to do right now is get you cleaned up. Get that bastard's blood off you. I'm going to run you a nice hot bath. Then we'll have to do something about those fingers."

"Like what?'

"I don't know. Maybe there's things under the sink we can make a couple of splints with."

"Do you know how to make a splint? Because I don't."

"Not really. But it can't hurt to try. How hard can it be?"

* * *

After the hot bath, Rebecca toweled Johnny dry. She had washed his back, chest, arms, and legs with the gentle touch of a caregiver. Searching beneath the sink for anything she could fashion into a splint, she found nothing except a box half-filled with bandages. She made Johnny sit on the lid of the toilet, a white towel wrapped around his waist. "Give me your hand."

Johnny held it out. "What for?"

Rebecca looked at the damaged fingers, turning his hand this way and that. "Maybe they're just, you know, dislocated. My brother dislocated a finger once, and it looked pretty much the same. Bent awkwardly at the knuckle. My father made me watch while he put it back in place. Told me it was something I needed to know. That it might come in handy someday. I guess he was right. Yes, I believe they're just dislocated."

Johnny attempted to pull his hand away.

Rebecca held it firm. "Don't be a baby. It'll only hurt for a minute or two. I promise." She took hold of the middle finger. "Ready?"

"About as ready as I'll ever be I guess. Are you sure you know what you're doing?"

"No, I'm not. Now take a deep breath and hold still."

Using all the strength she could muster, Rebecca pulled hard on the finger until the knuckle straightened, then, using her thumb to guide it, forced it back into place.

Gnashing teeth, Johnny winced, jerked his hand away. "Fuck, that hurt!"

"Yes. I'm sure it did. But look. It's as good as new. Just as I suspected. They're only dislocated. Now for the other one."

"Can you just give me a second?"

"Take all the time you need. But I think it's best that while you're in pain, we do the other one quickly. It'll hurt less."

"Thanks for the advice, Nurse White. But I guess you're right." Grudgingly he gave her his hand.

Taking his index finger in her fist, she asked, "Ready?"

Before Johnny could answer, Rebecca yanked hard on the digit, and righted its position.

"Jesus Fucking H. Christ on a Fucking Hockey Stick! You tricked me!"

"Yes. But you weren't expecting it, so I bet it hurt less." Raising his hand to her lips, she kissed the now-righted fingers. "There. Better now?"

Johnny let out a heavy breath, tried the fingers, flexing them back and forth. Though they still pained him, they moved to his will. "I wonder how long it's going to take Mr. Green to realize one of his accomplices is missing?"

"Probably not long. I'm sure they're keeping close contact with one another. With the cold and snow, I imagine they'll get back together pretty soon. Then they'll know. Mr. Green's going to be pretty pissed."

"Maybe they'll back off some."

"I doubt it, Johnny. They might go back to wherever it is they're staying and rethink their plan of attack. But they won't back off. If anything, they'll be even more vigilant in their attempts to track us down. At least now, with what you did, they'll be looking over both shoulders everywhere they go. That could be a good thing or a bad thing."

"What I would really like to know is how in the hell did they find us here in the first place? I was thinking about it on my way back here. The only thing I could come up with was one of two things. Either there's some kind of tracking device somewhere hidden in the money or, when we took the money, we were seen doing it. A security camera or something. It would certainly explain how the guy I just killed knew what I looked like. And it would explain why I had a notion someone was watching us while we did it."

"You're right. Okay, let's check the money first."

They went into the other room and dumped the money onto the bed. Carefully they went through it. Not once but twice, finding nothing. Johnny stuffed it back into the knapsack. "I guess that answers my question. Tony Millions must have had a security device that recorded the whole thing. That's how they knew to come to Destiny, Alberta. They must have heard you saying it."

Rebecca dropped onto the bed, and began to cry. "It's all my fault. I should have kept my big mouth shut. Here I go out of my way to disguise myself, and then I tell them exactly where they could find us. Stupid! Stupid! Stupid!"

Johnny sat next to her, took her into his arms. "Don't beat yourself up, Becca. How could you know there was a security camera? What's done is done. Nothing can change it. Yes, maybe we should have thought things through better. But we didn't. I'm just as much to blame."

Rebecca looked at him. "That's sweet of you to say." *Sniff.* "So what are we going to do now?"

"I've just killed a man and had my fingers repaired by the Marquis de Sade. I'm exhausted. What I would like to do is lie down for a while. We're probably safe for the time being. It'll be dark soon. They might know we're here in Destiny, but I don't believe they know where. And they're not going to continue searching once night falls. Not in this shit. I'm sure of it." Claiming their weapons, he placed them on the night table where and, for the first time, noticed Rebecca had removed the radio from its container. It sat next to the lamp. "Is it plugged in?"

"Yes, of course."

Johnny found the on-off switch and turned it on. Static hissed from the speakers. "What was that station we were listening to on the way in here?"

"I believe it was called the Eagle. Out of Okotoks. Move the dial to 100.9."

Moving the dial to the right, Johnny found the station quite easily. The DJ was telling his listeners the New Year's Eve gala at a place called the George was one hundred and fifty dollars per couple. This included a buffet, party favors, and a champagne toast at midnight. "Don't miss out."

"It would be nice if we could attend," said Rebecca.

"We'll have our own little party. Right here. If we're able."

"One day at a time my love."

"Yes," agreed Johnny for without a doubt, a great tragedy lay ahead. It had been foreseen. It had been told. "One day at a time."

The advertising ended and was replaced by an updated weather report.

Rebecca lay on the bed, and propped the pillows behind her head. The need for Percocet jabbed at her, but only a little. "Come here, my love."

Johnny slid next to her, rested his head on her bosom, then closed his eyes.

Tenderly, lovingly, Rebecca stroked his face. She could feel his heartbeat against hers and the lasting tension in his body. In a few short breaths, he succumbed to desperate sleep. Decreasing the volume on the radio, tears of empathy fell from her eyes. Taking hold of the .38, she laid it next to her. *How long could she keep it a secret between them that she knew the end of their brief love affair was near? That they would soon join each other in the afterlife. Was it Johnny's fate that he be brutally murdered by Mr. Green? Is that why she feared him from the second she laid eyes on him? More likely than not.*

A young Pat Benatar filtered through the speakers. Rebecca closed her eyes and listened while her heart ached for the man lying next to her.

Many times I've tried to tell you
Many times I've cried alone
Always I'm surprised how well you
Cut my feelings to the bone

Don't want to leave you really
I've invested too much time

To give you up that easy
To the doubts that complicate your mind

We belong to the light
We belong to the thunder
We belong to the sound of the words
We've both fallen under
Whatever we deny or embrace
For worse or for better
We belong, we belong
We belong together...

Without meaning to go with it, sleep carried Rebecca in its arms, and whisked her away to its address of dreams.

She found herself standing on the edge of a towering cliff, an endless blue sky above, raging river below. It was hot, yet the sky held no sun. The perfume of many flowers filled her senses. The screeching call of a hawk came from out of the blue. She looked up, only to find that the sky was empty. Then a sound rose from the river below. It lifted higher and higher until, finally, it reached Rebecca's ears in all its inherent innocence. It was the wail of an infant's plight. The stones beneath her feet gave way, and she was cast over the cliff's boundary, soaring in the air as if she had wings, as if she were meant to fly. She cried with joy; however, the sound that emanated from her lips was not that of her bliss, but the piercing shrill of a great bird.

* * *

Mr. Green's search for the Russian was futile. For a half hour, he visited the shops of the mini mall in case the Russian had taken refuge from the cold. Yuri Dimeniachuk was nowhere to be found. Furious, Mr. Green drove to Government Road and headed south. In less than a minute, he saw the small figure of Cracker, standing in the swirling snow in front of the automotive shop Koops. He pulled the Navigator even and stopped, wipers slapping time.

Cracker got in.

"We have a problem," Mr. Green told him.

"And that is?"

"Yuri is nowhere to be found. Do you know what that means?" He didn't wait for a response from his little friend. "It means they know we're here." He slammed the steering wheel with a fist. "Somehow, that fucking Indian got the upper hand on our friend. I guarantee you, dollars to donuts, Yuri is dead. You want to know what else it means? It means now we'll have to watch *our* backs. Tony was right. This guy's going to be a handful."

Cracker stared at the wipers arcing over the windshield and the snow drifting to anywhere all around. All he said was, "Let him come."

* * *

79

Tell Me No Lies

IT was the voice of the wind that shook Rebecca from slumber, the window trembling within the grasp of its holler. Her eyes were sticky with sleep. She rubbed them into focus. Darkness encompassed the room. "You're the One I've Been Waiting For" oozed from the radio. During her travels throughout the realm of dreams, she had taken the gun in hand, her index finger now locked around the trigger. *It's a good thing the safety was on.* She set it aside, turned on the light to find Johnny lying on his side, knees drawn to his chest like a child. *God, he was gorgeous.*

Being as quiet as she could, she rose from the bed, went to the darkened window, and drew apart the curtains. There was a light secured to the back of the hotel that revealed the intensity of the storm. Unrelenting snow was coming down at an acute angle. Reaching, she touched the glass. It was as cold as a sheet of ice.

"What are you looking at?"

Turning, she saw that Johnny was sitting upright. "Just the storm. How are you feeling?"

"Rested. And hungry. I wonder what time it is?"

"Let me rephrase that. How are your fingers?"

Johnny opened and closed his hand. "Still a little sore. But I'll manage." He reached for the remote and gave life to the television. Searching the directory, he found an all-news station. According to the digital readout in the right-hand corner, it was almost 10:00 p.m. The temperature, -22° Celsius. He clicked it off. "Do you think the kitchen is still open?"

"Probably." Rebecca returned to the bed and sat next to him. "You're not thinking of going down there, are you?"

"We've got to eat, Becca." He kissed her on the back of her neck. "We can't live on love alone."

"What about Mr. Green and that other man? Aren't you worried they're still out there?"

Johnny thought it over for a moment. "The way I see it, by now, Mr. Green and this other guy are fully aware their accomplice has disappeared. That their friend is probably dead and buried someplace, courtesy of yours truly. At least that's what I would be thinking. This changes everything. The tables have turned. Don't you see? The hunters have now become the hunted. Wherever they are right now, they're probably wondering what to do about it. They'll have to rethink their original intentions. That's going to take time. Time we can use to our advantage. They're going to be particularly careful about their next move. Another thing we have going for us is this storm. There's no way they're looking for us in this kind of weather at this time of night. No way. Whatever their next move is going to be, it won't take place until tomorrow. And I'll be ready for it."

"You sound so sure."

"I am. You didn't fall in love with an idiot you know."

"So what do you want to eat? I'll go down."

"Are you sure? I don't mind going."

"No. It's all right. I'll put my hood up just in case. Use the back door. I could use the change of scenery even if it's just for a few minutes. Besides, you're not dressed to go anywhere." She looked down at the towel barely concealing his manhood. "Now that you're rested, and after we eat, maybe we could, you know." Knowing what she knew, and regardless of the situation they were in, she would make love to him as often as she could.

"Then you better feed me. I'll have some wings, hot, and a cheeseburger with fries. Oh, and a Coke."

Rebecca rose from the bed, went to the table next to the window, and retrieved the handbag. Then she put on her coat, and drew the hood over her head. "I'll be back in ten, twenty minutes."

"I'll be right here waiting." Standing from the bed, the towel slipped from his waist. His stomach growled.

"At least put some pants on."

"What for? Nobody can see inside this room."

"So that I have something to take off after we've finished eating."

"You're bad."

"Would you have me any other way?"

"Not a chance."

Rebecca went to the door, opened it, stuck her head into the hall just in case, and left for the restaurant.

Concealing his nakedness in a pair of jeans, Johnny walked toward the frozen window. All he could see were the streaking slashes of snow crashing to the earth. The cold was coming right through the glass. Something was troubling him. Had been for the past few days now. He had no doubt Rebecca was hiding something from him. He could see it hidden in the depths of her green eyes. *Was she aware what the near future held for them? Was there a future? Did she know of the great tragedy Konahee Wolf spoke of?* He stared at the storm until the raining snow became hypnotic. Paul McCartney sang volumes of his dilemma.

Stuck inside these four walls
Sent inside forever
Never seeing no one
Nice... again
Like you...
Momma
You...

The bar was nearly empty. Only one person, an elderly gentleman, hunched by his formative years, was playing the VLTs. In the kitchen, three cooks were beginning the close-out, cleaning stainless steel surfaces and mopping the floor. The doorman was sitting at his station near the arched entrance, bored. He smiled at Rebecca. Rebecca smiled back. Brook the bartender stood behind the bar, speaking to someone on her cell. Of the three waitresses, two were wiping down tables, the other tallying a bill for one of four customers who remained.

Rebecca went to the bar. Brook smiled and held up a finger indicating she would be done with the call momentarily. A menu lay on the long bar's surface. Rebecca sat on one of the stools, opened it, and examined the list of food available. After a moment, she chose something light. Chicken quesadilla with salad.

"Hi Tiffany." Brook stood in front of her.

"Um, yes. Nice of you to remember," said Rebecca, offering a smile and silently thanking Keely for not revealing her true identity.

"It's a prerequisite in this kind of work."

"Is it too late to order food?"

"You're in luck. The kitchen doesn't close for another hour. The guys would be happy to fix you something."

"Good. Then I would like a pound of wings, hot. Cheeseburger and fries and a chicken quesadilla with Caesar salad to go please. Oh, and a Coke and a 7 Up. Hey? I could have sworn your eyes were brown last night. Now they're green."

"They do that. I don't know why. I was once told by a local clairvoyant that it meant I was special. That I have a gift. Though I have no idea what it is. As far as I know, I'm just plain Brook. Nothing special."

"Oh, but you are. Special I mean. Trust me. I can tell. You'll find out what your gift is one day. I assure you."

"I hope you're right." Brook turned and entered the order on a terminal. "Would you like something to drink while you're waiting?"

"That would be nice. An iced tea would be fine. Thank you."

Brook filled a tall glass with ice, then using the soda dispenser, filled it with iced tea and dropped in a red straw. "Would you like a lemon?"

"No, thanks. This will do fine." Rebecca took a long quenching drink. "How much do I owe you?"

"Thirty ninety-five. The iced tea is on the house."

Rebecca fished in her handbag for a few twenties. "Here you go. Keep five for yourself."

"Thank you," said Brook. She went to the cash register, made change, and handed it to Rebecca. "Have you and your boyfriend decided whether or not you're coming to the New Year's Eve party tomorrow?"

"We're not sure yet. Sounds like a good time though."

"Well, the band is great. They play everything from country to old rock. If you *do* decide to come, you should get here no later than eight, eight thirty. We fill up pretty quick on New Year's Eve. Even in this kind of weather."

"I'll remember that. Thanks again."

Each looked to the bank of windows and the raging storm outside.

"Is it always like this during the winter months?" Rebecca wanted to know.

"Not always. Sometimes it's worse." Brook laughed.

The bar phone rang.

"You'll have to excuse me. Duty calls."

Rebecca turned in the stool and watched the cooks in the kitchen. Through the glass partition, she could see her order was already being prepared. The silver-haired gentleman playing the VLTs started talking to the machine. He tapped the glass terminal with his drink and swore at it. "Fucking greedy bitch." Reaching into a pocket, he withdrew another twenty and slid it into the machine. "You better pay off." *Tap. Tap. Tap.*

Rebecca felt sorry for him. Putting hopes in Lady Luck was, more times than not, a one-sided relationship. She knew that better than anyone.

Within ten minutes, her order was ready.

"Your order is ready, Tiffany," said Brook. "Just go to the kitchen and they'll give it to you."

"Thanks again, Brook. Oh, do you serve breakfast?"

"Used to. Not anymore. But there's a place in Turner Valley, one town to the west of here and a short drive, called the Chuck Wagon. They serve breakfast all day."

"That's good to know, thanks again."

"Not a problem. Here's your drinks." She handed Rebecca two cans. "Stay warm."

The soda pops went into the side pockets of her coat and she went to the kitchen counter where one of the cooks was holding two white plastic bags.

"Here you go," he said in a thick Russian accent and smiled. "There are napkins in bags."

"Thank you."

Rebecca stepped out into the white storm and looked up and down Government Road. The town was asleep, the road as barren as a church on Mondays. Not a night fit for man or beast nor hired killers.

When she entered room 8, Johnny was standing by the window. The radio was off and the television was on. He turned when he heard the door open. *At least he was wearing jeans.* Setting the lock, she held up the plastic bags. Where do you want to eat? And you were right. Nobody's out in this shit storm."

"I knew there wouldn't be. Might as well make use of the table." He went to her, kissed her mouth, and relieved her of the bags. Rebecca shrugged out of the parka, and removed their drinks from the pockets.

Setting the bags on the table, Johnny asked, "Was the bar busy?"

"Not at all. Just a few die-hards and an old man fighting it out with one of the VLTs. An uninvited shiver racked her body. "God, it's cold out there." She set the cans on the table.

Removing the Styrofoam containers, Johnny opened them. The smell of hot sauce filled the room. "According to the local weather report, the highway between here and Okotoks, that's the town I went to earlier, is closed. So are parts of Highway 2 between Calgary and a town called Red Deer. They say it's not going to let up for at least two more days."

"Do you mind if I turn the TV off and put on some music?"

"Of course I don't. I've learned all I need to know anyway."

"Meaning what?" She turned off the television, clicked on the radio. The Four Seasons' "Oh, What a Night" rocked the airwaves.

"That we couldn't go anywhere even if we wanted to."

They sat at the table. Snow blistered the window. Rebecca opened the quesadilla container. "Those wings smell good."

"Yeah, they do." Taking one, Johnny striped it to the bone in one motion. Between chews, he said, "Becca? I want to ask you something, and I want you to be honest with me."

Rebecca picked up a triangle of quesadilla, took a bite, then a drink, the look on Johnny's face telling her he was going to ask the questions she dreaded to answer. "Okay."

"Something has been bothering me for the past few days. There's something you're not telling me. I can see it in your eyes every time I look at you. I would like to know what it is. I'll accept whatever it is you tell me."

Rebecca swallowed hard. Though they had been together for only a week, they had learned so much about each other. She could not deceive him anymore. He deserved to know the truth. She took another drink. Looking him in the eyes, she truthed in a flat tone, "You're going to die, Johnny. I've known for quite some time. Since the night we met. I'm sorry, I never should have kept that kind of knowledge from you."

Johnny blinked several times. Looking down at his wings, he found that he was suddenly not hungry. When he looked up again, there were tears in Rebecca's eyes. "I was also aware. Someone told me that a great tragedy was in store for me. I guess we had our reasons for keeping it a secret. Now that its out, do you know when? How?"

Rebecca lowered her eyes, releasing the tears pooled within. Shaking her head and with a sad tone, she said, "Soon I believe now. I was hoping we would have some time together. Just you and me. That fate would stop the clock for us. I was wrong. I'm sorry. That's why I'm so afraid of this desire you have to hunt Tony Million's men. Nothing good can come of it. I'm afraid you're going to go through that door and not come back."

"You know I have to at least try. I can't just sit here and let them find us. Like you said, they would convert you back into a life of debauchery or worse. I promised that I would protect you best I can, and I will. If I should go through that door and not come back, I want you to promise me you'll call the police. You have nothing to hide. You're not wanted for anything. You could start over. Promise me, Becca. Promise me right now!"

Rebecca wiped at her face. "I couldn't live without you, Johnny. You and I are meant to be together, forever. That's something else I know. No matter what happens, we will always be together. When you die, I have every intention of keeping the promise we made to each other. I would take my own life. Nothing you say will stop me from doing so."

"Don't talk like that, Becca. It was just a silly promise we made at a time when it seemed to suit the situation. We were love-drunk. People say the stupidest things when they're like that. It doesn't mean you have to go through with it."

"I know with all my heart another life waits for us, Johnny. A life where you and I will walk hand in hand. Forever and a day. Our destiny fulfilled. Where being happy will be all that exists for us. Where we'll never grow old. Where darkness is forbidden and sickness and worry no longer exist. You cannot deny what I know."

Johnny lowered his eyes. "You're right. I can't deny your abilities. But taking your own life, Becca. I can't bear to think of it."

"Then don't. We'll let fate run its course. We can't change what's going to happen, so let's not think about it anymore. When the time comes. You and I will both know it, and we'll accept it. *Okay?* I have nothing, Johnny. Only you."

Swallowing the lump in his throat, he looked at her. Rebecca's eyes implored him to accept fate for what it was. A numinous authority no one could alter. "Okay, Becca. We'll let fate run its course."

They ate their food. The mournful wind pushed against the window pleading to come in. Music played from the radio. When they were done, Johnny went to her and, in one loving motion, scooped her into his arms.

"What are you doing?"

"I'm taking you to the bed, and I'm going to love you, Becca. Love you like you never thought possible." Resting her on the comforter, he lay beside her, stroked her face with a gentle hand and told her how beautiful she was over and over. Together they discarded their clothing and stared at each other for a long tender moment before they kissed, the desire for each other all-consuming, as was their time.

"I love you, Johnny Black," she told him, breath soft against his face.

"And I adore you, Rebecca White," he told her with all his heart.

For the remainder of the night, nothing else existed or mattered. Not the raging storm outside, or the men who saw them as a means to financial gains. Not the days of past or the telling verses of the future. Just a single heartbeat of unencumbered passion for which time had no hold.

Sunshine, every single day
Helps to light my way
And, darlin', right before my eyes
It don't come as no surprise

That it's easy
Easy lovin' you

And, baby, till you came along
There was always something wrong
Around me
There was emptiness of course
But it's all right

And it's easy
Easy lovin' you...

* * *

80

December 31
Fade to Black

HALF-AWAKE, Rebecca reached for Johnny. When her hand found only mattress, fear took hold of her, forcing her upright. Immediately her body was covered in a fine coating of dread, heart beating rapidly. Instinctively her eyes went to the gun sitting on the night table. "Johnny?" Then she heard the shower running. He was still with her. *Thank God*. Surprisingly, sunlight was pouring through the window, and she could see that the snow had stopped, at least for the time being. Through the glass, she could hear the rumbling of a snow-removal vehicle as it cleared Government Road.

Crawling out from beneath the cover, she sat on the edge of the bed. The radio was low. Harry Chapin's "Taxi" evoked part of a journey past. Sky's bugeyed glasses. Mr. Chapin sitting in the back seat, singing with the radio. Carly Simon's signature.

When the song ended, replaced by an auto dealer's commercial, memories of the night before flooded her soul. Johnny had made love to her for most of the night, bringing her to and beyond the heights of her most secret fantasies. He had loved her body, savoring every inch of it, until she thought she could take no more. Then orchestrating a rhythm that could have only come from the most deepest regions of his essence, he played her as though she were a fine instrument, bringing her to orgasm again and again and again. When finally, a thunderous eruption shook his loins, he had collapsed on top of her, telling her once more before surrendering to sleep that he loved her, that he would love her forever and a day and that she was most beautiful.

The sound of running water stopped.

The time of day and weather report was tallied by the DJ, two fifteen, and the sunshine the foothills was enjoying would not last long due to another system quickly moving into the area. When he finished with the local news, he introduced the next five songs beginning with "Sweet City Woman" by the Stampeders.

A moment later, the bathroom door opened. Trapped steam billowed. Johnny stepped through it, a towel around his waist, long hair dripping, grey eyes sparkling. "Good afternoon, sleepyhead. Feeling rested."

"After last night, I think my body is going to need a week to recover. *If we have a week*. How are your fingers?"

"Good as new. I guess I owe you an apology about the whole Marquis de Sade comment."

Rising from the bed, she went to him, embraced him, kissed his mouth again and again. "Mmm. You smell good. Did you save me some hot water?"

"There seems to be an endless supply."

"Good. My turn." She released his neck. "Are you hungry?"

"Always."

"Well, you *did* expend a tremendous amount of energy last night."

"Hey, I had help you know."

"Maybe a little. The rest was all you, my love." She picked up the Pharmasave bag containing clippers, polish, razors and went into the still-steaming bathroom, closing the door behind her.

Releasing the towel from his waist, Johnny gave his hair the once-over and dressed. The feather hung just right. During the shower, he had contemplated what, he was going to do about Mr. Green and his accomplice. *I still have to at least try*, he'd told himself. He knew he had a much better chance at eliminating them one at a time. However, if they determined that two sets of eyes were better than one, then the difficulty in dealing with them would proliferate tenfold. He had to be very, very careful.

Walking to the window, he looked to the lane below. Ten, possibly twelve inches of snow had fallen over night. Everything was white. A young Asian fellow was doing his best to shovel it from the asphalt of the Esso. Hunkered in heavy coats, two female hotel staff were standing on the loading dock and smoking. Neither were Keely or Brook. A black pickup truck and a soft blue Kia were parked near the dock. *How ordinary everything seemed*. His stomach growled. Inspecting the takeout containers on the table for maybe a wing or a few cold fries, he saw they had eaten everything. At least he could quench his thirst. He went to the bar fridge, opened it, took out a Kokanee, twisted the cap, and consumed nearly half.

The sound of the shower stopped. A trice later, the buzz of the supplied hair dryer permeated through the door, drowning the low volume of the radio.

Johnny went to it and turned it up, his eyes focused on the gun and killing knife sitting side by side. They seemed to communicate their intent. The knife spoke of retribution, the gun vocalizing impending death. He sat on the edge of the bed, and took the .38 in hand. It was as cold as its intended purpose. *This would be the best method*, he heard Rebecca say. *A bullet to the brain*.

Retrieving another beer, he put the gun back on the nightstand, leaned into one of the pillows, and listened to the music, hoping it would chase away the pessimistic thoughts he was having.

In the third verse of "Welcome to My Nightmare," someone knocked on the door. Johnny sat rigid, and nearly dropped the beer, the hairs on the back of his neck standing to attention. He put the beer on the nightstand and lowered the volume on the radio as if doing so would make whoever was on the other side of the door go away.

Whoever it was knocked again.

"Just a minute," Johnny called out, collected the gun and wedged it between the waistband of his jeans and the small of his back. The knife, he jammed beneath one of the pillows. He went to the door, a finger looped through the trigger. "Who is it?"

A female's voice said, "I'm sorry to bother, sir. Do you need your room cleaned?"

Johnny blew out a breath. "No, that's okay. We're a little indisposed at the moment."

"Shall I come back later then?"

"I think we're okay until tomorrow. But thanks anyway." He listened. It wasn't until he heard her move away from the door and down the hall that he took his finger off the trigger and returned to the bed. He lifted the beer to his lips, drained the bottle, and wiped the trauma sweat from his forehead.

The bathroom door opened. Rebecca stood naked, legs shaved, fingernails and toes painted red, the light from the bathroom igniting the entirety of her beauty. A little of her natural color bled through the black. She immediately saw the look of concern on Johnny's face. "What is it? What's wrong?" She moved toward him, stopping inches away from his upturned face.

Johnny leaned his head against her abdomen. "The hotel maid came to the door just now. I nearly jumped out of my skin. My first thought was to protect us, so I armed myself. Is that what all this has come to? My being paranoid every time I hear a sound."

"I'm sorry, Johnny. I don't have an answer for that."

"Well, I think I do. I'm going to go out there today and find those bastards. Once I'm done with them, we can let fate decide which route to take."

Stroking the top of his head, Rebecca said, "Then I'm going with you."

Pulling away, he looked up at her as if she were crazy. "No, you're not! You're staying right here!"

"The hell I am. If you think I'm going to just stay in this room going crazy with worry while you're out there hunting these men, think again. I'm going with you and that's that." Turning from him, she folded her arms across her bosom like a stubborn child.

Rising from the bed, Johnny placed his hands on her shoulders. A much safer alternative than them walking the streets came to mind. "This town must have a taxi service, right?"

"Probably. Why?"

"Instead of us being vulnerable out in the open, we can hire a taxi, have him drive us from town to town, like we're a couple of tourists who want to see the sights. We can cover a lot more territory that way and possibly find out where Mr. Green and the other one are hiding out. Once we've accomplished that, what I have to do will be much easier. I'll definitely have the upper hand. They won't see me coming."

What Johnny was saying made sense. A lot more sense than being easy targets out in the open. She turned to face him. "So what are we going to do once we do find them?"

"*We're* not going to do anything. If we do find them, *I'm* going to take care of things. If I can draw them out some place, I might get lucky and finish them off. You know. Like killing two birds with one stone."

"It would have to be a place where you won't draw attention to yourself."

"There's lots of places around here. These towns are surrounded by woods and rivers."

Rebecca paced the floor, thinking. "Okay. We'll go to the bar and call a cab, *if* one exists. So let's say you do find them and manage to kill them, then what? It will only be a matter of time before Tony Millions sends more men after us. Like I said before, you can't kill them all, Johnny, and I'm done running."

"Who knows? Maybe once Tony Millions realizes his men have failed in their attempt to dispose of us, he might decide to leave us alone."

"That's pretty optimistic."

"Hey. You're always telling me how pessimistic I am. I thought I would try optimism for a change."

Rebecca knew everything they had just discussed bordered on the fantastic. Johnny was going to die. And he was most likely going to meet his end at the hands of Mr. Green and his accomplice. Nevertheless, she would support him in his decision making, frivolous as it may be. He was being what he had promised he would always be. Her guardian, without regard for himself. But she knew, deep down, that this was their final stand. Their last desperate act. And she would go with him. There was after all, another life waiting for them.

"I need a few minutes to let the nail polish dry and to dress. Why don't you go downstairs. Make sure you hide your face just in case. It's sunny. They could be driving around looking for us right now. Hopefully not. Hopefully they're still holed up someplace, scheming. We'll eat first before calling a cab. Then we'll do what you said. See if we can't find out where they're at."

"All right. Do you want me to order you anything?"

"I'd like to take another look at their menu."

Johnny slipped into his coat and put on his boots. Taking the gun, he dropped it into a side pocket. "See you in a few minutes." He kissed her then turned for the door.

"Johnny?"

"Yes."

"Be careful all right."

Johnny looked at her over a shoulder. "Hey. Careful is my middle name. Besides, if you recall, I'm an Indian. I can be invisible if need be. Runs in the blood."

By the time Rebecca had dressed and checked herself in the bathroom mirror because it was something all girls who were in love did before they went out, the snow began to fall again, though nowhere near as fierce as the night before. She went to the window, her eyes searching every square inch of what she could see. Except for the new snow, cars moving up and down Government Road and only a handful of pedestrians, there was no sign of Mr. Green, the Navigator, or the little man who accompanied him.

Shrugging into her coat, she drew the hood over her head. The Do Not Disturb sign she hung on the outside of room 8, locked the door, and took a deep breath.

* * *

As soon as she entered the bar, Rebecca knew something was amiss. Johnny was nowhere in sight. Tiny ants tickled her arms and legs. *No! No! No!* More than half the tables were occupied with people either eating or drinking or both, including the elderly regulars gathered around a pitcher of beer. "All I Need Is a Hero" bled through the speakers. A quick check of the entertainment and pool table area relinquished the same result. No Johnny. Keely the waitress was at the kitchen speaking to one of the cooks. Rebecca went to her. "Sorry to bother you, Keely, but have you seen Johnny?"

"No. I'm sorry. I haven't. Was he supposed to meet you here?"

"Yes. We were going to have some lunch."

"Maybe he stopped at one of the stores to pick up something. Why don't you have a seat. I'm sure he'll be along momentarily. You know how men are. Can't even depend on them to be on time. I'll bring you a coffee while you wait. There's a table open by the window." Her eyes leaned toward an empty table setting. "He'll be along. You'll see." Then in a whispered, concerned tone so that neither of the cooks could hear, she asked, "Are you guys all right? I mean, you know."

"I'll know as soon as I find Johnny," Rebecca whispered back. "You haven't seen that man again, have you?"

"Not a sign of him."

"Well. that's good."

"Remember, if there's anything I can do."

"Thanks, Keely." Rebecca went to the open table and took a seat in one of the wingbacks. Ants at her face now. *Johnny wouldn't just stray. It was too risky. Something is wrong. Something is terribly wrong.*

Keely sat a coffee and some creamers next to her elbow. "Here you go, Tiffany." She winked.

"Thank you," said Rebecca, her eyes focused on the falling snow, the people moving about.

"You're welcome. Gotta go. The old buggers are really thirsty today."

Blindly Rebecca added cream to coffee, kept one eye on the entrance, the other at the window. A few minutes of normal, small town life slipped by before her breath caught in her throat and the inevitable hand of fate turned a final page. A black Lincoln Navigator turned at the four-way, and stopped across the street at the Esso. The rear license plate was covered with snow, so she could not tell whether it bore the plate of Nevada. It just sat there for what seemed like an eternity before the driver door opened and the little man with big ears emerged. He headed straight for the hotel.

Rebecca wanted to be sick. *They had Johnny.* She knew it the moment she entered the bar though her mind would not, could not accept it. And now they were coming for her. She took a sip of coffee, worried eyes riveted to the arched entrance.

The little man walked into the bar and looked around, his eyes stopping on

Rebecca's. He smiled, walked right up to the table, and took a seat across from her. "Hello, Rebecca," he said as if they were old friends.

It took all of Rebecca's will not to leap across the table and pull his eyes out through his mouth. "Where's Johnny? What did you do with him?" she whispered.

Cracker held up Johnny's room keys. "If you ever want to see your boyfriend again, you'll follow me out of the hotel like we're old acquaintances. Don't try anything stupid. Your boyfriend's life depends upon it."

Rebecca took another swallow. *This is it. Once they had them together, there was nothing to stop them from killing us both or worse.*

The little man stood. "The least I can do is pay for your coffee." He fished for some change, tossed a handful onto the table. "Follow me," he instructed and turned.

Rebecca rose, reminded her self that another life waited for her and Johnny, and fearlessly followed him out of the hotel.

When they arrived at the Navigator, the little bastard had the audacity to open the door for her. "Buckle up," he told her. "The roads are slippery." Once he was behind the wheel, Rebecca asked. "Where are we going?"

"I thought I made that perfectly clear, Rebecca. We're going to see Johnny."

"You better not of hurt him or..."

"Or what? You'll kill me. If I had a nickel for every time I heard that, I'd be a rich man." He laughed. The sound of it like chalk on a blackboard. He directed the Navigator west on Center Street. "I have to hand it to the both of you. You did well to avoid us for as long as you have. Kudos. But it was only a matter of time you see. We're professionals. There *is* something I would like to ask you however. Mr. Green and I were wondering what you did with the body of our good friend?"

"Fuck you!" Rebecca spat at him. "I'm just glad he's dead."

"Feisty to the end, eh? I like that in a person. Shows you had a good upbringing."

"Where are we going?"

"Not far. You wouldn't believe the unobtrusive places these small towns offer in order for us to carry out our tasks."

They came to a bridge that crossed over a partially frozen river.

Rebecca glared at him. "What's your name?"

"All right. I'll play along. Most people call me Cracker."

"Well, Cracker. I'll make you a deal. You can have me and do whatever you want. I won't even complain. Then you can bring me back to Tony, and I'll go back to work for him without griping. Just let Johnny go. Sounds like a fair tradeoff, don't you think?" She pulled the hood from her head so the little man could see all of her features and smiled.

Cracker laughed. "You're barking up the wrong tree. little lady. I prefer the company of young strong studs to the camaraderie of women. But nice try. I will however inform Mr. Green of your generous offer. I'm sure he wouldn't mind getting a crack at what's between your legs. Tony did instruct us to have a little fun should we find ourselves in the position to do so. And well, we're in the position to do so." He laughed again, a sickening, twittering sound that sent shivers up Rebecca's spine.

She stared out the windshield. The snow was being aided by an easterly wind out of the Rockies, producing an effect that looked more intense than it actually was. The road they were on wound its way through low-lying hills with a river on the south side. A ReMax For Sale sign was nailed to a free-standing birch. Within a thicket of poplars on her near side, an assembly of four white-tailed deer stood at attention and watched them as they passed.

The drive between towns took less than a minute.

Cracker maneuvered the Navigator left, and it bounced as they came upon a side road covered in snow. Right away Rebecca saw where they were headed. A large Quonset sat off the road, looking as abandoned as a fire-ravaged forest. Behind it were metal buildings, domes, and stacks, a refinery or plant that had long since seen the last days of operation.

A ten-foot chain-link fence offered an entrance. Cracker stopped the Navigator in front of two large double doors at the rear of the Quonset. There wasn't a soul in sight. His signal to Mr. Green was a quick honk of the horn. A moment later, Mr. Green pushed one then the other. He ushered them in with the wave of an arm and an insufferable grin on his face.

Cracker drove the Lincoln inside. Mr. Green closed the doors, terminating the snow, wind, and all sound. The interior of the Quonset was lit by natural light seeping through several large grimy windows adjacent to the domed roof. Another vehicle was parked in its center. A baby blue Kia.

Johnny was sitting in a chair, spotlighted by a shaft of winter's glare, naked from the waist up, his hands bound behind his back, legs duct-taped to the front limbs of the chair, a gunnysack over his bowed head. Blood dripped from beneath the sack and onto his chest. On the wood floor were his coat, shirt, and new boots. A table with several tools, hammer, pliers, small handsaw, roll of duct tape, white plastic jug, and the .38 stood next to him. Another chair waited with Rebecca's name on it.

She did not need to be told to get out. In a shattered heartbeat, she ran to Johnny, and dropped to her knees in front of him. "Johnny! Johnny! Talk to me!"

When he issued no reply, Rebecca turned on her abductors. "What did you do to him, you bastards!"

Cracker exited of the Navigator, tossed the room keys to his accomplice. Mr. Green supplied her with an answer. "Well, you see, my dear Rebecca. While Mr. Cracker here was out fetching you, your boyfriend and I had a little misunderstanding. A misunderstanding that led me to knocking him out temporarily. You needn't worry. He should be coming around any moment now. Please, take a seat in that chair. You won't want to miss a thing."

"You fucking bastards! Johnny! Johnny! Can you hear me?! Please wake up! Please!"

Cracker grabbed her roughly by the arm and pulled her toward the empty chair where he forced her down with a strength impossible for his stature.

"Please don't do this," cried Rebecca. "If you're going to kill us, then get it over with."

"Oh, but we must. Mustn't we, Mr. Cracker?" Mr. Green moved toward Johnny. Cracker tied Rebecca's hands behind her back with a length of yellow nylon rope. Once the knot was tied, he put his hands on her shoulders as though to console her. "You know what she told me, Mr. Green?" he said.

"Do tell." Mr. Green removed the sack from Johnny's head.

Rebecca's gasp was cut short as Cracker quickly covered her mouth with duct tape, stifling her cries and the screams that wanted to purge from her lips.

Johnny's mouth was also covered with tape from which blood oozed, slick, redder than red. One of his eyes was severely lacerated and already turning black, his nose shifted awkwardly to the left.

Rebecca screamed regardless, the sound traveling no farther than the tape across her mouth, coming out through her eyes. They were going to torture Johnny to death and make her watch every excruciating moment. The wish she had made that his death be as painless as possible was not going to be granted.

"Our little darling here says you can have your way with her if you let him go."

"Is that a fact, Rebecca? Unfortunately, my dear, Tony Millions, you remember him, well, he's paying us a tremendous amount of money to rid the world of you both. Nevertheless, since you've so generously offered, I might just take you up on your proposal, of course, after I'm done with your boyfriend here." He went to Johnny, slapped him hard across the face. Johnny's head rocked side to side. His good eye fluttered for a second then closed again. "I think your boyfriend here needs a little encouragement." Taking the white container from the table, Mr. Green unscrewed the cap and began to pour its contents over Johnny's head. "I learned this method in the Navy. A little vinegar always does the trick."

Johnny's eyes shot open and he bucked in the chair as though he were being electrocuted. Rushes of air and bubbles shot through bloodied nostrils.

"There. That's better. Look at what we brought you, Johnny." Mr. Green moved so that he could see Rebecca sitting in the chair next to the table, her eyes bulged in horror, struggling against her binds, tape over her mouth. Cracker raised a fist and slammed it into the back of her head. Little blue lights twinkled.

Johnny's eyes went wild with rage.

"Ah. There. Now I've got your attention." Mr. Green drew back a fist and rammed it into Johnny's jaw. He did not move. All of his anger fueled attention was focused on Rebecca, a prisoner once more.

"That's better. Tony said you were one tough cookie. That'll make what I have to do all the more pleasurable." Turning so he was looking at his ally, he said, "Mr. Cracker, if Rebecca decides she doesn't want to watch and closes her eyes, I want you to break her kneecaps with the hammer."

"It'll be a pleasure."

"Now back to you, my friend." He looked to the table, reached for the pliers, and held them in front of Johnny's face while opening and closing them. "Let me see if I can straighten that nose for you." He sat on Johnny's lap, grabbed a fistful of hair, tilted his head back, and applied the business end of the pliers to Johnny's nose, twisting it one way, then the other.

Rebecca's screams could only be heard within the borough of her tortured mind.

She tried to turn her head; however, Cracker forced it straight, and reminded her in a creepy whisper that he would, and with utmost pleasure, break her kneecaps.

Mr. Green turned Johnny's head left and right as he examined his work. "You know. I do believe I've missed my calling. I would have made one hell of a plastic surgeon." He lifted himself from Johnny's lap.

Johnny's nose bled profusely. Regardless, he fought off the pain, drank it in, sent it to a place where dark angels lived and sheet-sodden nightmares were born.

Mr. Green set the bloodied pliers on the table, and turned his torturing methods onto Rebecca. With a solid fist, he struck her hard across the face. White blinding pain ignited, bringing with it a dizzying dance with the devil himself. "That was for killing our friend. And just a sample of what's going to happen to you."

Johnny bucked in the chair with so much fury he and the chair were sent sideways, his head striking the floor.

"Give me a hand for a moment, Mr. Cracker," said Mr. Green. Together they righted the chair.

Johnny glared at the men, his eyes propelling a message that if he got free from his binds, he would kill them.

"Isn't hatred a wonderful creature, Mr. Cracker?"

"Yes, it is. I do believe he now possesses enough of it that we could torture him for hours before he showed signs of wear and tear."

Johnny's eyes went to Rebecca's, and begged forgiveness.

Mr. Green took out an apparatus from his parka pocket, shrugged out of the coat, and rolled up his sleeves to the elbows. A dark V centered the back of his shirt. He showed the small device to Rebecca. "Isn't modernization wonderful, Rebecca? We keep inventing new and horrific ways in which to torment our fellowmen. By the way. Just in case you were wondering, it was this little device that enabled us to capture Johnny in the first place. It has several disciplinary settings. Of course we had to use the utmost level of potency in order to get him into the Kia. He's a pretty big boy. Bet he fucked you good." He drew a breath. "You see, after I spoke to the staff at the hotel, and once we exhausted all avenues, there really was only one place you could be. Just a process of elimination really. I know when someone is lying to me. It became apparent you knew we were here when you disposed of our friend. So this morning, we went out and rented that little beauty." He nodded toward the Kia. "All I had to do was wait you out, make you think we were driving around in circles looking for you. In a Navigator of course. I knew you were going to be brash enough to pop your heads out again. And voila. Here you are. Come to think of it, it's pretty ironic that you would choose Destiny, Alberta, to run to after you stole Tony Millions's money. So much so, it's laughable. I imagine the money is still in your hotel room. Tony will be very generous when we return it to him." He held the Taser in front of her eyes, and drew on its trigger. A blue electric current appeared between the contacts. "Right now this little baby is set at its lowest level. Even so, it is still quite effective." He went to Johnny, and pressed the device into the side of his neck.

Johnny's eyes went wild as five hundred volts of electricity charged through his being.

Rebecca watched in horror as Mr. Green hit him again and again, large red welts appearing on his neck and chest. He was having great difficulty breathing, his chest expanding to its full girth as he desperately sucked air through a nose that now looked like pounded hamburger. Though it was cold inside the Quonset, his body was covered in a heavy veneer of sweat.

"Would you like a go at him, Cracker?" asked Mr. Green.

"Definitely," the little man said.

Mr. Green moved aside, and placed the Taser on the table.

While slipping his hands into a pair of tight-fitting black leather gloves, Cracker circled Johnny. Without warning, he struck him in the temple with a mighty blow. Then he went to the table, picked up the hammer, and tapped the palm of his hand with it. "You're not going to like this very much I'm afraid," he told him.

Rebecca squeezed her eyes and turned her head.

"We'll have none of that" said Mr. Green, and struck her hard across the face. "Open your eyes, you little bitch, or I'll cut your eyelids away so you have no choice but to watch."

Reluctantly, Rebecca opened tear-filled eyes to see Cracker pull off one of Johnny's socks. Then he got down on one knee and took hold of Johnny's bare foot in a tight grip.

"Let me see. How does that nursery rhyme go again? Oh yes. I remember now. This little piggy went to market." He lightly tapped Johnny's big toe with the blunt face of the hammer. "This little piggy went home." He drew the hammer back, swung it down, and stopped before it made contact. "This little piggy had roast beef." He touched the next digit lightly. "And this little piggy had none." He raised the hammer to shoulder height, and turned it so the claw faced south. "And this little piggy went wee, wee, wee all the way home." The hammer came down.

Johnny's eyes rolled into the back of his head. His body jerked repulsively. A crimson pool grew beneath his foot.

Cracker picked up the severed digit, looked at it as though he were examining a rare find, turned, and tossed it into Rebecca's lap.

She fainted.

"Hey, that's not fair," said Cracker. "She must see all of my work. I won't continue until she's conscious."

"Maybe this would be a good time to get something to eat," suggested Mr. Green, slipping back into his parka. "Why don't you go to that restaurant we went to this morning and get us a couple of burgers and fries. What about you, Johnny? Want anything?"

Johnny's tear-filled eyes fired razors of odium at his captors.

"*No?* Suit yourself. Get me a couple of Cokes as well. I've got a feeling I'm going to be working up quite a thirst over the next while."

Cracker put the hammer on the table, got into the Navigator, drove it to the entrance, got out, opened the doors, and drove away.

It was snowing much harder. A strong, howling wind breached the Quonset sounding like an animal in distress. Mr. Green went to the doors, closed them, then returned to the table where he picked up the saw. "Nah. Too soon," he said. "You know. I'm not that bad of a guy really. I'm even going to give you a little break. Let you lick your wounds as they say." He looked to an unconscious Rebecca. "Your girlfriend doesn't seem to have the stomach for our work. We're artists just like any other you see. Only we use human flesh as our canvass, and your basic everyday run of the mill tools as our brushes and chisels. We're a rare breed and get paid very handsomely for our distinctive talents." Pacing back and forth, he stopped and added, "I would like to make one thing perfectly clear to you, Johnny. The both of you are going to die here today. Make no mistake about it. However, before we kill you, you are going to beg me to end it all. You will experience about as much pain a person can without going completely out of your mind. Then when I'm done torturing you to the brink of madness, you're going to watch me rape your girlfriend, repeatedly. I'm going to fuck her so many times she'll think she's being assaulted by a dozen men." He walked up to Rebecca and slapped her hard across the face. "Wake up, you little bitch!"

Rebecca moaned, the sting of the heavy-handed slap shaking her from insentience.

One bleary eye opened then the other. It took a few seconds for the indistinct, beaten figure of Johnny to come into focus. Their eyes met. Her body shuddered, fresh waves of tears spilled over her face.

"I was just telling Johnny here how much I'm going to enjoy raping you, Rebecca," said Mr. Green. He joined his fingers and cracked his knuckles.

Rebecca's pleas were nothing more than muted mumbles through the tape. Taking hold of one end, Mr. Green ripped it from her mouth. "You wish to say something?"

Rebecca stretched the numbness from her lips. She could taste the coppery flavor of blood working its way into her throat. She thought she might be sick. Quickly she swallowed the rising bile into her trembling stomach. "Please, Mr. Green. Please don't hurt him anymore. It was my idea to take the money, not his. Johnny's only mistake was that he fell in love with someone who was bent on revenge. Phone Tony. Tell him that I'm sorry. He can have all the money back. Tell him that I'll work very hard for him. I'll never complain. Please, Mr. Green. You have all the power to make this happen. Just call him. I'm begging you."

"You are right about one thing, my dear. I do possess all of the power. Unfortunately for you and Johnny, Tony wants you dead. To disappear without a trace as though you were never born. He was very specific about that." He looked to Johnny. "Trouble is, I'm enjoying what I'm doing immensely. Must be the sadist in me." He went to Johnny, closed his fist, and struck him hard across the jaw. "Oh. I forgot to tell you, Johnny. Before I kill you. I'm going to scalp you. Mr. Millions wants a souvenir of our work. He's going to pay me extra for that hair of yours. Pretty ironic when you think about it."

"You fucking bastard!" screamed Rebecca.

"That I am." Mr. Green drew his arm back again and again sent a solid fist into the side of Johnny's face. Then he went to the table, picked up the Taser, and applied it to Johnny's genitals.

Johnny's head reared back, mucus exploded from his nose.

"Fuck, that's got to hurt. Eh, Johnny?"

Tears of pure unabated loathing washed over Johnny's face. He roared with all of his inner defiance through the tape.

"I bet you would like nothing better than to kill me right now, wouldn't you, Johnny?"

Johnny's watery glare locked on to Mr. Green's sinister eyes.

"I'll take that as a yes. Then you're really going to hate me for this." He moved to within arm's reach of Rebecca and touched her forehead with the Taser.

Rebecca's screams echoed throughout the Quonset. Blood erupted from the lacerations within her mouth.

Johnny bucked in the chair, pulled with all his vigor against his restraints, finding that the rope binding his hands gave some though not enough to petition hope. The knots were just to good.

Mr. Green set the device on the table. From a pocket, he withdrew a switchblade, then depressed a button. A five-inch blade stood to attention. Holding it before his eyes, he turned it so that the cold steel-flashed in the light descending from the roof. "Did you ever see the movie *Reservoir Dogs*, Johnny?" He went to him and sat on his lap again, pushed the length of Johnny's wet hair behind his ears, and tore the feather from its tether and tossed it to the floor. "I'll leave the other one for Mr. Cracker. He would not be too happy if I were to have all the fun." He took hold of Johnny's left ear, and smiled, his eyes glinting with sightedness of a psychopath.

Time seemed to reverse itself for Johnny as the blade sliced through flesh.

"Use your mind to see something else, Rebecca."

The woman's voice came from all around her.

"I'm here to help you. But I need your resolve in order to do so. Concentrate hard, Rebecca. Use your gift to give me the strength I need to reach out to you. To free you from this madness. I'm sorry it took me so long to get to you, but I'm very weak."

Looking left then right, Rebecca could see no one. Using her mind to communicate with the woman who wished to help liberate them from certain death, she said, *"I need to know who you are."*

"My name is Lucy. Lucy Whitehead. You're the first person I've been able to communicate with since my life was taken from me so many years ago. I'm here to help you if I can."

"You can. I know you can, Lucy. These men will kill us if you don't."

"Then concentrate, Rebecca. Concentrate with all of your inner sanctum."

Lifting himself from Johnny's lap, Mr. Green held the severed ear like a trophy, his hands covered in blood. Laughing, he brought it to his lips. "Hello, hello," he said. "Can you hear me, Johnny?" He tossed the ear to the floor.

There was no more pain. No more anguish. Johnny was in shock, his eyes seeing only the inevitable veil of his quandary, blood washing his neck, his chest, his back.

Turning to Rebecca, Mr. Green said, "I'm surprised. You took that very well. I would have expected you would be screaming blue bloody murder seeing that." He put the scarlet-stained switchblade on the table.

Rebecca did not respond, all of her concentration focused on giving Lucy the strength she needed in order to alleviate them from these madmen.

The Quonset doors opened.

"Ah. Mr. Cracker has returned. And just in time. I'm famished." He went to the doors. Cracker drove the Navigator into the building. A ghostly wail embarked on a whirlwind journey throughout the open space. With it came twisting column of snow.

Mr. Green sealed doors. The storm seemed to grip the Quonset in its grasp, shaking the domed structure to its very foundation.

Cracker got out of the vehicle, went to the table, set a large brown bag down, and looked at a sedentary Johnny. "I see you've been busy while I was gone." From the bag, he produced two burgers, a couple of Styrofoam containers of fries, and four cans of Coke. He looked to a silent Rebecca whose attention seemed to be elsewhere. "What's up with her?"

Mr. Green joined him at the table, unwrapped one of the burgers, and took a bite. "She must be in shock," he said, chewing. "As a matter a fact, I think they both are. No matter. We'll bring them around once we're done eating. Hey, this burger is pretty good."

"It's a bison burger."

"You don't say."

While Mr. Green and Cracker discussed the benefits of the local cuisine, Rebecca was trying desperately to get Lucy Whitehead to draw energy from her as Caleb had in Ed and Hester's barn. *"See if you can become visible to me, Lucy. That would be a good start."*

"Okay. I'll try. It's just that I seem to be everywhere. Like I'm fragmented or something."

"When did you die, Lucy? How did you die? You said your life was taken from you. If you told me, maybe it would help me help you. Allow us to connect better."

"It was so long ago. I was a young wife. Married to a man who I thought would love me forever. Our home was where this building stands today. It was during the boom days at the beginning of this century. I learned that I was with child..."

As she spoke, Lucy's spirit became stronger. The apparition of her otherworldly self materialized, head first, then shoulders. She was young, no more than twenty-five, with long brown hair surrounding a face that appeared Asian in its ovate appeal. Eyes dark, and like Rebecca, she bore the design of many freckles.

"Keep talking, Lucy. I can see you now."

"You can?"

"Yes. And you're very pretty."

"Thank you, Rebecca. So are you." The spirit of Lucy Whitehead closed her eyes for an instant. When she opened them again, they were haunted with memory. *"I was anxious to share the news with my husband when he returned home from his job at the coal mines in the neighboring town. I waited and waited. It was wintertime, so darkness fell over us quite early. I'd put a candle in the window. I was in the mood to celebrate, so I had fixed him a dinner of roast chicken, potatoes, corn bread, and dumplings, his favorite foods. I fell asleep on the sofa while the meal I had prepared turned cold. When he finally came home, he was drunk, angry. He sat at our eating table mumbling incoherently. I imagined the news*

of our having a child might lighten his foul mood, so I told him while I reheated his dinner. Instead, he became even more distressed, calling me a whore. An aberration in the eyes of God, slamming his fists on the table. He pointed an accusing finger at me as though I had betrayed him. Then he went outside to the wood shed. All I remember after that is a great fire that didn't burn."

Lucy Whitehead's spirit came into full spectacle. She was small, naked, still bearing the mutilations of her wrongful death. Rebecca now knew why she felt so fragmented.

"Your energy is strong. And I understand what you have endured. Come to me, Lucy. Be one with me. Take from me what you will."

Lucy Whitehead moved toward Rebecca, joining with her in a conjugal visage of oneness. Rebecca's inner self filled with the sadness of her eternal grief. *"Try to be strong, Lucy. For me. For Johnny. They're killing him. Put aside yesterday's memories and focus on the now."* Rebecca could feel prickles of energy slipping from her physical self. *"That's it, Lucy. You're doing it. Take as much as you need."*

Pushing the last bite of burger into his mouth, Mr. Green said, "I guess we should snap him out of it before we continue." He took a swallow of Coke then wiped at his mouth.

"Allow me," said Cracker, picked up the jug of vinegar and poured a fair amount over Johnny's head.

The burn shook Johnny from the comatose state he was in, searing the raw flesh of his lost ear, blinding his eyes, igniting a pain that lit his mind in a sea of flames. All he could see of his tormentor was the distorted vagueness of his face. Because Cracker was in such close proximity, Johnny could not see Rebecca, and that distressed him to no end, not knowing what they might have done to her. He blinked over and over until the vinegar washed from his eyes and his vision cleared. Moving his head side to side, he tried to catch a glimpse of her.

"What's the matter, Johnny?" asked Cracker. "Do you want me to move so you can see what we're going to do to her? Fine by me." Cracker stepped aside. Rebecca was still in the chair, hands bound behind her back; however, there was a look about her Johnny found strangely comforting. Her beautiful green eyes were vacant, as though she had seen enough and escaped to a place where she wouldn't have to bear witness to the acts of Mr. Green and Cracker. *Good for you, Becca. Stay there. Stay there as long as you have to.*

Mr. Green took the jug of vinegar from Cracker, walked up to Rebecca, and poured the acrid liquid over her head.

She did not move.

"Fuck me. That's one tough girlfriend you've got there, Johnny." Mr. Green reared back a fist and sent it booming into Rebecca's temple. Her head rocked viciously; nonetheless, she remained as placid as a mannequin. Mr. Green snapped his fingers in front of her eyes. "Hello in there. Anybody home?"

Rebecca's gaze did not stray. She did not blink. Did not move. The only indication that she was even alive was the rise and fall of her chest.

"I've heard about people who can do this," Mr. Green told Cracker. "They have the ability to venture their mind to other places. Close out what's going on around them."

"Oh yeah. Let's see if she can ignore this." Cracker picked up the knife from the table, and drove it to the hilt into the musculature of Johnny's upper chest, deliberately missing the lung.

Rebecca gave no tangible response that she saw anything.

"Try hitting her again."

"I don't think it'll do any good. I'll only bruise my knuckles more. Let's work on the boyfriend. When we're done with him, we'll just shoot her in the head and be done with her. Of course, after I rape the living shit out of her."

Rebecca could feel Lucy's fingers begin to work. The nylon rope began to loosen, though very slowly. "*That's it, Lucy. You're doing it. Don't stop. A little more and I'll be able to get my hands free.*"

Cracker drew the blade across Johnny's chest again and again, creating an X that ran from his abdomen to his shoulders. "Have you ever heard the term *death by a thousand cuts*, Johnny?"

Mr. Green picked up the hammer. "Move over. Let's work him together." He swung it hard. The side of Johnny's right knee buckled. Something inside went pop.

Cracker pushed the tip of the blade between the bones of Johnny's ribcage, digging deep, knowing exactly when to stop before mortal wounds were inflicted. He worked it in and out, creating a xylophone of deep lacerations on both sides of his torso.

The nylon rope loosened enough that Rebecca could slip one hand through, then the other. The .38 sat on the table not more than three feet away. "*Thank you, Lucy. You've saved us.*"

"*I'm happy that I could,*" said Lucy, her voice weak. "*Though I am very tired from the effort. I must go back now, Rebecca. We could have been good friends, you and I.*" Then she was gone.

With their backs turned, Rebecca seized the opportunity, rose quietly from the chair, and picked the gun up from the table in time to hear Cracker say, "And now for the other ear."

She clicked the safety off, just as Johnny showed her, and aimed.

The interior of the Quonset roared. The first shot struck home, the slug passing through the skull of Cracker, back to front. He fell forward onto Johnny's lap, rolled, then slipped to the floor as dead as he could be, the knife skittering from his hand.

Mr. Green spun, a look of utter surprise etched on his face. "What the fuck?!"

"What the fuck indeed, you sadistic prick." Aiming at his chest, Rebecca squeezed the trigger. The second retort followed the first. The hammer in Mr. Green's hand dropped to the floor. He went down on both knees, staring at the stain of his own blood blossom on his shirt. He began to laugh.

Rebecca pocketed the .38. In a momentary dance with insanity, she picked up the knife, moved in behind Mr. Green, took hold of his red mane, drew his head back, and cut his throat with so much vengeance guiding her hand, she would have decapitated him if not for the blade striking vertebrae. Mr. Green's face hit the wooden floor with a thud, the last remnants of air within his lungs escaping through the gaping mutilation with a hiss. A wreath of gore unfurled beneath his face then seeped between the cracks in the floorboards.

Rebecca turned to see that Johnny was barely conscious, bleeding profusely from dozens of wounds. Falling to her knees in front of him, she cut the tape that bound his legs. "Oh god, Johnny!" Reaching at his mouth, she gently pulled the tape from his lips. Trapped blood spurted, dotting her face.

Johnny gasped for desperate air.

With the tips of shaking fingers, Rebecca touched his face, tears filling her eyes. She wiped them away. *Be strong,* she told herself.

Johnny mumbled incoherently.

"Shh. Don't try to speak, my love. I'll have you out of here in a moment." She moved behind him, the blade slicing through rope. Johnny's arms fell to his side. Rounding him, she put his arms in his lap and took hold of his biceps. "Johnny! Johnny! Listen to me!" She shook him hard as she dared. "You have to help me. I don't have the strength to carry you. You can't die. Not here. Please, Johnny. Snap out of it."

Johnny's eyes rolled within his head. "Becca." Blood lingered on his lips, dripped to his chest. He nodded. "Becca."

"Dig deep, Johnny. I know you can do it. You're the strongest man I know." She pulled on his arms.

"Yesss." Johnny began to rise from the chair, willing the strength back into his legs. Slowly he rose, and staggered forward.

Drawing one arm over her shoulder, Rebecca steadied him. His more than two hundred pounds was almost more than she could bear. She summoned every ounce of verve she had to support him. "That's it, my love. Now walk with me."

The Navigator was a mere twenty feet away. It might as well have been a mile.

Little by little they moved toward it, one painstaking step at a time. When they reached it, Johnny's physical and mental energies began to resume to a state where he was able to support himself. Leaning into the side of the SUV, he said, "Becca. You saved us."

Rebecca took all of him in, wanting to scream. They had mutilated him from top to bottom. He was still bleeding from all of his wounds, and she knew that if she didn't stem the flow, he would bleed to death in the Quanset. Retrieving his coat, she placed it over his shoulders then opened the passenger door.

Johnny fell into the seat. Rebecca took his legs, swinging them in while he righted himself. Closing the door, she went to the Quonset entrance, pushed the doors open, and was hit with a blast of snow and wind so fierce that, in her weakened state, nearly sent her reeling. She fought hard against it, stepped out into the open, and scooped as much snow into her hands as she could. While she ran back to the SUV, she packed the snow until it was a solid pie of cold, blotched red with Mr. Green's blood. Opening the door, she pressed the provisional ice pack against the raw tissue where Johnny's ear should have been. "Hold this, Johnny. I know it must hurt, but it will help."

Johnny's hand went over hers, his bloody and battered face stretching into a grotesque smile. "My savior," he muttered. "How badly… are… you hurt?"

Rebecca removed her hand and lied to him. The blows Mr. Green administered to her head had taken their toll. Her ears were ringing, and she had the world's worst headache. "I'm okay, my love. Just some bruises, that's all." Closing the door, she rounded the Navigator. About to get in and get the hell out of there, reflected movement caught her eye. Turning, she saw Johnny's feather caught in the vortex of wind, twisting upward toward the ceiling. She would have ignored it if not for her inner voice telling her to retrieve it. *It's more important than you can possibly understand.* Quickly she went to it, having to snatch at it several times, dodging Mr. Green's and Cracker's corpses before her fingers took hold. Another moment and it would have continued its upward spiral and she would have never been able to recover it.

She put it in the pocket with the gun, got into the Navigator, started the engine, dropped the gear into drive, and looked at Johnny. His eyes were closed. When she put a hand over his, they opened. They stared at each other for a brief, silent moment, sharing a difficult smile. Rebecca focused on the storm breaching into the cavernous space, her foot pressing fast on the accelerator.

The rented Lincoln roared out of the Quonset into the fading light of day.

Thank you, Lucy Whitehead.

* * *

According to the digital when Rebecca parked at the rear of the hotel, it was 5:05. Mr. Green and Cracker had tortured Johnny for nearly two hours. She killed the engine. Wipers stopped. The windshield immediately covered in a layer of snow. "Wait here. I'll be right back. I have to check and make sure the stairs and hallway are clear."

Leaving the vehicle, Rebecca pulled the hood over her head. A quick look around disclosed there was no one in the immediate area. Not even a waitress smoking a cigarette. Opening the metal door, she ran up the stairs, to find the hallway empty.

Quickly she returned to the vehicle, opened the door, and helped Johnny ease his way out. "I can manage," he told her when she tried to support him. Drawing the hood over his head to conceal his abused face, he pulled the coat tight against his wounds. The cold ground felt good against his bare, four digit foot. "Let's get inside," he said, his eyes darting back and forth as though Mr. Green and Cracker would miraculously reappear.

As soon as they were in their room, Rebecca went into the bathroom and began to fill the tub with cold water.

Johnny sat on the bed, head hanging south, Rush's "Fly by Night" played on the radio. He moved his shoulders in a circular motion until the coat fell from them. Staring into his hands, he did not see flesh and blood, instead, observed the ghostly images of his ordeal. Closing one hand over the other, he wiped them away. When he looked up, Rebecca stood over him, eyes brimming with tears, for she knew all she could do was try to ease his pain, that inevitably, as predicted, Johnny was going to die. *At least it won't be in a desolated Quonset with the likes of Mr. Green and Cracker.*

"Here. Let me help you with your clothes. We've got to get you into some cold water to see if the bleeding will stop." Taking hold of the remaining sock, she pulled it off, made Johnny stand, unfastened his jeans, and pulled them and his underwear to the floor.

Johnny stepped out from them, blood hemorrhaging from his wounds. "How do I look?"

Rebecca forced a smile. "You're a beautiful man, Johnny Black," she said, trying hard not to stare at a face that was now anything but. "Come on. Let's get you to the tub."

They went into the bathroom. Johnny caught a brief glimpse of himself in the mirror. *I'm hideous.*

"This might come as a shock to your system, but it's necessary," said Rebecca, supporting him as he stepped into the frigid water that turned quickly pink. "Holy shit, that's cold."

"I know, and I'm sorry, but if we don't stop the bleeding..." She didn't finish the thought.

Johnny took hold of the support handle, eased himself into the water, and stretched his legs best he could. Gooseflesh covered his body. Wrapping his arms around his chest, he winced. In seconds, the pink of the water turned to a more telling shade of red.

Rebecca went to the sink, washed the dots of Johnny's blood from her face and the lifeblood of Mr. Green from her hands. The air of vinegar overwhelming in the minimal space. Though she had taken several blows, her face was marginally swollen, and only a small red welt existed where Mr. Green had touched her with the Taser. She lathered a washcloth with soap, hot water, dropped to her knees, and gently began to wipe the blood from Johnny's face.

"That feels good," said Johnny, his eyes on hers. "I don't know how you got us out of there, but I'm glad you did. Those bastards would have tortured you to death."

"Let's just say I had a little help from a friend and leave it at that. Now stop talking so I can clean you up." She washed his neck and shoulders, staying clear of the gaping wound that used to be his ear. Her main concern were the lacerations up and down his ribcage and upper chest. They were still bleeding, and she didn't know how deep they were. What she needed to do, she ascertained, was to go to the drugstore and get some gauze and bandages. She squeezed the blood out of the cloth, adding to the now-vermilion water. "I'm going to go out for a few minutes. I want you to stay in here until I get back, okay?"

"What for?" asked Johnny, his body shuddering with an incessant shiver.

"I need to get some bandages and such. The cold water isn't going to be enough to stop the bleeding. You do understand that we have to stop the bleeding, don't you?" Voice rising.

"Yes. I understand."

"Good. Then bear with me. I'll only be a few minutes. But you have to stay put."

"Okay, I will Becca. Be careful."

She lowered her face to his, and kissed his ruptured lips. "They're gone, Johnny." Pushing herself to her feet, she went into the other room, removed the gun from her pocket, placed it on the nightstand, and took fifty dollars from her handbag then checked on Johnny once more before she left.

Johnny sat upright in the tub to examine the torture he had suffered. Running a finger along the X Cracker had carved, he found the wound wasn't too deep. His hand went to the side of his head and found only crude flesh. Lifting his disfigured foot from the cold water, Cracker's version of the popular children's nursery rhyme echoed in his mind, and he relived the drop of the hammer for a painful moment. *And this little piggy went wee, wee, wee, all the way home*. He let the foot and damaged knee slip back into the cold. Looking at the wounds climbing both sides of his torso, he saw that most of them were still haemorrhaging, albeit slowly. He sank back into the cold, rested his head against the porcelain and closed his eyes. He thought about his mother, his father, and Dallas. He could see them all together again, sitting at the dining room table, Dallas lying at his place on the floor waiting for any scraps that might come his way. The image gave him cause to smile and, for a brief stint, chased away the anguish, the pain, and put at bay the darkness he knew would soon envelope him.

He did not hear Rebecca enter the room until she stood next to the tub holding a Pharmasave bag. She placed it in the sink and shrugged out of her coat. "Okay, that's enough cold water. Let's get you out of there. You're turning blue."

She helped him out of the tub, steered him to the toilet and told him to sit down. Taking one of the white towels from the rack, she began to dry him off, starting with his face, working her way to his feet, all the while careful that she did not cause him further discomfort. When she was done, the towel was mottled red. She threw it into a corner, retrieved another, and spread it across his lap for warmth.

Rebecca examined his still-bleeding wounds. She needed to patch them quickly. "Raise your arms best you can," she told Johnny. He did, and winced. Rebecca removed a box of large square bandages from the bag, tore them open one by one, and gingerly placed them over the fourteen incisions. "Okay, you can put your arms down now."

"Where did you learn to do all this?" he asked, the chill in his bones beginning to relent.

"Call it maternal instinct." She regarded the mess on the side of his head, fought back the tears that threatened to spill from her eyes. Opening a packet that contained a thick square of gauze, she pushed his hair back and placed it over the wound. It held its place, the exposed flesh acting like an adhesive. "Does it hurt much?"

"Surprisingly, not that much."

"You're so brave, my love."

"Not me. You're the brave one in this relationship. What you did in that Quonset took a lot of guts."

"I was acting on pure adrenalin and a shitload of hatred."

"Still."

"Are you going to let me finish?"

"Okay, Nurse White. Carry on."

By the time Rebecca was done, Johnny resembled an accident victim. Most of his head was wrapped in gauze and his foot was bandaged up to his ankle. A patchwork of white climbed his torso. There was nothing she could do to alleviate the pain of his knee except to give him three extrastrength Tylenol she'd purchased with the bandages. She helped him to bed, told him to lie down, covered him to the chin with the comforter and sat next to him "Johnny?"

"I know what you're going to say, Becca. I was thinking about it while you were fixing me up. It's time. Isn't it?"

"Yes, my love. It's time. We can't run anymore, and you're slowly bleeding to death. I'm afraid all of my efforts have only prolonged the inevitable. You can't go to a hospital, and once Tony figures out that his men are missing, he'll send more. And then there's still Mr. Black to consider. He could be right behind us. There will always be someone lurking in the shadows, Johnny. If that's not enough to convince you, let's say you did survive your injuries. We've just killed three men, though they deserved it. We've left our signature everywhere. The police aren't stupid, Johnny. They would catch us. Then what? We would spend the remainder of our lives in prison, never to see each other again. I don't know about you, but for me, that's not an acceptable alternative."

Each looked to the .38 waiting on the nightstand.

"When?" asked Johnny, suddenly very tired.

"Tonight, my love. Just before midnight. We'll start our new lives in the new year. We'll be together forever, Johnny. Just as I promised."

"Then lie down next to me, Becca. Let's be as close as we can before it's time."

"Okay, but first there's something I need to do. I'll only be a moment or two." She kissed her fingers, and placed them over his pulverized lips. Rising from the bed, she picked up the knapsack and went to the table. When she turned to look at Johnny, he had fallen quickly asleep or was rendered unconscious from the loss of blood.

She flipped the knapsack upside down. All of the money fell onto the table. She tidied it up some, stacking the bills into uneven heights. Then she went into the bathroom and collected the notepad and pen she had also purchased at the drugstore, knowing full well they would not see the next day. At least not on this earth. Sitting at the table she began to write while "Have You Seen Her" by the Chi-lites cried from the radio.

Oh, I see her hand reaching out to me
Only she can set me free
Have you seen her
Tell me have you seen her

To those who find us.

This money was taken from a ruthless crime boss by the name of Tony Millions who resides in Las Vegas. This man is responsible for numerous murders, including the death of Mr. Benjamin Wong and a young girl named Kimberly Gagne whose parents live in Sacramento, California. They deserve finality to their grief.

Tony Millions is the coordinator of a white slave market also based in Las Vegas. I know this because I was an unwilling participant at the Shangri-La Palace. Kidnapped and forced into a life of debauchery. He should be punished for his crimes.

The man you find with me is Johnny Black and is guilty of only one thing: falling in love. Together we defended ourselves when need be.

We leave this world as we entered. Innocents. Our only crime is that we were caught in a web of despair at the pinnacle of our young lives.

For the record, my name is Rebecca White. And I'm in love with Johnny Black.

She put down the pen, and examined for a moment what she had written before slipping the note beneath one of the stacks of stolen bills. As she walked toward the bed, she removed all of her clothing, slipped beneath the covers and listened to the music until her lids closed on their own accord and she fell asleep next to the man she would spend an eternity with.

* * *

It was the sound of the band playing one floor below that woke Rebecca. She sat up, the comforter dropped to her waist. She looked at a still-sleeping Johnny then at the window. It was pitch outside. "Johnny?" She shook his shoulder. He did not move. "Johnny. Wake up." Drawing the comforter away from him, she gasped. The lacerations running up and down his sides had bled clean through the bandages. The sheets on both sides of him were wet with blood. "Oh my god! Johnny! Wake up!" For a moment she thought he had died in his sleep, gone on ahead of her, until one eye opened then the other. Selfish relief washed over her, for as strong as she might be, and as many times as she told herself she could do it, she knew deep deep deep, she did not possess the courage to end her life by putting the barrel of a gun to her head.

"How long have I been asleep?" he asked weakly.

Rebecca reached for the remote and turned on the TV. The screen came into focus. A countdown party was taking place in front of the city hall in Calgary. Thousands stood in front of a stage where a five-piece band played. The digital readout in the corner read 11:37. They watched the festive scene for a few minutes before she clicked it off.

Johnny could feel warmth running down his sides. He looked at his bandaged wounds, and saw he was bleeding heavily. "Holy shit!" He tried to sit up, found he was weak, and had to push with his arms to propel himself, the soaked sheet beneath him clinging to his back.

"You're bleeding out, Johnny. I'm sorry. I did all I could. How do you feel?"

"I feel kind of weak and really tired. And my knee and foot hurt like a son of a bitch."

Even with only a handful of minutes remaining before they joined each other in the afterlife, Rebecca hated to see him suffering. "I'm sorry, Johnny. I'm sorry that they hurt you so badly." Swinging her legs over the edge, she stood to find that everything around her seemed surreal. Like the sum of what had happened, and was about to happen, came right out of a poorly budgeted movie.

"Reelin' in the Years" by Steely Dan emitted from the radio. She turned up the volume and went to Johnny's side of the bed.

As if the band and revelers below were competing with the small radio sound, their vocal celebrations increased dramatically.

"Can you stand? I need you to be strong for us." Taking his hands, she helped him from the blood-soaked sheets. He wavered. She had to take hold of his arms to steady him.

Johnny's head went whoosh; he felt dizzy. He closed his eyes until the sensation subsided. When he opened them, Rebecca was staring up at him, tears dripping from her eyelashes. "I'm okay now, Becca. Please don't cry."

"It's just that… that, I'm so sorry it's come to this. If it weren't for me, you wouldn't be in the position you're in."

"Don't talk like that. I wouldn't trade the time I've spent with you for anything." He took her by the shoulders. "Not anything, Becca. Besides, we're going to be together forever and a day, just like you said." Lowering his face, he kissed her.

"Yes, my love. Forever and ever," she whispered against his punished lips.

"Reelin' in the Year" ended. The DJ announced it was only four minutes until midnight.

"It's time, my love." Reaching for the .38, she put it into Johnny's hands. "Be strong. For us." She went to her coat and retrieved the feather before lying on top of the comforter. She watched Johnny as he rounded the front of the bed, hobbling badly, her own body trembling with the sad reality of what she was forcing him to do.

The Eagles' "Heartache Tonight" appropriately pumped from the radio.

Somebodys gonna hurt someone
Before the night is through
Somebodys gonna come undone
There's nothing we can do…

Rebecca squeezed the feather in a tense grip and closed her eyes. "For me. For you. For us. I'll see you on the other side, my love." were her final words to him.

Johnny stepped up to her, the.38 a lead brick in his hand, and placed the barrel close to her temple. Tears rained over his battered face. Taking a deep breath, he looked into her face, and realized he could not do it. Not in the head. He could not destroy her beauty. He pointed it over her heart, the only other *true* kill shot he could think of. Trembling, eyes closed, he pulled the trigger, the sound of the retort louder than expected. Rebecca's body bucked once, then she was still. He looked to the outdated calendar hanging above the fridge, checked the chamber, walked to the window, and sat on the radiator, drowning.

* * *

Visiting Sergeant Ken Morrow from the RCMP detachment in Medicine Hat was hosting a private New Year's Eve party in room 9 when he and his guests heard the shot. "Somebody call 911," he yelled to no one in particular. "Get the police and an ambulance." He killed the music, hastily snatched his 9 mm from a nightstand drawer and went to the door. Drunkenly, his guests gathered quickly behind. Cautiously he opened it, checked the hall. All his eyes registered was the grey head of an old woman peering out from a door and her cat as it darted from the room. "I heard it too," the woman said quietly.

"Go back in your room! Lock the door!" He turned on his guests whose combined body weight were pushing him farther into the hallway. "Stay here."

His proficient ear told him the shot came from the room directly across from his. With duly trained stealth, he moved toward door number 8 from which music emanated. More curious than drunk, more drunk than curious, his guests took up the rear. "I told you to stay back. This could be very dangerous."

They abided his caution, but only by a step.

Officer Morrow leaned against the wall next to the door and pounded on it with a heavy hand. "This is Officer Morrow of the RCMP I need you to answer me."

* * *

Rebecca floated from her physical self through a vastness of white so bright and so all-encompassing it rivaled anything she had ever seen before, leaving her to feel as chaste as the day she was born. In the brilliance, there were many voices; however, one rose above the others. Her name was called over and over, Rebecca, Rebecca, Rebecca. She found she had the ability to move toward it without effort. It was the conversant voice of her mother.

"Momma. I'm coming."

"Wait, Rebecca. Do not come further. Now is not your time, daughter. You must go back. You still have a life to complete."

"I want to be with you. You and Johnny."

"And one day you will. You will be with all of us. But not now. You have so much to accomplish. Your destiny still awaits you." Then her mother's voice was gone, consumed by the many. The one. As before.

All around her, the immense whiteness faded, and Rebecca could feel herself being drawn back to whence she came. When unbounded brilliance surrendered completely to utter darkness, Rebecca White was reborn.

* * *

Officer Morrow's fist pounded on the door again. "If you don't answer me, I'm coming in."

"Mmmaybe you shhhould wait fffor more po . .police," slurred one of his guests.

"The hell with that. Someone could be really hurt or worse." Reversing a few feet, gun at the ready and using his body like a battering ram, he propelled himself hard against the wood.

The door crashed inward to reveal a horrific incident. A young Native, male, his face pummeled beyond recognition, head and upper body covered in bandages, lay on a bloodied bed, a gun pointed beneath his chin. A pretty girl who appeared to be already dead, a small leaking hole centering her chest was positioned next to him, a feather tightly grasped in hand. Aided by a squall bleeding through the open window, money danced about the room. A radio voice announced Gary Wright's "Dream Weaver" would be next.

"Jesus Christ, son! No! Don't do it!"

Bodies push. From between someone's legs, Mr. Jingles sauntered into the room, a quick paw claiming one of the dancing bills.

One of Morrow's female guests screamed, "Oh my god! Oh my sweet Jesus!"

"Don't do it, son. Give me the gun. Everything will be all right. You'll see."

The battered young man squeezed the girl's hand. His finger engaged the trigger. The top of his head erupted. A spray of red decorated the wall, the ceiling.

"HAPPY NEW YEAR!" ascended from the floor below.

Rebecca's eyes blinked. Once, twice, three times, her lungs swelling to their most extreme, and she drowned them with desperate air, gasping with the elixir of sweet life.

Ken Morrow ran to her side, taking the hand holding a feather in his. "Listen to my voice," he told her and stroked the top of her head. "Stay with me, sweetheart. An ambulance is on the way. You're going to be fine. I promise."

Sirens breached the room. The calendar fluttered. Mr. Jingles ran at liberty. Blood ran south on the wall, dripped from the ceiling. Officer Morrow turned his head to the gaping, horrified faces cramped within the doorway leading to room 8. "She's alive! Thank God! The girl is still alive!"

* * *

81

Three Years Later
Time after Time

REBECCA clears the last of the lunch plates, sprays the tables with cleanser, and wipes them down with anxious swipes of a cloth. She is wearing jeans, a blue blouse, and leather sandals on her feet. From her ears dangle precious ruby earrings.

It is a particularly beautiful July day in Valentine, and people had arrived in droves to sample Mr. Sonjee's tandoori chicken. Rebecca had been working for him part-time for the past two years much to his delight and he thanked the gods every day for returning her to him. In a very brief time, she had become such a welcome fixture that his business thrived beyond his wildest imagination.

The young men in town kept track of the days she worked and would flock to the small restaurant/grocery store to gaze upon her beauty in hopes that one day she might grant one of them an evening out. However, Rebecca humbly refrained from the affections bestowed upon her and would, for the remainder of her days, be true to the one and only person she could ever love, Johnny.

Carrying the bus bin full of dishes to the back of the store where Mr. Sonjee weighed steaks on a scale for Mabel Helpnot, Rebecca stops for a moment and says hello. She then deposits the dishes into the double sink where one of her young admirers worked as a dishwasher and busboy. "See you next week, Jason." Rebecca smiles, adding triumph to the young man's day.

Jason blushes, as he always did whenever Rebecca spoke to him. "Okay, Rebecca. Next week it is, unless of course I see you sooner."

"Yes. Well. Have a great day." Turning her attention to Mr. Sonjee who is mathematically calculating the total to Mabel Helpnot's bill, seeing the sum somewhere on the ceiling, she bids him a good day. "The tables are cleaned, Mr. Sonjee. If you don't need me for anything else, I think I'll go home and enjoy the rest of the day."

"Yes, yes. I am thanking you again for coming in on such short notice, Rebecca."

"That's okay. I just hope Masha will be feeling well soon."

"Oh yes. Her fever has already been broken. I am thinking she will be back to her good self any day now."

"I'm glad to hear it. Well, have a nice day. You too, Mabel."

Mr. Sonjee presses his hands together as if he were suddenly struck with the notion to pray and bows slightly from the hip. "You also. And may the gods be walking with you on this glorious day."

"And with you, Mr. Sonjee."

Leaving the store, Rebecca slides into Ed's truck parked in front of the store and in the searing afternoon sun. The interior is stifling hot, filled with thick, humid air. Retrieving sunglasses from under the visor, Rebecca slips them over her eyes and rolls down the window as quickly as possible. Gentle relief pours in, however, is quickly consumed by the soupy interior. Reaching for the radio, she turns up the volume and waits for the steering wheel to cool. Amanda Marshal's "I Believe in You" envelops her mind's ear.

Somewhere there's an angel
Trying to earn his wings
Somewhere there's a silent voice
Learning how to sing

Some of us can't move ahead
Paralyzed with fear
And everybody's listening
'Cause we all need to hear

I... believe in you
I can't even count the ways that
I believe in you
And all I want to do is help you
Believe in you...

A single tear carves Rebecca's cheek. It was their song, and every time she has heard it over the years, Johnny's voice penetrated her thoughts. "*We're a great couple.*" Closing her eyes, she listens to the words and comes face-to-face with the only man she could ever love until the song ends and is replaced with an advertising out of Louisville for big, big, big savings at Big Al's Furniture and Appliances. Testing the steering wheel, she discovers it has cooled enough to manage. Checking herself in the rearview, she sees that the feather she wears, braided within the trestles of her long red hair, is twisted outward. She rights it and focuses on the eye staring back at her. "I miss you so much, Johnny," she says to her reflection.

"*I will love you forever and a day,*" his cerebral voice reminds her.

Hanging over the middle of Main, the banner catches her eye as it surrenders lazily to a warm breeze. The Valentine's Day in July celebration was only two weeks away, and she was looking forward to the social affair that each year had brought the people of Valentine closer together.

She people-watches for a moment, having come to know everyone who resided within Valentine. She now knows their names, their children's names, what they did for a living, who was ill and whether or not a newborn resident would soon breathe the unspoiled air of small town America. What their favorite menu items were and who was cheating on whom and with whom and those who would soon breathe their last breaths.

Putting the truck in reverse, she heads back to the place she now calls home. The peaceful surroundings of Ed and Hester Hart's domestic bliss. She had returned to them after recovering from the bullet that should have ended her life, spending three weeks at the Rockyview Hospital in Calgary where she retold her story to the RCMP. After a collated investigation involving the FBI and the Las Vegas sheriff's department, they found everything she claimed to be accurate. There were no charges laid against her (the public's outcry would have been tantamount on both sides of the border because her story had become a major issue with the media) and the doors to the Shangri-La Palace and Club Paradise were closed forever.

You see, Rebecca had been born with a rare medical anomaly in that her heart, liver, and kidneys were displaced, her heart being two inches to the left, henceforth, the bullet had missed it completely, exiting through her back from behind a lung.

It was also revealed during the investigation that Rebecca White was the sole survivor of a deadly fire that had claimed the lives of her brother and father. Much to Rebecca's surprise, Ray White, the quintessential poster child for cheap, had left behind an insurance policy valued at one hundred thousand dollars for his children. With the aid of a lawyer, and not having to return to Bay Ridge Cove for the formalities, Rebecca inherited a small fortune, minus the taxes and legal retainer.

There really wasn't anything for Rebecca to return to. The intense heat of the fire had reduced Ben and Ray White to nothing more than a dust pan of ashes. Gifted as she was, to this day, she never saw them again and never would.

Tony Millions's assets were seized by the FBI, his bullet-riddled body cremated by the state. No one who remained of the Millions family willing to claim him.

Hillary Storm, alias Madame Olivia, was sentenced to fifteen years in the Florence McClure Correctional Center for aiding and abetting in the kidnapping of several young women. Coerced into testifying for the prosecution, Alvarita Amaranto aka Gypsy, ended her life once the trial was over by swallowing a bottle of pain killers and consuming a quart of Vodka. Li Ling, Hillary's lover, also took her life. Bath tub and razor. Brit, Brat and Tinker continued with the world's oldest profession, working the streets of Vegas.

The man Rebecca knew only as Mr. Black and the ex-Playboy pinup girl Pamela, were never apprehended.

None of the investigation reflected on the Santangello family. Twenty of the country's finest legal representatives saw to it, always.

While Rebecca recovered in hospital, Buck Black claimed the body of his only son, returning him to the Double B ranch. He buried him at the foot of Anvil Pine next to his beloved best friend Dallas where he situated a white cross inscribed with a single word: JOHNNY.

Having witnessed Johnny's eternal resting place before the final events of his destiny sealed his fate, there was no need for Rebecca to visit. He was in good company.

Once recovered, and after all the legalities with the authorities were concluded, Rebecca bounded a bus and headed back to Kentucky. The Harts had welcomed her with opened arms, treating her like their own daughter and converting Caleb's room into one more suitable to her needs. For three distant years, she has been waiting for Johnny's spiritual return as promised, missing him more and more with each passing day.

In less than a half hour, she pulls into the yard to find Ed and Hester sitting in the garden among the roses. Hester is reading; and Ed, with guarded eyes, is watching Elvis run about the yard. They wave as she parks, and Rebecca is more than happy to exit the oven on wheels.

Elvis, her son, is pursuing Caleb and Chase about the yard in a game Caleb called "catch me if you can." Elvis had been born nine months and three days after Johnny's death. On the day Rebecca birthed him into the world, two memories rushed forward in her thoughts. The enchanting occasion sitting beneath the wishing tree with Johnny's weary head resting on her lap and the night spent at Konahee's where, sheltered in the Ford, and with a little help from Konahee's lasting magic, a King had serenaded them.

Elvis John Black introduced himself to the world on September 9 in the privacy of Ed and Hester's home with Hester acting as midwife. When she laid him in Rebecca's arms, Elvis already possessed a full mane of jet-black hair like his father, skin the color of polished copper, and long dark lashes fringing eyes that were so grey they appeared transparent. Even before his first birthday, it was obvious he was brilliant, gifted like his mother, speaking full sentences and running about the yard, albeit wobbly, in an attempt to catch the free-range spirits of Caleb and Chase.

Seeing his mother, Elvis waves frantically. A Cleveland Indians baseball cap protects his head and eyes from the July sun. He is wearing a white T-shirt, blue shorts, and runners that flash whenever his feet hit the ground. An arm's length away from reaching the red ball Caleb had thrown, Chase snatches it, then proceeds happily toward the barn, bounding like a great red-and-white dream.

With a mother's love singing in her heart, Rebecca watches him for a moment before joining Ed and Hester. She sits on the bench between them. Decades of roses are in magnificent bloom, and the place she calls her forever home is encompassed in a shroud of numinous perfume.

"How was your day, my dear?" asks Hester from beneath the brim of her sun hat, resting the novel on her lap, allowing her reading glasses to slip to her breast.

"It was busy. I made forty dollars in tips."

"Mr. Sonjee must be very pleased with himself," said Ed.

"And how's his wife?" Hester wanted to know.

"Mr. Sonjee says she should be well very soon. Her fever has broke."

"Oh, that's such good news. She is such a dear woman. Mr. Sonjee must be relieved. Did you have a chance to eat?"

"Not yet. When the lunch crowd left, I just wanted to come home and enjoy the day."

"Then we must remedy that. I'll fix you a nice sandwich and some soup. How does that sound?"

"Sounds yummy. Has Elvis eaten?"

"Oh yes, my dear. He had a sandwich and two bowls of soup with a tall glass of milk. I swear, I've never seen a boy his age eat like he does. I don't know where he puts it."

"I'll help you, Mother, said Ed. "I could use a break from the sun. I think it's baking my already-baked brains." Lifting his huge frame from the bench, he helps Hester from her place. She is slow moving these days because osteoporosis had definitively settled into her aged bones. The novel slides from her lap, and lands open on the ground. Rebecca reaches down, picks it up, and hands it to her. "Is it a good book?"

"It seems to me that Stephen King is finally getting a little worn-out," Hester says with mock disapproval, for no matter what the King of fright puts out, she has always remained his number one fan. "This story doesn't quite have the fear factor he is so renowned for. Still, I don't know where he comes up with them. He must constantly tightrope the fine line between brilliance and insanity. Probably bipolar. I wish I could meet him someday."

It never ceased to amaze Rebecca that Hester's preferred reading were stories that smacked of blood and violence. "Perhaps you will someday," Rebecca tells her, realizing suddenly how much she sounded like her mother.

"I'm afraid I do not have many somedays left, my dear."

"Nonsense, Mother. I'll not have you talking like that," reprimands Ed, though his voice is tainted with truth.

Hester loops an arm through his and leans into his side for support. "I'll have your lunch ready in ten minutes. Would you like me to bring it to you, or will you be eating inside?"

"I'll be in in a few minutes. I'd like to change out of these clothes anyway. It's too hot for what I have on."

"As you wish, my dear."

Ed and Hester Hart begin what was now for them a long stroll back to the house. They were aging rapidly, and Rebecca's internal radar constantly expressed that Hester's time was near. She also knows, with absolute certainty, that when the inevitable comes, Ed will quickly follow, surrendering to an absent heart.

Six months previous, the Harts had confided that they had amended their wills and Rebecca would inherit the house, *sans* mortgage, the truck, and what little money remained, as if they too, understood what precious little time remained for them. "You and Elvis are the only family we have of this earth," explained Hester.

Rebecca watches them for a moment before directing her attention to Elvis as he nears the barn at a full gallop. Caleb and Chase have already disappeared behind the huge double doors, Caleb knowing full well that Rebecca does not like Elvis going in there alone. The barn has sagged further over the last couple of years and seems on the brink of collapse.

Standing and removing her sunglasses, she calls out to him, "Elvis! Don't you go in the barn! Elvis! Do you hear me? Mommy doesn't want you going in the barn!"

Elvis stops, turns, waves, then flashes a smile.

"Come to Mommy! I want to see you!"

"Okay, Mommy," Elvis calls out, his small voice swept silent by a breeze stemming from the trees. Taking one more look at the barn, he runs to his mother as fast as his little feet can carry him. When he reaches her, Rebecca leans forward, scoops him into her arms, and plants kisses all over his face. "Did you miss me, Elvis?"

"Yes, Mommy. Did you miss me?"

"Of course I did. I always miss you whenever we're away from each other." She stands her lovely son on the bench next to her, forgetting about the glasses. A soft crunching sound emits from beneath his left foot.

"Oh-uh. Sorry, Mommy," says Elvis, looking down, lifting his foot.

"It's okay, Elvis. It wasn't your fault. I just forgot I put my glasses on the bench. It was an accident."

Elvis sticks a finger into his nose, pulls it out, and examines what he has mined.

"You shouldn't pick your nose, Elvis."

"Why?"

"Because it's not polite."

"Caleb picks his nose."

"Well, he shouldn't."

Elvis wipes the booger onto his shorts and smiles with a mischievous light pricking from his eyes. "There. All gone."

"No, it isn't. Now it's on your shorts."

Elvis looks down. "Oh, sorry. It'll be gone when you do the laundry." He smiles proudly at his deduction.

Rebecca wants to burst with laughter, however, suppresses the urge and instead laughs within. "That's not the point, Elvis."

"What's the point? I can point." Extending a chubby arm, he aims a finger at the barn. "See. That's the barn. Can't go in the barn." He looks toward the house and the oven on wheels. "That's the house. That's the truck. Papa Ed's truck." Then he directs his attention to the double white crosses and points. "That's where Caleb and Chase sleep."

"Okay, okay. I get it. You can point."

"Told you I could." Regarding the shattered glass at his feet he adds, "Those damned glasses are broken."

"Elvis! You shouldn't say that word."

"What word?"

"You know very well what word."

"Papa Ed says it all the time."

"Well. It's not a word little boys should say. No matter how smart they think they are."

"What about *shit*? Papa Ed says that a lot too."

Disrupting the laughter threatening to burst from Rebecca's clenched lips, a shadow crosses her face. With a hand shielding her eyes against the brilliant sun, she looks into the vast sky. A hawk much larger than most is circling directly above them, its extended wings sharp against the blue. The magnificent bird appears to look down at them and ushers a piercing cry.

Elvis looks up and points again. "Daddy! Daddy!" he cries excitedly.

Rebecca looks to her son. "That's just a bird, silly. Mommy told you. Your daddy is like Caleb and Chase. Not like us."

"No, no, Mommy," said Elvis, still jamming his finger at the air. "It's Daddy!"

Rebecca gazes skyward. The bird circles, wider and wider, repeating its shrilling call. Something falls from it, a dark sliver, and it takes Rebecca several moments to realize the great bird has let loose a feather. It spirals downward, unhampered by the breeze, landing directly in front of her. Rising from the bench, she retrieves it. It appears a normal feather until she turns it over and gasps, the air in her lungs coming out all at once. Staggered by what she is seeing, she plops herself down on the bench again, her heart hammering within. Without taking her eyes away from what lay across her hand, she removes the feather from her long red hair with the other. Crisscrossing the two, she is staring unbelievably into the eyes of Johnny Black. Tears of a boundless joy spill from her eyes. "Johnny," she breaths softly, looking to the great bird.

Moving next to her, Elvis leans on her shoulder and, with his fingers, takes her chin and turns her head so that she was looking directly at him. He points to his face. "See, Mommy. My eyes." Then he points to the feathers in his mother's hands. "Daddy's eyes. Don't cry. Be happy."

"Yes, sweetheart. Daddy! And I am happy, Elvis. More than you can understand." Pressing the feathers to her bosom, she looks skyward once more.

The great bird has perched itself atop the nearest pine. Stretching its wings, it releases such an unusual cadence so loud and so heartwrenching Rebecca can feel it to the very essence of her soul. She now realizes Johnny's destiny did not end in a lonely hotel room. *No.* By way of powers beyond her own, his true fortune was to inherit the spirit that lived deep within, taking its shape, and all the mystery that came with it. She has no doubt time spent at Konahee's played a major role in this miraculous conversion of the two. Johnny had returned to her, and she knows unquestionably with all her heart he will remain with her forever and a day. Just as he promised.

From out of the thick forest comes a crow as black as sin, pursued by several sparrows. Rebecca watches as the small birds attack the crow's rear, one by one. The great hawk remains positioned atop the pine, its head moving, as it too watches the lesser species commence to do battle with the crow. Suddenly the crow turns in the air, its talons lashing out at one of the small birds. The tiny sparrow falls earthward, trying desperately to maintain flight; however, the crow has clipped one of its wings, causing it to obtrude from its body at an unusual angle. The brave little bird spirals helplessly down, landing soundlessly halfway to the barn.

Elvis jumps off the bench and runs toward it faster than Rebecca has ever seen him run.

"No, Elvis," she calls after him. "Leave it alone. It's gone now. We'll bury it later."

But Elvis will not listen. He stops next to the tiny creature and scoops it into his hands. Returning to his mother, he holds it out for her to see. The little thing's neck had been snapped when it hit the earth, its wing severely broken.

The great bird continues to watch from the pine, and lets loose another shrilling cry.

"It's dead, Elvis," said Rebecca, trying to make Elvis understand. "See. It's not moving."

Elvis puts one hand over the other so the bird is covered by his palms. He stares at his cupped hands for a moment, leans his face close, and whispers, "Be all better, birdie."

From out of the rose garden, like a floating dream, a monarch appears, flutters toward Elvis, and comes to rest atop his sealed hands. He repeats his wish. "Be all better now, birdie." Taking flight, the monarch floats to the final resting places of Caleb and Chase and settles on the tip of the cross representing Caleb Hart's grave.

In the following heartbeat, an amber glow, as bright as a sun beam, emanates from between Elvis's little fingers. Rebecca gasps and watches in unbounded amazement as the sparrow begins to stir. The brilliant glow fades until it returns to whence it came. When Elvis separates his palms, the darling thing stands on twig legs, ruffles its feathers, and chirps before taking flight, rising high into the air and disappearing into the woods.

Rebecca gently places her hands on Elvis's shoulders, and turns him so he is facing her, a part of her not wanting to believe what her eyes had just witnessed. "Did you do that, Elvis?" she asks, voice croaked with emotion, her eyes looking deep into her son.

"Yes, Mommy. I wanted it to be all better, and it is. Did I do something bad?"

"No, sweetheart," said Rebecca, stunned. "Have you ever done that before?"

"No, Mommy. This was the first time."

Rebecca regards her son as though seeing him for the first time. "You must promise me, Elvis. You know what a promise is, right?"

"Yes, Mommy. Don't tell nobody nothing."

"Good. You must promise me not to tell anyone about what you just did. Not Papa Ed or even Nana Hester. No one. Okay? It'll be our secret. At least for a while. When Mommy thinks the time is right, I will tell Papa Ed and Nana Hester."

"Okay, Mommy. I promise." Elvis looks up to his father perched atop the pine, watching, watching, watching. "Hi, Daddy," he calls out, the miracle he had just performed meaning nothing more to him than picking his nose.

The totality of everything that had happened since Rebecca left Bay Ridge Cove and found a love that would last her lifetime, came to an understanding she found difficult to grasp, yet accepted with utmost joy. What she perceived as the providence of two souls who had found each other at the most chaotic period of their lives was only the beginning of something much greater. What was meant to be was the child standing in front of her. Elvis John Black was the provident offspring of events that befell them. He was destiny's child. The fact that Johnny appeared just as Elvis revealed his gift was not a coincidence. The hand of fate had turned another page in the book that was Rebecca's life.

"Come on, Elvis. Mommy's lunch must be ready by now." Taking him by the hand, she looks to the top of the pine where her forever love sits regally. Where he will always remain, watching over her, and over the years, witness his son grow to be a man. A man who possesses the extraordinary ability to cure Mother's sick and injured creatures. A man who would change the mind-set of wealth-consumed men and begin a new understanding of the relationship between man and beast. Rebecca waves and, in return, receives an endearing cry of recognition. "I love you too, Johnny Black." Smiling, new life breathed into her being, she turns for the house, Elvis holding one hand, twinned feathers clutched tightly in the other.

* * *

After a lunch of salmon sandwiches and Hester's world-famous chicken noodle soup, Rebecca, Ed, Hester, and Elvis spend the remainder of the day sitting in the garden enjoying the summer sun. The great bird has kept his place atop the pine and watches over them with keen eyes. Rebecca knows in her heart of hearts that one day soon she would have to tell Ed and Hester about Elvis' special gift. She also knew they would accept it wholly and without prejudice. It was the rest of the community and those beyond she was concerned about. The world was a curious place. Its peoples prone to ignorance when it came to matters of the unknown. Justifiably, she feared for her son.

Caleb and Chase had joined in, more to tease Elvis who couldn't keep up no matter how hard he tried, than to make their presence known to Rebecca, which was now commonplace. With unrelenting energy, the trio ran about the yard until boy and bestest friend in the world momentarily returned to the dark place they had inherited in death, leaving Elvis curious with a procession of questions and exhausted as always.

By dinnertime, the little family gathered at the kitchen table to enjoy the roast Hester had prepared, courtesy of Mr. Sonjee, and to listen to Caleb play "Twinkle, Twinkle, Little Star" on the piano. As time passed, Caleb's abilities grew stronger, drawing energy from Rebecca, and he would often entertain his parents by tickling the ivories. The Harts would speak to him through her, and she realized over the past couple of years their faith in God had become more of a spiritual funnel they used for guidance than a belief that when their time came, there was only one afterlife to which they would endure.

When Rebecca finished the dinner dishes, she told Ed and Hester she needed to share something with them that was of the utmost importance and sent Elvis into the living room to watch television.

With the sound of the TV spilling from the other room, Hester asks anxiously, "Well, what is it, my dear?"

Rebecca takes her place at the table. Ed and Hester see a shine in her eyes they had not seen before. "It's about Johnny."

"Oh?" Hester looks to Ed. "Well, what is it, my dear? We're listening."

"Promise to have an open mind?"

"Of course, Rebecca," said Ed. "After everything we've experienced, it's hard not to."

"Well." She pauses for a moment. "He's come back to me."

Clapping her hands together, Hester said, "That's wonderful, my dear. When? Today?"

"Yes. This afternoon. While I was sitting in the garden and you were fixing lunch."

"So he's kept his promise to be with you," said Ed.

Rebecca had shared with the Harts every moment she and Johnny spent together. The good. The bad. And the promises they made. "Yes. But he's not like Caleb or Chase."

"Oh? Then what do you mean, my dear? How has he returned to you? We'll understand. Won't we, my love?" Hester puts a hand on Ed's arm.

"Yes. Absolutely."

Rebecca takes a deep breath. "He's come back to me in the form of his animal spirit." Unfastening the feathers she had braided in her hair, she sets them on the table so their significant features are obvious to the Harts.

"My god!" exclaims Hester, taking a quick breath. The hand resting on Ed's arm goes to her chest. She looks to Rebecca then back to the feathers sitting in front of her. "Those are Elvis's eyes."

"Yes. They're also his father's."

"You mean?"

A moment of silence fills the kitchen.

"Yes, Hester. Johnny has come back to me in the form of a hawk. A great bird who will watch over us all. He often told me about the dreams of flight he had. How had he searched for me in the form of a great bird. Now I know why."

"I'm... I'm... I'm... I don't know what I am." Hester falls silent and stares at her lifetime love.

Ed reaches across the table, picks up the feathers, and studies them for a moment before handing them to Rebecca. "Well, I'll be." He scratches the top of his head.

"So you both understand then? You accept what I've just told you?"

Hester blinks several times before a knowing smile creases her brow. "How can we not, my dear? You've opened our eyes to the wonders of the world. Why, if it weren't for you, we would still be swimming in our ignorance. Far be it from us to dismiss such things. I'm just a little taken back is all. It's not every day someone informs you that what was once a man is now a bird."

"Oh, thank you, Hester. Thank you, Ed. You don't know how much your understanding means to me. At least now you won't think I'm crazy when you see me talking to him."

"We would never think that of you, my dear. Would we, my love?"

"No. Of course not." Ed rises from his chair and limps toward the window overlooking the property, his eyes searching. When he looks up, he sees the great bird immediately. "Is that him? Is that Johnny? Sitting on top of that pine tree?"

Rebecca and Hester join him at the window and follow his gaze. "Yes," said Rebecca. "That's Johnny. Isn't he beautiful?" Tears of love spill from her eyes.

"Does Elvis know? Considering his gift?" inquires Hester.

"Yes. He recognized him right away. There was an instant bond between the two."

"Well, I'll be," said Ed.

"Isn't love grand," replies Hester, tears manifested by the wondrous moment and the maternal joy she feels for Rebecca washing her face.

* * *

That night, shortly after reading Elvis a story from one of his favorite books, telling him how beautiful life was going to be now that his father had returned, Rebecca tucked him into bed, and remained by his side until he fell asleep to the sounds of a lullaby recited countless years before. Nestled beside him, Bandit the bear would share his dreams and keep him safe as he had for Rebecca many a year.

Stripping out of her clothes, and getting comfortable in a pair of PJs, she goes to the window overlooking the bountiful rose garden and stares out into the night for a few moments, wondering if Johnny was near. Shadow upon shadow dance in the darkness. Opening the window ever so gently, she is greeted with the sound of trees moving in the silent breath of nocturnal bliss and the aura of rose perfume cast about the land.

Reading her thoughts, the great bird releases a gentle sound only Rebecca can comprehend. *"I love you, Becca,"* she hears.

"And I love you, Johnny. Always have. Always will."

Closing the window and crawling into bed, Rebecca pulls the floral sheet to her breast, her mind racing with memories of Johnny, and what life was going to be like now that he had returned and what lay in store for a child who had the gift to heal. *Would Elvis be accepted by society, or will I have to do everything in my power to keep his special purpose within the family? How long would it be before I can reveal to Ed and Hester his more than special gift before Elvis, not meaning to break his promise, shocks them with a display of his rare ability? Time will tell all,* she reminds herself. *It always has.*

Reaching for the radio on the nightstand, she dials it low like she always does, clicks off the lamp, and stares at the dark ceiling until her lids close on their own. It isn't long, regardless of the day's revelations, before she descends into a beautiful sleep. One filled with the wonder and dreams of a time since past. *"Time after time, Johnny."* She breathes a final conscious breath before falling into his strong arms.

* * *

Through the closed door, sometime in the wee hours of night, Caleb and Chase enter the room. *"Shhh,"* he cautions his bestest friend in the whole world, a finger pressed firmly against his lips. Caleb listens for a moment to the music emanating from the radio. He likes Rebecca's choice in music, even though, at first, it was very strange to him. Together boy and bestest friend move to where Elvis lay sound asleep. *"Good night, Elvis,"* says Caleb. *"We'll play again tomorrow. Maybe we'll even let you catch us."*

They float to where Rebecca lay lost in the land of imaginings, where a six-almost seven-year-old boy, once upon a time and a thousand dreams ago, used to rest his head. Chase sits tall by Caleb's side, tongue lolling from his mouth. Caleb would like her to be with him always, but understands it will be many years before she joins him in the world where he somehow exists. His mommy and daddy will come first, and very soon he knows. Mommy was sick and Daddy could not live without her. Then Rebecca would come, and one day so would Elvis and his daddy, and they would all be together, one big happy family. All he had to do was play and wait.

Reaching, he touches the soft flesh of Rebecca's face with his tiny fingers and kisses her cheek with his forever-boy lips. Rebecca stirs, smiles, and, in a dream voice, breathes, "*Johnny. I love you.*"

In a quiet, loving cadence, Caleb says good night like he does every night, "*Good night, Rebecca White. Sleep tight. Don't let the bed bugs bite.*"

Oh... my love,
My darling,
I hunger for your touch,
A long. Lonely time.
And time goes by, so slowly,
And time can do so much,
Are you still mine?
I need your love.
I need your love.
Godspeed your love... to me.

Lonely rivers flow to the sea, to the sea,
To the open arms of the sea.
Lonely rivers sigh, wait for me, wait for me,
I'll be coming home, wait for me...

END

Edwards Brothers Malloy
Thorofare, NJ USA
December 4, 2012